PENGUIN TWENTIETH-CENTURY CLASSICS

THE SEA OF FERTILITY

Yukio Mishin[illegible] graduated from the Pee[illegible] from the Emperor as t[illegible] highest [illegible] He then attended the Tokyo Imperial University School of [illegible]prudence until 1947. Starting in his teens, he became a prolific writer of great diversity, whose works include some fifteen novels (many of which have been made into films), thirty-three plays, two travel books, numerous essays and countless short stories. Among his books published in England are *After the Banquet*, *Confessions of a Mask*, *Death in Midsummer* and *The Sailor Who Fell from Grace with the Sea*. *The Sound of Waves*, published in Japan under the title *Shiosai*, won the 1954 Shinchosa literary prize.

Mishima revered and mastered the martial arts of Japan. He was a devotee of body-building exercises and also accomplished in the arts of *kendo* and *karate*. He always firmly upheld the traditions of Japan's imperial past – a legacy from his samurai forbears – and believed that these values were being eroded by Western materialism.

On November 25, 1970, at the peak of his brilliant literary career, he astonished the world by committing ritual suicide, or *hara-kiri*, by disembowelment. Mishima had written much about suicide and early death and often expressed the wish to die young. His last work was this tetralogy, which was finally completed on the morning before his death. Just before his suicide he wrote to friends that he felt empty, having put everything he thought or felt about life into this mammoth undertaking, later hailed as a masterpiece. His writing has been widely acclaimed, compared to that of Proust, Gide and Sartre, and Arthur Miller once said of him that 'He had the economy of means to create enormous myths – his novels are compressed visions.'

YUKIO MISHIMA

THE SEA OF FERTILITY

SPRING SNOW
RUNAWAY HORSES
THE TEMPLE OF DAWN
THE DECAY OF THE ANGEL

PENGUIN BOOKS

PENGUIN BOOKS

Published by the Penguin Group
Penguin Books Ltd, 27 Wrights Lane, London W8 5TZ, England
Viking Penguin, a division of Penguin Books USA Inc.
375 Hudson Street, New York, New York 10014, USA
Penguin Books Australia Ltd, Ringwood, Victoria, Australia
Penguin Books Canada Ltd, 2801 John Street, Markham, Ontario, Canada L3R 1B4
Penguin Books (NZ) Ltd, 182–190 Wairau Road, Auckland 10, New Zealand

Penguin Books Ltd, Registered Offices: Harmondsworth, Middlesex, England

Spring Snow (Haru no Yuki) First published in Tokyo 1968
This translation published in Great Britain by Martin Secker & Warburg Ltd 1972
Published in Penguin Books 1976

UNESCO COLLECTION OF REPRESENTATIVE WORKS/JAPANESE SERIES
This book has been accepted in the Japanese Series of the
Translations Collection of the United Nations Educational,
Scientific and Cultural Organization (UNESCO)

Runaway Horses (Homba) first published by Shinchosha Company 1969
This translation first published in Great Britain by Martin Secker & Warburg Ltd 1973
Published in Penguin Books 1977

The Temple of Dawn (Akatsuki no Tera) first published in Japan 1970
This translation published in Great Britain by Martin Secker & Warburg Ltd 1974
Published in Penguin Books 1977

The Decay of the Angel (Tennin gosui) first published in Japan 1971
This translation published in Great Britain by Martin Secker & Warburg Ltd 1975
Published in Penguin Books 1977

Published in Penguin Books in one volume as *The Sea of Fertility* 1985
10 9 8 7 6 5

Scanned and phototypeset by
Datasolve Information, London
Made and printed in Great Britain by
BPCC Hazell Books
Aylesbury, Bucks, England
Member of BPCC Ltd.
Set in 9/11 Times

CONTENTS

SPRING SNOW

Translated by
Michael Gallagher

1

When conversation at school turned to the Russo-Japanese War, Kiyoaki Matsugae asked his closest friend, Shigekuni Honda, how much he could remember about it. Shigekuni's memories were vague – he just barely recalled having been taken once to the front gate to watch a torchlight procession. The year the war ended they had both been eleven, and it seemed to Kiyoaki that they should be able to remember it a little more accurately. Their classmates who talked so knowingly about the war were for the most part merely embellishing hazy memories with tidbits they had picked up from grown-ups.

Two members of the Matsugae family, Kiyoaki's uncles, had been killed. His grandmother still received a pension from the government, thanks to these two sons she had lost, but she never used the money; she left the envelopes unopened on the ledge of the household shrine. Perhaps that was why the photograph which impressed Kiyoaki most out of the entire collection of war photographs in the house was one entitled 'Vicinity of Tokuri Temple: Memorial Services for the War Dead' and dated June 26, 1904, the thirty-seventh year of the Meiji era. This photograph, printed in sepia ink, was quite unlike the usual cluttered mementos of the war. It had been composed with an artist's eye for structure: it really made it seem as if the thousands of soldiers who were present were arranged deliberately, like figures in a painting, to focus the entire attention of the viewer on the tall cenotaph of unpainted wood in their midst. In the distance, mountains sloped gently in the haze, rising in easy stages to the left of the picture, away from the broad plain at their foot; to the right, they merged in the distance with scattered clumps of trees, vanishing into the yellow dust of the horizon. And here, instead of mountains, there was a row of trees growing taller as the eye moved to the right; a yellow sky showed through the gaps between them. Six very tall trees stood at graceful intervals in the foreground, each placed so as to complement the overall harmony of the landscape. It was impossible to tell what kind they were, but their heavy top branches seemed to bend in the wind with a tragic grandeur.

The distant expanse of plains glowed faintly; this side of the mountains, the vegetation lay flat and desolate. At the centre of the picture, minute, stood the plain wooden cenotaph and the altar with flowers lying on it, its white cloth twisted by the wind.

For the rest you saw nothing but soldiers, thousands of them. In the foreground, they were turned away from the camera to reveal the white sunshields hanging from their caps and the diagonal leather straps across their backs. They had not formed up in neat ranks, but were clustered in groups, heads drooping. A mere handful in the lower left corner had half-turned their dark faces toward the camera, like figures in a Renaissance painting. Farther behind them, a host of soldiers stretched away in an immense semicircle to the ends of the plain, so many men that it was quite impossible to tell one from another, and more were grouped far away among the trees.

The figures of these soldiers, in both foreground and rear, were bathed in a strange half-light that outlined leggings and boots and picked out the curves of bent shoulders and the napes of necks. This light charged the entire picture with an indescribable sense of grief.

From these men, there emanated a tangible emotion that broke in a wave against the small white altar, the flowers, the cenotaph in their midst. From this enormous mass stretching to the edge of the plain, a single thought, beyond all power of human expression, bore down like a great, heavy ring of iron on the centre.

Both its age and its sepia ink tinged the photograph with an atmosphere of infinite poignance.

Kiyoaki was eighteen. Nothing in the household where he had been born would account for his being so sensitive, so prone to melancholy. One would have been hard pressed to find, in that rambling house built on high ground near Shibuya, anyone who in any way shared his sensibilities. It was an old samurai family, but Kiyoaki's father, Marquis Matsugae, embarrassed by the humble position his forebears had occupied as recently as the end of the shogunate fifty years before, had sent the boy, still a very small child, to be brought up in the household of a court nobleman. Had he not done so, Kiyoaki would probably not have developed into so sensitive a young man.

Marquis Matsugae's residence occupied a large tract of land beyond Shibuya, on the outskirts of Tokyo. The many buildings spread out over a hundred acres, their roofs rising in an exciting counterpoise. The main house was of Japanese architecture, but in the corner of the park stood an imposing Western-style house designed by an Englishman. It was said to be one of four residences in Japan – Marshal Oyama's was the first – that one might enter without removing one's outdoor shoes.

In the middle of the park a large pond spread out against the backdrop of a hill covered with maples. The pond was big enough to boat on; it had an island in the middle, water lilies in flower, and even water shields that could be picked for the kitchen. The drawing-room of the main house faced the pond, as did the banqueting room of the Western house.

Some two hundred stone lanterns were scattered at random along the banks and on the island, which also boasted three cranes made out of cast-iron, two stretching their long necks to the sky and the other with its head bent low.

Water sprang from its source at the crest of the maple hill and descended the slopes in several falls; the stream then passed beneath a stone bridge and dropped into a pool that was shaded by red rocks from the island of Sado, before flowing into the pond at a spot where, in season, a patch of lovely irises bloomed. The pond was stocked both with carp and winter crucian. Twice a year, the Marquis allowed schoolchildren to come there on picnics.

When Kiyoaki was a child, the servants had frightened him with stories about the snapping turtles. Long ago, when his grandfather was ill, a friend had presented him with a hundred of these turtles in the hope that their meat would rebuild his strength. Released into the pond, they had bred rapidly. Once a snapping turtle got your finger in its beak, the servants told Kiyoaki, that was the end of it.

There were several pavilions used for the tea ceremony and also a large billiard room. Behind the main house, wild yams grew thick in the grounds, and there was a grove of cypresses planted by Kiyoaki's grandfather, and intersected by two paths. One led to the rear gate; the other climbed a small hill to the plateau at its top where a shrine stood at one corner of a wide expanse of grass. This was where his grandfather and two uncles were enshrined. The steps, lanterns, and torii, all stone, were traditional, but on either side of the steps, in place of the usual lion-dogs, a pair of cannon shells from the Russo-Japanese War had been painted white and set in the ground. Somewhat lower down there was a shrine to Inari, the harvest god, behind a magnificent trellis of wisteria. The anniversary of his grandfather's death fell at the end of May; thus the wisteria was always in full glory when the family gathered here for the services, and the women would stand in its shade to avoid the glare of the sun. Their white faces, powdered even more meticulously than usual for the occasion, were dappled in violet, as though some exquisite shadow of death had fallen across their cheeks.

The women. No one could count exactly the multitude of women who lived in the Matsugae mansion. Kiyoaki's grandmother, of course, took precedence over them all, though she preferred to live in retirement at some distance from the main house, with eight maids to attend to her needs. Every morning, rain or shine, Kiyoaki's mother would finish dressing and go at once with two maids in attendance to pay her respects to the old lady. And every day the old lady would scrutinize her daughter-in-law's appearance.

'That hairstyle isn't very becoming. Why not try doing it in the high-collar way tomorrow? I'm sure it would look better on you,' she would say, her eyes narrowed lovingly. But when the hair was arranged the Western way next morning, the old lady would comment: 'Really, Tsujiko, a high-collar hair-do simply doesn't suit an old-fashioned Japanese beauty like you. Please try the Marumage style tomorrow.' And so, for as long as Kiyoaki could remember, his mother's coiffure had been perpetually changing.

The hairdressers and their apprentices were in constant attendance. Not only did his mother's hair demand their services but they had to look after more than forty maids. However, they had shown concern for the hair of a male member of the household on only one occasion. This was when Kiyoaki was in his first year at the middle school attached to Peers School. The honour had fallen to him of being selected to act as a page in the New Year's festivities at the Imperial Palace.

'I know the people at school want you to look like a little monk,' said one of the hairdressers, 'but that shaved head just won't look right with your fine costume today.'

'But they'll scold me if my hair is long.'

'All right, all right,' said the hairdresser. 'Let me see what I can do to improve it. You'll be wearing a hat in any case, but I think we can arrange things so that even when you take it off, you'll outshine all the other young gentlemen.'

So he said, but Kiyoaki at thirteen had had his head clipped so closely that it looked blue. When the hairdresser parted his hair, the comb hurt, and the hair oil stung his skin. For all the hairdresser's vaunted skill, the head reflected in the mirror looked no different from any boy's, yet at the banquet Kiyoaki was praised for his extraordinary beauty.

The Emperor Meiji himself had once honoured the Matsugae residence with his presence. To entertain his Imperial Majesty, an exhibition of sumo wrestling had been staged beneath a huge gingko tree, around which a space had been curtained off. The Emperor watched from a balcony on the second floor of the Western house. Kiyoaki confided to the hairdresser that on that occasion he had been permitted to appear before the Emperor, and His Majesty had deigned to pat him on the head. That had taken place four years ago, but it nevertheless was possible that the Emperor might remember the head of a mere page at the New Year's festivities.

'Really?' exclaimed the hairdresser, overwhelmed. 'Young master, you mean to say you were caressed by the Emperor himself!' So saying, he slid backward across the tatami floor, clapping his hands in genuine reverence at the child.

The costume of a page attending a lady of the court consisted of matching blue velvet jacket and trousers, the latter reaching to just below the knees. Down either side of the jacket was a row of four large white fluffy pompons and more were attached to the cuffs and the trousers. The page wore a sword at his waist, and the shoes on his white-stockinged feet were fastened with black enamel buttons. A white silk tie was knotted in the centre of his broad lace collar, and a tricorn hat, adorned with a large feather, hung down his back on a silk cord. Each New Year, about twenty sons of the nobility with outstanding school records were selected to take turns – in fours – bearing the train of the Empress, or in pairs to carry the train of an imperial princess during the three days of festivities. Kiyoaki carried the train of the Empress once and did the same for the Princess Kasuga. When it was his turn to bear the Empress's train she had proceeded with solemn dignity down corridors fragrant with the musky incense lit by the palace attendants, and he had stood in attendance behind her during the audience. She was a woman of great elegance and intelligence, but by then she was already elderly, close to sixty. Princess Kasuga, however, was not much more than thirty. Beautiful, elegant, imposing, she was like a flower at its moment of perfection.

Even now, Kiyoaki could remember less about the rather sober train favoured by the Empress than about the Princess's broad sweep of white ermine, with its scattered black spots and its border of pearls. The Empress's train had four loops for the pages' hands, and the Princess's two. Kiyoaki and the others had been so exhaustively drilled that they had no trouble in holding firm while advancing at a steady pace.

Princess Kasuga's hair had the blackness and sheen of fine lacquer. Seen from behind, her elaborate coiffure seemed to dissolve into the rich white skin-textures of the nape of her neck, leaving single strands against her bare shoulders whose faint sheen was set off by her décolleté.

She held herself erect, and walked straight ahead with a firm step, betraying no tremor to her trainbearers, but in Kiyoaki's eyes that great fan of white fur seemed to glow and fade to the sound of music, like a snow-covered peak first hidden, then exposed by a fluid pattern of clouds. At that moment, for the first time in his life, he was struck by the full force of womanly beauty – a dazzling burst of elegance that made his senses reel.

Princess Kasuga's lavish use of French perfume extended to her train, and its fragrance overpowered the musky odour of incense. Some way down the corridor, Kiyoaki stumbled for a moment, inadvertently tugging at the train. The Princess turned her head slightly, and, as a sign that she was not at all annoyed, smiled gently at the youthful offender. Her gesture went unnoticed; body perfectly erect in that fractional turn, she had allowed Kiyoaki a glimpse of a corner of her mouth. At that moment, a single wisp of hair slipped over her clear white cheek, and out of the fine-drawn corner of an eye a smile flashed in a spark of black fire. But the pure line of her nose did not move. It was as if nothing had happened ... this fleeting angle of the Princess's face – too slight to be called a profile – made Kiyoaki feel as if he had seen a rainbow flicker for a bare instant through a prism of pure crystal.

His father, Marquis Matsugae, watched his son's part in the festivities, absorbing the boy's brilliant appearance in his beautiful ceremonial costume, and savouring the complacency of a man who sees a lifelong dream fulfilled. This triumph dispelled completely his lingering fears of still seeming an imposter, for all his attempts to establish himself as someone fit to receive the Emperor in his own home. For now, in the person of his own son, the Marquis had seen the ultimate fusion of the aristocratic and the samurai traditions, a perfect congruence between the old court nobles and the new nobility.

But as the ceremony continued, the Marquis's gratification at the praise people had lavished on the boy's looks changed to feelings of discomfort. At thirteen, Kiyoaki was altogether too handsome. Putting aside natural affection for his own son, the Marquis could not help noticing that he stood out even in comparison with the other pages. His pale cheeks flushed crimson when he was excited, his brows were sharply defined and his wide eyes, still childishly earnest, were framed by long lashes. They were dark and had a seductive glint in them. And so the Marquis was roused by the flood of compliments to take note of the exceptional beauty of his son and heir, and he sensed something disquieting in it. He was touched by an uneasy premonition. But Marquis Matsugae was an extremely optimistic man, and he shook off his discomfiture as soon as the ceremony was over.

Similar apprehensions were more persistent in the mind of young Iinuma, who had come to live in the Matsugae household as a boy of seventeen the year before Kiyoaki's service as a page. Iinuma had been recommended as Kiyoaki's personal tutor by the middle school of his village in Kagoshima, and he had been sent to the Matsugaes with testimonies to his mental and physical abilities. The present Marquis's father was revered as a fierce and powerful god in Kagoshima, and Iinuma had visualized life in the Matsugae household entirely in terms of what he had heard at home or at school about the exploits of the former Marquis. In his year with them, however, their luxurious way of life had disrupted this expectation and had wounded his youthfully puritanical sensibilities.

He could shut his eyes to other things, but not to Kiyoaki, who was his personal responsibility. Everything about Kiyoaki – his looks, his delicacy, his sensitivity, his turn of mind, his interests – grated on Iinuma. And everything about the Marquis and Marquise's attitude toward their son's education was equally distressing. 'I'll never raise a son of mine that way, not even if I am made a Marquis. What weight do you suppose the Marquis gives to his own father's tenets?'

The Marquis was punctilious in observing the annual rites for his father, but almost never spoke of him. At first, Iinuma used to dream that the Marquis would talk more often about his father and that his reminiscences might reveal something of the affection in which he held his father's memory, but in the course of the year such hopes flickered and died.

The night that Kiyoaki returned home after performing his duties as an imperial page, the Marquis and his wife gave a private family dinner to celebrate the occasion. When the time came for Kiyoaki to hurry off to bed, Iinuma helped him to his room. The thirteen-year-old boy's cheeks were flushed with the wine that his father, half as a joke, had forced upon him. He burrowed into the silken quilts and let his head fall back on the pillow, his breath warm and heavy. The tracery of blue veins under his close-cropped hair throbbed around his earlobes, and the skin was so extraordinarily transparent that one could almost see the fragile mechanism inside. Even in the half-light of the room, his lips were red. And the sounds of breathing that came from this boy, who looked as though he had never experienced anguish, seemed to be the mocking echo of a sad folksong.

Iinuma looked down at his face, at the sensitive darting eyes with their long lashes – the eyes of an otter – and he knew that it was hopeless to expect him to swear the enthusiastic oaths of loyalty to the Emperor that a night like this would have invoked in any normal young Japanese boy striving toward manhood, who had been privileged to carry out so glorious a task.

Kiyoaki's eyes were now wide open as he lay on his back staring at the ceiling, and they were filled with tears. And when this glistening gaze turned on him, Iinuma's distaste deepened. But this made it all the more imperative for him to believe in his own loyalty. When Kiyoaki apparently felt too warm, he pulled his bare arms, slightly flushed, out from under the quilt and started to fold them behind his head; Iinuma admonished him and pulled shut the loose collar of his night-gown: 'You'll catch cold. You ought to go to sleep now.'

'Iinuma, you know ... I made a blunder today. If you promise not to tell Father or Mother, I'll say what it was.'

'What was it?'

'Today, when I was carrying the Princess's train, I stumbled a little. But the Princess just smiled and forgave me.'

Iinuma was repelled by these frivolous words, by the absence of any sense of responsibility, by the tearful look of rapture in those eyes, by everything.

2

It was hardly surprising, then, that by the time Kiyoaki turned eighteen, his preoccupations had served to isolate him more and more from his surroundings. He had grown apart from more than just his family. The teachers at the Peers School had instilled in their pupils the supremely noble example of the principal, General Nogi, who had committed suicide to follow his Emperor in death; and ever since they had started to emphasize the significance of his act, suggesting that their educational tradition would have been the poorer had the General died on a sickbed, an atmosphere of Spartan simplicity had come to permeate the school. Kiyoaki, who had an aversion to anything smacking of militarism, had come to loathe the school for this reason.

His only friend was his classmate Shigekuni Honda. There were of course many others who would have been delighted to be friends with Kiyoaki, but he didn't like the youthful coarseness of his contemporaries; he shunned their rough, coltish ways and was further repelled by their crude sentimentality when they mindlessly roared out the school song. Kiyoaki was drawn only to Honda, with his quiet, composed, rational temperament, unusual in a boy of his age. Even so the two had little in common in appearance or temperament.

Honda seemed older than he was. Though his features were quite ordinary, he tended to assume a somewhat pompous air. He was interested in studying law, and was gifted with keen intuition, but it was a power he tended to disguise. To look at him was to believe that he was indifferent to sensual pleasures, but there were times when he seemed fired by some deep passion; at these moments, Honda – who always kept his mouth firmly shut, as he kept his somewhat near-sighted eyes severely narrowed and his brows in a frown – was to be caught with a hint of parted lips in his expression.

Kiyoaki and Honda were perhaps as different in their makeup as the flower and the leaf of a single plant. Kiyoaki was incapable of hiding his true nature, and he was defenceless against society's power to inflict pain. His still unawakened sensuality lay dormant within him, unprotected as a puppy in a March rain, body shivering, eyes and nose pelted with water. Honda, on the other hand, had quite early in life grasped where danger lay, choosing to shelter from all storms, whatever their attraction.

Despite this, however, they were remarkably close friends. Not content to see each other in school, they would also spend Sundays together at one or the other of their homes. And because the Matsugae estate had more to offer in the way of walks and other amusements, Honda usually came to Kiyoaki's house.

One October Sunday in 1912, the first year of the Taisho era, on an afternoon when the maple leaves were almost in their prime, Honda arrived in Kiyoaki's room to suggest that they go boating on the pond. Had this been a year like any other, there would have been a growing number of visitors coming to admire the maple leaves, but as the Matsugaes had been in mourning since the Emperor's death the previous summer, they had suspended normal social activities. An extraordinary stillness lay over the park.

'Well, if you want to. The boat will take three. We'll get Iinuma to row us.'

'Why do we need anybody to row us? I'll row,' said Honda, remembering the dour expression of the young man who had just needlessly escorted him with silent but relentless obsequiousness to Kiyoaki's room.

Kiyoaki smiled. 'You don't like him, do you, Honda?'

'It's not that I don't like him. It's just that, for all the time I've known him, I still can't tell what's going on inside his head.'

'He's been here six years, so I take him for granted now, like the air I breathe. We certainly don't see eye to eye, but he's devoted to me all the same. He's loyal, he studies hard, you can depend on him.'

Kiyoaki's room was on the second floor facing the pond. It had originally been in Japanese style, but had been redecorated to look Western, with a carpet and Western furniture. Honda sat down on the windowsill. Looking over his shoulder, he took in the whole sweep of the pond, the island and the hill of maples beyond. The water lay smooth in the afternoon sun. Just below him, he could see the boats moored in a small inlet.

At the same time, he was mulling over his friend's lack of enthusiasm. Kiyoaki never took the lead, though sometimes he would join in with an air of utter boredom only to enjoy himself in his own way. The role of exhorter and leader, then, always fell to Honda if the pair were to do anything at all.

'You can see the boats, can't you?' said Kiyoaki.

'Yes, of course I can,' Honda replied, glancing dubiously behind him.

What did Kiyoaki mean by his question? If one were forced to hazard a guess, it would be that he was trying to say that he had no interest in anything at all. He thought of himself as a thorn, a small, poisonous thorn jabbed into the workman-like hand of his family. And this was his fate simply because he had acquired a little elegance. A mere fifty years before, the Matsugaes had been a sturdy, upright samurai family, no more, eking out a frugal existence in the provinces. But in a brief span of time, their fortunes had soared. By Kiyoaki's time, the first traces of refinement were threatening to take hold on a family that, unlike the court nobility, had enjoyed centuries of immunity to the virus of elegance. And Kiyoaki, like an ant that senses the approaching flood, was experiencing the first intimations of his family's rapid collapse.

His elegance was the thorn. And he was well aware that his aversion to coarseness, his delight in refinement, were futile; he was a plant without roots. Without meaning to undermine his family, without wanting to violate its traditions, he was condemned to do so by his very nature. And this poison would stunt his own life as it destroyed his family. The handsome young man felt that this futility typified his existence.

His conviction of having no purpose in life other than to act as a distillation of poison was part of the ego of an eighteen-year-old. He had resolved that his beautiful white hands would never be soiled or calloused. He wanted to be like a pennant, dependent on each gusting wind. The only thing that seemed valid to him was to live for the emotions – gratuitous and unstable, dying only to quicken again, dwindling and flaring without direction or purpose.

At the moment nothing interested him. Boating? His father had thought the little green and white boat he had imported from abroad to be stylish. As far as his father was concerned the boat was culture; culture made tangible. But what of it? Who cared about a boat?

Honda, with his inborn intuition, understood Kiyoaki's sudden silence. Although they were the same age, Honda was more mature. He was, in fact, a young man who wanted to lead a constructive life, and he had made up his mind about his future role. With Kiyoaki, however, he always took care to seem less sensitive and subtle than he was. For he knew that his friend was quite receptive to his careful displays of obtuseness – the only bait that seemed to draw a rise from Kiyoaki. And this streak of deception ran through their whole friendship.

'It would do you good to get some exercise,' said Honda brusquely. 'I know that you can't have been reading all that much, but you look as if you'd read your way through a library.'

Kiyoaki smiled by way of reply. Honda was right. It was not his books that had drained him of energy but his dreams. A whole library wouldn't have exhausted him as much as his constant dreaming night after night.

The very night before, he had dreamed of his own coffin, made of unpainted wood. It stood in the middle of an empty room with large windows, and outside, the pre-dawn darkness was shading to a deep blue; it was filled with the sound of birdsong. A young woman clung to the coffin, her long black hair trailing from her drooping head, her slender shoulders wracked with sobs. He wanted to see her face but could make out no more than her pale, graceful forehead with its delicate peak of black hair. The coffin was half covered with a leopard-skin bordered in pearls. The first muted glow of the dawn flickered on the row of jewels. Instead of funeral incense, a scent of Western perfume hung over the room with the fragrance of sun-ripened fruit. Kiyoaki seemed to be watching this from a great height, though he was convinced that his body lay inside the coffin. But sure as he was, he still felt the need to see it there by way of confirmation. However, like a mosquito in the morning light, his wings lost all power and ceased beating in mid-air; he was utterly incapable of looking inside the nailed-down coffin lid. And then, as his frustration grew more and more intense, he woke up. Kiyoaki took out his secret journal and wrote all this down.

Finally, the two of them went down to the landing and unfastened the mooring rope. The calm surface of the water reflected the flaming scarlet maples beginning to turn on the hill beyond. As they stepped into the boat, its wild rocking evoked in Kiyoaki his favourite feelings about the precariousness of life. At that instant, his inner thoughts seemed to describe a wide arc, clearly reflected in the fresh white trim of the boat. His spirits rose.

Honda pushed against the stone landing with an oar and manoeuvred the boat out into the water. As the prow shivered the brilliant scarlet surface of the water, the smooth ripples heightened Kiyoaki's sense of liberation. The dark water seemed to speak in a deep, solemn voice. 'My eighteenth autumn, this day, this afternoon, this moment: never to come again,' he thought, 'something already slipping irrevocably away.'

'Shall we take a look at the island?'

'What's the fun in that? There's nothing to see.'

'Don't be a kill-joy. Come on, let's go and look,' Honda urged. His voice sounded deep in his chest as he rowed with a lively vigour that suited his years.

As Kiyoaki stared fixedly down into the pond, he heard the faint sound of the waterfall far away on the other side of the island; he could not see a great deal because of the cloudy water and the red of the maples reflected in it. There were carp swimming down there, he knew, and at the very bottom snapping turtles lurked in the shelter of the rocks. His childhood fears flared for a moment, then died.

The hot sun struck the backs of their close-shaven necks. It was a peaceful, uneventful, glorious Sunday afternoon. Yet Kiyoaki remained convinced that at the bottom of this world, which was like a leather bag filled with water, there was a little hole, and it seemed to him that he could hear time leaking from it, drop by drop.

They reached the island at a spot where a single maple stood among the pines, and climbed the stone steps to the grassy clearing at the top with the three iron cranes. The boys sat down at the feet of the pair that were stretching their necks upward in an eternal, mute cry, then lay back on the grass to stare up at the late autumn sky. The rough grass pricked through the backs of their kimonos, making Kiyoaki rather uncomfortable. It gave Honda, however, the sensation of having to endure an exquisitely refreshing pain that was fragmented and spread out under his back. Out of the corners of their eyes, they could see the two cranes, weathered by wind and rain and soiled by chalky-white bird droppings. The birds' supple, curved necks, stretched against the sky, moved slowly with the rhythm of the shifting clouds.

'It's a beautiful day. In all our lives, we may not have many like this – so perfect,' said Honda, stirred by some premonition.

'Are you talking about happiness?' asked Kiyoaki.

'I don't remember saying anything about happiness.'

'Well, that's all right then. I'd be much too scared to say the things you do. I don't have that kind of courage.'

'I'm convinced that the trouble with you is, you're horribly greedy. Greedy men are apt to seem miserable. Look, what more could you want than a day like this?'

'Something definite. What it might be, I've no idea,' the young man answered wearily, as handsome as he was indecisive. Fond as he was of his friend, there were times when Kiyoaki found Honda's keenly analytic mind and his confident turns of phrase – the very image of youthful promise – a severe trial to his capricious nature.

All at once, he rolled over on his stomach on the grass and raised his head, staring across the water at a spot some distance away, in the direction of the garden that fronted the drawing room of the main house. Stepping-stones set in white sand led from it to the edge of the pond, which was intricately scalloped with small inlets crossed by a network of stone bridges. He had noticed a group of women there.

3

He tapped Honda on the shoulder and pointed in that direction. Honda raised his head and peered across the water until he too spotted the women. And so they stared from their hiding place like two young snipers. His mother went for her daily walk whenever the mood struck her; but her company was not confined to her personal maids today; two guests, one old and one young, were walking just behind her. All except the young girl were wearing kimonos of muted, quiet colours. And although she was in pale blue, the material was richly embroidered. As she crossed the white sand to walk along the water's edge, it shone pale and silky like the sky at daybreak. The women's laughter, carrying on the autumn air, betrayed her uncertain footing on the irregular stepping-stones, but it rang too pure and sounded a little artificial. It always irritated Kiyoaki to hear the women of the household laughing like that, but he was well aware of the effect it had on Honda, who had a glint in his eye like a rooster alerted to the clucking of hens. The brittle stalks of dry autumn grass bent under their chests.

Kiyoaki felt sure that the girl in the pale blue kimono would never laugh that way. In a great flurry of merriment, his mother's maids were leading their mistress and the guests hand-in-hand from the edge of the pond to the hill of maples along a path deliberately complicated by a maze of stone bridges that threaded to and fro across the inlets. Kiyoaki and Honda soon lost sight of them behind the tall grass in which they lay.

'You certainly have a lot of women around your house. We have nothing but men,' said Honda, putting a good face on his interest, which was keen enough to make him get up and move to the other side of the island. Here, from the shelter of the pines, he was able to follow the awkward progress of the women. To the left of him, a hollow in the slope held the first four of the nine waterfalls. The stream then followed the curve of the hill and finally splashed down in front of it into the pool below the red Sado rocks. The women were now making their way below these last falls, testing their footing on the stepping-stones. The maple leaves here were especially beautiful, so thick as to blot out the white ribbon of the falls and stain the water at the edge of the pond a deep scarlet. The maids were leading the young woman in the aquamarine kimono across the stepping-stones, her head bent forward, and even at that distance the white of the nape of her neck was visible to Kiyoaki. It made him think of Princess Kasuga and her creamy white neck, something that was never far from his mind.

After the path crossed below the falls, it levelled out for a time, following the waterline as the shore began to come toward the island. Kiyoaki had followed the women's progress with concentration. But now he caught sight of the profile of the woman in the aquamarine kimono and recognized Satoko. His fantasies were shattered. Why hadn't he recognized her earlier? Probably his whim that the beautiful girl should be a total stranger.

Now that she had destroyed his illusion, there was no point in remaining hidden. Brushing the burrs from his kimono, Kiyoaki got to his feet and parted the lower branches of the pines that had been his cover.

'Hello,' he called.

This sudden cheerfulness took Honda by surprise, and he craned his neck for a better look. Aware that Kiyoaki's high spirits were by now a reflex response to the interruption of his dreams, Honda did not mind his friend seizing the initiative.

'Who is it?'

'Oh, it's Satoko. Did I never show you her picture?' answered Kiyoaki, speaking her name with cool indifference. Satoko, the girl on the shore, was certainly a beauty. Kiyoaki, however, seemed determined to ignore this. For he knew that Satoko was in love with him.

This instinctive rejection of anyone who showed him affection, this need to react with cold disdain, were a failing of Kiyoaki's that no one could have known better than Honda, who saw this pride as a kind of tumour that had taken hold of Kiyoaki when he was no more than thirteen and had first had to endure people making a fuss over his looks. Like a silvery bloom of mould, it would spread at the slightest touch.

Perhaps, in fact, the dangerous attraction that Kiyoaki's friendship held for Honda was rooted in the same impulse. So many others had attempted to befriend Kiyoaki, only to be rewarded for their pains with his mockery and contempt. In challenging Kiyoaki's caustic reserve, Honda alone had been skilled enough to escape disaster. Perhaps he was mistaken, but he wondered if his own acute dislike for Kiyoaki's gloom-faced tutor sprang from the latter's expression of perpetual defeat.

Although Honda had never met Satoko, Kiyoaki's stories were full of her. The Ayakura family, one of twenty-eight among the nobility that bore the lofty rank of Urin, was descended from an ancestor named Namba Yorisuke, a skilled player of *kemari*, the version of football popular at the Imperial Court in the time of the Fujiwaras. The head of the family was appointed a chamberlain of the Imperial Court when it established residence in Tokyo at the time of the Meiji Restoration. The Ayakuras moved to the city and lived in a mansion in Azabu formerly occupied by one of the retainers of the shogun. The family excelled in the sport of *kemari* and in composing *waka*. And since the Emperor had seen fit to honour the family's young heir with a court rank of 'fifth degree, junior grade', even the post of Grand Councillor of State now seemed within reach.

Marquis Matsugae, who was conscious of his own family's lack of polish and who hoped to give the next generation at least a touch of elegance, had entrusted the infant Kiyoaki to the Ayakuras after obtaining his own father's consent. And so Kiyoaki had been raised in the atmosphere of the court nobility with Satoko, who was two years older and lavished affection on him; until he went to school, she was his only companion and friend. Count Ayakura himself, a warm and personable man who still retained his soft Kyoto accent, taught the young Kiyoaki calligraphy and *waka*. The family would play *sugoroku*, an ancient form of backgammon, far into the night, as was the custom in the Heian era, and the lucky winners would receive traditional prizes, among them candies moulded like gifts from the Empress.

Moreover, Count Ayakura arranged for Kiyoaki to continue his early cultural training by going to the palace each New Year to attend the Imperial Poetry Reading Ceremony, in which he himself figured prominently. At first, Kiyoaki had seen this as a chore, but as he grew older, his participation in these elegant and ancient rituals came to hold a certain charm for him.

Satoko was now twenty. And thumbing through Kiyoaki's picture album, one could see the changes as she grew to maturity, from when she was a child with her cheek pressed affectionately to Kiyoaki's until the previous May, when she had taken part in the Matsugae Omiyasama festival. At twenty she had passed the stage that was popularly supposed to mark a girl's greatest beauty, but she was still unmarried.

'So that's Satoko. And the other one, the woman in the grey tunic everyone's making such a fuss over, who's she?'

'Her? Oh yes; that's Satoko's great-aunt, the Abbess of Gesshu. I didn't recognize her at first because of that curious hood.'

Her Reverence the Abbess was indeed an unexpected guest. This was her first visit to the Matsugaes, hence the conducted tour of the garden – something that Kiyoaki's mother would not have undertaken just for Satoko but was quite happy to do for the Abbess. Her great-aunt's visit to Tokyo being such a rarity, Satoko had no doubt brought her to see the maple leaves. The Abbess had taken great delight in Kiyoaki when he first came to the Ayakuras, but he could not remember that far back. Later, when he was in middle school and the Abbess had paid a visit to Tokyo, he had been invited to the Ayakuras, but he had had the opportunity to do no more than pay his respects. Even so, the Abbess's pale face with its air of quiet dignity and the calm authority in her voice had made a lasting impression on him.

Kiyoaki's voice had brought the group on the shore to an abrupt halt. Startled, they looked toward the island as if pirates had risen before their very eyes from the tall grass beside the decorative iron cranes.

Pulling a small fan from her obi, Kiyoaki's mother pointed toward the Abbess to indicate that a respectful greeting was expected. Kiyoaki, accordingly, made a deep bow from where he stood on the island. Honda quickly followed suit, and Her Reverence acknowledged them both. His mother then opened her fan and waved it imperiously, its golden sheen suddenly giving off scarlet reflections. Kiyoaki urged Honda to hurry up, knowing that they must come back from the island at once.

'Satoko never misses a chance to come here. She's taking advantage of her great-aunt,' grumbled Kiyoaki with a show of bad temper, while helping Honda by hurrying to cast off the boat. Honda, however, viewed Kiyoaki's haste and his grumbling with some scepticism. The way Kiyoaki had lost patience with Honda's steady, methodical movements and had seized the rough rope in his own unseasoned white hands to try to help with the unpleasant task of unknotting it was enough to raise doubts about the Abbess being the cause of his eagerness.

As Honda rowed back to the shore, Kiyoaki looked dizzy, his face picking up a red flush from the reflection of the maple leaves floating on the water. He nervously avoided Honda's eyes in an attempt to deny his vulnerability to Satoko. For each moment brought him closer to the young woman who knew altogether too much about him, about his childhood, even about his body's most intimate details, and to whom he seemed tied by almost overwhelming bonds of emotion.

'Why, Mr Honda! What a good oarsman you are!' said Kiyoaki's mother admiringly when they reached the shore. Her pale, classic face had a persistently melancholy cast, even when she laughed. Yet her expression was a façade rather than a true indication of her deeper emotions. She was in fact almost invariably insensitive. She had raised Kiyoaki to tolerate his father's dissipation and boorish energy, but she was quite incapable of grasping the complexities of her son's nature.

Satoko's eyes were riveted on Kiyoaki from the moment he stepped out of the boat. Strong and calm, affectionate from time to time, they invariably unnerved Kiyoaki. He felt, not without reason, that he could read criticism in their glance.

'Her Reverence has honoured us with a visit today, and we shall shortly have the pleasure of listening to her speak. But first we wanted to show her the maple leaves. Then you gave us such a fright by that rude shout of yours. What were you doing on the island in the first place?'

'Oh, just watching the sky,' Kiyoaki replied, being as enigmatic to his mother as possible.

'Watching the sky? And what's there to see in the sky?'

His mother was quite unembarrassed about her failure to grasp the intangible, which struck him as her sole admirable characteristic. He found it comical that she could adopt such a pious expression for the Abbess's sermons. The Abbess maintained her role of guest throughout this exchange, smiling unassumingly. And he would not look at Satoko, who gazed steadily at the thick, glossy, tousled black hair that brushed his smooth cheeks.

The group now started up the steep path, admiring the maples as they went and amusing themselves by trying to identify the birds singing in the branches above their heads. However much the two young men tried to check their stride, they inevitably drew ahead to walk some distance in front of the women around the Abbess. Honda took advantage of this to discuss Satoko for the first time, and admire her beauty.

'You think so?' Kiyoaki replied, well aware that although Honda's finding Satoko unattractive would have been a severe blow to his pride, he must make a show of cold indifference. He was firmly convinced that any young woman in Satoko's relationship to him would have to be beautiful, whether he chose to acknowledge her or not.

At last their climb ended at the bridge below the topmost waterfall, and they stood looking up toward its rim. Just as his mother was savouring the compliments of the Abbess, whose first view of the falls this was, Kiyoaki made an ominous discovery which cut across the mood of the day.

'What's that? At the top there, what's damming the water like that?'

His mother responded at once. Using her fan to shade her eyes from the bright sunlight that shone through the branches, she peered upward. The landscape artist had painstakingly built up walls of rock on either side of the rim to ensure a graceful fall of water, and could never have intended the flow to be diverted so awkwardly at the middle of the crest. A mere rock wedged up there could never have caused such a disruption in the flow.

'I wonder what can be the matter. Something seems to have lodged itself up there,' his mother said to the Abbess, openly puzzled.

The Abbess, though she seemed to be aware that something was wrong, said nothing and smiled as before. If anyone was to speak out clearly, regardless of the effect, it would have to be Kiyoaki. But he held back, fearing the impact of his words on the happy mood of the group. He realized that everyone must have recognized what it was by now.

'Isn't it a black dog? With its head hanging down?' said Satoko quite plainly. And the ladies gasped as if they were noticing the dog for the first time.

Kiyoaki's pride was hurt. Satoko, with a boldness that might be construed as unfeminine, had pointed out the dog's corpse, ignoring its ominous implications. She had adopted a suitably pleasant and straightforward tone of voice, which bore witness to her elegant upbringing; she had the freshness of ripe fruit in a crystal bowl. Kiyoaki was ashamed of his hesitation, and felt cowed by Satoko's capacity for directness.

His mother issued some quick orders to the maids, who left at once to look for the negligent gardeners. But her profuse apologies to the Abbess for such an unseemly spectacle were cut short by Her Reverence, who made a compassionate proposal that was totally unexpected.

'My presence here would seem to be providential. If you will bury the dog under a mound, I'll offer a prayer for it.'

The dog had probably been mortally sick or wounded when it came to the stream to drink, and had fallen in. The force of the current had wedged its corpse into the cleft of rocks at the top of the falls. Satoko's courage had excited Honda's admiration, but at the same time he felt oppressed by the sight of the dog hanging dead in the falls under a bright sky only faintly flecked with cloud. The dog's black fur glistened in the clear spray, its white teeth shining in the gaping, dark red, cavernous jaws.

Everyone adjusted quickly to the shift in attention from the red maple leaves to the dog's burial. And the maids in attendance suddenly livened up, becoming almost frivolous. They had all crossed the bridge and were resting in the arbour designed as a vantage point from which to view the falls when the gardener came rushing up, babbling every cliché of apology in his repertoire. Only then did he climb the steep, treacherous rock face to remove the dripping black body and bury it in a suitable spot.

'I'm going to pick some flowers. Kiyo, won't you help?' asked Satoko, effectively ruling out any assistance from the maids.

'What kind of flowers would one pick for a dog?' Kiyoaki countered, his obvious reluctance drawing a burst of laughter from the women.

Meanwhile the Abbess removed her drab tunic to reveal the purple habit beneath and the small stole that hung around her neck. She had a presence that radiated grace to those around her, her brightness dissipating the atmosphere of ill-omen.

'Goodness, the dog is blessed to have Your Reverence offering a requiem for it. Surely it will be reborn as a human being,' said Kiyoaki's mother with a smile.

Satoko did not bother to wait for Kiyoaki, but started up the hill path, stooping now and then to pick a late-flowering gentian that she had spotted. Kiyoaki found nothing better than a few withered camomiles.

Each time she bent to pick a flower, Satoko's aquamarine kimono was an inadequate disguise for the roundness of her hips, surprisingly generous on such a slim figure. All at once Kiyoaki felt unsettled, his mind a remote lake of clear water suddenly clouded by a disturbance deep below its surface.

After picking the gentians necessary to complete her bouquet, Satoko suddenly straightened up and stopped abruptly in Kiyoaki's path, while he did his best to look elsewhere. Her finely shaped nose and huge bright eyes, which he had never yet dared to look into directly, now confronted his vision at uncomfortably close range, a threatening phantom.

'Kiyo, what would you do if all of a sudden I weren't here any more?' Satoko asked, her words coming in a rushed whisper.

4

This was a long-standing trick of Satoko's for disconcerting people. Perhaps she achieved her effects without conscious effort, but she never allowed the slightest hint of mischief into her tone to put her victim at ease. Her voice would be heavy with pathos at such times, as though confiding the gravest of secrets.

Although he should have been inured to this by now, Kiyoaki could not help asking: 'Not here any more? Why?'

Despite all his efforts to indicate a studied disinterest, Kiyoaki's reply betrayed his uneasiness. It was what Satoko wanted.

'I can't tell you why,' she answered, deftly dropping ink into the clear waters of Kiyoaki's heart. She gave him no time to erect his defences.

He glared at her. It had always been like this. Which was why he hated her. Without the slightest warning she could plunge him into nameless anxieties. And the drop of ink spread, dull and grey, clouding everything in his heart that had been pellucid only a moment ago.

Satoko was still watching him intently, and her eyes, which had been sad, suddenly twinkled.

On their return, Kiyoaki's bad temper surprised everyone and gave the women of the Matsugae household something to gossip about.

Kiyoaki was so capricious that he tended to exacerbate the very worries that gnawed at him. Had it been applied to love affairs, his stubborn persistence would have been that of almost any young man. But in his case it was different. Perhaps this was why Satoko deliberately sowed the seeds of dark and thorny flowers, rather than brightly coloured ones, knowing what an unhealthy fascination they held for Kiyoaki. Indeed he had always been fertile ground for such seeds. He indulged himself, to the exclusion of all else, in the cultivation of his anxiety.

Satoko had caught his interest. Although a willing prisoner of his discontent, he was still angry with Satoko, who always had a ready supply of fresh ambiguities and riddles to disconcert him. And he was also angered by his own indecision when faced with finding a solution to her teasing.

When he and Honda had been resting in the grass on the island, he had indeed said that he was looking for 'something absolutely definite'. What it was he didn't know, but whenever this bright certainty seemed to shine within his grasp, the fluttering sleeves of Satoko's aquamarine kimono interposed themselves, trapping him once again in the quicksands of indecision. Though he had sensed something definite, a flash of intuition, distant, unattainable, he chose to believe that Satoko was the barrier that prevented him from taking a single step toward it.

It was even more galling to have to admit that his very pride, by definition, cut him off from all possible means of dealing with Satoko's riddles and the anxiety they provoked. If, for example, he were now to ask someone: 'What does Satoko mean about not being here any more?' it would only betray the depth of his interest in her. 'What could I do,' he thought. 'No matter what I did to convince them I wasn't interested in Satoko but only in an abstract anxiety of my own, nobody would believe me.' A multitude of such thoughts raced through his head.

Ordinarily a bore, school under these circumstances offered Kiyoaki some relief. He always spent his lunch hours with Honda, even though Honda's conversation had taken a somewhat tedious turn of late. On the day of the Abbess's visit, Honda had accompanied the others to the main house. And there Her Reverence had addressed them with a sermon that had completely seized his imagination. Now he couldn't wait to assault Kiyoaki's inattentive ears with his own exegesis of each point.

It was curious that while the sermon had left the dreamy Kiyoaki quite indifferent, it struck rationalistic Honda with the force of cogency.

The Gesshu Temple on the outskirts of Nara was a convent, quite a rarity in Hosso Buddhism. The gist of the sermon had strongly appealed to Honda, and the Abbess had been careful to introduce her listeners to the doctrine of Yuishiki* by using examples of no sophistication at all.

'Then there was the parable that Her Reverence said came to her when she saw the dog's body hanging over the falls,' said Honda, thoroughly caught up in

*The fundamental doctrine of Hosso Buddhism: all existence is based on subjective awareness.

himself. 'I don't think there's any doubt whatever that her use of it shows how fond she is of your family. And then her way of telling it – court phrases blending with old-fashioned Kyoto dialect. It's an elusive language that is filled with all sorts of subtle nuances. It certainly did a great deal to heighten the impact.

'You remember that the story is set in Tang China. A man named Yuan Hsaio was on his way to the famous Mount Kaoyu to study the teachings of Buddha. When night fell, he happened to be beside a cemetery, so he lay down to sleep among the burial mounds. Then in the middle of the night he awoke with a terrible thirst. Stretching out his hand, he scooped up some water from a hole by his side. As he dozed off again, he thought to himself that never had water tasted so pure, so fresh and cold. But when morning came, he saw what he had drunk from in the dark. Incredible though it seemed, what had tasted so delicious was water that had collected in a human skull. He retched and was sick. Yet this experience taught something to Yuan Hsaio. He realized that as long as conscious desire is at work, it will permit distinctions to exist. But if one can suppress it, these distinctions dissolve and one can be as content with a skull as with anything else.

'But what interests me is this: once Yuan Hsaio had been thus enlightened, could he drink that water again, secure in the knowledge that it was pure and delicious? And don't you think that the same would hold true for chastity? If a boy is naïve, of course, he can worship a prostitute in all innocence. But once he realizes that his woman is a slut, and that he has been living an illusion that merely serves to reflect the image of his own purity, will he be able to love this woman in the same way again? If he can, don't you think that would be marvellous? To take your own ideal and bend the world to it like that. Wouldn't that be a remarkable force? It would be like holding the secret key to life right there in your hand, wouldn't it?'

Honda's sexual innocence was matched by Kiyoaki's, who was therefore unable to refute his strange ideal. Nevertheless, being headstrong, he felt that he was different from Honda, that he already had the key to existence within his grasp as a sort of birthright. He did not know what gave him this confidence. Ominously handsome and a dreamer, so arrogant yet so much a prey to anxiety, he was certain that somehow he was the youthful repository of a peerless treasure. Because at times he seemed to wear a quite physical radiance, he bore himself with the pride of a man marked down by a rare disease, even though he suffered neither aches nor painful swellings.

Kiyoaki knew nothing about the history of Gesshu Temple and saw no need to remedy this lack. Honda by contrast, who had no personal ties with it at all, had taken the trouble to do some research in the library. Gesshu, he discovered, was a comparatively new temple, built at the beginning of the eighteenth century. A daughter of the Emperor Higashiyama, wishing to observe a period of mourning for her father, who had died in the prime of life, devoted herself to the worship of Kannon, the Goddess of Mercy, at the Kiomizu Temple. She soon came to be deeply impressed by the commentaries of an old priest from the Joju Temple on the Hosso concept of existence, and consequently she became a fervent convert to this sect. After her ritual tonsuring, she declined to accept one of the benefices reserved for imperial princesses, deciding instead to found a new temple, one whose nuns would devote themselves to study of the scriptures. And it still preserved its unique place as a convent of the Hosso sect. Satoko's great-aunt, however, though an aristocrat, had the distinction of being the first abbess who was not an imperial princess.

Honda suddenly turned on Kiyoaki.

'Matsugae! What's the matter with you these days? You haven't paid the slightest attention to anything I've said, have you?'

'Nothing's the matter,' Kiyoaki replied defensively, for once caught off guard. His beautiful clear eyes looked back at his friend. If Honda thought him insolent, it did not bother Kiyoaki in the least. What he feared was that his friend should become aware of his agony of mind. He knew that if he gave Honda the least encouragement in this direction, there would soon be nothing at all about him that Honda did not know. As this would be an unforgivable violation, he would have lost his only friend.

Honda was immediately alert to Kiyoaki's tension. He knew that to retain Kiyoaki's affection he must check the unthinking roughness that friendship ordinarily permitted. He had to treat him as warily as one would a freshly painted wall, on which the slightest careless touch would leave an indelible fingerprint. Should the circumstances demand it, he would have to go so far as to pretend not to notice Kiyoaki's mortal agony. Especially if such assumed obtuseness served to point up the elegance that would surely characterize Kiyoaki's ultimate suffering.

At such moments, Honda could even love Kiyoaki for the look of mute appeal in his eyes. Their beautiful gaze seemed to hold a plea: leave things as they are, as gloriously undefined as the line of the seashore. For the first time in their relationship – a protracted, warily transacted negotiation in the coin of friendship – Kiyoaki's composure was about to shatter; he was pleading. Honda was thus transformed into an aesthetic observer. Those who considered Kiyoaki and Honda to be friends were not mistaken, for as it stood, their relationship gave to each of them exactly what he desired.

5

One evening about ten days later, Marquis Matsugae happened to return home unusually early and so Kiyoaki had dinner with both his parents, something that happened very rarely. Since the Marquis was fond of Western food, dinner was served in the small dining room of the Western-style house, and he himself had gone down to the wine cellar to choose the wine. He had taken Kiyoaki with him and had gone to great lengths to expound on the characteristics of the various wines cradled in the shelves that filled the cellar. His father had gone on to explain what wine went with which foods, what wine should be served only on the occasion of the visit of a member of the Imperial Family, and so on, beaming all the while.

The Marquis never seemed as happy as when dispensing useless knowledge of this kind.

While they were sipping their aperitifs, his mother, who had been driven to Yokohama two days before by her young coachman, described the shopping expedition as if it were an event of great significance.

'I was simply astounded at the way people stared at my Western clothes, and in Yokohama of all places! Some dirty little children actually ran after the carriage shouting, "Foreign lady! Foreign lady!"'

His father ventured something to the effect that he was thinking of taking Kiyoaki with him to the launching of the warship *Hie*, but he spoke as though it were a foregone conclusion that his son would not be interested.

At this point, both parents were at a loss for viable topics of conversation and began to flounder, their discomfiture evident even to Kiyoaki. Somehow, however, they finally happened upon the congenial subject of Kiyoaki's Otachimachi, the divination ritual that had taken place three years before when he was fifteen.

This ancient ceremony fell on the seventeenth of August according to the lunar calendar. A large wooden basin filled with water was placed in the garden to catch the reflection of the moon, and appropriate offerings were made. If the sky was overcast on this August night of his fifteenth year, bad fortune was expected to dog the boy who stood before the basin, for the rest of his life.

As his parents talked, the scene came back to Kiyoaki vividly. Flanked by his parents and dressed in his *hakama*, a divided skirt, and kimono blazoned with the family crest, he had stood in the middle of the dew-drenched lawn, the new basin filled with water before him, and a chorus of chirping insects ringing in his ears.

The trees that encircled the now-darkened garden, the tiled roofs of the mansion itself beyond, even the maple hill – the reflection of all this, and more, had been fixed in jagged outline, compressed into the circle of water that was defined by the rim of the basin. That rim of blond cyprus wood had become a frontier where this world ended and another began. Since this ceremony during his fifteenth year was to determine his lifetime fortune, Kiyoaki felt as though his very soul, naked, had been set there on the wet grass. The wooden sides of the basin expressed his outer self; the disc of water, which they in turn defined, expressed his inner.

Everyone was silent, so the sounds of insects throughout the garden filled his ears as never before. He gazed earnestly into the basin. The water within was dark at first, shadowed by clouds as thick as clustered seaweed. A moment later the seaweed seemed to wave and he thought he had seen a faint glow suffuse the water, but then it faded. He could not remember how long he had waited after that. Then all of a sudden the black water in the basin, which had seemed impenetrably obscure, cleared, and there directly in its centre shone a tiny image of the full moon.

Everyone broke into exclamations of pleasure, and his mother, rigid all this time, was greatly relieved and began to wave her fan to drive away the mosquitos swarming around her skirt.

'Oh, I'm so glad! Now the boy will have a fortunate life, won't he?' she said.

Then Kiyoaki was congratulated by everyone present.

But still he felt a certain dread. He could not bring himself to look up into the sky at the moon itself, the origin of the image in the water. Rather he kept looking down into the basin and into the water contained by its curved sides, the reflection of his innermost self, into which the moon, like a golden shell, had sunk so deep. For at that moment he had captured the celestial. It sparkled like a golden butterfly trapped in the meshes of his soul.

Yet, he thought, were these meshes fine enough to hold it? Once caught, would the butterfly not slip out soon and fly away? Even at fifteen he feared its loss. His character was already formed, and each of his triumphs would bring this fear in its wake. Having gained the moon, how much then would he dread life in a world without it. The oppression of such fear! Even if this moon aroused nothing but hatred in him.

For even in the triviality of a single playing card missing from a deck, the world's order is inevitably turned awry. And for someone like Kiyoaki, the smallest incongruity took on the proportions of a watch deprived of one cogwheel. The order of his universe collapsed and he found himself trapped in terrifying darkness. The lost playing card, of no value in itself, would, in his eyes, assume the significance of a crown over which rival claimants were locked in a struggle that would plunge the world into crisis. His sensibility was thus at the mercy of every unforeseen occurrence, however trivial, and he had no defences at hand.

As he thought back to his Otachimachi, that night of August 17 three years before, he suddenly shuddered with the realization that Satoko had somehow impinged on his thoughts.

At that moment, to Kiyoaki's relief, the butler entered in his cool *hakama* with a rustle of Sendai silk to announce that dinner was ready. Kiyoaki and his parents went into the dining room, each to sit in front of a place set with fine English china decorated with the family crest. Since early childhood Kiyoaki had had to endure the tedium of his father's lessons in Western table manners. As it was, his mother had never become accustomed to the Western way of eating and his father still behaved with the ostentation of a man eager to seem at home abroad, so he was the only one who ate naturally and at ease.

When the soup course arrived, his mother lost no time in raising a new topic in her calm voice.

'Really, Satoko can be very trying. Only this morning I discovered that the Ayakuras sent a messenger with her refusal. And for a time she gave everyone the distinct impression that she had decided to accept.'

'She's twenty already, isn't she?' his father replied. 'If she continues to be so demanding, she may find herself left an old maid. I've been worried about her myself, but what can one do?'

Kiyoaki was all ears as his father went on casually: 'I wonder what's the matter with her? Or did they think he was too much beneath her? No matter how noble a family the Ayakuras once were, their present fortunes hardly allow them to turn down a young man like that, with a bright future ahead of him in the Ministry of the Interior. They should have been glad of him, shouldn't they, without bothering about what kind of family he came from?'

'That's exactly how I feel. And that's why I'm disinclined to do anything more to help her.'

'Well now, we owe them a great deal because of what they did for Kiyoaki. I feel obliged to do all I can to help them build up their family fortunes again. But what could we do to find a suitor whom she'd accept?'

'I wonder if such a man exists?'

As he listened, Kiyoaki's spirits rose. His riddle was solved. 'Kiyo, what would you do if suddenly I weren't here any more?' Satoko had asked. She had simply been referring to the offer of marriage then pending. At the time she had been inclined to accept but had dropped her hint out of concern for Kiyoaki's reaction. Now, ten days later, it would appear from his mother that she had formally refused. And her reason for doing this was clear to him. She had done so because she was in love with Kiyoaki.

And with that the clouds faded from his horizon. He was no longer beset by anxieties. The water in the glass was clear once again. For ten days he had been excluded from the small, peaceful sanctuary that was his only refuge. But now he could return to it and breathe easy.

Kiyoaki was enjoying a rare moment of acute happiness, a happiness that without question sprang from his regaining his clarity of vision. The card that had been deliberately concealed had reappeared in his hand. The deck was complete. And so once more it became a mere pack of cards. His happiness shone clear and unmarred. For a moment at least, Kiyoaki had succeeded in breaking the grip of his emotions.

The Marquis and Marquise Matsugae, however, were still looking at one another across the table, their insensitivity blinding them even to something as obvious as their son's sudden rush of happiness. The Marquis confronted the classic melancholy of his wife's face, and she, in turn, the coarseness of his. Features proper to a man of action had become blurred by the ravages of indolent living that spread beneath his skin.

Despite the seemingly erratic course charted in his parents' conversation, Kiyoaki had always been aware of adherence to a definite ritual; it was as set as the Shinto ceremony of offering the gods a branch of the sacred sakaki tree, a ceremony in which each syllable of the incantation is meticulously pronounced and each lustrous branch carefully selected.

Kiyoaki had observed the ritual countless times since early childhood. No burning crises. No storms of passion. His mother knew exactly what was coming next. The Marquis knew that his wife knew. Their expressions blank, innocent of foreknowledge, they glided downstream like twigs hand in hand on clear waters mirroring blue sky and clouds, to take the inevitable plunge over the crest of the falls.

Just as predictably, the Marquis left his after-dinner coffee unfinished and turned to his son, 'Now, Kiyoaki, what do you say to a game of billiards?'

'Well, then, please excuse me,' said the Marquise.

Kiyoaki was so happy tonight, however, that this kind of charade did not grate on him in the least. His mother returned to the main house and he went with his father into the billiard room. With its English-style oak panelling, its portrait of Kiyoaki's grandfather, and its large map done in oils depicting the naval battles of the Russo-Japanese War, this room was much admired by visitors. One of the disciples of Sir John Millais, famous for his portrait of Gladstone, had done the huge likeness of Kiyoaki's grandfather during his stay in Japan. And now his grandfather's figure loomed in ceremonial attire from the shadows.

The composition was simple, but the artist had evinced a high degree of skill in his judicious blending of idealization and realistic sternness to achieve a likeness that expressed not only the indomitable air expected of a Restoration peer but also those more personal traits dear to his family, down to the warts on his cheek. According to household custom, whenever a new maid came from the ancestral province of Kagoshima, she was taken before the portrait to pay reverence. Some hours before his grandfather's death, though the billiard room was empty and it was unlikely that the picture cord could have become so worn, the portrait fell to the floor with a crash that echoed throughout the house.

The room contained three billiard tables covered with layers of Italian marble. Though the three-ball game had been introduced at the time of the war with China, no one ever played it in the Matsugae billiard room; Kiyoaki and his father used four. The butler had already placed the red and white balls on the table in proper order and now he handed a cue to both the Marquis and his son. Kiyoaki looked down at the surface of the table as he rubbed the tip of his cue with the Italian chalk of compressed volcanic ash. The red and white ivory balls lay motionless on the green baize, each casting a round shadow like a shellfish making a hesitant foray into the open. They stirred not the slightest interest in him. He had the sensation of standing alone on an unknown street at the height of the day and suddenly finding himself face to face with these odd shapes devoid of all meaning.

The Marquis was always made uneasy by the boredom on his son's handsome face. Happy as Kiyoaki felt tonight, his eyes remained dull. 'Did you know,' said his father, hitting on a subject of conversation, 'that two Siamese princes are coming to Japan to Peers School?'

'No.'

'Since they'll be in your class, we might have them staying here with us for a few days. I've mentioned it at the Foreign Ministry. It's a country that's made great strides recently. They've abolished slavery and they're building railroads and so on. Be sure to keep that in mind when you deal with them.'

His father lined up his shot. Kiyoaki stood behind him and watched him crouch like a fat leopard twisting his cue with a show of fierceness. Kiyoaki could not suppress a sudden smile. His sense of happiness and the image of a mysterious tropic land fused in his mind with a soft click as appealing to him as the contact of the red and white ivory balls on the table. And then his elation, which had been as abstract as pure crystal, suddenly took on the green extravagance of the tropical jungle.

The Marquis was an expert at billiards, and Kiyoaki was never a match for him. After each had taken the first five shots, his father turned abruptly from the table with the suggestion Kiyoaki had long been expecting. 'I think I'll take a little stroll. What would you say to that?'

Kiyoaki did not answer. His father then made a totally unexpected proposal: 'You can come just as far as the gate, can't you? The way you used to when you were a child.'

Startled, Kiyoaki turned dark, flashing eyes on his father. In any event, the Marquis had scored a point over his son for surprise.

His father's mistress was installed in one of the houses just outside the gate. European families rented the other two. Each house had its own back gate in the fence that separated it from the Matsugae estate. The European children were free to make use of this opportunity and played every day in the grounds of the estate. The only gate with a lock on it – and this was covered with rust – was the gate behind his mistress's house.

From the front door of the main house to the front gate was half a mile. When Kiyoaki was a child, his father would take him by the hand and walk with him as far as the gate en route to his mistress's. There they would separate, and a servant would bring Kiyoaki back.

When his father went out on business, he invariably used the carriage. When he left the house on foot, therefore, his destination was obvious to everyone. Accompanying his father on these occasions had always been painful for Kiyoaki. While some naïve instinct of boyhood urged him to hold his father back for his mother's sake, the realization of his own helplessness stirred bitter frustration in him. His mother of course was not at all pleased at Kiyoaki's accompanying her husband on these evening strolls. But the more she resented it, the more her husband persisted in taking Kiyoaki by the hand. Kiyoaki had been quick to detect his father's covert desire to make him an accomplice in his mother's betrayal.

This walk, however, on a cold November night, was something quite new. As his father put on the overcoat proffered by the butler, Kiyoaki left the billiard room to fetch the uniform coat with metal buttons that he wore at school. As always, the butler was waiting at the door with the usual present wrapped in purple crepe; then he followed his master at the customary distance of ten paces.

The moon was bright, and the wind moaned through the branches of the trees. Although his father did not trouble to glance back at the wraithlike figure of Yamada the steward, Kiyoaki was concerned enough to look over his shoulder more than once. Without so much as a cape over his *hakama*, Yamada came along behind, swaying slightly on his unsteady legs, his hands, white-gloved as always, cradling the package in its purple wrapper. His glasses had a frosty sparkle in the moonlight. Kiyoaki wondered at this man, loyal beyond a doubt, allowing almost nothing to pass his lips. How many passions lay spent within his body like a tangle of rusted springs? Far more than the jovial, extrovert Marquis, his reserved and seemingly indifferent son was capable of detecting depth of feeling in others.

The hooting of the owls and the wind in the trees reminded Kiyoaki, still wine-flushed, of the branches blowing in the photograph of the memorial service. As they walked through the bleak, wintry night, his father was anticipating the moist warmth and intimacy of the rosy flesh that awaited him, while his son's thoughts turned toward death.

As the Marquis went along elated by the wine and scattering pebbles with the tip of his walking stick, he suddenly turned to Kiyoaki: 'You're not much of one for having a good time, are you? I couldn't tell you how many women I'd had at your age. Look here, suppose I take you with me next time? I'll see that there are plenty of geishas there and for once you can kick up your heels. And bring along some friends of yours from school if you want.'

'No, thank you.'

Kiyoaki shuddered as he blurted this out. He felt his feet suddenly glued to the ground. At this one remark of his father's, his elation shattered, like a vase striking the floor.

'What's the matter?'

'Please will you excuse me? Good night.'

Kiyoaki turned on his heel and walked rapidly back past the dimly lit entrance of the Western house in the direction of the main residence whose distant lights, burning at the front door, gleamed faintly through the trees.

Kiyoaki was unable to sleep that night. But it was no thought of his mother or his father that troubled him. On the contrary, he was absorbed in revenging himself on Satoko. 'She has been cruel enough to lure me into a petty trap. For ten days she let me suffer. She had just one thing in mind: to keep me in agony. I can't let her get away with it. But then I'm no match for her when it comes to inventing ways of torturing people. What can I do? What would be best would be to convince her that I have no more respect for female dignity than my father has. If only I could say or write something absolutely outrageous to her that would strike home. But my trouble is that I'm always at a disadvantage since I'm not bold enough to let people know bluntly how I really feel. It wouldn't be enough to tell her that she doesn't interest me in the least. That would still leave her plenty of room to scheme. I have to insult her. I have to humiliate her so completely that she'll never come back for more. That's what I have to do. For the first time in her life, I'm going to make her sorry for what she's done.'

Despite all this, Kiyoaki's resolutions were feeble. No specific plan had yet occurred to him.

A pair of threefold screens stood on either side of his bed, each decorated with poems of Han Shan. At the foot of the bed, a carved jade parrot looked down from its perch on a sandalwood display shelf. Kiyoaki had little interest in anything as currently fashionable as a Rodin or a Cézanne. His tastes were rather conservative. Sleepless, he stared at the parrot. Every detail of its clouded green jade, even down to the fine carving of the wing feathers, seemed to glow more clearly. Thus the figure of the bird appeared to hover, disembodied, in the dark, a phantom image that made Kiyoaki uneasy. Realizing that the phenomenon was caused by a stray shaft of moonlight coming in through the window, he pulled the curtain all the way open in an abrupt movement. The moon was high in the sky, and its light spilled over the bed.

It was dazzling enough to suggest frivolity rather than solemnity. He thought of the cold gleaming silk of Satoko's kimono. With unearthly clarity he saw her eyes there in the moon, those splendid large eyes which he had seen so disconcertingly close to his own. The wind had died.

The burning heat of Kiyoaki's body could not be explained by the mere warmth of the room, and something like fever seemed to tingle in his earlobes. He threw off the blanket and opened the collar of his nightgown. The fire still burned and seethed under his skin, and he felt that he would find no relief until he took off his nightgown and bared his body to the cold moonlight. Finally, wearied by his thoughts, he rolled over on his stomach and lay with his face buried in his pillow, his naked back to the moon and the hot blood still throbbing in his temples.

And so he lay, the moonlight washing over the incomparable smooth white of his back, its brilliance highlighting the graceful lines of his body to reveal the subtle but pervasive hint of firm masculinity that made it clear that this was the flesh not of a woman but of a still immature young man.

The moon shone with dazzling brightness on Kiyoaki's left side, where the pale flesh pulsed softly in rhythm with his heartbeat. Here there were three small, almost invisible moles. And much as the three stars in Orion's belt fade in strong moonlight, so too these three small moles were almost blotted out by its rays.

6

In 1910, His Highness King Rahma VI had succeeded his late father, Rahma V, to the throne of Siam. One of the princes now coming to study in Japan was his younger brother, Prince Pattanadid, whose titular name was Praong Chao. His companion, eighteen like himself and also his best friend, was his cousin Prince Kridsada, a grandson of King Rahma IV, whose titular name was Mon Chao. Prince Pattanadid nicknamed him 'Kri'. But Prince Kridsada, in deference to Pattanadid's place in the succession, addressed him more respectfully as 'Chao P.'.

Both princes were fervently devout Buddhists. But they not only dressed for the most part like young English gentlemen, they also spoke the language with perfect fluency. Indeed it was precisely because the new king had been concerned about their becoming too Westernized that he had decided upon Japan for their university studies. Neither of the princes had raised any objections, despite one unfortunate aspect to it. Leaving Siam entailed the separation of Chao P. and Kri's younger sister.

The love of these two young people for each other was the delight of the court, since their engagement at the end of Chao P.'s studies was a foregone conclusion and their future was secure in every way. Yet when he sailed, Chao P.'s grief was so intense as to give rise to alarm in a country whose customs did not favour such direct expressions of feeling.

The sea voyage and his cousin's sympathy had helped considerably to alleviate the young prince's distress, and when they arrived for a stay at the Matsugaes', Kiyoaki found their swarthy faces alight with happiness.

The princes were free to follow the school routine as they liked until the winter holidays began. Though they were to start attending classes in January, it was decided that they would not be officially enrolled until the new term began in the spring, by which time they would have had the chance to acclimatize and also to study the language intensively.

While they were at the Matsugaes', the princes were to occupy two adjoining guest rooms on the second floor of the Western-style house, which had been equipped with a steamheating system imported from Chicago. The period before dinner with the assembled Matsugae family was awkward for Kiyoaki and his guests, but when the three young men were left to themselves after the meal, stiff formality suddenly eased as the princes began to show Kiyoaki photographs of the golden temples and exotic scenery of Bangkok. Kiyoaki noticed that Prince Kridsada was no younger than his cousin and yet still retained a certain childish capriciousness, but he warmed to Prince Pattanadid in whom he sensed a dreamy nature like his own.

One of the photographs was a general view of the monastery of Wat-Po, famous for its huge sculpture of the reclining Buddha. Since a skilled artist had applied delicate tinting to the photo, it was almost like having the temple itself before one's eyes. Palm trees were blowing gracefully, every detail of their clustered leaves carefully etched in colour against a background of tropical sky whose vivid blue contrasted sharply with the sheer white of the clouds. The monastery buildings were incomparable; they overwhelmed the spectator with a brilliant sunburst of gold, scarlet, and white. Two golden warrior gods stood guard on either side of a scarlet gate outlined in gold. Delicately carved golden bas-relief climbed the temple's white walls and columns to form a kind of frieze at the top. Then there was the roof with its array of pinnacles, each one also covered with intricate bas-relief of gold and scarlet; from the treasure house in their midst, the gleaming spires of the triple tower soared up into the bright blue of the sky.

The princes were delighted with Kiyoaki's look of unfeigned admiration. Then Prince Pattanadid began to speak; there was a distant look in his fine, wide, sloping eyes, whose keen glance contrasted strongly with his soft, round face.

'This temple is special for me. On the voyage here to Japan, I often dreamed about it. Its golden roofs seemed to float up out of the night sea. The ship kept on moving, and even by the time the entire temple was visible, it was still a long way off from me. Having risen from the waves, it glistened under the stars the way the light of the new moon shines across the surface of the water. Standing on the deck of the ship, I put my hands together and bowed in reverence toward it. As happens in dreams, although it was night and the temple was so far away, I could make out the smallest details of the gold and scarlet decoration.

'I told Kri about this dream and said that the temple seemed to be following us to Japan. But he laughed at me and said that what was following me to Japan was not the temple but the memory of something else. He made me angry at the time, but now I'm inclined to agree with him. For everything sacred has the substance of dreams and memories, and so we experience the miracle of what is separated from us by time or distance suddenly being made tangible. Dreams, memories, the sacred – they are all alike in that they are beyond our grasp. Once we are even marginally separated from what we can touch, the object is sanctified; it acquires the beauty of the unattainable, the quality of the miraculous. Everything, really, has this quality of sacredness, but we can desecrate it at a touch. How strange man is! His touch defiles and yet he contains the source of miracles.'

'He certainly puts it in a difficult, roundabout way,' said Prince Kridsada, breaking in, 'but what he's really thinking about is the girl he loves back in Bangkok. Chao P., show Kiyoaki her picture.'

Prince Pattanadid flushed, but his dark skin hid the rush of blood to his cheeks. Seeing his guest's discomfiture, Kiyoaki turned the conversation back to their previous topic.

'Do you often dream like that?' he asked. 'I keep a diary record of my dreams.' Chao P.'s eyes flashed with interest as he replied: 'I wish my Japanese were good enough to let me read it.'

Kiyoaki realized that even though he was having to speak in English, he had just succeeded in conveying to Chao P. his fascination with dreams, something he had never dared reveal even to Honda. He felt himself liking Chao P. more and more. From then on, however, the conversation lagged, and Kiyoaki, noticing the mischievous twinkle in Prince Kridsada's eyes, suddenly realized the difficulty: he had not insisted on seeing the picture, which was what Chao P. had wanted him to do.

'Please show me the photo of the dream that followed you from Siam,' he hastened to ask.

'Do you mean the temple or the girl?' Kridsada interjected, as playful as ever. And although Chao P. scolded him for his frivolous bad manners, he was unrepentant. When his cousin finally took out the photograph, he thrust out his hand eagerly to point.

'Princess Chantrapa is my younger sister. Her name means "moonlight". But we usually call her Ying Chan.'

Looking at the picture, Kiyoaki was rather disappointed to see a much plainer young girl than he had imagined. She wore Western clothes, a dress of white lace. Her hair was tied with a white ribbon and she wore a pearl necklace. She looked modest and unsophisticated. Any student at Peers might well be carrying a picture of a girl like her. The beautiful, waving fall of her hair to her shoulders showed signs of care. But the rather strong brows over wide, timid eyes, the lips slightly parted like the petals of an exotic flower before the rains come – her features all gave the unmistakable impression of girlish innocence unconscious of its own beauty. Of course that had its charm, but much like a young nestling quite oblivious of its power to fly, she was too passively content.

'Compared with this girl,' Kiyoaki thought, 'Satoko is a hundred, a thousand times more of a woman. And isn't that why she is often so hateful to me – because she is so much a woman? Besides, she's far more beautiful than this girl. And she knows how beautiful she is. There's nothing she doesn't know, unfortunately, including how immature I am.'

Chao P., seeing how Kiyoaki was staring at the picture of his sweetheart and perhaps feeling slightly alarmed that he might be too attracted to her, suddenly reached out his fine-boned, amber-skinned hand and retrieved it. As he did so, Kiyoaki's eye was caught by a flash of green, and for the first time he noticed Chao P.'s beautiful ring. Its stone was a rich, square-cut emerald. On either side of it, the fierce beasts' heads of a pair of yaksha, the warrior gods, had been finely etched in gold. All in all, it was an immense ring of such quality that for Kiyoaki to have overlooked it until now was proof of how little he was inclined to take notice of others.

'I was born in May. It's my birthstone,' Prince Pattanadid explained, slightly embarrassed again. 'Ying Chan gave it to me as a farewell present.'

'But if you wore something as magnificent as that at Peers, I'm afraid they'd order you to stop,' warned Kiyoaki.

Taken aback by this, the two princes began to confer earnestly in their native language, but quickly realizing their inadvertent rudeness, they switched back to English for Kiyoaki's sake. Kiyoaki told them that he would speak to his father about making arrangements for them to have a safety deposit at the bank. After this had been settled and the atmosphere had warmed still further, Prince Kridsada brought out a small photograph of his own sweetheart. And then both princes urged Kiyoaki to do the same.

'In Japan we are not accustomed to exchanging pictures,' he said hastily, under the spur of youthful vanity. 'But I'll certainly introduce her to you very soon.' He did not have the courage to show them the pictures of Satoko that filled the album he had kept from early childhood.

It suddenly dawned on Kiyoaki that although his good looks had excited praise and admiration all his life, he had nearly reached the age of eighteen in the gloomy confines of the family estate without a single female friend other than Satoko.

And Satoko was as much an enemy as anything else; she was far from being the ideal of womanhood, sweetness and affection incarnate, that the two princes would admire. Kiyoaki felt his anger rising against the many frustrations that hemmed him in. What his somewhat tipsy father had said to him on that 'evening stroll' – though his tone had been very kind – now seemed in retrospect to contain a veiled scorn.

The very things that his sense of dignity had made him ignore up to now had suddenly gained the power to humiliate him. Everything about these lively young princes from the tropics – their brown skin, the flashing virility in their eyes, their long, slender, amber fingers, already so experienced in caresses – all this seemed to taunt Kiyoaki: 'What? At your age, not even a single love affair?'

Feeling his poise evaporating, Kiyoaki, with his last reserves of aloofness and elegance, hurriedly said, 'I'll introduce her to you very soon.' But how was he to arrange matters? How to show off Satoko's beauty before his foreign friends? For the very day before, after a long hesitation, Kiyoaki had finally sent a wildly insulting letter to Satoko.

Every phrase in that letter, a letter whose premeditated insults he had worked and reworked with the most painstaking care, was still vivid in his mind. He had begun by writing: 'I am very sorry to say that your effrontery toward me compels me to write this letter.' And from that curt opening, he had gone on:

When I think how often you have presented me with these senseless riddles, withholding any clues in order to make them seem more serious than they really are, numbness strikes this hand of mine holding its writing brush until it withers me. I have no doubt that your emotional whims have driven you to do this to me. There has been no gentleness in your method, obviously no affection whatever, not a trace of friendship. There are deep-seated motivations in your despicable behaviour to which you are blind, but which are driving you toward a goal that is only too obvious. But decency forbids me to say anything further.

But all your efforts and schemes have now become a mere froth on the waves. For I, unhappy though I once was, I have now passed one of life's milestones, a transition for which I owe you some debt of gratitude, however indirect. My father invited me to go with him on one of his excursions to the Gay Quarters, and now I've crossed a barrier that every man must cross. To put it bluntly, I spent the night with a geisha my father had chosen for me. Nothing but one of those exercises in pleasure that society sanctions for men.

Fortunately enough a single night was sufficient to bring about a complete change in me. My previous concepts of women were shattered. I learned to see a girl as nothing but a plump, lascivious little animal, a contemptible playmate. This is the wonderful revelation to be found in my father's kind of society. And having had no sympathy for his attitude toward women until that night, I now endorse it completely. Every fibre in my body tells me that I am my father's son.

Perhaps at this point you may feel that I am to be congratulated on having finally outgrown the dead old-fashioned views of the Meiji era in favour of more enlightened ones. And perhaps you are smiling contemptuously, secure in the knowledge that my lust for paid women will only serve to enhance my esteem for pure ladies like yourself. No! Let me disabuse you of any such notion. Since that night (enlightenment being exactly what it says) I have broken through all these standards into territory where there are no restraints. Geisha or princess, virgin or prostitute, factory girl or artist – there is no distinction whatever. Every woman without exception is a liar and 'nothing but a plump, lascivious little animal'. All the rest is makeup and costumes. And I must say that I see you as being just like all the others. Please believe that gentle Kiyo, whom you considered so sweet, so innocent, so malleable, is gone forever.

The two princes must have been somewhat taken aback when Kiyoaki said an abrupt good night and hurried out of their room fairly early in the evening, although he smilingly observed all the usual proprieties expected of a gentleman, such as checking that their bedding was correctly laid out, inquiring after any further needs, and finally withdrawing with the ritual courtesies.

'Why is it that at times like this, there is never anyone to rely on,' Kiyoaki muttered to himself as he fled through the long corridor that led back to the main house from the Western one. He thought of Honda, but his exacting standards of friendship made him dismiss that possibility.

The night wind howled at the windows of the passageway with its line of dim lanterns stretching into the distance. Suddenly afraid that someone might see him and wonder at his running and being out of breath like this, he stopped, and as he rested his elbows on the ornamental window frame and pretended to stare out into the garden, he tried desperately to put his thoughts in order. Unlike dreams, reality was not so easy to manipulate. He had to conceive a plan. It could not be anything vague and uncertain; it had to be as firmly compact as a pill, and with as sure and immediate a result. He was oppressed by a sense of his own weakness, and after the warmth of the room he had just left, the cold corridor made him shiver.

He pressed his forehead to the wind-buffeted glass and peered out into the garden. There was no moon tonight. The island and the maple hill beyond formed one mass in the darkness. In the faint glow of the corridor lamps he could make out the surface of the pond ruffled by the wind. He suddenly imagined that the snapping turtles had reared their heads out of the water and were looking toward him. The thought made him shudder.

As he returned to the main house and was about to climb the stairs to his room, he encountered his tutor Iinuma, and looked at him very coldly.

'Have Their Highnesses already retired for the night, sir?'

'Yes.'

'The young master is about to retire too?'

'I have some studying to do.'

Iinuma was twenty-three and in his final year of night school. In fact, he had probably just returned from class since he was carrying some books under one arm. To be young and in his prime seemed to have no other effect on him than to deepen his look of characteristic melancholy. His huge dark bulk unnerved Kiyoaki.

When the boy returned to his room, he did not bother to light the stove, but began to pace about anxiously, tossing up plan after plan after plan.

'Whatever I do, I must do it quickly,' he thought. 'Is it too late already? Somehow, in the very near future I have to introduce a girl to the princes as being on the fondest terms with me, when I have just sent her this letter. And furthermore, I have to do it in a way that won't cause gossip.'

The evening paper, which he had had no time to read, lay on the chair. For no good reason, Kiyoaki picked it up and opened it. An announcement for a Kabuki play at the Imperial Theatre caught his eye, and suddenly his heart began to thump.

'That's it. I'll take the princes to the Imperial Theatre. And as for that letter, it can't have arrived already since I sent it only yesterday. There's still hope. My parents won't allow Satoko to go to a play with me, but if we met by accident, there'd be nothing wrong with that.'

Kiyoaki rushed out of the room and down the stairs to the room beside the front entrance where the telephone was. Before he went in, however, he looked cautiously in the direction of Iinuma's room, which was emitting streaks of light. He must be studying.

Kiyoaki picked up the receiver and gave the operator the number. His heart was pounding; his customary ennui had been swept away.

'Hello, is this the Ayakura residence? Please may I speak to Miss Satoko?' Kiyoaki asked, after the familiar voice of an old woman answered. From distant Azabu, her voice expressed a certain displeasure, though remaining agonizingly polite.

'It's young Master Matsugae, I believe? I'm terribly sorry, but it's so late, I'm afraid.'

'Has Miss Satoko gone to bed?'

'Well, no, I don't believe she has retired yet.'

After Kiyoaki persisted, Satoko finally came to the phone. The sound of her warm, clear voice cheered him immensely.

'Kiyo, what in the world do you want at this time of night?'

'Well, to tell the truth, I sent you a letter yesterday. Now I must ask you something. When it comes, please, whatever you do, don't open it. Please promise me that you'll throw it right into the fire.'

'Well really, Kiyo, I don't know what you're talking about...' Something in Satoko's apparently calm voice told Kiyoaki that she had started to weave her usual net of ambiguities. And her voice on this cold winter night was as warm and ripe as an apricot in June. He said impatiently, 'I know you don't. So just please listen and promise. When my letter comes, throw it in the fire right away without opening it, please?'

'I see.'

'Do you promise?'

'Very well.'

'And now there's something else I want to ask you...'

'This certainly seems to be the night for requests, doesn't it, Kiyo?'

'Could you do this for me: get tickets to the play at the Imperial Theatre for the day after tomorrow for yourself and your maid.'

'A play ... !'

The abrupt silence at the other end made Kiyoaki afraid that Satoko might refuse, but then he realized that, in his haste, there was something he had forgotten. Given the Ayakuras' present circumstances, the price of a pair of tickets at two yen fifty sen apiece would represent quite an extravagance.

'No, wait, excuse me. I'll have the tickets sent to you. If your seats are next to ours, people might talk, but I'll arrange it so that they are somewhere nearby. I'm going with the two princes from Siam, by the way.'

'How kind of you, Kiyo! Tadeshina will be delighted, I'm sure. I'd love to go,' said Satoko, making no effort to conceal her pleasure.

7

The next day at school, Kiyoaki asked Honda to join him and the Siamese princes at the Imperial Theatre the following night; Honda was pleased, and accepted at once, although not without a vague sense of awkwardness. Kiyoaki, of course, did not choose to tell his friend the part of the plan that provided for the chance encounter with Satoko.

At home that evening during dinner, Honda told his parents about Kiyoaki's invitation. His father had some reservations about the theatre, but felt that he should not restrict the freedom of an eighteen-year-old in matters of this sort.

His father was a justice of the Supreme Court. He saw to it that an atmosphere of decorum reigned in his household. The family lived in a large mansion in Hongo with many rooms, some of which were decorated in the oppressive Western style popular in the Meiji era. Among his servants were a number of students, and books were to be found everywhere. They filled the library and study and even lined the hallways, in an expanse of brown leather and gold lettering.

His mother, too, was the opposite of frivolous. She held office in the Women's Patriotic League, and she was rather pained that her son should have struck up a close friendship with the son of Marquise Matsugae, a lady who had no taste for such worthwhile activities. Aside from this, however, Shigekuni Honda's school record, his diligence, his health, and his unfailing good manners were a source of constant pride to his mother, and she never tired of singing his praises to other people.

Everything in the Honda household, down to the most trivial utensil, had to meet exacting standards. Starting with the bonsai in the front entrance, the screen behind it with the painted Chinese ideogram for harmony, the cigarette case and ashtrays laid out in the drawing room, the tasselled tablecloth, and ending with the rice bin in the kitchen, the towel rack in the toilet, the pen holders in the study, and even the various paperweights in the study – each item was perfection of its kind.

And this same care extended to the conversation of the household. In the homes of Honda's friends, one or two old people could always be counted on to come up with absurd stories. In all seriousness, for example, they might recall the night when two moons had appeared at the window, one of them a badger in disguise who immediately resumed his normal shape on being roundly abused, and lumbered away. And there would always be an appreciative audience. But in his own home, a severe glance from his father would make it clear even to the oldest of the maids that to indulge in such ignorant nonsense was out of the question.

In his youth, his father had spent some years studying law in Germany, and he revered the German respect for logic.

When Shigekuni Honda compared his own home with Kiyoaki's one aspect of the contrast particularly amused him. Although the Matsugaes seemed to lead a Westernized life and although their house was filled with objects from abroad, the atmosphere of their home was strikingly and traditionally Japanese. In his own household, on the other hand, the day-to-day life-style might be Japanese, but the atmosphere had much that was Western in spirit. And then his father's regard for the education of his student houseboys was in marked contrast to Marquis Matsugae's attitude toward his.

As usual, once he had finished his homework, which tonight was French, his second foreign language, Honda turned to some law digests. These were written in German, French, and English, and he had had to order them through the Maruzen bookstore. He read these every night in anticipation of the future demands of college work, and also, more significantly, because he had a natural bent to trace everything to its source. Lately, he had begun to lose interest in the European natural law that had exercised such a fascination on him. From the day of the Abbess of Gesshu's sermon, he had become more and more aware of such a system's inadequacies.

He realized, however, that although natural law had been comparatively neglected in recent years, no other system of thought displayed such a capacity for survival: it had flourished in different forms suited to each of the many epochs in two thousand years of history – from its apparent origins in Socrates and its powerful influence on the formulation of law in the Roman era through the medium of Aristotle's writings, to its intricate development and codification during the Christian Middle Ages and its renewed popularity in the Renaissance; this indeed reached such a peak that the period could be called the Age of Natural Law. In all probability, it was this recurrent philosophy that preserved the traditional European faith in the power of reason. Still, Honda could not help thinking that despite its tenacity, two thousand years of its strong, bright Apollonian humanism had barely sufficed to hold off the assaults of darkness and barbarism.

Nor was the assault limited to these forces. Another, more blinding light had also threatened it, since natural law had to rigidly exclude the very possibility of a concept of existence based on romantic and irrational nationalism.

However that might be, Honda did not necessarily cling to the historical school of law, which was influenced by nineteenth-century romanticism, nor to the ethnic school. The Japan of the Meiji era, indeed, needed a nationalistic type of law, one that had its roots in the philosophy of the historical school. But Honda's concerns were quite different. He had first been intent on isolating the essential principle behind all law, a principle which he felt must exist. And this was why the concept of natural law had fascinated him for a time. But now he was more concerned to define the outer limits of natural law, which were inadvertently pointed up by its claims to universality. He enjoyed giving his imagination free rein in this direction. If the law, he thought, was to do away with the restrictions that natural law and philosophy had imposed upon man's vision of the world since ancient times, and break through to a more universal principle (granted that such exisits) would it not reach a stage where the law itself, as we know it, would cease to exist?

This was, of course, the kind of dangerous thinking that appealed to youth. And given Honda's circumstances, with the geometrical structure of Roman law towering so formidably in the background to cast its shadow over the modern operative law that he was now studying, it was no wonder that he found its orthodoxy rather tedious; from time to time, he therefore put aside the legal codes of Meiji Japan, so scrupulously based on Western models, and turned his eyes in another direction – to the broader and more ancient traditions of Asia.

In his present sceptical mood, a French translation by Delongchamps of the Laws of Manu, which had arrived from Maruzen at an opportune moment, contained much that he found strongly appealing.

The Laws of Manu, probably compiled over the period from 200 BC to 200 AD, were the foundation of Indian law. And among faithful Hindus, it maintained its authority as a legal code right up to the present. Within its twelve chapters and 2,684 articles were gathered an immense body of precepts drawn from religion, custom, ethics, and law. It ranged from the origin of the cosmos to the penalties for robbery and the rules for dividing an inheritance. It was imbued with an Asian philosophy in which all things were somehow one, in remarkable contrast to the natural law and world view of Christianity, with its passion for making distinctions based on a neatly corresponding macrocosm and microcosm.

However, the right of action in Roman law embodied a principle that contradicted the modern concept of rights. Just as Roman law held that rights lapse when there is no possibility of redress, so too the Laws of Manu, according to the procedural rules in force in the great courts of the rajahs and Brahmins, restricted the suits that might be brought to trial to cases of nonpayment of debts and some eighteen others.

Honda was fascinated by the uniquely vivid style of the Laws. Even details as prosaic as court procedure were couched in colourful metaphors and similes. During the conduct of a trial, for example, the rajah was to determine the truth and falsehood of the matter before him 'just as the hunter searches out the lair of the wounded deer by following the trail of blood'. And in the enumeration of his duties, the rajah was admonished to dispense favours on his people 'as Indra lets fall the life-giving rain of April'. Honda read right to the very end, including the final chapter, which dealt with arcane matters that defied classification either as laws or as proclamations.

The imperative postulated in Western law was inevitably based on man's power of reason. The Laws of Manu, however, were rooted in a cosmic law that was impervious to reason – the doctrine of the transmigration of souls. This was set out in the Laws as a matter of course:

'Deeds proceed from the body, speech, and the mind, and result in either good or evil.'

'In this world, the soul in conjunction with the body performs three kinds of act: good, indifferent, and evil.'

'That which proceeds from a man's soul shall shape his soul; that which proceeds from his speech shall shape his speech, and deeds that proceed from his body shall shape his body.'

'He who sins in body shall be a tree or grass in the next life, he who sins in speech shall be a bird or a beast, and he who sins in soul shall be reborn at the lowest level of caste.'

'The man who retains a proper guard over his speech, his mind, and his body with regard to all living things – the man who bridles his lust and his anger – shall achieve fulfilment. Total liberation shall be his.'

'It is fitting that every man should employ his inherent wisdom to discern how the fate of his soul depends on his adherence or nonadherence to the law and that he should exert himself wholeheartedly in the faithful observance of the law.'

Here, just as in the natural law, to observe the law and to do good deeds were taken as being the same thing. But here the law was based upon the principle of the transmigration of souls, a doctrine that short-circuited normal rational inquiry. And rather than making an appeal to human reason, the Laws seemed to play on the threat of retribution. And thus as a doctrine of law, it placed somewhat less trust in human nature than did the Roman law with its reliance on the powers of reason.

Honda had no desire to spend his time mulling over the problem like this, or to steep himself in the wisdom of the ancients. Being a law student, he was inclined to support the establishment of law, but he was persistently troubled by doubts and misgivings about the operative system that was his subject. His struggles with its painfully intricate and tangled structure had taught him that a broader view was sometimes necessary; this was to be found not only in natural law, with its apotheosis of reason that was at the heart of operative law, but also in the seminal wisdom of the Laws of Manu. From this vantage point, he could enjoy two worlds – the clear blue of midday or the star-filled night.

The study of law was certainly a strange discipline. It was a net with mesh so fine as to catch the most trivial incidents of daily life, yet its vast extension in time and space encompassed even the eternal movements of the sun and stars. No fisherman seeking to increase his catch could be more greedy than the student of law.

Lost for so long in his reading and oblivious to the passage of time, Honda at last realized with some anxiety that he had better go to bed if he was not to look exhausted when he met Kiyoaki at the Imperial Theatre the next night. When he thought of his friend, so handsome and so hard to fathom, and then considered how unlikely it was that his own future would be anything but ordinary and predictable, he could not suppress a slight shudder. He idly turned over in his mind the triumphs with which his classmates so proudly regaled him, such as using a rolled-up cushion to play rugby in a Gion teahouse with a flock of young geishas.

Then he thought of an episode in his own home this spring that would have been insignificant in a more worldly environment but which set off immense reverberations in the Honda household. A memorial service to commemorate the tenth anniversary of his grandmother's death had been held at the temple in Nippori where the family remains were buried, and afterwards the immediate family relatives had shared their hospitality. Shigekuni's second cousin Fusako was both the youngest of the guests, and the prettiest and most vivacious. In the staid Honda household, her loud peals of laughter caused a few raised eyebrows.

Despite the day's religious overtones, the awareness of death was not enough to hinder the contented babble of conversation among relatives who had not seen one another for so long. And so they talked, touching on the dead grandmother from time to time, perhaps, but much more concerned with telling one another about the children who were the pride of each family.

The thirty-odd guests wandered about the house from room to room, astonished at finding themselves confronted with books at every turn. A few of them asked to see Shigekuni's study and poked around his desk for a time, then they left one by one, until Fusako alone remained with him.

The two of them sat down on a leather couch by the wall. Shigekuni was wearing his school uniform, and Fusako a formal purple kimono. Once they became aware that they had been left alone, they became rather awkward with each other, and Fusako's peals of laughter ceased.

Shigekuni was wondering whether it would be the right thing to show Fusako a picture album or something like that, but unfortunately he had nothing of the sort at hand. To make matters worse, Fusako suddenly seemed displeased. Until now, he had not been particularly attracted to her, with her excess of physical energy, her loud, interminable laugh, her habit of teasing him although he was a year older than she, and her constant flurry of activity. Admittedly she had the warm bloom of a midsummer flower, but Shigekuni had already come to a private decision: he would rather not have a woman like her for his wife.

'I'm tired, you know. How about you, Shige, aren't you?'

Before he could reply, she seemed to fold at the waist and fall toward him in her wide obi, like a wall suddenly collapsing. An instant later, her head was snuggled in his lap, and he found himself contemplating the warm fragrant weight across his knees.

He was totally at a loss. He looked down at the supple burden settled in his lap and things remained that way for what seemed a very long time. He felt powerless to move even a muscle, and Fusako, too, once she had so contentedly buried her head in the blue serge of her cousin's uniform, gave no sign that she ever intended to remove it.

But then the door suddenly opened to reveal his mother and an aunt and uncle. His mother paled, and Shigekuni's heart gave a thump. Fusako, however, merely looked slowly in the direction of the newcomers, and then oh so languidly raised her head.

'I'm so very tired. And I have a headache too.'

'My goodness, we can't have that. Shall I get you something for it?'

Not for nothing did his mother hold office in the Women's Patriotic League, as she stepped into the breach as a volunteer nurse.

'No, thank you, I don't believe it's that serious.'

This episode added considerable spice to his relatives' conversation, and although it fortunately did not reach his father's ears, his mother took him severely to task for it. And as for Fusako, despite being his cousin, she was never invited to the house again. Honda, however, would never forget those few brief moments when her warm weight lay heavy in his lap.

And although he had supported her whole upper body in its kimono and obi, it was the subtly complex beauty of her head and hair that had most attracted him. Its luxuriant mass had pressed against him with the clinging heaviness of smouldering incense. The blue serge of his trousers could not conceal its constant, penetrating warmth. It was like the heat of a distant fire – what caused it, he wondered. It had radiated from her as if from coals in a fine china vase. It implied that her affection for him was somehow excessive. And hadn't the pressure of her head been a stinging reproof as well?

And then there were Fusako's eyes. While her cheek was on his lap, he had been able to look down into her wide, dark eyes. They were small and vulnerable, as glistening as raindrops, like dancing butterflies momentarily at rest. The flutter of her long lashes was the flutter of their wings, which were as beautifully speckled as the pupils of her eyes.

So insincere, so close to him yet so indifferent, so ready to dart away – he had never seen such eyes that roamed ceaselessly in discontent. First focused, then vacant, they were as unsettled as the bubble in a spirit level.

But she was not flirting. Her look conveyed even less than it had when she was chattering gaily a few minutes before. Her eyes seemed to express nothing more significant than the headstrong passion that surged in her. The unnerving force of such sweetness and fragrance sprang from something far more elemental than a desire for flirtation.

What, then, was the pervasive mood of those moments of physical contact which had seemed to stretch into an eternity?

8

The main production at the Imperial Theatre from the middle of November to the tenth of December was not a popular modern piece involving actresses, but two Kabuki plays featuring such masters of the craft as Baiko and Kojiro. Kiyoaki had picked the classical theatre because he felt that this kind of entertainment would have more appeal for his foreign guests. But as he didn't know much about Kabuki, he was unfamiliar with that evening's two offerings, *The Rise and Fall of the Taira* and *Lion Dance*. And so he persuaded Honda to spend his lunch hour in the library looking up the plays in order to explain them to the princes beforehand.

The two princes were inclined to bring no more than idle curiosity to bear on foreign plays. Kiyoaki had introduced them to Honda, who had come home from school with him. And now, after dinner, he noticed that they were not paying much attention to his friend's English summary of the evening's plays.

In such circumstances, Honda's loyalty and utter solemnity moved Kiyoaki to both guilt and pity. Certainly none of the theatre party that night was much concerned with the plays themselves. Kiyoaki, for one, was preoccupied; Satoko might have read the letter after all and hence might break her promise to come.

The butler came in to announce that the carriage was waiting. The horses neighed and their breath flared white from their nostrils, to swirl up into the black, wintry sky. Kiyoaki enjoyed seeing horses proudly displaying their strength in winter, when their usual musky smell was fainter and their hooves rang clearly on the frozen ground. On a warm spring day, a galloping horse was only too clearly a sweating animal of flesh and blood. But a horse racing through a snowstorm became one with the very elements; wrapped in the whirling blast of the north wind, the beast embodied the icy breath of winter.

Kiyoaki liked riding in a carriage, especially when he was oppressed by some concern or other. For the bouncing would jolt him out of the dogged, steady rhythm of his worry. The tails arching away from bare rumps close to the carriage, the manes trailing wildly in the wind, the saliva falling in a gleaming ribbon from the gnashing teeth – Kiyoaki liked to savour the contrast between the animals' brute strength and the elegant fittings in the interior of the carriage.

Kiyoaki and Honda wore overcoats over their school uniforms. The princes, though they themselves were huddled in immense, fur-collared overcoats, shivered miserably.

'We're not used to the cold,' said Prince Pattanadid, an unhappy look in his eye. 'Some cousins of ours studied in Switzerland, and they warned us that it was cold. But no one said anything about how cold Japan was.'

'But you'll get used to it in no time,' said Honda to console them; they were already on good terms despite their short acquaintance.

Since it was December, the season for the traditional end-of-year sales, the streets were bright with advertising banners and crowded with shoppers in heavy cloaks, all of which prompted the princes to ask what festival was being celebrated.

For the past two days or more, the faces of both Prince Pattanadid and even the heedless and irrepressible Kridsada had become more and more downcast, an unmistakable proof of homesickness. Naturally they were careful not to be too open about this, as they did not wish to affront Kiyoaki's hospitality. Yet he knew that their thoughts were elsewhere, adrift on some broad ocean. But he was pleased by it, for to him the idea of human emotions remaining steadfast and inextricably anchored in the body, in the here-and-now, was unbearably oppressive.

As they were passing Hibiya Park and approaching the moat of the Imperial Palace, the three-storied white theatre loomed up ahead in the early darkness of the winter evening.

When they entered the theatre, the new play that came first on the programme was already in progress. Kiyoaki picked out Satoko where she sat beside her old servant, Tadeshina. Their seats were two or three rows behind and somewhat to one side of the young men. Seeing her there and catching the hint of a flashing smile, Kiyoaki was ready to forgive her everything.

During the rest of the first play, while two rival generals of the Kamakura era marshalled their forces against each other on stage, Kiyoaki watched as though in a daze. Everything on stage paled before his self-esteem, now that he was delivered from any threat to it.

'Tonight Satoko is more beautiful than ever,' he thought. 'She has taken extra care over her toilette. She's come looking just as I hoped she would.'

Kiyoaki was delighted with the way things had turned out. He congratulated himself over and over again as he sat there secure in his contentment, unable to turn and look in Satoko's direction but basking in the warmth of her beauty so close at hand. He could not wish for anything more.

What he had wanted of her tonight was a beautiful presence, a demand that he had never previously made on her. On reflection, he realized that he had not been accustomed to thinking of Satoko in terms of beauty. Though he had never exactly considered her as a confirmed enemy, she was nevertheless like fine silk disguising a sharp needle, or rich brocade that hid an abrasive underside. Above all, she was the woman who loved him without having bothered to consult him at all in the matter. This Kiyoaki could not bear. Not for him the meek acceptance of favours granted. He had always firmly shuttered his heart against the rising sun, for fear that a single ray of its harsh, overcritical brilliance might pierce through.

The intermission came. Everything went off naturally. First Kiyoaki turned to Honda and whispered to him that, by a remarkable coincidence, Satoko was there. And although the look in his friend's eye, after a quick glance backward, left no doubt that he knew that something more than chance was at work, this, surprisingly enough, did not shake Kiyoaki's complacency in the least. For Honda's look was eloquent proof of Kiyoaki's concept of friendship, which never demanded an excess of honesty.

There was a bustle of talk and movement as everyone went out into the lobby.

Kiyoaki and his friends strolled under the chandeliers to meet Satoko and her maid in front of a window that looked out over the castle moat and the ancient stone walls of the shogun's castle. His ears burning with unaccustomed excitement, he introduced Satoko to the two princes. Realizing how inappropriate cold formality would be, he observed all etiquette, but put on the same show of naïve enthusiasm he had displayed when he had first mentioned Satoko to the princes.

He knew that the expansive surge of emotion, the liberating power of his newly won sense of security, enabled him to adopt an alien maturity. Abandoning his characteristic melancholy, he revelled in his freedom. For Kiyoaki knew that he was not at all in love with Satoko.

Tadeshina had retired to the shelter of a pillar with all sorts of deprecating gestures. Judging from the tightness of the embroidered plum-coloured collar of her kimono, one would gather that she had decided to treat these foreigners with circumspection. Her attitude pleased Kiyoaki, who was thus spared her high-pitched acknowledgement of his introduction.

Although the two princes were delighted to be in the company of such a beautiful woman, Chao P. was not too involved to notice the remarkable alteration in Kiyoaki's manner when he introduced Satoko. Never imagining that Kiyoaki was in fact modelling himself on his own boyish earnestness, the prince began to feel a real fondness for Kiyoaki, believing that for the first time he was seeing him behave as a young man should.

Honda, in the meantime, was lost in admiration for Satoko, who, although she did not speak a word of English, maintained exactly the right degree of poise before the two princes. Surrounded as she was with four young men, and wearing an elaborate formal kimono, she nevertheless carried herself without the least sign of constraint; her beauty and elegance were self-evident.

As Kiyoaki translated for the two princes, who were taking turns at plying Satoko with questions, she smiled at him as if to seek his approval. It was a smile that seemed to imply much more than the circumstances demanded. Kiyoaki became uneasy.

'She's read the letter,' he thought. But no, if she had read the letter, she would not be behaving like this toward him tonight. In fact, she would not have come at all. Surely she could not have received the letter before he telephoned. But there was no way of knowing whether or not she had read it after his call. It would be pointless to confront her with a direct question because she would be quick to deny it. But still, he grew angry with himself for not daring to do it.

Trying to sound as casual as possible, he did his best to discover if there were not some note in her voice that differed from the cheerful warmth of two nights before, or some suggestive change in her expression. Once more the clarity of his self-possession was becoming blurred.

Her nose was as well moulded as that of an ivory doll, without being so sharply defined as to give her a haughty profile. And her face seemed to glow and fall into soft shadow; alternating with the quick, vivacious movement of her eyes. Alertness of eye is usually considered a vulgar trait in women, but Satoko had a way of delivering her sidelong glances that was irresistibly charming. Her smile followed close upon her words, as her glance did upon her smile – the graceful sequence heightening the bewitching elegance of her expression. Her lips, although somewhat thin, concealed a subtle inner voluptuousness. When she laughed, she was always quick to hide the sparkle of her teeth with the slender, delicate fingers of one hand, but not before the young men had noticed a white brilliance that rivalled that of the chandeliers above.

As Kiyoaki translated the extravagant compliments of the princes for Satoko, he noticed a blush spreading to her earlobes. Almost hidden by her hair, they were shaped with the fluid grace of raindrops, and however hard he peered at them, he was unable to decide whether they owed their heightened colour to some cosmetic or to embarrassment.

One thing about Satoko, however, transcended all artifice. This was the force of her bright eyes. It unnerved him as it always did. He felt pierced by its uncanny keenness; its power sprang from her very essence.

The bell rang to announce the beginning of *The Rise and Fall of the Taira*, and the audience began to file back to their seats.

'She's the most beautiful woman I've seen since my arrival in Japan. How lucky you are!' said Chao P. in a low voice as he and Kiyoaki walked down the aisle. Judging by the look in his eyes, one could gather that he had recovered from his attack of homesickness.

9

Kiyoaki's tutor Iinuma had come to realize that the six years and more that he had spent in service to the Matsugae household had not only blighted the hopes of his youth but had dissipated the consequent indignation he had felt at first. When he brooded over his frustrating circumstances, he did so with a chill resentment quite different from the hot anger he had once felt. Of course the atmosphere of the Matsugae household, so unfamiliar to him, had had much to do with the changes in him. From the very beginning, however, the main source of contagion had been Kiyoaki, now eighteen years old.

The boy would be nineteen this coming year. If Iinuma could only see to it that he graduated from Peers with good marks and then that he was entered in the law school of Tokyo Imperial University when the autumn of his twenty-first year came round, he would be able to feel that his own responsibility had been properly discharged. However, for some reason that Iinuma could not fathom, Marquis Matsugae had never seen fit to take his son to task over his school record. And as things stood now, there seemed little chance of Kiyoaki's studying law at Tokyo University. After graduating from Peers, there seemed to be no other course open to him but to take advantage of his privileges as a member of the nobility and enter either Kyoto or Tohoku Imperial University without having to take an entrance examination. Kiyoaki's performance at school had been indifferent; he put no effort into his studies, nor did he compensate for this at all by trying to shine at athletics instead. Had he been an outstanding student, Iinuma could have shared in the glory, giving his friends and relatives in Kagoshima cause to be proud. But by now, Iinuma could only dimly recall the fervent hopes he had once entertained. And besides, he realized bitterly, no matter how far short of the mark Kiyoaki fell, he was still assured of a seat in the House of Peers.

The friendship between Kiyoaki and Honda was another source of irritation. Honda was close to the top of his class, but he made no attempt to influence his friend for the good, despite Kiyoaki's regard for him; quite the reverse, in fact. He behaved, in Iinuma's eyes, like an uncritical admirer, blind to Kiyoaki's every shortcoming.

Jealousy, of course, played its part in Iinuma's resentment. Being a friend and classmate, Honda was in a position to accept Kiyoaki as he was, whereas for Iinuma, he was an eternal monument to his own failure.

Kiyoaki's looks, his elegance, his diffidence, his complexity, his disinclination for any exertion, his languid dreaminess, his magnificent body, his delicate skin, his long lashes over those dreaming eyes – all of Kiyoaki's attributes conspired to betray Iinuma's hopes with a careless, elegant grace of their own. Iinuma saw his young master as a constant, mocking reproach.

So bitter a frustration, a sense of failure so gnawing in its intensity, can, over a long period, be transmuted into a kind of religious fervour directed at its cause. Iinuma became enraged at anyone who tried to slight Kiyoaki. By a sort of confused intuition of which he himself was unaware, he grasped something of the nature of Kiyoaki's almost impenetrable isolation. Kiyoaki's determination, in turn, to keep his distance from Iinuma doubtless sprang from the fact that he perceived all too clearly the nature of his tutor's burning fanaticism.

Of all the retinue in the Matsugae household, only Iinuma was possessed by this fervour, something intangible yet quite apparent as soon as one looked into his eyes. One day, a guest asked: 'Excuse me, but that houseboy of yours isn't a socialist is he?' The Marquis and his wife could not help bursting into laughter at this, for they were well aware of Iinuma's background, his present behaviour, and, above all, the zeal with which day in, day out, he performed his devotions at the 'Omiyasama' shrine. It was customary for this taciturn young man, who had no words to waste on anyone, to go to the family shrine early each morning; there he poured out his heart to Marquis Matsugae's renowned father, whom he had never known in his lifetime. In the early days, his pleas were shot through with a radical anger, but as he grew older, they began to be shaped by a pervasive discontent that now had spread to envelop every aspect of his world.

He was the first to rise every morning. He washed his face and rinsed out his mouth, then putting on his indigo-striped kimono and his *Okura hakama*, he set off in the direction of the shrine.

He walked along the path that led past the maids' quarters at the rear of the main house and through the grove of Japanese cypresses. In cold weather, like this morning's, the frost tortured the dirt of the path into tiny spiral mounds; when these were crushed by the blunt impact of Iinuma's wooden clogs, they shattered into pure, glittering fragments. The morning sun, lying bright and gauzy over the withered brown and green leaves that still clung to the cypresses, shone on his frosty breath rising in the winter air. He felt utterly purified. Incessant birdsong filled the pale blue morning sky. However, despite the stimulation of the cold air briskly striking his bare skin under his open-necked kimono, something wrung his heart with bitter regret: 'If only the young master would come with me, just once!'

He had never succeeded in communicating this vigorous, masculine sense of well-being to Kiyoaki. No one could hold him responsible for this failure. To force the boy to accompany him on these morning walks was out of the question, yet Iinuma continued to blame himself. In six years he had not been able to persuade Kiyoaki to participate even once in this 'virtuous practice'.

On the flat crest of the small hill, trees gave way to a fairly broad clearing of grass, now brown and dry, through which a gravel path led to the shrine. As Iinuma gazed at it and the full force of the morning sun struck the granite torii in front of it and the two cannon shells to either side of its stone steps, a feeling of self-possession came over him. Here in the dawn, he found a bracing air of purity, free from the stifling luxury penetrating the Matsugae household. He felt as if he were breathing in a new coffin of fresh white wood. Since early childhood, all that he had been taught to revere as honourable and beautiful was to be found, as far as the Matsugaes were concerned, in the proximity of death.

After Iinuma had climbed the steps and taken up his position before the shrine, he saw a small bird, a glimpse of dark red breast, as it hopped about the branches of a sakaki, rustling the gleaming leaves. Then, with a piercing cry, it flew away. A flycatcher, he thought.

He pressed his palms together and, as always, invoked Kiyoaki's grandfather as 'Reverend Ancestor'. Then in silence he began to pray: 'Why is our era one of decadence? Why does the world despise vigour and youth and worthy ambitions and single-mindedness? You once cut men down with your sword, you were wounded by the swords of others, you endured the most terrible dangers – all to found a new Japan. And finally, having achieved high office and esteemed by everyone, you died, the greatest hero in a heroic age. Why can we not recapture the glory of your era? How long must this age of the effete and the contemptible endure? Or is the worst still to come? Men think only of money and women. Men have forgotten everything that should be becoming to a man. That great and shining age of gods and heroes passed away with the Meiji Emperor. Will we ever see its like again? A time when the strength of youth will unstintingly give of itself once more?

'In the present day – when places called cafés are springing up everywhere, drawing in thousands of idle people with money to squander, when male and female students behave so shockingly in streetcars that it has become necessary to segregate them – men have lost all trace of that fervour that drove their ancestors to accept the most frightening challenges. Now they are good for nothing but to flutter their effeminate hands like dry, fragile leaves shaken by the merest puff of air.

'Why all this? How did such an age come about, an age which has defiled everything that once was sacred. Alas, Reverend Ancestor, your own grandson, whom I serve, is in every way a child of this decadent era, and I am powerless to do anything about it. Should I die to atone for my failure? Or have things taken their course according to some great design of yours?'

Oblivious to the cold in the fervour of his devotions, Iinuma stood there, a virile figure with his matted chest showing through his open kimono. In truth, he secretly regretted that his body did not correspond to the purity of his zeal. On the other hand, Kiyoaki, whose body he saw as a sacred vessel, lacked the single-minded purity required of all true men.

Then suddenly, at the height of his ardent outpouring, as he was getting warmer and warmer despite the chill morning air swirling under the skirt of his *hakama*, he began to feel sexually aroused. He immediately snatched a broom from its place under the floor and began to sweep out the shrine in a frenzy of energy.

10

Shortly after the new year, Iinuma was called to Kiyoaki's room. There he found the old lady, Tadeshina, whom he knew to be Satoko's maid.

Satoko herself had already been to the Matsugae house to exchange New Year's greetings, and today, finding occasion to bring some traditional Kyoto bran mash as her own New Year's present, Tadeshina had made her way inconspicuously to Kiyoaki's room. Though Iinuma was aware who Tadeshina was, this was the first time he had ever been brought together with her intentionally, and the reason for it was not yet clear to him.

The New Year was always lavishly celebrated in the Matsugae household. Some twenty or more people came from Kagoshima, and after going to the residence of the traditional head of the clan to pay their respects, they were entertained at the Matsugaes'. The New Year's dinners, cooked in the Hoshigaoka style and served in the black-beamed main hall, were famous, largely because of such desserts as ice cream and melon, which were delicacies almost never tasted by country people. This year, however, because the period of mourning for the Meiji Emperor was not yet over, no more than three guests came up from Kagoshima; among them, the principal of Iinuma's middle school, a gentleman who had the honour of having known Kiyoaki's grandfather.

Marquis Matsugae had established a certain ritual with the old teacher. As Iinuma waited on him at the banquet, the Marquis would speak graciously to the old man: 'Iinuma has done well here.' This year, too, the formula had been invoked and the principal had murmured the usual politely deprecating words, as predictably as someone stamping his seal on a routine document. But this year, perhaps because there was only a handful of guests present, the ceremony struck Iinuma as being insincere, a perfunctory formality.

Of course Iinuma had never presented himself to any of the illustrious ladies who came to call on the Marquise, so he was taken aback at being confronted in his young master's study by a New Year's guest who happened to be a woman, however elderly.

Tadeshina wore a black kimono patterned with crests, and though she sat upright in her chair with extreme propriety, the whisky that Kiyoaki had urged on her had evidently taken some effect. Beneath her greying hair, gathered neatly into a knot and still unruffled, the skin on her forehead glowed through the layer of white makeup with a shade of snowcovered plum blossom.

After acknowledging Iinuma with a brief glance, she returned to the story she had been telling about Prince Saionji.

'According to what everyone said, the Prince enjoyed tobacco and alcohol from the age of five onward. Samurai famllies are always so concerned to bring their children up impeccably. But in noble families – I think you know what I mean, young master – parents never discipline their children from the moment they're born; wouldn't you agree? For after all, their children receive the court rank of fifth degree at birth, which qualifies them to become retainers of His Imperial Majesty, and so out of reverence to the Emperor, their parents don't dare to be harsh with them. And in a court nobleman's house, nobody says anything about His Imperial Majesty that isn't absolutely prudent. Just as nobody belonging even to the household of a lord would ever dare to gossip openly about their master. And that's the way it is. And my mistress too has this same deep reverence for His Imperial Majesty. But of course it doesn't extend to foreign lords.' This last was Tadeshina's ironic jab at the hospitality extended to the Siamese princes by the Matsugaes. Then she hastened to make some amends: 'But then, thanks of course to your great kindness, I was privileged to see a play again after I don't know how long. I felt that it gave me a new lease of life.'

Kiyoaki let Tadeshina ramble on as she liked. In asking her to come to his study, he had had something quite definite in mind. He wanted to be free of the nagging doubt that had pursued him ever since that night. And so now, after plying Tadeshina with more whisky, he asked her abruptly if Satoko had in fact taken his letter and thrown it unopened into the fire as requested.

Her answer came more readily than he might have expected: 'Oh that! The young lady spoke to me immediately after her telephone conversation with you. So when the letter came next day, I took it and burned it unopened. Everything was taken care of. You need not worry about it at all.'

On hearing this, Kiyoaki felt like a man who has struggled for hours through tangled undergrowth and at last fights his way into the open. A multitude of delightful prospects unfolded before his eyes. Satoko's not having read the letter did two things: not only did it restore things to their former balance, but Kiyoaki was now happily confident that he had opened up a whole new perspective on life.

Satoko had already made an overture whose implications were dazzling. Her annual New Year's visit to exchange greetings fell on a day traditionally set aside by the Marquis for the children of his relatives. They would gather at his house, their ages ranging from three to twenty. And on this one day he would don the role of loving father, listening kindly to what each of them had to say and giving counsel when called upon to do so. This year, Satoko had brought some children out to see the horses.

Kiyoaki led them to the stable where the Matsugaes kept their four horses. It was decorated for the holidays with the twisted rope traditional in Shinto observance. The horses, with their powerful, smooth-muscled bodies, suddenly rearing back or kicking their hooves against the boards, struck Kiyoaki as having a pulsating life appropriate to the New Year. The children were enthralled. They asked the groom for each horse's name. Then, taking aim at the huge yellow teeth, they hurled salvos of squashed pieces of crumbling candy they had been clutching in their fists. The high-strung beasts glared sidelong at their tormentors with bloodshot eyes. This delighted the children even more since these baleful looks were proof that the horses regarded them as adults.

Satoko, however, was frightened by the saliva streaming from the horses' gaping mouths, and withdrew to the shelter of an evergreen some distance away. Kiyoaki walked over to join her, leaving the children to the groom.

Her eyes were showing the effects of the spiced saké that was traditional at New Year celebrations. What she said, therefore – to the accompaniment of the children's shouts of joy – might have been attributed to this stimulus. At any rate, as Kiyoaki came to her side, she looked at him far from demurely and began to speak with a lilt of excitement in her voice.

'I was so happy that night, you know. You introduced me as though I were your fiancée. I'm sure Their Highnesses were quite surprised that I should be so old. But do you know how I felt then? If I had had to die at that very moment, I would have had no regrets. My happiness lies in your hands. Be careful with it, won't you? I've never been so happy at a New Year as I am now. I never looked forward so much to what the year may bring.'

Kiyoaki did not know what to say. 'Why are you telling me all this?' he asked finally, in a strained voice.

'Oh, Kiyo, when I'm very happy, my words come tumbling out like the doves they release at a launching, flying up through a burst of confetti. Kiyo, you'll understand soon enough.' To make matters worse, Satoko had ended on that phrase calculated to irritate Kiyoaki: 'You'll understand soon enough.'

'How proud and self-satisfied she is!' thought Kiyoaki. 'So much older and wiser.'

All this had taken place some days before. And now today, after Tadeshina's account of the fate of the letter, Kiyoaki lost his lingering misgivings, now confident that he was embarking on a New Year under the most favourable auspices. He would be rid of the melancholy dreams that had plagued his nights. He was determined that from now on his dreams would be happy. His manner would never fail to be open, and since he would be free of depression and worry, he would try to communicate his own well-being to everyone. But dispensing goodwill to mankind is a hazardous business at best, and one that demands a considerable degree of maturity and wisdom. Nevertheless, Kiyoaki was driven by an extraordinary sense of urgency.

Whatever his sense of mission, however, he had not called Iinuma to his room solely out of the warm desire to dispel his tutor's gloom and see his face transformed with happiness.

The saké he had drunk combined with something else to provoke Kiyoaki to rashness. Tadeshina, despite her self-abasing manner and excruciating courtesy, had a certain air about her that put one in mind of the proprietress of a brothel, albeit one with an ancient and honourable reputation. An unmistakable distilled sensuality seemed to cling to the very wrinkles of her face. And having her so close at hand aroused Kiyoaki's natural wilfulness.

'As far as schoolwork goes, Iinuma has taught me all sorts of things,' said Kiyoaki, deliberately directing his remarks exclusively at Tadeshina. 'Still, there are a number of things he didn't teach me. Actually, the truth is that there are many things that Iinuma doesn't know. And it's just because of this that from now on you, Tadeshina, will have to become a teacher to Iinuma, you see.'

'Really now, young master, whatever do you mean by behaving like this,' said Tadeshina with heavy deference. 'This gentleman here is already a university student. And an ignorant old soul like myself...'

'Exactly. Because what I am talking about has nothing to do with what's learned in school.'

'Tch, tch, making such fun of an old woman!'

And so the exchange continued, still excluding Iinuma. Since Kiyoaki had not indicated that he might take a seat, he continued to stand, looking out over the pond. The day was overcast, and a flock of ducks swam near the island, from which the dark green crowns of the pines rose, cold and forbidding. The rough brown grass that covered the island reminded Iinuma of a farmer's straw raincoat.

Finally, at a word from Kiyoaki, Iinuma sat down stiffly in a chair. Until then, Kiyoaki had not appeared to notice him standing by the door, which seemed extremely odd to him. Perhaps, he thought, his master was making a show of his authority in front of Tadeshina. If so, it was something new in Kiyoaki, which pleased him.

'Well now, Iinuma, let's see. Tadeshina here has just been gossiping with our maids. And just by chance she happened to hear...'

'Young master, please! Don't.' Waving her arms in a show of frantic distress, Tadeshina tried to stop him, but to no avail.

'She happened to hear that the maids are convinced that when you go to the shrine every morning, you have more on your mind than mere devotion.'

'More on my mind, master?' Iinuma's face muscles tightened and his clenched hands resting in his lap began to tremble.

'Please, young master,' wailed Tadeshina, 'don't go into it with him.' She slumped back in her chair like a carelessly dropped porcelain doll, but despite her manifestations of acute distress, there was a faint but unmistakable gleam in her deepset eyes. And the lines around her mouth, with its badly fitting false teeth, were slack, witnesses to past sensuality.

'To reach the shrine, you have to pass the rear wing of the house, don't you? Which means, of course, that you walk right past the windows of the maids' quarters. And on your way every morning, you've also been exchanging looks with Miné. And finally, just the other day, you slipped her a note through the lattice. Or so they say. Is it true or isn't it?'

Before Kiyoaki had finished, Iinuma was on his feet. His pale face was contorted in rigid desperation as he struggled to control himself. It was as though a white heat were building within him, ready to explode into a terrible inferno. Kiyoaki was delighted by the look on his face, which was transformed from the dull phlegmatic expression he was used to. Though Iinuma was obviously in agony, to Kiyoaki his face, contorted into an ugly mask, was happy,

'If the master will be good enough to excuse me now . . .' said Iinuma, making a rapid turn toward the door. But before he could take another step, Tadeshina lunged from her chair to stop him with an alacrity that astounded Kiyoaki. In an instant she had changed from a decrepit old woman to a leopard making its kill.

'You mustn't go! Don't you see what will happen to me if you do that? I've served the Ayakuras for forty years, but if they find out that I'm to blame for somebody being dismissed by the Matsugaes because of an indiscretion on my part, they'll do the same to me. Please have a little pity on me. You've to think what will happen. Do you understand what I'm saying? Young people are so rash! But what can we do about it? It's one of the attractions of youth.'

And so Tadeshina clung to Iinuma's sleeve and spoke simply, and to the point, gently remonstrating, with the authority that comes with age.

Her manner of assured confidence had been perfected over the course of years, during which time she had convinced herself that she was indispensable to the running of the world. Her face was now composed again, and radiated the confidence of someone accustomed to supervising the smooth management of events from behind the scenes. In the middle of some solemn ceremony a kimono might tear at the seam with dismaying suddenness; someone might forget his copy of the speech of congratulation he had so painstakingly composed; Tadeshina's confidence was born of her proven ability to handle these and a thousand other crises with unflurried efficiency. Things that to most people were shattering bolts from the blue, to her were all in a day's work. And so, by her ready skill in warding off threats of sudden catastrophe, she had repeatedly vindicated her role in life. This tranquil old lady knew that nothing in human affairs could be counted on to turn out precisely as intended. A solitary swallow flitting across a cloudless blue sky might well be the harbinger of a surprise storm. Thus Tadeshina, with constant reserves of experience, need have no misgivings as to her worth.

Iinuma had plenty of time to reflect later, but very often a man's whole life alters course because of a moment's hesitation. That instant is like a fold made down the middle of a sheet of paper. In it, the underside becomes upmost, and what was once visible is hidden forever.

Standing there in the door of Kiyoaki's study, with Tadeshina clutching him, Iinuma experienced such a moment, and with it the matter was settled. Young and callow as he was, uncertainty cut into him the way a shark's fin cuts through the surface of the water. Had Miné laughed at his note and showed it to everyone? Or had it come to light some other way, causing her great shame? He desperately wanted to know.

Kiyoaki studied him as he sat down again. He had won a victory that gave him little cause for pride. He gave up all hope of extending his benevolence to Iinuma. There was nothing else to do but to give free reign to his own sense of happiness, he felt, and to work out the details as he went along. He had a new sense of power, and felt able to behave with the refinement of maturity.

'I didn't bring this matter up to cause you distress or to subject you to ridicule. Don't you see that Tadeshina and I are trying to work out the plan that is best for you? I'm not going to say a word to my father, and I'll make sure that it doesn't reach his ears from any other quarter. As for our immediate course of action, I'm sure that Tadeshina's vast knowledge and experience in these matters will be a great help, won't it, Tadeshina? True, Miné is one of the prettiest of the housemaids, and that presents a bit of a problem. But you just leave things to me.'

Iinuma's eyes glittered like those of a spy caught in a trap; he hung on Kiyoaki's every word, afraid to utter a sound. When he tried to penetrate the substance of Kiyoaki's words, he seemed to release in himself a surging flood of anxieties. On the other hand, when he sat there passively, Kiyoaki's words seemed to bore into his very soul.

Iinuma had never seen so authoritative an expression on the face of the younger man, who continued to speak with a magnanimity that was quite out of character. His great hope, of course, had been that Kiyoaki would some day acquire a mature poise such as this. But he had never dreamed that this would happen under circumstances like these. In losing to Kiyoaki the way he had – was it not his own lust that had defeated him, he wondered. And after his brief hesitation of a moment ago – had he not felt that his shameful pursuit of pleasure had now become inextricably bound up with loyalty and service to his master? That was the trap that they had laid for him so cleverly. However, even in his present depths of unbearable humiliation, a small, golden door had been opened for him in fulfilment of their unspoken bargain.

After Kiyoaki had finished, Tadeshina spoke up in tones as smooth as a peeled scallion. 'It's exactly the way the young master says it is. He has a wisdom far beyond his years.'

Iinuma had always considered Kiyoaki's wisdom to be quite the opposite, but now he listened to Tadeshina without surprise.

'And now, in return, Iinuma,' said Kiyoaki once again, 'you most stop lecturing me and join forces with Tadeshina to give me some help. If you do, I'll do the same for your romance. We three could become quite friendly.'

11

Kiyoaki took up the diary he kept of his dreams again, and wrote:

Even though I haven't known the Siamese princes very long, I dreamed about Siam recently. I was sitting on a splendid chair in the middle of a room. I seemed to be held there, unable to move. Throughout the dream, I felt as if I had a headache. And this was because I was wearing a tall, pointed gold crown set with all sorts of precious stones. Above my head, a huge flock of peacocks were perched on a maze of beams just under the roof. And from time to time white droppings fell on my crown.

Outside the sun was scorching. It was beating down in a desolate garden run wild. Everything was still except for the faint droning of flies and the occasional thud of the peacocks' feet on the beams above or sometimes the rustling of their wings. The garden was surrounded by a high stone wall, but there were large openings like windows let into it. And through these I could see the trunks of palm trees and, behind them, piled-up white clouds, dazzling and unmoving.

Then I looked down at my hand and saw that I was wearing an emerald ring. This, of course, was Chao P.'s, but somehow it had been placed on my finger. The design was certainly the same – the two weird faces of the guardian gods, the yaksha, carved into the gold on either side of the stone.

I stared at the ring glinting in the sun pouring in from outside, my eyes held by a pure, flawless white light that sparkled like frost crystals in the centre of the emerald. And as I did so, I became aware of the face of a woman, young and beautiful, which had gradually formed within it. I turned around, thinking that it was the reflection of someone behind me, but there was no one there. Now the face in the emerald moved slightly and its expression changed. Where it had been serious, it was now smiling. At that moment, the back of my hand began to itch as one of the swarm of flies hovering above me settled on it. Annoyed, I shook my hand to get rid of it and then looked at the ring again. But the woman's face had vanished. And then, as I began to feel an indescribable sense of bitterness and loss, I woke up...

Kiyoaki never took the trouble to add a personal interpretation to these accounts of his dreams. He did his best to recall exactly what had taken place, and he set it down as fully as possible, recording happy dreams or ominous ones just as they were. Perhaps this unwillingness to acknowledge specific meanings in dreams, and this compulsion for exact description, pointed to some deep misgivings of Kiyoaki's concerning life itself. Compared to the emotional instability he experienced when awake, his dream world seemed far more authentic. He could never be certain that these day-to-day emotions were part of his true self, but he knew that the Kiyoaki of his dreams, at least, was real. The former resisted all attempts at definition, whereas the latter had a recognizable form and character. Nor did Kiyoaki use his journal to pour out his discontent with the irritations of the world around him. Here, on the contrary, for the first time in his life, immediate reality corresponded exactly to his wishes.

Iinuma, his resistance utterly crushed, had become blindly obedient to his master. Together with Tadeshina, he frequently served as go-between to arrange meetings for Kiyoaki and Satoko. This sort of devotion was enough to satisfy Kiyoaki and, furthermore, made him wonder if such a thing as friendship was really so important. And in the meantime, without being wholly aware of it, he was growing apart from Honda. This saddened Honda, but he had always been keenly aware that he was only a marginal necessity in Kiyoaki's life. He thus knew that their relationship had lacked an element vital to friendship. The time he would have spent in idleness with Kiyoaki, therefore, he now spent on his books. Besides his study of law in German, French, and English, he read widely in literature and philosophy. And although he did not follow the great Christian leader, Kanzo Uchimura, he read and admired Carlyle's *Sartor Resartus*.

One snowy morning, as Kiyoaki was about to leave for school, Iinuma came to his study with conspicuous caution. His melancholy expression and bearing had not undergone any change, but his present obsequiousness robbed them of their power to annoy Kiyoaki.

He had, he said, just received a phone call from Tadeshina. The message was simply this: Satoko was so delighted by the snow that she would like Kiyoaki not to go to school, and come for a rickshaw ride through the snow with her instead.

No one had ever made so startlingly capricious a request of Kiyoaki. Ready for school, he stood with his book bag in his hand, appalled, and stared at Iinuma.

'What's this? Miss Satoko really suggested something like that?'

'Yes, sir. I heard it directly from Miss Tadeshina. There can be no mistake.'

Curiously enough, as he confirmed this, Iinuma seemed more like his former independent self, and he looked ready to lecture Kiyoaki if challenged about it.

Kiyoaki gave a quick glance over his shoulder at the garden, where snow was falling. This time, Satoko's forceful methods did not wound his pride. On the contrary, he felt a sense of relief, as though her scalpel had skilfully cut out a malignant tumour of arrogance. Since the surgery was over before he knew it, this bypassing of his own wishes gave him a kind of keen pleasure. 'I'll do just as she wants,' he said, gazing out thoughtfully at the thickly falling snow. Although it was not yet deep, it had already turned the island and the maple hill beyond to a shining white.

'All right, telephone the school for me. Tell them I've caught a cold and will be absent today. Make certain that no word of this reaches Mother or Father. Then go to the rickshaw stand and hire a large one pulled by two men. Make sure the men can be trusted. I'll walk there.'

'In this snow?'

Iinuma watched as his young master's face flushed crimson. Since Kiyoaki had his back to the window which looked out on to the storm, his face was in shadow, but his blush was no less apparent. This young man whom he had helped to raise was not at all inclined to heroism, yet he was startled to catch himself applauding the fiery glint in Kiyoaki's eyes, whatever his purpose. Once, Iinuma had had nothing but contempt for his young master and his ways, but whatever Kiyoaki was up to now, and however self-indulgent he might be, there seemed to be a hidden determination in him that had never shown itself before.

12

The Ayakura residence in Azabu was an old feudal mansion, and on either side of the wide main gate, the latticed windows of guard posts protruded from the wall. Now a household with very few visitors, however, there was no sign that the posts had been manned recently. The snow had not blotted out the massed ridges of the roof tiles, but rather seemed to have moulded itself faithfully to each of them as it fell.

A dark figure holding an umbrella, Tadeshina apparently, stood in front of the small door beside the gate, but as Kiyoaki's rickshaw approached, she vanished abruptly. As it drew up and he sat before the gate, Kiyoaki stared through it, seeing nothing in the garden through the snow.

Finally, protected by Tadeshina's half-open umbrella, Satoko appeared in the gateway wearing a purple robe, and as she bent her head before stepping out, her hands together at her breast, Kiyoaki felt his chest tighten at this sudden apparition of extravagant beauty, as though a billowing cloud of purple had burst out of the tiny gate into the falling snow.

Helped by Tadeshina and the rickshaw men, Satoko seemed to float up to meet Kiyoaki as he leaned over to push back the rickshaw hood, but when he suddenly faced her bright, warm smile and the whirl of snowflakes clinging to her hair and the collar of her robe, he was startled, as if he had been assailed by something nebulous in the torpor of his dreams. The sudden lurching of the light vehicle as Satoko climbed up doubtless strengthened this impression, as did the tumbled purple folds of her robe lying heaped beside him, and her heady perfume, whose fragrance seemed to draw the very snowflakes that swirled in, making them strike against his cold cheeks. As Satoko got into the rickshaw, her momentum carried her cheek close to Kiyoaki's for a second, and when she pulled her head back, disconcerted, to straighten up, Kiyoaki was caught by the supple strength of her neck. It made him think of the smooth, white neck of a swan.

'What's got into you all of a sudden?' he asked, trying desperately to keep his voice steady.

'Mother and Father took the train to Kyoto last night. One of our relatives is seriously ill. I was left all by myself, and I began to think how very much I would like to see you, Kiyo. After thinking about it all night, I saw the snow this morning, and then more than anything else in the world I wanted to go riding through the snow with you. I've never done anything so impulsive in all my life. You'll forgive me, won't you, Kiyo?' Satoko spoke rather breathlessly in a child's voice that was quite unlike her.

They had already started to move. Their ears rang with the shouts of the two rickshaw men, one of whom was pushing, the other pulling. The snow had splashed into patterns that turned from white to yellow in the confinement of the tiny front window of the enclosed cab. In the interior, the light flickered dimly in time to the constant swaying.

Kiyoaki had brought a green tartan blanket that now covered their legs. Since those forgotten days of childhood, this was the first time that they had ever been so close together, but Kiyoaki was distracted by the pale light flooding through the cracks in the bonnet of the rickshaw that narrowed and widened as a stream of snow filtered through them, by the snow itself turning to water on the green blanket, by the loud rustle of the snow pelting down on the hood as if on to dry banana leaves.

'Go wherever you like. Take us anywhere you can go,' said Kiyoaki in answer to the rickshaw man. He knew that Satoko's mood was his own.

As the men raised the poles, ready to start, both of them sat back in their seats, their bodies slightly tensed. As yet, neither of them had even attempted to hold hands. Yet the inevitable contact of their knees under the blanket was like a spark flaring secretly under the snow.

Kiyoaki's gnawing doubt persisted: had Satoko really not read the letter? 'Tadeshina denied it so emphatically she can't have,' he thought. 'But in that case, is Satoko just playing with me now, in the conviction that I am completely inexperienced with women? How could I tolerate such an insult? I was so anxious for her not to read the letter, but now I wish she had, because then to meet me in this insane way on such a snowy morning could mean only one thing: she'd be throwing down the gauntlet to a man of the world. And there'd be advantages for me in that. The only problem is that I am in fact inexperienced and I suppose there's no way to hide it.'

Kiyoaki's thoughts twisted and turned as he sat in the small, dark, square confines of the swaying rickshaw. Since he would not look at Satoko, there was nothing else to do but stare out at the snow, flashing brightly through the narrow window of yellow celluloid. Finally, however, he put his hand under the blanket, where Satoko's was waiting, already in possession of the one warm, narrow refuge available.

One of the snowflakes blew in and lodged itself on Kiyoaki's eyebrow. It made Satoko cry out, and without thinking, Kiyoaki turned toward her as he felt a cold trickle on his eyelid. She closed her eyes abruptly. Kiyoaki stared at the face with its closed lids; only the subdued crimson of her lips glowed in the shadows, and because of the swaying of the rickshaw, her features, like a flower held between trembling fingertips, were softly blurred.

Kiyoaki's heart thumped violently. He felt as if he were being choked by the high, tight collar of his uniform jacket. Never had he been confronted with anything as inscrutable as Satoko's white face, eyes closed, quietly waiting. Beneath the blanket, he felt her grip on his hand tighten slightly. He realized that she was telling him something, and so, despite his terrible sense of vulnerability, he felt that something gentle but irresistible was drawing him on. He pressed a kiss on her lips.

A moment later, the shaking of the rickshaw was about to force their lips apart, but Kiyoaki instinctively resisted the movement, until his whole body seemed to balance on that kiss, and he had the sensation that a huge, invisible, perfumed fan was slowly unfolding where their lips met.

At that instant, although totally engrossed, he was still keenly aware of his own good looks. Satoko's beauty and his: he saw that it was precisely this fine correspondence between the two that dissolved all constraint and allowed them to flow together, merging as easily as measures of quicksilver. All that was divisive and frustrating sprang from something alien to beauty. Kiyoaki now realized that a fanatical insistence on total independence was a disease, not of the flesh but of the mind.

Once his anxiety had been erased and he felt increasingly sure of the girl who was the source of his happiness, their kiss became increasingly, passionately intense; Satoko's lips were growing more pliant, and then just as he began to fear that his very essence might be melted and drawn into the sweet fragrance of her mouth, his fingertips stirred with the desire to touch her flesh. He pulled his hand out from under the blanket and passed it around her shoulders to hold her chin. He felt the small, fragile bones of a woman's jaw with his fingertips and so gained a renewed awareness of a physical presence quite outside his own. This realization, however, only intensified the passion of his kiss.

Satoko had begun to cry, as he realized when her tears wet his own cheeks. He felt a surge of pride, which owed nothing to his recent mood of altruism, the complacent desire to benefit mankind that had seized him; and in the same way, Satoko's manner had lost all trace of her former condescension, so like that of a critical older sister. As he moved his hands over her body, touching first her earlobe, then her breast, the softness under his fingers excited him. This must be the true nature of caresses, he thought. At last his sensuality, given to drifting away like a rising mist, had settled upon something tangible. His mind was now filled with nothing but his own joy. And this, for Kiyoaki, was the height of abandon.

The moment when a kiss ends – it was like awakening reluctantly from sleep, struggling drowsily against the glare of the morning sun as it struck their eyelids, as they yearned to hold on to the fragment of unconsciousness left to them. That is the moment when sleep is sweetest.

When their lips parted, an ominous silence seemed to fall, as though the birds had suddenly stopped their attractive song. They looked away from each other and stared fixedly into space. The movement of the rickshaw, however, saved the silence from becoming too oppressive. At least they could feel part of some other activity.

Kiyoaki dropped his eyes. Beneath the bottom of the green blanket, the toe of a woman's white *tabi* edged out timidly, like a nervous white mouse peeping out of its grassy burrow. It was already covered with a light dusting of snow. He felt his cheeks burning, and so he reached over as spontaneously as a child to touch her cheek, pleased to discover the same warmth in her. It was like a tiny promise of summer.

'I'll open it up.'

She nodded. He reached out and unfastened the front flap of the cab. The layer of snow that had collected on it to form a momentary square of solid white crumbled away without a sound.

The rickshaw men, noticing movement inside the cab, suddenly stopped.

'No, no! Keep going!' Kiyoaki shouted. Spurred on by the young man's tone, they broke into a trot again.

'Keep going! And as fast as you can!'

The cab glided through the snow, the rickshaw men giving cries of encouragement to each other.

'Somebody might see,' said Satoko, sitting back in the seat, unwilling to show her eyes still wet with tears.

'It doesn't matter.'

The decisive ring in his own voice took Kiyoaki by surprise. Suddenly he understood. What he really wanted to do was to challenge the world.

As he looked up, the sky above seemed to be a fury of boiling white. The snow was now lashing down right on their faces. If they opened their mouths, it lay on their tongues. To be buried in such a drift ... it seemed like heaven.

'Now there's snow in here?' she said dreamily. Apparently, she meant that it had melted in a trickle from her neck to her breast. There was nothing anarchic in the falling snow, however: it fell with the steady solemnity of an ordered ritual. He felt his cheeks grow cold, and gradually became aware that his heart was fading within him.

By now the rickshaw had climbed to the top of a hill in the fashionable Kasumi section of Azabu. The edge of the slope was skirted by a field that allowed a clear view of the parade ground and barracks of the Azabu Third Regiment below. On the white expanse of parade ground, there was not one soldier to be seen. Suddenly Kiyoaki had the illusion of seeing a huge mass of troops drawn up, just as in the familiar picture of the memorial ceremony near Tokuri Temple for the fallen of the Russo-Japanese War. With bowed heads, thousands of soldiers stood in groups around a white wood cenotaph and an altar covered with white cloths that were blowing in the wind. This scene differed from the photo only insofar as the soldiers' shoulders were covered with snow and the visors of their caps had turned white. The moment he saw these phantoms, Kiyoaki understood that they had all died in battle. The thousands of troops below had massed not only to pray for fallen comrades, but to mourn their own lives as well.

In a moment, the phantoms were gone. Behind a curtain of snow, scene after scene swept past them. The thick straw-coloured ropes that supported the pines on the steep side of the Outer Moat bore a dangerous weight of snow. And behind the tight-shut windows of the small houses, the lamps were burning faintly although it was mid-morning.

'Close it,' said Sakoto.

Kiyoaki shut the front flap, and they found themselves once more in the familiar half-light. The mood of ecstasy, however, was not to be so easily recaptured. Kiyoaki as usual was prey to misgivings. 'I wonder how she felt when I was kissing her,' he thought. 'She's probably angry about the way I did it. She knows that I get too carried away, that I was all wrapped up in myself – just like a child. And it's true. I couldn't think about anything except how wonderful it felt to me.'

Then Satoko's voice broke into his thoughts.

'Shouldn't we go home?' she said, her voice altogether too composed.

'There she goes,' he thought, 'leading me by the nose again.' But even as he grumbled to himself, he knew that he was letting pass by the moment when he had the chance to change things. He could say: 'No, let's not go back.' But to do that was to reach out and pick up the dice. And his unskilled hand would have frozen at the very touch of them. He was not ready.

13

He went home and concocted a story about leaving school early because of a sudden chill. His mother rushed up to his room to take his temperature. In the midst of this commotion, Iinuma appeared to say that Honda was on the phone. Kiyoaki had the greatest difficulty in persuading his mother not to take the call in his place, and when he had finally won his point and had gone downstairs to the phone, he was wrapped in a cashmere blanket, at his mother's insistence.

'It's all very simple: the story is that I did go to school today but came home early. No one here knows anything different. My cold?' Made uneasy by the glass door at his back, he continued in a low, muffled voice. 'Don't worry about that. I'll be at school tomorrow, and we can talk about it then. Don't start telephoning just because I wasn't at school – you do exaggerate!'

When Honda rang off, he was shaking with anger at Kiyoaki's icy response to his expressions of concern, but there was more to it than his unfriendly tone or his rudeness. Honda had never once put Kiyoaki in the position of having to share a secret.

Once he had recovered himself, however, he began to think: 'To telephone just because he wasn't at school today – that's not very like me.' And, indeed, something more than friendly concern had driven him to telephone so hurriedly. When rushing across the snow-covered schoolyard to the administration office at recess to make the call, he had been driven by a feeling of foreboding that he could not pin down.

Kiyoaki's desk had been empty all morning. Looking at it, Honda experienced the sense of dread of a man whose worst fears are confirmed. The old desk, with its scars under the new varnish, reflected the direct glare of the snow through the window. It made him think of an upright coffin draped in white, the kind used to bury ancient warriors in a sitting position.

His gloom persisted even after he had got home. Then there was a phone call; it was Iinuma with a message from Kiyoaki: he was sorry about the way he had spoken to Honda. If he sent a rickshaw to Honda's house tonight, would he please come to visit him? Iinuma's heavy, sepulchral tone depressed him still further. He curtly refused, saying that they could discuss things when Kiyoaki was well enough to go back to school.

When Iinuma delivered this message, Kiyoaki felt the discomfort of real sickness. Afterwards, he called Iinuma to his room late that night, but instead of ordering him to do something, he surprised Iinuma by unburdening himself of his vexations.

'Satoko causes nothing but trouble. It's true what they say, isn't it? A woman will destroy the friendship of men. If Satoko hadn't behaved so wilfully this morning, I wouldn't have given Honda such cause for anger.'

During the night it stopped snowing, and the next day was clear and pleasant. Prevailing over his mother and the rest of the household, Kiyoaki left for school. He intended to get there before Honda and be the first to say good morning. But as the sun rose in the sky, the dazzling splendour of this winter morning worked a change of mood. He was affected by a deep, insuppressible happiness that transformed him. Later, when Honda came into the classroom and returned his smile with a nonchalant one of his own, Kiyoaki in a sudden about-face abandoned his intention to tell him everything about the day before.

Honda had managed a smile, but no words. After putting his book bag down on his desk, he leaned on the windowsill for a few moments and looked out at the snow. Then after a quick glance at his watch that presumably told him there were still thirty minutes to spare before class, he turned without a word and walked out. Kiyoaki felt impelled to follow him.

A number of small flowerbeds were laid out geometrically along the side of the school, a two-storey wooden structure. In their midst was an arbour. Not far beyond the edge of the beds the ground dropped away sharply, and a small path led down the slope to a pond surrounded by a grove of trees. Kiyoaki was reasonably sure that Honda would not go down to the pond, since the melting snow would make walking extremely difficult. Just as he had guessed, Honda stopped in the arbour, brushed the snow off one of the benches and sat down. Kiyoaki, threading his way through the drifts in the flower garden, walked up to him.

'Why are you following me?' asked Honda, squinting into the brilliant light as he looked up.

'I behaved very badly yesterday,' Kiyoaki apologized smoothly.

'Never mind. Your cold was just an excuse, wasn't it?'

'Yes.'

Copying Honda, Kiyoaki brushed some snow off the bench and then sat down beside him. Because of the glare, the two of them had to squint painfully to look at each other, which greatly reduced the emotional charge in the atmosphere. The pond below was hidden from view, although they only had to stand up to see it through the snow-laden tree branches. They were surrounded by the sound of trickling water, proof that the mounds of snow on the school roof, on the arbour, and on the trees were now melting. The frozen crust that covered the flowerbeds had collapsed here and there, leaving coarse, layered chips of ice that glittered like split granite.

Honda expected Kiyoaki to divulge some portentous secret and yet he didn't want to admit to himself that he was curious, which almost made him hope that Kiyoaki would say nothing at all. Any confidence that smacked even remotely of condescension would be bitterly distasteful.

It was Honda, then, who spoke first, wishing only to find a subject that had no bearing on the issue between them.

'You know, I've been thinking a lot about personality lately. Take the times we live in, this school, this society – I feel alien to them all. At least I would like to think I did. And the same can be said for you too.'

'Yes, of course,' Kiyoaki replied, his tone as uninterested and aloof as ever, yet with a sweetness that was very much in character.

'But let me ask you this: what happens after a hundred years? Without us having any say in the matter, all our ideas will be lumped together under the heading, "The Thought of the Age". Take the history of art, for example: it proves my point irrefutably, whether you like it or not. Each period has its own style, and no artist living in a particular era can completely transcend that era's style, whatever his individual outlook.'

'Does our age have its style too?'

'I think I'd be more inclined to say that the style of the Meiji era is still dying. But how would I know? To live in the midst of an era is to be oblivious to its style. You and I, you see, must be immersed in some style of living or other, but we're like goldfish swimming around in a bowl without ever noticing it. Take yourself: yours is a world of feeling. You appear different from most people. And you yourself are quite sure that you have never allowed your personality to be compromised. However, there is absolutely no way of proving that. The testimony of your contemporaries has no value whatever. Who knows? It may just be that your world of feeling represents the style of this era in its purest form. But then again, there's no way of knowing.'

'Well, then, who does decide?'

'Time. Time is what matters. As time goes by, you and I will be carried inexorably into the mainstream of our period, even though we're unaware of what it is. And later, when they say that young men in the early Taisho era thought, dressed, talked, in such and such a way, they'll be talking about you and me. We'll all be lumped together. You detest that bunch on the *kendo* team, don't you? You despise them?'

'Yes,' Kiyoaki said, uncomfortably aware that the cold was beginning to penetrate the seat of his trousers, but gazing nevertheless at some green camellia leaves beside the frame of the arbour. Freshly bared by the melting snow, they were gleaming brightly. 'Yes, I not only dislike them, I despise them.'

Taking his perfunctory reply in his stride, Honda went on: 'All right, then, just imagine this if you can. In a few decades, people will see you and the people you despise as one and the same, a single entity. Your slow-witted friends – with their sentimentality, their vicious narrow-mindedness that condemns as effeminate anyone who is not like themselves, their harassment of the underclassmen, their fanatical worship of General Nogi, the frame of mind that lets them draw such incredible satisfaction from sweeping the ground every morning around the sakaki planted by the Meiji Emperor – you with all your sensitivity will be seen cheek-by-jowl with these people when they stop to think about our times in years to come. You see, this is the easiest way to establish the essence of our era – to take the lowest common denominator. Once the churning water has settled to a calm surface, you can see the rainbow oil slick floating there. And that's the way it will be. After we're all dead, it will be easy to analyse us and isolate our basic elements for everyone to see. And of course this essence, the thought that is the foundation of our era, will be considered quite benighted a hundred years from now. And you and I have no way of escaping the verdict, no way to prove that we didn't share the discredited views of our contemporaries. And what standard will history apply to that outlook? What do you think? The thoughts of the geniuses of our age? Of great men? Not at all. Those who come after us and decide what was in our minds will adopt the criterion of the uncritical thought patterns of your friends on the *kendo* team. In other words, they'll seize upon the most primitive and popular credos of our day. You see every era has always been characterized solely in terms of such idiocies.'

Kiyoaki was not sure where this was taking Honda, but as he listened, a germ of thought began to grow in his mind. By now several of their classmates were to be seen at the open windows of their second-floor classroom. The windows of the other rooms were shut, reflecting the glare of the morning sun and the brilliant blue of the sky. A familiar morning scene. When he thought of the events of the previous day, the morning of the snowstorm, he felt as if he had been drawn unwillingly from a dark world of sensuous excitement into the clear, bright courts of reason.

'Well, that's history,' he said. He was embarrassed by the immaturity of his remarks in contrast to Honda's, but he was finally making an effort to come to grips with the other's thought. 'In other words, no matter what we think, or hope for, or feel – all that has not the slightest bearing on the course of history? Is that what you mean?'

'That's it exactly. Europeans believe that a man like Napoleon can impose his will on history. We Japanese think the same of the men like your grandfather and his contemporaries who brought about the Meiji Restoration. But is that really true? Does history ever obey the will of men? Looking at you always makes me ponder that question. You're not a great man and you're not a genius either. But, nonetheless, you have one characteristic that sets you quite apart: you have no trace whatever of willpower. And so I am always fascinated to think of you in relation to history.'

'Are you being sarcastic?'

'No, not a bit. I'm thinking in terms of unconscious participation in history. For example, let's say that I have willpower –'

'You certainly have.'

'Say that I want to alter the course of history. I devote all my energies and resources to this end. I use every ounce of strength I possess to bend history to my will. Say I possess the prestige and authority so necessary to bring this about. None of this would ensure that history proceeded according to my wishes. Then, on the other hand, perhaps a hundred, two hundred, even three hundred years later, history might veer abruptly to take a course that was consonant with my vision and ideals – and this without my having had anything whatever to do with it. Perhaps society would assume a form that was the exact replica of my dreams of a hundred or two hundred years before; history, enjoying the new glory that had been my vision, would smile at me with cool condescension and mock my ambition. And people would say: "Well, that's history."'

'But there is such a thing as the time being ripe for everything, isn't there?' asked Kiyoaki. 'Your vision's time would finally have come, that's all. Maybe it wouldn't even take as long as a hundred years; maybe thirty or fifty. That sort of thing often happens. And perhaps even after your death, your will would serve as an invisible guideline, unknown to anyone, that would help bring about what you wanted to accomplish in your lifetime. Maybe if someone like you had never lived, history would never have taken such a turn, no matter how long it lasted.'

Even though such cold, uncongenial abstractions were a struggle for him,

Kiyoaki felt stirred by a certain warmth, an excitement that he knew he had Honda to thank for. He was reluctant to acknowledge satisfaction from such a source. But as he looked around the white-carpeted school grounds, with the bare branches of the trees casting shadows over the snow-covered flowerbeds, and the clear sound of trickling water in his ears, he knew he was happy that Honda had started this discussion. Even though he must have known that he was still engrossed in the memory of the happiness and fascination of the day before, Honda had chosen to ignore it, a decision that seemed appropriate to the purity of the snow around them. At that moment, some of it slid off the roof, baring a few square feet of wet tile, gleaming black.

'And so,' continued Honda, 'if society turned out as I wanted it to after a hundred years, you'd call that an accomplishment?'

'It must be.'

'Whose accomplishment?'

'That of your will.'

'You're joking. I'd be dead. As I just told you, all this came about without my having had anything to do with it.'

'Well, can't you say that it's the accomplishment of the will of history then?'

'So history has a will, eh? It's always dangerous to try to personify history. As far as I'm concerned, history has no will of its own and, furthermore, it hasn't the least concern for mine either. So if there is no will whatever involved in the process, you can't talk about accomplishments. And all the so-called accomplishments of history prove it. They're no sooner achieved than they begin to crumble away. History is a record of destruction. One must always make room for the next ephemeral crystal. For history, to build and to destroy are one and the same thing.

'I am fully aware of all this. Although I understand it, I cannot be like you and stop being a man of determination. I suppose it's probably a compulsion in my character. No one can say for certain, but I will say this much: any will has as its essence the desire to influence history. I'm not saying that human desires affect history, only that they try to. Then, too, some forms of will are bound up with destiny, even though this concept is anathema to the will.

'But in the long run, all human will is doomed to frustration. It's a matter of course that things turn out contrary to your intentions. And what conclusion does a Westerner draw from this? He says: "My will was the sole rational force involved. Failure came about by chance."

'To speak of chance is to negate the possibility of any law of cause and effect. Chance is the one final irrationality acceptable to the free will.

'Without the concept of chance, you see, the Western philosophy of free will could never have arisen. Chance is the crucial refuge of the will. And without it the very thought of gambling would be inconceivable, just as the Westerner has no other way of rationalizing the repeated setbacks and frustrations that he must endure. I think that this concept of chance, of a gamble, is the very substance of the God of Europeans, and so they have a deity whose characteristics are derived from that refuge so vital to free will, namely chance – the only sort of God who would inspire the freedom of human will.

'But what would happen if we were to deny the existence of chance completely? What would happen if – no matter what the victory or the defeat – you had to exclude utterly all possible roles of chance in it? In that case, you'd be destroying all refuge of free will. Do away with chance and you undermine the props under the concept of the will.

'Picture a scene like this: it's a square at midday. The will is standing there all alone. He pretends that he is remaining upright by virtue of his own strength, and hence he goes on deceiving himself. The sun beats down. No trees, no grass. Nothing whatever in the huge square to keep him company but his own shadow. At that moment, a thundering voice comes down from the cloudless sky above: "Chance is dead. There's no such thing as chance. Hear me, Will: you have lost your advocate forever." And with that, the Will feels his substance begin to crumble and dissolve. His flesh rots and falls away. In an instant his skeleton is laid bare, a thin liquid spurts from it, and the bones themselves lose their solidity and begin to disintegrate. The Will still stands with his feet planted firmly on the ground, but this final effort is futile. For at that very moment, the bright, glaring sky is rent apart with a terrible roar, and the God of Inevitability stares down through the chasm.

'But I cannot help trying to conjure up an odious face for this dreadful God, and this weakness is doubtless due to my own bent toward voluntarism. For if Chance ceases to exist, then Will becomes meaningless – no more significant than a speck of rust on the huge chain of cause and effect that we only glimpse from time to time. Then there's only one way to participate in history, and that's to have no will at all – to function solely as a shining, beautiful atom, eternal and unchanging. No one should look for any other meaning in human existence.

'You are not likely to see things this way. I wouldn't expect you to subscribe to such a philosophy. The only things you do put any faith in – and that without much thought – are your own good looks, your changing moods, your individuality and – not your fixed character, but on the contrary, your very lack of it. Am I right?'

Kiyoaki could not manage an answer. For want of anything better, he smiled, knowing that Honda was not trying to insult him.

'And that for me is the greatest riddle,' said Honda, sighing so earnestly that it seemed almost comical. His breath became a frosty cloud that hovered for a second in the clear morning air, and seemed to Kiyoaki to be a secret manifestation of Honda's concern for him. Deep down inside him, his sense of happiness intensified.

The bell rang to announce the beginning of classes, and the two young men stood up. Just then, someone scooped up some of the snow piled on the second floor window ledges and threw down a snowball. It struck the path at their feet, in a burst of sparkling fragments.

14

Kiyoaki's father had entrusted him with the key to the library. This was in a corner of the north side of the main house, and it was one room of the Matsugaes that received scant attention. The Marquis was not the man to devote much time to books. But here were gathered the Chinese classics that had belonged to Kiyoaki's grandfather, the Western books that the Marquis had ordered from Maruzen out of the desire to appear intellectual, and many others received as gifts. When Kiyoaki started high school, his father had handed over the key with the pomposity of one conferring the guardianship of a treasure trove of wisdom. Thus he alone was privileged to go there whenever he liked. Among the books in the library least likely to excite the Marquis's interest were many collections of Japanese classics and children's books. Prior to publication, each of their publishers had requested a brief recommendation from the Marquis together with a photograph of him in formal dress, and then in exchange for this privilege to print 'Recommended by His Excellency Marquis Matsugae' in gilt letters on the binding of each book, they presented him with the collections.

Kiyoaki himself was not inclined to make frequent use of the library. He preferred his own reveries to books. For Iinuma, who was given the key once a month by Kiyoaki so that he could clean the room, the library was the most hallowed place in the house, sanctified as it was by the Chinese classics dear to Kiyoaki's grandfather. When he spoke of it, he never referred to it merely as the library. It was always 'His Late Excellency's Library', and when he pronounced those words, his voice was choked with emotion.

On the evening after Kiyoaki had become reconciled with Honda, he called his tutor to his room just as Iinuma was about to leave for his night classes, and dropped the library key into his hand without a word. There was a set day for the monthly cleaning. Furthermore, this was a job that Iinuma never did at night. What, he wondered, was the reason for giving him the key now, on the wrong day and in the evening at that? It lay on the palm of his thick, blunt hand, blue and metallic like a dragonfly with its wings torn off.

Afterwards Iinuma would recall this moment time and again. How torn and naked the key seemed, like a ravaged body as it lay in his palm. He stood for some time trying to decide what it meant, but he could not. When Kiyoaki finally did explain, he seethed with anger directed not so much at his master as at himself for being at his mercy.

'Yesterday morning I didn't go to school and you stood by me. Tonight it's my turn to help you. Go out just as if you were leaving for school. Then go round to the back and come in by the door opposite the library. That key will open the room and you can wait inside. But don't turn on the light. And the safest course would be to lock the door from the inside.

'Tadeshina has given Miné full instructions. She'll telephone here with a message for her, asking when Miss Satoko's sachet will be finished. That will be the signal. Miné is skilled at such delicate work and people are always asking her to do something like this. Miss Satoko herself asked her to make a gold brocade sachet. So such a phone call won't arouse the least suspicion.

'Once Miné receives the message, she'll wait for the time when you're supposed to leave for school and then she'll go to the library and knock lightly on the door, hoping that you'll open it for her. And since it'll be just after dinner, when everyone is bustling around, no one will miss her for thirty or forty minutes.

'Tadeshina believes that for you two to meet outside instead would be too dangerous and hard to arrange. There would have to be all sorts of pretexts for a maid to go out alone without everyone having something to say about it.

'At any rate, I took the liberty of deciding the matter without consulting you. Tadeshina is going to call Miné tonight. And so you must go to the library. If you don't Miné will be terribly upset.'

As he stood listening, a bear at bay, Iinuma's hand shook so violently that he almost dropped the key.

The library was very cold. The heavy curtains of gold thread let in a little light from the lanterns burning in the garden behind the house, but not enough to allow one to decipher the titles of the books. The room was filled with the smell of mildew, like the odour hanging over the banks of a clogged canal in winter.

The darkness was no obstacle to Iinuma. He had memorized the place of almost every book in the library. Works such as the writings of Han Fei-tzu, *The Testimony of Seiken*, and *The Eighteen Histories* lined the shelves, including a Japanese-bound edition of the *Commentaries on the Four Classics* which had lost its protective cover. This was a book that Kiyoaki's grandfather had thumbed so often that its binding was worn out.

One day when Iinuma was turning over the pages of one of the books he was dusting, a poem by Kayo Honen had caught his eye. It was in a collection of famous Japanese and Chinese works, and Iinuma had carefully memorized the place. The title was 'Song of a Noble Heart'. One verse of it was particularly consoling as he performed his duties of cleaning the library:

Though now I sweep a little room
I will not do so forever
Can Kyushu hold my ambition?
Can flocks of chattering sparrows
Share the eagle's solitary path?

Iinuma now understood. Knowing his deep reverence for 'His Late Excellency's Library', Kiyoaki had deliberately chosen it for this tryst. There could be no doubt about it. When he had been explaining the plan that he had so considerately arranged, the cold satisfaction in his manner was proof enough that he grasped all its implications. He wanted events to take their course so that Iinuma himself would commit sacrilege in the place he worshipped.

When he thought about it, there had been a silent menace in Kiyoaki ever since he had been a beautiful child. A delight in sacrilege. And when Iinuma had thus defiled what was so precious to him, Kiyoaki would be as delighted as if he had taken a piece of raw meat and rolled it up in a sacred Shinto pendant. In legendary times, the savage god Susano, the brother of the Sun Goddess, had found satisfaction in the same way.

Ever since Iinuma had lost himself to a woman, Kiyoaki's power over him had grown immensely. Furthermore – and to Iinuma the injustice of it was baffling – the world would always accept Kiyoaki's pleasures as charming and natural, whereas it would condemn his own with unflagging severity as sordid, not to say sinful. As he brooded over this, Iinuma's self-loathing steadily deepened.

From the ceiling of the library came the rustle of scurrying rats, and an occasional muffled squeal. When he had done the cleaning the previous month, he had spread plenty of poisoned chestnuts up there, but apparently to no avail. Suddenly he shuddered, remembering what he most wanted to forget.

Every time he saw Miné's face, no matter how he tried to suppress it, the same evil thought stirred in his mind. Even now, as her warm body was coming to meet him in the evening darkness, this thought stood between them. It concerned something that Kiyoaki probably knew already, but since he had never mentioned it to him, Iinuma himself, without forgetting about it for a moment, had kept quiet about it. Actually, it was a rather open secret, which made Iinuma's distress increasingly hard to bear. He was tormented by it, as if a pack of rats were swarming over him in all their filth. The Marquis had slept with Miné and still occasionally did. His imagination was triggered by the rats above – their bloodshot eyes, their loathsome bodies...

The cold was biting. No matter how brave a figure Iinuma cut when he went out to perform his daily devotions, he shook now as the cold struck his back and crept through him until it covered his skin like an icy compress. Miné had probably been delayed until there was an opportunity to leave the table without attracting attention.

As he waited, his desire grew, sharp and insistent. Then a mass of disagreeable feelings combined with the piercing chill and the smell of decay to assault his already taut nerves. He had a sinking sensation as though the foul waters of a drainage ditch were rising against his legs, soiling his fine silk *hakama*. 'Is this my way of finding pleasure?' he thought – a man of twenty-four, capable of great bravery and ripe for the highest honours.

There was a light knock at the door. Iinuma reacted with such speed that he crashed painfully into a bookcase. Finally, however, he managed to turn the key in the lock. Miné turned slightly and slipped through the doorway. When Iinuma had turned the lock behind her, he took her by the shoulders and propelled her unceremoniously toward the back of the library. Whatever the reason, his mind was fixed on the dirty grey snow he had seen shovelled into piles along the outside wall of the library on his way there. Though he had no time or inclination to speculate about this, he was consumed with the need to violate Miné in the corner that was closest to the dirty snow.

Driven to savagery by his fantasies, he was brutal with the girl. The more he pitied her, the crueller he became. And when in the midst of it all he realized that his viciousness was a passion to revenge himself on Kiyoaki, he was overcome by an indescribable misery. Since time was short and silence imperative, Miné let Iinuma have his way without offering any resistance. But the meekness of her submission only tormented Iinuma the more, for her gentle manner bespoke a quiet understanding of himself as someone very similar to her.

Still, this was by no means the only reason for her gentle compliance. Miné was cheerfully promiscuous. And for her the total awkwardness of his manner – his attempt to intimidate her by his silence, his clumsy, fumbling hands – proved the reality of his desire. She never dreamed that he might be pitying her.

Lying there in the dark, Miné suddenly felt the cold like a sword thrust under the spread skirt of her kimono. Looking up through the gloom, she saw shelves laden with books, each tucked into its case, the gold of its title dulled by the passage of time. They seemed to be pressing in on her from all sides. Speed was essential. Tadeshina had briefed her down to the last detail so that she would be clear on every point, and all that was required of her in this brief moment was to act without hesitation. She saw her role in life as that of someone who was ready to give her body freely to soothe and comfort. This was enough for her. And her small ripe body, with its firm flesh and smooth, flawless skin, was pleased to give satisfaction.

It would be no exaggeration to say that she was fond of Iinuma. Whenever she was desired, Miné had a wonderful knack of discovering the good points in her suitor. She had never joined the other maids in their contemptuous mockery of Iinuma, and so his virility, so long harassed and ridiculed, at last received its due in her woman's heart.

She suddenly had a vision of a temple holiday in all its gaudy festivity: the acetylene lights with their glare and acrid smell, the balloons and pinwheels, the gaily coloured candies...

She opened her eyes in the darkness.

'What are you staring at?' asked Iinuma in irritation.

The rats were scurrying around in the ceiling again. Their movements were almost soundless, and yet they held a note of desperate urgency. They seemed to be rushing frantically through their dark domain in a frenzy that dashed them from one end of it to the other.

15

All the mail that was delivered to the Matsugae household was handled according to a fixed ritual: the steward Yamada took charge of it and stacked it neatly on a gold-laquered tray engraved with the family crest. This was then borne into the presence of the Marquis and Marquise. Since Satoko was aware of this procedure, she had taken the precaution of entrusting her note to Tadeshina, who, in turn, was to give it to Iinuma.

So it was that Iinuma, in the middle of studying for his final examinations, took the time first to meet Tadeshina and then to hand over Satoko's love letter to Kiyoaki.

Though the morning after the snowstorm was clear and bright, I just couldn't help thinking about what had happened the day before. In my heart it seemed as if the snow had not stopped, but was falling still. And the snowflakes seemed to merge into the form of Kiyo's face. How I wished that I could live somewhere where the snow fell every day of the year so that I would never stop thinking of you, Kiyo.

If we were living in Heian times, you would have composed a poem for me, wouldn't you? And I would have had to offer one of my own in reply. I am shocked to think that although I have been learning *waka* since my childhood, at a time like this I can't set down a single poem to express my feelings. Is it because I lack the talent?

Why do you believe that I'm so happy? Just because I have found someone who is kind enough not to be upset by whatever I say or do, no matter how capricious? That would be the same as thinking that I enjoy treating Kiyo however I choose – and nothing could cause me greater pain than to know that you believe this.

No, what really makes me happy is your gentleness. You were able to see through that whim of mine the other day. You could see how desperate I secretly felt. And without a word of reproach you came with me on that ride through the snow and you fulfilled the dream that I had buried deep inside me with so much embarrassment. That is what I mean by your gentleness.

Kiyo, even now, remembering what happened, I feel my body tremble with joy and shame. Here in Japan, we think of the spirit of snow as a woman – the snow fairy. But I remember that in Western fairy tales I read it's always a handsome young man. And so I think of Kiyo as the spirit of snow, so masculine in your uniform. I think of you as overwhelming me. To feel myself dissolve into your beauty and freeze to death in the snow – no fate could be sweeter.

At the end, Satoko had written: 'Please be kind enough not to forget to throw this letter into the fire.'

Up to this final line, the style was smooth and graceful, for Satoko never expressed herself other than with elegance. Nevertheless, Kiyoaki was startled by the sensuous vigour that seemed to flare up here and there.

After he had read it, his immediate reaction was that it was the kind of letter that ought to transport a man into ecstasy. On reflection, however, it seemed more of a textbook exercise from Satoko's classes in the art of elegance. He felt she wanted to teach him that elegance overrides any question of indecency.

If the two of them had really fallen in love that snowy morning, how could they bear to let a day pass without meeting, if only for a moment or two? What could be more natural? Yet Kiyoaki was not inclined to follow his impulses in such a way. Oddly enough, living only for one's emotions, like a flag obedient to the breeze, demands a way of life that makes one balk at the natural course of events, for this implies being altogether subservient to nature. The life of the emotions detests all constraints, whatever their origin, and thus, ironically enough, is apt eventually to fetter its own instinctive sense of freedom.

Kiyoaki delayed seeing Satoko again, though not to practise self-denial. Still less was he guided by a profound knowledge of the subtleties of emotion which are only open to those already experienced in love. His behaviour was simply the result of his imperfect grasp of the art of elegance, and was still so immature, almost bordering on vanity, that he envied Satoko her serene freedom, wantonness even, and was made to feel inferior.

Just as a stream returns to its normal course after a flood, Kiyoaki's predilection for suffering began to reassert itself. His dreamy nature could be as demanding as it was capricious, so much so, in fact, that he was angered and frustrated at the lack of obstacles to his love. The meddlesome assistance of Tadeshina and Iinuma provided a ready target, and he came to view their manoeuvres as inimical to the purity of his feelings.

His pride was hurt when he realized that this was all he had to rely on as the fierce pain and agony of love spun their coil. Such pain ought to be fit material for weaving a magnificent tapestry, but Kiyoaki had only a tiny domestic loom with nothing but pure white thread at his disposal.

'Where are they leading me,' he wondered, 'at this very moment when I am gradually, genuinely, falling in love?'

But even as he decided that what he felt was love, his contrary nature was asserting itself once more.

For any ordinary young man, the memory of Satoko's kiss would have been enough to lift him into ecstasies of joy and satisfaction. But for this young man, for whom complacency was already too common a condition, it was a memory that caused greater heartache with every passing day.

No matter what else might be true, the happiness he had felt at that moment had the brilliant fire of a rich jewel. There was no doubt about that. It was engraved on his memory. In the midst of a formless, colourless snowy desert, with his emotions in turmoil, not knowing how he had embarked on this journey or how it should end, the warm glow of that jewel had been like a compass point.

His sense of discrepancy between the memory of that happiness and his present heartache grew steadily, and its effect on him deepened: he finally lapsed into the black melancholy that had been so congenial before. The kiss ceased to be anything more than another reminder of Satoko's humiliating mockery.

He decided to write a reply to her letter as chill as he could make it. He tore up several sheets of stationery in the attempt, making a fresh start each time. When he had finally composed what he thought was the ultimate in unfeeling billets-doux and put down his writing brush, he suddenly became aware of the extent of his achievement. Without intending to, he had hit upon the style of a man of great worldly experience, having built on the letter of accusation he had once sent her. This time the very thought of such outright deception was so painful that he began yet another letter. In it, without any attempt at qualification, he conveyed the joy of experiencing a kiss for the first time. It was filled with boyish passion. He closed his eyes as he slipped it into an envelope and ran the tip of his tongue over the flap. The glue tasted vaguely sweet, like medicine.

16

The Matsugae estate was most famous for its autumn display of maple leaves, but its cherry blossoms were also the object of much admiration. Cherry trees were scattered among the pines in the long rows of trees that flanked the drive to the main gate for more than half a mile. The best view was from the second-floor balcony of the Western-style house. Standing there, one could take in all the cherry blossoms on the Matsugae estate in a single sweeping glance; some bloomed along the drive, several trees stood among the huge gingko trees in the front garden, some ringed the small grassy knoll where Kiyoaki's Otachimachi ritual had taken place, and a few grew on the maple hill beyond the pond. Many discriminating viewers preferred this arrangement to an overwhelming display of massed blossoms in the middle of a garden.

From spring to early summer, the three principal events in the Matsugae household were the Doll Festival in March, the cherry blossom viewing in April, and the Shinto festival in May. But since the prescribed year of mourning following the death of His Imperial Highness had not yet elapsed, it was decided that this year the March and April festivals would be curtailed to strictly family observances – much to the disappointment of the women of the house. For throughout the winter, as happened every year, all sorts of rumours had been filtering down from the quarters of the senior staff about plans for the Doll Festival and the blossom viewing – such as the story that a troupe of professional entertainers would be brought in. The house was always full of such tales, the kind of speculation that gave a thrill to simple souls accustomed to making a great deal out of the arrival of springtime. To have their expectations blighted in this way seemed like a blight on spring itself.

The full Kagoshima-style celebration of the Doll Festival at the Matsugaes' was renowned; thanks to appreciative foreign visitors invited in years gone by, it was now famous abroad as well, so much so in fact that every year a large number of Americans and Europeans who were in Japan at the festival time would use whatever influence they had to try to obtain invitations.

The pale cheeks of the two ivory dolls representing the Emperor and Empress shone cold in the early spring light, despite the gleam of the surrounding candles and the reflection from the scarlet carpet beneath. The Emperor doll was dressed in the splendid ceremonial robes of a Shinto high priest, and the Empress in the extravagantly rich Heian court costume. Despite the bulk of their countless skirts, their gowns dipped gracefully at the back to reveal the pale translucence of the napes of their necks. The scarlet carpet covered the entire floor of the huge main reception room. Countless wooden balls inside richly embroidered cloth hung down from the beamed ceiling, and bas-relief pictures of various kinds of popular dolls covered the walls. An old woman named Tsuru, famed for her skill at this sort of picture, came to Tokyo every February to throw herself wholeheartedly into the preparations; her pet refrain was a mumbled 'as madam wishes'.

Even though this year's Doll Festival lacked the usual gaiety, the women were nevertheless cheered by the prospect of the cherry blossom season; it would not be observed publicly, but it would still be celebrated with considerably more festivity than they had first been led to believe. This hope was warranted by a communication from His Highness Prince Toin announcing that he would deign to be present, though in a private capacity.

This had also cheered the Marquis immensely. He was happiest in the midst of extravagance and ostentation, and the restraints of polite society weighed heavily on his outgoing nature. If the Emperor's cousin himself saw fit to take a lax view of the observation of mourning, then no one would dare cast aspersions on the Marquis's own sense of what morality required.

Since His Highness Haruhisa Toin had been the Emperor's personal representative at the coronation of Rahma VI and so was personally known to the royal family of Siam, the Marquis decided that it would be proper to include the two young princes in the invitations.

Years before in Paris, during the Olympic Games of 1900, the Marquis had become rather intimate with the Prince while rendering him valued service as a guide to the night life of the city. Even now the Prince was fond of recalling those days with references that only the Marquis understood. 'Matsugae,' he would say, 'remember that place with the fountain that gushed champagne? That was a night to remember!'

April the sixth was the day set for the formal viewing of the cherry blossoms, and as soon as the rather subdued observance of the Doll Festival was over, the tempo of life in the household quickened as preparations got underway.

Kiyoaki, however, did nothing at all during his spring vacation. His parents urged him to take a trip somewhere, but even though he did not see Satoko very often, he was not in the mood to leave Tokyo while she was there.

As spring came gradually, day by day, despite the sharp cold, Kiyoaki struggled with a series of unsettling premonitions. Finally, when his ennui became overpowering, he decided to do something he did only rarely; he paid a visit to his grandmother's house on the estate. She seemed unable to shake off a lifetime's habit of treating him like an infant, and this, together with her fondness for cataloguing his mother's faults, was reason enough for his reluctance to visit her. Ever since the death of his grandfather, his grandmother, with her masculine shoulders and no-nonsense face, had turned her back on the world completely, and ate little but a handful of rice a day, as though living in anticipation of the death she hoped was soon to come. As it turned out, however, she thrived on this diet.

When people came from Kagoshima to visit her, she talked to them in the dialect of her home region, indifferent to what others might think. With Kiyoaki and his mother, though, she spoke in the Tokyo manner, however stiffly and awkwardly. Furthermore, since she had none of the nasal tone of Tokyo speech, the strong parade-ground quality of her voice was all the more apparent. He was convinced that she carefully preserved her Kagoshima accent as an implicit condemnation of the easy fluency of his own Tokyo inflections.

'So, Prince Toin is coming to see the blossoms, eh?' she said without preamble as he entered; she was warming her legs in the *kotatsu*.

'Yes, that's what they say.'

'I'm not going. Your mother asked me, but I prefer being here out of everybody's way.'

Then, showing concern over his idleness, she went on to ask him if he didn't feel inclined to take up judo or fencing. There had once been an exercise hall on the estate, but it had been torn down to make way for the Western house. She made the sarcastic comment that its destruction had marked the beginning of the decline of the family. This was one opinion, however, that was congenial to his own way of thinking. He liked the word 'decline'.

'If your two uncles were alive, your father wouldn't be carrying on the way he does. As far as I'm concerned, this being on familiar terms with the Imperial Family and pouring out money on entertainment is just a big show. Whenever I think of my two sons dead in the war without ever having known what luxury was, I feel I don't want to have anything more to do with your father and the rest of them – floating through life and thinking of nothing but having a good time. And as for the pension I receive for my two boys, that's why I put it up there on the shelf beside the household altar without ever touching it. It seems to me that His Imperial Majesty gave it to me for the sake of my sons and the blood they shed so gallantly. It would be wrong ever to use it.'

His grandmother enjoyed delivering herself of little sermons like this, but the truth was that the Marquis was unstintingly generous in granting whatever she wished, be it clothes, food, spending money, or servants. Kiyoaki often wondered if perhaps she was acutely ashamed of her rural origins and so was trying to avoid any kind of Western social life.

Still, whenever he visited her and only then, he felt that he was escaping from himself and from the artificial environment that suffocated him. He enjoyed the contact with a person who was so close to him but who still retained the earthy vigour of his ancestors. It was a pleasure of a rather ironic sort.

Everything about his grandmother was in physical harmony with his image of her character: her hands were large and her fingers blunt; the lines of her face seemed to have been laid there with the firm, sure strokes of a writing brush, and her lips were set with firm resolution. Once in a while, however, she was willing to allow a lighter note to creep into her conversations with him. Now, for example, she tapped her grandson's knee under the low table that covered the foot-warmer and teased him: 'Whenever you come here, you know, my women get flustered and I don't know what to do with them. To me, I'm afraid, you're still a little boy with a wet nose, but I suppose that these girls see things differently.'

Kiyoaki looked up at the faded photographs of his two uncles in uniform on the wall. Their military dress seemed to him to preclude any possible bond between them and himself. The war had ended a mere eight years before, yet the gap between them seemed immeasurable.

'I'll never shed real blood. I'll never wound anything but hearts,' he boasted to himself, although not without a slight sense of misgiving.

Outside, the sun shone on the shoji screen. The small room bathed him in cozy warmth, making him feel as if he were wrapped in a huge, opaque cocoon of glowing white. He felt as if he were basking luxuriously in the direct sunlight. His grandmother began to doze. In the silence of the room, he became aware of the ticking of the huge old-fashioned clock. His grandmother's head tipped forward slightly. Her forehead jutted out sharply under the line of her short hair which she wore bound and sprinkled with a black powder dye. He noticed the healthy sheen of her skin. More than half a century ago, he thought, the hot Kagoshima sun must have burned her brown each summer of her youth, and even now she seemed to have retained its mark.

He was daydreaming, and his thoughts, moving like the sea, gradually turned from the rhythm of the waves to that of the long, slow passage of time, and hence to the inevitability of growing old – and he suddenly caught his breath. He had never looked forward to the wisdom and other vaunted benefits of old age. Would he be able to die young – and if possible free of all pain? A graceful death – as a richly patterned kimono, thrown carelessly across a polished table, slides unobtrusively down into the darkness of the floor beneath. A death marked by elegance.

The thought of dying suddenly spurred him with a desire to see Satoko, if only for a moment.

He telephoned Tadeshina and then hurriedly left the house. There was no doubt that Satoko was full of life and beauty, as he himself was – these two facts seemed to be a strange twist of fortune, something to seize and cling to in time of danger.

Following Tadeshina's scheme, Satoko pretended to go out for a stroll and met Kiyoaki at a small Shinto shrine not far from her home. The first thing she did was to thank him for the invitation to the cherry blossom festival. She obviously thought that he had persuaded the Marquis to issue it. This was, in fact, the first he had heard of the matter, but with his usual deviousness, he did not disabuse her of the idea, and accepted her thanks in a vague, noncommittal way.

17

After a prolonged struggle, Marquis Matsugae succeeded in compiling a severely curtailed guest list for the blossom festival. His criterion was to invite the number of suitable guests most appropriate to the occasion, as the banquet that concluded it would be graced by the august presence of the Imperial Prince and his wife. Besides Satoko and her parents, Count and Countess Ayakura, he therefore included only the two Siamese princes and Baron Shinkawa and his wife, who were frequent visitors and great friends of the Matsugaes. The Baron was the head of the Shinkawa *zaibatsu.* His whole way of life was modelled on that of the complete English gentleman, whom he copied with scrupulous attention to detail. The Baroness, for her part, was on intimate terms with such people as the noted feminist Raicho Hiratsuka and her circle, and was also a patron of the Women of

Tomorrow. She could thus be relied upon to add a touch of colour to the gathering.

Prince Toin and his wife were to arrive at three in the afternoon and be shown around the garden after a short rest in one of the reception rooms of the main house. They would then be entertained until five o'clock at a garden party by some geishas, who would go on to perform a selection of cherry blossom dances from the Genroku era.

Just before sunset, the imperial couple were to retire to the Western-style house for aperitifs. After the banquet itself, there would be a final entertainment: a projectionist had been hired to show a new foreign film. Such was the programme devised by the Marquis with the help of Yamada, his steward, after pondering the varied tastes of his guests.

Trying to settle the choice of films gave the Marquis some agonizing moments. There was the one from Pathé featuring Gabrielle Robin, the famous star of the Comédie Française, that was indisputably a masterpiece. The Marquis rejected it, however, fearing that it might destroy the mood of the blossom viewing, created with such care. At the beginning of March the Electric Theatre in Asakusa had begun to show films made in the West, the first of which, *Paradise Lost*, had already become wildly popular. But it would hardly do to present a film that was readily available in a place like that. Then there was another film, a German melodrama filled with violent action, but that could hardly be expected to score a success with the Princess and the other ladies-in-waiting. The Marquis finally decided that the choice most likely to please his guests was an English five-reeler based on a Dickens novel. The film might be rather gloomy, but it did have a certain refinement, its appeal was fairly wide, and the English captions would help all his guests.

But what if it rained? In that case, the large reception room in the main house would not offer a sufficiently varied array of blossoms, and the only suitable alternative would be to hold the viewing on the second floor of the Western-style house. Afterwards, the geishas could also perform their dances there, and the aperitifs and the formal banquet would follow as planned.

The preparations got underway with the construction of a temporary stage at a spot near the pond, just at the foot of the grassy hill. If the weather turned out to be fine, the Prince and his party would undoubtedly make a full tour of the estate in order not to miss any of the blossoms. The traditional red and white curtains that must be extended along his route were far larger than those required by more ordinary events. The work of decking the interior of the Western-style house with cherry blossoms and decorating its banqueting table to suggest a rural spring scene demanded all the attentions of a large group of helpers. Finally, on the day before the party, the hairdressers and their assistants were driven into a frenzy of activity.

Happily, April 6 was clear, even if the sunshine left something to be desired. It came and went, and there was even a chill in the morning air.

An unused room in the main house was set aside as a changing room for the geishas and was filled with all the available mirrors. His curiosity aroused, Kiyoaki went there to take a look for himself, but the maid in charge quickly chased him away. His imagination, however, was caught by the room, scoured and swept in preparation for the women who were soon to come. Screens were set up, pillows scattered everywhere, and mirrors glinted through their brightly coloured covers of printed Yuzen muslin. At the moment there wasn't the faintest hint of the scent of cosmetics in the air. But within no more than half an hour, there would be a transformation; the place would be filled with lovely voices as the women gathered about the mirrors, donning and shedding their costumes with unflurried self-possession. Kiyoaki found the prospect fascinating. He was caught up by the seductive magic of the occasion, which did not emanate from the rough stage that had just been built in the garden, but rather was concentrated here in this room with its promise of intoxicating fragrance soon to come.

As the Siamese princes had very little concept of time, Kiyoaki had asked them to come as soon as lunch was over. They arrived at about one thirty. He invited them up to his study for the moment, startled to see that they were wearing their school uniforms.

'Is that beautiful girl of yours coming?' Prince Kridsada asked loudly in English before they were through the door.

Prince Pattanadid, always gently reserved, was affronted; he scolded his cousin for his unthinking rudeness and apologized to Kiyoaki in halting Japanese.

Kiyoaki assured them that she would come, but he caused surprised glances by asking that they refrain from speaking about him and Satoko in front of either the imperial guests or the Matsugaes and Ayakuras. The princes had apparently assumed that the relationship was common knowledge.

By now the two princes were showing no sign of their former homesickness, and they seemed to have settled into the rhythm of life in Japan. In their school uniforms, they struck Kiyoaki as being almost indistinguishable from his other classmates. Prince Kridsada, who was a gifted mimic, did an imitation of the dean that was good enough to make Chao P. and Kiyoaki laugh out loud.

Chao P. walked over to the window and looked out over the grounds of the estate at a scene quite different from what one saw on ordinary days. The red and white curtain that wound through it was waving in the wind.

'From now on it must surely get warmer,' he said forlornly, his voice filled with longing for the hot summer sun.

Kiyoaki was quite taken with his touch of melancholy. He stood up and was about to walk over to the window himself, but as he rose, Chao P. gave a sudden, boyish cry that aroused his cousin and brought him out of his chair.

'There she is!' he exclaimed, slipping into English. 'There's the beautiful lady we mustn't mention today.'

And indeed it was Satoko, unmistakable in her long-sleeved kimono as she came along the path beside the pond toward the main house with her parents beside her. Even at a distance, Kiyoaki could see that the kimono was a beautiful cherry-blossom pink, its pattern reminiscent of the fresh green profusion of a spring meadow. As she turned her head momentarily, pointing out the island, he caught a glimpse of her profile, the delicate pallor of her cheek set off by her shining black hair.

No red and white curtains had been hung on the island. It was still too early to see the first tinges of spring green, but the curtains that marked the twisting path up the maple hill beyond cast wavering reflections on the surface of the water, their colours putting Kiyoaki in mind of striped cookies. Although the window was shut, he felt that he could hear Satoko's warm, bright voice.

Two young Siamese and a Japanese . . . they stood in a trio at the window, each catching his breath. How strange, thought Kiyoaki. When he was with the two young princes, was it that he found their passionate natures so infectious that he could believe himself to be the same, and feel able to show it openly? At this moment he could tell himself without a qualm: 'I love her. I'm madly in love with her.'

Six years before, he had had all too brief a glimpse of the Imperial Princess Kasuga's beautiful profile as she turned to glance back at him; it had filled his heart with a hopeless and lingering yearning, but now as Satoko left the pond, she turned her face toward the main house with a graceful movement of the head, and although she was not looking directly at his window, Kiyoaki suddenly felt liberated from that former obsession. In one moment, he had experienced something that surpassed it. Six years later, he now felt that he had recaptured a fragment of time, sparkling and crystalline, from a different perspective. As he watched Satoko walking in the pale watery spring sunshine, she suddenly laughed, and as she did so, he saw her raise her arm in a fluid movement, hiding her mouth behind the graceful curve of her white hand. Her slim body seemed to vibrate like a superb stringed instrument.

18

Baron Shinkawa and his wife were uniquely matched as a couple: absentminded detachment was here quite literally wedded to frenzy. The Baron took not the slightest notice of anything his wife said or did, while the Baroness, oblivious to her effect on others, kept up a ceaseless outpouring of words. This was their customary behaviour, whether at home or in public. Despite his abstracted manner, the Baron was perfectly capable on occasion of mercilessly nailing a person's character with a single, incisive, pithy observation, on which, however, he never deigned to elaborate. His wife, on the other hand, no matter what torrent of words she might expend on that same individual, never succeeded in bringing him to life.

They owned a Rolls-Royce, the second ever purchased in Japan; it was a distinction they treasured as evidence of their social position. It was the Baron's custom to don a silk smoking jacket after dinner and, thus attired, to spend the rest of the evening ignoring his wife's inexhaustible flood of chatter.

At the Baroness's invitation, Raicho Hiratsuka's circle met at the Shinkawa residence once a month, calling themselves the Heavenly Fire Group after a famous poem by Lady Sanunochigami. However, since it invariably rained on the appointed day, the newspapers amused themselves by referring to them as the Rainy Day Club. Any sort of serious thought was beyond the Baroness, who was amazed at the intellectual awakening among Japanese women. She observed it with the same excited curiosity that might have been aroused in her by hens laying eggs of some novel shape – pyramids, for instance.

The Shinkawas were both irritated and flattered by the Matsugaes' invitation to the blossom viewing. Irritated because they realized how bored they would be. Flattered because it would give them an opportunity to display their authentically European manners in public. The Shinkawas were an old and wealthy merchant family, and while it was, of course, essential to maintain the mutually profitable relationship established with the men from Satsuma and Choshu who had risen to such power within the government, the Baron and his wife held them in secret contempt because of their peasant origins. This was an attitude inherited from their parents, and one that was at the very heart of their newly acquired but unshakable elegance.

'Well, now that the Marquis has invited Prince Toin to his house,' the Baron remarked, 'perhaps he'll organize a brass band to greet him. That family views the visit of an imperial prince as a sort of theatrical event.'

'We just have to keep our enlightened views to ourselves, I'm afraid,' was his wife's reply. 'I think that it's rather chic to remain au courant as we do without seeming to, don't you think so? In fact it's rather amusing, don't you agree, to mix unobtrusively with old-fashioned people like them. For example, I think it's frightfully amusing the way Marquis Matsugae is so obsequious in front of Prince Toin at one moment and then tries to behave as though they were old friends the next. But I wonder what I should wear? We'll be leaving early in the afternoon, so I imagine it wouldn't quite do to go in formal evening dress. When all is said and done, I suppose a kimono would be the wisest. Perhaps I should hurry and put in an order at Kitaide in Kyoto and have something made up, perhaps in that lovely blossoms-by-firelight pattern? But for some reason I never look well in a Suso pattern. I'm never sure if it's just me who thinks that the Suso pattern looks frightful on me and that it's really just the thing, or whether other people also think it looks frightful. So I just don't know what to do – but what do you think I should do?'

On the day itself, the Shinkawas received a note from the Matsugaes. They were respectfully requested to arrive some time before the time set for the imperial couple's arrival, and although they chose with cool deliberation to make their own appearance five or six minutes after the time the Toinnomiyas were expected, they were chagrined to discover that they were still early. The Marquis had apparently allowed for such manoeuvres. This display of country manners ruffled the Baron.

'Perhaps His Imperial Highness's horses had a stroke on the way,' he observed by way of a greeting. But no matter how biting the Baron's sarcasm, his speech was mumbled and his expression blank in true English fashion, so that no one heard him.

A dispatch from the distant main gate announced the appearance of the imperial carriage, and the host and his party immediately took up their positions at the entrance of the main house to welcome the Prince.

His carriage was splattered here and there with spring mud as the horses, the gravel spurting under their hooves, trotted up under the pine tree that stood in the drive in front of the house. They snorted irritably and tossed their heads, and for a moment their flying grey manes made Kiyoaki think of the seething crest of a huge wave about to break on the shore. At the same instant, the imperial chrysanthemum on the door blurred in a whirlpool of gold and then was still as the carriage came to a halt.

Prince Toin's fine grey moustache was well set off by a black derby. The Princess, following her husband, walked into the entranceway, crossing the threshold onto the white carpeting that had been spread over the floors of the main house that morning to obviate the necessity of changing into slippers. The imperial couple naturally gave a brief nod before entering the house, but the formal ritual of welcome was to be enacted in the reception room.

As the Princess passed him, Kiyoaki's eye was caught by the black tips of her shoes flashing beneath the frilly white material of her skirt. They were like pods of seaweed, he thought, bobbing in a rippling eddy. The elegance of it so fascinated him that he was even more reluctant to look up at her face, which was beginning to show signs of age.

In the reception room, Marquis Matsugae presented the other guests to the Toinnomiyas. The only person who was new to them was Satoko.

'What have you been up to, Ayakura,' the Prince chided her father, 'hiding such a beautiful young lady from me?'

Kiyoaki, standing to one side, was seized by a slight shudder that he could not explain. He felt that Satoko had suddenly been transformed into a rare work of art on public display.

Since the Prince was so close to the court of Siam, the two princes had been presented to him immediately on arrival in Japan. He now chatted with them familiarly, asking whether or not they liked their fellow students at Peers. Chao P. smiled brightly, his reply the very model of dutiful courtesy: 'They all help to make things easier for us in every way; it's as if we'd been friends for years. We lack for nothing.'

Since the Princes had hardly ever appeared at school until now and apparently had no friends at all there, except for himself, Kiyoaki found this enthusiastic testimony very funny.

Baron Shinkawa liked to think of his sensibility as being of polished silver. Its lustre shone unmarred in the congenial atmosphere of his own home, but no sooner was he plunged into the vulgar intercourse of the outside world than its carefully burnished surface began to tarnish. To suffer a single encounter such as this was enough to cast a light film over it.

Under the direction of the Marquis, the guests now went outside, on the heels of the Prince and Princess, to see the blossoms. Being Japanese, however, the couples did not permit themselves to mingle freely; each wife remained behind her husband. Baron Shinkawa had already fallen into a fit of abstraction that was noticeable to the others. Nevertheless, as soon as he and his wife had put a suitable distance between themselves and the other guests, he roused himself to remark to her: 'When the Marquis was studying in Europe, he took to foreign ways. Before that he kept his mistress in the same house as his wife, but afterwards he installed her in a rented house just outside the front gate, which is about half a mile from the house. That amounts to, say, one half-mile of Westernization. It's what I believe is called six of one, half a dozen of the other.'

'To be enlightened at all,' replied his wife, launching out, 'one must be enlightened all the way. Half measures just won't do. If the household is really to be run on European lines, then whether it's a matter of replying to a formal invitation or merely going out for a short evening stroll, husband and wife should do it together as we do, regardless of what others say. Oh, look over there! See how the hill's reflected in the pond, with two or three cherry trees and the red and white curtain? Isn't it pretty? And do you like my kimono? Looking at what the other ladies are wearing, I'd say that mine has the most elaborate, the boldest, the most enlightened pattern here. And so how gorgeous it would look to someone on the other side who saw it reflected in the water, don't you think? Oh, how frustrating! Why can't I be on both sides of the pond at once? One is so frightfully limited, isn't one, don't you think?'

Pairing each husband with his own wife was an exquisitely refined torture that the Baron endured with cheerful equanimity. It was, after all, one that he preferred and had, in fact, pioneered. He looked on it as the kind of ordeal that might well become general practice in advanced civilization a hundred years hence. The Baron was not the kind of man to desire a passionate rapport with life, and he was ready to welcome any form of behaviour that precluded this, however unendurable or tedious it might be to lesser men; he accepted his lot with the noblesse oblige of an English sophistication.

When the guests finally reached the top of the hill, from which they were to view the entertainment, they were greeted by the Yanagibashi geishas, already disguised as the traditional characters of the Genroku cherry blossom dances. Thus they found themselves mingling with the samurai in his padded costume, the female Robin Hood, the clown, the blind minstrel, the flower seller, the carpenter, the seller of woodcuts, the young hero, the town and the village maidens, the haiku master, and all the others. Prince Toin was gracious enough to be amused, letting the Marquis at his side see his smile of pleasure, and the Siamese princes gleefully thumped Kiyoaki on the shoulder.

Since his father and mother were busy entertaining the Prince and Princess respectively, Kiyoaki was left more or less alone with the two Siamese boys; he had enough to do fending off the geishas who clustered around him while he looked after the princes, who were still awkward in Japanese, and had little chance to worry about Satoko.

'Young master,' said the old geisha who played the poet, 'won't you please come and visit us soon? So many of the girls have fallen head over heels in love with you today; must they go unrequited?'

The young geishas and even the ones who took masculine roles wore a light touch of rouge around the eyes, which gave their laughing faces a slightly drunken cast. Though the growing chill in the air told Kiyoaki that evening was drawing on, he nevertheless had the feeling of being sheltered from the real night wind, surrounded by a folding screen of silk, embroidery, and white powdered skin.

He wondered how these women could laugh and play as happily as if they were bathing in water warmed to their liking. He observed them closely – the way they gestured as they told stories, the way they all nodded alike, as though each had a finely wrought gold hinge in her smooth white neck, the way they allowed themselves to be teased, letting mock anger flash for an instant in their eyes without ceasing to smile, the way they instantly assumed a grave expression to complement a guest's sudden sententious turn, their fleeting air of cold detachment as they adjusted their hair with a touch of the hand – and of all these many devices, the one that interested him most was their manner of letting their eyes rove incessantly. Without being aware of what he was doing, he was comparing it with Satoko's characteristic habit of casting sidelong glances. The geishas' eyes were certainly cheerful and alive, their only expression of independence, but Kiyoaki found them distasteful nevertheless. They darted here and there as aimlessly as buzzing flies, quite in contrast with their expressions. They had none of Satoko's delicate co-ordination, a gift that comes only with a sure sense of elegance.

Now as she stood talking with the Prince, Kiyoaki watched her profile. Her face was lit with a faint glow from the setting sun, and as he looked on from the other side of the group, he thought of a crystal sparkling far away, the faint note of a koto, a distant mountain valley – all alike imbued with that peculiar charm of the inaccessible. As the background of trees and sky gradually darkened, moreover, her profile became still more brightly etched, like Mount Fuji's silhouette, caught by the setting sun.

In the meantime, Baron Shinkawa and Count Ayakura were exchanging laconic observations quite unhindered by the attendant geisha whose ministrations they accepted with cool indifference. The lawn beneath their feet was thickly scattered with blossoms, and one of these petals, to the fascination of the Baron, was clinging to the polished toe of one of the Count's shoes as they gleamed in the rays of the setting sun. They were small enough to be women's shoes, he thought. And indeed, as the Count stood there holding a glass of saké, his hand seemed so small and white as to be doll-like. The Baron, faced with such manifest evidence of noble breeding in elegant decline, experienced a pang of jealousy. However, the Baron was convinced that the interplay of his own carefully nurtured 'English' absentmindedness with what was a natural condition of beaming abstraction in the Count imparted a quality to their conversation that no other pair could possibly match.

'As to animals,' said the Count unexpectedly, 'whatever one says, I maintain that the rodent family has a certain charm about it.'

'The rodent family...?' replied the Baron, not getting the drift at all.

'Rabbits, marmots, squirrels, and the like.'

'You have pets of that sort, sir?'

'No, sir, not at all. Too much of an odour. It would be all over the house.'

'Ah, I see. Very charming, but you wouldn't have them in the house, is that it?'

'Well, sir, in the first place, they seem to have been ignored by the poets, d'you see. And what has no place in a poem has no place in my house. That's my family rule.'

'I see.'

'No, I don't keep them as pets. But they're such fuzzy, timid little creatures that I can't help thinking there's no more charming animal.'

'Yes, Count, I quite agree.'

'Actually, sir, every charming creature, no matter what sort, seems to have a strong odour.'

'Yes, indeed, sir. I believe one might say so.'

'They tell me, Baron, that you spent a good deal of time in London.'

'Yes, and in London at tea time the hostess makes a great point of asking everyone: "Milk or tea first?" Though it all comes to the same in the end, tea and milk mixed together in the cup, the English place enormous importance on one's preference as to which should be poured in first. With them it seems to be an affair of greater gravity than the latest government crisis.'

'Very interesting. Very interesting indeed, sir.'

They gave the geisha no chance to contribute a single word, nor, despite the day's theme, did they seem to have the slightest interest in cherry blossoms.

Marquise Matsugae was talking with Princess Toin, who was extremely fond of *nagauta* and also played the samisen with great skill. Beside them stood the old geisha who was the best singer in Yanagibashi, contributing her share to the conversation. The Marquise was telling them how, some time before, at a relative's engagement party, she had played 'The Green of the Pines' on the piano to the accompaniment of a koto and samisen, an ensemble, she said, that all the guests found charming. The Princess followed the story with keen interest and exclaimed how much she regretted not having been there to take part herself.

Marquis Matsugae's loud laugh rang out frequently. Prince Toin, on the other hand, was pleased to laugh now and then, but he did so with due moderation, putting a hand to his handsomely trimmed moustache. The old geisha who played the blind minstrel whispered something in the Marquis's ear, and he immediately called out to his guests in his hearty voice. 'Well now it's time for the cherry blossom dances. Will you please be kind enough to move over close to the stage.'

This sort of announcement, in fact, belonged to the steward Yamada's sphere of authority. Shocked at having his master snatch his role from him without warning, the old man now blinked rapidly behind his spectacles. This reaction, which he concealed from everyone, was customary when he had to put up with the unexpected.

Yamada would never lay a finger on anything belonging to the Marquis, and he expected his master to show a like discretion toward him in return. There was, for example, an incident that had occurred the previous fall. The children of the foreigners who lived in the house outside the gate had gathered some acorns while playing on the grounds of the estate. Yamada's children had come out to join them, but when the foreign children had offered them a share of the acorns, they had refused in horror. Their father had warned them severely against touching anything that belonged to the master. The foreign children misunderstood their reaction, however, and later the father of one of them came to Yamada to complain. When he thus learned what had happened, he summoned his solemn, pinch-faced children with their mouths turned down in perpetual obsequious respect and praised them highly for their behaviour.

As he thought about this, he rushed forward with pathetic determination into the midst of the guests, the skirts of his *hakama* flapping about his unsteady legs, and directed them feverishly toward the stage.

Just at this moment, from behind the red and white curtain that was stretched in a semicircle at the back of the stage, there came the sharp crack of the two sounding sticks that announced the start of the programme; the report cut through the evening air and seemed to make the fresh sawdust that was scattered over the boards dance for an instant.

19

Kiyoaki and Satoko had no chance to be alone until there was a brief interval after the dance, just as darkness was finally beginning to settle. This was the time allotted for the guests to move toward the Western-style house where the banquet was to be held. The geishas mingled with the guests once more to hear high praise for their performance while everyone drank freely. It was that strange moment, poised on the edge of evening, when lights are still unnecessary, when even in the midst of a convivial gathering, one may be caught by a vague intimation of precariousness.

Kiyoaki deliberately glanced back in Satoko's direction and saw that she was being careful to follow him at a discreet distance. At a point where the path leading down from the hill came to a fork – one branch leading toward the pond, the other toward the front gate – there was an opening in the red and white curtain. A big cherry tree stood here, its trunk thick enough to give some protection from prying eyes. Kiyoaki stepped through the curtain and waited behind the tree. Before Satoko could join him, however, she was caught up in a group of court ladies, Princess Toin's attendants, as they came from the pond on their way back from a tour of the maple hill. Since Kiyoaki could not come out of hiding at this moment, there was nothing for him to do but wait in the shelter of the tree until Satoko was able to find a pretext for escape.

Left to himself, Kiyoaki looked up at the tree above him and for the first time that day gave some thought to the cherry blossoms. They hung in huge clusters from the black austerity of the branches like a mass of white seashells spread over a reef. The evening wind made the curtains billow along the path, and when it caught the tips of the branches, they bent gracefully in a rustle of blossoms. Then the great, widespread branches themselves began to sway with an easy grandeur under their weight of white. The pallor of the flowers was tinged here and there by pink clusters of buds. And with almost invisible subtlety, the star-shaped centre of each blossom was marked with pink in tiny, sharp strokes, like the stitches holding a button in place.

The sky had darkened, and the outline of the clouds began to blur as they merged into it, and the blossoms themselves, already turned into a single mass, began to lose their distinctive colouring for a shade that was almost indistinguishable from that of the evening sky. As he watched, the black of the tree trunk and branches seemed to grow steadily heavier and more sombre.

With every minute, every second that passed, the cherry blossoms sank into deeper, darker intimacy with the evening sky. Kiyoaki was plunged into feelings of foreboding.

Out of the corner of his eye, he thought he saw the curtain swell once more in the wind, but it was Satoko brushing against it as she slipped through the opening. He took her hand, cold to his touch from the chill of the night breeze.

She resisted him and glanced anxiously about when he tried to kiss her, but since she was also trying to protect her kimono from the dust-streaked moss on the tree trunk, he was able to embrace her with ease.

'This is breaking my heart. Please let me go, Kiyo.'

Satoko kept her voice low, afraid that others might hear. Kiyoaki was angered by her self-control, for he had set his heart on nothing less than an ecstatic, supreme consummation at that moment, there beneath the blossoms. The rising moan of the night wind had made him more and more uneasy, and now he was driven in desperation to seize one sure moment of happiness for them both, to the exclusion of all else. Hence his frustration when he discovered that her thoughts were obviously turned elsewhere. He was like a husband so jealous that he insists his wife have the very dreams he has.

Satoko had never looked more beautiful than now as she closed her eyes, still struggling in his arms. But although there was no feature, no contour that marred the delicacy of her face, it was nonetheless imprinted with a subtle, fleeting cast of wilfulness. The corners of her lips were slightly upturned. He anxiously tried to make out whether she was smiling or crying, but her face was already deep in shadow, an omen of the darkness almost upon them. He looked down at her ear, half-hidden by her hair. With its tinge of pink and its fine curve, the wonder of it made him think of a delicate coral recess that might appear in a dream, containing a tiny, beautifully carved Buddha. There was something mysterious about the hollow of her ear, now fading in the darkness. Was it there that her heart was hidden, he wondered, or was it concealed behind her slightly thin lips and sparkling teeth.

With a sense of nagging frustration, he wondered how he could ever penetrate Satoko's defences. Then suddenly, as though she could no longer bear his look, she thrust her face forward and kissed him. One of his arms was around her waist. He felt a warmth that insinuated itself through his fingertips resting on her hip and that reminded him somehow of the sweet, sultry atmosphere of a greenhouse whose flowers were dying.

There was a scent to it that struck his nostrils and gave him a delightful sensation of being smothered in it. Although she had not said a word, he was in the grip of his own images, and was quite convinced that he was on the verge of a moment of peerless beauty.

She pulled her mouth away, but this left the huge mass of her hair pressed against the front of his uniform jacket. Gazing over her head at the cherry trees some distance beyond the curtain as they became edged with silver, his head reeled from the perfume of her hair oil, which became indistinguishable from the scent of the blossoms themselves; they stood out against the last light of the sun like thick, shaggy white wool, but their powdery colour, shading almost to silver-grey, could not altogether blot out a faint, and to Kiyoaki ill-omened, pink. It made him think of an undertaker's cosmetics.

In the midst of this, he suddenly realized that tears were pouring down her cheeks. Afflicted by the spirit of pure research, he was prompted to try to identify these as tears either of joy or of grief, but she was too quick for him.

She shook herself free, and then without even pausing to wipe her eyes, she glared at him, her manner completely changed, and lashed out with stinging words that held no trace of compassion: 'You're just a child, Kiyo! A mere child! You don't understand a thing. You don't even try to understand. Why did I hold back so much? How I wish I had taught you what you know about love. You've got such a high opinion of yourself, don't you? But the truth is, Kiyo, you're no more than a baby. Oh, if only I had realized it! If only I had tried harder to help you! Now it's too late.'

After this outburst, she vanished back through the curtain, leaving the young man, utterly shattered, to his own devices.

What had happened? With unerring accuracy, she had marshalled just those words that were calculated to wound him most deeply, like arrows aimed at his weakest points. She had tipped them with a poison distilled from the misgivings that preyed on him most. He should have stopped to reflect on the extraordinary efficacy of this poison. He should have tried to decide just why such a crystallization of pure malice had occurred.

But his heart was thumping in his chest, and his hands shook. Bitter anger so overwhelmed him that he was close to tears. He could not be objective and coolly analyse the emotion that wracked him. Worse yet, he had to rejoin the guests. And later in the evening there would be no escape; he would have to make pleasant conversation as though nothing were troubling him. He could imagine no task that he felt less fit to perform.

20

As for the banquet, everything went off as planned and was brought to a successful conclusion without any slips being apparent to the guests. The Marquis's rude optimism was proof against all subtleties of misgiving. He himself was well satisfied, and he never dreamed that any of his guests might possibly feel otherwise. It was at such moments that his wife's dazzling worth was brought home to him, as their subsequent conversation revealed.

'The Prince and Princess seem to have had a good time from beginning to end, wouldn't you say?' the Marquis began. 'I think they went home quite happy, don't you?'

'That goes without saying,' replied the Marquise. 'Didn't His Highness the Prince deign to remark that he had not spent so delightful a day since the Emperor died?'

'That's not the best way he could have phrased it, but I know what he meant. But still – to go from mid-afternoon until late at night – don't you think it might have been too tiring for some of them?'

'No, no, not at all. You arranged things so cleverly, with a variety of diversions following one after the other, that it all flowed wonderfully well. I don't believe that our guests had a moment to spare in which they could have become weary.'

'There wasn't anybody asleep during the film?'

'Oh, no. They were all watching wide-eyed from beginning to end and following with the keenest interest.'

'But, you know, that Satoko is a tenderhearted girl. I did think the pictures were quite emotional, but she was the only one sufficiently moved to cry.'

Satoko had, in fact, been crying uncontrollably throughout the show. The Marquis had noticed her tears when the lights were lit.

Kiyoaki made his way up to his room, worn out. He was wide awake, and sleep became impossible. He opened the window and imagined that the snapping turtles were gathering together just at that moment, lifting their metallic green heads above the dark surface of the pond to peer in his direction. Finally he rang the bell that summoned Iinuma, who since graduating from night school was always home in the evening.

On stepping into the room, Iinuma needed no more than a single glance to realize that anger and frustration were contorting the face of the young master. In recent weeks he had gradually developed a certain skill in reading facial expressions, a talent that until recently had been totally beyond him. He had become especially adept with Kiyoaki, with whom he had daily contact and whose expressions reminded him of the whirling fragments of coloured glass that settled into continually changing patterns within a kaleidoscope.

As a result, his disposition and outlook began to alter. Not so long ago, the sight of his young master's face drawn in this way by anxiety and grief would have filled him with loathing for what he would have judged to be Kiyoaki's sluggish indolence. But now he was able to see it as a refinement.

Joy and exuberance did not, in fact, suit Kiyoaki. His beauty had a melancholy cast and so appeared most attractive when he was under the stress of anger or grief, and together with these there was always a forlorn suggestion of the spoiled child as a kind of shadow image. At times like this his pale cheeks became still whiter, his beautiful eyes bloodshot, his finely arched eyebrows were twisted into a frown, and his whole spirit seemed to waver as though his inner world were shattered. He seemed desperately to need something to cling to. And so the hint of sweetness lingered in the midst of his desolation, like the echo of a song over a barren waste.

Since Kiyoaki said nothing, Iinuma sat down on the chair he had made a habit of using recently even when Kiyoaki did not offer it to him. Then he reached out and began to read the banquet menu, which Kiyoaki had thrown down on the table. The dishes listed constituted a feast such as Iinuma knew he would never taste, no matter how many decades he might serve the Matsugaes.

The Evening Banquet of the Cherry Blossom Festival

April 6, 1913
The Second Year of the Taisho Era

SOUP

Turtle Soup *Finely chopped turtle meat floating in broth*
Chicken Soup *Broth with thin slices of chicken*

ENTREES

Poached Trout *Prepared in white wine and milk*
Roast Fillet of Beef *Prepared with steamed mushrooms*
Roast Quail *Stuffed with mushrooms*
Broiled Fillet of Mutton *Garnished with celery*
Pâté de Foie Gras *Served with assortment of cold fowl and sliced pineapple in iced wine*
Roast Gamecock *Stuffed with mushrooms*

INDIVIDUAL SALADS

VEGETABLES

Asparagus Green Beans
Prepared with Cheese

DESSERTS

French Custard Petits Fours
Ice Cream *A choice of flavours*

While Iinuma read the menu, Kiyoaki kept staring at him, one expression succeeding another on his face. One moment his eyes seemed full of contempt, the next brimming with pathetic appeal. He was irritated that Iinuma should sit there with insensitive deference just waiting for him to break the silence. If only Iinuma had been capable of forgetting the master–retainer relationship at that moment, and had put his hand on Kiyoaki's shoulder like an elder brother, how easily he could have started to talk.

He had no idea that the young man who sat in front of him was different from the Iinuma to whom he was accustomed.

What he did not realize was that the Iinuma who had once been obsessed with the rough suppression of his own passions had now developed a gentle forbearance toward him, and, inexperienced as he was, had taken his first tentative steps into the world of subtle emotions.

'I can hardly imagine that you have the least idea what's on my mind,' Kiyoaki said at last. 'Miss Satoko insulted me terribly. She spoke to me as if I were a mere child. And she as much as said that in everything up to now I've behaved like a foolish little boy. No, in fact she said it in so many words. She came at me with everything that would hurt me most, as though she had had it all carefully planned. I just don't understand how she could have brought herself to do it. Now I realize that the ride that snowy morning – which was her idea – now I know that I was nothing more than a toy she felt like playing with.' Kiyoaki paused for a moment. 'But you had no inkling at all of how things really stood? Tadeshina, for example, didn't say anything at all that sounded suspicious?'

Iinuma thought for a while before answering.

'Well, no, sir. I haven't heard anything.' But his awkward pause clung to Kiyoaki's nerves like a vine.

'You're lying. You do know something.'

'No, sir, I don't.'

Finally, however, under the pressure of Kiyoaki's questions, Iinuma poured out what he had been determined not to reveal. Being able to sense a man's mood is one thing, but to gauge his probable reaction is quite another. He did not realize that his words would strike Kiyoaki with the force of an axe.

'This is what Miné told me, sir. I'm the only one she told, and I promised faithfully not to breathe a word of it to anyone else. But since it concerns the young master, I think it's best that I tell it. It was on the day of the New Year's family party, when Miss Ayakura was here at the house. It's the day your father the Marquis is kind enough to invite all your relatives' children here to entertain them, talk to them and listen to their problems, as you know. And so it came about that your father the Marquis asked Miss Ayakura in a joking way if she didn't have any problems she wanted to discuss with him.

'She answered, also apparently as a joke: "Yes, as a matter of fact I have a very serious matter I want to discuss with you, Marquis Matsugae. I wonder if I might inquire about your views on education."

'At this point I must tell you, sir, that this entire incident was related to Miné by the Marquis as – well, a so-called bedtime story' – these two words cost Iinuma inexpressible pain – 'and so he told it to her in detail, like a bedtime story, laughing a great deal as he did so. And so she told it to me just as he said it happened. At any rate, Miss Ayakura had caught the interest of your father the Marquis, and he asked: "My views on education, you say?"

'And then Miss Ayakura said: "Well, according to what I've heard from Kiyo, his father seems to be a great advocate of the empirical approach. He told me that you treated him to a guided tour of the world of geishas so that he could learn how best to conduct himself there. And Kiyo seems to be very happy with the results, feeling that he's now quite a man. But really, Marquis Matsugae, is it true that you champion the empirical method even at the expense of morality?"

'I understand that the lady asked this awkward question with her usual effortless ease. He himself burst out laughing and then answered: "What a difficult question! That's just the sort of thing these moral reform groups ask in their petitions to the Diet. Well, if what Kiyoaki said were true, I could muster something in my defence. But the truth is this: Kiyo himself rejected that very educational opportunity. As you know, he's a late bloomer – he's so fastidious, it's hard to believe he's my son. Certainly I asked him to come with me, but I hardly had time to open my mouth before he bristled and stalked off in a high dudgeon. But how amusing! Even though that's what actually happened, he's made up a story so as to have something to boast to you about. However, I'm pained to think that I've raised a boy who would mention the red-light district to an aristocrat, no matter how close friends they are. I'll call him in now and let him know how proud I am of his behaviour. It might persuade him to go out and have a fling at a geisha house."

'But Miss Ayakura pleaded with your father the Marquis and finally convinced him to give up such a rash idea. And she also made him promise to forget what she had told him. And so he refrained from mentioning it to anyone else out of respect for his word. But he finally told Miné, laughing all the time and obviously very amused by the whole thing. But he gave her a strict warning not to say a word to anyone. Miné is a woman, of course, and so she couldn't keep it to herself; she finally told just me. I realized that the young master's honour was involved, so I threatened her in no uncertain terms, saying that if this story went any further, I would break off with her at once. She was so shaken by the way I said this that I don't think there's any danger of the tale spreading.'

As he listened to this account, Kiyoaki became even paler. He was like a man who has been groping wildly in thick fog, striking his head on one obstacle after another, until the fog suddenly lifts about him to reveal a line of white marble columns. The amorphous worry that had enveloped him now assumed a shape that was perfectly clear.

Despite her denial, Satoko had read his letter after all. It had of course dismayed her somewhat, but when she found out at the New Year's family party from the Marquis himself that it was a lie, she became ecstatic and exhilarated over her 'happiest New Year'. Now he understood why she had opened her heart to him so passionately and so suddenly at the stable that day. And finally, her confidence at its highest, she had thus been sufficiently emboldened to invite him to go for that ride through the February snow.

This revelation did not explain Satoko's tears today nor the severe tongue-lashing she had given him. But it was abundantly clear to him that she was a liar from first to last, that she'd been laughing at him secretly from beginning to end. No matter how one might try to defend her, it was undeniable that she had taken a sadistic pleasure in his discomfiture.

'On the one hand,' he thought bitterly, 'she accuses me of behaving like a child and on the other, how obvious it is that she has been behaving as though she wants me to remain that way forever. How shrewd she is! She gives the appearance of being a woman who needs to be dependent at the very moment when she's up to one of her unscrupulous tricks. She pretended to worship me, but she was really baby-nursing.'

Overcome as he was by resentment, he did not pause to reflect that it was his letter that had begun everything, that it was his lie that had initiated the train of events. All he could see was that his every misfortune sprang from Satoko's treachery.

She had wounded his pride at a stage in his life – the painful transition between boyhood and manhood – when nothing was more precious to him. Though the affair itself would seem trifling to an adult – as his father's laughter had so clearly demonstrated – it was a trifle that nevertheless bore upon his self-esteem, and for Kiyoaki at nineteen, nothing was more delicate nor more vulnerable. Whether she realized this or not, she had trampled on it with an incredible lack of sensitivity. He felt sick with disgrace.

Iinuma watched his white face in the lengthening silence with compassion, but he didn't realize how punishing a blow he had just delivered. This handsome boy had never missed an opportunity to discomfit him, and now, without the least trace of revenge in his intentions, he had crushed Kiyoaki. Furthermore, he had never felt anything so close to affection for him as at this moment, watching him sitting with his head bowed.

His thoughts took a still gentler, more affectionate turn: he would help Kiyoaki up and over to his bed. If the boy began to cry, he too would cry in sympathy. But when Kiyoaki raised his head, his features were hard and set. There was no trace of tears. His cold, piercing glance banished all Iinuma's fantasies.

'All right,' he said. 'You may go now. I'm going to bed.'

He got to his feet by himself and pushed Iinuma toward the door.

21

The next day Tadeshina telephoned repeatedly, but Kiyoaki would not go to the phone. She then asked to speak to Iinuma and told him that Miss Satoko wanted at all costs to speak directly with the young master and would Iinuma please convey this to him. Kiyoaki, however, had given him strict instructions, and so he could not act as a mediator. Finally, after a number of calls, Satoko herself telephoned Iinuma. The result, however, was the same: his unqualified refusal.

The calls kept up for some days, causing no little stir among the housemaids. Kiyoaki's response did not vary. At last Tadeshina came in person.

Iinuma received her at a dark side entrance. He sat on his heels on the entrance platform, every fold of his cotton *hakama* in place, determined not to let Tadeshina one step into the house.

'The young master is absent and so is unable to welcome you.'

'I don't believe that's altogether true. However, if you insist that it is, would you please call Mr Yamada.'

'Even if you were to see Mr Yamada, I'm afraid that it would make no difference. The young master will not see you.'

'All right then, if that's the way you feel, I'll just take the liberty of coming in uninvited and I'll discuss the matter directly with the young master himself.'

'You are, of course, quite free to enter as you like. But he has locked himself in his room, and there is no way of gaining access to him. And then, I presume that your errand is of a rather confidential nature. If you were to disclose it to Yamada, it might give rise to some talk within the house and eventually come to the ears of His Excellency the Marquis. However, if that prospect does not unduly concern you...'

Tadeshina said nothing. As she glared with loathing at Iinuma, she noticed how clearly his pimples stood out, even in the gloom of the entranceway. She herself stood against the background of a bright spring day, the pale green tips of the pine branches flashing in the sunlight. Her old face, its wrinkles barely subdued by their covering layer of white powder, reminded him of a figure painted on crepe. Malice glinted sharply from her eyes sunk deep in their nests of folded skin.

'Thank you very much. I presume that even though you are only following the orders of the young master himself, you must be prepared to take the consequences of addressing yourself to me in such a fashion. Up until now, I have been exercising my ingenuity to some considerable extent on your behalf as well. It would not be wise to depend on it too much from now on. Please be kind enough to convey my respects to the young master.'

Some four or five days later, a thick letter came from Satoko. Usually Tadeshina gave letters for Kiyoaki directly to Iinuma, so as to circumvent Yamada; but this time the letter was placed upon a gold lacquer tray with the family crest and delivered openly by Yamada to Kiyoaki's room.

Kiyoaki was at pains to call Iinuma to his room and show him the unopened letter. Then he told him to open the window. In his presence he put the letter into the fire of his hibachi. Iinuma watched his white hand darting about in the hibachi contained in paulownia wood, avoiding the small tongues of flame that flared up from time to time, stirring up the fire whenever the weight of the letter threatened to choke it. Iinuma had the feeling that a refined form of crime was being committed before his eyes. Had he helped, he was sure that the thing could have been done more efficiently, but he did not offer to, fearing a refusal. Kiyoaki had called him there to be a witness.

Kiyoaki could not avoid the smoke that rose from the smouldering paper, and a tear rolled down his cheek. Iinuma had once hoped that hard discipline and tears would help Kiyoaki to achieve a suitable attitude to life. Now he sat looking at the tears that graced Kiyoaki's cheeks, reddened by the fire, tears that owed nothing whatever to any efforts of his. Why was it, he wondered, that he always felt hopeless in Kiyoaki's presence?

One day about a week later, when his father came home unusually early, Kiyoaki dined for the first time in several weeks with both his parents in the Japanese reception room of the main house.

'How time passes!' the Marquis said exuberantly. 'Next year you will receive the fifth degree, junior grade. And once you have it, I'll have all the servants address you that way.'

Kiyoaki dreaded his majority, which was looming over him in the coming year. Possibly Satoko's faint influence was at the heart of his weary disinterest at the age of nineteen in the prospect of achieving adult status. He had left behind the childhood disposition that makes a boy count the time remaining to New Year on his fingertips and burn with impatience to grow to manhood. He heard his father's words in a cold and sombre mood.

The meal proceeded according to fixed ritual: his mother with her mask of classic melancholy and her never-failing gentility, his father with his red face and deliberately cheerful scorn for the niceties. Still, being perceptive, he was quick to notice something that surprised him: his parents' eyes met once, though not so that anyone could say they were exchanging glances. There seemed to be nothing more afoot than the usual silent conspiracy between the couple. As Kiyoaki looked into his mother's face, her expression wavered slightly, and she stumbled for a second over her words.

'Now ... Kiyoaki ... there's something I'd like to ask you which may not be altogether pleasant. Though it would be making far too much of things to call it unpleasant. But I would like to know how you feel about it.'

'What is it?'

'Well, the fact is that Miss Satoko has received another wedding proposal. And this time the circumstances are extremely complex and delicate. If it proceeds much further, there can be no question of a free and easy refusal being permissible. As always, Miss Satoko is disinclined to let anyone know how she really feels, but this time I doubt if she would feel like giving an outright refusal as she has done in the past. And then her parents are also disposed in favour. So now let's say something about you. You and Miss Satoko have been fond of each other ever since you were babies. About her getting married, you have nothing to say against it? All you have to do now is just to tell us how you feel. For if you have an objection, I think it would be most helpful if your father knew the exact reason.'

Kiyoaki answered expressionlessly and without hesitation, without even pausing in the use of his chopsticks. 'I have no objection at all. It's something that doesn't concern me in the least.'

A brief silence followed, after which the Marquis spoke in a tone that indicated how unruffled his good mood was. 'Well now, at this point it's still possible to go back. If just for the sake of argument we were to suppose that you might feel yourself involved somehow, even to the smallest degree, what would you say to that?'

'I feel no involvement whatever.'

'I said it was for the sake of argument, didn't I? But if that's the case, well and good. We have a long-standing obligation to that family, and therefore I intend to do all I can to help in this matter and to spare no expense in bringing it to a suitably happy conclusion. Well, at any rate, that's the way things stand. Next month is the Omiyasama festival, but if things keep progressing at this rate, I imagine that Satoko is going to find herself rather busy and won't be able to take part in it this year.'

'In that case, perhaps it would be a good idea not to go to the trouble of inviting her.'

'Well, this is a surprise,' the Marquis exclaimed with a loud laugh. 'I had no idea that you were at each others' throats.'

And the laugh was the end of the discussion.

In the final analysis Kiyoaki was a mystery to his parents. His emotional reactions were quite different from theirs. As often as they had tried to fathom what he was thinking, they had always been frustrated in their efforts. And so they eventually gave up. With regard to the present matter, they even bore the Ayakuras some resentment for having educated their son, although they themselves had entrusted them with him. They wondered if the courtly elegance that they had both yearned for did not, after all, consist in precisely the kind of fluctuating moods that made their son so difficult to understand. From a distance, such elegance had an undeniable attraction, but when they were confronted with it in the person of their own son, the effect was an enigma.

The Marquis and Marquise, whatever their intrigues, wore their emotions like clothes that were dyed in the vivid primary colours of the tropics. Kiyoaki's emotions, however, were as subtly complex as the layer upon layer of colour in the dresses of the court ladies; they were constantly merging – the drab brown of an autumn leaf shading into crimson, the crimson dissolving into the green of bamboo grass. His father was exhausted by the mere attempt at solving the riddle of his son's moods. He was exhausted by the mere sight of his handsome son's bored indifference and his cold silences. He searched the memories of his own youth, but he could not recall any torment that had given rise to the kind of instability that ruled his son. Kiyoaki was like a lake whose clear waters reveal the very pebbles on its bed at one moment, only to cloud over the next in a sudden squall.

After a few moments, the Marquis spoke to Kiyoaki again: 'By the way, I've been thinking of letting Iinuma go fairly soon.'

'Why's that?' Kiyoaki asked, looking genuinely surprised for the first time that evening. This really was unexpected.

'Well, he's been very faithful to you for a long time now, but you'll be grown up next year. And then he's graduated from college, so I think this is a good time. There's also a more specific reason. A rather unpleasant rumour about him has come to my attention.'

'What sort of rumour?'

'That his conduct within the house has been a bit irregular. Not to mince words, it seems that he's been carrying on with one of the maids, Miné. In the old days it would have been a matter of my having to cut him down with my own sword.'

As she listened to her husband's words, the Marquise's calm reserve was admirable. In every aspect of this matter, she would be her husband's staunch ally.

'From whom did you hear this rumour, Father?' Kiyoaki persisted.

'That's irrelevant.'

Kiyoaki had an immediate vision of Tadeshina's face.

'Yes, in the old days I would have had to cut him down. But times have changed. And then he came here with a fine recommendation from the people in Kagoshima, and I know his old middle-school principal, who comes up here to give us New Year greetings. It's best to let him go without creating any kind of stir that would damage his future. Not only that, but I want to handle it tactfully, so as to make things easy for him. I'll send Miné off on her own too. And then if they're both still in the mood and want to marry, well and good. I'm willing to find work for him. The main thing is to get him out of the house, so it would be best to handle it in a way that will give him no cause for resentment. That's the best thing. After all, he served you faithfully for such a long time, and we have no complaints about him in that regard.'

'How compassionate you are! And so generous!' the Marquise exclaimed.

Kiyoaki passed Iinuma in the corridor that night but said nothing to him.

As he lay with his head on his pillow, his head was a whirling mass of images. He was faced with the stark realization that from now on he would be alone. He had no friend but Honda, and he had told Honda nothing about his immediate problem.

He had a dream, and in the midst of it, the thought came to him that he would never be able to record it in his journal. The events were far too complex and irrational for that.

All sorts of faces appeared in it. The snow-covered parade ground of the Third Regiment seemed to be spread out before him. There stood Honda, dressed as an officer. Then he thought he saw a flock of peacocks settle suddenly on the snow. He saw Satoko. She wore a jewelled necklace, and on either side of her stood the two Siamese princes holding a golden crown that they were about to place on her head. In another corner, Iinuma and Tadeshina were having a heated argument. Then he saw their entangled bodies go rolling over the edge and down into a vast, gaping chasm. Miné came riding up in a carriage and his mother and father came out to meet her with obsequious smiles. Then he himself seemed to be sailing on a pitching raft over a vast ocean. 'I'm too involved in my dream-world,' he thought while still in the middle of this one. 'They've spilled over into reality. They're a flood that's sweeping me away.'

22

Prince Harunori, the third son of His Imperial Highness Prince Toin, had recently attained his twenty-fifth birthday and a generalcy in the Imperial Horse Guards. He had a magnanimous, sturdy nature, and on him rested most of his father's hopes. To select a bride for such a paragon, his father did not require anyone's mediation, and so a vast array of candidates had been brought directly to the young man's attention. None of these, however, had struck his imperial fancy. Thus the years went by, and just when his imperial parents were at their wits' end, Marquis Matsugae took a chance and invited them to the cherry blossom celebration at his estate. There Satoko Ayakura was casually presented to them. The imperial couple were quite taken with her, and when the Ayakuras later received a confidential request for a photograph, they hastily obeyed by sending a picture of her in a formal kimono. When Prince Harunori's parents showed it to him, he did not make his usual derogatory remarks, but stared at it for some considerable time. Satoko's advanced age of twenty-one became a matter of no consequence.

Marquis Matsugae was well aware of the debt he owed the Ayakuras for having taken care of Kiyoaki as a child and he had long been anxious to do something to help the Count's family regain something of its former grandeur. The best way to achieve this, short of marriage into the Emperor's immediate family, would be a marriage that united the Ayakuras with one of the princes, and the flawless lineage of the Ayakuras as a noble Urin family precluded any question of status being an obstacle. What the Ayakuras did lack, however, was the financial means for the incredible expenses they would incur in their new position. These ranged from a huge dowry to the money that would have to be disbursed regularly for the traditional seasonal gifts to all the retainers of the imperial household, an appalling sum to consider. The Marquis, nevertheless, was prepared to underwrite the cost in all particulars.

With cool composure, Satoko watched the bustle as these events went on around her. There was very little sun in April that year, and as one dark day gave way to another beneath the overcast sky, the fresh imprint of spring faded, to be replaced by the signs of approaching summer. Satoko looked out over the wide, neglected garden from a bay window of her austere room in the handsome, old-fashioned mansion that now retained its pretensions only in its imposing gate. She saw how the camellia blossoms had already fallen and new buds were pushing out from the thick dark clusters of leaves. The intricate tracery of branches and pointed leaves of the pomegranate, bristling with thorns, also showed reddish buds that were straining to burst. All the new buds grew vertical, so that the entire garden seemed to be standing on tiptoe and stretching upward to reach the sky. Indeed, every day seemed to bring it closer to its goal.

Tadeshina was deeply concerned that Satoko had become so subdued and that she should so often appear lost in thought. On the other hand, she listened attentively to all her mother and father had to say and followed their wishes as a quiet brook its banks. She now accepted everything with a faint smile, and there was no trace of her former wilfulness. But behind the screen of gentle compliance, Satoko was hiding an indifference as vast as the grey April sky.

One day early in May, Satoko was invited to tea at the summer villa of Their Imperial Highnesses, Prince and Princess Toin. Ordinarily, an invitation should have come from the Matsugaes by this time of year to attend their Omiyasama festival, but although all her hopes were now centred on it, it did not come. In its place, an official of the Prince's household appeared bearing the invitation to tea, handed it casually to a steward of the Ayakuras, and departed.

Despite the semblance of complete naturalness that attended this and similar incidents, they were in fact carefully plotted in the deepest secrecy, and though her parents said little, they were supporting the conspirators in their attempt to ensnare Satoko in the complex spell that was stealthily being woven around her.

The Count and Countess, of course, were also invited to tea at the Toinnomiya villa. Since it seemed that to go in a carriage sent by the Prince with all its appropriate trappings would be to create too much of a spectacle, the Ayakuras decided they would rather ride in one kindly lent by Marquis Matsugae. The villa, built just a few years before, toward the end of the Meiji era, stood on the outskirts of Yokohama. Had their purpose been different, a trip of this sort would have had the happy, carefree spirit of an all-too-infrequent family outing in the country.

For the first time in many days, the weather was pleasant, a good omen cheerfully noted by the Count and his wife. Since Boys' Day was approaching, nearly every house they passed along the way had hoisted its cloth or paper carps, one for each son, and they were flapping vigorously in the stiff south breeze. They ranged in size from huge black carp to tiny red ones that looked like goldfish. If five or more were hanging from the same staff, they seemed to bunch awkwardly together, unable to swim freely in the wind's powerful current. When the carriage passed one farmhouse on the edge of the mountains, the school of carp above the roof was so vast that the Count was moved to raise a white forefinger to count them from the window. There were ten in all.

'My, what a vigorous sort of fellow!' said the Count with a smile. To Satoko, this remark smacked of a vulgar humour uncharacteristic of her father.

The trees along the way bore evidence of a remarkable surge of growth with their clusters of new leaves and branches. The mountains were a mass of green that ranged from a near yellow to a dark tone verging on black. The bright young maple leaves stood out especially against the general outpouring of green that made the whole countryside glitter.

'Oh, a bit of dust...' the Countess exclaimed, gazing at Satoko's cheek. But just as she reached out with her handkerchief to wipe it off, Satoko drew quickly away and the speck of dust vanished. It was then that her mother realized that the dust on her daughter's cheek had been no more than a shadow cast by a spot on the window. Satoko gave a wan smile; she didn't find her mother's mistake particularly amusing. She disliked being given a special inspection today, as if she were a bolt of silk intended as a gift.

The windows had been kept shut in case the breeze rumpled Satoko's hair, and the interior of the carriage had become unpleasantly hot as a result. As it rocked unceasingly and the green of the mountains flashed up in reflections from the flooded rice paddies beside the road, Satoko could not remember what she was looking forward to with such yearning. On the one hand, she was letting a rash caprice sweep her with appalling boldness into a course of action from which there would be no turning back. On the other, she was waiting for something to intervene. For the moment there was still time. There was still time. Up until the very last instant, a letter of pardon might come – or so she hoped. And then again, she despised the very thought of hope.

The Toinnomiya villa, a palatial Western-style house, stood on a high cliff overlooking the sea. Stairs carved out of marble led up to its front entrance. As a groom took charge of the horses, the Ayakuras descended from the carriage and exchanged admiring remarks about the view of the harbour below, which was filled with all sorts of ships. Tea was served on a wide porch that faced south, looking down over the water. It was decorated with a number of luxuriant tropical plants, and on either side of the door that opened onto it hung a pair of giant curving tusks, a gift from the royal court of Siam.

Here the imperial couple welcomed their guests and cordially offered them chairs. The tea was, of course, in the English manner, complete with small, thin sandwiches, some cookies and biscuits – all neatly arranged on a tea table furnished with silverware engraved with the imperial chrysanthemum.

The Princess remarked how delightful the recent cherry blossom festival at the Matsugaes had been and then, by and by, her conversation turned to mahjong and *nagauta*.

'At home we still think of Satoko as a child, and we haven't let her play mahjong yet,' said the Count, wanting to save his silent daughter embarrassment.

'Oh, don't tell me!' the Princess laughed graciously. 'We sometimes spend a whole day playing nothing else, when we have time.'

Satoko could no longer bring up a topic such as the old-fashioned *sugoroku* and its set of twelve black and white pieces, with which they often played.

Prince Toin was relaxed and informal today in a European suit. Calling the Count over to the window beside him, he pointed down to the ships below and displayed his knowledge of things nautical as if he were instructing a child: that was an English freighter, that was a ship with a flush deck, that one was a French freighter, see the shelter deck on the one over there, and so on.

Judging by the atmosphere, one might well conclude that the imperial couple were making rather anxious efforts to hit upon some topic congenial to their guests. Anything at all that sparked a mutual interest – be it sports or wine or anything else – would suffice. Count Ayakura, however, received whatever subject came up with earnest but benign passivity. As for Satoko, she had never been so conscious as she was this afternoon of the uselessness of the elegance bred in her by her father's example. Sometimes the Count had a way of foolishly coming out with a stylish joke that had nothing to do with the conversation at hand, but today he was obviously restraining himself.

After some time, Prince Toin glanced at the clock and made a casual remark, as if something had just occurred to him.

'By a happy coincidence, Harunori will be coming home on leave from his regiment today. Though he's my own son, he has the look about him of a rough sort of fellow. But please don't be upset by it. He's truly quite gentle beneath it all.'

Soon after he said this, the sound of servants scurrying about at the front entrance heralded the arrival of the young prince.

A few moments later, sword clattering, boots squeaking, the martial figure of His Imperial Highness Prince Harunori appeared on the porch. He greeted his father with a military salute, and the immediate impression he gave Satoko was one of empty dignity. But how obvious the paternal pride of Prince Toin was in this display of military pomp, and how evident the young prince's conviction that he was fulfilling every detail of his father's projected image of him. The truth was that his two older brothers were, in fact, quite different. Unusually effeminate and sickly, they had been the despair of their imperial father.

Today, however, a touch of embarrassment at being confronted for the first time with Satoko's beauty may perhaps have had some effect on Prince Harunori's subsequent behaviour. At any rate, neither when she was presented to him nor at any time thereafter did he look at her directly.

Though the young prince was not particularly tall, he had an impressive physique. He moved briskly at all times, with an air of importance and decision that lent him a gravity extraordinary in one so young – all of which his father watched, complacent and happy, his eyes narrowed with pleasure. This paternal satisfaction, however, was giving rise to a growing impression among many that Prince Toin himself concealed a certain weakness of will beneath that grand and impressive exterior.

As for hobbies, His Imperial Highness Prince Harunori was devoted to his record collection of Western music. This seemed to be the one subject on which he had opinions of his own. When his mother asked: 'Would you play something for us, Harunori?' he was quick to agree and to turn toward the reception room, where the phonograph stood.

As he did so, Satoko could not resist raising her eyes to watch him. He covered the distance to the door with long strides, his brilliantly polished black boots sparkling in the sunshine that was pouring in through the porch windows. They were so dazzling that she imagined she could even see patches of the sky itself reflected in them like fragments of blue porcelain. She closed her eyes and waited for the music to begin. She felt the first stirrings of ominous premonition, and the faint sound of the phonograph needle falling into place echoed like thunder in her ears.

Afterwards, the young prince contributed little to the casual conversation that followed the musical interlude. As evening approached, the Ayakuras took leave of their hosts.

A week later, the steward of Prince Toin's household came to the Ayakura residence and had a long, detailed discussion with the Count. The upshot was a decision to begin the formal proceedings for obtaining the Emperor's permission for the wedding. Satoko herself was shown the document, which read:

To His Excellency the Minister of the Imperial Household:

Herein is a humble plea with reference to negotiations concerning a marriage between:

His Imperial Highness Prince Harunori Toin and Satoko, the daughter of His Excellency Count Korebumi Ayakura, Second Degree, Junior Grade; Bearer of the Order of Merit, Third Class;

That a petition as to whether such negotiations may proceed in accordance with the Imperial Pleasure may be vouchsafed to be brought before the Imperial Throne.

Offered upon this 12th Day of the Fifth Month of the Era of Taisho.

Saburo Yamauchi
Steward of the Household of
His Imperial Highness Prince Toin

Three days later a response came from the Minister of the Imperial Household:

To the Steward of the Household of
His Imperial Highness Prince Toin:

Relative to the disposition presented to the Officials of the Imperial Household concerning the marriage of His Imperial Highness Prince Harunori Toin and Satoko, the daughter of His Excellency Count Korebumi Ayakura, Second Degree, Junior Grade; Bearer of the Order of Merit, Third Class;

it is herein acknowledged that a petition destined for presentation to the Imperial Throne whereby such negotiations may proceed with the Imperial Pleasure has been duly and properly entered.

Given this 15th Day of the Fifth Month of the Era of Taisho.

The Minister of the Imperial Household

And so with the preliminary formalities observed, the petition for imperial sanction could be presented to the Emperor at any time.

23

Kiyoaki was now in his senior year at Peers. He was to begin his university studies in the coming fall, and there were those in his class who had been busy preparing for the entrance examinations for more than eighteen months. Honda, however, betrayed no such concern, a fact which pleased Kiyoaki.

The spirit of General Nogi lived on in the compulsory dormitory regime at Peers, but its harsh rules did, nonetheless, contain allowances for those whose health was not up to the demands made on them. Students such as Honda and Kiyoaki, whose families kept them out of the dormitories as a matter of policy, were provided with suitable medical certificates from their doctors. Honda's convenient ailment was put down as valvular heart disease and Kiyoaki's as chronic bronchial catarrh. Their nonexistent illnesses were the source of much amusement, with Honda pretending to be choking for breath and Kiyoaki putting on a hacking cough.

There was no real need for pretence, because no one believed they were sick. However, the noncommissioned officers in the military science department, all veterans of the Russo-Japanese War, vented their hostility by making a point of treating them like invalids. Then during drill period, the sergeants were fond of interspersing their rhetoric with oblique digs at the shirkers, asking what use they would be in the service of their country if they were too feeble to live under the dormitory regime, and other such questions.

Kiyoaki felt deep sympathy for the Siamese princes when he heard that they were to be put in the dormitory. He often visited them in their quarters and brought small presents. They felt very close to him, and so they took turns pouring out their complaints, lamenting in particular the restrictions on their freedom of movement. The other dormitory students, moreover, being rowdy and insensitive, were not the sort to make friends with them.

Though Honda had been neglected by Kiyoaki for quite some time, he welcomed him nonchalantly when he came dancing back to him, bold as a sparrow. It was as if he had completely forgotten his recent disregard of Honda. With the start of the new school term, he seemed to have changed character, now full of forced gaiety, or so it appeared to Honda. Naturally, he made no comment on this, and Kiyoaki himself, just as naturally, provided no explanation.

Kiyoaki was able to congratulate himself for at least one piece of wisdom – he had never let his friend know his innermost feelings. This now spared him any worry that he might appear to have let a woman manipulate him like a foolish child. He realized that this made him feel secure enough to behave with carefree good humour toward Honda. To him, the ultimate proof of his friendship was his desire to avoid disillusioning Honda and to feel easy and unconcerned in his presence – and this desire should more than make up for his countless moments of reserve.

He was so cheerful, in fact, that he surprised even himself. At about this time, his parents had begun to talk quite openly and matter-of-factly about the course of negotiations between the Ayakuras and Toinnomiyas. They seemed to take great amusement in recounting incidents such as how 'even that headstrong girl' became so tense that she could not say a word during the carefully arranged meeting with the young prince. Kiyoaki, of course, had no reason to suspect what grief the incident had caused Satoko. Those who lack imagination have no choice but to base their conclusions on the reality they see around them. But on the other hand, those who are imaginative have a tendency to build fortified castles they have designed themselves, and to seal off every window in them. And so it was with Kiyoaki.

'Well, once the imperial sanction is received, that should settle everything,' said his mother.

Somehow he was moved by her words, especially the phrase 'imperial sanction'. It made him think of a darkened corridor, long and wide, and at the end a door fastened with a small but impregnable padlock of solid gold. And suddenly, with a noise like the grinding of teeth, it opened of its own accord, a metallic rasp echoing clearly in his ears.

He was full of self-satisfaction that he could remain so calm while his mother and father discussed such matters. He had triumphed over his own rage and despair and so was relishing a sense of immortality. 'I never dreamed that I could be so resilient,' he thought, never more confident in his life.

Once he had been convinced that his parents' unfeeling coarseness was something totally alien to him, but now he took pleasure in the thought that he had not escaped his origins after all. He belonged not among the victims but among the victors.

He drew an exquisite pleasure from the thought that day by day Satoko's existence would recede further and further from his mind until it would finally pass beyond recall. Those who set a votive lantern afloat on the evening tide stand on the shore and watch its light growing fainter over the dark surface of the water as they pray that their offering may travel as far as possible and so attain the maximum grace for the dead. In the same way, Kiyoaki looked upon the receding memory of Satoko as the surest vindication of his own strength.

Now there was nobody left in the world who was privy to his innermost feelings. No further obstacle would prevent him from disguising his emotions. The devoted servants, ever at his elbow, with their customary words: 'Please leave everything to us. We know just how the young master feels,' had been removed. Not only was he happy to be free of that master conspirator, Tadeshina, but also of Iinuma, whose loyalty had become so intense as to threaten him with suffocation. The last of his irritants was gone.

As for his father's dismissal of Iinuma, however kindly done, he rationalized his own indifference with the argument that Iinuma had brought it upon himself. He made his self-satisfaction complete with the vow, faithfully kept, thanks to Tadeshina, never to mention to his father what had happened. And so he had brought everything to a successful conclusion out of his acuity and coldness of heart.

The day came for Iinuma's departure. When he went to Kiyoaki's room for his formal farewell, he was crying. Kiyoaki could not accept even such grief for what it was. The thought that Iinuma was emphasizing his fervently exclusive loyalty to him gave him no pleasure.

Inarticulate as ever, Iinuma merely stood there crying. By his very silence he was trying to tell Kiyoaki something. Their relationship had lasted some seven years, beginning in the spring when Kiyoaki was twelve. Since his recollection of his thoughts and feelings at that age were rather vague, he had the general impression that Iinuma had always been there beside him. If his boyhood and youth cast a shadow, that shadow was Iinuma, in his sweaty, dark blue, splashed-patterned kimono. The relentlessness of his discontent, his rancour, his negative attitude to life, had all weighed heavily on Kiyoaki, try as he might to feign immunity. On the other hand, however, the dark woe in Iinuma's eyes had served to warn him against those very same attitudes in himself, although they were normal enough in youth. Iinuma's particular demons had tormented him with manifest violence, and the more he wanted his young master to emulate him, the more Kiyoaki had shied off in the opposite direction, a predictable turn of events.

Psychologically, Kiyoaki had probably taken the first step toward today's parting when he had broken the power that had dominated him for so long and turned Iinuma into his confidant. Their mutual understanding was probably too deep for master and retainer.

As Iinuma stood before him with bowed head, the chest hair escaping from the neck of his blue kimono glistened faintly, caught in a ray of the evening sun. Kiyoaki stared gloomily at this matted tangle, depressed at the realization of what a distastefully coarse and heavy vessel Iinuma's flesh made for his overpowering spirit of loyalty. It was, in fact, a direct physical affront. Even the glow on Iinuma's rough-skinned, pimpled cheeks, mottled and unhealthy as it was, had something shameless about it that seemed to taunt Kiyoaki with Miné's devotion – Miné who was leaving with Iinuma, ready to share his fate. Nothing could be more insulting: the young master betrayed by a woman and left to grieve; the retainer believing in a woman's fidelity and going off triumphant. Iinuma, moreover, was quite secure in the conviction that today's farewell had come about in the line of duty – a presumption that Kiyoaki found galling.

However, deciding that noblesse oblige was the best course, he spoke humanely, if curtly.

'So then, once you're on your own, I presume you'll marry Miné?'

'Yes, sir. Since your father was gracious enough to suggest it, that's exactly what I shall do.'

'Well, let me know the date. I must send you a present.'

'Thank you very much, sir.'

'Once you have a permanent home, send me a note with your address. Who knows, perhaps I might come and see you some time.'

'I cannot imagine anything that would give me greater pleasure than a visit from the young master. But wherever I live, it will be too small and dirty to be a fit place to receive you.'

'Don't worry about that.'

'How gracious of you to say so...'

And Iinuma began to cry again. He pulled a piece of coarse tissue paper from his kimono and blew his nose.

During this exchange Kiyoaki had chosen his every word with care and an eye to its suitability for the occasion before smoothly giving voice to it. He made it patently clear that in a situation such as this, the emptiest words were those that aroused the strongest emotions. He professed to live for sentiment alone, but circumstances now compelled him to learn the politics of the intellect. This was an education that he would apply to his own life with profit from time to time. He was learning to use sentiment as a protective armour and how best to polish it.

Devoid of worry or annoyance, free of all anxiety, Kiyoaki at nineteen liked to see himself as a cold and supremely capable young man. He felt that he was now past some watershed in the course of his life.

After Iinuma had gone, he stood at the open window gazing down at the beautiful reflection of the maple hill, with its fresh green mantle of new leaves, as it floated on the water of the pond. Close to the window itself, the foliage of the zelkova was so thick that he had to lean out in order to see the place at the bottom of the hill where the last of the nine waterfalls plunged into its pool. All around the edge of the pond, the surface was covered with clusters of pale green water shields. The yellow water lilies had not yet flowered, but in the angles of the stone bridge that zigzagged a path close to the main reception room, irises were pushing their purple and white blossoms out from sharp-pointed clusters of green leaves.

His eye was caught by the iridescent back of a beetle that had been standing on the windowsill but was now advancing steadily into his room. Two reddish purple stripes ran the length of its brilliant oval shell of green and gold. Now it waved its antennae cautiously as it began to inch its way forward on its tiny hacksaw legs, which reminded Kiyoaki of minuscule jeweller's blades. In the midst of time's dissolving whirlpool, how absurd that this tiny dot of richly concentrated brilliance should endure in a secure world of its own. As he watched, he gradually became fascinated. Little by little the beetle kept edging its glittering body closer to him as if its pointless progress were a lesson that when traversing a world of unceasing flux, the only thing of importance was to radiate beauty. Suppose he were to assess his protective armour of sentiment in such terms. Was it aesthetically as naturally striking as that of this beetle? And was it tough enough to be as good a shield as the beetle's?

At that moment, he almost persuaded himself that all its surroundings – leafy trees, blue sky, clouds, tiled roofs – were there purely to serve this beetle which in itself was the very hub, the very nucleus of the universe.

The atmosphere of the Omiyasama festival was not the same as in previous years. For one thing, Iinuma was gone; every year, long before the day of the festival, he had thrown himself into the task of cleaning up and had done the arranging of the altar and chairs all by himself. Now it had all fallen to Yamada, and was the more unwelcome for being without precedent. Furthermore, it was work more befitting a younger man.

In addition, Satoko had not been invited. There was thus the sense that someone was missing from the group of relatives customarily present, but more significant than that – for Satoko was not really a relative after all – none of the women there was remotely as beautiful as she.

The gods themselves seemed to view the altered circumstances with displeasure. Midway through the ceremony, the sky darkened and thunder rumbled in the distance. The women, who had been following the priest's prayers, were thrown into a fluster, worried that they might be caught in a shower. Fortunately, however, when the time came for the young priestesses in their scarlet *hakama* to distribute the sacred offerings of wine to everyone, the sky lightened again. As the women bowed their heads, the bright sunshine on the napes of their necks drew beads of sweat despite the heavy coating of white powder. At that moment, the clusters of wisteria blossoms on the trellis cast deep shadows that fell like a benediction on those in the back rows.

Had Iinuma been present, the atmosphere of this year's festival would doubtless have angered him, since each year brought less reverence and mourning for Kiyoaki's grandfather. He now seemed to have been relegated to a vanished era, especially since the death of the Meiji Emperor himself. And so he had become a distant god who had no connection at all with the modern world. True, his widow, Kiyoaki's grandmother, took part in the ceremony, as did a number of other old people; their tears, however, seemed to have dried up long ago.

Each year as the painfully long ceremony went on, the women's whispering grew steadily louder. The Marquis did not go out of his way to manifest disapproval. He himself was finding the observance more tedious year by year, and he was hopeful of finding some way of making it a bit more cheerful and less depressing for himself. During the ritual, his eye was drawn to a young priestess whose pronounced Okinawan features were all the more striking under her heavy white makeup. As she held the earthenware vessel filled with sacred wine, he was fascinated by the reflection of her bold dark eyes on the surface of the liquid. As soon as the ceremony was over, he rushed over to his cousin, who was not only an admiral but also a drinker of no small fame, and apparently made a vulgar joke about the priestess, for the admiral's laugh was so loud and crude that it drew a number of stares. The Marquise, however, knowing how appropriate her mask of classic melancholy was to today's affair, did not alter her expression in the slightest.

Kiyoaki meanwhile was otherwise occupied. The women of the household, the whole vast array of them, many of whom he did not even know by name, were crowded together in the luxuriant shade of the late spring wisteria. They were whispering among themselves, their air of reverence vanishing with each passing moment. Their faces were expressionless, empty even of sadness as they stood dutifully grouped according to their instructions, waiting until they could disband once more, and full of heavy, sluggish reluctance. The sultry atmosphere that surrounded these women with white faces as blank as the moon at midday had a profound effect on Kiyoaki. Beyond a doubt, much of it had to do with their scent, from which there was no excluding Satoko herself. And this was something that even the Shinto priest, armed with the sacred sakaki branch with its weight of glossy dark green leaves and its string of white paper pendants, would have been hard put to exorcise.

24

Kiyoaki drew comfort from the peace of mind that comes with loss. In his heart, he always preferred the actuality of loss to the fear of it.

He had lost Satoko. And with that he was content. For by now he had learned how to quiet even his subsequent resentment. Every show of feeling was now governed with a marvellous economy. If a candle has burned brilliantly but now stands alone in the dark with its flame extinguished, it need no longer fear that its substance will dissolve into hot wax. For the first time in his life, Kiyoaki came to realize the healing powers of solitude.

The rainy season had begun. Kiyoaki, like a recuperating invalid who cannot resist endangering his health despite his fears, began to test his emotional stability by deliberately provoking memories of Satoko. He would open his album to look at the old pictures. He saw himself as an infant, standing next to Satoko beneath the pagoda tree on the Ayakura estate. Both of them were wrapped in children's white pinafores, but he took satisfaction in having been taller than she even at that early age. Count Ayakura, who was a superb calligrapher, had taken great pains to instruct the two children according to Tadamichi Fujuwara's Hosso Temple school of writing. Sometimes, when they tired of their usual exercises, he had rekindled their interest by letting them take turns copying verses from the Okura One Hundred Poets card game onto a scroll.

Kiyoaki had written a verse by Shigeyuki Minamoto:

I feel the wind's keen force
As waves break over rocks
Worn down by loneliness
I dream of days gone by.

Below it Satoko had written a verse by Yoshinobu Onakatomi:

When day gives way to night
And guards kindle fires
The thoughts of other times
Come alive within me.

The childishness of his handwriting was apparent at a glance. But Satoko's was flowing and precise, so much so that the brush hardly seemed to have been wielded by a little girl. In fact he rarely opened this scroll simply because he did not relish being confronted with the unhappy evidence of how much Satoko, two years older than he, had surpassed him even then. Now, however, as he studied the writing with a measure of objectivity, he felt that his own scrawl had a boyish vigour that made a pleasing contrast with the refined elegance of Satoko's smooth, flowing script.

But there was more to it than that. The very thought of himself that day boldly setting down the tips of his writing brushes, heavy with ink, against the fine, gold-flecked paper of the scroll, was enough to evoke the entire scene with the force of vivid immediacy. At that time, Satoko's long, thick black hair was cut straight across at the brow. As she bent over the scroll, she kept the handle of the writing brush tight in her slim, delicate fingers, concentrating with such passion that she was oblivious to the mass of hair that poured down her shoulders in a jet-black cascade, nearly flooding the scroll itself. Her small, white teeth bit ruthlessly into her lower lip, and although she was just a little girl, her nose was already well formed in her profile that stood out with sweet determination against the torrent of falling hair. Kiyoaki watched as if in a dream. Then there was the ink that smelled dark and solemn, and the sound made by the tip of the brush as it raced over the surface of the scroll, like the wind rustling through bamboo grass. And finally, there was the sea – the well of the inkstone was the sea, and above it rose the hill with the strange name. The sea fell away so sharply from its shore that it gave not so much as a glimpse of its shallow bed. The still black sea, without a single wave, a sea spangled with gold powder fallen from the ink stick, always made him think of the rays of the moon fragmented on the night sea of eternity.

'I can even enjoy memories of my past and it doesn't bother me at all,' he thought in silent boast.

Satoko did not even appear in his dreams. If he caught a glimpse of a figure in his sleep that seemed to resemble her, the woman quickly turned her back and disappeared. But then the scene was most often a broad crossroads at midday, totally deserted.

One day at school, Prince Pattanadid asked Kiyoaki a favour. Would he please return the ring that Marquis Matsugae had put in a deposit box for him?

General rumour had it that the two princes had not made a very favourable impression at school. The language barrier presented an understandable obstacle to their studies, but more than that, there could be nothing resembling friendly banter between them and their fellow students, who became impatient with the princes and as a result kept them at a respectful distance. Furthermore, being simple and boorish, their classmates were apparently quite put off by the smiles that the princes produced on all occasions.

It had been the foreign minister's idea that they live in the student dormitory, a decision, Kiyoaki heard, that had created considerable anxiety for the dormitory prefect since his was the responsibility for deciding upon the specific arrangements made for them. He gave them their own room, furnished with the best beds available, as befitted royalty. Then he made every effort to promote good relations between them and the other students, but as the days went by, the princes tended to isolate themselves more and more in their own little castle, frequently missing exercises like reveille and group callisthenics. The estrangement between them and the others thus grew still more pronounced.

There was good reason for this. The preparatory period of less than six months following their arrival was inadequate for the princes to have learned Japanese, even if they had applied themselves far more seriously than they had done. And then, even in the English classes, where their ability should have shown to advantage, the system of translating from English into Japanese and from Japanese into English thoroughly confused them.

Since Marquis Matsugae had arranged to have Pattanadid's ring placed in his personal vault at the Itsu Bank, Kiyoaki had to return home to get his father's seal before going to the bank to reclaim the ring. It was nearly evening before he returned to Peers and went to the princes' room.

It was a typical 'dry' day in the midst of the rainy season, overcast and humid, a day that was perfectly attuned to the frustration of the two princes, who were longing for the sparkling summer weather that was still beyond reach, though it seemed close enough. The dormitory itself, a rough-frame one-storey building surrounded by trees, seemed to be sealed in a gloom all its own.

The shouts coming from the direction of the athletics field indicated that rugby practice was still in full swing. Kiyoaki hated the idealistic cries that rose from those young throats. His classmates' rough-and-ready relationships, their untried humanism, their constant jokes and puns, their never-faltering reverence for the talent of Rodin and the perfection of Cézanne – they were no more than the modern equivalent of the old traditional shouts of *kendo*. And so, hoarse in voice and reeking of youth like green paulownia leaves, they went about wearing their arrogance much as the ancient courtiers wore their tall caps.

Life for the two princes was extremely difficult, having to swim in the midst of this riptide of old and new. When Kiyoaki thought about this, he rose above his own preoccupations and now was able, out of a new generosity, to sympathize with them. He walked down a dark, rough-finished corridor of the dormitory toward the princes' room at the end of it, selected with such care. Stopping in front of a battered old door, on which hung a wooden rectangle with their names on it, he knocked lightly.

The princes were overjoyed to see him, as though he had come as a saviour. He had always felt much closer to the serious and somewhat dreamy Pattanadid – Chao P. – but in recent months Kridsada too, once so frivolous and carefree, had become subdued. The two of them now spent much of their time here in their room, whispering to each other in their native language.

The room, bare of all decoration, was furnished austerely with two beds, two desks, and two cupboards for their clothing. The building itself was redolent of the barracks atmosphere so prized by General Nogi. The blank white expanse of wall above the panelling, however, was relieved by a small shelf holding a golden Buddha, before which the princes performed their worship morning and evening. The altar lent a hint of the exotic to the room. Wrinkled, rain-spotted muslin curtains hung at the window.

Now, in the approach of darkness, the smiling princes' teeth gleamed white against their dark skin and deep tans. They offered Kiyoaki a seat on the edge of one of the beds and then eagerly asked to see the ring.

Its brilliant green emerald, guarded on either side by the fierce beasts' heads of the yaksha, glowed richly in complete contrast to the atmosphere of the room.

With an exclamation of happiness, Chao P. took the ring and slipped it onto his dark, slender finger. Thin and supple, on a hand that seemed created for caresses, it made Kiyoaki think of a warm tropical moonbeam stretching a slender finger through a crack in the door and striking a mosaic floor.

'Now Ying Chan has finally returned to my touch,' Chao P. said, heaving a melancholy sigh.

In months gone by, such a reaction would have provoked Prince Kridsada to make fun of his cousin, but now he searched through the drawer of his clothes cupboard and took out a picture of his sister which he had carefully hidden between layers of shirts.

'In this school,' he said, nearly in tears, 'even if you tell them it's a picture of your own sister, they make jokes about you if you put it out on your desk. That's why we hide Ying Chan's picture in here.'

Chao P. was soon able to explain to Kiyoaki that no letter from Princess Ying Chan had come for more than two months. He had made inquiries about this at the Siamese legation but had not yet received a satisfactory answer. Moreover, the princess's brother Prince Kridsada himself had had no word about her. If something had happened to her, if she had fallen ill, he would normally have been informed by telegram. Chao P.'s imagination was exacerbated by the thought of what her family might be hiding even from her brother. It might well be that she was being pushed into another marriage, one that held greater political advantage. The very idea was enough to plunge him into gloom. Tomorrow, he thought, there might be a letter, but even if there were, what unhappiness might it not contain? With such thoughts preying on his mind, he was in no state to study. Since he had no other consolation, all he could think of was the return of the ring that had been a parting present from the princess, and all his intensity of longing became focused on its emerald, which shone with the brilliant green of the jungle at first light.

It now seemed that Chao P. had become oblivious to Kiyoaki as he stretched out his finger that bore the emerald ring and rested it on the desk beside the picture of Ying Chan that Prince Kridsada had placed there. He seemed to be about to make an effort of will that would not only dissolve the barriers of time and space but merge two separate lives into one.

When Prince Kridsada turned on the light that hung from the ceiling, the picture glass caught the reflection of the emerald on Chao P.'s finger, and a square of vivid green glowed on the white lace of the princess's bodice.

'Look at that – how does it strike you?' Chao P. asked in English, in a bemused tone of voice. 'Doesn't it seem as though her heart were a green flame? Perhaps it's the cold green heart of a small green snake, with a minute flaw in it, the kind of small green snake that slithers from branch to branch in the jungle, passing itself off as a vine. What's more, perhaps when she gave me the ring with such a gentle, loving expression, she wanted me to draw such a meaning from it some day.'

'No, Chao P. That's utter nonsense,' Prince Kridsada cut in sharply.

'Don't be angry, Kri. I don't mean to insult your sister for a moment. All I'm trying to do is find words for the strangeness of a lover's existence. Let me put it this way: although she is here in this picture, it shows her only as she was at a certain moment in the past. But I feel that here in this emerald she gave me when we parted is her soul, just as she is now at this moment. In my mind, the emerald and the picture – her body and her soul – were separated. But look now: the two are reunited.

'Even when we're with someone we love, we're foolish enough to think of her body and soul as being separate. Although I am apart from her now, I may be in a much better position than I was to appreciate the structure of the single crystal that is Ying Chan. Separation is painful, but so is its opposite. And if being together brings joy, then it is only proper that separation should do the same in its own way.

'But what do you think, Matsugae? As for me, I've always wanted to know the secret that enables love to evade the bonds of time and space as if by magic. To stand before the person we love is not the same as loving her true self, for we are only apt to regard her physical beauty as the indispensable mode of her existence. When time and space intervene, it is possible to be deceived by both, but on the other hand, it is equally possible to draw twice as close to her real self.'

Kiyoaki had no idea how profound the prince's philosophizing was intended to be, but he listened intently. Many of his words did, in fact, strike home. As for Satoko, Kiyoaki believed that he had now indeed drawn that much closer to her real self. He saw quite clearly that what he had loved had not been the real Satoko. But what proof did he have of that? Wasn't he liable to be deceived twice over? And wasn't the Satoko he loved once again the real Satoko after all? He shook his head slightly, almost unconsciously. Then suddenly he remembered the dream in which the face of a strangely beautiful girl had suddenly appeared in Chao P.'s emerald ring. Who was that woman? Satoko? Ying Chan, whom he had never seen? Someone else perhaps?

'Well anyway, will it ever be summer?' Prince Kridsada said sadly, gazing out of the window at the grove of trees surrounding the dormitory.

The three boys could see the lights burning in the other dormitory buildings as they flickered through the trees, and they also heard shouting and loud conversation coming from various directions. It was time for the dining room to open for the evening meal. One student making his way along the path through the grove was burlesquing an ancient song, to the raucous laughter of his companions. The princes' eyes widened as though in fear that at any moment monsters of the mountains or rivers would appear out of the darkness.

Kiyoaki's return of the ring on this occasion was to lead to an unpleasant incident.

A few days later, there was a telephone call from Tadeshina. The maid informed Kiyoaki, but he did not go to the phone. Another call came next day. He did not accept that one either.

The calls unsettled him to some extent, but he fell back on his established rule: he put Satoko out of his mind and concentrated on the anger Tadeshina's rudeness provoked in him. All he had to do was to think about the cunning, lying old woman who had deceived him outrageously time and time again, and his consequent fury was strong enough to outweigh any slight misgivings he might have had about not going to the phone.

Three days passed. It was well into the rainy season, and it poured without let-up. When Kiyoaki came back from school, Yamada came up to him carrying a lacquered tray and respectfully presented a letter that lay face down upon it. Glancing at it, he was startled to see that Tadeshina had brazenly put her own name on it. The thick, oversized envelope had been carefully sealed, and to go by the feel of it, so was the letter inside. He felt afraid that if left to himself he might not be able to restrain himself from opening the letter. So, steeling himself to act deliberately, he tore it to shreds intentionally in front of Yamada and then ordered him to dispose of what was left of it. He knew that if he threw it into the waste-basket in his own room, he would be tempted to take it out and reassemble the fragments. Yamada's eyes flickered with surprise behind his glasses, but he said not a word.

A few more days passed. The matter of the torn-up letter began to weigh on Kiyoaki and his reaction took the form of anger. This was more than mere irritation that a supposedly trivial letter should have such power to unsettle him. What was agonizing was the realization, impossible to ignore, that he now regretted the decision not to open it. At first he had been able to regard the letter's destruction as proof of his strength of will, but in retrospect he was now beset by the feeling that on the contrary he had acted out of sheer cowardice.

When he had torn up that thick, plain white envelope, his fingers had encountered stiff resistance, as though the letter had perhaps been written on paper reinforced with tough linen fibre. But it was not the paper's composition that mattered. He now realized that had it not been for his burst of will-power, it would have been impossible for him to tear it up. Why should he have been afraid? He had no desire to become painfully involved with Satoko again. He hated the very thought of being re-enveloped in that fragrant haze of anxiety that she could conjure at will, especially now that he had finally achieved command over himself again. But despite all this, when he had been ripping up that thick letter, he had had the feeling that he was tearing a gash in Satoko's skin with its soft white glow.

On his way back from school one torrid Saturday afternoon during an unseasonal break in the wet weather, he noticed a hum of activity at the entrance of the main house. The grooms had prepared one of the carriages and were now loading it with a bulky package whose purple silk wrapping immediately identified it as a present. The horses were twitching their ears, and bright streams of saliva dropped from their mouths as they gaped to reveal yellowed teeth. In the hot sunlight their dark coats glistened as if smeared with grease, and their throbbing veins stood out on their necks beneath the fine, thick coats.

Just as he was about to go up the steps into the house, his mother appeared dressed in bulky ceremonial robes marked with the family crest.

'Hello,' he said.

'Oh, welcome home. I'm just on my way to the Ayakuras to extend our congratulations.'

'Congratulations for what?'

Since his mother disliked discussing important matters in front of the servants, she did not answer at once but drew Kiyoaki over to a dark corner of the wide entrance next to an umbrella stand before beginning to speak in a low voice.

'This morning the imperial sanction was graciously granted at last. Would you like to go with me?'

Before her son replied, the Marquise noticed that her words had caused a flash of grim pleasure in his eyes. Naturally she did not have time to reflect what it meant. Furthermore, her next words there by the doorway were eloquent proof of how little she had derived from that moment.

'After all, a joyful event is a joyful event,' she said, her mask of classic melancholy on her face. 'So no matter how badly you are at odds with her, the only correct thing to do on such an occasion is to be polite and offer your congratulations.'

'Please send my regards. I'm not going to go.'

He stood at the entrance and watched his mother leave. The horses' hooves scattered the gravel with a noise like a sudden squall, and the gold crest of the Matsugaes on the carriage seemed to quiver in the air as it flashed through the pines that stood in front of the house as the vehicle disappeared. Their mistress had gone, and Kiyoaki could sense the consequent relaxation of the servants. The tension in their muscles dissolved with a fall like a noiseless snowslide.

He turned back toward the house, so empty without either master or mistress. The servants, their eyes cast down, stood waiting for him to enter. At that moment, he was certain that he was holding the seeds of a problem immense enough to fill the vast emptiness of the building. Without bothering to glance at the servants, he went inside and hurried down the corridor, anxious not to waste a single moment reaching his room where he could seal himself off from the rest of the world.

His heart was beating with a strange excitement, and he was feverishly hot. The solemn words 'imperial sanction' seemed suspended before his eyes. The imperial sanction had been graciously granted. Tadeshina's repeated phone calls, the bulky letter – they must have represented a last, desperate flurry before it came. Their object had clearly been to obtain his forgiveness, to be relieved of a feeling of guilt.

All that day, he let his imagination run loose. He was oblivious of the outside world. The clear, calm mirror of his soul had now been shattered. There was a turmoil in his heart that churned with the force of a tropical storm. He was now shaken by a violent passion that bore no trace of the melancholy that had been such a part of its feeble precursors. But what emotion now had him in its grip? It must be called delight. But it was a delight so irrational, so passionate, that it was almost unearthly.

If one were to ask what was its cause, the only possible answer would be that it sprang from an impossibility, a sheer impossibility. Just as the string of a koto cut by a sharp blade yields with an abrupt, poignant note, so the tie that bound him to

Satoko had been cut by the shining blade of the imperial sanction. In the midst of his wavering inconsistency, this was something that he had dreamed of and hoped for in secret ever since he had begun to grow out of boyhood.

To be more precise, the dream had begun to form in the moment when he had looked up from Princess Kasuga's train and had been dazzled by the nape of her white neck with its peerless beauty, forever unattainable. That instant certainly foreshadowed today's fulfilment of his hopes. Absolute impossibility – Kiyoaki himself had helped to bring it about by single-mindedly shaping events to the pattern of his every caprice, his every twist of feeling.

But what kind of joy was it? Something in it obsessed him; there was something sinister, ominously threatening about it. Long ago he had resolved to recognize his emotions as his only guiding truth and to live his life accordingly, even if this meant a deliberate aimlessness. That principle had now brought him to his present sinister feelings of joy, which seemed to be the brink of a racing, plunging whirlpool. There seemed to be nothing left but to throw himself into it.

He thought back once again to himself and Satoko all those years before, copying verses from the Hundred Poets during their writing exercises. He bent over the scroll trying to inhale a trace of Satoko's fragrance that might have remained from that day fourteen years earlier. As he did so, he caught a scent of incense that was not far removed from mildew, something faint and so distant that still evoked such a powerful nostalgia that he felt he had laid bare the very source of all his emotion, so aimless and at the same time so impetuous.

Each piece of the Empress's confection, the prize for winning at *sugoroku*, had been moulded in the form of the imperial crest. Whenever his small teeth had bitten into a crimson chrysanthemum, the colour of its petals had intensified before melting away, and at the touch of his tongue, the delicately etched lines of a cool white chrysanthemum had blurred and dissolved into a sweet liquid. Everything came back to him – the dark rooms of the Ayakura mansion, the court screens brought from Kyoto with their pattern of autumn flowers, the solemn stillness of the nights, Satoko's mouth opening in a slight yawn half-hidden behind her sweep of black hair – everything came back just as he had experienced it then, in all its lonely elegance. But he realized that he was now slowly admitting one idea that he had never dared entertain before.

25

Something sounded within Kiyoaki like a trumpet call: *I love Satoko.* And no matter how he viewed this feeling he was unable to fault its validity, even though he had never experienced anything like it before.

Then a further revelation released the flood of desire he had pent up for so long: elegance disregards prohibitions, even the most severe. His sexual impulses, so diffident until now, had been lacking just such a powerful impulse. It had taken so much time and effort to find his role in life.

'Now at last, I'm sure that I do love Satoko,' he told himself. And the impossibility of fulfilling that love was proof enough that he was right in his conviction.

He could not stay still. He rose from his chair and then sat down again. His thoughts had always been preponderantly melancholy and anxious, but now he was swept by a surge of youthful energy. He felt that everything previous had been mere delusion. He had allowed his sensitivity and melancholy to dominate, smother him.

Opening the window, he took a deep breath as he stood looking out at the pond, whose surface glinted in the bright sunshine. He smelled the strong fresh odour of the zelkovas. In the midst of the clouds that were massed to one side of the maple hill, he noticed a hint of brightness that told him summer had come at last. His cheeks were hot and his eyes bright. He had become a new person. Whatever this might hold in store, he was at least nineteen years old.

26

He gave himself over to passionate daydreams while he waited impatiently for his mother to return from the Ayakuras. Her presence there did not fit in with his plans at all. Finally he could wait no longer, and took off his school uniform, dressing in a Satsuma splashed-pattern kimono and *hakama*. Then he called one of his servants and told him to have a rickshaw waiting for him.

Following his plan, he left the rickshaw at Aoyama, 6-chome, which was the terminus for the streetcar that went to Roppongi. He boarded it and rode to the end of the line. Around the corner from Roppongi, at the turn to Toriizaka, were three huge zelkova trees, the remainder of the six that had given the Roppongi or Six Trees district its name. Beneath them, just as in old times before there were streetcars in Tokyo, a big placard with 'Rickshaw Stand' scrawled on it was fastened to a post, and rickshaw men in conical wicker hats, short jackets, and blue trousers were gathered waiting for customers.

Kiyoaki called one of them, immediately handed him an exorbitant tip and told him to take him at once to the Ayakura mansion, which was no more than a few minutes away on foot. The old-fashioned Ayakura gate would not admit the Matsugaes' English carriage, and so if it were still waiting outside with the gate open, he would know that his mother was still there. However, if it were gone and the gate closed, he could safely assume that she had already fulfilled her ceremonial obligations and left.

When the rickshaw passed the gate, he saw that it was shut and in the road in front he recognized the marks left by a carriage.

He instructed the rickshaw man to take him back to the top of Toriizaka. Once there he sent him back on foot for Tadeshina while he himself remained behind, making use of the cover provided by the rickshaw.

As it turned out, he had a long wait. Through an opening in the side of the rickshaw, he watched the setting rays of summer sun flood the new leaves clustered at the tips of the branches. It seemed to be slowly submerging them in liquid brilliance. A giant horse chestnut towered above the red brick wall that ran along the edge of the slope of Toriizaka. Its very topmost leaves made him think of a white bird's nest decorated with a loosely woven crown of white flowers tipped with pink. Then all at once he was thinking of that snowy morning in February, and for no obvious reason he was shaken by a violent wave of excitement. But nevertheless, his intention was not to force an immediate meeting with Satoko, for since passion had now found a definite course, he was no longer vulnerable to each new onrush of emotion.

Tadeshina came out of a side entrance, followed by the rickshaw man. When she reached the rickshaw, Kiyoaki pushed back its top to reveal his face and so startled her that she could only stand there gaping up at him. He reached down, seized her hand and jerked her up into the rickshaw.

'I've something to tell you. Let's go somewhere we can talk safely.'

'But, master ... this is such a shock! The Marquise your mother took her leave just a few minutes ago. Then tonight we're preparing for an informal celebration ... I'm really so busy.'

'Never mind. Hurry up and tell the boy where to go.'

Since Kiyoaki kept a firm grip on her hand, she had no choice but to comply.

'Go toward Kasumicho,' she told the rickshaw man. 'Near Number Three there's a road going downhill that turns toward the main gate of the Third Regiment barracks. Please take us just to the bottom of the slope.'

The rickshaw lurched forward and Tadeshina stared straight ahead with desperate concentration, nervously smoothing back a stray hair. This was the first time he had been so close to this old woman with her thick mask of white powder, and the experience was far from pleasant. Yet he could not help but notice that she was even tinier than he had imagined, hardly more than a dwarf in fact. Buffeted by the shaking rickshaw, she kept up a mumbled stream of protest that he could only barely understand.

'It's too late, too late ... no matter what, it's just too late.' And then: 'If only you'd sent one word of answer ... before this happened. Oh why...?'

Kiyoaki said nothing and so she finally said something about their destination just before they got there: 'A distant relative of mine runs an inn for soldiers near here. It's not a very presentable place but an annex is always available, and it will permit me to hear whatever the young master wishes to say in confidence.'

Tomorrow was Sunday, when Roppongi would be transformed suddenly into a bustling garrison district, its streets full of khaki-uniformed soldiers, many out strolling with their visiting families. But it was still Saturday afternoon, and this transformation was yet to take place. As the rickshaw carried him along through the streets toward Tadeshina's destination, he had the feeling that on that snowy morning too, he and Satoko had passed first this spot, then another. Just as he became convinced that he remembered the slope they were following, Tadeshina told the man to stop.

They were in front of an inn at the foot of the slope. Its main wing was two storeys high, and although it had neither gate nor entranceway, it was surrounded by a good-sized garden enclosed by a broad fence.

Standing outside this fence, Tadeshina glanced up at the second floor of the rough wooden structure. It showed no sign of life. The six glass doors facing the front were shut, and none of the interior was visible, The low-quality panes in the latticed doors mirrored the evening sky in their own warped fashion, even catching the reflection of a carpenter working on an adjacent roof and distorting his image as though it were lying across water. The sky itself bore a watery image as seen there, tinged with the melancholy of a lake at evening time.

'It would of course be awkward if the soldiers were back – but only officers take rooms here,' Tadeshina said as she pushed open a close-worked lattice door beside which there hung a plaque of the Goddess of Children. She then called out to announce their presence.

A tall, white-haired man who was on the verge of old age appeared.

'Ah, Miss Tadeshina! Please come in,' he said in a somewhat squeaky voice.

'Is the annex available?'

'Yes, yes, of course.'

The three of them went down the back hallway to the rear of the inn and entered a small room perhaps ten feet square, the kind often used for assignations.

'I can't stay very long, though,' said Tadeshina. 'Besides, being alone like this with such a handsome young man, I don't know what people would say.' Suddenly she was speaking casually and coquettishly, addressing herself to both Kiyoaki and the old innkeeper.

The room was suspiciously tidy. A small scroll suitable for a tea ceremony room hung in a little alcove, and there was even a sliding Genji screen. The atmosphere was quite different from what one would have expected from the exterior, that of a cheap inn frequented by the army.

'What then do you so kindly wish to communicate to me?' Tadeshina asked as soon as the innkeeper withdrew. When Kiyoaki did not answer, she repeated her question, making no further effort to hide her irritation.

'What is this all about? And why choose today of all days...?'

'Because it's so appropriate. I want you to arrange a meeting between me and Satoko.'

'What do you mean, young master? It's too late. After what's happened, how can you ask such a thing? From now on, there's nothing more to be done. Everything must be subordinated to the Emperor's pleasure. And now this – after all those phone calls and the letters I sent! You didn't see fit to give us any reply whatever. And today you make a request like this! It's not a joking matter.'

'Just remember this: everything that happened was your fault,' said Kiyoaki with as much dignity as he could muster, staring at the veins that throbbed under the white powder caking Tadeshina's forehead. Angrily he accused her of having allowed Satoko to read his letter and then to lie about it brazenly, and also of having spread malicious gossip that had lost him his faithful retainer Iinuma. Tadeshina finally contrived to burst into tears, and apologized abjectly on her knees.

She then pulled some tissue paper from the sleeve of her kimono and began to wipe her eyes, rubbing away the white powder around them to reveal the pink web of wrinkles over her cheekbones, unmistakable proof of mortality. There was hardly any difference in texture between that wrinkled skin and the crumpled, rouge-smeared piece of tissue. Finally, staring into thin air, she began to talk.

'It's true. It's all my fault. I know that no amount of apology can make up for what I have done. But I should apologize more to my mistress than to you. Tadeshina's grievous failure was not communicating to the young master exactly how Miss Satoko felt. Everything that I had planned so carefully, thinking it for the best, has failed terribly. Please be kind enough to bear with me for a moment, young master. Imagine Miss Satoko's distress when she read your letter. And think what effort of courage it cost her not to show any sign of it when she met you. And then, after she had decided to take my advice and put a direct question to His Excellency your father, imagine how profoundly relieved she was to learn the truth from him at the family New Year's party. And after that, morning, noon, and night, she thought of nothing but the young master, until finally she went so far as to issue that invitation to ride through the snow that morning, whatever embarrassment it cost her as a woman. For some time after that, she was happy every day and even whispered your name at night in her sleep. But then she realized that through the kindness of His Excellency the Marquis, she was going to receive a proposal from the Imperial Family itself, and though she was counting on your courageous decision and had staked all her hopes on it, you didn't say a word, young master, and just let things go on. Miss Satoko's anxiety and suffering became unspeakable. Finally, when the granting of the imperial sanction was becoming imminent, she said that as a last hope, she wanted to tell the young master how she felt. Despite all my pleas, she decided to write a letter under my name. But now that hope too is dead. Miss Satoko was just coming to consider it all as a thing of the past. And so your demand today is a piece of cruelty. As you know, my mistress was brought up since childhood to revere the wishes of His Imperial Majesty the Emperor. We cannot expect her to go back on her word now. It's too late . . . simply too late. If your anger is unappeased, hit Tadeshina, kick her – do whatever is necessary to quiet your heart. But there's no other solution – it's just too late.'

Listening to Tadeshina's speech, a thrill of joy went through him like a knife. Yet at the same time he felt somehow that he knew it all already, that he was hearing things repeated that were quite clear to him in his heart. He was now finding himself possessed of an acute wisdom he had never suspected before. Thus armed, he felt strong enough to overcome all that the world had to offer in the way of obstacles. His eyes were full of the fire of youth. 'She read the letter I begged her to destroy,' he said to himself, 'so why shouldn't I resurrect the letter of hers that I destroyed?'

He stared wordlessly and fixedly at the little old lady with the white-powdered face. Once more she dabbed her reddened eyes with a piece of tissue paper. The room was growing steadily darker with the onset of evening. Her hunched shoulders seemed so frail that he was sure that if he grasped them suddenly the bones would give way with a hollow crack.

'It's not too late.'

'But it is.'

'No it isn't. I wonder what would happen if I were to show Miss Satoko's last letter to the Prince's family? Especially when one considers that it was written after the formal request for imperial sanction.'

At these words the blood suddenly drained from Tadeshina's face.

Neither said anything for a long time. It was no longer the rays of the setting sun but light from the second-floor rooms of the main wing that lit up the windows. The lodgers were returning and there was an occasional flash of khaki uniform at a window. Outside the fence a beancurd-seller sounded his bugle. The evening air was characterized by the mild warmth, like flannel, of the few summer days that come before the final end to the rainy season.

From time to time, Tadeshina whispered something to herself which Kiyoaki heard only in snatches: 'This is why I tried to stop her ... this is why I said not to do it.' She was evidently muttering about having opposed Satoko's writing of that final letter.

He maintained his silence, with increasing confidence that he held the winning hand. A wild animal seemed to be gradually if invisibly rearing its head within him.

'Very well then,' said Tadeshina. 'I will arrange just one meeting. And now the young master will, I trust, be kind enough to return the letter.'

'Splendid. But a meeting of itself is not enough,' he answered. 'I want the two of us to be alone together – without your being there. And as for the letter, I'll return that afterwards.'

27

Three days went by. The rain did not cease. After class, Kiyoaki went to the boarding house in Kasumicho, hiding his school uniform under a raincoat. He had received a message from Tadeshina that today would be Satoko's sole opportunity to escape from the house, since both her parents would be away.

Even after being shown to the back room in the boarding house by the innkeeper, Kiyoaki felt hesitant about removing his raincoat. Noticing this as he poured out his tea, the old owner reassured him: 'Please feel quite comfortable, sir. There's no cause for concern with someone like me who has renounced the world.'

The innkeeper left him. He looked around the room and noticed that a bamboo blind was now covering the window through which he had looked up at the second floor of the main wing last time. The windows had been shut to keep out the rain, and a damp, oppressive heat filled the room. When he idly opened a lacquered box on the desk, its inside was covered with drops of moisture.

He knew that Satoko had arrived when he heard the rustle of clothing and the sound of whispers coming from the other side of the Genji sliding door.

The panel opened and Tadeshina made him a deep bow. Then without saying a word, she let Satoko into the room and quickly shut the panel again. Before it slid back into place, her upturned eyes momentarily flashed white in the sultry midday gloom of the hallway like a squid.

Satoko sat down on the tatami floor in front of Kiyoaki, her knees primly together. Her head was bent and she hid her face with a handkerchief, letting the other hand rest on the floor. Her body was turned sideways, so that the nape of her neck shone white like a small lake that one sometimes comes upon in the mountains.

He sat facing her in silence, feeling as though they were both submerged in the rain falling on the roof. He could hardly believe that the moment had finally come.

Satoko was bereft of words, and he himself had brought her to this. It had been his most fervent hope to see her reduced to this state, robbed of the power given her by her greater age to drop those little homilies she had been so fond of, capable of nothing but silent tears. At this moment she held an irresistible attraction for him, in her kimono the colour of white wisteria, but it was not merely that of a rich prize finally within his grasp; it was the lure of the forbidden, the utterly unattainable, the proscribed. He wanted her this way and no other. And she herself, on the other hand, had always wanted to keep him off balance by playing games. How things had changed now! She could have chosen this beautiful, sacred, inviolable position at any time, but she had always preferred the false role of elder sister, cherishing him with that affectionate condescension he so hated.

Now he realized why he had objected so strongly when his father had proposed to give him an introduction to the pleasures that the women of Yoshiwara had to offer. Just as one can discern the stirrings of a dark green chrysalis inside a cocoon, he had always foreseen the gradual distillation of some ineffably sacred essence in Satoko. And he could give his purity to that essence alone. From that moment on, a dawn of unimaginable brilliance would begin to flood the world of black, inchoate melancholy in which he had imprisoned himself.

The elegance he had absorbed from his infancy under Count Ayakura's tutelage now became a silken cord in his hands, a noose for his innocence and Satoko's sanctity. Now at last he had found a valid use for the shining rope whose purpose had puzzled him for so long.

He was sure that he loved Satoko. And so he edged forward on his knees and grasped her by the shoulders. He felt them tense in resistance. This firm rebuff to his fingers delighted him. It was resistance on the grand scale, a ritual of resistance with cosmic significance. The soft shoulders that aroused such desire in him were opposing him with a force that drew on the weight of imperial sanction. For this very reason it had the remarkable power to drive him mad, making his fingertips ache with feverish desire. Her fragrant, jet-black hair, carefully dressed and piled lightly above her forehead, had a full-bodied gloss; glimpsed so briefly at close range, it made him think of being lost in a forest on a bright, moonlit night.

He put his face close to one wet cheek that had escaped the protection of her handkerchief. Still wordless, she began to shake her head in an attempt to ward him off, but her struggles were so mechanical that he knew they were not heartfelt, but imposed from outside. He pushed aside the handkerchief and tried to kiss her, but whereas her lips had been willing on that snowy February morning, they resisted fiercely now, and finally she ducked her head and, like a sleeping fledgling, froze with her chin burrowed in the neck of her kimono.

The drumming of the rain grew louder. Maintaining his grip on her, he paused to assess the strength of her defences. Her kimono, its neckband embroidered with a design of summer thistles, was chastely gathered at the throat, revealing a tiny triangle of skin. Her wide, tight-wrapped obi was cold and hard to the touch, like the door barring entrance to a sanctuary, and in the centre there gleamed a golden clip like the ornamented head of a spike in a pillar of a temple courtyard. Nevertheless, her body gave off the warm scent of flesh. Passing through the inner sleeve openings at her shoulders, it escaped from the wide kimono sleeves, a warm breeze against his cheek.

He took one hand away from her back and gripped her chin firmly. It fitted there as smoothly as a small, rounded ivory chessman. Her nose was wet with tears, and her delicate nostrils flared. He was thus able to kiss her properly.

Suddenly she seemed consumed by a mysterious fire, much as the flame in a stove burns more fiercely when the door is open. Both her hands were now free, and she pressed them against Kiyoaki's cheeks, pushing hard against him, but her lips remained on his, even though she tried to thrust him away. As a result of her resistance, however, her lips, with an incredible, liquid smoothness that intoxicated him, kept twisting one way, then the other against his own. The firm edge of her resolve was melting away like a lump of sugar in hot tea, and now a wonderfully sweet dissolution had begun.

He had no idea whatever of how to unfasten a woman's obi. Its tightly fastened flared bow at her back defied the efforts of his fingers. But as he groped blindly, trying to undo it by force, she reached behind her and while giving every sign that she was trying desperately to check his fumbling efforts, she subtly guided them in a more profitable direction. Their fingers lay tangled for a few moments in its folds, and then as its clip suddenly fell away, the obi uncoiled in a rustle of silk and sprang away from her body as though it had a life of its own. It was the beginning of a confused riot of uncontrollable movement. Her entire kimono swirled in revolt as he tore frantically at the folds of silk that bound her breasts, rebuffed at every turn by a whole network of straps that tightened as others came loose. But then right before his eyes, he saw the tiny, well-guarded triangle of white below her throat spread into a rich and fragrant expanse of skin.

She did not actually utter a word of protest. There was nothing to prove whether it was silent resistance or silent seduction. She seemed to be drawing him on at the same time as she was fighting him off. He sensed, however, that the strength underlying his assault upon her sacred inviolability was not wholly his own.

What was its source, then? As he looked at her face, it gradually flooded crimson, and her desire was unmistakable. He had one hand under her back to support her, and felt her lean on it more strongly, though with shy subtlety, until, as if giving up all hope of resistance, she fell back on the floor.

He parted the skirts of her kimono and began pushing aside the printed silk of her Yuzen underskirts in a dazzling tangle of fretted patterns and brilliant phoenixes soaring above stylized cloud formations. A distant vision of her thighs wrapped in fold after fold of silk drew him on as he fought his way through more and more layers of the clouds. Some secret hidden core was cunningly maintaining the complex arrangements with which he was struggling, and the key to it kept eluding him as his breath grew harsher and more irregular.

Finally, however, he was drawing closer to her body, slowly lowering himself on to her thighs, which had the faint sheen of a pale dawn horizon, when she raised her hands and gently helped him; this intended kindness ruined the moment, for at the instant when he merged with the dawn, whether he was touching her or not, it all ended abruptly.

The two lay side by side on the tatami floor staring up at the ceiling. The rain had become torrential again and was beating on the roof. The pounding of their hearts had scarcely subsided. Kiyoaki felt an exaltation that overrode not only his momentary exhaustion but even the realization that something had come to an end. However, a lingering sense of shared regret still hung over them, as palpable as the shadows now gradually forming in the darkening room. He thought he heard the faint sound of an old woman clearing her throat on the other side of the Genji panel. As he was about to sit up, however, Satoko reached over to stop him with a gentle grasp of his shoulder.

And then, without a word, she dispelled every vestige of regret. He was delighted to follow her lead. From that moment on, there was nothing he could not forgive her.

He was young; his desire quickly revived, and this time she was receptive and everything went smoothly. Under her sure, feminine guidance, he sensed that for the first time every barrier was gone and that he had found himself in a rich new world. In the heat of the room he had already stripped off the last of his clothes and now he felt the immediacy of flesh on flesh, firm but yielding, with the resistance of water and clinging plants to the advancing prow of a boat. He saw that there was no trace of distress in her face. She was even smiling faintly but this gave him no misgivings now. His heart was completely at rest.

Afterwards, he took her, rumpled, in his arms and pressed his cheek against hers, feeling the wetness of fresh tears. He knew that they were tears of joy, but still, nothing could better convey in silence their mutual consciousness of having committed unpardonable sin than her tears quietly rolling down his cheek as well as her own. For Kiyoaki, however, this sense of sin increased his already rising courage.

'Here,' she said, picking up his shirt, 'it won't do for you to catch cold.'

Just as he was about to snatch it roughly from her, she checked him for a moment, and pressed the shirt to her face with a deep breath. When she handed it to him, it was wet with tears.

When he had put on his school uniform and finished dressing, he was startled by the sudden sound of her clapping her hands. Then, after a significant pause, the Genji panel slid open a fraction and Tadeshina's head appeared.

'Did you call me, Miss Satoko?'

Satoko nodded and with a quick glance indicated her obi, which lay on the floor in a tangle around her. Tadeshina slid the door shut behind her and edged across the tatami floor to Satoko without looking in Kiyoaki's direction. She helped her mistress to dress and fastened her obi. Then she brought over the mirror from a corner of the room and began to arrange Satoko's hair. Meanwhile Kiyoaki was in acute embarrassment, at a loss as to what he should do; so while the two women performed their long-drawn-out ritual in the now-lighted room, he felt quite superfluous.

When everything was finally in order, Satoko, more beautiful than ever, sat with drooping head.

'I'm afraid, young master, that we have to go now,' the old woman began. 'The promise I made has been kept. From now on, please, I beg you, try to forget Miss Satoko. And now if you would be so kind, would you please return the letter as you promised?'

Kiyoaki sat cross-legged in silence. He did not answer.

'As you promised, would you please return the letter?' Tadeshina asked again.

Kiyoaki remained silent, as if he were deaf. He was staring at Satoko, who sat calmly without a single hair out of place and her beautiful kimono in perfect order. All at once she raised her eyes. They met Kiyoaki's. A brilliant piercing flash passed between them and in that instant he knew just how she felt.

'I'm not returning the letter. Because I want to meet her again, just like this,' he said, drawing on his newfound courage.

'Young master!' Tadeshina made no attempt to hide her anger. 'What do you think will happen? Only a spoiled child would say such a thing! You know what terrible things will come about, don't you? It's not just Tadeshina who will be destroyed.'

Then Satoko stopped her, her voice so composed, so otherworldly, that the sound of it sent a chill down his spine.

'It's all right, Tadeshina. Until Master Kiyo wishes to return the letter, there's nothing we can do but agree to keep meeting him. There's no other way to save both you and me – that is, if you intend to save me too.'

28

Kiyoaki's visit to his house to confide in him in such detail was so rare an event that Honda not only asked his mother to invite his guest to stay for dinner but even went so far as to forgo the work for the entrance examinations that normally occupied his entire evening. The mere prospect of Kiyoaki's arrival somehow charged the sedate atmosphere of the house with expectancy.

Throughout the day the sun, engulfed in cloud, had shone like white gold and now in the evening the sultry heat it had left behind was not appreciably diminished. As they sat talking, the two young men wore light summer kimonos with a Kasuri pattern.

Honda had had some sort of premonition about Kiyoaki's visit, but it had by no means prepared him for what was to come. As soon as Kiyoaki began to speak, Honda was startled to realize that the young man sitting beside him on the old leather couch along the wall of the reception room was someone radically different from the Kiyoaki he had known before. He had never seen eyes flash so openly. They were unmistakably the eyes of a worldly adult, but Honda had a lingering regret for the melancholy look and the downcast eyes that he had grown used to in his friend.

Despite this, however, he was delighted that Kiyoaki had chosen to confide in him without reservation what was a secret of the gravest consequence. Honda had been hoping for a gesture like this for a long time, and it had come about without the slightest urging on his part. On reflection, he realized that Kiyoaki had kept his secrets even from his friend, as long as they had concerned nothing but his own inner struggles, but now that it was a matter of reputation and serious wrongdoing, he had poured it all out in an impetuous flood of words. Considering the gravity of the confession and the limitless trust it implied, Kiyoaki could hardly have given him greater cause for happiness. As he studied his friend, he found Kiyoaki noticeably matured, and some of the beauty that had belonged to the face of an irresolute young boy was gone from his features. They now shone with the determination of the passionate young lover, and his words and gestures were free of any hint of reluctance and uncertainty.

He was the very image of a man proud of his conquest. As he told his story to Honda, his cheeks glowed with colour, his teeth gleamed, and his voice was firm and clear, although he paused shyly at times and there was a new gallantry evident even in the set of his eyebrows. Almost nothing seemed more alien to him than introspection, or so it struck Honda, whether because the tale came so abruptly to an end or because of the incoherence of his outpourings.

'Listening to you, the oddest thing came to my mind – why, I don't know,' said Honda. 'One day, when we were talking – I'm not sure when it was – you asked me if I remembered anything about the Russo-Japanese War. And then afterwards, when we were at your house, you showed me a collection of war photographs. And I remember you telling me that the one you liked best had written under it "Vicinity of Tokuri Temple: Memorial Services for the War Dead" – a strange picture, in which all the soldiers looked as if they had been assembled like actors in a huge pageant. At the time it struck me as being an odd preference for you since you had so little taste for anything that smacked of military life.

'But at any rate, as I was listening just now, the memory of that dusty plain in the picture came to my mind and somehow seemed to fuse with your beautiful love story.'

Honda had managed to surprise himself. He was startled not only by the obscurity of what he had said and the fervour with which he had said it, but also by the admiration he felt for Kiyoaki's wanton disregard of commandment and precept – he, Honda, who had long ago decided to become a man of the law!

Two servants entered with small tables on which their dinners had been placed. His mother had arranged things like this so that the two could eat and talk as friends without any constraint. A saké bottle stood on either table, and Honda offered him some.

'Mother was rather worried. She didn't know how well you'd take to the food we serve, seeing as you're accustomed to such luxuries,' he remarked, turning the conversation to something more commonplace.

He was happy to see Kiyoaki starting to eat as though, in fact, he found the food much to his liking. So for a little while the two young men stopped talking and gave themselves over to the healthy pleasures of eating.

Enjoying the further brief silence that usually follows a good meal, Honda asked himself why, after hearing his classmate confess to so romantic an exploit, he had felt so happy about it, without a twinge of jealousy or envy. He was refreshed by it the way a lakeside garden is imperceptibly steeped in moisture during the rainy season.

'Well then, what do you intend to do?' he asked, breaking the silence.

'I don't have the least idea. I'm slow off the mark, but once I get started, I'm not the type to stop halfway.'

Honda stared at him wide-eyed. He had never dreamed that he would ever hear Kiyoaki say something like this.

'You mean you want to marry Miss Satoko?'

'That's out of the question. The sanction has already been granted.'

'But you've already violated the sanction. Why can't you marry her then? Couldn't the two of you run away – go abroad and get married there?'

'You just don't understand,' he answered. Then he lapsed into silence, and for the very first time that day, Honda noticed a trace of the old melancholy in the lines that suddenly appeared between his eyebrows.

Perhaps he had been expecting as much, but now that he had seen it, he felt a slight uneasiness cast a shadow over his own mood of exhilaration. As he sat staring at his friend's handsome profile, whose fine and delicate lines would defeat all but the most skilled artist, he wondered just what it was that Kiyoaki hoped to get from life. He felt a shudder pass through him.

Kiyoaki picked up his strawberries, got up from the couch and sat down in front of the scrupulously tidy desk where Honda worked. He propped his elbows on its austere surface and casually began to swing the swivel chair from side to side. As he did so, he put his weight on his elbows and restlessly eased the posture of his head and torso, his bare chest showing at the neck of his loose-fitting kimono. Then, after arming himself with a toothpick, he began lightly spearing the strawberries one by one and popping them into his mouth. It was a display of relaxed bad manners that showed how glad he was to escape the strict decorum of his own home. He spilled some sugar, which dropped down on to his light-skinned chest, but he brushed it off with no sign of embarrassment.

'You're going to attract ants, you know,' said Honda, laughing through a mouthful of strawberries.

Kiyoaki's delicate eyelids, usually too pale, were now diffused with colour, thanks to the saké he had drunk. As he kept turning the swivel chair from side to side, his bare flushed forearms still propped on the desk, he happened to move too far in one direction, and his body was oddly twisted. It was just as if he had suddenly been stricken by some vague pain of which he himself was unaware.

There was no mistaking the faraway look in those eyes beneath their fine, graceful brows, but Honda was well aware that their flashing glance was not directed toward the future. Unlike his usual self, he had a cruel desire to inflict his growing uneasiness on his friend – an urgent impulse to pretend to raise his own hand to destroy Kiyoaki's all-too-recent sense of happiness.

'Well, what *are* you going to do? Have you even thought about what will come of this?'

Kiyoaki raised his eyes and looked at him steadily. Honda had never seen a gaze of such burning eagerness and yet such gloom.

'Why must I think about it?'

'Because all those people around you and Miss Satoko are moving slowly but inexorably toward a dénouement. You don't think the two of you can hover forever in mid-air like two dragonflies making love?'

'I know we can't,' Kiyoaki replied, breaking off the exchange and casually glancing elsewhere. He gave himself over to an examination of the shadows in the various nooks and crannies of the room, such as the intricate patterns beneath the bookcases and the ones beside the wicker wastepaper basket – those elusive little shadows that crept into Honda's plain and functional study night after night, insidious as human emotions, to lurk wherever they could find cover.

As Honda watched him, he was struck by the prominence of his graceful eyebrows. They were like shadows themselves, bent into elegant bows. They seemed to be an embodiment of an emotion, yet nevertheless had force enough to check its expression. He imagined them guarding the dark, brooding eyes beneath, loyally following their master's glance wherever it went, like zealous servants with impeccable training.

Honda decided to come out directly with something that had been taking form in a corner of his mind.

'A bit earlier,' he began, 'I said something very odd. I mean about thinking of the picture from the Russo-Japanese War while you were telling me about you and Miss Satoko. I wondered why that came to me, and now that I've given it a little more thought, I have an answer. The age of glorious wars ended with the Meiji era. Today, all the stories of past wars have sunk to the level of those edifying accounts we hear from middle-aged noncoms in the military science department or the boasts of farmers around a hot stove. There isn't much chance now to die on the battlefield.

'But now that old wars are finished, a new kind of war has just begun; this is the era for the war of emotion. The kind of war no one can see, only feel – a war, therefore, that the dull and insensitive won't even notice. But it's begun in earnest. The young men who have been chosen to wage it have already begun to fight. And you're one of them – there's no doubt about that.

'And just as in the old wars, there will be casualties in the war of emotion, I think. It's the fate of our age – and you're one of our representatives. So what about it then? You're fully resolved to die in this new war – am I right?'

Kiyoaki's only answer was a flickering smile. At that moment a strong breeze, heavy with the rain's dampness, found its way in through the window and, in passing, cooled their foreheads, which were covered with a light film of sweat. Honda was perplexed at Kiyoaki's silence. Was his answer so obvious that no reply was necessary? Or had his words really struck a responsive chord in his friend, while his way of putting them had been so extravagant that there was no way for him to answer frankly? He thought that it had to be one or the other.

29

Three days later, when two cancelled classes gave Honda a free afternoon, he went to watch the district court in session, accompanied by a law student who was one of the family houseboys. It had been raining since morning.

Honda's father was a justice of the Supreme Court and, even within his own family, was a strict observer of principles. He was greatly pleased by the promise shown by his nineteen-year-old son, who had applied himself to the law even before entering college. His father thus felt confident enough to conclude that his son would eventually succeed him. Up to this year, the office of judge had been for life, but the previous April a large-scale reform of the juridical system had been put into effect. As a result, more than two hundred judges had been laid off or requested to hand in their resignations. Justice Honda, wanting to show his solidarity with his unfortunate old friends, had offered his own resignation, but it had not been accepted.

The experience, however, seemed to have marked a turning point in his views on life, which, in their turn, affected what had been a rather formal relationship with his son. From then on, he brought to it a warmth of generosity that resembled the affection shown by a high official to the subordinate he has selected to succeed him. Honda himself was determined to work harder than ever at his studies to try to be worthy of such unprecedented favour.

One result of his father's changed views was that he permitted his son to attend court sessions even though he was not yet an adult. He did not, of course, go so far as to let him come into his own court, but he gave him permission to watch whatever civil or criminal cases he liked, as long as he was accompanied by the young retainer who was also a law student.

His father explained to Shigekuni that since all his familiarity with the law came from books, it would be extremely valuable for him to come in contact with the actual process of law in Japan and to experience it at a practical level. Justice Honda had more than this in mind, however. Truth to tell, his main concern was to expose his still sensitive, nineteen-year-old son to those elements of human existence that were dredged up in all their shocking sordid reality in criminal court. He wanted to see what Shigekuni was able to draw from such experience.

It was a dangerous sort of education. Still, when the Justice considered the greater danger of allowing a young man to form his character out of an assimilation from careless popular behaviour, cheap entertainment and so on, from whatever might please or appeal to his immature taste, he felt confident of the advantages of this educational experiment. There was a good chance that it would at least make Shigekuni acutely aware of the stern and watchful eye of the law. He would see all the amorphous, steaming, filthy detritus of human passions processed right then and there according to the impersonal recipes of the law. Standing by in such a kitchen should teach Shigekuni a great deal about technique.

Honda hurried through the dark corridors of the courthouse on his way to the 8th District Criminal Court, a route lit only by the faint light that filtered through the rain soaking the ravaged grass of the quadrangle. The pervasive atmosphere of this building had absorbed the raw essence of the criminal spirit; the place struck him as being altogether too sinister for the palace of reason it was supposed to be.

His depression still clung to him after he and his companion had taken their seats in the courtroom. He glanced at the highly strung law student who had conducted him here with such anxious haste and was now engrossed in the case book he had brought with him, as though he had completely forgotten his master's son. Then he turned the same listless gaze on the still empty judge's bench, the public prosecutor's desk, the witness stand, the defence attorney's desk, and so on. Such universal emptiness struck him as being expressive of his own spiritual state on this damp, humid afternoon.

So young and so lethargic! As though he had been born to sit and stare like this. Ever since Kiyoaki had confided in him, Shigekuni, who would have been bright and confident, as befitted such an able young man, had undergone a change. Or rather, the friendship between him and Kiyoaki had undergone a strange reversal. For years, each of them had been extremely careful to intrude in no way on the personal life of the other. But now, just three days before, Kiyoaki had suddenly come to him and, like a newly cured patient transmitting his disease to someone else, had passed on to his friend the virus of introspection. It had taken hold so readily that Honda's disposition now seemed a far better host to it than Kiyoaki's. The first major symptom of the disease was a vague sense of apprehension.

What was Kiyoaki to do, he wondered. Was it right for himself, as Kiyoaki's friend, to do nothing more than sit by idly and let things take their course?

While he waited for the court session to begin at one thirty, he sat engrossed in the reflections provoked by his anxiety, his mind far from the hearings that he had come to attend.

'If I were really to act as a true friend,' he thought, 'wouldn't it be best to persuade him to try and forget Miss Satoko? Up until now I thought it best as his friend to pretend not to notice even if he were in his death agonies, out of respect for that elegance of his. But now that he's told me everything as he did the other day, shouldn't I interfere, as I have the right to do in an ordinary friendship, and do my best to save him from the clear danger that's threatening him? Moreover, I shouldn't hold back even if it makes him so resentful that he breaks our friendship. In ten or twenty years, he'll understand why I did it. And even if he never understands, it should make no difference to me.

'There's no doubt that he's heading straight for tragedy. It will be beautiful, of course, but should he throw his whole life away as a sacrificial offering to such a fleeting beauty – like a bird in flight glimpsed from a window?

'I know what I have to do. From now on I've got to put aside all the niceties and behave like an insensitive and imperceptive friend. And whether he likes it or not, I've got to do something to pour cold water on that raging passion of his. I've got to use every ounce of my strength to prevent him from fulfilling his destiny.'

This feverish rush of thoughts made Honda's head ache with the effort they cost. He no longer felt able to sit there patiently and wait for the start of the hearings, in which he had lost all interest. He wanted to leave at once, rush to Kiyoaki's house and pour out every argument at his command to persuade him to change his mind. And the frustration of realizing that this was impossible caused a new upsurge of anxiety that increased his discomfiture.

He glanced around and noticed that all the seats had been filled. Now he understood why the houseboy had brought him here so early. Among those present were young men who looked like law students, drab middle-aged men and women, and newspaper reporters with armbands who were coming and going with a great show of urgency. He watched as those who had been drawn by nothing more than base curiosity hid their interest behind masks of sober propriety, stroking their moustaches and passing the time with a genteel wave of a fan or using the long nails of their little fingers to dig sulphur-coloured deposits out of their ears. It was an instructive sight, and one that, more than anything seen previously, opened his eyes to the moral ugliness of the belief that 'Oh, I'm in no danger of ever committing a sin'. Whatever the future might hold, he was determined never to fall prey to that kind of attitude.

The windows were shut against the rain, and they admitted a dull, flat light that lay over all the spectators indifferently like a coat of grey dust; only the shiny black visors of the guards' caps were exempt from it.

The entrance of the defendant set up a flurry of comment. Flanked by two guards and dressed in a blue prison uniform, she made her way to the dock. He tried to get a look at her as she passed, but there was so much jostling and neck-craning going on among the spectators that he could do little more than catch a glimpse of plump white cheeks with conspicuous dimples. Then after she had entered the dock, all he could see was that her hair was pulled back in the cylindrical bun worn by female prisoners. Although she hunched forward respectfully, he noticed that there was a little sign of nervous strain in the way her plump shoulders were set beneath her uniform.

The defence lawyer had already come in, and now everyone was waiting for the public prosecutor and the judge himself.

'Just take a look at her, young master. Would you think she's a murderess?' said the young law student, whispering in his ear. 'It's true what they say about not being able to tell a book by its cover.'

The court ritual began with the presiding judge putting the usual questions to the accused about name, address, age, and social status. The courtroom was so hushed that Honda imagined he could hear the busy swish of the recorder's writing brush.

'Two-five, Nihonbashi Ward, Tokyo City. A commoner. Tomi Masuda,' the woman replied in a voice that was clear and steady but so low that the crowd of spectators pricked up their ears and leaned forward as one, afraid of missing something when the testimony reached matters that were crucial. The responses came smoothly enough until the accused came to her age, and there, whether intentionally or not, she hesitated. Then, after the urgings of her lawyer, she shook herself and said in a louder voice: 'I'm thirty-one.'

At that moment, she turned her head toward her lawyer and Honda caught a glimpse of her profile, her eyes wide and clear and a few stray hairs brushing her cheek.

The spectators stared at this small woman in fascination, as if she might perhaps have the translucent body of a silkworm that had somehow excreted a thread of inconceivable complexity and evil. Her slightest movement made them imagine the sweatmarks on the armpits of her uniform, her nipples tight with fear, the line of her buttocks, rather too full, dull, and a little cold. This body had spun threads without number until they were finally wrapping her in a sinister cocoon. For the spectators, there had to be a peculiarly intimate correspondence between her body and her crime. They would be dissatisfied with anything less. For the average man, driven as he is by lurid fantasies, there is almost nothing more deliciously titillating than the contemplation, from a safe distance, of evil laid out in its cause and effect. Had the woman been thin, her very thinness would have embodied this for them. But since she was plump, her plumpness served just as well. And so, satisfied that she was nothing less than evil incarnate, they eagerly exercised their harmless powers of imagination, fastening with delight on every detail down to the very beads of sweat that they were sure covered her breasts.

Honda's scruples would not let him follow the thoughts of the crowd, although these were quite clear to him, despite his youth; he focused his entire attention on the testimony of the defendant as she answered the judge's questions. Her account was now getting to the matter at issue.

Her way of telling things was tedious and confused, but it was clear enough that the chain of events leading up to this crime of passion had unfolded relentlessly in a manner that must lead inevitably to tragedy.

'When did you start living with Matsukichi Hijikata?'

'I ... it was last year, Your Honour. I remember it very well. June the fifth.'

Her retentive memory made the spectators laugh, but the guards quieted them at once.

Tomi Masuda was a waitress who had become enamoured of a cook named Matsukichi Hijikata, who worked at the same restaurant. The man was a widower who had only recently lost his wife. Spurred by affection, she had begun to take care of him, and the previous year they had started to live together. Hijikata, however, gave no sign that he wanted to make the arrangement official, and in fact after they had set up housekeeping, he became more and more energetic in his pursuit of other women. Then toward the end of the previous year, he had taken up with a maid who worked at an inn called Kishimoto in the same Hama district. Though Hidé, the maid, was only twenty, there was little she did not know about men. As a result, Hijikata's nights away from home became more and more frequent. Finally, this spring, Tomi had gone to confront Hidé and plead with her to leave her man alone. Hidé had treated her with contempt, and Tomi, unable to control her rage, had killed her.

It was, in brief, a triangle that ended in violence, a common affair of the streets with no particularly distinguishing feature. Yet under the close scrutiny of the court hearing, many undoubtedly authentic and totally unpredictable elements came to light.

The woman had found herself with a fatherless child, now eight years old, who had been left in the care of relatives in her home village, but she had asked them to send him to Tokyo so that he would have the benefit of a better school system. But although she had hoped to use the boy as an inducement to Hijikata to settle down, Tomi, even as a mother, had already embarked on the course that would force her to become a murderess.

And now her testimony came to the events of that night.

'No, Your Honour. If only Hidé had not been there that night, everything would have been all right. I know that this whole thing just wouldn't have happened. If only she had had a cold or something that night and had been in bed when I went to the Kishimoto to see her, everything would have been all right too.

'The knife I used was the one Matsukichi uses to cut *sashimi*. He's a man who takes real pride in his work and he has all kinds of good knives. "To me these are like a samurai's sword," he keeps saying, and he never lets any of the women at work touch them but always sharpens them carefully himself. But about the time I started to get jealous of Hidé, he hid them all away somewhere, thinking it was dangerous.

'When I realized the way his mind was working, it made me angry. After that I used to make jokes about it, pretending to threaten him. I'd say: "I don't need any of your knives. There're plenty of others around I can lay my hands on, you know." Then one day after Matsukichi hadn't been home for a long time, I was cleaning out a closet, and all of a sudden I came across a package with all his knives in it in a place you'd never expect. And what surprised me most, Your Honour, was that almost all of them were covered with rust. When I saw that rust, I just knew how much he'd got himself involved with Hidé, and I started to shake with one of the knives right there in my hand. But just then my boy came home from school, and I gradually calmed down. Then I thought to myself that maybe if I took his favourite knife, the one he uses to cut *sashimi*, to be sharpened, Matsukichi would appreciate it – trying to make myself think I was a real wife. I wrapped it up in a cloth, and then when I was going out, my boy asked me where I was off to and I told him I had a little errand to run and I'd be right back and he should be a good boy and watch the house. And then he said: "I don't care if you never come back. Then I can go back to my school back home." This gave me such a shock and when I stopped to ask him what he meant, I found out the children in the neighbourhood were making fun of him and saying: "Your old man couldn't stand your mother's nagging, and he ran out on her." This is something the children probably picked up from hearing their parents gossiping about us. And so now here was my boy wanting to get away from a mother who's been turned into a laughing stock and go back to his foster parents in the country. Suddenly I got so angry and before I knew it, I'd hit him across the face. As I rushed out of the house, I could hear him crying behind me.'

According to the testimony that followed, Tomi was not thinking about Hidé at this moment, but was hurrying through the streets with one thing only on her mind: to get the knife sharpened so that she would feel better. The knife sharpener had a great deal of other work to do, but she would not be turned away. After she had waited for over an hour, he finally sharpened it for her. When she left his shop, she had not felt at all like going back home, and finally had turned almost involuntarily in the direction of the Kishimoto Inn.

Shortly beforehand, Hidé had returned to the Kishimoto after enjoying a wild night with Matsukichi and had been lectured by the innkeeper's wife for leaving work. She had gone to the woman and apologized tearfully, just as Matsukichi had instructed. It was only a few minutes after this was over that Tomi arrived at the inn and asked to speak to Hidé for a moment outside. Hidé came out to see her and was surprisingly cordial. She had just changed into a stylish working kimono, and as she walked along the street with Tomi, her loose clogs scraped languidly along the ground in the manner affected by affluent prostitutes.

'I made a promise to the boss just now. From now on I'm going to have nothing more to do with men, I told her,' she said.

Tomi felt a rush of happiness when she heard this, but next moment Hidé, smiling brightly, robbed her words of all significance with a further remark: 'But I don't know if I can hold out even for three days.'

Making a great effort of self-control, Tomi then offered to treat her to a drink at a near-by *sushi* shop on the bank of the Sumida River. Once they had begun to drink, Tomi did her best to talk to her as though she were addressing her elder sister, but Hidé refused to be drawn; her only reaction was an ironic smile. And finally, when she was probably driven to melodramatic extremes by the saké, Tomi lowered her head in supplication, but the younger woman turned away in brusque contempt. They had been there for over an hour by this time, and it was dark outside. Hidé got up to go, saying that the manager would be angry at her again unless she returned immediately.

After they left the *sushi* shop, Tomi claimed that she did not know why they wandered into a badly lit vacant lot in Hama that lay by the river. She said that perhaps when she tugged at Hidé's kimono, trying to get her to stay and talk, Hidé had happened to begin walking in this direction as she pulled herself free. At any rate, Tomi denied any intention of having led her that way in order to kill her.

After walking for a short time, Tomi began to argue again, but Hidé only laughed. As she did so, her even teeth flashed white, although there was no more than a glint of light on the surface of the Sumida to relieve the darkness that engulfed the two of them.

'It's no use you keeping on like this,' Hidé replied at last. 'No wonder Matsukichi got so fed up with you.'

This, according to Tomi, was the decisive moment, as she went on to describe her reactions.

'When I heard that, the blood rushed to my head. I don't know how to describe it exactly . . . right then I felt like a baby crying desperately in the dark, waving its arms and legs because it had no words to say it wanted something – or because it was hurting somewhere. And then I started to swing my own arms about, and somehow they loosened the cloth, got hold of the knife, and while they were still waving it around, Hidé's body bumped into it in the dark – that's the only way I can say it.'

Her words had been so intense that the crowd in the courtroom, and Honda with them, could clearly see the phantom baby miserably waving its arms and legs.

After she had finished, Tomi Masuda covered her face with her hands and sobbed. Her shoulders under the prison uniform seemed the more pathetic for being plump. The mood of the spectators now seemed to be shifting gradually from undisguised curiosity to something else.

The rain was still falling outside the windows and veiled the courtroom in a bleak light which seemed to focus on Tomi Masuda. She stood there as though she was the sole representative of all the complex passions of man, living, breathing, grieving, and crying out in pain. She alone was endowed with the privilege of emotion. Until a few moments before, the spectators had seen nothing but a plump, perspiring thirty-one-year-old woman. But now with bated breath and staring eyes, they were looking at a human being wracked by her feelings, writhing like a fish carved up alive for the dinner table.

She had absolutely no protection from their gaze. The crime that she had once committed in darkness had now taken possession of her to reveal itself before the eyes of them all. For it was the vivid character of the crime itself, rather than any consideration of good intentions or moral scruples, that she had impressed with such cogent force upon the spectators. Tomi Masuda's self-revelation far surpassed the possible accomplishment of even the most skilled of actresses, who, after all, would have revealed no more than she had intended. It amounted to facing the whole world and turning it into one giant audience. Her lawyer, who stood beside her, seemed too shabby to have any capacity to help. She stood there, a short plump figure, with nothing to mitigate her drabness – no combs in her hair, no jewellery, no fine kimono to catch a man's eye – but the fact of being a criminal was enough to make them see her as a woman.

'If we had the jury system here in Japan, this is the kind of case where they might let her get away with it,' said the law student, whispering in Shigekuni's ear again. 'What can you do with a glib woman like that?'

Shigekuni sat thinking. Once passion was set in motion according to its own laws, then it was irresistible. This was a theory that would never be accepted by modern law, which took it as self-evident that conscience and reason ruled man.

Then his thoughts turned to more personal things. Although he had come to watch this trial as a thoroughly disinterested spectator, he was now fascinated. At the same time, however, it had made him realize something else: he would never plunge into the kind of molten red-hot passion that had come gushing out of Tomi Masuda.

Outside, the overcast sky had brightened further and the rain had slackened into brief, scattered showers. The raindrops coating the window shone eerily in the sunshine.

He hoped that his reason would always be like that sunlight. But a part of him was drawn irresistibly to the darkness of human passion. This blackness was a fascination, no more. And Kiyoaki, too, was a fascination that seemed to come surging up to shake the very fabric of life, but that instead of being life-giving, carried the seeds of a fateful end.

It was in this mood, then, that Honda decided not to interfere with Kiyoaki for the time being.

30

As the summer vacation grew closer, something happened that disturbed the atmosphere at Peers. Prince Pattanadid lost his emerald ring. The affair became very serious when it became generally known that Prince Kridsada had protested in anger that the ring had been stolen. More than anything else, Prince Pattanadid wanted the matter to be settled as quietly as possible, and he rebuked his cousin for his rudeness. Nevertheless, it was evident that in his heart, he, too, believed it to have been stolen.

Prince Kridsada's angry charge provoked a predictable response from the school administration. They said that such a thing as theft was unthinkable at Peers. The ensuing turmoil was eventually to reach such proportions that the princes, more and more homesick, were finally to decide that they wanted to return to Siam. The chain of events that was to put them on a collision course with the school began when the dormitory prefect, trying to be as helpful as possible, asked them to give him an account of the events immediately preceding the disappearance of the ring.

As he continued to question them, their stories began to differ. They both agreed that they had gone for a walk on campus in the early evening, returned to the dormitory for dinner, and then discovered the loss of the ring when they went back to their room afterwards. Prince Kridsada claimed that his cousin had worn the ring during the walk and then left it in the room before dinner, contending, therefore, that it must have been stolen during dinner. But Prince Pattanadid himself was not so sure on this point, as was evident from the vagueness of his testimony. He was sure that he had worn the ring when he went out for the walk but confessed that he could not remember whether or not he had left it in his room during the meal.

This, of course, was crucial to deciding whether the ring had been stolen or lost. Then, when the prefect asked about where they had been on their walk, he discovered that the two princes, drawn by the pleasant evening, had gone through the fence surrounding the Reviewing Mound and had lain down for a while on the grass at the top, an act forbidden by school rules. It was not until the next day, a muggy afternoon with intermittent showers, that the prefect heard their account of what had happened. Nevertheless, he decided that there was only one thing to be done, and he asked the princes to come with him at once so that all three of them could make a thorough search of the top of the mound.

The Reviewing Mound was in a corner of the drill field. Though it was small and undistinguished, the Emperor Meiji had once deigned to review a student parade from its flat, grassy top. And so it had afterwards been made into a memorial of the event, with several of the sakaki trees sacred to Shintoism planted at the top, one of them by the Emperor himself. It was considered the most venerable place at Peers, second only to the sanctuary where Emperor Meiji had planted a sakaki.

Accompanied by the prefect, the two princes passed through the fence again, this time in broad daylight, and climbed to the top of the mound. The grass had been soaked by the drizzle, and the task they faced of searching roughly two hundred square yards of the mound's surface was obviously not going to be an easy one. Since it did not seem adequate to search merely the spot where they had lain down, the prefect decided that they should divide the area into three, with each of them scouring a section. And so with the rain, now increasing somewhat, falling on their backs, they picked through the grass, blade by blade.

Prince Kridsada made little effort to hide his reluctance, and carried out his task with a certain amount of grumbling. Prince Pattanadid, however, being good-natured, began his search more willingly, recognizing that it did, after all, concern his own ring. He started at the bottom of the slope in his section and worked his way upwards with great precision.

He had never taken so close a look at each blade of grass. For nothing less than the most painstaking care would do, because despite the ring's gold setting, its large emerald would be next to invisible in the grass. The drizzle became raindrops on the back of his neck, finally slid under his tight collar and rolled down his back, a sensation that aroused a yearning for the warm monsoons of Siam. The light green at the roots of the grass gave the illusion that a ray of sunshine had broken through, but the sky remained overcast. Here and there, there were small white wildflowers in the grass, their heads drooping under the weight of the rain, but the powdery whiteness of their petals remained as bright as ever. Once Prince Pattanadid's eye was caught by a bright glittering spot under a sawtooth leaf of a tall weed. Sure that his ring could not have lodged there he nevertheless turned the leaf over to find a small, brilliantly coloured beetle clinging to the underside to escape the rain.

Peering at the grass at such close range made it loom up under his nose, immense and green, reminding him of the jungles of his homeland in the rainy season. With his eyes thus fixed on the grass, he could imagine the gathering cumulus clouds shining with such white intensity, the sky a deep azure blue in one quarter but dark and threatening in another, and he could even hear the violent rumble of thunder.

It was not really the ring that made him willing to expend such painful effort. He wore himself out searching through the grass that defied his exertions for the sake of recovering the image of Princess Chan, however slight the hope of success. He was near to tears.

A group of students on their way to the gymnasium walked by carrying umbrellas and wearing their sweaters draped over the shoulders of their gym uniforms. Seeing the activity on the mound, they stopped to watch.

A rumour about the lost ring had already spread through the school, but since the students considered it effeminate for a man to wear a ring, there were few who felt the least sympathy or concern for its loss or for the frantic search. They grasped its purpose, of course, as soon as they saw the two princes working their way through the wet grass on hands and knees. Prince Kridsada's charge of theft had obviously reached their ears and now they seized the chance to express their resentment by hurling bitter taunts at the two princes. But when they caught sight of the prefect getting to his feet to look in their direction, they were taken aback. When he requested them quietly to join the hunt, they fell silent, turned their backs, and scattered in all directions.

The two princes and the prefect, each working from a different direction, had almost met up in the centre of the mound, and so there was no escaping the realization that all their efforts were likely to prove in vain. The showers were now over, and some late afternoon sunshine had broken through the clouds. The wet grass sparkled as it caught the low-slanting rays, and the shadows cast by the leaves made complex patterns on its surface.

Prince Pattanadid thought he saw the unmistakable glint of an emerald in one clump of grass, but when he plunged his wet hands into it, he found nothing but a faint, unsteady gleam, blurred by the dirt, no more than a tangle of wet grass, glowing golden at the roots, with no resemblance at all to the ring.

Afterwards, Kiyoaki heard the story of the futile hunt. The prefect had certainly given evidence of goodwill by helping as much as he could, but there was no denying that the search had been an unnecessary humiliation for the two princes. Not too surprisingly, they chose to make an issue of it and so furnished themselves with a good excuse to pack their bags and move to the Imperial Hotel. They confessed to Kiyoaki that they had decided to return to Siam as soon as they could.

When he heard this news from his son, Marquis Matsugae was most distressed. He realized that to allow the two princes to return home in their present mood was to leave them permanently scarred. For the rest of their lives their attitude to Japan would be tinged by bitter memories. At first he tried to mitigate the antagonism that existed between them and the school, but he found that the princes' attitude had hardened to such an extent that there was little hope of any successful mediation at present. He therefore bided his time for the moment, having decided that the first thing was to persuade the princes not to go home, and then to work out the best plan for softening their hostility.

Meanwhile the summer vacation was almost on them. After conferring with Kiyoaki, the Marquis decided to invite the princes to the family villa on the seashore once the vacation had begun. Kiyoaki was to go with them.

31

The Marquis had already given Kiyoaki permission to invite Honda to the villa, and so, on the first day after school ended, the four young men boarded a train at Tokyo station.

Whenever the Marquis himself went to the Kamakura villa, there had to be a huge delegation, led by the major and the chief of police, at the station to greet him with the appropriate honours. Moreover, white sand was hauled up from the beach and scattered along the road from Kamakura station to the villa at Hasé. However, since the Marquis had told the town council that he wanted the four young men to be treated as mere students without any welcome committee whatever, despite the princes' status, they were able to get into rickshaws at the station and enjoy the ride to the villa in privacy.

The narrow winding road was overhung with branches heavy with greenery. As they neared the top of a steep hill, they saw the stone gate of the villa come into view, its name carved in Chinese characters on the right-hand pillar. It was called Chung-nan, from the title of a poem by the Tang poet Wang Wei.

The estate attached to this Japanese Chung-nan covered more than eight acres, taking up an entire wooded ravine that opened onto the beach. Kiyoaki's grandfather had once built a simple reed-thatched cottage there, but after it was destroyed by fire some years previously, his father had immediately seized the opportunity to put up a substantial summer home with twelve guest rooms, of combined Japanese and Western design. The garden, however, which spread out from the terrace on the south side of the house, had been landscaped entirely in the Western style. From this same terrace, one could see the island of Oshima, its volcano glowing at night like a distant bonfire. A walk of no more than five or six minutes through the garden brought one to the Yuigahama beach. In fact the Marquis, with the aid of binoculars, could sit on the terrace and watch the Marquise frolicking in the surf, an incidental diversion that amused him greatly. There was a narrow field of vegetables between the garden and the beach, however, and in order to suppress this element of discord, a line of pines had been planted along the southern edge of the garden. Once these trees were fully grown, they would destroy the uninterrupted view from the garden to the sea, and the Marquis would no longer be able to amuse himself with his binoculars.

On clear summer days, the beauty of the villa's setting was at its peak. The ravine spread out like a fan with the house at its apex, its two ridges bounding the garden on either side: the right-hand one ended in a promontory called Cape Inamuragazaki, and the left-hand one pointed to the island of Iijima.

The sweeping view was unobstructed and made one feel that all it encompassed – sky, land, and the sea embraced by the capes – was part of the Matsugae domain. No images obtruded on its sovereignty save those of the fantastically billowing clouds, the occasional bird, and the ships that passed by far out in the offing. In summer, when the cloud formations were at their peak, the whole thing seemed to be transformed into a huge theatre, with the villa for the spectators and the smooth expanse of the bay becoming the vast stage on which the clouds performed their extravagant ballets.

The outside terrace was floored in heavy teak, laid out in checkers. The architect had been against exposing a wooden floor to the ravages of the weather, but he yielded when the Marquis reminded him sharply that the decks of ships were made of wood. From the vantage point of this terrace, Kiyoaki had spent whole days last summer carefully observing each subtle nuance of the shifting clouds. The sunlight became awesome as it shone on the cumulus clouds, towering up over the offing like huge masses of whipped cream, and penetrated their deep, curving hollows. While the areas that lay in shadow resisted the probing sun, its bright rays threw the rugged force of their sculptured outlines into relief. In his imagination, the parts cut off from direct light were totally different in character from those that were dazzlingly exposed. They slumbered on uneventfully, while in contrast their brilliant counterparts fiercely enacted a swiftly unfolding drama of tragic proportions. But there was no place for the human element, and so both slumber and tragedy came to the same thing, an idle game at best.

If he gazed fixedly at the clouds, he noticed no alteration, but if he looked away for a moment, he found that they had changed. Without his realizing it, their heroic mane became ruffled like hair dishevelled in sleep. And as long as he kept his eyes on it, this new disorder persisted in just the same slow-moving way.

What had disintegrated? One moment their brilliant white shapes dominated the sky, and the next, they dissolved into something trivial, an enervated banality. Yet their dissolution was a kind of liberation. For as he watched, their scattered remnants gradually reformed and as they did so, they cast strange shadows over the garden as if an army were marshalling its forces in the sky above. Its might first overshadowed the beach and the vegetable field, and then, moving up toward the house, it overran the southern border of the garden. The vivid colours of the leaves and flowers that covered the garden slope, laid out in imitation of Shugakuin Palace, glowed like a mosaic in the dazzling sunlight – maples, sakakis, tea shrubs, dwarf cedars, daphnes, azaleas, camellias, pines, box trees, Chinese black pines, and all the others – and then suddenly it was all in shadow; even the cicada's song was hushed, as though in mourning.

The sunsets were especially beautiful. He imagined that as each one approached, every cloud knew in advance what colour it would take on – scarlet, purple, orange, light green, or something else – and then, under the strain of the moment, that it paled just before turning to its new shade.

'What a beautiful garden! I had no idea that summer in Japan could be so glorious,' Chao P. said, bright-eyed.

As the two brown-skinned princes stood on the terrace flooded with sunlight, Kiyoaki could not imagine anyone seeming more at home there. Today, their bleak mood was clearly gone.

Although he and Honda both thought the sunshine excessive for their taste, to the princes it was no more than pleasantly warm and exactly as they liked it. They stood on the terrace soaking it up as though they could not get enough of its heat.

'After you have washed and rested a little,' Kiyoaki said to them, 'I'll show you around the garden.'

'Why bother to rest? Aren't we all four young and energetic?' Kridsada replied.

More than anything else, Kiyoaki thought, more than Princess Chan, the emerald ring, their friends, their school, perhaps what the princes had needed had been sunshine. It seemed that summer had the power to heal all frustrations, soothe every grief, restore their lost happiness.

As he was ruminating in this way about the torrid heat of Siam which he had never experienced, he noticed in himself too a certain intoxication with the summer that had burst on them so suddenly. He heard the cicadas singing in the garden. The coolness of reason had evaporated like cool sweat from his brow.

The four of them stepped down from the terrace and gathered around an old sundial that stood in the middle of the wide lawn around it.

The legend '1716 Passing Shades' was carved in English on its face. Its upright bronze needle was a fantastic arabesque of a bird with its outstretched neck pointing directly at the Roman numeral twelve, just between the markers that designated northwest and northeast. The shadow it cast was drawing close to three o'clock.

As Honda rubbed his finger against the letter S in the inscription, he thought of asking the princes in which direction was Siam, but he decided not to take the needless risk of arousing their homesickness again. At the same time, without meaning to, he shifted his position slightly and blocked out the sun so that his own shadow overwhelmed the one that was about to mark three o'clock.

'That's it. That's the secret,' said Chao P. when he saw what Honda had done. 'If you did that all day, time would have to stop. When I get back home, I'm going to have a sundial set up in the garden. And then on days when I'm very, very happy, I'll have a servant stand next to it from morning to night and cover it with his shadow. I'll stop time passing.'

'But he'll die of sunstroke,' said Honda, stepping aside to let the fierce sunlight restore the hour to the dial.

'No, no,' replied Kridsada, 'our servants can stand all day in the sun, and it doesn't trouble them in the least. And the sun at home is probably at least three times as strong as this.'

The princes' skin, so richly brown and warm in the sunlight, captured Kiyoaki's imagination. He felt that such skin must surely seal within itself a cool darkness that constantly refreshed these young men, like a luxuriant shade tree.

He had only to make a casual reference to the enjoyment to be had from the walking trails in the mountains behind the villa; and immediately nothing would do but for all four of them to set out at once to explore, before Honda could wipe away the sweat brought on by the heat of the garden. Honda, moreover, was amazed at the sight of the once-indolent Kiyoaki taking the lead in this enterprise with such energy.

Despite his misgivings, however, when they had made their way up as far as the ridge, they were met by a delightfully cool sea breeze blowing through the shady pine forest, which made them forget the sweat of the climb as they enjoyed a panoramic view of the Yuigahama beach.

Kiyoaki led them along the narrow trail that followed the line of the ridge, and as they tramped energetically over last year's fallen leaves and crashed through the ferns and bamboo grass that nearly choked the path, they felt all the energy of youth. Then all at once, Kiyoaki stopped and pointed to the northwest.

'Look over there,' he called to them. 'This is the only place from which you can see it.'

A collection of shabby, nondescript houses stood in a valley that stretched out below, but towering above and beyond them, the four young men caught sight of the figure of the Great Buddha of Kamakura.

Everything about the image of this Buddha, from his rounded shoulders to the very folds of his robe, was on a grand scale. The face was in profile, and the chest partially visible as it protruded somewhat beyond the graceful lines of the sleeve that flowed smoothly down from the shoulder. The bright sunlight beat upon the glinting bronze of the rounded shoulder and struck brilliant lights from the broad bronze chest. It was already approaching sunset, and the rays caught the bronze snails coiled like hair on the Lord Buddha's head, and each stood out in relief. The long earlobe seemed to hang like dried fruit on a tropical tree.

The princes startled Honda and Kiyoaki by falling to their knees as soon as they saw the statue. With no thought for their freshly creased white linen trousers, they knelt unhesitatingly on the wet, mouldering leaves that covered the path and pressed their palms together in reverence toward the distant figure bathed in summer sunlight.

The other two were irreverent enough to exchange a quick glance. Faith such as this was so removed from their experience that they had never even thought of it ever touching their lives. Not that they felt the least inclination to mock the princes' exemplary devotion. But they felt that these two young men, whom they had come to regard as students much like themselves, had suddenly flown away into a world whose ideals and faith were quite alien to them.

32

The walk in the mountains behind the house was followed by a complete tour of the garden. All this exertion taxed their energy, so that the four of them were finally quite happy to rest for a while in the living room of the villa. There they enjoyed the sea breeze from the terrace while they sipped lemonade brought from Yokohama and cooled in the villa's well. They were soon ready to set off again, however. This time they gave in to the impulse for a quick swim before sunset and hurried to their rooms to dress for the occasion according to their individual taste. Kiyoaki and Honda put on the red loincloths used for swimming at Peers, and over them they threw the thin cotton tunics decorated with feather-stitching that completed the uniform. Then they put on straw hats and would have been on their way to the beach if they had not been delayed by the two princes. When these two finally appeared, they were dressed in striped English bathing suits that showed their brown shoulders to advantage.

Kiyoaki and Honda had been friends for a long time, but Kiyoaki had never before invited him to the family villa during the summer, though he came once in the fall to gather chestnuts. This was therefore the first time that he had gone swimming with Kiyoaki since they both were boys together at the school villa at Katasé beach, when their present intimacy had hardly begun.

The four of them plunged impetuously down the garden slope, broke through the border of young pines, and dashed across the narrow vegetable field on to the beach.

Here Honda and Kiyoaki paused to perform the prescribed pre-swimming callisthenics, a formality that made the two princes double up with laughter. Perhaps this was a mild form of retaliation against the two Japanese for not having joined them in kneeling to the distant Great Buddha. In the eyes of the princes, this modern, totally self-centred penance was the funniest thing in the world.

However, the very nature of their laughter showed that they were feeling more at ease than ever before; not for a long time had they looked so cheerful. After they had enjoyed themselves in the water to their hearts' content, Kiyoaki felt that he could forget about playing host for a while; the princes paired off to talk in their own language, and he and Honda talked Japanese until all four fell asleep on the beach.

The setting sun was blurred by a thin film of cloud. It had lost much of its earlier heat, but this was a pleasant time to lie in it, especially for someone whose skin was as white as Kiyoaki's. Dressed only in his red loincloth, he threw his wet body down on the sand and lay face up, his eyes shut.

To his left, Honda sat cross legged in the sand staring out at the waters of the bay. Though the sea was calm, its rolling waves fascinated him. As he watched, the crest of the sea seemed to be level with his eyes. How strange, he thought, that it should come to an abrupt end and give way to the land right in front of him.

He kept pouring dry sand from one palm to the other. When he had spilled a good part of it in the process, he reached down automatically and began again with a fresh handful, his thoughts completely taken up with the sea.

It ended a few feet from where he sat. The sea, broad and vast, with all its mighty force, ended right there before his eyes. Be it the edge of time or space, there is nothing so awe-inspiring as a border. To be here at this place with his three companions, at this marvellous border between land and sea, struck him as being very similar to being alive as one age was ending and another beginning, like being part of a great moment in history. And then too the tide of their own era, in which he and Kiyoaki lived, also had to have an appointed time to ebb, a shore on which to break, a limit beyond which it could not go.

The sea ended right there before his eyes. As he watched the final surge of each wave as it drained into the sand, the final thrust of mighty power that had come down through countless centuries, he was struck by the pathos of it all. At that very point, a grand pan-oceanic enterprise that spanned the world went awry and ended in annihilation.

But still, he thought, this final frustration was a gentle, soothing one. A small, lacy frill, the wave's last farewell, escaped from disintegration at the last moment before merging into the glistening wet sand as the wave itself withdrew, and vanished into the sea.

Starting a good way out in the offing at a point where the whitecaps thinned out, the incoming waves went through four or five stages, each of which was visible at any given moment – a swelling, a cresting, a breaking, the dissolution of its force and an ebbing – a constantly recurring process.

The breaking wave let out an angry roar as it showed its smooth, dark green belly. The roar tailed off to a cry and the cry to a whisper. The charging line of huge white stallions yielded place to a line of smaller ones until the furious horses gradually disappeared altogether, leaving nothing but those last imprints of pounding hooves on the beach.

Two remnants, streaming in from left and right, collided roughly, spread like a fan, and sank into the bright mirror of the sand's surface. At that moment, the reflection in the mirror came to life, catching the next white-crested wave just as it was about to come crashing down, a sharp vertical image that sparkled like a row of icicles.

Beyond the ebb, where other waves kept rolling in one after the other, none of them formed smooth white crests. They charged at full power again and again, aiming for their goal with determination. But when Honda looked out to sea in the distance he could not escape the feeling that the apparent strength of these waves that beat upon the shore was really no more than a diluted, weakened, final dispersion.

The farther out one looked, the darker the colour of the water, until it finally became a deep blue-green. It was as if the innocuous ingredients of the offshore water became more and more condensed by the increasing pressure of the water as it got deeper, its green intensified over and over again to produce an eternal blue-green substance, pure and impenetrable as fine jade, that extended to the horizon.

Though the sea might seem vast and deep, this substance was the very stuff of the ocean. Something that was crystallized into blue beyond the shallow, frivolous overlapping of the waves – that was the sea.

His staring and his thoughts were at length enough to tire both his eyes and his mind, and he turned to look at Kiyoaki, who was assuredly sound asleep by now. The light skin on his handsome graceful body seemed all the whiter in contrast to the red loincloth that was all he had on. Just above the loincloth, on his pale stomach that rose and fell lightly with his breathing, there had lodged some sand, now dry, and some tiny fragments of seashell. Since he had raised his left arm to put it behind his head, his left side, that ordinarily was hidden, lay revealed to Honda, and behind the left nipple, which made him think of a tiny cherry-blossom bud, a cluster of three small black moles caught his eyes. There was something odd about them, he felt. Why should Kiyoaki's flesh be marked like that? Though they had been friends for so long, he had never seen them before, and now they embarrassed him too much for him to keep looking at them, as though Kiyoaki had abruptly confessed to a secret better left untold. But when he closed his eyes, he saw the three black moles come into focus against his eyelids, as clear as the shapes of three distant birds flying across the evening sky, so brilliantly lit up by the setting sun. In his imagination he saw them draw closer, turn into birds with flapping wings, and then pass overhead.

When he opened his eyes again, a light sound was coming from Kiyoaki's well-formed nose, and his teeth glistened wet and pure white through his slightly parted lips. Despite himself, Honda's eyes fell on the moles on Kiyoaki's side again. This time he thought that they looked like some grains of sand that had embedded themselves in his white skin.

The dry area of the beach ended right at their feet, and here and there the waves had splashed up beyond their usual limit and left contracted patterns of wet sand behind them, a sort of bas-relief that preserved the trace of the wave. Stones, shells, and withered leaves were embedded here too, for all the world like ancient fossils, and the smallest pebble among them was backed by its own rivulet of wet sand to prove how it had fought the receding wave.

And there were more than stones, shells, and withered leaves. Tangles of brown algae, fragments of wood, pieces of straw, and even orange peelings had been cast up and lay fixed in the sand. He thought it possible that some fine wet grains might also have worked their way up into the white skin that stretched taut over Kiyoaki's side.

Since he found this idea very disturbing, he tried to think of some way to brush the grains away without waking Kiyoaki. But as he continued the watch, he realized that the black marks were moving in such a free and natural way with the rise and fall of his chest that they could not be foreign matter. They were part of him and so could be nothing other than the black moles he had first taken them to be.

He felt that they were a kind of betrayal of Kiyoaki's physical elegance.

Perhaps Kiyoaki sensed the intensity of his gaze, because he suddenly opened his eyes, catching Honda's stare directly. And then he raised his head and began to speak abruptly, as if to prevent his flustered friend from escaping him.

'Would you do something for me?'

'Yes.'

'I didn't really come here to play nursemaid to the princes. That's a good excuse, but actually I want to give everyone the impression that I'm not in Tokyo. Do you see what I mean?'

'I had guessed that you were thinking something of the sort.'

'What I want to do is to leave you and the princes here sometimes and go back there without anyone knowing. I can't go for as much as three days without her. So it will be up to you to smooth things over with the princes while I'm gone and also to have a good story ready just on the off chance that someone telephones from Tokyo. Tonight I'm going to go third-class on the last train and I'll be back on the first one tomorrow morning. So will you do it for me?'

'I'll do it,' said Honda emphatically.

Delighted at his friend's firm agreement, Kiyoaki reached up to shake his hand before he spoke again.

'I suppose your father will be attending the state funeral for Prince Arisugawa.'

'Yes, I think so.'

'It was good of the Prince to die when he did. As I heard just yesterday, the Toinnomiyas have no choice but to postpone the betrothal ceremony for a while.'

This remark reminded Honda that Kiyoaki's love for Satoko was inextricably bound up with the interests of the nation as a whole, and the danger of it sent a shiver through him.

At this point their conversation was interrupted by the two princes who came running over in such enthusiastic haste that they almost fell over each other. Kridsada spoke first, struggling both to regain his breath and to express himself in his scanty Japanese.

'Do you know what Chao P. and I were talking about just now?' he asked. 'We were discussing the transmigration of souls.'

33

When they heard this, the two young Japanese spontaneously glanced at each other, an instinctive reaction whose significance was lost on Kridsada, who was an impetuous sort, not given to gauging his listeners' expressions. Chao P., on the other hand, had learned a great deal from six months of dealing with the tensions brought on by living in a foreign environment. And now, although his skin was too dark to betray anything as obvious as a blush, he was clearly hesitant about continuing such a conversation. Nevertheless, he did so, using his fluent English, perhaps because he wished to appear sophisticated.

'You see, when Kri and I were children, we used to hear all sorts of stories from the *Jataka Sutra*. Our nurses would tell us how even the Lord Buddha underwent many rebirths while he was still a bodhisattva – as a golden swan, a quail, a monkey, a great stag, and so on. So we were speculating just now as to what we might have been in our previous existences. However, I'm afraid that we didn't agree at all. He maintained that he had been a deer and I a monkey. And I insisted that it was just the other way around: he was the monkey and I the deer. But what do you say? We'll leave it to you.'

Whichever way they answered, they ran the risk of offending somebody, so they just smiled, hoping that would serve as a reply. Then Kiyoaki, wanting to turn the conversation to other matters, said that he knew nothing about the *Jataka Sutra* and he wondered if the princes would be kind enough to tell him and Honda one of the stories from it.

'We'd be glad to,' said Chao P. 'There's the one about the golden swan, for example. It took place when the Lord Gautama was a bodhisattva, during his second reincarnation. As you know, a bodhisattva is someone who voluntarily travels the road of mortification and suffering before entering into the full enlightenment of buddhahood. And in his previous existence the Lord Gautama himself was a bodhisattva. The austerities they practise are the works of *paramita*, one's good deeds to others, by means of which one crosses from this sphere to the sphere of total enlightenment. As a bodhisattva, Buddha is said to have lavished abundant grace on mankind. He was reincarnated in many guises and there are all sorts of stories about the good works he performed.

'For example, in very ancient times, he was born to a Brahmin family. He married a woman of another Brahmin family and after having three daughters by her, he died, forcing his bereaved wife and daughters to make their home with strangers.

'But after his death as a Brahmin, the bodhisattva took on another life in the womb of a golden swan. And he carried within him the knowledge that would in due course make him fully aware of his previous existence. And so the bodhisattva grew into an adult swan, covered in gold feathers and unrivalled in beauty. When he glided over the water, he glowed like the rising full moon. And when he flew through the forest, the very leaves that he brushed looked like a golden basket. And when he rested on a branch, it seemed as though the tree had borne some fabulous golden fruit.

'The swan came to realize that he had been a man in his previous existence and also that his wife and children were compelled to live with strangers, eking out their existence by doing whatever work they could find.

' "Any one of my feathers," he said to himself one day, "could be hammered out into a sheet of gold and sold. And so, from time to time, I'll give a feather to my poor companions whom I've left behind to lead such hard lives in the world of men."

'And so the swan appeared at the window of the house where his wife and daughters of times gone by were living. And when he saw how wretched their condition was, he was overcome with pity.

'Meanwhile, his wife and daughters were amazed at the sight of the glittering figure of the swan on their window ledge.

'"What a beautiful bird!" they cried. "Where have you come from?"

'"I was once your husband and father. After I died, I came to life again in the womb of a golden swan. And now I have come to change your poor lives into ones of happiness and plenty."

'So saying, the swan dropped one of its feathers and flew off. Afterwards he came back at regular intervals and left a feather in the same way, and soon life had greatly improved for the mother and her three daughters.

'One day, however, the mother spoke to the girls.

'"We can't trust that swan," she said to them. "Even if he's really your father, who knows if he might stop coming here one day? So next time he comes, let's pluck every one of his feathers."

'"Mother, how cruel!" said the girls, very much opposed to this.

'Nevertheless, the next time the swan appeared at the window, the greedy woman pounced on him, took him in both hands, and plucked out every single one of his feathers. But strangely enough, each gold feather turned as white as a heron feather as she pulled it out. Still undaunted, his former wife then took the helpless swan and thrust him into a large empty container and fed him while she waited doggedly for his golden feathers to grow again. But when the feathers did appear, they were ordinary white ones. And once they had grown, he flew off and his shape grew smaller and smaller in the sky until it became a white dot lost in the clouds, never to be seen again.

'And that was one of the stories that our nurses used to tell us from the *Jataka Sutra*.'

Honda and Kiyoaki were surprised to find that many of the fairy tales that had been told to them were very similar to the prince's story. The conversation then turned into a discussion of reincarnation itself and whether or not it was credible as a doctrine.

Since Kiyoaki and Honda had never talked about anything like this before, they were naturally somewhat perplexed. Kiyoaki glanced at Honda with a questioning look in his eyes. Usually headstrong, he always began to look forlorn whenever abstract discussions took place. His look now urged Honda to do something, as if he were prodding him lightly with silver spurs.

'If there is such a thing as reincarnation,' Honda began, betraying a certain eagerness, 'I'd be very much in favour of it if it were the kind in your story, with the man himself being aware of his previous existence. But if it's a case of a man's personality coming to an end and his self-awareness being lost so that there's absolutely no trace of them in his next life, and if a completely new personality and a totally different self-awareness come into being, well, in that case I think that various reincarnations extending over a period of time are no more significantly linked to one another than the lives of all the individuals who happen to be alive at the same given moment. In other words, I feel that in such a case the concept of reincarnation would be practically meaningless. Something has to be passed on in transmigration, but I don't see how we can take any number of separate and distinct existences, each with its own self-awareness, and bracket them together as one, claiming that a single consciousness unites them. Right now, each one of us has no memory at all of even a single previous existence. And so it's obvious that it would be pointless to try to produce any proof of transmigration. There's only one way that it could be proved: if we had a self-awareness so independent that it could stand aside from both this life and previous lives and view them objectively. But as it is, each man's consciousness is limited to the past, the present, or the future of that single life. In the midst of the turmoil of history, each one of us builds his own little shelter of self-awareness and we can never leave it. Buddhism seems to hold out a middle way, but I have my doubts: is this middle way an organic concept which a human being is capable of grasping?

'But to go back just a bit . . . Granted that all human concepts are mere illusion, in order to distinguish the various illusions arising from other reincarnations from the illusion of the present reincarnation of that same life, you must nevertheless be able to observe them all from a thoroughly independent viewpoint. It's only when one stands aside in this way that the reality of reincarnation would be apparent. But when one is in the midst of a reincarnated existence oneself, the whole must remain an eternal riddle. Moreover, since this independent standpoint is probably what is called full enlightenment, only the man who has transcended reincarnation can grasp its reality. And wouldn't it then be a case of finally understanding it at a time when it was no longer relevant?

'There is an abundance of death in our lives. We never lack reminders – funerals, cemeteries, withered commemorative bouquets, memories of the dead, deaths of friends, and then the anticipation of our own death. Who knows? Perhaps in their own way the dead make a great deal of life. Perhaps they're always looking in our direction from their own land – at our towns, our schools, the smokestacks of our factories, at each of us who has passed one by one back from death into the land of the living.

'What I want to say is that perhaps reincarnation is nothing more than a concept that reverses the way that we, the living, ordinarily view death, a concept that expresses life as seen from the viewpoint of the dead. Do you see?'

'But how is it,' replied Chao P. quietly, 'that certain thoughts and ideals are transmitted to the world after a man's death?'

'That's a different problem from reincarnation,' Honda said emphatically, with a trace of the impatience to which intelligent young men are susceptible showing in his voice.

'Why is it different?' asked Chao P. in the same gentle tone. 'It seems that you are willing to admit that the same sense of self-awareness might inhabit various bodies successively over a period of time. Why then do you object so strongly to differing senses of self-awareness inhabiting the same body over a similar period of time?'

'The same body for a cat and a human being? According to what you said before, it was a matter of becoming a man, a swan, a quail, a deer, and so on.'

'Yes, according to the concept of reincarnation, the same body. Even though the flesh itself might differ. As long as the same illusion persists, there is no difficulty in calling it the same body. However, rather than do that, perhaps it would be better to call it the same vital current.

'I lost that emerald ring that was so rich in memories for me. It wasn't a living thing, of course, and so it won't be reborn. But still, the loss of something is significant, and I think that loss is the necessary source of a new manifestation. Some night I might see my emerald ring appear as a green star somewhere in the sky.'

The prince abruptly abandoned the problem, apparently overcome with sadness.

'Chao P., maybe the ring was actually a living thing that underwent a secret transformation,' Kridsada responded with earnest naïveté, 'and then it ran off somewhere on legs of its own.'

'Then, round about now it might be reborn as someone as beautiful as Princess Chan,' Chao P. said, now completely absorbed in thinking about his loved one. 'People keep telling me in their letters that she's well, but why don't I hear anything at all from her herself? Perhaps they're all trying to protect me from something.'

Honda, meantime, had ignored the prince's last words, as he was lost in thought about the strange paradox that Chao P. had brought up a few minutes earlier. One could certainly think of a man not in terms of a body but as a single vital current. And this would allow one to grasp the concept of existence as dynamic and on-going, rather than as static. Just as he had said, there was no difference between a single consciousness possessing various vital currents in succession, and a single vital current animating various consciousnesses in succession. For life and self-awareness would fuse into a whole. And if one were then to extrapolate this theory of the unity of life and self-awareness, the whole sea of life with its infinity of currents – the whole vast process of transmigration called *Samsara* in Sanskrit – would be possessed by a single consciousness.

While Honda organized his ideas, the beach had gradually been growing darker, and Kiyoaki became absorbed in building a sand temple with Kridsada. The sand did not lend itself to moulding the tall pointed towers and the upswept roof-corner tiling that distinguished Siamese temples. Nevertheless Kridsada skilfully added wet sand and built up the slender peaks, and carefully moulded up the corners of the roof as if he were drawing a woman's dark, slender fingers from her sleeve. They curved out into the air for an instant, and then as soon as they dried out, the black sand-fingers twisted convulsively, crumbled, and fell down.

Honda and Chao P. stopped talking to watch the others playing with the sand in childlike glee. Their sand temple needed lanterns. All the care they had lavished on the fine detail of the facade and the tall windows now went for nothing, for darkness had already reduced the temple to a small, dim outline silhouetted against the white foam of the breakers,which seemed to reflect what lingering light there was, much as the last flickers of life show in the eyes of a dying man.

Unnoticed, the sky over their heads had become filled with stars, dominated by the brilliance of the Milky Way. Honda did not know much about them, but even he could make out the Weaver Maid and her lover the Herd Boy, separated by the broad stream of the Milky Way, and also the Northern Cross of the Swan constellation, which stretched its huge wings in flight as it acted as go-between for the two lovers.

The roar of the waves seemed to have grown much louder than it had been during the day. The beach and the water had each been part of their own sphere in daylight, but now they seemed to have merged under cover of darkness. The inconceivable array of stars above overwhelmed the four young men. To be surrounded by such majestic massive power was like being shut up within a vast koto.

Indeed, it was precisely that. They themselves were like four grains of sand that had somehow found their way into its base, an enormous world of darkness, outside which all was light. Above them were stretched thirteen strings from one end to the other. And fingers of a whiteness that was beyond words were touching these strings, making the koto come alive with the grand and solemn music of the spheres, its immense vibrations shaking the four grains of sand within.

A breeze came in off the night sea. The salty fragrance of the tide and the smell of seaweed thrown up on the beach made their bodies tingle with emotion, bare to the cool night air. The sea breeze, heavy with the smell of salt, coiled against their naked flesh, but made them burn rather than shiver.

'Well, it's time we went back,' said Kiyoaki abruptly.

It was meant, of course, as a reminder that it was time for them to get ready for dinner. Honda, however, knew that Kiyoaki's mind was fixed on the departure of the last train for Tokyo.

34

Kiyoaki made secret trips to Tokyo at least once every three days, and on his return, he would give Honda all the details of what had gone on. The Toinnomiyas had indeed postponed the betrothal ceremony, but that by no means meant that there was any significant obstacle to Satoko's marriage to the young prince. She was, in fact, often invited to their home, and the Prince's father, His Imperial Highness himself, had started treating her with cordial affection.

Kiyoaki was not at all satisfied with the way things stood. Now he was thinking of having Satoko down to Kamakura to spend the night at the villa, and he asked Honda if he had any idea about how to carry out such a dangerous plan. But on even the most cursory reflection, one grave difficulty after another was brought to light.

One hot sultry night, as Kiyoaki was settling into an uneasy sleep, he began to dream. It was quite unlike his previous experiences. If one flounders in the shallows of sleep, wading where the water is tepid and full of all sorts of flotsam that has come in from deeper water to pile up with the land debris in a tangled heap, one is liable to slash one's feet.

Kiyoaki was standing in the middle of a road that led through open fields. For some reason he was wearing a white cotton kimono and matching *hakama*, a costume he had never worn, and he was armed with a hunting rifle. The land around him was rolling country, but it was not deserted. He could see a cluster of farmhouses up ahead, and a cyclist passed him on the road. A strange, sombre light permeated the entire scene. It was no brighter than the final traces of daylight, and was so diffuse that it could more easily have sprung from the ground rather than the sky, for the grass in the rolling fields gave off a green glow from its very roots and bathed the bicycle in a hazy silver gleam as it vanished into the distance. He looked down and saw that even the thick thongs of his clogs and the veins of his bare feet stood out with brilliant, uncanny clarity.

At that moment, the light filmed over and a huge flight of birds appeared in the sky. When they reached a point above his head, filling the air with their squawking cries, he aimed his rifle upward and pulled the trigger. He did not fire in cold blood. It was rather that he was seized by an unfathomable anger and grief, and he fired, aiming not so much at the birds as at the great blue eye of the sky itself.

The whole flock plummeted earthward in a single mass, a tornado of screams and blood that linked heaven and earth. Countless shrieking birds, their blood spurting out, tumbled down in an unending stream, gathered into one thick column that formed the cone of the whirlwind. The cascade of blood and fury never slackened.

As he watched, the whirlwind suddenly solidified before his eyes and became a giant tree that stretched to the heavens. Its trunk was a forbidding rust colour, devoid of leaves or branches. As soon as this giant tree took shape and the screaming died away, the same sombre glow that had lit up the fields before the storm spread out over them once more. Down the road appeared a new silver bicycle without a rider and made its way unsteadily toward him.

He was proud to have been the one to sweep away the obstacle that had blocked the light of the sun.

But then in the distance he saw a group coming his way along the road. They were all dressed in white just as he was. They checked their solemn, measured advance a few yards away. He saw that each of them carried a shining sakaki branch in his hand.

They pointed their branches toward him and began to wave them in the rite of purification, the rustle of leaves echoing clearly in his ears. As they did so, he was startled to recognize the face of his former retainer Iinuma in their midst. Iinuma himself spoke to him.

'You are heedless and intractable. You have proved it beyond all question.'

He looked down at his chest when Iinuma spoke. A necklace of crescent-shaped stones, dark maroon and purple, now hung around his neck. The stones were cold and as they touched his skin they sent a chill through his body. His chest felt like a flat, heavy rock.

Then the white-clad group pointed to the tree, and when he looked at it, he saw that the massive trunk of dead birds was now covered with branches, all of which were laden with glossy green leaves. The whole tree was a vivid green, down to its lowest branches.

Then he woke up.

Since the dream had been so extraordinary, he reached out to open his dream journal, which he had neglected for some time now. He began to write, trying to record the events as accurately and as objectively as he could. Even now that he was awake, however, he was torn by the fierceness and antagonism of the dream. He felt as if he had just returned from battle.

Kiyoaki's problem was to bring Satoko from Tokyo in the dead of night and get her home again by dawn. A carriage was no good. Nor was the train. A rickshaw would be quite out of the question. Somehow he had to get the use of a car.

Obviously it could not be one belonging to anyone who knew the Matsugaes. And, even more important, anyone in the Ayakuras' circle had to be ruled out. And the car would have to be driven by someone completely ignorant of the situation and the people involved.

The villa area was large enough, but precautions still had to be taken to avoid a chance meeting between Satoko and the princes. Kiyoaki and Honda had no idea whether or not the princes were aware of the circumstances of her engagement, but even if they were not, a meeting could only lead to disaster.

Without the least experience in such things, Honda had to find a way through these difficulties somehow. For he had promised Kiyoaki to see to it that Satoko would be able to come down from Tokyo and return in safety.

As he began to size up the problem, he thought of a friend of his named Itsui, the eldest son of a wealthy commercial family. Since Itsui was the only one in his class at Peers who had his own car to use as he liked, Honda had no choice but to go up to Tokyo to visit him in Kojimachi and ask if he would lend him the Ford and a driver for a night.

High-living Itsui, whose career at Peers continually veered toward the shoals of academic shipwreck, was astounded. That the class genius, who was notorious for his sobriety and application moreover, should come to him with such a request! When he had recovered a little, he decided to make the most of the opportunity, and so with no more arrogance than befitted the occasion, he said that if Honda would tell him honestly why he wanted the car, he might be willing to lend it to him.

With that, Honda began to stutter through the confession he had concocted for the loutish Itsui's benefit, and as he did so, was conscious of an unaccustomed and pleasurable sensation. This was provoked by the rapt expression of total belief on Itsui's face; he obviously took Honda's stumbling manner not as an indication of an outright lie, but as testimony to his classmate's brooding sense of shame.

A man may be hard to persuade by rational argument while he is easily swayed by a display of passion, even if it is feigned. Honda was amused at the spectacle, but his amusement was tinged with disgust. He wondered if Kiyoaki had used him in much the same way as he was using Itsui.

'Well, you are turning out to be altogether different from what I imagined. I never thought I'd see this side of you. But you're still being secretive. Won't you at least tell me her name?'

'Fusako,' said Honda, spontaneously coming up with the name of the second cousin he hadn't seen in months.

'I see. So Matsugae is going to provide a place to spend the night and I'm going to provide the car. And in return, when the exams come round, you'll remember old Itsui, won't you?' he said, bowing his head in mock supplication that was still meant in earnest.

The light of friendship shone in his eyes. Despite Honda's awesome brain, Itsui now felt on a par with him in many respects. He was vindicated in his unimaginative view of human nature.

'After all, people are all alike,' he said, summing it up, his voice expressing the fact that he felt at one with the world, which was exactly the state of mind Honda had been intent on inducing from the beginning.

And so, thanks to Kiyoaki, Honda could soon expect to enjoy a romantic reputation that any boy of nineteen would envy. All in all, this transaction would benefit each of them: Kiyoaki, Honda, and also Itsui.

Itsui's car was a 1912 Ford, the newest model. It was one of the first equipped with a self-starter, the recent invention that had eliminated the nuisance of the chauffeur having to get out each time it happened to stall. It was the ordinary Model T, with a two-speed transmission, painted black with a crimson line around the doors. The driver's seat was open and the rear enclosed, an arrangement that seemed to preserve something of the air of a carriage. A speaking tube in the back seat led to a trumpet-shaped device next to the driver's ear. A rack fastened onto the roof, besides holding a spare tyre, could also carry baggage. The car seemed altogether capable of making a long journey.

Mori, the driver, had been the Itsuis' coachman and had learned his new trade from a master driver. He had pointedly arranged for the man to accompany him to the police station to get his licence. Every time Mori ran into a difficult question on the written examination, he went into the lobby to consult with his master before returning to the examination room to continue.

Honda went to Itsui's house very late at night to borrow the car. In order to conceal Satoko's background from Mori as much as he could, he had him park the car near a boarding house for military officers where they waited until Satoko and Tadeshina appeared according to plan, arriving inconspicuously in a rickshaw. Kiyoaki had hoped that Tadeshina would not make the trip to Kamakura, but she could not possibly come even if she wanted to, for it was up to her to stay behind and pretend that Satoko spent the night fast asleep in her room, a task of crucial importance. Her face betrayed her worry. She cautioned Satoko at great length before finally surrendering her to Honda's care.

'I'll call you Fusako in front of the chauffeur,' he whispered in her ear.

Mori started the Ford with a blast that shattered the midnight silence of the residential neighbourhood.

Satoko's calm and resolution surprised Honda. She was in Western clothes, and the white dress she had chosen seemed to enhance her air of quiet determination.

Riding through the night like this in the company of the woman claimed by a friend was an odd experience for Honda. There he sat as the car bounced over the rough road, friendship personified, while the scent of Satoko's perfume wafted around him in the summer night.

She belonged to another man. Her very femininity, moreover, seemed to be mocking him. The unprecedented trust that Kiyoaki had shown in him made him more sharply aware than ever before of the cold, subtle poison that permeated their relationship. His friend's contempt and trust were as closely linked as a fine leather glove and the hand inside it. But Kiyoaki had an aura about him that made Honda forgive him.

The only way he could cope with contempt of this sort was to hold on to a belief in his own nobility, and this he did with moderation rather than with the blind traditionalism of so many young men. This meant that he would never come to think of himself as ugly, as Iinuma did. For if this ever happened, there would be nothing left but for him to become Kiyoaki's slave.

Although the breeze blowing in through the window naturally ruffled her hair, Satoko maintained her poise throughout the trip. Kiyoaki's name had become a sort of taboo word between them, quite of its own accord. And the name 'Fusako' served as a mild, fictional term of endearment.

The return trip was quite different. 'Oh, there's something I forgot to tell Kiyo,' she said soon after they had left the villa. But if they turned back, there would be no hope of her getting home before the early summer dawn.

'Could I tell him for you?' Honda asked.

'Well...' Satoko hesitated. Then she seemed to make up her mind, and gave him the message: 'Please tell him this: Tadeshina talked with Yamada, the Matsugaes' steward, some time ago, and she's found out that Kiyo was telling a lie. She discovered that he actually tore up the letter he was pretending still to have a long time ago in Yamada's presence. But ... tell him not to worry about it. Tadeshina has resigned herself to everything. She said she would keep her eyes shut. Would you please pass that on to Kiyo?'

Honda memorized it as she spoke, and didn't ask any questions about its cryptic meaning. From then on, impressed perhaps by his good manners, she became very talkative.

'You've done all this for his sake, haven't you, Mr Honda? Kiyo should think himself the luckiest man in the world to have a friend like you. You see, we women have no real friends at all.'

Satoko's eyes still burned with passion, but her coiffure was in perfect order, with not a hair out of place. When he did not reply, she bent her head, and after a time, spoke in a subdued voice.

'But Mr Honda ... I know what you must think of me... What else am I but a slut?'

'Don't talk like that,' he replied with considerable force. He certainly had not been thinking of her with such contempt, but even so, her words had accidentally hit a nerve with uncanny accuracy.

He had gone without a night's sleep to be loyal and fulfil the duty with which he had been entrusted, of bringing Satoko down from Tokyo, turning her over to Kiyoaki, and now taking charge of her again to get her back. But his real source of pride was in keeping himself emotionally uninvolved. Nothing good would come of that sort of thing. It was a gravely dangerous situation, for which he was sufficiently responsible already.

When he had stood watching Kiyoaki take Satoko by the hand and run down through the shadows of the moonlit garden to the beach, he had felt that he too was sinning by helping them. But if it was sin, it was also indescribably beautiful; a recurrent image of loveliness running away from him and disappearing.

'You're right,' said Satoko. 'I shouldn't talk like that at all. I can't think of what I've done as being something nasty. Why is that? Kiyo and I have committed a terrible sin, but I still don't feel defiled in any way. In fact I feel as if I'd been purified. You know, when I saw those pines by the beach tonight, I knew that I'd never see them again no matter how long I lived. And when I heard the sound of the breeze that blew through them, I knew that I'd never hear that again as long as I lived. But every moment I was there felt so pure that now I have no regrets about anything at all.'

As she spoke, she tried to convey something to Honda, some essence of everything that happened between her and her lover during their meetings, each of which had felt like the final one – she longed to throw discretion aside and try to make Honda understand by telling him how on this last night, in the midst of such a tranquil, natural setting, she and Kiyoaki had soared to dazzling heights that were almost terrifying. But it was the kind of experience – like death, like the glow of a jewel, like the beauty of a sunset – that is almost impossible to convey to others.

Kiyoaki and Satoko wandered over the beach, trying to avoid the uncomfortably dazzling brightness of the moon. Now, in the middle of the night, there was no trace of human life along the deserted shore, apart from a beached fishing boat, whose tall prow cast a black shadow on the sand. Because of the brilliant moonlight all around, it seemed to offer a reassuring darkness. The moon's rays washed over the boat, making its planks glisten like bleached bones. When Kiyoaki rested his hand against the side for a moment, his skin seemed to become translucent in the moonlight.

They embraced immediately in the shadow of the boat as the sea breeze swirled around them. She hardly ever wore Western clothes, and now hated the glaring white of her dress. Forgetting the whiteness of her skin, she had only one thought: to tear the dress off as quickly as possible and hide herself in the darkness.

No one was likely to see them, but the rays of moonlight, infinitely fragmented over the surface of the sea, were like millions of eyes. She gazed up at the clouds suspended in the sky and the stars that seemed to graze their edges. She could feel Kiyoaki's small, firm nipples touching hers, brushing against them playfully, then finally pressing against them, pushing down into the rich abundance of her breasts. It was a touch far more intimate than a kiss, something like the playful caress of a young animal. An intense sweetness hovered on the edge of her awareness. The unexpected familiarity when the very edges, the extremities of their bodies brushed together made her think of the stars sparkling among the clouds, even though her eyes were closed.

From there it was a direct path to a joy as profound as the sea. But even as she felt herself dissolving gradually into the darkness, she felt afraid that this was nothing more than a shadow that was dependent in turn on the fishing boat beside them. They were not lying in the protection of a solid structure or a rocky ridge, but of something fortuitous, that in a few brief hours might be far out to sea. Had the boat not happened to be beached there at that moment, its heavy shadow would have been no more real than a ghost. She was afraid that this huge old fishing boat might begin to slide noiselessly across the sand even now and plunge into the water and sail away. To follow its shadow, to remain forever within it, she herself would have to become the sea. And at that moment, in a single great surge, she did.

Everything that framed the two of them – the moonlit sky, the sparkling water, the breeze that blew across the sandy beach to rustle the pines at its edge – all these boded destruction. Just beyond the merest flicker of time there boomed a monstrous roar of negation. Its message was carried in the sound of the pines. She felt that she and Kiyoaki were hemmed in, observed, guarded by an unforgiving spirit, just as a single drop of balm that has fallen into a bowl of water has nothing to sustain it but the water itself. This water was black, vast, silent, and the single drop of balm floated in a world of total isolation.

That 'No!' was all-embracing. Was it a creature of the night – or the approaching dawn? To them it seemed incomprehensible. But even though it hovered threateningly over them from moment to moment, it had not yet struck at them directly.

They both sat up. Their heads were just out of the shadow now and the sinking moon shone directly into their faces. She felt that it was somehow the emblem of their transgression, fixed there so bright and full and conspicuous in the sky.

The beach was still deserted. They stood up to fetch their clothes, which they had placed in the bottom of the boat. Each of them stared at the other, at the remnant of darkness that was the black area just below their white bellies so brilliantly lit by the moon. Although it lasted only for a moment, they gazed with intense concentration.

When they had dressed, Kiyoaki sat dangling his legs over the edge of the boat.

'You know,' he said, 'if we had everyone's blessing, we would probably never dare to do what we've done.'

'You are awful, Kiyo. So that's what you really want!' she replied in mock affront. Their banter was affectionate enough, but it had an indefinably gritty taste. They sensed that the irrevocable end of their happiness was not far away. She was still sitting in the sand, hiding in the shadow of the boat. His foot, shining in the moonlight, hung in the air in front of her. She reached out, took it in her hand, and kissed his toes.

'I suppose it's uncalled-for – my telling you all this. But you see, there's no one else I could even think of telling. I know that I'm doing something terrible. But please don't say anything against it, because I do realize that it will come to an end sometime. But until then, I want to live each day as it comes. Because there's nothing else to be done.'

'Then you are quite prepared for whatever may happen?' Honda asked, his voice unable to conceal the deep pity he felt.

'Yes, I'm quite ready.'

'Matsugae is too, I think.'

'That's why it's not at all right for him to involve you so deeply in our problems.'

Honda suddenly felt an unaccountable desire to understand this woman. It was his subtle form of revenge. If she intended to assign him the role of truly understanding friend, rather than one of mere compassionate supporter, then he would have the right to know everything. But it was a formidable challenge to try to understand her – this graceful woman overflowing with love, who was sitting by his side with her heart elsewhere. Nevertheless, his bent for logical inquiry began to gain the upper hand.

The car jounced a great deal, and tended to throw the two of them together, but she protected herself so skilfully that their knees never so much as brushed, a display of agility that reminded him of a pet squirrel making its exercise wheel whir. He was slightly annoyed. If Kiyoaki were beside her, he thought, she would not be so nimble.

'You just said that you were prepared for anything, didn't you?' he asked, not looking at her. 'Well then, I wonder how that acceptance of the consequences squares with the realization that it will have to end some day. When it does end, won't it be too late to make a decision about the consequences? Or alternatively, will your acceptance of the consequences somehow gradually bring about the end, of itself? I know I'm asking you a cruel question.'

'I'm glad you did,' she replied calmly.

Despite himself, he glanced at her earnestly. Her profile was beautifully composed, and showed no sign of distress. While he was looking at her, she suddenly shut her eyes, and the long lashes of her left eye cast a still longer shadow over her cheek in the dim light of the roof lamp. The trees and shrubbery glided past in the pre-dawn darkness like black clouds swirling about the car.

Mori, the driver, kept his reliable back to them, wholly intent on his driving. The thick sliding glass behind him was shut. Unless they went out of their way to put their mouths close to the speaking tube, there was no chance that he would overhear.

'You say that I'm the one who should be able to end it some day. And as you're Kiyo's best friend, you have the right to say it. If I can't end it and stay alive, then dying...'

She might have wanted to startle Honda into interrupting with a command to stop saying such things, but he doggedly kept silence and waited for her to continue.

'...but the moment will come sometime – and that time is not too far off. And when it does – I can promise you right now – I shan't shrink from it. I've known supreme happiness, and I'm not greedy enough to want what I have to go on forever. Every dream ends. Wouldn't it be foolish, knowing that nothing lasts forever, to insist that one has a right to do something that does? I've nothing in common with these "new women". But ... if eternity existed, it would be this moment. And perhaps you, Mr Honda, will come round to seeing it this way some day.'

Honda was at last beginning to understand why Kiyoaki had once been so terribly in awe of Satoko.

'You said that it wasn't right of Matsugae to involve me in your problems. Why not?'

'You're a young man who set himself worthwhile goals. It's wrong to get you entangled with us. Kiyo has no right at all to do it.'

'I wish you wouldn't think of me as such a saint. You're unlikely to find a more grimly moral family than mine. But despite that, I have already done something that makes me an accomplice in sin.'

'Don't say that. It's not true,' she broke in angrily. 'This is our sin, Kiyo's and mine ... and nobody else's.'

Of course she only meant to convey that she wanted to protect him, but her words had a cold, proud glitter that could not tolerate the intrusion of a third party. In her own mind, she had fashioned their sin into a tiny, brilliant, crystal palace in which she and Kiyoaki could live free from the world around them. A crystal palace so tiny that it would balance on the palm of one's hand, so tiny that no one else could fit in. Transformed for a fleetingly brief instant, she and Kiyoaki had been able to enter it and now they were spending their last few moments there, observed with extraordinary clarity in all their minute detail by someone standing just outside.

She suddenly leaned forward with bent head. He reached over to support her and his hand brushed against her hair.

'Excuse me,' she apologized, 'but I think I just felt some sand in my shoe, even though I was so careful. Tadeshina doesn't look after my shoes, and so if I took them off at home with sand left in them that I didn't notice, I'd be afraid of what some startled maid might blurt out.'

He had no idea how to behave while a woman was inspecting her shoes, so he turned away and began to look out of the window with intense concentration.

They had already reached the outskirts of Tokyo. The night sky had turned to a vivid dark blue. The dawn showed the clouds spread low over the roofs of the houses. Though he wanted to get her home as soon as possible, he still felt regret that the morning light would put an end to what was probably the most extraordinary night of his life. Behind him he heard the sound – so faint that he thought he must be imagining it at first – of Satoko pouring the sand from the shoe she had taken off. To Honda, it sounded like the most enchanting hourglass in the world.

35

The Siamese princes were thoroughly enjoying themselves at Chung-nan Villa. One evening shortly before dinner the four young men had rattan chairs brought out and placed on the lawn so that they could enjoy the cool evening breeze before eating. The princes chatted in their native language, Kiyoaki was lost in his own thoughts, and Honda had a book open on his lap.

'Would you like some twist?' asked Kridsada in Japanese, walking over to Honda and Kiyoaki holding out a pack of gold-tipped Westminster cigarettes. The princes had been quick enough in picking up 'twist', the slang word for cigarettes at Peers. The school rules forbade smoking, but the authorities allowed the upperclassmen a certain amount of laxity, provided they did not go so far as to smoke openly. The boiler room in the basement had thus become a haven for smokers and was known as 'the Twist Room'.

Even now, as the four of them puffed on their cigarettes beneath the open sky without fear of being observed, they sensed the lingering, secret pleasure that went with smoking in the Twist Room. The smell of coal dust that filled the boiler room, eyes flashing white in the gloom as their classmates kept careful watch, the deep, luxurious puffs of smoke, the recurring restless glow of the red tips – these and many other impressions now enriched the fine flavour of their English cigarettes.

Kiyoaki turned away from the others, and as he watched the smoke trailing away into the sky, he saw how the cloud formations out over the ocean were beginning to dissolve, their clear outlines now blurred and tinged with a pale gold. At once he thought of Satoko. Her image, her scent, were mingled with so many things. There was no alteration of nature, however slight, that did not bring her to mind. If the breeze suddenly dropped and the warm atmosphere of the summer evening pressed in on him, he felt Satoko brush naked against his own nakedness. Even the gradually deepening shadow cast on the lawn by the dense green foliage of the silk tree held a hint of her.

As for Honda, he could never be quite at ease unless there were books within easy reach. Among those now at hand was a book he had been lent in secret by one of the student houseboys, a book proscribed by the government. Entitled *Nationalism and Authentic Socialism*, it had been written by a young man named Terujiro Kita, who at twenty-three was looked upon as the Japanese Otto Weininger. However, it was rather too colourful in its presentation of an extremist position, and this aroused caution in Honda's calm and reasonable mind. It was not that he had any particular dislike of radical political thought. But never having been really angry himself, he tended to view violent anger in others as some terrible, infectious disease. To encounter it in their books was intellectually stimulating, but this kind of pleasure gave him a guilty conscience.

In order to be prepared for any further discussions on reincarnation with the princes, he had stopped off at his own home that morning after accompanying Satoko back to Tokyo and had borrowed a book from his father's library, *A*

Summary of Buddhist Thought by Tadanobu Saito. Here for the first time he was treated to a fascinating account of the varied origins of the doctrine of Karma, and he was reminded of the Laws of Manu which had so absorbed him at the beginning of the winter. But at that time his examination ambitions had forced him to postpone a more thorough study of Saito's book.

This and several others were spread out on the arms of his rattan chair. After dipping at random into one or another of them, Honda looked up at last from the one that was now open on his lap, his slightly short-sighted eyes narrowed a little. He turned to look at the sharp slope that marked the western border of the garden. Though the sky was still bright, the slope was in deep shadow, and the heavy growth of trees and shrubbery on the ridge stood out blackly against the white glare of the sky. However, the light was breaking through here and there like silver thread skilfully woven into an otherwise dark tapestry. Behind the trees, the western sky was like a sheet of isinglass. The bright summer day had been a gaudy scroll which was tapering off into blankness.

The young men savoured the delicious hint of guilt that added spice to their cigarettes, as a swarm of mosquitoes towered up in one corner of the sunset garden. They felt the golden heaviness that comes from a day of swimming, their skin still warm from the midday sun ... Though Honda sat there in silence, he felt that the day would be counted as one of the happiest of their youth.

The princes seemed to feel similarly content. They were obviously pretending to take no notice of Kiyoaki's amorous pursuits. On the other hand, Kiyoaki and Honda both chose to ignore the princes' lighthearted forays among the fishermen's daughters along the beach, though Kiyoaki was careful to follow them up with suitable sums of compensation to the girls' fathers. And so, under the protective eye of the Great Buddha, whom the princes worshipped every morning on top of the ridge, summer waned in languorous beauty.

Kridsada was the first to notice the servant who came down on to the lawn from the terrace bearing a letter on the gleaming silver tray that he doubtless spent most of his free time polishing, lamenting the while that he had so few occasions to use it at the villa, compared with the house in Shibuya.

Kridsada jumped up to meet him and took the letter. Then, when he saw that it was a personal letter to Chao P. from his mother the Queen Dowager, he walked over to where Chao P. was sitting and presented it to him facetiously with a deferential flourish.

Kiyoaki and Honda had, of course, noticed this piece of byplay, but they restrained their curiosity and sat waiting for the princes to come over to them in a rush of nostalgic happiness. As Chao P. took the thick letter from its envelope, they heard the crinkle of paper, and white stationery flashed like the feathers of an arrow winging through the darkness. Then suddenly they were on their feet staring at Chao P., who had let out an agonized cry and collapsed in a faint.

Kridsada stood looking down at his cousin with astonishment on his face as

Kiyoaki and Honda rushed over to help. Then he bent over to pick up the letter, which had fallen on the grass, and had just started to read when he burst into tears, throwing himself to the ground. The two young Japanese could understand nothing of what Kridsada was sobbing to himself in a rush of Siamese, and since the letter, which Honda now picked up, was in the same language, it furnished no clues either, apart from the glittering golden seal of the royal family of Siam at the top, with its intricate design of pagodas, fabulous beasts, roses, swords, sceptres and other devices grouped around three white elephants.

Chao P. regained consciousness while he was being carried back to his bedroom by servants, but he was obviously still dazed. Kridsada trailed after him, still moaning.

Though they were ignorant of the facts, it was obvious to Kiyoaki and Honda that some terrible news had arrived. Chao P. lay silent, his head on his pillow and his eyes, as cloudy as two pearls, staring up at the ceiling. The expression on his swarthy face grew less and less discernible by the minute as the room grew rapidly darker. After some time, it was Kridsada who was finally able to explain in English.

'Princess Chan is dead. Chao P.'s love, my sister . . . . If I had been told first, I could have watched for a chance to tell him in a way that would spare him such a shock, but I suppose his mother, the Queen Dowager, was more afraid of upsetting me and so wrote to Chao P. If so, she miscalculated. But then she may have had a deeper concern . . . to strengthen his courage by making him confront his sorrow head-on.'

This was more judicious than anything they usually heard from Kridsada. The princes' violent grief, as powerful as a tropical cloudburst, affected Kiyoaki and Honda profoundly. But they sensed that after the thunder, the lightning, and the rain, their grief would be a wet and glistening jungle that would recover all the more quickly and luxuriantly.

Dinner that evening was brought to the princes' room, but they did not touch their food. Some time later, however, Kridsada evidently recalled the duties of politeness to one's host, and called Kiyoaki and Honda back to their room to translate the entire letter into English.

Princess Chan had, in fact, fallen ill in the spring, and though she was too sick to write, she had pleaded with everyone not to tell her brother and cousin. Her lovely white hand grew more and more emaciated until she could no longer move it. It lay there as cold and still as a single moonbeam coming in through a window.

The English doctor in charge tried everything he knew, but he could not prevent the relentless paralysis of her whole body. Finally it became a great strain for her even to speak. But in order perhaps to leave Chao P. with the image of her in full health as she was when they parted, she repeatedly insisted to everyone that nothing should be said about her illness. It reduced them to tears.

The Queen Dowager went to see her very often, and she could never help crying when she saw the young princess. When Her Majesty was informed of Chan's death, she restrained the others and said immediately: 'I myself will tell Pattanadid.'

'What I have to tell you is very sad,' the letter began.

> Please bear it as bravely as you can. Your beloved Chantrapa has died. Later I will tell you just how much her thoughts were of you at the end. As your mother, what I most want to convey to you right away is that you must resign yourself to all this as the will of the Lord Buddha. I pray that you will always be mindful of your princely dignity and accept this tragic news with good bearing. How well I know what your feelings must be on learning of this away in a foreign land, and how I regret that I am not at your side to comfort you as a mother should. But now where Kridsada is concerned, please behave as an elder brother and tell him of his sister's death with the deepest solicitude. I have given you the tragic news like this without warning only because I believe that you have sufficient fortitude not to give way to grief. And then do please take consolation at least that the Princess had thoughts for you alone until she breathed her last. No doubt you regret not having been there when she died, but you must make every effort to appreciate how she felt in wanting you to preserve forever in your heart the image you had of her as a girl in the bloom of youth...

Chao P. lay listening intently until Kridsada had translated the very last word. Then he sat up in bed and turned to Kiyoaki. 'I'm rather embarrassed,' he began. 'I neglected my mother's admonition, and just collapsed. But do please try to understand.

'What I've been struggling with these past few hours is not the riddle of Princess Chan's death. In the period that began with her illness and lasted until her death – no, that lasted in these twenty days since the moment of her death – I have of course been in constant anxiety. But even so, having no idea of the truth, I lived calmly enough in a false world through all that time. That's the riddle.

'I clearly saw the bright sea and the shining beach just as they were. Why wasn't I able to see the subtle change that had occurred deep in the substance of the universe? The world was constantly and imperceptibly changing, just like wine inside a bottle. And I'm like a man who sees no farther than the dark red liquid glowing warmly inside the glass. Why did it never occur to me to taste it, if only once a day, and try to gauge if some small change had taken place. The soft morning breeze, the rustling trees, the flutter of birds' wings and the sound of their calls – all these were constantly in my eyes and ears. But I merely took them all to be an embodiment of the joy of being alive, the beautiful essence of life itself. It never occurred to me that under the surface something was changing day by day. If I had stopped one morning to taste the world and so discovered that it had subtly altered on my tongue ... oh, if only I had done that, then it couldn't have escaped me that this world had suddenly become a world without Princess Chan.'

As he said this, his voice gradually became choked and his words were muffled in tears.

Leaving him in Kridsada's care, they returned to their own room. They found, however, that they were in no mood for sleep.

'The princes will want to go back to Siam as soon as they can. Whatever the others may say, they certainly won't feel like going on studying here,' Honda said as soon as the two of them were alone.

'Yes, I'm sure they'll go home,' Kiyoaki answered gloomily. The princes' grief had evidently had a deep effect on him, and he was sunk in a mood of vague foreboding. 'And after they've gone, you and I won't have any good reason to stay here just by ourselves,' he went on, almost to himself. 'Or perhaps Mother and Father will be coming down, and then it'll be a matter of spending the summer with them. Whatever happens, our happy summer is over.'

Although Honda was well aware that a man in love has no room in his heart for anything but his feelings and loses even his ability to sympathize with the sorrows of others, he could imagine no heart more naturally suited than Kiyoaki's to be such a vessel of pure passion, cold and tough as tempered glass.

A week later, the two princes began their homeward journey on an English ship, and Kiyoaki and Honda went to Yokohama to see them off. Since it was in the middle of the summer vacation, none of the princes' other classmates were on hand. In deference to his close ties with Siam, however, Prince Toin sent his steward to represent him. Kiyoaki greeted the man coolly, exchanging no more than a word or two.

As the huge cargo-passenger liner pulled away from the pier, the trailing streamers parted and were carried away by the wind. The two princes stood on the fantail to one side of the Union Jack snapping in the breeze, and waved their handkerchiefs unceasingly.

Long after the ship was far out into the channel and all the other well-wishers had gone, Kiyoaki stayed on, despite the torrid heat of the afternoon sun that beat down on the pier, until Honda could not help urging him to leave. Kiyoaki was not parting with the two princes from Siam. He felt, rather, that it was his youth, or the most glorious part of it, that was about to vanish below the horizon.

36

When autumn came, classes started once more, and meetings between Kiyoaki and Satoko became more and more restricted. Tadeshina had to take the most extreme precautions to enable them to go walking together in the early evening without being discovered.

They had to be careful to avoid even the lamplighters who still made their rounds in that one part of Toriizaka. With their tight-collared uniforms they carried long poles which they thrust under the protective mantle of each streetlight into the gas jet below. By the time this hurried ceremony was completed daily at dusk, the streets of the neighbourhood were emptied of passers-by. It was therefore a time when Kiyoaki and Satoko could walk through the crooked back lanes in comparative security. The chorus of insects grew louder at this hour, but the lights in the windows were not unduly bright. Many houses had no gates to separate them from the street, and the two of them could even hear the footsteps of a returning husband and then the noise of a door being shut.

'Everything will be over in a month or two. The Toinnomiyas will certainly not be willing to delay the betrothal ceremony longer than that,' Satoko said rather mildly, as if she were talking about someone else. 'Every night when I go to bed, I think: it will end tomorrow, something irrevocable will happen tomorrow. And then, strangely enough, I sleep peacefully. That's just what we're doing now – something that can't be undone.'

'Well, suppose even after the engagement ceremony ...'

'Kiyo, what are you saying? If we increase our sins any more than we have, your gentle spirit will be crushed. Instead of thinking of things like that, I would rather keep counting how many times I will still be able to see you.'

'You've made up your mind, haven't you? In due course, you're going to forget everything, aren't you?'

'Yes. Though I don't yet know just how I'll be able to do it. The path we're taking is not a road, Kiyo, it's a pier, and it ends someplace where the sea begins. It can't be helped.'

That was indeed the first time they had talked about the end. And confronted by it, they felt no more responsibility than a pair of children. They had no plans in mind, nothing to fall back on, no solution, no plan of action – and they felt that all this testified to the purity of their intentions. Still, once they had mentioned the final separation, the idea clung to their minds like rust.

Had they embarked on all this without considering the end? Or had they begun their affair precisely because they had thought about its end? Kiyoaki did not know. He thought that if the two of them were suddenly charred to ashes by a bolt of lightning, well and good. But what was he to do if no dreadful punishment fell from the skies and things remained as they were? It made him uneasy. 'If that were the case,' he wondered, 'would I be able to go on loving Satoko just as passionately as I do now?'

It was the first time that he had experienced an anxiety of this sort. It made him take Satoko by the hand. But when she linked her fingers with his in response, he was irritated and tightened his grip with almost paralysing force. She did not let out the smallest cry of pain. He maintained his hold with the same force, and when the light of a stray beam from a distant second-storey window showed him a trace of tears in her eyes, he felt a black satisfaction.

This, he knew, was further proof of the hidden, savage essence of the elegance he had cultivated for so long. Surely the simplest solution was for them to die together, but he felt that something far more agonizing was called for. The taboo that they were violating even now with every fleeting moment of this secret meeting, and that was growing more formidable with each violation, fascinated Kiyoaki and drove him on, like the peal of a distant, forever unattainable golden bell. The more he sinned, the more the sense of sin eluded him. And the end? How could things end otherwise than in a gross deception, he thought with a shudder.

'It seems that you don't much enjoy walking with me like this,' she said in her usual clear and untroubled tones. 'I am drinking in every passing moment of happiness, but ... you seem to have had enough of it.'

'It's just that I've come to love you too much. And happiness is something I've left far behind me,' he answered gravely. Even as he uttered this rationalization, he realized that he need no longer worry about any trace of childishness in the way he spoke.

The lane they were in was now approaching Roppongi and its clustered shops. A faded flag bearing the character for ice hung in front of an ice house with closed shutters, a forlorn sight on this street echoing with the cries of insects. When they had gone a little farther, they came to a window that spilled light into their path. The shop belonged to a dealer in musical instruments named Tabé, who, according to his sign, was accredited to the band of the Azabu Regiment. He was apparently working late on some sort of urgent order.

They skirted the pool of light, but even so a dazzling glare of brass from the window lit up the corners of their eyes for a moment. A line of new bugles hung there, and they flashed with a brilliance more suited to a midsummer parade ground under the extravagance of the lights above them. From inside the shop came the sudden, melancholy note of a bugle, a single, experimental blast that ceased as soon as it was heard. It struck Kiyoaki's ears like the prelude of doom.

'Please turn back. There'll be too many people up ahead,' Tadeshina whispered to Kiyoaki. She had slipped up close behind them unnoticed.

37

The Toinnomiyas made no attempt to intrude on the course of Satoko's life. Prince Harunori was taken up with his military duties, and no one else among those concerned troubled to arrange a meeting between the Prince and Satoko, nor did Prince Harunori himself give any sign that he wanted one. All this, however, by no means implied that the Toinnomiyas were treating her coolly. In terms of the progression of such betrothals, everything was going smoothly. Those around the Prince believed that frequent meetings between the two young people whose marriage was a foregone conclusion could yield no profit and might well engender some mishap.

In the meantime, there were those accomplishments expected of a young lady who was about to become a princess. Had she been the daughter of a family whose quality might be even slightly in question, she would have had to undergo a varied course of training that conceded little to any previous education. But the tradition of good breeding maintained in Count Ayakura's household was so strong that a daughter of his could rise with ease to the status of princess. Such elegance had become so much a part of Satoko that she could, whenever she wished, compose poems worthy of a princess, write in a hand suitable for a princess, arrange flowers as befitted a princess. There would have been no obstacle to her becoming a princess at any time after her twelfth birthday.

Count Ayakura and his wife, however, were both concerned about three accomplishments that so far had not been featured in her education. They were therefore anxious that she should familiarize herself with them as soon as possible.

These were singing *nagauta* and playing mahjong, of which Princess Toin was so fond, and listening to European records, the favourite diversion of Prince Harunori himself. After the Count had explained the situation to him, Marquis Matsugae immediately arranged to have a *nagauta* master come and give lessons to Satoko, and he also had a German gramophone delivered to the Ayakuras, together with all the available records. Finding an instructor for something like mahjong, however, presented him with a harder task. Though he himself was an avid player of English-style billiards, he was nevertheless scandalized that a noble family of such exalted rank could take pleasure in so plebeian a game as mahjong.

It so happened that the proprietress of the geisha house in Yanagibashi and her oldest geisha were both skilled mahjong players. And so the Marquis arranged for them to pay frequent visits to the Ayakura residence and make a foursome with Tadeshina to introduce Satoko to the game. He himself, of course, paid the extra fee for the trips they made.

One would expect that this foursome, including two professionals, would have brought an unaccustomed touch of frivolity to the austere atmosphere of the Ayakura household. Tadeshina, however, was immovable in her opposition. She pretended that it was an affront to her dignity, but she was in fact terrified that the keen eyes of these two women of the world would uncover Satoko's secret. And even if this did not happen, these mahjong games would nevertheless offer the occasion for Marquis Matsugae to plant paid spies in the Ayakura residence.

The proprietress and the old geisha lost no time in interpreting Tadeshina's unyielding arrogance as a calculated insult, and their reaction took less than three days to reach the ears of the Marquis. He bided his time, and at the first favourable opportunity, gently reproved Count Ayakura.

'Indeed it's most admirable that a faithful old servant of yours should value your family dignity so highly, but surely in this case the whole object is to cater to the pleasure of the Prince's family, so some degree of forbearance may be in order. And then these Yanagibashi women look upon this as a glorious opportunity to be of service, and so, busy as they are, they're willing to take the time to come.'

The Count conveyed all this to Tadeshina, putting her in an extremely awkward position.

Satoko and the two women had in fact met before. On the day of the cherry blossom garden party, the proprietress had been in charge behind the scenes and the old geisha had played the part of the haiku master. When they had come for the first mahjong session, the proprietress had delivered a speech of congratulation to the Count and Countess on the engagement and had also brought an extravagant present:

'What a beautiful lady your daughter is! And as she is possessed of the gracious dignity of a born princess, how pleased you must be at this betrothal. The memory of your permitting us to be associated with it will remain with us forever, and we will pass it on from generation to generation – in the utmost secrecy of course.'

After this commendable expression of their esteem, however, the proprietress and her companion had not been quite up to maintaining the proper veneer when they retired to another room and sat down at the mahjong table with Tadeshina and Satoko. The eyes so overflowing with damp devotion to Satoko would, from time to time, run dry, exposing the shoals of criticism beneath. Tadeshina was distastefully conscious of the same look turned upon her and her old-fashioned silver obi clip. But still more disturbing than that was an incident that occurred at the very beginning.

'I wonder how Marquis Matsugae's young son is?' the old geisha remarked offhandedly as she shuffled the mahjong tiles. 'I don't believe I ever saw a better-looking young gentleman.'

Thereupon, with remarkable skill the proprietress casually turned the conversation to other things. She might have done this merely to chide her companion for introducing an unsuitable topic, but the exchange had set Tadeshina's nerves on edge.

In accordance with her advice, Satoko tried to say as little as possible. But over-concentration on guarding her inner thoughts in front of these two women, who were unsurpassed in their skill at interpreting the subtleties of a woman's outward behaviour, gave rise to another danger. If she showed herself to be too subdued, this might start a scandalous rumour that she seemed unhappy about her coming marriage. To conceal her feelings was to risk betrayal by her behaviour, and to dissemble in her behaviour was to risk revealing her feelings.

As a result, Tadeshina was compelled to draw on all of her considerable tactical ability to put an end once and for all to the mahjong sessions.

'I'm simply astounded,' she said to the Count, 'that His Excellency Marquis Matsugae should deign to accept the slanders of these two women at face value. They say that I'm to blame for Miss Satoko's lack of enthusiasm. If they did not do so, her indifference would otherwise be blamed on them. I'm sure that was why they said I was haughty with them. However much it conforms with the wishes of His Excellency the Marquis, having women of that profession coming and going here in the master's house is a disgrace. Furthermore, Miss Satoko has already learned the rudiments of mahjong. And so if she only plays after her marriage to be sociable, and always loses, it will make her very appealing. I would therefore be very opposed to any further lessons, and if Marquis Matsugae will not desist, then I will request that Tadeshina be dismissed from the master's service.'

Count Ayakura had little choice but to bow to an ultimatum delivered with such force.

The moment she had learned from the steward Yamada that Kiyoaki had lied about Satoko's letter, Tadeshina had found herself at a fork in the road. She had the choice either of becoming Kiyoaki's enemy or of doing whatever he and Satoko wanted her to do, in full awareness of the consequences. And she had chosen the latter course.

Although her main motive in this was a genuine affection for Satoko, she was at the same time afraid that keeping the lovers apart could drive Satoko to suicide. She had decided that the best course was to guard their secret and let them do as they liked, waiting until the affair ended of its own accord. And in the meantime, she would exert herself to the utmost to maintain secrecy.

She prided herself on knowing all there was to know about the workings of passion. A firm advocate, moreover, of the philosophy that what is unknown does not exist, she did not think of herself as betraying either her master the Count or the Toinnomiyas or anyone at all. She was able to help along this love affair and be the lovers' ally, just as if she were conducting an experiment in chemistry, and at the same time she could deny its existence by covering up any betraying details. She knew very well that she had charted a dangerous course, but she believed that she had been born into this world to fulfil the role of saviour of every critical situation. And she could thus lay a wealth of obligations on others that would eventually force them in turn to do exactly as she wished.

She was intent on making the meetings as frequent as possible to hasten the wane of their passion, but she failed to perceive that her own passions had become involved. This had nothing to do with revenge on Kiyoaki for his cruel behaviour. True enough, she was waiting for the day when he would tell her that he wanted to leave Satoko and would she please gently read the funeral rites for him. And when that happened, she would remind him forcefully of how ardent his now cooled desires had once been. But she already only half-believed in this dream. And if it did come true, how agonizing for Satoko.

Why was it that this self-possessed old woman, who should have followed her philosophy that nothing in this world was safe by putting her own self-preservation first, let it prompt her instead to throw aside all thoughts of safety? How could she have brought herself to use this very philosophy as a pretext for adventure? In some unguarded moment, she had, in fact, submitted to a joy that defied rational analysis. To be the means of uniting two young people of such beauty, to watch their hopeless love burn more and more passionately – bit by bit she gave way to an agony of delight that ignored every single danger.

Thus possessed, she felt that there was something so sacred about the physical union of two beautiful young people that it could be judged only by extraordinary criteria. The way their eyes flashed when they met, the way they throbbed as they drew close – this was a fire to warn Tadeshina's frozen heart. For her own sake, she wanted to keep its glow from dying. Each time before they met, their cheeks were pale and sunken with melancholy, but as soon as they saw each other, their faces began to shine as brightly as glossy heads of barley in a June field. For Tadeshina that moment was a miracle, no less than the lame walking or the blind restored to sight.

Her actual role, of course, was to protect Satoko from all evil. But something that flamed like this was not evil; something that was transformed into poetry was not evil – surely this tenet subtly permeated the ancient tradition of elegance in the Ayakura family?

And yet Tadeshina was waiting patiently for something to happen. In some ways she was like a woman who has let her pet bird fly free to forage and now waits for a chance to recapture it and return it to its cage, but there was something in that expectation that reeked of blood and doom. Every day she scrupulously applied the thick white makeup affected by the court ladies of long ago. She hid the nests of wrinkles under her eyes with white powder and those around her lips with vivid Kyoto rouge. And while she was doing this, she avoided studying her face in the mirror, and stared sombrely, questioningly, into space instead. The brilliance of the high autumn sky seemed to condense into clear, bright drops in her eyes, but in their depths one could see a desperate thirst for the future. Then, in order to give her makeup a final inspection, she would pick up a pair of old-fashioned spectacles, which she ordinarily avoided wearing, and put them on, hooking the slender metal side pieces over her ears. As she did so, their pointed ends pricked her earlobes, white with makeup, making them burn.

At the beginning of October the Toinnomiyas sent the prescribed notification that the betrothal ceremony was to take place in December, and attached to this was an informal listing of the presents: five rolls of dress material, two barrels of refined saké, and one carton of fresh sea bream. The last two items were, of course, readily available, but as for the dress material, Marquis Matsugae himself had undertaken to arrange for that. He sent a long telegram to the Itsui Corporation's London office to have the finest English cloth specially ordered and sent at once.

One morning when Tadeshina went to wake Satoko, she noticed that her face was drained of colour when she roused her. Then Satoko pushed her hand aside, got out of bed and rushed into the hallway. She had barely reached the washroom before she vomited, slightly soiling the sleeve of her nightgown. Tadeshina helped her back into the bedroom and made certain that the door was shut.

Some ten or more chickens were kept in the back yard of the house, and their clucking and crowing pierced the shoji screens as they began to lighten each morning, announcing the beginning of a new day to the Ayakura household. Nor did the chorus cease once the sun was high. In the midst of this crowing, Satoko laid her face back on her pillow and shut her eyes.

'Please listen,' said Tadeshina, her mouth close to Satoko's ear. 'It wouldn't do to mention this to anyone. Please don't give your nightgown to the maid to wash under any circumstances. I'll take care of it myself, so that nobody will know. And from now on, I'll make all the arrangements for your food. I'll see to it that you eat only what agrees with you so that your maid won't suspect a thing. What I'm telling you is only for your own good. So it will be best to do exactly as I say.'

Satoko agreed uncertainly as a single tear rolled down her lovely face.

Tadeshina was filled with delight. First of all, she was the only one to have received this initial sign. And then, the moment it occurred, something had dawned on her: this was just what she had been waiting for. Now Satoko was in her hands!

All things considered, Tadeshina was far more at home in the area of life represented by Satoko's present condition than in the realm of passion. Just as she had been prompt to notice and advise Satoko years before when she began to menstruate, so now she showed herself a practised specialist in all things physical. By contrast, Countess Ayakura, who maintained only a nodding acquaintance with the everyday, learned that her daughter had begun to menstruate a full two years later, and only then from Tadeshina.

Tadeshina, who had never failed to note Satoko's every physical sign, intensified her vigilance after that first morning sickness. And once she recognized the signs one by one – the way Satoko put on her makeup, the way she frowned as though anticipating another bout of nausea from a distance, her capricious appetite, the vague heaviness in her movements – she unhesitatingly made her decision.

'It's not healthy to stay indoors all the time like this. Let's go for a walk,' she said to Satoko.

This was usually the hint that a meeting with Kiyoaki had been arranged, but since the sun was still high in the sky, Satoko was somewhat puzzled and looked up questioningly. Tadeshina's customary expression was gone, replaced by a look of stern aloofness. She was well aware that she held a matter of honour in her hands that was of national concern.

As they went out through the rear yard, Countess Ayakura was standing there, her arms clasped to her breast, watching one of the maids feeding the chickens. The bright autumn sun picked out the shiny feathers of the clustering birds and struck the wash hanging out to dry, turning it into a pageant of whiteness. As Satoko walked along, trusting Tadeshina to clear a path through the chickens, she nodded politely to her mother. She noticed the strutting legs thrusting out so abruptly from their feathers, and for the first time in her life she thought of these creatures as being hostile – a natural enmity born of the antagonism of species. It was a dire feeling. A few loose, white feathers floated toward the ground. Tadeshina greeted Satoko's mother.

'I'm just taking Miss Satoko for a little walk.'

'A walk? Well, thank you for your trouble,' the Countess answered. But since her daughter's wedding was drawing closer by the day, she seemed, naturally enough, to be feeling rather nervous. On the other hand, she was becoming more and more polite and reserved toward her daughter. As was customary in the families of court nobles, she never uttered a single word of criticism to her, as she was already like a member of the Imperial Family.

The two of them walked through the streets of Ryudo until they came to a small shrine surrounded by a granite wall and dedicated to the Sun Goddess. They entered its narrow precincts, deserted now that the autumn festivals were over, and after bowing before the inner shrine draped with purple curtains, Tadeshina led the way to the rear of the little pavilion used for sacred dances.

'Is Kiyo coming here?' Satoko asked hesitantly. For some reason, she found herself intimidated by Tadeshina's manner today.

'No, he won't be coming. Today there's something I'd like to ask you, Miss Satoko, and that's why we've come here. We needn't worry that anyone will overhear us.'

Three or four huge rocks had been placed to one side of the pavilion for the convenience of anyone who might want to sit down and watch the ritual dances. Tadeshina now took off her *haori*, folded it, and placed it on the moss-covered surface of one of them.

'Here, now you won't catch a chill,' she said, as Satoko sat down.

'Well now, young mistress,' she said formally, 'I know that I have no need to remind you now, but you are, of course, well aware that loyalty to the Emperor must take absolute precedence. It's a foolish kind of sermon for someone like Tadeshina to make to Miss Satoko Ayakura, whose family has been blessed down the centuries with the imperial favour for twenty-seven generations. But even leaving all that aside, once a marriage is proposed and ratified by imperial sanction, there is no question of having second thoughts. And to spurn it is to spurn the beneficence of His Imperial Majesty. In all the world, there is no sin more terrible than this.'

Tadeshina went on to a detailed explanation. Despite what she had to say, she was by no means blaming her for anything that had already occurred. For she herself had been equally guilty. Furthermore, whatever escaped the notice of the public need not be agonized over and considered as a sin. However, she insisted, there had to be a limit somewhere, and now that Satoko had become pregnant, the time had come to put an end to it. She had been a silent observer up to now, but with matters in their present state, she felt that it would not do to let things slide and permit this love affair to go on and on. So now was the time to muster her determination. She had to make it clear to Kiyoaki that they must part. And she was to do everything according to Tadeshina's instructions. And thus, making each of her points in their proper sequence, and deliberately excluding every emotional consideration, she said what she had to say.

Thinking that this was enough to convince Satoko and that she would obey, Tadeshina cut short her lecture and, with a neatly folded handkerchief, dabbed lightly at the sweat that had gathered on her brow.

Rational as her argument had been, she had spoken with a sadly sympathetic expression and a hint of tears in her voice. This girl was dearer to her than a daughter, but she was aware that her sorrow was not genuine. She was conscious of a barrier between her sorrow and her love. Since her affection for Satoko was so great, she hoped that the girl would share the unfathomable and frightening joy that lurked in her own terrible resolve. To wash oneself clean of one sin that was so permeated with sacrilege, one must commit another. In the end, the two would cancel each other out, as if neither had ever existed. One must merge one form of darkness with another, and then wait for the darkness to be tinged with the rosiness of the fateful dawn to come. And above all, maintain secrecy.

Since Satoko was still silent, Tadeshina began to feel uneasy and asked: 'You'll do everything just as I say, won't you? How do you feel about it?'

Satoko's expression was blank. She gave no sign that Tadeshina's words had startled her. The truth was that her stilted remarks had held no meaning for her whatsoever.

'But what am I to do?' she replied. 'You must be specific.'

Tadeshina looked around her before replying, satisfying herself that the faint sound of the gong that hung before the shrine had been caused by a gust of wind and not by a chance worshipper. The halfhearted chirping of a cricket came from beneath the wooden floor of the pavilion.

'You must get rid of the baby – as soon as possible.'

Satoko caught her breath.

'What do you mean? They'll send me to prison.'

'Don't talk like that. Please leave it to me. Even supposing that it did somehow leak out, it would be impossible for the police to punish either you or me. Your wedding has already been arranged. Once the betrothal gift is presented in December, things will be all the safer. Because in matters like this, the police understand. However, Miss Satoko, this is what I want you to realize: if you dilly-dally and everyone can see that you're pregnant, of course His Imperial Highness and the rest of the world as well would never be able to forgive you. The engagement would be broken off without delay, His Excellency your father would have to hide himself from the eyes of the world, and Master Kiyoaki would also be in a terrible situation. To put it frankly, his future hopes as well as those of the Matsugae family would be so threatened that there would be no course for them but to pretend that he was in no way involved. And so everything would then be lost where you are concerned. Would you want that to happen? There's only one thing you can do now.'

'If it did come out somehow, even supposing that the police said nothing, the Toinnomiyas might still hear something about it. Then how would I be able to show myself at the wedding? And afterwards, how would I dare go on serving the Prince? Tell me that?'

'There is absolutely no need to get upset over what's only a rumour. As for what the Toinnomiyas think, that will depend entirely on you. So if you behave at all times like a chaste and beautiful princess, that's what they'll take you for. The rumours and the rest – they'll be forgotten in no time.'

'Then you can assure me that there's no chance I'll be punished, that I'd go to prison?'

'Let me try to explain it this way, so that you will understand. First of all, the police have the greatest reverence for the nobility. And so there is not the slightest possibility of their allowing something like this to become public. If you're still worried, we could always ask Marquis Matsugae for his kind assistance. His Excellency has a great deal of influence and he can accomplish anything. After all, it would be to cover up for the young master.'

Satoko cried out sharply: 'No! You're not to do that. That's something I shall not allow. You're not under any circumstances to ask either the Marquis or Kiyo for help. I'd be completely disgraced if you did.'

'Well . . . I only mentioned it as a mere possibility. But secondly, even in strictly legal terms, I am determined to shield you. We would make it a matter of you having done as I said without any idea of what scheme I had in mind, of breathing in the anaesthetic without realizing what it was, and so becoming helpless. And if we did that, no matter how public a matter it became, it would end with me bearing the punishment.'

'So you say that whatever happens, then, I shan't go to prison?'

'You can rest assured about that.'

However, her reply brought no look of relief to Satoko's face. 'I want to go to prison,' she said.

Tadeshina's tenseness dissolved as she burst out laughing.

'You sound like a little girl. Why do you say that?'

'I wonder how women prisoners have to dress. What would Kiyo do if he saw me like that . . . would he still love me or not? I'd like to know.'

As she made this absurd remark, her eyes, far from being filled with tears, flashed with such fierce satisfaction that Tadeshina shivered.

However great the difference in status between these two women, there was no denying that they shared the same strength and courage. Whether for deception or for truth's sake, there could never be a more severe demand on their joint bravery than now.

Tadeshina felt that she and Satoko were matched like a boat advancing against the current and the current itself, so well matched that the boat was held immobile for a time, bound together with it from moment to moment in impatient intimacy. At this instant, moreover, the two of them felt the same joy. It had the sound of the beating wings of a flock of birds fleeing overhead before an approaching storm. Their violent emotion, though it had something of sorrow, of fear, of anxiety, was different from all of these and could be called by no other name than joy.

'Well, at any rate, you'll do as I say, won't you?' Tadeshina asked, watching Satoko's pale cheeks flush under the autumn sun.

'I want you to say nothing at all about this to Kiyo,' Satoko replied. 'About my condition, I mean. Whether or not I do just as you say, don't worry. Without bringing anyone else into it, I'll talk everything over with you, and eventually I'll decide what's best.'

Her words already held the dignity of a princess.

38

Kiyoaki was having dinner with his father and mother in early October when he learned that the betrothal ceremony would at last take place in December. His parents displayed the keenest interest in the etiquette for this occasion and vied with each other to show how much they knew about ancient court rites and observances.

'Count Ayakura will have to prepare a chamber of state for the Prince's steward when he comes,' his mother remarked. 'Which room do you suppose it will be?'

'Well, since everyone will stand for the ceremony, a grand Western-style room would be nice, if they had one. As it is, they'll have to spread cloth on the floor of the drawing room and in the corridor leading to it from the entrance, to receive the steward. He will come in a carriage with two attendants, and Ayakura will have to be ready with the letter of acceptance, written on fine, thick crepe paper, in an envelope of the same paper and tied with two ropes of twisted paper knotted together. The steward will be dressed in ceremonial robes and so when Ayakura makes the acceptance speech, he too will have to wear the uniform of a count. But he's an expert on all these little details and there's no need for me to say anything. Only when money becomes a problem, that's when I can be of help.'

Kiyoaki was deeply shaken, and spent a restless night. He imagined that he could hear the dull clank of chains dragging across the floor, coming closer and closer to imprison his love. Now he felt none of the exhilarating energy that had fired him when the imperial sanction was granted. What had so aroused him then, the idea of utter impossibility, had appeared to him like an exquisite piece of white porcelain. But now it was covered with a network of hair-fine cracks. And so in place of the wild joy that had flowed from his sense of resolution at that time, he now felt the sadness of a man who watches the dying of a season.

Had he given up, then, he asked himself. No, he had not. But nevertheless he felt that while the force of the imperial sanction had served to throw him and Satoko wildly into each other's arms, this official announcement of the betrothal ceremony had the power to tear them apart, despite the fact that it was no more than the extension of the first. Dealing with the other had been extremely simple: he had had to do no more than follow his desires. But how was he to cope with this new force? He had no idea.

The next day, using his customary method of contacting Tadeshina, he phoned the owner of the officers' boarding house and told him to tell Tadeshina that he wanted to see Satoko as soon as possible. Since he could not expect any answer before evening, he dutifully went to school, but the lectures he heard that day made no impression on him. After classes were over and he was able to phone the inn from a place close to the school, the innkeeper conveyed Tadeshina's answer. The situation being what it was, Kiyoaki must surely realize that for the present there seemed to be no possibility of arranging a meeting for at least ten days. As soon as an opportunity arose, however, Tadeshina would inform him at once. And so would he please wait until then?

Those ten days were spent in an agony of impatience. He felt that he was now suffering for his behaviour in the past, especially for the time when he had showed such coldness to Satoko.

Autumn became more and more evident. It was still a little early for the maples to have reached their full colour, though the leaves of the cherry trees had already turned a smouldering scarlet and begun to fall. He was in no mood to seek out the company of friends, but to spend the days alone was trying. Sundays were especially difficult, he thought, as he stood looking out over the pond, whose surface reflected the moving clouds. Then he gazed blankly toward the distant waterfall and wondered why the water that flowed unceasingly down its nine levels never ran dry. How strange that this smooth continuity should never be broken! He felt it to be like an image of his emotions.

He was oppressed by a mood of empty frustration that made him feel both feverish and chilled. It was as though he were afflicted with a disease that turned his movements sluggish and heavy, but nevertheless made him feel restless. He roamed alone through the huge family estate, and turned onto the path that led through the grove of Japanese cypresses to the back of the house. He passed by the old gardener hard at work digging up wild potatoes with yellowed leaves.

Blue sky was showing through the cypress branches, and a drop of yesterday's rain fell from them to strike his forehead. He suddenly felt that he had received a message of devastating clarity, as if this raindrop were gouging a furrow down his brow. It rescued him from the anxiety he thought he had left behind him, forgotten. He was only waiting, and nothing was happening. It seemed as if he were standing at a crossroads, where his doubts and misgivings were parading to the hollow beat of a multitude of footsteps. He was so tense that he became oblivious to even his own beauty.

The ten days passed. Tadeshina kept her promise. But the meeting was hedged about with so many restrictions that it tore his heart.

Satoko was going to the Mitsukoshi department store to order new kimonos for the wedding. Her mother was to have gone with her, but since she was in bed with a slight cold, Tadeshina would accompany her alone. They were to meet at the store, but not under the eyes of the salesclerks, which wouldn't do. So Kiyoaki was to be waiting at the entrance decorated with the lion's statue at three o'clock. When Satoko and Tadeshina came out, he was to pretend to ignore them, but follow them at a distance. Finally, when they had entered a small bean-soup restaurant nearby, where they were unlikely to be seen, he could follow and speak to her for a short time. In the meantime, their rickshaw man, waiting at the front entrance of Mitsukoshi's, would think they were still inside.

He left school early, and at three o'clock he was waiting in the crowd of shoppers at the entrance of Mitsukoshi's, wearing a raincoat over his uniform so that it concealed even his collar insignia. He had put his cap inside his bag. Satoko came out, cast an unhappy but burning glance at him, and walked down the street with Tadeshina. Doing as he was directed, he followed and sat down with them in a corner of the almost deserted restaurant.

Satoko and Tadeshina seemed to be somewhat vexed with one another. He noticed that Satoko's makeup was not as becoming as usual, and he realized that she was using it to make herself look healthy at all costs. Her voice, moreover, sounded dulled, and her hair had lost its lustre. He felt that he was looking at a fine painting whose colours, once brilliant, were fading horribly before his very eyes. What he had spent ten days praying to see in an agony of expectation had undergone a subtle change.

'Can we meet tonight?' he asked impetuously, but even as he did so, he sensed that the answer would be no.

'Please don't be so unreasonable.'

'Why am I being unreasonable?'

His words were aggressive enough, but his heart was empty. Her head was drooping and her eyes were now filled with tears. Tadeshina, fearful that the other customers would notice, took out a white handkerchief and shook Satoko by the shoulder. Her gesture struck Kiyoaki as harsh, and he glared at her angrily.

'Why are you looking at me like that?' she retorted, her words full of rudeness. 'Don't you realize, young master, that I've been driving myself frantic for you and Miss Satoko? And not just you, young master – Miss Satoko, you don't understand what I've been through either. It would be better if old people like me had already departed this earth.'

A waiter had placed three bowls of red bean soup on the table in front of them, but nobody touched them. A bit of hot bean paste clung to the edge of the small lacquer cover on one of them like a daub of slowly hardening mud.

Their time together was short. The two parted with no more than a vague promise to meet again in ten days.

That night his agony of mind raged unchecked. He wondered if Satoko would ever agree to meet him at night again, and felt rejected by the whole world. Now that he was plunged in despair, he could no longer doubt his love for her.

When he had seen her tears today, he saw that she belonged to him wholeheartedly. But at the same time he understood that a mere rapport no longer had the strength to sustain them.

What he was experiencing now was genuine emotion. When he compared this to the various sentiments of love that had once occupied his imagination, he knew that this was something crude and blunt, violent and sinister, an emotion that was altogether far removed from elegance. It was hardly the stuff that poems are made of. For the first time in his life, he accepted raw ugliness as indeed being part of him.

After a sleepless night, he went to school next day with his face pale and haggard. Honda noticed this at once and questioned him; his eyes filled with tears in response to his friend's shy kind-heartedness.

'This is what's the matter: Satoko's not going to sleep with me any more, I think.'

Honda's face flushed with virginal consternation.

'What do you mean?'

'It's because the betrothal ceremony's finally been arranged for December.'

'And so she feels she can no longer ... ?'

'That seems to be it precisely.'

Honda could think of nothing to say to console his friend. This was a situation outside his range of experience, and he was saddened to think that he had nothing to offer but his usual generalizations. Even if it were futile, he would have to climb to a vantage point in place of his friend, survey the lay of the land, and then offer a psychological analysis.

'That time when she was with you at Kamakura, didn't you say that you happened to get a feeling that you might tire of her someday?'

'But that was only for an instant.'

'Perhaps she's only putting you off like this because she wants you to love her more fiercely and more deeply.'

For once, however, Honda had miscalculated in attempting to make use of Kiyoaki's delusions of vanity as a means to console him. For he had not the slightest interest in his own attractiveness any more, nor even in Satoko's love for him.

He was only concerned with when and where the two of them could meet without anxiety, as freely as they liked, regardless of anyone else. And he feared that by now it could only happen in some place beyond this world, and only when this world had been destroyed. The vital issue was not feeling but circumstance. In his weary, desperate, bloodshot eyes there was a vision of a world thrown into chaos for their sake.

'If only there were a great earthquake! If so, then I could rescue her. Or a major war would do just as well. If it broke out, what couldn't I do then! ... But no, what I'm after is something that will shake the whole country to its foundations.'

'And who is going to bring about this great event of yours?' asked Honda, looking at this elegant young man with pity in his eyes. He knew that irony and a touch of scorn were now the best means of strengthening his friend. 'Why don't you give it a try yourself?'

Kiyoaki made no attempt to hide his distress. A young man obsessed with love had no time for such things. But there was more than that in his expression. Honda felt a shiver of fascination when he saw the destructive gleam momentarily kindled in Kiyoaki's eyes by his taunt.

It was as if a pack of wolves went raging through the darkness of a sacred precinct. The malevolence fell short of realization: it escaped the notice of Kiyoaki himself: it was born and died in his eyes – but for an instant they flashed with the image of a savage destroyer.

'How am I going to break out?' Kiyoaki muttered as if to himself. 'Would power do it? Or money?'

Honda thought it more than a little ridiculous for the son of Marquis Matsugae to be talking in these terms.

'Well, as far as power goes, what are your prospects?' he asked coldly.

'I'll do everything I can to acquire some. But still, that takes time.'

'There has never been the slightest chance that either power or money would be of any use. You're not forgetting, are you? From the very beginning you've been bewitched by *impossibility* – something which is outside the scope of authority and money. You were drawn in precisely because the whole thing was impossible. Am I wrong? And if it were to become possible now, would it have any value for you?'

'But it did once become possible.'

'You saw an illusion of possibility. You saw the rainbow. What else do you want now?'

'What else...?'

Kiyoaki faltered and his words came to a stop. Beyond this interruption spread a vast great void, unfathomable to Honda. He shuddered.

'These words we exchange,' he thought, 'they're like a mass of building blocks lying scattered over a construction site in the dead of the night. With the immense, starry sky spread out about them and its awful pressure of silence, what else can they do but be mute?'

The two of them were talking at the end of the first period of the school day as they walked along the path that led through the grove surrounding Chiarai Pond. Since the second period was almost upon them, they now turned and retraced their steps. A vast variety of objects had come to rest on the path underfoot as it wound its way through the autumn woods – tangled heaps of wet, brown leaves, their skeletons conspicuous, acorns, green chestnuts, split open and rotting, cigarette butts. Then in the midst of all this, Honda saw something that made him stop and stare at the ground. It was a whitish, crumpled lump of fur, sickly white. By the time he had recognized it as the body of a young mole, Kiyoaki had also stopped and squatted down to study it in silence as it lay in the sunlight filtering down through the branches overhead. The dead animal was lying on its back, and the whiteness that had caught Honda's attention was the fur of its belly. The rest of its body was a sleek, velvet black. Mud was worked into the lines of its tiny, intricately formed white paws, proof of strenuous digging. As it was lying on its back, they could see its pointed beaklike mouth. Its death rictus revealed the soft, pink interior of its mouth behind the two delicate incisors.

At the same moment the two young men thought of the black dog whose dead body had hung over the edge of the waterfall on the Matsugae estate until sent on its way with altogether unexpected funereal solemnity.

Kiyoaki picked the young mole up by its almost hairless tail and laid it gently in his palm. It was already rather shrivelled, and so there was nothing distasteful about it. What was disturbing, however, was that this wretched little animal was condemned to labour blindly and without purpose. The very care and delicacy that had gone into the shaping of its tiny paws were odious.

Kiyoaki took the animal by the tail again as he stood up. At this point the path passed close to the pond, and he casually turned and threw the animal into the water.

'Why did you do that?' demanded Honda, frowning at his friend's offhandedness. This rough behaviour, typical of a student, allowed him to read at a glance the depth of his friend's desolation.

39

Seven days passed, then eight, but there was still no word from Tadeshina. After ten days Kiyoaki telephoned the innkeeper in Roppongi and was told that Tadeshina was apparently ill and confined to her bed. More days went by. Then when the innkeeper told him that she was still ill, his suspicions were aroused.

Hounded by wild desperation, he went to Azabu alone one night and walked aimlessly round the streets near the Ayakura mansion. When he passed underneath the light of the gas lamps in Toriizaka, he stretched out his hands. He was shaken to see how pale their backs looked, for he remembered once hearing that invalids near to death look at their hands constantly.

The gate in front of the Ayakura mansion was shut fast. The faint light above it was scarcely enough to read even the lettering of the weather-beaten nameplate that loomed up out of the darkness. This house was always poorly lit. He knew that there would be no chance of seeing a light in Satoko's room from the street.

He looked at the latticed windows of the empty lodges that flanked the gate. He remembered how he and Satoko had stolen in there as children, and become frightened by the gloom and smell of mould in the deserted rooms. Yearning for the sunlight outside, they had rushed to the windows and grasped the wooden latticework covered with dust. The same layer of dust was still there. The leaves of the trees around the house opposite had been so lush and green that it must have happened in May. Close-worked as the lattice was, it had not shut out this greenery, perhaps because the two young faces peering through it were so small.

Just then, a man selling seedlings had gone by, and the two of them, giggling to themselves, had mimicked him as he cried 'Morning glories, eggplants,' comically dragging out the syllables.

He had learned much in this house. The smell of ink used in calligraphy invariably had melancholy associations for him. Melancholy, in fact, was inseparably bound up with the elegance that had become part of him. All of the beautiful things that the Count had shown him – sutras copied in gold on purple scrolls, screens with the autumn flower design favoured in the imperial palaces in Kyoto – must have emitted a bright ray of carnal desire, he now realized, but in the Ayakura mansion the smell of ink and mould had lain heavy on everything. But now, within these walls that shut him out tonight, that elegance and seductive brilliance had come to life again after the lapse of many years. And he was completely cut off from it.

A faint light went out on the second floor of the house, which was fairly visible from the street. Perhaps Count and Countess Ayakura had gone to sleep. The Count had always gone to bed early. Maybe Satoko was still lying awake. But her light could not be seen. He walked along the wall until he came to the rear gate. There, without thinking, he stretched out his hand to push the cracked and yellowed doorbell, but then drew back.

Stricken with shame at his cowardice, he turned and went home.

More days passed, a terrible period of dead calm. Then still more days. He went to school, but only as a means of somehow getting through each day. When he came home, he gave no thought to his studies.

All around him at school were constant reminders that many of his classmates, Honda among them, were totally absorbed in preparations for the next spring's university entrance examination. It was no more difficult to recognize the behaviour of those who were planning to take the easier route of entering schools that did not have entrance requirements. These students were zealously pursuing their favourite sports. Since he had nothing in common with either camp, Kiyoaki became more and more lonely. If someone spoke to him, he often did not answer, and so his classmates began to be rather unfriendly.

One day when he returned from school, he found Yamada the steward waiting for him at the entranceway.

'His Excellency came home early today, and he expressed a desire to play billiards with the young master. He now awaits him in the billiard room,' Yamada announced.

Kiyoaki felt his heart beat faster as he heard this altogether extraordinary summons. True, the Marquis did sometimes feel the whim to have Kiyoaki's partnership in a game of billiards, but this was customarily restricted to the mellow period after dinner when the Marquis still savoured the effects of the wine he had been drinking.

If his father were seized by such a mood while it was still no more than midafternoon, he must, Kiyoaki thought, be either in exceptionally good or exceptionally bad spirits.

He hardly ever entered the billiard room during the day. He pushed open the heavy door and walked in. The sun was shining in through the west windows, its rays slightly distorted by the glass. When he saw how the oak panelling gleamed in the sunlight, he had the feeling that he had entered this room for the first time.

The Marquis, cue in hand and face pressed close to the baize, was in the act of taking aim at a white ball. The fingers of his left hand, cradling the tip of his cue, made Kiyoaki think of the bridge under a koto string.

'Shut the door,' said the Marquis to Kiyoaki, who had stopped just inside the half-opened door, still in his school uniform. His father's features were tinged by reflections from the green surface of the billiard table so close to his face, so Kiyoaki found it difficult to gauge his expression.

'Read that. It's Tadeshina's farewell,' said the Marquis, straightening up at last and using the tip of his cue to indicate an envelope that was lying on a small table by the window.

'Is she dead?' asked Kiyoaki, feeling his hand shake as he picked up the envelope.

'No, she's not dead. She's recovering. She's not dead – which makes the whole thing that much more disgraceful.' As he answered, the Marquis appeared to be making an effort not to march over to where his son was standing.

Kiyoaki hesitated.

'Hurry up and read it!' For the first time, there was a cutting edge to the Marquis's voice.

He unrolled the long sheet of paper on which Tadeshina had written what was intended as her deathbed testimony, and began to read, still standing in front of the window.

When the time comes for Your Excellency to deign to take forbearing note of this letter, I would beg you to think of Tadeshina who writes it as one who has already departed this world. But before I cut the slender thread that binds this wretched creature to life – the just reward for what I contritely acknowledge to be my heinous and sinful deeds – I am writing this in anxious haste both to confess the gravity of my sins and to offer a dying plea to Your Excellency.

The truth of the matter is that it has recently become evident that, due to Tadeshina's negligence in her entrusted duties, Miss Satoko Ayakura is pregnant. Being overcome with dread when I learned of this, I endeavoured to persuade her that something must be done about her condition at once, but try as I might, my words were of no avail. Realizing that the matter would become more crucial as time went by, I went to Count Ayakura on my own initiative and told him everything in full detail. But my master did no more than say 'What am I to do? What am I to do?' and he did not deign to give the least indication of his intention to take definite action. Finally, knowing full well that it would become more difficult to settle this matter as each month passed, and that it might become a grave affair of state, it became clear that Tadeshina, whose disloyalty was the source of all this tribulation, now had no other course open to her but to sacrifice herself and to cast herself in supplication at the feet of Your Excellency.

I fear that this will anger Your Excellency, but since this matter of Miss Ayakura's pregnancy may be something that could be termed 'within the family' please, please, I beg of Your Excellency that you bring to it your gracious wisdom and discretion. Please have pity on an old woman hurrying toward death, and deign to intercede in this matter of my mistress. This I beg of you from the shadow of the grave.

Humbly yours.

When he had finished reading the letter, Kiyoaki suppressed the momentary rush of cowardly relief that he had not been named in it, and hoped that his look would not express a dishonest denial to his father. Nevertheless, he noticed that his lips were dry and his temples were throbbing feverishly.

'Did you read it?' asked the Marquis. 'Did you read the part that says she requests my gracious wisdom and discretion because this is a matter "within the family"? No matter how close we've been to the Ayakuras, one would hardly describe anything between us as a "family matter". But Tadeshina dared to put that on paper. If you can possibly make a case for yourself, go ahead and make it. Say it right here before the portrait of your grandfather! If I happen to be wrong, I'll apologize. As your father, I have every reason in the world not to want to make such conjectures. Beyond any doubt it's a detestable thing, a detestable conjecture.'

His frivolous hedonist of a father had never been capable of inspiring such awe in Kiyoaki before. Nor had he ever seemed possessed of such dignity. Irritably striking the palm of one hand with his billiard cue, the Marquis stood flanked by the portrait of his father and the painting of the Battle of Tsushima. This huge oil painting, which showed the vanguard of the Japanese fleet deploying before the Russians in the Sea of Japan, was more than half taken up with the massive, dark green billows of the ocean. Kiyoaki was accustomed to seeing it only at night, and the meagre lamplight had prevented him from appreciating the fine detail of the waves, which merged at night into the dark irregular shadows that covered the wall. But now in daytime, he saw how the sombre blue of the waves towered up in the foreground with ponderous force, while in the distance a lighter green blended in to brighten the dark water, and here and there foaming white crests topped the waves. And then the trailing wakes of the manoeuvring squadron spread out with smooth uniformity over the surface of this turbulent northern sea with terrible impact. The line of the Japanese main fleet heading farther out to sea was painted horizontally on the canvas, with its plumes of smoke drifting to the right against a sky whose chilly blue contained a touch of pale green as befitted a northern May.

In contrast, the portrait of Kiyoaki's grandfather in ceremonial robes was imbued with a human warmth, despite his evident sternness. Even now he did not seem to be chiding Kiyoaki, but rather admonishing him with both dignity and affection. He felt that he could confess anything at all to this portrait of his ancestor. Here in front of his grandfather – the face with the heavy eyelids, the cheeks with their warts, the thick lower lip – he had the exultant feeling that his indecisiveness was being cured, if only temporarily.

'There's nothing for me to say. It is as you suppose,' he said, speaking the words without even dropping his eyes. 'It's my child.'

Despite the Marquis's threatening pose, his actual mood on finding himself caught up in such a situation was one of desperate confusion. Handling such things had never been his strong point. So now, although the stage was set for him to proceed to a stinging rebuke, he instead began to mutter to himself.

'Once wasn't enough for old Tadeshina,' he muttered. 'She had to have a second little secret for me. Well and good the first time – nothing but a naughty houseboy. But this time it had to do with no less than the son of a marquis. And yet she could not even kill herself off successfully. Intriguing old bitch!'

The Marquis had always eluded life's more subtle problems with a hearty burst of laughter, and now that one had cropped up calling for indignation, he was nonplussed. This beefy, red-faced man differed strikingly from his own father in that he was vain enough to try not to appear harsh and unfeeling to others, including his own son. He was thus anxious to prevent his anger from appearing as old-fashioned wrath, but his consequent bewilderment made him feel that the sustaining forces of unreason were draining away. At the same time, there was an advantage in anger: it made him quite incapable of reflection.

His father's momentary hesitation gave him courage. Like pure water spurting from a cleft in a rock, words came out of this young man's mouth as the most natural and spontaneous he would ever utter: 'However that may be, Satoko is mine.'

'Yours, did you say? Say that again, would you? Yours, did you say?' demanded the Marquis, happy to have his son relieve him of the task of giving vent to his outrage. Now, his heart at peace, he could air his rage blindly. 'How dare you speak like this now! When it first became a probability that Satoko might become engaged to Prince Toin, didn't I try to ensure that you had no objection? Didn't I say to you, "At this stage things can still be reversed. If your feelings are at all involved, tell me"?'

The Marquis tried to alternate between scorn and conciliation, but in his fury he botched the attempt. Moving along the edge of the billiard table, he came so close that Kiyoaki could see his hand trembling around the cue it held. For the first time, he felt a touch of fear.

'And what did you say then? Eh? What did you say? "I'm not at all involved" – that's how you answered me. That certainly amounted to a man's word, didn't it? But are you a man, I wonder? I regretted raising you in such a soft and easy way, but I never realized you'd turn out like this. To lay hands on someone betrothed to an imperial prince after the Emperor himself has sanctioned the marriage! To go so far as to make her pregnant! To stain your family honour! To throw mud in your father's face! Could there be any disloyalty, any breach of filial piety worse than this? If it were in times gone by, I as your father would have had to cut my belly open and die in atonement to the Emperor. You've behaved like an animal. You've done something that's rotten through and through. Do you hear me? Just what do you have to say for yourself, Kiyoaki? You won't answer me? You'll still defy me, will you?'

The instant that he perceived the panting urgency in his father's words, Kiyoaki dodged to one side to avoid the brandished billiard cue, but he nevertheless caught a solid blow across the back. His father followed that up at once with another that numbed the arm that had tried to protect his back. And as he frantically sought his only escape, the library door, a third blow, meant for his head, missed its target and struck across the bridge of the nose. At this point Kiyoaki collided with a chair in his path and stumbled to the floor, grasping the arm of the chair as he did so to break his fall. As the blood began to spurt from his nose, his father finally held off with his cue.

Each blow must have provoked a sharp cry from Kiyoaki, and now the library door opened to reveal his grandmother and mother in the doorway. The Marquise stood trembling behind her mother-in-law as her husband, still grasping his cue and panting heavily, went rigid.

'What's this?' asked his grandmother.

With that, Marquis Matsugae seemed to notice his mother's presence for the first time, though it was clear from his expression that he found it hard to believe she was actually standing in the doorway. Far less was he capable of guessing how she had got there: that his wife, grasping the drift of events, had probably gone to fetch her. His mother's setting foot outside her retreat was by no means an everyday occurrence.

'Kiyoaki has been a disgrace. You'll understand if you read Tadeshina's farewell on the table there.'

'Did Tadeshina kill herself?'

'The letter came in the mail. Then I phoned the Ayakuras to find out...'

'And what did you find out?' asked his mother, now seated in a chair beside the small table as she slowly pulled out of her obi the black velvet case that contained the glasses she wore to boost her failing sight. She carefully opened the purselike case.

As the Marquise stood watching her mother-in-law she suddenly realized why she had not yet spared so much as a glance for her grandson. It was a sign of her determination to cope with the Marquis single-handed. Sensing this, she rushed in relief to Kiyoaki's side. He had already taken out his handkerchief and was holding it to his bloody nose. The wound hardly seemed to be grave.

'And what did you find out?' repeated the Marquis's mother, unrolling the scroll.

Her son felt that something inside him was already crumbling.

'I phoned and inquired about Tadeshina. They caught her in time and she's recovering. And then the Count asked me suspiciously how I happened to know about it. Apparently he didn't know about her letter. She took an overdose of sleeping pills and I warned the Count that he had to prevent any word of it leaking out. But since, all things considered, my son was at fault, I could not possibly put all the blame on the Count. So the whole conversation became thoroughly pointless. We have to meet as soon as possible to talk it over, I told him, but ... At any rate, one thing at least is clear; unless I come to a decision myself, nothing at all will be done.'

'Very true. Very true indeed,' said the old lady absentmindedly as she ran her eyes over the letter.

Oddly enough, her unsophisticated country vigour – the heavy forehead glowing with health, the blunt, powerful lines of the face, the skin still ruddy with the hot sun of a generation gone by, the bobbed hair dyed a simple, glossy black – her every trait harmonized perfectly with the Victorian setting of the billiard room.

'Well, it doesn't seem that Kiyoaki is mentioned anywhere here by name, does it?'

'Please, that part about "within the family". One glance should be enough to tell you it's an insinuation. But, whatever else, I heard it from his own lips. He confessed that it was his child. In other words, you're on your way to becoming a great-grandmother, Mother, and of an illegitimate child at that.'

'Perhaps Kiyoaki is protecting someone and his confession is false.'

'You'll say anything at all, won't you, Mother? Please go ahead and ask Kiyoaki yourself.'

She turned to Kiyoaki at last and spoke to him affectionately, as if he were a child of five or six.

'Listen, Kiyoaki. Look at me straight, now. Look Granny straight in the eye and answer my question. Then you can't tell fibs. Now, what your father said – is it the truth?'

Kiyoaki turned toward her, mastering the pain he still felt in his back and clutching the now blood-soaked handkerchief to his nose, which was still bleeding. With tears in his eyes and careless streaks of blood clinging to the tip of his prominent nose, he seemed pathetically young, like a wet-nosed puppy.

'It's true,' he said quickly in nasal tones, immediately seizing the fresh handkerchief proffered by his mother and clapping it to his face.

His grandmother then made a speech that seemed to echo the hoofbeats of horses galloping free, a speech that eloquently tore to shreds the conventional niceties.

'Getting the betrothed of the Imperial Prince pregnant! Now there's an achievement! How many of these simpering lads nowadays are capable of anything like that? No doubt about it – Kiyoaki's a true grandson of my husband's. You won't regret it even if you are jailed for it. At least they surely won't execute you,' she said, obviously enjoying herself. The stern lines around her mouth were gone now, and she seemed aglow with a lively satisfaction, as if she had banished decades of stifling gloom, dispersing at a single stroke the enervating pall that had hung over the house ever since the present Marquis had become its master. Nor was she laying the blame on her son alone. She was speaking now in retaliation against all those others, too, who surrounded her in her old age, and whose treacherous power she could sense closing in to crush her. Her voice came echoing gaily out of another era, one of upheavals, a violent era forgotten by this generation, in which fear of imprisonment and death held no one in check, an era in which the threat of both was part of the texture of everyday life. She belonged to a generation of women who had thought nothing of washing their dinner plates in a river while corpses went floating past. That was life! And now, how remarkable that this grandson, who seemed so effete at first glance, should have revived the spirit of that age before her very eyes.

The old lady stared off into space, a look of almost drunken satisfaction on her face. The Marquis and Marquise stared at it in shocked silence – the face of an old woman too stern, too full of rough country beauty to be presented to the public as the matriarch of the Marquis's household.

'Mother, what are you saying?' said the Marquis weakly, finally shaking himself out of his stupor. 'This could mean the ruin of the House of Matsugae – and it's also a terrible affront to Father.'

'That's very true,' she replied at once. 'And so what you've got to think about now is not punishing Kiyoaki but how best to protect the House of Matsugae.

The nation is important, of course, but we must think of the family too. After all, we're not like the Ayakuras, who have enjoyed the imperial favour for more than twenty-seven generations, are we now? So what do you think must be done?'

'Well, we have no choice but to go through with it as if nothing had happened, right up to the betrothal ceremony and the marriage.'

'That's all very fine and clear, but something has to be done about Satoko's baby as quickly as possible. And if it's done anywhere near Tokyo and the newspapers somehow find out, then you'll have a fine mess. Don't you have anything practical to suggest?'

'Osaka would be the place,' replied the Marquis, after a moment's thought. 'Dr Mori would do it for us in the strictest secrecy. And I'll make it worth his while. But Satoko will have to have some plausible reason for going to Osaka.'

'The Ayakuras have all sorts of relatives down there. So wouldn't it be a perfect chance to send Satoko down to visit them and tell them in person about her engagement?'

'But if she has to visit a number of relatives and they notice her condition ... that wouldn't do at all. But wait. I have it. How about having her go to Gesshu Temple in Nara to pay her final respects to the Abbess before her marriage? Wouldn't that be best? It's a temple that's always been closely associated with the Imperial Family, and so it would only be proper to show the Abbess this honour. All things considered, it would be perfectly natural. The Abbess has been fond of her ever since she was a little girl. So first she goes to Osaka to receive the attentions of Dr Mori. Then she rests for a day or two, then she goes to Nara. That would be best. And her mother should go with her, I suppose...'

'Not just her mother. That wouldn't do,' said the old lady sternly. 'Count Ayakura's wife can't be expected to have our interests at heart. Someone from here has to go along with them and look after the girl both before and after Dr Mori's treatment. And it has to be a woman. So...' she pondered and then turned to Kiyoaki's mother: 'Tsujiko, you go.'

'Very well.'

'And you've got to keep your eyes open all the time. You don't have to go to Nara with her. But once you've seen that the crucial thing is done, come back to Tokyo as quick as you can to give us a full report.'

'I understand.'

'Mother's right,' said the Marquis. 'Do just as she says. I'll talk to the Count and we'll decide what day she's to leave. Everything will have to be done so that no one gets the least hint of what's going on.'

Kiyoaki felt that he had become part of the background and that his life and love for Satoko were being treated as things already terminated. Before his very eyes, his father and mother and grandmother seemed to be carefully planning the funeral, quite unconcerned that the corpse could hear every word. Even before his funeral, something seemed already to have been buried. And so on the one hand he was like an attenuated corpse and, on the other, a severely scolded child who had no one to turn to.

Everything was thus proceeding smoothly to an altogether satisfactory conclusion, although the person most intimately concerned had no role in it and the wishes of the Ayakuras themselves were being ignored. Even his grandmother, who just a moment before had been speaking so daringly, now seemed to be basking in the pleasures of coping with a family crisis. Her character was essentially different from his, with its delicacy, and while she was endowed with the intelligence to perceive the savage nobility that lay at the root of his dishonourable behaviour, once family honour was at stake, this same intelligence enabled her to put aside her admiration and adroitly conceal any such noble manifestations. This faculty, one might well suppose, she owed not to the summer sun that beat down on Kagoshima Bay but to the tutoring of her husband, Kiyoaki's grandfather.

The Marquis looked directly at Kiyoaki for the first time since he had aimed his billiard cue at him.

'From now on, you are confined to this house, and you are to fulfil your duties as a student. All your energy is to go into studying for the examinations. Do you quite understand? I shall say nothing further about this matter. This is the turning point: either you will become a man or you will not. As for Satoko, I need hardly say that you are not to see her again.'

'In the old days, they called it house arrest, you know,' said his grandmother. 'If you get tired of studying sometimes, come over and see Granny.'

And then it dawned on Kiyoaki that his father could never disown him now – he was much too afraid of what the world would say.

40

Count Ayakura was a hopeless coward in the face of such things as injury, sickness, and death. There was quite a disturbance on the morning that Tadeshina did not get up. The suicide note left on her pillow was brought to the Countess at once, and when she in turn handed it over to her husband, he opened it at fingertips' length, as if it were germ-ridden. It turned out to be nothing more than a simple farewell note apologizing for the many defects that had marred her service to the Count and Countess, and to Satoko, and thanking them for their never-failing benevolence, the sort of note that could fall into any hands at all and still not excite suspicion.

The Countess sent for the doctor at once. The Count, of course, did not go to see for himself, but was content to receive a full report from his wife afterwards.

'She took more than a hundred and twenty sleeping pills. She hasn't recovered consciousness yet, but the doctor told me what she'd done. My goodness, she was flailing her arms and legs and her body was convulsed like a bow – what a commotion! No one knew where the old woman could find such strength. But then, all of us held her down together and there was the injection and then the doctor pumped out her stomach – that was frightful and I tried not to look. And the doctor finally assured me that she was going to live. How wonderful to have such expertise! Before we said anything at all, he sniffed her breath and said: "Ah, a smell of garlic. It must be Calmotin tablets." He knew right away.'

'Did he say how long it would take her to recover?'

'Yes, he was kind enough to tell me that she would have to rest for at least ten days.'

'Be sure that nothing of this becomes known outside the house. You'll have to warn the women to keep their mouths shut and we'll have to speak to the doctor too. How is Satoko taking this?'

'She's shut herself in her bedroom. She won't even go and see Tadeshina. In her present condition I think it might not be good for her to visit Tadeshina right now. And then, she hasn't said a word to her since Tadeshina raised that matter with us, so she probably feels disinclined to rush in to see her. The best thing would be to leave Satoko alone.'

Five days before, Tadeshina, at her wit's end, had broken the news of Satoko's pregnancy to the Count and Countess, but instead of flying into a rage and subjecting her to the expected torrent of rebukes, the Count had in fact reacted so listlessly that she had been driven in desperation to write the letter to Marquis Matsugae and then to take an overdose of sleeping pills.

Satoko had persisted in rejecting Tadeshina's advice. Although the danger was growing more acute with each day that passed, she not only ordered Tadeshina to say nothing to anyone, but she gave no slightest indication that she herself was ever going to come to a decision. And so, unable to bear this any longer, Tadeshina had betrayed her mistress by telling her secret to her mother and father. But the Count and Countess – perhaps because the news was such a stunning blow – had shown no more perturbation than if the news had been of a cat running off with one of the chickens in the backyard.

The day after she told him, and the day after that too, Tadeshina happened to cross paths with the Count, but he gave no sign of being concerned about the problem. He was, in fact, profoundly shaken. But since the problem was at once too vast to deal with on his own and too embarrassing to discuss with others, he made every effort to put it out of his mind.

He and his wife had agreed to say nothing to Satoko until they were ready to take some kind of action. Satoko, however, whose perceptions were now at their keenest, subjected Tadeshina to a cross-examination and so found out what had happened. And with that, she shut herself in her room and would have no more to do with her, and an uncanny silence fell over the house. Tadeshina stopped receiving any communications from the outside world, telling the servants to say that she was sick.

The Count avoided the problem even with his wife. He was fully aware of the fearful nature of the circumstances and of the necessity for immediate action, but he continued to procrastinate nonetheless. This did not mean that he believed in miracles either.

Count Ayakura's paralysis did have a sort of refinement. Although one could hardly deny that his chronic indecisiveness involved a certain scepticism about the value of any decision at all, he was by no means a sceptic in the ordinary sense of the word. Even though he was plunged in meditation from morning to night, he was loath to direct his immense emotional reserves toward a single conclusion. Meditation had a great deal in common with *kemari*, the traditional sport of the

Ayakuras. No matter how high one kicked the ball, it would obviously come down to earth again at once. Even if his illustrious ancestor Namba Munetate could excite cries of admiration when he picked up the white deerskin ball by its thongs of purple leather and kicked it to such incredible heights that it topped the ninety-foot roof of the imperial residence itself, it must inevitably fall back again into the garden.

Since all the solutions left something to be desired in terms of good taste, it was better to wait for someone else to make the unpleasant decision. Someone else's foot would have to stretch out to intercept the falling ball. Even if one kicked the ball oneself, it was quite possible that it might be seized by some unexpected whim of its own as it reached the high point of its arc, and come sailing down in a new and unpredictable trajectory.

The spectre of ruin never rose before the Count. If it was not a grave crisis to have the fiancée of an imperial prince, whose engagement had been sanctioned by the Emperor himself, carrying another man's offspring in her womb, then the world would never know a grave crisis. Still, the descending ball would not inevitably be his to kick; surely someone else's turn to cope with it would come. The Count was never one to be long vexed by worries, and as an inevitable consequence, his worries always ended up by vexing others.

And then it happened that on the day after the tumult of Tadeshina's attempt on her life, the telephone call came from Marquis Matsugae.

That the Marquis should have known what had happened despite all efforts to hush it up was simply incredible to the Count. He would not have been surprised to learn that there was an informer in his household. But since his prime suspect, Tadeshina herself, had been unconscious throughout the previous day, all his most likely speculations were left with the ground cut out from under them.

Having heard from his wife that Tadeshina was recovering at a good rate, that she could talk and that her appetite had even returned, the Count therefore summoned up his extreme reserves of courage and decided to visit the sickroom all by himself.

'You needn't come with me. I'll go and see her on my own. Perhaps the woman will be more inclined to tell the truth that way,' he told his wife.

'But the room is in a terrible state, and if you visit her without warning, she'll be upset. I'll go and tell her first, and help her to get herself ready.'

'As you wish.'

The Count had to endure a two-hour wait. When the patient heard the news from the Countess, she immediately began to apply her makeup.

She had been granted the exceptional privilege of a room in the main house, but it was not more than four and a half mats large, and never caught the sun. When her bedding was laid out, it occupied almost the whole floor. The Count had never been in there before.

Finally, a servant came to escort him to the room. A chair for him had been placed on the tatami floor and Tadeshina's bedding had been put away. Dressed in a sleeved coverlet and with her elbows supported on a pile of pillows on her lap,

Tadeshina bowed in reverence as the master entered. As she did so, her forehead seemed to press down on the pillows in front of her, but he noticed that, perfect as her bow was, she overcame her weakness sufficiently to preserve a slight gap between her forehead and the pillows. She was concerned about her makeup, that smooth expanse of thick, congealed white that extended right up to her scrupulously groomed hairline.

'Well, you've had quite an ordeal,' the Count began, after sitting down. 'But you pulled through, and that's the main thing. You shouldn't worry us so.'

Although he found nothing awkward in looking down at her from his position in the chair, he felt that for some reason neither his voice nor his meaning was reaching her.

'How unworthy I am to receive Your Excellency's visit! I am altogether in a state of dread. Never can I express adequately the deep shame that I feel...'

Her head still bowed, she seemed to be dabbing her eyes with the tissue paper she had pulled from her sleeve, but he realized that in so doing she was again being careful to preserve her makeup.

'According to the doctor, ten days' rest and you'll be your old self again. So just relax and take a good long rest.'

'Oh thank you so much, Your Excellency. I am covered with shame, having failed so miserably in trying to die.'

As the Count looked down at the old woman cowering in her russet chrysanthemum-patterned bedjacket, he sensed the offensive aura that surrounds someone who has gone down the road of death only to turn back. He smelled the breath of defilement that clung to everything in the small room, even to its cabinet and drawers, and he grew more and more uneasy. The very care and skill that had gone into the application of the liquid white makeup on the nape of her neck, still visible as she bowed her head, and that had arranged her coiffure so that not a single hair straggled out of place, only served to intensify his indefinable sense of fear.

'Actually,' he said, putting the question as casually as he could, 'I was rather taken aback to receive a telephone call from Marquis Matsugae today. He already knew what had happened. And so I thought I might ask you if you did not have some explanation for it.'

But there are questions that answer themselves as soon as they are formulated. The words had hardly passed his lips before the answer came to him with startling suddenness, just as she raised her head.

The old court-style makeup covering her face was thicker than ever. She had painted her lips a bright red that covered even their innermost edge. Not content merely to subdue her wrinkles with makeup, she had applied layer upon layer of white to create a smooth surface which did not, however, blend into her skin, roughened by her recent ordeal. The effect was as if the makeup were clinging to her skin as though the pores had sprouted a white mould. The Count furtively looked away before he started to speak again.

'You wrote to the Marquis beforehand, didn't you?'

'Yes, Your Excellency,' she answered, her head still raised, her voice quite steady. 'I really intended to die, and so I wrote to him begging him to do what was necessary after I was gone.'

'You told him everything in that letter?'

'No, sir.'

'There are things you left out?'

'Yes, Your Excellency, there are many things I left out,' she replied, now cheerful.

41

Although the Count had no very clear-cut idea of anything he might wish to keep from Marquis Matsugae, he had only to hear Tadeshina mention her omissions to feel suddenly uneasy.

'And the things you left out – what were they?'

'What does the master mean? I answered Your Excellency as I did, simply because you were pleased to ask me if I had told the Marquis *everything* in the letter. There must be something on the master's mind to make him ask such a question.'

'This is no time to talk in riddles. I've come here alone like this because I thought we could talk freely without regard for others. So it would be as well if you said clearly what you meant.'

'There are many, many things I did not discuss in that letter. Among them is the matter that the master was pleased to confide to me some eight years ago at Kitazaki's. I intended to die with that sealed in my heart.'

'Kitazaki's?'

The Count shuddered as he heard that name, which rang like doom in his ears. He now understood what Tadeshina had been hinting at, and as he did so his anxiety deepened. He felt driven to tear away any vestige of doubt.

'What did I say at Kitazaki's?'

'It was an evening during the rainy season. The master can hardly have forgotten. Miss Satoko, though she was slowly growing up to be a young lady, was still only thirteen. Marquis Matsugae came here that day to pay one of his rare visits. And when he was leaving, the master's mood seemed to be not what it should be. And so he went to Kitazaki's house for a little recreation. And that night he was pleased to tell me something.'

The Count was fully aware of the drift of Tadeshina's remarks. She intended to forge a weapon from his words that night and to make her own dereliction entirely his responsibility. He suddenly doubted that she had ever really intended to kill herself.

Her eyes now regarded him from the heavily powdered face above the pile of pillows like two loopholes cut into the white walls of a fortress. The darkness behind that wall was teeming with things from the past and out of it could come flying an arrow, aimed at him as he stood exposed in the bright light outside.

'Why do you bring that up now? It was something I said as a joke.'

'Was it really?'

Suddenly those loophole eyes seemed to narrow still further. He had the feeling that darkness itself in all its intensity was pointed at him. Then she went on, her voice heavy, 'But still ... that night, at Kitazaki's house ...'

Kitazaki, Kitazaki – that name, bound up with memories the Count had been trying to ignore, came to the lips of this sly old woman again and again. Though eight years had passed since he last set foot there, every detail of the house now sprang vividly to mind once again. The inn stood at the foot of a slope, and although it had no gate nor entranceway to speak of, it was surrounded by quite a large garden with a wooden fence. The gloomy, damp front hall, a spot favoured by slugs and snails, had been preempted by four or five pairs of black boots. Even their blotched, yellowish brown leather linings, greasy and mouldy with sweat, now flashed before his eyes, as did the broad-striped name-tabs that hung out of them. That night the sound of rude and boisterous singing had greeted him at the front door. The Russo-Japanese War was at its height, and the quartering of soldiers was a respectable and sure source of income. It had given the inn a reputable appearance along with the smell of a stable. As he was led to a room at the rear, he walked along the corridor as if passing through a quarantine ward, fearful even that his sleeve might brush against a pillar along the way. He had a profound aversion to human sweat and all that related to it.

On that night in the rainy season eight years ago, the Count had been unable to regain his usual composure after ushering out his guest the Marquis. And that was the moment that Tadeshina, shrewdly gauging her master's mood from his expression, had chosen to speak.

'Kitazaki tells me that something very amusing has come his way and that he would like nothing better than to offer it to the master for his enjoyment. Would the master not consider going there tonight, just for a little recreation?'

Since she was free to do such things as 'visiting her relatives' once Satoko had gone to bed, there was no obstacle to her going out and then meeting the Count at a prearranged spot.

Kitazaki received the Count with extreme obsequiousness and served him saké, then left the room to return carrying an old scroll which he laid deferentially on the table.

'It is indeed noisy here tonight,' he said apologetically. 'Somebody is about to leave for the front, and is having a farewell party. It's terribly hot, but perhaps it would be well to close the rain shutters, Your Excellency.'

Kitazaki meant that by so doing, the din that echoed from the second floor of the main wing would be somewhat lessened. The Count agreed and he closed the shutters. However, the falling rain immediately seemed to sound more insistently on every side, caging him into the room. The brilliant colour of the Genji sliding door gave it a kind of suffocating, panting sensuality, as though the room itself were a picture rolled up within a forbidden scroll.

Sitting opposite the Count, Kitazaki reached respectfully across the table with his wrinkled but honest-looking old hands and unfastened the purple cord that bound the scroll. Then he began to unroll it for the Count, revealing first the pretentious inscription at the top. It was a koan:

Chao Chu went to a nun one day to say, 'Do you have it? Do you have it?' And when the nun in turn raised her fists at him, Chao Chu went on his Way at once, declaring: 'Shallow water affords poor anchorage.'

The oppressive heat of that night! Its sultry torpor, only aggravated by the breeze stirred at his back by Tadeshina's fan, seemed to the Count to equal that of a rice-steaming basket. The saké had begun to take effect; the Count heard the drumming of the rain outside as if it were striking the back of his skull; the world outside was lost in innocent thoughts of victory in war. And thus the Count sat looking down at the erotic scroll. Suddenly Kitazaki's hands flashed through the air to clap together on a mosquito. He apologized at once for the disturbance of the noise, and the Count caught a glimpse of the tiny black smudge of crushed mosquito in his dry white palm, together with a red smear of blood, an unclean image that unsettled him. Why had the mosquito not bitten him? Was he really so well protected from everything?

The first picture on the scroll was that of an abbot in a brown robe and a young widow seated facing each other in front of a screen. The style was that of haiku illustrations, done with a light, humorous touch. The face of the abbot was drawn in caricature to look like a large penis.

In the next picture the abbot sprang upon the young widow without warning, intent on raping her, and although she was putting up a fight, her kimono was already in disarray. In the next they were locked in a naked embrace and the woman's expression was now blissfully relaxed. The abbot's penis was like the twisted root of a giant pine, and his brown tongue stuck out in great delight. In accordance with this artistic tradition, the young widow's feet and toes were painted with Chinese white, and curved sharply inward. Tremors ran the length of her white, clinging thighs and ended finally at her toes, as though the tension there embodied her straining effort to hold back the flood of ecstasy that was about to gush out into eternity. The woman's exertions were altogether admirable, thought the Count.

On the other side of the screen, meantime, a number of novice monks were standing on a wooden drum and a writing table, and boosting one another on to their shoulders, desperately keen to see what was going on behind the screen while simultaneously engaged in a comic struggle to keep down those parts of their anatomy that had already swollen to massive proportions. Finally the screen fell over. And as the stark-naked woman attempted to cover herself and escape, and the abbot lay exhausted with no strength left to reprimand the novices, a scene of total disorder began to unfold.

The monks' penises were drawn to appear nearly as long as their owners were tall, the usual proportions being inadequate for the artist to convey the magnitude of their burden of lust. As they set upon the woman, the face of each of them was a comic study in indescribable anguish, and they staggered about under the weight of their own erections.

After such punishing toil, the woman's entire body turned deathly pale and she died. Her soul flew out of her and took refuge in the branches of a willow tree blown by the wind. And there she became a vengeful ghost, her face drawn in the image of a vulva.

At this point, the scroll lost whatever humour it had once had, and became permeated with fearful gloom. Not one but many ghosts, all similar, assaulted the men, hair streaming wildly, crimson lips gaping. Fleeing in panic, the men were no match for the phantoms, who swarmed over them in a whirlwind, tearing out their penises as well as the abbot's with their powerful jaws.

The final scene was by the seashore. The emasculated men lay naked on the beach, howling desperately, while a boat weighed down with their mutilated penises was just setting sail on a dark sea. The ghosts crowded the deck, hair streaming in the wind, pale hands waving derisively, their vaginal faces mocking the wretched cries of their victims on the shore. The prow of the boat, too, was carved in the form of a vulva, and as it pointed toward deep water, a tuft of hair clinging to it waved in the sea breeze.

When he finally looked up from the scroll, the Count felt inexplicably depressed. The saké, far from soothing him, had only increased his feelings of apprehension. But he had Kitazaki bring more of it, and drank it in silence. His mind was still filled with the vivid image of the woman in the scroll, her toes bent inward. The lewd whiteness of her painted legs still flashed before his eyes.

What he did next could only have been due to the languid heat of that night in the rainy season and to his own disgust. Fourteen years before that wet evening, when his wife had been pregnant with Satoko, he had favoured Tadeshina with his attentions. Since even then she had been past forty, this had been an extraordinary whim, and did not last long. Fourteen years later, with Tadeshina well into her fifties, he never dreamed that anything of the sort would happen again. At any rate, because of what took place this time, he was never to set foot across the threshold of Kitazaki's inn again.

Events and circumstances – the Marquis's visit, the crushing blow to his pride, the rainy night, the isolated rear parlour of Kitazaki's house, the saké, the sinister pornography – all crowded in on the Count, intensifying his mood of resentment and (it could hardly have been otherwise) inflaming him with a desire to debase himself, which drove him to do what he did. Tadeshina's response, devoid of any reproach, set the seal on his feelings of self-loathing.

'This woman,' he thought, 'she'll wait fourteen, twenty, a hundred years – it makes no difference to her. And no matter when she hears the voice of her master, she'll never be caught unawares.'

Through circumstances which had been none of his doing, he was driven by his seething resentment to plunge into a dark wood where the ghost from the pornographic scroll was lying in wait for him. Moreover, Tadeshina's unruffled composure, her deferential flirting, the evident pride she took in her exhaustive knowledge of sexual technique, all worked on him just as coercively as they had fourteen years earlier.

Perhaps there had been some collusion between her and Kitazaki who left the room and did not return. Afterwards, in the darkness, shut in by the pervasive sound of falling rain, neither of them spoke. Then the soldiers' voices broke through once more, and this time the Count clearly heard the words of their song:

To the battlefield
Torn with steel and fire,
The fate of the nation's defence
Falls on you.
Forward, brave comrades!
Forward, Imperial Army!

The Count suddenly became a child again. He felt the need to unburden himself of the anger that was devouring him, and he gave Tadeshina a detailed account of something that belonged to a sphere from which servants were excluded. For he felt that his anger was not merely his alone, but rather an emotion that incorporated the wrath of his ancestors.

Marquis Matsugae had paid a visit that day. And when Satoko had come into the room to pay her respects, he had stroked her bobbed hair. And then perhaps under the influence of the saké he had drunk, he spoke abruptly in front of the child: 'What a beautiful little princess you have become! When you grow up, you will be so beautiful that nobody will find words to describe you. And as for finding a handsome husband, you just leave that to Uncle, and don't worry about a thing. If you trust Uncle completely, I'll get you a bridegroom without equal anywhere in the world. Your father won't have a thing to worry about. I'll line up a trousseau on golden satin for you when you become a bride. What a long, long, proud procession that will be! – such as has never been seen in all the generations of Ayakuras.'

The Countess had given the slightest of frowns at that moment, but the Count had merely smiled. Instead of smiling in the face of humiliation, his ancestors would have revealed just enough of their elegance, and struck back. But these days – when, for example, the ancestral game of *kemari* was no more than a memory – there were no means left to dazzle the vulgar. And when such men as this imposter, overflowing with goodwill and innocent of any intention to wound a genuine aristocrat, offered their unwitting insults, there was nothing to do but laugh vaguely. However, there was a faintly mysterious element lingering in the smile that came to the lips of the cultured when confronted with the new ascendancy of money and power.

The Count had remained silent for a while after telling Tadeshina all this. If elegance was to have its revenge, he was thinking, how was it to be accomplished? Wasn't there a revenge proper to court nobles, like the revenge in which incense was inserted into the flowing sleeve of a court robe and allowed to burn slowly to a fine ash while showing hardly a trace of flame? A revenge such as this, that would leave a subtle, fragrant poison permeating the material, so that its potency would remain undiminished down the years?

At last the Count turned to Tadeshina and said: 'I am going to ask you, long in advance, to do something. When Satoko grows up, I am afraid that everything will go exactly according to Matsugae's wishes, and so he will be the one to arrange a marriage for her. But when he's done that, before the marriage takes place, I want you to guide her into bed with some man she likes, a man who knows how to keep his mouth shut. I don't care about his social position – just so long as she is fond of him. I have no intention of handing Satoko over as a chaste virgin to any bridegroom for whom I have Matsugae's benevolence to thank. And so I'll give Matsugae's nose a twist without his knowing a thing about it. But nobody is to know about this, and you're not to consult me about it. It's something you must do just as if it were a sin committed on your initiative alone. And there's one more aspect to it: since you are the equivalent of a master of arts in all sexual matters, it's not asking too much, is it, for you to instruct Satoko thoroughly in two rather different accomplishments? The first is to make a man think he's taking a girl as a virgin when he's not. And the second, on the contrary, is to make him think that she's already lost her virginity when in fact she has not.'

'You need say no more, master,' Tadeshina replied, her voice betraying no sign of hesitation or dismay. 'There are such effective techniques with regard to both that there is no danger of arousing the suspicions of even the most experienced and libertine gentlemen. And so I will take great pains to educate Miss Satoko in them. However, might I be permitted to wonder what the Marquis has in mind as concerns the second of these?'

'So that the person who makes a conquest of someone else's bride before the wedding doesn't become too exultant about it. If he knows that she's a virgin, he may become presumptuous about his conquest, and that just won't do. And so I'm entrusting you with this as well.'

'Everything is quite understood,' answered Tadeshina. Instead of a simple 'As the master wishes,' she undertook her appointed task with a grave and formal agreement.

And Tadeshina was now alluding to what had happened that night eight years before. The Count was only too aware of what she wanted to say. But at the same time, he was quite sure that the significance of the unforeseen course of events after she had accepted her commission could not have been lost on a woman of Tadeshina's shrewdness. The prospective bridegroom had turned out to be a prince of the Imperial Family, and although credit was due to the Marquis, a marriage as fortunate as this would mean the resurgence of the House of Ayakura. In short, the circumstances were very different from those he had envisaged eight years before when he had given Tadeshina his instructions in a burning rage. If, despite all this, she had carried out her task in scrupulous accordance with that ancient promise, the reason must lie in her own desire to do so. Furthermore, the secret had already been spilled to Marquis Matsugae.

Was it possible that she had taken aim against the House of Matsugae out of some grand design, intended to bring down a disaster that would achieve the revenge the Count's own timidity and listlessness had put beyond his reach? Or was it that her revenge was directed not at the Matsugaes but at none other than the Count himself? Whatever he did, he was at a disadvantage – he could not afford to let her tell the Marquis that bedtime story of eight years before.

He felt it best to say nothing. What was done was done. And as for the Marquis knowing about it, he had to be prepared for a more or less severe rebuke on that score. Still, he reflected, the Marquis would use his immense influence to devise some ploy that would save the situation. Now was the time to entrust the whole matter to somebody else.

About one thing, however, he was quite certain: Tadeshina's state of mind. However much she professed her guilt she was in fact quite disinclined to beg forgiveness for what she had done. There she sat, the old woman who had tried to kill herself, still indifferent to his pardon, the russet coverlet about her shoulders, the white makeup clinging to her face as thickly as if she were a cricket that had tumbled into a box of powder. And tiny as her figure was, it somehow seemed to fill the whole wide world with melancholy.

He suddenly noticed that this room was the same size as the rear parlour of Kitazaki's inn. All at once he could hear the rustling murmur of the rain and, quite out of season, the stifling heat that brings decay struck his cheek as it had done before.

She raised her whitened face once more to say something. Her dry, wrinkled lips were slightly parted and the wet, red cavern of her mouth gleamed in the light of the electric bulb as brightly as the deep scarlet of her court lip rouge.

He could guess what she was about to say. Wasn't what she had done the result, just as she herself had said, of the events of that night eight years before? And hadn't she done it for no other reason than to give the Count a forcible reminder of what had occurred that night, since he had never again shown the slightest interest in her?

Suddenly he felt the urge to ask the sort of ruthless question of which only a child is capable.

'Well, happily your life was saved ... but did you honestly mean to kill yourself?'

He thought that she might either become angry or burst into tears, but instead she merely laughed politely.

'Well now, if the master had deigned to say to me, "Kill yourself", perhaps I would really have been in the mood to die. And if he should so order me even now, I would try once more. Eight years from now, however, the master might naturally enough have forgotten what he had said, once again.'

42

When Marquis Matsugae met with Count Ayakura, he was taken aback to see how little concern the Count evinced at the course of events. But when the Count readily agreed to the proposal he had so strongly urged, high spirits returned. The Count assured him that everything would be done just as he wished. He was immensely heartened, he said, to hear that the Marquise herself would accompany

Satoko to Osaka. And as for being able to entrust everything to Dr Mori in the strictest confidence, this was an undreamed-of blessing. Everything would be carried out in accordance with the Matsugaes' instructions, and he therefore begged that the Marquis be so gracious as to continue his kind efforts on behalf of the Ayakuras. Such was the tenor of his reply.

The Ayakuras had but one, extremely modest request, which the Marquis could hardly help but grant. This was that Satoko and Kiyoaki be allowed to see each other just before she left for Osaka. There was of course no question of permitting them to be alone together. But if they could meet face to face for a brief moment with their parents at hand, that would satisfy the Ayakuras. And if this request could be granted, the Ayakuras would give every assurance that Satoko would never be allowed to see Kiyoaki again. The request originated with Satoko herself, but, as the Count explained with some embarrassment, he and his wife felt that it would be best to grant her this much.

The circumstance of the Marquise accompanying Satoko to Osaka could now be utilized to give the meeting with Kiyoaki an uncontrived appearance. Nothing would be more natural than a son coming to the station to see his mother off, and at such a time no one would have any cause to look askance if Kiyoaki exchanged a word or two with Satoko.

With matters thus concluded, the Marquis, at the suggestion of his wife, secretly summoned Dr Mori to Tokyo, even though he was fully occupied with his Osaka practice. The doctor stayed with the Matsugaes for a week prior to Satoko's departure on November 14, always in reserve in case she should need him. For if a message came from the Ayakuras, he was ready to rush over there at once. It was the danger of a miscarriage, looming from moment to moment, that made these precautions necessary. If such a thing did occur, Dr Mori himself would have to attend to it and in such a way that no word would escape. Furthermore, he was to be on hand during the long and extremely perilous train trip to Osaka, travelling inconspicuously in another car.

A renowned obstetrician thus surrendered his freedom and put himself at the beck and call of the Matsugaes and Ayakuras, something that only the Marquis's money could have achieved. And if things progressed as he hoped, the trip to Osaka would itself greatly contribute to keeping the truth hidden from the world. For who would imagine a pregnant woman undertaking any venture such as a train journey?

Although Dr Mori wore suits tailored in England and was the very model of a Western gentleman, he was a stumpy little man, and there was something about his face that put one in mind of a clerk. Before he examined each of his patients, he spread a fresh layer of high-quality paper over the pillow for her, and would carelessly crumple it up and throw it away afterwards, a practice that enhanced his reputation. He was flawlessly polite and his smile never waned. He had numerous patients among women of the upper class. His skill was unsurpassed and his mouth as tight as an oyster.

He enjoyed talking about the weather, and apart from this, there seemed to be no topic capable of capturing his interest. However, he was able to muster enough charm for his patients merely by remarking how terribly hot it was today or that it was getting warmer after each shower. He was skilled in Chinese poetry and had expressed his impressions of London in twenty Chinese poems in the seven-line form, which he had published privately under the title *London Poems*. He wore a huge, three-carat diamond ring, and before examining a patient he would screw up his face ostentatiously and pull off the ring with apparent difficulty, throwing it brusquely on whatever table was close at hand. However, no one ever noticed him forgetting to pick it up again. His stiff moustache had the subdued lustre of a fern after rain.

It was incumbent on the Ayakuras to accompany Satoko to the Toinnomiya residence so that she could pay her respects before her trip to Osaka. Since a trip by carriage would increase the risks involved, Marquis Matsugae furnished them with an automobile. Moreover, Dr Mori accompanied them disguised as a butler, sitting up beside the driver and wearing an old suit of Yamada's. By a stroke of good fortune, the young prince himself was away on manoeuvres. Satoko was able to greet Princess Toin just inside the entranceway and then withdraw. The perilous expedition was thus completed without mishap.

Though the Toinnomiyas planned to dispatch a household official to the station to see Satoko off on November 14, the Ayakuras politely declined this favour. Everything was going exactly according to Marquis Matsugae's plan. The Ayakuras would meet Marquise Matsugae and her son at the Shimbashi station. Dr Mori was to board a third-class carriage without so much as a glance in their direction. Since the purpose of the trip was supposedly the perfectly laudable one of paying a farewell visit to the Abbess of Gesshu, the Marquis did not hesitate to reserve the entire observation car for the Ayakuras and his wife. This belonged to a special express bound for Shimonoseki which left Shimbashi station at nine thirty in the morning and arrived at Osaka eleven hours and fifteen minutes later.

Shimbashi station, designed by an American architect, had been built in 1872 at the beginning of the Meiji era. It had a timber frame, but its walls were of dark, speckled stone cut from quarries on the Izu Peninsula. Now, on this clear, bright November morning, the sunshine sharply etched the shadows cast by the projecting cornice onto their austere surface. Marquise Matsugae, rather tense at the prospect of setting out on a trip from which she would have to return on her own, arrived at the station having said hardly a word on the way either to Yamada, who was carrying her baggage with his usual deference, or to Kiyoaki. The three of them climbed the long flight of stone steps that led to the platform.

The train had not yet pulled in. The slanting rays of the morning sun poured down on the broad platform and the tracks to either side of it, and motes of dust stirred in the brilliant air. The Marquise was in such a state of anxiety about the trip that confronted her that she heaved deep sighs at frequent intervals.

'I don't see them yet, I wonder if something has happened?' she said from time to time, but she could get no response from Yamada but a reverent and meaningless 'Ah!' Although she had known what to expect, she could not refrain from her question.

Kiyoaki realized how disturbed his mother was, but being in no mood to alleviate her distress, he stood some distance away. He felt faint, and his stiff posture was expressive of the effort he was making to keep a grip on himself. It seemed as if he might topple over still rigid like a statue, cast in one piece but lacking any vital strength to sustain it. The air on the platform was chilly but he threw out his chest under his braided uniform jacket. The bleak distress of waiting seemed to have frozen him to the marrow.

The train backed into the station with ponderous dignity while the sun streaked the tops of the cars with brilliant ribbons and flashed from the rail at the rear of the observation car. Just at this moment, the Marquise picked out Dr Mori by his neat moustache, in the midst of a group waiting some way down the platform. She felt a measure of relief. It had been agreed that, barring some emergency, the doctor would keep to himself throughout the trip to Osaka.

The three of them climbed into the observation car, Yamada carrying the Marquise's luggage. While she was giving Yamada further instructions, Kiyoaki stared out of the window at the platform. He was watching Countess Ayakura and Satoko approaching through the crowd. Satoko was wearing a rainbow shawl wrapped around her shoulders. When she reached the bright flood of sunlight that poured past the edge of the platform roof, her expressionless face looked as white as curds.

His heart beat wildly both with distress and joy. And as he watched her, with her mother at her side, drawing steadily closer but moving at a slow and measured pace, he was taken for a moment with the fancy that he was the bridegroom waiting there to receive his bride. And the solemn ceremonial march, like a cumulative weariness that settled over him particle by particle, stirred a joy that was painfully intense and left him quite enervated.

Countess Ayakura stepped up into the car, and, leaving the servant to carry Satoko's luggage, offered her apologies for being late. Kiyoaki's mother naturally greeted her with the utmost courtesy, but a certain contraction still visible in her forehead gave adequate expression to the haughty displeasure she felt.

Satoko covered her mouth with her rainbow shawl and kept herself hidden behind her mother. She exchanged the normal greetings with Kiyoaki and then, urged by the Marquise, sat down promptly in one of the deep scarlet upholstered chairs which furnished the car.

Kiyoaki then realized why she had arrived so late. She must have delayed her arrival at the station for no other reason than to shorten, even by a fraction, the length of their parting. In the light of this November morning, clear as bitter medicine, they would have no time to say anything to each other. While their mothers were talking, he stared down at her as she sat with bowed head, and in so doing, he began to be concerned about the rising intensity of passion that must be evident in his gaze. His whole heart was in it, but he feared that, like too powerful sunlight, it might scorch Satoko's fragile pallor. The forces at work within him, the emotion he wanted to communicate, had to have subtlety and grace, and he realized how crude a shape his passion had given it. He now felt something that had never touched him before, and he wanted to beg her forgiveness.

As for her body, now covered by her kimono, he knew all there was to know about it, even its tiniest recesses. He knew where her white flesh would first flush crimson with embarrassment, where it would yield, where it would throb with the wingbeat of a snared swan. He knew where it would express joy and where it would express sorrow. Because he knew it in its totality, it seemed to give off a faint glow which could be sensed even through her kimono. But now something he didn't recognize within that body, deep within her very heart, which she seemed to be protecting with the flowing sleeves of her kimono, was pushing its way into life. His nineteen-year-old imagination could not deal with a phenomenon such as that of a child, something that, however intimately bound up with dark, hot blood and flesh, seemed altogether metaphysical.

But even so, the only thing of his that had entered Satoko and become part of her had to be a child. Soon, however, this part would be torn from her and their flesh would become separate once again. And since he had no means whatever of preventing this, there was nothing to do but stand by and let it happen. In a way the child involved here was Kiyoaki himself, for he was still lacking in the power to act independently. He trembled with the bereft loneliness and bitter frustration of a child forced to stay at home as a punishment for a misdeed while the rest of the family went happily off on a picnic.

She raised her eyes and stared vacantly out of the window on the platform side of the train. She seemed entirely absorbed in the vision of what would be cast out from her and he was sure that there was no hope he would ever be reflected in them again.

A piercing whistle sounded a warning. She stood up. It seemed to him that her action was a decisive effort that had demanded all her strength. Her anxious mother reached out and seized her arm.

'The train's about to leave. You'll have to get off,' Satoko said to him. Her voice sounded almost cheerful, but it was a trifle shrill.

Inevitably there ensued a hurried conversation between him and his mother, consisting of the usual admonitions and good wishes exchanged between mother and son before she goes off, leaving him behind. He wondered at the skill he was able to bring to supporting his role in this little skit.

When he had finally freed himself from his mother, he turned to the Countess and quickiy ran through the correct formulas of farewell with her. Then, as though nothing could be more casual, he said to Satoko, 'Well, take care of yourself now.' At that moment he felt able to lend lightness to his words, and this was reflected in an impulse to put out his hand and lay it on her shoulder. But at the next moment, his arm seemed stricken with paralysis and hung useless at his side, for he had met her gaze in its full intensity.

Her large, beautiful eyes were certainly wet with tears, but tears quite different from those he had been dreading up to now. They were something living that was being cut to pieces. Her eyes held the terrible glance of a drowning man, and he could not bear this gaze. Her lovely long eyelashes spread wide, like a plant bursting into flower.

'You too, Kiyo. Good-bye,' she said in one breath, her tone quite proper.

He fled from the train as if pursued, just as the station-master, wearing a short sword at the belt of his black five-button jacket, raised his hand in signal. Once more the conductor's whistle sounded. Although restrained by Yamada's presence beside him, he called her name in his heart again and again. The line of cars gave a brief shudder and then, like a length of yarn being unwound from a spool, the train began to move. In a few brief moments the observation car and its rear railing were far away, and neither Satoko nor the two mothers had shown themselves. The trailing smoke that poured over the platform testified to the power unleashed in the train's departure. Its acrid smell filled the untimely darkness that it had left behind.

43

On the morning after two days in Osaka, Marquise Matsugae left the inn where she was staying and went to the nearest post office to send a personal telegram. Her husband had given her strict instructions that she was not to delegate this task to anyone. This being the first time in her life that she had entered a post office, she was thoroughly flustered, although in the midst of her confusion she somehow happened to recall a princess, recently deceased, who was convinced that money was filthy and passed her life without even laying hand on it. But willy-nilly, she sent a telegram couched in the wording agreed on with her husband: 'Visit safely accomplished.'

She felt a surge of relief sweep through her as if a heavy burden had slipped from her shoulders. She returned to the inn to pay her bill and then went to Osaka station, where Countess Ayakura was waiting to see her off on her solitary return trip to Tokyo. In order to pay her these respects, the Countess had momentarily slipped away from Satoko's bedside in the hospital.

Satoko had entered Dr Mori's private clinic under an assumed name, in conformity with the doctor's insistence on two or three days of complete rest. The Countess had been with her constantly, but although her physical condition was excellent, she had not said a word to her mother since the operation, an attitude that pained the Countess deeply.

Since the comfortable stay in the hospital was prescribed merely as a precautionary measure, when Dr Mori gave his permission for her to leave, she was quite fit to move about, almost as if in perfect health. Now, with her morning sickness a thing of the past, she should have become more buoyant both physically and mentally, but she obstinately held to her silence.

According to the plan arranged for them, they were to go to Gesshu Temple next for Satoko's farewell visit to the Abbess. They would stay there one night and return to Tokyo the next morning.

In the middle of November 18, then, the two of them got off a Sakurai Line train at Obitoké station. It was a warm and beautiful autumn afternoon, and despite her uneasiness over her taciturn daughter, the Countess felt more at rest.

Since she had wanted to avoid putting the old nuns to any inconvenience, she had not informed the convent of their time of arrival. Now, however, though she had asked a station attendant to call two rickshaws for them, there was still no sign of them. While they were waiting, the Countess, who had a fondness for exploring unfamiliar places, went for a stroll in the quiet vicinity of the station, leaving her daughter to her own reflections in the first-class waiting-room. Just outside, she came across a signboard directing visitors to the Obitoké Temple nearby.

OBITOKÉ TEMPLE OF MT KOYASU.
The Bodhisattva Obitoké Koyasu Jizo is revered here. Japan's most ancient and hallowed place of prayer for obtaining the favour of children and their safe birth. Sanctified by the imperial prayers of the Emperors Montoku and Seiwa and the Empress Somedono.

She felt it just as well that these words had escaped Satoko's eye. To lessen the chance of her daughter seeing the signboard, she would have to let the rickshaw pull in deep under the station roof and help her in. It seemed to her that the words were unexpected drops of blood tainting this lovely scenery underneath so brilliant a November sky.

Obitoké station had a well beside it, and white walls under a tiled roof. Opposite it stood an old-fashioned house surrounded by a roofed-in mud wall and boasting an imposing storehouse at the back. Although the white storehouse and mud wall made the bright sunlight dance, an eerie silence hung over the scene. The road surface was grey with thawing mud and glinted with traces of frost, which made for difficult walking. However, her eye was caught by an attractive splash of yellow in the distance. This lay at the approach to a small bridge; it crossed the railway line at a spot where the tall bare trees that bordered the track in ascending ranks came to an end, although they seemed to file on into infinity. So she gathered up her skirts and began to make her way up a slight gradient in the direction of this diversion.

As it turned out, the bridge approach had been decorated with flowerpots of trailing chrysanthemums. Any number of them were dotted about haphazardly in the shelter of a pale green willow that stood beside the path leading onto the bridge. Though it served its purpose as an overpass, it was unpretentious, made of wood, and seemed barely larger than a saddle. Some checkered quilts, hung out to air, were draped over its railing, soaking up the sun and fluffed out as they swung gracefully in the breeze. In the yard of a house close by, diapers were drying in the sun and a length of red material was stretched out and secured by clothespins. The dried persimmons that lined the eaves still had a lustre like the glow of sunset. And there was no one to be seen anywhere.

Far down the road, she caught sight of the swaying black hoods of two rickshaws coming in her direction. She hurried back to the station to tell Satoko.

Because the weather was so pleasant, she had the men lower the rickshaw hoods. They left the town and its two or three inns behind them and travelled for a time along a road bordered with rice paddies. If one looked carefully at the mountains, one could pick out Gesshu Temple at the very heart of them.

Some distance farther on, the road was lined with persimmon trees, whose branches, although bare of almost all their leaves, were heavy with fruit. All the rice fields looked festive, decked all over with a maze of drying racks.

The Countess, in the first rickshaw, turned around from time to time to look back at her daughter. Satoko had folded her shawl and laid it in her lap. When her mother saw that she was looking around her as though she were enjoying the scenery, she felt somewhat relieved.

As the road entered the mountains, the pace of the rickshaw men slowed down. Both of them were old men, and their legs were evidently not what they had been. However, there was no reason to hurry. On the contrary, thought the Countess, she and Satoko were fortunate to be able to have such a leisurely view of the countryside.

They were approaching the outer stone gate of Gesshu, and once they had passed through it, the scenery became limited to the gently sloping path itself, a broad expanse of pale blue sky partially obscured by the tall, white-bearded grass along the path, and a low range of mountains far in the distance.

The rickshaw men finally stopped for a rest, and as they talked and wiped away their sweat, the Countess raised her voice to carry over theirs and called back to Satoko: 'You'd better take your fill of the scenery from here to the convent. People like me can come here at any time, but you will soon be in a position where you won't be able to go on outings so easily.'

Her daughter did not reply, but she gave a slow smile and nodded her head slightly.

The rickshaws moved on again, and the path continued to slope upwards, which slowed the pace still further. After they had entered the convent grounds, however, the trees on either side of them grew denser, lessening the heat of the sun.

The Countess's ears still echoed faintly with the autumn midday humming of the insects she had been listening to while the rickshaw men were having their rest. But then the persimmon trees that had begun to appear on the left-hand side of the road caught her eye and enchanted her with their clear, glowing fruit. Flashing in the sunlight, some of the persimmons that weighed down each branch were casting lacquered shadows on the others. One tree was rich with orange-red fruit which, unlike flowers, resisted the wind and left only the dry leaves to stir. Its mass of ripe fruit was thus spread out against the sky as if fixed firmly to the spot against a field of blue.

'I don't see any maple leaves at all. I wonder why,' she called back to Satoko, nearly shrieking with the effort but not drawing any response.

Even scrub maples were scarce along the road. There was little to catch the eye now but the green of radish fields to the west and bamboo thickets to the east. The radish fields were covered with a thick growth of leaves that filtered the sunshine into subtly complex patterns. Then they gave way to a line of tea bushes separated from the road by a marsh. Red-berried vines of magnolia covered this tea hedge, and beyond appeared the still waters of a larger marsh. A little farther on, the road darkened abruptly as the rickshaws passed into the shade of some ancient cedars. The sun spilled down in flecks of light on the bamboo grass beneath the trees, and one tall, isolated stalk flashed with a singular intensity.

She felt a sudden chill in the air. Turning again toward the rickshaw behind her, she mimed the clutching of her shawl about her shoulders. Although she hardly dared hope for a response, when she glanced backward a few minutes later, she caught the iridescent colours of Satoko's shawl in the corner of her eye, fluttering in the breeze. Although her daughter still had no inclination to talk, the Countess could at least take consolation in her obedience.

Once the rickshaws had passed through a black-painted gate, the scenery around them took on the more formal aspect of a garden, as might be expected of the immediate surroundings of the convent. Its red maple leaves – the first she had seen along the way – caught the Countess by surprise, and she gasped with admiration.

There was nothing gaudily charming about the colours of these maples here within the black gate. Their deep scarlet was a shade that was blended only in the depths of the mountains, a colour that seemed to speak to the Countess of sins as yet unpurged. She suddenly felt a chill edge of anxiety cut into her, and thought of Satoko in the rickshaw behind.

The screen of slender pines and cedars that formed a backdrop to the maples was not thick enough to shut out the broad, bright expanse of sky. Its brilliance flooded through them, striking the maples from behind and turning their extended red-leaved branches to scattered clouds caught in the radiance of the morning sun. As she looked up at the sky from beneath the branches, she admired the subtly delicate way the leaves were interwoven, and imagined that she was seeing the heavens through a tracery of deep scarlet.

Finally the rickshaws stopped and the Countess and Satoko stepped down in front of a Tang Dynasty gate, behind which was a stone-paved lane and the main entrance to the convent of Gesshu.

44

A full year had gone by since Satoko and her mother had last paid their respects to the Abbess on the occasion of her trip to Tokyo. And now, as they waited in a large parlour, the senior nun assured them that Her Reverence had been delighted at the prospect of this visit. She was still speaking as the Abbess herself entered, the junior nun leading her by the hand.

After the Countess had imparted the news of Satoko's engagement, Her Reverence congratulated her, saying, 'The next time you are kind enough to honour us with a visit, it will not do for you to be lodged anywhere but in the pavilion.' The pavilion was a villa in the convent grounds reserved for members of the Imperial Family.

Now that she was here at Gesshu, Satoko could not very well keep silent any longer, and she answered, however briefly, whenever she was spoken to. Her withdrawal might have been taken for mere shyness. The Abbess, of course, being a woman of immense discretion, gave no sign that she noticed anything amiss.

'A man in the village who cultivates them brings some every year,' said the

Abbess in response to the Countess's lavish praise of the potted chrysanthemums that were standing in rows in the courtyard. 'He gives us such a lecture about them.' Then she made the senior nun repeat the chrysanthemum enthusiast's explanations – this was a crimson single-fold chrysanthemum, bred to blossom in a pattern of parallel stripes; this a yellow tubular chrysanthemum bred in the same way, and so on. Finally Her Reverence herself led Satoko and her mother into the drawing room.

'Our maples seem to be late in turning this year,' she said after the senior nun had pulled open the sliding door to reveal the beauty of the inner garden, with its simulated mountains and its now fading grass. It contained several huge maple trees that were crowned with red, but as one looked down at the lower branches, this paled to an orange that gave way to a yellow that finally merged into a light green. The red at the very top was dark, with a quality suggestive of congealed blood. The sasanquas had already begun to bloom. And in one corner of the garden, the smooth curve of a dry branch of crape myrtle added a beautiful touch of lustre.

They returned to the parlour, and while Her Reverence and the Countess engaged in polite conversation, the short autumn day drew to a close.

Dinner was a festive affair, complete with the rice and red beans reserved for holidays, and the two nuns did their best to enliven the company but nothing seemed able to lighten the mood of the evening.

'This is the day of the fire kindling at the Imperial Palace,' said the Abbess. The fire kindling was a court observance built around the kindling of a huge flame in a hibachi while a court lady stood in front of it chanting an incantation. The senior nun, who had seen it during her years of service at the palace, chanted it from memory.

It was an ancient ritual that took place in the presence of the Emperor on the eighteenth of November. After a flame was struck in the hibachi and soared almost to the ceiling, a court lady, swathed in white ceremonial robes, would begin the chant with the words: 'Upwards! Upwards! Let the holy flame be kindled! If these tangerines and these *manju* should please you . . .' The tangerines and bean-jam dumplings were then thrown on to the fire, heated through, and then offered to the Emperor.

One might well feel that the nun's reenactment of so solemn an observance was bordering on the sacrilegious, but the Abbess realized that the old woman's sole intention was to provide some badly needed cheer, and she did not utter a word of reproof.

Night came early at Gesshu. By five in the evening, the front gate was already bolted. Shortly after dinner, the nuns retired to their sleeping quarters, and the Countess and her daughter were led to their room. They would stay until the following mid-afternoon, allowing for a leisurely farewell. Then they were to board a night train that evening for Tokyo.

The Countess had intended to reprimand Satoko once they were alone together for having let her sadness affect her good manners during the day. But after some reflection on her state of mind after the Osaka experience, she decided against it and went to bed without a word to her daughter.

Even in the unrelieved darkness of the night, the sliding door's paper panelling loomed white and insistently mournful in the guest parlour of Gesshu. It was as if the frost air of the cold November night had penetrated the thin skin of the paper. The Countess could easily distinguish the paper patterns of sixteen-petal chrysanthemums and white clouds that decorated the door catches. Up in the direction of the darkened ceiling, metal rosettes of six chrysanthemums grouped around kikkyo blossoms masked each of the pegs, accentuating the blackness around them. Outside there was no wind at all, with not even the sound of a breeze stirring in the pines to be heard. Nevertheless, one was distinctly aware of the expanse of forest and mountain.

The Countess was overcome with a sense of relief. Whatever the cost, she and her daughter had faithfully carried out the painful duty that was their lot, and now she felt that everything would be calm and serene. And so, despite her consciousness that her daughter was tossing and turning beside her, she soon fell asleep.

When she opened her eyes, Satoko was no longer at her side. Stretching out her hand in the pre-dawn darkness, she came upon her daughter's nightgown neatly folded on top of the quilt. Anxiety surged through her, but she told herself that Satoko had merely gone to the lavatory, and she determined to do nothing for a few moments. But although she tried to wait, her chest was tight with a dull coldness and she got up to make sure. The lavatory was empty. There was no sign of anyone else about. The sky was now tinged with an uncertain blue.

Just then she heard the sound of movement coming from the kitchen. A few moments later, an early-rising serving maid, startled at the Countess's sudden appearance, went down on her knees.

'Have you seen Satoko?' she asked her, but the maid was terrified and could do nothing but shake her head frantically, nor would she budge an inch to help in the search.

After this, however, while the Countess was pacing the convent passages in aimless desperation, she happened to meet the junior nun. The nun was startled at her news and began at once to guide her in her search.

At the far end of a connecting corridor, the flickering glow of candles came from the main hall of worship. It was hardly likely that a nun would already be at her devotion at this hour of the morning.

Two burning candles traced with the flower-wheel pattern were illuminating the image of Buddha before which Satoko was sitting. Seeing her daughter from the rear, the Countess did not recognize her for some moments. For Satoko had cropped short her hair. She had placed the shorn strands on the sutra stand, as though in offering, and, beads in hand, was lost in prayer.

Her mother's first reaction was relief at finding her daughter alive. She then realized that until that moment she had been certain that Satoko was dead.

'You've cut off your hair,' she cried as she embraced her.

'Yes, Mother. There was nothing else to do,' Satoko answered, finally looking her mother directly in the eye. The small, wavering candle flames flickered in her pupils, but the whites of her eyes already held the brilliance of the dawn. Never had the Countess seen so fearful a daybreak as she now saw mirrored in her daughter's gaze. And the same white glow, growing stronger by the minute, shone in each of the crystal beads of the string wrapped around her fingers. Like a force of will so intense that it transcends mere willing, the dawn light seemed to flow with equal force from every one of the cold crystals.

The junior nun hurried off to break the news to her senior. And then, having completed her report, she withdrew, leaving it to the senior nun to conduct Countess Ayakura and her daughter to the Abbess.

'Your Reverence, have you arisen yet?' she called from outside the door of the Abbess's quarters.

'Yes.'

'Please forgive us.'

The old nun then slid open the door to reveal the Abbess sitting upright on her quilted mattress. The Countess began haltingly.

'What has happened, Your Reverence, is that Satoko, just now, in the chapel, cut off her hair.'

The Abbess gazed out into the corridor as her eyes absorbed the change that Satoko had worked on herself. But her features betrayed no sign of surprise.

'Well, well. I was wondering if things might not turn out something like this,' she said. After a pause, as if a new thought had just struck her, she went on to say that as the circumstances appeared to be rather involved, she thought it best for the Countess to be kind enough to leave her daughter alone with her so that she and Satoko could have a heart-to-heart talk. The Countess and the senior nun acquiesced, and withdrew.

The nun, left alone with Countess Ayakura, did her best to entertain her, but the Countess was so distraught that she could not eat a bite of breakfast. The nun could well imagine her distress and was unable to think of any topic of conversation that might divert her. A long time passed before a summons finally came from the Abbess's quarters. And there, in Satoko's presence, the Abbess informed the Countess of a piece of news of shattering significance: since there was no mistaking the genuineness of Satoko's desire to renounce the world, Gesshu Temple would receive her as a novice.

For most of the morning so far, the Countess's mind had been wholly involved in concocting a variety of stopgap measures. She could not doubt that Satoko's decision was firm. And then some months or even half a year would be required to restore her daughter's hair to normal, but if only she could be dissuaded from taking the tonsure, these months could be accounted for a period of convalescence from some illness incurred during the trip, and the Ayakuras could thus obtain a postponement of the betrothal ceremony. Then the persuasive powers of her father and Marquis Matsugae could be brought to bear on her in the interval, and perhaps she could be induced to change her mind.

And now, hearing the Abbess's words, her determination, far from weakening, became all the more set. The usual procedure, when one was to be accepted as a novice, was to undergo a year of ascetic discipline before receiving the tonsure at the formal induction ceremony. Whatever else, the restoration of Satoko's ravaged hair was of prime importance. Then, in the event that she could be persuaded fairly soon to reject her vocation . . . the Countess's mind was filled with marvellous ploys: if events quickly took a favourable turn, perhaps Satoko could get through the betrothal ceremony safely with the help of a carefully made wig.

Countess Ayakura came to her decision: for the present, her only course was to leave Satoko here and return to Tokyo as quickly as possible to work out a plan of action.

'I appreciate the sentiments expressed by Your Reverence,' she said in reply. 'However, not only has this come up suddenly in the midst of a journey, but it is also a matter that involves disturbing the Imperial Family. I therefore think it best to beg your indulgence to return temporarily to Tokyo to consult my husband before coming back here. And in the meantime I will entrust Satoko to your care.'

Satoko heard her mother out without so much as a raised eyebrow. The Countess was now afraid even to speak to her own daughter.

45

Upon his wife's return, when Count Ayakura learned of this astonishing development, he let an entire week pass without doing anything at all, a procrastination that was to provoke the wrath of Marquis Matsugae.

The Matsugae household was resting secure in the assumption that Satoko had already returned to Tokyo and that due notice of this had been conveyed to Prince Toin's family. A miscalculation of this sort was out of character for the Marquis, but once his wife had come back from Osaka and told him that his meticulous planning had been carried out without a hitch, complacency got the upper hand, and he felt assured of a successful conclusion.

Count Ayakura's abstraction persisted. He believed that only a vulgar mentality was willing to acknowledge the possibility of catastrophe. He felt that taking naps was much more beneficial than confronting catastrophes. However precipitous the future might seem, he learned from the game of *kemari* that the ball must always come down. There was no call for consternation. Grief and rage, along with other outbursts of passion, were mistakes easily committed by a mind lacking in refinement. And the Count was certainly not a man who lacked refinement.

Just let matters slide. How much better to accept each sweet drop of honey that was Time, than to stoop to the vulgarity latent in every decision. However grave the matter at hand might be, if one neglected it for long enough, the act of neglect itself would begin to affect the situation, and someone else would emerge as an ally. Such was Count Ayakura's version of political theory.

Once back at the side of such a husband, the Countess became daily less concerned with the anxiety that had oppressed her at Gesshu. In the present circumstances, it was lucky that Tadeshina was away and unable to act blindly on one of her rash impulses. The Count had been kind enough to send her off for a leisurely convalescence at the hot springs of Yugawara.

After a week, however, there was a phone call from Marquis Matsugae, and even Count Ayakura could no longer keep the matter secret. The Marquis was temporarily struck dumb when he heard the Count tell him that as a matter of fact Satoko had not yet returned and he felt the stirrings of all sorts of nasty premonitions.

The Marquis and his wife lost no time in paying a visit to the Ayakuras. At first the Count offered one vague response after another as he was questioned. And then when the truth finally came out, the Marquis was so furious that he struck the table in front of him with his fist.

So it came about that this ten-mat parlour awkwardly redone to become the sole Western-style room in the mansion became the scene for the first occasion in their long acquaintance that these two couples confronted each other stripped of all niceties. The women averted their eyes and each from time to time stole a look at her husband. Though the two men faced each other, Count Ayakura tended to hang his head. His hands, resting on the table, were small and white, the hands of a doll in a puppet play. In contrast, despite his essential weakness, the Marquis's coarse, florid features could have served as a Noh mask of the angry devil with the fiercely contorted eyebrows. Even in the eyes of the wives, the Count appeared to have no chance.

As it turned out, the Marquis's anger swept all before it for a time. But even while he was letting himself rage, he began to feel a little embarrassed over his display of self-righteousness. For after all, his own position in this affair was safe from first to last. Moreover, he could hardly have been matched with a weaker, more pitiful antagonist than the one who now confronted him. The Count's colour was unhealthy. As he sat there in silence, an expression, part sorrow, part dismay, came over his face, which seemed to be carved out of yellow ivory, the features delicately chiselled and quite composed. The crinkled eyelids emphasized the deep-set cast of the habitually downcast eyes as well as their melancholy. The Marquis had the feeling, not for the first time, that they were women's eyes.

Count Ayakura's languid reticence, his manner of slumping casually in his chair, clearly bespoke the graceful elegance of ancient tradition – something that was nowhere to be found in the Marquis's pedigree – now displayed at its most deeply injured. It had something of the soiled plumage of a dead bird, a creature that had once sung beautifully but whose flesh was tasteless and so inedible after all.

'It's quite unbelievable! A positively wretched thing to happen. What apologies could we offer to the Emperor, to the entire nation?' the Marquis declaimed heedlessly, intent on letting his anger sweep along on a stream of orotund syllables but aware that its supporting lifeline might snap at any minute. Anger was useless against the Count, who was neither acquainted with logic nor remotely inclined to initiate any course of action. Worse still, the Marquis gradually came to realize that the more enraged he became, the more the force of his passion was turned relentlessly back against itself.

He could not believe that the Count had plotted just such a result from the very beginning. But nonetheless he now saw with painful clarity that the Count had been able to use his endemic listlessness to forge so impregnable a position that, however monumental the catastrophe, the blame for it would come to rest not on himself but on his ally.

After all, it was the Marquis who had asked the Count to give his son an upbringing that would imbue him with a sense of elegance. It was undoubtedly the desires of the flesh in Kiyoaki that had brought on this misfortune, and one might well argue that this was the consequence of the subtle poison that had begun to infect his spirit after his arrival in the Ayakura household as an infant. But the ultimate instigator of this was none other than the Marquis himself. Furthermore, in this latest twist of the crisis, it was the Marquis who had insisted on sending Satoko down to Osaka without any forethought that something like this might occur. Everything thus conspired to turn the force of the Marquis's wrath against himself.

Finally worn out by his exertions and unnerved by his growing anxiety, the Marquis held his tongue. The ensuing silence lengthened and grew more profound until it seemed as if the four of them had gathered in this room to practise group meditation. The noonday clucking of the chickens came from the yard behind the house. Each time the early winter wind blew through the trees outside, the pine needles that stirred at the slightest touch flashed brightly. There was no sound of human activity from anywhere else in the house, and the silence seemed to be in deference to the eerie atmosphere in the parlour.

The Countess finally broke the spell.

'It was my negligence that caused this. There is no way that I can apologize sufficiently to you, Marquis Matsugae. However, things being as they are, wouldn't it be best to try and make Satoko change her mind as soon as possible and have the betrothal ceremony take place as planned?'

'But what about her hair?' was the Marquis's immediate retort.

'Well, as to that, if we are quick and arrange to have a wig made, it would mislead the public eye for a while...'

'A wig!' the Marquis exclaimed, breaking in before the Countess had finished with a slightly shrill note of joy in his voice. 'I never thought of that.'

'Yes, of course,' said his wife, chiming in at once. 'We never thought of that.'

And from then on, as the others were infected with the Marquis's enthusiasm, the wig was all they could talk about. For the first time, laughter was heard in the parlour as the four of them competed to pounce first on this bright idea as if it were a scrap of meat.

Not all of them, however, placed the same degree of faith in the Countess's novel idea. The Count, for one, did not trust its efficacy. The Marquis may well have shared his scepticism, but he was capable of feigning belief with dignity. And the Count himself hastened to profit by his example.

'Even if the young prince gets a bit suspicious about Satoko's hair,' said the Marquis, lowering his voice to a forced whisper while he laughed, 'he's certainly not going to touch it to see for himself.'

An atmosphere of cordiality pervaded the room, however fragile the fiction that sustained it. For the fiction supplied them with that tangible element so vital at this moment. No one considered Satoko's soul; it was her hair alone that pertained to the national interest.

The Marquis's father had dedicated all of his fierce strength and passion to the cause of the imperial restoration. His mortification would have been bitter had he known that the glory he had earned for the family name would one day depend on a woman's wig. This sort of intricate and shady manoeuvring was hardly the forte of the House of Matsugae. It was, in fact, far more characteristic of the Ayakuras. But the present Marquis, instead of leaving elegantly refined deceptions to the Ayakuras, who were bred to that kind of thing, had become fascinated by it, and so the House of Matsugae was now compelled to share an unaccustomed burden.

The truth of the matter was that this wig as yet only existed in their imaginations and was totally irrelevant to Satoko's intentions. However, once they succeeded in dressing her in a wig, they would be able to construct a flawless picture from the pieces of a shattered jigsaw puzzle. Everything thus seemed to depend on the wig, and the Marquis gave himself over to the project with enthusiasm.

Each of the foursome in the parlour contributed wholeheartedly to the discussion of the nonexistent hairpiece. Satoko would have to wear one dressed in a long, straight hairstyle for the betrothal ceremony, but for everyday use, a wig done in the Western fashion would be necessary. And since there was no telling when someone might catch sight of her, she must not take if off even when she took a bath. And each of them began to use his or her imagination to picture this wig with which they had already decided to crown her: abundant, jet-black hair, even more glossy than her own. Such sovereign power would be hers despite herself, the grandeur of a towering, gracefully arranged coiffure radiating a dark fascination moreover that would imbue the flat brightness of midday with something of the essence of night. Each of the four was well enough aware that it would be no simple matter to achieve this – that beneath this peerless wig there would be a face marked with unhappiness, but no one was willing to dwell for long on this aspect of the problem.

'This time I would appreciate it greatly if you yourself, Count, went down there to impress upon your daughter how firmly your mind is made up. Countess, I'm so sorry that you must go to the trouble of a second trip, but I'll arrange for my wife to accompany you again. Of course, I, too, should really go. However...' Here, the Marquis, who was sensitive to appearances, faltered slightly. 'If I should go, you see, it might well make people wonder. So I'll stay here. I would like the whole trip to be accomplished in the greatest secrecy this time. As far as my wife's absence is concerned, we can let it be known that she's ill. And in the meantime here in Tokyo, let me look around and I'll hire the best craftsman available to make us a fine wig without anyone being the wiser. If a newspaper reporter should get wind of it, we'd have a pretty situation on our hands. But just you leave that question to me.'

46

Kiyoaki was surprised to see his mother once again getting ready for a trip. However, she refused to tell him either the destination or the purpose of her journey, saying only that he was not to mention it outside the house. He sensed that something alarming was afoot and that it had to do with Satoko, but with Yamada constantly at his side to keep an eye on him, there was no way he could find out any more.

When the Ayakuras and Marquise Matsugae arrived at Gesshu Temple, they were met with an appalling state of affairs. Satoko had already received the tonsure.

The circumstances that had led so rapidly to her renunciation of the world were as follows. When the Abbess had heard the entire story from Satoko that first morning, she had known at once that she must allow the girl to become a nun. Keenly aware that each of her predecessors at Gesshu had been an imperial princess, she felt bound to revere the Emperor above all else. And so she had come to the decision that she had to allow Satoko to enter even if this involved a temporary thwarting of the imperial will. She had concluded that, given the circumstances, there was no other way to discharge her loyalty to the Emperor. She had happened to uncover a plot directed at him, and she could not allow it to proceed unchecked. She was not one to countenance a breach of loyalty, no matter how elegant the cunning that disguised it.

Thus it was that the normally so discreet and gentle Abbess of Gesshu made up her mind, determined to give in neither to the force of authority nor the threat of coercion. Even if all the world should be ranged against her, even if she were forced to ignore a particular imperial decree, she would persist in what she had to do – to be a silent guard of the sacred person of His Majesty.

Her resolve had a profound effect on Satoko, who became all the more determined to turn her back on the world. She had not expected the Abbess to grant her request so readily. She had had an encounter with the Lord Buddha, and the Abbess, her eye as keen as a crane's, had immediately discerned the firmness of the girl's decision.

Although it was customary for a novice to undergo a year of ascetic discipline before her formal induction as a nun, both Satoko and the Abbess felt that in the present circumstances this period should be dispensed with. But the Abbess could not bring herself to disregard the Ayakuras so completely as to allow Satoko to take the tonsure before the Countess returned from Tokyo. Moreover, there was the matter of Kiyoaki. Would it not be wise, she thought, to allow him and Satoko to bid each other a long farewell before she sacrificed what hair she had spared so far?

Satoko could hardly endure the delay. She came to the Abbess every day and, like a child teasing her mother to give her candy, begged to be allowed to take the tonsure. Finally, the Abbess found herself prepared to yield.

'If I were to allow you to take the tonsure,' she asked Satoko, 'you would never be allowed to see Kiyoaki again. That wouldn't trouble you?'

'No.'

'Well, once you make the decision not to see him ever again in this world and so advance to initiation, any later regrets would indeed be bitter ones.'

'I will have no regrets. In this world I shall never set eyes on him again. As for parting, we've had farewells enough. So please...'

Her voice as she replied was clear and firm.

'Very well. Tomorrow morning, then, I will preside at the tonsure ceremony,' the Abbess replied, allowing one more day of grace.

Countess Ayakura did not return in the interval.

From that first morning at Gesshu, Satoko had plunged herself, of her own volition, into the disciplined routine of convent life. The distinctive character of Hosso Buddhism was in placing greater emphasis on the cultivation of the mind than the practice of religious austerities. Gesshu Temple, furthermore, was traditionally dedicated to praying for the welfare of the whole nation, and there were no households registered with it as parishioners. Sometimes the Abbess would observe with gentle humour that the 'Grace of tears' was something never encountered in Hosso Buddhism, thus underlining the contrast with the more recently arisen Amida cult of Pure Land Buddhism, with its great stress on ecstatic prayers of gratitude.

Then, too, in Mahayana Buddhism in general, there were no precepts to speak of. But for the rules of its monastic life the precepts of Hinayana Buddhism were often borrowed. In convents such as Gesshu, however, the rule was the 'Precepts of a Bodhisattva' contained in the *Brahamajala Sutra*. Its forty-eight prohibitions began with ten major injunctions against such sins as the taking of life, stealing, excess of any sort, and lying, and it concluded with an admonishment against destroying Buddhist teachings.

Far more severe than any commandment, however, was the monastic training. In the brief time she had been at Gesshu, Satoko had already memorized both the 'Sutra of the Enlightened Heart' and the 'Thirty Verses' expounding the doctrine of *Yuishiki*. Each morning she got up early to sweep and dust the main hall of worship before the Abbess came for her morning devotions, in the course of which she then had an opportunity to practise the chanting of the sutras. She was no longer treated as a guest, and the senior nun, whom the Abbess had placed in charge of her, was now a changed woman in her severity of manner.

On the morning of the initiation ceremony, she carefully performed the prescribed ablutions before putting on the black robes of a nun. In the hall of worship, she sat with her string of beads wrapped around her hands, which she held clasped together in front of her. After the Abbess herself had first taken the razor and begun the tonsuring, the old nun in charge of her took over. And as she shaved steadily with a skilled hand, the Abbess began to chant the 'Sutra of the Enlightened Heart', accompanied by the junior nun.

When she had consummated the works of perfection,
The Five Aggregates of living became as
Things void before the Bodhisattva Kannon's eyes,
And stricken from her was the yoke of human suffering.

Satoko, too, took up the chant, her eyes closed. And as she did so, her body became like a boat that is gradually lightened of all its cargo and freed of its anchor, and she felt herself being swept along on the deep swelling wave of chanting voices.

She kept her eyes shut. The main hall had the penetrating chill of an ice house and so, although she herself was floating free, she imagined a vast expanse of pure ice gripping all the world about her. Suddenly the cry of a shrike came from the garden outside, and a crack raced across this icy plane with the swiftness of a jagged streak of lightning. But it sealed itself almost at once, and the ice became whole once more.

She felt the razor working its way with scrupulous care across her scalp. Sometimes she imagined the frenetic gnawing of a mouse's tiny white incisors, sometimes the placid grinding of the molars of a horse or cow.

As lock after lock fell away, she felt her scalp begin to tingle with a refreshing coolness that was quite new to her. The razor was shearing off the black hair that had separated her from the world for so long, sultry and heavy with its sorry burden of desire; but her scalp was now being laid bare to a realm of purity whose chill freshness had not been violated by any man's hand. As the expanse of shaved head broadened, she began to feel the skin coming more and more alive, just as if a cool solution of menthol was spreading over it.

She imagined that the chill must be like the surface of the moon, directly exposed to the vastness of the universe. The world she had known was falling away with each strand. And as it did so, she became infinitely removed from it.

In one sense, it seemed as though her hair were being harvested. Shorn black clumps, still saturated with the stifling brilliance of the summer sun, piled up on the floor around her. But it was a worthless crop, for the very instant that the luxuriant black handfuls ceased to be hers, the beauty of life went out of them, leaving only an ugly remnant. Something that had once been an important part of her, an aesthetic element of her innermost being, was now being relentlessly thrown aside. As irrevocably as the amputation of a limb, the ties that bound her to the world of transience were being severed.

When her scalp at last shone with a bluish glint, the Abbess addressed her gently.

'The most crucial renunciation is the one that comes after formal renunciation. I have the utmost trust in your present resolution. From this day on, if you seek constantly to purify your heart in the austerities of our life, I have no doubt that one day you will become the glory of our sisterhood.'

This was how Satoko's premature tonsuring came about. Neither Countess Ayakura nor Marquise Matsugae, however, was prepared to give up, no matter how shattered they were by Satoko's transformation. After all, there remained the wig, a potent weapon still held in reserve.

47

Count Ayakura alone among the three visitors maintained an appearance of affability from first to last. He engaged the Abbess and Satoko in casual, unhurried conversation about the world in general, and at no time gave the slightest hint that he might want Satoko to change her mind.

A telegram arrived every day from Marquis Matsugae demanding a report on the situation to date. Finally the Countess broke down and wept as she pleaded with her daughter, but this gained her nothing, and so on the third day after their arrival, the Countess and the Marquise left for Tokyo, putting all their trust in the Count, who remained at Gesshu. The strain had worked such ravages in the Countess that she took to her bed as soon as she returned home.

As for the Count, he spent a week at Gesshu doing nothing at all. He was afraid to return to Tokyo. Since he had made no attempt whatever to persuade Satoko to return to secular life, the Abbess relaxed her guard and gave him and his daughter the chance to be alone together. The senior nun, however, kept a casual eye on them from a distance.

The two of them sat facing each other in silence on a veranda that caught some share of the winter sunshine. Beyond the dry tree branches, some scattered clouds reemphasized the blue of the sky. A flycatcher called timidly from a crape myrtle. They had been sitting without a word for a long time. Finally Count Ayakura spoke, with a hint of an ingratiating smile.

'I won't be able to mix much in society from now on, because of you.'

'Be kind enough to forgive me,' Satoko answered calmly, without a trace of emotion.

'My, you have all sorts of birds in this garden, haven't you?' he said after a few moments.

'Yes, we have all sorts.'

'I took a little stroll around this morning. By the time the persimmons here are ripe enough to fall, it looks as though the birds have already been at them. There seems to be no one to pick them up.'

'Yes, that's exactly what happens.'

'I should think we'll have some snow before too long,' he added, but there was no answer. And so the two of them sat in silence, gazing down at the garden.

The following morning Count Ayakura finally left Gesshu. And when he confronted Marquis Matsugae in Tokyo, having failed completely in his mission, he found that the Marquis was no longer angry.

It was already December 4, which left a mere week until the betrothal ceremony. The Marquis secretly summoned the superintendent-general of the metropolitan police to the Matsugae residence. His plan was to invoke the power of the police to effect Satoko's forcible removal from the convent.

The superintendent-general sent a confidential order to the Nara police. Since this was a matter of setting foot in a convent whose Abbess was traditionally an imperial princess, however, the Nara police were afraid of incurring the wrath of the Imperial Household Ministry. As long as the temple was receiving assistance from imperial funds – be it only a thousand yen a year – the slightest violation of its autonomy was unthinkable. The superintendent-general himself therefore went down to Nara in private, accompanied by a trusted subordinate in civilian clothes. The Abbess did not show the slightest sign of alarm when the senior nun handed her his card.

After spending an hour chatting with the Abbess over tea, he finally had to withdraw, yielding to the force of her massive dignity.

The Marquis had played the last card in his hand, and had come to the realization that there was nothing else to do but to request the Toinnomiyas to accept Satoko's withdrawal from the proposed marriage. In recent weeks, Prince Toin had sent an official to the Ayakuras several times, and was concerned over their strange behaviour.

The Marquis summoned the Count to his home and told him that they had no choice but to accept the situation. Then he outlined the strategy they were to follow. They would present the Toinnomiyas with a certificate signed by a reputable doctor testifying that Satoko had been stricken by a severe nervous breakdown. The shared responsibility of preserving this secret might unite the Toinnomiyas with the Ayakuras and Matsugaes in mutual trust, and this might soften the Prince's anger. As for the general public, all that need be done was to spread the rumour that the Toinnomiyas had released a curt, vaguely worded statement that the engagement was at an end and that Satoko had turned her back on the world and fled to a convent. As a result of this inversion of cause and effect, the Toinnomiyas, although obliged to some extent to play the villain, would nonetheless maintain face and prestige. And the Ayakuras, while incurring a measure of shame, would nevertheless benefit from public sympathy.

It would never do, however, to let things get out of hand. If that were to happen, altogether too much sympathy would accrue to the Ayakuras, and the Toinnomiyas, faced with the stirrings of unjustified hostility, would be compelled to clarify matters, and so have to make public Satoko's medical certificate. It was essential to present the story to the newspaper reporters without making too much cause and effect out of the Toinnomiyas' breaking of the engagement and Satoko's becoming a nun. They must be presented as separate events – but their chronological sequence would have to be reversed. The reporters themselves, however, would hardly be content with such an explanation. Should this be the case, a bare hint would be dropped to them that there was indeed a causal relationship but the families involved requested that they refrain from disclosing this.

As soon as he obtained Count Ayakura's agreement to this plan, the Marquis immediately put in a call to Dr Ozu, the director of the Ozu Mental Clinic, and requested that he come to the Matsugae residence at once to conduct an examination in the strictest secrecy. The clinic had an excellent reputation for protecting the privacy of its eminent patients when emergencies of this sort arose. Dr Ozu took a long time to arrive, however, and in the interval the Marquis was no longer able to hide his irritation from the Count, who was forced to wait for the doctor with him. But since it would have been improper in the circumstances to send a car from the Matsugae residence, the Marquis could do nothing but grit his teeth.

When the doctor arrived, he was brought to the small second-floor parlour of the Western-style house, where a fire was burning brightly in the fireplace. The Marquis introduced himself and the Count in turn and offered the doctor a cigar.

'And where would you like me to examine the patient?' asked Dr Ozu. The Marquis and the Count exchanged glances.

'Well,' the Marquis replied, 'the truth of the matter is that the patient isn't here at the moment.'

As soon as he learned that he was being asked then and there to sign a medical certificate for a patient he had never set eyes on, the doctor went red with anger. What particularly provoked him was the look that he was sure he had caught in the Marquis's eyes: a flicker of presumption that his signature would indeed be forthcoming.

'What's the meaning of this preposterous request?' he demanded. 'Do you by any chance take me for one of your society doctors who can be bought and paid for?'

'Believe me, Doctor,' the Marquis replied, 'we have by no means mistaken you for a gentleman of that sort.' He took his cigar out of his mouth and began to pace the room. Then, gazing across at the doctor and noting how his plump, healthy ruddy cheeks were quivering in the firelight, he addressed him in a deep, solemn tone: 'As for this medical certificate, it is something that is essential to the continued tranquillity of His Sacred Majesty.'

When the Marquis had the signed certificate in his hand, he at once requested a meeting with Prince Toin at his earliest convenience, and went next night to the Prince's residence.

Fortunately enough, the young prince was away again on regimental manoeuvres. Since the Marquis had specifically requested an audience with Prince Haruhisa, the Princess was not at her husband's side when he greeted the Marquis.

Prince Toin seemed to be in a jovial mood as he urged a fine French wine on his guest and spoke of this and that, not forgetting to declare once again how fine the entertainment had been at the blossom festival the previous spring. Quite some time had passed since the two had had a chance to talk together like this, and the Marquis again recalled the experiences they had shared during the Paris Olympics of 1900 and went on to entertain the Prince with a variety of anecdotes about their well-remembered cabaret at the champagne fountain. It seemed as if neither had a care in the world.

Nevertheless the Marquis was well aware that beneath the Prince's dignified and unruffled composure, he was in fact waiting with anxiety and misgiving to hear what he had to tell him. The Prince had not said a word about the betrothal ceremony, now only a few days distant. Like sunlight falling on a sparse grove of trees, the lamplight on the handsome grey moustache revealed a fleeting expression of uneasiness which from time to time contorted the mouth beneath.

'Well now, as regards my intruding on you here tonight...' the Marquis said, broaching the crucial topic in a deliberately frivolous tone, as agile as a bird that darts straight to its nest after flying around for a time with careless ease. 'I have the unpleasant task of imparting some unfortunate news that is not at all easy to express. Ayakura's daughter has gone out of her mind.'

'What?' The Prince's eyes opened wide with shock.

'Ayakura, being the sort of fellow he is, kept it completely hidden. Without even consulting me, he put Satoko into a convent, hoping to avoid a scandal, and yet up until now he hasn't been able to summon enough courage to inform Your Highness of what has happened.'

'Why, this is incredible! Waiting until now!'

The Prince pressed his lips firmly together, and the edges of his moustache dipped downward. He stared for some moments at the pointed toes of his shoes glinting in the light cast by the fireplace.

'This is a medical certificate signed by Dr Ozu. Indeed, as you see, it's dated a month ago, but Ayakura didn't show it to me. All this is due to my failure to keep a sharp eye on everything, and there is no way for me adequately to express my sorrow...'

'If she's ill, she's ill. It can't be helped. But why didn't he tell me about it earlier? And so that's what the trip to the Kansai was about! Now that you mention it, when they were here to pay their respects before leaving, her colour wasn't good at all, and Princess Toin was concerned about it.'

'Her mind hasn't been right since last September, and she's been doing all sorts of odd things, they say, until finally her behaviour was brought to my attention.'

'Well, that's how the situation stands; nothing can be done about it,' said the Prince. 'I'll go to the palace early tomorrow to express my apologies to the Emperor. I wonder how His Majesty will take it? You'll let me take this certificate, then, won't you? I'll have to show it to him.'

Prince Toin's exquisite breeding was evident in that he said not one word about young Prince Harunori. As for the Marquis, he kept his shrewd eyes fixed throughout the interview on each shift of expression in the Prince's face. In it, he had seen dark threatening waves rise and fall and rise again. And after he had watched the process for some time, he felt his own anxiety receding. The moment of greatest danger had passed.

The Prince summoned his wife, and after the three of them had gone well into the night discussing the best plan to follow, Marquis Matsugae finally took his leave.

The following morning, Prince Harunori happened to return from manoeuvres just at the awkward moment when his father was about to leave for the Imperial Palace. Prince Toin took his son aside and broke the news to him. There was no trace of emotion on his young, sturdy face as he replied that he would behave entirely according to his father's wishes in the matter. And so, far from being resentful, the young man showed no signs even of being perturbed at the course of events.

Since he was tired after the all-night manoeuvres, he went to bed as soon as he had seen his father off. His mother, however, feeling sure that he would be unable to sleep after such news, came to his room.

As he raised his eyes to her, she noticed that they were slightly bloodshot from lack of sleep, but his look was as direct and unflinching as ever.

'So it was just last night,' he said to her, 'that Marquis Matsugae came to tell us about it.'

'Yes, just last night.'

'You know, Mother, I just happened to think of something that took place a long time ago, when I was a lieutenant at the palace. I told you about it then, didn't I? Anyway, I was going for an audience with the Emperor and I happened to run into Marshal Yamagata in the corridor. I'll never forget it, Mother. It was the corridor that ran along the side of the front reception room. The Marshal was just coming from an audience, I think. As usual, he was wearing that uniform overcoat with the wide lapels, the peak of his cap was down over his eyes, and his hands were sticking in his pockets as if he didn't give a damn about anybody. He was coming toward me down that dark corridor with his sword almost dragging at his side. I instantly stepped aside, stood to attention and saluted him. He glanced at me quickly from under the peak of his cap with those eyes that never smiled. Surely, Mother, Marshal Yamagata must have known who I was. But he turned his head away abruptly, looking annoyed, threw back his shoulders inside that overcoat at the same time, and swaggered away down the corridor without so much as returning my salute. Now why, Mother, do you suppose I happened to remember that just now?'

An article in next day's paper informed the general public that they were going to be deprived of the festivities they had been anticipating with such pleasure. There would be no betrothal ceremony. The engagement had been dissolved 'because of circumstances in the family of His Imperial Majesty Prince Harunori'. And so it came about that Kiyoaki, who had been told nothing at all about recent events, finally learned what had happened from a newspaper.

48

After the broken engagement became known, the family watched over Kiyoaki even more closely, and the steward Yamada accompanied him even to school. His classmates, having no inkling of the circumstances, did not know what to make of such solicitude, ordinarily shown only to the youngest of the grade-school boys. Furthermore, his father and mother no longer uttered a word about the affair in his presence, and everyone else in the household behaved in front of him as though nothing had happened.

Society, however, was agog. Kiyoaki was surprised to find that even the sons of the most prestigious families at Peers were so much in the dark over this event that some of them asked him, of all people, what he thought of the affair.

'Everybody's so sympathetic toward the Ayakuras, but do you know what I think?' one student demanded. 'I think that this is going to undermine people's reverence for the Imperial Family. Isn't everybody saying that they found out later that this Miss Ayakura wasn't quite right in her mind? But I want to know why this only came out right now.'

While Kiyoaki was wondering how best to answer, Honda, who was standing beside him, stepped into the breach.

'Even if someone is sick, there's no way of knowing until the symptoms appear, is there? Why don't you stop gossiping like a schoolgirl?'

But this kind of appeal to masculinity was ineffective at Peers. To begin with, Honda's family did not have the status to qualify him as a person in the know, who could provide a plausible ending to this sort of exchange. In order to qualify as a person in the know, one had to be able to say something like: 'She happens to be my cousin,' or perhaps, 'He is the son of my uncle's mistress.' A boy such as this had to show that he was proud to have faint blood ties to crime and scandal, and yet at the same time parade his own noble aloofness intact. And so with a slight curl to his lip, he would drop enough of a hint to indicate that, unlike the rumourmongering rabble, he had access to behind-the-scenes information. At this school, mere boys of fifteen or sixteen were apt to put on airs and say: 'It's given the Home Minister quite a headache, you know. He called up last night to talk to Father about it'; or again: 'Everyone thinks that the Home Minister is laid up with a cold, but the truth is that he was in such a hurry to get to an imperial audience that he missed the step getting out of his carriage and sprained his ankle.'

Strangely enough, Kiyoaki's habitual secretiveness seemed to have worked to his advantage in this business. For other than Honda, none of his classmates had any idea of his relations with Satoko, nor was anyone aware of Marquis Matsugae's role in the matter. There was, however, a son of the ancient court nobility who was related to the Ayakuras and vehemently insisted that someone as beautiful and gifted as Satoko could not possibly have gone mad; but all he provoked were scornful smiles from his classmates, who thought him simply anxious to defend his own kind.

All of this caused Kiyoaki constant pain. In comparison with Satoko's public humiliation, however, he did not even have a slighting remark to contend with. And however acute his private agony, it was, after all, the torment of a coward.

Whenever this business came up with his classmates or he heard Satoko's name on their lips, he would look out of the window of the second-floor classroom as though absorbed in the view of the distant mountains, now wholly in the grip of winter, their snow-covered slopes sparkling in the clear morning air. He would imagine Satoko herself, now remote and unapproachable, presenting a similar purity to the world at large, without a word in her own defence. The brightness, distant yet almost painful, was visible to Kiyoaki alone. Its flawlessness struck him to the heart. By accepting everything – sin, shame, the imputation of madness – she had absolved herself. But what of him?

There were times when he wanted to shout out his guilt at the top of his voice. But then her terrible self-sacrifice would be in vain. Would it really be an act of courage to nullify that for the sake of quieting his conscience? Or did true courage demand rather that he silently endure his present existence as a virtual prisoner? It was too complex an evaluation for him. But at any rate, to continue as he was, despite the worsening pain, in other words to submit to the will of his parents and the whole household, was to persist in a course of action that was becoming more and more difficult.

There had been a time when idleness and melancholy seemed to be the intrinsic elements of life as he wanted it to be. How had he happened to lose his capacity for such enjoyment, his ability to luxuriate in it without ever getting bored? It was gone, as unnoticed as an umbrella forgotten at someone's house.

Now he needed something to hope for if he was to endure idleness and melancholy. And since there was nothing even remotely encouraging about this situation, he began to construct a hope of his own.

'The rumour about her insanity is too incredible even to bother discussing,' he thought. 'I just don't believe it. So why couldn't it be true that her running away from the world and becoming a nun is only a trick? Maybe she staged this daring comedy just to gain time and get out of that marriage – for my sake, in other words. If it's true, then we must unite to keep perfect silence, even though such a distance separates us. That accounts for her not even writing me so much as a note. It's obvious! What else could her silence mean?'

If Kiyoaki had truly understood her character, he would have known immediately that his fiction was an impossibility. After all, wasn't the image of a domineering Satoko no more than an illusion he had created out of his own timidity? If so, then she was perhaps no more substantial than a flake of snow that had melted in his arms. His eyes had been fixed on one single aspect of the truth. So much so, that now he almost believed in the eternal validity of the pretence in whose shadow this truth had found a precarious existence. Thus his hope made him a prey to self-deception.

It was a hope tinged with baseness. For if he had really surrendered to the vision of her beauty, he could not have left any room for hope. Without his noticing it, his coldly glittering heart had begun to melt with pity and tenderness, like ice under the rays of the setting sun. He felt the urge to be gentle with people. And he began to take a closer look at the world about him.

There was a student at Peers, the son of a marquis whose family lineage was extremely ancient, who had been nicknamed 'the Monster'. Rumour had it that he was a leper, but since it was unthinkable that a leper would be allowed to attend classes, it could only be that he had some other disease, which was not contagious. Half his hair had fallen out. His complexion was ashen and his skin lacklustre. His back was hunched. No one knew what his eyes were like because he kept them well covered with the peak of his school cap which he had special permission to wear even in the classroom. He snivelled constantly, and made a noise like water at a low boil. As he never talked to anyone, he would take a book during recess and walk to the far edge of the lawn in front of the school before he sat down to read it.

Kiyoaki too, of course, had never had anything at all to do with this student, who, besides everything else, was in a different course. Even though their fathers were nobles of the same rank, Kiyoaki seemed to embody beauty more than any other boy in the school, whereas the other was like the chosen emissary of ugliness and sinister shadow.

Although the dry grass in the corner of the lawn that was the Monster's chosen spot caught more than its fair share of sun on this particular early winter day, everyone else avoided it. When Kiyoaki came up and sat down beside him, he shut his book and went tense as he prepared to flee, as he always did. Only the muffled sound of his snivelling, like the steady dragging of a light chain, broke the silence.

'What's that you're always reading?' asked the Marquis's son who was beautiful.

'Nothing...' replied the Marquis's son who was ugly. He thrust the book behind him, but not before Kiyoaki's eye caught the name Leopardi printed on the spine. The gilt lettering cast a faint reflection that flashed over the dry grass and was gone.

Since the Monster was not disposed to talk, Kiyoaki edged away from him without getting up, then stretched out his legs and lay on his side, supporting himself on one elbow and ignoring the numerous blades of dry grass now clinging to his woollen uniform. Still directly opposite him, the Monster sat huddled in obvious distress, shutting the book that he had once more spread out in front of him. Kiyoaki felt that he was looking at a caricature of his own misery, and his gentleness began to give way to indignation. As the unseasonably warm sun continued its prodigality regardless, Kiyoaki saw the ugly figure of the Marquis's son begin to undergo a gradual transformation. His crumpled legs cautiously stretched out as he lay down on the grass and propped himself on his elbow opposite Kiyoaki. His form became Kiyoaki's own, down to the very angle of the head and the set of the shoulders. They had become as like as a pair of lion-dogs guarding a temple gate. Beneath the lowered brim of his cap, the other's lips, though not exactly smiling, at least gave a hint that their owner was in a cheerful mood.

And so the two Marquis's sons, one ugly, one beautiful, made a pair. The Monster had handled Kiyoaki's whim of pity and solicitude by showing neither gratitude nor resentment but by calling on his profound self-awareness, the mirror-image of Kiyoaki's own, and by so doing, he had acquired a form that was somehow a match for Kiyoaki's. If one disregarded their faces, the two of them presented a remarkable symmetry there on the warm, dry grass, from the braid that trimmed their jackets to the cuffs of their trousers.

Kiyoaki's attempt to penetrate the other's reserve could hardly have been rebuffed more completely, yet with greater gentleness. He felt enveloped in the warmth and kindness that had accompanied it.

From the nearby archery range came the twang of a bowstring – a sound that made him think of the cold bite of the winter wind – followed by the dull thud of the arrow striking home as if the target were a slack-tuned drum.

His own heart seemed to him to be much like an arrow stripped of the flashing white feathers that gave it direction.

49

When school ended for the winter vacation, the studious among Kiyoaki's classmates devoted themselves to studying for the pre-graduation exams, but the mere prospect of opening a book filled him with horror. No more than a third of his class, including Honda, intended to go on after the spring graduation to sit for the university entrance exams that were held in the summer. Most of them intended to use their privilege as graduates of Peers to receive dispensation from the entrance examinations and either apply to those departments of Tokyo Imperial University that were always under-subscribed, or perhaps enter one of the other imperial universities, such as Kyoto or Tohoku. Kiyoaki too, regardless of what his father might think, would probably follow the line of least resistance. If he entered Kyoto University, he would be that much closer to Satoko's convent.

For the present, therefore, he was free to drift in privileged idleness. There were two heavy snowfalls in December, but he was in no mood to feel boyish glee at the sight of the snowcovered grounds that greeted him one morning. He pushed aside the curtain of the window beside his bed and looked out with indifference at the winter scene, the island now a patch of brilliant white in the middle of the pond. He did not stir from his bed for hours. At other times an idea would strike him and his eyes would flash at the prospect of getting back at Yamada, who supervised him even while he was walking around the estate. He chose a night when a particularly gusty north wind was raging, and went for a brisk climb up the maple hill. Yamada, flashlight in hand and neck buried in the collar of his overcoat, had to come striding after him despite his feebleness. The creaking of the branches, the crying of the owl, the treacherous footing underneath – everything filled him with delight as he felt himself moving onward and upward as irresistibly as a devouring flame. With each step he imagined himself crushing the darkness beneath his heel as if it were something soft and alive. At the crest of the hill, the brilliant, star-filled winter sky was spread wide.

Just before the year's end, a gentleman came to the Matsugae residence to call the Marquis's attention to a newspaper article written by Iinuma. The Marquis was enraged at this evidence of his disloyalty to the family.

The paper had a small circulation and was the organ of a right-wing group. The Marquis protested that it was the kind of muckraking sheet whose practice was to extort money from those in high society under the threat of exposing some scandal or another. It would have been quite something else if Iinuma had degraded himself to the extent of coming to ask for money before publishing the article. But to go ahead and write such a thing without even attempting this was nothing less than an open and provocative breach of his obligations.

Under a heading with a decidedly patriotic flavour, 'A Disloyal and Unfilial Marquis', the burden of the indictment was as follows: the man intimately involved behind the scenes in the present affair of the broken engagement was, in fact,

Marquis Matsugae. Any marriage involving a member of the Imperial Family had to be subjected to close scrutiny in accordance with the provisions of the Imperial Household Code because such a marriage, no matter how remote the possibility, might affect the imperial succession. These then were the grave circumstances under which Marquis Matsugae had taken it upon himself to sponsor the daughter of an ancient family, a girl whose mental instability he claimed to have been unaware of at the time, going so far as to obtain an imperial sanction for her marriage, only to have his plans fall through, almost on the eve of the betrothal ceremony. Despite all this, however, simply by being lucky enough to have succeeded in keeping his name out of the affair, Marquis Matsugae today was going tranquilly about his business, thus displaying not only a brazen disloyalty to His Majesty the Emperor, but also a lack of reverence toward his own father, one of the pillars of the Meiji Restoration.

If the article provoked the Marquis to fury, it aroused misgivings in his son. He noticed at once that Iinuma had made a point of appending his name and address to it and also that, although he was fully aware of what had happened between Kiyoaki and Satoko, he had written as though he really believed Satoko had had a nervous breakdown. Up to then, Kiyoaki had had no idea where he was living. And now the thought struck him that Iinuma had written this in the knowledge that he would incur the stigma of someone dead to all sense of obligation, because he had wanted Kiyoaki to read it at all costs and know where he was, without seeming to inform him directly. At any rate, he was sure that the article contained a hidden message that was aimed at him alone: Don't be like your father.

All at once, he felt a rush of nostalgia at the thought of Iinuma. To have his awkward devotion once more, to mock it playfully – he could think of nothing that would cheer him more in his present mood. However, to try to see him now while his father's anger was at its peak, would be to court further reprisals, and his sense of nostalgia was not strong enough to make him want to run that risk.

On the other hand, he knew that arranging a meeting with Tadeshina would be far less dangerous. Ever since the old woman's thwarted suicide, however, he could only think of her with indescribable disgust. To judge by her having betrayed him to his father in her farewell letter, he was convinced that some twist of character made her derive a peculiar pleasure from betraying all those without exception whom she had brought together. He had come to realize that she was like those people who would tend their gardens scrupulously just for the pleasure of tearing up their flowers once they had bloomed.

His father almost never spoke to him. And his mother, not wishing to cross her husband, tried her best to leave her son alone.

The reality at the heart of his father's anger was worry and fear. He hired a private policeman to stand guard at the front gate, and had two more posted at the rear. The old year ended, however, with neither private threat nor the rise of public antagonism to confront the Matsugaes. Iinuma's disclosure had apparently failed to set off any repercussions in official circles.

It was customary for the two foreign families who rented from the Matsugaes to send over invitations for Christmas Eve. But since to gratify one family would be to disappoint the other, the Marquis made it a practice to accept neither invitation, but rather to send over presents for each family's children. This year, however, feeling that he might find something to divert him in the holiday mood of a foreign household, Kiyoaki asked his mother if she would intercede with his father to let him go. But the Marquis would not hear of it.

The reason he gave was not the usual one of being unwilling to disappoint one family or the other. Instead he said that it was beneath the dignity of the son of the nobility to accept an invitation from a tenant family. One of the implications in this was clear enough to Kiyoaki: his father still had little faith in his son's ability to maintain his dignity.

The Matsugae household was in a flurry of activity during the last days of the year, as the traditional massive housecleaning that preceded the New Year's holidays could not be completed in a single day. Kiyoaki had nothing to do. The feeling that the year was ending was a knife in his heart – this year above all years – for it would never come again. In these last, waning days, he had come to realize that this year had seen the peak of his life.

He left the house and all its bustle behind him and walked alone toward the pond, in the mood to go rowing. Yamada came hurrying after him with an offer of company that was harshly rebuffed.

As the prow of the boat pushed through dry reeds and broken remains of lotus leaves, a small flock of wild ducks took to the air. In the midst of their frantic flapping, he saw their small, flat bellies flash for a second in the clear winter air with not a drop of water to mar the silken sheen of their feathers. A reflected gleam raced crookedly across the tangled reeds.

He looked down at the cold image of clouds and blue sky reflected in the surface of the water, and wondered at the sluggish ripples stirred by his oars. As the reflection broke up, the dark, muddy water seemed to be telling him something quite alien to the crystalline clouds and winter sky.

He rested his oars and looked toward the main reception room of the house, watching the servants busy at work as if they were actors scurrying about on a distant stage. The waterfall had not frozen, but its sound was muffled and discordant. His view of its lower reaches was blocked by the island, but farther up, on the north side of the maple hill, the bare tree branches revealed the dirty remnants of snow on the banks of the stream.

He finally steered his boat into the tiny island inlet, fastened it to a stake, and made his way up to the faded green pines that crowned the knoll. As he looked at the three metal cranes, the beaks of the two that had outstretched necks seemed like a pair of blunt arrowheads aimed at the December sky.

He threw himself down at once on the dry brown grass warmed by the heat of the sun, and lay there, face up, knowing that he was completely alone, secure from every eye. Then as he sensed the numb chill that came from rowing in the fingers that cradled his head, he was suddenly overwhelmed by a wild rush of misery that he had been able to fend off while he was in the presence of other people.

'This year was mine – and now it's gone,' he cried out to himself. 'It's gone!

Just like a cloud dissolving.' The words poured out of him, cruel and unrestrained, lashing him, intensifying his agony. Never before had he given way to such wildness. 'Everything has turned sour, I'll never be carried away with joy again. There's a terrible clarity dominating everything. As though the world were made of crystal so that you only have to flick part of it with your fingernail for a tiny shudder to run through it all ... And then the loneliness – it's something that burns. Like hot thick soup you can't bear inside your mouth unless you blow on it again and again. And there it is, always in front of me. In its heavy white bowl of thick china, dirty and dull as an old pillow. Who is it that keeps forcing it on me?

'I've been left all alone. I'm burning with desire. I hate what's happened to me. I'm lost and I don't know where I'm going. What my heart wants it can't have ... my little private joys, rationalizations, self-deceptions – all gone! All I have left is a flame of longing for times gone by, for what I've lost. Growing old for nothing. I'm left with a terrible emptiness. What can life offer me but bitterness? Alone in my room ... alone all through the nights ... cut off from the world and from everyone in it by my own despair. And if I cry out, who is there to hear me? And all the while my public self is as graceful as ever. A hollow nobility – that's what's left of me.'

A huge flock of crows was perched in the bare branches of the maples on the hill. He listened to their discordant shrieks and to the beating of wings as they flew overhead toward the low hill where Omiyasama was enshrined.

50

Early in the new year it was customary for the Imperial Poetry Recitation to be held at the palace. Ever since Kiyoaki was fifteen, Count Ayakura had sent him an invitation each year without fail, a kind of abiding token of the training in elegance he had once received from the Count. And this year too, though one would hardly have been surprised if it had been otherwise, an invitation came as usual through the Imperial Household Ministry. The Count was going to assume his role as an imperial lector once again, unhindered by any shameful scruples, and it was clearly he who had arranged Kiyoaki's invitation.

When he showed his father the invitation, the Marquis frowned at the sight of the Count's signature among those of the four lectors. He was seeing elegance in a new light: it confronted him with tenacity and impudence.

'Since it's a regular event, you'd better go,' he said at last. 'If you didn't this year, it might start people talking about some rift between the Ayakuras and us. In essence, we are not supposed to have any connection with them where that affair is concerned.'

Year by year the poetry ceremony had grown on Kiyoaki, and he had come to appreciate it greatly. At no other time did the dignity of Count Ayakura's bearing show to such advantage as it did on these occasions, nor could Kiyoaki imagine any role more suited to him. Now of course, the sight of the Count would be a painful one, but even so he felt that he wanted to see him. He felt the desire to take a steady look at the shattered fragments of a poem that had once been alive inside him too, until he had grown weary of looking. He thought that if he attended, the image of Satoko would fill his mind.

He no longer believed himself to be a thorn of elegance jabbed into the sturdy fingers of the Matsugaes. But he had not changed to the point of thinking that he actually was one of those fingers either. Only the elegance that had been so conscious a part of him had withered. His heart had become desolate. Nowhere in himself could he find the kind of graceful sorrow that inspires poems. He was empty now, his soul a desert swept by parching winds. He had never felt more estranged from elegance and from beauty as well.

Yet perhaps all this was essential to his attaining true beauty – this inner emptiness, this loss of all joy, even this utter inability to believe that the oppressive weight of each moment was something real, that his pain, at least, was something that was his. The symptoms of a man afflicted by true beauty are much like those of leprosy.

Since he no longer looked in the mirror, he had no way of knowing that the sad and haggard cast of his features had evolved into the classical expression of youth pining away for love.

One evening when he was eating dinner at a table laid for him alone, the maid set down a small wineglass beside his plate, with cut-glass sides that were darkened by the crimson liquid they contained. Without bothering to ask the girl, he presumed it to be wine and drained the glass without hesitation. But then a strange sensation, a thick, slippery aftertaste lingered on his tongue.

'What was this?'

'The blood of a snapping turtle, sir,' the maid answered. 'I was ordered not to tell you unless you asked what it was. It was the cook, sir. He said that he wanted to make the young master fit and healthy again. So he caught a turtle from the pond and prepared it for you.'

As he felt the unpleasantly smooth liquid sliding down his throat, he remembered the story the servants had so often used to frighten him when he was a child. Once again he saw the disturbing picture he had formed at that time of a snapping turtle raising its head like a sinister ghost from the dark waters of the pond, its eyes fixed on him, a creature that usually lay buried in the warm mud on the bottom, but never failed to force its way up to the surface time and again, pushing through the hostile weeds of dreams that conquered time, to fix its eyes on him at every stage of his life. But now, suddenly, the spell was broken. Death had overtaken the turtle, and he had just drunk its blood without knowing it. And with that, a whole era seemed suddenly at an end. Inside him, the terror was being docilely transformed into this unfamiliar energy that was coursing through him with a force whose intensity he could only guess.

The order of procedure each year at the Imperial Poetry Recitation was to read the selections according to the status of the writer, beginning with poems written by those of lower rank. With these first poems, the lector began by reading the poet's brief words of introduction, and then gave his office and rank. With the later poems, however, the lector first gave office and rank and then immediately began to recite the poem itself.

Among those who functioned as imperial lectors, Count Ayakura held the honoured position of chief. Once more today both their Imperial Majesties and His Imperial Highness the Crown Prince graced him with their attention as the clear tones and beautifully modulated voice sounded through the chamber.

No tremor of guilt blurred its clarity. On the contrary, it was so brilliant as to stir sadness in the hearts of his audience. As he read each poem, the languid cadence of his words kept the pace of a Shinto priest's gleaming black-shod feet climbing, one by one, the stone steps of a shrine bathed in the strange warmth of the winter sun. It was a voice whose tone was neither masculine nor feminine.

Not a single cough marred the silence of the audience. But although his voice was supreme in the palace chamber, it was never sensual, nor called attention to itself at the expense of the poem itself. What poured smoothly from his throat was the very essence of elegance, impervious to shame, and its paradoxical blend of joy and pathos flowed through the room like the rolling mist in a picture scroll.

Up to now, each of the poems had been repeated only once, but when the Count concluded the Crown Prince's poem with the formula, 'Such being the most eminent composition of His Majesty the Heir to the Imperial Throne', he went on to recite it twice more.

The Empress's poem was recited three times. The Count read the first verse, and then from the second verse on, all four lectors recited it in unison. With the exception of the Emperor himself, the rest of the Imperial Family, including the Crown Prince, and of course everyone else in the audience, stood up to listen.

This year, Her Imperial Majesty had composed a poem of exceptional grace and nobility. As he stood listening to it, Kiyoaki stole a glance at Count Ayakura, who was standing some distance from him. He noticed how the paper bearing the poem rested folded in the Count's small, white hand, so like a woman's. The fine tissue was a light plum colour.

Although an affair that involved the Count and that had shaken the whole country was barely concluded, Kiyoaki was not surprised to hear no trace of a nervous quiver in his voice, much less the deep sorrow of a father whose only daughter has been lost to the world. The voice went on, clear, beautiful, never strident, performing exactly what had been entrusted to it. Let a thousand years go by, the Count would still be serving his Emperor as he served him now, like the rarest of songbirds.

The Imperial Poetry Recitation came to its climax at last. It was the moment for the reading of the poem of His Imperial Majesty himself.

Count Ayakura made his way reverently into the immediate vicinity of the Emperor and gravely took the imperial composition, which had been placed on the cover of an inkstone case in the traditional manner, and raised it to the level of his forehead. He then recited it five times.

As he read, the purity of his voice became, if anything, more pronounced, until he came at last to the end of the fifth recitation and concluded with the words 'Such being the most august composition of His Sacred Majesty'.

Kiyoaki, meantime, glanced up fearfully at the Emperor's face, his imagination quickened by the memory of the late Emperor's having patted him on the head when he was a boy. His Majesty seemed to be rather more frail than his imperial father had been, and although he was listening to the reading of his own composition, his face showed no sign of complacency, but retained an icy composure. Kiyoaki suddenly shook in fear at the totally improbable notion that His Imperial Majesty was in fact suppressing an anger that was directed at him.

'I've dared to betray His Majesty. There's nothing to do but to die.'

He held fast to that one thought as he stood there, the atmosphere around him heavy with the rich fragrance of incense, feeling as though he might collapse at any moment. A thrill ran through him, but whether of joy or dread he could not tell.

51

It was February. With the pre-graduation exams looming over them, all Kiyoaki's classmates were now wholly caught up in their work. And he, who was indifferent to anything of the sort, stood more aloof than ever. Honda was certainly willing to help him with the preparation for his tests, but he held back, feeling that Kiyoaki would have none of it. He knew only too well how Kiyoaki reserved his keenest displeasure for any excessive show of friendship.

One day, just at this time, the Marquis suddenly presented his son with the suggestion of entering Merton College, Oxford. His admission could be arranged with no great difficulty, especially since the Marquis was on good terms with the dean of this famous institution founded in the thirteenth century, but in order to qualify, Kiyoaki would at least have to get through the final exams at Peers. The Marquis had, in fact, been painfully aware that Kiyoaki was becoming more pale and haggard by the day, and he had finally devised this means of saving his son, who was to attain a court rank of at least fifth degree, junior grade, before long. Since the plan of salvation was so unexpected, Kiyoaki's interest was certainly aroused. He therefore decided that he would give every appearance of being delighted with his father's proposal for the present.

Prior to this, he had cherished a moderate sort of desire to see something of the West. But now that his whole existence was focused on a single object, a tiny, exquisitely beautiful part of Japan, he could look at the map of the world spread out before him, and be filled with a sense of crudity, not only by the vast array of foreign countries, but even by the red-painted image of his own, curving like a shrimp against the flank of Asia. His Japan was light green, a country without shape, full of a pathos, as pervasive as rising mist.

His father bought a huge new map and had it hung on the wall in the billiard room. His intention was obviously to arouse great thoughts in Kiyoaki. However, its flat, lifeless seas failed to excite him. What came to his mind instead was the memory of a night sea like a huge, black beast with a living warmth, a pulse of its own, and blood that cried out – the sea at Kamakura, whose awesome rumbling had tormented him to the limit of endurance on a summer night.

Though he had mentioned it to no one, he had recently been troubled with frequent headaches and dizzy spells. He slept less each night. As he lay in bed, he told himself that the next day would surely bring a letter from Satoko. She would set a time and place for them to meet so that they could run away together. He would find her in some small, unfamiliar town, perhaps on a corner in front of an old-fashioned storehouse converted into a bank. She would run up to him and he would take her in his arms and hold her as he had been longing to do. Over and over again, he visualized the scene down to its last detail. But the image he cherished in this way was formed in a mirror backed with thin, brittle foil that was easily torn away to reveal nothing but a dismal blankness. His tears soaked his pillow and he called her name again and again through the night in helpless frustration.

As he did so, there were moments when her image was suddenly there beside him, somewhere between dream and reality. His dreams ceased to tell stories objective enough to be recorded in his journal. Hope and despair, dream and reality, now came together to cancel each other out, the border between them as vague as the shoreline against which the rolling waves break without cease. There for an instant, on the surface of the water that lapped back over the smooth sand, he saw the reflection of her face. Never had she seemed more lovely nor more grief-stricken. And when he put his lips close to this face that glimmered like the evening star, it vanished.

A frantic desire to break out of his plight grew more intense every day. Although everything had one single message for him – be it every hour, every morning, every noon and night, or the sky, the trees, the clouds and wind all telling him to give her up – he was still tormented by uncertainty. He felt a desperate need to lay hands on one thing at least that was sure and certain, to hear no more than a single word from her own lips, if he could only know that it was true. And if a word was too much to ask, he would be satisfied with just a glimpse of her face. He could no longer endure his racking anxiety.

In the meantime, the storm of rumours had quickly subsided. People did not take long to forget even so unprecedented and inexplicable an affair as an engagement sanctioned by imperial decree being broken on the very eve of the betrothal ceremony, especially since a naval bribery scandal had recently come to light to attract their indignation.

He made up his mind to leave home. Since his parents were on their guard, however, they had stopped giving him any allowance, and so he didn't have so much as a sen of his own.

Honda was taken aback when Kiyoaki approached him for money. In accordance with his father's ideas, he had been given a bank account of his own, which he was free to manage as he saw fit. He now withdrew the entire amount and gave it to Kiyoaki without asking a single question about what he intended to do with it.

It was the morning of the twenty-first of February when Honda brought the money to school and handed it over to his friend. The sky was bright and clear, but the morning air was bitterly cold.

'You've about twenty minutes left before class,' said Kiyoaki after taking the money. His voice sounded a little timid. 'Won't you come along and see me off?'

'Where are you going?' asked the startled Honda. He knew that Yamada must be standing guard at the front gate.

'That way,' Kiyoaki answered, smiling and pointing toward the woods.

Honda was pleased to see his friend showing signs of energy for the first time in months, but no healthy glow had returned to his face. On the contrary, his gaunt features were pale and strained, making Honda think of a thin sheet of ice in early spring.

'Do you feel all right?'

'I think I have a cold. Otherwise I'm fine,' Kiyoaki replied, leading the way cheerfully along the path that ran through the woods.

It had been a long time since Honda had seen him walking so briskly. Moreover, he had a good idea where his steps were leading, but said nothing. They passed a marsh whose icy surface, laced with intricate designs of frozen driftwood, dully reflected the slanting rays of the morning sun. And then, leaving the wood and its chattering birds behind, they came to the eastern edge of the school property.

They were now at the top of a slope, across the bottom of which stretched a line of factories. Strands of barbed wire had been carelessly strung along here in place of a fence, and the neighbourhood children often slipped through the breaks into the campus. Beyond the wire, the grassy hill extended as far as the road, where a rough wooden fence had been put up over a low stone wall.

At this point the two of them came to a halt. Off to the right was a streetcar line. Directly below, the sun glinted from the jagged slate factory roofs as they caught the force of its morning rays. The motley collection of machines gathered under these roofs, already running at full throttle, set up a dull roar like the sea. The smokestacks stretched bleakly toward the sky. The smoke that poured from them left a shadow that crawled over the tops of the factories and shut out the sun from the washing that was hung out beside a row of hovels. But there were also some houses with makeshift shelves hung from the roof to display a number of bonsai. Here and there, one saw constant flashes of light. Once it was the reflection from a pair of pliers on the hip of an electrician climbing a pole. Another time it was the eerie glow of a flame seen through the windows of a chemical plant. In one factory, when the roar of machines ceased, there arose the sustained din of hammers beating on steel plating.

Far away, there was the clear sun. Below, skirting the school property, ran the road over which Kiyoaki was about to escape. The shadows of the small houses that lined it were etched upon its dusty white surface. A man was riding a dull, rusted bicycle past a group of children who were kicking a stone about.

'Well, I'll be seeing you,' said Kiyoaki.

These were clearly words of farewell. They were graven on Honda's mind: for once, Kiyoaki had come up with a cheerful expression typical of a young man.

Kiyoaki had even left his book bag in the classroom. All he had on was his uniform and his overcoat trimmed with two rows of brass buttons and the cherry-blossom insignia running down the front of it. He had stylishly spread the collar open, exposing the tight, navy-style collar of his jacket, together with the strip of white celluloid inside it, pressed against his young throat as he now smiled at Honda, his faced shadowed by the peak of his cap. Then still smiling, he turned and, bending apart some broken strands of wire with his gloved hands, climbed through the barrier.

His disappearance was immediately reported to his parents, who were thoroughly upset. Once again, however, it was his grandmother's decisiveness that restored order.

'Don't you see the way it is? He's happy about going to school in England. And since he intends to go, he wants to see Satoko first and say good-bye to her. But since you wouldn't have let him do it if he'd told you about it first, he's gone down there without telling you. Is there any other likely explanation?'

'But surely Satoko won't see him.'

'If that's what happens, he'll give up and come home. Kiyoaki's a young man. You've got to let him have his head until he gets this out of his system. It's because you tried to keep too close a rein on him that this sort of thing had to happen.'

'But Mother! After what's happened the precautions we took were only to be expected.'

'All right, and this was only to be expected too.'

'That's as may be, but it will be just terrible if this gets out. What I'll do is get in touch with the superintendent-general at once and have him start a search in absolute secrecy.'

'A search! Why a search? You already know where he's going.'

'But unless he's caught and brought back ...'

'You'll regret it!' the old woman shouted, her eyes burning with anger. 'He might do something really terrible this time. It's quite all right for safety's sake to have the police look into things quietly. If they let us know just where he is as soon as they find out, that will be useful. But since we know perfectly well where he's going and why, they're to keep their distance, and they must absolutely not let him suspect anything. Right now the boy is to be left completely free, and not to be interfered with. Everything must be done quietly. We must get through this without turning it into a big drama. That's what's essential. If there's any blunder now, the results could be disastrous. That's what I want you to understand.'

The night of February 21, Kiyoaki stayed at a hotel in Osaka. The next morning he paid his bill and took a Sakurai Line train to Obitoké, where he rented a room at a merchant's inn called the Kuzonoya. No sooner had he done this than he hired a rickshaw to go to Gesshu. He hurried the rickshaw man through the temple gate and up the slope that led to the Tang front entrance, where he got out. Confronted by a blank expanse of tightly shut sliding door, he called out. The convent janitor appeared, asked him his name and business, and then left him standing there. After a short wait, the next to appear was the senior nun. And she, without even allowing him to step up into the front hallway, rebuffed him by saying with thinly veiled displeasure that Her Reverence the Abbess would not see him and that furthermore it would be unthinkable for a novice to be permitted to do so. Since he had more or less expected this reception, he did not press the issue, but left then and there and returned to the inn.

He deferred his hopes to the next day, and when he thought over his initial failure in solitude, he concluded that it was due to his presumption in taking the rickshaw right up to the very entrance of the convent. He had been driven to it by his anxiety and haste, of course, but since seeing Satoko again was a kind of supplication, he decided that he should have got out at the gate and walked from there, whether the nuns took note of this show of devotion or not. He had better do some kind of penance.

His room at the inn was dirty, the food was tasteless, and the night cold. But the thought of Satoko now nearby gave him a feeling of deep contentment. That night, for the first time in months, he slept soundly.

The next day was the twenty-third; he felt more energetic and went to the convent twice – once in the morning and again in the afternoon – leaving the rickshaw at the gate and climbing the long sloping path as a pilgrim would. However, his reception was no warmer than the day before. On the ride back, he began to cough, and felt a slight pain deep inside his chest. He decided against using the hot bath at the inn.

His dinner that night proved to be of a quality wholly unexpected at a country inn of this sort. Furthermore, not only had everyone's behaviour toward him markedly improved but despite his protests, he had been moved into the best room the inn had to offer. When he demanded an explanation from the maid, she tried to put him off. Finally, however, when he became angry with her, the mystery was solved. She told him that while he had been out that day, a local policeman had come and questioned the innkeeper closely about him. The policeman then said that Kiyoaki was from an extremely exalted family. He was therefore to be treated with the utmost deference, but on no account was he to learn of the policeman's visit. Furthermore, should he move out of the inn, the police were to be informed immediately. Kiyoaki felt a rush of fear. He realized that he had no time to lose.

When he got up next morning, the twenty-fourth of February, he felt very much out of sorts. His head was stuffy and he was listless. Nevertheless, his mind was made up. If he was ever to see Satoko again, he had to commit all his strength to the penance he must undergo, whatever hardship it entailed. In this mood he set out from the inn, and, without hiring a rickshaw, started on the more than two miles to Gesshu. Fortunately it was a beautiful morning. The road itself, however, was none too easy. Moreover his cough grew worse as he walked, and he had a sensation in his chest like the settling of metallic dust. A severe fit of coughing overtook him at the very entrance to Gesshu. The expression on the face of the senior nun who met him remained unaltered as she refused his request in precisely the same terms.

The next day, the twenty-fifth, he began to have chills and fever. Although he realized that it was unwise to go out, he hired a rickshaw once more and went to the convent, only to be rebuffed just as before. His hope at last began to fail. Hindered by the fever that clouded his mind, he tried to evaluate the situation, but no feasible course of action occurred to him. Finally, he told the clerk at the inn to send a telegram: 'Please come at once. Am at the Kuzonoya in Obitoké on Sakurai Line. Not a word to my parents. Kiyoaki Matsugae.'

This done, he passed an uncomfortable night before waking groggily on the morning of the twenty-sixth.

52

It was a morning when light flakes of snow danced in the brisk wind that swept over the plain of Yamato. They seemed too fragile even for spring snow, but were rather more reminiscent of a swarm of summer insects. When the sky remained overcast, they disappeared against the clouds. Only when the sun shone through did one become aware of the powdery, swirling snow. The cold in the air was worse than it would have been on a day of heavy snow.

As he lay with his head on his pillow, he considered how he could prove his ultimate devotion to Satoko. The night before he had at last decided to appeal to Honda for help, and he was sure that his friend would come today without fail. With Honda to sustain him, perhaps he might be able to soften the Abbess's unyielding attitude. But before that there was one thing he had to do. He had to try it. All by himself, with no one's help, he had to demonstrate the purity of his devotion. On looking back, he realized that up to now he had not even once had the opportunity of proving this devotion to Satoko. Or perhaps, he thought, his cowardice had made him flee any such opportunity until now.

Today, there was only one thing for him to do. To go out, ill as he was, to risk worse illness, was a significantly great penance. Devotion so overwhelming might stir a response from Satoko, or then again it might not. Whatever the result, even if there were not the faintest hope of her being moved, he had now reached a state of mind where he would have no peace until he had done this thing, done it as a penance that he demanded of himself. He had begun his journey completely obsessed by a single thought: to have even a single glimpse of her face. In the meantime, however, his heart had formed another resolution of its own, that overrode his intentions and desires.

The only force to counter this wayward urge in his heart was his body itself. He was in the grip of an aching fever. A heavy gold thread had been strung through every part of it, embroidering his flesh with pain and heat. The strength had gone out of him. If he lifted his arm, the pale skin immediately turned blue and cold, and the arm itself became as heavy as a full bucket in a well. His cough seemed to come from deeper and deeper in his chest, like the constant rumble of distant thunder on a darkened horizon. His body balked at his demands, weak and enervated to the very fingertips under the assault of the burning fever that shot through him.

He called Satoko's name more and more desperately. The empty hours dragged by. This morning, for the first time, the servants at the inn realized that he was ill. They warmed his room and anxiously set about doing all they could to make him comfortable, but he stubbornly refused to allow them either to treat him themselves or call a doctor.

Finally in the afternoon, he told the maid to hire a rickshaw for him. She hesitated, and went to tell the innkeeper. When the man came up to his room and tried to persuade him to stay indoors, he struggled to his feet, got into his uniform and put on his overcoat without help, to put on a show of health. A rickshaw came. He set out in it, his legs wrapped in a blanket that the inn maids had thrust in after him. Despite its protection, however, he was attacked by the terrible force of the cold.

His eye was caught by the stray snowflakes swirling in through the openings left by the black canvas rickshaw cover. Suddenly the vivid memory of the ride through the snow with Satoko just a year before came to him, and his chest tightened with emotion and a grating pain.

He could no longer cower in the gloom inside the swaying rickshaw, doing nothing but trying to endure the pain in his head. He loosened the front flap of the bonnet and then pulled his muffler up over his mouth and nose and looked out at the passing scenery, his eyes watering with fever. He wanted to rid his mind of any image that would drive his thoughts back upon the pain that racked him.

The rickshaw had already passed out of the narrow lanes of Obitoké. Powdered snow fell on the fields and paddies to either side of the flat road that led directly to where Gesshu stood among the mountains shrouded in cloud. It fell on the rice shocks left in the paddies, on the withered mulberry leaves, on the blurred green of the pak-choi leaves that separated the rice and mulberry fields, on the rust-coloured reeds and bulrushes on the marshes. It kept falling noiselessly, but was not enough to cover the ground. Even the flakes that fell on his blanket vanished without leaving obvious drops of moisture.

He saw the flat white of the sky grow gradually brighter until a pale sun at last shone through the clouds. The falling snow blended into this new brightness more and more, until it was like a fine white ash floating in the air.

All along the road, the tall, dry grass swayed in the light wind, its feathery plumes having a faint glint of silver in the cold sunlight. Just beyond the fields, the foothills were shrouded in grey, but in the distance was a corner of clear blue sky and the snow-capped mountains were dazzling white.

As he gazed out at the scenery around him, his ears ringing with fever, he felt that he was really in touch with external reality for the first time in long months. The world around him was absolutely still. The swaying of the rickshaw and the heaviness of his eyelids may well have confused what he saw out there, but whatever the incidental distortion, this was a clear enough confirmation. And since he had been floundering about for so long in a chaotic darkness of sorrow and worry, the experience struck him with all the force of novelty. Wherever he looked, moreover, there was no sign of human life.

The rickshaw was already getting close to the thick growth of bamboo that covered the mountainside and surrounded Gesshu itself. Up ahead, towering over the bamboos, stood the pines that lined the road as it began its upward climb inside the gate. When he saw the austere stone gate posts at the end of the winding length of road that led out of the fields, he was convulsed by a spasm of poignant fear.

'If I go in through the gate in the rickshaw,' he told himself, 'and then the four hundred or so yards up to the front door – if I ride all the way, I have the feeling that they won't let me see Satoko today either. Maybe things have changed a little since last time. Maybe the old nun took my part with the Abbess, and now she's relented a bit. And then if they see that I've walked up through the snow, she might let me see Satoko, if only for a moment. But if I ride all the way, that could make a bad impression on them and provoke an instinctive reaction against me. Then the Abbess might decide never to let me see Satoko. All my efforts should bring about some change of heart in them. It's like a fan made with hundreds of thin, delicate slats held together by a single rivet. If I'm at all careless, the rivet will come loose, and the whole thing will fall apart. And then, if I rode all the way to the front door and wasn't able to see Satoko, I'd feel it was my fault. I'd tell myself it was because I was insincere. I'd know in my heart that if only I had got out of the rickshaw and walked, no matter how weak I felt, then such sincerity – even if she was unaware of it – would have affected her, and she would have seen me. That's it then. There's no reason to have such regrets. I have no other choice but to risk my life if I want to see her. To me, she's the essence of beauty. And it's only that which has brought me this far.'

He himself no longer knew whether his reasoning was ordered or wildly disturbed by fever.He told the rickshawman to stop at the gate. Then after getting out and telling him to wait there, he began to walk up the slope. The sun was coming through again, and the snowflakes danced in its pale rays. From the bamboo groves on either side of him he heard a chirping that sounded like a lark. Green moss grew on the trunks of the bare cherry trees that were scattered among the pines along the roadside. A single plum tree bloomed white in the midst of the bamboos.

Having come this way six times in the last five days, it would seem that there was nothing left to catch him unawares. But as he began to make his way upward from where he had left the rickshaw, with unsteady legs and stumbling feet, he looked around him and the world took on a mournful clarity in his fevered eyes. The scenery that had become familiar in recent days now had a strange novelty about it that was almost unnerving. And at every moment, sharp-pointed silver arrows of cold shot through his spine. The ferns along the road, the red-berried spearflowers, the pine needles rustling in the wind, the bamboos with their green trunks and yellowed leaves, the abundance of tall dry grass, the road itself, rutted and white with frost as it passed through the midst of it all – Kiyoaki's eyes followed everything until it finally merged into the black shadow that lay across the road ahead as it rose through a grove of cedars. Surrounded by unbroken silence and utter clarity was a world untouched by blemish of any kind. And at its centre, so inexpressibly poignant, at its innermost heart, he knew, was Satoko herself, her figure as quiet and still as an exquisite gold statue. But could such a still and perfect world, which eschewed all intimacy, really bear any relation to the familiar world he knew?

His breath grew harsh as he walked. Stopping to rest, he sat down on a large rock beside the road, only to be struck to the bone immediately by its intense chill, as though his layers of clothing could do nothing to hinder it. He coughed deeply, and as he did so, he saw that the handkerchief he held over his mouth was covered with rusty phlegm.

After his fit had gradually subsided, he looked up dizzily at the distant snow-covered mountain peaks that rose up beyond the sparse growth of trees. As his eyes were filled with tears from his coughing spell, his blurred vision seemed to heighten the sparkle of the snow. At that instant a memory of his thirteenth birthday came back to him. He was an imperial page once more, looking up at Princess Kasuga ahead of him as he held her train. The snowy peaks before his eyes today were the very image of the white that had dazzled him that day – the pure colour of the nape of her neck under the lustrous black of her hair. That had been the moment in his life when a divine female beauty had first moved him to adoration.

The sun disappeared once more. Gradually the snow came down more heavily. He took off his glove and caught some flakes in one hand. His palm was hot with fever, and they melted before his eyes as soon as they touched it. How well he had looked after his beautifully shaped hand, he reflected – it had never been dirtied, never known a blister. He had used it, but only in emotion.

Finally he got to his feet and started walking again, wondering whether he would be able to plod through the snow and reach the temple. By the time he had climbed as far as the cedar grove, the wind had grown much worse and its harsh whine throbbed in his ears. The cedars thinned to reveal a small pond, its chill surface a froth of ripples under the leaden winter sky. Once past the pond, the gloomy darkness of the thick old cedars closed in on him again, their branches deflecting the force of the pelting snow.

By now he had but one objective: to keep putting one foot in front of the other. All his recollections of the past had crumbled away. He now knew that the future would only reveal itself at this pace, foot by foot, yard by yard, as he painfully struggled forward.

He went through the black gate without realizing it, and when he looked up, he saw the Tang entrance itself in front of him. Snow clung to the row of chrysanthemum tiles that formed its eaves.

Collapsing in front of the sliding door, he broke into such a violent fit of coughing that there was no need to call out.

The senior nun opened the door and immediately began to rub his back to relieve his spasm. In a kind of trance, he had the indescribably blissful feeling that Satoko had come, that her hands were now caressing him.

The old nun did not refuse him at once today as she had before. Instead she left him there after a few moments and went back inside. He waited for a long time, feeling the minutes stretch out interminably. And as he waited, a mist seemed to cloud his sight. His pain, his joyful hope, both dissolved gradually into a single vague state of consciousness.

He heard women's voices in a flurry of conversation. Then silence again. More time passed. When the door slid open once more, the senior nun was alone.

'I'm sorry. Your request for a meeting cannot be granted. No matter how many times you come here, sir, I shall be forced to give you the same answer. I will arrange for a servant of the convent to accompany you, so please be kind enough to leave.'

Helped by the janitor, who was fortunately a strong man, he went back down the road to where his rickshaw was waiting.

53

Honda arrived at the inn in Obitoké late on the night of February 26. As soon as he saw how critical Kiyoaki's condition was, he was all for taking him back to Tokyo at once, but his friend would not hear of it. He discovered that the local doctor who had been summoned earlier in the evening had said that the symptoms indicated pneumonia.

Kiyoaki pleaded with him desperately. He wanted his friend to go to Gesshu next day, to talk to the Abbess, make every effort to soften her attitude. Since Honda was not involved, his words might perhaps have some effect on Her Reverence. And if she should relent, he wanted Honda to take him up to the temple.

Honda resisted for a time, but finally gave in, agreeing to delay their departure by one day. At all costs he would try to obtain an interview with the Abbess next day and do all he could on Kiyoaki's behalf. But he made his friend promise faithfully that if she should still refuse, he would go back to Tokyo with him immediately. Honda stayed up all that night, changing the wet dressings on Kiyoaki's chest. By the light of the dim lamp in the room, he saw that his skin, white as it was, now had a slight tinge of red from the dressings that covered it.

The final exams were only three days away. He had had every reason to expect his parents to be opposed to his making any trip at all right now. But when he had shown Kiyoaki's telegram to his father, surprisingly he had told him to go ahead, without asking any further details. And his mother had quite agreed. Justice Honda had once been ready to sacrifice his career for the sake of his old colleagues who were being forced to retire because the system of life tenure was being abolished. Now he intended to teach his son the value of friendship. During the train ride to Osaka, Honda had worked intently, and even now, as he held watch at Kiyoaki's bedside, he had his logic notebook open beside him.

In one circle of pale yellow light the lamp above them caught the ultimate symbols of two diametrically opposed worlds to which these young men had given themselves. One of them lay critically ill for the sake of love. The other was preparing himself for the grave demands of reality.

Kiyoaki, half asleep, was swimming in a chaotic sea of passion, seaweed clutching at his legs. Honda was dreaming of the world as a creation securely based on a foundation of order and reason. And so throughout a bitter night in early spring, in the room of an old country inn, these two young men's heads were close together under the light, one coolly rational, one burning with fever, each in turn finally bound by the rhythm of his own particular world.

In all their friendship, Honda had never been more aware than he was now of the utter impossibility of seeing into Kiyoaki's thoughts. He lay in front of him, but his spirit was off racing somewhere else. Sometimes he would deliriously call Satoko's name, and his cheeks would flood with colour. His face lost its haggard look and instead seemed more than normally healthy. His skin glowed as if it were fine ivory with a fire inside it. But Honda knew that there was no way for him to reach that essence. Here before him, he thought, was passion in its truest sense. The kind of thing that would never take possession of him. But more than that, he thought, wasn't it true that no passion whatever would succeed in sweeping him away? For he realized that his nature seemed to be lacking in the quality that made this possible. It would never assent to such an invasion. His affection for his friend was deep, he was willing enough to weep when required – but as for feelings, he was lacking in something here. Why did he instinctively channel all his energies into the maintaining of a suitable inner and outer decorum? Why, unlike Kiyoaki, had he been somehow unable to open his soul to the four great inchoate elements of fire, wind, water, and earth?

His eyes returned to the notebook in front of him and his own neat, precise handwriting.

> Aristotle's formal logic dominated European thought until almost the end of the Middle Ages. This is divided into two periods, the first of which is called 'Old Logic'. The works expounded were the 'Theses' and the 'Categories' from the *Organon*. The second is called 'New Logic'. It may be said that this period received its initial impetus from the complete Latin translation of the *Organon* which was finished by the middle of the twelfth century...

He could not help thinking that these words, like inscriptions cut into stone exposed to the weather, would fall from his mind, flake by flake.

54

Honda had heard that the convent day began early, so he shook himself out of a brief doze just as dawn was breaking. After a hasty breakfast, he told the maid to hire a rickshaw and got ready to leave.

Kiyoaki looked up at him from his bed, tears in his eyes. All he could manage was a look of entreaty as he lay with his head on the pillow, but it pierced Honda like a knife. Up until that moment, his intention had been to make a perfunctory visit to Gesshu and then get his gravely ill friend back to Tokyo as quickly as he could. But once he had seen the look in Kiyoaki's eyes, he knew that whatever the cost, he had to make every effort to effect a meeting between his friend and Satoko.

Fortunately it was a warm springlike morning, perhaps a good omen. As his rickshaw approached the convent entrance, he noticed that a man who was sweeping there took one look at him from a distance, abruptly put down his broom and rushed inside. His school uniform, which was the same as Kiyoaki's, must have put the man on guard, he thought, making him hurry in to sound the warning. The nun who appeared at the door had an expression of forbidding determination even before he could say who he was.

'Excuse me, Sister. My name is Honda. I am sorry to intrude, but I have come all the way from Tokyo because of this matter of Kiyoaki Matsugae. I would be extremely grateful if the Reverend Abbess would consent to see me.'

'Please wait for a few moments,' the nun replied.

He stood there for a long time on the front step, and then while he was involved in turning over in his mind the various counter-arguments to be used in the event of a refusal, the same nun surprised him by coming back and conducting him to a parlour inside. Hope, however faint, began to stir in him.

In the parlour he was again left to himself for a long time. The song of warblers came from the inner garden, though the sliding door was fully shut and he had no view. In the shadows he could just make out the intricate paper crest design of cloud-and-chrysanthemum on each door catch. The flower arrangement in the *tokonoma* alcove combined rape blossoms and peach buds. The bright yellow flowers seemed to pulse with the vigour of the spring countryside, and the dull bark and pale green leaves of the peach branch brought out the beauty of its swelling buds. The sliding doors were plain white, but he noticed a folding screen by the wall that seemed to be something precious, and he walked over to it.

He inspected it in detail. It was a screen depicting scenes of each of the twelve months of the year, done predominantly in the style of the Kano school, but enriched with the vivid colours that were traditionally Yamato.

The flow of the seasons began with spring at the right-hand edge of the screen. Courtiers enjoyed themselves in a garden beneath pines and white plum trees. A mass of golden cloud hid all but a fraction of a pavilion surrounded by a cypress hedge. A little to the left, young colts of various colours frolicked about. The pond in the garden at some point became a paddy and here young girls were at work planting rice shoots. A small waterfall burst from the golden cloud and tumbled down in two stages into another pond. The green shade of the grass at the water's edge bespoke the arrival of summer. Courtiers were hanging white paper pendants for the Midsummer Purification on the trees and bushes round the pond, with minor officials and crimson-robed servants in attendance. Deer were grazing contentedly in the garden of a shrine, and a white horse was being led out through its red torii gate. Imperial guards, bows slung over their shoulders, were busy making preparations for a festival procession. And the red maple leaves already reflected in the pond foretold the chill of winter that would soon take its toll. Then a bit farther on, still more courtiers were setting out on a day's falconry in gold-tinted snow. The sky too was golden, shining through the snowy branches of a bamboo grove. A white dog was in baying pursuit of a partridge with a touch of red at its neck; it streaked through the dry reeds like an arrow and escaped up into the winter sky. The hawks at the courtiers' wrists kept their arrogant eyes riveted on the fleeing partridge.

He returned to his place after a leisurely examination of the Tsukinami screen, but there was still no sign of the Abbess.

The nun returned, knelt down, and served him with tea and cake. She told him that the Abbess would be with him in just a few minutes, and asked him to make himself comfortable while he waited.

A small box decorated with a picture relief lay on the table. It must have been a product of the convent, and furthermore, there was something unskilled about its workmanship that made him wonder if Satoko's inexperienced hand had been at work on it. The paper glued to the sides and the padded picture mounted on the lid were both highly coloured after the taste of the old Imperial Court, lavish and oppressively gaudy. In the picture, a boy was chasing a butterfly. As he raced after the red-and-purple-winged insect, his face, his satiny white skin and his plump nakedness all suggested the sensuous grace of a court doll. After his ride through the dark, early spring fields and up the mountain through the still desolate woods, he felt that here in this shadowy parlour at Gesshu he had finally experienced the heavy, syrupy sweetness that was the essence of womanhood.

He heard the rustle of clothing, and then Her Reverence herself came in through the doorway, leaning on the arm of the senior nun. He stood up straight, but was unable to control the beating of his heart.

The Abbess must certainly have been advanced in years, but the small features in the clear-skinned face above the austere purple robe seemed to be carved out of fine yellow boxwood and showed no trace of age. They had a warm expression as she now sat down opposite him. The old nun took a seat to one side.

'So, they tell me that you have come all the way from Tokyo?'

'Yes, Your Reverence.' He had difficulty in getting his words out in front of her.

'This gentleman says that he is a school friend of Mr Matsugae,' said the old nun by way of contribution.

'Ah yes!' said the Abbess. 'To tell the truth, we have been feeling so sorry for the Marquis's son. However...'

'Matsugae has a terrible fever. He's in bed back at the inn. I received a telegram from him and I came down here as quickly as I could. Today I've come here in his place to make the request he asked me to make.' At last Honda found himself able to talk freely.

This, he thought, was most probably the way a young lawyer felt when he stood before the court. Regardless of the mood of the judges, he must plunge ahead, wholly intent on his plea and concerned only with the vindication of his client.

He told the Abbess of his friendship with Kiyoaki, he described his illness, and made it clear to her that Kiyoaki was risking his life for the sake of even the briefest of meetings with Satoko. He did not hesitate to say that if all this came to a tragic end, Gesshu itself would not be free of cause for remorse. He grew hotter and hotter as his fervent words poured out, and although the room was rather cold, he felt his ears and forehead burning.

As might be expected, his speech seemed to move the Abbess and the senior nun but they both remained silent.

'And then I do wish you would be kind enough to try to understand my own position. I lent my friend money because he told me he needed it. And that's what he used to come down here. Now he's fallen ill. I feel responsible to his parents for all this. And furthermore, as you must be thinking yourselves, the proper thing for me to do is obviously to get him back to Tokyo as soon as possible. I also realize that it's the only sensible solution. But I haven't done it. Instead, without even daring to contemplate how upset his parents are going to be with me, I've come to you now like this to beg you to grant Matsugae's request. I'm doing it because after seeing the look of desperate hope in his eyes, I do not feel that I have any other choice. If Your Reverence could only see that look, I'm sure that you too would be moved. As for me, I can't help but believe that it's far more important now to grant him what he wants than to worry about his illness. It's a frightening thing to say, but I somehow feel that he's not going to recover. So I am really giving you his dying request. Would letting him see Satoko for just a moment or two be quite outside the scope of the Lord Buddha's compassion? Won't you please permit it?'

Her Reverence still did not answer. Although he was completely wrought up, he stopped there, afraid that if he said anything further his words would only make it less likely that the Abbess would change her mind. The chilly room was hushed. The light that filtered through the pure white paper of the latticework doors made Honda think of a thin mist.

At that moment he thought he heard something. It was not by any means so close as to be in the next room, but close enough, coming perhaps from a corner of the hallway or from the next room but one. It sounded like a muffled laugh, as faint as the opening of a plum blossom. But then after a moment's reflection, he was sure that unless his ears had deceived him, the sound that had carried to him through the chill convent atmosphere on this spring morning was not a muffled laugh, as he had thought, but a young woman's stifled sob. It did not have the weight of a woman fighting down her tears. What he had heard, as dark and faint as the sound of a cut bowstring, was the trailing echo of a hidden sob. But then he began to wonder if it was no more than a momentary quirk of his imagination.

'Ah,' said the Abbess, breaking her silence at last, 'no doubt you think me unduly severe. You may feel that I am the one who is using every means to keep these two apart. However, surely it may well be that some superhuman agency is at work here. It began when Satoko herself made a vow before the Lord Buddha. She swore never to meet this man again in this world. I therefore think that the Lord Buddha in his wisdom is making sure that she does not. But for the young master, what a tragedy it is.'

'Despite everything then, Your Reverence will not give permission?'

'No.'

Her voice had an inexpressible dignity, and he felt quite powerless to answer her. The simple *no* seemed powerful enough to tear apart the very sky like fragile silk.

After that, seeing his deep distress, the Abbess's beautiful voice began to direct an exalted monologue at him. Although he was by no means eager to leave and have to face Kiyoaki's dejection, his distress prevented him from paying more than half-hearted attention to what she was saying.

The Abbess referred to the net of Indra. Indra was an Indian God, and once he cast his net, every man, every living thing without exception was inextricably caught in its meshes. And so it was that all creatures in existence were inescapably bound by it.

Indra's net symbolized the Chain of Causation or, in Sanskrit, *pratitya-samutpada. Yuishiki* (Vijñaptimātrata or Consciousness), the fundamental doctrine of the Hosso Sect, to which Gesshu belonged, was celebrated in *The Thirty Verses of Yuishiki*, the canonical text attributed to Vasubandhu, whom the sect regarded as its founder. According to the Verses, *Alaya* is the origin of the Chain of Causation. This was a Sanskrit word that denoted a storehouse. For within the *Alaya* were contained the karmic 'seeds' that held the consequential effects of all deeds, both good and evil.

Deeper within man than the first six forms of consciousness – sight, hearing, smell, taste, touch, and mind, with which sentient beings are endowed – there was a seventh called *Mana* or self-awareness. But *Alaya*, the ultimate form of consciousness, lay deeper yet.

Just as *The Thirty Verses* expressed it, 'Like unto a violent torrent, ever flowing, ever changing,' this eighth form of awareness, like a raging river, changed incessantly, never ceasing to flow onward. In constant flux, *Alaya* is the source of all sentient beings and the sum of all effects on them.

Asanga, the co-founder along with Vasubandhu of the Yuishiki school, in a doctrinal work called *The Providence of the Greater Vehicle*, evolved, on the basis of the eternally mutative nature of *Alaya*, a unique theory of the Chain of Causation in terms of time. It dealt with the interaction of the *Alaya* consciousness and the Law of Defilement that gave rise to what was termed 'the ever-recurring cycle of annihilation and renewal of causality'. According to the doctrine of *Yuishiki*, 'awareness only', each of the various dharmas, which were actually nothing other than consciousness, far from enjoying permanence, existed purely for the moment. And once the instant was past, they were annihilated. At the present moment, the *Alaya* consciousness and the Law of Defilement exist simultaneously, and their interaction gives rise to the causality of the present moment. Once this moment is past, both *Alaya* and the Law of Defilement are annihilated, but with the next moment, both are reborn, and both once again interact to give rise to a new causality. Beings in existence thus are annihilated from moment to moment, and this gives rise to time. The process whereby time is engendered by this moment-to-moment annihilation may be likened to a row of dots and a line.

As the minutes passed, Honda gradually found himself being drawn into the Abbess's profound doctrinal exposition. But his present circumstances prevented any stirring of his instinctive spirit of rational inquiry. The sudden burst of complex Buddhist terminology put him off, and then there were many difficult points over which he had doubts. Karma, he thought, should operate eternally, a process without beginning, that by its nature contained within itself elements of time. It seemed contradictory to him that, on the contrary, time was to be understood as arising from the dissolution and regeneration of each present moment's causality.

His various misgivings thus prevented him from giving wholeheartedly respectful attention to Her Reverence's learned discourse. The old nun also irritated him with her interjections. At appropriate intervals, she would chime in with 'How very true!' ... 'Indeed, just so!' ... 'How could it be otherwise?' and the like. So he contented himself by memorizing the titles of *The Thirty Verses* and *The Providence of the Greater Vehicle* and thought that he could look into them when he had the leisure and then come back here to ask questions. Given his present mood, then, he did not realize from what perspective and with what clarity the Abbess's words were illuminating Kiyoaki's fate as well as his own, though on the face of it they might seem remote and irrelevant. It was just the same way that the moon, at its zenith, subtly lights up the dark waters of a lake.

He murmured a polite farewell and took his leave of Gesshu as quickly as he could.

55

During the train ride back to Tokyo, Kiyoaki's all too evident pain was a constant source of distress to Honda. He put aside his books entirely, his sole concern now to get his friend home as soon as possible. As he looked down at Kiyoaki lying gravely ill on his berth, being carried back to Tokyo without having achieved the meeting he had so desired, he felt a gnawing regret. He was now wondering if it had really been the act of a friend to give him that money.

Kiyoaki had fallen into a doze. Honda, on the other hand, was more alert than ever, despite having gone without sleep for so long. He allowed a multitude of thoughts to come and go unchecked. Among these, the memory of the Abbess's sermons on two occasions came to him, each with an entirely different effect. In the autumn of the previous year, he had heard his first sermon from her, the parable of drinking the water from the skull. He had taken that principle and made a parable of his own from it, one dealing with human love. And he had concluded by thinking that it would unquestionably be wonderful if a man could really make the substance of the world truly conform to that of his innermost heart. Later, in the course of his legal studies, he had given considerable thought to the doctrine of reincarnation as expressed in the Laws of Manu. And this morning, he had heard the Abbess speak again. He now felt as though the only key to the riddle that had been vexing him had dangled momentarily on a cord before his eyes, swinging back and forth with so many confusing jumps and twists that the riddle itself seemed to have become all the more complex.

The train was due at Shimbashi Station at six in the morning. The night was already well advanced. The heavy breathing of the passengers mingled with the rumble of the wheels. He would stay awake until dawn, watching Kiyoaki in the lower berth directly opposite him. He had left the curtains open so that he would know at once if there was any change at all in Kiyoaki's condition, and now he stared out of the window at the fields clothed in darkness.

Though the train was racing through the night, the darkness was so thick and the sky so overcast that the fields and mountains beyond were almost blotted out, leaving nearly nothing to mark the forward progress of the train. From time to time, a tiny flash of light or the brief glow of a lantern tore a brilliant rent in the curtain of blackness, but these could not provide any orientation. It was not the train that made this rumbling noise, Honda mused. It was something else. Something that enveloped this little thing as it made its insignificant way through the night. The roaring issued from the massive darkness itself.

While Honda had been hurriedly packing to leave the inn at Obitoké, Kiyoaki had obtained a few sheets of cheap stationery from the innkeeper and had written a note which he had then given to Honda, asking him to deliver it to his mother the Marquise. Honda had placed it carefully in the inside pocket of his jacket. Now, for want of anything better to do, he took it out and read it by the poor light of the bulb hanging from the roof of the car.

It was written in pencil, and the hand was unsteady, quite unlike Kiyoaki. He had never drawn his figures with much grace, but there had always been an abundantly vigorous touch to them:

Dear Mother,

There is something that I would like you to give Honda for me. The dream journal in my desk. He'd like it. And since nobody else would want to read it, please see that he gets it.

Kiyoaki

Honda could see that he had used his last reserves of strength to write this as a kind of will. But if it really had been that, he should surely have included a word or two for his mother herself, instead of addressing her in this curt and businesslike fashion.

A groan came from the opposite berth. He quickly put away the note and was beside Kiyoaki in a flash, looking down at his face.

'What is it?'

'My chest hurts. It feels as if I'm being stabbed here.'

Kiyoaki's breathing was harsh. His words came in spurts. Honda, not knowing what else to do, gently began to massage the lower left side of his chest, the spot where he said the pain was most intense. But in the faint light, he saw that his friend's face was still contorted.

Despite the contortions, however, it was beautiful. Intense suffering had imbued it with an extraordinary character, carving lines into it that gave it the austere dignity of a bronze mask. The beautiful eyes were filled with tears. Above them, however, the eyebrows were tightly puckered, and the masculine force they conveyed made a striking contrast with the pathos of the flashing dark, wet pupils. As he fought the pain, his finely chiselled nose jutted upward as if he were trying to probe the darkness around him, and his lips, parched with fever, were drawn back to reveal the palely gleaming mother-of-pearl of his teeth.

Finally, the racking pain seemed to subside.

'You're asleep? Good. It's what you need,' said Honda. He wondered about the tortured look he had seen on his friend's face just a moment before. Hadn't it in fact been an expression of intense joy, the kind to be found nowhere but at the extremity of human existence? Perhaps Kiyoaki had seen something, and Honda envied him that, an emotion that in turn stirred an odd shame and self-reproach in him.

He shook his head slightly. He had begun to feel the numbing weight of grief. Deep within him, as subtly and persistently as the spinning of a silkworm's thread, an emotion had gradually taken shape. Its significance eluded him, and he was disturbed by it.

Then Kiyoaki, who seemed to have dozed off for a moment, suddenly opened his eyes wide and reached for Honda's hand. He grasped it tightly as he spoke.

'Just now I had a dream. I'll see you again. I know it. Beneath the falls.'

His dream, Honda thought, had taken him to the park around his father's house. And there, the most vivid of all the images must have been the falls, tumbling down from the crest of the hill in its nine stages.

Two days after his return to Tokyo, Kiyoaki Matsugae died at the age of twenty.

RUNAWAY HORSES

Translated by
Michael Gallagher

1

It was 1932. Shigekuni Honda was thirty-eight.

While still a law student at Tokyo Imperial University, he had passed the judicial civil service examination, and after graduation he had been given a probationary assignment as a clerk in the Osaka District Court. Osaka was his home from then on. In 1929 he became a judge, and last year, having already advanced to senior associate judge of the District Court, he had moved to the Osaka Court of Appeals to become a junior associate judge.

Honda had married at twenty-eight. His wife was the daughter of one of his father's friends, a judge who had been forced to retire in the legal reform of 1913. The wedding was held in Tokyo, and he and his wife came to Osaka immediately afterwards. In the ten years that followed, his wife had borne him no children. But Rié was a modest and gentle woman, and their relationship was harmonious.

His father had died three years before. At the time, Honda had considered disposing of the family home and having his mother come to Osaka. She had been opposed to this, however, and now she lived alone in the large house in Tokyo.

Honda's wife had one maid to help her care for the rented house in which they lived. There were two rooms on the second floor and five on the first, including the foyer. The garden covered somewhat more than seven hundred square feet. For this Honda paid a monthly rent of thirty-two yen.

Aside from three days a week at the court, Honda worked at home. To go to the Court of Appeals he took a streetcar from Abeno in Tennoji Ward to Kitahama in downtown Osaka. Then he walked across the bridges spanning the Tosabori and the Dojima rivers to the Courthouse, which stood close by Hokonagashi Bridge. It was a red brick building with the huge chrysanthemum of the imperial crest glittering above its front entrance.

A *furoshiki* cloth was indispensable to a judge. There were always documents to take home, usually more than a briefcase would hold, and a cloth-wrapped bundle could be either large or small. Honda used a medium-sized muslin *furoshiki* from the Daimaru department store, and, to be on the safe side, carried a second one folded up within it. For the judges these *furoshiki* bundles were vital to their work; they would never trust them to a luggage rack. One of his colleagues would not even stop off for a drink on the way home without passing a cord under the knot of his *furoshiki* and then looping it around his neck.

There was no reason why Honda could not use the judges' chambers to compose his decisions. But on a day when court was not in session the crowded room would be ringing with vigorous legal arguments, as the probationary clerks stood about respectfully assimilating all they could learn. Little hope of his being able to write his decisions in peace. Honda preferred to work at home late into the night.

Shigekuni Honda's specialty was criminal law. He felt no concern that Osaka, because of its small criminal law division, was said to offer only limited advancement in this field.

Working at home, he would spend the night reading the police reports, the prosecutor's briefs, and the accounts of the preliminary examinations relating to the cases to be tried at the next session. After he had made extracts and taken notes he would pass the material along to the senior associate judge. Once a decision had been reached, it was up to Honda to draft it for the Chief Judge. The sky would already be growing light in the east by the time he finally plodded his way to 'All of which having been considered, the judgement of this court is as has been hereinbefore stated.' The Chief Judge would revise this and give it back to Honda, who now had to take up his writing brush and make the final copy. The fingers of his right hand had scrivener's calluses.

As for geisha parties, Honda attended only the traditional end-of-year celebration which was held at the Seikanro in the red-light district of Kita Ward. On that night superiors and underlings caroused freely together, and occasionally somebody or other, emboldened by saké, expressed himself to the Chief Justice with unwonted frankness.

Their usual diversion was drinking in the cafés and *oden* shops clustered around the streetcar junction of Umeda-Shimmichi. The service at some of these cafés knew no limits. If one were to ask the waitress what time it was, she would lift her skirt to consult a watch strapped to a plump thigh before answering. Some judges, of course, were altogether too dignified for this sort of thing, and even believed that cafés were merely places for drinking coffee. One of them happened to be presiding over an embezzlement trial, when the defendant testified that he had squandered all of the misappropriated thousand yen in cafés. The judge interrupted indignantly.

'How can you say that?' he demanded. 'A cup of coffee is only five sen. Are you trying to tell us you drank that much?'

Even after the general reduction of civil service salaries, Honda had an ample income of nearly three hundred yen a month, the equivalent of a regimental commander. His colleagues gave their leisure to various pastimes: some read novels, others took up the chants and Nō plays of the Kanzé School, and still others gathered to write haiku and make sketches illustrating the poems. Most of these diversions, however, served as pretexts for getting together to do some drinking.

Then there were some judges, especially enthusiastic for things Western, who went to dances. Honda did not care for dancing, but he often heard his colleagues talk about it. Since a city ordinance forbade dancing in Osaka itself, devotees had to go to Kyoto, where the Katsura and the Keagé dance halls were popular, or else to Amagasaki, where the Kuisé stood isolated in the midst of rice paddies. The taxi ride to Amagasaki cost one yen. As one approached the gymnasium-like building on a rainy night, the shadows of dancing couples flickered past the lighted windows, and the strains of the foxtrot took on an uncanny quality across the flooded paddy fields gleaming in the rain.

Such was Honda's world about this time.

2

How oddly situated a man is apt to find himself at age thirty-eight! His youth belongs to the distant past. Yet the period of memory beginning with the end of youth and extending to the present has left him not a single vivid impression. And therefore he persists in feeling that nothing more than a fragile barrier separates him from his youth. He is forever hearing with the utmost clarity the sounds of this neighbouring domain, but there is no way to penetrate the barrier.

Honda felt that his youth had ended with the death of Kiyoaki Matsugae. At that moment something real within him, something that had burned with a vibrant brilliance, suddenly ceased to be.

Now, late at night, when Honda grew weary of his legal drafts, he would pick up the dream journal that Kiyoaki had left him and turn over its pages.

Much that it contained seemed like meaningless riddles, but some of the dreams recorded there gracefully foreshadowed Kiyoaki's early death. His dream of looking down in spirit upon his own coffin of plain wood while the pre-dawn blackness gave way to deep blue at the windows was fulfilled with unforeseen swiftness in less than a year and a half. The woman with the widow's peak who clung to the coffin was evidently Satoko, but there had been no sign of the actual Satoko at Kiyoaki's funeral.

Since then eighteen years had passed. The border between dream and memory had grown indistinct in Honda's mind. Because the words contained in this journal, his only souvenir of his friend, had been traced there by Kiyoaki's own hand, it had profound significance for Honda. These dreams, left like a handful of gold dust in a winnowing pan, were charged with wonder.

As time went by, the dreams and the reality took on equal worth among Honda's diverse memories. What had actually occurred was in the process of merging with what could have occurred. As reality rapidly gave way to dreams, the past seemed very much like the future.

When he was young, there had been only one reality, and the future had seemed to stretch before him, swelling with immense possibilities. But as he grew older, reality seemed to take many forms, and it was the past that seemed refracted into innumerable possibilities. Since each of these was linked with its own reality, the line distinguishing dream and reality became all the more obscure. His memories were in constant flux, and had taken on the aspect of a dream.

On the one hand, he could not definitely recall the name of a man he had met yesterday, but on the other, the image of Kiyoaki came to him fresh and clear whenever he called it up, much as the memory of a nightmare is more vivid than the look of the familiar street corner that one passes the next morning. After reaching the age of thirty, Honda had begun to forget people's names, just as paint flakes away bit by bit. The reality that these names signified became more fleeting and more insignificant than any dream, a waste substance thrown off by each day's life.

Honda felt that the future had no shocks in store for him. Whatever new turmoil rocked the world, his function would remain the same, and he would bring to bear upon each disturbance the rational scrutiny of the law. He had become thoroughly acclimatized to a sphere whose atmosphere was logic. And it was logic, therefore, that Honda took as valid – more than dreams, more than reality.

The vast number of criminal cases tried before him had, of course, brought him into constant contact with the more extreme forms of passion. Though he himself had never experienced such emotion, he had seen many human beings whom a single passion held fatally in thrall.

Was he really so secure? Whenever the thought occurred to him, Honda had the feeling that long ago a glittering danger had threatened him, a danger that had been destroyed in a final flash of brilliance. And from that moment, he felt, he had become invulnerable to any temptation, however compelling – a freedom that he owed to the armour that had encased him ever since. The danger of that distant past, and its temptation, had been Kiyoaki.

Honda had once enjoyed talking about the days that he had shared with Kiyoaki. But as a man grows older the memory of his youth begins to act as nothing less than an immunization against further experience. And he was thirty-eight. It was an age when one felt strangely unready to say that one had lived and yet reluctant to acknowledge the death of youth. An age when the savour of one's experiences turned ever so slightly sour, and when, day by day, one took less pleasure in new things. An age when the charm of every diverting foolishness quickly faded. But Honda's devotion to his work shielded him from emotion. He had fallen in love with his oddly abstract vocation.

When he came home in the evening, he had dinner with his wife before going to his study. Though he usually ate at six on the days that he worked at home, on court days the hour varied since he sometimes remained at the Courthouse as late as eight o'clock. Now, however, he was no longer called out in the middle of the night as he had been when he had presided over preliminary hearings.

No matter how late he came home, Rié always waited to eat with him. When he arrived late, she would hurry to warm up dinner. Honda read the newspaper as he waited, conscious of the purposeful bustle of his wife and the maid in the kitchen. Thus the dinner hour was for Honda the most relaxing of the entire day. The pattern of his own household was different, to be sure, but the image of his father enjoying the evening paper often came to his mind. Somehow he had come to resemble his father.

Still, there were differences. He was sure he did not have any of the rather artificial sternness of his father, so characteristic of the Meiji era. For one thing, he had no children to be stern to, and, for another, his household, of its own accord, functioned in a simple and orderly manner.

Rié was quiet. She never opposed her husband, nor was she inquisitive. She was bothered by a touch of inflammation of the kidneys, and occasionally her features would be swollen. Then her sleepy eyes would seem to smoulder with passion, an effect heightened by the somewhat heavier makeup she wore at these times.

Now on this Sunday evening in the middle of May, Rié's face was swollen again. Tomorrow would be a court session. Honda had begun his work in the afternoon, thinking he would be able to complete it by dinnertime, and so he had told his wife before going into his study that he wanted to keep at it until he was finished. He was not through until eight. It was unusual for him to eat at so late an hour on a day spent at home.

Although refined tastes meant very little to Honda, during his long residence in the Kansai area he had developed an interest in ceramics, and he allowed himself the modest luxury of using good-quality dishes for even ordinary meals. They ate from bowls of Ninsei porcelain and their evening saké was served in Awata ware by Yohei III. Rié took great pains to prepare such delicacies as a mustard-flavoured fish salad made with young trout, eels broiled unseasoned in the Kanto manner, and sliced winter melon spread with a sauce thickened with arrowroot starch. She was concerned about her husband's health, bound as he was to his desk throughout the day, and planned her menus accordingly.

It was the time of year when the fire in the brazier and the steam whistling from the copper kettle began to seem disagreeable.

'It won't do any harm to take a bit more saké than usual tonight,' said Honda, as if to himself. 'All my work is done now, since I gave up my Sunday to it.'

'How nice to have finished,' said Rié, filling his cup. A simple harmony co-ordinated the movements of their hands, his holding out the cup, hers the bottle from which she was pouring. An invisible cord seemed to link them, tugged back and forth almost playfully in accordance with the spontaneous rhythm of life. Rié was not a woman to disturb such rhythms. Honda could be certain of that, just as he could tell from the rich scent of the blossoms that the magnolia in his garden was in bloom that night.

Thus everything that Honda wanted was tranquilly arranged within his view and within easy reach. This was the domain established in less than twenty years by the young man of promise. Then he had had almost nothing over which his fingers might close with a sense of possession, but because the lack had stirred no anxious irritation in him, all these things had now come securely into his grasp.

After sipping his saké, he took up a steaming bowl of rice in which scattered green peas gleamed brightly. Just then he heard the jingle of a newspaper-boy's bell announcing an extra. He had the maid run out to buy a copy.

The paper, whose ragged cut edges and barely dry ink showed the haste in which it had been put out, conveyed the first news of the May Fifteenth Incident, the assassination of Prime Minister Inukai by Navy officers.

Honda sighed. 'As if it weren't enough to have had the Blood Oath Alliance.' Honda felt that he was above the usual run of indignant men who arose, their faces dark with passion, to condemn the corruption of the times. He was persuaded that his own world was one of reason and clarity. Now that he was a little intoxicated, its clarity seemed to shine with even greater brilliance.

'You'll be very busy again, won't you?' asked Rié.

Honda felt a surge of affectionate condescension on hearing the daughter of a judge betray such ignorance.

'No, no. This will be a matter for a military court.'

The affair by its very nature was outside civilian jurisdiction.

3

For some days, of course, the May Fifteenth Incident was the sole topic of conversation in the judges' chambers at the Courthouse. But by the beginning of June there was such a crush of cases pending that all the judges were too busy to concern themselves any longer with the affair. They were already well aware of the facts left out of the newspaper accounts and had exchanged every scrap of information among themselves. Everyone knew that the Chief Justice of the Court of Appeals, Judge Sugawa, a kendo enthusiast, was very much in sympathy with the defendants, but no one was rash enough to allude to this.

Incidents of this sort, arising one after another, were like waves rolling in from a night sea to break upon the beach. First a small crest like a wavering line of white out upon the deep. Then as the wave came rushing in, it swelled enormously, only to crash down upon the sand and melt back into the depths. Honda remembered the sea at Kamakura on that night nineteen years before, when he and Kiyoaki and the two princes of Siam had lain upon the beach and gazed out at the waves as they rolled in and receded.

As for waves such as the May Fifteenth Incident, Honda thought, the beach was innocent. It was only obliged to force them back into the deep with inexhaustible patience, preventing them from rolling over the land. To force them back each time into the abyss of evil from which they had arisen, back into the primeval realm of remorse and death.

What did Honda himself think of evil? What did he think of sin? Such thoughts were really not his responsibility. He had but to guide himself by the established legal code. Somewhere deep within him, however, Honda did harbour a secret concept of sin, a concept as fragrant and stimulating as a pungent lotion soaking into dry, chapped skin. No doubt he owed this to Kiyoaki's lingering influence.

Still, this 'unwholesome' notion was not so strong that he felt he had to combat it. Dominated as he was by reason, Honda lacked anything like a blind devotion to justice.

One day in early June, when the morning court session had ended earlier than usual, Honda returned to the judges' chambers with some time on his hands before lunch. He took off his black cap with its purple piping and his black legal robes with the arabesque design of purple embroidered across the front and put them away in the mahogany cabinet that reminded him of a Buddhist household altar. Then he stood looking absently out of the window as he smoked a cigarette. A misty rain was falling.

'I'm not a beginner at this any more,' Honda mused. 'I've done my work without being swayed by the opinions of others, and I can say that I've met the prescribed standards. I've become thoroughly adept at my profession – like a potter whose clay seems to shape itself, taking the form that he wants it to.'

Suddenly he realized that he was on the verge of forgetting the face of the defendant who had just stood trial before him. He shook his head. Try as he might, he could no longer clearly visualize the man's features.

Since the Public Prosecutor's Office occupied the third-floor rooms facing the river on the south side of the Courthouse, the view left to the judges' chambers, whose windows faced north, was a dismal one. The prison took up most of it. A passageway through the red brick wall separating the Courthouse and prison allowed defendants to go to court without being exposed to the public gaze.

Honda noticed that the painted wall of the room was dripping with moisture, and he opened the window. Beyond the red brick wall the roofs of the various wings of the white-brick two-storey prison were clustered together, with a guard tower shaped like a silo rising at their point of juncture. Only in this tower were the windows without bars.

The tile roofs of the prison wings and the little tile shields over the ventilation stacks all gleamed with the wet blackness of an inkstone. In the background a huge chimney towered up into the rainy sky. The view from Honda's window extended no farther than the stack.

The sides of the prison buildings were pierced at regular intervals by windows, each covered with white-painted iron bars and a screen of wooden slats. Below each window, on the rain-wet wall the colour of soiled linen, a large Arabic number was painted: 30, 31, 32, 33, and so on. The first- and second-floor numbers were staggered so that directly below window 32 of the second floor was window 31 of the first. There was a line of oblong air vents, and on the first floor, just at ground level, were openings for toilet drainage.

All at once Honda found himself wondering which of those cells contained the defendant who had just appeared before him. Such knowledge had no bearing upon his role as a judge. The man was a poverty-stricken farmer from Kochi Prefecture in Shikoku. He had sold his daughter to an Osaka brothel, and then, having received less than half of what he had been promised, he had gone to see the madam. Enraged by her insults, he had begun to beat her and had become so carried away that he had killed the woman. Still, Honda could not clearly recall the defendant's face, a face as impassive as stone.

The smoke from his cigarette rose through his fingers and yielded to the misty rain. This cigarette would be a precious treasure in that other world separated from him by only a wall. For a moment Honda was struck by the absurd contrast of values between these two worlds whose borders the law defined. Over there the taste of tobacco was infinitely desirable; here a cigarette was nothing more than a means to while away an idle moment.

The exercise ground within the cluster of prison buildings was divided into a number of fan-shaped enclosures. From this window one often saw the blue uniforms and blue-shaven scalps of the prisoners as, two or three at a time, they were given callisthenics or allowed to walk around. Today, however, perhaps because of the rain, the exercise ground was as empty and still as the yard of a hencoop after all the birds had been slaughtered.

Just then the heavy, sultry silence was shattered by a noise from below, like rain shutters slammed together.

Then the silence closed in once more. A faint breeze caught the misty rain, and Honda felt a touch of moisture on his brow. As he was closing the window, his colleague, Judge Murakami, came into the room from his own morning court session.

'I just heard the sound of an execution,' Honda said abruptly, as though apologizing.

'I heard one too a few days ago. Not a very pleasant noise, is it? I don't think it was a good idea to put the gallows close to the wall there.' Murakami took off his robes. 'Well, shall we go to lunch?'

'And what are you going to have today?'

'What else? An Ikematsu *bento*.'

The two of them walked down the dark corridor that led to the dining room reserved for high officials, which was here on the third floor. It was the custom of Honda and Murakami to devote their lunch to discussing current cases. Just over a door marked 'Senior Officials' Dining Room' was a stained-glass window whose intricate art nouveau floral pattern shone brightly from the lights inside.

The dining room contained ten long, narrow tables each furnished with kettles and teacups. Honda looked to see if the Chief Justice was among those already eating. He often came here for lunch in order to talk things over with his fellow judges. On such occasions, the woman in charge of the dining room, well aware of the Chief Justice's preferences, always hurried over to his table with a small kettle. This contained not tea but saké. Today, however, the Chief Justice was not present.

Seated across from Murakami, Honda opened his own lacquered *bento* box and took out the top section containing fish and vegetables. As usual its bottom was moist and sticky from the hot, steaming rice in the lower section, and grains of rice clung to its chipped red lacquer. Honda, disturbed at the very hint of waste, carefully picked off the rice grain by grain and put it into his mouth.

This scrupulous display amused Murakami.

'You were raised the same way I was,' he said, laughing. 'Every morning you had to bow and offer a few grains of rice to a little bronze farmer sitting cross-legged with a straw rain coat between his legs. So did I. If I dropped a single grain on the floor during dinner, I had to pick it up and put it in my mouth.'

'Samurai realized that they ate without working,' said Honda. 'The effects of being brought up that way still remain. How do your children behave?'

'They follow Papa's lead,' answered Murakami, a cheerfully complacent expression on his face. Murakami was aware that he lacked the dignified countenance proper to a judge, and at one time he had tried cultivating a moustache, only to give it up when his colleagues and superiors made fun of it. He was fond of reading, and often talked about literature.

'You know, Oscar Wilde said there's no such thing as a pure crime in the present-day world. All crimes spring from some necessity. Take most of these recent assassinations. I feel as if I'd have to disqualify myself from presiding.'

'Yes, I see what you mean,' replied Honda prudently. 'You might call them crimes resulting from social maladjustment. Most of these incidents seem to be social problems crystallized into crime, don't they? Furthermore, the men involved are hardly ever intellectuals. They don't know what it all means, but they come to personify the very problems.'

'The farmers in the North, for example. There's a terrible situation.'

'We can be thankful we have nothing that bad in our district.'

The jurisdiction of the Osaka Court of Appeals was constituted in 1913 to include Osaka, Kyoto, Hyogo, Nara, Shiga, Wakayama, Kagawa, Tokushima, and Kochi – two urban districts and seven prefectures, a generally prosperous area.

The two went on to discuss at length the rapid growth of ideological crime, the policy of the Public Prosecutor's Office, and the like. As they talked, the clap of the execution still echoed in Honda's ears with a fresh, vibrant quality that would satisfy a carpenter. Nevertheless, he ate with a good appetite. Rather than disturbing him, the noise made him feel as if a thin wedge of crystal had pierced his awareness.

Chief Justice Sugawa entered to the respectful nods of greeting of all present. The woman in charge rushed to get the special kettle as His Honour sat down by Honda and Murakami. A huge, florid-faced kendo expert, the Chief Justice was a qualified instructor in the Hokushin Ittoryu school of kendo and served as an adviser to the Martial Arts Association. He was fond of quoting a classic kendo book in the course of his legal addresses and was consequently referred to behind his back as 'the referee'. But he was a very pleasant gentleman, and a warm humanity always informed his judicial decisions. Whenever there was a kendo meet or tournament within his district and he was asked to make the congratulatory address, he was happy to comply. And since many Shinto shrines sponsored the martial arts, the Chief Justice naturally developed ties with these and was always an honoured guest at their festivals.

'I don't know what to do!' sighed the Chief Justice as he sat down. 'I told them I'd come a long time ago, and now there's just no way of my being there.'

His distress surely had something to do with kendo, Honda thought, and so it turned out. There was to be a kendo tournament at the Omiwa Shrine in the town of Sakurai in Nara Prefecture on the sixteenth of June. The shrine had worshippers all over the country, and even the universities in Tokyo were sending their best athletes to participate. Chief Justice Sugawa had agreed to give the main address, but, as it now happened, he had to go to Tokyo on that very day for a conference of district court heads. Since this was a matter that in no way involved official duty, he told Honda and Murakami, he had no right to ask one of them to go in his place, but did either of them, by chance, feel like lending him a hand? Faced with such a humble request, the two judges immediately consulted their appointment books. A court session on the sixteenth ruled out Murakami, but Honda was to work at home for a few days and the cases he would be reviewing were simple ones.

The Chief Justice's face glowed. 'I don't know how to thank you,' he told Honda. 'This will keep me in their good graces, and there's no doubt they'll be quite happy about it at the shrine, knowing your father too. You'd better make it a two-day trip. You can stay at the Nara Hotel the night of the tournament. It's very quiet, and it will be a good place to work. The next day is the Saigusa Festival of Izagawa Shrine, the branch shrine of Omiwa right there in Nara itself, so you can see that too. I saw it once myself, and there isn't a more beautiful old festival anywhere. How does the idea suit you, Honda? If you think you'd like to see it, I'll send a letter off today. No, no two ways about it. It's something you can't afford to miss.'

Pressed as he was by the Chief Justice's well-meaning enthusiasm, Honda somewhat reluctantly agreed. As for a kendo match, he had not seen one since twenty years before at Peers School. In those days both he and Kiyoaki had detested the kendo team and the fanatic yelling that accompanied their practice sessions. Neither of them could hear those cries without feeling their youthful sensitivity painfully affronted. Savage, strangled, revolting cries that seemed bent on exalting brazen madness to the level of something holy. Of course Honda and Kiyoaki had different reasons for loathing them. To Kiyoaki, the screams were a shock to his refined sensibility. To Honda, they were an assault upon reason itself. A reaction of this sort, however, was something that belonged to Honda's past. By now he had become so disciplined that he could hear or see anything at all without betraying himself by so much as a flicker of his eyebrow.

On days when there was a fairly long interval between lunch and the beginning of the afternoon session, Honda would take a walk along the bank of the Dojima River if the weather was pleasant. He liked to watch the lighters towing timber down the river, the logs churning up white water as though frothing at the mouth. But today it was raining. And the judges' chambers would be bustling with far too much activity for him to relax there. After leaving Murakami, he stood idly for a time by the front entrance, where the pale green and white light from a stained-glass window depicting an olive grove shone faintly upon the polished, mottled granite of the pillars that lined the lobby. A thought struck him, and he went to the accounts department to get a key. He had decided that he would climb the tower.

The red brick Courthouse tower was one of the landmarks of Osaka and, seen from the opposite bank, its reflection lying across the Dojima River, made for an aesthetically pleasing view. On the other hand, it was referred to as the Tower of London and was the subject of fables such as the one alleging that there was a gallows at its top upon which executions were carried out.

No one had ever been able to devise a use for this extraordinary whim of the English architect who had designed the Courthouse, and so the tower was kept locked and left to gather dust through the years. Sometimes a judge would climb it for the sake of the view. On a clear day one could see as far as Awaji Island.

Honda turned the key in the lock and went in. He was confronted with a vast white emptiness. The base of the tower was the ceiling of the front lobby of the Courthouse. From there to the very top was nothing but unobstructed space. The white walls were soiled with layers of dust and the rain that had seeped in over the years. There were windows only at the top, around which was a narrow balcony. One reached this by means of an iron stairway which crooked its way up the walls with the tenacity of ivy.

Honda knew that if he touched the stairway railing its thick coat of dust would blacken his fingertips. Though it was raining, the light let in by the windows above was enough to fill the interior of the great tower with an eerie illumination like an ill-favoured dawn. Whenever he entered this tower and found himself enveloped in its blank expanse of walls and its absurdly twisting stairway, Honda had the impression of coming into a bizarre world whose dimensions had been deliberately expanded. Such a space, he felt, must house some gigantic statue hidden from his eyes, a huge figure whose invisible features were set in stern anger.

Were it not so, Honda thought, nothing would justify this extravagant spaciousness. It would be altogether devoid of meaning. Even the windows, fairly large close up, seemed no bigger than matchboxes from where Honda stood.

He climbed step by step, occasionally glancing downward through the iron grating that supported him. Each footstep stirred thunderous echoes within the tower. Though he had no reason to doubt the safety of the stairway, every step he took made its long metal frame shake from top to bottom with a giddy trembling, like a shiver passing down a man's spine. And dust drifted silently down toward the distant floor.

When he reached the top and looked out through the various windows, the scene spread out below him offered little that Honda had not already discovered. Although the rain cut his field of vision considerably, he could see the Dojima River following its leisurely southern course to its confluence with the Tosabori. On the opposite bank of the Dojima, directly to the south, stood the Public Hall, the Prefectural Library, and the Bank of Japan with its round bronze roof. Honda looked down at the office buildings that covered this broad strip of land between the two rivers, all of them dwarfed by the tower. To the west of the Courthouse, the Dojima Building rose up as a near neighbour, and in its shadow, the Gothic front of Resurrection Hospital. The wings of the Courthouse stretched out to either side below, its red brick lent charm by the rainy wetness. The small lawn of its inner courtyard seemed fitted in place as carefully as the green felt of a billiard table.

From such a height, Honda could not make out any human figures below. He saw nothing but the lines of buildings, lights burning at midday, passive beneath the falling rain. In the pervading coolness, the consolation of nature, Honda began to reflect.

'Here I am in a high place. High enough to make one giddy. And I am here not because of power, not because of money, but simply because I represent reason for the nation. A height upheld by logic, like a tower formed of steel girders.'

Whenever Honda came up here, far more than when he was seated upon the mahogany bench, he felt possessed of that all-encompassing vision that should belong to a judge. Now as he looked from this vantage point, all the phenomena below and all the phenomena of the past seemed to lie before him on a single rain-soaked map. If even reason had a childish playfulness, perhaps no diversion would be more natural for it than to gather all within a single view.

All sorts of things were going on below him. The Minister of Finance shot to death. The Prime Minister shot to death. Leftist teachers rounded up. Wild rumours flying about. The crisis of the farming communities deepening. Party government tottering along, no more than a step away from collapse. And what of Honda? He stood upon the height reserved for justice.

Honda, of course, was a man who could sketch all sorts of mental caricatures of himself in this role. Here he was, for example, upon the tower of justice, holding up in turn with a pair of tweezers each variety of human passion for evaluation. Here he was wrapping them up in the snug *furoshiki* of reason so that he could carry them home to use as the raw material of his decisions. Day after day, Honda's task was to thrust aside every element of mystery and set himself single-mindedly to the work of firming up the mortar that held the bricks of the law in place. Still, he thought, to stand upon a high place, to encompass human nature in a single view, from the clear upper reaches to the lower depths – there certainly was something to it. To possess an affinity, not with phenomena, but with the principles of law – there was something to it. Just as a groom smells of stables, so Honda, at age thirty-eight, had become permeated with the aroma of legal justice.

4

June sixteenth turned out to be unusually hot, even from early morning. The sun blazed down with an extravagant flourish as though announcing the midsummer heat to come. Honda left his house for Sakurai at seven a.m. in a car sent by the Chief Justice.

Omiwa Shrine ranked extremely high among national shrines. Most local people referred to it as Miwa Myojin, after Mount Miwa, which was considered to embody the divinity worshipped at the shrine. Mount Miwa itself was called simply the Holy Mountain. It rose fifteen hundred feet above sea level, with a circumference at its base of about ten miles, and it was covered by a thick forest of cedars, cypresses, red pines, and oaks. Not one of the trees growing here could be cut down. No defilement whatsoever was permitted. This primary shrine of the land of Yamato was the oldest shrine in all of Japan, and was reputed to have transmitted the Shinto faith in its purest form. And so all who reverenced the ancient rituals felt compelled, at least once in their lifetime, to make the pilgrimage to Omiwa.

The principal god enshrined at Omiwa was the major deity Nigimitama, 'the mild god', who was worshipped throughout Japan as the patron of saké brewing. And the name of the shrine itself came, perhaps, from that of a vessel in which rice was fermented. Within its precincts stood the small Sai Shrine. This was consecrated to Aramitama, 'the harsh god', towards whom military men had a warm devotion, and vast numbers of them came to pray for good fortune in battle. Five years before, the head of a veterans' association had proposed holding a kendo meet here each year as an act of worship. Because the grounds of Sai Shrine itself were too small, however, the wide court in front of the main shrine was finally chosen as the site.

All this the Chief Justice had explained to Honda. The car pulled up before the huge torii gate, and Honda got out in front of the signpost instructing pilgrims to proceed on foot.

The gravel pathway leading up to the shrine curved gently. White paper pendants hanging at prescribed intervals from cords linking the branches of the cedar trees on either side swayed in the faint breeze. The moss that covered the roots of the pines and oaks beyond the cedars, still soaked from yesterday's rain, gleamed with the wet greenness of seaweed. For some distance a brook paralleled the path just off to the left, and the sound of splashing water came up through the ferns and bamboo grass. From the clear sky overhead, the sun's torrid rays sought out the undergrowth, little hindered by the sheltering cedar branches. Just as Honda was crossing the sacred bridge he caught a glimpse of the curtain, white with a design of purple, that hung before the shrine. It was well beyond the crest of the winding stone steps that now confronted him. After climbing the steps, Honda stopped to wipe his forehead. Omiwa Shrine rose imposingly before him, at the foot of Mount Miwa.

The broad courtyard before the shrine had been swept free of gravel to form a square lightly covered with sand that was tinged red by the clay beneath. Here the kendo matches were to be held. Chairs and folding stools lined three sides, and a large canopy covered a portion of the spectators' section. His own seat as an honoured guest, Honda thought, was there beneath the canopy.

A welcoming delegation of white-robed priests appeared and told him that the head of the shrine would be honoured to receive him. Honda glanced quickly over his shoulder at the white disc of the morning sun blazing down upon the kendo ground as he followed the priests to the shelter of the shrine office.

Though he usually wore a grave expression, Honda was not an especially pious man. As he looked beyond the shrine at the towering cedars of Mount Miwa shining in the awesome brilliance of the morning sky, he had the feeling of being in the presence of divinity. Nevertheless, he was far from being possessed by a mood of devotion.

The feeling that the mystical enwraps the world like a pure atmosphere differs considerably from an outlook that, while acknowledging the mystical, simply does not think of it as having anything to do with ordinary affairs. Honda was of course sympathetic to the mystical. It was somewhat like affection for a mother. But from about the age of nineteen he had felt he could get along quite well without it, a feeling that had by now become second nature to him.

After Honda and the various local dignitaries had greeted one another at length and exchanged cards, the chief priest brought them all to the entrance of the corridor leading to the shrine itself where two *miko* were waiting. The guests put out their hands for the young girls to pour water over them according to the Shinto purification ceremony. Within the shrine were the fifty participating athletes, a cluster of blue-clad figures. Honda was accorded the place of honour as the guests seated themselves.

Ritual flutes sounded, and then a priest in tall cap and white robe advanced to the altar and began to recite a dedicatory prayer: 'Here in the terrible presence of the great divinity of Omiwa, the Sacred Prince, Omononushi Kushimigatama, forever enthroned beneath the heavens, forever favoured by the light of the sun, here upon this holy ground of Omiwa...'

As he prayed, the priest waved above the heads of everyone the sacred green sakaki branch hung with strips of white paper. Taking his turn after a member of the sponsoring association, Honda, as representative of the guests, accepted the sakaki branch and raised it reverently before the altar of the gods. Next to make the offering was the representative of the athletes, an old man of about sixty, whose kendo uniform was a faded blue. In the course of all this solemn ritual the heat grew ever more intense, and Honda was uncomfortably aware of the rolling beads of sweat like a swarm of insects under his shirt.

When the formal worship was at last completed, the whole group went down into the forecourt. The guests took their seats in the chairs beneath the canopy, and the athletes sat down upon mats, which were also covered with a canopy. The unsheltered seats were already filled with spectators. Since these sat facing the shrine, they were in the direct rays of the morning sun climbing behind Mount Miwa and had to shield themselves as best they could with fans and hand towels.

Next on the programme was a long series of welcoming and congratulatory speeches. Honda, too, got to his feet and expressed appropriate sentiments. The fifty athletes, he had been told, were divided into the traditional two groups of red and white. Today's meet honouring the gods of Omiwa, then, would have five rounds, each consisting of at least five matches between the two camps. The veterans' association head rose to speak after Honda, and in the course of his address, which went on and on, the chief priest leaned over and whispered into Honda's ear.

'Do you see that boy first from the left in the front row beneath the canvas? He is only in his first year at the College of National Studies in Tokyo, but he is the lead-off man for the whites in the first round. I think that Your Honour would do well to mark this lad. The kendo world expects much of him. At nineteen, he has already achieved the third rank.'

'What's the boy's name?'

'It is Iinuma.'

The name stirred Honda's memory. 'Iinuma? Is his father a kendoist?'

'No, he is Shigeyuki Iinuma, the head of a well-known patriotic group in Tokyo. He has always been most devoted to our shrine. But he himself has never engaged in kendo.'

'Is he here today?'

'He wanted very much to see his son perform in the tournament, he told me, but unfortunately he has to attend a meeting in Osaka today.'

It was Iinuma, then, beyond a doubt – the Iinuma that Honda had known. For a long time now, his name had been rather prominent, but Honda had identified him with Kiyoaki's former tutor only two or three years before. At that time, when the current ideological ferment was becoming a popular topic in the judges' chambers, Honda had borrowed some journals from a colleague making a study of it. Among the articles he read was one entitled 'A Survey of Right-Wing Personalities' which mentioned Iinuma as follows: 'An increasingly conspicuous figure is Shigeyuki Iinuma, a living embodiment of the Satsuma spirit. During the time he was a middle school student he was esteemed by his masters as the most promising boy in the entire prefecture. His family was poor, but, being highly recommended, he came to Tokyo to enter the household of Marquis Matsugae and serve as tutor to the Marquis's young heir. He devoted himself wholeheartedly to the furthering of both his own education and that of the young master. However, he fell passionately in love with one of the maids, a girl named Miné, and he abandoned the Marquis's service. Today this hot-blooded man has survived a time of hardship to attain eminence as the head of his own academy. He and his wife – Miné, of course – have one son.'

Thus Honda learned what had become of Iinuma. He had never had much to do with Kiyoaki's tutor. The only impression of Iinuma that lingered in his mind was that of a stern figure in a sombre dark-blue kimono with a pattern of white splashes leading him silently through the long, dark corridors of the Matsugae mansion. To Honda, Iinuma remained an inscrutable figure against a background of darkness.

The shadow of a horsefly darted over the clean-swept surface of the forecourt. Suddenly the fly buzzed loudly, approaching the long table covered with a white cloth behind which Honda and the others sat. One of the guests opened his fan and brushed it away. His gesture was so elegant that Honda at once remembered seeing from his name card that this man was a kendoist qualified to the seventh rank. The tedious address of the leader of the veterans' group went on and on.

From the square before him – but also from the overhanging gable of the shrine, the green of the holy mountain, the radiant sky – came the scorching breath of violence. Stray gusts of wind stirred the dust in the silent kendo square, soon to be filled with the shouts of antagonists and the crack of bamboo staves, as if the unseen breeze were a lithe phantom flexing its limbs to presage a brave combat.

Honda's eyes were somehow drawn to the face of Iinuma's son, who happened to be seated directly opposite him across the courtyard. The Iinuma of twenty years before must have been five years older than Kiyoaki and Honda. Even so, the realization that the earnest young tutor from the provinces had now become the father of a boy so mature forcibly reminded Honda, childless as he was, of the years that had slipped by unnoticed.

The boy had sat bolt upright throughout the long-winded speeches without making the least movement. Honda could not be sure whether he was really listening. His eyes glittered and he glared straight ahead, an image of steely imperviousness.

The boy's eyebrows were prominent. His complexion was dark. The line of his tight-shut lips was as straight as a blade's edge. Certainly he resembled Iinuma, but the features that had been blunted with heavy melancholy were now strikingly refashioned to express a keen vivacity.

'Here's a face,' Honda thought, 'that knows nothing of life. A face like new-fallen snow, unaware of what lies ahead.'

The athletes sat with their masks and gauntlets arranged carefully in front of them, mask over gauntlet, a small towel partly covering each mask. Sunlight striking the metal bars of the masks flashed along the line of blue-clad knees, heightening the feeling of danger and tension that preceded combat.

The two referees took their positions, one to the front, one to the rear.

'White team: Isao Iinuma.'

As soon as his name was called out, Iinuma's son arose, his body girded with protective gear, and strode forward over the hot sand in his bare feet. He made a deep bow of reverence before the enshrined gods.

For some reason or other, Honda found himself hoping that this boy would win. Then the initial shout broke from young Iinuma's mask, a wild cry like that of an enraged bird. Honda suddenly felt his own youth rushing back upon him.

He had once told Kiyoaki that in later years the two of them, their subtle emotional complexities lost sight of, would be lumped together with the members of the kendo team in the general estimate of the youth of their era. History would say they were dominated by callow faith. And now all had turned out as he had said. What was surprising, however, was that Honda's feeling towards this callow faith was now one of nostalgia. At some point in his life he had come to feel that the 'foolish gods' were more beautiful than the exalted deities that he had once vaguely acknowledged. And in fact the cave of youth into which he had now stumbled was different from the one he had known before.

When that first cry tore the silence it was as though the burning soul of youth had flared out through the rent. The sharp pain that Honda had felt in the days when there were wild flames in his own breast now gripped him once again, as intensely as ever, though at his age he should have been immune to it.

So it is that time reenacts the most curious yet earnest spectacles within the human heart. The past makes its appearance again, with all its mingled dreams and aspirations, the delicate tarnish of falsehood left undisturbed upon its silver. And a man may thus come to a much deeper understanding of himself, a realization that was beyond him in his youth. If one looks down on one's old village from a distant mountain pass, whatever details of that era may have faded from memory, the significance of having lived there becomes vividly apparent. Even the rain-filled hollow in the stone paving of the square, once so disturbing, now merely has a simple, obvious beauty as it glitters in the sun's rays.

The instant that young Iinuma shouted out his challenge, the thirty-eight-year-old judge perceived that there was some pain tearing at this boy's breast, as though an arrowhead had pierced it and remained fixed there. Never had Honda tried to fathom in this manner what went on within the heart of any young man who appeared before him in the prisoner's dock.

The opponent from the red team, his neck pads bouncing against his shoulders like a fish's distended gills, hurled back his own challenge fiercely.

Young Iinuma now was quiet. The two squared off, staves half-raised, and, thus confronting each other, circled once, then once again. When the boy turned toward Honda, the streaked shadow of his mask bars could not obscure the black, well-defined eyebrows, the brilliant eyes, and the line of white teeth that flashed when he shouted. And then when he turned his back, the shaven nape of his neck, below the neatly folded towel inserted beneath the blue mask straps, conveyed a sense of pure, youthful power.

Then suddenly there was a clash, like the collision of two boats buffeted by storm waves. The slender white pendant attached to young Iinuma's back flashed in the sunlight, and the same instant Honda heard the sound of a crashing blow. The boy from the red team had taken it upon the mask.

The spectators applauded. Young Iinuma had eliminated one of the opposition. Now as he faced another man from the red team, first squatting down, then swiftly drawing his stave from his hip, his virile grace persuaded one that he was already master of his new antagonist. Even to Honda, as little as he knew of kendo, young Iinuma's perfect form was evident. However violent the action, he maintained his poise throughout, his flawless bearing at each moment fixed in space like a classic pattern cut from blue cloth. He always kept his balance, unhindered by the clinging heaviness of the air. Though for others the atmosphere might be hot, sticky mud, for young Iinuma it seemed a light, congenial element.

He took a step forward out of the area shaded by the canopy, and his black cuirass shone with the lustre of the clear sky above.

His opponent retreated a step. The blue of his kendo tunic and *hakama* was faded and uneven from many washings, especially where the cords that secured his cuirass had rubbed against his back to form a worn x-shaped pattern. A bright red pennant was attached here.

As young Iinuma advanced one step farther, Honda, whose eye was becoming accustomed to the action, recognized the ominous tension the set of his gauntlets conveyed. The forearm visible between the flaring cuffs of the gauntlets and the sleeves of his tunic showed a thickness unexpected in so young a man, the tendons straining beneath the light skin of the inner arms. The white leather of the gauntlet palms shaded into a bluish tint from their cloth backs, colour as lyrical as the dawn sky.

The tips of the two staves moved cautiously together, like the noses of two wary dogs confronting each other.

'Ee-yaah!' his opponent shouted furiously.

'Ah-ree-yah, ah-ree-yah, ah-ree-yaah!' young Iinuma shouted back at him, his voice sonorous.

He swung his stave to the right to block the other's thrust at his waist, and there was a crack like a bursting firecracker. Then they closed with each other, grappling face to face until their sword arms locked together. The referee separated them.

At the official's signal to resume combat, young Iinuma, without pausing for breath, moved upon his opponent like a blue whirlwind, delivering a combination attack aimed at the head. Each blow struck with force and precision, each more intense. So overwhelming was their combined effect that the other boy, after parrying to right and to left to ward off the first and second blows, seemed to take of his own volition the third, which crashed down directly upon his mask. Both referees flung up their small triangular white pennants at the same moment.

The young athlete had thus eliminated his second opponent, and this time there were shouts of appreciation as well as applause from the spectators.

'The tactic of pressing with vigour and driving him back for the kill, you see,' the kendo instructor next to Honda observed in an affected tone. 'Red there was watching the tip of white's stave. No better way to lose. It just doesn't do to eye the other man's stave. You do it, and you get flurried.'

Though he knew almost nothing of kendo, Honda grasped that there was something like a coiled spring within this young boy that gave off a dark blue glow. The vigour of his spirit manifested itself without a trace of disorder, and, whatever the resistance, created a vacuum within his opponent's resolve, if but for an instant. And the usual result was that, just as air is drawn into a vacuum, so this weak spot of his opponent drew Iinuma's stave. Thrust with perfect form, that stave, Honda thought, would no doubt pierce the guard of any opponent as easily as one enters through an unlocked door.

The third red opponent confronted young Iinuma, advancing with a weaving motion, as though reluctant. The edge of his towel, held in place across his forehead by his mask, was sloppily arranged. Instead of forming a white line straight across his brow, one of its edges dipped down, almost touching his right eye. He hunched his back slightly, like some sort of strange, erratic bird.

This, however, was a man to be reckoned with. Every dip and rise of his stave told something of a tough and shrewd competitor. Like a bird who snatches up the bait and then quickly darts to safety, this opponent would take distant aim for the forearm, strike home in most cases, and then withdraw swiftly to give a shout of victory. And to defend himself, he would not scruple to use any tactic at all, no matter how graceless.

Matched with such an opponent, young Iinuma's very grace, like that of a swan gliding confidently across the water, seemed vulnerable. This time his beauty and skill appeared likely to be his downfall.

His opponent disrupted the rhythm of movement and striking by constantly slipping away. He meant to infect him with his own awkwardness, his own unruliness.

Honda had forgotten the heat. He had even forgotten the cigarettes he liked so well. He realized that he had stopped discarding butts into the ashtray in front of him. Just as he put out his hand to smooth the badly wrinkled tablecloth, the priest beside him uttered a cry of alarm.

Looking up, Honda saw that both referees were waving crossed pennants.

'That was lucky,' said the priest. 'He was almost struck on the gauntlet.'

Young Iinuma was trying to decide how to pursue an opponent who kept at such a distance. If Iinuma took a step forward, the other retreated. His opponent's defence was formidable. He protected himself artfully, as clinging as seaweed.

Then, when Iinuma suddenly attacked with a fierce cry, he countered his thrust derisively, and the two of them came together. Their two staves pointed almost straight upward, shaking slightly, like the masts of two boats side by side, and their cuirasses glistened like wet hulls. Antagonists though they were, their staves were now locked together as though united in reverence to a sky that offered no hope. The hard breathing, the sweat, the straining muscles, the force of their contention compressed into burning frustration ... Such were the elements that went into their immobile symmetry.

Just as the referee was about to call out to put an end to this, young Iinuma, using the strength his opponent was mustering against him, suddenly broke free in a swift backward leap accompanied by the slapping sound of his stave landing a clean blow. He had struck the other's chest as he came away.

Both referees raised their white pennants, and the spectators applauded enthusiastically.

Honda finally lit a cigarette. It glowed feebly, its fire almost imperceptible within the pool of sunlight creeping over the table, and soon he lost interest in it.

Drops of young Iinuma's sweat sprinkled the dust at his feet like a libation of blood. When the boy arose from his squatting position, there was supple vigour in the way his pale Achilles' tendons stretched beneath the dusty hems of his blue *hakama*.

5

Isao Iinuma, kendoist of the third rank, scored five victories in succession, bringing the first round to an end. When the fifth and final round of the match was completed, the officials declared the white team the winner. Furthermore, the silver cup for outstanding individual achievement was to go to Iinuma. As he advanced to receive his award, the sweat of combat wiped away but his cheeks still flushed, he showed the cool modesty suited to a victor. Honda could not recall ever having encountered so manly a young man.

He wanted to talk with the boy and to inquire about his father, but the priests were eager to escort him to the lunch being served in an adjacent building. During the meal the chief priest turned to Honda.

'Would Your Honour care to go up the mountain?' he asked.

Honda hesitated for a moment as he gazed out at the courtyard which lay at the mercy of the blazing sun.

'Of course ordinary visitors are not permitted to go all the way,' the priest added. 'Beyond a certain point the mountain is normally restricted to those who have been devoted to our shrine for many years. To enter there is truly a solemn experience. Gentlemen who have worshipped at the peak say that it gave them a sudden feeling of awesome mystery, as stunning as if they had been struck by lightning.'

Honda looked once more at the summer sunlight shining on the foliage of the courtyard. Could mystery indeed be so bright? His imagination was stirred and he felt himself tempted.

Honda was only willing to sanction a mystery that could flourish in the clear light of day. Thus, if there could be mystery shot through with brightness, he would gladly accept it. A miraculous phenomenon with no link to reality had only a shadowy, dubious existence. But any mystery that could maintain itself beneath the pitiless glare of the sun was a mystery fit to occupy a place beside clearly acknowledged principles. Honda was willing to make room for it in his world.

After a short rest following lunch, one of the younger priests led Honda along the path taken by pilgrims, and after a five- or six-minute walk up a gentle slope covered with lush greenery, they arrived at Sai Shrine, the subordinate shrine within the Omiwa precincts. Its formal title was the Sai Shrine of Omiwa Aramitama. Here pilgrims customarily underwent the rite of purification before proceeding farther up the mountain.

A grove of cedars encircled the unpretentious shrine, whose roof was thatched with cypress bark. So tranquil was its atmosphere that Honda felt that the harsh god whom it honoured must have grown serene. Behind the shrine some red pines rose high above the roof, evoking for Honda the long, agile legs of an ancient warrior.

After Honda's purification, the young priest relinquished him to the care of another guide, a man of about forty wearing rubber-soled climbing shoes. His manner was extremely deferential. Just as they were to begin the formal climb of the sacred mountain, Honda noticed his first wild lily of the day.

'There's a lily they'll be picking for tomorrow's Saigusa Festival, I imagine.'

'Indeed, sir, they will. But they'll never find three thousand on this mountain, so they've already gathered lilies from all the related shrines around here and put them in water in the sanctuary. The young men who fought in the match today will be pulling a cartload of lilies to Nara tomorrow as a sacred offering.' And then, cautioning Honda that yesterday's rain had made the clay underfoot treacherous, the guide turned abruptly and started up the mountain path.

Almost a hundred valleys radiated from the forbidden area of Mount Miwa, including Omiya Valley, which opened out behind the main shrine to the west. After they had climbed a short distance, Honda could see the forbidden zone itself beyond a fence to his right. The trunks of the red pines growing there, in the grip of a tangle of vegetation, glowed like agate beneath the afternoon sun.

Within this area the trees, the ferns, the bamboo thickets, even the sunlight that spilled over everything seemed, to Honda at least, to create an air of purity and solemnity. The fresh colour of the soil at the roots of a cedar, where the guide told him a boar had been digging, made him think of the stories from the old chronicles about the odd forms that the boar could assume.

Still, as he made his way up the sacred mountain, he had no strong feeling that it was either itself divine or the abode of divine beings. A little disconcerted by the swiftness of his middle-aged guide, Honda was hard-pressed to keep up. He felt grateful that the trees along the stream they were following warded off the afternoon sunlight, which was now even hotter.

Though sheltered by the trees, the path was becoming more and more difficult. There were many sakaki on the mountain-side. Even the young trees had far broader leaves than the sakaki Honda had seen elsewhere, and in the midst of their dark green they showed a wealth of white blossoms. The current of the stream grew more rapid as they climbed until they at last reached Sanko Falls. The view of the falls, however, was half hidden by a shelter at the foot for those who came to undergo the water purification. Honda had heard how dark the woods were at this spot, but since sunlight was glinting all around, the impression was of being in a basketwork cage of light.

From here, the path led directly to the peak, and this was by far the hardest part of the climb. Wherever the path gave out, the two of them had to make use of jutting rocks and pine roots to scale the sections of bare cliff that blocked their way. And whenever Honda allowed himself to hope that a relatively easy portion would last for a time, yet another rock wall loomed up ahead in the brilliant glare of the afternoon sun. Honda was soaked with sweat and panting for breath. It was the intoxicating force of such harsh mortification, he supposed, that prepared a man for the mystery that he was approaching. That indeed was a divine law.

Honda looked down on a silent valley with red pines and black pines over ten feet in diameter. He saw withered pines choked with ivy and twisted vegetation, all their needles the colour of dull brick, and a lone cedar halfway up a cliff, around whose trunk some pilgrim, sensing the tree's divinity, had wound a length of sacred rope. Offerings were placed before it, and a growth of lichen had turned one side of its trunk a greenish bronze. The closer they drew to the peak of the sacred mountain, the more every shrub and tree seemed to have its own divinity, as if it had naturally become a god.

When, for example, the wind caught the tips of some tall oaks and scattered their blossoms in a cloud of pale yellow floating down through the lonely mountain forest, Honda felt that the scene was charged with divinity, like a sudden charge of electricity.

'Just a little more effort, sir,' said the guide, his voice unaffected by the strenuous climb. 'There's the top ahead. You can see the Iwakura and Konomiya Shrine.'

The Iwakura – the seat of the gods – had suddenly appeared at the end of the steep slope in front of them. Its circumference marked by sacred rope, it was a huge, irregular rock formation, now sharp-pointed, now jagged and blunted, like a great ship whose back had been broken. Since ancient times this mass of rock had defied comprehension, had never submitted to the general order, its bulk an awesome image of pure chaos. Rock had fused to rock to form the mass that now lay broken and shattered. Below it more rock stretched out in a broad, flat surface slanting downward. Rather than a tranquil seat of the gods, the whole impression was that of the aftermath of battle or of something incredibly terrible. But then, perhaps any place visited by the gods would undergo a similar transformation.

The sun beat pitilessly down upon the moss that crept over the rock surface like an infection. But, as one might expect at this height, a refreshing breeze stirred the forest.

Konomiya Shrine, at the very top of the Iwakura, was 1,534 feet above sea level. The simplicity of this little shrine alleviated the wild, awesome mood of the Iwakura itself. The small cross-beams that formed a sharply acute angle over the peaked roof stood out from the green pines around it like a headband gallantly knotted across a warrior's forehead.

After Honda had paid his reverence, he wiped away his sweat, and, begging the guide's indulgence, lit a forbidden cigarette and drew hungrily upon it. Many years had gone by since he had last put his legs to such a test. Now that he had come through the ordeal, he took satisfaction from it and found himself very much at peace. In the midst of divinity of this sort, a divinity filled with brightness and the sound of pine needles rustling in the breeze, he felt as if he might be willing to believe in anything.

All at once Honda was reminded of another time, probably by the terrain and the altitude. He remembered climbing the mountains behind Chung-nan Villa at Kamakura on a summer day nineteen years before. They had come upon a distant view of the Great Buddha of Kamakura through the trees, and he and Kiyoaki had exchanged amused glances at the expense of the two Siamese princes, who had knelt in reverence at the first sight of the Buddha. Honda would never again feel inclined to mock such a display.

In the intervals between gusts of wind through the pines, the silence could come stealing back. His ear caught the buzz of a passing horsefly. The cedars pointed upward like so many spears thrust at the brilliant sky. The clouds were moving. The cherry trees were in full leaf, a study in light and shadow beneath the sun's rays. Honda was happy without knowing why. And this happiness had a trace of indefinable sadness, a light, poignant sting. It must have been the first time in years that he had felt this way.

The descent was not as easy as he had expected. He tried to use the tree roots to keep his footing, but the red clay around them was even more slippery. When they finally reached the tree-lined path that circled Sanko Falls, Honda found his shirt wringing wet once more.

'Would Your Honour care to make use of the water purification? It's very refreshing.'

'But it wouldn't be right to bathe for that purpose, would it?'

'On the contrary, sir. When the falling water strikes a man, it clears his head. That's what makes it a religious exercise, so you needn't worry.'

When they entered the shelter at the base of the falls, Honda noticed two or three kendo uniforms hanging from nails. Someone had preceded them.

'The students who were in the match today, sir. They'll be making the offering of the lilies, and they must have been told to come here to purify themselves.'

Honda stripped to his undershorts and went through the door that faced the falls.

Sacred rope stretched across the falls high up at its crest, where a lush growth of vegetation shone in the afternoon sun. Up there were brightness and colour, the green of trees and shrubbery ruffled by the wind, the white Shinto pendants dancing along the length of the rope, but as Honda looked downward, the scene before him was enveloped in the dark shadow cast by the rock walls to either side. A small shrine to the stalwart God of Fire occupied a grotto beside the falls, and ferns, spear flowers, and sakaki trees, all of them wet with spray, grew in the half-light at its foot. The gloom was relieved only by the slender white ribbon of falling water. Its sound echoed from the encircling rock walls with a full-throated roar.

Three young men in undershorts were standing side by side beneath the falls, water spilling in all directions over their heads and shoulders. Honda could hear the water beating on their resilient young flesh. Through the swirling spray he saw the reddened flesh of their gleaming wet shoulders.

When one of the young men noticed Honda, he nudged his companions, and they stepped back, bowing politely as they yielded the falls to him. It was then that he recognized young Iinuma among them.

Honda moved forward beneath the falls. But the water struck the upper part of his body with such clubbing force that he hastily drew back. Young Iinuma, laughing pleasantly, came up beside him, raised both hands high to demonstrate how to break the force of the falling water, and plunged himself beneath it. He stood there for a few moments, catching the violently tumbling water upon his palms and outspread fingers as if bearing a heavy flower basket aloft. Then he turned to Honda and smiled.

Honda was about to follow his example, when he happened to glance at young

Iinuma's left side. There back from the nipple, at a place ordinarily hidden by the arm, he clearly saw a cluster of three small moles.

A shiver ran through Honda. He stared at the gallant features of the boy who looked back laughingly from beneath the falls, brows contracted against the water, eyes blinking.

Honda remembered Kiyoaki's dying words: 'I'll see you again. I know it. Beneath the falls.'

6

Only the voices of the frogs of Sarusawa Pond were audible in his quiet room at the Hotel Nara, as Honda, the legal documents untouched on the desk in front of him, passed a sleepless night lost in thought.

He had left Omiwa Shrine towards evening, he recalled, and had encountered a cart laden with lilies just as his car was passing flooded rice paddies ablaze with the scarlet glow of the setting sun. The wild lilies piled high upon the cart and held in place with sacred rope were a faint pink, as if they had been cut just at the flush of dawn. Two students with white headbands over the school caps were pushing the cart, and another was pulling it. A white-robed priest walked ahead, holding a purification wand hung with paper pendants. The student pulling the cart was young Iinuma, and as soon as he noticed Honda in the car, he stopped and raised his cap in greeting. His companions followed suit.

Ever since he made his incredible discovery beneath the falls, Honda had been unable to regain his equanimity. He had barely acknowledged the various courtesies that the priests of the shrine had shown him afterwards. And then when he had again come upon the three students, their offering of lilies and their white headbands brilliant in the sunset glow mirrored upon the surface of the rice paddies, he became still more abstracted. The young man left behind in the dust raised by the speeding auto, much as his features and his complexion differed, was assuredly in his essential being no one but Kiyoaki.

Once Honda was left to himself at the hotel, he was beset by the thought that from that day on, his world would be drastically changed. He went down to the dining room at once, but ate his dinner as if in a daze. He went back to his room. The sheets on the freshly made bed were folded back to form a lustrous white triangle. Like the pages of a book lying wide open, they gleamed in the faint light of a table lamp.

He turned on all the lights, trying in vain to keep mystery at a distance. The miraculous had invaded his own ordered world, and he had no idea what might happen in the future. Furthermore, though he had seen the marvel of reincarnation with his own eyes, it was a secret he could never reveal. If he were to speak of it to someone, he would immediately be thought insane, and the rumour would pass from mouth to mouth that he was no longer qualified to be a judge.

Still, mystery had a rationality of its own. Just as Kiyoaki had said eighteen years before ('I'll see you again. I know it. Beneath the falls.') Honda had indeed met beneath a waterfall a young man whose side was marked with the same pattern of three moles. He was reminded of what he had read about the four successive existences in the books on Buddhism that he had studied after Kiyoaki's death, following the teachings of the Abbess of Gesshu. Since young Iinuma was eighteen years old, his age as Kiyoaki reincarnated fitted precisely.

These four existences, marking the progression of every sentient being, were conception, life, death, and then an intermediate period of existence, a state midway between the previous life and the reincarnation to come. At its shortest this lasted seven days, and it could extend for as long as seventy-seven. Honda did not, of course, know the date of Iinuma's birth, but it was altogether possible that it fell somewhere within the period of from seven to seventy-seven days after Kiyoaki's death in the early spring of 1914, the third year of the Taisho era.

In this intermediate state, according to Buddhist lore, one existed, not as a merely spiritual being, but in the form of a fully sentient young child of five or six. Now, however, all the ordinary powers were marvellously heightened. The eye and ear became incredibly keen. One heard the most distant sounds, one saw the most hidden objects, one was immediately present wherever one wished to be. The childlike figures thus gifted, though invisible both to men and to beasts, could be seen hovering in the air by the rare clairvoyant who had attained sufficient purity.

These invisible children nourished themselves on the fragrance of burning incense as they went about their rapid journeys through the air. Hence this intermediate state was also known as 'seeking fragrance', after the divinities called Gandharva in Sanskrit.

In the course of his far-ranging flights, such a child would come upon the overwhelming sight of his future father and mother in the very act of copulating. A male child would be fascinated by the shameless disarray of his future mother's body, and yet, though he burned with resentment towards the man who was to be his father, no sooner had this man made his impure ejaculation than the child would be seized with a passionate joy as though the act were his own, and give up his free existence to take life up within the woman's womb. This instant was the next stage of existence.

Such was the Buddhist explanation. Honda, of course, had once looked upon it as a mere fairy tale. And now all at once it had come to his mind. The process, he thought, was certainly what mystery should be: something that arbitrarily made its appearance, independent of the wishes of any man. A dangerous gift. Like a shimmering sphere of changing colours, it came plunging into the midst of the cold but well-regulated structure of order and reason. Its colours, indeed, changed according to principle, but a principle that was entirely different from human reason. Hence the sphere had to be somehow hidden from human eyes.

Whether Honda was willing to acknowledge it or not, mystery had already irrevocably altered his outlook. He could not escape it. Perhaps the best course was to find an ally, someone to share the secret. There was young Iinuma himself for one. And then, too, there was the boy's father. But what assurance had he that either one was aware of the presence of mystery? It might well be that Shigeyuki

Iinuma, who must have had occasion to see Kiyoaki naked, realized that the mark on his son's side strikingly resembled the one that his young master had borne. Even so, he might wish to conceal it. How could Honda question father and son about such a matter? Would not the very act of questioning them be ill-advised? Even if they were aware of the presence of mystery, would they be willing to share their secret? If they refused, the mystery might weigh heavily on him for the rest of his life.

Once more Honda felt racing through him the keen excitement that Kiyoaki had brought to his youth. Though Honda had never yearned to exchange lives with anyone, the brief beauty of Kiyoaki's life, like delicate blossoms on a branch, seemed joined to his own, the tree that for those few years had provided the needed support. And thus Kiyoaki's life gave meaning to Honda's, having flowered with a beauty that Honda's itself would never attain. Could this happen again? What was the meaning of Kiyoaki's reincarnation?

Beset though he was by the riddles that surrounded him, Honda nonetheless felt joy stirring deep within him like a subterranean spring. Kiyoaki was alive once more! The tree cut down in its youth had sprung up once more. Eighteen years ago both he and Kiyoaki had been young. Now Honda's youth was gone, but his friend's shone with undiminished brilliance.

Young Iinuma might lack Kiyoaki's beauty, but he compensated for that with the manly force that Kiyoaki had lacked. Though Honda could not be certain from so brief an acquaintance, it seemed to him that young Iinuma, in place of Kiyoaki's arrogance, possessed simplicity and fortitude, qualities hardly apparent in Kiyoaki. The two were as different as light and shadow, but they shared one characteristic: both of them strikingly personified youth.

When Honda thought about those years he had spent with Kiyoaki, he felt mingled grief and nostalgia, but now also an unexpected rush of hope. He would have to pay a price for the excitement that was building within him, but he was ready to do so without regret, no matter how severe the consequences for his once unswerving commitment to reason.

And then how strange a turn of fate that he made the incredible discovery of Kiyoaki's rebirth in Nara, a place so intimately involved with Honda's last memories of his friend!

'I'll wait until morning,' Honda thought, 'but there's something I should do before going to Izagawa Shrine. I'll have my driver rush me to Obitoké for an early morning visit to the convent. I'll apologize to Satoko for not having come to see her in the years since Kiyoaki's death, and then I'll tell her about his reincarnation, even if she won't believe it. She should be the first to know. Now she's the Abbess of Gesshu, after the death of the former Abbess, and I've heard that she is greatly revered. Probably the years have touched her only lightly, and I'll be able to see that beautiful face of hers lit up by pure joy.'

For a time Honda felt a youthful impulsiveness. Finally, however, he prudently decided to suppress that hasty notion.

'No, I shouldn't do it,' he told himself. 'After all, she didn't even attend his funeral. She made her decision to turn her back on the world, and I have no right to disturb her. No matter how often Kiyoaki was reborn, it would not concern her

– it would always be something that happened in the world of deceitful illusion which she has abandoned. No matter how unmistakable the proof, she would turn coldly away. For me it may be a miracle, but miracles no longer exist for Satoko in the world in which she now lives. It won't do to let myself be carried away by excitement over this. I'll not go to see her. If this strange reincarnation is the work of providence, I needn't rush to see her. Some occasion will arise for her to meet him. It's better that I wait and let events mature in their own way.'

After pondering all this, Honda found sleep still more remote. The warmth of his pillow and spread became oppressive, and he gave up all hope of a pleasant night's rest.

The window was beginning to whiten. In the pane of glass enclosed by a frame carved in Momoyama style, the reflection of Honda's night lamp shimmered like a dawn moon. Against the faint light of the sky he could already make out the five-storeyed pagoda of Kofuku Temple rising up beyond a grove of trees encircling a pond. Only the three top storeys and the spire thrusting itself upward into the dawn were visible. As he gazed at the pagoda, hardly more than a shadow in a corner of the grey sky, Honda felt as if he had awakened only to fall into another dream, like a man who thinks that he has escaped from one kind of irrationality only to find himself in the midst of another, even more persuasive. Thus did the pagoda affect him – the subtle curvature of those three upper roofs – as if it were the image of a many-layered dream. A smoky mist seemed to be rising from the topmost roof to swirl through the nine rings circling the spire and up past the flame-shaped device at its peak, finally to fade into the dawn sky. Even as he was watching this happen, Honda had no assurance that he was in fact awake. For all he knew, he might be in the midst of another dream, a dream so vivid that not even the keenest perception could distinguish it from reality.

The song of the birds became louder. Suddenly the thought struck him that it was not just a matter of Kiyoaki's returning to life. Had not Honda himself risen from death? From the death manifested by a chilled spirit, by a rigorous order like a file jammed with thousands of entries, by the tedious refrain, 'Youth is gone'?

Perhaps it was exactly because his own life had once been so far encroached upon by Kiyoaki's life, so deeply buried with it, that life was now being restored to Honda too, just as the first rays of dawn brighten one branch of a tree and then the next.

At this point Honda felt a curious relief, and at last, as if falling into a light faint, succumbed to sleep.

7

Honda awoke with a start, realizing that he had forgotten to ask to be called, and by the time he arrived at Izagawa Shrine the solemn ritual of the Saigusa Festival had already begun. Bending forward, he made his way through the hushed crowd to the seat reserved for him beneath the canopy. He sat down quietly, without even looking around, and fastened his gaze on the ceremony before him.

Izagawa Shrine was in Nara itself, not far from the railway station. To the rear of the shrine precincts stood three sanctuaries. The centre sanctuary enshrined the goddess Himetataraisuzu, and, to either side, as though to protect her, were her goddess mother and her father, the latter the principal deity of Omiwa Shrine. A scarlet railing encircled the three small, beautifully fashioned structures, which were linked together by white screening partitions decorated with paintings of pines and bamboos done in rich turquoise and gold.

Each sanctuary was fronted with three stone steps which were swept clean of impurity. And then to reach the sanctuary door itself, one had to ascend ten wooden steps. The white paper pendants that hung from the sacred rope at the eaves seemed to stand out like fragments of pure ivory against the scarlet railing and the yellow and gold-flecked bracketing in the dark shadow of the roof.

Fresh mats had been spread upon the stone steps for today's ritual. The gravel of the courtyard had been raked into a neat pattern. To the front of the precincts was the scarlet-pillared outer hall of the shrine, an open gallery in which priests and shrine musicians were sitting on either side. Through this gallery the worshippers would observe the ceremonies.

A priest had already begun the purification ritual, and the three small bells attached to the base of a large sacred branch tinkled as he waved it over the bowed heads of the crowd. After the prayer ended, the chief priest of Omiwa Shrine, bearing a gold key hung with a crimson cord, advanced towards the centre sanctuary and knelt upon the wooden steps, the back of his white robe half in sunlight and half in shadow. As he was kneeling, the assistant priests at his side twice chanted a long, drawn-out 'Oh!'. The chief priest then climbed the steps, inserted the key into the lock of the sanctuary doors, and reverently drew them open. The dark purple Sacred Mirror flashed from within. The stringed instruments were sounding a repeated tremolo of almost ludicrous intensity.

The assistant priests spread fresh mats before the sanctuary. Then, together with the chief priest himself, they bore oblations covered with oak leaves to a table of bark-covered wood hung with white paper pendants. And now began the most beautiful part of the Saigusa Festival.

The next offerings would be a cask filled with white sake and an earthen jar filled with black saké, both of them beautifully adorned. The cask was of plain wood and the jar was unglazed, but both were entirely covered with lilies, like two sheaves of flowers. Thus the body of the cask was completely wrapped around with the tough green stems of lilies, bound by fresh white hempen cord. Since their stems formed such a tight sheath, the flowers and leaves and buds were thrust all together in a promiscuous tangle. The greenish red buds had a rustic vigour, and there was a trace of green left even in the fully opened flowers, whose petals were streaked with a delicate pink. Their inner surfaces were dusted with red, and the tips of their petals, bent back in utter disarray, were translucent in the sunlight. Huddled together in such a mass, the lilies stood with drooping heads.

The most beautiful of the three thousand wild lilies brought by young Iinuma and his companions had been selected to adorn the cask and the jar, but the rest were also brilliantly in evidence, arranged in vases before the sanctuaries. Lilies were everywhere. The breeze carried the scent of lilies. The theme of lilies was persistent and inescapable, as though lilies had come to express the very essence of life. Now the priests advanced with the cask and the earthen jar. White-robed, with black ceremonial headgear, they solemnly held these offerings aloft, and the bound lilies trembled in beauty over their heads. The bud of one especially long-stemmed lily seemed as pale as a tense young man on the verge of fainting.

The wail of the flutes filled the air. The drums throbbed. Placed before a dark stone wall, the lilies seemed to flush crimson. The priests crouched down beside the cask and the jar, parted the stems of the lilies, and dipped out saké. Other priests approached to receive it in their plain wood flasks, and then raised them in oblation before each of the three shrines. This ritual, with its musical accompaniment, seemed quite in the spirit of a cheerful banquet of the gods. Within the doorway of the sanctuary the noon shadows evoked a vaguely growing sense of divine intoxication.

Meanwhile a group of *miko*, four beautiful young girls, had begun the Cedar Dance in the outer hall. Their heads were bound with cedar leaves, and their black hair was braided with red and white paper fastened with gold thread. Over pale crimson *hakama*, they wore gossamer robes of pure white with a silver pattern of rice leaves. The five robes worn beneath the white outer one revealed themselves at the neckline in an alternating white and red pattern.

The young girls made their appearance in the midst of lilies, lilies standing upright, petals wide open, amber-coloured stamens out-thrust. And each of these *miko*, too, held a bunch of lilies in her hand. As the musicians played, the girls formed a square facing inward and began to dance, their upraised lilies starting to shake with fearful abandon. The dance progressed, the lilies now elegantly rising, now dipping to come together, now separating once more. Again and again, like the passes of a keen sword blade, a graceful edge of whiteness cut through the air. As they were thus whipped about, the lilies gradually wilted, cruelly handled, it seemed, for all the quiet elegance of the music and the dance.

As Honda looked on, he felt a kind of intoxication overcoming him. He had never seen such a beautiful ritual. The effects of his sleepless night made the spectacle begin to blur, and the lily festival he was now watching started to merge with the kendo match he had seen the previous day. The girls' lilies became bamboo staves and then, in another moment, flashing sword blades. As the *miko* circled about with easy grace in the sunlight, the shadows of their long eyelashes on their white-powdered cheeks became for Honda the shadows cast by the glittering bars of the kendo mask.

After the guests and other worshippers had lifted the pendant-festooned sakaki branch in reverence before the sanctuary, the doors were shut once more. By noon the ritual was over.

The Naorai, the sacred banquet following a ritual, was to take place in an adjacent hall. The chief priest came over to Honda with a middle-aged man he wanted to introduce. As soon as Honda saw young Iinuma in his school cap walking along behind him, he realized that the man was Shigeyuki Iinuma. Iinuma's slender moustache had thrown him off for a moment.

'This must be Mr Honda,' Iinuma said. 'What memories this brings back! Has it really been nineteen years? My son Isao told me about yesterday, how kind you were to him. What a strange turn of fate!'

Iinuma pulled a sheaf of calling cards from his pocket, picked out one of his own, and presented it to Honda. As he read it, the fastidious Honda could not help noticing that one corner of the card was slightly soiled and bent:

THE ACADEMY OF PATRIOTISM
SHIGEYUKI IINUMA
HEADMASTER

What startled him about Kiyoaki's old tutor was his talkative and open manner, so unlike the Iinuma Honda remembered. Years before he had been quite different. As Honda looked more closely, he saw that some things about him were unchanged: the uncouth tuft of hair just visible at the neck of his kimono, his square shoulders, the dark, brooding eyes, with a tendency to waver. His outward bearing, however, was altogether different.

'Forgive me for addressing you so familiarly!' said Iinuma, looking up from Honda's card. 'You certainly have attained eminence. The truth is, your fame came to my notice some time ago, but it seemed rude for someone like me to presume upon past acquaintance, so I restrained myself. Now that I look at you, you haven't changed a bit. If the young master were alive, you would be his most trusted friend. Anyway, as I learned afterwards, you proved the depth of your friendship by what you did for him. Everyone said how wonderful you were.'

As Honda listened, feeling as though he were being slightly mocked, it occurred to him that Iinuma would not speak so openly of Kiyoaki if he were aware of his young master's reincarnation in his own son. Then again, possibly Iinuma's apparent frankness was a means of seizing the initiative and warning Honda not to intrude into this mystery.

Still, when Honda looked at Iinuma in his crested *hakama* and at young Isao standing behind him, he could only see everyday reality. Iinuma's face was marked by the years and by the common tribulations. The smell of day-by-day existence was so strong that the wild thoughts that had pursued Honda from the dreams of the night before seemed no more than ephemeral fantasy. He began to wonder if even the moles he had seen on Isao's side might have been no more than a trick of vision.

Nevertheless, despite the urgency of the work that awaited him that evening, Honda found himself asking Iinuma: 'How long will you be in the Kansai?'

'I'm afraid I'll be taking the train back to Tokyo tonight.'

'That's too bad.' After a moment's thought, Honda made his decision. 'What do you say to this? Before you leave tonight, won't you and your son have dinner at my home? It's a rare chance for us to have a leisurely talk.'

'You do me too much honour. I couldn't think of imposing myself and my son upon your hospitality.'

Honda turned directly to Isao: 'It will be my pleasure. You and your father must come. You'll be returning to Tokyo on the same train, won't you?'

'Yes, sir,' answered Isao, somewhat inhibited by his father's presence.

Iinuma, however, now said that he would accept Honda's kind invitation, and promised that, after attending to a few matters in Osaka, both of them would come to his home that evening.

'Your son was superb yesterday in the kendo match. It's really a pity that you couldn't be there. It was a performance to take one's breath away.' As he spoke, Honda looked from one to the other.

Just then a lean but erect old man in Western clothes approached them. He was accompanied by an extremely attractive woman of about thirty.

'General Kito and his daughter,' Iinuma whispered into Honda's ear.

'General Kito, you say? The poet?'

'Yes, yes. That's right.'

Iinuma had become tense, and his hushed, respectful tone made Honda think of a courtier sent to prepare the way of a lord.

Kensuké Kito was a retired major-general of the Imperial Army, but his fame came from his poetry. Honda, urged by friends, had read his highly praised *Hekiraku*, a collection of poems that, according to critics, revived the bold spirit and style of the thirteenth-century poet Sanetomo. Such classical elegance and simple beauty were wholly unexpected from a contemporary military man, and Honda had found his poems so moving that he could recite two or three of them from memory.

Iinuma greeted the General with the utmost deference and then turned to introduce Honda: 'This gentleman is Judge Honda of the Osaka Court of Appeals.'

Honda would have preferred to be presented merely as an old friend, but now that Iinuma had seen fit to introduce him with such a flourish, Honda had no choice but to assume his role as an official and stand on his dignity.

The General, however, seemed quite equal to the occasion, his military background having accustomed him to distinctions of rank. He smiled, crinkling the corners of his eyes, and said quietly: 'My name is Kito.'

'I am a great admirer of your poetry, especially of *Hekiraku*.'

'You'll have me blushing.'

General Kito had the affability and utter lack of arrogance of a man who has spent his life as a soldier. Having survived a profession that offered ample opportunity to die young, he inspired a feeling of strength and steadfastness. His old age shone with cheerful detachment, like the winter sun shining through white paper stretched over a latticework of fine, aged wood, not in the least warped, beyond which patches of snow lay here and there on the ground.

As he and Honda were exchanging a few words, his beautiful daughter spoke to Isao: 'I hear that you defeated five men in succession yesterday. Congratulations.'

Honda glanced over toward her, and the General introduced them: 'My daughter, Makiko.' Makiko bowed her head politely.

During that moment Honda found himself eagerly waiting to look into the lovely face beneath her Western-style hairdo. Now that he saw her close at hand, Honda noticed by both the whiteness of her skin, almost devoid of makeup, and the faint, tell-tale signs, like the grain of thick Japanese paper, that she was no longer a young girl. Her smooth features seemed somehow to express a distant sorrow. The tautness at the corners of her mouth gave a disturbing hint of disdainful resignation but her eyes were brimming with a soft, gentle light.

As Honda and Iinuma stood talking with the General and his daughter about the beauty of the Saigusa Festival, young priests in white robes and pale yellow *hakama* came out and urged all the guests to take their places at the Naorai.

The General and his daughter met other friends, walked ahead with them towards the reception hall, and were soon lost in the crowd.

'What a lovely young woman!' said Honda, half to himself. 'And she's still not married?'

'She's divorced,' Iinuma replied. 'I suppose she must be in her early thirties. It's hard to think a man would let a beauty like that get away from him.' His voice sounded muffled, as if the lips beneath the neat moustache were reluctant.

The worshippers crowded the entrance of the hall, jostling together as they struggled to remove their shoes and enter. Honda let himself be carried along by the flow of people, and, looking ahead through the crowd, caught his first glimpse of the tables set up for the banquet. A mass of wild lilies was spread over the white tablecloths.

Somewhere Honda had become separated even from Iinuma. As the crowd surged by, it occurred to him that Kiyoaki himself, alive again, was caught in this same press of humanity. How wild a fancy this seemed here at midday beneath the early summer sun! He was dazzled by the excessive brightness of the mystery.

Just as sea and sky blurred together at the horizon, so, too, dream and reality could certainly become confused when viewed from a distance. But here, at least around Honda, everyone was clearly subject to the law and, in turn, guarded by the law. His role was that of a guardian of the order established by the operative law of this world. This operative law was like a heavy iron lid upon the pot in which the multifarious stew of the day-to-day world simmered.

Human beings eating, digesting, excreting, reproducing, loving and hating ... Honda reflected that these were the human beings under the court's jurisdiction. If worst came to worst they would appear before it as defendants.

They alone had reality. Human beings who sneezed, laughed, human beings who went about with absurdly dangling reproductive gear. If all human beings were like this, there was no basis whatsoever for Honda's fearful mystery. Even if a single reborn Kiyoaki might be hidden in their midst.

Honda sat at the place of honour to which the priests directed him. On the table before him were wooden boxes of various delicacies and jars of saké as well as plates and small bowls. At appropriate intervals stood vases of wild lilies. Makiko was sitting on the same side of the table, and he was occasionally able to catch a glimpse of her lovely profile and the wisps of hair that fell over her cheek.

The rays of the early summer sun, scattered by tree branches, fell upon the garden. Now it was the turn for humans to feast.

8

After Honda had returned home in the afternoon, he asked his wife to arrange for dinner guests and then took a short nap. He had a dream that Kiyoaki suddenly appeared and began telling him how joyful he was at their being reunited. When Honda awoke, however, he did not allow this to excite him. He accounted for it as merely an illustration of the lingering thoughts that had occupied his fatigued mind since the previous night.

Iinuma and his son arrived at six o'clock. Intending to leave directly by train afterwards, they had brought their luggage with them. When Honda and Iinuma sat down together, they felt awkward about immediately returning to their talk of the past, and instead began to discuss recent politics and social conditions. But Iinuma, apparently in deference to Honda's position, refrained from voicing any outright complaints about the evils of the times. Isao sat upright, hands on knees, as he listened.

Those eyes of his, which had flashed brightly even from behind a kendo mask yesterday, seemed extravagantly brilliant here in an ordinary room. They seemed to express intense determination. To have such eyes close to one, to be gazed at intently by such eyes was an extraordinary experience.

Honda sensed Isao's eyes on him as he talked with Iinuma, and he felt uneasy. 'It's quite uncalled for to stare like that during a conversation,' he thought, feeling tempted to say a word of remonstrance. Eyes of that kind should not be brought to bear upon the petty doings of everyday life. Honda felt somehow accused by their clear brilliance.

Two men may talk together enthusiastically for an hour or so about shared experiences, and yet not have a true conversation. A lonely man who wants to indulge his nostalgic mood feels the need of someone with whom to share it. When he finds such a companion he starts to pour out his monologue as though recounting a dream. And so the talk goes on between them, their monologues alternating, but after a time they suddenly become aware that they have nothing to say to each other. They are like two men standing at either side of a chasm, the bridge across which has been destroyed.

Then at last, since they cannot bear to remain silent, their conversation turns again to the past. For some reason, Honda found himself yielding to the urge to ask Iinuma why he had published an article in a right-wing newspaper accusing Marquis Matsugae of being disloyal and unfilial.

'Ah, that!' answered Iinuma. 'I hesitated before making an attack on the Marquis, who was so kind to me, but I felt I had to write that article regardless of the consequences. I did it solely out of concern for the nation.'

Such a smooth, ready answer naturally did not satisfy Honda. He remarked that Kiyoaki, after reading the article and sensing its significance, told him he missed Iinuma.

A startling surge of emotion swept over Iinuma's face, which had already begun to show the effects of the saké they were drinking. The neat moustache trembled slightly.

'Is that right? The young master said that? He must have known how I felt. My motive in writing that article – how should I put it – was to make a public complaint, even though it meant sacrificing the Marquis, so that no one could blame the young master himself. I was afraid the young master's involvement might somehow become known, and the scandal would do him irreparable harm. By taking the initiative and exposing the Marquis's disloyalty, I could shield the young master. And then, too, wouldn't any good father want to bear the brunt of the scandal himself? That was what I expected. Perhaps it was inevitable that the Marquis would become enraged at me, but when I think how the young master understood my intentions, I feel an overwhelming gratitude.

'Judge Honda, please listen to what I have to say. It's the saké that gives me the courage to tell you this, but I'm not exaggerating. When I heard that the young master had passed away I wept for three whole days and nights. I thought that I would at least attend the wake, and I went to the Matsugae mansion, only to be turned away at the door. It seems that the arrangements concerning me were very thorough. Even on the day of the public funeral service I was kept out by their police. And so I could not offer incense for the departed young master.

'Of course I brought it on myself, but it's a grievance that I'll bear for the rest of my days. Even now I sometimes speak bitterly about it to my wife. What an unhappy fate for the young master! To die without achieving what he wished, and at barely twenty.' Iinuma pulled a handkerchief from his pocket and wiped away his tears.

Honda's wife had come in to pour the saké, and sat there speechless. Young Isao, who had apparently never seen his father so overcome with emotion, had stopped eating and was looking down. Honda stared at Iinuma across the brightly lit, dish-laden table as if he were gauging the distance between them.

Honda did not doubt the genuineness of Iinuma's sentiment. Thus, since his grief expressed such finality, he could hardly have known of Kiyoaki's re-incarnation. Otherwise his emotion would surely have been far more ambiguous and uncertain.

As he reflected, Honda found himself scrutinizing his own inner thoughts. Why did the sight of Iinuma's grief provoke no tears from him? For one thing, there was the tempering his emotions had undergone in a profession that prized reason. And for another, there was the newfound hope that Kiyoaki lived again. A mere hint of the possibility of reincarnation made even the keenest grief suddenly seem to lose its freshness and reality, and begin to scatter like dry leaves. Somehow that was related to man's unwillingness to tolerate any injury to the dignity that he achieved through sorrow. In a sense, such a loss was more fearful than death.

When Iinuma had gained control of himself, he at once turned to his son and asked him to go to send a telegram for him. He had forgotten to tell the students of the academy to come to meet them at Tokyo Station the next morning. Rié suggested sending the maid, but Honda, realizing that Iinuma wanted his son out of the way for a time, quickly sketched a map to show Isao how to find the nearest post office that was open at night.

After Isao left, Rié went back to the kitchen. At last Honda had a chance to question Iinuma closely, but, while he was wondering how to broach the subject, Iinuma himself began to speak of Kiyoaki.

'I failed wretchedly in educating the young master, so I intended to do my best to give my own son what I considered an ideal education. But again something was missing. When I look at my grown son, it's incredible how the young master's good qualities come to my mind. In spite of how I failed with him.'

'But you have a wonderful son. From what I've seen of him, he's quite superior to Kiyoaki Matsugae.'

'Judge Honda, you're being too polite.'

'Well, consider Isao's physical fitness. Kiyoaki neglected his body completely.' Honda felt the excitement rising within him as he tried to lead Iinuma to the crucial point of the mystery. 'It's no wonder he died so early from pneumonia – he was handsome, but he had no strength. But you were with him ever since he was a chlld. You must have been thoroughly familiar with his body.'

'By no means!' Iinuma hastily protested. 'I never so much as washed the young master's back.'

'Why not?'

Embarrassment contorted Iinuma's blunt features, and the blood rushed to his swarthy cheeks.

'When the young master was undressed, I could never bring myself to look at him directly.'

After Isao's return from the post office, it was soon time to leave. Honda, whose profession had not equipped him to deal with the young, realized that he had yet to exchange a word with Isao.

'What sort of books do you like to read?' he asked, rather awkwardly.

'Let me show you, sir.' Isao, who was just putting something into his suitcase, took out a thin paperbound book and showed it to him. 'I bought this last month after a friend recommended it, and I've already read it three times. I've never been so moved by a book. Have you read it, Your Honour?'

Honda looked at the title and author's name printed in old-style characters on the plain cover: *The League of the Divine Wind* by Tsunanori Yamao. He turned over the small book, hardly more than a pamphlet, and noted that even the publisher was unfamiliar. He was about to give it back without a word when he found his hand checked by Isao's strong hand, calloused from the kendo stave.

'If Your Honour is interested, please read it. It's a splendid book. I'll lend it to you. You may send it back later.'

His father had just gone out to the lavatory, or he would have scolded him for his presumption. As Honda looked at the flashing eyes of the enthusiastic young man, he saw at once that Isao believed that lending his favourite book was the only way he could express his gratitude for Honda's kindness. Honda accepted the book, and thanked him for it.

'It's good of you to part with a book that means so much to you.'

'No, no, I'm delighted to have Your Honour read it. I'm sure, sir, that you too will be moved by it.'

The force of Isao's answer gave Honda a glimpse into a world where the pursuit of idealism was easy, where youthful enthusiasms were readily shared – a world as simple as the endlessly repeated pattern of white splashes on the coarse blue kimono of his student days. He felt a twinge of envy.

One of Rié's merits was that she never gave a critique of guests immediately after their departure. Though not in the least credulous, she had a kind of languid, bovine steadiness. Still, even two or three months after the visit of a particular guest, she would sometimes surprise Honda with a casual allusion to a shortcoming she had noted.

Honda was extremely fond of Rié, but she was not the sort of woman to whom he could pour out his fantasies and dreams. No doubt she would be delighted if he did. Certainly she would not ridicule them, but neither would she believe in them.

Honda made it a rule never to discuss professional matters with his wife, and he had no difficulty being just as secretive about the products of his by no means fertile imagination. As for the events that had so bewildered him since the day before, he intended to keep them as hidden as Kiyoaki's dream journal at the back of his desk drawer.

Honda entered his study to confront the work that had to be done before morning, but the stack of thick Mino paper on which the court proceedings had been recorded in hard-to-read brush strokes gave such a severe check to his sense of duty that he was unable to begin.

He reached out absently, picked up the pamphlet that Isao had left, and, without any eagerness, began to read it.

9

The League of the Divine Wind
by Tsunanori Yamao

PART THE FIRST
The Rite of Ukei

One day in the summer of 1873 – the Sixth Year of the Meiji era – four stalwart men of high ideals gathered at the Imperial Shrine in Shingai Village five miles south of Kumamoto Castle to offer worship under the direction of Tomo Otaguro, adopted son and heir of the former chief priest. The Shingai Shrine was a branch of the Grand Shrine at Isé, and was known locally as Isé Shingai. Sheltered by a grove of tall trees and surrounded by paddies, this simple thatched-roof shrine was the most sacred place within the prefecture.

Their worship done at last, the four left Otaguro alone in the shrine and retired to the parlour of the priest's dwelling. Now Otaguro was to perform the secret rite of Ukei.

As for these four: Harukata Kaya was at the height of his powers, a man of stern visage. Kengo Ueno was past sixty. Kyusaburo Saito and Masamoto Aikyo were men in their fifties. Kaya wore his hair long and tied at the back of his head. Each of them bore a sword at his side.

Taut with emotion as they awaited the issue of the Ukei, the four of them sat erect in silence, neither wiping away their sweat nor looking at one another.

Again and again, the cicada's untiring cry pierced the sultry summer air like a needle at work on thick cotton cloth. A pine bent like a reclining dragon shaded the pond in the garden upon which the parlour opened. Though not the faintest breeze reached the veranda, the irises at the pond's edge, some upright like sword blades, others gracefully bent, trembled slightly. The reflection of the water glimmered upon the white branches of the delicate-blossomed crape myrtle.

Greenness was heaped up abundantly, even the leaves of the bush clover giving way to green. Yellow butterflies fluttered about. At the edge of the garden, between the trunks of a row of half-grown firs, the blue sky shimmered.

Kaya, his emotion evident in the glitter of his eyes, turned in the direction of the shrine. What he hoped for from this Ukei ran counter to the wishes of the others.

The fore-hall of Isé Shingai was appointed thus: in its centre, mounted within a frame, hung the sword of Lord Tadatoshi Hosokawa in its white sheath. To the left was a votive picture of a dragon, and to the right was another depicting the white cock and hen of Lord Nobunori Hosokawa. The inscription 'The Third Year of the Manji Era' was in the calligraphy of Sekki Obaku. A raised platform stood ever in readiness for the clan lord, whether he chose to worship in person or through a retainer.

The white-robed figure of Tomo Otaguro lay prostrate in the Divine Presence. The priest's neck was thin and his face as pale as an invalid's. It was his practice, whenever he was to address a petition to the gods, to fast for a period of seven or ten days and to do without cooked food for fifty or a hundred days.

The Ukei, through which the will of the gods was consulted, was accorded the utmost reverence by Otaguro's late master, Oen Hayashi, who had passed away three years before at this very shrine. Indeed, Oen had written *A Treatise on the Ukei.* His vision of Shinto went beyond Atsutané Hirata's principle of continuity between the Revealed World and the Hidden World. Oen wrote, for example:

> Divinity is the source. The visible world is its issue. He who has charge of affairs, he who governs men, must view Divinity as source and the visible world as issue. For the ruler who rightly integrates source and issue, the governing of the whole world will be of small concern.

And Oen taught that the Ukei, by means of which the divine will became manifest, was of prime importance within the arcane canon.

A Treatise on the Ukei began with these words:

> Of all the rites of Shinto, the Ukei is the most wondrous. As to its origin, the ineffably awesome goddess Amaterasu, together with Lord Susano, conducted the first Ukei in High Heaven, whence it was transmitted to our land of Yamato.

Among the offspring brought forth by Lord Susano in the course of the Ukei that he undertook in order to demonstrate his innocence was Lord Amenooshihomimi, who is none other than the Divine Parent of Lord Ninigi, first of the everlasting Imperial Line. Hence the Ukei was the central mystery of the Divine Ritual. Its practice, however, had fallen into abeyance for centuries, and thus it was that Oen had striven for its revival so that, in this confused world, men might once more attain the guidance of the gods and have the divine will manifested to them.

Thus the Ukei ritual was 'worship of the awesome and exalted gods', and the Emperor's Land was a land whose good fortune sprang from the wondrous power of words. For it was evident that when the priest intoned the ritual, his words, fraught with sacred power, invariably called down the protection of all the gods of heaven and earth. Thus the Ukei was 'worship by words fraught with sacred power'.

At the clan school at Kumamoto, when someone drew upon a treatise of Neo-Confucian learning called *Eight Steps of Self-Discipline* to express contempt for the mystery of the Ukei, Oen replied in the following manner:

> In this world both he who rules and he who is ruled are but men. If a mere man as a mere man attempts to rule another, he is like one who, having no boat, plunges into the sea to rescue one who is drowning. But the Ukei is what can bear up both of them. It is the boat without which the drowning man cannot be saved.

In Shinto learning Oen favoured the works of Mabuchi and Norinaga. As for Chinese learning, he was versed in sutras as well as Confucius and other philosophers. His knowledge of Buddhism embraced both the Greater and Lesser Vehicles. Indeed, he even engaged in Dutch studies to some extent. Cherishing as he did the ideal of glorifying the Imperial Tradition within the land and upholding the rational honour in the face of foreign incursion, he was appalled by the vacillation of the Shogunate officials at the time of Perry's arrival and also by the tactics of those who turned away from the policy of 'Expel the Barbarians' but tried to use it to overthrow the Shogunate. He became a recluse and gave himself over to the contemplation of occult wisdom.

Oen hoped for the restoration of the rule of the gods in this world. Not content with the exegeses of Mabuchi and Norinaga, he resolved to make known to all the ancient Shinto ritual as preserved in the classics and, by so doing, to set right the hearts of men and restore the pure land of the gods, a land blessed with the divine favour. The practice of the ancient worship, then, the achievement of restoration, had been his goal. He went so far as to bring Socrates of Greece into his writings, approving the view that, though Socrates did well to preach morals in a country lacking them, the superior state of the Emperor's Land precluded the need for moral teaching.

The Way of the Gods meant that worship and government were one. To serve the Emperor, the shining vicar of the gods in the world of men, was to serve the distant gods of the world hidden to men. To govern was to act always in accordance with the divine will, and to ascertain that will was a most sacred task, a task that could only be accomplished by the rite of Ukei.

The example of this man whose zeal for the gods was so notable inspired a host of pure-minded disciples, foremost of whom was Tomo Otaguro. The attitude of Oen's followers mourning his passing could be likened to that of Buddha's disciples seeing him entering Nirvana.

Now three years after his master's death, it had come to pass that Tomo Otaguro, purified in body and in spirit, felt compelled to perform the rite of Ukei.

At the time of the Decree of Imperial Restoration, the indications had been altogether favourable that the august wish of His Late Majesty Komei to expel the barbarians would be fulfilled. But clouds soon cut off the light of Heaven, and month by month, year by year the policy of opening the land to foreign influence had grown stronger. In Meiji 3, permission was granted to an imperial prince to study in Germany, and at the end of the same year, swords were forbidden to the common people. In Meiji 4 it was decreed that samurai could cut off their topknot and that they might go without swords. Treaties were concluded with various foreign countries, and just the previous year, Meiji 5, the Western calendar was adopted. At the beginning of the current year, six army garrisons were established with an eye towards curbing popular unrest, and, indeed, a disturbance did break out in Oita Prefecture. The world was moving further and further away from the late Master Oen's central doctrine of government and worship as one. Far from being progress, this was a heedless rush to destruction. Thus were the Master's hopes betrayed. Men delighted in defilement rather than purity. Base ambition gained the victory over lofty idealism.

What would be the late Master's thoughts if he were still in this world? And what would be the thoughts of His Late Imperial Majesty?

Though Otaguro and his companions were, of course, unaware of it, at the time of Prince Iwakura's mission to Europe and America in Meiji 4, there had been intense discussion on ship board among such subordinate ministers as Koin Kido, Toshimichi Okubo, and Hirobumi Ito with regard to changing the national polity, and many voices were raised to argue that Japan should become a republic in order better to confront the power of America and the nations of Europe.

In the meantime, hopelessly contrary to the late Master's teaching about restoration and the oneness of government and worship, the Ministry of Shrines was reorganized in Meiji 5 as the Ministry of Religion, and soon after was abolished entirely, its functions delegated to the Department of Shrines and Temples. Thus were the places of worship revered and the most ancient traditions put on the same level with the temples of a religion brought from abroad.

Now Otaguro was about to offer two Ukei formulations to the divine scrutiny. The first of these was in accordance with the wishes of Harukata Kaya and read as follows: 'To bring an end to misgovernment by admonishing authority even to the forfeiture of life.'

Kaya was bent upon the use of argument, of subduing their enemy without shedding any blood but his own. He wished to ensure that his admonition achieved its goal by emulating Yasutaké Yokoyama, the samurai of the Satsuma Clan who, in Meiji 3, set the seal upon his heroic remonstrance by slaying himself with his sword as soon as he had delivered his petition. Kaya's comrades, however, had misgivings about the efficacy of such a course. The second formulation, to be proposed in the event of the first's not gaining the divine sanction, read as follows: 'To cut down the unworthy ministers by striking in darkness with the sword.'

Otaguro, too, if this resolution was favoured by the divine will, would see it through to the last.

Although Oen's *Treatise on the Ukei* recommended the use of a saké flask and rice honey in the manner of the Emperor Jimmu, Otaguro preferred to follow the Ukei procedure preserved in the arcane tradition of the Grand Shrine of Isé, into which he had become initiated at the Sumiyoshi Shrine in Udo. He therefore selected a peach branch, and, after paring it to a straight stick, cut heavy Mino paper into strips and fastened these to the branch as sacred pendants, save for four, upon each of which he inscribed the first Ukei formulation, allowing space for a positive or negative response. Then he took up one of these, and after the words 'To bring an end to misgovernment by admonishing authority even to the forfeiture of life,' he wrote: 'is propitious.' He crumbled these into small wads and placed them upon a three-legged stand. Carrying this with him, he went down from the fore-hall and climbed the stairs leading to the sanctuary. Reverently he opened the sanctuary doors and made his way upon his knees into the midday darkness within.

It was high noon, and the heat of the sanctuary was intense. The drone of mosquitoes filled the darkness. The rays of the sun touched the skirt of Otaguro's white robe as he knelt, head bowed, just inside the threshold. Bathed in sunlight, the folds of his white raw silk *hakama* shone like bunched hibiscus flowers. Otaguro began by reciting the Great Prayer of Purification.

In the midst of the darkness, the Sacred Mirror glinted faintly. That the gods were present therein, that their eyes were upon him, Otaguro felt with the same certainty that he felt the very sweat that trickled down over his forehead and temples and past his ears. The beating of his heart became the divine life pulsing within him, and enclosed as he was by the four walls of the sanctuary, this seemed to grow to a rumble. Then with his whole body withering in the heat and his heart bursting with an intensity of yearning, he sensed that from somewhere in the darkness before him, an unseen force, as pure and fresh as spring water, was pouring out upon him.

When Otaguro picked up the branch, the sacred pendants rustled like the wings of doves. At first he waved it slowly from side to side above the stand in the manner of purification, and then, quieting his heart, lowered it till the pendants gently brushed the surface. Two of the four crumpled papers were caught by the pendants and swept from the stand. He spread out each of these and held it to the light. On the wrinkled paper of the first, he clearly saw the words 'is not propitious'. And on the second, too, was written: 'is not propitious.'

After reciting the prescribed prayer once more, he began the second Ukei rite, this time to put to the divine scrutiny the formulation 'To cut down the unworthy ministers by striking in darkness with the sword'. His procedure was as before, this time but a single paper being swept from the stand. When he had uncrumpled this, Otaguro read thereupon the words 'is not propitious'.

Three of the four comrades received Otaguro with bowed heads, awaiting the judgement of the gods. Harukata Kaya alone sat erect, looking full into the priest's pale countenance which was moist with sweat. If the gods favoured his petition, the thirty-eight-year-old Kaya was resolved to take sole responsibility for admonishing the authorities, on behalf of his comrades, and then to slay himself with his own sword.

Otaguro sat without uttering a word. At length, Ueno, the eldest of the four, asked him the outcome. Thus it was learned that neither of the two had secured the divine sanction.

Though the gods had not looked with favour upon their endeavour, the will of the four to offer themselves up for the Imperial Land remained unaltered. They therefore decided to devote themselves all the more earnestly to prayer, while awaiting the approval of the gods, and to vow in the Divine Presence to make a joint oblation of their lives whenever the proper time might come. The four went back to the shrine, and, after burning to ashes the paper inscribed with the vow offered in the Divine Presence, they sprinkled these into a flask of holy water, from which each drank in turn, leaving not a drop.

As for the name of the League of the Divine Wind, 'league' was a common term in Kumamoto to designate a party or group, such as the Tsuboi League, the Yamazaki League, and the Kyomachi League, local groups founded to foster the samurai spirit. The patriotic samurai who gathered about Oen, however, came to be called the League of the Divine Wind under different circumstances. In Meiji 7, when some of their number took the examination for the Shinto priesthood at the prefectural office, each of them, as though by prearrangement, responded as follows in the course of his examination: 'If men were pure of heart, if they revered the Emperor above all else, the Divine Wind would rise at once, just as in the time of the Mongol Invasion, and the barbarians would be swept away.'

Their examiners were quite taken aback and for the first time Oen's disciples were called the League of the Divine Wind.

Among these patriotic samurai, youths such as Tsuguo Tominaga, Tomo Noguchi, Wahei Iida, Saburo Tominaga, and Mikao Kashima sought to realize the ideals of their brotherhood in every aspect of daily life, and so they shunned defilement and loathed all innovation.

Tomo Noguchi, because telegraph lines were something brought from abroad, refused to walk beneath them. (The telegraph system was established in Meiji 6.) When Noguchi made his daily pilgrimage to the shrine dedicated to Lord Kiyomasa, he took special care not to pass under any telegraph lines, even though this meant taking a roundabout way. If he found it impossible to avoid them, he passed beneath while shielding his head with a white fan.

It was the custom of these young men to carry salt in a pocket of their sleeve, and scatter it about to purify themselves if they met a Buddhist priest, a man dressed in Western style, or a funeral procession. Herein may be seen the influence of the famous work *The Jewelled Sash* of Atsutané Hirata, which even Masahiko Fukuoka, foremost of the group in his contempt for books, had read with appreciation.

Again, Saburo Tominaga once went to the Shirakawa Prefectural Office to cash his brother Morikuni's bonus bond and, unwilling to touch paper currency defiled with a foreign-style design, carried it home between chopsticks.

Master Oen was fond of the uncouth vigour of these young men. Most of them did not take to refinement. They loved the moon shining on the banks of the Shirakawa with the love of men who believed that it was the last harvest moon they would see in this life. They prized the cherry blossoms like men for whom this spring's blossoms were the last that would ever bloom. And so they would sing together the song of Ichigoro Hasuda, the patriotic samurai of Mito:

I look upon the moon
Beyond my upright spear,
Wondering when its rays
Will fall upon my corpse.

According to Master Oen's teaching, in the world hidden from men there is neither life nor death. The life and death of this world about us took its origin from the Ukei of the gods Izanagi and Izanami. Since men are the offspring of the gods, however, if they preserve themselves from all polluting transgression and, upright, just, and pure of heart, worship in the ancient manner, they can put off the death and corruption of this world and ascend to heaven to become one with the gods.

Master Oen was wont to recite this poem:

As the white swan soars to heaven,
Leave no traces here below.

In February of Meiji 7, the Saga Rebellion broke out, the rebellious forces having been raised by those who had cast their lot with the supporters of the Subdue Korea Policy. To aid in its suppression, government forces were dispatched from various encampments, including Kumamoto. And thus, for the moment, the troops left guarding the castle numbered a mere two hundred. Otaguro deemed it improper to let such an opportunity slip by.

In Otaguro's mind a strategy for sweeping away misrule had already taken form. To unseat corrupt advisers and enhance the grandeur of the Imperial Throne, there was no better way to begin than by raising a force of loyal men and seizing the camps at Kumamoto. With this stronghold as a focal point, a number of like-hearted men could be rallied to the cause from both east and west, and a vast force could be put together for an advance to the east. The first step was the seizure of the Kumamoto camps. It was a time when the enemy had become extraordinarily vulnerable, and it behoved Otaguro and his comrades to turn this to their advantage.

Thus it was that Otaguro once more consulted the will of the gods through the Ukei rite. Again, after fasting for a number of days he made his way reverently into the Divine Presence, and, raising the branch adorned with the sacred pendants, executed the rite of Ukei with a devout heart.

This time the darkness was not filled with the heat of midsummer. The chill of early spring held possession of the sanctuary. Then, too, it was just before dawn, and from the rear of the priest's house could be heard the crowing of roosters. Their cries seemed to shatter the darkness like streaks of crimson lightning. They were rending cries, as if the dark throat of night had been burst asunder and was spurting blood.

The sage Atsutané Hirata talked endlessly of the pollution caused by death, but, as to blood pollution, he mentioned only the loss of a trivial amount of blood. Now there took form in Otaguro's mind, here before the gods, the image of pure, seething blood. As his thoughts dwelt upon this blood which was to purify the Imperial Court, he felt that the gods would not take offence. There flashed through Otaguro's prayerful entreaty terrible phantasms: glinting swords cutting down the wicked, blood spilling out on every side. And beyond the blood, what was pure, just, and honest took form, like the blue line of the distant sea.

The candles burning before the Divine Presence flickered in the dawn breeze. As Otaguro began to wave the branch with its sacred pendants, the candles guttered and nearly went out.

The eyes of the gods were fixed upon him. They evaluated the doings of men by a standard of their own, a standard beyond human knowledge. Alone able to foresee all consequences, only the gods could sanction or forbid.

Otaguro picked up the wad of paper that the pendants had caught. He opened it and read it by the candlelight. The words 'not propitious' met his eye.

The patriotic samurai of the League of the Divine Wind were not unreasonably still men to whom the usual human motions were foreign. Each of them yearned with all his heart to prove himself upon the field of combat, but otherwise they were simply vigorous young men.

Haruhiko Numazawa had unusual strength and excelled in wrestling. One day when he was pounding rice outside his door, a sudden shower began to fall. He immediately picked up both mortar and pestle, carried them indoors, and set calmly to work once more.

Hironobu Saruwatari had a two-year-old daughter named Umeko, upon whom he lavished his affection. One night, coming home somewhat drunk, he placed a large saké bottle in the arms of the sleeping girl and cried out: 'Look, a melon! A melon!' Umeko loved melons. Still half-asleep, she began to caress the bottle. But when his wife Kazuko laughing remarked: 'You keep saying "Don't lie even to a child" – how can you do such a thing?' Saruwatari was stricken with remorse. He went out and searched until he was able to buy an out-of-season melon, which he brought home and gave to Umeko.

Kisou Onimaru, along with Gensai Kawakami and his companions, had once been committed to prison for a year for a political offence. He loved saké dearly, and throughout his sentence his friends regularly brought bean curd steeped in saké. On New Year's Day, they carried a large box of it to the prison, having on this occasion emptied three bottles of saké into the bean curd. When the warders called attention to the powerful aroma, Onimaru satisfied them with the explanation that the bean curd had been simmered in saké.

Gitaro Tashiro was a devoted son. Since the doctor had told his father to eat beef, which the League shunned, Gitaro went each day to the slaughterhouse at Kamikawara to buy beef for him. However, in the summer that the patriotic force was raised, when his father arranged a match without consulting him and urged him to marry, Gitaro refused again and again with tears in his eyes. He had already resolved to die.

Tomo Noguchi was a man of inborn integrity, not fond of books but devoted to martial skills, especially archery from horseback. Each spring and fall at the festival of military arts held in the gardens of the Lord of Kumamoto he drew his bow with unerring accuracy. Then, too, he was not one to forget a promise. Once a friend happened to complain that all year long he had been unable to find any radishes for pickles. Late that very night Noguchi and his brother came to this man's gate carrying on their shoulders a huge barrel of fragrant pickled radishes.

In the summer of Meiji 7, the governor, Nagasuké Yasuoka, appointed various members of the League of the Divine Wind to shrines of greater and lesser importance throughout the prefecture. Tomo Otaguro was of course appointed chief priest of the Imperial Shrine at Shingai, with Mitsuo Noguchi and Wahei Iida as his assistant priests. Yasuoka designated Harukata Kaya as chief priest of Kinzan Shrine and Yasuhisa Koba, Tateki Ura, and Chuji Kodama as his assistants. In this manner the comrades of the League came to have custody of some fifteen shrines in all. Besides the beneficial effect that their fervent zeal had upon the general piety, shrines in every part of the province became main or subordinate bases of operations for the League.

All this had the result of strengthening the dedication of the men of the League. The more they revered the gods, the more anxious they were over the state of national affairs. As time passed, they grew ever more resentful at seeing those in authority draw the nation further and further from Master Oen's ideal of a land in which the gods would once more be worshipped as of old.

In Meiji 9 they suffered a crushing blow to their aspirations. On the eighteenth of March, the governor promulgated the Edict Against Wearing Swords, which was followed soon after by an edict forbidding the traditional samurai hair style. Yasuoka stringently enforced both of these.

Otaguro, in order to restrain the violent indignation of the League's young men, instructed them that the decree against wearing swords could be circumvented by going about with one's sword concealed in a bag. But this did not suffice to stem their anger. Together, the young men came to Otaguro and demanded to know when they would be permitted to sacrifice their lives.

If their swords were snatched from them what means would be left to guard the honour of the gods they revered? Each of them was determined, whatever the odds, to fight to the death in the Divine Cause. To worship the gods, the sacrosanct Divine Ritual was the essential means. Thus if this sword were torn away from them, it was inevitable that the gods of Japan, so utterly disdained by the new government, would become powerless spirits, worshipped only by the ignorant masses.

Meanwhile, month after month, year after year, the gods Master Oen had said were so close at hand, the gods who had enflamed their hearts with such devotion, were being degraded. The young men felt certain that a conspiracy was afoot to rob the gods of their dignity, to thrust them off into the distance, to make them as insignificant as possible. Thus, out of fear that the Christian West might look upon Japan as an ignorant heathen land, the ideal of worship and government as one would be slighted more and more. The gods would finally sink to the level of feeble spirits, ephemeral beings who clung to life in the shelter of sprouting reeds rippling in the wind beside remote streams.

And the sword was to suffer a like fate. The defences of the land would no longer be entrusted to the manly warrior bearing at his side the swift thunderbolt of the immortal gods. The national army created by Aritomo Yamagata gave no preference to the samurai class, nor did it honour the ideal of the Japanese as individuals rallying spontaneously to the defence of their native land. Rather, it was a Western-style professional army which, in ruthless disregard of all tradition, ignored class distinctions and depended upon a draft system to supply its manpower. The Japanese sword, giving way to the sabre, had lost its soul. Now it was fated to become a mere decoration, an ornament.

It was at this time that Harukata Kaya resigned his priestly office at Kinzan Shrine and presented a formal petition of several thousand words concerning the wearing of swords to the prefectural governor. This was a superb composition in praise of the Japanese sword, and Kaya's heart's blood had nourished every word. To it he later added a preamble, intending to present the revised document to the highest authorities in Tokyo:

A Petition Concerning the Proclamation of the Edict
Prohibiting the Wearing of Swords

I, Harukata, a lowly subject, holder of no office, though at the hazard of my own life, hereby submit with utmost humility a statement to the honourable members of the Council of Elders.

Edict Number Thirty-eight, issued from the office of the Prime Minister in March of this year, prohibits the wearing of swords by any citizen except military police and government officers in full-dress uniforms, as prescribed by regulations. With all due respect, I must point out that such a proclamation is not in accord with the unique national character of our glorious land, unchanged since the time of the Emperor Jimmu.

The intensity of my patriotic zeal forbade my keeping an awe-struck silence and clinging stealthily to my office. Thus on April 21 I submitted to the governor of Kumamoto a detailed protest, in much the same terms as below, and also requested that he promptly relieve me of every main and subsidiary duty pertaining to my office. On June 7, however, this memorial was sent back to me on the grounds that a prefectural office could not concern itself with the matter therein since it was urged in opposition to the law of the land.

Alas, an untutored rustic such as I cannot cope with the formalities of an advanced civilization! I realize that my expression is crude, and that I am unable to marshal my thoughts adequately, and this has for some time given me pause. Nevertheless, the spirit of dogged devotion and humble loyalty ever surges up within me, and I can no longer hold back. Thus do I dare, in all humility, to present my arguments once more.

In this preamble we see the full measure of Harukata's long-stifled rage and anguish, and of his irrepressible 'dogged devotion' and 'humble loyalty'.

In my view, the bearing of swords is a custom that characterized our Land of Jimmu even in the ancient era of the gods. It is intimately bound up with the origins of our nation, it enhances the dignity of the Imperial Throne, solemnizes the rites of our gods, banishes the spirit of evil, puts down disorders. The sword, therefore, not only maintains the tranquillity of the nation but also guards the safety of the individual citizen. Indeed, the one thing essential to this martial nation that reveres the gods, the one thing never to be put aside even for an instant, is the sword. How, then, could those upon whom is laid the burden of fashioning and promulgating a national policy that honours the gods and strengthens our land be so forgetful of the sword?

Thus did Harukata, drawing from sundry sources, attest ample proof of the importance of the sword in the history of Japan from the time of the early chronicles, and of the significance of its role in exalting the Japanese Spirit. And he went on to explain how the wearing of a sword by people of all ranks was a custom that fulfilled the divinely inspired precepts of Japan's ancient rulers.

A recent rumour in the town would have it that this edict prohibiting the wearing of swords was recommended by the supreme commander of the Army, it being alleged that it would be a matter of grave consequence to the authority of the military if those outside its scope were permitted to bear swords. After much thought, I have come to the conclusion that such an outrageous statement could not have issued from an Army commander but was rather the fabrication of street-corner idlers.

Those who guide the Army are the fangs and claws of the Imperial Throne and the very salvation of the Land of the Gods. To their benevolence, their authority, their magnanimity, their severity the populace must ever give respectful heed. Thus, with all those in military service as the winged limbs of their commanders, even if the whole people of the Divine Emperor should go about with swords and spears throughout the land, this would but magnify the power of the Army, strengthen national policy, and temper the nation for the shocks of greater and lesser trials. How could it possibly obstruct the workings of government? For it would manifest the glory of a land where the splendour of arms is abundantly nourished . . .

In the light of all this, I cannot forbear to observe that never has the honour of the Land of Jimmu fallen so low as in these present times. How could any citizen, in the least eager to serve the nation, pass his day in idle pursuits, heedless of national policy, and not bend his efforts to aid in promoting good and suppressing evil? Now is the time for those loyal subjects close to the Throne, the men who are the Emperor's claws and fangs, to ponder deeply, to agonize, to labour unremittingly . . .

This edict is in opposition to the Imperial Decree on the Abolition of Clans and the Establishment of Prefectures, and turns its back on the understanding of duty, the search for justice, the preservation of domestic tranquillity, and the defence of the nation against foreign incursion. Thus it contradicts the Imperial Will. Beyond doubt it would speedily verify the proverb that a nation must ravage itself before foreigners can ravage it, a man must despise himself before others can despise him.

As stated in the preamble, Kaya's original petition had been returned from the governor's office without acknowledgement. He had supplemented it and put it in suitable form, having resolved to go alone to Tokyo, present it to the Council of Elders, and disembowel himself on the spot. Thus he was far from eager to join his comrades in armed resistance.

Meanwhile Otaguro had been holding in check the hot-blooded youths who came to him protesting: 'The warrior bereft of his sword is wretched. When, Master, will you give us an opportunity to lay down our lives?' But at last he assembled the seven leaders of the League at the shrine in Shingai. These were Morikuni Tominaga, Masahiko Fukuoka, Kageki Abé, Unshiro Ishihara, Kotaro Ogata, Juro Furuta, and Tsunetaro Kobayashi. The plan that they devised was as follows: since their comrades in other parts of the land seemed to lack the courage to set matters in motion, they themselves would strike the first blow in the righteous cause by cutting down every major military and civilian official in the prefecture and seizing the camps at Kumamoto. Placing as they did the deepest trust in Otaguro, the whole group then waited as, at their bidding, he left them to consult the gods for a third time through an Ukei.

It was late on a May night in the Ninth Year of Meiji, with all gathered together at the imperial shrine of Shingai. Otaguro, having purified himself, entered the sanctuary.

The seven leaders sat in a row in the fore-hall of the shrine, waiting to hear the will of the gods.

When Otaguro clapped his hands, the sound echoed loudly from within the sanctuary.

Otaguro's hands were large, though emaciated, and the sharp report of their clapping was as if the palms, like hollowed, rough-hewn cedar planks, had entrapped pure atmosphere, and crushed it with an explosive burst of divinity.

Thus Tominaga, for one, felt that the clapping of those dedicated hands, hands purified by sacred ablution, echoed as if in a forest glen deep in the mountains.

Especially on a night like this, in the darkness of the small hours with the spring rains not far off, the reverberating echo of Otaguro's clapping seemed charged with yearning and devotion, and the seven heard it as striking upon the very doors of heaven.

Otaguro next began the prayer of purification. His loud, clear voice seemed to herald the dawn that would break through the curtain of night and whiten the eastern sky. To the eyes of those waiting in the fore-hall, there was perfection even in the straight seam running down the back of his white priestly robe. His clear voice seemed like a blade cutting through evil:

'... When these entreaties are heard, all the land under heaven, beginning with the court of the offspring of the gods, will be free of every defilement. As the winds of heaven scatter the towered clouds, as the breezes of morning and evening sweep away the mists of morning and evening, as a great ship moored in a wide harbour is freed at the prow and at the stern, and pushed out towards the deep as the scythe blade forged in fire cuts away yonder tangled growth – so shall all defilements be purged and purified...'

The seven leaders held their breath in awe as they beheld the arcane ritual from the fore-hall. Unless they received the divine sanction this time, they would perhaps never be able to strike their blow.

Silence fell with the conclusion of Otaguro's chant. His tall cap seemed to sink into the darkness of the inner sanctuary as he prostrated himself in prayer.

The shrine was surrounded by open country. The night scent of fresh young leaves, of manured fields, of oaks in blossom floated in upon the breeze, an oppressive heaviness to the mingled odours. Since they sat in darkness, there was not even the drone of swarming insects.

Suddenly a sound from the roof above shattered the silence. It was the cry of a night heron taking flight. The seven regarded one another. They knew that each had felt the same shudder.

Soon the candles burning in the sanctuary were hidden for a moment as Otaguro rose to make his return. The seven awaiting him heard the very sound of his footsteps as a favourable omen. Otaguro announced that the gods had blessed their undertaking. The divine approbation thus gained not only freed them to act but designated them the army of the gods.

Matters having reached such a stage, Otaguro set about forming a secret coalition with patriots in other areas, and dispatched comrades of the League to Yanagawa in Chikugo, to Fukuoka, to Takeda in southern Bungo, to Tsuruzaki, to Shimabara, as well as to Saga, to Hagi in Choshu, and elsewhere. As for the comrades in Kumamoto itself, they were to enter into a seventeen-day period of mortification, during which they would pray for the success of their long-cherished enterprise. The day to strike, the grouping of the comrades – nothing was determined without consulting the will of the gods. As for the day, the divine will ordained thus: 'At the start of the Eighth Day of the Ninth Lunar Month, when the moon hides herself behind the mountain.' In like manner, the comrades were assigned in accordance with the sacred casting of lots.

Thus the entire group was divided into three units, the first of which was then further divided into five bands. The first of these five, led by Unki Takatsu, had the task of assaulting the residence of the commander of the Kumamoto post, Major-General Masaaki Taneda. The second band, with Unshiro Ishihara at its head, was to attack the residence of the chief of staff at Kumamoto, Lieutenant-Colonel of Artillery Shigenori Takeshima. The third band, led by Kagesumi Nakagaki, had as its target the home of the commander of the Thirteenth Infantry Regiment, Lieutenant-Colonel Tomozané Yokura. The fourth band, with Yoshinori Yoshimura commanding, was to direct its attack upon the residence of Nagasuké Yasuoka, the governor of Kumamoto prefecture. The fifth band, led by Tateki Ura, was to slay the chief of the Kumamoto Prefectoral Assembly, Korenobu Otaguro. The total force thus committed was some thirty men and was designated the First Unit. Once they had taken these enemy heads, they were to signal by fire and rejoin the main body.

The next group was the main force, and its commanders were Tomo Otaguro and Harukata Kaya. The two elders, Kengo Ueno and Kyusaburo Saito, were among the secondary commanders, who also included Kageki Abé, Kotaro Ogata, Kisou Onimaru, Juro Furuta,

Tsunetaro Kobayashi, and Gitaro Tashiro, aided by such stalwarts as Goichiro Tsuruda. Designated the Second Unit, its mission was to assault the Sixth Artillery Battalion. Its strength was some seventy men.

The last group, whose command was entrusted to Morikuni Tominaga and Masahiko Fukuoka, was to attack the Thirteenth Infantry Regiment, spurred on by the zeal of its elder, Masamoto Aikyo, together with such men as Tsuneyoshi Ueno, Gengo Shibuya, and Tomo Noguchi. Its strength was some seventy men, and it was designated the Third Unit.

There was one, however, who had not yet declared himself willing to join in this armed rising. This was Harukata Kaya. Kaya was a man of rigorous moral character. His heart was filled with courage and his eyes flashed with the purity of his zeal. He was skilled in literature, composing both Japanese and Chinese poems and having an excellent prose style. As for martial accomplishments, he was adept in the Shiten School of kendo.

Since his decision would greatly affect the morale of all, Tominaga and the other leaders went in turn to try to persuade him to join them. Finally, a mere three days before the event, he told them that if the Divine Will were consulted and a favorable response elicited, he would commit himself to the enterprise.

Kaya himself having resigned his priestly office, he designated Tateki Ura to present to the gods the question of his participation. And thus at Kinzan Shrine on the Plateau of Kinzan, with Kimpo rising to the west and the haze-covered peak of Aso to the east, Ura fervently performed the rite of Ukei on his comrade's behalf. The gods indicated their approval. Earlier, with regard to Kaya's proceeding to Tokyo to present his petition to the Council of Elders at the sacrifice of his life, they had indicated disapproval.

Kaya realized that his reluctance to support the rising was something that had sprung from his own will. Now the will of the gods clearly took precedence. He believed firmly that they had enjoined him to commit himself to this seemingly hopeless resort to arms, and that, after its violence, they would somehow lay a banquet for him and his comrades upon a cloth of pure white, unmarred by the least wrinkle. And so, without vacillation, Kaya submitted to the divine will and joined the enterprise.

How did the men of the League prepare for combat? Most of all, night and day alike, by imploring the blessing of heaven. The shrines allied to them were thronged with comrades come to offer worship.

The troops opposing them numbered two thousand, and they themselves less than two hundred. One of the elders, Kengo Ueno, proposed that some firearms be obtained, but the comrades as a whole were hotly opposed to arming themselves with the weapons of the barbarians. Thus they would carry into battle nothing but swords, spears, and halberds. In order to destroy the post, however, they secretly made several hundred grenades by joining two bowls packed with gravel and gunpowder and attaching a fuse. For the same purpose, Masamoto Aikyo purchased and laid away a supply of kerosene.

How would they garb themselves for combat? Some of them would don helmets and cuirasses, some even the tall caps and ceremonial robes of the ancient nobility, but most would wear short *hakama* over their everyday dress, with two swords thrust into their sashes. Each would wear a headband of white cloth and bind up his sleeves with strips of white cotton. And every man would fasten on a white cloth shoulder-strap bearing the character *victory*.

More than their arms and equipment, however, more than their banners, they put their trust in the Divine Simulacrum that Tomo Otaguro was to bear upon his shoulder. The god whom Otaguro would carry into battle, the Divine Simulacrum of the war god Hachiman of Fujisaki Shrine, would be their unseen commander, the one who would mysteriously direct their efforts. And herein would be the fulfilment of their late Master's dying wish.

For when in his youth Master Oen heard of the incursion of the American warships and set out for Edo in great wrath to avenge this profanation, he bore upon his shoulders this same Divine Simulacrum.

PART THE SECOND
The Combat of the Ukei

The entire force was to meet at the home of the elder Masamoto Aikyo, directly behind the Fujisaki Hachiman Shrine with its guardian rows of huge camphor trees. This house stood on high ground at the western edge of the second defence perimeter of the old castle, adjoining the Kumamoto garrison.

So that nearly two hundred armed men could gather here without being noticed, small groups met at dusk at various rendezvous and thence made their way to the marshalling point under cover of night.

Here, by Aikyo's house, they could see Kumamoto Castle rising into the night sky beneath the moon of the Eighth Day of the Ninth Month. The Great Tower, bathed in moonlight, thrust itself up at the castle's very centre, and to its left rose the lesser tower. Still further to the left the outline of the level roofs of the main hall and the women's quarters stretched out for a short way before giving place to the Udo Turret, whose dark outline jutted skyward. To the right of the Great Tower, at the end of an irregular line of roofs, rose two final towers of more modest height, the Sangai Turret and the Tsukimi Turret, their tile roofs glistening in the moonlight. The Tsukimi Turret looked down upon the riding ground of Sakuranobaba just to the west of the castle, where slept the artillerymen upon whom would fall the assault of the Second Unit.

The moon set.

The First Unit whose object was the residences of major officials made its departure. The hour was drawing on to eleven. There were stars in the sky, and the deep grass of Fujisaki Heights was covered with dew.

Next to leave was the Second Unit, led by Otaguro and Kaya. And as it set out in the direction of the artillery battalion, the Third Unit also departed, bound for the infantry encampment.

The seventy-odd men of the Second Unit, the main force of the rising, went up the Slope of Keitaku, and divided into two sections, one of which was to assault the east gate of the artillery encampment and the other, the north. They found both gates firmly barred. At the east gate two expert young swordsmen, Wahei Iida, twenty-two, and Gitaro Tashiro, twenty-six years old, scaled the wall with gallant exuberance and, shouting 'First over!' plunged into the camp and at once cut down the sentries who challenged them. They were followed over the wall by Tsunetaro Kobayashi and Tadajiro Watanabé. Then Tashiro, seizing a pestle from the nearby mess hall, rushed up and smashed the bolt of the gate, and the entire force came pouring in like an avalanche.

Just inside the gate, Kango Hayami overpowered a soldier and bound him with a rope, intending to press him into service as a guide.

Meanwhile, the north gate, too, had fallen, and the other section of the Second Unit dashed forward to join forces in cutting their way into the two barracks of the artillerymen. Roused from deep sleep by fierce battle cries, the troops were thrown into a panic by the sight of blades flashing in the darkness. Utterly routed, they sought safety by cowering in various corners of the barracks. The battalion headquarters duty officer on this night, Second Lieutenant of Artillery Keiichi Sakaya, ran downstairs from the second-floor duty room and engaged the onrushing swords with drawn sabre. Quickly wounded, however, he escaped through a rear door and watched the scene from the shadows.

Leaderless, the soldiers fled like terrified women and children. As the lieutenant looked on, flames sprang up from the east barracks. Pressed by the billowing black smoke, the soldiers who had hidden in the barracks came tumbling from the windows, to be driven and scattered by the swords of the oddly garbed insurgents. Seeing this, the young officer grated his teeth.

The fire had been set with grenades and kerosene in the east barracks by Tsunetaro Kobayashi, Wahei Iida, and their comrades, and in the west barracks by Katsutaro Yonemura and his. Neither Iida nor Kobayashi were carrying matches, and they had had to shout out to their companions for 'phosphorus', as they were called, to light the fuses.

Avoiding the glare of the flames, Lieutenant Sakaya made his way to the garrison dispensary and hurriedly bandaged his wounded right arm. Then, plunging once more into the fray, he confronted some fleeing soldiers, and tried to take command of them. The terrified soldiers would not heed his orders. When he firmly put heart into a few of them, his efforts caught the eye of Kyusaburo Saito, renowned for his skill in fighting with the spear, who came running to the attack.

Lieutenant Sakaya raised his sabre with his wounded arm, but was instantly pierced by Saito's spear, and fell, uttering a bitter cry. He was the first officer of the government forces to perish in the struggle.

Meanwhile Yoshinori Yoshimura and his comrades of the fourth section of the First Unit had wounded Governor Yasuoka grievously in wild fighting but failed to take his head. They then withdrew from the Governor's residence and hastened across Geba Bridge, attracted by the battle cries and the leaping flames within the castle walls. Kageki Abé turned aside from the final routing of the enemy to greet them, thereupon learning of the outcome of their battle and of the loss of Motoyoshi Aikyo at the tender age of seventeen, the first of the League of the Divine Wind to fall.

The garrison artillerymen had not been issued small arms. Those who had been tardy in fleeing either perished in the flames or were slain by the flashing blades of the comrades of the League, and now their corpses lay heaped about. Kisou Onimaru, who had cut down the foe with exuberant zeal, happened to come up at that moment and, seeing Yoshimura, broke into a broad smile. Raising his bloodied sword so that it glittered in the noonday brightness cast by the flames that enveloped the two barracks, he gazed at it with cheerful mockery as he declared: 'Indeed, such is the worth of garrison troops!' Even his garments, drenched in enemy blood, glowed crimson in the flames. Then Onimaru rushed off in pursuit of the remnants of the enemy.

The comrades of the League had crushed all resistance here. A single hour had brought them victory.

Otaguro and Kaya re-formed their force, but as they were withdrawing they saw a red blaze lighting the sky above the infantry camp within the castle's second perimeter. Realizing the fierceness of the battle there, Kaya called out to his men to help in the assault on the infantry garrison, to which they responded eagerly. Behind them flames ravaged the artillery barracks. The black bulk of Kumamoto Castle loomed up against a crimson sky. In Yamazaki, Motoyama, and other parts of the city were still more conflagrations. These flames, dancing skyward on all sides, gave witness to the fury with which their comrades had struck. In their mind's eye they saw the brave figures of their brothers in arms, forever faithful, moving through the swirling fire, each one smiting the foe with flashing blade. This was the hour for which they had so long checked their fierce rage and whetted their sword blades in secret. Otaguro's bosom heaved with an ineffable surge of joy. 'Every man is fighting,' he murmured. 'Every man.'

As for the Third Unit, led by Morikuni Tominaga, Masamoto Aikyo, Masahiko Fukuoka, and Hitoshi Araki, the seventy men of this group had left the precincts of Fujisaki Shrine at the same time as the main force commanded by Otaguro and Kaya. Its objective, the Thirteenth Infantry Regiment's camp, lay within the same castle perimeter as the shrine, though at the eastern edge of it, whereas Fujisaki Shrine was at the western. The foe's strength was close to two thousand men.

Finding the west gate of the infantry camp shut fast before them, twenty-year-old Haruhiko Numazawa clambered atop the palisades and, shouting 'First over', leapt down on the other side, to be followed immediately by several other young men. The lone sentry fled across the drill field intending to sound the alarm with his bugle, but he had no more than put it to his lips when he was cut down where he stood.

Hitoshi Araki had come equipped with a rope ladder. He flung this up so that it caught upon the top of the palisade, then hastened to mount it, but so many others grasped it too that the ropes gave way. Kyushichi, Araki's loyal servant, thereupon offered his shoulders to his master, and several men, one after the other, scaled the wall by this means and opened the gate from the inside. With a great battle cry, the entire company rushed in to the attack.

Masahiko Fukuoka, wielding a massive sledgehammer, shattered one barrack's door after another, and his comrades hurled in grenades. Soon the regimental headquarters barrack as well as those housing the first, second, and third companies of the second battalion were engulfed in flames.

According to current military practice, no ammunition was distributed to individual soldiers in time of peace. Thus the only weapons of use were sabres for the officers and fixed bayonets for their men. Beset as they were by battle cries, swirling flames, billowing black smoke, and sword blades flashing about them, the troops had no means to resist. The captain who was regimental duty officer was cut down before he could rally his forces, and the corpses of his men soon lay in heaps, some clad only in their shirts, still others stark naked, and the flames and the black smoke rolled over them.

A lone survivor, Second Lieutenant Ono, still wielded his sabre and fought on with bitter tenacity. But then just as two sergeants had come rushing to his assistance, all three men were cut down.

It was at this moment that the third section of the First Unit poured into the camp through the second perimeter gate to join forces with the Third Unit. In their assault on the residence of Lieutenant-Colonel Yokura, the regimental commander, the third section's prey, had slipped through their grasp, but now the morale of the combined forces soared to new heights.

With a full infantry regiment, however, the combat was of a different order from that waged in the artillery compound. There was a limit to the number of men that could be felled by blades alone. Though each attack threw that part of the camp into disorder, it took time for the waves of panic to spread. Thus some were able to regain their wits. With clearer vision, they could correctly assess the situation. And now the grenades that had served so well to terrify the foe worked against the men of the League. For as the flames soared up from the barracks and the men of the League leapt about in the noonday brilliance, it became all too clear how incredibly few they were.

One officer, having observed this, took command of some troops and formed them into two rings on the drill field with their bayonets pointing in every direction like the spines of a thistle, in order to counterattack. To confront this threat, the elder Masamoto Aikyo grasped his spear, whose use he had so well mastered, and marshalling some ten of his comrades, who aligned their spears with his, charged into the massed infantrymen. The troops broke formation at once and fled. One man alone held his ground, Cadet Lieutenant Tarao, and he fell with spears through his body.

Earlier, two officers who had been quartered off post, First Lieutenant of Infantry Sataké and Cadet Lieutenant Numata, were hastening back to camp, aroused by the sight of the flames. At Hoké Slope they met some of the routed troops and learned how the issue stood. The waters of the moat which lay to the north of the slope shone scarlet from the fiery sky overhead. As the officers questioned the men, more straggled up in twos and threes, the inferno of the burning camp at their backs, and their shadows merged with those of the others.

The two officers hotly chastised the troops for being out of uniform and almost speechless with terror. Thus they managed to rally a platoon of sixteen soldiers, but one which lacked both rifles and ammunition.

It happened, however, that a man named Kichizo Tachiyama, a shrewd merchant who dealt with the military, made his appearance and proffered from his storehouse sufficient rifles, 180 rounds of ammunition, and one thousand percussion caps. The officers rejoiced immensely at this, and the morale of their battered troops rose at last. Thereupon, the two officers each took command of one half of their platoon and secretly made their way into the camp by different routes, Lieutenant Sataké by the rear gate and Cadet Numata by the emergency gate. Coming together once more, their number swelled by other survivors, the troops took up position in a still unburned barrack and commenced firing.

Lieutenant-Colonel Tomozané Yokura, the regimental commander, was at his residence in Kyomachi Heights when the assault of the third section of the First Unit fell upon it. The Lieutenant-Colonel's wife, Tsuruko, woke her husband the instant she heard the men of the League storming in through the front entrance, and he immediately grasped the situation and fled to the quarters occupied by his grooms. There he snatched a workman's jacket off a hook and hurriedly donned it just as two or three of the League burst into the room. One struck him a blow on the shoulder with his sword, but when he pleaded: 'Spare me! I am a groom,' he was able to extricate himself from his foes.

The commander thereupon fled to a restaurant, the Ichijitsu, which stood to the rear of Kinzan Shrine. There his wound was hastily seen to by the proprietor, and the commander then shaved off his moustache and further disguised himself by putting on a servingman's jacket. So attired, he made his way once more through the enemy force and at length reached the rear palisade of his infantry command.

After he had climbed to the top and looked down within the camp, he caught sight of the hurrying figures of an officer and two enlisted men. Recognizing Captain Takigawa, the commander hailed him. The Captain stopped and stared for an instant in shocked surprise at the sight of his disguised commander atop the palisade. But then realizing that it was indeed he, the Captain hurried over as the commander descended and gave him a report on the battle. By that time the duty officer of the Second Battalion, Lieutenant Sazuki, had marshalled one company and was seeking to stave off defeat, but had run desperately short of ammunition. Captain Takigawa himself, together with the two soldiers, was now on his way to the magazine to obtain the ammunition left over from manoeuvres.

'Very well. Be quick about it,' replied Lieutenant-Colonel Yokura abruptly. Then he rushed into the midst of his scattered troops, issuing orders and rallying his routed command. With their leader restored to them, the will to carry on flared up among the common soldiers.

The supply of ammunition obtained by Lieutenant Sataké and by Captain Takigawa was augmented by that brought from general headquarters. Thus strengthened the regiment was at last in a state to give an account of itself.

At general headquarters Major Gentaro Kodama, a staff officer and later a general, had already arrived on the scene. Flinging wide the doors of the magazine, he supplied the soldiers dispatched by Lieutenant Colonel Yokura with ammunition. Then he himself led a company up to a high point on the castle's innermost perimeter, where they were able to look down on the burning camp and see the figures of the men of the League clearly lit by flames in the fighting on the drill field. His troops took aim at the glittering armour, the ancient court robes, and the white headbands, and he gave the command to fire a volley.

*

The Third Battalion of the regiment had been quartered separately in the gardens of the castle, and had escaped the onslaught of the League. Also, the previous day it had been supplied with Snider rifles and ammunition. Now these were issued to the troops of both its companies, who at once went to the relief of their comrades, the First Company hastening up Keitaku Slope, the Second Company penetrating the camp by crossing Geba Bridge.

In the meantime, the Second Unit of the League under the command of Otaguro and Kaya, who had gone to the aid in the assault upon the infantry garrison, smashed through the south gate into the camp only to find the tide of battle turned and themselves now entrapped. Under cover of buildings and stone walls they strove to come to grips with their foes, but helpless against the volleys of bullets they could only grit their teeth and clench their fists. The arrival of the Second Unit had given the other men of the League their last hope. If a man exposed himself, he was struck at once. But if all clung to their cover, defeat was inevitable. There was no way to launch an attack upon the massed rifles.

Sixty-six-year-old Kengo Ueno spoke out as he crouched in hiding and surveyed his comrades around him: 'Though I insisted that we equip ourselves with firearms, no one would heed me, and now we have come to this pass.' In their hearts, all of them agreed.

Yet what the men of the League had been willing to risk by renouncing the use of firearms had clarified their intent. Divine aid was to be theirs, and their very purpose was to challenge the Western arms hateful to the gods with swords alone. Western civilization would, as time went by, search out weapons still more terrible, and would direct them at Japan. And then might not the Japanese themselves, in their anxiety to counter these, fall into bestial fighting and lose all hope of restoring the ancient worship so revered by Master Oen? To rise to the combat bearing only the sword, to be willing to risk even crushing defeat – in no way but this could the fervent aspirations of each man of the League take expression. Here was the essence of the gallant Yamato Spirit.

A fierce will inflaming the heart of each one, they broke from cover to charge across the fire-lit drill field.

Raising his sword crafted by Rai Kunimitsu, Eiki Fukami, his comrade Haruhiko Numazawa at his side, dashed headlong through a hail of bullets. Almost at once Numazawa was hit in his right arm. Taking cover he tore a strip from his tunic with his teeth and hastily wrapped it about his wounded arm. Fukami, after advancing another fifteen yards or so, went down with a bullet in his chest. Masahiko Fukuoka hastened to him, but as soon as he lifted him in his arms he realized that his comrade was dead, and he cried out with anguished rage. Forthwith he brandished his sword in fury and charged the massed foe, only to fall before a murderous volley. Then Numazawa, apparently unhampered by his wound, leapt to the assault once more, but a bullet pierced his left temple from the side. This time, he did not rise.

Harukata Kaya was a master in the combined use of long sword and short. Now he raised his swords, nicked in countless desperate combats and covered with blood, and glared at the enemy. He saw his younger brother Shiro in his mind's eye, Shiro who had disembowelled himself on Mount Tenno after the abortive assault of the Choshu samurai upon the Imperial Palace. Now he too, at age forty-one, would die impelled by the same spirit. Kaya had been unwilling to make common cause with the League in the venture, until the gods had indicated their approval only three days before. Yet he was without regrets. Here on this field he would join his fate forever with that of his comrades.

Kaya brandished his swords and led the men around him in a fierce charge, drawing upon himself the concentrated fire of the enemy. Mortally wounded, he gave one last cry, 'Hachiman, God of Battles!' and fell headlong.

It was around this time that eighteen men of the League perished, among them the elder Kyusaburo Saito, together with Hitoshi Araki, Hironobu Saruwatari, and Tomo Noguchi.

Some twenty others were wounded, including Masamoto Aikyo, Yoshinori Yoshimura, Kengo Ueno, and Yoshio Tominaga.

Otaguro, glaring furiously and ignoring those who shouted to him to withdraw, plunged toward the enemy line. A bullet pierced his chest.

Gunshiro Yoshioka, trusting in the keen blades of Onimaru and his comrades to check the assault of the bayonet-wielding government troops, bore up Otaguro on his shoulders and carried him down Hoké Slope, whence, with the aid of Otaguro's brother-in-law Hideo Ono, he brought him into a house.

Otaguro's wound was mortal. He kept losing and regaining consciousness, but even so managed to ask Yoshioka and Ono in which direction his head lay. They answered, in turn, that it lay to the west. 'His Divine Majesty dwells in the east. Make haste to have me sit with head poised accordingly,' Otaguro told them. They did so.

Then Otaguro ordered Ono to strike off his head. His voice faint, he asked them to bear it to Shingai Shrine together with the Divine Simulacrum of Hachiman.

The foe might well have come storming in at any moment. Hideo Ono had no will to strike his brother-in-law such a blow. But upon the exhortation of Yoshioka, he at last unsheathed his sword. Carefully wiping off the enemy blood that stained it, he purified its blade. Then he lifted it above his head and took aim at his brother-in-law's neck. Yoshioka had helped Otaguro to sit up, head sagging, but facing toward the east. At the very instant that his brother-in-law's torso, thus awkwardly positioned, was about to pitch forward, Ono's blade came sweeping down.

PART THE THIRD
One with the Gods

Mount Kimpo is less than four miles west of Kumamoto Castle, and, like the mountain in Yamato from which it takes its name, is revered as a sacred peak. At its crest stands a shrine dedicated to the deity Zao.

Though small, the shrine has a long history. In 1933 – the Third Year of the Genko era – Lord Takeshigé Kikuchi ascended to it in order to implore the divine favour before going into battle. Victory was his, and in gratitude he had the shrine rebuilt. According to tradition, he himself carved the Worship Image, reciting a triple prayer after each stroke. This represented the god as standing on the mountain peak with one hand raised, gazing at the armed host he had blessed. It was an image of victory.

Now, however, the morning after the rising, early on the auspicious Ninth Day of the Ninth Month, the time of the Chrysanthemum Festival, there were gathered around the shrine forty-six hunted survivors of a defeated force. Some standing, some sitting, they stared blankly about them, though the penetrating autumn chill made their wounds sting. The clear light of the rising sun cast a striped pattern as it shone down through the branches of the few old cedars that surrounded the shrine. Birds were singing. The air was fresh and clear. As for signs of last night's sanguinary combat, these were visible in the soiled and bloodstained garments, the haggard visages, and the eyes that burned like live embers.

Among the forty-six were Unshiro Ishihara, Kageki Abé, Kisou Onimaru, Juro Furuta, Tsunetaro Kobayashi, the brothers Gitaro and Gigoro Tashiro, Tateki Ura, Mitsuo Noguchi, Mikao Kashima, and Kango Hayami. Every man was silent, sunk deep in thought, looking off at the sea, or at the mountains, or at the smoke still rising from Kumamoto.

Such were the men of the League at rest on the slope of Kimpo, some with fingers yellowed from brushing the petals of wild chrysanthemums that they had plucked while staring across the water at Shimabara Peninsula.

Before the break of day, the way leading to the sea had lain open to them in their flight. A man of the League, Juro Kagami, had been offered six boats by a family powerful in clan days, but these had become stuck fast in the mud left by the morning's ebb tide and no amount of tugging or pushing could free them. Since they were being hotly pursued, the men of the League had no choice but to abandon the boats and make their way up Mount Kimpo.

The foothills around them were interlaced with small valleys dotted with villages, and there were terraced fields and paddies far up the steep slopes. Some sort of white-flowered bush grew here and there, along with the ripening crops of rice plants. The mountain forest spread out over the undulating terrain around the patchwork of small villages scattered like so many cushions set out to dry, and the foliage of the trees, still a deep green in this early autumn, entrapped the subtle morning light to form delicate tracings of brightness and shadow. In these villages were the homes of men whose upbringing had been different from that of the men of the League. At some time in their lives, would they too feel the powerful emotions of a decisive battle? They whose lives now seemed so peaceful, so without incident?

To the west of Kochi, a cape in the form of a seahorse stretched a green neck out into the sea. Still farther west was the fan-shaped muddy delta of the Shirakawa. If a man shifted his gaze down from the kites circling in the sky over the mountain villages nearby, he saw the mud flat swarming with the huge birds, flapping their soiled-looking mottled brown wings.

As for the sea below, Shimabara Peninsula opposite thrust itself out between Ariaké Bay and Amakusa Channel, its tip pressing upon the strait at Kimpo's base. The water's colour was dark blue everywhere, except for a casual stroke of black at mid-strait, the effect of a tidal current. To the men of the League this seemed to be a divine omen, of uncertain significance.

Nature had never been more beautiful than on this morning after defeat. All was clear and fresh and tranquil.

Across the water on Shimabara Peninsula, the skirts of Mount Unzen stretched out wide to either side. Rows of tiny houses were clearly visible amid the foothills. The peak of Unzen lay concealed behind towering clouds. Off to the southwest, in Saga, the crest of Tara was shrouded in mist that but faintly revealed its outline. The clouds massed in the sky were shot through with a brightness that seemed to bode divinity.

The sight vividly reminded the men on Mount Kimpo of the mystic teaching on the ascent to heaven that they had heard from Master Oen.

According to the Master, there were but two means of ascent to heaven, and these were similar in nature. A man had to use either the Pillars of Heaven or the Floating Bridge of Heaven. Though these still existed unchanged from ancient days, ordinary men given over to defilement could not even see them, much less ascend by them to heaven. If men purged themselves of pollution and with pure hearts returned to the ways of old, then like the godlike beings of those times, they would be empowered to see the Pillars of Heaven and the Floating Bridge of Heaven before their eyes and avail themselves of the means thus offered to mount to the high place where the gods dwell.

Now divinity seemed so embodied in the bright-flecked clouds upon the mountain peaks that the watching men felt that they were viewing an epiphany of the Floating Bridge. Should they not turn their swords joyfully upon themselves and make an end to their lives? There were those, however, who had taken up a position on the cliff edge facing east and kept their gaze fastened upon Kumamoto Castle, around which thin smoke still rose.

Before them was the bulk of Mount Arao, rising to the left, and, beyond a forest of cedars, the close-packed forms of Mount Tengu, Mount Hommyoji, Mount Mibuchi, and others. Still farther stood Mount Ishigami, like a guardian lion-dog seen from the rear, its foothills projecting well into the city. Kumamoto was well endowed with greenery. The view from Kimpo afforded more the prospect of dense forest than of human dwellings, and the castle's Great Tower rose sharply from the midst of clustered trees. There was also a sweeping view of the region of Fujisaki Heights.

The watchers felt as if last night's battle, erupting at eleven and raging but three hours, and the wretched flight that followed, were being reenacted before them. Once more they were storming about with upraised blades within the camp. Or rather it was ghostly warriors and ghostly flames that now held sway on a field of combat flooded with morning light – of more substance, though, than they, the fugitives on Kimpo, who looked down upon the scene of last night's combat as though upon an ancient battleground.

Beyond the city, far to the east, the smoke that poured up from the crater of Mount Aso, merging with the clouds drawn by it, blotted out that whole portion of the sky. It seemed to hang there peacefully, but was changing from moment to moment. Smoke kept rising from the crater to thrust ever upward the smoke that had preceded it, and the swelling clouds drank it in unremittingly.

The sight of the rising smoke put heart into the watchers, and the will to strike another blow quickened within them.

Just then some of their comrades returned from a successful forage in the villages below with a cask of saké and rations for the day, and all fell to eating and drinking lustily. Every man felt his vigour returning, whether he had set his mind upon death or yearned to make another assault, and before long a resolution was formed that took into some account their actual circumstances. With Kisou Onimaru urging another assault upon the garrison and Tsunetaro Kobayashi counselling against this, it was finally determined with near-unanimity that a scouting party should first be dispatched to probe the enemy's strength and disposition.

After the departure of the scouting party, those remaining upon the mountain took counsel once more, this time to determine what should be done about the youngest members of the group. For seven were mere boys of around sixteen or seventeen: Kataro Shimada, Tadao Saruwatari, Saburohiko Ota, Tamonta Yano, Kakutaro Motonaga, Susumu Morishita, and Kango Hayami.

These seven had been whispering among themselves with the irrepressible verve of youth: 'What are the old fellows up to with their constant delays? Why do they not decide at once? Let us commit seppuku or let us attack again!' But when they learned of the sudden decision that they were to withdraw from the mountain under the command of forty-eight-year-old Goichiro Tsuruda, who had been lamed by a swollen leg, they were appalled by this unforeseen turn of events and protested fiercely.

Yielding at last to the fervent arguments of their elders, they glumly followed Tsuruda down the mountain. Tsuruda's son Tanao, since he was already twenty, stayed behind with the others. Soon it was night.

The report of the scouting party was to be heard in the house of a sympathizer in Shimazaki Village. The men on the mountain slipped down by twos and threes. Their comrades returned from their reconnaissance. According to the news they brought, troops and police were keeping a strict watch in Kumamoto and its environs, the government had issued orders forbidding all vessels to leave harbour, and the foe's patrols had penetrated even to the edge of Shimazaki.

They all made their way secretly to the beach of Chikozu, where they sought the aid of a fisherman, a former servant of Juro Furuta, in order to cross the bay. The fisherman, however, could do no more than offer them his only boat. This was wholly inadequate to the more than thirty comrades who remained.

Accordingly they decided to disband their force, letting each go his own way to seek whatever succour he could. Furuta himself, Kagami, the Tashiro brothers, Teruyoshi Morishita, and Shigetaka Sakamoto availed themselves of the precious boat and set out for Konoura. And with this the uprising came to an end.

*

The number of those who had retreated to Mount Kimpo was less than a third of those under arms at the time of the muster. All the rest either had been slain outright in battle or, wounded and hard-pressed in their places of refuge by government troops, had perished heroically by turning their own swords against themselves. One of the elders, Masamoto Aikyo, fled as far as the mountain pass of Mikuni, but, with three police officers closing in upon him, he abruptly sat down by the side of the road, cut open his stomach, and died. He was fifty-four years of age.

Saburo Matsumoto, twenty-four, and Suehiko Kasuga, twenty-three, returned to their homes and killed themselves. Tatenao Arao, twenty-three, returned to his home and, revealing to his mother his intent to kill himself apologized for the grief he would cause her. However, she had only praise for him. Arao, weeping tears of joy, thereupon went to do reverence at his father's grave, and, at the graveside, valiantly committed seppuku.

As for Goichiro Tsuruda, who had been entrusted with leading the seven boys down from Mount Kimpo, he saw the youngsters to their various homes and then returned to his own home and prepared to take his life.

After his wife Hideko had set out food and drink, he exchanged a last cup of saké with her, wrote a death poem, and told her that she should not lose heart, since their only son, Tanao, was still alive. It was now the night of the second day after the uprising. Tsuruda also had two daughters, aged ten and fourteen. His wife wished to wake them so that they might say farewell to their father, but Tsuruda insisted on letting them sleep. And having unfastened his garments, he cut open his stomach and then thrust his blade into his throat. With his own hand he drew it out again, and he toppled over just as his older daughter, awakened by chance, came into the room and burst into bitter sobs.

Around dawn, word was brought that Tanao, the only son, had also committed seppuku. Thus on the morning after her husband had died telling her to place all her trust in her son, the news of that son's death came to Hideko's ears.

After the disbandment at Chikozu, Tanao had made his way to Shingai Shrine accompanied by Buichiro Sugé and Masura Ito. Parting from his friends, he journeyed on alone to the village of Kengun. His plan was to escape to Choshu.

He had an uncle named Tateyama in Kengun, and when he came to him for assistance, Tanao learned that his father had visited his uncle earlier that very afternoon, and had explained his own intentions, and had asked him to look after his family. No doubt his father had already killed himself. When he heard this, Tanao lost all desire to escape.

Granted the use of the garden in front of his uncle's house, Tanao spread a mat of fresh straw beneath a tall tree there. Facing the east, he bowed in worship three times to the distant palace of the Emperor, after which he turned in the direction of his parents' house, not far away, and bowed again. Then he took up his short sword, cut open his stomach with it, and plunged it into his throat. This word was carried to the Tsuruda home at once.

After Masura Ito and Buichiro Sugé had parted from Tanao Tsuruda, they headed towards Udo, a region just to the south of Kumamoto. The village of Mikka in Udo was the home of Ito's elder brother, Masakatsu. When he saw his younger brother, however, he berated him harshly for his rashness, and would not let him enter his house. The two young men had no choice but to go away. That night they sat down facing each other on the bank of a clear stream behind the village and carried out their ritual suicides with extraordinary grace. People who lived nearby heard the echo of repeated clapping coming from the direction of the stream late in the night. Tears filled their eyes as they realized that it was someone clapping in reverence to the gods and the Emperor before committing seppuku.

Ito was twenty-one. Sugé was eighteen.

*

Then as to the seven youths whom Goichiro Tsuruda had conducted to their homes, three among them, Ota, Saruwatari, and Shimada, slew themselves heroically with their own swords.

Just before the uprising, the sixteen-year-old Tadao Saruwatari had composed the following poem, writing it upon the white headband that he would wear the night of the battle:

> Our land divided, sold to barbarians,
> The Sacred Throne in peril.
> May the gods of heaven and earth
> Behold our loyal devotion.

When he reached home he learned of the suicides of many of his comrades. Disregarding all attempts to dissuade him, he exchanged a farewell cup of saké with his father and mother and relatives and then retired alone to another room. There he cut open his stomach, and thrust his sword into his throat. The blade hit the bone and was slightly nicked. Saruwatari called for one of his family to bring him another sword, and this time, cleanly pierced by the blade, he fell forward.

Saburohiko Ota was seventeen. As soon as he returned home he threw himself upon his bed and began to snore. When he awakened the next morning his face was glowing with health. He announced his intent to his sister and asked her to invite two young friends of his, Shibata and Maeda, to the house. When these two came, he told them that he was saying farewell forever and requested that they attend to whatever matters he would leave unresolved.

After the young men had left, Ota rose and went into another room alone. An uncle, Fusanori Shibata, waited in an adjoining room with only a sliding paper door between them. He became aware that Ota had cut himself open. Then he heard his nephew cry out in a heartrending voice: 'Uncle, Uncle! Please help me a little.' When Shibata flung open the sliding door, Ota's dagger was already thrust into his throat. With Shibata's hand guiding his own, the youth brought his life to a brave conclusion.

Kataro Shimada was eighteen. As soon as he arrived home, his family wanted him to escape by disguising himself as a Buddhist monk, but he would have none of it. He had determined to kill himself, and after the farewell saké, he entreated Juzo Uchishiba, a man renowned for his skill in judo, to come to his house and instruct him in the ritual of seppuku.

After Shimada had cut open his stomach, he pressed his blade to his throat.

'Master, is this the correct place?' he asked. When Uchishiba answered that it was, the youth plunged the blade in with graceful dispatch.

After the defeat of the uprising, three men, Kazuo Jugé, Namihei Imura, and Hisaharu Oda, were sheltered in the village of Kakihara by a prominent family named Oyano. Having gone to Abumida one day they met two of their comrades, who were among those just come down from Mount Kimpo, Tateo Narazaki and Taketsuné Mukunashi. These two they asked to join them, and all five were kept hidden by the Oyano family. Their place of shelter was the grotto of Rakugen Temple and the Oyano family attended to all their needs.

Seven days had passed since the uprising. In the interval the five men in the cave began to get word from various sources of the suicides of their comrades, and they came to the decision that to hide themselves further was unthinkable. Accordingly they left the grotto and went to the Oyano home to make their last farewells. The family, struck with grief at such a parting, set out food and drink for them.

Jugé ate very little, thinking how unseemly to have the food pour out when the sword cut into his stomach. Such considerations, however, hindered the lusty Narazaki not at all as he ate and drank his fill. Afterwards these two begged some cosmetics of a woman of the family, and brushed their cheeks lightly with rouge. They wished the glow of health to remain there even after death.

The five waited until nightfall to leave the house, and then went to a place close by called Nariiwa. It was the Fifteenth Day of the Ninth Month, a night on which the moon was full. Its bright beams seemed to scatter jewels through the dewy grass. The five men sat upright upon the grass, and after each had recited a farewell poem, Oda, the youngest at twenty, cut open his stomach, after which each of the others in turn fell forward over his own sword. Imura was thirty-five, Narazaki and Mukunashi twenty-six. Jugé was twenty-five.

Tsunetaro Kobayashi, who had parted from Kageki Abé and Unshiro Ishihara at Abumida, returned to his home late the evening of the Eleventh Day of the Ninth Month, accompanied by Kisou Onimaru and Mitsuo Noguchi.

Though he was but a youth, Tsunetaro Kobayashi combined courage and intelligence to a remarkable degree. He had generally taken a position opposed to the rash counsels of the extravagantly bold Onimaru, but these two comrades of opposite temperament chose to meet death at the same time and place. Now that the three of them had learned of the immense obstacles in the way of a second rising and of the utter dissolution of the League, they all committed seppuku side by side the evening of the following day.

Before doing away with himself, Kobayashi expressed his regrets to his mother for preceding her in death, and then withdrew to a separate room with his wife Mashiko, a girl of nineteen, whom he had just married the previous spring. Out of pity at causing her to pass the rest of her life as a widow, he offered to divorce her. But Mashiko burst into tears and refused.

The three men went into a room at the back of the house while the family waited in the kitchen. Kobayashi called out: 'Let no one enter here. Draw some water and put it on the veranda.' Then the three took up a tatami mat in the centre of the room and laid it over another. Onimaru sat down facing the east upon the double mat and unfastened his kimono.

Those in the kitchen heard Kobayashi call out again: 'Noguchi has perfomed the service of severing Onimaru's head.' At length no further sound came from the room.

When the members of the family entered, they found the three facing the east, Onimaru in the middle, the act of ritual disembowelment carried out to perfection.

Onimaru was forty years of age. Kobayashi was twenty-seven. Noguchi was twenty-three.

Ikiko Abé was the wife of Kageki Abé. The eldest daughter of Kishinta Torii, she was born in Kumamoto in 1851, the Fourth Year of the Kaei era. Her elder brother Naoki studied the Japanese classics under the tutelage of Master Oen, learned military tactics from Teizo Miyabé, and so became an ardent patriot with the slogan 'Honour the Emperor and expel the barbarians' ever on his lips.

Ikiko grew up hearing the opinions of her brother and his comrades, which made a deep impression upon her. The family was poor, and she worked hard to aid her mother.

When she was sixteen, a certain wealthy man desired her as his bride, but since Ikiko had resolved to marry only a militant patriot, she was not at all inclined to assent. Her brother and her mother were of like mind. However, the village headman was the matchmaker, and moreover the family was in the rich man's debt. Thus there was no avoiding the marriage.

Ikiko asked her mother, 'Well, then, if I marry this man, will that fulfil all obligations?' Her mother replied that it would. The wedding took place. That night Ikiko sat upright and did not allow her husband to approach her, and when dawn came, she fled to her mother's house. Bowing low before her mother she said: 'I have gone through with the marriage. Is anything else required of me?' That very day her husband divorced her.

She reached the age of eighteen. In 1868, the First Year of the Meiji era, her brother, Naoki, was appointed to serve at the Imperial Court.

It happened at this time that Kageki Abé, together with his comrade, Morikuni Tominaga, went to do worship at Hommyo Temple, sacred to the memory of Lord Kiyomasa. As they were approaching the black gate, they encountered a nubile young beauty. Perceiving that she was the sister of their comrade Naoki Torii, they bowed courteously. After they had walked on for a bit, Tominaga abruptly asked: 'What would you say to marrying that girl?' Abé replied that he would have no objections. With Tominaga as go-between, the marriage soon took place. Abé at that time was twenty-nine. Ikiko's hopes had been fulfilled. She had become the wife of a patriot. But no child was born of the marriage.

Ikiko became twenty. A comrade in Kurumé named Kii Kagamiyama escaped from prison and was given shelter by Abé. Then after Kagamiyama had left, Abé himself was taken into custody, examined severely, and thrown into prison.

As long as her husband was imprisoned, Ikiko would eat no food in the morning, she prayed constantly to the gods that this unjust punishment be lifted from her husband, and at night she did without a mosquito net, though it was the height of summer, and slept upon bare boards so that her husband's sufferings would be ever in her mind.

After he had been freed Abé was taking a stroll through the town when in one shop he came across a fine belly band. But the price was so high, as he told his wife, that he gave up all thought of buying it. Ikiko secretly sold a kimono and sash and presented her husband with the amount of money he needed. He thanked her and bought the belly band. And this is what girded his body the night of the rising.

As the rising drew nearer and nearer, the Abé house became a kind of headquarters. Ikiko and her mother-in-law spared no efforts in treating their guests with the utmost hospitality. And when some ten men gathered to prepare to take to the field, the women assisted them in every way, making ready food and drink. Noticing with a shrewd eye that one of the group was somewhat flurried, Ikiko admonished him quietly: 'One must go into battle with a tranquil heart.'

On the night itself, when Ikiko and her mother-in-law, Kiyoko, saw from a distance the angry flames flaring up from Kumamoto over the castle, the fires burning at five places in the Kyomachi, Yamazaki, and Motoyama districts, she leapt with joy, crying: 'It's done! It's done.' She lit vigil lamps before the household shrine and implored the gods for the success of the rising and her husband's good fortune in battle.

But with the morning, reports of setbacks came in thick and fast, and there were endless rumours of men falling in battle or perishing upon their own swords. With her husband's whereabouts unknown, Ikiko prayed to the gods yet more fervently for his welfare.

Three days were to intervene before his return. It was just before daybreak on the Twelfth Day of the Ninth Month.

After the disbandment of their force at the beach of Chikozu, Kageki Abé, accompanied by Unshiro Ishihara, left there to spend the following day, the tenth, in hiding in the mountain vastness of Shioya. As soon as it was dark they set out for the shrine of Kitsuki in Abumida and arrived in the middle of the night at the home of Oki Sakamoto, the shrine priest. There they were reunited with Tsunetaro Kobayashi, Onimaru, and Noguchi and, staying the night of the eleventh, they debated their future course of action. When a response of the gods to a question put by Oki Sakamoto held out hope for a second rising, all took heart, and Abé and Ishihara left Kobayashi and his party and made their way each to his own home.

Ikiko awoke to the sound of a voice calling softly through a chink in the wooden shutters. It was her husband. Her heart leapt as she slid open the shutters. He came in without a word, and then, facing Ikiko and his mother, who had risen and joined them, gave a brief account of the defeat. Ikiko stripped off her husband's blood-stained kimono and buried it in a bamboo grove behind the house. In the days that followed, Abé spent the daylight hours hiding beneath the floor of his study, a dagger grasped in his hand. When the sun had set he came up into the study. He sent Ikiko secretly to the Ishihara house so that she could consult with Ishihara's wife, Yasuko.

Ikiko and Yasuko made a frantic search for a boat for the passage to Shimabara Peninsula, but the ban on leaving harbour was stringently enforced, and all hope of an escape by sea vanished.

On the dawn of the fourteenth, Unshiro Ishihara, determined to break through the police cordon that blocked the roads or to die at his own hand, said farewell to his wife and children and left his house.

Abé had invited his uncle, a man named Baba, to his house, and in the dawn hours, the three men, Ishihara, Abé and Baba, discussed a plan of action. Baba explained that the strict measures taken by the police seemed to make flight impossible. And with that he departed.

Yasuko Ishihara went to the home of her husband's elder brother, Kimura, to beg for help. She had heard the thump of the boots of a search patrol coming along the road towards her house, then Kimura advised her to hurry to the Abé house to tell them that the time was past for flight.

Yasuko hired a rickshaw but got off just before reaching the Abé house, where she knocked softly at the rear door and asked that Ikiko come out. She explained to Ikiko briefly that a patrol was approaching their house in Ishihara's absence.

Ikiko made a gesture of striking at her own throat, and Yasuko nodded. Ikiko urged Yasuko to see her husband once more, but Yasuko said she had no wish to become an obstacle on her husband's path to the other world. Then she left as though fleeing.

Ikiko immediately reported all this to her husband and Ishihara. For their part, from the time they had heard Baba's intelligence, both leaders had cast away all hope for a second rising and had set their minds upon death.

Reverently the two bowed and offered worship before a scroll depicting the Grand Shrine of Isé. Ikiko placed three earthen cups upon a three-legged stool of plain wood. Urging the men to partake of the final draught of saké, she herself took up one of the cups.

Abé and Ishihara opened their kimonos and took their short swords in hand. As for Ikiko, she quietly drew a small dagger from within her sash.

Her action provoked consternation in Ishihara as well as her husband, and they tried to stop her, but Ikiko would not turn aside from her resolve. She had no children, she told her husband, so why should he prevent her from accompanying him? Since she gave no sign of retreating, Abé did not venture to deny her her will.

At the same moment that the two men cut open their stomachs with a precise thrust of their swords, Ikiko struck her throat with her dagger.

It was the Fourteenth Day of the Ninth Month. The time was shortly past noon. Abé was thirty-seven years of age. Ikiko was twenty-six. Ishihara was thirty-five.

Hardly a moment after their suicides the door of the Abé house shook with a violent knocking. The patrol had come. Abé's old mother called out in a loud voice: 'They have just committed seppuku.' An officer flanked by his troops forced his way into the house and was confronted with the three fresh corpses.

When the force had disbanded at Chikozu, the group of those who embarked in the lone fishing boat and made their way to Konoura in Udo, just south of Kumamoto, numbered six men.

There was the twenty-eight-year-old Juro Furuta, who together with Tsunetaro Kobayashi was one of the most youthful of the leaders. In the struggle within the garrison walls, he broke two swords, took up a third, and kept on fighting. It was he who cut down Lieutenant-Colonel Kunihiko Oshima as well as many others, though he himself also sustained a wound.

There was Juro Kagami, forty years of age and a master of the ancient court music.

There was Gitaro Tashiro, twenty-six years of age and a master swordsman. He was the first man upon the palisade of the artillery-men's camp.

Tashiro's younger brother Gigoro was twenty-three and had fought valiantly in the combat with the infantrymen.

Teruyoshi Morishita was twenty-four. He struck down Major-General Taneda, and then joined the struggle at the infantry garrison and slew another officer, greatly distinguishing himself.

Shigetaka Sakamoto was twenty-one.

The six had placed their hopes in the aid of the priest of Konoura Shrine, their comrade and fellow-disciple of Master Oen, Takeo Kai. He most certainly would have joined in the rising, but word of it had not reached him in this distant place. Kai gave them a cordial welcome.

They passed the night at Kai's house, taking counsel with one another as to a second rising. Kagami offered a suggestion for procuring funds for travelling and military supplies. He had learned that his former lord, Eijiro Mibuchi, happened to be staying at the Matsui residence in Ueyanagi, and so he entrusted a letter to Kai, asking Mibuchi to provide funds for their journey. Kai set out with the letter at once.

Everyone waited anxiously for Kai to come back. The following day, the Twelfth Day of the Ninth Month, passed without his return.

When Kai arrived at the Matsui residence, not only was Mibuchi no longer there, but Kai himself was recognized by the police on guard as one of those in sympathy with the League, and he was taken into custody.

The six who waited realized that every moment that Kai's return was delayed heightened their peril. And once a certain limit was reached, they knew they would have to prepare to meet their fate.

Three of them, Gigoro Tashiro, Morishita, and Sakamoto, racked by impatience, climbed to the top of the nearby peak of Omigataké just as the sun was setting. They gazed at distant Kumamoto Castle. Seen thus from afar, the castle tower's appearance gave no hint of any extraordinary activity within. But when the comrades casually questioned the mountain folk, they were told that by night the castle was ablaze with lights and by day search patrols were dispatched without let-up in every direction. When the three came down from the mountain, they urged their three comrades to resign themselves to the inevitable.

They set their minds upon death. As for the place, they chose Omigataké. As for the time, they chose dawn of the following day.

Not long after the first cockcrow, the six climbed to the crest of Omigataké. The previous evening, the Tashiro brothers had selected there a level portion of unspoiled ground and marked it off into a square bordered with sacred rope which they hung with Shinto pendants. Now at dawn these white pendants fluttered in the breeze. Gazing up at the trailing clouds as daylight broke over the mountains, Juro Kagami composed his farewell poem:

> I have lived long in this world
> By the grace of the gods of Yamato,
> And today I at last set foot
> On the Floating Bridge of Heaven.

As need hardly be said, his poem was based upon the mystic teaching of Master Oen on the ascent to heaven. Kagami told his comrades that he would very much like to have played for them in this final hour the ancient music in which he had been schooled, and that the lack of an instrument grieved him.

The six stepped within the sacred rope, they partook together of the farewell cup of saké, and Gitaro Tashiro, singled out by the others, agreed to administer the finishing stroke to each of them. Whereupon Kagami, thinking it a pity that Tashiro should undergo the last agony alone, said that he would wait and die with him.

Juro Furuta was the first to expose his flesh to the autumn breeze of morning and to cut his stomach straight across. Tashiro then severed head from body.

After that, Morishita, Gigoro Tashiro, and Shigetaka Sakamoto committed seppuku in turn. Finally Gitaro Tashiro and Kagami, performing the ritual together, cut open their stomachs and thrust their blades into their own throats.

Inspector Yoshitaka Niimi, alerted by an informer, began leading several policemen up the mountain. While still on the middle slopes, he met a hunter rushing down excitedly, who told him that six members of the League of the Divine Wind were committing seppuku on the mountaintop. Halting his impatient group with the words, 'We will rest here before going on,' Niimi sat down at the base of a tree and lit a cigarette. He did not wish to disturb the last moments of these men.

When the police reached the crest of the mountain, the last traces of the night's darkness were gone. Within the square cordoned with sacred rope, the corpses of the six patriots lay slumped forward in perfect fulfilment of the ritual. The white paper pendants that hung from the rope, many of them flecked with fresh blood, shone in the rays of the morning sun.

After the rising had been suppressed, one of its leaders, Kotaro Ogata, consulted the gods and was told that he should surrender. Ogata did so, and, while in prison serving a life sentence, wrote a short book entitled *The Romance of the Divine Fire*. In it he addressed himself to the problems of why the Divine Wind had not blown and why the Ukei had proved fallible.

With dedication of such unparalleled intensity, with wills so purged of impurity, how was it that divine assistance was not forthcoming? Such was the riddle with which Ogata struggled vainly in his prison cell for the rest of his life. Ogata's thoughts, as he recorded them in the following passage, merely represent his own interpretation, his personal conjecture. The will of the gods is hidden, and, indeed, it does not lie in man's province to know it:

> How wretched and pitiable that men so splendidly faithful should, counter to all expectation, perish in a single night, like blossoms scattered by a storm, like the fleeting frost and dew, and in an enterprise conceived and executed under the guidance of the divine will! Thus in my foolish heart did I wonder why it was that events had so come to pass, and I even began to feel doubt and bitterness. But I came to believe that the end was foreordained, that it was what the divine will had intended.
>
> Had the gods once more frowned upon the enterprise for which these hardy men, so fierce and bold, had sought their approval, what they had planned would no doubt become known to the world, and a most perilous situation would have come about. Even if that danger could have been surmounted, surely some of them would have taken their own lives, out of sheer frustration and despair.
>
> And so the great gods, moved to pity, fashioned a marvellous providence whereby these men would vindicate their honour at one stroke and thereafter render their service in the world to come.
>
> Though stricken with awe, so do I reason with myself.

A keen regret lies hidden in these words that Ogata wrote to console both himself and the souls of his comrades. And in the simple exclamation that follows, one that truly expresses the mind of this group of men who let no obstacle deter them, Ogata may be said to have given voice to the spirit of the samurai: 'Were we to have acted like frail women?'

10

The rainy season had already begun. Isao Iinuma paused before leaving home for his morning classes to glance inside the large envelope that had just arrived bearing Honda's name. After seeing that it contained a letter as well as his *League of the Divine Wind*, he put the envelope into his bookbag, intending to read it at his leisure once he had reached school.

He passed through the gate of his school, the College of National Studies. Just inside the entranceway of his classroom building stood a huge drum which well embodied the spirit of the school. It was a venerable-looking drum with the inscription 'Yahachi Onozaki, drum-maker, Temma', and had a large iron ring hanging from its cylinder. The broad circle of taut-stretched leather was like an expanse of early spring sky hazy with yellow dust. And the spots of wear inflicted by numerous blows were like clusters of white clouds floating in such a sky. But on a muggy rainy-season day like this, Isao thought, the drum, its vigour gone, would probably give off a sluggish, muffled sound.

As soon as he entered his second-floor classroom, he heard the drum being beaten to announce the beginning of the school day. His first class was ethics. Since neither that subject nor its decrepit teacher roused Isao's enthusiasm, he stealthily took out Honda's letter and began to read it.

My dear Mr Iinuma:

I am returning to you your copy of *The League of the Divine Wind*. I read it with keen appreciation indeed. Thank you.

I well understand why this book stirred such admiration in you. And rest assured that I, too, who had regarded this uprising as nothing more than an affair of discontented samurai fanatically dedicated to the gods, have had my horizons broadened by learning of the purity of motive and feeling of those involved. My appreciation, however, probably differs from yours, and it is about this difference that I would like to write in more detail.

That is to say, when I reflect upon whether, were I your age, the emotions aroused in me would be the same, I cannot help but doubt this. Rather I think that, whatever regrets, whatever envy I might have concealed within my heart, I would have smiled derisively at these men who staked everything upon a single blow. When I was your age I thought of myself as on the way to becoming a useful and proper member of society. At that age, my emotional balance was carefully preserved, and my intellect had come to function in a more or less clear if prosaic manner. I was convinced that the usual passions were altogether 'unsuitable' for me. Just as one cannot take on a body other than one's own, so I believed that one could not speak any lines other than those allotted one in human life. When I saw passion in others, it was my practice to search out the incongruity there as quickly as I could, the necessary contradiction, however small, between the man himself and his passion, and then to smile a little derisively – to protect myself. When one has this bent, it is easy to discover 'unsuitability' anywhere. This kind of derision was not necessarily malicious. I might even venture to say that my very derision contained a kind of cordiality and tolerance. Why? Because at that age, the realization had begun to take form in me that passion by its very nature is something born of man's failure to perceive this kind of incongruity in himself.

It happened, however, that a close friend of mine, Kiyoaki Matsugae, whom your father, too, has spoken to you about, put a great strain upon this so carefully ordered awareness of mine. He fell passionately in love with a girl, and I, with the eyes of a friend, perceived this from the first as the most extraordinary of incongruities. For I had thought of him up to that time as having no more warmth than a glittering crystal. He was maddeningly capricious, he was given to sentiment, but I, as an observer, had concluded that his all too exquisite sensitivity would preserve him from heedless and simple-minded passion.

Things did not proceed as I had thought, however. Even as I watched, I saw this naïve, heedless passion changing my friend. Love was feverishly at work, transforming him into a person suited for love. His passion, altogether foolish, altogether blind, made him into one altogether suitable. Just at the moment of his death, I saw his face become the very face of one who had been born to die for love. All incongruity was wiped away at that moment.

I, whose eyes had witnessed so miraculous a transformation, could myself hardly remain unchanged. My callow faith in my own indomitable nature became a prey to misgivings, and I had to work to maintain it. What had been an act of faith now became an act of will. What had been something natural now became something to be sought after. This was an alteration that brought with it a certain profit valuable to me in my role as a judge. When I deal with a criminal I am able to believe, unswayed by theories of retribution or re-education, or by optimism or pessimism towards human nature, that any man, regardless of his situation, is capable of being transformed.

At any rate let me return to the emotions I felt after reading *The League of the Divine Wind.* Strangely enough, I, who now am thirty-eight, discovered myself capable of being stirred by this narration of an historical event shot through with irrationality. What came to my mind most vividly was Kiyoaki Matsugae. His passion was no more than a passion dedicated to one woman, but its irrationality was the same, its violence, its rebelliousness was the same, and its resistance to all remedies but that of death was the same. Still, even in the midst of my excited appreciation, I felt secure in knowing that at my present age I can be aroused by such accounts without incurring any risk. Perhaps precisely because of the immutable truth of my never having done such things myself, I am now able to contemplate with safety everything that I might have done in the past. Thus, with no danger at all, I can fix my imagination upon such events, and I can let myself bathe in the poisonous rays of my own reveries reflected from them.

At your age, however, every excitement is dangerous. Every excitement that can send one pitching headlong is dangerous. And some are especially dangerous. For example, judging from that light that flashes from your eyes to disconcert those around you, I would think that your very nature makes a tale of this sort 'unsuitable' for you.

Having reached my present age, I find myself no longer adverting to the incongruity between men and their passions. When I was young, concern for my own welfare certainly made such fault-finding a necessity, but now not only is this necessity gone but the disharmony in others resulting from their passion, which in the past I would have considered a weakness worthy of scornful laughter, has become but an allowable imperfection. And with that perhaps I have lost the last vestige of my youth, whose vulnerability made it fearful of the wounds incurred by reacting emotionally to the erratic conduct of others. Now, indeed, it is the beauty of danger rather than the danger of beauty that affects me with the utmost vividness, and there is nothing comical to me about youth. Probably this is because youth no longer has any claim on my self-awareness. When I consider all this for a moment, there is something frightening about it. My own enthusiasm, innocuous as it is for me, may well have the result of further stimulating your dangerous enthusiasm.

Because I realize this, I want very much to admonish you in this regard, to urge restraint upon you – though my efforts may well be useless.

The League of the Divine Wind is a drama of tragic perfection. This was a political event so remarkable throughout that it almost seems to be a work of art. It was a crucible in which purity of resolve was put to the test in a manner rarely encountered in history. But one should by no means confuse this tale of dreamlike beauty of another time with the circumstances of present-day reality.

The danger of this account lies in its leaving out the contradictions. The author, Tsunanori Yamao, seems to have written in accordance with historical fact. But for the sake of the artistic unity of this slim volume, he has, without doubt, excluded a number of contradictions. Furthermore, he focuses so insistently upon the purity of resolve that pertained to the essence of this affair that he sacrifices all perspective. Thus one loses sight not only of the general context of world history but also of the particular historical necessities that conditioned the Meiji government which the League chose as its enemy. What the book lacks is contrast. To give an example, you yourself are aware, are you not, of the existence at the same time in the same Kumamoto Province of a group called the Kumamoto Band?

In the 1870s, a retired American captain of artillery named L. L. Janes, who had distinguished himself in the Civil War, came to take an assignment as a teacher at the school of Western learning founded in Kumamoto. He began to give Bible classes, and to slip into the role of a Protestant missionary. In the same year of the rising of the League of the Divine Wind, 1876, thirty-five of his students, led by Danjo Ebina, gathered on Mount Hanaoka on January thirtieth. And under the title of the Kumamoto Band they took a vow 'to Christianize Japan, to build a new nation based upon this teaching'. Persecution arose, of course. The school was finally closed, but the thirty-five comrades were able to flee to Kyoto, where they helped Jo Niijima build up Doshisha University. Though their ideals were diametrically opposed to those of the League, here, too, do we not see another example of the same purity of resolve? In the Japan of that day even the most eccentric and unrealistic ideas were not without some faint possibility of realization, and diametrically opposed concepts of political reform manifested themselves with the same naïveté and lack of sophistication. One should realize how much different that era was from the present when the structure of government has taken on a definite form.

I am no advocate of the novelties of Christianity, nor am I one to scorn the zeal for the past and the stubborn narrow-mindedness of the men of the League. However, if one is to learn from history, one should not concentrate solely upon a single portion of an era but rather make a thorough investigation of the many complex and mutually contradictory factors that made the era what it was. One must take the single portion and fit it into its proper place. One must evaluate the various elements that went into giving it its special character. Thus one must look at history from a perspective that offers a broad and balanced view.

This, I believe, is what is meant by learning from history. For any man's view of his own era is limited, and he has great difficulty in trying to obtain a comprehensive picture of his time. Precisely because of this, then, the comprehensive picture offered by history both provides information and constitutes a pattern for one's guidance. A man who lives bound by the limits of the minute-to-minute present is able, by means of the broad vision offered by time-transcending history, to avail himself of a comprehensive picture of his world and so correct his own narrow view of things. Such is the enjoyable privilege that history offers men.

Learning from history should never mean fastening upon a particular aspect of a particular era and using it as a model to reform a particular aspect of the present. To take out of the jigsaw puzzle of the past a piece with a set form and attempt to fit it into the present is not an enterprise that could have a happy outcome. To do so is to toy with history, a pastime fit for children. One must realize that yesterday's sincerity and today's sincerity, however much they may resemble each other, have different historical conditions. If one seeks a kindred purity of resolve, one should seek it in a 'diametrically opposed ideology' of the present day, existing under the same historical conditions. A modest attitude of this sort is appropriate for the characteristically limited 'present-day me'. For thus one is at last able to abstract this purity of resolve as a historical problem, and to make this 'human motive' which transcends history the object of one's study. Then the historical conditions common to the era become no more than the constant factors in the equation.

What a young man like you should be especially warned against is the blurring together of purity of resolve and history. The immense esteem, then, that you have for this book on the League of the Divine Wind makes me fearful. I think it would be well if you would try to think of history in terms of a vast stage of events, and of purity of resolve as something that transcends history.

All this has probably been a show of excessive solicitude, but such is my advice and admonition. I suppose that, without realizing it, I have arrived at the age of pouring out advice to anyone younger than myself. But, beyond that, I value your intelligence. Why should I admonish at such length a young man whom I expected to amount to nothing?

As for the almost sublime strength that you displayed in the kendo match, as for your own purity of resolve and passionate feelings, I cannot withhold my admiration. But placing still more reliance upon your intelligence and your zeal for truth, I would like to express the deeply felt hope that you will be ever aware of your primary duty as a student, ever assiduous in your studies, and so turn out a man valuable to your country.

Again, whenever you come to Osaka please take the opportunity to visit me. You will always be welcome.

Finally, though there should be no need for such concern with a man as excellent as your father always at hand, nevertheless, should any especially grave problem arise to trouble you and you feel the need for consulting with someone else, I would be willing at any time to talk things over with you. Please do not have the least hesitation in this regard.

Sincerely yours,
Shigekuni Honda

The young man sighed when he came to the end of the long letter. What was written there did not please him. He was opposed from first to last to what it said. Then there was something else. Even though this man was an old friend of his father's, Isao could not fathom his motive in sending a letter of such length, one furthermore which was so cordial, so carefully fashioned, so obviously sincere, to a boy whom he, a judge of the Osaka Court of Appeals, had met only once.

To be so singled out was a unique privilege, but what impressed Isao was not the letter itself but the frankness and warmth of its style. Never before had an eminent man demonstrated so sincere a regard for him.

Isao could draw but one conclusion: 'There's no doubt that he was moved by the book. His age and his profession have turned him into a coward, but Judge Honda, too, must be a man of "purity".'

Though the letter was filled with phrases that offended his feelings, at least his boyish eyes could find no corruption lurking there.

But even so, had not Honda's skilful freezing of history, stripping it of time, had the effect of reducing everything to a map? Was that how a judge's mind worked? The history of an era in terms of his 'comprehensive picture' would become no more than a map, a scroll, a thing with no life.

This man understands nothing at all of the blood that flows in Japanese veins, of our moral heritage, of our will, the boy thought.

Isao looked up to find the lecture still drowsily in progress. The fall of rain outside the window had intensified. The damp and sultry atmosphere of the classroom was filled with the heavy acid odour given off by the young flesh of growing boys.

The lecture ended at last. There was the same feeling of relief with which one sees a frightfully squawking chicken suddenly breathe its last and become tranquil.

Isao went out into the corridor, which was damp from the rain. Izutsu and Sagara were waiting for him.

'What's on your minds?' asked Isao.

'Lieutenant Hori said he wasn't on duty today and he'd be back at his quarters by three o'clock,' Izutsu told him. 'The place will be quiet at that time, and we'll be able to talk. He said we're to have dinner with him too.'

Isao answered without hesitation: 'Well, I'll skip kendo practice today.'

'Won't the captain have something to say about that?'

'He can say what he likes. He doesn't dare put me off the team.'

'How wonderful to have such power!' replied Sagara, who was small and wore glasses.

The three of them walked together to the next class, since all three had chosen German for their foreign language.

Izutsu and Sagara both deferred to Isao's leadership. It was Isao who had roused their enthusiasm by letting them read *The League of the Divine Wind.* Having by chance received his book that morning from Osaka, Isao decided to lend it next to Lieutenant Hori, whom he would meet that afternoon. It was hardly likely that the Lieutenant's reaction would be anything like the temporizing response of Judge Honda.

'A perspective that offers a broad and balanced view,' Isao thought, the phrase from the letter he had just read coming to his mind. He smiled slightly: 'That man would never touch hot fire tongs. He'd touch only the hibachi. But how different fire tongs and the hibachi. One is made of metal, the other of clay. He's a man who is pure, but he belongs to the clay category.'

The concept of purity was something that came from Isao and entered deeply into the minds and hearts of the other two. He had composed a motto, 'Learn from the purity of the League of the Divine Wind,' which had become the motto of their group.

Purity, a concept that recalled flowers, the piquant mint taste of a mouthwash, a child clinging to its mother's gentle breast, was something that joined all these directly to the concept of blood, the concept of swords cutting down iniquitous men, the concept of blades slashing down through the shoulder to spray the air with blood. And to the concept of seppuku. The moment that a samurai 'fell like the cherry blossoms', his blood-smeared corpse became at once like fragrant cherry blossoms. The concept of purity, then, could alter to the contrary with arbitrary swiftness. And so purity was the stuff of poetry.

For Isao, to die purely seemed easy. But what about laughing purely? How to be pure in all respects was a problem that disturbed him. No matter how tight a rein he kept upon his emotions, there were times when some trivial thing would arise to make him laugh. Once, for example, he had laughed at a puppy frolicking at the side of the road, with a woman's high-heeled shoe, of all things, in its mouth. It was the kind of laugh that he preferred others not to see.

'Do you know how to get to the Lieutenant's place?'

'Trust me. I'll get you both there.'

'I wonder what the Lieutenant is really like.'

Isao spoke up: 'I think he is someone who will give us a chance to die.'

11

The three boys, carrying their umbrellas and wearing their school caps with the white piping, got off the streetcar at Roppongi and walked down the street that began its descent at No. 3 Kasumi-cho and led around towards the main gate of the Azabu Third Regiment.

'That's it,' said Izutsu, pointing his finger at a house at the foot of the slope. All three stopped to look.

It was a two-storey house so worn with age that one wondered how it could have survived the disastrous earthquake. Its garden seemed rather large, but there was no gate, the board fence that surrounded it opening immediately upon the door. At the front a narrow porch ran along the second storey backed by a line of six glass doors, which seemed to brim over with the twisted reflection of the dark, wet sky. As soon as he had observed the rain-soaked bulk of this house from the slope above, Isao had had an eerie impression. This could not be the first time he was looking upon it, he thought. There the house stood wrapped in falling rain like a ludicrously oversized cabinet too old to be of any use and so abandoned to the elements. The trees and shrubs of its garden, unpruned and unclipped, flourished immoderately, and made the fence seem like a trash box stuffed with weeds. Isao felt that this place of so melancholy an aspect was connected with a past event of ineffable sweetness, a memory of which stirred deep within him like the bubbling of dark honey. How odd it seemed that he should have such an uncanny but distinct impression of having been here before. Perhaps this was founded upon the actual experience of having been brought to this neighbourhood by his parents when he was a child. Then, too, he might have once seen a photograph of this house. Whatever the case, he felt that the form of this house had remained perfectly preserved within his heart like a tiny but fully detailed garden wreathed in mist.

In another moment, Isao shook off these reflections which the dark shadow of his umbrella might have provoked. Ahead of the other two, almost running, he hurried down the steep slope awash with muddy water.

They stood before the entranceway. There was a nameplate fastened at the top of the closely worked lattice of the door, but the wind and the rain had taken such a toll of its wood that only the part inked over with the name 'Kitazaki' seemed to have any substance left. The rain had penetrated even the mouldering threshold.

An officer cousin of Izutsu had introduced him to Lieutenant Hori, the infantry officer whom they had come to see today. Izutsu could well expect the Lieutenant to be especially receptive to his bringing with him the son of the headmaster of the Academy of Patriotism.

Isao's mood was that of a vigorous young man newly enrolled in the League of the Divine Wind on his way to meet Harukata Kaya, and his heart thumped furiously. Now, however, the era was one in which the League was a thing of the distant past, and Isao well understood that the situation today was not that of sword-wielding samurai of the League clashing with the soldiers of the Meiji government, with friend and foe clearly marked like opposing pieces set up on a chessboard. He knew that today the samurai spirit was alive deep within the Army, and that those who had it viewed with sorrow and indignation the 'Meiji mentality' of the militarists and the important ministers who were their allies. That one of these possessed of the samurai spirit should live within such a wretched house seemed to Isao as though a scrub citrus tree hidden in the shadowy dampness of a forest should bear a single, bright-coloured orange.

Isao completely lost the cool reserve that he was able to maintain even before a kendo match. The man he was about to meet was someone capable perhaps of lifting him to the heavens – though every dream and hope that he had up to now placed in someone else had been betrayed.

The old man who answered the door sent a chill through the three youths. He was tall but bent forward so that, with his white hair and his deep-set eyes, he materialized in the gloom of the entranceway as though swooping down upon them. He was the sort of birdlike creature one might expect to meet in a mountain fastness, an ancient with broken wings folded.

'The Lieutenant eagerly awaits your visit. Please come this way,' said the old man, pressing his palms to his knees. Then he went off through the darkness of the damp corridor as though using his hands to direct the motion of his legs. Though the materials that had gone into the house seemed no different from those of any other lodging house, the very walls were permeated with the smell of leather, and the distant sound of the morning and evening bugle calls of the Third Regiment seemed to have been compounded with the fibre of its sliding panels. Apparently no other lodger but the Lieutenant had yet returned, so deep was the silence throughout the house. The old man's breath grew laboured as he began to climb the creaking stairway. Then he stopped halfway up, and, as if to gain a moment's rest, called to the second floor: 'Lieutenant Hori, your guests have come.' There was a youthful, almost insolent vigour to the voice that shouted in response.

The room that Lieutenant Hori lived in was a single one of eight mats, and, aside from a desk and a bookcase, it had no furnishings at all. Spartan surroundings altogether suited to a bachelor officer.

He had already changed into a splashed-pattern summer kimono with a carelessly fastened sash, and, so dressed, he seemed an ordinary young man of dark complexion. His uniform was neatly arranged upon a hanger which hung from a beam. The red tab at the collar and the brass numeral '3' gave the room the only bit of colour that caught the eye.

'Well, come right in. I was duty officer this week, and I was relieved at noon. That's why I'm home early.' The Lieutenant's voice rang with self-confidence.

His head was close-cropped, and his scalp was like a text proclaiming the rough vigour of his spirit. And though his eyes were clear and his glance penetrating, yet, dressed as he was, there was nothing to set him apart from any other young man of twenty-six or -seven from the provinces. Save, perhaps, for the thick forearms which told of his mastery of kendo.

'Now make yourselves comfortable. Don't bother about the tea, old fellow. We'll take care of it.'

When the old man's footsteps on the creaking stairs had grown faint, the Lieutenant began to talk cheerfully as he leaned forward to take up a thermos bottle containing the hot water for the tea. His words were obviously meant to put the tense boys at ease.

'This place looks like a haunted house, but both it and that old man there have a momentous history behind them. He was a hero of the war with China, and then, during the Russo-Japanese War, he opened this lodging house. Many great military men started to make their own way in life right here. So it's a house with good associations. Then it's cheap and it's also handy because it's close to the barracks, and so there's never an empty room in it.'

As the Lieutenant laughed, Isao watched his face. A visit about the time the cherry blossoms had begun to fall would have been preferable, he thought. How much better if the Lieutenant had come home after drilling on a windswept parade ground beneath a dusty yellow sky, had pulled off soiled boots to which clung cherry blossom petals, and had greeted the boys dressed in a khaki uniform that gave off the scent of spring and of manure, a gleeful flash of red and gold at the shoulders and collar.

The Lieutenant was evidently a man who cared little about the impression he made upon others. His tone was free and easy as he began to talk about kendo.

Izutsu and Sagara held their breath, intent on saying something. What they both wanted to say was that Isao, already a third-level kendoist, was a young man from whom the world of kendo expected much. At length, Sagara, small and bespectacled, stammered out this information. Isao's face reddened, and the Lieutenant's expression suddenly took on a kind warmth as he looked at Isao.

This is what Izutsu and Sagara had been hoping for. In Isao they saw the perfect embodiment of their hopes, and so, with the aggressiveness which is the privilege of youth, they wanted him to be on an equal footing in any confrontation with an outsider. Of course Isao would never resort to verbal trickery, but only bring to bear upon his opponent the piercing force of the purity to which they all were dedicated.

Suddenly the Lieutenant changed his tone and, eyes sparkling, put a direct question. Izutsu and Sagara felt their hearts throb; it was the moment they had been awaiting.

'All right, let me ask Isao here. What ideal do you hold?'

Isao, still sitting erect though he had been told to make himself comfortable, threw out his chest and answered succinctly: 'To form a Showa League of the Divine Wind.'

'The rising of the League failed. Doesn't that trouble you at all?'

'That was not a failure.'

'No? All right, what are you going to put your trust in?'

'Our swords,' answered Isao, not mincing a word.

The Lieutenant said nothing for a moment. He seemed to be rehearsing the next question in his mind: 'Well and good. But let me ask you this: what do you wish for more than anything else?'

This time Isao was silent. He had been keeping his eyes fixed upon the Lieutenant's, but now he turned them slightly away. His glance went from the damp wall to the tight-fast window of ground glass. That was as far as he could see. He knew that beyond the close-worked lattice of the window was a thick curtain of rain. Even if the window had been opened, there would have been nothing but rain in view. Still Isao seemed about to speak of something that was not close at hand but far off.

When he spoke, though his voice stammered slightly, his words were bold: 'Before the sun ... at the top of a cliff at sunrise, while paying reverence to the sun ... while looking down upon the sparkling sea, beneath a tall, noble pine ... to kill myself.'

'Hmm,' said the Lieutenant.

Izutsu and Sagara looked at Isao in shock. Though he had never before made such a momentous confession, certainly not to his two friends, he had expressed himself in these terms to a man whom he was meeting for the first time.

Fortunately for Isao the Lieutenant did not respond with harsh scepticism but gave every indication of weighing with the utmost seriousness this declaration which seemed little short of madness. Finally, he spoke: 'So that's how it stands. But it's not easy to die beautifully, you know. Because it's not up to you to choose the moment. Even for a military man, there's no guarantee that he'll be able to die exactly the way he wants.'

Isao gave no heed to the Lieutenant's words. Subtle discourse, exegesis, the 'on the one hand this, on the other that' approach – all these were foreign to his way of thinking. His ideal was drawn upon pure white paper in fresh black ink. Its text was mysterious, and it excluded not only translation but also every critique and commentary.

Isao's manner now became very tense, and, fully prepared to receive perhaps a slap across the face, he looked directly into the Lieutenant's eyes and spoke, his shoulders square.

'Would it be permissible to ask a question?'

'Go ahead.'

'Is there any truth to the rumour that before the May Fifteenth Incident Lieutenant Nakumura of the Imperial Navy made a visit to Lieutenant Hori?'

For the first time, a cold, hard expression flickered across the Lieutenant's face.

'Where did you hear a rumour like that?'

'Someone said it at my father's school.'

'Was it your father himself?'

'No, it was not my father.'

'It doesn't matter. Everything will come out at the trial. You shouldn't let yourself be taken in by stupid rumours.'

'Is it a stupid rumour?'

'A stupid rumour, yes.'

The Lieutenant lapsed into silence, and the anger which he had checked seemed to tremble in the interval like a compass needle.

'Trust us. Please tell us the truth. Did you meet with him?'

'No, I didn't. I never meet with any of them from the Navy.'

'Did you meet with Army men?'

The Lieutenant attempted a carefree laugh.

'I meet with them every day. I'm a soldier after all.'

'That does not answer my question.'

Izutsu and Sagara looked fearfully at each other. How far would Isao dare to go?

'Do you mean with comrades?' asked the Lieutenant after a pause.

'Yes.'

'That's something that doesn't concern you.'

'Please, we really must know.'

'Why must you?'

'Because if ... if we should ever come to ask something of you, we have to know ahead of time whether or not Lieutenant Hori is a man who will try to restrain us.'

Even before hearing the other's answer, Isao, taught by what had happened so often before, felt the unpleasant time had come when a chill would isolate him from the man sitting opposite him. The personality of his companion, which a moment before had seemed so radiant, would lose all its lustre. This was a change that was perhaps painful enough for the one who underwent it but decidedly more painful for the one who witnessed it. As though the tension of a drawn bow were suddenly relaxed, the arrow unreleased, the bow-string slack again before one's eyes. As though the heaped-up duration of day-to-day living, like a pile of rubbish, were manifested at one stroke. Was there not one man among their elders who would throw aside discretion and the caution brought on by his years and respond at once to the keen thrust of their purity with a sharp-pointed purity of his own? If there were definitely none, the purity that Isao envisaged had to be something that the bonds of age strangled. (This despite the example of the men of the League of the Divine Wind.) If it was in the nature of purity to fall victim to age, then purity was something destined to waste away before his eyes. No thought could make Isao more fearful. If this was true, he had no time to lose.

The way for elders to cure the impetuosity of youth is to give it their unqualified approval, but this is a bit of wisdom that they never seem to learn. And so the young put all their trust in the fierce purity which they feel will of its very nature vanish on the morrow, and they go to extremes in their pursuit of it. And the fault lies with no one but their elders.

*

Isao and his two friends stayed in Lieutenant Hori's room until nine that evening, the Lieutenant treating them to a dinner brought in by a caterer. Once he had abandoned his subtle questions, Lieutenant Hori's conversation became both interesting and profitable, quite capable of arousing their zeal. The shameful state of foreign affairs, the government's economic programme which was doing nothing to relieve rural poverty, the corruption of politicians, the rise of communism, and then the political parties' halving the number of Army divisions and, by championing the cause of arms cutbacks, bringing constant pressure to bear upon the military. In the course of this conversation, the Shinkawa *zaibatsu*'s exertions in purchasing American dollars came up, something of which Isao had already heard from his father. According to the Lieutenant, Shinkawa's group had been making a great show of restraint ever since the May Fifteenth Incident. However, the Lieutenant went on to say, there were no grounds at all for placing any trust in the self-control of people of that sort.

Japan was sorely beset. Storm clouds were piling up in an ever-growing mass, and the situation was enough to make a man despair. Even the august person of His Sacred Majesty was affronted. The boys' knowledge of current evils to be deplored was greatly expanded. In any event, the Lieutenant was a good man.

As they were leaving, Isao said: 'Our ideals in their entirety are contained in this.' He then handed *The League of the Divine Wind* to the Lieutenant. Since he had not made it clear whether he was giving the book or just lending it, if he ever wanted to visit the Lieutenant again, he thought, it would suffice to say that he was coming to get the book.

12

Early on Sunday morning, Isao conducted a kendo practice for young boys in the drill hall of the neighbourhood police station. The officer in charge was an admirer of his father, and from time to time visited the Academy of Patriotism. With his father as go-between, Isao could hardly refuse the officer's request. As for the boys' regular instructor, since he was thus able to sleep late on Sunday at least, he welcomed the opportunity to turn his charges over to Isao, whom the boys were not only fond of but looked upon as a hero.

The grade-school youngsters formed a line, their thin arms thrust out from the sleeves of their drill uniforms with the hemp-leaf pattern stitched in black on the white cloth, and one by one they charged at Isao with reckless abandon. As each pair of earnest young eyes behind their mask came rushing at him, Isao felt that he was being assaulted by a hail of brightly polished stones. Bending his body in accordance with the height of each antagonist and deliberately remiss in maintaining his guard, he dodged back and forth, taking blow after blow from the bamboo swords of the boys, much as though he were being whipped by young branches springing at him as he made his way through a thick grove. Isao felt his own youthful body glow pleasantly as the torpid mood of the rainy-season morning was shattered by the ever more fierce cries of the boys.

While Isao was wiping off his sweat after practice, a detective named Tsuboi, a man in his early fifties, who had been an interested spectator, came over to talk to him.

'You know, when I was watching you,' said Tsuboi, 'I realized what they mean about no kind of kendo practice demanding as much of you as when you're working with young boys. What a splendid sight! And then at the very end, the final reverence to the gods, when the oldest boy shouted out the order, "Divine Presence!" with such force even though he's so young, I saw right there the effect of good education. I tell you, it was a splendid sight!'

Tsuboi was a second-level kendoist, but his technique had no flexibility and power, all of his strength being in his shoulders. Sometimes when Isao would practise with the policemen at the station, Tsuboi would very affably put himself under his tutelage, a youth some thirty-five or six years younger. With his sunken eyes, which were devoid of expression, his long nose with its florid, unsightly tint, the garrulous and sentimental Tsuboi scarcely looked like a detective assigned to thought control.

Just as the boys were leaving by twos and threes through the gate in front of the drill hall, a patrol wagon turned into the yard. When it had stopped, a group of long-haired young men, bound and fastened to one another, got down from it. One was dressed like a workman, the two behind him wore drab business suits, and the fourth was dressed in a fashionable kimono.

'Well, well! Looks like we have some visitors this Sunday morning,' said Tsuboi, getting sluggishly to his feet. He gripped a kendo sword with his bare hands and executed a few strokes as he was about to leave. Isao could not help noticing that his hands were distastefully soft and weak, their veins standing out as though under nervous tension.

'Who are they?' he asked Tsuboi, impelled by no more than normal curiosity.

'Reds. You couldn't tell just by looking at them? Your Reds today don't dress like they used to. They make it a point either to dress so you don't notice them or to look like foppish playboys, one or the other. The one in work clothes is probably an organizer. The rest of them are most likely college students. Well, we'll have to make them feel right at home.' So saying, he twisted his weak hands suggestively about the handle of the sword, then put it aside and went out.

Isao felt a touch of envy toward these young men being thrown into prison. Sanai Hashimoto had been imprisoned at twenty-five and executed at twenty-six.

Was it possible that Isao himself might one day become a prisoner like Sanai? For a number of reasons, he found himself discontented that prison seemed so remote from him. Yet would he not choose to kill himself rather than submit to imprisonment? Very few of the League of the Divine Wind had been imprisoned. Surely, once he had plunged into a heroic enterprise, he would not await capture and all its indignities, but would put an end to himself with his own hand.

He wished that some morning, were it possible, the death that he was intent upon – to die atop a cliff swept by a breeze fresh with the scent of pine overlooking a sea bright in the morning sun – would somehow partake of the atmosphere reeking of urine that the rough and clammy concrete walls of a prison enclosed. But how could the two be mingled?

He was always thinking of death, and this had so refined him that the physical seemed to fall away, freeing him from the pull of earth and enabling him to walk about some distance above its surface. Indeed he felt that even his distaste and hatred for the affairs of the world no longer stirred him deeply. That was what Isao feared. Perhaps then the dampness of prison walls, the bloodstains upon them, the stink of urine, might serve to quicken his hatred. Perhaps prison was something he needed.

Since his father and the students had already finished breakfast when he returned home, Isao ate alone, served by his mother.

His mother had grown rather fat, so much so that her movements had become cumbersome. The blithe young girl with a roving eye and imperturbably sunny outlook now lay concealed beneath a melancholy burden of excess flesh which seemed to give expression to a temperament as cheerless as a heavily overcast sky. There was a sharpness to her gaze that suggested constant anger, but, even so, the erotic movement of her eyes had not changed from what it had been years before.

Since Miné's function at the Academy of Patriotism was to attend to the needs of some ten or more students, she surely had much to do. As demanding as her duties were, however, she had reached an age where playing the role of mother to so many young men should have given her a certain amount of pleasure, but Miné had built a wall around herself, as though for some reason she had rejected all intimacy. Whatever leisure she had she fervently devoted to the sewing of bags, and every corner of the house was filled with examples of her handicraft. The spectacle of brocade and Yuzen work scattered throughout an institution as purposefully austere as the Academy was like bright-coloured seaweed twined around the unpainted hull of a fishing boat.

Here in the kitchen, the base of a large saké bottle was jacketed with red brocade. The rice tub from which Miné now was serving her son was wrapped in a quilted cover of gaudy purple Yuzen muslin. It was obvious that her husband disliked this affectation more suited to a lady in waiting, but he had never gone so far as to reprimand her for it.

'I can't rest even on Sunday, you see. Master Kaido's lecture will be at one o'clock. Since the boys are sure to overlook something, I'll have to be there too to see all the arrangements.'

'How many will be coming?'

'Maybe about thirty. But there seem to be more every time.'

The Academy of Patriotism served as a kind of church on Sundays. Besides the students, all those in the neighbourhood who were interested came to attend the lectures of Kaido Masugi on the history of imperial decrees, which were prefaced by a welcoming address by the headmaster himself. These sessions ended with all present chanting in unison the prayer for prosperity, and provided an occasion for inviting donations to the school. This afternoon Master Kaido was to take up a decree of the Emperor Keiko, 'The Empowering of Yamoto Takeru to Subdue the Eastern Barbarians'. Isao had memorized a text from this: 'Then, again, evil spirits infest the mountains, devils ravage the countryside, roadways are blocked, pathways cut off, and multitudes are made to suffer.' He thought of it as a passage that could be well applied to his own era. The evil spirits in the mountains and the ravaging devils were flourishing.

From across the table Miné gazed fixedly at the face of her eighteen-year-old only son as he silently disposed of one serving of rice and then another. She was quite taken with the masculinity evident in the line of his jaw beneath the cheeks so vigorously occupied with the rice. Miné turned to look out into the garden at the cry of a passing pedlar hawking morning glory and eggplant seedlings. A hedge bounded the gloomy luxuriance of the shrubbery beneath an overcast sky, but it was too thick to afford a glimpse of the man. There was a heat-induced weariness to the pedlar's voice, and in Miné's mind his morning glories were drooping. The man's lethargic tone conveyed the feel of the garden, teeming with tiny snails at this hour of the morning.

All at once Miné found herself thinking of her abortion, the time she lost the first child that she conceived. This was a decision that Iinuma had forced upon her because no amount of calculation of the time involved had been able to satisfy him that the child was his own and not Marquis Matsugae's.

'This boy, Isao,' she thought, 'he doesn't smile. Why not, I wonder. He almost never jokes. And lately he'll go for a long time without saying a word to me.'

She was reminded of the young Iinuma in the Matsugae household, but there was a significant difference. The Iinuma of that period could hardly hide his tortured soul from even a casual observer, but Isao, whatever the circumstances, had an awesome poise. And this in the period of pimply adolescence when most boys were like puppies panting beneath the summer sun.

An abortion in first pregnancy makes the birth of the second child difficult, but Isao was delivered with remarkable ease, and it was not until afterwards that Miné suffered ill effects. Whether or not Iinuma had meant to show pity by finding fault with her feelings rather than with her physical disability, sometimes, as they lay beside each other at night, he berated her more severely and more sarcastically than ever about her former liaison with Marquis Matsugae. All of this was a severe mental and physical strain for Miné, but, instead of growing thin, she put on her gloomy burden of flesh.

The Academy of Patriotism had flourished. When Isao was twelve years old, Miné became altogether too friendly with one of the students. When Iinuma learned of this, he gave her a frightful beating. She was in the hospital for nearly five days.

From that time on, as far as anyone could tell, relations between husband and wife were tranquil. Miné lost all her vivacity, the price that had to be paid for the severe restraint she laid once and for all upon her wayward heart. Iinuma himself, as though freed from a spell, did not mention the Marquis again. The past had become something never to be touched upon.

Nevertheless, Miné's stay in the hospital could not have helped but make some sort of lasting impression upon Isao. He had never said a word about it to his mother, of course, but his failure to refer to it even in passing showed all too clearly that he had something stored up within him.

Miné was sure that someone must have told Isao of her old misdemeanour. Oddly enough, she found herself provoked by the desire to hear an accusation from Isao's own mouth. That her son entertained doubts about her qualifications as a mother was not without some satisfaction for her. The prospect had a certain sweetness. Troubled by a headache that made her imagine that she had a shallow pool of stagnant water somewhere at the back of her head, she kept gazing at her son from beneath her heavy eyelids, which crinkled when she was tired. His cheeks were still filled with rice.

Iinuma had enjoined her by no means to let Isao know how much the financial situation of the household had brightened immediately following the May Fifteenth Incident. Nor did Iinuma himself inform Isao of the school's circumstances, insisting that, when his son became an adult, there would be time enough to tell him whatever ought to be told. Miné, however, with the advent of this new prosperity, could not keep herself from increasing the allowance that she secretly gave him.

When Isao had finished eating, Miné took a folded five-yen note from her obi and, saying, 'Don't tell your father, now,' stealthily passed it under the table to him.

Isao smiled slightly for the first time and said thank you as he quickly slipped the money into his kimono. He seemed to begrudge the smile.

The Academy of Patriotism stood in the Nishikata section of Hongo. Iinuma had obtained possession of the building ten years before. It had belonged to a well-known Western-style painter, and a separate wing that had served as a studio of massive proportions had been redesigned as a meeting hall and shrine. The main house, which had evidently been occupied by a number of the artist's apprentices, was now given over partly to the students of the Academy. The pond in the garden to the rear had been filled in and left that way, with the thought that it would eventually become the site of a drill hall. Until such time the students made do with the meeting hall for the practice of their martial arts. The floor, however, lacked the proper resilience, and Isao disliked practising there.

To avoid setting his son apart from the other pupils, Iinuma had him join in mopping the floor each morning before he went off to school. Exercising a careful control, Iinuma did not permit Isao to be treated either as the master's son or as one altogether on the same footing with his fellow students. He tried to keep him from becoming too friendly with any of them. And though he trained the students to confide in himself the headmaster, in all matters whatsoever, he discouraged them from opening their hearts to his wife and son.

Despite this, however, Isao spontaneously established a cordial rapport with the oldest of the students, a man named Sawa. Since he was forty, and had left his wife and children in his native place to come to Tokyo, Sawa's case was extraordinary enough to provoke astonishment. He was stout and droll, and, whenever he had even a few moments free, his head was buried in a swashbuckling adventure magazine, *Kodan Club*. Once a week he would go to the courtyard before the Imperial Palace, where he would sit down in a formal position on its gravel surface and bow until his forehead touched the ground. Believing that a man must be ready to offer his life for the fulfilment of the Imperial Will at any moment, he washed out his clothes energetically every day, to keep himself scrupulously clean. On the other hand, he gambled with the young students, and, in the course of one bet, sprinkled flea powder on his rice before eating it, with no ill effects. Whenever the headmaster sent him with a message, Sawa would relay it in such an absurd way that the person it was meant for would be utterly confounded, for which offence Sawa was always being scolded by the headmaster. Still, he had no equal for his reliability in confidential matters.

Isao, leaving his mother to her work of cleaning up after him, walked down the connecting corridor to the meeting hall. The shrine, with its doors of plain wood, stood upon a raised platform in the middle of the far end of the hall. Above it hung the curtain that concealed the portraits of Their Imperial Majesties the Emperor and Empress. From where he stood at the door of the hall, Isao faced in that direction and bowed reverently.

Though Iinuma was some distance away, giving directions to a group of students within the hall, his son's act of reverence caught his eye. It seemed to him that Isao always spent too much time at it. Also, in the course of the monthly pilgrimage to Meiji Shrine and Yasukuni Shrine, Iinuma had had occasion to notice how much longer than the others Isao took in offering his worship. And he had never confided any reason for it to his father. When he looked back on his own youth, Iinuma tried to recall those things that he had prayed for with such angry anathemas during his morning devotions before Omiyasama on the Matsugae estate. Compared to himself at the same age, Isao was a boy whose status was secure and so had no cause to resent the world and call down curses upon those around him.

Isao looked on as the students were busy rearranging chairs in the dim light filtering down through the broad skylight. Since the sky was heavily overcast, the patch of light above gave the hall the subdued glow of an aquarium.

The boys had by now put the chairs and benches in good order, but Sawa, alone among them, was still at work in his own inefficient way, pushing the same chair this way and that, eyeing its position, then moving it once more, a good portion of his plump torso visible as usual at the neck of his loose kimono.

Sawa escaped the headmaster's wrath only because Iinuma was busy overseeing the arrangement of the platform, taking pieces of chalk from the blackboard tray and lining them up neatly. The students, wearing Kokura *hakama*, carried in the desk that was to serve as a lectern, covered it with a cloth, and then placed a pine bonsai upon it. As they did so, light from the skylight caught the tree and caused its green porcelain vase to flash and its needles to brighten as though life had suddenly quickened within it.

'What are you doing there?' Iinuma called out as he turned around on the platform to face in his son's direction. 'Are you going to be quick and give us a hand or not?'

Isao's friends Izutsu and Sagara came to hear the lecture on imperial decrees, and he brought them to his room afterwards.

'Show it to us,' said little Sagara, pushing back his over-large glasses with his forefinger, his nose pointed and quivering with curiosity like that of an eager ferret.

'Just a minute. First let me tell you I happen to have plenty of money on hand, so I'll stand you to a treat later,' said Isao, tantalizing his friends ingenuously. The eyes of the two boys sparkled. Isao's manner made them feel that something was about to be accomplished then and there.

His mother came with some fruit and tea, and as soon as the sound of her footsteps had faded in the corridor, Isao unlocked and opened a drawer. He took out a folded map, and spread it out on the floor. It was a map of Tokyo, parts of which were heavily shaded with a purple pencil.

'Here's how it is,' said Isao, with a sigh.

'That bad?' asked Izutsu.

'Yes, that bad. The corruption has already gone this far.' Isao took a shaddock from the bowl and began to rub its bright yellow lava-like skin with his hand. 'If the inside of this fruit was as rotten, it wouldn't be fit to eat, and you'd have to throw it out.'

Isao had used the purple pencil to indicate the presence of corruption, marking every critical spot. From the vicinity of the Imperial Palace to Nagata and throughout the entire Marunouchi area near Tokyo Station the colour was a deep purple, and even the palace area itself was not without a purple tinge. The Diet Building wore a heavy coat of it, and this saturation area was linked by a dotted line to the purple mass that covered Marunouchi, the home ground of the *zaibatsu*.

'What's that?' asked Sagara, pointing to a spot of purple a little distance removed in the neighbourhood of Toranomon.

'The Peers Club,' Isao answered coolly. 'They like to call themselves the Emperor's "Shield of Flesh", but they're just parasites on the Imperial Household.'

In the Kasumigaseki area, as was hardly surprising, the avenue lined with government bureaux, whatever the variations of shade, was purple from one end to the other. The Foreign Ministry, the chief architect of the weak and vacillating foreign policy, had taken such severe punishment from Isao's pencil that it gave off a purple glow.

'So, this is how far the corruption has spread! And the Army Ministry, and the General Staff too!' Izutsu exclaimed, his eyes flashing and his voice surprisingly harsh and loud for his age. Izutsu's voice, however, expressed true belief, its tone one of quick and ready affirmation surging up through a channel free of all impurity.

'Of course. I put my pencil to work only where I had certain knowledge.'

'I wonder what we could do to purify this all with one sweep?'

'The men of the League of the Divine Wind would disapprove perhaps, but if you want to do it all at once there is no other way but this,' Isao answered. He lifted the shaddock in his hand above his head and let it fall upon the map. The shaddock struck with a dull plop and bounced heavily a single time before rolling to one side and coming to rest upon Hibiya Park. When it stopped rolling, its reflection sluggishly took form as a broad circle of pale yellow over the cocoon-shaped pond of Hibiya Park and the winding paths that surrounded it.

'I see,' exclaimed Sagara, so excited that he nearly let his glasses slip from his nose. 'We drop bombs from an aeroplane.'

'That's it,' answered Isao, smiling easily.

'Of course, what else?' said Izutsu. 'In that case, though Lieutenant Hori is a wonderful man, we must make contact with somebody in the Air Corps. If we tell the plan to the Lieutenant, he'll introduce us to the right man. I'm sure Lieutenant Hori will soon be one of our most valuable comrades.'

Izutsu's credulity was almost a thing of beauty, and Isao allowed himself a moment to savour it. Izutsu would be obedient to the end, to any decision Isao made. His character was such, however, that he became completely taken up with whatever good qualities he discovered in those whom he met. This credulity turned the world of his ideals into something as bright and level as a meadow. Izutsu had no fear of encountering contradictions, and, in his world which was without complexities, evil, as he conceived it, took the flattest imaginable form. He thought of himself, no doubt, as crushing evils like so many wafers, and here lay the source of his rash boldness.

'All very well,' said Isao, after letting Izutsu's credulity sink in, 'but as for bombs, let me remind you that Kengo Ueno of the League of the Divine Wind wanted to use firearms, but his plan was rejected. Our ultimate reliance too must be upon the sword. Never forget that. We can only rely on our swords, and on bombs made of our flesh.'

13

Lieutenant-General Kito's home in Hakusanmaé was within easy walking distance of the Academy of Patriotism. Isao knew by heart the number of the thirty-six stone steps that one climbed to reach the house after crossing the stone bridge that lay at the foot of the rise upon which it stood. In the surroundings of his home, the General's manner was especially gracious. He was a widower, and he was content to entrust the running of his household entirely to his daughter Makiko, who had returned home after an unsuccessful marriage. His relations with the Academy were cordial, and since he had always shown special fondness toward Isao, Iinuma did nothing to prevent his son spending a great deal of time at the General's home, beyond warning him not to make too much of a nuisance of himself.

Whenever Isao went there with his friends, the task of entertaining the young men always fell to Makiko. Her kindness was extraordinary. The General and his daughter both assured them that, though they were to come whenever they liked, they were especially welcome just before dinner since nothing could give them greater pleasure than to feed young men whose appetites so well showed their appreciation.

Makiko's manner was one of unvarying impartiality. Cheerful, gently graceful, coolly reserved, she never had a single hair out of place or the slightest disarray in dress.

Since it was a Sunday night and Isao, Sagara, and Izutsu had no particular place to go in mind, they decided to spend the evening at General Kito's. Izutsu and Sagara had persuaded Isao to forget about his promise to treat them, and to put aside the money, however little, so that it could be of some use when the time came to carry out their plan. And so the three had to go somewhere that did not require money.

Makiko met them at the entranceway, wearing a kimono of light purple serge. Isao felt a sudden chill at the sight of it, hoping that it did not recall to Izutsu and Sagara the map splotched with corruption which he had just shown them.

'Good evening. Please come right in,' Makiko greeted them, her arm curved gracefully about a hall post like a handle on a delicate vase. 'Father is away on a trip, but that doesn't matter. Do come in. You haven't eaten yet, I hope?' Her manner was as cordial as ever. Then, as rain suddenly began to fall, she peered outside into the dusk and said: 'What lucky young men you are!' her soft tone blending with the light rustle of rain. When she spoke like this, she sometimes seemed to be talking to herself. Isao, feeling that it would be impolite to attempt any sort of clever response, said nothing as he stepped up into the dark house.

Makiko turned on a hanging ceiling lamp in the guest parlour. But just as she was reaching up for the switch above the shade, the lamp swayed and her hand slipped. The light went on and off for an instant, and then on again. During the brief time that she stood there on tiptoe, the seductive whiteness of her *tabi*-shod feet attracted Isao's eye. He somehow felt as though he had penetrated one of this woman's secrets.

The ability of the Kito household to have ever on hand an ample selection of dishes no matter how unexpected their guests was always a source of surprise to the boys. This, however, was a long-standing custom of the household dating from the time when they had had to be prepared for the appearance at any moment of young officers with hearty appetites. Dinner was served immediately. Makiko ate with them, having the maid do the serving. Isao had never seen anyone who could eat with Makiko's grace. She bent her head supply and moved her chopsticks with a fluid grace, holding but the smallest portion of rice or fish between them. And, furthermore, even while laughing at the boys' jokes, she nimbly finished her dinner as though skilfully attending to some small task suited to a woman.

'Shall we listen to some records?' asked Makiko when dinner was over.

The atmosphere was hot and humid, and so, despite the light shower, Makiko had the maid open the glass doors facing the porch, and they sat down by them. A mahogany-coloured cabinet phonograph stood in one corner of the room. Although electric phonographs had become popular everywhere, the Kito household clung stubbornly to its imported wind-up model. Izutsu undertook the work of winding it up. Isao might well have done so himself, but Makiko was at that moment standing near the phonograph as she looked over the records, and the thought of going beside her made him hesitate.

Makiko selected a twelve-inch record with a red label, a Chopin 'Nocturne' played by Cortot, and put it on the turntable. Though this was something outside the boys' cultural background and they made no pretence of being familiar with it, they meekly gave themselves over to the selection offered to them. They began to feel as if they had slipped into agreeably chilly water and were swimming about in it. When Isao compared the quiet passivity of spirit he experienced now with his customary state at his father's Academy, he felt that the latter was like a constant masquerade.

As though to confirm this insight, the music set his mood drifting one way and then another. Vivid memories of things seen and heard during his visits to the Kito home flowed through his mind one by one, carried along by the current of piano music, each one, as though marked with a crest, bearing a small image of Makiko.

Once, on a spring afternoon while the General, Makiko, and Isao were talking, a pheasant flew down into the garden. 'Oh, look! It most be from the Botanical Gardens,' Makiko had exclaimed. Her cheerful voice still echoed clearly in Isao's ears. As the memory flashed before him, the womanly voice seemed to come from the crimson-winged pheasant itself. 'It must be from the Botanical Gardens' – her tone seemed to suggest a luxuriantly wooded spot such as he had never seen, a domain of women.

Then the piano music caught Isao's memory again and swept it along this way and that.

On an evening in May the same voice had spoken: 'I was just on my way to flower-arranging class the other morning. It had been raining for days, so I opened my umbrella and was going down the stone steps when a swallow darted by and almost flew into the umbrella. It was a close call, believe me.' But when the General replied that it was indeed fortunate that she had not taken a bad tumble down the steps, Makiko protested that that was not what she meant. She had been concerned, rather, lest the swallow injure itself upon the umbrella's pointed ribs. And Isao, listening to her, instantly re-created in his mind this critical moment and its captivating circumstances. The face of a woman flashed before him, somewhat pale in the faint green light that shone through the oiled paper of her sheltering umbrella, her cheeks moist from the misty rain, her expression taut with concern. Here was the quintessential woman, a woman standing upon the precipice of womanhood. And then the swallow, secure in the woman's concern, revels in her pity, risking the ultimate as it flirts with death. Intent on wounding though it will itself be wounded, the swallow obeys a rebellious impulse, like a blade cutting through the purple irises of May, its eye upon the supreme moment. But the moment does not come. The anxiety resolves into a gentle poetic mood: a beautiful woman on her way to practise flower arranging, a darting swallow – they brush past each other and go their separate ways.

'Are you taking good care of the lilies that you received at Izagawa Shrine?' Makiko asked Isao, and her question was so direct and unexpected that Isao could only say 'I beg your pardon?' in response. The record had finished.

'The lilies I was given there, the lilies you brought from Omiwa Shrine.'

'No, no. I gave them all away.'

'You kept not even one for yourself?'

'No.'

'What a shame! No matter how withered they get, one should keep them until lay them reverently on the family altar.'

'Did you press them?' asked Sagara without thinking.

'No, I didn't think it would be proper to crush the flowers of the gods under a heavy object, so I put them on the altar just as they were and I've been giving them fresh water ever since.'

'But they're already a month old!' Isao retorted.

'It is a marvellous thing, but they never wither to an unsightly colour. I will show you. There can be no doubt that they are the flowers of the gods.'

So saying, Makiko went out of the room to return in a few moments, her step slow and reverent, bearing in upraised hands a vase of white porcelain filled with a profusion of lilies. She placed them on the table for the boys to look at. The lilies certainly had withered, as cut flowers would, but they had not turned the usual ugly colour as though scorched by fire. Their white had become a sombre ivory. As though anaemia afflicted them, the green shading of their veins had become sharply etched. Each blossom seemed to have shrunk in the same proportion. They were as though transfigured into flowers of some yet undiscovered species.

'I will give one to each of you, and you must take them home and carefully preserve them. They will guard you from sickness.' With a small pair of scissors Makiko began to clip off a lily for each of them, cutting the stems close to the blossoms.

Izutsu laughed. 'Even if you didn't do us this favour, we wouldn't have to worry about getting sick.'

'You shouldn't talk like that, after Isao showed such devotion in bringing these lilies from Omiwa Shrine. And besides, it's not only for sickness,' replied Makiko cryptically, still snipping with her scissors.

Embarrassed at the prospect of having to go over to accept a flower from a woman, Isao remained obstinately by the porch. He sensed something he could not define about the now-silent Makiko, and, without realizing what he was doing, he looked at her. As she leaned upon the rosewood table that held the vase, her profile was turned toward him. At that moment, Isao knew she was fully aware that his eyes were upon her profile.

Seeing his two friends standing close to her, ready to take their lilies, he spoke out as though threatening them, his outlandish tone altogether unsuited to the setting: 'Listen to me, you two. If in Japan today you could kill only one man, who do you think it would be best to kill? The sort, that is, whose murder would be at least a step toward the purification of Japan.'

'Jugoro Itsui?' replied Sagara, turning the lily Makiko had given him in his fingertips.

'Don't be stupid. He has money, but he's unimportant.'

'What about Baron Shinkawa?' asked Izutsu as he came over to Isao to hand him the lily that he had taken for him. His eyes were flashing.

'If you could kill ten, I rather think he'd be one of them. But he's only an opportunist. He's learned something from the May Fifteenth Incident, and he trims his sails to suit whatever wind is blowing. Naturally, he deserves punishment as a traitor.'

'Premier Saito?'

'He'd surely be one if you killed five. But Saito stands in front of a black curtain that hides the world of big money. And who's behind that curtain?'

'Oh! Busuké Kurahara?'

'He's the one,' answered Isao decisively, as he quickly slipped the lily Izutsu had given him into his kimono. 'Kill him and Japan is much the better for it.'

Even as he spoke, Isao's eyes held fast to the sight, as though at a far distance, of a woman's slender white hand curved upon a rosewood table and a pair of scissors giving off a sparkle like flashing water beneath the lamp. Makiko's practice was never to obtrude upon the boys' conversation among themselves, but she could hardly fail to note from Isao's manner that he wanted her to be aware of what he was saying. The look she turned towards him was warm with a maternal affection, but her eyes had a distant focus to them, as though she was perhaps looking beyond him into the garden outside, seeking out the last of the blood-red glow of the setting sun all but concealed by the wet foliage of the garden shrubbery.

'Evil blood,' said Makiko, 'is blood that cries to be shed. And those who shed it may indeed heal our country's sickness. Those cowards who now stand at the bedside of our stricken nation do nothing but wring their hands piteously. Japan will die if the issue is left to them.'

Makiko's tone was as light as if she were reciting a poem. Isao felt his grim tautness ease.

Hearing the sound of heavy panting behind him and of something coming through the grass, Isao glanced back over his shoulder. He felt embarrassed at the quickening of his heartbeat. A stray dog had probably slipped into the rainy garden. The unpleasant snuffling noise it made as it pushed its muzzle through the vegetation confirmed this impression.

14

Little rain marked the latter half of the rainy season. Day after day the skies, heavy with brownish grey clouds, persisted in trapping the sunshine, but finally they cleared. The colleges began their summer vacation.

Isao received a postcard from Lieutenant Hori with a message scrawled with a thick, coarse lead pencil. He had found *The League of the Divine Wind* quite stimulating, he wrote, and since he wanted to share it with his friends, he was keeping the book at the regimental headquarters. He would be happy to see Isao any time that he wished to come to retrieve it.

Isao went one afternoon to visit the Lieutenant at the garrison of the Azabu Third Regiment. The barracks and parade ground lay transfixed by the glare of the summer sun.

Off to the right of the main gate as one entered stood the conspicuously modern barracks that the regiment so prized. But, rather than this, the dust that swirled up beyond the trees by the drill field and the smell that came drifting from a stable somewhere were the qualities that most conveyed the sense of *army* that permeated all that Isao saw spread out before him, qualities that merged with the consecrated fame of the regiment to rise up into the dust-laden sky.

As Isao passed through the gate, a platoon drilling in a distant corner of the parade ground caught his eye at once, the figures of the men like so many upright khaki crayons beneath the blazing afternoon sun.

A private first class on guard showed him the way. 'Lieutenant Hori is drilling some trainees over there. They should finish in about twenty minutes,' he said. 'You can watch if you like.'

Isao followed the private across the parade ground, feeling the sun's heat pressing down upon him. Everything lay sharply etched beneath its rays. When the two at length came up to the platoon, the brass of the soldiers' buttons and regimental '3s' flashing in the sun and the massed red collar patches of the infantry stood out in vivid contrast from the khaki mass.

The men were now marching straight ahead and the thumping echo of their booted feet was like the champing of massive teeth. Lieutenant Hori held his drawn sabre at his right shoulder, and as he bellowed the commands of close-order drill, his voice soared over the ranks of silent men like a fierce bird of prey.

'Platoon right...' came the warning command, followed a moment later by the command to execute: 'March!' At that instant, the pivot man on the inside file immediately turned his sweaty face to the right, and for the next few paces marched in place as he waited for the outside file to perform its wide turn. The other files in the meantime seemed to open up like wide-spaced picket fences only to come together again with the ease of a folding fan closing.

'Squads on line left ... march!'

At the Lieutenant's shouted command, the formation dissolved without an instant's delay, and the troops rushed forward with mathematical precision to form a single rank pivoting upon the guidon bearer. And when the manoeuvre was completed with the file on the outside flank moving up into position, the platoon resumed its forward march.

'By the right flank ... march!'

The Lieutenant's virile shouts, accompanied by the flashing of his sabre, were like shots discharged into the summer sky. The long rank changed its line of march again. Now as the men drew away from him, Isao could see their backs, the shirts stained and darkened with sweat. From the strain so evident in the set of their shoulders, Isao realized what frantic effort they were putting into checking the harsh breathing provoked by the manoeuvre just accomplished.

'Fall out!' shouted the Lieutenant. And with that he turned and ran back to Isao's direction before pulling up abruptly to shout: 'Fall in!' While the Lieutenant was running, Isao saw beneath his black visor, which was glinting in the sunlight, beads of sweat flying from the sunburnt bridge of his nose and from his tight-set lips.

The soldiers, too, in accordance with their officer's new position, came rushing towards Isao as though racing one another, and, after the manoeuvres that had taken them so far off, formed up in two ranks right before Isao, jostling one another in their eager haste.

After inspecting their order with severe thoroughness, the Lieutenant once more barked out the commands 'Fall out!' and 'Fall in!' Clutching their rifles, the men dashed over the sun-baked earth. The commands were repeated over and over. Sometimes the area just beside Isao and the private was ravaged by a whirlwind of dust and sweat and the smell of leather and the labouring breaths of some twenty men. Afterwards the dry ground lay darkened with drops of sweat. Dark splotches also covered the Lieutenant's back where he now stood some distance away from Isao.

Beneath a summer sky encircled by a low bank of distant, dreamlike clouds, oblivious to the thick and lovely shade cast by the trees bordering the drill field, the little band of soldiers performed like a finely tuned engine as they fell in, fell out, changed direction, and altered formation. They seemed to be moved by a giant, unseen hand reaching down from above. That hand could only belong to the sun itself, Isao thought. The Lieutenant was no more than a lone representative of that hand which manipulated the soldiers as it willed, and when one thought in such terms, even his powerful voice took on a hollow ring. The unseen hand which shifted pawns about on a chessboard – in the very sun above was the force that guided it, the blazing sun which dealt out death, too, whenever it wished. Here was the power of the Emperor himself.

Only on this drill ground was the hand of the sun working with a mathematical clarity and precision. Only here! The will of the Emperor penetrated the sweat, the blood, the very flesh of these young men, piercing their bodies like X-rays. From high above the entranceway of regimental headquarters, the golden chrysanthemum of the imperial crest, brilliant in the sunshine, looked down upon this beautiful, sweaty, intricate choreography of death.

And elsewhere? Elsewhere throughout Japan the rays of the sun were blocked.

When the drill was finished, Lieutenant Hori, his creaking leather puttees white with dust, came over to Isao. 'Glad to see you here,' he said and then dismissed the private: 'Very good. I'll take over now.'

They began to walk toward a huge, yellowish oval-shaped building.

'What do you think of it?' asked the Lieutenant proudly. 'The most modern barracks in Japan. It even has an elevator.'

As they were going up the stone steps that led to the entrance facing the stables, Lieutenant Hori remarked: 'I gave them quite a workout today. But I imagine you could tell they were recruits.'

'No, I didn't notice anything at all go wrong.'

'Oh? Well, we let them take a siesta in the summer. And afterwards when you give them a workout like that, you really wake them up.'

As a company officer, Lieutenant Hori worked in the third-floor room assigned to the officers of the First Battalion. The room was austere, with five or six sets of the protective gear used in bayonet practice hanging upon one of its walls. His desk was by a window, and the straw stuffing had begun to project from the upholstery of his chair. While the Lieutenant stripped off his jacket and went out to wipe away his sweat, Isao looked down from the window at the oval inner courtyard of the building. An orderly brought in tea and left it on the desk.

A detachment of soldiers was at bayonet practice in the courtyard, and the sound of their exertion seemed to thrust itself up past the window. Six exits fronted by stone steps opened into the courtyard. On this side the building had four floors with one level half underground, but on the opposite side there were only three, including the one half underground. Large white numerals were painted over each of the doors. Three gingko trees stretched out their full leafed branches, something almost menacing in their manner. White buds hung from the tips of the branches of the many Himalayan cedars with not a breeze to stir them.

The Lieutenant made his appearance again, dressed in a short-sleeved white shirt, and after he had thirstily gulped down his tea, he called the orderly and told him to bring more.

'All right then,' he said to Isao, 'let me give you back your book.' He casually reached into the drawer of his desk, took out *The League of the Divine Wind*, and laid it down in front of Isao.

'And what did you think of it?'

'It really moved me. And now I understand more how you feel. You've got that same spirit, haven't you? But I'd like to put one question to you,' said the Lieutenant with a faintly ironic smile. 'When it comes time for you to fight somebody, are you going to be like the League and pick the Imperial Army?'

'Of course not.'

'All right, who then?'

'I thought that, if nobody else, Lieutenant Hori at least understood us. The real foe of the League was not the Army. There was something that lurked behind the troops of the garrison – and that was the budding military clique. It was the militarists whom the men of the League saw as their enemy and took the field against. For they firmly believed that the army of the militarists was not the army of the gods. They believed that their own League of the Divine Wind was the Emperor's army.'

Before replying, the Lieutenant glanced around the room. He and Isao were alone.

'All right, all right, but one doesn't shout out things like that for everyone to hear.' The loyalty and affection evident in the Lieutenant's words made Isao's spirits soar.

'But there's no one else here. Now that I'm with you, sir, I can't help pouring out all the things that have been building up within me. The men of the League fought only with the Japanese sword, and we, too, I feel, when the supreme test comes, must depend upon the sword alone. Still, if our plan is going to be on a large scale, there's room for other approaches ... Would there be any chance of your introducing us to an officer in the Air Corps?'

'Why?'

'So that we can have support from the sky, to have the key points bombed.'

The Lieutenant only snarled in response, but he did not seem especially angry.

'Somebody must take action. If not, Japan is lost. There is nothing else to be done if the heart of the Emperor is to be put at rest.'

'Don't jabber about grave matters,' said the Lieutenant, his voice suddenly harsh.

Isao realized, however, that the Lieutenant had no animosity towards him, and meekly apologized: 'I was wrong. I'm sorry.'

Had the Lieutenant, Isao wondered, perceived something that lay within him? Yes, the Lieutenant's fierce gaze must have penetrated the very soul of a boy not long out of high school. And Lieutenant Hori, from what Isao had heard of him, was no man to be swayed by considerations of age or rank.

Isao well knew that his words were immature, but his determination made up for their deficiency. He had been supremely confident that his own inner fire would provoke flames in the man opposite him. And then, too, it was summer. The two of them sat facing each other in heat as smothering and oppressive as a heavy wool garment. It was as though even a spark would set off a conflagration or, for want of a spark, the heat would simply melt everything down to a pitiful remnant like metal in a furnace. Isao had to seize this opportunity.

'Since you were kind enough to visit me,' said the Lieutenant, breaking the silence, 'suppose we do something to forget the heat. How about going over to the drill hall and running through the kendo forms without masks? Sometimes I practise that way with one of the sergeants. There's nothing better for strengthening your will.'

'Yes, sir, I like that kind of practice,' Isao readily agreed.

Among the military, winning or losing took on critical significance, and so Lieutenant Hori no doubt rarely competed seriously, because of his comrades' eyes upon him. At any rate, the thought that the Lieutenant wished to communicate with him through the sword was pleasant to Isao.

Surrounded by the aged wooden walls of the drill hall, Isao felt a congenial shiver. Three pairs of men were practising kendo, but he could tell at once that they were novices. Their handling of the staves was flurried, and their footwork erratic.

'Take a break, all of you,' the Lieutenant shouted unceremoniously. 'I'm going to do the forms with this visitor. Watch us and you'll learn something.'

Isao stepped out on the floor wearing a borrowed kendo suit and holding a borrowed stave of hard wood. The six reduced to spectators took off their masks and sat down on the floor attentively in a neat line. After he had made his obeisance to the gods, he stepped forward to face the Lieutenant. Lieutenant Hori was to take the offensive role and Isao the defensive.

The rays of the sun poured down from the high windows on the western side of the hall and the polished floor beneath shone as though spread with a glistening oil, as the insistent chant of cicadas outside wound round the building. The boards, hot beneath the soles of the feet, had a good spring to them, their smooth resilience like that of pounded rice cake.

The two squatted down facing each other for the opening ritual of touching the tips of their kendo staves together. Then they rose and held their staves at middle position. Though blending with the song of the cicada, every sound seemed to strike the ear with an intense clarity, even the faint rustle of the pleats of their *hakama*.

Isao quickly sized up the Lieutenant's stance. The impression he received was one of hearty magnanimity. Somehow, too, there was a touch of bold negligence to his bearing which saved it from being rigidly orthodox. And the glimpse of his chest visible at the loosely fastened neck of his faded blue jacket increased the sense of vitality that the Lieutenant gave off, as fresh as the early morning air of a summer's day. His ease and lack of strain marked him as an outstanding swordsman.

Each of them moved his stave to his right, retreated five short paces, and lowered it to complete the salutation. Then began the first round. Once again they faced off, and, after the initial confrontation at middle position, the Lieutenant raised his sword to high left and Isao, his to high right, and they advanced steadily toward each other.

'Yaah!' Lieutenant Hori shouted as he moved forward on his right foot and swung straight for the head with his stave.

This first vigorous blow came down towards Isao's head with the suddenness of a burst of hailstones. The wooden stave concentrated all its power on a single spot, and it was there that the heavy, thick, woolly garment of heat was ripped asunder. An instant before Isao would have taken the Lieutenant's blow he moved his left foot to retreat a step, drew his own stave back further in the upper right position, and then brought it down toward his opponent's head as he shouted: 'Toh!'

The Lieutenant's eyes glared fiercely. Isao's stave came whistling down, aimed directly at the top of the Lieutenant's close-cropped head. At the same moment, their eyes met, and Isao sensed a communication pass between them too swift for any words. The Lieutenant's jaw and the bridge of his nose had been burnt relentlessly by the sun day after day, but the skin of his forehead, protected by the visor of his cap, was light, which made his eyebrows more prominent. And it was this white forehead that Isao's stave threatened with a stroke of shattering force. Just before the blow would have landed, at the instant the stave stopped in midair, an intuitive force swifter than light passed between the two of them.

After checking the blow aimed at the Lieutenant's head and making a thrust at his throat, Isao coolly raised his sword to the upper left position, showing himself prepared to receive another attack.

So ended the first round. The two faced off once more at middle position, and the second round began.

After they had poured water over themselves to wash away their sweat and were on their way back to the barracks, the Lieutenant, still young himself and at the moment feeling especially cheerful and vigorous, spoke to Isao as though they were equals. His newly gained experience of Isao's kendo ability no doubt further prompted this familiarity.

'Have you ever heard much about Prince Harunori Toin?'

'No, sir.'

'He's now a regimental commander in Yamaguchi. He's a splendid man. He was trained in the Imperial Horse Guards, and so I was in a different branch, but just after I was commissioned, a classmate at the Academy took me along to an audience with the Prince, and he showed me real cordiality. It was "Hori this" and "Hori that". He's a man of determination, and he especially likes to hear about young men's aspirations. He takes good care of those who serve under him, and there's nothing arrogant about him – a prince of the Imperial Family and a brave and splendid soldier. What do you say – should I ask for an audience for you? If we could let him see that there were young men like you around, I'm sure His Highness would be delighted.'

'Yes, sir. Please do.'

Isao was not especially exhilarated at the prospect of meeting such an august personage. But because he realized that this was a mark of the Lieutenant's special favour, he acquiesced.

'His Highness will be in Tokyo for four or five days during the summer, and he's told me to come see him then. When I do, I'll take you along,' said Lieutenant Hori.

15

Marquis Matsugae, who had some time before disposed of Chung-nan Villa in Kamakura and now spent his summers at Karuizawa, received an invitation to a banquet at the huge Karuizawa villa of Baron Shinkawa. Its arrival provoked but a single thought in the Marquis, one that he was extremely reluctant to face. Though all of the other invited guests were 'targets', Marquis Matsugae alone among them was no one's target.

No anonymous threatening letters or even letters of a milder sort had come to Marquis Matsugae from radicals on either the right or left. Past sixty and a member of the House of Peers, the Marquis had always been quick to lend a hand in shelving whatever proposed bills had the least radical flavour about them, but no one seemed to have noted this. When the Marquis looked back upon the past, he realized that, strangely enough, the only attack that he had sustained had been the peculiar essay that Iinuma had published and signed nineteen years before in a right-wing paper. As he reflected upon the unnatural period of calm that had continued uninterrupted since then, the Marquis was drawn to speculate that someone was working behind the scenes to protect him, someone who was none other than his former attacker, Iinuma.

It was a line of reasoning injurious to the Marquis's pride. Then, too, the more he thought about his situation, the more absurd it seemed to him. Because of the influence his rank commanded, it would be a simple matter for him to discover the true circumstances. But if his speculation was correct, he would find himself greatly in Iinuma's debt, and his position would become still more untenable. And if the speculation was unfounded, he would be shamed by the realization that he had, after all, been capable of provoking rancour in no one.

Baron Shinkawa's banquets were always showy affairs. The bodyguards assigned to guests were served their own meal during the banquet in a room immediately adjoining, and they made almost as large a group as those invited. Thus in the Shinkawa villa two meals progressed at the same time, so different in the number and quality of courses as to make ordinary comparisons impossible. Of these two banquets, when one took into consideration such points as the indescribably seedy look of the suits worn by the detectives, their sharp, restless eyes and coarse features, their manner of eating in silence and turning thir heads like surly hunting dogs in the direction of the slightest noise, the uninhibited way in which they rushed to take up toothpicks after the meal and poke earnestly about their mouths, one would have to judge the detectives' banquet a superior spectacle. But, sadly enough, a bodyguard for Marquis Matsugae was not there among them.

The Marquis had no hopes of remedying this shameful situation by resorting to artifice. For the police had declared in unequivocal terms that there was no threat to the Marquis's personal welfare, and so if he demanded a guard on his own initiative, he would only make himself look ridiculous.

The matter had implications that the Marquis found extremely distasteful. For the era was such that a man's power was measured in terms of the danger that stalked him.

And so, though the Shinkawa villa was within easy walking distance, the Marquis took pains, at least, to be driven there in his Lincoln. Marquise Matsugae carried folded upon her lap a small wool blanket on account of the arthritis that affected her husband's right knee. For the Shinkawas liked to entertain their guests by serving the before-dinner drinks outside until the sun had set and the air grown chilly. And all this time, scattered among the white birches that filled the Shinkawas' broad garden laid out to exploit the view of Mount Asama, the bodyguards would stand until their figures faded to crudely cut silhouettes. They had been instructed to remain inconspicuous, but this only made them seem like lurking assassins intent upon the guests who were sipping apéritifs in the garden.

Baron Shinkawa had already passed his fiftieth year. In the surroundings of his Edwardian villa, the Baron was accustomed to reading the editorials in *The Times* each morning before turning to the Japanese newspapers. And like an English colonial official he would wear one or another of his half-dozen white linen suits every day. As for the Baroness, her intrinsic bent for chattering about herself had remained unchanged through the years. The lady was blessed with the ability to discover in herself ever fresh sources of wonder, though she was at the same time able to forgo discovering that she was in fact little by little growing fat.

The Baroness had had quite enough of 'New Thought'. The Heavenly Fire Group too, which had championed the Blue Stocking movement, had long since disbanded. The occasion for her perceiving the danger of 'New Thought' was the suicide of her niece, who came out of a women's college to join the Communist Party and, the very evening she returned home after being released from prison on bail, slashed her jugular vein.

However, since Baroness Shinkawa was as overflowing with energy as ever, she simply could not think of herself as being a member of a class 'on its way to destruction'. When her husband, a chillingly cynical man who saw nothing as worth fighting for, was put on the right-wing blacklist, and she found that both far right and far left looked upon the two of them as their sworn foes, she felt as if she and her husband were fair-skinned people of a higher civilization compelled to live in some barbarian land. On the one hand she found the situation stimulating, on the other, she longed 'to go home' to London.

'This Japan, it's an altogether distasteful place, don't you think?' the Baroness had taken to observing from time to time. Once a friend of hers who had been to India told her that an Indian acquaintance had lost her son when the boy plunged his hand into a toy box and was bitten by a poisonous snake hiding in the bottom of it. 'That's just how things are here in Japan,' the Baroness had commented. 'All one has to do is plunge one's hand in, intent only on a bit of amusement, and there's a poisonous snake in there waiting. Ready to bite and kill a person who has done nothing to it, an innocent, harmless person.'

The evening was clear, and as the cry of cicadas echoed quietly across the lawn a distant rumble of thunder came from one corner of the sky. The guests, five married couples, were gathered in the garden. Marquis Matsugae sat in a rattan chair, and the brilliant red of the plaid blanket that his wife was arranging over his knees gave a touch of colour to the dusk sweeping over the garden.

'I think it's hardly likely that one or two more months will pass without the government's recognizing Manchukuo,' said one man, who was the Minister of State. 'For the Prime Minister really intends to do just that.' After which, turning to Marquis Matsugae, he remarked pleasantly: 'That matter of Count Momoshima's son which we spoke of, is it proceeding well?'

The Marquis uttered a noncommittal grunt. 'This fellow,' he thought, 'he talks to the others about Manchukuo, and then asks me about my adopting a son. What effrontery!'

After Kiyoaki's death Marquis and Marquise Matsugae would not hear of adopting an heir, but lately they no longer felt the will to resist the arguments of the Bureau of Estates. Preliminary negotiations were now under way.

Mount Asama rose in the failing light, visible through a break in the trees where a path led down to a stream. It was hard to determine from which direction the distant thunder came. The guests, however, enjoyed watching the shadow of evening steal over their hands and faces while the thunder afforded the further pleasure of thrilling to a peril far removed from them.

'Well, since all the other ladies and gentlemen have arrived, I imagine that it must be just about time for Mr Kurahara to make his appearance,' Baron Shinkawa remarked to his wife, loudly enough for everyone to hear and join in the laughter.

It had become Busuké Kurahara's invariable practice to arrive last, a never-excessive tardiness that bespoke the immensity of his power.

He seemed totally indifferent to his personal appearance, without a hint that this might be a pose, and his inability to speak otherwise than with a stiff formality was rather appealing. He certainly in no way resembled the monopolistic capitalist who appeared in left-wing cartoons. When he sat down, he had the habit of choosing the chair upon which he had just laid his hat. The second button of his suit coat had a great affinity for the third buttonhole. He left off arranging his tie well before it was tucked beneath his collar. At the banquet table, he inevitably reached out to his right to seize the roll on his neighbour's bread dish.

Busuké Kurahara spent his summer weekends in Karuizawa and all the others at Izusan, where he owned a tangerine orchard of five or six acres. He took pride in the lustre of his tangerines and their sweet taste, and derived much pleasure from making gifts of them not only to his friends but to orphanages and welfare hospitals. It was hard to realize that he was indeed the object of widespread resentment.

No doubt it seemed astonishing that a man so cheerful in his private life could hold such dourly pessimistic views on public affairs. The guests gathered in Baron Shinkawa's garden, however, were always thrilled and titillated to hear from the mouth of Japan's supreme capitalist accounts of tragedy, of dire foreboding, and of evils to come.

More than the death of Prime Minister Inukai, Kurahara mourned the retirement of Finance Minister Takahashi. Prime Minister Saito, of course, had no sooner formed his cabinet than he was paying a call on Kurahara and protesting, perhaps a bit too much, that he could do nothing without Kurahara's cooperation. Nevertheless, Kurahara sniffed something unsavoury in the new prime minister's manner.

Takahashi had indeed been an insider of the Inukai Cabinet which had imposed another embargo on the export of gold as one of its first acts, but, secretly influenced by classical hard-currency advocates, he acted to sabotage this new-fangled government policy so that he could then contend that since this policy had not lived up to expectations and provided quick relief, since conditions were no better and prices still in the doldrums, failure to such a degree proved that the old ways were after all the best.

Baron Shinkawa, on the other hand, who avidly kept up with all that went on in London, had closely studied in *The Times* the details of England's going off the gold standard in September of the previous year and had made up his mind at once. The Wakatsuki Cabinet had kept proclaiming that it would never enact an embargo on the export of gold, but with every government proclamation, dollar speculation had increased, despite the anger of the right wing, who branded all dollar buyers as plunderers of the nation. The Baron himself had been a dollar speculator, but after he had stored away all the money that would not bear scrutiny into Swiss banks, he was unwilling to wait for an overnight shift in government policy, and came to the side of those supporting the gold export embargo and the policy of 'reflation'. Thus he had had enough of the half-way economic measures of the previous cabinet, and his hopes were bound up with the new cabinet. Beyond the issue of internal recovery through reflation lay the glittering prospect of the industrialization of Manchuria. Though the Baron's air was as abstracted as ever, here in the midst of Karuizawa, whose volcanic soil was so barren of resources, the image of the underground wealth of Manchukuo rose up in his mind like a seductive phantom, those resources that were as rich and varied as a menu of the Café Royal. Surely, the Baron thought, he could even kindle an affection for stupid soldiers.

*

Years before, Baroness Shinkawa had found it hard to countenance men carrying on a discussion all to themselves, but, as she grew older, her feelings altered. Now she was quite willing to let the men carry on with their talk, provided that the women were able to function as overseers.

'Well, they're already well into it,' she said, turning to Mrs Kurahara, Marquise Matsugae, and the other ladies, after noticing the men gathered around Kurahara. Marquise Matsugae's eyebrows, whose tilt gave her face its sorrowful look, grew almost over to her hair, now noticeably grey and brushed down over her ears.

'Just this spring,' Baroness Shinkawa chatted on, 'I wore a kimono to an affair at the British Embassy, and the Ambassador, who had only seen me in Western clothes, simply could not get over it. He outdid himself with his compliments, protesting how becoming a kimono was to me and all that. Really, how frustrating! Even a man of his refinement – he never notices Japanese women except as Japanese women. Of course, the kimono I wore that night, at the suggestion of my designer, was like a Momoyama Nō costume, red with a snow-covered willow and butterfly circle pattern, the whole thing worked in gold and silver lacquer thread, obviously quite showy. Because it flashed so brightly, I felt no more Japanese than if I were wearing Western clothes.' Intent on being hospitable, the Baroness began by offering herself as a topic of conversation.

'Junko, perhaps the Ambassador meant stunning clothing was becoming to you,' said the wife of the Minister of State. 'When you wear Western clothes you're not so daring, indeed you tend to be rather restrained.'

'How true!' replied Junko Shinkawa, quick to agree. 'The colours of Western clothes are really so sober. And if one does wear some sort of gaudy flower pattern, it only makes one look older, like some grandmother from Wales.'

'But that dress is such a lovely colour, Junko,' said Marquise Matsugae, offering the flattery that circumstances made imperative. The truth was that all that concerned the Marquise at the moment was the pain in her husband's knee. This was a pain that seemed to her somehow associated with the pain that affected the entire Matsugae household, a malady that seemed on the verge of discommoding the joints of everyone involved. The Marquise gave a quick glance in the direction of her husband sitting with the blanket over his knees. The man who in the past had seemed so frank and unconstrained, so fond of monopolizing the conversation, now listened quietly to what people had to say.

Since it was Baron Shinkawa's practice scrupulously to avoid controversy, he prodded Viscount Matsudaira to take on Kurahara. The Viscount was a young man who agreed with him and who, furthermore, was not in a position of real responsibility. And so this naughty boy, a member of the House of Peers and on friendly terms with the military, turned to Kurahara, his manner one of calm challenge.

'I don't especially care for all this talk about whatever we do, we're in danger, that this is a time of crisis, and so on,' said Viscount Matsudaira. 'Everything has started to take a turn for the better. The May Fifteenth Incident was a tragic event, of course, but it has given the government the strength to act decisively so that Japan can be pulled out of this economic slump. And in the last analysis, I think that it will have the effect of putting Japan upon the right course. It will be this affair that changes our fortune from bad to good. Isn't it in such a manner, after all, that history moves forward?'

'We will indeed be happy if it turns out as you say,' answered Kurahara plaintively, a quiet gruffness to his voice. 'I, for one, have no such expectations. What is this reflation, after all? It can be termed a controlled inflation, the idea being that although the fierce beast of inflation is let out of his cage we can still breathe easily because he has a chain fastened to his neck. But that chain is not going to hold long. The vital thing is not to let the beast out of the cage. I can well imagine how things might go – save the farmer, rescue the unemployed, introduce reflation – all of which seem splendid at first, and no one wants to sing a contrary tune. But soon reflation will turn into an inflation based on the demand for military supplies. The fierce beast will snap his chain and run wild. And once he starts, no one will be able to stop him. When the military itself finally awakes to the peril, it will be too late to catch him again. The wise course, therefore, is to keep him shut in the shiny cage of gold reserves. For nothing could be more secure than such a golden cage. It has a tough flexibility. If the beast grows larger, the space between the bars grows larger. If he grows smaller, it narrows. If we keep our specie reserves adequate, we prevent a falling off of our exchange rate, and we gain the confidence of other nations. That is the only way for Japan to get along in the world. If you let the fierce beast out of his cage as a means of bringing about a recovery, you achieve only the most transitory of results and you dash Japan's long-range hopes. However, even though what should be done, given this enactment of a second gold embargo, is to adopt a vigorous policy of strengthening the currency by supporting it with specie, with the aim of promptly returning to the gold standard, still, the government has been scared out of its wits by the May Fifteenth Incident and is rushing in the opposite direction. That is why I worry.'

'This is merely my opinion,' said the Viscount, unwilling to be shaken off, 'but if the hardship of the farmers and the discontent of the workers continue as they are, it won't be a matter of anything as mild as the May Fifteenth Incident. A revolution may well break out, and then it will be too late for all remedies. Did you see the farmers who pushed their way into the special session of the Diet in June? Are you aware of the strength embodied in the groups that presented the petition demanding an immediate moratorium on farmers' debts? Furthermore, when they didn't get what they wanted from the Diet, they went to the Army, and the result was that a joint petition of farmers and military men was drawn up and a report of it carried to the Throne itself by a regimental commander.

'And then you said, sir, that attempting recovery through reflation would offer only a temporary advantage, but if the economy does become inflated, effective domestic demand will increase. Then with the drop in the interest rate, small businessmen and manufacturers will get a new lease on life. By opening up Manchuria, our development will proceed on the continent. With the increase in military expense, the construction of heavy industry and chemical plants will be stimulated. The price of rice will go up, and the rural communities will be saved and the jobless farmers put back to work – all in all, a multitude of good effects, don't you think? Wouldn't it be well for us, while taking pains to avoid the danger of war, to advance our industrialization step by step? If I were to propose the plan I thought ideal, this would be it.'

'The young are optimistic,' said Kurahara. 'But older men, because of the knowledge that the years have brought them, find it hard to entertain such bright expectations. I hear "the farmers, the farmers", from you, but that's mere sentimentality and has no bearing on the nation's plight. At a time when every citizen must grit his teeth and endure hardship, these complaints that disrupt the national unity – "Oh, the villainy of the upper classes! Oh, the villainy of the financiers!" – all come from the mouths of self-seeking men.

'Just think for a moment. The rice riots of 1918 made us aware that the Country of Abundant Rice could be imperilled by want, but now, with the increased yield from the crops of Taiwan and Korea, there's more than a generous supply of rice throughout the country, is there not? And since all our citizens, aside from the farmers, have benefited from the sharp drop in farm prices and so have no worries about buying what food they need, there's been no upsurge of the revolutionary spirit preached by the left wing, despite the high unemployment rate that this severe depression has brought about. As for the farmers themselves, they're not at all the sort to listen to the blandishments of the left wing, no matter how much threatened they are by starvation.'

'But aren't incidents always begun by military men?' the Viscount retorted. 'And isn't the Army an Army sprung from the farming villages?'

Though the young man's assertive manner might well have struck the onlookers as somewhat lacking in deference, Kurahara was not one to be provoked into an emotional response. His words, ever controlled, ever preserving the same inflection, flowed from his lips like the white pennants issuing from the mouths of the saints and sinners in medieval religious prints. Since Kurahara was drinking a Manhattan, the moisture that wet his lips served to smooth and sweeten his hoarse voice. A smile seemed to be on the verge of flickering over his stern features, and when he put the red cherry on its toothpick between his lips, he seemed to be swallowing with it the batch of concerns that were then troubling society.

'But on the other hand,' said Kurahara, in gentle rebuttal, 'isn't the Army feeding the able-bodied sons of poor farmers? Comparing last year's disastrous crop with the record harvest of two years ago, I cannot help but suspect a touch of sabotage on the part of those farmers vehemently opposed to the use of foreign-grown rice.'

'If they did anything of the sort, wouldn't they risk starving themselves to death?' the smooth-cheeked Viscount asked.

'Well, at any rate,' said Kurahara, not answering the question put to him, 'however one may analyse the present situation, I have been talking with an eye to the future. The citizens of Japan – what sort of a people are they? I imagine that, depending upon whom you ask, you would receive all sorts of definitions. But as for me, I would reply that the citizens of Japan constitute a race blind to the dire perils of inflation. A race that, when inflation strikes, lacks even the wisdom to turn its money into property to protect itself. It behoves us never to forget for a single moment that this people with whom we have to deal constitute a naïve and ignorant, a passionate and emotional citizenry. There is a certain beauty in a nation's lacking even the wisdom to preserve itself. Indeed, an undeniable beauty. And because I love the people of Japan, I cannot help but hate those who would exploit this beautiful ignorance in order to gain popular favour.

'Stringent economic measures are never popular, and any government policy that embraces inflation is sure to gain the favour of the people. For our part, however – we who know what is the ultimate happiness of this ignorant race of ours – we must strive with this ever in mind even if a certain number of people unavoidably are victimized.'

'The ultimate happiness of the people, you say. What is that?' asked the Viscount aggressively.

'Don't you know?' asked Kurahara tantalizingly, tilting his head slightly to one side as a smile lit his features. His intent listeners, under his spell despite themselves, tilted their own heads. The trunks of the white birches outside seemed restless in the long twilight, like the pale shins of a row of young boys. The evening darkness was a huge throw-net cast over the lawn. At that moment all present confronted the glittering phantom of ultimate happiness like men about to receive a revelation. When Kurahara spoke, it was as though, before their very eyes, a giant fish leapt up vigorously from the tightening net of evening, its golden scales flashing.

'You don't know, eh? Well ... it happens to be a stable currency.'

So struck was his audience that they stood speechless as shudders of uncertain dread ran down the backs of their necks. Kurahara took no notice of the reaction that he had provoked. Like a thin varnish, a light coat of sadness seemed to spread gradually over his compassionate expression.

'It's peculiar about secrets. For the very reason that certain things are so simple, so well known, they become secrets. Be that as it may, those of us who know this secret have, indeed, a heavy responsibility laid upon us.

'And though we lead this ignorant people, persisting in their ignorance, step by step along the path that leads to the ultimate happiness, they become disheartened by its steepness. They give ready ear to the devil that whispers: "Look here, see how much easier this path is." And when they look and see how delightful a path the other is with a profusion of flowers blooming along it, they make a headlong rush for it and end by plunging down into the abyss of ruin.

'Since economics is not a benevolent enterprise, one must foresee that some ten per cent will become victims while the remaining ninety per cent will be saved. But if we take no hand at all, the full hundred per cent will go happily to their destruction.'

'I presume, then,' replied Viscount Matsudaira, 'that the ten per cent who are the farmers must reconcile themselves to death by starvation?'

The Viscount had been rash enough to speak of starving to death, and such a choice of words before such a gathering was not likely to have the effect he wished. Certain words seem empty but forbiddingly moral. Even without an adjective, they contain an intrinsic element of exaggeration. From the standpoint of taste, they leave much to be desired, being far too strident and having by their very nature the ring of radicalism. As well he might, the Viscount felt embarrassed for having been so imprudent.

While Kurahara had been eloquently holding forth, the French maître d'hôtel had come to whisper in the Baroness's ear that dinner was ready to be served, but the Baroness had no choice but to wait until Kurahara's zest for his own conversation began to pall. When she was at last able to break in, Kurahara rose from his chair. And there on the seat, visible despite the thickening darkness, was a silver cigarette case which lay open to reveal its contents arrayed like a row of white teeth, thoroughly crushed, however, by Kurahara's bulk.

'Oh no! Not again!' cried his wife when she saw this, and everyone laughed heartily, as they always did at Kurahara's idiosyncrasies.

'Really,' said Mrs Kurahara, picking up the crushed cigarettes, 'how could you!'

'I've had trouble before with its coming open so easily.'

'But, my goodness! Couldn't you feel it underneath you?'

'That's the sort of thing only Mr Kurahara could carry off, I believe,' said Baroness Shinkawa teasingly as she made her way through the patches of brightness that spilled out onto the lawn from the windows.

'I still don't understand. Surely it must have hurt you, open like that,' said Mrs Kurahara.

'I thought it was just the rattan chair.'

'Yes, yes, that's true. Our rattan chairs do cause some pain,' exclaimed the Baroness, provoking more laughter from the guests.

'Still and all,' offered Baron Shinkawa, his manner abstracted as ever, 'they're far better than the ones in that motion picture house.' There was an old movie theatre in Karuizawa in a converted stable.

Marquis Matsugae had no place in such conversation. And when he had taken his seat at the dinner table the wife of the Minister of State, who sat beside him, found herself short of suitable topics.

'Have you spoken recently,' she ventured, 'with Marquis Yoshichika Tokugawa?'

The Marquis thought for a moment. It seemed that he had not talked to Tokugawa for a very long time. Then, again, it seemed that he had spoken with him just two or three days before. And in any case, Marquis Tokugawa had never at any time discussed anything significant with Marquis Matsugae. Whenever they had met, either in the lobby of the House of Peers or at the Peers Club, they had never done more than exchange a few words about wrestling.

'Well,' replied Marquis Matsugae, 'I haven't seen too much of him recently.'

'He's been rather active lately among the veterans, getting together groups like the Moral Light Society,' said the lady. 'He's quite fond of that sort of thing, Marquis Tokugawa.'

'Yes,' agreed a gentleman across the table, 'he seems to take great delight in letting right-wing malcontents use him as a figurehead. Bit by bit his playing with fire is turning into something earnest.'

'If a man must play with fire, women are preferable, I suppose,' declared Baroness Shinkawa in a voice that seemed loud enough to split the petals of the flowers that decorated the table. When she spoke of playing with fire, without a trace of feeling of innuendo, it was immediately obvious that she was a woman incapable of misconduct.

Once the soup course had been served, the conversation turned to the kind of topic that the upper classes were more accustomed to talk about. A discussion arose as to what sort of costumes would be suited for incognito participation in the villagers' Bon Festival that year. In Karuizawa the Bon Festival was celebrated in August in accordance with the old calendar. Marquis Matsugae was reminded of the Bon Festivals at his mansion in Tokyo when the eaves outside the parlour were hung with Gifu lanterns. And then he remembered how his mother had been vexed by something up until the moment of her death. It had been she who had bought the hundred and twelve acre Matsugae estate in Shibuya for three thousand yen which she had obtained from the sale of stock. Midway through the Taisho period, about 1920, she sold seventy-five acres of it for five million yen, but the buyer, the Hakoné Realty Company, was extremely tardy in making good the money due, a cause of grief that stayed with his mother until she drew her last breath.

'Have they paid yet? Do we have the money?' she asked again and again during her final illness. Those who were with her, wanting to put an end to such a scandalous show of concern, told her that the payment had indeed been made, but the woman on her deathbed would not be deceived.

'It does no good to lie,' she said. 'If all that money came walking into this house, the floor would creak and groan under its feet. I haven't heard anything like that, have I? I want to hear its footsteps so that I can die in peace.'

After his mother's death, with the passage of time and after many vicissitudes, the account was at last paid in full. In 1927, however, at the beginning of the Showa period, the Marquis lost more than half of this in the failure of the Fifteenth National Bank. The lame steward, Yamada, oppressed by his sense of responsibility, hanged himself.

Because his mother had said not a word about Kiyoaki but had spoken of nothing but money, her death, as far as the Marquis was concerned, was robbed of all that was lyric and exalted. In his heart, he could not avoid the presage that there would be little noble afterglow left to light his own decline and death.

Since the Shinkawa household was governed according to the English manner, the male guests remained in the dining-room after dinner to be presented with cigars, while the ladies retired to the parlour. Furthermore, according to Victorian custom the gentlemen did not rejoin the ladies until they had enjoyed their post-prandial drinking to the full. This was a source of acute distress to Baroness Shinkawa, but, since it was an English custom, she accepted it as something that could in no way be amended.

Rain had begun to fall halfway through dinner. And since the evening had grown more chilly than normal, the servants quickly kindled a fire of white birch logs in the fireplace. The Marquis then had no need of his blanket. The lights in the room were extinguished, and the men relaxed around the fireplace.

The Minister of State began to speak, addressing Kurahara and returning to a topic that excluded Marquis Matsugae.

'With regard to what you were saying before, I'd like very much to see you give so exhaustive an explanation to the Prime Minister. Though he would like to remain above such matters, he cannot help but find himself under pressure from the flow of events.'

'Exhaustive explanations are my forte,' replied Kurahara. 'And I haven't spared the Prime Minister. What a bother I must be to him.'

'Ah, but it's not by being a bother to prime ministers that you run risk,' replied the Minister of State. 'There was something I had to refrain from saying before out of consideration for the nerves of the ladies, but really, Kurahara, I'd like to see you have a proper regard for your safety. Since you are a pillar of our economy, it would indeed be catastrophic if you were to go the way of Inoué and Dan. However much you take precautions, there's no possibility of your being over-careful.'

'Since you're kind enough to tell me this, I presume that you're well acquainted with the actual circumstances,' replied Kurahara in his hoarse voice, his features without expression. Even if a wave of distress had swept over his face, the restless flames that made the shadows dart across his fleshy cheeks would have concealed it. 'All sorts of declarations from would-be assassins come to my home, and the police show much concern. However, having lived as long as I have, I am not the least worried about my personal safety. What fears I have pertain not to myself but to the future of our nation. I take the greatest delight, just like a child, in slipping away from my guards and doing whatever I like. There are those who are so fearful they urge bothersome measures upon me, and there are also those who tell me to use money to protect myself, offering to act as go-betweens. But I have no inclination to do anything of the sort. At this late date, I'm not going to start buying life.'

So confident was Kurahara's declaration that his companions became ill at ease, but he was not a man to take ready notice of such reactions.

Viscount Matsudaira was warming his smooth white hands over the fire. They had turned a delicate pink, all the way back from the well-trimmed nails. Gazing intently at the ash of the cigar he held at his fingertips, he began a story whose evident intent was to dismay.

'This is something I once heard from a fellow who was a company commander in Manchuria. It impressed itself on my memory because I had never heard such a tragic story. One day this officer received a letter from the father of a private in his company who came from a poor farming district. The family, the father wrote, was crushed by poverty and tormented by hunger. Though there was no way that the father could make amends to his dutiful son for so wishing, he nevertheless hoped for his death in battle as soon as possible. For, without the bereavement payment they would then receive, the family had no means of surviving. As might well be expected, the company commander didn't dare to show this letter to the son but hid it away. And just a short time later, he told me, it happened that the son died a heroic death in battle.'

'This really happened?' asked Kurahara.

'I have the story from the company commander himself.'

'Really!'

The sap from the logs sputtered in the flames of the fireplace in the silence that followed Kurahara's response. After a few moments, Kurahara took out his handkerchief, and the sound of his blowing his nose attracted the attention of the others. They saw several tears, bright in the firelight, rolling down over the heavy flesh of Kurahara's creased cheeks.

These enigmatic tears had a strong emotional effect on all present. The man most startled to see them was Viscount Matsudaira, but he was content to congratulate himself on his story-telling ability. From Marquis Matsugae, however, Kurahara's tears drew still more tears. That so unsentimental a man would weep in sympathy with another could perhaps be explained only by concluding that his thoroughly egoistic cast of character had been unable to maintain itself before the advance of age. But as for Kurahara's tears, which would remain something of a mystery in the face of all explanation, perhaps Baron Shinkawa alone was able to view them accurately. Since the Baron's heart was cold, he ran no risk in any situation. Tears, however, were dangerous. Supposing they did not necessarily proceed from the approach of senility.

The Baron, then, was somewhat moved, somewhat taken aback, and as a consequence, though he made it a practice to discard his cigars half-smoked, neglected to toss the one he was holding into the fire.

16

Isao made up his mind that, when he had his audience with Prince Toin, rather than express himself in personal terms, he would bring with him *The League of the Divine Wind.* Since there could be no question of merely lending this to the Prince, he would buy a new copy to present to him. For the first time, he found his mother's talents to be of some use. He asked her to make a brocade cover for the presentation copy, choosing a pattern as conservative as possible. She went to work with her needle at a pitch of enthusiasm.

The matter, however, came to the ears of his father. Iinuma summoned his son and told him that he was not to see the Prince.

'But why not?' asked the startled Isao.

'Because I said so. There's no need for an explanation.'

His son had no way of knowing how tangled was the skein of Iinuma's emotions and to what deep and obscure region it led. Still less could he know the part that Prince Toin had played in the events leading to the death of Kiyoaki.

Since he realized that his anger was impossible to explain, Iinuma himself grew more and more uncomfortable with it. Though he was well aware that the Prince's role in the affair was obviously that of an injured party, nevertheless, whenever Iinuma traced events back to the remote causes of Kiyoaki's death, he invariably found himself vexed with the image of a man he had never met, Prince Toin. If there had been no Prince, if the Prince had not been present at that particular time and place ... Iinuma's complaint always moved toward this same conclusion. The truth was that if there had been no Prince Toin, Kiyoaki's irresoluteness would have been still more likely to prevent him from winning Satoko even for a time, but, knowing little of the particulars, Iinuma tended to fasten his resentment doggedly upon the person of the Prince.

Iinuma was still tormented by the long-standing discrepancy between his political tenets and the turbulent emotions that were their source. For the burning, emotional loyalty that had taken form in Iinuma in his boyhood – a loyalty that at times had been shot through with anger and contempt, at times had poured down like a waterfall, at times had erupted like a volcano – this loyalty that was so much a part of him was a loyalty wholly to Kiyoaki. To define it still more precisely, one might well say that it was a loyalty dedicated to Kiyoaki's beauty. It was a loyalty swerving almost to betrayal, a loyalty ever choked with a dark anger. And for that very reason it was an emotion to which one could give no other name.

He called it loyalty. Well and good. Yet it was something quite other than being dedicated to an ideal. He struggled against the ineffably beautiful temptation that would lure him far from his idealism. He was intensely eager to reconcile idealism and beauty, both of which had such a hold upon his heart, and moreover his emotion flowed from a kind of powerful need to reconcile the two. His was a loyalty that from its inception had the character of a lonely, single-minded fidelity. It was an emotion fated for him from boyhood, a dagger that had been thrust into his grasp.

In teaching his classes, Iinuma was fond of using the expression 'love for the Emperor'. Whenever these words passed his lips he felt a surging power go out of him which made his students tremble with emotion and their eyes sparkle. Clearly the source of this inspiration was some experience of his own boyhood. Otherwise, where could it have come from?

Since Iinuma had little self-awareness, he was quite capable of forgetting all that pertained to the distant source of his emotions. Freely transcending time, he directed the fire within him wherever he wished, setting blazes where it pleased him, letting himself rest in the flames, letting himself taste the burning ecstasy and suffering no significant pain in the process. Yet if Iinuma had been more honest with himself, he would undoubtedly have noticed that he used an excessive number of metaphors having to do with emotion. He would undoubtedly have recognized himself as one who had indeed once lived out the original poem but who now made do with mere echoes of it, constantly applying the images of the moon, snow, and blossoms of long ago to scenes that were altering with every passing year. What he did not realize, in short, was that his eloquence had grown hollow.

Thus with regard to reverence for the Imperial Family, though he, Iinuma, should have been ready to cut down on the spot anyone who cast doubt upon this virtue, a chill shadow, like the wavering but constant image of rain flowing down a glass roof, fell upon his own sense of reverence – the name of Prince Toin.

'Who is it that was going to take you to see Prince Toin?' asked Iinuma in a somewhat quieter and roundabout manner. The boy said nothing.

'Who? Why don't you answer?'

'I can't answer that question.'

'Why can't you answer?'

The boy fell silent once more. Iinuma grew furious. To say 'Don't see Prince Toin' was for him an order from father to son. There was no need for explanation. But, to Iinuma, for Isao not to tell him the name of his intermediary was equivalent to rebellion against his father. The truth of the matter was that Iinuma, as Isao's father, should have been able to explain the basis of his repugnance for the Prince so that his son could have readily understood it. He should have been able to say that Isao was not to see the Prince because he had been involved in the circumstances that had driven to his death the young master whom Iinuma had served. Shame, however, like a rock glowing red with heat, blocked Iinuma's throat and prevented all explanation.

And for Isao to go against his father like this was most extraordinary. In his father's presence, Isao had always been reticent and deferential. For the first time Iinuma realized that there was an inviolable core within his son, and now he, who had failed in attempting to form Kiyoaki, in another time and in quite different circumstances, felt the same enervating frustration with Isao and could not stem a sudden rush of anguish.

As father and son thus sat confronting each other, the light of the setting sun, brilliant after an early evening shower, shone from the puddles scattered through the garden outside the room, and the green foliage sparkled as though the trees and shrubbery were growing in the Pure Land. The breeze was cool and refreshing as it blew across their faces. Isao's anger was sharply defined, like something lying at the bottom of a clear brook. He sensed its presence like a stone that he could place on a Go board wherever he wished. But the emotions that raged within his father were, as always, opaque to Isao, beyond his understanding. The cicadas kept up their solemn chant.

The copy of *The League of the Divine Wind* in its sober rust-and-green brocade cover lay on the table. Isao abruptly picked it up and got to his feet, intending to leave the room without another word. His father was too fast for him. He snatched the book away from his son, and he, too, got to his feet.

For one instant their eyes met. Isao saw that his father's eyes were utterly cowardly, that no courage shone in them. But in those eyes, like distant pounding hoofs drawing closer, anger was rushing up from the depths of his heart.

'Have you a tongue in your head or not?'

Iinuma threw the book into the garden. The gleaming orange surface of one of the puddles was rent as the book meant for a prince splashed into it and came to rest. The instant that he saw the muddy water close over the object that he had invested with so sacred a character, Isao felt a shock of anger, as if a wall had suddenly burst before his eyes. He clenched his fists without realizing it. His father trembled. He slapped Isao across his face.

At the sound, Isao's mother came into the room. To Miné the figures of the two men standing there seemed gigantic. The next instant she noticed that her husband's kimono was in disarray, while that of her son, whom he had just slapped, was not. She looked beyond into the garden sparkling in the glow of the setting sun. Miné remembered her husband's violent passion at the time that he had beaten her half to death.

Slithering across the tatami floor, Miné interposed herself between the two of them and cried out: 'Isao! What are you doing? Apologize to your father. How dare you show such a face to him! Bow down before him and apologize this instant.'

'Look at that,' said Isao, paying no attention to the blow he had taken on his cheek. He knelt on one knee, and, tugging at his mother's sleeve, directed her gaze toward the garden. Above her head, Miné heard her husband panting like a dog. Contrasted with the bright garden, the interior of the house was very dark. Miné had the feeling that something was floating in that darkness, filling it – something so uncanny that she could not bear to keep open her upturned eyes. Half in a dream, Miné was thinking of that long-ago time in the library of Marquis Matsugae. And still, as though in a delirium, she kept saying: 'Apologize. Apologize at once.'

Slowly she opened her eyes. The object that took clear form before them was of glittering green-and-rust brocade half-sunk in a puddle of water. Miné was aghast. The brocade that sparkled in the evening sun from the midst of the muddy water affected her so that she felt it was she herself who was being punished. As for what kind of book it might be, not the faintest inkling crossed Miné's mind.

The Prince had informed Lieutenant Hori that he would receive them on Sunday evening, and the Lieutenant took Isao with him to pay their respects at the Toinnomiya residence in Shiba. The Prince's family had been visited by a series of misfortunes. After his elder brother, who had never enjoyed good health, passed away, so also, within a short time, did his father and mother. Thus the sole heir of the Toinnomiya family was the vigorous Prince Harunori. When he was away on duty, his wife and children had the mansion to themselves. And since his wife was a lady of extremely quiet disposition who came from a family of the court nobility, a lonely stillness, as might be expected, hung over the residence most of the time.

Isao had had great difficulty in obtaining a third copy of *The League of the Divine Wind*, but at last had found one in a secondhand bookstore, and he carried it under his arm as he walked along in his Kokura summer uniform beside Lieutenant Hori. He had taken care to wrap it in good paper at least and to draw in ink the characters designating it as a gift. In leaving the house this evening, he had used deception against his father for the first time.

The huge gate of the Toinnomiya mansion was closed, and only a dim light burned before it. There was no indication that the master of the house was in residence. A small door beside the gate was open, and a guard light shone down on the gravel. When the Lieutenant stepped through this door, the scabbard of his sword rattled as it brushed lightly against the frame.

Though the guard had been informed ahead of time of their coming, he took care to inform the house by an inside phone, and in the interval Isao, noticing how clearly he could hear the wings of the moths, the small beetles, and the other insects fluttering about the light that hung from the eaves of the old guard post, became aware of the profound silence that brooded over the trees surrounding the mansion and the sloping gravel road that shone a brilliant white beneath the moon.

A few moments later, they were climbing the gravel road. The heavy, sucking noise of the Lieutenant's boots echoed as though he were on a night march. Isao felt a faint warmth still in the gravel, a reminder of the torrid heat of midday.

In contrast to the altogether Western-style Yokohama villa of the Toinnomiyas, this mansion was in Japanese style. Above the broad expanse of gravel, white in the moonlight, where vehicles pulled up, there rose the heavy roof of a Chinese gable over the entrance.

The mansion's administrative office was apparently to the side of the entranceway, but no lights were burning there this late. The old steward came out to meet them and, after taking charge of the Lieutenant's sword, escorted them into the house. There was no sign of life anywhere within. The corridor was spread with a maroon rug, and one of its walls was wainscoted in Western style. After opening a door to a darkened room, the steward flicked a switch. Light struck Isao's eyes, the radiated brilliance of a massive chandelier hanging in the centre of the room. Its countless fragments of glass floated in the air like a glittering mist.

Isao and the Lieutenant sat stiffly in linen slipcovered armchairs as the breeze from a sluggish fan brushed their cheeks. They heard the rustling sound of the insects that fluttered against the window. Since the Lieutenant kept silent, Isao, too, kept silent. After a short wait, a servant brought them some chilled barley tea.

A huge Gobelin tapestry depicting a battle scene hung upon the wall. A mounted knight was thrusting his lance through the breast of a foot soldier bent back by the force of the blow. The tapestry had faded with age, and the gushing blood that blossomed at the man's breast was tinged with the russet colour of an old *furoshiki*. Blood and flowers were alike, Isao thought, in that both were quick to dry up, quick to change their substance. And precisely because of this, then, blood and flowers could go on living by taking on the substance of glory. Glory in all its forms was inevitably something metallic.

The door opened and Prince Harunori, wearing a white linen suit, came into the room. Though there was nothing pretentious about his entrance, and though its very lack of ceremony brought a measure of warmth and ease into the somewhat tense atmosphere of the room, the Lieutenant at once leaped from his chair to a position of rigid attention, and Isao followed his example. For the space of a moment, Isao studied the Prince, the first member of the Imperial Family whom he had ever been so close to. His Highness was not especially tall, but his physique gave a decided impression of sturdiness. His suit bulged at the midsection, putting a strain upon his jacket buttons. His shoulders and chest were so well fleshed that his white-suited figure with its knotted tie of reddish yellow might at first glance seem to be that of a politician. But the beautifully tanned complexion, the close-cropped head, the splendid, rather aquiline nose, the majesty that shone from the long, slender eyes, and the carefully trimmed jet-black moustache all revealed that, beyond a doubt, here was a man who combined a commanding martial presence with the graceful bearing of the nobility. The Prince's eyes were bright and lively, but he gave the impression of seldom shifting his penetrating gaze.

The Lieutenant introduced Isao at once, and he bowed deeply.

'Is this the young man you spoke to me about? Well! Sit down then, make yourself comfortable,' said the Prince affably. 'As far as young men today go, I haven't met a single one outside the military. And so I thought, if this lad's a civilian and truly a young man worthy of the name, then I want very much to meet him. Isao Iinuma, is it? I've heard of your father.'

Since the Lieutenant had told Isao to say whatever came into his mind, he asked abruptly: 'Your Highness, has my father ever had an audience with you?'

When the Prince replied that he had not, the riddle of his father deepened and became more complex. Why should he harbour such feelings toward a man whom he had never met?

The Prince and the Lieutenant began to tell old stories with a freedom that came of their both being military men. Isao watched for an opportunity to present his book. He had little hope that the Lieutenant would make the effort to offer him such an occasion. Lieutenant Hori seemed to have forgotten all about the book.

Consequently, Isao remained silent, having no choice but to sit stiffly correct while he observed the Prince across the table engaging in pleasant conversation. The whiteness of the Prince's untanned forehead gave off a serene brightness beneath the chandelier. The light shining upon his close-cropped head showed the newly cut hair bristling in perfect order.

Perhaps becoming aware of Isao's piercing look, the Prince suddenly turned his gaze, which had been fixed on the Lieutenant, toward Isao. For a moment their eyes met. It was as if the clapper of an old, rust-covered iron bell, long silent, had been loosened by some errant tremor and struck an unexpected note. What the Prince's eyes said at that moment Isao could not comprehend, nor in all likelihood could the Prince himself. But that fleeting moment of communication was charged with an emotion that transcended ordinary love and hate, an emotion that sprang from some uncanny tie. For an instant some far-off sorrow seemed to pour from the Prince's unmoving eyes, as though he meant to quench Isao's burning gaze with the water of his sadness.

'The Lieutenant, too, looked at me in just this way during kendo drill,' Isao thought. 'But that time, down deep, there was something definite that he conveyed to me without words. And in the Prince's gaze, there's nothing of the sort. Perhaps His Highness's impression of me is unfavourable.'

By then the Prince, who had turned back to his conversation with the Lieutenant, was nodding in vigorous assent to something the latter had said that had escaped Isao.

'You're right,' the Prince said. 'The nobility, too, is guilty. It sounds splendid to call the nobility the "living ramparts" of the Imperial Family, but there are those among them who, sure of their power, tend even to make light of His Sacred Majesty. This is nothing new. There have been examples of it since ancient times, you know. And as for the necessity of chastising the overweening pride of those who should be the mirror of conduct for the common people, here, especially, I am entirely of the same opinion as you.'

17

Isao was surprised at the intensity of the hatred that the Prince reserved for the nobility, with whom he had such close affinity. But when one took into consideration the Prince's position, he thought, there were no doubt numerous occasions when the corruption of the nobility offended His Highness's nostrils. As for that of the politicians and the entrepreneurs, no matter how far off it was, it struck the nose as squarely as the stink of a dead animal's carcass drifting across the fields in summer. But the nobility were capable of disguising their unsavoury odour with the fragrance of incense. Isao wanted to hear from the Prince the names of those he considered the worst among the nobility, but His Highness prudently refrained from mentioning them.

Since he now felt somewhat at ease, Isao took up the book in its paper wrapping and addressed the Prince: 'Desiring to present this to Your Highness, I have brought it with me. Though it is an old and soiled book, all our spirit is contained within it, and my hope is to be one who carries on this spirit.' The words now came easily to his lips.

'Oh? *The League of the Divine Wind*, is it?' said the Prince, unwrapping the book and looking at its cover.

'I believe the book gives an excellent presentation of the spirit of the League,' said the Lieutenant, coming to Isao's assistance. 'These students seem to have vowed to establish a like brotherhood for the Showa era.'

'Indeed? Well, then, instead of the garrison at Kumamoto, have they been slashing into the Third Regiment at Azabu, I wonder?' said the Prince. Though he joked, he showed no trace of disdain as he courteously turned over the pages. Then, suddenly lifting his eyes from the book, he looked at the boy sharply as he spoke to him: 'I'll ask you something. Suppose ... suppose His Imperial Majesty had occasion to be displeased with either your spirit or your behaviour. What would you do then?'

A question like this could only have come from a member of the Imperial Family. And then, too, even among the Imperial Family, certainly no one but Prince Harunori could have been expected to ask it. The Lieutenant and Isao once more became rigid with tension. They intuitively grasped something from the quality of the moment: the Prince's question, though seemingly directed to Isao alone, really included the Lieutenant. The Lieutenant's as yet unspoken aspirations, his intention in deliberately bringing this unknown boy with him to the Toinnomiya residence – these were some of the things the Prince must have had in mind in asking his question. Isao perceived that the Prince, though not a direct superior, found it awkward as a regimental commander to question a lieutenant point-blank, and he suddenly awoke to his own situation. Both the Prince and the Lieutenant were using him as an interpreter, or a puppet that conveys another's intent, or a piece on a chessboard. Although the dialogue in progress was disinterested and offered no advantage to those involved, Isao, for once in his young life, felt himself in the midst of something like the whirlpool of partisan politics. Even if this left a somewhat unpleasant taste in his mouth, Isao would not have been true to his character if he had not responded as frankly as was in his power. The Lieutenant's scabbard rattled lightly as it struck against the arm of his chair.

'Like the men of the League, I would cut open my stomach.'

'Indeed?' The martial prince's expression indicated that he had grown used to hearing such answers. 'Well, then, if he was pleased, what would you do?'

Isao replied without the least hesitation: 'In that case, too, I would cut open my stomach at once.'

'Oh?' For the first time a gleam of interest flashed from the Prince's eye. 'And what would be the meaning of that? Explain yourself.'

'Yes, Your Highness. It refers to loyalty. Suppose I make steaming rice balls with rice so hot it burns my hands. My sole purpose is to present them to His Majesty, to offer them in his sacred presence. Now as to the outcome. If His Majesty is not hungry, he will curtly refuse my offering or perhaps he may even be pleased to say: "Am I to eat food so tasteless?" and hurl it into my face. In which case I will have to withdraw, the grains of rice still clinging to my face, and gratefully cut open my stomach at once. Then, again, if His Majesty is hungry and is pleased to eat the rice balls with satisfaction, there will still be no course of action open to me but to withdraw at once and gratefully cut open my stomach. Why? To make rice balls to serve as food for His Sacred Majesty with hands so common is a sin worthy to be punished with a thousand deaths. But, then, suppose I were to make rice balls as an offering but keep them in my hands and not present them, what would happen then? After a while the rice would certainly rot. This, too, would be an act of loyalty, I suppose, but I would call it a loyalty without courage. Courageous loyalty belongs to the man who, with no fear of death, dares to present the rice balls that he has thus made with single-minded devotion.'

'While knowing he's sinning? Is that what he's to do?'

'Yes, Your Highness. The gentlemen of the military, Your Highness foremost among them, are indeed fortunate. For the soldier's loyalty rests in casting away his life in obedience to the Emperor's commands. But in the case of an ordinary civilian, he must be prepared to sin by reason of his unsanctioned loyalty.'

'"Obey the law" – isn't that a command of His Majesty? And the law courts – they are, after all, His Majesty's courts.'

'The sins I refer to have nothing to do with the law. And the greatest sin is that of a man who, finding himself in a world where the sacred light of His Majesty is obscured, nevertheless determines to go on living without doing anything about it. The only way to purge this grave sin is to make a fiery offering with one's own hands, even if that itself is a sin, to express one's loyalty in action, and then to commit seppuku immediately. With death, all is purified. But as long as a man goes on living, he can't move either right or left, or take any action whatever, without sinning.'

'Ah, this has become a very complex matter indeed,' said the Prince, smiling as though somewhat taken aback by Isao's sincerity.

Gauging the situation, the Lieutenant restrained Isao: 'That's enough. You've made your point.'

But the excitement aroused in Isao by this examination of his ideals persisted. The exchange was with a prince of the Imperial Family. To face such a personage and to respond with utter frankness to his questions had made Isao feel that he was facing a brilliance not of this world shining from behind the Prince, and was giving full expression to his innermost self. He had been able to give an immediate answer to whatever question the Prince asked, proof that for some time his thoughts had been refined and tempered within him.

When he pictured himself standing, arms folded, doing nothing at all, Isao shuddered as though he had imagined himself a leper. The easy course was to accept such a posture as man's ordinary, sinful condition, as inescapable as the earth upon which one walked or the air one breathed. But if he himself would become pure in the midst of this, his sin had to take another form and he had, in any event, to draw his nourishment from the very source of sin. Only by doing so would he join together sin and death, seppuku and glory, atop the precipice swept by the pine breeze before the rising sun. His reason for not wanting to enter either the army or the naval academies was that there ready-made glory would be provided, there the sin of inaction would be purged. But perhaps, in order to attain the glory that he alone had in mind, he had begun to love sin for its own sake.

Isao did not think of himself as being pure and immaculate in accordance with the doctrine of Oen Hayashi, the beloved Master of the League of the Divine Wind, who taught that all men were sons of the gods. But he burned with a constant impatience to draw near enough to purity to touch it with his hand. So that his fingertips could reach it, he was making use of stepping stones that offered but treacherous footing, aware all the time that the next instant these might give way beneath him. He knew that Master Oen's rite of Ukei had no relevance to the present age. Still, this rite by which one asked the will of the gods seemed to contain an element of danger not unlike a footing that could give way at any moment. And what was this element of danger but sin? Surely nothing could so resemble sin as did the inevitability of danger.

'Well, well, so a young man like this has turned up,' said the Prince as he turned back to the Lieutenant, his voice filled with emotion. The thought struck Isao that he was like a model on display before the two of them, and a painful shock ran through him as the desire seized him to fashion himself to fit the pattern that he saw reflected in the Prince's eyes. To do so he would have to die.

'When I realize that Japan has produced students like this, I have somewhat more hope for the future. One never hears such an outburst from those in the military. You've done me a favour in bringing so fine a lad here.' Since the Prince deliberately ignored Isao and expressed gratitude to the Lieutenant, the Lieutenant gained honour, and Isao himself felt the warmth of the Prince's benevolence far more than if he had been praised directly.

The Prince summoned his steward and had him bring in some fine Scotch and some caviar. Pouring with his own hand, he urged the Lieutenant to drink, and Isao too: 'I don't suppose you're of age, Iinuma, but you've just given such a display of perceptiveness that I consider you a grown man. So drink up. And don't worry. If you overdo it, I'll send you home in my car.' Though the Prince spoke most graciously, Isao shuddered. For at that moment there arose in his mind the image of his father's face as he received his son coming home dead drunk in a car from the Toinnomiya residence. It was enough to jolt the hand that held his glass as he stood up to receive the Scotch from the Prince. The whisky spilled out of the tipped glass and fell onto the delicate lace cloth that covered the table.

'Oh!' Isao cried. He pulled out his handkerchief and desperately wiped the spot.

'Please forgive me,' he said, his head hanging low as tears of shame welled up in his eyes.

Isao remained standing there with bowed head, and the Prince, seeing his tears, spoke to him humorously: 'That will do now. Look up. Don't carry on as though you're going to cut your stomach open right here and now.'

'Permit me to apologize for him, Your Highness,' said the Lieutenant at Isao's side. 'I believe that it was the excitement of the occasion that made his hand shake.'

Isao sat down at last, but, altogether taken up with thoughts of his blunder, he was unable to say a single word. At the same time, however, despite his mortification, the Prince's words were like a warm current coursing through his body, affecting him far more than did the whisky. The Prince and the Lieutenant then began to discuss the political situation in detail, but Isao, occupied as he was with his shame, could not attend to what they were saying. While the Prince was thus enthusiastically engaged in discussion and apparently paying no attention at all to Isao, he suddenly turned to him and spoke in a loud, cheerful voice which to some degree showed the effect of the Scotch he had drunk: 'Come now! Pull yourself together. You're quite a disputant yourself, aren't you?'

Having no other choice, Isao took a modest role in the discussion. He now felt that he realized why, just as the Lieutenant had told him, the Prince enjoyed such immense popularity among the military.

It was getting very late. After the Lieutenant, surprised at the hour, had expressed their gratitude, the Prince presented him with a bottle of excellent whisky and some cigarettes in a box with the imperial crest. To Isao he gave a package of cakes, also bearing the imperial crest.

'It looks as if His Highness was quite taken with you,' said the Lieutenant on the way home. 'I think he'll be willing to help you, when the time comes. Considering his position, though, it would be quite improper to give the appearance of wanting anything from him. At any rate, you're a lucky fellow. And don't worry about that little faux pas.'

When he left the Lieutenant, instead of going straight home, Isao stopped at Izutsu's house. After a servant had roused Izutsu, who was already in bed, Isao handed him the package of cakes.

'Take good care of this. Don't let anyone in your house see it.'

'All right.'

Izutsu stuck his head out through the entranceway door in the dead of night, the nape of his neck stiff with tension, and took the package. A look of uncertainty crossed his face as he felt its lightness. He was sure that any package received from his comrade at such an hour would have to contain explosives.

18

That summer the number of Isao's recruits grew to twenty. Only the most trustworthy students with the highest principles were allowed to enter his circle, after having been screened by Izutsu and Sagara and then interviewed and approved by Isao. Of foremost use in the process was *The League of the Divine Wind.* After reading this, each candidate had to write an essay describing how it affected him, which served as the basis for his first evaluation. There were those among them who, though their style and their comprehension were superior, left too much to be desired with regard to their strength of character.

Isao came to lose his fervour for kendo. When he announced that he was not going to participate in the summer training camp, he narrowly missed the unpleasant experience of being dealt with summarily by those upperclassmen who had been counting upon him to win the coming tournament for the school. One upperclassman was particularly aggressive in demanding to know the reason for Isao's change of heart.

'Are you plotting something? Is there something that fascinates you more than kendo?' he asked. 'I hear you've been getting students to read some kind of pamphlet. You're involved in some ideological movement, aren't you?'

Isao forestalled him by answering: 'I imagine that was *The League of the Divine Wind.* What I'm doing is talking with people about organizing a group to study Meiji history.'

In fact, Isao's kendo career was of great help in secretly gathering new comrades. When a student was confronted with his laconic presence and his brilliant, piercing glance, respect for his reputation was immediately transformed into devotion to him.

Having advanced thus far, Isao decided to gather all his comrades together at the same time so that he could test their maturity and enthusiasm. During the summer vacation, accordingly, when most of them were away from Tokyo, he sent them telegrams ordering them to return, deliberately choosing a time a full two weeks before the new semester began. During vacation the school grounds would serve as an ideal place to preserve their secrecy. The students were to meet before the shrine on campus at six in the evening, a time when the heat of the day would still be lingering.

All the students at the College of National Studies referred to this as simply 'the shrine', and a gathering of students in front of this small place of worship dedicated to the myriad gods was not at all unusual. Students from the Shinto department, destined to succeed their fathers as priests of the family shrine, always came here to practise their chants, and members of the athletic teams would come either to pray for victory or to ponder defeat.

One hour before the time set for the meeting, Isao was waiting for Sagara and Izutsu in the woods just to the rear of the shrine. He wore *hakama* over a white splashed-pattern summer kimono, and a school cap with white piping. When Isao sat down on the grass, the bright rays of the evening sun, coming from beyond the precincts of Hikawa Shrine as it sank towards the heights of Sakuragaoka in

Shibuya, struck the chest of his white kimono and the black trunks of the oaks. Despite this, Isao did not seek the shade, but rather, pulling the peak of his cap down over his eyes, sat facing the sun. The heat given off by his sweat-covered flesh built up beneath his kimono and crept up toward his brow, melding with that which radiated from the sun-soaked grass. The whirring song of the cicadas filled the woods.

The bicycles that moved along Hakadori Street, just below him, gleamed in the sun. The bright rays seemed to stitch together the low roofs that lined the street. At one point among the eaves, there glittered as bright as the sun itself something that resembled a tilted mass of glass. When Isao looked more closely, he saw that an iceman's truck was parked there. He could sense the peril of the ice catching the full force of the evening sun. He felt as if he could hear distant, shrill cries of pain as it was being ruthlessly dissolved by the final heat of summer.

When Isao looked over his shoulder, the drawn-out shadow of one oak seemed to him the very image of his ambition here beneath this end-of-summer sun, a thing he had been dragging behind him to no purpose. The slipping away of summer affected him keenly. This parting with the sun. He dreaded seeing that massive, scarlet-glowing symbol of ideal devotion begin to fade with the change of seasons. This year too he had let slip the chance to die one morning before the blazing summer sun.

Again he raised his eyes, and he saw great swirling clusters of red dragonflies, as if the glow of the gradually reddening sky overhead, filtering down through the closely bunched branches of the oak, had given wings to every crevice. This was yet another presage of autumn. These signs of a cool reason, slowly, leisurely taking form from out of the midst of hot passion, would make some men happy, but to Isao they brought sadness.

'Why wait in such a hot place?' said Izutsu in surprise, as he and Sagara came up, wearing white shirts with their school caps.

'Look there!' said Isao, sitting up straight in the grass. 'There in the evening sun is the face of His Majesty the Emperor.' His words had a magical effect upon Izutsu and Sagara. As always, they were quick to fall in with his mood even while feeling intimidated. 'And His Majesty's face is troubled.'

Izutsu and Sagara sat down in awed silence beside Isao, and for the moment, as they twisted blades of grass between their fingers, they steeped themselves in the feeling that was theirs whenever they were close to him – that of having drawn near to a naked sword. At times Isao seemed frightening to the two boys.

'I wonder if they'll all come?' said Sagara, pushing up his glasses as he broke the silence, hoping to account for a misgiving he did not understand.

'They'll come. What other choice have they?' answered Isao with casual assurance.

'You finally escaped the kendo training camp, eh? Good for you!' said Izutsu, expressing his admiration to a somewhat embarrassing degree. Isao was about to explain his reason, but changed his mind. Their activities had not yet become so busy that he had to deny himself the least diversion. Rather his reason for not participating was simply that he had had enough of the bamboo sword. He had grown weary because victories came too easily with it, weary because the bamboo sword was no more than a symbol; weary, finally, because it carried with it *no real danger*.

The three of them began to talk earnestly among themselves about how remarkable it was that they could enlist as many as twenty comrades. At that very time, at the Olympic Games in Los Angeles, the Japanese swimming team was gaining glory for the homeland, and so it was quite easy at any school to get swimming candidates to turn out. But what Isao and his friends were doing was a different story from the recruitment of the sports clubs. The appeal of their group had nothing to do with faddish popularity. For each student whom they had selected had to be asked to entrust his life to them. Furthermore, until he unqualifiedly trusted his life to them, they could give him no clear concept of their purpose.

Finding young men willing to give their lives and getting them to declare their intention was not so difficult. Each and every one one of them, however, was eager to embrace a cause that he could brag about to others and hoping for the most exquisite of funeral wreaths to mark his passing. Some of the students had secretly read Ikki Kita's *An Outline Plan for the Reorganization of Japan*, but Isao had sniffed out the odour of a devilish pride there. This book, far, far removed from the 'dogged devotion and humble loyalty' of Harukata Kaya, certainly stirred up the hot blood of many of the students, but such young men were not the kind that Isao wanted.

Beyond a doubt, Isao's comrades would be chosen not for what they had to say but because of something deep and inscrutable, manifested only when their eyes met his. This was something not in the realm of thought but of a more distant origin. Further, it gave rise to a clear, outward expression that would yet pass unrecognized by anyone who did not hold a like aspiration. It was this element alone that would cause Isao to choose his comrades.

The candidates had come not just from the College of National Studies but from various schools, some of them from Nihon University and some even from high school. One Keio University student had been introduced to Isao as a candidate, but, though this boy had a ready facility with words, his dilettantish manner made him unsuitable. There was even one student who, after professing the greatest enthusiasm for *The League of the Divine Wind*, gave himself away in more casual conversation as a fraud, odds and ends of vocabulary revealing him as a left-wing activist intent on spying.

A quiet and unsophisticated manner and a cheerful smile went in most cases with a character that could be relied upon, a brave disposition, and, as a consequence, a spirit that had little regard for death. Talkativeness, high-sounding words, an ironic smile, and the like all too often went with cowardice. A pale face and a sickly body were in some cases the source of extraordinary zeal. Fat youths in general were not only cowardly but indiscreet, while lean and logical-minded ones lacked intuition. Isao thus became aware of how much the face and outward bearing could communicate.

There was, however, nothing about the city-bred students to indicate kinship with the more than two hundred thousand children then suffering privation in farming and fishing villages. The very term 'undernourished child' had become an expression popularly used to ridicule gluttons and had lost almost all of its old deep-seated anger. Yet it had been reported that even in Tokyo, at an elementary school in Fukagawa, school inspectors were disconcerted to find that pupils who received the rice balls supplied to undernourished children took them home at once for their younger sisters and brothers. In Isao's college, however, no one was from this part of Tokyo. Many were the children of provincial middle school teachers and Shinto priests, and while few came from wealthy families, still fewer came from families hard put to lay food upon the table. As members of the families of moral leaders they were well acquainted with the severity of the conditions in the desolate and impoverished villages. Their fathers, for the most part, were grieved at what they saw and angry at what they did not see. All they could do was become angry. For as schoolteachers and priests they had no responsibility for the dreadful poverty or for the fact that it was ignored.

The government was skilled in relegating rich and poor to separate boxes, from which they could hardly see each other. Party politics, keeping to an accustomed rut that excluded any changes either for better or worse, had lost the power to deal the kind of killing blow to the spirit that had been embodied in the ordinance of the Ninth Year of the Meiji era that forbade the wearing of swords. Its methods left its victims still half-alive.

Isao had not drawn up any statement of principles. Since the world was such that all that was evil in it applauded inertia and weakness, the determination to act, whatever the act, would be their only principle. Consequently, when Isao interviewed his candidates, he said not a word to them about his intentions nor did he make any promises. When he had reached the point with one of these young men where he felt that he might admit him, he relaxed his hitherto unremitting sternness, and, looking him full in the eye with a kindly expression, asked simply: 'What do you say? Are you with us?'

Izutsu and Sagara, following Isao's directions, had made up a dossier with a picture for each of the twenty students who had been admitted in this way. Although the information, of course, came from the candidate himself, it included full details on his family, the occupations of his father and brothers, his own character, his physique, his particular skills, his favourite books, and even the state of his relationship with girls. Isao was quite pleased that eight of the twenty were the sons of Shinto priests. The affair of the League of the Divine Wind was by no means something terminated long ago by death. The average age of the twenty was eighteen.

As Izutsu presented him with one dossier after another, Isao read each of them once again, storing the data in his head and making it a point to join each name in his memory with the proper picture. Even in regard to a comrade's personal affairs, he had to be prepared to speak sympathetically at the proper moment, in words that would reach his heart.

The firm conviction that the political situation was in sorry shape was, in fact, very well suited to the youthful tendency to think that reality itself was in sorry shape. Isao never worried about confusing the two. As far as he was concerned, whenever the slovenly beauties that covered the garish kiosks on the street corners troubled his thoughts on the way to school, this for him was an indication of the corrupt state of politics. He and his comrades had formed a political union that was necessarily based upon their boyhood sense of shame. Isao was ashamed of the present state of things.

'Only a month ago you couldn't even tell a fuse from a detonator,' said Sagara in the midst of a minor dispute with Izutsu.

Isao smiled and said nothing. He had told his two friends to investigate thoroughly the manner of dealing with explosives. Sagara had asked a cousin who was an engineer to instruct him, and Izutsu had made the same request of a cousin in the Army.

'And you,' Izutsu retorted, 'I'll bet even you didn't know whether you cut a fuse straight across or diagonally.'

The two then plucked blades of the pampas grass at their feet to represent fuses, and broke off a section of a thin and hollow dry branch for a percussion cap. They were ready to practise setting off a charge.

'Here's a well-made percussion cap for you,' said Sagara boastfully as he packed dirt into the short branch with his fingertips. 'You leave half of it hollow, and you stuff as much powder as you can into the other half.' The wooden branch lacked, of course, the ominous fascination of a red brass percussion cap, like a metallic caterpillar, which concealed with capricious unreliability enough explosive power to blow off one's hand. It was no more than a thin branch reduced to its dry and withered shell. However, the lingering beams of the warm summer sun sinking into the woods of Hikawa Shrine shone through the busy, soiled fingers of the two boys, and from the direction toward which time was slipping came the distant, burnt odour of the inevitable killing to come. The odour, which might well have been nothing but the smoke from the kitchen fires of the nearby houses, combined with the sunlight to effect the sudden transformation of dirt into gun-powder and dry branch into percussion cap. Izutsu carefully inserted a thin blade of grass into the percussion cap and drew it out to gauge the length of the section not filled with gun-powder. He marked it with his fingernail and then laid it against the stalk of pampas grass that was to be the fuse and measured off an equal length. Finally, he slowly inserted this fuse into the percussion cap to the proper depth. Were he carelessly to thrust it too far, the percussion cap would explode.

'We don't have a crimper.'

'Use your fingers. And no nonsense while you're doing it,' said Sagara.

The colour that suffused Izutsu's sweat-covered face showed his earnestness. Just as he had been taught, he grasped the percussion cap with his left hand, his forefinger at its tip, middle finger against the powder-filled portion, and his third finger and thumb close to the opening at the hollow end. Then as he placed the thumb and forefinger of his right hand, doing duty as a crimper, at this opening, he brought both hands down firmly to his left side and turned his face sharply to the right. Twisting his right hand, he skilfully performed the function of securing the fuse to the percussion cap. He kept his face turned away during this process, not looking at what he was doing, in order to protect his face on the off-chance of the cap's exploding.

'You're overdoing it, looking away like that,' said Sagara teasingly. 'You've got your body so twisted that your hands won't be able to do the important job they're supposed to. And why so much bother to protect a face like yours?'

All that was left was to insert the cap securely into an explosive charge and light the fuse. Sagara, looking serious, helped with this, a clod of dirt serving as the explosives. Now to put a match to it. The flame of the match held against the still-green stalk of pampas grass quite obviously lacked the power to set it afire. The flame, all but invisible in the sunset light, burned halfway down the stem of the match before going out. A thirty-inch fuse allowed some forty or forty-five seconds. The stalk of pampas grass had been broken off at a length of thirty-five inches and so the two boys gazed at the second hand of their watches as it measured off fifty seconds.

'Hurry, run!'

'It's all right. I'm already a hundred metres away.'

Still seated as before, the two made as if they had fled far from the spot, acting as though they were short of breath and laughing as they looked at each other.

Thirty seconds passed. Then ten seconds more. Thanks to their imagination, and to the time elapsed, the explosive charge with the cap thrust into it was now far from them. But the fuse had been lit, and all the conditions necessary for the explosion had been fulfilled. The flame crawled along the fuse like a ladybug with set purpose.

Finally the imagined charge, at its imagined distance, detonated. Something ugly and corrupt suddenly heaved as though giving a violent hiccough, and the evening sky was rent for a moment. The oaks shook in the surrounding grove. Everything became transparent. The very report itself was transparent as it beat against the red sky and spread its force. At last all was still.

'Better the Japanese sword,' said Isao abruptly, looking up from the dossiers he had been scrutinizing. 'We need twenty swords without fail. Some of our friends can surely slip them out of their homes for us.'

'Wouldn't it be good to learn how to draw and strike at close range, and how to test a sword on a dead criminal?'

'We don't have that much time,' said Isao. His voice was quiet but his words had a poetic fervour for the two boys. 'Instead, before the end of vacation if possible, or else after the fall term begins, we should all attend Kaido Masugi's training camp on the rites of purification. We can talk about anything there, and he won't object to whatever kind of training we do. And if that's where we're going, we'll have a good reason for leaving our houses.'

'It's not much fun to listen to Master Kaido from morning to night on the evils of Buddhism.'

'That's something you'll have to bear with. He's a man who understands us thoroughly,' Isao replied. He looked at his watch and got to his feet at once.

Isao and his two companions, deliberately waiting until somewhat past the designated hour of six o'clock, peered towards the shrine through the low door beside the already-shut main gate. The light of the evening sun fell upon a group of students. They faced uncertainly in various directions, their uneasiness quite apparent.

'Count them,' said Isao in a low voice.

'Every one of them is there,' said Izutsu, unable to restrain his happiness. Isao, however, knew how imprudent it would be to let himself steep in the satisfaction of being the object of such trust. Every man being present was certainly preferable to having absentees. But they were gathered there because of a telegram. Because they expected action. Because, in other words, of the reckless courage of youth. In order to temper their resolution, he would have to take this opportunity to plunge it into cold water.

With the setting sun behind it, the shrine's copper-tiled roof was dark, but the sun's rays caught the splendid ornamental crossbeams of its gable among the glossy branches of the surrounding ilexes and zelkovas. The slanting sunlight fell upon the black granite gravel spread within the shrine fence, catching a little of each pebble and giving it its own shadow, black as grapes at the end of autumn. Two sakaki trees were half in the shadow of the shrine while their upper branches shone brilliant.

The twenty young men were grouped around Isao, who stood facing them with the shrine to his rear. As they watched him silently, he felt the brightness of their eyes, due as much to their inner fire as to the sun striking their faces, he felt their longing for some incandescent power that would lift them up to the heavens, he felt their almost frantic dependence upon him.

'You have performed well in assembling here today,' he said, breaking the silence. 'Nothing could have made me happier than your coming here like this, from as far away as Kyushu, with not a man missing. But my summons was not, as you thought, because I had some purpose. There was no purpose whatever. From all over Japan you've come, holding fast to the vision within your hearts, and you've gathered here utterly in vain.'

Suddenly there was agitation among the group, and a murmur arose.

Isao raised his voice: 'Do you understand? This meeting today is absolutely meaningless. There's no purpose to it. I have no work at all for you to do.'

He said no more, and the murmuring subsided. Silence settled upon the gathered boys even as the night was overtaking them.

Then a single angry voice shouted out. It was a boy named Serikawa, the son of a Shinto priest in the far north-east: 'What are you doing to us? If I thought I was being mocked, I couldn't stand it. I drank the farewell cup of water with my father before leaving home. My father has never ceased being indignant over the plight of the farming villages, and he told me that the time had come for the young to take action. So when the telegram arrived, he said nothing but raised the farewell cup with me and sent me off. If he learns I've been made a fool of, do you think my father will have nothing to say?'

'That's right,' another boy chimed in promptly. 'Serikawa is right.'

'What kind of nonsense is this? I don't recall making any promises. You took my telegram telling you only to meet here, and you let your imaginations run wild. Isn't that what you did? Was there anything else in that telegram – anything other than the time and the place? Tell me,' Isao demanded, keeping his voice calm as he ridiculed them.

'There's such a thing as common sense. If you decide to take some important action, are you going to tell people about it in a telegram? We should have decided on a code and a clear commitment from you. If we had, this wouldn't have happened,' said Seyama, a student at the First High School, who was the same age as Isao. Since he lived in Shibuya, however, coming here could hardly have been much trouble for him.

'Just what wouldn't have happened? Isn't that simply going back to a situation where nothing will occur?' said Isao, quietly refuting him. 'Isn't that simply realizing that what you all imagined was mistaken?'

The twilight was deepening so that it was becoming harder and harder to make out one another's features. There was a long silence. Only the chirping of insects filled the darkness.

'What are we to do then?'

When someone asked this in a pathetic whisper, Isao's response was immediate: 'Whoever wants to go home, go home.'

One white-shirted figure at once detached itself from the group and hurried towards the college gate. Then two more drew away and walked off. Serikawa did not leave. He squatted down by the shrine hedge and held his head in his hands. In a few moments, the others heard Serikawa's sobs. The sound seemed to penetrate the gloom in their hearts like a chill, white stream, a tiny Milky Way.

'I can't go back! I can't!' Serikawa muttered as he wept.

'Why don't all of you go home?' Isao shouted. 'Despite what I've told you, you still don't understand?'

Not a single voice answered him. Furthermore this silence differed markedly from the one that had preceded it. It was a silence that gave the feeling that some huge, warm-blooded beast had risen up in the darkness. For the first time, Isao sensed firm response. It was hot, it had an animal smell, it was filled with blood, its pulse throbbed.

'All right then. You that are left, with no hopes, no expectations whatsoever, are you willing to throw away your lives on an act that probably will amount to nothing at all?'

'Yes,' one voice spoke out with a forceful dignity.

Serikawa rose to his feet and began to walk toward Isao. His eyes, wet with tears, approached through the darkness so thick that a face could barely be seen until it was very close. His voice was choked from weeping, and when he spoke out boldly, its tone was frightfully low: 'I'm still here too. I'll follow anywhere at all, and I'll keep quiet.'

'Good enough. All right, let us make our vows together before the gods. Let's offer worship. Then I'll recite the vows. Say each one of them after me, all together.' The sound of Isao, Izutsu, Sagara, and the remaining seventeen clapping their hands in worship echoed sharply through the darkness, as regularly as the night sea slapping a wooden gunwale.

Isao intoned: 'Be it thus that we, emulating the purity of the League of the

Divine Wind, hazard ourselves for the task of purging away all evil deities and perverse spirits.'

The youthful voices of the others responded as one: 'Be it thus that we, emulating the purity of the League of the Divine Wind, hazard ourselves for the task of purging away all evil deities and perverse spirits.'

Isao's voice reverberated from the dimly visible plain wood doors of the inner shrine. Strong and deep, it rose up from his chest with all the poignance of the misty fantasies of youth. The stars were already out. The noise of streetcars jangled from far off. Isao chanted again: 'Be it thus that we, forging deep friendship among ourselves, aid one another as comrades in responding to the perils that confront the nation.'

'Be it thus that we, never seeking power and giving no thought to personal advancement, go forth to certain death to become the foundation stones for the Restoration.'

As soon as they finished reciting the vows, one boy grasped Isao's hand and held it with both of his own. Then all of them were clasping each other's hands, and jostling in their haste to clasp Isao's. Beneath the starry sky, as their eyes grew more accustomed to the darkness, they thrust out their hands again and again on all sides, seeking other hands still ungrasped. No one spoke. Any words would have been inadequate.

Grasping hands were everywhere as though a growth of tenacious ivy had sprung up from the darkness. Each tendril, whether sweaty or dry or hard or soft to the touch, was filled with strength as it held fast for a brief moment marked by a mutual sharing of the warmth of their bodies and their blood. Isao dreamed that he would some night stand like this with his comrades upon the field of battle, taking wordless farewell before their deaths. Bathing in the marvellous satisfaction of having seen the task through to the finish and in the blood that flowed from his own body, yielding his consciousness to that peak of sensitivity where the scarlet and the white threads of ultimate pain and ultimate joy are woven together...

Since there were twenty of them in all, they could not safely meet at the Academy of Patriotism. His father's eye would be likely to search out Isao's plans. On the other hand, Izutsu's home was too small and Sagara's, too, was unsuitable. This had been a concern of the three of them from the beginning, but no workable plan had suggested itself. Even if the three were to put their pocket money together, they could not cope with the cost of all twenty meeting at a restaurant. And then a coffee shop would hardly be the place to speak of grave matters.

Now, after the handclasps beneath the stars that sealed their alliance, it was Isao who felt a reluctance to put an end to things that night without something further. Then, too, he was hungry. No doubt all the boys were hungry. He turned perplexed eyes toward the main gate, where a dim light was burning.

Below the gate light, a little to one side, was something like a moonflower that seemed to be floating in the air. It was the face of a woman who was standing there, her head slightly bowed, not wanting to be seen. Once his eyes had discovered her, he found he could not turn away,

Somewhere in his heart he had recognized who she was. His dominant wish, however, was to go on a little longer without recognizing her. The woman's face floating in its dark seclusion, no name yet attached to it, had the character of a mysterious, lovely apparition. It was like the scent of the fragrant olive which, as one walks along a path at night, tells of the blossoms before one sees them. Isao wanted to keep things just as they were, if only for an instant more. At this moment a woman was a woman, not someone with a name attached to her.

And that was not all. Because of her hidden name, because of the agreement not to speak that name, she was transmuted into a marvellous essence, like a moonflower, its supporting vine invisible, floating high up in the darkness. This essence which preceded existence, this phantasm which preceded reality, this portent which preceded the event conveyed with unmistakable force the presence of a substance yet more powerful. This presence which showed itself as gliding through air – this was woman.

Isao had yet to embrace a woman. Still, never so strongly as at this moment, when he keenly sensed this 'womanliness that preceded woman', had he felt that he too knew what ecstasy meant. For this was a presence that he could even now embrace. In time, that is, it had drawn near with an exquisite subtlety, and in space it was only a little distant. The affectionate emotion that filled his breast was like a vapour that could envelop her. And yet once she was gone, Isao, like a child, could forget her entirely.

However, after Isao had for some time let his thoughts dwell upon this presence, he found himself, despite his earlier wish to preserve the moment, unable to bear the uncertainty any longer.

'Wait for me,' he ordered Izutsu in a voice loud enough for all to hear, and sprinted toward the gate. There was a dry, faint stutter of scampering clogs as his white splashed-pattern kimono disappeared into the darkness.

Isao went through the low door beside the gate. Just as he had imagined, the woman standing there was Makiko.

Makiko's hair was arranged in a different manner, something that even the inexperienced Isao noticed at once. It was a stylish hairdo that covered her ears, leaving only a wavy border about her temples and cheeks, pressing in upon her features and giving her face a heightened air of mystery. Although she was not one to use much makeup, the nape of her neck seemed to stand out like a carving in relief above the crepe of her Akashi kimono, which seemed a solid navy blue in the darkness. A whiff of some fragrant scent from her body struck Isao with unnerving force.

'Miss Makiko! What are you doing here?'

'What am I doing? All of you came here at six, didn't you, to recite your vows?'

'How did you know that?'

'Don't be stupid!' Makiko's teeth gleamed as she laughed. 'Didn't you yourself say so?'

Thus challenged, Isao had to conclude that a few days ago, concerned as he was with the ever-present worry of not having a place to meet, he had probably happened to let slip the time and place of the vows in her presence. He had always been willing to confide anything to Makiko, but he felt ashamed at the thought of revealing something important and then forgetting about it, with her of all people. Perhaps he lacked some quality essential in one who was to lead men and bring about events. In his carelessness in so grave a matter, Isao could not fail to detect a certain unmanly dependence upon her. Though quite different before his comrades, in Makiko's presence he felt a subtle desire to seem a heedless young man.

'Well ... it's just that you took me by surprise. But why have you come?'

'I thought that, after gathering a large group of students together, you might be hard put for a place to bring them. First of all I imagine you are quite hungry, aren't you?'

Isao scratched his head with a fresh, boyish candour.

'We'd be happy to offer all of you dinner at our house, but since it's a long way from here, Father suggested that I treat you to a sukiyaki dinner in Shibuya, and he gave me the money for it. He was invited to a poetry composition party tonight, and so I'm here in his place to offer you gentlemen our hospitality. Don't worry, I can take care of the bill.'

Then Makiko, as though drawing up a fresh-caught fish, held up a large Panama handbag with a quick motion of her white hand. Despite the fragile grace of the slender wrist that appeared from the sleeve, however, it was a hand that seemed to convey something of the fatigue of late summer.

19

About this same time, Honda was attending a performance of *Matsukazé* at the Osaka Nō Theatre in Tennoji-Dogashiba at the invitation of a colleague fond of performing Nō chants himself. It was a production featuring Kanesuké Noguchi from Tokyo as *shité* with Yazo Tamura assisting him as *waki*. The theatre stood upon the eastern slope of Uemachi Hill between Tennoji and Osaka Castle. This had been a section of fine villas at the beginning of the Taisho period and was still a secluded area containing high-walled mansions. One of these functioned as a Nō theatre under the auspices of the Sumitomo family.

Most of the guests were merchant princes, and Honda recognized many of them. As for the famous actor, the harsh-voiced Noguchi, Honda's colleague had warned him beforehand that, although his intonation might sound like a goose being strangled, Honda was not by any means to laugh. And he predicted that, ignorant of Nō though Honda was, once the play was underway he would suddenly find himself emotionally aroused.

Honda had reached the age at which advice of this sort did not provoke any childish antipathy. Although the reason that had been his foundation had begun to crumble when he met Isao Iinuma at the beginning of the summer, his usual habits of thought had not changed. Once again he found himself believing that, just as he had never contracted venereal disease, neither had he ever experienced emotional arousal.

As soon as the exchange was finished between the *waki* as a priest and the clown, the *shité* and his companion made their entrance along the passageway at the left rear. Honda's colleague explained to him that the serene and tranquil accompaniment now being played was ordinarily limited to that entrance scene in god plays. *Matsukazé* contained the sole exception to this rule. Such was the high regard, it seemed, in which this music was held as expressing the full force of the occult.

Matsukazé and Murasamé, both clad in white robes revealing scarlet underskirts spilling out beneath, faced each other on the entrance bridgeway, and then began to chant in unison as quietly as the rain falling and sinking into a sandy beach: 'Drawing our brine cart along, how briefly we live in this sad world, how fleetingly!'

Though Honda was distracted by the reflection of the pointed pines falling on the highly polished cypress floor of the stage, gleaming too brilliantly beneath the rather harsh lighting of this Nō theatre, the final 'how fleetingly!' rang clear in his ear, as the lighter and brighter tones of the companion entangled the deeper and more melancholy voice, ever on the verge of breaking, of Kanesuké Noguchi.

Since there was, of course, nothing to interfere with listening, the words were easily recalled.

'Drawing our brine cart along, how briefly we live in this sad world, how fleetingly!'

No matter how lean, how slender of body, the graceful figure of the verse took on significant form in Honda's mind. At that moment he shuddered without knowing why.

Then the companion began to chant the second verse: 'The waves beat close to us, here at the Bay of Suma. Even the moon moves us to tears that wet our sleeves.'

After the two had joined together to chant the concluding words, the *shité*, as Matsukazé, began a vigorous soliloquy: 'The autumn wind saddens the heart. A little away from the sea...'

Although Kanesuké Noguchi wore the mask of a beautiful young woman, his voice had nothing that would recall a woman's charm. It was a voice that made one think of the rasping together of rusty, discoloured metal. Furthermore, his recitation was broken by interruptions, and his style of chanting seemed to be tearing the beauty of the words to shreds. But despite all this, the mood inspired was like the outpouring of a dark and ineffably elegant mist, like the sight of a moonbeam shining into a corner of a ruined palace to fall upon a mother-of-pearl furnishing. Because the light passed through a worn and ravaged bamboo blind, the elegance of the shattered fragments shone all the more.

Gradually, then, his harsh voice became far from irritating. Rather, one had the feeling that only through this harsh voice could one for the first time become aware of the briny sadness of Matsukazé and the melancholy love that afflicts those in the realm of the dead.

Honda at some point began to find it hard to tell whether the images that shifted to and fro before him were reality or illusion. On the gleaming cypress surface of the stage, like the mirroring sea at the shoreline, was reflected the glittering embroidery of the white robes and scarlet underskirts of two beautiful women.

Mingling with the words of the soliloquy, the first line still held stubborn sway in Honda's heart: 'Drawing our brine cart along, how briefly we live in this sad world, how fleetingly!'

What came to his mind was not the meaning of this line but the significance of the unaccountable shudder that he had felt when the *shité* and his companion had stood together on the bridgeway and recited it, the moment of recitation imbued with perfect stillness, the chant falling like quiet rain.

And what was that significance? Just then beauty itself had begun to walk before him. Like the beach plover, strong in flight but unsteady on the ground, the white *tabi*-shod feet moved on tiptoe as though come for a few brief moments to make their way through the world known to man.

This beauty, however, would occur but once. A man could do nothing but commit it to memory immediately and reflect upon it thereafter. Then too it was a beauty that preserved a noble futility, a purposelessness.

Keeping pace with Honda's thoughts, the Nō drama of *Matsukazé* flowed on, a small stream of never-failing emotion.

'Dwelling in this world we find thus so wretched, even while envying the carefree moon clear above us, come let us ladle out the tidewater she summons.'

That which chanted and moved about on the stage bathed in moonlight was now no longer the ghosts of two beautiful women but something beyond description. One might call it the essence of time, the pith of emotion, the dream that stubbornly obtrudes upon reality. It had no purpose, no meaning. From moment to moment it fashioned a beauty not of this world. For here what hope is there that one moment of beauty will follow at once upon another?

Thus did Honda gradually become drawn into a mood of sombre detachment. His thoughts had now become clearly focused. Kiyoaki's existence, his life, its consequences – Honda realized that it was a long time indeed since he had concentrated so intently on all this. It was easy to think of Kiyoaki's life as a breath of fragrance that had wafted faintly over a single era before vanishing. Even so, Kiyoaki's sin, Kiyoaki's heartbreak remained. And Honda himself would never be able to make reparation.

Honda recalled a morning of melting snow on the campus of the Peers School before classes began. He and Kiyoaki, sitting in an arbour encircled by flowerbeds and listening to the fresh sound of trickling water, were deeply involved in a long conversation, something rare with them.

That was early spring in the second year of Taisho, 1913. Kiyoaki and Honda were both nineteen. Since then nineteen years had passed. Honda remembered insisting that like it or not, a hundred years later he and Kiyoaki would be included in the thought of the era, lumped together with those they had the least regard for, classified with them on the basis of a few meagre similarities. He remembered also that he had talked of the irony of the human will's relationship to history, vehemently maintaining that every strong-willed person was in the last analysis frustrated and that there was only one way to participate in history: 'To function as a shining, forever unchanging, beautiful nonwilling particle.'

His terms had been entirely abstract; yet as he had been speaking on that morning of melting snow, his eyes had been resting upon the shining, beautiful features of Kiyoaki. Obviously, with Kiyoaki before him, a youth so lacking in will, so single-mindedly devoted to the vagaries of emotion, Honda's words had of their own accord fashioned a portrait of Kiyoaki himself: 'To function as a shining, forever unchanging, beautiful nonwilling particle' – a clear definition of Kiyoaki's manner of living.

When a hundred years had passed since that morning, the perspective would, no doubt, once more be altered. Nineteen years before was too recent a time for generalizations and too distant for minute assessment. Kiyoaki's image was not yet confused with the rough, wholly insensitive image of boys of the kendo team pursuing their cult of toughness. Nevertheless, Kiyoaki's particular kind of 'heroic figure', as a forerunner of that brief and fleeting period at the beginning of the Taisho era when a wholehearted surrender to the emotions enjoyed favour, had already, viewed from across the years, lost much of its vividness. The earnest passion of that time, except for its fond persistence in a man's memory, had now become something to provoke laughter.

Each passing year, never failing to exact its toll, keeps altering what was sublime into the stuff of comedy. Is something eaten away? If the exterior is eaten away, is it true, then, that the sublime pertains by nature only to an exterior that conceals a core of nonsense? Or does the sublime indeed pertain to the whole, but a ludicrous dust settles upon it?

When Honda reflected upon his own character, he had no choice but to conclude that he was a man possessed of a will. At the same time, however, he could not avoid misgivings as to the ability of that will to change anything or to accomplish anything even in contemporary society, let alone in the course of future history. Often his courtroom decisions had determined whether a man lived or died. Such a verdict might have seemed of extreme significance at the time, but as the years passed – since all men were fated to die – it turned out that he had merely hastened a man's fate; and that the deaths had been neatly consigned to one corner of history, where they soon disappeared. And as for the disturbing conditions of the present world, though his will had had nothing to do with bringing these about, he as a judge was ever at their beck and call. How much the choices made by his will proceeded from pure reason and how much, without his realizing it, they were coerced by the prevailing thought of the period was a question he was unable to decide.

Then again, when Honda looked at the world around him, no matter how searchingly, nowhere did he see any effect traceable to a youth called Kiyoaki – to his violent emotion, to his death, to his life of beauty. Nowhere was there evidence that anything had come about as a result of his death, that anything had changed because of it. It seemed to have been smoothly expunged from history.

In the course of such reflections, Honda came to realize that his exposition of nineteen years before had contained an odd presage. For, after explaining the frustration in store for a will that insisted upon having an effect on history, Honda had at last discovered that his own usefulness lay exactly in the frustration of that will. And now, nineteen years later, he found himself envying Kiyoaki's lack of anything remotely like it, envying Kiyoaki's having left not a single trace in the world. He could not help but recognize in Kiyoaki, whose image had become lost to history, an inner substance superior to Honda's for participating in history.

Kiyoaki had been beautiful. His life had been useless, devoid of any purpose whatsoever. He had passed swiftly through the world, his beauty severely limited to but a single lifespan, to an instant like that depicted in the chanted line: 'Drawing our brine cart along, how briefly we live in this sad world, how fleetingly!'

The truculent face of another young man rose sharply into view amidst the swirling froth of vanishing beauty. It was Kiyoaki's beauty alone that would truly occur but once. Its very excess made a renewed life essential. There had to be a reincarnation. Something had remained unfulfilled in Kiyoaki, had found expression in him only as a negative factor.

The face of that other young man ... He had ripped off his kendo mask, its bars glittering in bright summer sunlight. Sweat poured down over his features. His nostrils flared as he breathed violently. His lips formed a line as straight as a sword.

The figures that Honda gazed upon on a stage misted with light were no longer the gorgeous figures of the *shité* and his companion as two women dipping up seawater. The two who were there carrying out a task imbued with futility, now standing, now sitting with a singular elegance in the moon's rays, were two young men of diverse eras. Two young men the same age. From a distance, they looked alike, but, seen closer, their diametrically opposed characters became evident. The sturdy hands of one of them callused from the sword handle, the white hands of the other soft from indolence – these hands were devoted in turn to dipping up water of the sea of time. At intervals the sound of a flute, like a moonbeam darting through a break in the clouds, pierced the mortal forms of the two young men. By turns, they were drawing the brine cart, its two fourteen-inch wheels hung with scarlet damask, through the mirroring water at the sea's edge. This time, however, what sounded in Honda's ear was not the elegant, somewhat wearied verse 'Drawing our brine cart along, how briefly we live in this sad world, how fleetingly!' The lines suddenly altered to a sutra verse: 'Six paths for reborn sentient beings to tread, like the turning wheel, without respite.' And on stage the wheels of the brine cart began turning round and round.

Honda thought of the various doctrines of transmigration and reincarnation that he had encountered when he had on occasion given himself over to this study. The word for both transmigration and rebirth was 'samsara' in Sanskrit. According to the doctrine of transmigration, mankind's lot was to traverse the six states of the Sphere of Illusion without surcease – the Earth Hell, the Hell of Starvation, the Hell of Beasts, the Hell of Pandemonium, human existence, and ethereal existence. The term 'rebirth', however, was sometimes used to designate the transition from the Sphere of Illusion to the Sphere of Enlightenment. In that event, transmigration would be at an end. Transmigration necessarily involved rebirth, but rebirth did not necessarily involve transmigration.

At any rate, Buddhism recognized that there was a subject who underwent this transmigration, but it did not recognize this subject as constituting a constant and unchanging core. Since Buddhism denied the existence of the self, there was no place in it for the existence of the soul either. There was nothing but an extremely subtle nucleus at the centre of mental activity, something that pertained to the innermost functioning of the phenomena surrounding the continual birth and death that accompanied transmigration. This, then, was the subject – something that the doctrine of *Yuishiki*, 'awareness only', designated 'Alaya Awareness'.

Since none of the things of this world, even sentient beings, had souls as their core subject, and since insentient beings, emerging through causality, lacked even a core subject, there was nothing within the universe truly possessed of its own substance.

If the subject of transmigration was the Alaya Awareness, then the mode of activity of transmigration constituted its Karma. The theories thence grew quite numerous, the 'one hundred thousand diverse exegeses' that characterized Buddhism. One theory held that the Alaya Awareness was already defiled by sin and was therefore itself Karma. Another held that the Alaya Awareness was half-defiled, half-undefiled, and hence could serve as the bridge to salvation.

Honda remembered having, in the course of his study, gone through these intricate theories of Karma and of the origin of things as well as through the difficult metaphysics of the Five Aggregates, which were the source of continuation, but the truth of the matter was that his grasp of them had grown uncertain.

In the meantime, *Matsukazé* had advanced to the climax of its first half.

SHITE′: Into this pail, too, has the moon's image entered.
CHORUS: Fortunate event! Into it, too, has the moon's image entered.
SHITE′: The moon is but one.
CHORUS: Two are its images. We bear the moon itself, shining in the floodtide, on our cart tonight. Now this toil no longer seems wretched, as we draw our burden home.

For Honda it was once more the beautiful Matsukazé and Murasamé who held the stage. The *waki*, in the role of a priest, arose from his position by the *waki* pillar. Honda could now clearly distinguish the face of each spectator and hear each beat of the drum.

That sleepless night at the Hotel Nara after he thought he had been confronted with proof of Kiyoaki's reincarnation now seemed to Honda like a vaguely remembered event of the distant past. A crack had certainly appeared in the foundation of reason. But earth had filled the crack at once, and the lush grass of summer sprouted from it, completely hiding the memory of that night. As in the Nō drama before him, a phantom had confronted his reason, and his reason had for a brief time suspended its function. Isao was not necessarily the only young man to have a cluster of moles in the same spot as Kiyoaki. The meeting beneath the waterfall was not necessarily beneath the falls that Kiyoaki had spoken of in his delirium. Two chance occurrences of this sort provided but a flimsy basis for concluding that Kiyoaki had been reincarnated.

Now it appeared extremely rash to Honda, versed as he was in the procedural methods of criminal law, to have come to that conclusion on no stronger evidence.

The desire to believe in Kiyoaki's reincarnation shone within him like a small puddle of water at the bottom of a dry well, but Honda's reason had already told him in unequivocal terms that the well was dry. Whether or not there was something dubious about the very foundation of his reason was a matter that was certainly better left unexamined. The wisest course was to let matters stand as they were.

'How foolish!' he exclaimed, feeling as if he had suddenly come to his senses. 'How very foolish! Hardly a thing to be expected from a thirty-eight-year-old judge.'

However subtle the systems that Buddhism constructed, they pertained to problems outside Honda's jurisdiction. He felt refreshed, as though he had that instant skilfully solved the vexing riddle that he had been mulling over these many months. He had regained his clarity of soul. He was now not at all unlike those accomplished men around him, who had come to this Nō theatre to escape for a time the urgent demands of their work.

The Nō stage, so close at hand, shone like the world beyond. Spirits walked there, and Honda was stirred. That was sufficient. When he thought of how, that night in Nara, the pain of a bereavement incurred nineteen years before had quickened again within him and caused him to succumb to a delusion of such proportions, he saw that what had been reborn in all likelihood was not Kiyoaki himself but merely his own sense of loss.

When he returned home, Honda, for the first time in long months, felt the urge to read the dream journal that Kiyoaki had left to him.

20

October began with a stretch of fine weather. Isao was returning from school and had almost reached home when, drawn by the sound of the wooden clappers used to attract children to a storyteller's 'paper theatre', he turned into a side lane, making a slight detour. A crowd of children had gathered at a street corner.

The warm rays of the autumn sun struck the curtain of the tiny stage mounted on the rear of a bicycle, where a succession of pictures would illustrate the tale. It was clear at a glance that the storyteller was a man out of work. He needed a shave. He wore a wrinkled jacket over his dirty shirt.

The unemployed of Tokyo – as though acting in concert, it seemed – affected an appearance that made obvious their being out of work, giving not the least indication that they wanted to hide their condition. Some kind of invisible pock-mark covered their faces. Those who had caught the disease of unemployment, like men struck by a secret plague, seemed anxious to be recognized as set apart from others. The storyteller, striking his sticks together, glanced hastily in Isao's direction. Isao knew that the man saw him as a naïve, sheltered schoolboy.

The children, eager for the storyteller to open the curtain, were imitating the laugh of the Golden Bat. Isao did not stop, but as he passed, the image that appeared through the parting curtain caught his eye: the glaring yellow skull mask of the Golden Bat, who, in green tunic and white tights, trailed his crimson cloak as he flew through the sky. It was a crude and distorted image. Isao had once heard that pictures of this sort were drawn by poor boys, who were paid the considerable wage of one yen, fifty sen a day.

The storyteller cleared his throat and began his preliminary narration: 'Well now, the Golden Bat, the champion of justice . . .' The sound of his gravelly voice followed Isao as he walked on, leaving the paper theatre and the crowd of children behind him.

As he turned into a quiet street in Nishikata with a wall running along one side of it, that gold-skulled phantom who soared through the sky pursued him. How grotesque an image of justice was that bizarre golden figure!

He found no one at home when he got there, and he walked around to the back yard. Sawa was doing his laundry at the side of the well, humming the while. He was quite pleased that the weather was so suited to drying.

'Welcome home. Nobody's here. They all went to help with Mr Koyama's seventy-seventh birthday celebration. Your mother too.'

The old gentleman was a luminary of the world of the right, and Iinuma was one of those who had long enjoyed his patronage. Sawa, for fear of committing some breach of etiquette, had probably been ordered to remain behind to look after the house.

Since Isao had nothing better to do, he sat down on a ragged clump of grass. Now, at noontime, the faint chirping of insects gave way to the noise of Sawa's splashing. The sky, piercingly clear, was mirrored, then shattered again and again in the tub water belaboured by Sawa. Everything was right with the world. The elements seemed to be doing their best to reduce Isao's design to a flight of fancy. The trees, the bright sky joined in cooling his burning will, calming the torrent of his violent passion. They were trying to make him seem to himself like one altogether out of touch with reality, possessed by the illusion of a reform that was unwanted. His youthfulness, however, was like a steel blade, and the autumn sky, dazzling blue to no purpose, was at least in harmony with that.

Sawa seemed to have no difficulty in sensing what was behind Isao's silence.

'Have you been going to kendo practice lately?' he asked as he bunched up a white wad in the tub and kneaded it with his thick hands as though making rice balls.

'No.'

'That so?' Sawa did not ask why.

Isao stole a glance into the tub. The amount of Sawa's laundry seemed hardly in keeping with his extravagant efforts. For Sawa would wash no one's clothes but his own.

'As hard as I work to keep myself clean,' he said, somewhat out of breath, 'I wonder if the day will ever come when I'll be of service.'

'Maybe tomorrow will be the day,' said Isao, baiting him gently. 'And where will Mr Sawa be but bent over his washtub?'

Sawa never explained what he meant by 'be of service' beyond an unswerving insistence that when the hour struck it would be unfitting for any man to be clad in other than dazzling white underwear.

He wrung out his clothes at last. The water struck the dry ground in glittering black drops. Without looking at Isao, he began to speak in a droll tone of voice. 'Well, it seems to me that, rather than wait for the master, it might be best to look to young Mr Iinuma for an early opportunity.'

When he heard this, Isao's first concern was whether his expression had changed. There could be no doubt that Sawa had sniffed out something. Had Isao himself been guilty of some lapse?

Not giving the least sign that he had caught Isao's reaction, Sawa draped his laundry over one arm and hastily wiped off the drying pole with a rag.

'When will you be going to Master Kaido's training camp?' he asked.

'Well, I'm assigned to the week beginning the twentieth of October. It's all filled up until then. I hear that nowadays a lot of businessmen are attending.'

'Who's going with you?'

'I asked the ones in my study group at school.'

'You know what? I'd like to go too. Let me see if it's all right with the master. After all, what good am I but to watch the place when everybody's gone? So I think he might let me go with you. It would toughen me up and do me a lot of good to get in with you young fellows. When you get to be my age, no matter how eager your spirit is, your body's got a will of its own. Come on now, what do you say?'

Isao found himself without an answer. Indeed, if Sawa did ask his father, the reply certainly would be yes. And if he were to go with them, it would spoil the chance for the crucial talk with his comrades that Isao had gone to such trouble to arrange. Sawa might even be aware of what was up and be trying to draw him out. Furthermore, if Sawa meant to convey his dedication, his request might well be nothing but a roundabout way of communicating his desire to be numbered among Isao's comrades.

Turning to Isao, Sawa ran the pole through his undershirt and drawers and then fastened his Etchu loincloth to it by its string. Since he had not wrung them out as well as he might, water from his clothes ran down the slanted pole and dripped from its end, but this did not trouble him at all. While he was thus occupied, the back that bulged beneath the khaki shirt, the whole heavy, insensitive mass of flesh before Isao's eyes, seemed to be pressing him for an answer. Still, Isao did not know what to say.

Just as he had set the drying pole at a convenient level, a gust of wind caught a corner of the wet cloth and slapped it against Sawa's cheek. Startled as though a huge white dog were licking his face, he pushed it away and stepped hurriedly back. Then, turning to Isao in a carefree manner, he asked: 'Is there any reason why you really wouldn't want me to come along?'

Had Isao been a youth of some sophistication, he might have turned Sawa aside with a light answer. But since he was indeed thinking that Sawa's coming would cause difficulty, joking was out of the question.

Sawa did not pursue the matter. Instead, he asked Isao to come to his room to share some delicious cakes he had. The room was a full three mats and Sawa had it to himself in deference to his age. There were no books to be seen, only a few tattered copies of *Kodan Club*. When chided on this point, Sawa would reply that those who read books to imbibe the Japanese Spirit were 'pseudopatriots'.

He poured Isao a cup of tea and offered him the rice cakes, of a kind called higomochi, which his wife in Kumamoto had sent.

'Anyway,' said Sawa with a sigh, apropos of nothing, 'there's no doubt that the master loves you.'

Then after rummaging through the debris that littered the floor he came up with a fan decorated with a picture of a pretty woman, but when he tried to present Isao with this holiday gift from a neighbourhood saké dealer, whose name and phone number were prominently displayed on it, he was rebuffed. The slender lady with a faraway look somewhat resembled Makiko around the eyes, and this was what lent an undue severity to Isao's abrupt refusal. Sawa, however, had not meant to imply anything, apparently, and his proffering the fan was but another example of his idiosyncratic behaviour.

'Would you really like to go to the training camp?' Isao asked, regretting the harshness of his rebuff and wanting to end at once the lingering tension between them.

'No, not really,' answered Sawa, putting him off casually as though he had lost interest in the matter. 'I'd probably be busy and couldn't go anyway. I was just asking.' Then, as though to himself, he repeated his irrelevant remark. 'Yes, there's no doubt that the master loves you.' He wrapped both of his hands, their plump flesh dimpled at the joint of each finger, around the sturdy mug that held his tea and began a story that was wholly unsolicited.

'This is something I think young Master Isao is old enough to know. It's only recently that the Academy has been so well off. When I started here, we had all we could do to make ends meet. You were never told, and I know that this was in keeping with the master's theory of education. But if I might say so, it's getting to be time for you to learn some unpleasant things. Because if your education leaves out anything that you should know, then later on you'll be scandalized.

'It was three years ago, I think, that the *New Japan* came out with a piece attacking Mr Koyama, the very one whose birthday it happens to be today. The master said it wouldn't do to let this go by and say nothing. He went to see Mr Koyama, but I never found out exactly what decision they came to. Anyway, the master told me to go to the newspaper office and demand that they print a thoroughgoing apology. The instructions he gave me were certainly strange. "If they offer money, don't take it. Throw it back at them angrily and leave," he said. "But if they don't offer any money, it's a sign that you've handled things badly."

'It's rather fun to pretend to be angry when you really aren't. And I don't mind seeing a frightened look on people's faces. Especially in this case, it helped matters that the one they picked to deal with me was a rather cheeky young editor.

'The master's strategy was wonderfully worked out. He sends somebody like me to begin the negotiations. If I do say so myself, I seem to be a likeable sort of person, and nobody takes it too seriously even if I'm boiling with rage, so this fellow thinks he can settle the matter with a little money. Then when to his surprise I break off the meeting, the other side starts to get a bit uneasy.

'The master arranges matters so there's never a direct meeting with Mr Koyama, and in the course of the negotiations he puts five actors on the stage, five hurdles, each steeper than the one before. Each one of these gentlemen is more formidable and prestigious than the last. The other side gets in deeper and deeper without having any idea how far we're going to go before we settle. Furthermore there can be no question of extortion, since we keep insisting that "This isn't a matter of money", and so they have no grounds for going to the police. The second actor to take the stage is Mr Muto, who was involved in the June Incident. And it's at this point that the *New Japan* becomes aware, to its great surprise, that this is no simple matter.

'Furthermore, in going from the second actor to the third, the interval is made as indefinite as possible, and while offering the hope that a settlement can be had by a meeting with the third actor, the master arranges it so that this meeting seems as though it's never going to take place. And then when it finally does come off after all the anxiety, authority has been switched to a fourth party, unknown to them. At this stage, the number of "young men who can't contain their wrath" soars to far more than a mere one or two hundred, though none of them makes an appearance.

'As might be expected, the newspaper loses no time in hiring a former detective, and this fellow comes rubbing his hands obsequiously, carrying his letter of sanction from the publisher. The master was also very careful in picking out just the right meeting places, and when our fourth actor, Mr Yoshimori, goes on stage, the setting is perfect. He has connections with a construction company, and so the master makes it the shanty office on a building site.

'After four months of harassment, a smooth big shot who looks easygoing finally appears on the scene as our fifth actor. I can't tell you his name, but thanks to his hard bargaining, an agreement was reached. The place was in Yanagibashi. The publisher of the *New Japan* himself was there, and kowtowed to us, but with all that, they handed over something like fifty thousand yen. It seems the master got ten thousand as his share. That took care of the Academy very well for a year.'

Isao had been trying to suppress his irritation as he listened. Vanity compelled him to show that petty evils of this sort could by no means upset him. What was hard to bear, however, was the realization that he himself had up to now been enjoying the fruits of such petty evils.

Nevertheless, to suppose that Isao was having his eyes opened for the first time to the true state of affairs would be an exaggeration. Isao himself would not deny that his unwillingness to look into certain fundamental aspects of his life had somehow been the basis for his sense of purity, as well as the source of the strange anger and disquiet that troubled him. To plant one's feet upon evil and yet render justice was an over-blown concept flattering to the vanity of youth. The problem was that Isao's imagined evil had been of somewhat greater dimensions. But, whatever the case, this did not offer adequate cause for Isao to have misgivings about his purity.

Calming himself with an effort, he asked: 'Does my father still make a practice of doing this?'

'Now things are different. Now he's an important man. That kind of struggle isn't necessary any more. What I wanted you to know is what the master had to go through before he got where he is.'

Then Sawa, after a slight pause, made still another incongruous statement, and though he tossed it off carelessly, it stunned Isao: 'You can go after whoever you want. But don't go after Busuké Kurahara. If anything should happen to him, the one who'll suffer most will be the master. Go ahead out of a sense of loyalty, and you'll find yourself utterly betraying your father.'

21

Isao left Sawa's room abruptly and, determined to probe the significance of his words, shut himself in his own room.

Just as hot pepper becomes less pungent as it numbs the inside of the mouth, so the shock of the words 'Don't go after Busuké Kurahara' was not that intense after a time. They did not necessarily imply that Sawa had penetrated Isao's secret. For Busuké Kurahara was in the eyes of many men the very personification of capitalistic evil.

If Sawa had perceived that Isao had some plan or other in mind he might well imagine that Kurahara's name would, as a matter of course, come up as one objective. And his advice not to single out Kurahara would not really depend upon his knowing that Isao had already done so.

There remained a single problem: Sawa's implication in linking his father's name to Kurahara. Was Kurahara actually an important financial backer of his father? A secret patron of the Academy of Patriotism? The thought seemed unbearable. But since this was a problem that Isao was unable to solve in his present circumstances, the truth or falsity of the allegation was a matter that would have to be set aside for a time. The irritation that burned greedily within him came more from this uncertainty than from anger.

Actually, Isao knew nothing of Kurahara other than what he had gained from studying photographs of him in newspapers and magazines and carefully reading about what he said and did. Kurahara was the unmistakable incarnation of a capitalism devoid of national allegiance. If one wished to portray the frightening image of a man who loved nothing, there was no better model than Kurahara. At any rate, in an era when everyone was choking, the fact that this man alone could evidently breathe with ease was in itself grounds enough for suspecting that he was a criminal.

One of his best-known comments, quoted by a newspaper, displayed a heedlessness that seemed carefully contrived: 'Naturally, having a large number of unemployed is unpleasant. However, to equate this immediately with an unsound economy is fallacious. Common sense tells us that the contrary is true. The welfare of Japan is not bound up with there being good cheer in everybody's kitchen.' Such words stirred anger and resentment and were never forgotten.

The evil of Kurahara was that of an intellect that had no ties with blood nor with native soil. In any case, though Isao knew nothing of Kurahara the man, Kurahara's evil was vividly clear to him.

There were the bureaucrats of the Foreign Ministry, anxious to please England and America, oozing charm, only able to play the coquette. The financiers, giving off the stink of profit and greed, sniffing along the ground for their dinner like giant anteaters. The politicians self-transformed into lumps of corruption. The military cliques, so armoured with the cult of careerism that they were like immobilized beetles. The scholars, bespectacled, sodden white grubs. The speculators eager to exploit Manchuria, their beloved bastard child. And the sky itself reflected a panorama of poverty, like sunrise colours spread wide over the land. Kurahara was a cold, black silk top hat placed in the midst of this piteous landscape. Without saying so, Kurahara looked forward to many deaths, he welcomed them.

The sorrowful sun, the sun glittering with a chill whiteness, could give no touch of warmth, yet rose up sadly every morning to begin its course. This was indeed the figure of His Majesty. Who would not long to look up again to behold the joyful countenance of the sun?

If this Kurahara...

Isao opened the window. He spat. If the food he had eaten at breakfast, if his lunch, too, had come through Kurahara's bounty, then, in his ignorance, he had already corrupted his innards and his flesh with poison.

Suppose he confronted his father and questioned him severely. But would his father tell him the truth? Rather than hear skilful evasions, he preferred to keep silent and pretend to know nothing.

If only he did know nothing, if only he could have gone on without learning of this, thought Isao, stamping his feet and cursing himself for having heard it. He also felt resentment toward Sawa for having sprinkled the poison into his ears. And however much Isao feigned ignorance, Sawa might sometime tell the father what he had revealed to the son. Then, too, he would become a son who knowingly betrays his own father. He would be a traitor who kills the benefactor of his family. The purity of his conduct would be subject to question. An act conceived as bold and pure seemed in danger of becoming most impure.

How was Isao to guard his purity? Do nothing at all? Remove Kurahara's name from the list of those to be assassinated? No. If he did that, would not the cost of his being an unhappy but dutiful son be to overlook something that threatened the entire nation? Would it not be the betrayal of His Sacred Majesty as well as the betrayal of his own sincerity?

When Isao reflected, he saw that his not knowing Kurahara well was a circumstance that augmented the justice of his action. The evil of Kurahara should be kept as distant and abstract as possible. Only when the murderer could put aside not only all thought of favours granted or personal enmity but even the most elementary human considerations of liking or disliking did his act have a foundation in justice. Thus Isao's distant awareness of the evil of Kurahara was quite enough.

Killing a hateful man was an easy matter. Cutting down a despicable person was a pleasure. But Isao had no desire to seize upon an enemy's lack of humanity in order to steel himself to the act of killing. The massive evil of Kurahara as fixed in Isao's mind had nothing to do with such petty and inconsequential evils as buying off the Academy of Patriotism as a safeguard against assassination. The young men of the League of the Divine Wind had not killed the Kumamoto garrison commander for any incidental human failings.

Isao groaned with pain. How easily such a beautiful act could be destroyed! The possibility of his carrying out this beautiful act had arbitrarily been torn from him. All because of a few words!

The sole possibility left to him, if he were to act, was to become evil himself. But Isao was committed to justice.

A wooden kendo stave was leaning against the wall in one corner of the room. He seized it and rushed out to the back yard. Sawa was nowhere to be seen. Advancing step by step over the bare, flat ground next to the well, Isao made one stroke after another with furious abandon. The scolding whine of the wooden sword cutting through the air chafed his ears. He tried to make his mind a blank. He raised the sword high above his head, then brought it down. Like a man who hastily gulps saké to make himself drunk, he wanted this burning, oppressive exertion to race through his body. Though his breath was a searing flame, now trapped, now released from his heaving chest, the sweat that should have covered him would not come. All was in vain. He thought of an old poem that a senior kendoist had taught him:

> To try to avoid thought
> Is of itself to think.
> Thus even 'Think not!'
> Is not to be thought.

And then another:

> Since rising and setting
> Are one to the unthinking moon,
> No mountain ridge
> Can vex its heart with shadow.

But these brought no relief. The lovely sky of early evening shone through the worm-eaten leaves of a chestnut tree. Sawa's laundry seemed to be growing lighter by degrees, as though whiteness were seeping through it.

Still carrying the stave, Isao went to Sawa's room a second time and knocked on the door.

'What is it?' asked Sawa, opening his door. 'Are you hungry? Tonight we could send out for something to eat. What do you say?'

Isao thrust his face abruptly against Sawa's.

'Was what you said before true?' he demanded. 'Is Kurahara somehow connected with the Academy?'

'Don't threaten me, bringing a bamboo sword like that with you! Anyway, come in.'

In the course of his energetic sword drill, Isao had come to the conclusion that no matter how passionate he might grow in cross-examining Sawa, he need have no fear that he would give away his true state of mind. For it was only natural that an innocent young man would become thoroughly indignant upon learning that Kurahara had aided the Academy.

Sawa was silent.

'Tell me the truth,' said Isao. He had placed the sword at his left side and sat down in a stiffly formal position.

'And if I tell the truth, what do you intend to do?'

'I don't intend to do anything.'

'Nothing, eh? Then this business needn't bother you.'

'It bothers me. You suppose it makes me happy to hear someone say that my own father is in league with the scum of the earth?'

'But if he isn't, are you going to give it to that fellow?'

'It's not a matter of giving it or not giving it to anybody,' answered Isao, attempting a touch of sophistry. 'What I want to do is to preserve the images I have of my father and of Kurahara. Of Kurahara as the perfect villain.'

'Will that make you perfect too?'

'Perfection is no concern of mine.'

'If it isn't, why do you let things bother you so?'

Isao was finding himself outmatched.

'Mr Sawa, only cowards beat around the bush. I want to get at the truth. I want to confront it as it is.'

'Why? Could the truth shake that strong faith of yours? Have you been following some kind of mirage all this time? If your dedication is so weak, then you're well rid of it. I just thought I'd put a little doubt into your world of faith. If that makes the whole thing start to shake, there's something missing in your dedication. Where is that indomitable conviction that a man should have? Do you really have it? If you do, speak up right here and now.'

Isao once more found himself at a loss for words.

Sawa no longer seemed to be the man who read nothing but *Kodan Club*. He was attacking Isao; he was twisting his arm to make him spew up the burning lump lodged in his throat. Isao felt the blood rush to his cheeks, but, with an effort, he suppressed his emotion as he replied: 'I'm going to stay here until Mr Sawa tells me the truth.'

'I see.' Sawa remained silent for a time, as the small room was darkening in the twilight. A stout, forty-year-old man, he sat cross-legged in a baggy-kneed pair of the headmaster's old flannel pants. His head drooped forward so that the flesh of his shoulders swelled beneath his khaki shirt as though he were wearing a quiver across his back. The keen aggressiveness seemed suddenly blunted. Isao could not tell whether he was pondering or drowsing.

Sawa stood up abruptly. He opened a drawer and searched through it. Then he returned to sit upright across from Isao once more, and placed on the floor before him a dagger in a plain wooden sheath. He drew it out. A pale, sharp-edged crevice split the darkness of the room.

'I said what I said because I wanted to talk you out of it. You're the heir of the Academy of Patriotism, and so your life's too important. The master loves you very much.

'But as for myself, it doesn't make any difference. I have a wife and children, but I'd have no regrets on that account. And: on their side too, they've already given me up. So I feel apologetic for going on living, when I could have died at any time. In my case I wouldn't have to involve the master, I could just hand in my withdrawal notice and be free to stab Kurahara. I could stab him, all on my own. Anyway, I know one thing: that fellow's the very source of the evil. Even if worst comes to worst, as long as he gets it, all those politicians and industrialists that are doing his dirty work will be choked off. No matter what, he's one man that has to die. This is the conclusion I came to a while ago. So, please, since someone is going to get the job of cutting him down, let it be me. Let it be this short sword that does it. Please turn this Kurahara over to me. And then, once he's dead at my hand, if Japan still doesn't improve, that's the time for you young men to gather together and do whatever you have to.

'But if you think you've got to kill Kurahara yourselves, then let me be one of your comrades. I know I can help you. I'm the only one who can do the killing without any harm to the Academy. Please take me. Look, I bow down and beg you. Please tell me your mind.'

Sawa's sobbing plea rang in Isao's ears as he watched him wipe his eyes with the sleeve of his khaki shirt. Isao had now lost all chance of further pressing Sawa about Kurahara and his father. Sawa's words and his whole manner seemed to imply the existence of a relationship between the two men, and yet, depending upon how one interpreted them, Kurahara may well have been no more than a means used by Sawa to set the stage for his fervent plea. In any case, the one who was now hard-pressed was Isao.

He had no idea what to do, but at least there was no longer any danger of his losing control of himself. Now Isao was the one who stood in judgement. While he gazed down at the rather thin hair on the top of the weeping Sawa's bowed head, he had time to make a carefully formulated decision.

In those few moments, profit and loss, benefit and harm, like the sharp-pointed pales of a bamboo palisade jabbing the sky, stood lashed together. Isao could make Sawa one of his comrades or he could refuse. He could open his mind to Sawa or he could shut him out and persist in the course he had set for himself. He could hold fast to beauty and purity or he could let them go.

Were he to make Sawa one of his comrades, he would open his mind to him. And in return he could ask him the truth about Kurahara. From that moment Isao's intended Restoration could hardly remain the unblemished ideal it had been, but Sawa's rash thrust towards action could be thereby checked, the consequent danger avoided, and Sawa's energies channelled into the blow that Isao intended to strike.

If he did not make Sawa one of his comrades, there would be no need to open his mind to him, and, as a consequence, no need for Sawa to divulge what could be an ugly truth. But if Sawa rushed headlong to assassinate Kurahara, other enemies would be put on their guard, and the Restoration itself might suffer a setback.

Isao came to a cruel decision. In order to guard the beauty, the purity, the justice of his own conduct, it was best to let Sawa cut down Kurahara, but without a word of approval. Never would he give the least indication that he was delegating this task to Sawa. For if he were to do this, Isao would be one who used impure means to guard his purity. Everything had to come about naturally. Perhaps, by the time he had reached this decision, Isao had unconsciously begun to hate Sawa.

He let the smile of an adult form upon his lips. He was now the leader.

'Mr Sawa, we've talked enough,' Isao said. 'I got excited a while ago over something trifling, and perhaps I gave you the wrong impression. You talk about my "comrades"! My friends and I have no plot in mind. We meet to study the history of the Meiji period, and there are some great talkers among us, that's all. Since we're young men, it's only natural, isn't it? You've misinterpreted all this, Mr Sawa. But now you'll really have to excuse me. A friend has invited me over to dinner tonight, and I have to be going. So please don't trouble yourself about getting anything to eat for me.' He dreaded the strain of having dinner alone with Sawa. Isao got to his feet, leaving the naked dagger gleaming upon the floor like a rivulet in the darkness. Sawa made no move to stop him.

Isao had decided to go to Izutsu's house. Suddenly he found himself concerned about whether or not Izutsu had been taking proper care of the lily that Makiko had given him. But what of his own lily?

So that it would not be thrown out in his absence, Isao had placed his lily in a slim vase which he then put into a bookcase with a glass door. At first he had changed the water every day, but recently, he was ashamed to recall, he had become careless and forgotten to do so. He opened the glass door of the bookcase, removed the books he had put in front of the vase, and peered in. The lily drooped in the darkness.

When he took it out to hold it under the light, he saw that the lily had been reduced to the mummy of a lily. Were he to touch his finger to the brownish petals even a little ungently, they would surely crumple to dust at once and drop from the stem, which still kept a slight tinge of green. It could no longer be called a lily, but the memory, the shadow of a lily. It was like an abandoned cocoon after the immortal, lustrous lily itself had gone its way. Nevertheless, there was a hint of fragrance which told that it had once been a living flower. The rays of the summer sun had once poured over it, and now, like a dying ember, it still held a faint warmth.

Isao gently touched his lips to the petals. If he were to feel their texture clearly, he would have gone too far. The lily would crumble. His touch had to be like that of the dawn upon a mountain ridge.

Isao's young lips had yet touched no other lips, and he brushed them delicately against the petals of this withered lily with all the exquisite sensitivity that they possessed.

'Here is the source of my purity, the warrant for my purity,' he told himself. 'I am certain that it is here. When the time comes for me to turn my sword against myself, lilies will surely rise from the morning dew and open their petals to the rising sun. Their scent will purify the stench of my blood. So be it! How can I have any more doubts?'

22

The Current Affairs Club met once a month at the Courthouse, and it was here that Honda learned something about the revolution in Siam of the previous June which brought a constitution to that country. Since the club had been formed at the suggestion of the Chief Justice, a sense of obligation ensured a large turnout at the beginning, but gradually more and more of its members, busy with their work, failed to make an appearance. At this meeting in the small auditorium an outside lecturer had been brought in, and his talk was followed by informal discussion.

Even though Honda had never communicated with the Princes Pattanadid and Kridsada after their return to their homeland, the memory of former friendship made him extremely interested in the lecture, for once, and he listened attentively to the speaker, the head of the foreign branch of a large corporation who had happened to find himself in Siam at the time of the revolt.

The revolution began and ended quietly on the bright morning of June twenty-fourth without the citizens of Bangkok being aware of it. Launches and sampans thronged the Mae Nam River as usual and the shouts of hagglers filled the market place. In the government buildings, affairs crept on at the usual torpid pace.

Only those citizens who went by the palace and noted how its appearance had altered during the night were aware that something was amiss. Tanks and machine guns commanded every approach, and soldiers with fixed bayonets halted any car that drew near. The lofty windows of the upper storeys of the palace bristled with machine-gun barrels glittering in the sunlight.

The King, Rama VII, was at the seaside resort of Pa-In together with the Queen. The country was an absolute monarchy, but the actual ruler was the regent, the King's uncle. The regent's residence had been attacked at dawn by a single armoured car, and the pyjama-clad Prince meekly allowed himself to be brought to the palace in it. One policeman was wounded in this incident, the only blood shed in the revolution.

Besides the Prince himself, the members of the royal family and the officials who constituted the main support of the monarchy were brought to the palace one after another, where they were gathered together to hear Colonel Pahon Ponpayuhasena, the leader of the coup d'état, explain the ideology of the new government. The National Party had seized power, and a temporary government had been set up.

This information was conveyed to the King himself, and after he had sent a wireless dispatch the following morning indicating that he favoured a constitutional monarchy, he returned to the capital by special train to be greeted by the cheers of the crowd.

On June twenty-sixth Rama VII issued a proclamation approving the new government, immediately after receiving in audience the two young leaders of the National Party, Luang Pradit, a civilian, and Pya Pahon Ponpayuhasena, a colonel who was the representative of the young officers. The King showed himself altogether disposed in favour of the constitutional draft they presented to him, and at six o'clock that evening he bestowed the royal seal upon it. Siam had become a constitutional monarchy in both name and reality.

Honda had been anxious to hear something of Prince Pattanadid and Prince Kridsada. But since the only blood shed was that of the wounded policeman, he felt sure that no harm had come to either of them.

Though they gave no outward sign of it, those who listened to this account, aware as they were of the deplorable state of Japan, could not help but make comparisons and wonder why attempts at political reform in their own country had to be abortive affairs such as the May Fifteenth Incident, marked by senseless bloodletting and never proceeding temperately to a successful conclusion.

Soon after this lecture, Honda was ordered to attend a judicial conference in Tokyo. It was not an especially demanding assignment, and indeed one of the Chief Justice's intentions in sending him was to bestow some reward for his long service. He was to leave on the evening of October twentieth, the night before the conference. The day after it, the twenty-second, was a Saturday, and there was no need for him to return to Osaka until Monday. His mother would no doubt be happy to have her long-absent son spend a weekend in Tokyo.

It was early in the morning when Honda stepped down upon the platform in Tokyo Station. Since there was not enough time for him to go to his mother's house to freshen up after his trip, he decided to take a hot bath at the Shoji Inn within the station as soon as he had paid his respects to the delegation that came to meet him. Perhaps it was the early hour, but the Tokyo atmosphere, which he had not breathed for so long, now seemed to have something unfamiliar about it.

The crush of people moving between the platforms of the station and the lobby was just as before. Women in oddly long skirts caught Honda's eye from time to time, but this was already being seen in Osaka. He could not put his finger upon the exact difference. But something like an unseen gas seemed to have enveloped everything without anyone having noticed. People's eyes were moist. They walked as though in a dream. It seemed as if everyone was waiting anxiously for some impending event. The underpaid white-collar workers with their briefcases, the men in formal Japanese dress, the women in Western clothes, the girls at the cigar stands, the shoe-shine boys, the station personnel in their uniform caps – the mood of all alike made them seem bound together in a secret communication. And what was this mood?

When society was waiting fearfully for some event to occur, when the time had become fully ripe and the circumstances such that nothing could possibly prevent its occurrence, did not an expression of this sort appear on every man's face?

It was something not yet to be seen in Osaka. Honda felt as though he were listening to the spasmodic laughter of a frightened, goose-fleshed Tokyo, a city confronted with a huge, bizarre phantom which as yet revealed but half its bulk. Honda could not suppress a shudder.

His work done, Honda spent most of Saturday relaxing at his mother's house, and that evening it suddenly occurred to him to telephone the Academy of Patriotism. It was Iinuma who answered. His voice rang with exaggerated nostalgia.

'What a surprise to find you here in Tokyo! I am honoured that you should take the trouble to call. And you've already shown me such hospitality at your home, even including that boy of mine – I was quite overwhelmed.'

'How is Isao?'

'He left Tokyo the day before yesterday. He's at a place called Yanagawa. Kaido Masugi is conducting a training camp there on the rites of purification. In fact, I myself must pay a visit to Yanagawa tomorrow, Sunday, to thank Master Kaido for taking care of my son. If Your Honour has sufficient leisure, what would you say to accompanying me? I'm sure that the trees in the mountains will be in full colour.'

Honda hesitated. His past tie with Iinuma was reason enough for a visit to his home, but he was afraid that if he, as a judge, were deliberately to attend a right-wing training camp, even if he refrained from taking part in the purification rites themselves, it might give rise to untoward rumours.

And then too, either the next night or early the morning after, he would have to catch a train for Osaka. Honda refused, but Iinuma grew insistent. Perhaps it seemed his only way to show hospitality. Finally Honda agreed to go along on condition that he remain incognito. Since Honda wanted to sleep late, at least during his stay in Tokyo, they arranged to meet at Shinjuku Station at eleven o'clock the next morning. Iinuma told him that it would take two hours by the Chuo Line to get to Shiozu and from there they would have to proceed on foot along the Katsura River for about two and a half miles.

Yanagawa was in the district of Minamitsuru in what was once Kai Province. In a section of it called Motozawa, the Katsura River formed a right angle and turned into rapids, and here it was that Kaido Masugi owned some six acres of rice land which projected out into the river like the apron of a stage. Facing the rice land was a drill hall which also served as a dormitory for a considerable number of students. And there was a shrine. To the west of the drill hall stood a hut at a point where a suspension bridge crossed the river, and from here steps led down to the place of purification. The students of his academy cultivated the rice fields.

Kaido Masugi's aversion to Buddhism was celebrated. Since he was an admirer of Atsutané, this was only to be expected, and it was his practice to make Atsutané's diatribes against Buddha and Buddhism his own and to deliver them unchanged to his students. He condemned Buddhism for denying life and, as a consequence, denying that one could die for the Emperor, for knowing nothing of the 'abundant life of the spirit' and, as a consequence, shutting itself off from the essential, life-giving source that was the object of true devotion. And as for Karma, that was a philosophy of evil that reduced everything to nihilism.

'Siddhartha was the name of the founder of Buddhism, a very foolish man who buried himself in the mountains and gave himself over to all manner of austerities, without succeeding in discovering a way to escape the Three Calamities, age, sickness, and death ... But he had the perverse inspiration to stay on in the mountains for many years longer, during which time he became adept at sorcery. And with this occult lore to bolster him, he became the so-called Buddha ... and he concocted the theory that Buddha is a being to whom all reverence is due. So this founder of Buddhism, by virtue of his blasphemous fallacy, opened to men a path to destruction and turned himself into a devil racked with the Three Torments . . . Even before the coming of Buddhism, the advent of the so-called Confucianism had already made men's hearts cunning and corrupt. And then with the extravagant fable of retribution that Buddhism brought with it, all traces of manliness were wiped away, and it was not long before high and low alike became enslaved to false doctrine. Moreover, as this belief grew more flourishing, men naturally drew away from that vital source that was theirs from olden times, the oracles of our ancestral gods, and they began to neglect the ancient rites. And even these rites became corrupted by Buddhist influences . . .'

Such were the Atsutané sermons that Master Kaido poured into the ears of his students with a never-flagging zeal, and so Iinuma instructed Honda during the journey not to let slip any casual remark that was at all favourable to Buddhism.

Kaido Masugi turned out to be a different sort of person from the imposing elder with the long white beard that Honda had pictured from the bits of information that had come his way. He was an amiable little old man with several teeth missing, but his eyes were the eyes of a lion, and the impression he made upon Honda was a strong one.

After Iinuma had introduced Honda as a government official who had shown him great kindness years before, Kaido's lion's eyes looked fixedly into Honda's eyes as he responded: 'You seem to be a man who has had dealings with all sorts of people. And yet your eyes are not clouded with the least impurity. That is a rare thing. I do not wonder at the respect that Iinuma here has for you. Yet you still seem young.' And then, the compliments out of the way, he immediately began to lash out at Buddha: 'I realize that we have only just met, but, really, that fellow Buddha was a fraud. I suspect he's the rascal that robbed the Japanese of their Yamato Spirit, and their manly courage. Doesn't Buddhism deny all spirit?'

Since Iinuma had hastily gone off to perform the ritual of purification, Honda found himself sitting alone with Kaido in the drill hall, left for the time being to bear the brunt of his sermon.

When he saw Iinuma reappear in white robe and white *hakama*, accompanied by Kaido's chief disciple, Honda felt a surge of relief.

'Your water is indeed fresh and pure,' Iinuma said. 'I have been cleansed in mind and body. I thank you. And now I wonder where I can find my son.'

Kaido ordered his chief disciple to call Isao. Honda's interest was aroused by the prospect of seeing Isao appear clad in the same type of white robe and *hakama* that his father wore.

But there was no sign of Isao. The disciple reappeared and knelt at the threshold.

'According to the students, Isao was very angry over your taking him to task a little while ago, and he borrowed a hunting gun at the gatekeeper's house and said he was going to shoot a dog or a cat to get it off his mind. It seems he headed out towards the mountains, probably to Tanzawa.'

'What? Shedding the blood of animals after being purified? Such infamy!'

Kaido stood up, his lion's eyes blazing. 'Assemble every man in that study group of Isao's. Tell them that each is to take an oblation branch in his hand and go out to confront Isao. He'll be as bad as Lord Susano himself, defiling our sacred precincts.'

Strength seemed to drain out of Iinuma as his consternation deepened, a plight that the bystander Honda had to view with some amusement.

'But what could my boy have done? Why was it that you had to scold him?'

'For nothing serious. Don't worry. But in that son of yours the harsh god is too strong. I reprimanded him because unless he works hard to be more receptive to the mild god, he'll stray from the right path. In your son it's the heedless and intractable spirit that's dominant. Since he's a boy, that's fine, but he goes much too far. When I admonished him, he hung his head dutifully and listened, but then, afterwards, it must have been the harsh god suddenly breaking loose.'

'I must take an oblation branch myself and go along to purify him.'

'That would be well. Go quickly then, before he defiles himself.'

Hearing all this, Honda at first felt somewhat cowed by the uncanny atmosphere, but suddenly his intelligence was affronted by the utter absurdity of it. These people around him took no thought of the flesh but were altogether absorbed in the spirit. Here was a quite ordinary incident of an independent young man becoming furious when reprimanded, but they viewed it as a manifestation of the dread power of the realm of spirits.

Now Honda regretted that his strange sense of rapport with Isao had made him come to such a place. But some unknown peril to Isao seemed to be taking form before him, and he felt that he should do whatever lay in his power to hold it back.

When they went outside, some twenty young men, each holding a sakaki branch hung with white paper pendants, stood gathered there with tense expressions. Iinuma raised his branch and started to walk. The entire group fell in behind him. Honda, who alone was wearing a suit, took his place immediately behind Iinuma.

At that moment Honda had a peculiar feeling. What he was doing seemed somehow linked to a distant memory despite its being not all likely that he had ever found himself in the midst of a white-clad group such as this. Yet he seemed to hear a metallic sound, as though a hoe were at work unearthing a memory of inestimable value and striking against the first rock that lay in its way. The sound echoed strongly within his head, but then it was gone like a phantom. The impression had held him but for an instant. What had caused it?

It was as though a length of beautiful, thick golden thread had arched its graceful way past the needle of Honda's perception, barely grazing it. It had touched the needle, but, just as it seemed about to pass through the eye, it had turned aside and was gone. As though fearful of being woven vigorously into the embroidery material, blank but for the faint pattern sketched upon it, the thread had slipped to one side of the needle's eye and passed it. The fingers that guided it were huge yet slender and extremely supple.

23

It was about three o'clock on a late October afternoon, an hour when the sun had already begun to conceal itself behind the surrounding mountains. The light from the cloud-streaked sky enveloped the wooded ridges like mist.

The procession led by Iinuma crossed the old suspension bridge in silence, three or four men at a time. As Honda looked down, he saw that to the north of the bridge the water was still and deep, but on the south side, where the place of purification was located, the river ran swift and shallow between gravelled shores. It was this rotting bridge that marked the division between the depths and the shallows.

After he had crossed, Honda turned and looked back at the young men solemnly marching behind him on the bridge, their oncoming footsteps sending shudders along its planks.

The young men, each holding up his sakaki branch, moved forward against a background formed of the oaks on the opposite side, the mulberry fields, the ravaged red leaves of the nurudé trees, the hut atop the bank, and one black-trunked persimmon from which a single red fruit hung with sensuous grace. Their figures shone in the few rays of the setting sun that just then broke through the clouds hovering over the mountain ridges. The sunlight threw into sharp relief the pleats of their *hakama*, and gave such brilliance to their white robes that each marcher seemed to be his own source of brightness. The leaves of the sakaki branch he carried gave off a dark green lustre, and the white pendants hung upon it were flecked with delicate shadows.

There was some delay before the entire group of almost twenty men had crossed. Honda gazed around him once more at the autumn mountain scenery that he had already had leisure to study on the two-and-a-half-mile walk from Shiozu to Yanagawa.

Since this was in the heart of the mountains, the varied dark and light colours of near and distant slopes were superimposed one upon the other and seemed to press in on the viewer. Every mountain had a generous share of cedars that stood out darkly with severe aloofness from the mild red warmth that surrounded them. Autumn was not yet advanced, and the seasonal colouring, though apparent, was like a mantle of shaggy yellowish wool mottled with rust red. A listless mood seemed to weigh upon the reds, yellows, greens, and browns, muting their brilliance. The smell of wood smoke and the mistlike sunlight enwrapped everything. The more distant slopes were sharply etched in pale blue beneath their shrouds of light mist. None of these mountains, however, offered a forbiddingly steep aspect.

When everyone had crossed the bridge, Iinuma set out in the lead again, Honda still behind him. The ground beneath their feet had been covered with fallen oak leaves on the other side of the bridge, but now, along this high, rocky road, it was the leaves of the cherry trees that predominated. From the bridge on, these lay like fallen red flowers. Some wet leaves, already decaying, had faded to a pink that was the colour of the dawn. Why should decay take the colour of the dawn?

Honda wondered, the pointless question nagging at him. A fire tower stood at the top of the cliff, its small bell silhouetted against a pale blue sky. Now it was the leaves of persimmon trees that covered the path. On either side there were cabbage fields and farmhouses. Reddish purple wild chrysanthemums were everywhere, and each yard had its persimmon trees, bare except for a remnant of fruit which hung from their branches like New Year's ornaments. The path wound this way and that, between the hedges of the farmhouses.

Just as they had passed one of these houses, a much wider view abruptly opened before them. The path too, at a point where a Buddhist requiem stone from the Kaei era stood overgrown with weeds, suddenly turned into a broad road amid the farmland.

To the south-west there was but one small mountain. Directly in front of the marchers, tall Mount Gozen, together with the other mountains that filled the northern horizon, rose up beyond the river and the road. So far in their journey, except for this village in the foothills of Gozen, there had been no sign of a human dwelling.

Clusters of red-flowered knotgrass bloomed along the straw-littered side of the road. The chirping of crickets could be heard faintly. Rice-drying racks lined many of the fields, and in others the new-cut sheaves were spread out upon the dark, cracked ground. A young boy, proud of his new bike, turned to gawk at the strange procession as he slowly pedalled by.

Autumn tints, like smudged powder, covered the small mountain to the south-west. Before them, the way lay open to the north as far as the bank of the Katsura. A lone cedar, torn by lightning, stood in a nearby field, its rent trunk bent back and its withered needles the colour of dried blood. Its roots were partially pulled up out of the ground, and bearded grass sprung out in all directions from them.

It was then that a figure dressed in white appeared ahead on the road, and one of the young men called out: 'There he is.'

Honda felt an unaccountable shiver run down his spine.

A half hour earlier, Isao, his eyes bloodshot, had ranged over this same area with a Murata rifle in his hand. He was not angry at Master Kaido's scolding. But in the course of it an intolerable idea had come to him. He found he could not help thinking that the crystal vessel of beauty and purity he sought had already fallen to the ground and lay in fragments, and that he was stubbornly refusing to acknowledge it. Was it not true, he wondered, that if he wanted to take action he now had no choice but somehow to make secret use of the thrust of evil and let its strength drive him forward? Just as his father had done? No, certainly not. This had nothing in common with his father's behaviour. For him there would be no diluting righteousness with evil and evil with righteousness. The evil that he wanted to store within himself had to be pure evil, no less pure than the righteousness within him. In any event, once he had attained his purpose he would turn his sword against himself. At that moment, he felt, the pure evil within him would also die in the clash with the pure righteousness of his act.

Isao had never felt like killing anyone out of personal hatred. How was the desire to kill stirred up, he wondered. And what connection did it have with the sober events of everyday life? It was a problem that had long troubled him. He would first have to perform a small act of pure evil, commit a minor sacrilege.

Master Kaido, as a devoted follower of Atsutané, had lectured on the defilement brought about by the flesh and blood of beasts. And so Isao had borrowed a rifle and set out, hoping to hunt down a deer or a boar in the autumn mountains or, if that proved too difficult, to shoot a dog or a cat and bring the bloodied carcass back to Yanagawa. If that meant that he and his followers would be expelled from the camp, he was prepared to accept it. Indeed it would no doubt instill in them a new kind of courage and resolution.

He walked towards the south-west, his eye fixed upon the small mountain wrapped in scarlet leaves. He could see that a mulberry field encroached upon the gentle western slope of the mountain, and that a narrow path led uphill between the field and a bamboo thicket. The cedars were dense above the mulberry field, but someone had told him that the path climbed on up through them.

The Murata rifle, about two and a quarter feet in length, was like an iron bar in his hand, and the autumn air chilled its metal so that it squealed beneath the touch of his fingers. It was hard to believe that the bullet already in the chamber had the power to give heat to the metal. And the three bullets he carried in his robe, their chill, metallic touch pressing against his chest as he walked, seemed not so much murderous pellets as three cold eyes focused upon him.

Since there was no dog or cat to be seen, Isao decided to follow the path between the bamboo thicket and the mulberry field up the mountain. The interior of the thicket was a tangle of red-berried creeper vines and ivy. A moss-grown heap of mulberry roots, dug up and piled beside the field, stood in his way. From somewhere close at hand, he heard the song of a green finch. Isao imagined the figure of an unwary stag lazily taking form before the muzzle of his rifle. He was sure that he would fire without hesitation. He would have the will to kill. The victim would be unaware of it. There was no need for hatred. And in dying the stag would for the first time expose the full force of evil. It would shine in the dark gleam of the blood pouring out from the heart of the beast.

Isao pricked up his ears. There was no sound of movement over the fallen leaves. He stared at the path ahead. There was nothing that looked like a deer's track. If something was holding its breath, it was, Isao felt, not in fear, not out of hostility, but in derision of his intent to kill. The teeming silence of the scarlet-leafed forest, of the bamboo thicket, of the rows of cedars – he felt it ridiculing him.

He climbed to where the cedars began. The very spaces between the trees were packed with a dark silence. There was no sign of life. He began to walk across the slope and found himself in a sparse, sunlit grove. Suddenly a pheasant burst into flight from under his feet. It was an explosive target that preempted his field of vision. This had to be the moment to 'let go', as the gatekeeper had instructed him. He raised the gun at once and fired.

The mingled yellows and reds of the leaves above his head were suffused with the glow of the setting sun. A heavy, flashing crown of green seemed to hang poised for an instant against a patch of melancholy evening sky. This hurled crown dissolved in a flapping of wings, its glory shattered. The violent beating seemed to churn the air into a thick, sticky liquid which immediately clung to the wings like birdlime and took its toll. The bird, all unaware, was suddenly no longer a bird. The struggle to keep its wings going caused it to veer off its intended course, and it plunged abruptly downward, disappearing among the trees. The spot was not far distant. Isao estimated that the bird had fallen into the thicket which he had passed earlier.

Intent upon that spot, he ignored the path as he rushed down out of the grove, holding the rifle under his arm, black smoke still seeping from its barrel. Thorns caught at the sleeves of his robe and tore them.

An underwater glow filled the bamboo thicket. He used the gun to thrust aside the vines that clutched at him. He stared intently at the ground, anxious lest the pheasant be lost amid the colours of the fallen bamboo leaves. At last he found it. Isao knelt down, and as he picked up the lifeless body of the bird, blood spurted from its breast and fell upon his white *hakama*.

The bird's eyes were tight shut. The plumage that surrounded the closed eyes had the scarlet speckles of a toadstool. It was a sombrely plump bird with a metallic sheen that seemed to turn soft feathers into armour, its colour a rainbow against a black sky. As its head hung down over his arm, he noticed that the plumage of its bent body was less thick and the lustre of a different sort.

The feathers about the head were a purple almost as deep as black grapes and they clustered as close as scales. From the breast to the belly, dark green feathers meshed as though to form a protective tunic that glinted in the fading light. It was down these dark green feathers that the blood was flowing from an unseen wound.

Judging the location of the wound, Isao inserted his finger. It encountered no resistance as he plunged it deep into the breast torn by the bullet, and when he drew it out, it was covered with a red wetness. How does it feel to slaughter? he asked himself, burning for an answer. The action, that instant of aiming the gun and pressing the trigger, had been a rapid flow of movement, with only the barest feeling of wanting to kill. That had amounted to even less than the wisp of black smoke that later trailed from the muzzle.

A bullet certainly substituted for an intent. He had not begun to climb the mountain with the thought of killing this pheasant, but the gun itself would not let such a dazzling opportunity pass. And so a small shedding of blood and a small death had instantly taken place, and there was this stilled pheasant lying across his arm, a matter in no way out of the ordinary.

As for righteousness and purity, these he coolly rejected like bones left upon a plate. His appetite was not for bones but for meat. He wanted this thing that was quick to decay, this thing that shone, this thing that was so soft. It was no more than a savour barely caught by the tongue. He had experienced this taste, and from it had come the almost numbing rapture that he now felt, and the repose of fulfilment. This was what engaged his senses.

Had the pheasant been transformed into the embodiment of evil? By no means. As Isao looked closer, he saw that tiny winged insects were moving in its feathers. And if it were left lying there, ants and maggots would certainly soon be swarming over it.

He was irritated at the bird's tight-shut eyes. Like an arbitrary refusal, they seemed to shut him out coldly from something that he was desperately eager to know. But this thing that he wanted to know – Isao found himself unable to tell whether it was, after all, the sensation of killing or that of his own death.

He picked the bird up roughly by the neck, and, using his gun to slash at the undergrowth, made his way with difficulty out of the thicket. He cut away one hanging vine laden with red berries which fell around his neck and draped itself, its fruit trembling, about his chest and shoulders. Since neither hand was free to dislodge it, Isao left it as it was.

He came down to the mulberry field and began to cross it on a path along one of its ridges. Lost in thought, he paid no attention to the profusion of red flowers that he was trampling underfoot.

Ahead stood a shattered cedar, its needles already half brown. At a right angle to this path, he had noted before, was the road he had come by, a broad road through open fields. He turned onto it.

Some distance ahead a white-clad group was approaching. Though he could not yet make out their faces, the pendant-hung branches that each carried gave him an odd feeling. White robes in such a place had to indicate Master Kaido's students, but Isao would not have expected his own comrades to come marching out solemnly in this manner led by another. The leader seemed older, and behind him walked one man dressed in a suit. Isao was startled when he saw at last that the man in the lead had the neat moustache of his father.

At that moment the sky above, still lit by the sunset glow, was suddenly filled with the cries of a vast flock of small birds that had appeared from the shelter of the mountain. The white-clad marchers seemed distracted by this, and halted briefly until the birds had passed over.

As the distance separating Isao and the group lessened, Honda somehow began to feel excluded from the tableau taking form in the fading light of the open fields. Gradually he veered off the road until he was separated from the column and threading his way through rice-drying racks. Some moment of extreme significance was drawing near. What it was he did not know. Isao's figure was now clearly discernible. Honda saw upon his chest something that looked like a necklace of red crescent beads, apparently a kind of berry.

Honda's heart throbbed violently. An irresistible power was approaching, a power that would deal a smashing blow to his rational outlook. He could already feel the rush of its wings and its breath as it came bearing down. He did not believe in premonitions, but if there were something that could come to warn a man of his own death or the death of one close to him, would it not, he wondered, be a sensation like this?

'So you only bagged a pheasant, eh? Well, that's not too bad.'

Iinuma's voice rang in his ears. Honda, standing there in the field, could not help looking towards them.

'That's not too bad,' said Iinuma again. And then, as though in jest, he raised his sakaki branch and waved it over Isao's head. Its paper pendants flashed a pure white in the dusk. Their rustling sound had a poignant freshness.

'What a way to behave! Even taking a gun with you! Master Kaido had you sized up all right: You are heedless and intractable. You have proved it beyond all question.'

The instant Honda heard these words the memory that lay within him was at last revealed with pitiless clarity. Beyond any doubt, what had been fulfilled before his very eyes was the dream that Kiyoaki Matsugae had dreamed one summer night in the second year of the Taisho era. Kiyoaki had recorded this extraordinary dream in great detail, and Honda, just the previous month, had re-read that section of the dream journal. It had been vividly realized in every particular before his very eyes, becoming part of reality after the passage of nineteen years.

That Isao was Kiyoaki reborn, even if Isao himself was unaware of it, was now, as far as Honda was concerned, something impervious to all the power that reason could bring to bear against it. It was a fact.

24

The next evening, after classes, Isao led his comrades to the place where they had their secret meetings every day. There no one would see them, or even if someone did, the circumstances would resemble nothing more than a group of boys getting together for some carefree exchange. At a spot where the farmland that belonged to Kaido's Academy faced the cliff of Motozawa stood a huge rock covered with vegetation, like the artificial mountain of a landscaped garden. Once behind it, one was hidden from the eyes of anyone looking from the direction of the lecture hall. Right below were the rapids, and on the opposite side rose the towering cliff wall. The small grassy spot behind the rock was ideally suited for sitting in a circle and holding a discussion. In summer it would have been quite pleasant, but in Kai in late October the evening wind was extremely chilly. But so enthusiastic were the boys who gathered here that the cold did not trouble them.

As Isao led them along the path that crossed the fields, he noticed the charred traces of a fire which had not been there the previous day. The fine ash of burnt straw had traced a grey pattern upon the path, but where it had gathered in a rut it was a dense black. This black mingled with the red of the loam in a way that captivated Isao. Oddly, it was not the mixture of grey ash and a few remnants of fresh straw that stirred thoughts of the bright fire at its peak, but the black rut crushed into the earth by a wheel. The strong, barbaric red of the flames, the vulgarly strong black of the rut – here was the perfect expression, the perfect contrast. To flame up, then to be trampled out – both had the same vivid power. The near association that all this provoked in Isao's mind, obviously enough, was the spectre of revolt.

The group followed Isao in silence to the huge rock with its sheltering trees at the south end of the fields and sat down in a circle. They could hear the rushing water of the rapids below them, where the Katsura River made its sharp bend. The grey rock surface of the cliff that soared up on the opposite bank seemed to embody a stern and enduring fortitude. The red leaves that hung from the trees clinging to the face of the cliff, the first trees to be lost to the sun, had a gloomy tinge, while far up, through the trees that lined the top of the cliff, the evening sky could be seen in a turmoil of bright-flecked clouds.

'Today the time has come to decide when we will strike. We're all resolved, aren't we? But first we'll confirm the general plan and each man's responsibility, and Sagara will report on our funds. As for the exact time we strike, it would certainly be fitting if we could decide it by an Ukei, like the comrades of the League. Anyway, let's take it up later.' Isao's tone was businesslike as he opened the meeting. However, the trifling affair of the day before still affected him. His father and Honda had had a light supper and returned to Tokyo immediately. But even though it was supposed to be a courtesy to Master Kaido, what had prompted his father to make such a long trip to see how things were here? Could it be that he had had a talk with Sawa? And then what of the odd behaviour of Honda? There had been no sign yesterday of the detached and well-modulated kindness so evident in the first conversation and in the long letter, but, rather, Honda had said hardly a word to Isao, and his complexion had been very pale. Then later, in the course of supper, Isao had noticed that Honda kept staring at him from where he sat in the place of honour.

Isao wrenched away this dark lever that had forced his thoughts back to the past, and he spread the written plan out on the grass before him:

1. The month, date, and hour:
2. A summary of the plan:

Our objective is to throw the capital into disorder, bring about a state of martial law and thereby promote the establishment of a Restoration government. We are fully resolved to sacrifice ourselves for such a Restoration, hoping to achieve the maximum result with the minimum number of men. We believe that others who share our ideals will rise in response throughout the country. We will have copies of our declaration scattered from an aeroplane, contending that an imperial command has been issued to Prince Toin, and we will see to it that in short order this will in fact be the case. With the proclamation of martial law, our mission will be accomplished, and no later than the following dawn, whether we have succeeded or failed, we will commit seppuku honourably together.

The purpose of the Meiji Restoration was to return the governing power and the control of the military functions to His Imperial Majesty. The purpose of our Showa Restoration is to place finance and industry under the direct control of His Imperial Majesty, to uproot capitalism and communism, those doctrines of Western materialism, and thus deliver our people from their misery, and here beneath the bright light of the sun to seek the direct rule of the Emperor that will glorify the Imperial Way.

As for throwing the capital into disorder, we will first blow up every transformer substation throughout the city and in the dead of night we will assassinate the ringleaders of industrial capitalism: Busuké Kurahara, Toru Shinkawa, and Juemon Nagasaki. At the same time, we will occupy the Bank of Japan, the kingpin of the Japanese economy, and set it afire. We will then gather by sunrise at the latest before the Imperial Palace and put an end to ourselves by committing seppuku as one. Should we be unable to meet, there is nothing to prevent our turning our swords against ourselves in whatever place each man happens to find himself.

3. Table of Organization:

A. First Unit (The attacks upon the Tokyo Electric transformer substations)

Kamedo Substation:	Hasegawa
	Sagara
Kinuden Substation:	Seyama
	Tsujimura
Hatogaya Substation:	Yoneda
	Sakakibara
Tabata Substation:	Horié
	Mori
Mejiro Substation:	Ohashi
	Serikawa
Yodobashi Substation:	Takahashi
	Ui

B. Second Unit (The assassinations)

Toru Shinkawa:	Iinuma
	Miyaké
Juemon Nagasaki:	Miyahara
	Kimura
Busuké Kurahara:	Izutsu
	Fujita

C. Third Unit (The occupation and burning of the Bank of Japan)

The action will be carried out by fourteen men under the command of First Lieutenant of Infantry Hori, with two men, Takasé and Inoué, joining the twelve men who will assemble rapidly by bicycle immediately after the destruction of the transformer stations.

D. Special Assignment

An aeroplane piloted by First Lieutenant Shiga will drop flares and scatter leaflets.

The truth of the matter was that Isao was still disturbed about the assignment to kill Kurahara. It was a task that he really wanted to reserve for himself, but something prevented him from doing so. Sawa's words had somehow struck home.

Isao felt that even now as they were talking, Sawa might take it into his head to go out and kill Kurahara on his own initiative. If he did, they would have no choice but to delay their full-scale plan until the public outcry had died down. Then again, perhaps Sawa had been merely bluffing, trying to force Isao's assent, and would actually do nothing at all.

If Isao were to kill Kurahara, disregarding all that Sawa had said, he would be fulfilling the role he had always seen for himself. Obviously Kurahara would be the man most closely guarded. Isao had used the pretext of friendship in yielding Kurahara to Izutsu, that cheerful and credulous young man of extravagant bravery. Izutsu had been overwhelmed with gratitude, but Isao, deep within him, felt that for the first time in his life he had flinched from something.

As for using the aeroplane, it had been Lieutenant Hori's counsel that caused the substitution of flares and leaflets for bombs. Hori, however, had guaranteed that his staunch friend Lieutenant Shiga would participate.

Weapons were a problem. Of the twenty young men, ten of them had access to a Japanese sword, but, in the assaults upon the transformer stations, a sword might perhaps prove a hindrance. If they carried concealed daggers, that would suffice. As for the various explosives to be used, their aim was to obtain some of the most recently developed kind.

'Sagara. Read us the list of the items we need.'

'All right,' said Sagara, and he began to read in a low voice, as if fearful of being overheard:

'1. A large piece of bleached cotton: one length of about sixteen feet to be used for a banner proclaiming our ideals, to be set up at the place where we commit suicide. The rest of the material to provide a belly band for each man.

2. Headbands, armbands, pins for armbands, and rubbersoled footwear to equip twenty men.

3. Paper: one ream of white, two or three of varicoloured, a large enough supply for printing the leaflets.

4. Benzine: for incendiary use. One or two cans each to be purchased from three or four dealers by different men.

5. One mimeograph machine and accessories.

6. Writing brushes, ink, etc.

7. Bandages, styptic drugs, strong liquor to be used as a restorative.

8. Canteens.

9. Flashlights.

'That's about all. We'll buy everything individually and then assemble it in a good hiding place somewhere. Once we're back in Tokyo we'll get busy finding a place.'

'Do we have enough money set aside?'

'Yes. Iinuma has saved eighty-five yen in all, and putting this with the savings of the rest of us, we have a total of three hundred and twenty-five yen. And then, just before we came up here, I received a letter to the "Meiji History Study Club" with no return address. I brought it along so that I could open it in front of everybody. It might be money. I feel a little uneasy about it.'

Sagara opened the envelope to find ten one-hundred yen bills. A shock ran through the group. Sagara read aloud the single sheet of stationery with two or three lines upon it: 'I had some forest land at home sold off, and that's where this money came from. It's clean. Please use it as you like. Sawa.'

'Sawa?' Isao felt his heart thump when he heard the name. Sawa was again behaving in incomprehensible fashion. Even if Isao were to believe that the money was indeed 'clean', Sawa's purpose in giving it eluded him. Did he intend this gift as a substitute for his offer to assassinate Kurahara? Or did he mean this vast sum of one thousand yen as an apologetic farewell contribution before acting alone?

But Isao had to give an immediate answer. 'It's from Mr Sawa at the school,' he said. 'He's secretly one of us. So it's all right to take it.'

'Well, what a windfall! There's no need to worry about finances now. The

Divine Assistance is with us.' Sagara gleefully raised the money up to the level of his glasses as though offering thanks to the gods.

'Now we have to get down to details. First, let's settle the time of day and the date. Naturally, the time is critical to our plan. If it's too late at night, the effects of the power stoppage will be insignificant. So ten p.m. would be the limit, I think. And, within an hour after that, the attack on the bank. Now for the date...' As he spoke, Isao saw in his mind's eye the vague image of Tomo Otaguro in the shrine at Shingai, prostrate before the gods as he awaited their will.

The priest had offered two Ukei formulations in the midday summer heat of the sanctuary:

To bring an end to misgovernment by admonishing authority even to the forfeiture of life.

To cut down the unworthy ministers by striking in darkness with the sword.

The gods had favoured neither, however. Now it was their latter wish that Isao and his comrades were presenting to the gods.

Summer and fall, Kumamoto and Kai, the Meiji era and the Showa era – such were the differences. But the swords of these young men were thirsty for blood, and they indeed wanted to strike in the darkness of night.

The story told in that small pamphlet had at some point or other burst through the dam of literary convention and poured out upon the present. Reading that story had ignited a flame in the hearts of these young men, and now they could not be content until the fire within them had set off a conflagration.

As the white swan soars to heaven,
Leave no traces here below.

The poem of Master Oen suddenly came to Isao's mind, as freshly and vividly as if it had been composed only the day before.

No one ventured an opinion. The boys sat in silence, earnestly studying Isao's expression. He himself had raised his eyes to the sky above the cliff on the other side of the river. The brightness that edged the cloud fragments was now somewhat more subdued. But the streaked pattern, as though a fine-toothed comb had been at work, still held firm. Isao felt that the eyes of the gods might glance down through this.

Evening darkness had already claimed the cliff's rock face. Only the white water of the rapids below stood out in the gloom. He himself had become a character in a romance. Perhaps he and his comrades were on the verge of a glory that would long be remembered. True or not, the cold evening wind conveyed the chill of a bronze memorial tablet. The moment seemed suited to a manifestation of the gods...

No revelation came. Nothing at all about a date or a time. Nothing came down out of the lofty brilliance of the cloud-streaked evening sky to seize hold of him. No immediate communication of wordless feeling. It was as though a koto's strings had snapped and not a single note could be plucked from them.

But even so, the gods had not expressed their disapproval as clearly as they had to Tomo Otaguro. They had not made their rejection obvious.

Isao struggled with the implications. Now at this moment a group of young men, all of them under twenty and vibrant with youth, had their eyes fixed upon him, their eyes sparkling with fervour, while he himself kept gazing up at the divine brightness above the towering rock wall. Matters had moved relentlessly to this point, and never would the moment be more apt. Some sort of revelation had to take place. Yet the gods had neither consented nor denied. They had abandoned the decision, like a sandal casually let slip there in the brightness of the heavens, as if imitating the uncertainty and imperfection of this world.

Isao had to answer immediately. Something in his heart closed up for a moment, just as a clam closes its shell, for a time covering over its 'pure' flesh which should always be open to the cleansing waters. A tiny evil concept had scampered like a sea louse across one corner of his heart. Though the memory of closing up in defence may be vague, once done it would no doubt take on the force of custom. After two or three times, it must seem as common as eating and drinking.

Isao did not think of himself as lying. If something was not designated by the gods as either true or false, then it would be highly presumptuous for a human being rashly to think of it as a lie. Isao's case was no different from that of a bird that had to give nourishment to its young. They had to be fed, and had to be fed at once.

'It's December third, ten o'clock at night. That seems to be the will of the gods. Let's make it definite. There's over a month remaining, so I think we'll have plenty of time to prepare. And now, Sagara, you're forgetting something important. Our struggle will be pure and without blemish, like a white lily. And so in order that men in years to come can speak of the "War of the Lilies", I want each of you, when you go into battle, to make certain that you carry in your breast pocket a petal from one of the Saigusa Festival lilies that General Kito's daughter distributed to us. The protection of the harsh god of the Sai Shrine will surely be with us. Now, as to the date being December third, a Friday, is there anyone who objects? If so, speak up. Maybe it's inconvenient for someone.'

'If we're all going to die,' one boy responded in a loud voice, 'how could it be inconvenient?' Everyone laughed.

'All right then, let's go on to the reports on individual projects. Ohashi, Serikawa, let's hear the report on your investigation of the Mejiro station and your plan for bombing it.'

At Isao's order, Ohashi and Serikawa tried to defer to each other, but finally the articulate Ohashi began the account. Whenever Serikawa spoke to Isao he squared his shoulders and was as tense as a raw recruit, but because his strong feelings choked the flow of his words, the others had difficulty understanding him. Still, his reliability in performance was peerless. Never had he failed to carry out to the letter any order. When he spoke passionately of something, his voice sounded as if he were weeping. Presenting clearly detailed reports was not his forte, and so the task fell to the clever and articulate Ohashi, with Serikawa standing beside him and nodding vigorously at every significant point.

'When we arrived at the Mejiro transformer station, there was a man dressed in overalls at the entrance. He was repairing some copper wire. Now when Serikawa and I went to other stations and told them we were night school students in an electrical school and asked to inspect the station, someone always wanted to see our identity cards or made some other objection, and we were quickly sent on our way. But this man in overalls was surprisingly friendly, and had us come up to the second floor. When we climbed the stairs, there were three clerks working in an office, and one of them told the man in overalls to show us around. So this fellow got out of his regular work, and cheerfully showed us all over the place. He seemed to take great pride in it. Whenever we asked about the equipment or anything, he gave us a full explanation. And so we found out that that station had both a water-cooled and an oil-cooled transformer.

'In general, the most critical parts of a transformer station are the transformer, the switchboard, and the water pump for cooling. Just to destroy the water pump, all you'd have to do would be to smash the pump motor switch with a hammer or something, and then toss in a hand-grenade. But that wouldn't be too effective. Of course if you destroy the water pump it'll stop the flow of water to cool the transformer, the equipment will overheat, and it'll become useless. But that would take a certain amount of time – in the first place, the other oil-cooled transformer would go on working.

'However, from the standpoint of ease of attack, since the pump is outside the main building and there's no one guarding it, it would be the simplest. For a really crippling attack, the best thing would be to have one man kill the guard and go into the building itself. Then the other man would set the explosives by the switchboard, and once the fuse was lit, they could withdraw. But if some unforeseen obstacle should arise, all you could do would be to destroy the pump.

'Now as for those men who are going to investigate other stations, we think that the best way for you to get inside would be to see if you know somebody who is a student in an electrical school and borrow his identity card. And that's all we have to tell you.'

Isao was pleased with the clarity and succinctness of their report.

'Good. Next, Takasé. Give us your report on getting a plan of the interior of the Bank of Japan.'

'All right,' answered Takasé, whose partner, Inoué, was absent. His voice was hoarse from his lung affliction, but his shoulders were powerful, and his reddened, feverish eyes were fixed piercingly on Isao. 'To tell the truth, I puzzled over this for quite a while and couldn't come up with a good plan. Then I decided that the only way would be to get taken on as a night security guard, but before they'll hire you, the bank has you investigated thoroughly and you have to pass a very demanding physical examination. Since I had no hope of passing the physical, I approached Inoué on it. He's second degree in judo, you know. And so Inoué, ready to lay down his life at any time, set about it without the least fear or hesitation. He went to see the dean of student activities and told him that he wanted to work as a night security guard in order to help with his tuition, and the dean wrote a recommendation for him. With this and his certificate of the second degree in judo, he went to the bank and was hired with no difficulty. When he goes to work, he takes along some harmless books and pretends to be studying them. I went to see him once; the other guards seem to have a very good opinion of him. He told me that at their night supper they sometimes treat him to a bowl of noodles. And though Inoué is the man he is, he said he couldn't help feeling a little guilty to think that the time was coming when he was going to burn all this down.'

The sound of youthful laughter rose in the dark.

'Until the day we go into action, Inoué will continue to work as a security guard at the bank, keeping up an innocent appearance. And since we'll have assistance from the inside, Lieutenant Hori and the rest of us should work out some kind of signal so that Inoué will know when to open the door. As for the plan of the interior, Inoué and I will take the responsibility of having that drawn up by two weeks before the day itself, and we intend to show it to Lieutenant Hori. Inoué says that, instead of letting himself seem suspicious by investigating the layout of the bank too hastily, he makes a point of learning all about it in a natural way while being diligent in his work. He's certainly a grim sort of fellow. But his eyes are narrow and he looks very amiable when he laughs, so people take to him easily.' Takasé glanced at his watch. 'Oh, it's about time for the tellers and clerks to go home, and Inoué will be starting his shift. He was really sorry he couldn't come up here, but the work he's doing now is absolutely vital. That's the end of my report.'

While other such reports were being delivered in rather meandering fashion, Isao, who had heard them all before, was able to let his thoughts wander. But as he did, names that he would prefer to avoid thinking about – his father, Sawa, Honda, Kurahara – rose up at once in his mind to harass him like a cluster of swirling moths. Isao took forcible hold of the tiller and turned the vessel of his mind towards more desirable thoughts, thoughts that flashed, thoughts that provoked rapture: at the top of a cliff at sunrise, while paying reverence to the sun ... while looking down upon the sparkling sea, at the base of a tall, noble pine ... to kill myself. Yet, after the uprising, it would be difficult to get from Tokyo to an ideal seaside cliff. If the attacks on the transformer stations were successful, all transportation would be disrupted, even escape by train might be out of the question. There seemed little hope that an adroit withdrawal from the assassination locales followed by a flight of some distance would indeed be possible.

Nevertheless, Isao would not give up his dream: somewhere a place awaited him where all the elements that belonged to an unblemished enactment of seppuku came together. The vision he clung to, of course, was the scene atop Omigataké when the six comrades of the League of the Divine Wind turned their swords against themselves. The vision of dying on a mountain peak, as the sky gradually lightens to reveal trailing clouds and white pendants fluttering in the morning breeze.

Isao had no desire to decide now upon a place for himself. To make a choice beforehand that the events following the rising might frustrate would be pointless. He would leave himself free. He would let himself be guided by the Divine Will, whose signs would ever be at hand. Surely somewhere the wind would blow through the pines at daybreak, somewhere, when he loosened his kimono, the keen winter air of the seashore would set his flesh tingling, somewhere the blood that stained his corpse and the trunk of the red pine beside which it lay would soon gleam brightly in the rising sun.

Suppose he succeeded in fleeing to the plaza before the Imperial Palace ... An awesome thought took form in Isao's mind. He might even swim the palace moat, shattering the film of ice that covered it, and climb the steep bank on the other side. There, hidden among the pines atop the bank, he could wait for morning to come. Perhaps he could look out beyond the vast array of ships at anchor off

Tsukishima to see the dawn breaking over the bay, and then, just before the Marunouchi skyline opposite him stood out in the first rays of the sun, he could thrust his blade home!

25

Honda was not unaware of the gossip that he was somehow a changed man after his return from Tokyo. For him the once so imposing façade of present reality had fallen away. And his profession, involving as it did the minute analysis of the stuff of present reality, seemed suddenly to have lost all its savour.

Honda was frequently sunk in thought and failed to answer remarks made to him by his colleagues. When word of this reached the ears of the Chief Justice, he became concerned that the strain of overwork might have clouded his subordinate's peerless clarity of mind.

Though he dutifully considered the work spread before him on his desk in the judges' chambers, Honda, more often than not, would shudder as his thoughts returned still once more to the scene that evening in Yanagawa, the moment when Kiyoaki's dream of so many years before was realized in every detail. And he also recalled what had happened the following morning, shortly before he took the train back to Osaka, when he yielded to a strange impulse to go to Aoyama Cemetery to visit Kiyoaki's grave.

His mother seemed startled as he hurried out the door that morning earlier than necessary to catch his train. But Honda had the driver take him to Aoyama first. The car went up a road through the huge cemetery to the circular drive that lay in its very centre. After getting out of the car here and telling the driver to wait, he walked quickly along the road toward the Matsugae family plot. Even if he had forgotten the way, the great torii that marked the Matsugae plot would have been visible.

Honda walked along the road for only a short distance before turning off on a path that wound among the graves, the morning light at his back. When he turned to look over his shoulder he saw the late autumn sun shining but weakly through a thin screen of pines. The rays that filtered through the dark evergreen branches and fell among the pointed stone shafts seemed to subdue rather than heighten the lustre of the new marble gravestones.

Honda followed the path. In order to reach the Matsugae plot, whose torii seemed already to be looming up over him, he had to turn right on a still narrower path covered with moss and fallen leaves. The massive white marble torii of the Matsugaes towered over the small gravestones as if they were courtiers gathered in attendance. It had been modelled after the 'Omiya-sama' torii on the grounds of the Matsugae estate. This example of Meiji grandeur now struck Honda's eye as somewhat tasteless.

The first thing that caught his attention after he passed beneath the torii was a memorial stone, an enormous slab of rock which seemed about fifteen feet high. The seal-style characters of the title of the epitaph had been drawn by Prince Sanjo and engraved by a famous Chinese artist, who, besides carving the details of Kiyoaki's grandfather's life, praised himself with the words:

> Gazing up at this monument,
> A myriad generations will be struck with awe.

In the shadow of the memorial stone were the graves of all the Matsugaes, each one with its own epitaph, but so overpowering was the enormous stone that one hardly noticed them. To the right of this stone, on a level reached by climbing a few steps, was a section set off by a marble fence, and here, side by side, were the graves of Kiyoaki and his grandfather. Since the place was familiar to Honda, he hardly glanced at the memorial slab as he at once turned to his right and climbed the stone steps.

Though the two graves were side by side, they obviously had a different rank. His grandfather's huge gravestone rose up in the very centre of the fenced area, and four Nishinoya stone lanterns kept solemn watch at either side of the path approaching it. To the right stood Kiyoaki's more modest gravestone, an evident intrusion upon the symmetry of his grandfather's domain. Kiyoaki's seemed small beside the mass of stonework that was his grandfather's, though it rose to the respectable height of six feet from its foundation. But the stone itself, the water urn, the flower vase with the family crest – everything was in exactly the same design as his grandfather's, cut from the same kind of stone, only the scale altered. Chiselled gracefully upon the darkened marble in the ancient square-cut characters was: KIYOAKI MATSUGAE. There were no flowers in the vase, but there were some glossy sprigs of Chinese anise.

Honda stood before the grave for a few moments before offering a prayer. He could conceive of nothing less fitting than that a young man who had given his life so wholeheartedly to emotion should now rest beneath this mound of stone. The Kiyoaki of Honda's memories certainly had the hint of death about him. But even that aura of death was like a transparent flame, as if in him death itself was brilliant and volatile. This cold stone had nothing at all to say of Kiyoaki.

Honda looked away, letting his gaze wander over the stretch of cemetery beyond the grave of Kiyoaki's grandfather. Among the wintry trees the circular drive where his car stood was white beneath the morning sun. And in the midst of dark-hued evergreens there were the gravestones of other families, facing away from him, that seemed to be heaped up to overflowing on either side with floral offerings of yellow and purple chrysanthemums.

Oddly enough, Honda felt a protest stirring within him. Rather than press his palms together, he wanted to summon Kiyoaki rudely and then take him by the shoulders and shake him. In his frustration Honda let his eyes stray to the marble fence that marked off the grave site with such precision, and there, atop a railing, he caught sight of a very small tendril of red-tinged ivy. When he walked over for a closer look, he saw how it had worked its way stealthily up the polished marble, clinging firmly to the surface so as not to slip, and had at length climbed to the top of the railing, whence it now was reaching out toward Kiyoaki's gravestone.

Yellow veins were delicately sketched upon the spread-open red leaves, which were like fine candies, their tips dyed a deep scarlet. At the sight of this, Honda's heart at last became somewhat more tranquil, and he turned back once more to Kiyoaki's grave. He bowed his head deeply. He pressed his palms together. He shut his eyes. No sound came to disturb him.

All at once, an intuition struck him with unmistakable force. Honda shuddered. No one, the intuition told him, was within this grave.

26

Isao had not yet shown Lieutenant Hori either the summary of the plan for the rising or the draft of the declaration to be dropped from an aeroplane. The Lieutenant was fully taken up with the fall manoeuvres, and he had not acceded to Isao's request for a meeting. More than a month remained before the appointed day. Once into November, the Lieutenant was supposed to spend all his spare time in directing their efforts.

After he had returned home, Isao had been warmly welcomed as usual by his mother, and by Sawa and the other students. Sawa, perhaps because there was no chance to talk with Isao alone, had not once referred to the problem that he had recently discussed with such heat. And so Isao had not yet found an opportunity to thank him for the money.

The evening of his return, his father had gone out to attend some meeting, and, since the Academy students had told Isao that they would like to hear about the training camp at Yanagawa, he decided that he would eat with them in the dining hall that night. His mother took special pains to prepare a fine meal for them.

'With just you and the boys there, you'll be able to talk a lot more freely,' said his mother, handing him a colourful porcelain platter of sashimi as he stood in the hallway. The house custom forbade boys in the kitchen. 'So please take this in for me.' Slices of halfbeak, sea bream, mackerel, flounder, and yellowtail lay beautifully arranged upon the platter, the kind of treat that hardly ever brightened a schoolboy's diet. He felt suspicious of this unlooked-for generosity. As for Miné herself, she was struck by the icy look on her son's handsome face as he reluctantly took the platter. In the darkness of the corridor his features seemed set and unresponsive.

'Why are you being so extravagant?' he asked her.

'It's just a little celebration on your coming home.'

'But I was only gone a week, to the next prefecture. What would you do if I had been overseas?'

Isao could not keep his mind free of Kurahara and his money. Nothing made him so miserable in his own home as being under the constant menace of that name. The name was like a toxin that lay heavy in the atmosphere of the Academy of Patriotism, in the water, in every particle of food.

'Here I go to great lengths to give you a nice dinner, and you're not the least bit happy about it!'

Isao looked full into the eyes of his grumbling mother whose pupils were wavering uneasily like the bubble in a spirit level. As he did so, her expression went blank, and she suddenly shifted her gaze away from him.

Perhaps, Isao thought, this treat was no more than one of his mother's whims. But his underlying anxiety was such, he realized, that his mood could be nothing but suspicious. Anything out of the ordinary in the household, whether good or bad, was enough to make him uneasy. The least alteration pained him.

'Master Kaido scolded you, didn't he?' she said, her tone jocular and even coquettish. 'I heard all about it from your father.' As she spoke, it seemed to Isao that droplets of her saliva sprayed over the limpid slices of halfbeak sashimi, and he felt a twinge of revulsion. The thought of his mother's saliva falling like a sudden shower upon the fresh sashimi and green seaweed garnish almost distracted him from the other uncleanliness that was troubling him.

'It was nothing of importance.'

Isao's answer, given without the trace of a smile, was hardly satisfactory to her.

'Why must you be like this? You talk to me as if I'm a stranger, no matter how much I worry about you.'

With a sudden movement, Miné picked up a slice of sashimi from the platter and thrust it into Isao's mouth. He was holding the platter, and could not block the rapid thrust of her hand. Probably opening his mouth to take it was an automatic reaction to the urgency of her gesture. His eyes watering from this forced feeding, he watched as she turned hastily as though to hide her tears and went back into the kitchen. Being thus treated like a son going off to war stirred his resentment.

His mother's sorrow lay in his mouth like a foreign body. He was annoyed at the way the sashimi clung to his teeth.

What was going on? Everything had been knocked from its proper course. Still, it was hard to believe that his mother's intuition had discerned in his eyes the determination to die.

When he walked into the dining hall carrying the platter of sashimi, the students greeted Isao with loud cheers. The usual faces around the table suddenly seemed quite alien to him. He was the only one there who was set upon action. But this crew went on as before, doing nothing but composing their poems about loyal devotion, about noble resolves, about Restoration, about seething passions. And Sawa's face, too, had its place among them, Sawa who was smiling like an indolent Zen monk. Sawa had taken no action even up to now, and it seemed clear that the decision not to admit him to their group had been a wise one.

Isao felt keenly that he must develop the knack of masking his feelings in dealing with others. He had now become a man quite out of the ordinary. Even if nothing in his bearing showed this, the least carelessness might let people get wind of it. They might detect that within him was the odour of a burning fuse.

'We hear that Master Kaido severely chastises his favourite students, the ones he loves the most, and that you had the experience yourself,' said one of the students, making it plain to Isao that they all knew about the incident.

'What did you do with that pheasant?'

'We all ate it for dinner.'

'I'll bet it tasted good. But, Isao, we had no idea you were such a good shot.'

'Oh, I didn't do the shooting,' Isao answered cheerfully. 'Just as Master Kaido said, it was the "harsh god" in me that shot, and so there was no question of missing.'

'One of these days I hope some pretty young thing will bring out the "mild god" in Isao.'

Everyone went on eating and talking, except for Sawa. His smile persisted, and he said not a word. During the cheerful exchanges, Isao found himself unable to keep his eyes from straying in this man's direction. Then, suddenly, Sawa broke in to check the flow of chatter.

'I would like to recite a poem in celebration of Isao's having completed his training camp and become an even stronger man,' he said.

As he chanted the poem, Sawa's voice reverberated loudly in the hushed dining hall. It was pitched somewhat high, his lungs straining from the force of his passion, like a horse neighing as it senses an approaching storm:

'Purging away the evils of the West
Let us be faithful to our land.
Stalwart, giving no ear to traitor's pleas,
We shall hand down our great cause
Without the least fear of death.'

Isao immediately recognized the poem as one written by Inokichi Miura, but these last words of the young company commander involved in the Sakai Incident were not at all suited to a festive occasion.

As soon as he had acknowledged the applause, Sawa went on: 'Now just one more. This is something that would rejoice the heart of Master Kaido.'

After this introduction, he recited a poem of Kohei Tomobayashi:

'We who were a people
Of a land pure and holy
Foolishly became Buddha's lackeys
And preached that we were all one.
Now we shall throw out Buddha,
(Grieve not too much, Buddha!)
We who were a people
Of a land pure and holy.'

At the words 'Foolishly became Buddha's lackeys' everyone laughed, the image of Master Kaido's face before them. And the admonition 'Grieve not too much, Buddha!' also provoked laughter.

Though he laughed with the others, in his heart Isao was still responding to the emotion latent in Sawa's first poem beneath its clarity and openness, which was that of a young man's angry death. This Sawa, who had vowed to die, showed not the least sign of shame at being still alive, but seemed instead to be trying to implant in Isao the fervour of a youth who had brought his life to a furious conclusion at the dawn of the Meiji era. Isao felt the keen thrust of shame. Rather than Sawa himself suffering from a shame that was rightly his, that shame pierced Isao.

It was a shame that came from the conviction that Sawa, and Sawa alone, had seen in him both the pleasure and the arrogant pride of a young man luxuriating in the sweet feeling of having made up his mind to die. Sawa, in a sense, had purchased Isao's shame with his money.

27

On November seventh Lieutenant Hori sent word that Isao was to come at once to his billet. Isao went there. The Lieutenant was sitting down, still in uniform. Something was different about him. As soon as he entered the room, Isao had a premonition of trouble.

'How about having supper with me? I told them downstairs that you would.' As he spoke, the Lieutenant stood up and turned on the lamp.

'I'd rather hear what you have to say.'

'Don't be in such a rush.'

Devoid of furnishings as it was, the austere eight-mat room had taken on the aspect of a brightly lit empty box. It was cold inside, but there was no trace of fire in the hibachi. From the hallway outside the closed door came the sound of a consciously military tread. The footsteps passed, turned back again, and then, apparently from the head of the staircase there was a shout: 'Hey, old fellow! Hurry up and bring my supper.' The footsteps passed again and retreated down the corridor.

'That Lieutenant's in the room at the end of the hall on the other side. He can't hear what you say, so don't worry. The man next door is gone today. He's duty officer this week.'

These words sounded somehow evasive in Isao's ears. He had not come here to say anything himself but to listen to the Lieutenant.

Lieutenant Hori lit a cigarette. A piece of tobacco clung to his lip, and as he dislodged it with the tip of one of his large fingernails, he crushed the now empty Golden Bat cigarette pack with his other hand. For the briefest of moments, the openings between the Lieutenant's fingers revealed bat wings, golden against a green background, being crushed ruthlessly within his fist. He had some time or other mentioned to Isao that his monthly salary was eighty-five yen. And now this memory, together with the cold of the room, together with the loneliness of billet life, rose up from the noise of the paper being crumpled.

'Has something happened?' asked Isao, taking the initiative.

The Lieutenant only grunted.

Finally Isao gave voice to his worst fear: 'I see. It's gotten out.'

'No, that's not it. Rest easy on that point. The fact is, I'm suddenly being sent off to Manchuria. An order came down from headquarters. I'm the only one going from the Third Regiment. It's very hush-hush. I haven't told anyone else, but I'm assigned to an independent Manchurian security force.'

'When do you leave?'

'November fifteenth.'

'But ... that's only a week away.'

'That's right.'

Isao felt as if the sliding doors before his eyes were about to come falling in upon him. The Lieutenant's leadership was now lost to them. They had been by no means intending to leave everything up to him, but the expert guidance of a military man would be of inestimable help in the assault upon the Bank of Japan. Furthermore, they had been looking forward to the Lieutenant's detailed tactical and organizational instructions during this final month. Isao had the spirit but he lacked the technique.

'Is there no way for you to stay longer?' asked Isao, unable to keep the regret out of his voice.

'It's an order. You can't change a thing like that.'

After this final word, both of them remained silent for some time. Image after image passed through Isao's mind as he kept trying to settle upon the role that now would best suit the Lieutenant. As he gave himself over to such wishful thinking, throwing aside common sense, he felt as though the Lieutenant were about to change himself into an ideal figure. There was the example of Harukata Kaya, who made his heroic decision just before the rising. The image that held Isao's mind was that of the Lieutenant abruptly resigning his commission and becoming just another man from the provinces, sacrificing himself to lead Isao and his comrades in the rising. Isao felt, on that summer afternoon when they practised the kendo forms in the drill hall amid the cries of cicadas, that this was the very spirit that had flashed from the Lieutenant's eyes.

But perhaps the Lieutenant had already made this decision, and, after letting Isao be sufficiently distressed, would declare his intention.

'In that case, the Lieutenant will not be participating?'

'I didn't say that...'

Isao's eyes flashed as he heard the Lieutenant's prompt denial.

'You will take part then?'

'In the Army, an order is an order. But if you move the date up before the fifteenth of November, I'll be happy to take part.'

As soon as he heard this, Isao was struck by the absurdity of the Lieutenant's words, and realized at once that he had no intention of taking part. The Lieutenant was well aware that it was impossible to have the rising within a week, and so his offer had been meaningless. Isao was even more bitterly disappointed at the Lieutenant's sophistry than at his failure to join in the rising.

Now Isao began to suspect that the Lieutenant had had a good reason for remaining in uniform. When he made his announcement, he had to be clothed with unassailable dignity. Indeed, as he sat opposite Isao across the rough table, he kept himself in a stiffly formal position, his shoulders squared in his military tunic. His insignia glittered on the broad shoulders that inspired such confidence, and he held his firm and powerful chin rigid above the red infantry badge at his collar with the golden '3' affixed to it. He was deliberately showing off his strength, to announce that he could not lend it to their cause.

'That's out of the question,' answered Isao, but with no hint of defeat. By so answering he felt that, quite unexpectedly, he had moved into a broader and freer position.

The Lieutenant, apparently not noticing the sudden change in him, began lecturing Isao as if he had been crushed: 'If you think it's out of the question, give it up. All right? From the very beginning I had certain doubts – about deficiencies in planning, the inadequate number of men involved and therefore the absurdity of trying to bring about martial law, the project's premature timing ... I believe it has become quite hopeless. Now neither heaven nor the times seem to be with us. Your resolve is a splendid one. I was aware of that, and that's why I helped you, but to act now would be utterly in vain. You see? Wait for the right time. This business here of my sudden transfer – that's the voice of heaven speaking, telling you "Stop!" I won't be in Manchuria long. Wait till I come back. And then I'll be glad to take part. So the thing to do until then is to go over your strategy and tighten up the loose ends, and do more research. Even in Manchuria, I'll be thinking of you young men and the pleasant times we had together ... Well, how about it? Will you take my advice and tell me straight out that you're not going through with it? Don't you think that the real man is the one who can be decisive, and check his forward rush?'

Isao was silent. He was surprised to find himself not at all surprised by the Lieutenant's words. And he was well aware that the longer his silence, the more uneasy the Lieutenant would become.

Somehow Isao had grown accustomed to the idea that when one reality crumbles, another crystallizes and a new order comes into existence. The Lieutenant had already been cast out by the new order. And so his gallant uniformed figure spun aimlessly about the edges of this impenetrable mass of pellucid crystal. Isao had made his way to a higher degree of purity, to a nobler level of tragedy.

Perhaps the Lieutenant had imagined that this young man would be thrown into a panic and would cling to his knees and plead tearfully. Isao, however, sat stiffly upright, saying nothing, his features even colder and more composed than before. When he spoke, his words were so far removed from his customary sincerity that there was danger that the Lieutenant might perceive that he was being mocked.

'But would you at least be so kind as to put us in touch with Lieutenant Shiga? I do want to beg his assistance in distributing the leaflets.'

As he spoke, Isao was determined that the Lieutenant's eyes would never look upon the draft for the leaflet that lay within his briefcase. Lieutenant Hori, however, still failing to notice any change in him, gave a candid answer.

'No. That won't do. Give it up, I told you. You haven't even answered me yet. Do you think I enjoy saying this? The project just won't work, that's all, so I have to swallow my own feelings and warn you against going on. It's not the result of any spur-of-the-moment decision. And now that I've told you to give it up, I'll tell you also that I don't want you to count on any assistance whatsoever from the Army. I shouldn't have to mention that I didn't decide without consulting Lieutenant Shiga. You can understand that much, can't you?' The Lieutenant paused for a moment. 'Of course if you yourselves want to carry it through on your own, that's up to you. But insofar as I was once your adviser, I warn you against it from the bottom of my heart. I can't bear to see you throw away your young lives. Don't you understand? Give it up!' the Lieutenant shouted as though issuing a command on the drill field, his eyes fixed on Isao's face.

What he might do, Isao thought, was simply to promise then and there to abandon his plans. That was it! For if the Lieutenant were left with a vague answer, he might become anxious and use the week remaining before his departure to devise a means to frustrate the project. But would not this sort of deception violate his own purity?

What the Lieutenant said next worked a sudden change in Isao's mood.

'You understand? And I don't want even the smallest scrap of notepaper remaining with either my name or Shiga's on it. I put this to you all the more strongly if you have any intentions of going against my advice to give it up. Get rid of our names as quick as you can.'

'Yes, sir. We shall do that,' Isao answered smoothly. 'I understand all that you have said. I guarantee that no trace of your names will remain. As for abandoning the plan, it would be impossible to persuade everyone, so I will delay the date indefinitely. The effect will be the same.'

'You'll do that? I've gotten across to you?' The Lieutenant's expression suddenly turned jovial.

'You have, sir.'

'Good for you! There's no need for another episode of the League of the Divine Wind. We will bring about a Restoration, at whatever cost. And, without fail, there'll come a day when we'll have the chance to fight side by side. What do you say to a drink?' The Lieutenant took a bottle of whisky from the wall cabinet as he made his offer, but Isao firmly refused and got up to leave. Because he did not want to give the impression of sulking, he had to do his best to seem cheerful.

Isao left the inn through the latticework door with the nameplate 'Kitazaki' beside it. The rain was not falling as hard as it had the first afternoon that he had come there, but the pavement glistened beneath a winter shower. He was without rain gear, but, wanting to walk alone for a while to collect his thoughts, he turned in the direction of Ryudo. The high brick wall of the Third Regiment's compound rose on the left side of the street, and its smooth red surface gleamed wetly in the feeble glow cast by the street lights. No one else was out walking. Up to this moment he had been resolved to marshal firmly all of his mental power, but just then his will was betrayed by sudden tears.

He remembered an incident that had occurred when he was a fervent member of the kendo team and had been privileged to practise with the famous kendo master Fukuchi, who happened to visit the drill hall. Frustrated at every turn by the master's fluid defence, Isao had attacked with reckless force, only to be thwarted once more. Just as he was instinctively pulling back, a hoarse voice spoke quietly from behind the bars of his opponent's mask.

'Don't retreat. You need some work here, I think.'

28

Isao's comrades had gathered to wait for him at their secret headquarters, the newly rented house in Yotsuya Samon. Since Lieutenant Hori had asked to see Isao alone, everyone had presumed that the Lieutenant had some rather important instructions for him.

They had named their hideaway Kamikazé, divine wind, as a symbol of their link with the League. To meet in Kamikazé, therefore, meant to meet in this two-storey, four-room house reached by getting off the streetcar at Samon and walking about a hundred and twenty yards. The landlord had been happy to rent it to them even though they were students, and it was only lately that they learned the reason: a suicide had been committed there last summer and no one else was willing to take it. The entire south face of the house was covered with siding held by split-bamboo verticals, with only two small windows, and the veranda faced east, another unusual feature. When the previous tenants were moving out, an old woman of the family, her heart set against leaving, fastened a rope to the railing of the stairway and hanged herself. Sagara had heard the story at the neighbourhood bakery and reported it to the others. The woman at the bakery had told him that much as she stuffed a paper bag with poppyseed-covered bean jam buns, grasped the two top corners of the bag with her fingers, nimbly twirled it once to close it, and passed it across the counter to him.

When Isao slid open the door of the entranceway and stepped in, the group on the second floor, hearing the noise, gathered at the head of the stairs, the skirts of their blue splashed-pattern kimonos rustling against one another in the dim corridor.

'What's the news?' asked Izutsu, his voice filled with a joy born of his own optimism. When Isao merely made his way past him on the stairway without answering, everyone felt the setback as if it were an electric shock. A locked cabinet at the end of the second-floor hallway was used to store their arms. Whenever Isao came here, he would have Sagara unlock it so that he himself could immediately check the number of swords. But today, forgetting even that, he went directly into the parlour. The shoulders of his jacket were soaked from the rain, and after he sat down, he felt a chill run through his body. His friends had been eating peanuts and shells were scattered over spread-out newspapers. Lying there in the lamplight, the shells seemed dull and pale, contorted with tension.

Seated cross-legged, Isao nervously picked up a peanut and cracked it as the others were gathering around him. The shell gave way, squeaking beneath the pressure of his fingertips, and split into two parts, a peanut in each.

'Lieutenant Hori has been transferred to Manchuria. Not only does he refuse to give us any further help, but he insists that we drop everything. As for our aeroplane, Lieutenant Shiga too has abandoned us. So we have no link with the military. I think it's time to consider what we should do.'

Isao delivered all this in a single burst. The impression reflected in the faces around him was like that of brimming water abruptly receding. He sought out each one, compelled by the feeling that he had to make visual contact with them all. Now was the moment when purity was stripped naked. And no one but Isao embodied it.

Izutsu showed his lovely recklessness. He spoke out gallantly, his face flushed and glowing, as though Isao's news had been the best possible.

'I say: rework our plan, well and good. But there's no need to put off the date. Spirit is what counts – determination! These soldier boys! When it comes right down to it, all they're concerned about is their careers.'

Isao strained his ears to catch any adverse reaction to this, but he heard nothing. The silence was like that of a number of small animals, each holding its breath within the shelter of its own thicket. Not unnaturally, Isao was tempted to be a little ruthless. He felt that he had no choice but to act with arbitrary force.

'It is just as Izutsu says. We strike on the day set. Aside from the problem of leadership, all that we've lost is the chance to drop our leaflets by aeroplane and to get our hands on some light machine guns. We'll print the declaration, at any rate, and then we can decide how to distribute it. Have we already bought a mimeograph machine?'

'We'll do it tomorrow,' answered Sagara.

'Good. We have our swords. And so it has turned out that for the Showa League of the Divine Wind, too, the ultimate reliance will be upon the Japanese sword. Nothing could be more fitting. Let's reduce the scope of our attack, but double its intensity. We have all made our vows, and I know every man here will be loyal to the end.'

His words were indeed greeted with loud shouts of approval, but the blaze did not leap up as high as Isao had expected. If this sort of flame falls only a trifle short of what one had hoped for, then one's heart cannot help but sense a proportionate measure of coldness.

Serikawa alone showed high excitement.

'We'll do it! We'll do it,' he shouted, kicking about and scattering the shells that littered the floor. He gripped Isao's hand firmly and shook it. As usual, he was on the verge of tears. This young man affected Isao like a match girl who uses blatant emotional appeal to force a sale. It was a manifestation he had little need for at the moment.

That night all stayed until late discussing the means of cutting back on their plans. Two factions formed, one in favour of giving up the assault on the Bank of Japan, the other, of following through on it. Since no agreement was reached, another meeting was set for the following night, and they adjourned.

As everyone was leaving, three boys, Seyama, Tsujimura, and Ui, told Isao that they had something further to discuss with him. Sagara and Izutsu were going to stay too, but Isao sent them home, also dismissing Yoneda and Sakakibara, who were supposed to have been on night watch at the house.

The four returned to the room, which had no touch of fire to warm it. Though he was yet to hear their story, Isao well knew what they were going to say to him.

The high school student, Seyama, began to do all the talking. With a pair of fire tongs, he chipped at the crusted ash in the cold hibachi, and the scars of pimples showed on his cheeks, as, head down, he spoke in a numbed voice.

'As for what I've got to say, please understand that it's out of friendship. Anyway, I think we should postpone the attack for a while. I didn't bring it up in front of everybody because I thought it might give the wrong idea, as if I were throwing cold water on the discussion of the attack itself. Now as far as that goes, we made our vows too at the shrine in the presence of the gods. But a vow – a vow with the condition that there won't be any big change in the circumstances – isn't that made in the same spirit as a promise?'

'A vow and a promise are different!'

It was Tsujimura who broke in indignantly. The effect of his words was to anticipate the response expected from Isao and seem to act as his spokesman, a device that hinted of a subtle sycophancy towards Seyama. And the way Seyama took this as a cue irritated Isao still more.

'Oh, they're different? I shouldn't have confused them like that. Please disregard my slip of the tongue. But if we have any idea of bringing about martial law, the cooperation of the military is essential. What's really needed is not just dropping a declaration from an aeroplane but, as you said in the beginning, bombing the Diet. And wouldn't whether or not we had professional help be the big factor in coordinating local attacks? Wouldn't going ahead without it, depending only upon our spirit and our swords, be much too risky? We ought to be careful not to get carried away by spirit, I think.'

'It would be a risk,' said Isao, speaking for the first time, his voice low. 'That's certain. The comrades of the League took a risk.' So composed was his manner, so evident the fact that he had already given up trying to persuade them, that the three fell silent and exchanged glances.

A sombre waterfall was falling within Isao's heart. His self-esteem was being slowly worn away. But he acted as he did because the precious thing that concerned him now was not his self-esteem. As a consequence, however, the abandoned self-esteem took its revenge upon him with a pain that could not be shunted aside. And beyond that pain lay his purity, like the clear evening sky seen through rifted clouds. As though in prayerful reverie, Isao saw the faces of those plunderers of the nation who deserved to be assassinated. The more isolated and bereft of strength he became, the more oppressive grew their fleshy, opulent reality. The stench of their evil worsened every moment. Isao and his comrades were plunged into a world of ever-growing uncertainty and anxiety, a world like the reflection of the moon adrift on a night sea. It was the plunderers' crimes that did this, their crimes that had changed his world into something so unsure, so unworthy of belief. The grotesque reality of these men who confronted Isao – there lay the source of all the world's perfidy. When he killed them, when his untarnished blade cut cleanly into that flesh swollen with fat and ravaged by high blood pressure, only then, for the first time, could the world be put to rights again. And until then...

'If you want to quit, I'm not going to stop you.'

Isao would have had no chance to check these words, so readily did they pass his lips.

'Just a minute,' protested Seyama, flustered and swallowing hard. 'All we meant was, if our proposal wasn't accepted we'd have no choice but to quit.'

'Your proposal isn't accepted.' As he answered, Isao's voice seemed to him to be coming from a long way off.

*

There was a meeting every day thereafter.

On the first day, no one followed the three deserters. On the second, after a violent argument between the two factions, the four men of the smaller one withdrew. Then two men quit the day after that. Thus the number of the comrades, Isao included, was reduced to eleven. The day set for the rising was a bare three weeks ahead.

Isao came thirty minutes late to the meeting of November twelfth, the sixth meeting since Lieutenant Hori's abandonment of them on November seventh. When he climbed to the second floor, his ten comrades were already assembled. And seated there also was one uninvited guest. Isao did not see this man at first because he had settled himself in a corner, somewhat removed from the others. It was Sawa.

Sawa had obviously taken into consideration Isao's surprise and anger at his coming, and Isao realized that there would be no point in making a childish display that would give Sawa the advantage. The first thought that crossed his mind was that everything was finished now that Sawa knew their hideaway. For if one of the ten had secretly gone to Sawa for help, he could no longer trust any of them. But then he quickly ruled this out as an unworthy thought. It was much more likely that one of the deserters had gone to Sawa, hoping to soothe the pangs of conscience by asking him to take his place.

'I thought all of you would be hungry, so I brought some Osaka sushi,' said Sawa, his squat figure like a wooden temple drum as he sat cross-legged upon the only pillow in the house. He was dressed, to his evident discomfort, in an old Western-style suit, and the man who was so scrupulous about the state of his underwear had fastened his bulging necktie around a sweat-stained collar.

'Thank you,' said Isao, as calmly as possible.

'Surely it's all right, my coming here, isn't it? After all, what am I but a backer, so to speak? Come on, help yourself to some of this. All of them were stubborn. They held out, wouldn't take up their chopsticks until you came. They're good comrades, I tell you. And what greater joy can a man have than having comrades who'll stand fast for him?'

Since he could do little else, Isao replied with a touch of false enthusiasm: 'All right. Let's go ahead.' He reached out to take the first piece.

As he was eating, Isao tried to think how best to deal with Sawa, but chewing interfered with his calculations. Besides, the silence while they ate the sushi was a relief to him. Three more weeks. How many more times before he died, he wondered, would he experience this untidy pleasure of eating? He thought of the episode in *The League of the Divine Wind* of Tateo Narazaki eating and drinking heartily before he cut open his stomach. When he looked around, he saw that all the others too were eating in silence.

'Are you going to introduce me to your comrades?' asked Sawa, beaming. 'I see two or three familiar faces from the Academy.'

'This is Izutsu. This is Sagara. And then Serikawa, Hasegawa, Miyaké, Miyahara, Kimura, Fujita, Takasé, and Inoué,' answered Isao, introducing each of them.

Now that he thought of it, Isao realized that of the unit assigned to attack the transformer stations, only three men, Hasegawa, Sagara, and Serikawa, were still with him. As for the Bank of Japan unit, Inoué remained steadfast together with Takasé, though their assignment would be different. Not a man was missing from the assassination unit. Isao's intention had been to assign the more daring of his comrades to these two latter units, and his judgement of character had proved unerring.

The cheerfully rash Izutsu, the clever little Sagara with his glasses, the boyish son of a country priest Serikawa, the taciturn but often droll Hasegawa, the sincere Miyaké with his long head, Miyahara with the hard and sombre expression of a dried insect, Kimura with his love of literature and his profound reverence for the Emperor, the ever-silent but passionate Fujita, Takasé whose strong, broad shoulders belied his tuberculosis, the huge but mild-looking Inoué with his second degree in judo ... These were his true comrades, the ones who had survived every test. These youths who were left knew what confronting death meant. Here beneath a ceiling lamp whose dim light fell upon tatami mats smelling of mould, Isao saw before him the corroboration of his own burning conviction. The petals of a drooping flower decay and fall away, leaving not a single one, but the hardy stamens stand firm together, still lustrous. And these keen-tipped stamens can pierce the blue of the sky. The more hopeless their dream became, the more stubbornly he and his comrades thrust their bodies together, leaving no opening for rational argument, forming themselves into a block of chalcedony shaped for killing.

'You're fine young men,' said Sawa. 'Those young people at the Academy of Patriotism should hang their heads.' Then, having tried a bit of the *Kodan Club* style on them, he went at it in earnest: 'Gentlemen, this is what it's come to: either this very night you number me among you or else you've got to kill me here and now. There're no two ways about it. And watch it that you don't let me walk away. For then you'd never know what I might spread about. I never took a single vow yet, remember. Well, then, gentlemen, either you trust me all the way or you don't trust me a bit. You can only do one or the other. And from the standpoint of your own advantage, I think that the clever thing to do would be to trust me. Getting rid of me would only do you harm, believe me. Well, gentlemen, what do you think?'

When Isao hesitated before answering, Sawa startled them by beginning to recite the vows in a loud voice: 'Be it thus that we, emulating the purity of the League of the Divine Wind, hazard ourselves for the task of purging away all evil deities and perverse spirits. Be it thus that we, forging deep friendship among ourselves, aid one another as comrades in responding to the perils that confront the nation.'

As he listened to Sawa's recitation, the words 'forging deep friendship' struck Isao to the heart.

'Be it thus that we, never seeking power and giving no thought to personal advancement, go forth to certain death to become the foundation stones for the Restoration.'

'How do you know our vows?' Isao asked accusingly, a touch of boyish grievance in his voice despite himself. With the keen instinct of the hunter, unexpected in a body so blunt and massive, Sawa seized upon Isao's weakness at once.

'Divine inspiration! Well, now I've made my vows. If you want me to seal them in blood, I'm ready.'

Isao glanced briefly at the faces of his comrades, and then a smile formed on his lips around which there was a light trace of beard.

'There's no way of getting the best of you, Mr Sawa. So ... please join us.'

'Thank you.'

The joy evident in Sawa's face was overwhelming. He radiated the innocence that marks the absolute rejection of prudence. Isao now, for the first time, noticed that Sawa's teeth were no less white than the underwear that he washed so unremittingly.

The meeting that evening turned out to be productive. Sawa spoke earnestly and persuaded the others to abandon such exalted hopes as the proclamation of martial law and to concentrate their full force upon the assassinations.

The sword of justice need flash but once in the darkness. The light that shone from its blade would tell the world that the dawn was not far off. But men knew that a single glint from a Japanese sword was like the pale blue of daybreak along a mountain ridge.

Assassins had to be lone wolves, argued Sawa. There were twelve of them in the room, and therefore they had to make the chillingly bold decision to kill twelve. The date of December third could remain unchanged, but, having ruled out the attacks on the transformer stations, they should aim for a time just before dawn, rather than at night. Dawn was when these rich men, poor sleepers because of their years, lay awake in their beds. This was when the faint light would reveal their faces and so prevent mistakes. This was when they listened, heads on their pillows, to the twittering of the first sparrows of the morning, and calculated how best that day to spray all of Japan with the poisonous breath of their rule. This was the time to aim for. Now each man had to investigate the sleeping accommodation of his victim and then carry through his task with a burning sincerity that flamed up to the heavens.

Such was Sawa's counsel, and its adoption resulted in the assassination plan being altered as follows, in order to wipe out the principal figures of the economic world:

Busuké Kurahara – Sawa
Toru Shinkawa – Iinuma
Juemon Nagasaki – Miyahara
Nobuhisa Masuda – Kimura
Shonosuké Yagi – Izutsu
Hiroshi Teramoto – Fujita
Zembei Ota – Miyaké
Ryuichi Kamiya – Takasé
Minoru Gota – Inoué
Sadataro Matsubara – Sagara
Genjiro Takai – Serikawa
Toshikazu Kobinata – Hasegawa

This was a plan that struck at every great capitalist family in Japan. All the *zaibatsu*-controlled heavy industries, iron and steel, light metals, shipbuilding – an illustrious name from each of these sectors was on the list. That morning of mass killing would, beyond any doubt, send a severe shock through the economic structure of the nation.

Isao was amazed at the skill in persuasion shown by Sawa, who had set aside Kurahara for himself. Izutsu's boldness had been aroused by the very strength of Kurahara's guard, but Sawa easily turned him aside, saying: 'The Kuraharas dismiss the police on guard at their home every night at nine and don't let them return until eight the next morning. He'll be the easiest one to attack, so leave it for an old man like me.'

Sawa reached down inside his trousers and drew out the dagger in its plain wooden sheath that he had shown to Isao. 'From now on, I'll come here every day, and I'll show you how to go about killing a man,' he said. 'It would be good to make a straw dummy. The most important thing is practice. I'll show you how it's done ... All right? There's your enemy. He's shaking with fear. A pitiful fellow, ordinary-looking, on the old side – a Japanese just like you. Pity is taboo! The evil of these men has taken such deep root inside them that they're not even aware of it themselves. You've got to keep your eye on that evil. Do you see it? Whether you see it or not will decide whether you succeed or fail. You've got to destroy the flesh that's blocking your way. You've got to get at the evil that's festering inside. Here, let's try this. Look!'

Sawa faced towards the wall and gathered his strength, his shoulders hunched.

As Isao watched he realized that before one could attack with one's whole being like Sawa, there were many rivers to be leaped over. And one clouded stream that never ran dry was that choked with the scum of humanism, the poison spewed out by the factory at its headwaters. There it was: its lights burning brilliantly as it worked even through the night – the factory of Western European ideals. The pollution from that factory degraded the exalted fervour to kill; it withered the green of the sakaki's leaves.

So be it then. The leaping, head-on attack! The body, bamboo stave held high, breaking through an invisible barrier all unaware and coming out on the other side. The quick and marvellous emotional abrasion gives off sparks. One's enemy, as though of his own accord, presses heavily against the point of one's sword and impales himself. Just as prickly seeds cling to the sleeves when a man makes his way through a thicket, so the assassin's kimono becomes splotched with blood without his noticing it.

Sawa pressed his right elbow against his lower side, and then, with his left hand pushing down upon his right wrist to prevent the blade from turning up, his icy blade seeming to spring directly from his fat body, he screamed: 'Yaaah!' and struck the wall with full force, slashing through it.

The following day Isao began to investigate the layout of the Shinkawa house. The house stood on a knoll and was surrounded by a high wall. Isao discovered, however, one place at the top of a slope behind the house where a portion of the upper wall had been cut out to accommodate an ancient pine in the garden, a branch of which curved out over the street. Here it would be easy to get a footing, climb up into the tree, and then slip down into the garden. The trunk had, of course, been surrounded with barbed wire as a guard against burglars, but, if one disregarded a few cuts, this was nothing to be concerned about.

The Shinkawas often went away on the weekends, but would no doubt be found sleeping at home on Friday night. Since the Baron and his wife were so fond of English customs, perhaps they slept in a double bed; in any case, they surely shared the same bedroom. A mansion so large would have many bedrooms, but it seemed likely that the Shinkawas would naturally take advantage of the pleasant southern exposure. The view of the sea was from the east, however, and therefore Isao felt that their room would be in the south-east corner of the house, thus combining comfort with the beauty of the view.

Trying to sketch the plan of the house, with its many wings, was no easy matter. By chance Isao happened to come across an old issue of the magazine *Bungei Shunju* in which an affected essay by Toru Shinkawa caught his eye. Shinkawa was one who had long prided himself on his literary ability, but phrases such as 'my wife this', 'my wife that' were conspicuous in his style. Perhaps this was merely an unconscious affectation, but possibly he was insinuating a criticism of the Japanese custom of avoiding direct references to one's spouse.

The essay was entitled 'Gibbon Through the Night', and from it Isao was able to draw this essential portion:

> By any standard Gibbon's work is a masterpiece. It goes without saying that I am far too deficient in scholarship and intellect to comprehend its wisdom, but I may safely contend that no Japanese translation can possibly convey the monumental significance of *The Decline and Fall of the Roman Empire*. The lavishly illustrated 1909 edition edited by Professor Bury, seven volumes, unabridged, is absolutely without peer. When I give myself over to the pleasure of reading Gibbon by the light afforded by my bedside lamp, the hour inevitably grows far advanced. The breathing of my sleeping wife beside me, the rustle of the pages of my Bury edition of Gibbon, and the ticking of the antique clock purchased from LeRoi's of Paris become by and by the only sounds that occupy the silence of my bedroom, forming a kind of delicate nocturnal trio. And the small lamp that illumines Gibbon's pages is, within the whole house, the last torch of the intellect to be extinguished each night.

When he read this, Isao pictured to himself how, once he had slipped into the garden under cover of darkness, he could take up a position at the south-east corner of the mansion. Then if he saw a light shining through a window curtain, and if the light kept burning after all the others had gone out, he would be able to tell the Baron's room. To accomplish this he would have to slip into the garden late in the evening and conceal himself there until the last light had disappeared. This kind of residence would no doubt have night watchmen patrolling its garden, but the shelter of the trees would certainly offer him ample place to hide.

After having considered the problem up to this point, Isao experienced doubt from another quarter. How strange it was that the Baron, whom everyone knew to be in constant peril, should deliberately write in a public journal in a fashion to expose himself to further danger. Could it be possible that this essay was meant as a trap?

29

As November was drawing to a close, Isao found himself fighting with the desire to say farewell to Makiko Kito in a way that would seem casual. He had neglected her recently. He had been busy, for one thing. The circumstances of his enterprise had been frequently altered, and he had been able to spare little time or feeling for anything else. And then there was something about saying farewell after making the decision to die that embarrassed him. Besides, he was afraid he might become so tense before Makiko that his powerful emotions would get the better of him.

He felt that the most beautiful thing would be to die without seeing her, but, as the world viewed it, to do so would be a breach of etiquette. Furthermore, each of the young men would go to his death carrying a petal from the sacred lilies Makiko had given them. Makiko, then, was the *miko* who would preside over the divinely sanctioned conflict that was the War of the Lilies. How could it be otherwise, then, but that Isao, as the emissary of his comrades, go to Makiko to take an inconspicuous leave of her? This thought finally gave him courage.

Isao shuddered at the possibility that he might not find her at home if he paid a sudden visit. Given his mood, he would hardly be able to force himself to come a second time to say farewell. She had to appear at the door that night to greet him, allowing him a last glimpse of that beautiful face.

Though it was not in accordance with custom and though he realized that it violated the casualness he wanted, Isao ventured to telephone to make sure that Makiko was home. It happened that his family had received a gift of oysters that day, and he was able to say that he wanted to bring some of them over.

One of his father's old students, who lived in Hiroshima, sent oysters every year in season, and it would be only natural for his mother to have him take some of them to the Kitos, who had treated him with such kindness. The coincidence was fortunate.

Dressed in his student uniform with his feet thrust into clogs, Isao left the house carrying a little keg of oysters. Since it was already long past the dinner hour, there was no reason to hurry.

As one who was sworn to die and about to take an unspoken farewell, Isao resented the incongruity of his gift. The splashing sound that came from the keg as he walked was like low waves lapping at the base of a sheer cliff. He imagined the sea as crammed into that small dark space, its freshness giving way to pollution.

Probably it was the last time he would follow this familiar path. It would also be his farewell to the thirty-six stone steps he knew so well. As he climbed them, the steps seemed to cascade down through the darkness like a waterfall. The cold of the night was bone-chilling even though there was no wind. Suddenly he had an odd feeling that he wanted to turn and look back at the way he had come. Two or three hemp palms grew on the slope on the south side of the house. The hairy fibre that covered their trunks seemed to entangle the stars in the winter sky. There were only a few lights in the houses below, but the eaves of the stores by the

Hakusanmaé street-car stop shone brightly. He saw no streetcar, but the scraping noise of one echoed in the night like an old drawer being pulled out.

The scene was quite ordinary. There was nothing that had to do with death and the spilling of blood. Even the sight of the four or five bonsai in a neat row upon the drying frame outside a house whose shutters were already closed brought to his mind how life would go on along its ordinary course after his death. His death, he was sure, would ever be beyond the grasp of the people living in that house. The turmoil that he and his comrades stirred would not disturb their sleep.

He entered the gate of the Kito home. He pressed the bell. Makiko slid open the door at once as though she had been lying in wait in the entrance hall.

Any other time, he would have slipped off his clogs and stepped up into the house, but he was afraid that if he talked to Makiko too long, his expression would betray his emotions. And so he merely handed her the small keg and said: 'My mother asked me to bring you this. It's a few of the oysters we received from Hiroshima.'

'Thank you. This is certainly not an everyday present! Well then, do come in.'

'Today I can't. Please excuse me.'

'Why not?'

'I've got to study.'

'What a fibber! When did you start grinding away so at your books?'

Makiko insisted upon Isao's staying and then disappeared into the house. He heard the General's voice telling her to invite him in.

Isao shut his eyes and gave himself over greedily to the image of Makiko before him a moment ago. Her beautiful smiling face with its fair skin – he wanted to store this image in his heart just as it was, unflawed. But if he were too eager, it would shatter like a mirror that has slipped from one's grasp.

What was best, he thought, was to leave at once. If he did so, the Kitos would, he was sure, take his abrupt departure as nothing more than a bit of boyish rudeness and would later perceive its true significance as his farewell. The dim light of the entrance hall served well to hide Isao's expression.

The whiteness of the flat stone where one removed one's shoes stood out in the chill pool of darkness that pressed against the floor platform, which seemed to Isao like a quay where a ship might berth. He himself was a ship that was about to cast off. The floor's edge, then, was the trim quay where people were finally received or denied, or bade farewell. And he was a ship loaded down with a full cargo of emotion, riding low in the dark winter sea of death.

Isao turned to leave the entrance hall, just as Makiko reappeared. She cried out: 'What's this? Why are you going? After Father said to have you come in.'

'Please excuse me,' answered Isao, pulling the sliding door shut behind him. His heart pounded as if he had accomplished something difficult. He felt like running, but then he reflected that to run would be unfitting and ruin everything. Departing by a different route would be enough. Instead of going back down the stone steps, he could turn towards the rear of the house, in the direction of Hakusan Shrine. He could return home by going through the shrine precincts. But as Isao was about to turn on to the path, deserted this late at night, that led through Hakusanmaé to the shrine itself, he caught a glimpse over his shoulder of Makiko's white shawl.

She was coming along behind him, not pursuing at all but keeping the same pace.

Isao went on walking. He had made the decision never to see Makiko again. He was on a path along the edge of Hakusan Park, which was at the rear of the shrine. To pass through the shrine grounds he would have to stoop and go beneath an elevated passageway just ahead, that joined the forehall with the shrine office. Light shone faintly through the close-worked lattice of the passageway.

Makiko finally called out. Isao had to stop. But he felt that if he looked back at her some ill-omened event might occur.

Instead of answering her, Isao turned away and walked to the top of the small hill opposite the park. A flagpole stood on the crest. The front of the hill was a steep drop covered with a growth of trees and shrubbery.

Finally he heard Makiko's quiet voice at his shoulder.

'Why are you angry?'

Her voice hung in the darkness, charged with anxiety. Isao had to face her.

Her silvery white shawl concealed her mouth. But the faint light coming from the distant shops revealed tears shining in her eyes. Isao felt as if he were choking.

'I'm not angry at anything.'

'You came to say farewell. It's true, isn't it?'

Makiko pronounced this non sequitur with assurance, as though she were placing a white chess piece upon a new square.

Isao said nothing as he kept his eyes upon the scene below. A tall, sinewy zelkova tree, its upper roots exposed, lifted its branches to spread a delicate tracery across the face of the night and dim the stars caught within its branches. Two or three persimmon trees stood on the edge of the cliff, their scanty leaves black against the sky. Beyond the valley the land rose again, and the brightness of the shopping district misted the eaves of the houses along the hilltop. From here, a good many lights still seemed to be burning, but the effect was not at all that of a bustling city. Rather, the bright points were like small stones lying at the bottom of a brook.

'It's true, isn't it?' said Makiko once again.

This time her voice was very close to him, inflaming his cheek. It was then that he felt Makiko's hands pressing upon the back of his neck. Her cold fingers were like a sword blade against the close-cropped nape. When the time came to receive the finishing stroke, when his neck shivered in anticipation of the falling blade, no doubt he would feel a chill like this. Isao shuddered, but his eyes told him nothing.

And yet for Makiko to have stretched out her arms and clasped his neck as she was doing, she had to be standing before him. This is what Isao had not perceived. Whether she had been incredibly quick or incredibly slow, she must have moved in front of him. And he did not see her.

Makiko's face was no more visible than before. What he could see was something blacker than the night, the rich abundance of her hair just at the level of his chest. She had buried her face there. The perfume that rose from her seemed to screen his vision. His senses were fully taken up with that scent. Isao's feet trembled in his clogs and the thongs creaked faintly. His footing seemed to be giving way, and like a man seized by a drowning person, he reached out in self-protection and clasped Makiko in his arms.

He embraced her, but what he felt beneath her light coat was no more than the firmness of her bulky, tight-wound obi with its padded layers and its huge bow. This was a substance that seemed to put him at a greater distance from Makiko than before he had embraced her. And yet what this sensation conveyed to Isao was the reality behind all his mental images of a woman's body. No nakedness could seem so utterly naked.

Here began his rapture. Suddenly it was like a runaway stallion breaking free of the yoke. A wild strength flowed into his arms as he held the woman. He clasped her tighter, feeling their two bodies shake like the mast of a plunging ship. The face that had been buried in his chest was lifted. Makiko had lifted her face! Her expression was just what he had dreamed night after night that it would be when he said his last farewell. Tears sparkled on that lovely white face that was without a trace of makeup. Her tight-shut eyes looked at Isao with a force stronger than that of vision. Her face was like a delicate bubble that now floated before his eyes after having risen from some unimaginable depth. In the darkness her lips trembled as she sighed again and again. Isao could not bear having her lips so close to his. To banish them, all he could do was touch his own to hers. As naturally as one leaf falls and comes to rest upon another, Isao came upon the first and final kiss of his life. Makiko's lips reminded him of the red leaves of the cherry trees that he had seen in Yanagawa. He was startled by the sweetness that began to flow gently through him once their mouths were joined. The world trembled at the point of contact between their lips. From this point radiated a transformation that altered his very flesh. The sensation of being steeped in something indescribably warm and smooth reached a climax when he realized that he had drunk in some of Makiko's saliva.

When they finally drew their lips apart, they clung to each other and wept.

'Tell me just one thing. When will it be? Tomorrow? The day after?'

Because he realized that, were he in possession of himself, he would never answer such a question, Isao told her at once.

'It's December third.'

'Only three days from now. Will I see you again?'

'No. I'm afraid that's impossible.'

They began to walk in silence. Makiko chose a roundabout route, and Isao had to follow her through a small open space in Hakusan Park and down a dark path along the outbuildings where the shrine's sacred palanquins were kept.

'I know what I'll do,' said Makiko in the darkness beside him. 'I can take the train to Sakurai tomorrow and go to Omiwa Shrine. I'll pray for your good fortune in battle at the Sai Shrine. I'll bring back a talisman for each of you, and see that you have them by December second. How many should I get?'

'Eleven ... No, there's twelve of us.'

A kind of shyness kept Isao from daring to tell Makiko that each man would undertake his mission with a petal of her lilies hidden upon him.

The two of them entered the lighted area in front of the shrine, but there was no sign of anyone else being there. Since she did not want to cause any trouble at the Academy, Makiko asked him how to get to their hideaway, and he wrote the directions on a slip of paper and gave it to her.

Such light as there was had only one source, a small night lantern donated by a

Hakusanshito photo studio. It cast a feeble glow over the stone guardian dogs, the gold-lettered tablet, the embossed carving of a dragon breathing fire, and the wooden steps leading to the shrine. Only the white pendants that hung from the sacred ropes stood out with any clarity. Weak though the light was, it reached as far as the white wall of the shrine office, some twenty feet away. Shadows of sakaki leaves made a lovely pattern upon it.

Each of them prayed silently. Then they passed beneath the torii and parted at the top of the long stone stairway.

30

On the morning of December first, Isao, pretending that he was off to school, went directly to the hideaway. Sawa had been sent on an errand by the headmaster and was unable to attend the meeting, but the other ten were all present. The action was now only two days away, and, though it was necessary to work out some details, the main purpose of the meeting was to renew everyone's resolution to take his own life, whatever difficulty he might find himself in, immediately after the blow had been struck.

The expressions on the faces of his comrades seemed to Isao to be clear and determined. The group had sold two regular swords and bought six short swords. Thus each now had his own sharp-bladed dagger. But someone made the suggestion that, as an extra precaution, it would be well if they all had a hidden dagger too, and the others agreed. They knew that poison was the most effective way to commit a hasty suicide, but they spurned this womanish means of putting an end to life.

The practice was to lock the door of the house when the group was assembled. When a knock sounded, everyone presumed that Sawa had come after all, stealing time from the task he was sent to do.

Izutsu went downstairs and called out: 'Mr Sawa?'

'Yes,' came the answer in a low voice, but when Izutsu slid the door open, a stranger entered, pushed his way past, and began running up the stairs, still in his street shoes.

'Get away!' Izutsu shouted, as a second and third man rushed in and twisted his arms behind him.

The comrades who tried to escape by jumping down into the backyard from the overhanging roof were seized by detectives who had moved in from the rear. Isao snatched up one of the daggers in front of him to thrust it into his own stomach, but a detective caught his wrist. In the struggle that followed, the officer suffered a cut finger. Inoué grappled with the detectives and threw one of them, but two or three others brought him down.

And so the eleven were handcuffed and brought to the Yotsuya police station. On the afternoon of the same day, Sawa was arrested as he was returning to the Academy.

31

TWELVE ULTRA-NATIONALIST RADICALS ARRESTED IN HIDEOUT

SWORDS AND SEDITIOUS LITERATURE SEIZED SERIOUS PLOT SAY AUTHORITIES

Honda's first reaction when he saw the headlines in the morning paper was 'Again, eh?' and nothing more, but his calm was abruptly shattered when his eye caught the name Isao Iinuma on the list of those arrested. He wanted to place a call to Tokyo at once and talk to Iinuma at the Academy, but worldly prudence prevented this. The headlines the following morning were even larger:

FULL DETAILS ON 'SHOWA DIVINE WIND' AFFAIR
AIM TO DELIVER CRUSHING BLOW TO
FINANCIAL WORLD
EACH MEMBER TO ASSASSINATE ONE MAN
RINGLEADER NINETEEN-YEAR-OLD YOUTH

A picture of Isao appeared for the first time. The reproduction was very coarse, but there was no mistaking those incredibly clear eyes whose brilliance had so affected Honda when the boy and his father had come to dinner, those eyes with their piercing gaze, which could never blend into the pattern of ordinary amenities. No doubt they had been looking forward to this day.

Belatedly Honda regretted his tendency to be capable of discernment only after a matter had been strained through the meshes of the law.

Isao was already past eighteen and would therefore not be treated as a juvenile before the law. According to the article, the entire group, except for the middle-aged eccentric named Sawa, was made up of youths in their late teens or early twenties, and so some no doubt would be tried as juveniles. But for Isao there was no chance of this.

Honda visualized the worst possible legal situation. Something seemed missing from the vague newspaper articles. On the surface this affair was merely the rash assassination plot of some heedless boys, but the investigation might well turn up a far wider and deeper conspiracy.

As a matter of fact, the military authorities, wanting to refute wild rumours and to allay the prejudice provoked by the May Fifteenth Incident, had made a statement carried in that day's paper: 'No Army officers had any connection whatsoever with this recent incident. Unfortunately, every time an incident of this sort occurs there are those ready to believe that young officers must be involved. Ever since the May Fifteenth Incident, the greatest concern has been shown for the rigid enforcement of discipline in every unit throughout the Armed Forces. The extraordinary energy that we have displayed in putting our house in order is a matter of public knowledge.'

Such was the statement, but its effect, however groundless, was to excite the suspicion that some greater power was indeed at work behind the plotters.

If the scope of the affair broadened, and any intent were revealed that would come under Article 77 of the Criminal Code, 'Subverting the Constitution', the situation would become critical. The newspaper accounts were not clear as to whether the unconsummated aspect or rather the element of premeditation would be uppermost when the case was brought to trial. Honda remembered *The League of the Divine Wind*, which he had read at Isao's urging. He could not help but feel a sense of ill omen at Isao and his comrades' choice in calling themselves the Showa League of the Divine Wind.

He dreamed of Kiyoaki that night. Kiyoaki seemed to be asking for help, and also to be lamenting his premature death. When Honda awoke, his mind was made up.

Honda's reputation at the Courthouse seemed not quite as high as it had been. When he talked with his colleagues, their manner since his return from Tokyo in the fall had somehow cooled. The rumours in vogue alleged that either family trouble or woman trouble had made Honda a changed man. And his once highly regarded discernment was no longer so esteemed. The Chief Justice, though he kept it to himself, was grieved when he became aware of the situation. For no one had been more appreciative than he of Honda's rise to eminence.

For the vast majority of men, romantic dreams are inevitably bound up with a woman. And so when his colleagues intuitively diagnosed the affliction lodged within him since his fall trip to Tokyo as involvement with a woman, they were at least correct in giving it a romantic colouring. Their intuition was indeed remarkable in shrewdly picturing Honda as one who had strayed from the way of reason and was now wandering aimlessly along some overgrown path of emotion. But what might have been expected in a twenty-year-old youth was deemed improper in a man Honda's age, entirely human though the failing was. And this was where most of the disapproval was focused.

Members of a profession in which reason was of the essence, his colleagues could hardly be expected to view with respect any man who, unknown to himself, had contracted the disease of romanticism. And then from the viewpoint of national righteousness, though Honda had not gone so far as to commit any crime, he had certainly defiled himself with an 'unwholesome' attitude.

But most surprised of all at this state of affairs was Honda himself. The eagle's nest that he had constructed at a dizzying height in the structure of legalism, which by now had become second nature to him, was – something wholly unforeseen! – threatened with the floodwaters of dreams, with the infiltration of poetry. More awesome yet, the dream that assaulted him did not destroy either the transcendence of human reason, which he had always believed in, or his proud pleasure at living with more concern for principles than for phenomena. The effect was rather to strengthen his beliefs, to heighten his pleasure. For he could now glimpse towering up brightly beyond the principles of this world an unbreachable wall of principle. Once he saw it, so dazzling was this glimpse of the ultimate that he was unable to go back to the placid, everyday faith he had known before. And this was not to retreat but to advance. It was not to look back but to look ahead. Kiyoaki had certainly been reborn as Isao, and from this fact, beyond one kind of law, Honda had begun to see into the essential truth of law.

He suddenly remembered that in his youth, from the time he had heard the sermon of the Abbess of Gesshu, the European philosophy of natural law had lost its appeal for him, and he had been much attracted by the ancient Indian Laws of Manu, whose provisions extended even to reincarnation. Something had already taken root in his heart then. A law whose nature was not to impose order upon chaos but to point to the principles that lay within chaos and so give form to a legal code, just as the surface of the water caught the reflected image of the moon – such a law could well have sprung from a source more profound than the European worship of reason that undergirded natural law. Honda's instinctive feeling, therefore, may have been sound, but this was not the kind of soundness looked for in a judge, the guardian of the operative law. He could easily imagine how unsettling it must have been to his colleagues to have a man of this sort working with them in the same building. To have one dust-covered desk in a room filled with the spirit of good order. From the viewpoint of reason, nothing so resembled the stains on an untidy man's clothes as an obsession with dreams. Dreams somehow turn one into a slovenly figure. A soiled collar, the back of the shirt wrinkled as though slept in, trousers baggy – something similar overtakes the garment of the spirit. Though he had done nothing, though he had said nothing, Honda had, at some time or other, come to violate the code of public morality, and so he knew that, in the eyes of his colleagues, he was like wastepaper scattered along the path of a neatly kept park.

As for his home life, his wife Rié said nothing at all. Rié was not a woman who would intrude curiously into her husband's private thoughts. She must have realized that he had changed, and that he seemed preoccupied. But Rié said nothing.

It was not any fear of ridicule or insult, then, that kept Honda from confiding in his wife, but a certain sense of shyness. This subtle kind of bashfulness gave a special character to their marriage. Perhaps this was the most beautiful aspect of their rather quiet and old-fashioned relationship. And though Honda himself may have been faintly aware that something in his recent discovery and change of outlook infringed upon it, husband and wife made use of this extremely beautiful characteristic to preserve silence and the unrevealed secret.

Rié must have wondered why her husband's work had recently become so burdensome. The dishes that she took such pains to prepare for his evening meal failed to give him the pleasure that they had before. She did not grumble. She did not wear a sad expression. Nor did she punish him by putting on a brave cheerfulness. At some point or other a childish court-doll face, the vague look she had whenever her kidneys troubled her, had become her everyday face. Though always smiling and amiable, she never showed any expectation. The force that had shaped Rié into the woman she was belonged in part to her father, in part to her husband. At least, Honda had never given his wife cause to suffer from jealousy.

Although the affair of Isao was widely covered in the newspapers, her husband said nothing about it, and so Rié too said nothing. But then one night at dinner, when further silence seemed unnatural, she spoke out casually: 'That's a terrible thing about Mr Iinuma's son. When I saw him here, I thought he was such a serious and well-behaved boy...'

'Well, with this kind of crime, it's the serious and well-behaved ones you're most likely to find involved,' said Honda in rebuttal. But so gentle and bemused was his manner that Rié became concerned.

Honda's mind was in turmoil. Because his failure in trying to save Kiyoaki was the keenest regret of his youth, he felt that he must succeed this time. He had to rescue *him* from danger and scandal no matter what the cost.

The favour of the public would be something to count on. The extraordinary youth of the conspirators seemed to keep people from becoming too aroused against them, and, beyond that, Honda sensed that a feeling of sympathy was already in the air.

Honda made his decision the morning after he had dreamed about Kiyoaki.

When Iinuma met Honda at Tokyo Station on his arrival from Osaka, he was wearing an inverness with a seal collar and his moustache seemed to be quivering in the late December cold. The weariness of his long wait on the platform was evident in his voice and in his watery and bloodshot eyes. As soon as Honda descended, Iinuma clasped his hand, commanded a student to relieve him of his bags at once, and then began to pour an insistent stream of thanks into Honda's ear.

'How grateful I am that you chose to come! I feel that I have all conceivable power aligned with me. No boy could be luckier than that son of mine. But what a momentous resolution, Judge Honda, you have made on our behalf!'

After instructing the student to take his luggage to his mother's house, Honda accepted Iinuma's invitation and went to have dinner with him at a Ginza restaurant called the Gincharyo. The streets were gay with Christmas decorations. Honda had heard that Tokyo's population was now 5,300,000, and when he looked at the crowded streets, it seemed that hunger and depression were like conflagrations burning in some corner of a distant land, things too far off to be visible from here.

'When my wife read your letter, she too wept tears of joy. We put it upon the altar of the gods, and we pay it reverence each morning and evening. But wasn't your judgeship a life-time appointment? Why did you resign it?'

'Illness. No one can help that. However much they tried to keep me on, I had the doctor's certificate to defend myself.'

'But what kind of illness?'

'A nervous breakdown.'

'Not really?'

Iinuma said nothing further, but the frankness of the momentary misgiving that showed in his eyes gave Honda a warm feeling toward him. Honda knew that a flash of frankness from an unsavoury defendant could create a measure of goodwill in a judge, no matter how much care he took to avoid emotion. He tried to get some idea of the feeling that a lawyer would have for his client. No doubt it ought to be more theatrical. The goodwill that passed through a judge's mind would naturally have some ethical motivation, but a lawyer's feelings had to be fully exploited.

'It was a matter of being relieved of duty at my own request. So I'm still a judge as far as that goes, but now my status is that of a retired judge. Tomorrow I'm going to join the Bar Association, and then my career as a lawyer will begin. It's the work that I've decided to do, and so I intend to put everything I have into it. The truth is that since I rose no higher before resigning, I'm not going to bring too much prestige to my career as a lawyer. But the whole thing was my choosing, and I have to accept the consequences. After all, it's up to you to select your own lawyer. But as for compensation, I explained to you in my letter...'

'Oh, Judge Honda! How can you be so benevolent towards us? It would be despicable of me to take advantage of your good nature, but under the circumstances...'

'Very well then. Let us agree that I receive nothing at all. I'll undertake it on that condition only.'

'Judge Honda ... I am at a loss for words.' Sitting in a stiff, formal position, Iinuma bowed his head again and again. 'But after a decision of such grave consequences, wasn't your wife taken aback? And your mother too, wasn't she upset? It seems to me that they would be greatly opposed.'

'My wife was perfectly calm about it. When I phoned my mother to tell her, she caught her breath for a moment, but then she simply said that I should do as I thought best.'

'Really? What a fine mother! What a fine wife! Judge Honda, your wife and your mother are remarkable women. My wife, now, couldn't possibly match it. Sometimes you must teach me the secret of wife-training. I have to try to instil in my wife a little of what yours has. But I suppose it's too late for that.'

For the first time, the formality between guest and host gave way, and both of them laughed. As they did, a nostalgia welled up in Honda's heart. He felt as though twenty years had been rolled back and the student Honda and the tutor Iinuma were meeting to discuss how best to come to the rescue of the absent Kiyoaki.

The lights of the Ginza flashed beyond the frosted glass of the windows. But just as the gaudy night life could not altogether escape the reality of famine and bad times, so inside the night had a double aspect all too evident. Even the colourful scraps of fish that they had left uneaten upon the platter suggested a link to the cold darkness of a detention cell at night. And the past too, its unfulfilled hopes acknowledged with some reluctance, was linked to the present of these two men now in their prime.

Never again in his life, Honda thought, would he make a renunciation of such magnitude, and he determined to fix in his memory the bizarre passion that now seethed within him. He could recall nothing comparable to the inner fervour and exhilaration he felt after making the decision that all the world would call foolish, a decision made at a time of life when his powers of discretion should have been at their height!

It was for him to thank Isao rather than for Isao to thank him. If he had not been electrified by Kiyoaki's rebirth in Isao and by Isao's conduct, Honda might have turned into a man who would be delighted to live on an iceberg. For what he had looked upon as tranquillity had been a kind of ice. His concept of perfection had been a kind of desiccation. His ability to view things in an unorthodox fashion had seemed to him merely immature, but the truth was he had had no idea of what maturity meant.

Iinuma, as though spurred on by something, had drunk one cup of saké after another, wetting the ends of his neat moustache. As Honda studied those drops of saké, he thought of them as bits of ideology innocently clinging to the moustache of this man who had earned his living by commercializing a passionately held belief. Having made faith his livelihood, ideology his means of support, Iinuma's follies and excesses had given his face a certain fatuous look of self-deception. Still sitting in a formal position and drinking heavily, with a vigour that showed no sign of concern for his son shivering in a cold cell, he played up his emotion and his very affectation of emotion as a kind of role. His driving manner seemed as stereotyped as a painted black dragon on a screen in the entrance hall of an inn. He had chosen to cultivate his beliefs as a mannerism. A long period had passed since his youth when, with his dark, deep-set eyes, he had given such an overpowering, almost physical, impression of gloom. Now it was not surprising that his worldly reverses, his agonies, and, above all, his humiliations, made him throw out his chest in pride at his son's glory.

As Honda sat musing, he saw that Iinuma had wordlessly committed something to his son. The old humiliations of the father entrusted to the purity of the son, who goes against the powerful of this world with fiery cry and drawn sword.

Honda felt that he had to hear a frank word about Isao from Iinuma.

'Would you say,' he asked, 'that the truth is that your son fulfils a dream that you've had ever since the days when you were Matsugae's tutor?'

'No,' answered Iinuma with a touch of defiance. 'He's my son. That's all he is.' But then after this denial, he began to talk of Kiyoaki. 'When I stop and think today, the young master dying the way he did was probably the only thing that could have happened. It must have been the will of heaven. As for Isao, well, he's pretty much like his father. He's young, and the times are different, so he's got involved in something like this. Yes, I tried to instil the samurai virtues in the young master, but maybe it was my own boorishness that pushed me to do it. I suppose the young master did die of frustration...' Here Iinuma's voice broke as his emotions got the better of him. As soon as he yielded in the least to his feelings, the result, it seemed, was like a dam giving way. 'But still... he acted as his heart told him to act, and I'm sure that, if nothing else, he had that much satisfaction. At least, as time goes by, that's what I find myself wanting more and more to believe. Otherwise, I would find it unbearable, though that's my own selfish view. At any rate, the young master lived and died in a way suited to himself. As for me, an outsider, and all my anxiety, everything I tried was pointless and a waste of effort.

'Isao, though, is my own son. I raised him very strictly in accordance with my beliefs. And his response was all that I could have wanted. I was delighted at his reaching the third degree in kendo before he was out of his teens, but since then, needless to say, he's gotten out of hand. Perhaps he was too deeply influenced by my own life. But there was more to it than that. He was too anxious to be freed from his father's guidance. He put too much trust in himself, and this was the root cause of his going astray. Now in this affair, if through your great effort, Judge Honda, the sentence imposed is somehow a light one, the chastisement will do that boy a world of good. Surely there's no chance of the death penalty or life imprisonment, is there?'

'You needn't worry about that,' said Honda in laconic reassurance.

'Ah, Judge Honda! Thank you for everything. Father and son, Isao and I have had no greater benefactor in our lives than you.'

'You'd do well to spare your gratitude until after the trial.'

Iinuma bowed his head again. Now that he had let himself indulge in sentiment, the conventional vulgarity of his expression suddenly vanished. As he became drunker, his eyes began to water in an unsettling manner, and his whole body seemed to give off the feeling, like an invisible vapour, that there was something he wanted to say.

'I know what you're thinking, Judge Honda,' Iinuma finally declared. The pitch of his voice rose somewhat as he went on. 'I know, I tell you. It's that I'm impure beyond words and my son is pure. That's what you're thinking.'

'Not really.' Somewhat irked, Honda made his reply vague.

'No, that's it. There's no doubt about it. And since I've gone so far, let me go further: my boy was arrested just two days before they were to strike. Who do you think he has to thank for that?'

'Well now...' Honda knew that Iinuma was on the verge of saying something better left unsaid, but there was no way to stop him.

'You're doing so much for us, Judge, I find it painful to make this revelation after all your kindness, but I suppose a client shouldn't keep anything from his lawyer. So I'll make a clean breast of it. I'm the one. I secretly reported my son to the police. At the last possible moment I saved my son's life.'

'Why did you do it?'

'Why? Because if I hadn't, my son's life would have ended.'

'But, putting aside the good or evil of what had been planned, didn't you feel in any way that perhaps you should let your son achieve what he set out to do?'

'It was because I looked ahead. I'm always looking ahead, Judge.' Flushed from drink, Iinuma abruptly reached for his seal-collared inverness which lay upon a clothing box in the corner of the room. Heedless of the dust he scattered, he shook open the coat with a flapping noise and held it up like a mantle. 'Here,' he said. 'This is me. This inverness is myself. There is no sleight-of-hand involved. The inverness is the father. It's like the dark sky of a winter night. So the folds of the inverness reach far and wide, covering whatever spot the son might place his foot upon. The son runs about wanting to see the light, but he cannot. The huge black inverness is spread wide over his head. As long as the night continues, the inverness sternly makes him acknowledge the night. When the morning comes, the inverness falls to earth and lets the son's eyes be dazzled by the light. Such is the father. Am I not right, Judge Honda? My son didn't want to acknowledge this inverness, and he did what he wanted to do. Therefore it's only natural that he be taken to task. For it's still night, and the inverness knows this and wants to prevent the son from going to his death.

'These leftist scum – the more pressure you put on them, the stronger they get. Japan is invaded by their germs and those who made Japan so weak as to be susceptible to them are the politicians and the businessmen. I knew all about it without my son telling me. And those in the advance guard ready to leap to the defence of the Imperial Family when a crisis threatens the nation are, as hardly needs saying, we ourselves. But there's the matter of picking the time. There's such a thing as the favourable moment. Determination alone counts for nothing. Thus I have to conclude that my son is too young. The necessary discernment is still beyond him.

'I, the father, have the determination. Indeed, I may say that my patriotism, my agony of soul, exceeds that of my son. My son tried to hide everything from me that he was intent on carrying out – wouldn't you say he was blind to his father?

'I always look ahead. Rather than take action, the best course is to achieve results without acting. Am I right or not? I heard that at the time of the May Fifteenth Incident there was a flood of petitions asking leniency. So the naïve purity of the young defendants will surely evoke public sympathy. We can count on that. And my boy, rather than losing his life, will come home covered with glory. His whole life long, he'll have no worries as to where his next meal is coming from. Because the world will forever hold him in awe as Isao Iinuma of the Showa League of the Divine Wind.'

Honda was at first struck dumb, but then he wondered if Iinuma was being altogether candid.

By Iinuma's account, the primary saviour of Isao was Isao's father, and Honda, in coming to the son's rescue, was merely an agent assigned to bring about the realization of Iinuma's plan. No words could more effectively negate the goodwill shown by Honda in throwing aside his career and undertaking Isao's defence without a fee. Nor could any words more defile the nobility in Honda's action.

But, oddly enough, Honda was not angered. The person he was concerned about defending was Isao, not his father. However blemished the father, his blemishes had nothing to do with his son. They had not the least effect upon the son's purity of intention.

Beyond this, Honda, who should have been offended to some degree by Iinuma's boorish display, had another reason for remaining unperturbed. For as Iinuma, having said all this, kept hastily pouring himself more to drink in this little room from which he had long since excluded the waitress, Honda was aware of a tremor in his hairy hands. And here Honda perceived a sentiment that Iinuma would never voice, something that was probably the deepest motive of his betrayal. The son, in other words, had been on the verge of achieving a bloody glory and a sublime death, and the father had been unable to restrain his jealousy.

32

His Highness Prince Harunori Toin was another to whom the affair had been a severe shock. He was not apt to remember those who came once or twice to pay their respects, but the memory of Isao's visit that night was still vivid in his mind. And, especially since Lieutenant Hori had brought the boy, he could not take a detached view of this incident. Naturally, as soon as the affair broke, the Prince made a long-distance telephone call to his steward to seal his lips about Isao's visit. But since the steward was, in effect, a minion of the Imperial Household Ministry, the Prince could put little trust in him.

For some time now, the Prince had found in the Lieutenant a like-minded companion with whom he could deplore the times. The gentlemen of the Imperial Household Ministry were not amused at this. They frequently admonished him for granting audiences indiscriminately, without regard to rank. But this very conduct grew out of resentment at the Ministry's constraints, requiring him to report even the shortest trip, and so he could hardly be expected to listen meekly to this advice.

Since his appointment as regimental commander in Yamaguchi, the Prince had shown a certain intemperance in speech and action which had not gone unnoticed by the Imperial Household Minister and the Director of the Division of Special Affairs. Waiting until Harunori came up to Tokyo, they arranged to call on him for a friendly visit, in order to admonish him gently. The Prince heard them out without a word, and made no reply even after they were finished. A long silence ensued.

The Minister and the Director had expected the Prince to charge them angrily with meddling in military affairs. If he did so, their resources were at an end.

The Prince's expression was extremely subdued, however, and the moment for him to lash out at them was already past. Finally, his slender eyes half open but radiating dignity, the Prince looked from one official to the other and then said: 'This is not the first time I have had to suffer your interference. If you must interfere, I hope you will devote equal attention to the rest of the Imperial Family. How is it that I alone have long had to bear the brunt of this?'

Before the Minister could so much as protest, the Prince, struggling to keep his deep anger in check, began to deliver a tirade.

'Years ago, when Marquis Matsugae affronted me with the greatest impertinence regarding the woman who was to be my wife, the Imperial Household Ministry supported the Marquis and gave me no help whatsoever. It was a blatant case of the Imperial Family being insulted by one of its own subjects! Who is the Imperial Household Ministry meant to serve? Should it be any cause for wonder that since then I have viewed the manoeuvrings of you gentlemen with suspicion?'

The Imperial Household Minister and the Director of the Division of Special Affairs could offer nothing in reply, and they hastily took their leave.

Lending an ear to the violent words of Lieutenant Hori and two or three other young officers had been a great diversion for the Prince, and he enjoyed being looked up to as the blue sky showing through the dark clouds that hung over

Japan. A grievous wound lay deep within his heart. He was happy that this was a kind of beacon to some men, and that his sad, maverick spirit had become the source of hope for many. However, he was not at all inclined to take action.

Once the affair of Isao and his companions had come to light, nothing more was heard from Lieutenant Hori in Manchuria. The Prince had only his memory of that single audience granted Isao to draw on, but now, when he recalled the light blazing in the young man's clear eyes on that summer night, he realized that they had been the eyes of one sworn to die.

The copy of *The League of the Divine Wind* given to him by Isao, which he had read only hastily at the time, was still on the book shelf in the commandant's room. And so the Prince, hoping to search out the true meaning of the affair, took up the book again and read through it during his spare moments away from his military duties. More than the force of the story itself, what seemed to flare out from every line of the book was the intensity of Isao's eyes that night and the fire of his words.

The rough simplicity of a shared military life was something of a boon to the Prince, who had been altogether sheltered from the world, and he found it extremely congenial. Yet here too, there was deference and regard for rank. Not until he met that young civilian had he encountered such burning purity, and at searingly close range. And so the conversation of that night had been unforgettable.

What was loyalty? Soldiers had no need to wonder about that, the fiery young man had said. Their loyalty as soldiers was part of their duty.

Those words, the Prince realized, had struck home. Adopting a gruff, martial manner, the Prince had fitted himself to the obvious standard of loyalty of the soldier. Probably he had sought refuge in it in flight from a host of threatening sorrows. He knew nothing first-hand of the kind of loyalty that burns and destroys the flesh.

Nor had he had any reason to take notice of its possible existence. The night Isao was brought to him was the first time that the Prince had had an authentic encounter with such fiery loyalty, with such raw and uncontained loyalty. The experience had thrilled him.

Prince Harunori was, of course, ready at any moment to give his life for the Emperor. Some fourteen years older than His Majesty, who was thirty-one, the Prince had a love for the Emperor like that of an affectionate older brother. But these were serene, quiet feelings, a pleasant loyalty like the shade cast by a huge tree. Then too, the Prince habitually viewed with some suspicion the loyalty of those beneath him, and kept his distance from it.

Deeply impressed by Isao, Prince Toin had dedicated himself more gladly than ever to the simplicity of the military spirit. And now it occurred to him that the reason no evidence of military involvement in this incident had come to light was that the accused had kept silent to protect Lieutenant Hori. This speculation increased his sympathy all the more.

Prince Toin recalled a passage from *The League of the Divine Wind* that Isao must have read with keen appreciation, applying it to himself: 'Most of them did not take to refinement. They loved the moon shining on the banks of the Shirakawa with the love of men who believed that it was the last harvest moon they would see in this life. They prized the cherry blossoms like men for whom this spring's blossoms were the last that would ever bloom.' The hot blood of such young men made the forty-five-year-old regimental commander's heart stir excitedly within his breast.

Prince Toin began to ponder earnestly whether or not he could save these boys. All his life, whenever he became weary of thinking, whenever a problem seemed to have no solution, his practice had been to listen to Western-style music.

He called his orderly and had him light a fire in the chilly parlour of his large official residence. Then he selected a record and laid it on the turntable with his own hand.

Because he wanted to listen to something pleasant, he had chosen Richard Strauss's 'Till Eulenspiegel' performed by the Berlin Philharmonic under the direction of Wilhelm Furtwängler, and he dismissed his orderly so that he could enjoy it alone.

'Till Eulenspiegel' was a satiric sixteenth-century folk tale. Hauptmann's play and Strauss's tone poem based upon it were famous.

The late December wind whistled through the broad, dark garden outside the commandant's residence, and seemed to blend with the sound of the flames in the stove.

Without so much as loosening the collar of his Army tunic, Prince Toin settled himself in an armchair with a white linen slipcover that was cold to the touch. He crossed his legs in their military breeches, and the tip of one foot in its white cotton sock hung motionless in mid-air. The buttons at the knee of breeches like these constricted the upper calf, and so one usually unfastened them when one's boots were off, but the Prince paid no attention to the slight discomfort of this congestion. He caressed the waxed and curled tip of his moustache lightly, as if touching the tail feathers of some fierce bird.

It was a long time since he had listened to this record. He wanted something entertaining, but when he heard the first weak sounds of the horn that played Till's theme he had the immediate feeling that his choice had been wrong, that this was not the kind of music he would enjoy hearing now. For this was not a gay and mischievous Till, but a sad and lonely one, as transparent as crystal, a character fashioned by the conductor himself.

But Prince Toin kept on listening. From Till's going into a frenzy when he seemed to make the silvery bundle of his nerves into a duster that beat its way throughout the parlour, up until the end, when he received his sentence of death and was executed, Prince Toin heard it all. When the record was done, he got to his feet abruptly and rang the bell summoning his orderly. He instructed him to put in a long-distance call to Tokyo and to get his steward on the line.

The Prince had come to a decision. On the occasion of his return to Tokyo for the approaching New Year's holidays, he would request a few minutes with His Majesty, during which he would make bold to bring to the Imperial attention the unparalleled loyalty of Isao and his companions. And when some gracious response had come forth from His Majesty, the Prince would convey this in strictest confidence to the Chief Justice of the Supreme Court. But first, before the year ended, he had to invite the lawyer in charge of Isao's defence to discuss with him all the ramifications of the case.

By telephone, then, he ordered the steward to find out the name of the lawyer and to have him come to the Toin residence on a date immediately following the Prince's arrival in Tokyo on December twenty-ninth.

Until he was able to find a suitable place of his own, Honda had established himself in a room that was part of the office of a friend of his on the fifth floor of the Marunouchi Building. The friend was also a lawyer, and a college classmate.

One day an official came from the Toin residence to convey a confidential request from His Highness. Since this was indeed something unprecedented, Honda was startled. When he saw the little man in a black suit walking stealthily across the brown linoleum floor without making a sound, Honda felt an indescribable distaste, and, after he had led him into the conference room, the sensation grew more acute. The little man had a frozen yet uneasy expression as he looked around the small conference room, which was separated from the office by a wall of rippled glass. He was anxious about being overheard.

His face was like that of a pale fish fitted with gold-rimmed glasses. It told of living in a habitat of cold, dark waters never visited by the light of the sun, of breathing only with trepidation beneath the tangled seaweed of red tape.

Honda, who still had a little of the haughtiness of a judge, started off by brusquely neglecting the civilities.

'As far as guarding secrets goes, that's our business, and so I would urge you to put your mind at rest. And, especially since your errand has to do with such an august personage, I will exercise the greatest care imaginable.'

The official spoke in an extremely low voice, as if he had a lung ailment, and Honda was obliged to lean forward from the edge of his chair to hear him.

'No, no, there's no question of any sort of secrecy being involved. His Highness is pleased to take some interest in this affair, and he merely requests that you be gracious enough to visit his residence on December thirtieth. And if you would then have the goodness to tell him frankly whatever lies within the scope of your knowledge, he would be more than gratified. However...' Here the little man stammered spasmodically, as though trying to choke back an attack of hiccups. 'However, as to ... that is, if His Highness were to learn of what I have to say next, a grave problem would result, and I would therefore beg you refrain from mentioning it to him.'

'I understand. Please speak freely.'

'Well ... since this is an opinion that is by no means held by me alone, I would be pleased if you would be sensitive in this regard. But in the event, as it were, of your happening to catch a cold on the appointed day and being thus prevented from coming, and if you were to notify us of it, that too would be entirely agreeable. Since His Highness's desire has been duly communicated to you.'

Honda stared in amazement at the expressionless face of this delegate sent by Prince Toin. His mission was to deliver an invitation, but he hinted that Honda should contrive to slip out of it. To receive such an invitation from Prince Toin, nineteen years after his indirect involvement in Kiyoaki's death, was a strange turn of fate, and Honda had become ill at ease as soon as he had heard His Highness's request. But now, confronted with so odd a message. he became determined to pay his respects at the Toin residence.

'Very well. Then, if on that day I am without the least trace of a cold and the very picture of health, I am to present myself to His Highness. Is that correct?'

For the first time the official's face showed a slight expression. A sad discomfiture lingered briefly on the cold tip of his nose. But then, as though nothing had happened, the voice like the breeze blowing through bamboo grass went on.

'Yes, of course, of course. So please be good enough to come to the Shiba Residence at ten o'clock on the morning of December thirtieth. I will have informed the guard at the main gate, and you need merely give your name.'

Though Honda had been a student at Peers School, he had never had the experience of visiting the home of a member of the Imperial Family, perhaps because no personage so exalted had happened to be in the same class with him. Nor had he ever sought the opportunity.

Honda knew that the Prince had been involved in Kiyoaki's death, but no doubt the Prince was unaware that Honda had been Kiyoaki's friend. Since, in all justice, Prince Toin had been an injured party in that affair, the best course was to say nothing about it unless His Highness brought it up. A mention of Kiyoaki's name would in itself be an insult. Honda, of course, well realized this and knew how he must conduct himself.

On the basis of the official's manner the previous day, however, Honda's intuition told him that Prince Toin, for whatever reason, seemed to have a sympathetic attitude toward this most recent affair – never dreaming that Isao was none other than Kiyoaki reborn!

Whatever the official might think of it, Honda made up his mind that, just as the Prince had requested, he would tell him everything he knew, giving a true picture of the affair without saying anything that bordered upon disrespect.

Thus when he went out on the day set, his mind was tranquil. The winter rain, begun the previous day, was still falling, and the rivulets that streamed down through the gravel of the sloping path that led to the Toin residence wet Honda's shoes. The official himself greeted him at the entrance hall, but though courtesy informed his every word and action, the coldness of his manner was strikingly apparent. Indeed the white skin of this little man seemed to secrete coldness.

The visitors' parlour was a strange little room. Two of its walls formed an obtuse angle containing a door and a window which opened upon a rain-soaked balcony. A third wall was fitted with a *tokonoma*-like alcove, and the incense burning in it filled the room with a tenacious fragrance intensified by the heat coming from the glowing gas stove.

At length Prince Toin, the stately figure of a regimental commander in a dark brown suit, made his appearance, his cheerful manner calculated to put his guest at ease.

'Well, here I've brought you out in mid-morning. How kind of you to come!' said the Prince in a voice much too loud for the occasion.

Honda offered his card and bowed low.

'Please make yourself comfortable. My reason for asking you to come has to do with this affair that you are concerned with. I am told you have gone so far as to resign your judgeship in order to undertake the defence of these youths.'

'That is correct, Your Highness. One of them is the only son of an acquaintance of mine.'

'Iinuma, I take it?' asked Prince Toin with the straightforwardness of a soldier.

The window was clouded with drops of moisture from the heat. The winter rain seemed a mist as it fell upon the bleak trees in the broad garden and upon the pine and hemp palms outside the window, each of which was wound with straw mats to protect it from frost. A white-gloved butler served English-style tea. He filled the white china cups with a graceful amber stream issuing from the slender spout of a silver teapot. Honda withdrew his fingers from the sudden heat that his silver spoon transmitted. The too keen warmth all at once reminded him of the punishment provisions of the Imperial Code, which seemed to vibrate there in the silver.

'The fact is, someone once brought Isao Iinuma to my house,' said the Prince calmly. 'At that time he made a strong impression upon me. He expressed himself very passionately; he seemed absolutely sincere. And he has quite a head on his shoulders. A superior mind. No matter what tricky questions I put to him, his response was invariably to the point. A somewhat dangerous boy, but one with nothing frivolous about him. That such a worthy youth should stumble like this is indeed cause for regret. And so when I heard that you had cast aside your profession to become his lawyer, I was delighted and wished to meet you.'

'The boy, Your Highness, is wholly devoted to the Emperor. On the occasion of his coming here, did he express himself in such terms to Your Highness?'

'Yes. He said that loyalty was presenting to the Emperor steaming rice balls made with his own hands. And after that, whatever the result, loyalty demanded cutting open his stomach. He gave me a book called *The League of the Divine Wind* ... But surely he won't kill himself, will he?'

'Both the police and the prison authorities are alert to that possibility, so there seems to be no need for concern. But, Your Highness...' said Honda, gradually growing bolder and turning the conversation in the direction he wanted, 'Your Highness, to what degree do you countenance the conduct of these boys? How far would you go in supporting them, not only in the actions that have already come to light but in their entire plot? Or, indeed, would you deign to countenance whatever came forth from their burning sincerity?'

'That's not an easy question,' said the Prince. There was a disconcerted expression on his face as he halted his teacup in front of his moustache, a wavering ribbon of steam rising from the cup. At that moment Honda felt an unaccountable urge to inform the Prince of the circumstances of Kiyoaki's sorrowful death.

The Prince's self-esteem must have suffered a severe wound from the incident involving Kiyoaki, but Honda was uncertain as to whether or not passion had been the cause of the Prince's vulnerability. If, however, years before, the Prince's whole being had indeed become suffused with the splendour radiated by that bright phantom that draws all men – high and low, rich and poor alike – to death, to hell, if he owed his wound to that passion, altogether ignorant, altogether noble, that blinds men with its splendour ... And then as to Satoko, if it had been she herself and no one else who had turned the Prince's passion to ashes ... If that could be made known here and now ... no more consoling requiem could be offered for Kiyoaki. Nothing, Honda thought, could more comfort Kiyoaki's soul. Love and loyalty sprang from the same source. If Prince Toin would give some clear evidence of this, Honda would find in himself the sincere dedication to risk everything to protect the Prince. Thus, though Kiyoaki's name was a forbidden word, Honda, using this present issue as a metaphor of the storm of passion that had brought Kiyoaki to his death, now had the courage to test the Prince by speaking of something that up to now he had kept back for fear of showing disrespect. It might perhaps be to Isao's disadvantage in the trial, and perhaps, as a lawyer, he should leave it unsaid. But he could not suppress the thought that the voice of Kiyoaki and Isao were crying out together within him.

'The truth is, Your Highness, that according to what the investigation brought out, though this is still a matter of the deepest secrecy, it seems that the Iinuma group had something more in mind than the assassination of certain men of the financial world.'

'Something new has come out?'

'Their plot was, of course, nipped in the bud, but, as might be expected of such youths, they were moved by the earnest desire to see the governing power in the benvolent hands of His Majesty.'

'That's understandable.'

'Their primary objective was, I believe, the formation of a cabinet headed by a member of the Imperial Family. I find it very difficult to say this, but the police discovered leaflets secretly printed by them in which Your Highness's name has a prominent place.'

'My name?' exclaimed the Prince, his expression abruptly altered.

'The leaflets had been mimeographed with the intention of distributing them speedily after the assassinations, in order to make the populace believe the falsehood that the Emperor had vested Your Highness with authority to take action. Once the Prosecutor's Office became aware of them, their attitude hardened immeasurably. And my task is now all the more difficult. Depending upon how they handle it, this could result in the charges becoming extremely grave.'

'That is an offence against the Emperor! It's absurd. It's a shocking thing.'

Though the Prince's voice grew louder, this did not conceal a note of fear. Honda, still intent on testing the Prince's state of mind, quietly asked another question. He looked steadily into the Prince's almond eyes.

'It is rude of me to ask this, Your Highness, but could it be that in the military too there was similar sentiment?'

'Not at all. The military was not in the least involved. It's absurd to try to link it to the military. The whole thing came out of the fevered brains of schoolboys.'

Prince Toin, Honda realized, was angrily shutting the door in his guest's face to protect the Army. Honda's most cherished hope was shattered.

'Imagine a boy that intelligent coming up with such nonsense!' said the Prince as though muttering to himself. 'I am profoundly disappointed. And of all things, to use my name! To exploit my name that way after a single meeting, the name of an imperial prince! He's lost all sense of obligation – at least he doesn't know where to stop. He doesn't understand that there could be no greater disloyalty than an offence against the Emperor. Is this his concept of loyalty? Of sincerity? How distressing that young men are like that!' There was no longer any trace of the magnanimity of a leader of troops. His heart had suddenly turned cold. And Honda, as he listened, had easily perceived the instant change in His Highness's zeal. The fire that had burned in the imperial breast had been extinguished, embers and all.

Prince Toin was thinking how well it was that he had decided to meet with this lawyer. Now when he paid his respects to His Majesty at the New Year, he would make no mention of this to him, and thus he would avoid later mortification. But misgivings swarmed in his mind. It hardly seemed possible that such an offence could have been planned by schoolboys. How strange that he had heard nothing at all from Lieutenant Hori since this affair! Prince Toin had felt sorry to learn of his transfer to Manchuria, but now, as he considered the matter, he began to wonder if the Lieutenant might not have volunteered to go, fleeing before the affair broke. If that was the case, the Prince had been used, had been betrayed by this officer in whom he had placed such trust.

Since his hatred had its root in fear, it kept growing. For a long while Prince Toin's attitude towards those in the Imperial Household Ministry and towards that little group who made up the upper class had been one of distrust and revulsion. And now the odour of treachery had risen even from the one place where his mind had been at rest. That smell was all too familiar. He had only to reflect, and the memory came to him of how, ever since his childhood, it had been on all sides of him. The odour of a fox's den. No matter how he tried to banish it, this odour permeated his exalted surroundings, sinister, affronting the nostrils, an excremental stench of treachery.

Honda glanced through the window at the falling rain. The glass was becoming more and more clouded. The colour of the fresh mats wrapped protectively around the hemp palms in the foreground shone dully amid the rain-soaked scene, giving the impression of khaki-uniformed men crowding about the window. Honda knew that he was about to take a dangerous gamble, one that never would have occurred to him during his years as a judge. Of course he had not arrived at the Prince's residence with such a strategy already in mind. But with the pitiful ashes of His Highness's passion before his eyes, a sudden, reckless hope sprang up within him. This approach would be entirely different, no longer a matter of the Prince's interest in saving Isao. The approach left to Honda, one that was far more cogent, would have the effect of smoothly diverting Prince Toin to an effort to save Isao without his having the least intention of doing so. At this moment there was no one but Honda to instil such a resolution in the Prince, nor would there be another opportunity like this. And so, though with much trepidation, he felt obliged to urge this skilfully upon the Prince. The incendiary literature in question was in the hands of the prosecution, still unknown to the general public.

Trying to speak as calmly as possible, Honda said: 'With regard to those pamphlets in which Your Highness's name occurs, if they are allowed to remain as they are, and if this results in any awkward consequences for Your Highness, I am afraid that an extremely unfortunate situation will arise.'

'Awkward consequences? From something with which I had no connection?'

For the first time the Prince turned eyes upon Honda in which anger showed clearly. He raised his voice only a little, however, revealing that he felt some fear about giving way to anger. But his anger was precious to Honda. He felt that he had to make the most of it.

'I beg your pardon, Your Highness. But it seems to me that this material is dangerous, and in spite of my concern for Your Highness's welfare, I haven't the power to see that it's suppressed. Unless you take action speedily, it will sooner or later become public knowledge, and though you are involved in no way in this affair, grounds will be given for speculation that you are involved.'

'Do you mean that I have the power to suppress it?'

'Yes, Your Highness. You do have that power.'

'How?'

'It is simply a matter of Your Highness so directing the Imperial Household Minister,' Honda answered without hesitation.

'You're telling me to bend my knee to the Imperial Household Minister?' The Prince's voice finally became as loud as before. The fingers with which he tapped the arm of his chair trembled with anger. His impressive eyes, their pupils fixed, were wide open. He looked as stern as if shouting orders to his troops from horseback.

'Not at all, Your Highness. If you but give the order, the Minister will arrange things in an agreeable manner. For when I was a judge and an occasion arose that had some bearing upon the Imperial Family, I always treated the matter with extreme deference. The Imperial Household Minister will confer with the Minister of Justice, the Minister of Justice will give orders to the Attorney General, and the existence of those leaflets may well be totally disregarded.'

'Could that be done so easily?' the Prince asked with a little sigh. Before him was the face of the Imperial Household Minister, wearing that disagreeable soft smile of his.

'Yes, Your Highness. Given Your Highness's authority...' Honda's tone was so earnest and decisive that Prince Toin seemed much encouraged.

With this, Honda thought, one dangerous and ominous shadow hanging over Isao's crime had been swept away. But this happily accomplished, what was now to be feared was the Public Prosecutor's subtle revenge.

33

After having spent the New Year's in a police cell, Isao was transferred to Ichigaya Prison at the end of January when he was indicted. Through the weave of the basketlike headcover that prisoners wore he glimpsed the dirty remnants of a two-day snowfall piled in shaded spots along the streets. The many colours of the advertising banners hanging before the market stalls were heightened by the afternoon rays of the winter sun. The fifteen-foot iron door of the south entrance to the prison opened with a high screech from its hinges, admitted the car carrying Isao, and closed again.

Ichigaya Prison had been completed in 1904, and was of frame construction, its exterior covered with grey mortar and its interior walls almost all of white plaster. After entering through the south gate, the prisoners awaiting trial got out of their vehicle and walked through a covered passageway which brought them to an inspection room called 'Central'.

This bare room was more than sixty feet square. One wall was lined with narrow wooden cubicles like telephone booths. Here prisoners waited their turn. On the other side was a toilet with a glass door. The officer in charge sat on a high platform surrounded by a wooden enclosure, and just beyond, its floor covered only with a thin matting, was a place to change clothes.

The cold was severe. Isao was led with the others to the changing place, and there he was made to strip to the last stitch. He had to open his mouth and have even his back teeth examined. Guards carefully peered into the orifices of his ears and his nose. His arms were spread, and the front part of his body was scrutinized. Then he had to get down on all fours and be examined from the rear. Handled in this rude fashion, one's own body began to seem alien, and only one's thoughts remained secure. This state of mind was already a refuge from humiliation. Stripped of clothing, goose flesh over his entire body, Isao was feeling the lash of cold sparing no part of him, when a brilliant red and blue phantom appeared to him. What was it? He had happened to recall the tattoo artist, a habitual gambler, with whom he had found himself in a common detention cell. The man had been taken with Isao's skin and had repeatedly begged him to let himself be tattooed, free of charge, once they were out of prison. He told Isao that he wanted to cover the fresh skin of his back with lions and peonies. Why lions and peonies? Perhaps because that sort of red and blue pattern, like the reflection of glowing evening clouds upon the dark waters of a marsh covering a valley floor, was a sunset burst of colour that rose out of the very nadir of humiliation. No doubt the tattoo artist had seen the setting sun reflected deep in some valley. And nothing but lions and peonies would suffice to capture it...

However, when Isao felt a guard's hand touch the moles on his side and squeeze them momentarily, he realized once again that he could never commit suicide out of humiliation. During his sleepless nights in the detention cell he had toyed with the thought of killing himself. But the concept of suicide remained for Isao what it had always been, something extraordinarily bright and luxurious.

Prisoners awaiting trial could wear their own clothes, but since Isao had to hand over his present clothing to be steam-fumigated, he was obliged to wear blue prison garb for a day. He also had to gather together his personal belongings and, aside from what he needed for everyday use, turn these over to a guard. Then from the officer in charge, high upon his platform, he heard various instructions, on gifts sent in, interviews, letters, and the like. It was already night.

Other than the times he was led before the District Court for preliminary hearings, handcuffed and with a rope around his waist, Isao spent his days in a cell all to himself in Block 13 of Ichigaya Prison. At seven in the morning, a steam whistle blew, the signal to rise. The whistle was located above the kitchen, drawing its energy from the boilers. Though its noise was piercing, it seemed filled with the cheerful, steamy warmth of life. At seven thirty in the evening the same whistle gave the signal for retiring. One night Isao heard a cry while the whistle was blowing and shouts of abuse immediately afterwards. This was repeated the following night. On the second night, Isao realized that that cry, under cover of the whistle, was a prisoner shouting 'Long live the revolution!' in unison with a comrade whose cell window was in the wall opposite him. The shouts of abuse were those of a guard who had overheard them. Isao never heard this prisoner's voice again, perhaps because he had been removed to a punishment cell. Human beings, Isao realized, could descend to communicating their feelings like dogs barking in the distance on a cold night. It was as though he could hear even the restless shuffling about of chained dogs and the scratching of nails upon a concrete floor.

Isao too, of course, missed his comrades. But even in the common detention cell where he was put after being taken by bus to await his preliminary hearings, he was unable to learn anything about them, much less look upon their faces.

The gradual lengthening of the days was the only sign of the approach of spring. The straw matting that covered the floor of his cell still seemed to be woven of frost. And the chill made his knees stiff.

Isao longed to see his comrades who had been arrested with him; and as for those who had slipped so effortlessly away right before they were to strike, when he thought of them, rather than anger, he felt something mystical. Their sudden falling away had brought with it a sense of tranquillity, the lightness of a tree newly pruned. But what was at the heart of this mystery? What had brought about this reverse? The longer he pondered these questions, the more he avoided the word 'betrayal'.

Before he was thrown into prison, Isao was never one to dwell upon the past. If he thought about it at all, his mind would instantly turn to the League of the Divine Wind and the sixth year of the Meiji era. Now, however, everything forced upon Isao a consideration of the most recent past. The immediate cause of so swift a downfall for him and his sworn companions was Lieutenant Hori, of course, but, from the outset, his comrades had made their vows without waiting to assure themselves that the enterprise was possible. Something had abruptly given way, an avalanche within the heart, something that could not be stemmed. Isao himself had not been unaware of that interior avalanche. At that time, however, not one of the vowed group who had remained true would have been able, Isao was quite sure, to foresee their present situation. What they had thought of then was death. They were completely given over to fighting and dying. Indeed they had lacked the caution necessary to accomplish their aims. They had been confident in the thought that their rashness could bring on nothing other than death. How had they come to this humiliating and agonizing end? Isao's concept of purity had been that of a noble bird meant to perish by flying so high that the sun would sear its wings. He had never dreamed that any hand could capture that bird alive. As for Sawa, who was not with them at the time of their capture, Isao had no idea how he was faring now, but, even though he did not want to think of him, Sawa's face flashed disagreeably from somewhere deep among the emotions that clogged Isao's breast.

Article 14 of the Peace Preservation Laws put the matter bluntly: 'All secret organizations are forbidden.' And loyalist organizations such as that of Isao and his companions, firmly bound together in a blood brotherhood, ready to spill their hot blood so that they could rise up to the heavens, were proscribed by their very nature. But as for political organizations bent upon further enriching the bellies of vested interests, as for corporations bent on profit, there was no objection to forming any number of these. It was in the nature of authority to fear purity more than any sort of corruption. Just as savages fear medical treatment more than disease.

Isao finally came to the questions that he had up to now been avoiding: 'Does a blood brotherhood in itself invite betrayal?' This was a most dreadful thought.

If men brought their hearts together beyond a certain degree, if they were intent upon making their hearts one, did not a reaction set in after that brief fantasy had passed, a reaction that was more than simply alienation? Did it not inevitably provoke a betrayal that led to complete dissolution?

Perhaps there was some unwritten law of human nature that clearly proscribed covenants among men. Had he impudently violated such a proscription? In ordinary human relationships, good and evil, trust and mistrust appear in impure form, mixed together in small portions. But when men gather together to form a group devoted to a purity not of this world, their evil may remain, purged from each member but coalesced to form a single pure crystal. Thus in the midst of a collection of pure white gems, perhaps it was inevitable that one gem black as pitch could also be found.

If one took this concept a bit further, one encountered an extremely pessimistic line of thought: the substance of evil was to be found more in blood brotherhoods by their very nature than in betrayal. Betrayal was something that was derived from this evil, but the evil was rooted in the blood brotherhood itself. The purest evil that human efforts could attain, in other words, was probably achieved by those men who made their wills the same and who made their eyes see the world in the same way, men who went against the pattern of life's diversity, men whose spirit shattered the natural wall of the individual body, making nothing of this barrier set up to guard against mutual corrosion, men whose spirit accomplished what flesh could never accomplish. *Collaboration* and *cooperation* were weak terms bound up with anthropology. But *blood brotherhood* ... that was a matter of eagerly joining one's spirit to the spirit of another. This in itself showed a bright scorn for the futile, laborious human process in which ontogeny was eternally recapitulating phylogeny, in which man forever tried to draw a bit closer to truth only to be frustrated by death, a process that had ever to begin again in the sleep within the amniotic fluid. By betraying this human condition the blood brotherhood tried to gain its purity, and thus it was perhaps but to be expected that it, in turn, should of its very nature incur its own betrayal. Such men had never respected humanity.

Isao, of course, did not pursue the idea that far. But he had obviously reached the point where he had to make some sort of breakthrough by thinking. He felt resentment that his intellect lacked keen and ruthless canine teeth.

Seven thirty was too early for retiring, and his sleeplessness was worsened by the twenty-watt light that burned all night long, by the faint rustle of lice beginning to stir, by the stink of urine from the oval wooden pot in the corner, by the cold that brought a flush to the face. But soon the whistles of the freight trains that passed through Ichigaya Station told Isao that it was the dead of night.

'Why, why?' he thought, gritting his teeth. 'Why are people not allowed to do what is most beautiful, when ugly, shoddy acts, acts for the sake of gain, are all freely allowed?

'At a time when there is no doubt that the highest morality lies concealed only in the intent to kill, the law that punishes that intent is exercised in the sacred name of His Majesty, the sun without blemish. And so the highest morality itself is punished by the very personification of the highest morality. Who could have put together such a contradiction? Could His Majesty have any knowledge of such an appalling contrivance? Is this not a blasphemous system that a skilled disloyalty spent much time and effort to create?

'I don't understand. I don't understand it at all. And then, after we did the killing, not one of us would have disregarded his vow to kill himself at once. So if we could have done as we had meant to, not a single branch, not a single leaf of the tangled thicket of the law would have brushed so much as the tip of our sleeve or the hem of our kimono. We would have slipped marvellously through the thicket and gone rushing headlong up into the bright sky of heaven. So it was with the League of the Divine Wind. Though, I know, the tangled underbrush of the law didn't grow as thick in the sixth year of Meiji. The law is an accumulation of tireless attempts to block a man's desire to change life into an instant of poetry. Certainly it would not be right to let everybody exchange his life for a line of poetry written in a splash of blood. But the mass of men, lacking valour, passed away their lives without ever feeling the least touch of such a desire. The law, therefore, of its very nature is aimed at a tiny minority of mankind. The extraordinary purity of a handful of men, the passionate devotion that knows nothing of the world's standards ... the law is a system that tries to degrade them to "evil", on the same level as robbery and crimes of passion. This is the clever trap that I fell into. And because of nothing else but somebody's betrayal!'

The whistle of a freight passing through Ichigaya Station stabbed through his thoughts. It brought to his mind a man racked with an emotion so intense that he was like one rolling about on the ground to put out his flaming kimono. The heart-rending cry of the man tumbling in the blackness was wrapped in a swirl of its own fiery particles and glowed red with its own blaze.

This train whistle, however, differed from the prison whistle with its false warmth of life. This voice, though twisted with anguish, somehow pulsated with a limitless freedom and offered a smooth access to the future. Another part of the country, another day – even the rust-covered phantom of a white, sour-faced morning suddenly appearing in the line of mirrors above the sinks on some station platform did not suffice to dispel the powerful attraction of strangeness the whistle conveyed.

Then the dawn came at his prison window. From the window of the easternmost cell on the right of the three rows in Block 13, after a night without sleep, Isao watched the red winter sun rise.

The horizon was a high wall, and the sun clung to that line like a soft, warm rice cake before gently climbing. The Japan that that sun shone upon had refused the help of Isao and his comrades, and lay prey to sickness, corruption, and disaster.

It was after this that Isao, for the first time in his life, began to have dreams.

Of course, it was not actually the first time he had dreamed. But his earlier dreams had been the kind that a healthy youth forgot with the coming of morning. Never once had a dream lingered to affect his waking hours. Now it was different. Not only through the morning but through his entire day, last night's dream would persist, sometimes linked with the memory of the dream of the night before, or to be continued in the dream of the next night. His dreams were like bright-coloured garments put out to dry and left forgotten in the rain, hanging on the clothes pole without ever drying. The rain continued. Perhaps a madman lived in the house. And more printed silk robes were added to the drying pole, bright splotches of colour against the sombre sky.

One night he dreamed of a snake.

The setting was the tropics, perhaps the garden of a large mansion somewhere, which was surrounded by jungle so thick that the walls that bordered it could not be seen.

He seemed to be in the middle of this jungle garden, standing upon a terrace of crumbling grey stone. The house to which the terrace belonged could not be seen. There was nothing but this small, square terrace which defined a grey rocky zone of stillness, the curving stone images of cobras rising up from pillars set at each of its corners, like four outspread hands pushing back the heavy tropic air. A hot square of silence cut from the heart of the jungle.

He heard the whine of mosquitoes. He heard the buzzing of flies. Yellow butterflies flew about. The cries of birds came down to him like drops of blue water ever falling. And, now and again, came still another bird cry, a frenzied cry that seemed to tear through the very midst of the intricate tangle of green vegetation. Cicadas were shrilling.

Rather than these varied sounds, however, what most affronted the ear was a roar like that of a sudden rainstorm. It was not, of course. A passing wind was shaking the jungle growth that bound the treetops together, far above the shaded terrace, but since its effect was not felt below, the only visible sign of its passing was the movement of the flecks of sunlight that dappled the cobras' heads.

Leaves high up, caught by the wind, slipped down through the foliage, and the noise they made sounded like falling rain. Not all of them were newly torn from their branches. Tree limbs were thrust against each other to undergird the nearly impenetrable mass of vines that caught up leaves as they dropped away. A fresh wind would cause these to fall a second time, working down through the branches with a sound like heavy rain. Since the leaves were broad and parched, they made an echoing din. Each one that fell upon the stone terrace, overgrown with moss white as leprosy, was large.

The tropical light was like thousands of massed spearheads of marshalled troops. Reflections fell everywhere about Isao, as patches of sunlight filtered through the branches above. To look at that light directly would be blinding, to touch it would be to scorch one's fingers. From beyond the jungle growth, it held everything in siege. Isao felt its presence crowding in even upon the terrace.

At that moment Isao noticed a little green snake put its head through the railing. What had seemed to be an outstretched vine there suddenly grew longer. The snake was quite thick, like a waxwork figure coloured in light and dark shades of green. Its lustrous, artificial-looking body was not a vine, something Isao discovered too late. Its fangs had already found their mark by the time he realized that it had coiled itself to strike at his ankle.

The chill of death came to him through the tropic air. Isao shivered.

He was suddenly cut off from the torrid heat. The venom had driven all warmth from his body. Each of his pores awakened fearfully to the coldness of death. He could breathe only with difficulty, and each breath became more shallow. Soon the world had no more breath to put into his mouth. But the movement of life went on throbbing keenly within him. Against his will, his skin, like the surface of a pond struck by a shower, grew puckered. 'I was not meant to die like this. I was meant to die by cutting open my stomach. I never expected to die this way, a passive, miserable death by a chance of nature, a small touch of malice.' Even as he thought this, Isao seemed to feel his body freezing into a block as solid as a fish so frozen that a hammer blow could not shatter it. When he opened his eyes, he saw that he had kicked off his quilt and was lying in his cell in the glimmering dawn light of an unusually chilly early spring morning.

Another night he had this dream.

This one was so strange and disagreeable that he tried afterwards again and again to banish it from his mind. This was a dream in which Isao was transformed into a woman.

He was not at all certain, however, what sort of woman his body had been changed into. Perhaps because he seemed to be blind, he could only grope with his hands to try to find out. He felt as if the world had been turned inside out, and he was sitting languidly in a chair by a window, his body lightly covered with sweat, possibly just after awakening from an afternoon nap.

Perhaps his previous dream of the snake was impinging upon this one. What he heard were the cries of jungle birds, the buzzing of flies, the rainlike patter of falling leaves. And then there was an odour like sandalwood – he recognized it because once he had lifted the lid and sniffed inside a sandalwood tobacco box that his father prized – a melancholy, lonely odour, the sweet, bodylike odour of old wood. Suddenly he thought of something that resembled it: the odour of the blackened embers that he had seen on the path through the rice fields in Yanagawa.

Isao felt that his flesh had lost definite form, turned into flesh that was soft and swaying. He was filled with a mist of soft, languid flesh. Everything became vague. Wherever he searched, he could find no order or structure. There was no supporting pillar. The brilliant fragments of light that had once sparkled around him, ever drawing him on, had disappeared. Comfort and discomfort, joy and sorrow – all alike slid over his skin like soap. Entranced, he soaked in a warm bath of flesh.

The bath by no means imprisoned him. He could step out whenever he liked, but the languid pleasure kept him from abandoning it, so that staying there forever, not choosing to go, had become his 'freedom'. Thus there was nothing to define him, to keep him under strict control. What had once wound itself tightly round and round him like a rope of platinum had slipped loose.

Everything he had so firmly believed in was meaningless. Justice was like a fly that has tumbled into a box of face powder and smothered; beliefs for which he had meant to offer up his life were sprayed with perfume and melted. All glory dissolved in the mild warmth of mud.

Sparkling snow had melted away entirely. He felt the uncertain warmth of spring mud within him. Slowly something took form from that spring mud, a womb. Isao shuddered as the thought came to him that he would soon give birth. His strength had always spurred him with violent impatience towards action, had always responded to a distant voice that conjured up the image of a vast wilderness. But now, that strength had left him. The voice was silent. The outer world, which no longer called to him, now, rather, was drawing closer to him, was touching him. And he felt too sluggish to get up and move away.

A sharp-edged mechanism of steel had died. In its place, an odour like that of decaying seaweed, an entirely organic odour, had somehow or other permeated his body. Justice, zeal, patriotism, aspirations for which to hazard one's life – all had vanished. In their place came an indescribable intimacy with the things around him – clothing, utensils, pincushions, cosmetics – an intimacy in which he seemed to flow into and merge with all the minutiae of gentle, beautiful things. It was an intimacy of smiles and winks, one that was almost obscene, outside the range of Isao's previous experience. The only thing that he had been intimate with had been the sword.

Things clung to him like paste, and, at the same time, lost all their transcendental significance.

Trying to arrive at some goal was no longer a problem. Everything was arriving here from elsewhere. Thus there was no longer a horizon, no longer any islands. And with no perspective at all evident, voyages were out of the question. There was only the endless sea.

Isao had never felt that he might want to be a woman. He had never wished for anything else but to be a man, live in a manly way, die a manly death. To be thus a man was to be required to give constant proof of one's manliness – to be more a man today than yesterday, more a man tomorrow than today. To be a man was to forge ever upward towards the peak of manhood, there to die amid the white snows of that peak.

But to be a woman? It seemed to mean being a woman at the beginning and being a woman forever.

The smoke of incense came to him. There was the echo of gongs and whistles – apparently a funeral procession passing by the window. He caught the muffled sound of people sobbing. But nothing clouded the contentment of the woman dozing on a summer afternoon. Fine beads of sweat covered her skin. Her senses had stored up a vast variety of memories. Her belly, swelling slightly as she breathed in her sleep, was puffed like a sail with the marvellous fullness of her flesh. The delicate navel, which checked that sail by tugging from within, its colour the fresh, rosy tinge of the bud of a wild cherry blossom, lay quietly beneath a tiny pool of sweat. The lovely tautness of the breasts of so regal an aspect seemed all the more to express the melancholy of the flesh. The skin, stretched fine, seemed to glow as though a lantern burned within. The smoothness of the skin extended as far as the tips of the breasts, where, like waves pressing in upon an atoll, the raised texture of the areolas emerged. The areolas were the colour of an orchid filled with a quiet, pervasive hostility, a poisonous colour meant to attract the mouth. From that deep purple, the nipple rose up piquantly, like a pert squirrel lifting its head. The effect was mischievously playful.

When he clearly saw the figure of this sleeping woman, even though her face was shrouded with sleep and its contours blurred, Isao thought that it had to be Makiko. Then a strong whiff of the perfume Makiko had worn when they parted came to him. Isao shot out his semen, and he awakened.

An indescribable sorrow remained. Though the sensation that he had been transformed into a woman had persisted in his dream, he could not recall the point at which the course of the dream had shifted so that he seemed to be gazing at the body of a woman whom he took to be Makiko. And this confusion was the source of his disturbed feeling. Furthermore, though it was a woman, Makiko apparently, whom he had defiled, he, the defiler, strangely enough could not rid himself of the vivid sensation that he had felt before, that the whole world was turned inside out.

The fearfully dark emotion that had enveloped him in sadness – never before had he experienced such an incomprehensible emotion – lingered on and on even after his eyes were open, and hung in the air under the dim light cast down by the feeble bulb in the ceiling like a yellow pressed flower.

Isao did not catch the sound of the guard's hemp-soled sandals coming down the corridor, and, taken by surprise, he had no time to shut his eyes before they met the guard's peering in through the observation slot.

'Go to sleep,' the guard said hoarsely, and then moved on.

Spring was drawing near.

His mother came often with packages for him, but she was never allowed to see him. She told him in a letter that Honda was going to defend him at the trial, and Isao wrote a long reply. Such good fortune was more than he had hoped for, he wrote, but he would have to refuse it unless Honda agreed to defend him together with his comrades as a group. No answer to this ever came. Nor was he given the opportunity to meet with Honda, something that should have been readily granted. In the letters he received from his mother there were many words and phrases deleted with black ink – no doubt the news of his comrades that he wanted so much to hear. No matter how he scrutinized the portions blotted out with black ink, he could not make out a single letter, nor could he deduce anything from the context.

Finally Isao began a letter to the man he felt least inclined to write to. He did his best to suppress all emotion, and he chose his words with the intent of not bringing further trouble upon Sawa, whom the authorities must at least have questioned about his contribution of money. Yet he hoped that the pangs of conscience would drive Sawa to do what he could to better their situation. He waited and waited, but no answer came, and Isao's anger took a despairing turn.

Since he had heard nothing further by way of his mother, Isao wrote a long letter of appreciation to Honda himself, addressing it in care of the Academy. In it he gave fervent expression to his desire that Honda act as defence counsel for the entire group. A reply came at once. With well-chosen words, Honda expressed his sympathy for the way Isao felt. He said that, since he had gotten into this affair, he might as well go all the way, and so he would be willing to defend them as a group, except, of course, for those who would be tried as juveniles. Nothing could have strengthened Isao more in his prison cell than this letter.

Isao was moved by the way in which Honda responded to his expressed desire to take all the punishment upon himself and have his comrades absolved: 'I understand your wanting to do this, but neither judges nor lawyers conduct themselves on the basis of their emotions. Since tragic feelings are certainly not of long duration, what is important now is to remain calm. I think that I can count upon you, as an expert in kendo, to understand what I mean. Leave everything to me – that is what I am for – take earnest care of your health, and bear your lot with patience. During the exercise periods, by all means give your body a vigorous workout.' Honda had correctly perceived that the sense of tragic heroism in Isao's heart, like the colours of a sunset, was gradually fading.

One day, since there was still no indication that he would be allowed to see Honda, Isao put his trust in the sympathetic manner of the judge in a preliminary hearing, and asked casually: 'Your Honour, when will I be allowed to see someone?'

The judge hesitated for a moment, obviously uncertain whether or not to reply. Then he said: 'Not as long as the prohibition against it is in force.'

'And who has laid that down, Your Honour?'

'The Prosecutor's Office,' the judge answered, his intonation conveying his own discontent with this measure.

34

His mother's letters kept on coming frequently, but no other letters had so many blotted portions. Sometimes a section would be clipped out, or even a whole page removed. His mother obviously lacked the wit to write in such a way as not to run afoul of the censor. But one day there was a change. The censor's job had apparently been taken over by a new man. The blotted portions were noticeably fewer, but, since his mother wrote under the impression that everything in her previous letters had been conveyed to him, his impatience was aggravated by the difficulty of deciphering. It was as though he were receiving later letters before their predecessors. But then there was one line, reading: 'The letters ... are piled up like a mountain. They say there are at least five thousand of them, and when I think ... my eyes fill up with tears,' in which, even though two sections had been inked over, the ink had been lightly applied as though the censor had been careless. Isao realized that the man had done so deliberately, to encourage him. In one section Isao was able to read without difficulty 'letters *asking for leniency*', and in the other, though it was more obscure, 'when I think *of the sympathy people have*'. For the first time Isao learned about the public reaction to the affair.

He was loved! He who had never in the least wanted to be loved. Perhaps a gentle, sympathetic concern had been stirred by his youth, by the immature purity that people naturally expected in the young, by considerations of his 'promising' future, and this had inspired the clemency letters. It was a conjecture that caused Isao some pain. The mass of petitions sent in after the May Fifteenth Incident must have been of a different nature.

'The world does not take me seriously.' Ever since his imprisonment Isao had been haunted by that single relentless thought. 'If people ever suspected the fearful, blood-smeared purity I revere, they'd hardly be able to feel any love for me.'

Not feared nor, much less, hated, only loved, he found himself in a situation that wounded his pride. It was spring. Most of all, he yearned for the letters from Makiko that arrived one after another at regular intervals, well aware though he was how ill such a desire became that resolve, tough as hardened glass, that he had long embraced.

In fact, I have always been peculiarly favoured, thought Isao. Something murky lay in the depths of that favour.

Was it not that the nation, the laws of the nation, perhaps in just the same way as the public, refused to take him seriously?

Then too, when he was being questioned in an interrogation room on a cold day, the police would urge him to sit closer to the hibachi, and, if he was hungry, they would bring him a dish of noodles with fried bean curd. Once an assistant inspector pointed at the flowers on the table and said, 'What do you think of these camellias? Aren't they pretty? There are winter camellias blooming in my garden, and this morning I cut these and brought them here. During interrogation, you see, it's most important to be at ease, and flowers make everyone feel more congenial.' The odour of a vulgarized refinement bent on using nature clung to the inspector's words, much like that given off by the white shirt that he wore day after day despite its cloud pattern of grime. Still, three pure white camellias pushed aside tough, dark green leaves with their outspread petals. Drops of water lay upon them as though upon white lard.

'This sunshine is nice, isn't it?' said the inspector, as he asked the policeman standing by to open the window. From where Isao was sitting, the winter camellias occupied half of his field of vision. The iron bars of the window let pass the warm, abstract winter sunshine, their shadows cutting through it with a precision that made it seem still more devoid of substance.

The probing ray of sunshine like a warm hand upon his shoulder – this for Isao was something quite different from the brilliant summer sun that he had seen pressing down with glittering authority upon the heads of the troops drilling upon the Azabu Regiment parade ground. This ray spoke of the kindliness of the judicial system come down to touch him upon the shoulder after many a twist and turn. It had nothing at all to do with the summer sun of the Imperial Benevolence, Isao thought.

'With patriots like you and your friends, I don't need to worry about the future of Japan. You shouldn't have violated the law, of course, but that shining sincerity of yours is something that even we can understand. And now, about you and your friends making your vows, when and where was that?'

Isao responded automatically. That evening of the summer before, in front of the shrine ... there arose in his mind the memory of all twenty of them clasping each other's hands, one hand over another, like white fruit whose weight bent the branches that bore it. Yet to call up the memory had become painful. As Isao answered, he looked away from the inspector, who kept watching him intently, and he gazed at the sunlight and one of the white camellias by turns. Dazzled by the sun, his eyes saw the whiteness of the camellias as pitch black, the flower a small, lustrous knot of hair. And, in the same way, the dark green leaves seemed to form a collar of pure white. He had a secret need for this play of the senses to help him withstand the discordance within him. For when he spoke the 'truth' – 'Yes, sir. There were twenty of us. We bowed twice and clapped twice before the shrine. And then I recited the vows, one part at a time, and the others repeated it in unison' – giving an account that was totally unembellished, the words no sooner passed his lips than, here before the judicial authorities, they seemed to grow scales and become wrapped in a falsehood that made him shudder.

And then all at once Isao heard the white winter camellia groan.

Startled, he looked back at the inspector. There was no surprise in the inspector's eyes. It was only later that Isao realized that chance had not dictated the choice of this second-floor room, with its open window, for the interrogation on this particular day. The room was across a narrow alley from a drill hall, its windows shuttered even at midday, but with lights visible through transoms.

'You're third degree in kendo, I hear. You know, if you hadn't got yourself involved in this business and stayed with your kendo, you and I might have had a pleasant match in that hall down there.'

'Are they practising kendo now?' Isao asked, feeling sure that they were not. The inspector did not answer.

Some of the sounds that carried up to the room were like kendo yells, but the groans that had seemed to come from the white camellia had nothing of kendo about it. The crash of staves on thick-padded kendo gear was different. This was the dull, sombre sound of blows striking upon flesh.

Isao recalled that the white camellia, which seemed to be sweating in the heat generated by the clear winter sunshine, had somehow become sacred after the cries and groans of the tortured had filtered through it. Free of the inspector's debased refinement, the flower began to give off the scent of the law itself. His eyes could not help looking beyond the lustrous leaves of the camellia, through the transom where lights burned at midday, at the thick ropes swinging back and forth with what must have been a heavy burden of flesh.

Isao looked into the inspector's eyes once more, and the latter answered his unspoken question: 'Yes. It's a Red. Stubborn ones bring this kind of thing on themselves.'

Obviously the police intended to make him realize that, in contrast, he was being treated with the utmost gentleness, that the kindly law was showering benefits upon him. But it had the opposite effect. At that moment Isao felt a choking of anger and humiliation. 'My ideas – what do they amount to?' he asked himself in a rage. 'If real ideas have to be beaten like that, are mine supposed to be unreal?' Isao was vexed with frustration: despite the enormity of what he had plotted, there had been no adequate reaction. If they realized the core of terrible purity within him, he thought, they would surely hate him. Though officers of the Emperor, they could not help but hate him. On the other hand, however, if their ignorance persisted, his ideas would never gain the weight of flesh, never grow wet with agonized sweat. And, as a consequence, they would never give out the loud cries of beaten flesh.

Isao glared at his cross-examiner and shouted: 'Torture me! Torture me right now. Why can't you do the same thing to me? Can you tell me why not?'

'Easy now. Calm down, don't be foolish. It's very simple. You don't give us any trouble.'

'And that's because my ideas are rightist?'

'That's part of it. But rightist or leftist, anyone who gives us trouble is going to pay for it. Still, when all is said and done, those Reds ...'

'Is it because the Reds won't accept our national structure?'

'That's it. In comparison to them, Iinuma, you and your friends are patriots. Your thoughts are in the right direction. It's only that you're young. The trouble is, you're too pure, so you went to extremes. Your purpose is good. It's your methods. What about making them more gradual, toning them down a bit? If you made them a little more flexible, everything would be fine.'

'No,' Isao retorted, his body trembling all over. 'If we made them a little more flexible, it wouldn't be the same. That "little" is the point. Purity can't be toned down a little. If you make it a bit flexible, just a bit, it becomes a totally different idea, not the kind we hold. So if our ideas can't be watered down, and if they're a threat to the nation the way they are, that means our ideas are just as dangerous as those of the Reds. So go ahead and torture me. You have no reason not to.'

'You're quite a debater, aren't you? Now, don't get so excited. I'll tell you just one thing that would be good for you to know. There's not a man among those Reds that asked to be tortured, as you're doing. They take it if they have to. They're not like you, they don't respond to us even if we torture them.'

35

Makiko's letters, though she naturally avoided straightforward expressions, were filled with assurances that her feelings towards Isao were just as before, and she always took care to include two or three poems that her father had revised for her. The censor's cherry blossom seal affixed in red to the letter was no different, but when Isao considered how easily her letters alone came through, without any significant deletions, he suspected some help from General Kito. Still, there was hardly any sign that his own replies had reached their destination.

Never questioning nor responding to questions, neither alluding to present circumstances nor ignoring them, neither conveying information nor withholding it, Makiko wrote of this and that, of beautiful or entertaining things, or things altogether innocent, in keeping with the changing seasons. Thus she wrote of a pheasant from the Botanical Gardens flying into their yard, as one had the previous spring; of the records she had bought recently; of often going for a walk in Hakusan Park with thoughts of a particular night in mind; of seeing there one night the soiled petals of rain-scattered cherry blossoms clinging to the children's log swing as it moved gently back and forth beneath the faint light of a lamp post, as though an adult couple had been sitting on it just before; of the deep darkness around the Shinto pavilion, brightened once, however, by a running white cat; of the early-blooming peach blossoms that she used in practising her flower arranging; of freesia; of finding some starworts on a visit to Gokoku Temple and plucking them until her sleeves were heavily laden ... Since poems accompanied all this, Isao often felt as though he had been there to share her mood.

Makiko had in abundance the talent that his mother lacked, and she seemed to have easily learned a style of writing that enabled her to slip by the stern guard of the censor. Be that as it might, the Makiko that appeared here had all too little resemblance to Ikiko Abé, who, together with her mother-in-law, leapt with joy as she saw the fires of insurrection spring up in the distance, the work of her husband and his comrades of the League of the Divine Wind. He read Makiko's letters again and again. She never touched upon politics. Then, while he was striving earnestly to decipher certain passages that seemed to him to have double meanings or to hint at passion, he suddenly felt the need to resist the sensual attraction that these letters had for him. He was bent on finding something other than tender regard and goodwill. But how could Makiko have written to him with hostility? Even if there had been something like that hidden here, he was sure that it was not intentional.

Her smooth, vivacious style was clearly a kind of tightrope walking. How could he blame in her the exultation that an increasingly skilful tightrope walker found in the very act of risking danger? But, to go one step further, Isao could not but think that Makiko had an almost indecent zest for tightrope walking, and, under the pretext of fear of the authorities, was indulging a passion for emotional mischief.

Nowhere in her letters was there a phrase of this sort. But there was a certain scent. A playful feeling. At times Makiko seemed to be enjoying his being in prison. Cruel separation guarded the purity of emotion. The pangs of being apart were transformed into quiet joy. Danger aroused the sensual. Uncertainty fostered dreams.

Makiko conveyed in artless phrases the pleasure she felt at knowing how his heart trembled, as if from the seductive breeze blowing in through his cell window. This relationship between the two of them, though it verged on cruelty, was for Makiko the fulfilment of a cherished dream. Once Isao thought in such terms, he could see proof everyhere in her letters. Apparently Makiko had discovered in this kind of situation a kingdom of her own.

His senses, sharpened by prison life, told him this was true, and Isao suddenly became furious. He wanted to tear the letters to shreds.

In order to turn his mind in another direction and to strengthen his will, he asked that his parents be allowed to send him *The League of the Divine Wind*, but he was, of course, refused. Prisoners could purchase some magazines, but these was limited to such as *Science for Children, Today, Eloquence*, *Kodan Club, King*, and *Diamond.*

Whether a prison book or not, only one book a week was allowed, and none of those made available by the authorities were the sort to set his heart afire. When, therefore, he was allowed to receive a book that he had asked for some time ago from his father, Dr Tetsujiro Inoué's *The Philosophy of the Japanese Wang Yang-ming School*, Isao was indescribably happy. He had been loooking forward to reading about Chusai Oshio in it. Heihachiro (known as Chusai) resigned his position as a police official in 1830, at the age of thirty-seven, and devoted himself to writing and lecturing. He became famous as a scholar of the Wang Yang-ming school, and he was also an expert in the use of the spear. During the great famine from 1833 to 1836, no statesman or wealthy merchant came forward to aid the starving people; moreover, when Chusai sold all of his prized books to alleviate distress, it was viewed as an act to curry public favour, and his foster son, Kakunosuké, was subjected to reprimand. Finally, on February 19, 1837, he raised an armed force and, with this body of a few hundred men, burned down the storehouses of rich merchants and distributed gold and grain to the people. More than a fourth of Osaka was ravaged by fire, but Chusai's men were at last defeated, and he himself died by blowing himself up with an explosive charge. He was forty-four years old.

Chusai Oshio realized in his own person the Wang Yang-ming concept of unity of thought and action, embodying the dictum: 'To know and not to act is not to know.' What appealed to Isao, however, even more than Chusai's Wang Yang-ming fusion of thought and action, spirit and reason, was his concept of life and death.

Dr Inoué explained that: 'With regard to death, Chusai's view was quite similar to the Buddhist nirvana.'

'The "Great Void", according to Chusai's teaching, was not a negative condition in which all the workings of the human spirit were obliterated. He taught, rather, that here the light of intuition was able to shine in all its brilliance, simply by means of the elimination of personal appetite. To become a part of the Great Void, Chusai said, to give oneself over wholly to the ever-present and ever-lasting Great Void, was to enter the sphere of eternity.

'Once the spirit is given over to the Great Void,' Inoué wrote, 'even though the body perish, there remains something that does not. Thus there is no fearing the death of the body but only the death of the spirit. Knowing that the essential spirit will not die, one need fear nothing in the world. This, then, is the basis for one's resolution. And no matter what arises, it has no power to shake this resolution. Thus it might be said that this is to recognize the will of heaven.'

In the course of his discussion, Dr Inoué drew many quotations from *An Account of the Purification of the Heart*. One of these particularly struck Isao: 'There is no fearing the death of the body, but only the death of the spirit.' To Isao, in his present condition, these were words like hammer blows.

On May twentieth the preliminary hearing was concluded and a decision handed down, the main part of which read: 'This case is to be brought to trial before the Tokyo District Court.' Honda's hopes for a dismissal at the preliminary hearing were dashed.

The trial would most likely begin at the end of June. The prohibition against visitors remained in force during the period preceding this, but a present came from Makiko, which Isao opened in a state of high excitement. It was a wild lily from the Saigusa Festival.

Since it had been subjected to the guards' handling at the end of its long journey, the lily was a little withered and drooping. Still, it had a freshness and lustre far greater than those that Isao and his comrades had intended to conceal on their persons on the morning of their attack. This lily still seemed to have a trace of the morning dew that fell upon the open place before the shrine of the gods.

Makiko must have made a special trip to Nara in order to give this one lily to him. And, from all the lilies that she brought back, she must have chosen this one for its superb whiteness and beauty.

Isao reflected. The previous year at about this same time, he had been filled with a sense of freedom and strength. Beneath Sanko Falls on the holy mountain of the gods, he had snuffed out the fire still smouldering from the victorious kendo combat before the shrine. And with a purified heart, he had then given himself over to his act of worship, gathering the mass of lilies that were to be offered to the gods. Sweat had covered his forehead wrapped with a white *hachimaki* as he pulled the laden cart along the road to Nara. The village of Sakurai had been bright in the summer sun. Isao's youthfulness and the green of the mountainside had been in harmony.

Lilies were like a crest marking that memory. And afterwards they had become the symbol of his resolution. Since that day, lilies had been at the centre of everything – his fervour, his vows, his anxiety, his dreams, his readiness for death, his yearning for glory. The pillar that supported his dark plan, the soaring pillar of his resolution – always shining in the gloom at its top were the ornamental lilies that concealed the bolts holding it fast.

He gazed at the lily he held in his hand. He rolled the bent stem between his palms, feeling the leaves rubbing against his skin as the drooping lily revolved. Then it abruptly fell away from him, scattering a bit of dull golden dust. The sunlight at his window had become stronger. Isao felt that the lilies of the last year had been reborn.

36

When the ruling of the preliminary hearing was delivered to Isao, he saw Sawa's name among the defendants, and he felt ashamed of the suspicions that he had been entertaining for so long. He had only to think of Sawa's face, of his name, for that shameful, unpleasant feeling to surge up irresistibly. Sometimes in this mood he felt that he had to have someone to play the role of informer. If not Sawa, who then? His suspicions, since they could not be dismissed, required an object. Otherwise, how could he sustain himself?

What was most frightening, however, was what came next if Sawa, by far the most likely, was no longer to be considered. Isao was fearful of transferring the suspicion he had felt towards Sawa to some other person. At the time of his capture, ten others were with him: Miyahara, Kimura, Izutsu, Fujita, Miyaké, Takasé, Inoué, Sagara, Serikawa, and Hasegawa. Of these, the absence of the names of Serikawa and Sagara from the list of defendants was but to be expected because, being under eighteen, they would be tried as juveniles. Isao thought about Sagara and Serikawa: the one always so close at hand as if he were Isao's shadow – small, alert, bespectacled Sagara; the other the boyish son of a Shinto priest in the Tohoku region – Serikawa, who had burst out in tearful protest before the shrine: 'I can't go back!' Under no circumstances could Isao think of those two as betraying him. Someone on the outside then? Isao feared pursuing this further. For he felt that something lay hidden, the same sort of feeling that checked one from searching through a clump of grass in which one fears to discover white bones.

Those who had fallen away knew, of course, that December third was the date set. But the last man to desert them knew nothing more than what they had had in mind three weeks before that day. Since the plan had thereafter been drastically altered, there was no reason why the date set could not have been either postponed or moved up or simply cancelled. Even if one of the deserters had informed on them, Isao still could not fathom why the police had refrained from intervening until two days before they were to strike. Should not the simplification of the plan have made it likely that they would strike at an earlier date?

Isao kept struggling not to think about these things. But even as he did, just as the moth drawn to the flame must turn its eyes back upon it, no matter how it tries to look away, his mind returned to the foreboding thoughts he wanted most to avoid.

The day of the opening of the trial, June twenty-fifth, was fair. The heat was intense.

The patrol wagon carrying the defendants passed by the moat surrounding the Imperial Palace, its waters glittering in the sunlight, and entered the confines of the red brick Courthouse through the rear gate. The Tokyo District Court was on the first floor. Isao came into the courtroom wearing a white splashed-pattern kimono and *hakama*, which had been brought to the prison for him.

The amber lustre of the judges' bench struck his eyes. When the guard removed his handcuffs at the door, he made Isao turn, out of kindness, so that he had a momentary look in the direction of the spectators. There sat his father and mother, whom he had not seen for half a year. When his eyes met his mother's, she covered her mouth with a handkerchief. She seemed to be choking back sobs. Makiko was nowhere to be seen.

The defendants formed a single line, their backs to the spectators. Thus arrayed with his comrades, Isao felt his courage mounting. Izutsu was right beside him. Though they could neither exchange words nor look at each other, Isao sensed that Izutsu's body was trembling. He knew this was not due to his friend's standing before the bench. The excitement of seeing Isao after so long was conveyed by every tremor of his friend's hot, sweaty body.

Right before Isao and the others was the defendants' box. Beyond it was the dazzling light mahogany of the judges' bench, the grain visible in the wood of its panels. It was majestically proportioned, and to its rear stood a doorway of the same light mahogany, a gable in the baroque manner crowning its solemnity. The three judges, the Chief Judge in the centre, sat upon chairs, each of which had a corolla carved upon its back. The court stenographer sat to the right of the defendants, and over on the left was the prosecutor. The purple arabesque embroidered upon the front and spreading to the shoulders of the judges' black robes glinted dully. And there was also purple piping upon the haughty black judges' caps. Obviously this was like no other place in the world.

When he was somewhat more composed, Isao glanced to the right, where the defence counsel sat, and saw Honda staring full at him.

The Chief Judge asked his name and age. Since his arrest, Isao had become accustomed to being addressed authoritatively from above, but this was his first experience of being summoned by a voice from such an eminence, a voice that seemed to embody the rationale of the entire nation and to fall like distant lightning from a sky filled with brilliant mist.

'Isao Iinuma, Your Honour. Twenty,' he answered.

37

The second session of the trial was held on July nineteenth. The weather was fair, but an occasional breeze through the courtroom fluttered the legal papers, and so the attendants shut the windows halfway. Again and again Isao had to resist the temptation to scratch a bedbug bite on his side, which was aggravating his sweaty discomfort.

As soon as the session began, the Chief Judge rejected one of the witnesses that the prosecutor had requested at the first session. Delighted, Honda rolled a red pencil quietly across the papers that covered his desk. This was an idiosyncrasy that he had somehow acquired around the time he became a judge in 1929, and one he had been making an effort to suppress ever since. Now, four years later, it had reasserted itself. It was a bad habit for a judge, because of its disturbing effect upon defendants, but in his present position Honda could indulge it to his heart's content.

The rejected witness was Lieutenant Hori. Here indeed was a witness that would have presented problems.

Honda noted the sudden look of disappointment that darkened the prosecutor's face, as though a gust of wind had ruffled the surface of a pond. Hori's name appeared any number of times in the minutes of the preliminary examinations and hearings, as well as in the hearings to which the deserters had been summoned to give information. Isao alone had never mentioned the name. To be sure, Hori's function in the plan was extremely vague, and his name did not appear on the final list seized by the police. This was in the form of a chart upon which each of the names of the twelve major financiers was joined by a line to the name of one of the twelve defendants. The police had found it at the hideaway in Yotsuya. Still, there was nothing in it that clearly indicated assassination.

Most of the twelve defendants said that Lieutenant Hori had been an inspiration to them, but only one of the twelve testified that he had exercised any leadership. Among the deserters, many testified that they had never met Hori nor even heard his name mentioned. Essentially, then, aside from the confused testimony of the defendants, the prosecutor had no evidence whatsoever to back up his suspicion of a large-scale plot prior to the massive defections.

As to the leaflets falsely proclaiming that imperial authority had been granted to Prince Toin, the dangerous evidence that the Prosecutor's Office had set eyes upon, darkness had swallowed them up. Once the prosecutor had seen the disproportion between the ambitious proclamation and the scanty resources of the would-be assassins, it was obvious how vital a witness the Lieutenant had become for him. Honda perceived Sawa's hand at work in this turn of events which so irritated the prosecutor. Iinuma had hinted as much.

'That Sawa's a good fellow,' Iinuma had said. 'He wanted to join his fate with Isao's, whatever the consequences. He was going to help Isao carry out his plan, without a word to me, and then follow him in suicide. So perhaps the one that was hurt the most by my informing was Sawa. But he's a mature man, after all, and must have made careful preparations in case of failure. Since deserters are the greatest source of danger in this kind of activity. I'm sure he sprang into action as soon as they dropped out. He must have gone around to give each one a thorough talking-to. Maybe he said: "If this affair is nipped in the bud, you're going to be called to give testimony. It takes hardly anything to change a witness like you into an accomplice. Just in case you don't want this to happen, you'd better say that the military influenced you only in spirit. Otherwise this is going to turn into a big affair, you'll all be implicated, and you'll be sticking your neck into the noose."

'Sawa was all for going through with the action, but, on the other hand, I'm sure he was prepared for any eventuality, and had taken prudent means to do away with evidence. This is the kind of wisdom that's hard to find in young people.'

At the beginning of the session, when the Chief Judge, singularly expressionless, rejected Lieutenant Hori as a witness on the grounds that he had no direct connection with the case, Honda had immediately told himself: 'Ah! This is thanks to the statement by that "highly placed military authority" that came out in the paper.'

Ever since the May Fifteenth Incident, the military had been extremely sensitive to the public reaction stirred by this sort of event. And they would be especially nervous in this case because Lieutenant Hori was an officer marked indelibly in connection with the May Fifteenth Incident. Since he had been rushed over to Manchuria for this among other reasons, it would be most distressing if he should be called back, himself under suspicion, to testify before a civilian court. If he did appear, whatever the content of his testimony, the credibility of the 'highly placed military authority' who issued that statement immediately after the arrests would henceforth be open to question, and, consequently, the dignity of the military itself would be injured.

Given this state of mind, the military was without doubt keeping a sharp eye on this trial. And so as soon as the motion had been made to summon Lieutenant Hori, they had quite evidently been disgruntled with the prosecutor and were counting upon the judge to give the motion that expressionless dismissal.

In any case, the Prosecutor's Office had learned from the questioning conducted by the police that the students had met with the Lieutenant in the 'Kitazaki' lodging house for military personnel, at the rear of the compound of the Azabu Third Regiment.

Thus Honda read beyond the irritation and impatience on the prosecutor's features to deduce the sources of his frustration.

His conclusions were as follows: the prosecutor was not at all happy with the simple indictment for preparation to commit murder that came out of the preliminary hearings. What he wanted, however it could be attained, was to make the affair bigger, to make it become, if possible, an indictment for conspiracy to commit insurrection. Only by so doing, the prosecutor believed, could the evil root of this affair be torn out. This state of mind, however, seemed to have disturbed the logic of his procedure. By taking so many pains to prove that the defendants had curtailed an original plan that had been large-scale, the prosecutor had been remiss in gathering the essential elements for proving preparation to commit murder.

'To aim for this weak spot,' thought Honda, 'and, with one thrust if possible, render even the murder preparation charge unproved – that's what I must do. And so my greatest worry will be Isao's purity and honesty. I have to confuse him. My witnesses will be directed both against our opponents and against our own side.'

Honda felt his heart calling out to Isao's clear eyes, exceptionally beautiful and gallant, even among those of all his fellow defendants. When he had heard of the affair, Honda had thought that Isao's furiously gazing eyes were most appropriate, but now, seeing them again, he felt that they were unsuited to these circumstances.

'Beautiful eyes!' Honda exclaimed to himself. 'Clear and shining, forever disconcerting others. Peerless young eyes radiating a censure that seems from another world, as if one were suddenly plunged beneath the waters of Sanko Falls. Go ahead, express what you like. Confess to anything at all. Be deeply wounded. You're at the age when you should be learning the means to defend yourself. By speaking out without restraint, you will at last learn that no one is willing to believe the truth, one of the most valuable lessons a man can learn about life. This is the only wisdom that I have to convey to eyes as beautiful as yours.'

Then Honda began to study the face of Judge Hisamatsu, who sat in the Chief Judge's place upon the bench. The Chief Judge was somewhat past sixty, and faint splotches marked the dry, white skin of his handsome features. He wore gold-rimmed glasses. Despite the clarity of his enunciation, now and then, as he spoke, one heard inorganic sounds like the elegant click of ivory chess pieces striking together. Though this lent his speech something of the chill dignity of the glittering chrysanthemum crest above the door of the Courthouse, it was apparently merely due to his false teeth.

Judge Hisamatsu's character was in high repute, and Honda too admired his probity. But the reason why he was still a judge of the lower court at his age was that he could hardly be called brilliant. According to what lawyers had to say among themselves, though he looked as if reason reigned supreme in him, he was in fact easily moved, and his efforts to affect a cold exterior in order to combat his inner flames were given away by the sudden reddening of the old man's dry, white cheeks when he felt violent anger or deep emotion.

Honda, however, knew something about what went on inside a judge. And how intense were a judge's inner struggles! Emotion, sentiment, desire, personal concern, ambition, shame, fanaticism, and all sorts of other flotsam – the fragments of planks, the wastepaper, the oil slick, the orange peel, the fish, the seaweed filling the sea of human nature that was ever pushing against the lone seawall that kept it in check: legal justice. Such was the struggle.

Among the indirect evidence supporting the indictment was the defendants' having sold their swords in exchange for daggers, a matter to which Judge Hisamatsu seemed to attach considerable importance. As soon as he had ruled that the Lieutenant could not be summoned, he began the examination of the evidence.

JUDGE HISAMATSU: I have some questions for Isao Iinuma. You sold your swords and bought daggers in exchange preparatory to acting. Was that because you had assassination in mind?

IINUMA: Yes, Your Honour. That was the purpose.

JUDGE: What day and what month was that?

IINUMA: It was November eighteenth, as I remember it.

JUDGE: You sold two swords on that day and purchased six daggers with the money. Is that correct?

IINUMA: Yes, Your Honour.

JUDGE: Did you yourself go to do the exchanging?

IINUMA: No, Your Honour. I asked two of my comrades to do so.

JUDGE: Who were they?

IINUMA: Izutsu and Inoué.

JUDGE: Why did you give each of them a sword to exchange like that?

IINUMA: I thought that if someone saw a young man bringing in two swords to sell, it might attract attention. I picked the two men who would have the most cheerful and well-behaved appearance, and I sent them to dealers who were some distance apart. If the sword buyer asked why they were selling, I told them to say that they had been practising swordsmanship but had given it up, so they wanted to exchange their swords for some daggers with plain wooden sheaths for themselves and their brothers. If exchanging the two swords would bring six daggers, these and the six we already had would give us enough for the twelve of us.

JUDGE: Izutsu. Tell us what happened when you brought the sword in to exchange it.

IZUTSU: Yes, Your Honour. I went to a shop called Murakoshi's Swords at Number Three Koji-machi. I tried to look as nonchalant as I could as I said I wanted to sell my sword. A little old lady holding a cat was behind the counter. And I thought to myself how uneasy that cat would be if this was a samisen shop.

JUDGE: That is not to the point.

IZUTSU: Yes, Your Honour. When I told the old lady what I wanted, she went to the back of the shop right away, and the dealer himself came out, a grumpy-looking fellow with a bad complexion. He unsheathed the blade and examined it. With a contemptuous expression on his face, he looked at it from all different angles, finally removing the hilt fasteners and examining the part of the blade that fitted inside. 'Just as I thought,' he said. 'The maker's name was added later.' Without even asking why I wanted to sell it, he set a price and gave me three wooden-sheathed daggers in exchange. I took a good look at their blades and then walked out.

JUDGE: He didn't ask your name or address?

IZUTSU: No, Your Honour. He didn't ask me anything at all.

JUDGE: What do you say, Mr Honda? Do you wish to ask Iinuma or Izutsu any questions?

HONDA: I'd like to question Izutsu, Your Honour.

JUDGE: Very well.

HONDA: When you went to sell the sword, had Iinuma told you that swords would be awkward for an assassination and that it was therefore necessary to exchange them for daggers?

IZUTSU: Well, no, sir, he didn't say it in so many words as I remember.

HONDA: So he didn't specify anything of the sort but merely told you to go and exchange the swords, and you went without knowing the purpose?

IZUTSU: Well ... yes, sir. But I certainly had a good idea of it. It seemed obvious.

HONDA: Then it wasn't a matter at that time of a sudden change in the nature of your resolution?

IZUTSU: No, sir. I don't think that was it.

HONDA: The sword you brought to the dealer, was it your own?

IZUTSU: No, sir, it was not. It was Iinuma's sword.

HONDA: What kind of weapon was in your own possession?

IZUTSU: I had a dagger right from the beginning.

HONDA: When did you obtain it?

IZUTSU: Well, sir ... yes, it was last summer. It was after we had made our vows before the shrine on the campus. I felt that it would be unmanly of me not to have a dagger at least. So I went to my uncle who is a collector, and I got one from him.

HONDA: I see. And at that time, then, you had no clear and definite idea of the use to which you would put it?

IZUTSU: No, sir. I only felt that someday, somehow I would like to use it...

HONDA: Very well. Now when was it that you came to a clear realization of the definite use to which it could be put?

IZUTSU: I think it was when I was given the mission of assassinating Mr Shonosuké Yagi.

HONDA: What I'm asking is when the realization first came to you that, in order to commit an assassination, a dagger was indispensable.

IZUTSU: Well, sir ... as for that, I don't remember too well.

HONDA: Your Honour, I would like to ask Iinuma a few questions.

JUDGE: Very well.

HONDA: What kind of sword did you have?

IINUMA: The sword that I gave Izutsu to sell was signed by Tadayoshi of Bizen. When I reached the third rank in kendo the year before last, my father gave it to me as a present.

HONDA: Did you not exchange that valuable sword for daggers in order to use one of them to commit suicide?

IINUMA: Pardon, sir?

HONDA: You testified as to your fondness for the book *The League of the Divine Wind* and said how the suicides of the men of the League had aroused your admiration. And you further testified that you wished to die in that manner, and that you had praised such a death to your comrades. On the battlefield the men of the League fought with their swords, but, when it came to suicide, they used daggers. And so judging from this...

IINUMA: Yes, sir. Now I remember. At the meeting on the day of the arrest, someone said: 'In case of emergency, each one should carry a second dagger hidden on his person.' Everyone agreed. This emergency dagger would be definitely for committing suicide, but we were arrested before we could buy more.

HONDA: In that case, up to that time you had not considered buying weapons for such emergency use?

IINUMA: No, sir.

HONDA: But before that you had been firmly resolved upon suicide?

IINUMA: Yes, sir.

HONDA: In that case, this exchanging swords for daggers, might one say that you had killing yourselves in mind as much as killing others – that is to say, a double purpose?

IINUMA: Yes, sir, you could say that.

HONDA: Your action, therefore, in exchanging your ordinary weapons for daggers had a twofold purpose: assassination and suicide. And at the time in question these deadly weapons were not exclusively bound up with the idea of assassination. Is that right?

IINUMA: Ah ... yes, sir.

PROSECUTOR: Your Honour, I object. The defence's line of questioning is obviously tendentious.

JUDGE: That should be enough questions from the defence. The matter of exchanging the swords has now been sufficiently covered. The prosecution may therefore call its witnesses.

Honda, as he sat behind his desk, was fairly content. By his questions he had somewhat confused the logic of linking the obtaining of the daggers to the intent to murder. Honda was concerned, however, about Judge Hisamatsu's apparent lack of interest in the ideological aspect of the case. Right from the opening of the trial, the judge, by virtue of his authority, could have elicited from Isao any number of statements about his political beliefs, but he had made no attempt to do so.

The spectators looked over to the entrance of the courtroom, towards the uncertain tapping sound of a cane. An old man appeared. He was very tall but bent, shielding himself by clutching the front of his linen summer kimono, as though he were striving desperately to catch hold of something. The sunken eyes alone, beneath the white head of hair, were directed upwards. He made his way to the witness box, where he stood supporting himself on his cane.

The judge rose and read the written oath. The witness signed this with a trembling hand and put his seal upon it. A chair was provided for him before his testimony began.

In a voice so low the spectators could hardly hear him, the old man answered the judge's questions: 'My name is Reikichi Kitazaki. I am seventy-eight years old.'

JUDGE: The witness has been the proprietor of the place in question for some time, I understand.

KITAZAKI: Yes, Your Honour, I have. I opened my rooming house for military personnel at the time of the war with Russia, and I have continued to operate it up to the present time. Among my officer guests were many who went on to fame, becoming major-generals and lieutenant-generals. My establishment has a reputation for being a fortunate lodging house. It's a rather shabby, dilapidated place, but I have been honoured with the favour of military gentlemen, especially the officers of the Azabu Third Regiment. I have no wife, and, though it be frugal, I make my living without being a burden upon anyone.

JUDGE: Does the prosecution have any questions to ask?

PROSECUTOR: Yes, Your Honour. How long has First Lieutenant of Infantry Hori been a guest at your house?

KITAZAKI: Well, sir ... let me see now. Three years ... no, two years ... My memory is not what it used to be. Oh my ... yes, it's been about two years, I think...

PROSECUTOR: Lieutenant Hori was promoted to first lieutenant three years ago. In March of 1930, that is. When he became a guest at your house, then, he was already a first lieutenant. Is that correct?

KITAZAKI: Yes, sir, of that I'm sure. The gentleman wore two stars from the very beginning. And I have no memory of there being a promotion celebration.

PROSECUTOR: In that case, it's a matter of less than three years and more than one?

KITAZAKI: Yes, sir. That is correct.

PROSECUTOR: Did Lieutenant Hori have many visitors?

KITAZAKI: Yes, sir, very often indeed. Not once was there a woman guest, but young men, students, were forever coming and going. They liked to hear him talk. And the Lieutenant, for his part, was fond of them. If dinner time came, he would send out to the neighbourhood shops for food. He treated them well and would empty out his pockets for them.

PROSECUTOR: How long has he shown such a predilection?

KITAZAKI: That, sir, was from the very beginning. Yes.

PROSECUTOR: Did the Lieutenant have much to say to you concerning his visitors?

KITAZAKI: Oh, no. In that regard he was not at all like Lieutenant Miura. He was not affable with me and hardly had a word to say. So there was no likelihood at all of his confiding in me about his guests...

PROSECUTOR: One moment please. What about this Lieutenant Miura?

KITAZAKI: A gentleman who has been a long-time guest. His room is on the second floor – at the opposite end of the corridor from Lieutenant Hori. He has a rough manner, but he is good-natured.

PROSECUTOR: Please tell us whether or not there is anything special that you remember about Lieutenant Hori's visitors.

KITAZAKI: Well, sir, I will. On this particular night, I was bringing Lieutenant Miura his dinner, and when I was passing Lieutenant Hori's room, the door was closed, and, all of a sudden, from the inside I heard the Lieutenant shouting as though he were giving an order on the drill field. It rattled me considerably.

PROSECUTOR: What did Lieutenant Hori say?

KITAZAKI: That I remember clearly. 'Don't you understand? Give it up!' he shouted angrily.

PROSECUTOR: Do you have any idea what he meant by 'Give it up'?

KITAZAKI: Well, no, sir. After all, it was something shouted as I was just going by, and I was hard put to keep from dropping my tray. And since, as you see, I'm not good on my feet anyway, it was all I could do to hurry on to Lieutenant Miura's room. You see, Lieutenant Miura was really famished that night. Earlier he had called down to me: 'Hey, old fellow! Hurry up and bring my supper.' And now if I dropped his tray, I thought, I'd have Lieutenant Miura shouting at me. When I put the tray down in front of Lieutenant Miura, he grinned and said: 'He's going at it, isn't he?' And that was all. He didn't say another word about it. I think that's one of the good things about military men.

PROSECUTOR: How many visitors were in Lieutenant Hori's room on the night in question?

KITAZAKI: Well, I believe there was one. Yes ... that was it, one.

PROSECUTOR: And when was this night that Lieutenant Hori said, 'Give it up'? This is an extremely critical point, so please try to remember exactly. What year, what month, what day? Do you keep a diary?

KITAZAKI: No, sir. No chance of that.

PROSECUTOR: Perhaps you didn't understand my question?

KITAZAKI: Pardon?

PROSECUTOR: Do you keep a diary?

KITAZAKI: Oh, a diary? No, sir, I do not keep one.

PROSECUTOR: Well, then, what year, what month, what day was it?

KITAZAKI: Well, I'm fairly sure it was last year. Yes, it was. And because I didn't think it was at all strange that the sliding door should be closed, I know it wasn't summer – maybe not even early summer or early fall. The weather must have been cold, but it wasn't too cold out, so it could have been last spring as late as April, or else from October on. The time of day was dinner time, at night, but as for the day itself ... well, sir, on that, I'm not quite sure.

PROSECUTOR: So it was April or October, or perhaps March or November. Can't you be more specific?

KITAZAKI: No, sir. But I'm trying hard to remember. Let's see ... Yes, it was October or November.

PROSECUTOR: But which was it: October or November?

KITAZAKI: On that point, I'm not sure.

PROSECUTOR: Could one say that it was either the end of October or the beginning of November?

KITAZAKI: Yes, sir. That's fine with me. Forgive me for being so useless.

PROSECUTOR: Who was the visitor that night?

KITAZAKI: I don't know his name. Lieutenant Hori would only tell me how many young visitors he was expecting, and when they were supposed to come.

PROSECUTOR: His visitor that night was also young?

KITAZAKI: Yes, sir. It was a student, I believe.

PROSECUTOR: Would you be able to recognize him again?

KITAZAKI: Well, sir ... perhaps.

PROSECUTOR: Please turn around, Mr Kitazaki. Is the one who visited the Lieutenant that night there among the defendants? You may if you like get up and examine each of their faces.

Isao let the tall, bent old man come over to him and stare full into his face. The sunken eyes were clouded like an oyster. A web of dark red veins encroached upon the whites, and the pupils were so beset by their surroundings that they seemed shrunk to lustreless black moles.

Isao was forbidden to speak, but his eyes challenged the old man: 'It was me that time, wasn't it?' Even with Isao's face right before him, however, Kitazaki's gaze seemed somehow to be hindered, as though some shadowy, undefined presence were hovering between the two of them and he were being drawn into it.

The cane scraped lightly against the floor. The old man was now studying

Izutsu's face. Since he had spent much more time in front of Isao than anyone else, Isao was sure that Kitazaki had recognized him.

The old man returned to the witness stand. His elbow resting upon his cane, his hand pressed to his forehead, he stared blankly, as though worn out by the effort to chase down the memory, as elusive as mist, that fled before him.

The prosecutor took up the questioning again, a note of irritation evident in his tone.

'Well now, did you recognize him there?'

Kitazaki did not look at the prosecutor as he answered in a barely audible voice but seemed to be addressing his own image faintly reflected in the panelling of the judges' bench.

'I can't be sure, sir. But that first defendant...'

'Iinuma, you mean?'

'I do not know his name. But the face of that young man on the far left... I am certain that he came to my house at some time. It may have had nothing to do with Lieutenant Hori, though.'

'In that case, maybe he was a guest of Lieutenant Miura?'

'No, sir. It was not that. Quite some time ago, there was a young man who came to stay with a woman in the rear parlour. I think he is the one...'

'Iinuma brought a woman to your house?'

'I cannot be certain. But it was someone like him,'

'And when was this?'

'Well, as I look back now, I think it was, yes, some twenty years ago.'

'Twenty years? Iinuma brought a woman to your house twenty years ago?'

So taken aback was the prosecutor that the spectators burst into laughter. But this reaction did not unsettle the old man in the least. He doggedly repeated his answer.

'Yes, sir. That is correct. I think it was some twenty years ago.'

The incompetence of the witness was now clear to everyone. People were laughing at Kitazaki's senility. Initially, Honda too had the same reaction, but then when the old man earnestly repeated 'some twenty years', his amusement suddenly gave way to a shiver.

Honda had once heard from Kiyoaki the details of his tryst with Satoko in the back room of Kitazaki's lodging house. Other than their being the same ages there were no outward similarities between Kiyoaki and Isao. But still this Kitazaki, so close to death himself, had confused in his mind the memories of the two. Only the intensities of hue of all the things that had happened in his old house were blended together, transcending time. Passionate love of years past, passionate dedication in the present – these two had merged vaguely together in exceeding normal bounds, in becoming early failures. From the marsh of memories of a lifetime rose two superb lotuses, red and white, and these must have been seen as a single flower. But through this misapprehension, Honda was sure, in Kitazaki's senile old mind a stagnant, grey marsh had suddenly been lit up by strange, clear beams of light. The old man, eager to seize this extraordinary brilliance, had stubbornly repeated what he had said, undismayed by either the ridicule of the spectators or the anger of the prosecutor.

Having grasped this, Honda then had the feeling that the dazzlingly polished brown judges' bench and the robes of solemn black were suddenly fading before the intense brilliance of the summer sun pouring down outside the windows. As though struck by those powerful rays, the awesome, finely tuned mechanism of the legal order seemed to be melting swiftly away before him like an ice castle. Honda knew that Kitazaki had glimpsed that great bond of light, invisible to ordinary eyes. The summer brightness, which gave a sparkle to each needle of the pines outside the windows, surely had as its source a rope of light more forbidding, more magnificent than the legal order on display within this room.

'Does the defence wish to examine the witness?'

When he heard the judge's question, Honda, still dazed, could only reply: 'No, Your Honour.'

'Very well. Thank you, Mr Kitazaki. The witness is dismissed,' said the judge.

'... At this time I would like permission to call as a witness someone present who has not been formally summoned,' said Honda. 'Her name is Makiko Kito. For the sake of the defendant Iinuma and the other defendants too, I would like to have her questioned with regard to Iinuma's change of mind three days before the day set for their action. And since I will present as evidence the diary entries made by the witness at this time, I hope that the questioning can be based upon these.'

There was no provision for the calling of witnesses in this manner in criminal proceedings, but, depending upon the nature of the testimony to be given, a judge would usually grant permission after conferring with the prosecutor and the assistant judges, and Honda intended to take advantage of this custom.

The judge asked the prosecutor's opinion, and he acquiesced coldly, as though he considered it unworthy of his concern. After turning first to the judge on his right, consulting in a whisper, and then doing the same with the judge on his left, Judge Hisamatsu replied to Honda.

'Very well. You may do so.'

Accordingly, Makiko appeared at the entrance to the courtroom. She wore a dark blue, waterfall stripe Akashi kimono bound with a Hakata obi. In the midst of summer, Makiko's naturally white complexion, cool as ice, gave a tranquil, distant look to her face, framed in a border of the jet-black hair hiding her ears and the blue neck of the kimono. Below her lively, moist eyes, her skin was faintly touched, like the coming on of twilight, with the signs of ageing. Affixed to the slightly slanted cord that held her obi in place was the figure of a trout done in dark jade. Its hard green lustre seemed to impose a crisp firmness upon the easy flowing lines of Makiko's attire. There was a subtle tension beneath her unruffled exterior. But no one could tell whether the cold expression on her face concealed sorrow or contempt.

Makiko made her way to the witness stand without so much as glancing in Isao's direction. All that he saw of her then was the cool seam that ran down the back of her kimono and the huge bow in which her obi was fastened.

'I hereby swear that, in accordance with my conscience, I will speak the truth, neither concealing nor adding anything thereto.'

The judge read the oath as before, and Makiko signed the book, which was brought to the witness stand, with a hand that showed no sign of trembling. Then she drew from her sleeve the small case containing her seal, and, taking the slender ivory seal, she pressed it firmly to the paper so that her lovely fingers bent back. Watching from the side, Honda caught a glimpse of red ink between her fingers like a splash of blood.

On Honda's desk was the diary that Makiko had been willing to make public. Just as he had requested, Honda had offered this as evidence. Just as he had requested, he had called Makiko as a witness. But Honda could only guess at what the intent of the judge was in allowing this.

JUDGE: What are the circumstances of your being acquainted with the defendant?

MAKIKO: My father, Your Honour, is a friend of Mr Iinuma's father. And furthermore, since my father enjoys the company of young men, Mr Iinuma was a frequent guest at our house. And the relationship was much closer than that with relatives.

JUDGE: When was the last time you saw the defendant, and where was it?

MAKIKO: The evening of last November twenty-ninth. He came to the house.

JUDGE: The content of your diary that is being offered as evidence is altogether accurate?

MAKIKO: Yes, Your Honour, it is.

JUDGE: The defence may now question the witness.

HONDA: Yes, Your Honour. Miss Kito, this is your diary of last year, isn't it?

MAKIKO: Yes, sir.

HONDA: This diary is the sort in which the pages are not marked with dates, allowing you to write as much as you like, and you've kept such diaries faithfully for years. Is that correct?

MAKIKO: Yes, sir, that is correct. And so I can at times put in *waka* and the like.

HONDA: Your method from long past has been to leave a blank line between entries and not begin a new page each day?

MAKIKO: Yes, sir. In the last two or three years I've been writing so much that if I started a new page each day, even in a diary without printed dates, I would run out of pages by fall. So it doesn't look neat, but that is how I make entries every day.

HONDA: Very well, then. Last year, 1932, that is, as to the entry of November twenty-ninth, this was not something that you wrote later, but you can testify that it was written that very night?

MAKIKO: Yes, sir. I've never let a day go by without writing in my diary. That day too I made an entry before going to bed.

HONDA: Now, in that entry of November twenty-ninth, 1932, I shall read aloud just that portion that pertains to the defendant Iinuma:

> ...Tonight at around eight o'clock, Isao paid an unexpected visit. Though I had not seen him in quite some time, I was thinking of him tonight, why I don't know, and perhaps it was my odd faculty for premonition that impelled me towards the entrance hall before the bell rang. As usual, he was wearing his student uniform and had clogs on his feet, but when I looked at his face I sensed that something had happened. He seemed stiff

and formal. He suddenly thrust toward me a small keg he was carrying and said: 'My mother asked me to bring you this. It's a few of the oysters we received from Hiroshima.' In the darkness of the entrance hall the water inside the barrel made a sound like a clucking tongue.

Fidgeting about, he made the excuse that he had studying to do and so had to go, but the lie was written all over his face. I never would have expected such a thing from the Isao I knew. Pressing him to stay, I accepted the keg and went to tell Father, who cordially said: 'Have him come in.'

I rushed back to the entrance hall. Isao was already slipping out of the door. I hurried out after him. I wanted at all costs to find out what was troubling him.

I am sure he knew that I was following him, but he neither turned around nor altered his pace. When we had reached the front of Hakusan Park, I called out to him: 'What are you angry about?' and he finally stopped. He turned around to face me, and he smiled in a grim, embarrassed manner. We then sat down upon a bench in the park, and we talked there, in the cold night wind.

I asked him how he and his group were getting on. For some time he and his comrades have been gathering at the house and talking about how intolerable are the present circumstances of Japan, and I too have been a part of this, often treating them all to a supper of sukiyaki and the like. And I had been thinking that it was the activity of this group that had been keeping Isao away from the house in recent days.

Isao answered me with a woeful expression: 'What I really meant to do in coming to your house was to talk to you about the group. But when I saw your face, since I had said such brave things before, I was embarrassed and couldn't say anything. And so I stole away.' The words were spoken slowly and painfully.

The story that came out from my questions was as follows: Without my having been aware of it, the direction of his group's activities had gotten altogether out of hand, and the truth of the matter was that each of those involved, to hide his own fears and to measure the courage of the group, had grown ever more violently vocal, and as the numbers increased of those who fell away because this bravado unnerved them, the handful who remained bluffed all the harder. And while their actual resolution grew even weaker, their words and their plans kept mounting toward a fantastic bloody retribution. They no longer knew what to do with each other. Since none of them could show a trace of weakness in his words, an outsider would no doubt have been appalled by what went on at their meetings, but in fact no one any longer really wanted to take action. With the situation as it was, however, not one of them had the courage to insist on giving up their plan, for fear that he would be branded a coward. Furthermore, if things went on this way, the danger would grow more acute. All unwillingly, they would rush ahead on a collision course with the deed that they had no intention of performing. Isao himself, their leader, no longer wanted to go through with it. Was there no way of drawing back? And the real purpose in his coming to the house tonight had been to ask advice. Those were the circumstances.

I used every argument I could think of to urge him to give it up. The manly thing to do was to put an end to things. And so, even if his comrades turned their backs on him now, the time would certainly come when they would understand. There were many other ways to serve one's country. And, if he didn't mind, I would be willing to try to persuade his comrades from a woman's standpoint. But when he replied that that would only embarrass him, I thought he was right and I acquiesced.

When we parted before Hakusan Shrine, Isao turned to me after we had prayed together and said: 'Thanks to you, I feel good again. I have no intention of going through with it. As soon as I find the chance, I'll tell everyone that it's off.' He laughed cheerfully when he said this, and so I was somewhat relieved. But still, in my breast there was a lingering uneasiness.

As I write this my head is clear and alert, and I shall not be able to sleep tonight. If some misfortune should overtake that fine young man in whom my father, too, has placed such hope, I think I can say that Japan herself will suffer a great loss. My heart is heavy tonight. I am in no mood to write poems.

That is the entry. Can you assure us that you are the one who wrote it?

MAKIKO: Yes, sir. I wrote it.

HONDA: And afterwards, you neither changed anything nor added anything?

MAKIKO: No, sir. It was just as you see it.

JUDGE: If that's the case then, according to your observation, the defendant Iinuma, on the night in question, gave up all intention of committing a crime?

MAKIKO: Yes, Your Honour, that is correct.

JUDGE: Did Iinuma say anything to you about the day chosen or anything similar?

MAKIKO: No, Your Honour. He did not.

JUDGE: Do you think perhaps that he might have wished to conceal that from you?

MAKIKO: He had already told me, Your Honour, that he had given up his project, so he would consider it pointless, I think, to talk about such things as the day he had once set for it. He was always so honest that I feel sure I would have known if he had been lying.

JUDGE: Your relationship with the defendant seems to be a rather close one.

MAKIKO: I suppose I thought of him as a younger brother.

JUDGE: Well, if you two were so close then, didn't you, considering the lingering uneasiness that you mentioned in your diary, feel any urge to work secretly to make sure that they turned back?

MAKIKO: I felt that a woman's meddling would only make matters worse, so I just kept praying. And while I was doing this, I learned of the arrests. It was a shock to me.

JUDGE: Did you speak of the events of that night to your father or to anyone else?

MAKIKO: No, Your Honour.

JUDGE: Wouldn't it have been natural to tell your father – considering that the matter was so grave, and considering, moreover, how the circumstances had changed?

MAKIKO: When I returned that night, my father asked me no questions. In the first place, my father has a military man's point of view, and he had always held the sincere fervour of youth in high regard. So I had no desire to speak to my father of Isao's change of heart. I felt that he might take it amiss because of his affection for Isao. And, even without my saying anything, I felt that it would come to his knowledge. So I kept the matter sealed in my heart.

JUDGE: Does the prosecutor wish to question the witness?

PROSECUTOR: No, Your Honour.

JUDGE: The witness is hereby dismissed. Thank you, Miss Kito.

Makiko bowed, and, after turning her back with the huge bow in which her white Hakata obi was tied, she walked out of the courtroom without a glance in the direction of the defendants.

Isao clenched his fists. Sweat simmered inside them.

Makiko had committed perjury! The most brazen kind of perjury! She had given testimony that Isao knew to be an outright lie, risking the danger that, if discovered, she would be liable not only to the charge of perjury but also, according to circumstances, to that of criminal complicity.

As for Honda, undoubtedly he must have summoned Makiko without knowing that she was lying. Honda would surely not go so far as to jeopardize his whole career by conspiring with Makiko. Honda, therefore, believed the story Makiko told in her diary!

Isao felt at a loss. If Makiko was not to be indicted for perjury, he had no other course open to him but one that involved the sacrifice of that purity he so valued.

And then, too, if Makiko had actually made such an entry that night (and it would seem that here, at least, she was telling the truth), how could she, immediately after that tragically beautiful farewell, have changed their encounter into a scene so surpassingly ugly? Was that cunning trick prompted by hostility? By an unaccountable desire to defile herself? No, it could be nothing of the sort. Wise Makiko, perceiving the advent of a day like today, had come home from parting with him to prepare her defences against the moment when she would be called as a witness. And why? For no other reason but to save him.

There was no longer any question about Makiko having been their betrayer, Isao thought. Then it occurred to him that the court was not likely to allow an informer to be called as a witness to support indirect evidence for the defence. Had Makiko been the informer who had brought them to trial, the contradiction between the information she had given them and her testimony today would have been apparent. Amid the unpleasant scenes that his imagination flashed before him as his heart beat fast, he could at least discard the image of Makiko as informer. And this brought him momentary relief.

Makiko's only conceivable motive was love, a love that dared to face danger in full view of the public. Such a love! For this love Makiko did not hesitate to besmirch that which was most precious to him. Moreover, what was bitterest of all, he had to make a response to her love. He could not designate Makiko as a perjurer. On the other hand, no one but he knew the circumstances of that night, and so there was no one in the world but Isao who could call her testimony a lie. And Makiko was well aware of this. She testified as she did precisely because she was aware of it. The trap that she had set for him was that he had no choice but to save himself if he was to save her, however repugnant the means. Furthermore, he was sure, Makiko knew that Isao would do nothing else ... Isao struggled to shake off somehow the bonds that were constricting him.

He considered a further aspect. How did Makiko's false testimony strike the ears of his comrades beside him? Isao was confident that they trusted him. Still, they could hardly dismiss testimony so openly given as a tissue of lies!

The silence of his comrades while Makiko was testifying was like that of beasts tied up in their pens at night, their secret snarlings and their stealthy scratching at palings sharply intensifying an atmosphere of inexpressible discontent and the smothering stink of urine. Isao knew that his comrades were reacting with every fibre of their bodies. Even the noise of one of them scraping his heels against the back of the chair Isao heard as a reprimand directed at him. The anxiety about betrayal that had oppressed him in prison – that formless anxiety one feels in groping for a needle lost in the darkness – now its circumstances were reversed. Isao sensed a black poison spreading rapidly through the heart of each of his comrades. He could hear a network of cracks beginning to cover the entire surface of the white porcelain vase of his purity.

Let them be disgusted with him. Let them condemn him. That he could bear. What he could not bear was what they would naturally infer from Makiko's testimony: that so sudden arrest – might it not have resulted from Isao's betraying them to the authorities?

There was but one means to clear away this intolerable suspicion. There was but one person to clear it away. Isao himself, in other words, had to take the stand and expose Makiko's perjury.

Meanwhile, Honda himself was far from satisfied of the truth of Makiko's diary entry. He did not believe that the judges would accept the evidence of the diary at face value. He knew, however, that Isao would never do anything to cause Makiko to be charged with perjury. Isao, too, Honda was sure, clearly realized that Makiko's sole concern was to save him.

He hoped to bring about a struggle between his client and his witness. Isao's secret chamber – his clear purity of dedication – would be aglow with a woman's burning passion, as with the scarlet rays of the setting sun. Each of them, armed with the sword of ultimate truth, would have to destroy the power of the other's world – there was no other way. This was a kind of struggle that Isao in his twenty years of life had never imagined, had never dreamed of. It was, furthermore, a battle one had to learn to fight, a certain necessity of life.

Isao had an inordinate belief in his own world. Honda had to smash this for him. Why? Because this was the most dangerous of faiths. A thing that was endangering Isao's life.

If Isao had executed his plan as he wished, suicide following upon assassination, he would perhaps have brought his life to a conclusion without ever having encountered 'another person'. The 'big shots' he killed would never have been other persons whom he had to confront. He would have viewed these men as nothing more than ugly dummies to be destroyed by the pure zeal of youth. Indeed, when Isao's sword blade cut into such ugly old flesh, Isao would probably have felt a fondness for his victim, more so than if he were a blood relative, since this man would have been like an icon that embodied the concept that Isao had cherished for so long. For in his written testimony also, he had stated that he 'would never kill out of hatred'. His crime would have been one of pure abstraction. To say, however, that Isao knew nothing of hatred would be to say that he had never loved anyone at all.

Just now, perhaps, he was knowing hatred. The shadow of something alien had for the first time entered his world of purity. No matter how keen his blade, how quick his footwork, how swift his blows, this was something alien and powerful from the other world, something he could neither control nor suppress. He was, in short, learning that the 'outside' existed in the very substance of the flawless sphere in which he lived.

As he watched the retreating figure of the witness, the Chief Judge slipped off his reading glasses. The bright summer sunlight that spilled into the courtroom lit his face with its bad complexion and paperlike skin.

'He is thinking something. What is he thinking?' Honda asked himself with a quiver of interest as he watched the judge.

It was not plausible that a venerable judge would allow himself, in public, to be captivated by the crisp loveliness of a rear view of Makiko. Judge Hisamatsu on his high bench seemed, rather, to be keeping a lonely watch from the high tower of age and legal justice. With his farsighted old eyes he could command a wide, distant view, a gift that his superiors esteemed in him. Consequently, Honda was certain that, beyond Makiko's flawless conduct and attitude under questioning and during the reading of the diary entry, the judge's intention was to weigh more heavily the composure with which she walked away. To look beyond a desolate, barren plain of feeling, to where a view of a summer obi was growing distant ... Now, surely, he has inferred something. Though Judge Hisamatsu had no reputation for brilliance, it was not strange that he was thoroughly versed in human nature.

The judge turned to Isao: 'Is the testimony that Miss Kito just gave correct?' he asked. With a firm thrust of his forefinger Honda held fast the red pencil which he was about to roll down his desk, and pricked up his ears.

Isao stood up. Honda felt a little apprehensive as he noted that Isao's fists were tightly clenched, and even trembling slightly. At the neck of his somewhat loosely wrapped summer kimono, drops of sweat glistened upon the white skin of his chest.

'Yes, Your Honour,' Isao answered. 'It is correct.'

JUDGE: You visited the home of Makiko Kito the evening of November twenty-ninth, and you told her of your own volition that you had changed your mind about your resolution?

IINUMA: Yes, Your Honour.

JUDGE: And the conversation took place just as she described it?

IINUMA: Yes, Your Honour ... However ...

JUDGE: However? What do you mean 'however'?

IINUMA: I did not tell her what I really felt.

JUDGE: And what do you mean by that?

IINUMA: What I really felt ... The truth is, Your Honour ... that both Miss Kito and General Kito have been very kind to me for a long time. And so I wanted to make a brief farewell before I carried out my resolution. And since, for some time now, I had been letting her know something of my thoughts, I wanted to prevent her from becoming involved in any way whatsoever in the aftermath of our action. Therefore I deliberately acted as though my nerve had failed, and, in order to make her believe that, I told her nothing but lies. I wanted to see her gravely disappointed in me . . . and, by that means, break off my – attachment. Everything I said to her that night was a lie. She was completely taken in.

JUDGE: I see. Well, then, do you mean to say that on the night in question your resolution was as firm as ever?

IINUMA: Yes, Your Honour.

JUDGE: Aren't you just saying this in a hasty attempt to redress matters in front of your companions, who just heard from the mouth of Miss Kito testimony that portrayed you as weak and irresolute?

IINUMA: No, Your Honour. That's not it at all.

JUDGE: It seems to me that the witness, Miss Kito, is not the sort of person who is easily deceived. On the night in question, while Miss Kito heard you out, didn't you have the impression that she was merely pretending to be deceived?

IINUMA: Not at all, Your Honour. I was being very serious about it.

As Honda was listening to this exchange, he secretly applauded the desperate means that Isao had unexpectedly seized upon to extricate himself. Hemmed in as he was, Isao had at last learned the sophistication of adults. He had now discovered on his own the one device by which he could save Makiko and yet save himself. For the moment at least, Isao was not a young and heedless beast that knows nothing but how to hurl itself forward.

Honda calculated. When the charge was preparation to murder, the prosecution could not merely show intention but had to demonstrate that some concrete preparatory action had been taken. Since, therefore, Makiko's testimony pertained only to intention and had nothing to do with acts, in the broader context of the trial, it was neither a plus nor a minus. But when one considered the judges' own state of mind with regard to the defendants, that was a different matter. For article 201, which dealt with preparation to murder, had a provision specifying that punishment could be remitted, depending upon the circumstances.

How each judge assessed the circumstances would vary according to his character. Honda could find nothing in previous decisions of Judge Hisamatsu that would enable him to be confident of understanding his character. The wise course, accordingly, was to offer for the formation of the judge's assessment two kinds of mutually opposed data.

If the judge was psychologically inclined, he would base his opinion on Isao's renunciation of criminal intent, which Makiko's testimony alleged. If the judge was one who favoured commitment to a belief, an ideal, then perhaps the unswerving purity of resolution, which Isao's own testimony insisted upon, would move him. The essential thing was to be prepared to offer adequate material of both kinds, whichever view the judge might take.

'Say what you like. Insist as much as you like,' said Honda again in the depths of his heart to Isao. 'Pour out your sincerity. Let the thoughts you describe reek of blood, but don't by any means let yourself go beyond the realm of concepts. That's the one way that you can save yourself.'

JUDGE: Well now, Iinuma . . . you have talked of 'the action' and of your 'belief'. You had much to say on this in the written testimony. But what do you think about the connection between thought and deed?

IINUMA: Pardon, Your Honour?

JUDGE: Put it like this: why isn't belief enough? Can't patriotism simply remain a belief? Why must one go beyond that toward illegal acts, such as you had in mind? I would like to hear your opinion on this.

IINUMA: Yes, Your Honour. In the philosophy of Wang Yang-ming there is something that is called congruity of thought and action: 'To know and not to act is not yet to know.' And it was this philosophy that I strove to put into practice. If one knows of the decadence of Japan today, the dark clouds that envelop her future, the impoverished state of the farmers and the despair of the poor, if one knows all this is due to political corruption and to the unpatriotic nature of the *zaibatsu*, who thrive on this corruption, and knows that here is the source of the evil which shuts out the lights of our most revered Emperor's benevolence – with such knowledge, I think, the meaning of 'to know and to act' becomes self-evident.

JUDGE: That's extremely abstract, I'd say. Take as much time as you need, but explain the development of your feelings, your indignation, your resolution.

IINUMA: Very well, Your Honour. I gave myself over to the practice of kendo from boyhood, but when I realized that around the time of the Meiji Restoration youths had swords with which they fought actual combats, struck down injustice, and fulfilled the great task of the Restoration, I felt an indescribable dissatisfaction with the bamboo sword and the kendo of the drill halls. But as yet I had formed no definite idea of the sort of action that was right for me.

In 1930 there was the London Naval Conference, and even in school I was told what humiliating conditions had been forced upon us and how national security was imperilled. Just as my eyes were being opened to the dangers threatening the nation, there occurred the incident of Sagoya shooting Premier Hamaguchi. I then realized that the dark cloud that covered Japan was not something to be lightly shrugged off, and from that time on, I listened to what the teachers and older students had to say about current events, and, on my own, I began to read all sorts of things.

Gradually, I became acquainted with the problems of society. I was shocked at the inaction of the government in the face of the chronic depression that had been dragging on since the world-wide panic.

A mass of jobless wage-earners that reached two million, men who had formerly worked away from home and sent money back, now returned to their farming villages to aggravate the poverty already reigning there. I learned that there were great crowds at Yugyo Temple in Fujisawa where the monks dished out rice gruel to the unemployed who were walking home to the country, lacking the money for train fare. And yet the government, despite the gravity of the situation, responded only with nonchalant indifference, Minister of the Interior Antachi declaring: 'Relief measures for the unemployed would make people frivolous and lazy, so I will do all I can to avoid such a harmful policy.'

Then in 1931, bad harvests struck Tohoku and Hokkaido. Whatever could be sold was sold, land and homes were lost, and the situation was such that whole families lived in stables, and people held starvation at bay by eating acorns and roots. Even in front of the township hall one saw notices such as:

'Anyone wishing to sell his daughters, inquire within.' It was not at all rare for a soldier on his way off to war to bid a tearful farewell to his younger sister being sold to a brothel.

Beyond the hardship of the bad harvests, the stringent economic policy of the government after the lifting of the embargo on the export of gold laid ever heavier burdens on the farmers, and the panic in agriculture mounted to new heights. The Land of Abundant Rice, which was ancient Japan, was transformed into a wasteland populated by people sobbing from the pangs of hunger. And then the importing of rice, when there was more than enough rice within Japan, caused the price of rice to plunge disastrously. Meanwhile tenant farming grew by leaps and bounds, and more than half the crop a tenant produced had to go as rent, with not a single grain of rice going into the mouth of the farmer himself. The farmers had not one yen of currency. Trade was carried out by bartering. A pack of Shikishima cigarettes went for two quarts of rice, a haircut was four quarts, a pack of Golden Bat cigarettes was a hundred bunches of turnips, and twenty-six pounds of cocoons would bring in ten yen. That was the situation.

As you know, Your Honour, the farmers are breaking out in protest everywhere. There is danger that the farming villages will go Red. Even in the breasts of the young men who are being called to the imperial colours as loyal subjects one cannot find unalloyed patriotism, and that evil is beginning to infect the armed forces.

Giving no thought to these crises, the government plods along in the path of corruption. The *zaibatsu* has amassed vast sums through dollar buying and other policies ruinous to the nation, and no one pays any heed to the wretched misery of the masses. As a result of my varied reading and other research, I came to feel strongly that what had debased Japan to this extent was not just the sins of politicians. Much of the responsibility lay with the *zaibatsu*, who manipulated these politicians to satisfy their greedy craving for profit.

I never thought, however, of going over to the leftists. For the ideology of the leftists bore hostility towards the most revered person of His Sacred Majesty.

Japan from ancient days has been a land whose character was to reverence His Sacred Majesty, a harmonious land where the Emperor was held to be the head of the vast family that was the Japanese people. Here, I need hardly say, is the true image of the Emperor's Land, a national character as everlasting as heaven and earth.

But what of this decadent Japan filled with people suffering from hunger? Why has this become such a degenerate age despite the revered person of the Emperor? Isn't it the unparalleled virtue of the Emperor's Land that the exalted ministers who serve at his side and the starving farmers in the remote villages of Tohoku are alike his children without difference or distinction? At first I firmly believed that the day would certainly come when the poor would be saved by the benevolence of His Sacred Majesty. Japan and the Japanese had for the time being gone somewhat astray. With the passage of time, the Yamato Spirit would reawaken in the hearts of her loyal subjects, and the whole nation working together would make the Emperor's Land what it had been before.

Such were the hopes that I once held. I had faith that the dark clouds would one day be blown away and that a bright and clear future lay ahead for Japan.

Wait as I might, however, that day did not come. The longer I waited, the darker the clouds became. Then I happened to read a book that struck me with the force of a revelation. This was the book of Tsunanori Yamao: *The League of the Divine Wind.* After I finished it, I was a different person. I realized that to go on merely sitting and waiting was hardly the behaviour proper to a loyal man. Till that moment I had known nothing of desperate loyalty. Nor had I known that, once the flame of loyalty blazed up within one, it was necessary to die.

Over there the sun is shining. We cannot see it from here, but even the turgid grey light around us surely has the sun as its source, and so in one corner of the sky the sun must be shining. This sun is the true image of His Sacred Majesty. If the people could only bathe themselves in its rays, they would shout with joy. The desolate plain would then become fertile at once, and Japan, beyond any shadow of a doubt, would become once more the Land of Abundant Rice.

But the low-lying cloud of darkness covers the land and shuts off the light of the sun. Heaven and earth are cruelly kept apart, heaven and earth, which have but to meet to embrace smilingly, cannot even view each other's sad faces. The sorrowful cries of the people cover the land but cannot reach the ears of heaven. To scream out is in vain, to weep, in vain, to protest, in vain. But if their voices could reach the ears of heaven, the power of heaven, as easily as you move your little finger, could clear away those dark clouds, could transform a marshy wasteland to a shining countryside.

Who was to carry word to heaven? Who, mounting to heaven through death, was to take upon himself the vital function of messenger? I perceived that this was what the valiant men of the League of the Divine Wind intended by their faith in the Ukei.

If we look on idly, heaven and earth will never be joined. To join heaven and earth, some decisive deed of purity is necessary. To accomplish so resolute an action, you have to stake your life, giving no thought to personal gain or loss. You have to turn into a dragon and stir up a whirlwind, tear the dark, brooding clouds asunder and soar up into the azure-blue sky.

Of course I thought of gathering a vast number of arms and men and sweeping the sky clear of darkness before mounting to heaven. But I gradually came to realize that that was unnecessary. The valiant men of the League, wielding their Japanese swords, fought their way into a camp of infantry armed with modern weapons. All I had to do was to direct myself at that spot where the clouds were darkest, that point where their soiled texture was thickest and most filthy. All I had to do was to tear open a hole there, with all my might, and soar to heaven alone.

I never thought in terms of killing people, only of destroying the deadly spirit that was poisoning Japan. And to do so I had to tear away the robe of flesh with which this spirit was garbed. By this action the souls of those whom we cut down would also become pure, and the bright, wholesome Yamato Spirit would come alive in their hearts again. And they, with my comrades and me, would rise to heaven. For we in turn, after destroying their flesh, had to commit seppuku immediately. Why? Because if we did not cast aside our own flesh as soon as possible, we could not fulfil our duty as bearers of an urgent message for heaven.

Even speculating on the Imperial Mind is disloyal. Loyalty, I think, is nothing else but to throw down one's life in reverence for the Imperial Will. It is to tear asunder the dark clouds, climb to heaven, and plunge into the sun, plunge into the midst of the Imperial Mind.

This, then, is what my comrades and I pledged within our hearts.

Honda watched the face of the Chief Judge with unblinking gaze. As Isao had gone on with his explanation, the white, splotched skin covering the judge's old cheeks, Honda observed, had gradually taken on the red glow of youth. When Isao had finished and took his seat, Judge Hisamatsu began to shuffle busily the papers before him, but obviously this was a device to hide his emotion. After a time the judge spoke.

JUDGE: So that's it then? Does the prosecution have anything to say?

PROSECUTOR: Yes, Your Honour. To take things in proper order, I would like to say something with regard to the witness Miss Kito. I am sure that, when she was summoned, this court was exercising due consideration. Nevertheless, in my own view, I must not only say that her testimony was entirely irrelevant but, without going so far as to declare it perjury, contend that the credibility of the diary seems extremely questionable. As for the value of the diary as written evidence, then, I would register a forceful doubt. Now, with regard to the witness's testimony that she was as fond of the defendant as if he were 'a younger brother', one would expect emotional involvement, in view of the long and cordial relationship between the Iinuma and Kito families. The defendant Iinuma himself spoke of an 'attachment', and so one might well imagine that a tacit understanding existed between these two. Consequently, I regret to say that, in both Miss Kito's testimony and the defendant Iinuma's account of that night, one can detect a kind of unnatural exaggeration. In short, I believe that the summoning of this witness was not a proper step.

Now to consider the long account that the defendant Iinuma has just given us: elements of fantasy and abstraction predominate in it. At first it would seem that he was fervently pouring out all that he had intended, but one has the impression that he deliberately obscured some significant aspects. For example, how did he come to abandon the plan to gather a large number of arms and men and sweep away the dark clouds altogether, thinking it would be sufficient to tear open the clouds at one spot only? That is a gap in his account that cannot be ignored. I believe that the defendant deliberately omitted the particulars of the matter at this point.

On the other hand, though the witness Mr Kitazaki's memory was not clear with regard to the time, he testified that Lieutenant Hori had shouted angrily, 'Don't you understand? Give it up!' either towards the end of October or the beginning of November of last year. I submit that this testimony contributes vitally relevant evidence. For it clearly has a bearing upon the defendant

Iinuma's account of the weapon exchange which he describes as having taken place on November eighteenth. If this weapon exchange had taken place earlier, if the night on which the Lieutenant shouted 'Give it up' had been after it, the affair would be different. It is otherwise, however, and so the various parts fit together.

The judge, after conferring with the prosecutor and the defence counsel about the date and time of the next session, announced that the second session was at an end.

38

The verdict was handed down on December 26, 1933, just before the year-end holiday. Though it was not the 'not guilty' decision Honda had hoped for, it read: 'The punishment to which the defendants are liable is hereby dismissed.' It was a decision that utilized a provision in Article 201 of the Criminal Code, pertaining to preparation for murder: 'Dependent upon the circumstances, however, punishment may be remitted.'

The verdict acknowledged that preparation to commit murder had indeed taken place, but the defendants, with the exception of Sawa, were extremely young, their motives were pure, and they had obviously been carried away by excessive patriotism. Furthermore, there was inadequate evidence that, after plotting, they had not indeed turned aside from their criminal intent. The logic behind the remission of punishment for all the defendants was thus set forth in detail.

Then as to the older Sawa, had he been an initiator of the conspiracy, he would not have escaped, but since he had joined when it was already under way and seemed to have taken no particular leadership role, he benefited from the same remission of sentence.

Had there been a 'not guilty' decision, the probability would have been strong that the prosecutor would have appealed, but as matters stood, Honda was hopeful that he would not do so. In any case, they would know within a week.

All the defendants were released, and they returned home to their parents.

On the evening of the twenty-sixth, there was a private dinner at the Academy of Patriotism to celebrate Isao's return. Honda was the guest of honour, and Iinuma and his wife, Isao, Sawa, and the student body took part in the conviviality. Makiko was invited but did not come.

Up until the time the banquet began, Isao sat listening to the radio as though in a stupor. He heard the six o'clock Fairytale Theatre, Hanako Muraoka's Children's Newspaper at six twenty, a talk by the chief surgeon of the Konoe Division on 'Means to Be Taken by the Citizenry in the Event of Poison Gas Attack' at six twenty-five, and while he was listening to Harold Palmer's six fifty-five Current

Topics, he was compelled to get up and hurry to the dining room. Since returning home, he had merely smiled and said nothing.

His mother had met him at the door, weeping without restraint, and then, after putting on a shiny, freshly laundered apron, she retired into the kitchen and threw herself into the task of chopping vegetables. The kitchen was crowded with rejoicing housewives who had come to help her. As his mother gave orders, her busy fingertips seemed to send forth unseen rays directed at the platters everywhere, and these were instantly filled with multicoloured sashimi and broiled fish and meats. Women's laughter from the kitchen echoed in Isao's ears like sounds from another world.

Iinuma and the Academy students had met Isao and Sawa, and, on the way home, all had stopped to offer reverence before the Imperial Palace at Meiji Shrine, and as soon as they had returned to the Academy, they went to worship as one family in the shrine located in one wing. Only after this was Isao able to enjoy the leisure of a hot bath. All the gods had been thanked, and now at this banquet it remained to thank the one who, in the world of humans, deserved the most thanks: Honda. Iinuma, in his formal kimono with family crest, rose from his seat, moved down to a humble place with his son and Sawa on either side of him, and, turning to Honda, bowed low.

Isao did as he was told. Even his smile appeared to be one demanded of him. Sounds were ringing in his ears. Things were stirring and bustling. Things were glittering and dancing before his eyes. Things he had long dreamed of were being conveyed to his mouth. His senses were surely operative yet they diffused reality. The food seemed as insubstantial as delicacies tasted in dreams. The twelve-mat room in which he sat seemed to become permeated with a painful brilliance and suddenly transformed into a vast hall of a hundred or two hundred mats, where, far in the distance, a throng had gathered for a festive banquet. They were people with whom he had nothing to do.

It was Honda who quickly noticed that Isao had lost that piercing stare of his.

Iinuma smiled at Honda's concern. 'Naturally he's still somewhat numb,' he said in a low voice. 'I had a similar experience. Of course in my case it wasn't so long, but even at that, I was in a state of collapse for a week or so afterwards. I couldn't really feel free ... There's nothing to worry about, Mr Honda. But here now, do you know why I'm having this party for the boy? It's just to make this the day to celebrate his becoming an adult. He won't be twenty-one for a while yet, but there's no doubt that this day will be one of the most memorable of his life, the day of his rebirth. From now on tonight I'll be giving him rather rough treatment, but I intend to really open Isao's eyes and treat him as a full-fledged adult. And I know, sir, that you understand how I feel as a father and won't try to stop me.'

Isao, in the meantime, sat drinking with Sawa, both of them surrounded by students. Sawa was entertaining everyone by recounting prison experiences in a loud voice while Isao merely smiled and remained silent.

The youngest student, Tsumura, who idolized Isao, grew irritated as one funny story followed another, wanting to hear the icy severity of Isao's words. His attention never wavered from him, but, since Isao offered nothing at all, Tsumura finally took the initiative and whispered to him: 'Isao, did you hear the disgusting thing Kurahara did?'

The name Kurahara struck Isao's ears like a peal of thunder. As soon as he heard that name, the realm of reality which had seemed so distant suddenly impinged itself upon his senses like sweat-drenched underwear clinging to one's skin.

'Kurahara? What about him?'

'Something I saw in yesterday's paper. The *Imperial Way* gave its whole front page to it,' Tsumura answered, citing the name of a right-wing newspaper. 'It was really disgusting.' He pulled a folded-up tabloid newspaper from his jacket pocket and showed it to Isao. Then he peered intently over Isao's shoulder as he read the article, his breath hot, his angry eyes seeming to burn holes through the paper. 'It was really disgusting,' he repeated.

The newspaper was crudely printed, with broken type evident here and there. The story it carried did not appear in major newspapers but was an article reprinted by permission of a Shinto publication connected with the Grand Shrine of Isé.

According to the article, Kurahara had, on December fifteenth, attended a session of the Kansai Bankers Association, and on his return had stopped at Isé, where he had stuffed himself with a dinner of Matsuzaka beef, which he especially favoured. And on the following morning, he went together with the Prefectural Governor to offer worship at the Inner Shrine of Isé.

With them were their secretaries and a number of other underlings, but Kurahara and the Governor were accorded special treatment by having two folding chairs set up for them on the gravel pathway. At the sacred branch ceremonial too, two previously prepared sakaki sprigs were handed over to them. Both stood and, holding their sprigs aloft, listened to the ritual prayers. Then suddenly Kurahara, apparently feeling an itch on his back, transferred the sprig to his left hand and tried to scratch the spot, but could not reach it. He took the sprig in his right hand once more and this time reached behind him with his left. Again he failed to reach it.

The ritual prayers continued, still without any hint of coming to an end. Kurahara hesitated a moment, then, hindered as he was by the sakaki branch, decided to lay it down on the chair. Then he put both hands behind his back and scratched. At that moment the prayers finally ended, and two assistant priests indicated that the two men were to offer their sprigs.

Kurahara, forgetting that he had put aside his sprig, joined issue with the Governor in a contest of mutual deferring. Finally the Governor yielded, and stepped forward to make his offering. At this moment the priests were shocked to see that the sakaki sprig was gone from Kurahara's hand, but it was too late. For Kurahara, relieved that the Governor had preceded him, had sat down for the time being, crushing beneath his buttocks the sprig that lay on his chair. In the midst of the Shinto music accompanying the ritual, this faux pas was quickly passed off without attracting too much attention. Before many people had noticed, Kurahara, furnished with a fresh sprig, was stepping forward to offer worship. But, among the young priests who witnessed this, there was one who could not restrain his indignation. It was he who wrote about it in the Shrine journal, an article that came to the attention of the *Imperial Way*.

Kurahara could not have committed a greater sacrilege. Tsumura's indignation was reasonable enough. Even though it was a simple blunder on Kurahara's part, the night before he was to offer worship he had filled his belly with the flesh of beasts, and, furthermore, rather than begging forgiveness for the breach that he had committed before the gods, he had dared to advance with his second sakaki sprig into the very presence of divinity, and, as men looked on, had committed the still greater sin of glossing over his previous transgressions with a solemnly enacted sacrilege. Still, Isao concluded, this was not reason enough to kill him. But then, turning to look at young Tsumura, he noticed the boyish anger in those clear eyes. Somehow Isao felt ashamed.

This momentary misgiving seemed to rob the hand that held the newspaper of its strength. Sawa reached out the next instant and snatched the paper away.

'Forget it. Forget it. Don't bother your head about it,' said Sawa. Isao could not be sure how drunk the man really was as he wrapped a fat, too white arm around his shoulder and urged saké upon him. For the first time Isao noticed how sombrely pale Sawa's skin had become.

The saké bottle made its rounds, everyone sang and clapped, some stood up to entertain, and, at length, the headmaster declared that the party was over. Then Iinuma suggested that Honda, Isao, and Sawa join him around the *kotatsu* table in his own room to resume drinking while his wife served them.

This was the first time Honda had set foot in this room. It was ten mats in size, and in its centre he was startled to find, spread in bright splendour, a Yuzen silk *kotatsu* quilt of sensuous beauty with a palace oxcart pattern. Perceptive as he was, Honda immediately guessed that this was a product of the taste for aristocratic indulgence that Miné still clung to. At the banquet too, Honda had been taken aback to see how the wooden rice tubs were covered with quilted blue cotton.

When he observed the interchanges between husband and wife, Honda's intuition told him that Iinuma, somewhere in his heart, had never forgiven his wife's past. Whether it was the distant past, which involved Marquis Matsugae, or some event in the more recent past, he did not know. For Iinuma's unrelenting attitude was somehow evident in his manner, and, correspondingly, Miné had a certain obsequiousness that seemed to keep on begging her husband's forgiveness. Nonetheless, it was odd that Iinuma should tolerate, all over his house, reminders of the source of his wife's youthful lewdness, that gaudy style of beauty, so contrary to his own tastes, that could be seen in this sort of *kotatsu* quilt. Perhaps, Honda thought, Iinuma himself, in the depths of his heart, concealed a nostalgia for this kind of taste appropriate to a maid in the service of a noble household.

Honda was invited to sit in front of the *tokonoma*. Miné kept her gaze fastened to the large bottle of saké resting in the copper kettle on the hibachi, from time to time touching it quickly with the tips of her long, skilful fingers as though it were an easily aroused animal. No matter how extreme her politeness, Honda felt, she had something of the mischievous young girl about her. The four men, warming themselves in the *kotatsu*, began to drink saké, taking some dried mullet roe with it.

'Tonight, Isao, drink as much as you want.' As Iinuma offered the bottle to his son, he darted a stealthy glance at Honda. Apparently this was the start of the 'rough treatment' that he had given notice of earlier. 'Tonight, in front of Mr Honda here, I am going to say something that will probably set you back on your heels. I'm doing it because from today on, you're an adult in mind and body, and, as your father, I'm going to treat you as a full-fledged man so that you'll know all the ins and outs of life, and can become a worthy successor to me. I'll put it to you bluntly: it's obvious that the police got you a year ago because somebody had informed. Who do you think that somebody was? If you have any idea, tell me.'

'I have no idea.'

'Don't hold back. If you think you know, tell me. It's all right.'

'I don't know.'

'I'll tell you. It was your father here. Well, are you surprised?'

'Yes...'

Honda noticed with a sense of foreboding that at that moment Isao's expression bore not a trace of real surprise. That same instant Iinuma turned his eyes away from Isao and hurried on with what he was saying.

'Well? What do you think? Do you think there could be a father so cold-hearted as to hand over his own beloved son to the police? A father who, with a laugh, could turn his son over to the police? Eh? Well, I dared to do just that. But ... I did it weeping. It's the truth. Isn't it, Miné?'

'Yes, it's the truth. Your father was weeping as he did it,' said Miné, chiming in from across the hibachi. Coolly, but with no sign of disrespect, Isao put a question to his father.

'I see now that it was you who reported us to the police, Father. But who reported what we were planning to you?'

Iinuma's neat moustache trembled slightly. Startled, he put a hand to it as though pressing down a butterfly that was trying to fly away.

'I started keeping a close watch on it long ago. It was your mistake to think your father's eyes were like two knotholes.'

'Is that right?'

'Of course that's right. But why in the world did I hurry out and get you arrested? That's what I really want you to understand.

'To tell the truth, I was greatly impressed by what you intended to do. I thought it was magnificent. I even envied you. I wanted to let you go through with it, if only I could. But that meant sitting and watching you rush to your death. If I'd left you alone, you'd have gone through with it. You'd have died.

'But you've got to understand that I'm not like other fathers, not wanting to lose their boys, who would even frustrate their sons' greatest hopes just to save their lives. Get this point straight. I wanted to save your life, and I wanted to see your plan go through. But what should I do? I thought about it all night long, and finally I arrived at a solution. Saving you like this means, in the long run, taking everything into consideration, the fulfilment of your plan in an even greater way.

'Do you understand, Isao? Just to die isn't everything. Just holding your life cheap isn't loyalty. In the eyes of The Most Revered Son of Heaven, the life of each of the Emperor's treasures is a precious thing.

'It's been obvious since the May Fifteenth Incident, people are fed up with political corruption. They have admired and applauded incidents like this. Then, too, you and your companions were young. You were pure. You had everything needed for sympathy and appreciation. Furthermore, if you were apprehended one step away from your goal, people would have a sense of relief, all the more reason to applaud you. Not by committing the act, but by being caught on the verge of it, you could become greater heroes. And because of this, to strike in the future will be easier. When a truly large-scale Restoration takes place, you will be a force to be reckoned with, and then you can fight magnificently. I was right. The number of letters that came in asking for a reduction of sentence after your arrest, the tenor of the newspaper accounts – everything showed how much people were on your side. I did what was best, Isao.

'What I did, in other words, was in imitation of the lion who heaves the cub he loves so much down into a deep ravine in order to toughen him up. Now you've made your way from the bottom of the ravine in splendid fashion. You've proved yourself a man. Isn't that right, Miné?'

'Yes, it's just as your father says, Isao. You've come through in splendid fashion. It's all due to your father's love, like the love of the lion for its cub. You must thank him for what he did. It was all done out of love for you.'

Just as, when one digs a hole in the sand by the water's edge, however hard one tries, the sides give way before the water that wells up, so the elaborate speech that Iinuma had begun to deliver so triumphantly, Honda thought, was giving way before the uncomfortable silence of the listener at his side. Indeed as soon as the words had passed Iinuma's lips, the sands of silence were already trickling down upon the watery surface gleaming in the sun. Honda looked at Isao. He looked at Sawa. Shoulders squared, Isao was letting his head hang forward. Sawa was taking a surreptitious drink from his saké cup.

Honda had no idea whether or not Iinuma had intended from the beginning to say what he said next, but, whatever the case, Iinuma feared silence.

'Now listen. Up to now, I've been talking about something that you could understand well. But, Isao, here is something more you need to know to become an adult. You've got to swallow the bitter wisdom that women and children never taste. There's a gate that every man has to go through. With your experience this past year, you've gone through it in body. Now your soul has to go through it too.

'Up to now I have said nothing about this, but . . . the Academy of Patriotism – who do you suppose is the man responsible for its present prosperity? Whom do we have to thank, do you suppose?'

'I don't know.'

'If I say it, the name is going to set you back on your heels. But it is nobody else but Baron Shinkawa. Don't either you or Sawa ever mention a word of this to the students. This is the Academy's greatest secret. This building – the truth is that it's due to an anonymous contribution of Baron Shinkawa. And I in my turn, of course, have had to hustle in various ways on his behalf. The Baron, on his part, has not thrown money away in vain. Otherwise, how do you think he could have pulled through the recent storm of abuse over dollar buying?'

Honda looked at Isao's face once again. This time the coldness and utter lack of surprise made Honda shudder. Iinuma was still talking.

'So that was the relationship with Baron Shinkawa, and shortly before the May Fifteenth Incident I got a summons from the Baron. Since the money was passed to me every month secretly through his secretary, it was something extraordinary that made him want to meet with me face to face.

'I won't mention the amount, but he handed over to me a huge stack of bills and said: "This money has nothing to do with my safety. I'll tell you frankly: it's to protect Busuké Kurahara. Because he's the sort of person he is, you see, he'd never pay out money for his safety. I have received many favours from Mr Kurahara which I should repay. And so, without telling him, I'm giving you this on my own. So please, then, let this money act as a safeguard for Kurahara. If it's not enough, just let me know, and I'll give you more." And so, then, I–'

'So you took it, Father?'

'I did. I took it. Because I was so moved by Baron Shinkawa's feeling for his old friend. From then on, things went very well indeed with the Academy, as you and Sawa know.'

'That's why you reported us to the police then, to protect Kurahara?'

'So you'd think, I imagine. That's the way a child would see it. No matter how much money they gave me, whom do you think I'd put first: a big shot of the world of finance who is no relative of mine, or my own boy?'

'I see. You took the best possible course, one that ensured saving your son's life as well as saving Kurahara's and honouring your obligation to Baron Shinkawa.'

Honda was finally heartened to see for the first time in Isao's eyes the fire that had once been there.

'No. That shows how naïvely you look at things. Do you understand me? You've got to learn that in this world of ours everything is tangled and twisted together. You'll never get free of all that until you go up to heaven. The harder you try to shake it off, the tighter it will cling to you. But as long as you keep your faith, the tangle is nothing to worry about. It doesn't worry me a bit, Isao.

'As far as I was concerned, no matter how much money I took, you could have cut down Shinkawa and Kurahara, and it wouldn't have bothered me. Afterwards I'd make amends by cutting open my own belly. I was prepared for something like that from the moment I took the money. If a merchant doesn't hand over the goods when he receives payment, that's fraud. But it's different with a patriot. Money is money, fidelity is fidelity. Two different things. Money is used in money matters, and fidelity can be kept by seppuku. That's all.

'You see, I want you to be prepared for these situations. That's why I'm telling you all this. To defile yourself, yet not really be defiled – that's true purity. If you're fastidious about defilement, you're not going to do anything. You'll never become a real man, Isao.

'Having said this much, I think you must understand my intentions. I didn't turn you in to save Kurahara's life. Nor was it to save your own life either. If I had thought that that was the way to eternal glory for you, to throw away your life in that action, I would have rejoiced and let you go to your death. I didn't do that simply because I didn't think it was. Do you understand me? I said it before, so I won't repeat myself. I prized your goal, I cherished you as my son – and precisely because of this I took the step of denouncing you. I took the step, drinking tears of blood. Didn't I, Miné?'

'Isao, you'll suffer for it, if you don't show gratitude for your father's affection.'

His head hanging, Isao said nothing. The saké he had drunk had brought a rosy flush to his cheeks. His hands on the *kotatsu* quilt trembled slightly.

Honda, looking at Isao, suddenly realized what it was that he had been wanting so earnestly to tell him. Throughout Iinuma's long, self-seeking admonition, Honda had been bursting to say something. Once he said it, Isao's world would crumble, and his eyes might be opened, so that he could race across the wide fields in the bright light of the sun, afraid of nothing. And yet, if he said it to console Isao, who sat there with drooping head, there was the danger that what he told him might instead turn Isao's supreme moment of suffering, never to be lived again, into something altogether meaningless. What Honda wanted to communicate was the secret of Kiyoaki's rebirth in Isao. But when Isao raised his head and there were tears running down his cheeks, Honda completely lost the urge to free the secret he had guarded until now and let it beat its wings like a released bird.

Isao spoke out, like a dog yelping with eager restlessness: 'I've lived for the sake of an illusion. I've patterned my life upon an illusion. And this punishment has come on me because of this illusion ... How I wish I had something that's not an illusion.'

'If you become an adult, you'll get it.'

'An adult? I'd rather ... Yes! Maybe I ought to be reborn a woman. If I were a woman, I could live without chasing after illusions. Couldn't I, Mother?'

Isao laughed suddenly, as if something had cracked.

'What are you saying?' Miné answered, rather angrily. 'Reborn a woman! How silly of you! You're drunk, aren't you – to come out with something like that.'

Soon, after more saké, Isao fell asleep with his cheek upon the quilt that covered the *kotatsu*. Sawa took charge of him and led him to his room. The concerned Honda, deciding to make this the occasion for his own going, got up and followed them.

Showing a tender solicitude, Sawa, without a word, put Isao to bed for the night. When he had done so, Iinuma called him from the other end of the corridor, and Honda found himself alone with the sleeping Isao.

Isao's sleeping face, his skin flushed from drink, showed signs of distress, and his breathing was harsh. But even as he slept, his brows were contracted in manly fashion. Suddenly, as he tossed about on his *futon*, Isao shouted out in his sleep, loudly but too indistinct for Honda to hear clearly: 'Far to the south. Very hot ... in the rose sunshine of a southern land ...'

At that point Sawa returned for Honda. And so, even though this confused message cried out from a drunken sleep lingered in his mind, Honda begged Sawa to look after Isao, and turned his steps toward the entrance hall. He had risked everything in coming to Isao's rescue, and today he had at last won his gamble. Honda wondered, therefore, why he felt such a sense of futility.

39

The following day was fair.

In the morning there was a visitor, Detective Tsuboi from the neighbourhood police station. This middle-aged man, who had risen to second degree in kendo, relayed to Isao the message that the police chief hoped once again that Isao would be kind enough to come to the drill hall on Sundays to instruct the neighbourhood boys in kendo.

'Yes, indeed,' he said, 'though his position prevents him coming out to praise you publicly, the Chief tells us in private that he's struck with admiration for you. And the parents of the boys too are anxious for somebody like you to instruct their sons in kendo, so that the true Japanese spirit will be instilled in them. If there's no appeal, we would like you to come as soon as the new year is under way. Of course I don't think there's much chance of an appeal.'

Isao studied the trousers of the plainclothes man, in which a crease was only dimly visible, and, as he did, he thought of himself as he might look teaching children kendo, with age overtaking him. His white hair in a purple headband would shine wherever it was not covered by the towel bound in Kansai manner behind his mask.

After the detective had gone, Sawa asked Isao to come to his room, and said: 'It certainly feels good to flop down on a tatami again, with a cushion under my head, and skim through a whole year's stack of *Kodan Club*. By the way, even if you're supposed to be on your good behaviour, a young fellow like you can't stay around the house like this. You're allowed to go out as long as I accompany you. So what do you say to us going to see a movie or something tonight?'

'Well, maybe,' said Isao vaguely. Then he added, to be more polite, 'I could go to visit my friend, though.'

'Oh, no, not that! The best thing is for you not to see each other for the time being. You might say something that's better left unsaid.'

'I suppose so.' Isao had not mentioned the name of the person he wanted very much to see.

'Is there anything you'd like to ask me?' Sawa said after a somewhat uncomfortable silence.

'Yes. There's one thing I still don't understand in what my father said. Who told my father what we were up to? It must have been just before we were arrested.'

Sawa's hitherto carefree manner vanished. The sudden, withdrawn silence made Isao uneasy. It was a silence that seemed to poison the atmosphere. Isao found it hard to bear, and he stared intently at the faded brown binding of the tatami where the bright sunshine that poured through the clear glass of the window seemed to dig its claws into the fabric.

'Do you really want to know? If I tell you, you'll have no regrets?'

'No, I want to know the whole truth.'

'All right. I'll tell you what I know. I'm saying this because the master himself went as far with you as he did. What happened was that the night before the arrest, on the night of November thirtieth of last year, that is, a call came for the master from Miss Makiko. I answered the phone. The master came to the phone, and what they talked about, I don't know. But afterwards, the master got ready to go out, and he left without taking anybody with him. And that's all I know.'

As he continued, Sawa's kindliness took on the steadfast warmth of a blanket draped over the shoulders of a shivering man.

'I realize that you're fond of Miss Makiko. And that Miss Makiko is fond of you. Maybe on her side the fervour is a good deal stronger. But it's because she feels the way she does that we have this terrible result. I sized up her true nature when she stepped into the witness box during the trial. A frightful woman, I thought to myself. That was my honest feeling, I tell you. She was gambling all she had on saving your life, but, at the same time, the truth is that she was happy to see you in a prison cell. Do you follow me?

'What I mean is, that marriage of hers – you've got to understand why it ended so tragically in divorce. Her husband loved Makiko, but at the same time he was quite a playboy. The ordinary wife would have put up with it, but this one was proud, and she wouldn't have it. She loved him, and that made it even harder to bear. So, not caring what people might say, she went home to her family's house.

'Because she's that kind of person, then, when she falls in love with another man, it's no ordinary matter. The more she loves, the more anxious she becomes about the future when she might lose her lover. Because she's had an unhappy experience, she'll never believe in a man again. And so naturally, when a man she loves does come along, she wants to make sure that he stays hers and hers alone, even if he is put out of her reach, even if she has to bear the infinite suffering of not being able to be with this man. And as for a place where a man has no chance at all to play around, a place where, as far as a woman's concerned, there's the least cause for worry – where would that be, do you think? Jail, where else? She fell in love with you, so you landed in jail. What more could a man want, come to think of it? I wish I were in your shoes.'

Not looking at Isao, Sawa chattered on heedlessly as he rubbed the pale skin of his swollen cheek.

'Keep clear of a dangerous woman like that from now on. I'll see that you meet lots of lovely women. The master said something to me about this, and he's given me plenty of spending money. Sure, it must have come from Kurahara, indirectly, but it's just as the master said: Money is money; fidelity is fidelity. You've never been with a woman, I bet.

'Will you come along to a movie tonight? At the Shibazono there's a foreign film. Or there's the Hikawa Theatre, near the college, where we could see a movie starring Chiezo. Then we could have a drink at Hyakkendana and head for Maruyama. We've got to perform the "coming of age ceremony", just as the master said. If there's an appeal, the game will be up. So now's the time to get it over with.'

'Let's talk about this once the appeal is dropped.'

'But look, if there is one, what then?'

'We'll worry about that when the time comes,' Isao answered stubbornly.

40

On December twenty-eighth too the sun was shining. Isao held back. The next day, December twenty-ninth, was the day on which the ceremonies attending the naming of the Crown Prince would take place, and rather than darken the morning papers with an ominous headline on such a festive day, it would be more excusable to act later on the festive day itself, as long as the ceremonies were completed and the celebration at an end. Because of the possibility of an appeal, it was dangerous to wait any longer.

December twenty-ninth was still another clear day.

He asked Sawa to participate with him in a lantern procession to the Imperial Palace, and when the two left the house, Isao was wearing his overcoat over his school uniform, and they both were carrying lanterns decorated with the characters for 'celebration'. While they were eating an early dinner in a Ginza restaurant, they watched a streetcar float decorated with chrysanthemums making its way through the crowds in the street outside, the sign 'CONGRATULATIONS' glowing in lights, and its motorman standing with his chest thrust out proudly beneath his blue uniform and brass buttons.

The human wave of lantern-bearers surged forward from Sukiyabashi towards the Imperial Palace. The lanterns with the sun emblem that each one held above his head were reflected in the waters of the moat, and lit up the pines standing in the winter twilight. The many lanterns massed in the plaza before the palace put to flight the shadows lingering beneath the trees and filled the whole area with a shifting brightness at variance with the time of day. The shouts of Banzai went on, never abating. The flames in the uplifted lanterns of the marchers highlighted the shadows of their mouths and throats. Now the faces were steeped in shadow; now they were suddenly lit with shimmering brilliance.

Before long, Sawa was torn away from Isao. After searching hopelessly in the vast throng for some four hours, Sawa returned to the Academy to report what happened.

Isao went back to the Ginza, and at a shop there he bought a dagger and a knife, both with plain wooden sheaths. The knife he put into the inside pocket of his jacket, and the dagger he concealed in his overcoat pocket.

In a hurry, he hailed a cab to Shimbashi Station, where he boarded a train for Atami. It was empty. He had a four-passenger compartment all to himself as he pulled a clipping from his pocket and read it once again. It was a page taken from the New Year's issue of *Kodan Club* borrowed from Sawa, and on it was a boxed item entitled 'How the Big Shots in Politics and Finance Greet the New Year'.

'Busuké Kurahara customarily sees the old year out in very simple fashion,' read the portion that Isao was concerned with. 'Having no liking even for golf, at the end of every year, as soon as offices are closed, he slips away to his villa at Inamura in Izusan. His greatest pleasure is looking after the tangerine orchards there in which he takes such pride. The orchards in the neighbourhood are usually harvested before the year is out, but Kurahara likes to leave the tangerines hanging in bunches so that he may admire them up until the New Year's holidays are well underway. Then, except for giving some to his friends, he donates the entire harvest to welfare hospitals and orphanages. This amply bespeaks the unassuming personality and the admirable warmth of this man, who could be called the Pope of the world of finance.'

Isao took a bus from Atami Station and got off at Inamura. It was already past ten o'clock. The night was still, and he could hear the sound of the sea. The village was beside the road, but wooden shutters were closed everywhere, and no light shone through. Isao turned up his overcoat collar against the chill wind from the ocean. Halfway down the slope, which fell away toward the sea, stood a large stone gate. A light burned outside it, and Isao could easily make out KURAHARA on the name-plate. On the other side, beyond a huge front garden, was a house wrapped in stillness, which, here and there, showed lights burning. There was a walled embankment topped with a hedge all the way around.

On the other side of the road was a mulberry field. At the edge of it, fastened to a mulberry bush, was a tin sign: TANGERINES FOR SALE. The tin rattled in the wind. Isao hid behind the sign. He had heard footsteps coming up the twisting path from the ocean.

A policeman was climbing the slope. He made his way up slowly, stopped in front of the gate for a moment, and then, the noise of his sabre trailing behind him, disappeared along the narrow path that followed the wall.

Isao came out from behind the sign, and, exercising great caution, crossed the road. As he did so, he caught a glimpse of the sea, black beneath a moonless sky.

Scaling the wall presented no problem, but the hedge at the top concealed barbed wire which tore at his overcoat.

Besides plum trees, hemp palms, and pines, the garden of the villa held many tangerine trees planted right up to the house itself, presumably so that the master could appreciate them. The darkness was filled with the fragrance of their ripe fruit. The dried leaves of one giant palm, blown by the wind from the ocean, startled Isao with its sound like wooden clappers.

The ground beneath his feet yielded at every step, as if nourished by an abundance of fertilizer. Bit by bit, he drew closer to a corner of the house from which bright light was coming. The tiled roof was of Japanese design, but the window and siding indicated that the room within was Western style. The window was hung with lace curtains. Isao leaned against the wall, raised himself on tiptoe, and was able to see part of the room.

There was a chimney opening on one side of the room, indicating a Western-style fireplace. A woman was standing with her back to the window, revealing the bow of her obi. When she moved away, there appeared the somewhat plump but stern-looking face of an old man of small stature, dressed in kimono and a greenish brown sleeveless jacket. Isao knew that it had to be Kurahara.

There was some exchange with the woman. When she left, Isao saw the flash of a tray. She had brought Kurahara his tea, it seemed. With the woman gone, Kurahara was alone in the room.

Kurahara apparently sat down in a deep armchair facing the fire. All that could be seen from the window now was his bald forehead that seemed to shimmer from the flames burning in the grate. Perhaps he was reading something while he sipped the tea left at his side, or perhaps he was deep in thought.

Isao looked around for an entrance. A stairway of two or three stone steps led up from the garden to a doorway. He saw a faint light coming from the crevices of the door. The door was secured with only a metal latch. Isao took his dagger out from his overcoat and then threw off the coat, letting it fall to the soft ground in the darkness. At the foot of the stone steps he drew the dagger and discarded its sheath. The naked blade, as though giving off light of its own, shone pale.

He climbed the steps stealthily, and slid the tip of his dagger between the door and its frame, slipping it underneath the latch. The latch was extremely heavy. When it finally snapped upward, the noise it made echoed like the tick of a grandfather's clock. There was no way of knowing if anything had changed within the room, but the noise must have attracted Kurahara's attention. Isao twisted the doorknob and rushed inside.

Kurahara stood up with his back to the fireplace. He did not cry out, however. A thin film of ice seemed to have spread across his features.

'Who are you? What are you doing here?' demanded the hoarse, weak voice.

'Take the punishment you deserve for profaning the Grand Shrine of Isé,' said Isao. The clarity and modulation of his voice assured him of his self-possession.

'What?' An expression of altogether unfeigned incomprehension came to Kurahara's face. For a moment he was obviously groping for a memory, but without success. And at the same time he was looking at Isao with eyes that revealed the terror of being confronted in dreadful isolation with a madman. Avoiding the fire behind him, Kurahara shrank back against the wall beside the fireplace. This decided Isao's next movement.

As Sawa had once taught him, Isao bent his back like a cat, pressed his right elbow firmly into his side, and, gripping his right wrist with his left hand so that the blade would not go upward, plunged the blade into Kurahara with all his strength.

Rather than the feel of the dagger piercing the other's body, the main sensation was the shock of the butt of the hilt striking his own stomach with reflexive force. Then, determined to make sure of his man, Isao gripped his shoulder and pressed down, wanting to stab more deeply, but he was taken aback to discover how much lower that shoulder was than he had thought. And then the flesh that he was pressing down had none of the softness that goes with plumpness but was as rigid as a board.

As he looked down at him, the face of his victim seemed relaxed, rather than in pain. The eyes were open, the mouth gaped carelessly. The upper set of false teeth had come loose and was jutting out.

Tugging at the dagger, Isao became furious in his frustration. His victim's whole weight now lay upon the blade. Kurahara collapsed. growing heavier still, the blade at his centre of gravity. Finally, gripping the other's shoulder with his left hand, Isao raised his right knee, and, pushing against Kurahara's thigh, he pulled the dagger free. The blood that spurted out splashed Isao's knee. Kurahara, as though in pursuit of his own blood, toppled forward.

Turning swiftly, Isao was about to run from the room when a door leading to the hallway opened, and he was face to face with the woman whom he had seen a little while before. The woman screamed. Isao darted aside and raced out into the garden through the door that he had entered by. He could still see the after-image of the terrified woman's eyes, with their prominent whites.

He ran at full speed down through the garden towards the sea. Behind him the household was in turmoil, as one cry after the other was raised. He felt the sounds and lights were fixing themselves upon him and rushing in pursuit.

As he ran, he reached inside his jacket to make sure that his knife was there. The dagger in his hand, however, gave him greater assurance, and he gripped it tightly while he rushed headlong. His breath was laboured, and he had twisted his knee. He was made well aware of how his legs had weakened during his year in prison.

Tangerine orchards by the ocean were usually cultivated in terraced fields. Each of Kurahara's tangerine trees, as though on a platformed stage, was set upon a level of its own. The innumerable, varied levels, bound by the stone walls, each received its share of sunlight at its subtly varied angle, and, though each level slightly differed from the others, all of them fell away down to the shoreline. The average height of the tangerine trees was eight or nine feet. The roots were heavily mulched with straw, and the branches reached upward in all directions from a point quite near the ground.

Isao ran from one level to another. The fruit-laden branches blocked his way at every turn in the darkness. As though in a maze, he struggled not to lose his way. The sea could not be far off, but he was unable to reach it.

He burst out of the trees at last, however, and his field of vision suddenly widened. Before him were the sky and the sea. A flight of stone steps descended clinging to the sheer face of the cliff, and a gate at the edge of the orchard gave access to it.

Isao tore off a tangerine. It was then that he realized that he no longer held his dagger. He must have dropped it when he was running through the trees, and clutching and dodging branches.

The orchard gate opened easily. At the bottom of the steps, he saw the white spray leaping high as the waves worried the rocks. For the first time he became conscious of the echo of the sea.

Whether the land beyond the orchard was Kurahara's or not, Isao did not know. It was a cliff covered with an old growth of trees, and a path threaded its way through the grove. Isao was weary from fleeing, but, once more, he rushed headlong down the path, as the tree branches lashed his face and the undergrowth clutched at his running feet.

Finally he came to a place where the cliff was gouged out to form something like a cavern. A greenish, twisted mass of rock had been partly eroded away, and from its top the branches of a great evergreen tree hung low over this ledge. A slender stream of water, sheltered by ferns, meandered over the rock surface, flowed through the grass, and apparently fell off into the sea below.

Here Isao hid himself. He quieted his throbbing pulse. There was nothing to be heard but the sea and the wind. Since his throat was painfully dry, he tore the skin off his tangerine and roughly thrust the fruit into his mouth all at once. He smelled blood. It had splotched the tangerine skin and half-dried there. But the odour did not much alter the sweetness of the juice that was running down his throat. Beyond the dry weeds, beyond the tall pampas grass, beyond the low-hanging evergreen branches, with their clustered needles and entangled vines, lay the night sea. Though there was no moon, the sea reflected the faint glow of the sky, and the waters gleamed black.

Isao sat upright upon the damp earth, his legs folded beneath him. He removed his uniform jacket. From the inside pocket, he took out the knife. His whole being experienced such relief at finding it safe there that he almost lost his balance. Though he still wore his wool shirt and undershirt, the wind from the sea chilled his body as soon as his jacket was off.

'The sun will not rise for some time,' Isao said to himself, 'and I can't afford to wait. There is no shining disc climbing upward. There is no noble pine to shelter me. Nor is there a sparkling sea.'

He stripped off the remainder of his upper garments, but, as his body tensed, the cold seemed to vanish. He unfastened his trousers, exposing his stomach. As he drew his knife out of its sheath, he heard cries and the sound of running footsteps from the direction of the orchard above.

'The ocean. He must have got away in a boat,' one pursuer called out shrilly.

Isao drew in a deep breath and shut his eyes as he ran his left hand caressingly over his stomach. Grasping the knife with his right hand, he pressed its point against his body, and guided it to the correct place with his fingertips of his left hand. Then, with a powerful thrust of his arm, he plunged the knife into his stomach. The instant that the blade tore open his flesh, the bright disc of the sun soared up and exploded behind his eyelids.

THE TEMPLE OF DAWN

Translated by
E. Dale Saunders and Cecilia Segawa Seigle

PART ONE

1

It was the rainy season in Bangkok. The air was saturated with a continuous fine drizzle, and often drops of rain would dance in a brilliant ray of sunlight. Rifts of blue were always visible here and there; and even when the clouds clustered most thickly round the sun, the sky at their circumference was dazzlingly blue. Before an approaching squall, it would turn ominously dark and threatening. A foreboding shade would shroud the predominantly green, low-roofed city dotted with palms.

The name of the city dates from the Ayutthaya dynasty, when it was first called *bang*, 'town', *kok*, 'olives', because of its many olive trees. Another ancient name is Krung Thep, or 'City of Angles'. The metropolis, situated less than six feet above sea level, is completely dependent on canals for transportation. When roads are constructed by piling up dirt, canals are inevitably created. And when ground is excavated in building a house, ponds immediately form. Such pools connect up naturally with streams; and thus these 'canals' run in every direction, all flowing into the mother waters of the Menam, gleaming the same brown as that of the inhabitants' skin.

In the centre of the city there are European-style three-storeyed buildings with balconies and numerous two- and three-storeyed brick constructions in the foreign concession. The roadside trees, once the city's most beautiful feature, have been felled here and there in the path of highway construction, and some streets have been partially paved. Mimosa trees, intercepting the strong rays of the sun, form pools of deep shade on the roadways, covering them with black veils of mourning. After a thunder squall the leaves, shrivelled in the heat, suddenly revive and, refreshed, raise their heads.

In its prosperity the town reminds one of some southern Chinese city. Numberless two-seated pedicabs ply their way with shades drawn on the sides and in back. Sometimes buffaloes from the rice paddies near Bangkap are led through the streets, crows still perching on their backs. Here and there the luminous skin of a leprous beggar glows in the shade like a dark smudge. The boys run about quite naked, while the girls wear a metal pleating over their sex. Exotic fruits and flowers are on sale in the morning market. In front of the Chinese banks glitter chains of pure gold suspended like bamboo jalousies.

But when evening falls, Bangkok is left to the moon and the star-filled sky. Apart from hotels with independent electric systems, only the homes of the wealthy, which are provided with generators, sparkle festively here and there. For the most part, people resort to lamps and candles. A single taper burns throughout the night at the Buddhist altars in all the low-lying houses along the river, and only the gilt of the Buddhist images gleams dimly in the depths of the bamboo-floored structures. Thick, brown incense sticks burn before the statues. Candlelight from the houses on the opposite bank glimmers in the river and is interrupted now and then by the silhouette of a passing boat.

In 1939 – last year – Siam officially changed its name to Thailand.

The reason why Bangkok is called the Venice of the East does not stem from any external resemblance between the two cities, which cannot be compared either in design or in scale. First of all, both employ a plethora of canals for maritime transportation, and then both contain many holy edifices. There are seven hundred temples in Bangkok.

Buddhist pagodas soar up through the greenery and are the first to receive the light of dawn and the last to retain the rays of the evening sun, changing with the light into a multitude of colours.

Wat Benchamabopit, the Marble Temple, constructed by Rama V Chulalongkorn in the nineteenth century, though a modest edifice, is the newest and certainly the most sumptuous temple.

The present monarch, Rama VIII, or King Ananda Mahidol, succeeded to the throne in 1935 at the age of eleven, but he soon went to study in Lausanne; and now at the age of seventeen, he is still there devoted to his research. During his absence, the Prime Minister, Luang Phiboon, assumed totalitarian powers, and now the nominal parliament serves merely in an advisory capacity. Two regents were set up: the first, Prince Achitto Apar, was pretty much of a decoration, while the second, Prince Prude Panoma, held the real power.

Prince Achitto Apar, a devout Buddhist, often visited one or another of the sanctuaries in his spare time. One evening it was announced that he intended to go to the Marble Temple.

The edifice stood on the bank of a stream bordered by the mimosa trees of Nakhon Pathom Road.

The reddish brown portals of the Marble Temple, protected by a pair of stone horses with mandorlas like white crystal flames in the ancient Khmer style, stood open. On either side of the straight flagstone walk leading from the entrance to the main building set in glistening emerald-green grass, stood a pair of pavilions in classic Javanese style with upturned roofs. The mimosa trees on the greensward were cut in round shapes and blossoming; frolicking white lions on the eaves of the pavilions trampled flames underfoot.

The white columns of Indian marble directly in front of the main building, the pair of guardian marble lions, the low European-type balustrade, and the façade, also of marble, reflected the dazzling rays of the westering sun and formed a pure white canvas that served to bring out the rich decorative patterns of gold and vermilion. The inner frames of the pointed-arch windows were limned in scarlet and encircled by ornate golden flames that rose, engulfing them. Even the white columns of the façade were decorated in brilliant gold with coiled *naga*-serpents that sprang abruptly from the capitals. Rows of golden snakes with raised heads edged the upsweeping roofs, composed of tier upon tier of red Chinese tiles, and the tips of each subordinate roof were formed of thin, golden serpent tails, like the spike heels of a woman's shoe, thrusting upward, as if in competition, to the blue sky, to the very heavens. All this gold shone rather darkly in the sun, enhancing the white of the pigeons that idled along the gables.

But when the white birds, startled, suddenly flew up into the gradually darkening sky, they were as black as particles of soot. The soot from the golden flames, repeated in the ornaments of the temple, became birds.

In the garden the towering palms seemed petrified in amazement, arboreal fountains like bows, shooting their greenery farther and farther skyward.

Plants, animals, metal, stone, and Indian red, mingling in harmony, frolicked in the light. Even the marble heads of the white lions guarding the entrance appeared to be for all the world like sunflowers. Serrated seedlike teeth lined their gaping mouths; their lion faces were angry white sunflowers.

Prince Achitto Apar's Rolls-Royce drew up in front of the gate. The Young Men's Military Band, dressed in red uniforms, had lined up on the lawn by the pavilions and were playing their instruments, brown cheeks puffing. The polished mouths of the horns reflected minutely the figures of the youths in their bright uniforms. Under the tropical sun no instrument was more appropriate.

A servant clad in a white coat and red sash followed the Prince, holding a grass-coloured parasol over the royal head. The Prince, wearing decorations on his white military jacket, entered the temple escorted by a chamberlain in a blue sash, holding offerings, and ten royal guardsmen.

His visits usually lasted some twenty minutes. During this period spectators waited on the grass, roasting in the sun. At length came the sound of a Chinese viol in the inner precincts, mingled with delicate chimes, and the footman bearing the parasol moved to the entrance. He raised the umbrella, to the tip of which was attached a delicate golden pagoda, to his shoulder, and four guardsmen wearing monk-like hats with flaps hanging down over the napes of their necks lined up on the stone steps. The interior, hidden from view, was so dark that one could barely glimpse the flickering of the candles inside. Voices chanting a sutra rose rapidly to a crescendo, then stopped at the sound of a single bell.

The servant opened the green umbrella, respectfully holding it over the departing Prince, and the guardsmen saluted by hoisting their swords. The Prince passed quickly through the gate and entered his Rolls-Royce.

After a while the spectators who had watched the departure scattered, the military band left, and the quiet of evening gently settled over the temple. Some of the saffron-garbed priests strolled out to the riverbank; some read books, others conversed. Withered red flowers and dead fruit floated in the water that reflected the mimosa on the opposite bank and the beautiful clouds in the evening sky. The sun sank behind the temple, and the grass darkened. At length only the marble pillars, the lions, and the façade of the temple retained a fading evening whiteness.

Wat Po.

There one must push one's way through the crowds streaming among the late-eighteenth-century pagodas and the central hall constructed under Rama I.

Blazing sun. Azure sky. Still the great white columns of the gallery in the main temple are stained like the legs of a white elephant.

The pagoda is decorated with small fragments of porcelain, whose smooth glaze reflects the sun. In the purple Great Pagoda are chiselled tiers of blue mosaic, and innumerable pieces of ceramic, on which are painted countless flowers with petals of yellow, red, and white on a bluish purple ground: a ceramic Persian carpet towering high in the sky.

To one side stands a green pagoda. A pregnant bitch, black-spotted pink teats hanging pendulously, staggers down the flagstone walk as if crushed by the hammer of the sun.

In the Nirvana Hall a great gilded statue of Shakyamuni reclining rests its mass of golden curls on a box-pillow of blue, white, green, and yellow mosaic. His golden arm is stretched far out to support his head, and at the other end of the sombre hall gleam his golden heels.

The soles of his feet are inlaid with fine mother-of-pearl; and in each segment, against a finely wrought black background in gleaming iridescent shellwork, are depictions of the Buddha's life, all decorated with peonies, shells, altar accessories, rocky crags, lotus flowers rising from swamps, dancers, strange birds, lions, white elephants, dragons, horses, cranes, peacocks, ships with three sails, tigers, and phoenixes.

The open windows shine like polished brass panels. Under the lime trees a group of priests passes by in shimmering orange robes, their brown right shoulders bare.

Outside, the air itself seems stricken with some tropical fever. Over the stagnant pond between the pagodas, glistening green mangrove trees let fall their mass of aerial roots. Pigeons while away the time on a centre island with rocks painted blue. An immense butterfly is depicted on the rocky façade, and at the crest stands a small, inauspicious black pagoda.

And Wat Phra Keo, guardian temple of the royal palace, famed for its principal statue – an emerald Buddha.

It has never been damaged since its construction in 1785.

A golden *garuda*, half woman, half bird, flanked on either side by gilded spires, glistens in the rain at the top of the marble stairs. The green-bordered tiles of Chinese red sparkle more brilliantly than ever in the luminous rain.

The gallery walls of the Mahamandapa are covered with a series of murals illustrating episodes in the *Ramayana*.

Rather than the virtuous Rama himself, the monkey god, Hanuman, the flamboyant son of the wind god, appears throughout the painted story. The golden beauty, Sita, with teeth of jasmine flowers, is being kidnapped by the fearful *rakshasa* king. Rama fights his many battles with fixed, bright eyes.

Colourful palaces, monkey gods, and battles of monsters appear against mountains painted in the manner of the southern Chinese school or in that of the sombre early Venetian landscapes. Above the tenebrous *paysage* soars a god in the seven colours of the rainbow, mounted on a phoenix. A man in golden robes whips a clothed horse that sits motionless. A monstrous fish, rearing its head far above the sea, is about to attack some soldiers standing on a bridge. There is a faint blue lake in the distance; and Hanuman, sword unsheathed, lurks in a bush as he stalks a white horse with a golden saddle that paces silently through the dark forest.

*

'Do you know the real name for Bangkok?'

'No, I don't.'

'It's *Krung thep phra mahanakorn amon latanakosin mahintara shiayutthaya mafma pop noppala rachatthani prilom.*'

'What does all that mean?'

'It's almost impossible to translate. Thai names are like the temple decorations, unnecessarily pompous and flowery, ornate purely for the sake of ornateness.

'Well, *Krung thep* means roughly "capital", and *pop noppala* is "a nine-coloured diamond"; *rachatthani* is "a large city"; and *prilom* means something like "pleasant". They choose exaggerated and ostentatious nouns and adjectives and string them together like beads on a necklace.

'In answering a simple "yes" to the king, protocol of the country demands that you say: *phrapout chao ka kollap promkan saikrao sai klamon*, which roughly translates as: "Your humble and obedient servant makes reverent obeisance to Your Majesty".'

Honda, ensconced in a rattan chair, listened to Hishikawa's words with detached amusement.

Itsui Products Limited had sent this encyclopedic but somewhat strange and seedy character – doubtless a one-time artist – to serve as interpreter and guide for Honda. Already at forty-six, the latter considered it a kind of courtesy to himself to leave things to others, especially in such a sweltering country as this.

He had come to Bangkok at the request of Itsui Products. If a business transaction based on Japanese law has been closed in Japan and a dispute with a buyer arises abroad, even though the suit is brought before a foreign court, it is settled according to international civil law. Furthermore, foreign lawyers are invariably ignorant of Japanese law. In such cases, some eminent Japanese counsellor is invited to explain Japanese legal intricacies to the native lawyers and thus to help settle the suit.

Itsui Products had exported one hundred thousand cases of Calos anti-fever pills to Thailand in January. Of them thirty thousand had been damaged by damp and had been discoloured, thereby losing their effectiveness. The cases were dated, indicating a reduction in potency after a given time limit, but that served no purpose now that they were spoiled. Such civil problems should have been solved by reference to the law concerning default of obligation, but the buyers had brought charges of criminal fraud. According to article 715 of the Civil Code, Itsui Products should, of course, have assumed responsibility for indemnifying a non-negligence default for any flaw in merchandise issued by a subcontracting drug company. But they could do nothing without the assistance of a capable Japanese lawyer like Honda in matters of this nature which involved international civil law.

Honda had been assigned a room in the Oriental Hotel – the natives pronounced it Orienten Hoten – with a lovely view of the Menam River. The room was ventilated by a large white ceiling fan, but at nightfall it was better to go out to the garden along the river and enjoy the slightly cooler breezes there. As he sipped his aperitif with Hishikawa, who had come to guide him for the evening, he let his companion take over the conversation. Honda was overcome with weariness;

even the spoon felt too heavy for his fingers to raise, and conversing was even more burdensome than a silver-plated spoon.

On the opposite bank, the sun was sinking behind Wat Arun, the Temple of Dawn. An all-pervading evening glow filled the vast sky over the flat vista of the Thon Buri jungle, broken only by two or three spires silhouetted against the horizon. Like cotton the green of the forest absorbed the glow, changing it to a truly emerald hue. Sampans passed by, crows gathered in great numbers, and a soiled rose colour lingered in the river water.

'All art is like the evening glow,' said Hishikawa, watching as he always did when he was preparing to express an opinion, for the effect his words would have on his listener. Honda felt annoyed by these points of silence even more than by Hishikawa's continuous chatter.

Hishikawa's profile with its cheeks of Siamese swarthiness and the non-Siamese pasty, taut skin gleamed in the last rays of the sun that came from the opposite bank.

'Art is a colossal evening glow,' he repeated. 'It's the burnt offering of all the best things of an era. Even the clearest logic that has long thrived in daylight is completely destroyed by the meaningless lavish explosion of colour in the evening sky; even history, apparently destined to endure forever, is abruptly made aware of its own end. Beauty stands before everyone; it renders human endeavour completely futile. Before the brilliance of evening, before the surging evening clouds, all rot about some "better future" immediately fades away. The present moment is all; the air is filled with a poison of colour. What's beginning? Nothing. Everything is ending.

'There's nothing of substance in it. Of course, night has its own intrinsic nature: the cosmic essence of death and inorganic existence. Day too has its own entity; everything human belongs to the day.

'But there's no substance in the evening glow. It's nothing but a joke, a meaningless, but impressive joke of form and light and colour. Look ... look at the purple clouds. Nature seldom offers a banquet of such a lavish colour as purple. Evening clouds are an insult to anything symmetric, but such destruction of order is closely connected with the break-up of something much more fundamental. If the serene white daytime cloud may be compared to moral exaltation, then these riotous colours have nothing to do with morality.

'The arts predict the greatest vision of the end; before anything else they prepare for and embody the end. Gourmets and good wines, beautiful forms and sumptuous clothes – every extravagance human beings can dream up in one era is crammed into the arts. All such things have been awaiting form. Some form with which to pillage and destroy in the shortest time all of human living. And that is the evening glow. And to what purpose? Indeed, for nothing.

'The most delicate thing, the most fastidious aesthetic judgement of the minutest detail – I refer to the indescribably subtle contours of one of those orange-coloured clouds – is related to the universality of the vast firmament; its innermost aspects are expressed in colour, and uniting with external aspects, they become the evening glow.

'In other words, evening glow is expression. And expression alone is the function of the evening glow.

'In it, the slightest human shyness, joy, anger, displeasure is expressed on a heavenly scale. In this great operation the colours of human intestines, ordinarily invisible, are externalized and spread over the entire sky. The most subtle tenderness and gallantry are joined with *Weltschmerz*, and ultimately affliction is transformed into a short-lived orgy. The numerous bits of logic which people have so stubbornly cherished during the day are all drawn into the vast emotional explosion of the heavens and the spectacular release of passions, and people realize the futility of all systems. In other words, everything is expressed for at most ten or fifteen minutes and then it's all over.

'The evening glow is swift and possesses the characteristics of flight. It constitutes perhaps the wings of the world. Like the wings of a hummingbird which change into rainbow colours as it flutters about sucking the honey from flowers, the world shows us a brief glimpse of its potentiality for soaring; all things in the evening glow fly rapturous and ecstatic ... and then in the end fall to the ground and die.'

As Honda listened desultorily to Hishikawa's words, the sky above the opposite bank was already slowly sinking into dusk, leaving a faint gleam on the horizon.

Had he claimed that all art was evening glow? Yet there stood the Temple of Dawn!

Honda had crossed over to the other bank on a hired boat early the previous morning and visited the Temple of Dawn.

He had done this precisely at sunrise, a most fitting time. It was still darkish, and only the very tip of the pagoda caught the first rays of the rising sun. The Thon Buri jungle beyond was filled with the piercing cries of birds.

As he approached, he realized that the pagoda was all inlaid with countless fragments of Chinese porcelain of either red or blue glaze. Each tier was marked by a balustrade; the one on the first storey was brown, on the second green, and on the third a purplish blue. Countless porcelain dishes that had been placed there formed flowers: yellow ones represented the cores from which extended petals of plates. Some had a core of inverted lavender wine cups and here colourful golden dishes formed the petals. Chains of such flowers ascended to the summit. The leaves were all tile; and from the top, four white elephant trunks hung down at the four cardinal points.

The repetitiveness and sumptuousness of the pagoda were almost suffocating. The tower with its colour and brilliance, adorned in many layers and graduated toward the peak, gave one the impression of so many strata of dream sequences hovering overhead. The plinths of the extremely steep stairs were also heavily festooned and each tier was supported by a bas-relief of birds with human faces. They formed a multicoloured pagoda whose every level was crushed with layers of dreams, expectations, prayers, each being further weighted down with still other stories, pyramid-like, progressing skyward.

With the first rays of dawn over the Menam River, the tens of thousands of porcelain fragments turned into so many tiny mirrors that captured the light. A great structure of mother-of-pearl sparkling riotously.

The pagoda had long served as a morning bell tolled by its rich hues, resonant colours responding to the dawn. They were created so as to evoke a beauty, a power, an explosiveness like the dawn itself.

In the eerie, yellowish brown morning light reflecting ruddily in the Menam River, the pagoda cast its shining reflection, presaging the coming of still another sweltering day.

'I'm sure you've had enough of temples. Tonight I'll take you someplace amusing,' said Hishikawa. Honda was gazing absently at the Temple of Dawn, now completely enveloped in darkness.

'You've seen Wat Po and Wat Phra Keo. And when you went to the Marble Temple, you were lucky enough to see the Regent's visit. And yesterday morning you saw the Temple of Dawn. There's no end to temple-visiting if you've got a mind for it, but I think you've had enough.'

'Hm. I suppose I have,' Honda replied vaguely, reluctant to let the thoughts in which he was so deeply absorbed be interrupted.

He had been musing about Kiyoaki's old Dream Diary, which he had not glanced at for so long, but which he had brought along in the bottom of his suitcase, thinking he might read it again to help pass time during his journey. Because of the intolerable heat and his weariness, he had not had the opportunity to do so until now. But the brilliant tropical colours in the description of a dream about which he had read long ago were still vivid in his mind.

Indeed, being so busy, Honda had not accepted the trip to Thailand for purely business reasons. In his school days, at a most sensitive age, he had, through Kiyoaki, become acquainted with two Siamese princes and had witnessed the pathetic end of Chantrapa's love story and the loss of Prince Pattanadid's emerald ring. Because of the overwhelming realization that he was destined to be an observer, the hazy picture in his memory had been ultimately preserved in a strong and solid frame. Long ago he had firmly resolved that he must visit Siam one day.

Yet on the other hand, Honda at forty-six had become most wary of his slightest emotions; unconsciously he had fallen into the habit of detecting deceit and exaggeration in them. He mused that his last passion had been for saving Isao, the boy whom he had discovered to be the reincarnation of Kiyoaki. He had even given up his judgeship. It had led to naught, and he had experienced only a shattering failure that had borne home to him the total futility of altruism.

Having abandoned altruistic ideals, he had become a much better lawyer. No longer having any passions, he was successful in saving others in one case after the other. He accepted no assignment unless the client was wealthy, no matter whether the case was civil or criminal. The Honda family prospered far more than in his father's time.

Poor lawyers who acted as though they were the natural representatives of social justice and advertised themselves as such were ludicrous. Honda was well aware of the limitations of law as far as saving people was concerned. To put it candidly, those who could not afford to engage lawyers were not qualified to break the law, but most people made mistakes and violated the law out of sheer necessity or stupidity.

There were times when it seemed to Honda that giving legal standards to the vast majority of people was probably the most arrogant game mankind had thought up. If crimes were often committed out of necessity or stupidity, could one not perhaps claim that the mores and customs upon which such laws were based were also idiotic?

After the incident with the League of the Divine Wind in the Showa period that ended in Isao's death, many similar events had taken place, but internal turmoil in Japan had stopped with the events of February 26, 1936. The China Incident, which had begun shortly thereafter, remained inconclusive even after five years of fighting. And now the pact binding Japan, Germany, and Italy had provided a strong stimulus; and the danger of war between Japan and the United States had become a frequent topic of discussion.

But as Honda was no longer interested in the passage of time, political battles, or the imminence of war, he no longer felt any emotion about them. Something had collapsed in the innermost recess of his heart. He knew that he was powerless to arrest events which went storming on like rain squalls, drenching every insignificant person, beating indiscriminately upon the individual pebbles of fortune. But it was not clear to him whether all fortunes were ultimately pathetic. It was history's wont to progress by granting the wishes of some and by denying those of others. No matter how distressing the future might prove to be, it did not necessarily disappoint everyone.

However, one must not suppose that Honda had become a complete nihilist and cynic. Compared to the past he was quite cheerful and gay. His manner of speech, which he had been so careful of throughout the period of his judgeship, had changed considerably; and his taste in clothes was more liberal. He even wore a checkered hound's-tooth sports jacket and had begun telling jokes and acting more magnanimously. But since he had come to this sweltering country pleasantries no longer came readily to his lips.

His face now displayed a grave dignity suited to his years. He had long since lost the clean-cut profile of his youth, and his skin, once as plain as washed-out cotton, having known the taste of luxury, had taken on the texture of satin damask. As he was well aware that he had never been handsome, he was not altogether displeased with the opaque veil age had imposed.

Furthermore, he now possessed his future much more surely than any youth could. The reason why young men pattered on about the future so was simply that they didn't yet have it. Possessing by letting go of things was a secret of ownership unknown to youth.

Just as Kiyoaki had not influenced the times in which he had lived, Honda too did not affect his. In place of the era when Kiyoaki had perished on the battlefield of romantic emotions, a new period was coming when young men would die on real battlefields. Its forerunner was the death of Isao. In other words, Kiyoaki and his reincarnation, Isao, had died contrasting deaths on contrasting battlefields.

And Honda? There was no sign of death in him! He had never desired death passionately, nor had he ever tried to evade its onslaught. However, now that he had suddenly become the target of the fiery shafts of the tropical sun that poured down on him the livelong day, the beautiful, dense, luxuriant greenery all about seemed possibly the stunning luxuriance of death itself. 'A long time ago, perhaps twenty-seven or twenty-eight years, when two Siamese princes came to Japan to study, I was privileged to know them for some time. One was the younger brother of Rama VI, Prince Pattanadid; and the other was Prince Kridsada, his cousin, a grandson of Rama IV. I wonder what they're doing now. I had hoped to see them when I got to Bangkok, but it seems presumptuous to impose myself on people who have surely forgotten me.'

'Why didn't you tell me before?' said the omniscient Hishikawa, hastening to reproach Honda's reserve. 'Whatever you ask, I can find a solution.'

'Well, then, do you think I might be able to see the two princes?'

'I shouldn't go so far as to say that. Rama VIII, their uncle, depends very much on them, and they are both in Lausanne with him now. Most of the important members of the royal family have gone to Switzerland and the palace is empty.'

'I'm sorry to hear it.'

'But there's a possibility of seeing a member of Prince Pattanadid's family. It's a strange story. His Royal Highness's youngest daughter, a little girl about seven, is staying in Bangkok alone with her ladies-in-waiting. The poor thing is practically a prisoner in a small mansion they call the Rosette Palace.'

'Why is that?'

'It would be an embarrassment to the family if they took her abroad; she's thought to be retarded. Ever since the Princess was able to talk, she's been saying: "I'm not really a Siamese princess. I'm the reincarnation of a Japanese, and my real home is in Japan." She won't change her story no matter what people say. If anyone objects, she throws a tantrum. So the rumour is that all her attendants have gone along with her delusion and brought her up to believe whatever she wishes. An audience is rather difficult, but since you have relations with the royal princes, I think I can do something – depending on how I approach those responsible for her.'

2

Having heard the story of the poor little mad Princess, Honda was not at once moved to seek an audience.

He knew that she would be within his reach like some brilliant, little golden temple. And just as temples never fly away, he felt that the Princess too would always be there. Madness in this country would surely be like its architecture or its monotonous, elegant dances that went on and on in their eternal splendour. Another day, he thought, when his mood had changed, he would request an audience.

Perhaps this procrastination came in part from the listlessness one experienced in the tropics and in part from his advancing years. His hair was turning grey, and his sight would have been growing less acute too were it not, fortunately, that he had been slightly near-sighted since childhood. He still managed well without the assistance of an old man's spectacles.

His age enabled him to use the laws taught him by experience as measurements, and he could foretell the outcome of most situations. Actually, except for natural calamities, historical events occurred, no matter how unexpected they might seem, only after long maturation. History is as hesitant as a young maiden before a romantic proposal. For Honda there was always a hint of the artificial in any event that corresponded precisely to his own wishes and that approached at a pleasing speed. Therefore, if he wanted to entrust his actions to the laws of history it was always best for him to adopt a reserved attitude toward everything. He had seen too many instances where one could get nothing one wanted and where determination had ultimately been quite futile. Even things which one should have been able to obtain if one had not craved them managed to slip away simply because they had been coveted too much. Suicide seemed so completely dependent on one's own desire and resolve, yet Isao had had to spend a whole year in prison in order to carry it out successfully.

However, on reflection, Isao's act of assassination and his suicide seemed like brilliant evening stars, harbingers, in a night filled with glittering constellations, that led the way to the February Twenty-Sixth Incident. To be sure, the assassins had hoped for dawn, but what materialized was night. And now, be the times what they may, that night was almost spent, and an uneasy, stifling morning had settled in, one that none of those activists would have imagined.

The treaty drawn up by Japan, Germany, and Italy had angered a segment of the nationalists and those who were pro-French and pro-English; but the great majority of those who liked Europe and the West and even the old-fashioned proponents of a pan-Asia were pleased about it. Japan was to be married, not to Hitler, but to the German forests; not to Mussolini, but to the Roman pantheon. It was a pact joining German, Roman, and Japanese mythology: a friendship among the beautiful, masculine, pagan gods of East and West.

Honda, of course, had never submitted to such romantic prejudice, but he sensed that the times were somehow tremulously ripening and it was clear that some dream was forming. And now that he was here, away from Tokyo, the sudden rest and leisure resulted curiously in fatigue, and he could do nothing to prevent this plunge into reminiscing about things past.

He had not abandoned his idea, the one he had stressed long, long ago when talking with the nineteen-year-old Kiyoaki: the will to engage oneself in history is the essence of human purpose. Yet the instinctive fear that a nineteen-year-old boy has about his own character turns out, at times, to be extremely prophetic. While proclaiming such a concept, Honda at the time was in reality expressing despair in his own makeup. This despondency increased as he grew older and finally became a chronic ailment. But his personality had never changed in the slightest. He recalled a most terrifying passage from the chapter on the Three Recompenses* in the

*That is, recompensation in the present life for deeds already done, in the next rebirth for deeds now done, and in subsequent lives. (Translators' note.)

Treatise on the Establishment of Reality, which was among the two or three Buddhist texts recommended by the Abbess of the Gesshu Temple:

> That one takes pleasure in doing evil
> Is because that evil is not ripe.

Thus, Honda took a listless, tropical pleasure in the gracious reception he had met in Bangkok, in what he heard and saw, and even in what he ate and drank. But that was not really proof that he had been guiltless of evil acts in the nearly fifty years of his life. His evil was surely not yet so ripe as the fragrant fruit ready to fall of itself from the branch.

In Thai Theravada Buddhism with the artless concept of causality found in the Southern Buddhist Canon, Honda recognized the causality of the Laws of Manu that had impressed him so deeply in his youth. Throughout, Hindu deities show their grotesque faces. The sacred *naga*-serpent, the mythical *garuda*, half giant, half eagle with golden body, white face, and red wings, which adorn the eaves of the temples, still recount the stories of the *Nagananda*, the seventh-century Indian epic, and the filial piety of *garuda* is acclaimed by the Hindu Vishnu.

Since coming to this land, Honda's former intellectual curiosity had been piqued, and he was eager to discover how Theravada Buddhism explained the mystery of transmigration. It was this concept that provided him the opportunity of casting aside half a lifetime of rationality.

According to scholars, Indian religious philosophy is divided into six periods:

1. The period of the *Rig Veda*.
2. The period of the *Brahmanas*.
3. The period of the *Upanishads*, which extends from the eighth to the fifth centuries BC, an era of self-conscious philosophy, establishing as its ideal the unity of Brahma, the ultimate ground of all being, and atman, 'self'. The idea of a cycle of births and deaths – samsara – appeared clearly for the first time in this period, and when linked to the concept that acts (karma) bring inevitable consequences the law of causality came into being. By coupling that with the idea of atman, a philosophical system emerged.
4. A period of schism among various schools of thought.
5. The period of perfection of Theravada Buddhism, occurring between the third and first centuries BC.
6. The ensuing five hundred years which saw the rise of Mahayana Buddhism.

The problem is the fifth period, in which the Laws of Manu were compiled. Honda had been surprised when in his youth he had discovered that the concept of samsara was applied even to law codes. The idea of karma as it appears later in Buddhism was distinctly different from that in the *Upanishads:* the difference lay in Buddhism's denial of atman, for such denial is the essence of this religion.

One of the three characteristics which differentiate Buddhism from other religions is that of the selflessness of all the dharmas. Buddhism advocated selflessness and denied atman, which had been considered to be the main constituent of life. It followed that Buddhism rejected the idea of 'soul', which is the extension of atman into the hereafter. Buddhism does not recognize the soul as such. If there is no core substance called soul in beings, there is, of course, none in inorganic matter. Indeed, quite like a jellyfish devoid of bone, there is no innate essence in all of creation.

But then the troublesome question arises: if good acts produce a good subsequent existence and evil acts a bad one, and if, indeed, everything returns to nothingness following death, what then is the transmigrating substance? If we assume there is no self, what is the basis of the birth-and-death cycle to start with?

The three hundred years of Theravada Buddhism constitute a period of dispute and conflict among many schools which resulted in no satisfactory logical conclusion for any given one. All were embarrassed by the contradictions and inconsistencies that existed between the atman, that Buddhism denied, and karma, which it inherited.

For a credible philosophical answer to this question, mankind had to await the Mahayana school called Yuishiki, or 'consciousness only'. But when the Theravada Sautrantika school evolved, the concept of 'seed perfuming' was established, according to which the effect of a good or bad deed remains in one's consciousness, permeating it as the fragrance of perfume permeates clothes, and thus forms character. This power of forming was the origin of the causal theory. The doctrine was the precursor of later Yuishiki ideas.

And now Honda realized what was behind the constant smile and the melancholy eyes of the two Siamese princes. It was a feeling of heavy, golden listlessness, of lulling breezes beneath the trees – the constant evasion of any organized logical system; oppressed and languid in the sun, the people of this land of sumptuous temples and flowers and fruits faithfully worshipped the Buddha and believed implicitly in reincarnation.

Prince Kridsada aside, the intelligent Prince Pattanadid had had, surprisingly, the sharp mind of a philosopher. Yet the violence of his emotions swept away any dispassionate intellectualism. Honda still remembered most vividly, more than any words the Prince had spoken, the sight of him fainting that end of summer on the lawn chair at Kiyoaki's southern villa on hearing the news of Chantrapa's death. His tanned arm dangled limply from the white arm-rest. Honda could not see if the Prince's face, resting against his shoulder, had turned pale, but his brilliant white teeth were visible between slightly parted lips.

His long, elegant brown fingers, meant for the subtle caresses of love, hung loosely, almost touching the green summer grass, as though all five had momentarily followed in death the deceased object of his desire.

However, Honda feared that the princes' recollection of Japan might not be very pleasant, though the passage of time could well have made them miss it even more. Their isolation, their language difficulties, the different customs, Prince Pattanadid's loss of his emerald ring, and the death of Princess Chantrapa had made their stay in Japan something less than enjoyable. But what had ultimately turned away their understanding was the intimidating Swordsmen's Team spirit at the Peers School. This had alienated not only the princes but also ordinary students like Honda and Kiyoaki and the liberal and humanistic young men of the White Birch literary society. Unfortunately, the real Japan was not easily found among the friends of the princes, but was much more present among their enemies; the princes themselves were probably vaguely aware of this. An uncompromising Japan, as proud as a young warrior in scarlet silk, and yet as sensitive as a young boy challenging to battle before he is taunted and charging to his death before accepting insult. Isao was different from Kiyoaki, for he lived in the centre of this radical world and believed in the existence of the soul.

Approaching fifty, Honda now possessed one advantage: he was probably free of prejudice. Of authority too, for he himself had once been authority; and even of reason, since he had once been the personification of cerebration.

Even the spirit of the Swordsmen's Team in the second decade of the century was one of youth in uniform; it pervaded the entire era. And Honda too, who had never been a part of it, now that he was older did not hesitate to identify in his memory those youthful days with an aggressive spirit.

This temper, further distilled and purified, formed Isao's world, one Honda had not shared with him in his younger days, one he had observed only as an outsider. Noting how Isao's youthful Japanese mind, struggling in absolute isolation, had destroyed itself, Honda could not but realize that what had permitted him to live the way he had was the strength of Western thought, imported from the outside. Unfertilized thinking brings death.

If one wished to live, one must not cling to purity, as Isao had done. One must not cut oneself off from all channels of retreat; one must not reject everything.

Nothing had ever forced Honda to probe the question of an unadulterated Japan more deeply than had Isao's death. Was there any way to live honestly with Japan other than by rejecting everything, than by rejecting present-day Japan and the Japanese people? Was there no other way of living than this most difficult one, in which ultimately one murdered and then committed suicide? Everyone was afraid to say, but had not Isao given proof by his acts?

On reflection, in the purest of tribes there was the smell of blood and the taint of savagery. Unlike the Spaniards, who preserved their national sport of bullfighting despite the accusations of animal lovers throughout the world, the Japanese, when the nation had embraced a new culture and ethic at the end of the last century, turned their efforts to eliminating the barbaric customs of preceding generations. As a result, the genuine, unadulterated national spirit was subordinated, its energy erupting from time to time in explosions of violence which repelled and alienated the people even more.

However, whatever frightening mask it might assume, the national spirit in its original state was of pristine whiteness. Travelling through a country like Thailand, Honda realized more clearly than ever the simplicity and purity of things Japanese, like transparent stream water through which one could glimpse pebbles below, or the probity of Shinto rites. Honda's life was not imbued with such spirit. Like the majority of Japanese he ignored it, behaving as though it did not exist and surviving by escaping from it. All his life he had dodged things fundamental and artless: white silk, clear cold water, the zig-zag white paper of the exorciser's staff fluttering in the breeze, the sacred precinct marked by a torii, the gods' dwelling in the sea, the mountains, the vast ocean, the Japanese sword with its glistening blade so pure and sharp. Not only Honda, but the vast majority of Westernized Japanese, could no longer stand such intensely native elements.

But if Isao, who believed in the soul, had indeed gone to heaven – and this was an example of a good cause producing a good effect – if he had entered the cycle of births and deaths and been reborn as a human, what could the process be?

Now that he thought about it, Honda wondered if Isao, when he had determined to die, had not indeed secretly held some premonition of another life. There seemed to have been some indication of this. When a man strove to live his life in so pure and extreme a fashion, was he not naturally led to the supposition of another existence?

Honda recalled the Japanese shrine, and in the heat the very thought made him feel drops of clear cool water on his forehead. To the visitor climbing the stone steps, the torii, that seems merely a well-defined frame for the main shrine building, on his exit seems to change into a frame of clear blue sky. Strange that one frame should contain a lofty shrine from one side and empty blue sky from the other. The form of the torii seemed like that of Isao's soul.

For Isao had lived a well-defined life that resembled a torii, lofty, beautiful, simple. And inevitably it was ultimately filled with clear blue sky.

No matter how far the dying Isao's mind had drifted from Buddhism, this very paradox seemed to point up to Honda the relationship between the Japanese and Buddhism. It was as though the muddy waters of the Menam were to be filtered through a sieve of white silk.

Late the same night that he had heard the story of the Princess from Hishikawa, Honda rummaged through his suitcase in the hotel room and brought out Kiyoaki's Dream Diary wrapped in purple silk.

The diary had been read and reread and the binding had begun to fall apart; Honda had clumsily but carefully mended it himself. Kiyoaki's hasty, youthful writing was still vibrant, but the colour of the ink had faded during the thirty years since it had been written.

Yes, just as Honda remembered, Kiyoaki had had a vivid dream of Siam which he had entered in the diary shortly after the Siamese princes had visited his home.

Kiyoaki was seated in a fine chair in a palace with a ruined garden. He wore 'a high, pointed, gold crown inlaid with jewel clusters'. In the dream he was a member of Siamese royalty.

Many peacocks were perched on the beams, letting fall their white droppings, and Kiyoaki wore Prince Pattanadid's emerald ring on his finger. 'The lovely face of a small girl' was mirrored in the stone. This must have been the face of the little mad Princess he had not yet seen, and the reflection in the emerald with its downcast eyes was presumably Kiyoaki's own. It seemed beyond question now to Honda that the Princess was indeed the reincarnation of Kiyoaki by way of Isao.

It was not unexpected that he should have had such a dream after receiving the Siamese princes in his house and listening to the fascinating tales of their country. But after several experiences, Honda was forced to accept the fact that Kiyoaki's dream was another manifestation of his transmigration.

It was now self-explanatory. Once he had surmounted the problem of faulty logic, everything fitted together. Isao had never told Honda, nor had Honda ever discovered, whether Isao had had any other omens; Isao too might well have dreamed during his prison nights about the girl in the tropics.

Hishikawa diligently looked after Honda's needs during the latter's stay in Bangkok. And the lawsuit was going well, thanks to Honda's efforts. He had uncovered an oversight on the part of the buyers.

According to article 473 of the Thai Civil Code, which was founded on Anglo-American law, sellers need not assume responsibility for flaws in their merchandise in one or more of the following instances:

1. If the buyer was aware of the flaw at the time of purchase, or could have been had he been ordinarily observant.

2. If the flaw was evident at the time of the delivery of the merchandise, or if the buyer accepted the merchandise without reservation.

3. If the merchandise was sold at public auction.

As Honda investigated further, it became clear to him that the buyers could have been guilty according to either the first or second instance. If he could follow this up and get sufficient proof, they might well drop the charges.

Needless to say, Itsui Products were grateful, and Honda himself was quite relieved. He felt inclined to ask Hishikawa to get on with arranging an audience with the Princess. But he was such a bore.

Honda had never had any desire to make friends with artists, and indeed, he had never had a friend who could be called one. Nor had he ever expected to be introduced to an arty dropout in such a remote place as this.

It was all the more exasperating then that Hishikawa should be so helpful as a guide for the unaccustomed traveller, never the slightest reluctant to do whatever Honda asked. Furthermore, he possessed all sorts of back-door entrées in this country where any entrance through the front was strictly impossible. He was indeed a priceless guide, and he himself knew it.

But Hishikawa had retained the disagreeable affectations of an artist, whatever the work was he had produced in the past. He depended on guiding travellers to earn his living, and yet in his heart he was contemptuous of the Philistines whom he squired about. As this was transparently clear to Honda, he amused himself by being the very image of the Philistine Hishikawa thought him to be. He talked intentionally about his wife and mother in Japan, about his unhappiness in having no children. He enjoyed observing as Hishikawa unsuspectingly acted out the role of being sympathetic.

In fact, artists who were not only immature, but who made it a practice to flaunt immaturity as a dishonest alibi to fend off criticism of their works were hideous beyond measure when compared to the guileless immaturity which Kiyoaki or Isao had displayed. Artists dragged this immaturity throughout their lives ... into their eighties. It was as if they made the swaddling clothes they hauled along into merchandise.

If there was anything worse it was the pseudo-artists; their indescribable arrogance together with their particular brand of obsequiousness gave off an odour peculiar to lazy men. Hishikawa was simply a sloth living by hanging on to others, but he pretended to be the elegant, listless aristocrat living in the tropics. Honda was irritated by his habit of saying at restaurants, wine list in hand: 'Since Itsui Products are footing the bill anyway . . .', and of then proceeding to order the more expensive wines. Honda was not all that fond of wine.

While he hoped he would never be put in the position of defending such a man, it would be a breach of etiquette on his part, as an invited guest, to ask to have his guide replaced.

Every time the obese branch manager asked Honda in the waiting room at court or at a dinner party: 'Is Hishikawa doing all right by you?' Honda would answer: 'He's very capable, yes,' concealing in his words a certain bitterness. The manager seemed satisfied to take his reply at face value, and Honda was irked that he made no attempt to read behind the words.

Familiarity with the covert human relationships in this country, which were like the dank jungle undergrowth rapidly rotting away beneath the surface green that shone in the blistering sun, had enabled Hishikawa to develop his talent for smelling out rottenness in human matters faster than anyone else. And that was the source of his income. He would have rested his powerful, housefly wings of gold on the left-overs in the manager's plate.

'Good morning!'

Honda was awakened from deep sleep by a familiar voice on the interphone at his bedside, a voice he heard every morning – Hishikawa.

'Did I wake you? Forgive me. The court people think nothing of making you wait for hours, but they're terribly fussy about visitors being punctual. I called early to be on the safe side. Take your time shaving. What? Breakfast? No, no, don't worry about that. Well, to tell the truth, I haven't yet, but I can do without. Oh? In your room with you? Well, thank you very much indeed. I'll accept the invitation and come on up. Shall I let you have five minutes? Or ten? Well, since you're not a lady, perhaps I don't have to be so punctilious.'

This was not the first time that Hishikawa had partaken of the Oriental Hotel's sumptuous, multicourse English breakfast in Honda's room.

Shortly, dressed in a well-cut white linen suit, Hishikawa walked in, busily fanning his chest with a panama hat. He stopped squarely under the large, white, sluggishly rotating blades of the fan.

'Before I forget,' said the pyjama-clad Honda, 'what shall I call the Princess? Is it proper to say "Your Highness"?'

'No, no!' replied Hishikawa with assurance. 'She's the daughter of Pattanadid and he's half brother to the king. His title is Pra Ong Chao; you address him as "Your Royal Highness" in English. But the daughter is Mon Chao, and you should call her "Your Serene Highness". Anyway don't worry. I'll take care of everything.'

The unrelenting heat had already invaded the room. Having left his sweat-dampened bed and standing under the cold shower, Honda felt for the first time the morning on his skin. The experience was a strangely sensuous one. He who never contacted the external world without first filtering it through rational thought, here felt through his skin; only through his skin sensing the brilliant green of the tropical plants, the vermilion of the mimosa flowers, the golden decor adorning the temples, or the sudden blue lightning could he come into contact with the world about him. This was a totally exotic experience for him. The warm rains, the tepid showers. The external world was a richly coloured liquid, and it was as if he were constantly bathing in it. How could he have anticipated all this in Japan?

While waiting for breakfast, Hishikawa paced back and forth around the room like a European, scoffing at the mediocre landscape that hung on the wall. The heels of his freshly polished black shoes reflected the patterns of the carpet as he outrageously postured. Honda was suddenly tired of the game where Hishikawa played the artist and he the Philistine.

Abruptly turning, Hishikawa removed a small purple velvet-case from his pocket. Handing it to Honda, he said: 'You mustn't forget this. Hand it directly to the Princess.'

'What is it?'

'A present. Royalty has made it custom here never to receive a visitor who arrives empty-handed.'

Honda opened the case and discovered a fine pearl ring.

'Oh, I see. I never thought of that. Thank you for reminding me. How much do I owe you?'

'Oh, nothing. Really it's not necessary. I told Itsui Products you needed it for a royal audience. Anyway the manager probably picked it up cheap from some Japanese. You don't need to worry.'

Honda immediately understood he should not ask further about the price for the time being. But Itsui Products should not be expected to pay for his private expenditures. He would repay the manager. Hishikawa had probably charged them a fat commission. He would have to overlook that and reimburse the local representative, whatever the cost.

'Well then, I accept your kindness with gratitude.' Honda arose, and slipping the small case into the pocket of the jacket he was going to wear, casually asked: 'By the way, what is the Princess's name?'

'Princess Chantrapa. I hear that Prince Pattanadid named his last daughter after a fiancée who died long ago. Chantrapa means "moonlight". What a coincidence she's a lunatic,' Hishikawa commented smugly.

3

On the way to the Rosette Palace, Honda saw from his car window some boys in the Yuwachon Movement marching in khaki uniforms reputedly modelled on those of the Hitler Jugend. Hishikawa, seated next to him, complained that American jazz was rarely heard in town those days, and that Prime Minister Phiboon's nationalism seemed to be taking effect.

It was the kind of transformation Honda had already witnessed in Japan. Just as wine slowly turns to vinegar or milk to curd, matters long neglected slowly change in response to the various forces of nature. People have long lived in fear of too much freedom, too much carnal desire. The freshness of the morning after an evening when one has abstained from drinking wine. The pride one feels on realizing that water alone is essential. Such refreshing, new pleasures were beginning to seduce people. Honda had a vague idea where such fanatical ideas would lead. It was a realization that had been born of Isao's death. Single-mindedness often gives rise to viciousness.

Honda suddenly recalled Isao's drunken, incoherent words two days before his death. 'Far to the south ... Very hot ... in the rose sunshine of a southern land...' Now, eight years later, he was hastening to the Rosette Palace to meet him.

His was the joy of a parched and feverish land awaiting the drenching rains.

It seemed to Honda that in experiencing such emotions as these he was brought face to face with his innermost self. As a youth he had judged his fears, his sorrows, and his rationality to be his true inner core, but none was real. When he heard about Isao's suicide, he had felt a kind of sudden frustration instead of the sharp pain of sorrow; but with the passage of time, this had changed into the expectant pleasure of meeting him again. Honda realized in his heart that in moments like this, his emotions contained not one human element. His inner self was ruled perhaps by some extraordinary pleasure not of this world. It must be so, for he alone, in Isao's case, had escaped the sorrow and pain of parting.

'Far to the south ... Very hot ... in the rose sunshine of a southern land...'

The car drew up before an elegant gate beyond which lay a stretch of greensward. Hishikawa got out first and spoke to the guard in Siamese as he handed him a calling card.

From the car window Honda could see an iron gate of repeating octagon and arrow motifs, while beyond, the smooth green lawn quietly soaked up the intense sun. Two or three bushes with white and yellow flowers, trimmed into round shapes, cast their shadows on the grass.

Hishikawa escorted Honda through the gate.

The building was too insignificant to qualify as a palace; it was merely a small two-storey structure with a slate roof, painted a faded yellowish rose. Except for a large mimosa tree to one side, soiling the wall with its severe black shadow, only the expanse of yellow soothed the harsh brilliance of the sun.

They met no one as they walked along the winding path over the lawn. As Honda approached his goal, and despite the joy that he knew was metaphysical, he felt as though the sound of his footsteps was that of the sharp claws of some jungle beast stalking its prey with drooling fangs. Yes, he had been born for just this pleasure.

The Rosette Palace seemed confined in its own stubborn little dream. The impression was enhanced by the shape of the building itself. It was a little box with neither wings or extensions. The ground floor displayed so many casement windows that it was difficult to discern which was the entrance. Every one was panelled in wood carved into roses, above which octagons of yellow, blue, and indigo glass encircled small, five-petalled, purple rose-shaped windows in the Near Eastern style. The french windows facing the garden were half open.

The second floor bore a panel of fleur-de-lis, and three windows opening on the garden formed a triptych. The central one was higher than its neighbours, but all were bordered with carved rosettes.

The entrance itself at the top of three steps consisted of a french window of the same design. As soon as Hishikawa rang the bell, Honda indiscreetly peeped through the small rose pane of purple glass. Inside all was dark violet, like the ocean floor.

The french door opened and an old woman appeared. Honda and Hishikawa removed their hats. The white-haired brown face with its flat nose wore a smile of friendly greeting in the characteristic Thai manner. But the smile was a formality, nothing more.

The woman spoke with Hishikawa for a few moments. Apparently there had been no change in the appointment he had arranged.

Four or five chairs were lined up in the foyer that was too small for a reception hall. Hishikawa handed a package to the woman and she accepted it after joining her hands respectfully. Opening the central door, she at once led them into a spacious audience hall.

After the morning heat outside, the musty, stagnant coolness of the room was pleasant. The two men were invited to sit in red and gold Chinese chairs supported by legs in the form of lion paws.

While waiting for the Princess, Honda took the opportunity to scrutinize the room. There was no sound save the faint buzzing of a fly.

The reception hall did not give directly onto the windows. A pillared gallery supported a mezzanine; only the throne was heavily draped. And directly above it a portrait of King Chulalongkorn was displayed in the upper gallery. The Corinthian pillars of the gallery were painted blue with vertical incisions inlaid with gold, while the capitals were adorned with golden roses in the Near Eastern style instead of the usual acanthus leaves.

The rosette pattern was tenaciously repeated throughout the palace. The gallery, painted gold and bordered in white, had openwork balustrades of golden roses. An immense chandelier suspended from the centre of the lofty ceiling was also decorated with gold and white roses. When Honda looked down at his feet, he saw that the red carpet had a rosette pattern.

A pair of gigantic ivory tusks placed behind the throne – an embracing pair of white crescent moons – was the sole traditionally Thai decoration. The impressive polished ivory gleamed yellowish white in the gloom.

Upon entering, Honda discovered that the french windows occupied only the forepart of the house facing the front garden. The open ones looking out on the rear garden, barred by a corridor, were only chest high. It was through the northern windows that a light breeze entered.

As his eyes wandered toward the windows, he suddenly glimpsed a black shadow flitting by the window frame. He shuddered. It was a green peacock. The bird perched on the sill, stretching its long elegant neck that glittered a greenish gold. The plumed crest on its proud head was like the delicate silhouette of a miniature fan.

*

'I wonder how long they're going to make us wait,' Honda whispered into Hishikawa's ear, thoroughly bored.

'It's always like this. It doesn't mean anything. They're not trying to impress you particularly by making you wait. You know by now that you mustn't rush things in this country. In the days of Chulalongkorn's son, King Urachid, His Majesty used to go to bed at dawn and arise in the afternoon. Everything was slow and easy-going; day and night were reversed. The Minister of Palace Affairs put in his appearance about four in the afternoon and returned home only in the morning. But in the tropics perhaps that's the best way. The beauty of these people is the beauty of fruit; fruit should ripen lazily and gracefully. There's no such thing as diligent fruit.'

Honda was annoyed with Hishikawa's typically long, whispered disquisition, but before he could turn away to avoid his bad breath, the old woman reappeared. Joining her hands respectfully, she indicated the approach of the Princess.

There was a hissing from the window where the peacock perched. It was not the warning sound used in the ancient Japanese court to signal the arrival of royalty. They were simply chasing the peacock away. There was a flutter of wings at the window, and the bird disappeared. Honda saw three old ladies coming down the northern corridor. They walked in a straight line, keeping an equal distance between them. The Princess was led by the first lady-in-waiting, her one hand held by the woman, the other toying with a garland of white jasmine. As the little seven-year-old Princess Moonlight was led toward the great Chinese chair before the ivory tusks, the old woman who had first met the guests at the door immediately knelt down on the floor and kowtowed in the manner called *krab* in Thai. She was presumably of low rank.

The first lady-in-waiting put her arm around the Princess and sat down with her in the centre Chinese chair. The other two seated themselves in small chairs to the right of and facing the throne. The third lady was now next to Hishikawa. The woman who had knelt down had already vanished when Honda looked around.

He imitated Hishikawa, who stood up and bowed deeply, then sat down on the red and gold Chinese chair. The women seemed to be close to seventy, and the little Princess appeared more their charge than their mistress.

The little girl was not wearing the old-fashioned *panun*, but a Western-style blouse of some white material embroidered in gold, and a printed Thai cotton skirt called *passin* that resembled a Malayan sarong. On her feet she wore a pair of red shoes decorated in gold. Her hair was cut short in the characteristic Thai style. This traditional coiffure honoured the brave maidens of Khorat who long ago, dressed as men, had fought against an invading Cambodian army.

Her lovely, intelligent face showed no sign of insanity. Her delicate, well-shaped brows and lips were commanding, and her short hair made her look more like a prince than a princess. Her skin was a golden tan.

Audience to her was receiving the two men's obeisance; this over, she toyed with her jasmine wreath and swung her legs over the edge of the high chair. She looked intently at Honda and whispered to the first lady-in-waiting; the latter rebuked her with a single word.

At Hishikawa's signal Honda brought out the purple velvet case with the pearl ring. It was passed to the third lady, then by way of the second and the first, respectively, it finally reached the Princess's hand. The time spent as it made its way to her seemed to deepen the torpor of the summer heat. As the case had been examined by the first lady, the Princess was deprived of the childish delight in opening it herself.

Her lovely brown fingers carelessly discarded the jasmine garland and took up the pearl ring. She inspected it intently for some time. Her unusual quietness that signified neither emotion nor lack of emotion lasted so long that Honda began to think this might be one of the symptoms of her madness. Suddenly a smile, like a bubble in water, broke out on her face, showing her white, childishly irregular teeth. Honda was relieved.

The ring was returned to the case and given back to the first lady-in-waiting. The Princess spoke for the first time in a clear, intelligent voice. Her words were then transmitted through the three ladies like a green snake slithering from branch to branch in the sun-touched shade of the palms and finally, translated by Hishikawa, reached Honda. The Princess had said: 'Thank you.'

Honda asked Hishikawa to translate for him. 'I have for long been an admirer of the Thai royal family, and I understand Her Serene Highness likes Japan too. If I may, I should like to send her a Japanese doll after I return. Would she accept it?' The Thai sentences spoken by Hishikawa were rather simple, but as they were passed on by the third and the second ladies-in-waiting, they grew longer and more numerous, and by the time the first-lady-in-waiting conveyed the import to the Princess, they seemed endless.

And the Princess's words when they returned to Honda were devoid of any sparkle of emotion or charm after they had travelled through the ladies' dark and wrinkled lips. It was as though the meat of the young Princess's vivacious expressions had been sucked out in the process, chewed up by their ancient dentures, leaving only unsightly refuse for Honda.

'They say that Her Serene Highness is pleased to accept Mr Honda's kind offer.'

Then a strange thing happened.

Catching the first lady off-guard, the Princess jumped off the chair, covered the three feet that separated her from Honda, and clung to his trouser legs. Honda rose in alarm. Quivering and still clinging to him, the Princess cried out, weeping loudly. He bent over and put his arms around the fragile shoulders of the sobbing girl.

The ladies-in-waiting, nonplussed, were unable to pull her away. They clustered together, whispering uneasily among themselves as they stared at her.

'What does she say? Translate!' Honda called to Hishikawa who was standing in amazement.

Hishikawa translated in a shrill voice: 'Mr Honda! Mr Honda! How I've missed you! You were so kind, and yet I killed myself without telling you anything. I have been waiting for this meeting to apologize to you for more than seven years. I have taken the form of a princess, but I am really Japanese. I spent my former life in Japan, and that is really my home. Please, Mr Honda, take me back to Japan.'

*

Finally the Princess was brought back to the chair and somehow the propriety of an audience was restored. Honda looked from where he stood at the black hair of the girl who was still weeping, now leaning against the first lady-in-waiting. He cherished the child's warmth and fragrance which still lingered on his knee.

The ladies requested that the audience be terminated since the Princess was not feeling well; but Honda begged, through Hishikawa, to be permitted two brief questions.

'What year and what month was it that Kiyoaki Matsugae and I learned about the visit of the Abbess of the Gesshu Temple on the central island of the lake in the Matsugae estate?' was the first.

When the question was conveyed to her, the Princess partly raised her wet cheeks from her attendant's lap as though still cross and pushed back a strand of hair that adhered to her cheek.

'October of 1912,' she answered readily.

Honda was secretly surprised, but he was not sure whether, like an illuminated picture scroll, she kept in her mind a clear and detailed record of the events of two former lives. He was not certain either, despite Isao's words of apology spoken so fluently, whether she knew the background details and circumstances. As a matter of fact, the accurate words had dropped from the Princess's emotionless lips as though numerals picked and arranged at random.

Honda asked the second question: 'What was the date of Isao Iinuma's arrest?'

The Princess seemed to be growing sleepy, but she answered unhesitatingly: 'December first, 1932.'

'That should be enough,' said the first lady, rising and thus pressing her charge to leave immediately.

The Princess suddenly sprang to her feet, climbed up on the chair in her shoes, and shouted to Honda in her shrill voice. The first attendant scolded her in whispers. The Princess, still shouting, clutched at the old woman's hair. She was evidently repeating the same words, judging from the similarity of the syllables. As the second and the third ladies ran over to hold her arms, the Princess started to cry madly, her piercing voice echoing from the high ceiling. From among the old women who were trying to pull her down, her smooth, pliant arms shot out, catching hold here and there. The old women withdrew, crying out in pain, and the Princess's voice rose even higher.

'What was that?'

'She insists on inviting you to the Detached Palace of Bang Pa In when she goes there for a visit day after tomorrow, and the ladies are trying to prevent it. This is going to be some show,' said Hishikawa.

A discussion began between the Princess and her attendants. Finally she nodded and stopped crying.

'The day after tomorrow,' said the first lady, still out of breath, straightening her dishevelled clothes and speaking directly to Honda, 'Her Serene Highness will drive to the Bang Pa In Palace for amusement. Mr Honda and Mr Hishikawa are invited. We should very much like them to accept. As we shall lunch there, it would be well if they were here by nine o'clock in the morning.'

The formal invitation was immediately translated by Hishikawa.

In the car returning to the hotel, Hishikawa kept up his interminable chatter, ignoring the fact that Honda was lost in thought. The lack of consideration for others displayed by this self-styled artist bespoke his threadbare sensitivity. Had he deemed sensitivity to be an unnecessary, Philistine characteristic and had he adhered to this view, at least he would have had the virtue of consistency; but in truth Hishikawa took pride in his delicacy and sensitivity in human relationships, which he thought far exceeded those of other guides.

'It was very astute of you to ask those two questions. I didn't understand what it was all about. But you were putting her to a test because she showed you a special closeness in pretending to be the reincarnation of your friend. Isn't that right?'

'Quite,' Honda replied perfunctorily.

'And were both the answers right?'

'No.'

'Was one, at least?'

'No. I'm sorry to say both were wrong.'

Honda lied to be let alone, and his despairing tone conveniently concealed the deception, whereupon Hishikawa broke into loud laughter, believing Honda was telling him the truth.

'Is that right! All of them wrong? She said the dates so seriously. Well, too bad. The transmigration business wasn't very convincing then. You're not very kind, though, testing such a lovely little princess as if you were examining a quack fortune-teller on some street corner. By and large, there's no mystery in human life. Mystery remains only in the arts, and the reason is that mystery makes sense only in art.'

Honda was again surprised by Hishikawa's one-track rationalism. He glimpsed something red outside the car window, and looking out, saw a river and among the coconuts with trunks of flaming red bordering the road baboon-like, the smoky scarlet of poinciana along the bank. Heat waves were already quivering around the trees.

Honda turned to the problem of how he could get to the Bang Pa In Palace without Hishikawa, even though that meant he would be unable to communicate with the Princess.

4

Honda's wish materialized unexpectedly. 'I'm not in the mood for another session with the mad princess,' Hishikawa said patronizingly, 'but if I don't go, you'll have trouble. The attendants speak only a few words of English.' Contrary to his wont, Honda replied: 'I shall enjoy the Thai language as if it were music, even though I don't understand it. I'd rather do that than be bothered with the nuisance of a translation each time.' He hoped that this would more or less bring to a close his dealings with Hishikawa.

Subsequently Honda would recall again and again the delightful outing that day.

The car could approach only partway to the Bang Pa In Palace. The remaining distance was covered on a court-style pleasure boat, which moved along a waterway consisting of both the river and flooded rice fields. From time to time a water buffalo would awaken from his nap in a paddy and suddenly rear up, his muddy back glinting in the sun. When the boat skirted a forest of tall trees, the Princess was delighted at the sight of numerous squirrels scurrying up and down the branches along the riverbank. On one occasion a small green snake, his head erect, could be seen leaping from one low branch to another.

Golden spires rose above the jungle, each one freshly gilded, thanks to the donations of believers. Honda knew that the gold leaf was made in Japan and exported to Thailand in considerable quantity.

He vividly recalled the few moments during which Princess Moonlight ceased her constant childish chatter and motionlessly leaned against the side of the boat, staring blankly into the distance. The female attendants, engrossed in their own merriment, were quite accustomed to such whimsical action on the part of the little girl and paid her no attention. Honda noticed immediately what it was she was watching and was quite shaken.

A great cloud that had appeared from beyond the horizon now hid the sun. The sun was already high, and the cloud had to stretch its tentacles far to cover it. The black cloud reached out to overlay just the sun and, with some difficulty, succeeded. The highest part in the blue sky over the disc was a dazzling white, giving the lie to the ominous black density of the thicker area. Nor was that all; the extension had made the cloud too thin and resulted in a large rift in the lower portion, through which a radiant light streamed, as though the shining effulgence were blood endlessly spurting from a great wound.

The distant horizon was covered by low-lying jungle. The foreground sparkled in radiant green, as though it were part of another world, grasping the sunshine that poured from the rift in the cloud. But the jungle farther away under the lower black portion was drenched by rains of such violence that fog seemed to be rising. The rain hung like some elaborate fungoid network, wrapping the dark jungle in its misty vapour. The rain net, which covered only a part of the distant horizon, was distinctly visible, and one could discern the horizontal movement of the drops whipped by the wind. The heavy shower, as if imprisoned, seemed concentrated in that area alone.

Honda knew immediately what the child was looking at: she was seeing simultaneously time and space. That is to say, the area beneath the squall belonged to some future or past undetectable by the human eye. To be beneath a clear blue sky and perceive so clearly a world of rain meant that different time periods and different spaces coexisted. The rain cloud permitted a glimpse of the gap between separate times, and the vast distance involved testified to the hiatus between the two spaces. The Princess was staring into the deep chasm of the universe.

Her tiny, pink, wet tongue was absent-mindedly but earnestly licking the pearl ring Honda had given her – the lady-in-waiting would have scolded if she had noticed. It was as if the tiny Princess, by licking the pearl, were testifying to the revelation of such a miracle.

Bang Pa In.

The name had become unforgettable.

The Princess insisted on holding Honda's hand as she walked along; and ignoring the ladies' frowns, he let himself be guided by the tiny, damp fist. Thoroughly familiar with the land, the Princess led him to a Chinese villa, then to a French arbour, a Renaissance garden, an Arabian tower, to one spot after another, all of which pleased his eye.

The floating pavilion in the centre of a spacious artificial pond was particularly beautiful, like a fine *objet d'art* set upon the water.

The stone stairs at the water's edge had been invaded as the water rose and the bottom step was hidden in the depths of the pool. The white marble in the water was green with algae. Waterweed had wrapped itself around, covering it with tiny silver bubbles. Princess Moonlight wanted to dip her hands and feet into the water, but her attendants repeatedly forbade her to do so. Honda could not understand her words, but she seemed to think that the bubbles, like her ring, were pearls she wished to gather.

When Honda stopped her, she calmed down immediately and seated herself on the stone steps beside him and looked out at the chapel that seemed to float in the centre of the pond.

It was not really a chapel, but a small pavilion used merely as a resting place while boating. Inside, it was quite empty, as one could see when the breeze parted the faded buff-yellow curtains.

The simple building was enclosed by walls of thin black rods decorated in gold. Through the interstices the greenery of the opposite shore, the curling clouds, and the sky heavy with light were all visible. As Honda stared at the panorama, the magnificent clouds and the forest visible through the screen of rods took on the appearance of a picture composed of strangely long, vertical strips of colours. And, of course, the roof of the small pavilion was highly decorative, being constructed of four tiers of thick layers of brick-red, yellow, and green Chinese tiles and a brilliant thin spire of gold which pierced the blue sky.

Whether he had thought of it then or whether the vision of the pavilion overlapped with that of the Princess later, Honda could not remember. But in his mind the slim black rods of the pavilion somehow turned into the ebony bodies of dancing girls momentarily poised for dance, adorned with many gold filigree ornaments and wearing their pointed headgear.

5

All recollected events that happen without any verbal communication – especially those during which there is no special attempt made to establish such communication – become effortlessly so many beautiful miniature paintings, all equally edged in ornate golden frames. The time Honda had spent at the Rosette Palace was indelibly etched in his memory because of those moments of aesthetic pleasure. Segments of such sunny instants would suddenly well up, at times forming a momentary portrait of the little Princess: the childish roundness of her hand stretched out to the pearl bubbles on the steps submerged in the water; the delicate, clean lines on her fingers and her palms; the deep black of her short hair hanging against her cheek; the long, almost melancholy eyelashes; and on her dark forehead the reflection of water, flickering like mother-of-pearl against black ebony. The time was aglow, the air in the garden was filled with the humming of bees, and the mood of the strolling ladies was cheerful too. The essence of the moment was like coral, beautiful and exposed. Yet, in those moments, the Princess's innocent, unclouded happiness and the series of agonizing and bloody events of her former two lives were combined like the clear and rainy skies of the distant jungle they had seen on their way to the palace.

Honda felt as if he were standing in the centre of time, as if in some enormous hall in which all partitions had been removed. It was spacious and free, not like the mundane dwellings to which he was accustomed. There, black pillars stood in serried ranks and he felt almost as if his eyes and voice could reach areas normally unattainable. In this great expanse created by the Princess's happiness, behind the multitude of black pillars stood Kiyoaki and Isao and a myriad of other transmigrated shades lurking breathlessly as though in a game of hide-and-seek.

The Princess laughed again. Rather, in her merry-making she smiled constantly, but frequently her moist pink gums would suddenly flash in real laughter. With each outburst she would look up into Honda's face.

Once at the Bang Pa In the old ladies quickly put aside their formality. Forgetting their stiff decorum, they giggled and ran about in high spirits. The formality gone, their age was all that remained of their ceremoniousness. They occupied themselves in picking at betel nuts together, quite like greedy, wrinkled parrots clustering around a bagful of seeds. They also scratched wherever they itched, thrusting their hands under the hems of their skirts. They would cackle noisily as they strutted sideways in imitation of young dancing girls. One mummied dancer with wig-like white hair shining over her brown face stretched her betel-stained mouth in gaping laughter and raised her sharp elbows, thrust sideways as she danced; the exposed, dry bones of her angular arms cut sharp shadow-pictures against the background of blue sky with its layers of dazzling clouds.

The Princess spoke, and at once the ladies stirred about. They surrounded the child and bustled off with her like a rolling whirlwind, leaving a surprised Honda alone. He grasped the meaning of their actions when he saw the small building that was their destination. She wanted to go to the bathroom.

A princess going to the toilet! Honda was aware of a sharp pang of affection.

He had previously imagined having a small daughter and feeling a fatherly love for her, but having never had any child, his imagination had always been limited. His response to the charming idea of the little Princess going to the bathroom was an intimation of flesh and blood and a totally new emotional experience. He wished it was possible for him to hold the Princess's smooth brown thighs in his hands as she urinated.

She was shy for a while upon returning, saying nothing and avoiding looking at him.

After lunch they played games in the shade.

Now Honda could not recall how the games went. They had sung simple, monotonous songs over and over, but he was ignorant of their meaning.

He could recall only the scene where the Princess stood in the centre of a sun-dappled lawn under the trees, and around her the three old ladies were sitting at ease, one with one knee raised, the others with their legs crossed. One of them seemed to have entered the play just to be sociable; she kept smoking tobacco wrapped in lotus petals. Another had a lacquered water bottle inlaid with pearl shells by her knee in readiness for the Princess who complained so often of thirst.

Probably the game had something to do with the *Ramayana*. The Princess resembled Hanuman when she wielded a tree branch like a sword, assuming a hunchbacked stance and holding her breath in a comical way. Each time the ladies clapped their hands and chanted something, she changed her stance. By tilting her head slightly she was a delicate flower nodding to a fleeting breeze or a squirrel stopping to cock its head in the midst of its travels through the tree branches. Again, transformed into Prince Rama, she pointed gallantly heavenward with the sword held by a dark, slender arm extending from her gold-embroidered white blouse. At that instant a mountain pigeon swept down in front of her, obscuring her face with its wings. But she did not move. Honda discovered that the towering tree behind her was a lime. The broad leaves hanging at the tips of the long stems on the gloomy growth rustled at every soft touch of the breeze. Each green leaf was stamped with distinct yellow veins, as though tropical sunbeams had been woven into it.

The Princess grew warm. Rather peevishly she asked something of the old ladies. They consulted together, and standing up, signalled to Honda. The party quit the shade of the woods and moved on to the boat landing. Honda gathered they must be going home, but he was wrong. They gave the boatman an order, whereupon he brought out a large piece of printed cotton.

Holding the fabric, they moved along the shore with its coiling mangrove roots until they found a more secluded spot. Two of the ladies lifted their skirts and walked into the water, holding either end of the cloth, which they completely opened when the water was hip high, so as to provide a screen that shut out the view from the opposite shore. The remaining lady accompanied the now naked Princess. The light reflected from the water on the emaciated thighs of the old women.

The Princess cried out in delight when she caught sight of some small fish that had gathered round the mangrove roots. Honda was surprised that the ladies-in-waiting should act as though he were simply not there, but he assumed that that too must be some aspect of Thai etiquette. Seating himself at the base of a tree on the bank, he watched the Princess bathe.

She was never quiet. Lit by the sunbeams dancing through the stripes in the cotton print, she smiled constantly at Honda. She made no effort to conceal her quite plump, childish belly as she splashed water on the ladies. When she was scolded she dashed away. The stagnant river water was not clear, but rather a yellowish brown, similar to the Princess's skin. But even that turned into limpid, sparkling droplets when splashed in the light that filtered through the cotton print.

Once the little girl raised her arm. Involuntarily Honda looked intently at her left side, at her small flat chest usually hidden by her arms. But he did not see the three black moles that should have been there. Whenever he could, he stared at the area until his eyes watered, thinking that perhaps the light moles were indistinct against the tan skin.

6

The lawsuit Honda was handling came to an unexpected conclusion when the plaintiff, realizing he was at a disadvantage, suddenly dropped charges. Honda could have gone home at once, but as a token of their gratitude Itsui Products wanted to present him with a bonus in the form of a pleasure trip. He wished to go to India and expressed this desire. The administration replied that it would probably be the last opportunity for anyone to go to India since there were signs of approaching war; they promised that all Itsui offices would do their best to assure his every comfort. Honda prayed that that would not entail the kind of consideration they had imposed upon him by assigning Hishikawa as his guide.

Honda sent word to his family in Japan. At once he took pleasure in scheduling his itinerary with the aid of an Indian timetable featuring steam engines that travelled only fourteen or fifteen miles an hour. Upon consulting a map, he saw that the places he wished to visit – the Ajanta caves and Benares on the Ganges – were so far apart that he almost felt faint. Yet each attracted equally the magnetic needle of his desire for the unknown.

His intention of taking leave of Princess Moonlight was dampened as he was faced with the nuisance of asking Hishikawa to interpret for him. Using the urgent preparations for his trip as an excuse, he simply wrote a thank-you note on hotel stationery for the outing to Bang Pa In. He sent it off to the Rosette Palace by messenger moments before his departure.

Honda's trip to India was marked with colourful experiences. But it is enough to describe one profoundly moving afternoon spent in the Ajanta caves and the soul-shaking sight of Benares. In these two places, Honda witnessed things extremely important, things essential to his life.

7

His itinerary included a voyage by boat to Calcutta; then one whole day by train to Benares, which was 350 miles from there; a trip by car from Benares to Mogulsarai; then two days by train to Manmad; and finally another car trip to Ajanta.

Calcutta in early October was bustling with the annual Durga festival.

The goddess Kali, the most popular of the Hindu pantheon and especially venerated in Bengal and Assam, had innumerable names and avatars, as did her husband Shiva, the god of destruction. Durga is one of Kali's metamorphoses, but her bloodthirstiness is less pronounced. Gigantic effigies of the goddess had been erected everywhere in the city. They showed her in the act of punishing the deity of water buffaloes, and beautiful, angry eyebrows were depicted on the valiant face. At night the statues, standing out sharply against the bright lights, received the adulation of the crowds.

Calcutta is the centre of Kali worship, with its temple, the Kalighat; and the activity there during these festivals defies the imagination. As soon as he arrived in the city, Honda hired an Indian guide and paid a visit to the temple.

The core of Kali is *shakti*, the original sense of which is 'energy'. This great mother goddess of the earth imparts to all female deities throughout the world her sublimity as mother, her feminine voluptuousness, and her abominable cruelty, thereby enriching their divine nature. Kali is depicted in an image of death and destruction, doubtless the two essential elements of *shakti*, and she represents pestilence, natural calamities, and various other powers of nature which bring death and destruction to living things. Her body is black, and her mouth is red with blood. Fangs protrude from her lips and her neck is adorned with a necklace of human skulls and freshly severed heads. She dances madly on her husband's body which lies prostrate in fatigue. This bloodthirsty goddess brings epidemics and calamities as soon as she feels thirst, and constant sacrificial offerings are necessary to keep her appeased. It is reputed that the sacrifice of a tiger quenches her thirst for one hundred years, that of a human for a thousand.

Honda visited the Kalighat one sultry, rainy afternoon. Before the entrance, hordes of people were noisily jostling about in the rain while beggars everywhere pleaded for alms. The temple precinct was extremely small, and the temple itself was packed with people. A throng had congregated around the high shrine with its marble base, jostling, eddying back and forth, packed so closely together that there was no place to stand. The marble base, wet with rain, gleamed especially white, but it was daubed with brown mud by the feet of the worshippers who were trying to climb up and with spatterings of the cinnabar that was to be applied to their foreheads along with a blessing. It seemed like a sacrilegious turbulence, but the intoxicating din went on and on.

A priest, his black arm extended outside the temple, was painting small, round holy dots of red cinnabar on the foreheads of the devout who had thrown a coin in the box. In the pressing crowd of those wishing to be so decorated were a woman with a blue, rain-drenched sari that clung to her body, moulding the contours of her round back and buttocks, and a man in a white linen shirt, whose neck was a pile of shiny black wrinkles. They were all jostling toward the red-stained black fingertip of the priest. Their movements, their paroxysms, and their devotion reminded Honda of the crowd depicted in the 'Almsgiving of Saint Rocco' by Annibale Carracci, a painter of the eclectic Bolognese school. However, in the inner part of the temple, sombre even in the day, a statue of the goddess Kali, with her protruding red tongue and her necklace of fresh heads, quivered in the candlelight.

Honda followed his guide to the back garden, with its irregular, rain-drenched flagstones, that occupied an area of less than four hundred square yards. He found only a few people there. A pair of pillars stood like low, narrow gateposts, with a trough of carved stone at their base. There was also a small, partitioned enclosure like a sort of washing place. Then immediately beside them stood smaller but exact replicas. The shorter pair of posts was wet with rain; and in the trough at their base lay a pool of blood, and dots of blood smudged the rainwater on the stone floor. The guide explained to Honda that the larger one was the altar where water buffalo were sacrificed and that it was no longer in use. The smaller replica was one used to sacrifice goats; and particularly during important festivals like that of Durga, four hundred goats would be slaughtered there.

When Honda looked at the back of the Kalighat which had previously not been clearly visible because of the crowds around it, he found that only its base was constructed of pure white marble, the central stupa and surrounding chapels being decorated with a mosaic of brilliantly coloured tiles reminiscent of the Temple of Dawn in Bangkok. The rains had washed the dust from the exquisite floral patterns and arabesques of affronted peacocks, and the brilliantly coloured edifices towered arrogantly over the gory mess below.

Large raindrops fell in sporadic flurries; and the water-laden air, carried inside, created a misty warmth.

Honda saw a woman unprotected by her umbrella come to kneel reverently in front of the smaller altar. She had the round, sincere, intelligent face found so frequently in middle-aged Indian women. Her light green sari was drenched. She carried a small brass kettle containing holy water from the Ganges.

The woman poured the water over the pillars, lit the oil burner which functioned even in the rain, and scattered miniature vermilion java flowers around it. Then she knelt on the blood-stained stone floor, and pressing her forehead against the post, began fervently to pray. The holy red spot on her forehead was visible through her rain-plastered hair all during the ecstatic prayer, as though it were a spot of her own blood offered in sacrifice.

Honda was deeply moved, and at the same time his emotions were mixed with an indescribable abhorrence close to rapture. As he examined his own feelings, the scene about him receded and only the figure of the praying woman was sharply, almost uncannily focused. Just as the clarity of detail and his horror became so overwhelming that he felt unable to cope with either, the woman suddenly vanished. For a moment he thought it must have been an illusion, but no. He saw her walking away past the unclosed back gate of openwork wrought-iron arabesques. However, there was no connection between the woman who had been praying and the one walking away.

A child led in a young black kid. A vermilion holy spot shone on its shaggy, wet forehead. As holy water was poured on the daub, the kid shook its head and kicked its hind legs, struggling to escape.

A young man with a moustache, wearing a soiled shirt, appeared and took the animal from the boy. As he placed his hand on its neck, the goat began to bleat pathetically, almost irritatingly, writhing and backing away. The black hair on its rump was dishevelled in the rain. The youth forced the goat's neck between the two posts of the altar, face down, and inserting a black bolt between them, he pushed it home over the imprisoned animal. The victim reared its hips and struggled desperately, bleating piteously. The youth poised his crescent-shaped sword, its edge glittering silver in the rain. It descended accurately, and the severed head rolled forward, eyes wide open, its whitish tongue protruding grotesquely. The body remained on the other side of the posts, its front quivering delicately while the hind legs kicked wildly around its chest. The violent movements gradually weakened, like those of a pendulum abating with every swing. The blood flowing from its neck was relatively scant.

The young executioner grasped the headless kid's hind legs and ran out through the gate. Outside the sacrificed goats were hung on pickets where they were then dismembered and swiftly disembowelled. Another headless kid lay in the rain at the youth's feet. Its hind quarters were still trembling as though in the throes of some dreadful nightmare. The borderline between life and death, which had just been drawn so skilfully, so painlessly, had been passed almost unconsciously; only the nightmare remained to torment the animal.

The young man's skill with the sword was remarkable; he was following faithfully and unemotionally the practice of this holy, yet abominable profession. Holiness dripped in the most ordinary way, like perspiration, from the blood spotting his soiled shirt, from the depths of his deep, clear eyes, and from his large, peasant-like hands. The festival-goers, accustomed to the sight, did not even turn around, and holiness with its dirty hands and feet sat confidently in their midst.

And the head? The head was offered on an altar protected by a crude rain cover inside the gates. Red flowers had been scattered in the fireplace burning in the rain, and some of their petals were scorching; it was the fire of the shrine dedicated to the worship of Brahma. Seven or eight black goat heads were arranged by the fireside, each red, open end blooming like a java flower. One of these was the one that had been bleating just a few minutes ago. Behind them an old woman, crouching low, appeared to be intently sewing, but her black fingers were earnestly stripping away the smooth, gleaming entrails from the inner lining of the skin of a carcass.

8

During his trip to Benares, the sight of the sacrifice came again and again to Honda's mind.

It was a bustling scene as if in preparation for something else. He felt that the sacrificial rite did not end there at all; it was as though something had begun, and a bridge had been built to something invisible, more sacred, more abominable, more sublime. In other words, the series of rituals was like a strip of red carpet unrolled in welcome for some indescribable being who was approaching.

Benares is the holy of holies, the Jerusalem of the Hindus. At the point where the Ganges curves in an exquisite crescent, accepting the melted Himalayan snows where the god Shiva resides, is situated on its western bank the city of Benares, the Varanasi of old.

It is a city dedicated to Shiva, husband of Kali, and has come to be considered the main portal to paradise. It is also the destination of pilgrims from throughout the country. The bliss of paradise is achieved on earth by bathing in the waters at this juncture of the five holy rivers: Ganges, Dutapapa, Krishna, Jamna, and Sarasvati.

The *Vedas* contain the following passage concerning the efficacy of the water:

> The waters are medicine.
> The waters cleanse sicknesses of the body
> And fill the body with vitality.
> Indeed the waters are healing
> And will cure all sickness and evil.

And again:

> The waters are filled with eternal life.
> The waters are the protection of the body.
> The waters have miraculous efficacy for healing.
> Forget not ever the awful powers of the waters,
> For they are medicine for body and soul.

As eulogized in these passages, the ultimate of Hindu rituals, which start with the cleansing of the heart by prayer and the ablution of the body by water, is enacted on Benares's innumerable ghats.

Honda reached Benares in the afternoon and immediately unpacked and bathed in his hotel room. Then he arranged for a guide. He felt no fatigue after the long train ride, and he found his strangely youthful inquisitiveness had put him in a gay and restless frame of mind. The stifling light of the setting sun pervaded everywhere outside the hotel windows. He felt as if he could instantly grasp its mystery by dashing out into it.

Yet, Benares was a city of extreme filth as well as of extreme holiness. On both sides of the narrow, sunless alleys stalls for fried food and cakes, astrologers, grain and flour vendors were all crowded together; and the area was filled with stench, dampness, and disease. As one passed through and emerged on the flagstone square by the river, clusters of crouching leprous mendicants had gathered; they had come from all parts of the country as pilgrims, and now they begged for alms while awaiting death. Flocks of pigeons. Sultry late-afternoon sky. A leper was sitting in front of a tin can containing a few coppers; his one eye was red and festered and his fingerless hands like the stumps of felled mulberry trees were raised to the evening sky.

There was deformity of every kind. Dwarfs were running about, and bodies were arranged like some undeciphered ancient writing, lacking any common symbol. They appeared deformed not because of corruption or dissipation, but because the wretched, twisted shapes themselves, with freshness and feverishness, spewed out a repulsive holiness. Blood and pus were carried like pollen by thousands of fat, shiny, green-gold flies.

On the right-hand side of the slope that led down to the river, a colourful tent with holy insignia on it had been pitched, and cloth-wrapped corpses had been deposited beside the crowd listening to a sermon by some priest.

Everything was afloat. Under the sun lay exposed multitudes of the most ugly realities of human flesh with their excrement, stench, germs, and poisons. Everything hovered in the air like steam evaporating from ordinary reality. Benares. A piece of carpet, hideous to the point of brilliance. A riotous carpet joyously hoisted day and night by temples and people and children – fifteen hundred temples, temples of love with red pillars and black ebony reliefs illustrating all the possible positions of sexual intercourse, the House of Widows whose inmates earnestly await death, loudly chanting sutras night and day . . . inhabitants, visitors, the quick, the dead, children covered with pox, dying children clinging to their mother's breast . . .

The square sloped down to the river, leading visitors naturally to the most important ghat: the Dasasvamedha, the 'Sacrifice of Ten Horses'. Tradition has it that the creator Brahma once made a sacrifice of ten horses at this spot.

The river with its opulent ochre waters was the Ganges! The precious holy water which filled the small brass kettles to be poured on the foreheads of devotees and sacrificial victims in Calcutta was now flowing down the vast river before Honda's eyes. An unbelievably generous feast of holiness.

It was only reasonable that here the sick, the healthy, the deformed, the dying should all be equally filled with golden joy. It was only reasonable that the flies and vermin should be plump and besmeared with bliss; that the characteristically dignified and suggestive facial expression of the Indians here should be so filled with reverence as to verge on blankness. Honda wondered how he could fuse his reason with the blazing evening sun, the unbearable odour, with the river breezes like faint swamp vapours. It was doubtful he could immerse himself in the evening air which was everywhere like some thick woollen fabric woven with chanting voices, tolling bells, the sound of beggars, and the moaning of the sick. He was afraid his reason might, like the sharp edge of some knife he alone concealed in his jacket, slash this perfect fabric.

The important thing was to discard it. The edge of the knife of reason, which he had regarded as his weapon since youth, had barely been preserved, considering the nicks already inflicted on it by each substantiation of transmigration. Now he had no choice but to abandon it unperceived in the perspiring crowds covered with germs and dust.

Numerous mushroom-like umbrellas for bathers stood on the ghat, but for the most part they were unoccupied now that evening sunbeams darted deep beneath them. It was long after bathing time, which had reached its peak at sunrise. The guide went down to the shore and started to negotiate with a boatman. Honda could do nothing but wait to one side throughout the interminably long dickering, feeling the hot iron of the evening sun scorching his back.

Finally the boat carrying Honda and his guide put out from the shore. The Dasasvamedha was located approximately in the centre of the many ghats along the western bank of the Ganges. Sightseeing boats for the most part went downstream to the south to see the other ghats, then turned upstream to reach those north of the Dasasvamedha.

Whereas the western shore was considered to be holy, the eastern bank was sorely neglected. It was said that people who lived there would transmigrate into the body of an ass, and therefore all avoided that side. There was not so much as the shadow of a house, just the low jungle green in the distance.

Once the boat started downstream, the bright evening sun was at once cut off by buildings and provided only a brilliant halo for the magnificent view formed by the many imposing ghats with their columns at the back and the mansions supported by pillars. Only the Dasasvamedha ghat, backed by the square, allowed the setting sun its way. The evening sky was already casting its gentle rose colour over the river; passing sails dropped dusky shadows on the water.

It was a time of opulent, mysterious luminescence before the dusk of evening. A time controlled by light, when the contours of all things were perfect, every dove painted in detail, when everything was dyed a faded yellow-rose, when a languid harmony reigned with the exquisiteness of an etching between the reflection on the river and the glow in the sky.

The ghats are great architectural structures suitable precisely to this sort of light. They consist of colossal staircases, like those of palaces or great cathedrals, that lead down to the water, and behind each one stands a great monolithic wall. The columns and arches forming the background for the ghats are only pilasters, and the arcades have blind windows. The staircase alone has the dignity of a sacred place. Some capitals are Corinthian in style, others are quite syncretic in the Near Eastern fashion. On the pillars white lines are drawn as high as forty feet, the heights reached in the yearly flood disasters, especially the notorious ones of 1928 or 1936. Above the staggeringly lofty pilasters, cantilevered arcades jut out for the people who live at the top of the walls, and rows of pigeons perch on the stone balustrades. Over the rooftops a halo of evening sun paused, gradually fading in brilliance.

Honda's boat was nearing one of the ghats called Kedar. There a man was fishing with a net near his boat. Kedar ghat was quiet, and the thin, ebony bathers as well as the spectators on the steps were all lost in prayer and meditation.

Honda's attention was caught by a man who had come down the centre of the great staircase and was about to bathe. Behind him stood a line of magnificent ochre columns, and in the fading glow everything was clear and distinct, even to the ornamented crannies in the capitals. He was standing in the midst of holiness, yet it was questionable whether he could be called a man at all, so great was the contrast of his skin with that of the black bodies of the tonsured priests about him. A tall, stately old man, he alone was a radiant pink.

He wore a small topknot of white hair on his head, and with his left hand he held a heavy scarlet loincloth around his hips. The rest was an ample expanse of slightly slackened pink nudity. His eyes were rapturously transfixed, as though no one existed about him, and he gazed vacuously at the sky above the opposite bank. His right hand slowly stretched heavenward in adoration. The skin of the face, chest, and abdomen was a fresh pinkish white in the evening light, and his nobility completely removed him from his surroundings. But remnants of the black skin of this world remained here and there on the upper half of his arms, on the backs of his hands, or on his thighs, almost peeling off, but still forming blotches, marks, and stripes. These remnants made his glowing pink body appear even more sublime. He was a white leper.

A multitude of pigeons took flight.

As the boat started upstream, the movement of one startled bird was instantly transmitted to the others, and the sudden flutter of many wings took Honda by surprise. His attention was drawn from the foliage of the lime trees stretching out over the river surface between the many ghats. Each leaf was said to house for ten days the soul of one just deceased while it waited to be reborn.

The boat had already passed the Dasasvamedha ghat and was alongside the House of Widows, a building of red sandstone by the river. The window frames were decorated with green and white mosaic and the interior was painted green. Incense wafted from the windows, and bells and the chanting of *kirtana* could be heard echoing from the ceiling and spilling over the river surface. Here widows gathered from all corners of India to await their death. Emaciated by sickness and anticipating the salvation of extinction, for these people their last days in Mumukshu Bhavan, or the 'House of Happiness', in Benares were their happiest. Everything was conveniently close. The crematory ghat was situated to the immediate north, while just above rose the golden spire of the Nepalese Temple of Love, on which the sculptures honoured the thousand postures of sexual intercourse.

Honda's eyes picked out a package wrapped in cloth floating beside the boat. He remarked that the shape, bulk, and length suggested the corpse of a two- or three-year-old child and was told that that was precisely what it was.

Honda glanced at his watch. It was forty minutes past five. The evening dusk was gathering. At that instant, he distinctly saw a fire in front of him. It was the funeral pyre of the Mani Karnika ghat.

Facing the Ganges, it consisted of five-tiered platforms of varying widths on a Hindu-style base. The temple was formed of a group of stupas of different heights that surrounded a large central one, and every structure had a Mohammedan-style arched balcony in the shape of a lotus petal. As this gigantic brown cathedral was smoke-stained and stood on high colonnades, the closer Honda's boat approached the more its gloomy, imposing silhouette, uninhabited and smoke-swathed, loomed like an ominous hallucination in the sky. But a vast muddy stretch of water still lay between the boat and the ghat. On the darkening surface of the water, a profusion of flower offerings – including the red java flowers he had seen in Calcutta – and incense came floating down like trash; and the inverted reflection of the towering flames of the funeral pyre played clearly on the water.

The pigeons inhabiting the stupas fluttered about in confusion, mingling with the sparks that rose high in the sky. The heavens had turned a dark indigo touched with grey.

A sooty stone grotto stood near the water, and flowers had been placed before the statues of Shiva and one of his wives, Sati, who had flung herself into a fire in order to uphold her husband's honour.

Many boats piled high with wood for the funeral pyres were moored in the area, and Honda's craft hung back from the centre of the ghat. Behind the brightly burning fire a small flame was visible deep under the temple arcade. It was the sacred, eternal flame, and every funeral pyre received its fire from it.

The river breeze had died and a suffocating heat hung over the area. Like everywhere else in Benares, noise rather than silence prevailed here too; it mingled with the constant movement of people, cries, children's laughter, and the chanting of sutras. People were not the only bathers; emaciated dogs followed the children into the water; and from the dark depths away from the fires, there where the extremity of the ghat steps lay submerged, the sinewy, shiny backs of water buffalo suddenly emerged one by one, herded on by the cackling shouts of their keepers. As they teetered up the steps, the funeral fires were mirrored on their wet black backs.

Sometimes the flames were enveloped in white smoke and flickering red tongues would appear through rifts. The smoke wafted up to the temple balconies and eddied like some living thing in the dark recesses of the building.

The Mani Karnika ghat offered the ultimate in purification: it was the outdoor, public crematorium in which all was out in the open in Indian fashion. Yet it was full of nauseous abomination, the inevitable ingredient of all things deemed sacred and pure in Benares. Beyond question this location marked the end of the world.

A corpse wrapped in red cloth was propped against an easy slope of steps adjoining the grotto of Shiva and Sati. It had been soaked in the waters of the Ganges and now awaited its turn for cremation. The red wrapping around the human form showed that the body was that of a woman. White cloth was reserved for men. Relatives waited with tonsured priests under the tent in order to fulfil their duty by throwing butter and incense upon the corpse after the pyre was lit. Just then another white-swathed corpse arrived, borne on a bamboo litter and surrounded by chanting priests and all the relatives. Several children and a black dog chased each other around their feet. As observable in any Indian town, the living were all very much alive and making considerable noise.

It was six o'clock. Flames suddenly rose in four or five places. As the smoke was blown away in the direction of the temple, the offensive odour did not reach Honda in the boat, but he could see everything clearly.

To the extreme right all the ashes were gathered together and left to soak in the river water. Individual characteristics that had so obstinately clung to each body were no longer, and the ashes of all, conjoined and finally dissolved in the holy water of the Ganges, thus returned to their four elemental constituents and the vast Universe. The under part of the ash mound was inextricably mixed with the damp earth of the area before being soaked in the Ganges. The Hindus do not build tombs. Honda suddenly recalled the shudder that had gone through him at the Aoyama Cemetery when he had visited Kiyoaki's grave, the horror he had felt that Kiyoaki was quite definitely not under the gravestone.

The corpses were laid on the fire one after the other. As the binding cords burned away and the red and white shrouds were consumed in the fire, a black arm would suddenly rise or a body would curl up in the fire as though turning over in sleep. The corpses that had been placed on the pyre first turned a dark grey. Sizzling sounds, like those of a pot boiling over, could be heard across the water. The skulls did not burn easily, and a cremator constantly walked about, poking a bamboo pole through the ones that were still smouldering well after the bodies had been reduced to ash. The sinews in his strong black arms that powerfully drove the pole through the skulls reflected the flames, while the crunching sounds he made reverberated against the temple walls.

The slow progress of purification of the human body, returning its parts to its four elemental constituents ... the resistant human flesh and its useless odour lingering after death ... something red opening in the flames, something shiny writhing, black powdery particles dancing up with the fiery sparks. There was a flashing animation in the flames, as though something were being created. From time to time, when suddenly the firewood noisily collapsed and part of the fire disappeared, the cremator would pile on more wood; and from time to time unexpectedly lofty flames would leap upward, almost licking at the temple balcony.

There was no sadness. What seemed heartlessness was actually pure joy. Not only were samsara and reincarnation basic belief, but they were actually accepted as a part of nature, constantly renewing itself before one's eyes, the rice paddy and its growing plants, the trees bringing forth their fruit. Some assistance from human hands was necessary, just as harvest and cultivation required human intervention; people were born to take their turns in this natural progression.

In India the source of everything that seemed heartless was connected with a hidden, gigantic, awesome joy! Honda was afraid of grasping such delight. But having witnessed the extremes he had, he knew that he should never recover from the shock. It was as though all of Benares were afflicted with a holy leprosy and that his very vision had been contaminated by this incurable disease.

But his impression of having seen the ultimate was incomplete until the following moment arrived, one that struck Honda's heart with a crystalline thrill of fright.

It was the moment when the sacred cow turned toward him.

In this crematorium there was a white cow, one of those sacred animals permitted anything anywhere in India. The sacred cow, accustomed to the fires, had been chased off by the cremator and stood just out of reach of the flames in front of the dark temple arcade. Inside was total blackness; and the white of the animal seemed awe-inspiring and full of sublime wisdom. The white belly reflecting the flickering flames appeared like cold Himalayan snow bathed in moonlight. It was a pure synthesis of impassible snow and sublime flesh in the body of an animal. The flames were smoke-logged; sometimes flashes of red dominated, again to be hidden by the swirling smoke.

Just then the sacred cow turned its majestic white face to Honda through the vague smoke rising from the burning bodies and looked directly at him.

That night, as soon as he finished dinner, Honda left word that he would be leaving before dawn the next morning, and fell asleep with the help of a nightcap.

Legions of phantasmagoria cluttered his dreams. His dream fingers brushed a keyboard they had never touched before, producing strange sounds. They examined like an engineer all corners of the structured universe so far known to him. The limpid Mount Miwa suddenly appeared, then the Offing Rock, reclining rock of horror on the peak of which dwelt the gods; blood spouted from a crevice and the goddess Kali emerged, her red tongue protruding. A burned corpse rose in the form of a beautiful youth, his hair and loins covered with the brilliantly pure leaves of the sacred sakaki tree. Then the obscene scene at the temple instantly turned into the cool precincts of a Japanese shrine covered with clean pebbles. All ideas, all gods were jointly turning the handle of the gigantic wheel of samsara. The great disc like a spiral nebula was slowly turning, carrying masses of people who, unaware of the effects of samsara, were simply happy, angry, sad, or joyful, quite like those who lived their daily lives totally unaware of the rotation of the earth. It was like a ferris wheel at night all decorated with lights in the amusement park of the gods.

Perhaps Indians knew all this. This fear had followed Honda into his very dreams. Just as the fact of the earth's rotation is never detected through any of the human senses and is barely recognizable by scientific reasoning, samsara, karma, and reincarnation too were perhaps not discernible through ordinary perception and reason, but only through some supernatural power, some extremely accurate, systematic, intuitive super-logic. And perhaps this perception made the Indians appear so listless, so resistant to progress, and so devoid of all those human emotions – joy, anger, sorrow, and pleasure – that are common standards for measuring ordinary human beings.

Of course, these were the rough impressions of a traveller who had barely scratched the surface of the land. Dreams often combine the highest level of symbols and the most vulgar of thoughts. Perhaps Honda was following in his dreams the old habit of his judgeship days: a cold, prosaic, speculative process had inadvertently put in its appearance. His professional habits and his character seemed like a cat's tongue, too sensitive to hot food, forcing him to cool at once any warm, unidentified elements and to transform them into conceptually frozen food. He was probably using this same old automatic defence mechanism, exactly like so many others who are particularly cautious in their dreams.

Far more than the ambiguity and strangeness of the dream, what he saw in reality was a much greater mystery to him, one that stubbornly rejected understanding or interpretation. When he awoke he perceived that the heat of this fact lingered clearly in his body and mind. He felt as though he had contracted a tropical fever.

Near the dim light of the front desk at the end of the hotel corridor, his bearded guide stood joking and chuckling with the bellboy on night duty. He recognized Honda approaching in his white linen suit and bowed respectfully from a distance.

Honda's reason for leaving the hotel before the dawn was to see the crowds waiting to worship the sunrise at the ghats.

Benares was dedicated to the concept of the one from the many, the unity of Brahma, who was a transcendent godhead, being the One that contained the many. The solar disc was the embodiment of his divinity, and his godliness was greatest at the moment the sun rose above the horizon. The holy city of Benares and the heavens had been treated as equals in Indian religion. The pundit Shankara once said: 'When God put the heavens and Benares on the scale, heavy Benares sank to the land and the lighter heavens rose.'

Hindus perceive the highest consciousness of the godhead in the sun and consider it the symbol of ultimate truth. Thus Benares is filled with devotion to prayer and for the solar disc. People's consciousness frees itself from the rules governing the earth, and thus Benares itself, like a floating carpet, is elevated by the efficacy of prayer.

Unlike the day before, Dasasvamedha ghat was now swarming with masses of people, and the candles under countless umbrellas were flickering in the dusk before sunrise. In the sky above the jungle on the opposite side of the river, there was a hint of the approaching dawn below the tiers of clouds.

People had placed benches under each large bamboo umbrella and decorated the lingam stone, symbol of Shiva, with red flowers. Some were mixing red cinnabar powder in small mortars, preparing to paint their foreheads after the bath. Beside them attendant monks were mixing the paste with Ganges water in brass jugs which had been dedicated and blessed at the temple. Some people had already descended the stairs in order to be in the water to meet the sunrise. After worshipping the water, which they scooped up in their hands, they slowly immersed their entire body. Some awaited the sunrise kneeling under the umbrellas.

As the first light of dawn broke over the horizon, the scene on the ghat instantly assumed outline and colour; women's saris, their skin, flowers, white hair, scabies, brass vessels – all began to cry out with colour. The tortured morning clouds, slowly changing shape, gave way to the expanding light. Finally, just as the tip of the vermilion morning sun appeared above the low jungle, all at once a reverent sigh escaped from the lips of the people who had filled the square almost rubbing shoulders against Honda. Some of them knelt in devotion.

Those who were in the water pressed their hands together or opened their arms, praying to the red sun which gradually rose to display its full disc. The shadows of their torsos, cast far across the purplish golden river waves, reached to the feet of the people on the steps. Great rejoicing was heard, all directed toward the sun over the opposite shore. And all the while, one after the other, people stepped into the water, as though guided by some invisible hand.

The sun hung now above the green jungle. The scarlet disc, which had permitted itself to be looked upon, now turned in a trice into a cluster of brilliance that rejected even a momentary glance. It had already become a pulsating, threatening ball of flame.

Suddenly Honda knew! The sun which Isao had constantly seen in his suicide dream was this!

9

Buddhism suddenly deteriorated in India sometime after the fourth century of the Christian era. It has been rightly said that Hinduism stifled it in its friendly embrace. Like Christianity and Judaism in Judea and Confucianism and Taoism in China, Buddhism had to be exiled from India for it to become a world religion. It was necessary for India to turn to a more primitive folk religion. Hinduism perfunctorily retained the name Buddha in a far corner of its pantheon, where he was preserved as the ninth of the ten avatars of Vishnu.

Vishnu is believed to assume ten transfigurations: Matsya, the fish; Kurma, the land tortoise; Varaha, the boar; Narasimha, the man-lion; Vamana, the dwarf; Parashurama; Rama; Krishna; the Buddha; and Kalki. According to the Brahmans, Vishnu, assuming the form of the Buddha, purposely introduced a heretical religion so that believers would be led astray, thus presenting the opportunity for the Brahmans to lead them back to their true religion – Hinduism.

Thus, along with the decline of Buddhism the cave temples at Ajanta in western India fell into ruin and became known to the world only twelve centuries later, in 1819, when a British Army corps chanced upon them.

The twenty-seven stone caves in the cliffs of the Wagora River were originally excavated in three different periods: in the second century BC and in the fifth and seventh centuries AD. With the exception of caves 8, 9, 10, 12, and 13 constructed during the Hinayana period, all the rest belong to the age of Mahayana Buddhism.

After visiting the living holy land of Hinduism, Honda wanted to seek out the ruins of Buddhism, now extinct in India.

Ajanta was where he must go. Somehow it was his destiny.

This idea was substantiated by the fact that the caves themselves and the hotel and its surroundings were extremely quiet and simple, devoid of surging crowds.

As there were no facilities for lodgings around Ajanta, Honda registered in a hotel in Aurangabad with the thought of visiting the famous Hindu site of Ellora. Aurangabad was only eighteen miles from there, but sixty-six from Ajanta.

The best room in the hotel had been reserved for him by Itsui Products, and the finest car placed at his disposal. These advantages along with the Sikh chauffeur's deferential attitude turned the English tourists in the hotel hostile. That morning in the dining room before setting out on the all-day tour, Honda had already felt the silent pact of antagonism that united the Britishers against the lone Asian tourist. It was even expressed overtly when the waiter brought a plate of bacon and eggs to Honda's table before serving anyone else. An arrogant old gentleman with a handsome beard, doubtless some retired Army officer, seated with his wife at the next table, called the waiter over and admonished him sharply and curtly. After that, Honda was served last.

An ordinary traveller would have at once taken umbrage at such a situation, but Honda was obstinately impervious to trivia. Since Benares, some incomprehensible, thick membrane overlay his heart and everything slipped off its surface. Since the excessive respect of the waiter was surely the result of a generous tip paid in advance by Itsui Products, such incidents never affected the withdrawn dignity he had acquired during his term as judge.

The beautiful black car, assiduously cleaned and polished by more than five hotel employees with nothing else to do, stood in readiness for Honda's departure, the various flowers of the front garden reflecting in its shining surface. Soon, with Honda as passenger, it was rolling over the lovely plains of western India.

The vast expanse revealed not a single human figure. Sometimes the supple, dark-brown forms of mongooses splashed in the swamp water beside the road or scurried across in front of the car; or a group of long-tailed monkeys would peer out at him from the branches.

Hope for purification arose in Honda's heart. Purification in the Indian manner was too disgusting, and the sacraments he had witnessed in Benares were still in him like a raging fever. He craved a ladle of clear, cool Japanese water.

The expansiveness of the plains comforted him. There was no rice paddy nor other field under cultivation: only endless, beautiful plains stretching away, dotted with the deep indigo shadows of mimosa trees. There were swamps, streams, yellow and red flowers, and over it all, a brilliant sky hung like some colossal canopy.

There was nothing miraculous or extreme in this natural setting. The dazzling greenery radiantly exuded idle sleepiness. The plain itself had a tranquillizing effect on Honda whose heart had been seared by frightening and ominous flames. Instead of the spatter of sacrificial blood, a virginally white heron fluttered up from the jungle. The whiteness sometimes darkened when it passed before the deep green shade, but would emerge pure white again.

The clouds in the sky ahead were delicately convoluted, and their irregular borders gave out a silken sheen. The blue was fathomless.

Needless to say, a large component of the comfort Honda felt came with his awareness that soon he was to enter Buddhist territory, even though Buddhism had long been extinct.

To be sure, after experiencing the weird and variegated mandala of Benares, the Buddhism he dreamed of was as refreshing as ice, and already he felt a presage of the familiar Buddhist quietude in the bright stillness of the plains.

Suddenly Honda felt nostalgic. He was returning from a noisy kingdom dominated by living Hinduism to a familiar country of temple gongs, a land which had been destroyed but which had taken on a purity by that destruction. As he thought of the Buddha waiting for him to return from the Absolute he had experienced in Benares, he felt he had perhaps never expected an Absolute in Buddhism. In the tranquillity of the home-coming he had dreamed of, he felt an unremitting closeness to what was gradually perishing. Beyond the beautiful, radiantly blue sky, the graveyard of Buddhism itself, the site of its oblivion was soon to appear. Even before seeing it, Honda clearly felt the sombre coolness soothing his overheated mind, the coolness of the rock caves, and the limpidity of the water there.

It was a kind of weakening of intent. Perhaps the odiousness of colour and the deterioration of flesh and blood had driven him to seek another religion which had petrified itself in solitude. Simple, pure extinction was suggested even by the shapes of the clouds beyond. Here was the illusion of shade, perhaps a reward from a former life, in the beautiful, luxuriant foliage. In this world of absolute morning quiet, still except for the lazy vibration of the car engine, the smooth vista of the plains slowly unfolded beyond the window and slowly but surely carried Honda's heart home.

After a time the car reached the edge of a ravine cutting sharply into the flat plain. This was the first indication of Ajanta. They drove along the meandering road descending toward the bed of the Wagora which glistened at the bottom of the gorge like the sharp blade of a knife.

The teahouse where Honda stopped to rest was aswarm with flies. He looked out of the window immediately before him across the square toward the entrance to the caves. Going in now, giving in to his impatience, he felt, might infringe on the tranquillity he was seeking. He bought a postcard, and taking his fountain pen in a clammy hand, he scrutinized for some time the picture of the caves crudely printed on the front.

Again there was a suggestion of noise here as in Benares. Black people in white clothes with suspicious eyes were standing around, and skinny children were shouting in the square, selling souvenir necklaces. The space was filled with bright yellow sunlight that reached to every cranny. On a table in the dark room lay three small dried-up oranges with flies crawling over them. The heavy, acrid odour of fried food wafted from the kitchen. He addressed the postcard to his wife Rié, to whom he had not written for some time. Then he wrote:

I'm here to see the cave temples at Ajanta. The tour's about to start. I can't drink the orange drink in front of me, because I see the edge of the glass is all dotted with fly spots. But don't worry, I'm being very careful about my health. India's really astonishing. You're taking care of your kidneys, I hope. Love to Mother.

Could this be thought of as affectionate? He always wrote the same. The nostalgia and affection that had begun to gather like a haze in his heart had suddenly made him resolve to write. But when he tried to put his feelings into words, his sentences invariably turned out ordinary and dry.

Rié would always welcome his return with the same quiet smile she had displayed at his departure, no matter how many years he might leave her alone in Japan. Though her hair might bear a few more strands of white since he had left, the face which had seen him off and the one which would greet his return would coincide as perfectly as the two identical crests on the sleeves of a formal kimono.

A touch of kidney trouble had made her profile somewhat vague, like a moon in daytime; and this countenance, now that he called it to mind, seemed more suitable for being visualized in memory than seen in reality. Of course, no one could dislike such a woman. In his heart Honda felt deep relief as he wrote the postcard, and he offered thanks to an unnameable something. It was a relief altogether different from the assurance of being loved.

Having written the card, Honda placed it in the pocket of the jacket which he had taken off and stood up. He would mail it at the hotel. As he set out across the sunny square, the guide sidled up like an assassin.

The twenty-seven stone caves had been excavated at midpoint in the cliffs overlooking the Wagora, where there were several layers of rocky outcrops. Starting from the river, the slope gradually steepened, going from rocks to grass; then it became a precipitous cliff covered with coppice. A white stone walkway connected the entrances to the caves.

The first cave was a *chaitya*, or 'chapel'. There were the ruins of four chapels and twenty-three *vihara*, or 'monks' dwellings'; the first cave was one of the four.

Just as he had expected, the air inside had the musty coolness of dawn. A large image of the Buddha in a central recess was clearly visible; the smooth figure was seated in the lotus posture in the reflection from the entrance from which a patch of light the size of a doormat penetrated. There was not enough radiance to make out the frescoes on the ceiling and the surrounding walls. The ray of the guide's flashlight unsteadily flitted here and there like a bat of light hovering about the cave. Again and again, depictions of an unexpected motley of worldly desires flashed into view.

Half-naked women with golden crowns on their heads and colourful sarongs wrapped around their hips appeared in various postures in the spot of the flashlight. Most of them held the stalk of a lotus flower in their hands. Their faces were all alike, like those of sisters. The extremely long, slanting eyes were half open and new-moons of eyebrows curved above them. The coolness of their intelligent, straight noses was softened by slightly flaring nostrils. The lower lip was voluptuous, while the mouth was pinched as though tied at both ends. Everything reminded Honda of what the face of Princess Moonlight in Bangkok would be when she grew up. The difference between these women in the frescoes and the little Princess lay clearly in their mature bodies. Their breasts were cloves of ripe pomegranate ready to burst, with necklaces of fragile gold, silver, and precious stones hanging loosely over them like ivy clinging to fruit. Some were half reclining, with their back turned, showing the voluptuous curve of their hips; some revealed an overflowing sensual abdomen barely covered by scant sarongs. Some women were dancing and others were on the verge of death. And as the flashlight shifted from one spot to another, to the incessant prattle of the guide spouting his usual lines, the women again disappeared one by one into the darkness.

As Honda emerged from the first cave, the tropical sunlight, like a violently struck gong, at once changed the murals into illusions. Musing in the daylight, one felt as if one had visited the caves in some long-forgotten memory. The only thing that offered reality was the Wagora gleaming below and the barren look of the rocks.

As usual, Honda was annoyed with the guide's indifferent prattle. Thus, letting the others pass on, he remained for some time alone in the deserted ruins of a *vihara* which the guide had coldly passed by and which the other sightseers ignored completely.

The absence of any object enabled him to give free rein to his rich imagination. The *vihara* served this purpose well. There was no statue, no fresco, only thick, black columns standing at either side of the cave. A pulpit was situated in the centre of a particularly dark recess inside, while a pair of large stone tables facing each other ran from the entrance to the back. Light streamed in and it seemed as if the monks had just risen to take the fresh air outdoors, leaving the stone tables which they used both for studying and eating.

The absence of colour relaxed Honda's mind, although by searching carefully he found a faint red spot of faded paint in a small depression on the stone table.

Had there been someone here who had just left?

Who could it have been?

Standing alone in the cool of the cave, Honda felt as though the darkness around him suddenly began to whisper. The emptiness of the undecorated, colourless cave awakened in him a feeling of some miraculous existence, probably for the first time since he had come to India. Nothing was more vividly real to his skin – clear proof of a fresh existence – than the fact that this existence had declined, perished, and was extinct. No, existence had already begun taking shape among the odour of the mildew that covered every stone in the cave.

He experienced an animal-like emotion. It was the mixture of joy and anxiety which he always felt when something was about to take shape in his mind; it was the excitement of a fox, who, having caught the distant scent of prey, slowly approaches his victim. He was not sure what it was, but the hand of his distant memory had already grasped it firmly in the back of his mind. Honda's heart was turbulent with expectation.

He came out of the *vihara* and began walking in the outside light toward the fifth cave. The path described a wide curve and a new vista lay before him. The walkway before the caves passed inside some columns inserted in the rocks. The columns were wet, as they were located behind two waterfalls. Honda knew that the fifth cave was close by, and he stopped to look across the valley at the cascades.

One of the two waterfalls was interrupted as it ran over the surface of the rock, while the other streamed down in an unbroken silver cord. Both were narrow and precipitous. The sound of the cascades falling down the yellowish green rock cliff of the Wagora resounded clearly on the surrounding cliffs. Except for the dark hollows of the cave entrances, everything behind and to either side of the falls was bright: the light green clumps of mimosa, the red flowers bordering the water, the brilliant light playing on the falls, and the rainbow formed in the mist. Several yellow butterflies fluttered up and down, as though clinging to the straight line of Honda's gaze as he watched the water.

Honda looked to the top of the falls and was surprised at the amazing height. They were so lofty that he felt as if he were in a world belonging to another dimension. The green of the cliff to either side of the falls was dark with moss and fern, but at the top it was a pure light green. There were some bare rocks too; the softness and brightness of the green foliage was not of this world. A black kid was grazing there; and above, in the absolute blue of the sky, an abundance of luminous clouds rose in magnificent disorder.

There was sound, but complete soundlessness dominated. No sooner was Honda overwhelmed by the silence than the noise of the waterfalls came wildly to his ears. He was enchanted by the alternate stillness and the sound of water.

He was impatient to get to the fifth cave where the water splashed, but a strange feeling of awe held him back. It was almost certain that nothing was waiting there. Yet Kiyoaki's feverish and delirious words fell like drops of water in his mind.

'I'll see you again. I know it . . . beneath the falls.'

Since then, he had believed that Kiyoaki had been referring to the Sanko falls on Mount Miwa. Probably so. But it occurred to Honda that the ultimate waterfall he had meant must be these cascades at Ajanta.

10

The S.S. *Southern Seas*, of Itsui Shipping Ltd, on which Honda left India, was a six-cabin freighter. The rainy season was over, and the ship headed across the Gulf of Siam, which lay in the cool north-east monsoon breeze. After passing by Paknam at the mouth of the Menam, the ship made its way upstream to Bangkok, watching for propitious tides. The sky without rain this November twenty-third was a ceramic blue.

Honda was relieved to be returning to the familiar city from a land of such pestilence. His mind was at rest, but he carried a heavy load of terrifying impressions from his journey, and he remained leaning against the railing of the upper deck throughout the voyage, the cargo groaning deep in the hold of his heart.

They passed a destroyer of the Thai Navy, but there was no sign of human life along the quiet bank covered with coconut, mangrove, and reeds. Finally, when the ship began its approach, with Bangkok to the right and Thon Buri to the left, tall stilted houses with palm-thatched roofs could be seen on the Thon Buri side, and the dark skins of orchard workers were visible under the sparkling leaves, cultivating bananas, pineapple, mangosteen, and other fruits.

Betel nut trees, which the climbing fish preferred, thrived in one corner of the orchard. On seeing them, Honda remembered the old lady-in-waiting who chewed on betel wrapped in *kimma* leaves that tinted her mouth all red. The modernist Phiboon had already forbidden its use. The old ladies had apparently dispelled the gloom of the regulation by chewing the nuts away from the capital at Bang Pa In.

Sculled boats carrying water became more numerous, and at length the masts of commercial and naval ships formed a forest in the distance. It was Khlong Toei, the port of Bangkok.

The setting sun added a strange brilliance to the muddy waters, making them appear a smouldering rose colour; it added further iridescence to the patches of oil, reminding Honda of the smooth texture of the lepers' skin he had so frequently seen in India.

As the ship drew up to the pier, Honda recognized the obese branch manager of Itsui Products, two or three clerks, the director of the Japan Club, and behind them, Hishikawa, who looked as though he were hiding among the people waving their hats in welcome. Immediately he felt depressed.

As soon as Honda came ashore, Hishikawa grabbed the briefcase from his side before the Itsui clerks had the chance. He acted with unprecedented obsequiousness and diligence.

'Welcome back, Mr Honda. I'm relieved to see you looking so well. The trip to India must have been very hard on you.'

This seemed to be a very impolite greeting to the branch manager, so Honda ignored the comment and thanked the manager.

'I was amazed at the thoroughness of your arrangements for me every place during the trip. Thanks to you, I travelled like a king.'

'Now you know well enough that Itsui's not going to be stopped by anything like Britain and America freezing our credits.'

In the car on the way to the Oriental Hotel, Hishikawa was quiet, holding the briefcase in the seat next to the driver, while the manager talked about the worsening public feeling in Bangkok during Honda's absence. He advised Honda to be careful, for the populace, taken in by English and American propaganda, had grown extremely antagonistic toward the Japanese. Honda saw from the car window crowds of poor he had not habitually seen before swarming in the streets.

'With the rumours of impending invasion by the Japanese Army and the deterioration of local order, a staggering number of refugees have come into Bangkok from the French Indochina border.'

But the English-style businesslike curtness of the hotel management had not changed in the slightest. After getting himself settled in his room and taking a cold bath, Honda felt better.

The manager's party was waiting in the lobby facing the garden to join Honda for dinner, sitting under the large, slowly rotating fan against which beetles sometimes collided noisily.

On the way down from his room, Honda reflectively observed the arrogant behaviour of some so-called Japanese gentlemen in South-east Asia, a group to which he too belonged, he reminded himself. They were quite devoid of any redeeming feature.

Why? he wondered. It would be more appropriate to say that in that instant Honda really recognized for the first time their ugliness ... and his own. It was hard to believe that they were the same Japanese as those beautiful youths, Kiyoaki and Isao.

With their excellent English linen suits, white shirts, and neckties, their attire was above reproach. And yet each was fanning himself with inelegant haste, the Japanese cord with its single black bead attached to the fan hanging from their hands. Their gold teeth flashed when they smiled and they all wore glasses. The head man was talking with false modesty about some episode connected with his work, and his inferiors were listening to the old story they had heard so many times, nodding and repeating their perpetual comments: 'That's what I call real courage ... real pluck.' They gossiped about vagrant women, the possibility of war, and then, in whispers, about the high-handedness of the military. Everything had the tone of the listless, repetitive sutra chanting of the tropics, and yet was curiously imbued with simulated vivacity. Despite the listlessness they constantly experienced within, despite an itching or the trickling of sweat, they held themselves stiffly erect, occasionally recalling in some corner of their consciousness the pleasures of the night before with its concomitant fear of some disease with sores like red swamp lilies. Perhaps it had been because of his fatigue from the trip, but Honda had not recognized himself as being one of them when, minutes before, he had looked into the mirror in his room. He had seen only the reflection of a forty-six-year-old man, who had once been engaged in matters of righteousness, who had then made a living on the back streets of justice, the face of a man who had lived too long.

'My ugliness is special,' he thought, clinging to the confidence which he quickly retrieved, as he descended the red-carpeted steps between the elevator and the lobby. 'At any rate, I'm a recidivist of justice; I'm not like those tradesmen.'

*

That night, after a few cups of wine had been downed at a Cantonese restaurant, in front of Hishikawa, the manager said in a loud voice to Honda: 'Hishikawa here is terribly worried about having caused you so much trouble and hurt your feelings. He seems overly sensitive about it, and after you left he told me every day how wrong he had been, how he had been at fault. He's almost neurotic about it. I know he has his weaknesses, but I assigned him to you because he's very useful. I feel responsible for causing you any unpleasantness. You will be leaving in only four or five days – we've booked a seat in an Army plane – and Hishikawa has done a lot of soul-searching. He says he will do his best to please. I'm going to ask you, Mr Honda, to be generous enough to forgive him and accept his services for the rest of your stay.'

Hishikawa immediately spoke up from the other side of the table, as though beseeching Honda: 'Sir, please take me to task as much as you will. I was wrong.' He bowed his head almost to the table.

The situation was extremely depressing for Honda.

The manager's words could be interpreted that he still believed he had chosen a good guide for Honda; but that, judging from Hishikawa's attitude, Honda must have been extremely hard to please, that if he changed guides, Hishikawa would lose face. Therefore, there was nothing to do but to let Hishikawa swallow the humiliation and continue to work for the rest of the time until his departure. To achieve this, it was best to pretend that everything had been Hishikawa's fault. Thus, Honda would not be disgraced.

Honda felt a momentary surge of anger, but in the next instant he realized that it would not be to his advantage to reject the manager's suggestion. Hishikawa could not himself have confessed actual instances of his being at fault. Furthermore, Hishikawa was congenitally incapable of realizing why he was disliked. However, he must have sensed that he was and, having thought it over in his own limited way, must have decided to do something to ease his lot. He must have got the manager on his side for him to say such insensitive things.

Honda could forgive the obese manager's lack of sensitivity, but he could not pardon Hishikawa's impudent, hypersensitive play-acting which he had quickly thought up on sensing Honda's antipathy.

Suddenly he wanted to go back home the very next day. But a change of schedule at this point would obviously be interpreted as a childish plan for revenge because of his dislike for Hishikawa, and he realized he had no other choice. By showing generosity in the beginning, he was forced to be even more generous now.

Well, the only thing he could do was to treat Hishikawa like a machine. He protested smilingly that the manager's apology was quite unnecessary and that for the next few days he would have to depend totally on Hishikawa to help him purchase gifts, go book-hunting, and make arrangements for visiting the Rosette Palace to say goodbye. At least he felt satisfaction with his excellent deception in skilfully concealing his true emotions from the manager.

Hishikawa's attitude did change.

First he took Honda to a bookstore where, as at a poorly stocked vegetable vendor's, crudely printed paperbacks in English or Thai were sparsely arranged on a display board. Before, Hishikawa would have contemptuously discussed the level of Thai culture, but he let Honda make his choice without a word.

He could not find any books on Thai Theravada Buddhism, much less any in English concerning samsara and reincarnation. But he was attracted by a thin pamphlet of poetry, apparently a private publication printed on poor-quality paper, its white cover browned by the sun and its corners curled by handling. He read the English preface and realized that it was a collection of poems written shortly after the bloodless revolution of June, 1932, by a young man who seemed to have participated in it. The poet expressed the disillusionment that followed the revolution for which he had been so ready to give his life. By coincidence the collection was published the year after Isao's death. As Honda turned the pages, he saw in the faded print that the poet's English was immature.

Who would have known?
From the sacrifice of youth dedicated to the future
Only the vermin of corruption come forth.
Who would have known?
In debris-strewn fields that once promised rebirth
Only plants of venom and thorn are burgeoning.
The vermin will soon stretch their golden wings,
And the wind passing over the grasses will spread
  pestilence.
In my heart the love I bear my land
Is redder than mimosa flowers in the rain;
Suddenly after the storm, on eaves, pillars, balustrades
The white mildew of despotism reaches out.
Yesterday's wisdom is beclouded in luxurious baths
  of profit,
And yesterday's activist is ensconced in a
  palanquin of embroidered brocade.
There would be nothing better
In the regions of Kabin and Patani,
Where the flowering pear and rosewood and the
  monifan's luxuriant foliage,
The creeping ivy and the thorny rose and the pinks
  mark the byways;
Where the sun and the rain fall upon deep jungles;
Where rhinoceros, tapirs, and buffaloes dwell;
If, at times, a herd of elephants in quest of water
Would trample my bones underfoot.
There would be nothing better than
To rip with my own hands the red crescent of my throat
Shining in the dewy underbrush.
Who would know?
Who would know?
I sing my song of sorrow.

Honda was deeply moved by this political poem of despair and thought that he could find nothing better with which to comfort Isao's spirit. Was it not true? Isao had died without bringing about the revolution he had dreamed of for so long, but there was no doubt that he would have experienced even greater disillusionment if one had taken place. Death in success, death in failure – death was the basis of Isao's acts. But the unfortunate human lot is that one cannot take oneself out of time and dispassionately compare two deaths at two different points for the purpose of choosing one or the other. One cannot choose by giving equal priority to a death after experiencing disillusionment in the aftermath of revolution and to one before experiencing it. If one died before experiencing disillusionment, dying afterward would be impossible; and conversely, if one died after experiencing disillusionment, dying before would be out of the question. Therefore, all that one could do was to project oneself into the two deaths in the future and select the one one's intuition commanded. Isao had chosen death before disillusionment could set in. His prophetic choice showed the unclouded youthful wisdom of one who had never wielded the slightest political power.

But the feeling of disillusion and despair – as if one had seen the other side of the moon – which overtakes the sucessful revolutionary makes death merely an escape from a wilderness worse than death itself. Therefore, however sincere the poet's death was, it must surely be regarded as a pathological suicide that took place in the weary afternoon of revolution.

For this reason Honda wanted to dedicate this political poem to Isao. At least Isao had died dreaming of the sun, but the morning in this poem had opened a festering wound under a cracked orb. However, an endless thread stretched between Isao's brave death and the despair of this political poem, both by chance occurring during the same period. The very best, the very worst, the most beautiful and the most ugly illusions about the future for which people sacrificed their lives were probably to be found in the same place and, what was even more frightening, were probably the same thing. What Isao had dreamed of and had been willing to give his life for had to be the despair expressed in this poem, for the shrewder his foresight, the purer his death.

Honda knew full well that he tended to see things in this way because India had cast its spell on him. India imposed on his thinking a many-layered structure, like lotus petals, and no longer let him think in a direct and simple way. The time he willingly put aside his judgeship in order to help Isao – although he was strongly motivated by remorse for not having been able to help Kiyoaki – was probably the first and last occasion in his life that he had been so altruistic and dedicated. Yet despite his efforts, he had not been able to prevent Isao's futile death, and after that nothing remained but for him to reverse his ideas on reincarnation and see his future outside samsara. And it was India, terrifying India, that had dropped the final hint to Honda, who found it increasingly difficult to entertain 'human' emotions.

Whether in success or in failure, sooner or later time must lead to disillusionment; and if foresight of this disillusionment remains only that, it is mere pessimism. The important thing is to act on this foresight even by dying. Isao had achieved that magnificently. Only by action can one see through the glass walls erected at various points in time – glass walls insurmountable by human effort, but which can be seen through equally from both sides. In eager desire, in aspiration, in dreams, in ideals, the past and future become equal in value and in quality: they are co-ordinate.

Whether or not Isao had glimpsed such a world at the moment of his death was a question Honda could not put off now that he was growing older, if he would discover what he should have to face at the moment of his own death. At least it was certain that at that instant the existing Isao and the Isao to be had looked directly into each other's eyes. By his foresight the existing Isao had grasped the splendour of the unseen on the other side and his eyes there saw through to this side with craving. It was certain that the existing Isao had foreseen the glory of the future Isao, and the eyes of the Isao to come had looked back yearningly at the innocent being that had not yet experienced this glory. By passing through two unrelivable existences the two Isaos were connected through the glass wall. Isao and the political poet suggested the eternal link between the poet who, having passed through life, yearned for death, and the youth who, rejecting the passing, died. If that were true, what had become of that which they had so ardently desired, each in his own way? Honda's theory, unchanged since his youth, was that history could not be advanced by human volition, but that the intrinsic nature of human will was to become involved in history.

How, he wondered, could he dedicate these poems, a most suitable gift, to Isao's soul?

Would it be best to take the book back to Japan and offer it at his grave? No, Honda knew all too well that Isao's tomb was empty.

Surely the best way would be to dedicate it to the little Princess who openly claimed herself to be Isao's reincarnation. She would be the fastest and most dependable messenger. Honda now became the fleet-footed courier easily passing through the wall of time.

But no matter how intelligent, could a girl of seven understand the despair of such poems? Besides, as Isao's reincarnation had taken such an obvious form this time, Honda had experienced a twinge of suspicion. And then, he had not been able to see the three little moles on the Princess's lovely, dusky body even in the bright sunlight.

Having decided to take as gifts an Indian sari of excellent quality and the book of poems, Honda asked Hishikawa to contact the Rosette Palace. He was informed that the Princess would grant an audience in the Hall of Queens at the Chakri Palace, which she would have opened especially for him, as it had been closed for some time because of the King's absence.

However, one strict condition was imposed by the ladies-in-waiting. During his trip to India, the Princess had been anxiously waiting for Honda's return to Thailand, insisting that she was going to accompany him to Japan when he returned. She had complained that her attendants had done nothing in preparation for the trip, and they had soothed her by pretending to make arrangements. Therefore, they desired that at the time of the audience Honda make no mention of his departure, much less of the date, and that he pretend that he was staying on in Thailand.

11

The next day, the one before Honda was to leave for Japan, was beautifully clear, but the wind had fallen and it was extremely hot.

Honda and Hishikawa passed by the royal guard house about nine forty for their ten o'clock audience, suffering in necktie and jacket.

The palace, designed by an Italian architect, had been built in 1882 under King Chulalongkorn and was in style a magnificent mixture of neo-Baroque and Siamese.

It featured an amazingly complex, almost hallucinating façade set against the blue tropical sky. No matter how European the style, the brilliant and overly ornate front possessed the dazzling and intoxicating quality characteristic of tropical Asian architecture. The marble staircases which ascended gracefully to the left and right were guarded at their base by bronze elephants. The main entrance was in the style of the Pantheon in Rome, and the imposing pediment above the arches contained a colourful portrait of King Chulalongkorn. Up to this point, it was purely European neo-Baroque with marble and bas-reliefs and gold. But as one's gaze mounted to the storey above, one saw a pavilion in the Siamese style standing in the centre of a gallery of pink marble Corinthian pillars. The ceiling was checkered, alternately maroon and gold on a white base, and the whole structure jutted out impressively like a ship's turret. It bore the candelabrum-like coat of arms of the Chakri dynasty. The upper storeys to the very peak of the golden spire rose in pyramids of intricate, authentic Siamese intercalary roofs in red and gold, the ornate end-tiles of the ridges pointing to the blue sky like the raised shoulders of dancers. It seemed as if the whole point of the Chakri Palace was to have the solid, rationally cold European base crushed by the royal dreams of the tropics – superfluously complex, unnecessarily colourful ... maddening. It was as though a beaked nightmare with sharp talons and bristling gold and red wings were bent over the torso of a recumbent king, dignified, cold, white.

'Is this supposed to be beautiful?' said Hishikawa, stopping and wiping the perspiration from his upturned face.

'Whether it's beautiful or not, what's that to us? We've been invited only to see the Princess.'

Honda's unexpected curtness instantly intimidated Hishikawa, who looked at him with fear in his eyes; nothing further was said. Honda regretted that he had not used this effective method at the very beginning of his visit to Bangkok.

The officer of the guards who served as guide intimated that it had been considerable trouble for them to open the long-closed palace just to humour the whimsical Princess. Honda, at a wink from Hishikawa, quickly slipped a suitable amount of money into the officer's pocket.

Once the gigantic doors were open, a dark hall was revealed, on the black, white, and grey mottled mosaic floor of which some twenty rococo chairs edged in mahogany had been arranged. A familiar-looking lady-in-waiting took over from the officer and guided the two guests to a large door on the right. Beyond it was a well-lit room with a high ceiling, a purely European palace hall complete with chandeliers, Italian marble tables inlaid with floral patterns, and red and gold Louis Quinze chairs placed around them.

On the walls hung life-sized portraits of the four royal consorts of King Chulalongkorn and the Queen Mother. Hishikawa explained that three of the consorts were sisters. All the portraits had been painted in Victorian style by some Western painter. Their faces revealed the painter's artistic integrity, his fearful courage, his shameless lies, his malice, his sincerity, and his flattery – all coexisted like waves and sand at the water's edge in the margin of realism. The somewhat melancholy grace suitable to royalty matched the heavy sensuality of the subjects' dark skin, and the tropical feeling of the clothes and the background inadvertently blurred the seemingly realistic surface picture with an illusory quality.

The Queen Mother, Thep Sirin, was a wizened aristocrat, and her face showed the most dark and savage dignity of all. Honda walked slowly, carefully examining each painting as he passed by; he learned from Hishikawa that the first consort, Queen Prephaiphim, was the youngest of three sisters. Next came Queen Sawaeng Watana, and then the eldest sister, Queen Sunantha. It was unquestionable to anyone that the eldest was the most beautiful.

Queen Sunantha's portrait hung in one corner of the room, half concealed in the shadows. She was standing by a window, one hand resting on a table. Outside one could see the hazy blue sky filled with evening clouds and orange branches heavy with fruit.

On the table stood a rose-bud vase in cloisonné containing a small lotus flower, a gold ewer, and wine cups. The queen's beautiful bare feet were visible below her gold *panun*, and from one shoulder of her embroidered pink jacket hung a wide cordon. A large medal glistened at her breast, and she held an ivory fan. The tassel of the fan and the carpet both reflected the scarlet of the evening glow.

Honda was struck by her most charming small face. Of the five portraits it somehow bore a marked resemblance to that of Princess Moonlight. There were the same ripe, plump lips, the somewhat stern eyes, and the short-cropped hair. The resemblance faded after he had gazed at the portrait for a while. But after a time the impression like evening dusk crept back from some corner of the room, and again he was convinced of the likeness – the small, dark, quick fingers holding the fan, the curved hand resting on the table, and finally the eyes and lips that were the exact duplicate of those of the Princess. But just as the likeness became most apparent, like the sand of an hour-glass, it would once more begin irresistibly to slip away.

At that instant an inside door opened and the three old ladies-in-waiting emerged escorting the Princess. Honda and Hishikawa stood where they were and bowed deeply.

The afternoon at the Bang Pa In Palace seemed to have melted the ladies' hearts, for no one stopped the Princess as she ran toward Honda with a cry of joy. Like a dove picking up scattered peas, Hishikawa busily translated the torrent of words that spurted forth.

'It was a long trip . . . I was lonely. Why didn't you write me more often? Which country has more elephants, Thailand or India? I don't want to go to India, I want to go back to Japan.'

Then the Princess took Honda's hand and led him to a spot in front of the portrait of Queen Sunantha.

'This is my grandmother,' she said proudly.

'Her Serene Highness has invited Mr Honda to the Chakri Palace because she specifically wanted to show him this beautiful portrait,' offered the first lady-in-waiting.

'I inherited only my body from Queen Sunantha. My heart came from Japan, so really I should leave my body here and only my heart should go back. But to do that I should have to die. So I'll just have to take my body along, like a child with her favourite doll. Do you understand, Mr Honda? The pretty me you see is really only the doll I carry with me.'

Judging from the childish manner of her speech, she must have spoken less sophisticatedly than Hishikawa had translated, but as she spoke, the clarity in her serious eyes moved Honda's heart even before he understood what she was saying.

'There's another doll.' The Princess as usual paid no attention to what the adults were thinking; and now she left Honda's side and moved swiftly to the centre of the hall, where the sunlight took the shape of the grilled casement windows. She solemnly traced the outline of the creeping vines; then the flowers in the complex floral pattern – there were gaps in the inlay – on the table to which her chest scarcely reached. 'There's another doll,' she continued as if singing, 'which looks just like me in Lausanne. But she's my elder sister and she's not a doll really. Her body's Thai and so's her heart. She's different from me; I'm really Japanese.'

She accepted the sari and the poetry collection with delight, but she merely leafed through a few pages of the book and looked no further. One of the attendants explained apologetically that the Princess could not yet read English. Honda's test had not worked.

Entreated by the Princess, Honda talked for a while of his trip to India in the stiff formality of the hall. He noted tears and sadness in the eyes of the Princess as she listened rapturously to him, and he was conscience-stricken at the thought of concealing the news of his departure the next day.

He wondered when he would be able to see the Princess again. Surely she would mature into a very beautiful woman, but he would probably never have the opportunity of seeing her. This might be his last chance. Soon the mystery of reincarnation, like the shadow of a butterfly crossing a tropical garden of an afternoon, might vanish from her memory. Perhaps the soul of Isao, regretful of dying without a word of farewell to Honda, had borrowed the lips of the mad little Princess to deliver an apology. It was easier for Honda to leave Bangkok believing this.

Gradually the Princess's eyes became more moist as she listened to Honda's stories; she must have had some premonition of his departure. He had carefully chosen childish, entertaining episodes to relate, but the sorrow in her eyes kept deepening.

Honda spoke one sentence at a time which Hishikawa would then translate with gesticulations. Suddenly the Princess's eyes opened in astonishment. The ladies glared angrily at Honda who had no idea what had happened.

The Princess suddenly uttered a piercing cry and clung to Honda. The attendant rose and attempted to tear her away, but the child put her cheek to his legs and sobbed loudly.

The drama of the other day was re-enacted. At length the ladies succeeded in separating the two and signalled Honda to leave the room. As Hishikawa was translating the sign, Honda was again on the verge of being caught by the sobbing Princess. He ran among the tables and chairs with the little girl in pursuit, and the ladies scrambling after her from three sides. Louis Quinze chairs crashed to the floor, and the palace hall was transformed into a terrain for blind-man's buff.

Finally Honda freed himself, passed quickly through the anteroom, and ran down the marble staircase of the central entrance. There he hesitated to make his final departure, as he listened to the sharp cries of the little girl echoing from the high ceiling of the palace. 'The ladies are telling us to go quickly,' said Hishikawa, urging him on. 'They'll take care of her somehow. Let's go!'

Honda dashed through the spacious front garden, soaked in perspiration.

'I'm sorry. You must have been surprised,' said Hishikawa to the still panting Honda when the car had started to move.

'No. It happens every time,' he replied, trying to freshen up by wiping away the perspiration with a large white handkerchief.

'You told the Princess that you wanted to fly back from India but that you couldn't get a seat on an Army plane.'

'I did indeed.'

'I made a bad translation there,' Hishikawa explained coolly, obviously feeling no guilt. 'I didn't think and told her the truth. I said that you were going back to Japan, but as you were taking an Army plane you couldn't get a seat for her and so couldn't take her with you. That's why she made such a fuss. She begged you either not to go or to take her with you. The ladies looked so angry because you broke your promise. It was all my fault. I don't know how to apologize.'

12

Regular air transportation between Japan and Thailand had commenced the year before, in 1940. But after Japan had begun to send observers into French Indochina in order to control the supply routes to Chiang Kai-shek, the Indochinese no longer resisted, and a new southern air route was opened via Saigon, this in addition to the already existing Taipei–Hanoi–Bangkok run.

It was a civilian line administered by Greater Japan Air Lines. But Itsui Products considered military planes more sophisticated in handling important guests. The planes did not provide the most comfortable transportation, but they were speedy and powered by an excellent engine. Furthermore, a military plane gave the impression of an important official tour to friends of the traveller who might come to the airport to meet him or to see him off, and it would simultaneously demonstrate the extent of Itsui's influence with the military.

Honda was sorry to leave the tropics. When the golden pagodas had faded away in their distant jungle setting, his chancing on indications of reincarnation there began to seem like a fairy tale or a dream. Because of the Princess's extreme youth, it could all be no more than a children's song, in spite of the many proofs he had had. He did not know the life story or the cause-and-effect element in the Princess's dramatic beginning nor how she would end, as he had in the case of Kiyoaki and Isao. He had merely witnessed episodes in the life of the little girl as though he were watching the outlandish floral float of some festival passing before a traveller's curious eyes.

How strange it was that even a miracle required the commonplace! As the plane approached Japan, Honda realized with relief that he was returning to the familiar daily routine and had escaped the miracle of Benares. Finally, he had lost not only the process of reason, but even measure for his feelings. He felt no particular sorrow in leaving the Princess, and he felt neither annoyance nor any other emotion toward the officers on the plane who were heatedly discussing the approaching war.

He was naturally pleased to see his wife at the airport. Just as he expected, he felt that the Honda who had left Japan and the one who had come back had immediately fused into the same unchanged person. His wife's sleepy face, somewhat swollen and white, had acted as a catalyst to effect this fusing. The time interval between his two phases disappeared, and the deep raw wound inflicted by the Indian trip seemed to vanish without a trace.

His wife stood at the rear of the crowd of friends who had come to meet him. She removed the dull-hued shawl from her shoulders.

'Welcome home.'

She bowed to him, thrusting under his nose her familiar bangs, which she always rearranged herself after each permanent done at a beauty parlour whose styling she did not like. Her hair gave off the faint scorched odour of some chemical that had been used.

'Mother is well, but the nights have turned chilly and I didn't want her to catch cold. She's impatiently waiting at home.'

Honda experienced a surge of tenderness when Rié talked about her mother-in-law without being asked, yet there was no touch of obligation in her tone. Life was again exactly as it should be.

'I want you to go to a department store as soon as possible, maybe tomorrow. and get a doll,' said Honda on the way home in the car.

'All right.'

'I promised the little princess I met in Thailand to send her a Japanese doll.'

'An ordinary one with a little girl's haircut?'

'That's right. I don't think I'd send a very big one . . . one about so,' he said, holding his hands in front of his chest and abdomen to indicate the size. Momentarily he thought of sending a boy doll to stand for the transmigration of a boy's soul, but he thought it might seem strange, and decided against it.

His mother was there to greet him in the vestibule of the house in Hongo, her old hunched shoulders clad in a dark silk striped kimono. She had dyed her bobbed hair a pitch black and the thin gold earpieces of her glasses passed over it. Honda thought he would suggest sometime that she should not wear her glasses in that way, but whenever it occurred to him the time never seemed right.

He walked along the matted corridor to the inner room of his familiar spacious house, now dark and cold, accompanied by his mother and wife. He realized that his manner of walking resembled that of his deceased father when the latter had used to return home.

'I'm so relieved you could get back before war broke out. I was worried.' His mother, once a zealous member of the Women's Patriotic League, panted as she walked through the corridor swept by chilly night draughts. The old woman feared war.

After two or three days of rest, Honda resumed the trip to his office in the Marunouchi Building, and his busy but peaceful days recommenced. The Japanese winter rapidly awakened his reason that resembled a seasonal winter bird – he naturally had not seen that in South-east Asia – some crane that had again migrated to the frozen bay of his heart as it returned to Japan.

On the morning of December eighth, his wife came into the bedroom to awaken him. 'I'm sorry to wake you earlier than usual,' she said quietly.

'What is it?'

Thinking that his mother's health might have taken a turn for the worse, he scrambled to his feet.

'We're at war with the United States. Just now, on the radio . . .' Rié seemed still apologetic for having awakened him so early.

That morning, excited over the news of the attack on Pearl Harbor, no one in the office could settle down to work. Honda was amazed at the ceaseless and irrepressible laughter of the young office girls and wondered if women knew no other way of expressing patriotic exultation except through physical joy.

Lunchtime came. The staff discussed going to the Imperial Palace Square together. After sending them off, Honda locked the office and set out alone for an afternoon stroll. His steps led him of their own accord toward the square in front of the palace.

Everyone in the Marunouchi area seemed to have had the same idea, and the wide boulevard was jammed with pedestrians.

He was forty-six, Honda mused. Nothing of youth, power, or pure passion remained in either his physical or spiritual being. He would have to prepare for death, perhaps in another ten years. More than likely he would not die in the war. He had had no military training; and even if he had, there was no danger of being called to the battlefield.

All he had to do was to stay behind and applaud the patriotic acts of the young. So they had gone to bomb Hawaii! It was a glamorous action from which his age had absolutely excluded him.

But was it only age? No. He was basically unsuited for any physical action.

Like everyone else, he had lived by approaching death step by step, but he did not know any other way. He had never run. Once he had tried to save a man's life, but he had never been placed in any position where the efforts of another had been required to save him. He lacked the requisite quality for being saved. He had never given people the feeling of impending crisis where they would feel compelled to extend their hand in help, where they would be forced to try to rescue that certain glorious something that was in danger. The quality was charisma, and regrettably Honda was totally self-reliant and completely devoid of that.

It would be an exaggeration to say that he was jealous of the excitement about the attack on Pearl Harbor. He had simply become the captive of the egoistic and melancholy conviction that henceforth his life would definitely end and he would never achieve greatness. But had he ever really desired that in life?

On the other hand all glamorous and heroic acts faded away against the hallucination of Benares. Was it perhaps because the mystery of transmigration had warped his mind, robbed him of courage, made him recognize the futility of all brave actions, and in the end taught him to utilize all his knowledge of philosophy merely for the sake of self-love? Like a man skirting around the lighting of firecrackers, Honda felt that his mind shrank violently from the sight of such mass paroxysms.

The little flags waving and the shouts of *banzai* sounding in front of the Imperial Palace could be seen and heard from a considerable distance. Honda maintained a good stretch of the pebbled square between himself and the demonstrators; from a distance he noted the colour of the dead grass covering the banks of the moat around the palace and the wintry hue of the pines. Two girls in dark blue office smocks passed by laughing, holding hands, running toward the bridge at the entrance to the palace, their white teeth flashing and glistening moistly in the winter sun.

The beautiful, bow-shaped winter lips of the women created a momentary crevice, attractive and warm, in the clear air as they passed by. The heroes in the bombers must dream at times of just such lips. Young men were always like that, seeking the most rigorous and yet attracted to the most tender. Could the tenderest thing they seek be death? Honda himself had once been a young man of promise, but not one attracted to death.

Suddenly the expanse of pebbled space beneath the winter sun became in Honda's eyes a vast and barren field. The image in the photograph labelled 'Memorial Service for the War Dead, Vicinity of the Tokuri Temple', shown him by Kiyoaki thirty long years ago, returned vividly to his mind. It was Kiyoaki's favourite picture from the entire collection of photographs of the Russo-Japanese War. It now superimposed itself upon the scenery before him and finally occupied his entire consciousness. That was the end of one war, and here was the beginning of another. At any rate, it was an ominous illusion.

A mountain range in the distant left rose in the haze, trailing its long skirt of spacious plains; the horizon on the opposite side dotted with clumps of trees disappeared in yellow dust, and instead of mountains, a line of trees rose to the right, through which peeked a yellow sky.

Such was the background of the photograph. The centre was occupied by a small altar covered with white cloth fluttering in the breeze, on which had been placed a bouquet of flowers and an unpainted wooden grave marker. Thousands of soldiers with bent heads surrounded it.

Honda saw the image most vividly. Again the voices shouting *banzai* and the waving flags returned to his consciousness. The vision left an indescribable sorrow in his heart.

13

During the war Honda used his spare time entirely for his own study of samsara and transmigration and found pleasure in hunting for old books on these subjects. As the quality of new publications gradually deteriorated, the dusty luxury of war-time second-hand bookshops increased. Only there were freely available the knowledge and the pursuit of a hobby that transcended the times. And compared to the increase in the cost of everything else, the price of both Japanese and Western books remained low.

Honda gleaned considerable information from these tomes which expounded on Western theories concerning life cycles and reincarnation.

One theory was attributed to Pythagoras, the Ionian philosopher of the fifth century BC. But his ideas on life cycles had been influenced by the earlier Orphean mysteries that had swept all of Greece in the seventh and sixth centuries. Orphean religion had in turn evolved from the worship of Dionysus that had ignited fires of madness throughout the preceding two hundred years of war and instability. The fact that the god Dionysus had come from Asia and fused with the Earth Mother and agricultural rituals throughout Greece suggested that the two had really originated from one source. The Earth Mother's vibrant figure still lived in the Kalighat in Calcutta that Honda had seen. Dionysus embodied the life cycle of nature that was manifest in the northern country of Thrace. He arrived with the beginning of winter, died at its height, and was resurrected with spring. No matter what lively, wanton figure he might simulate, Dionysus was the personification of young spirits of grain, of whom Adonis was one – beautiful youths who died prematurely. Just as Adonis indubitably had united with Aphrodite, Dionysus too unvaryingly united with the Earth Mother in mystic rituals observed in various lands. At Delphi, Dionysus was enshrined with the Earth Mother, and the chief deity in the mystic worship of Lerna was the holy ancestor of both.

Dionysus had come from Asia. His worship, which brought frenzy, debauchery, cannibalism, and murder, had its roots in Asia and posed the all-important problem of the soul. The paroxysms of this religion permitted no transparency of reason and no firm, beautiful form for either man or god. It was a religion that attacked the fertility of Greek fields in their Apollonian beauty like a swarm of grasshoppers darkening sun and sky, ravaging them, consuming their harvests. Honda could not but compare this to his own experience in India.

Everything abominable – debauchery, death, madness, pestilence, destruction ... How was it that such things could so entice the heart and allure the soul outward. Why did souls have to 'exist', discarding easy, dark, and quiet dwellings? Why was it that the human heart rejected tranquil inertness?

That was what happened in history and with individuals. If men did not do thus, it was because they surely felt that they could not touch the wholeness of the universe. Inebriated, dishevelled, tearing their clothes, and exposing their genitals, blood dripping from the raw flesh in their mouths – by such actions, they must have felt they could scratch the surface of that wholeness.

This was indeed the spiritual experience of *enthusiasmus*, being god-possessed, and *extasis*, exiting from self, which had eventually been refined and ritualized by the Orpheans.

What had turned Greek thought to the concept of samsara and reincarnation was this *extasis* experience. The deepest psychologic source of reincarnation was 'ecstasy'.

According to Orphean mythology, Dionysus was called Dionysus Zagreus, Zagreus being the child born to Zeus and Persephone, daughter of the Earth Mother. He was the favourite of his father and destined to be his successor and the future universal ruler. It is said that when Zeus, Heaven, fell in love with Persephone, Earth, he transformed himself into a great serpent, betokening the essence of earth, in order to make love to her.

His love for the maiden aroused the wrath of his jealous wife, Hera. She summoned the subterranean Titans, and they enticed the baby Zagreus with a toy. Once captured, he was murdered, dismembered, cooked, and eaten. Only his heart was offered to Zeus by Hera. In turn, Zeus gave it to Semele, and a new Dionysus was reborn.

Meanwhile, Zeus was infuriated by the Titans' act and he attacked them with thunder and lightning. When they were completely destroyed, man was born of their ashes.

Thus, mankind was given the evil character of the Titans and at the same time possessed godlike elements transmitted by Zagreus's flesh that the Titans had consumed. Accordingly, the Orpheans proclaimed that man must worship Dionysus by *extasis* and re-establish his holy origin by self-deification. The ritual of the sacred feast persists in the Christian sacrament of the holy eucharist.

Orpheus the musician, murdered and dismembered by Thracian women, seems to re-enact the death of Dionysus; and his death, rebirth, and the mysteries of Hades became significant Orphean doctrines.

As wandering souls who left their bodies by *extasis* were thought to be able to make contact for a short time with the mysteries of Dionysus, men were clearly aware of the separation of body and soul. Their flesh was formed of the evil ashes of the Titans and their soul embraced the pure fragrance of Dionysus. Furthermore, the doctrine of Orpheus taught that earthly suffering did not end with corporeal death; the soul, having escaped its dead body, was obliged to spend some time in Hades before reappearing on earth and transmigrating into another human or animal body. Thus was it destined to traverse limitless 'cycles of life'.

The immortal soul, originally holy, must traverse such a dark passage because of the original sin of the flesh: namely, the Titans' murder of Zagreus. Man's earthly life added new sins and they renewed themselves. Thus, mankind is eternally incapable of escaping from the suffering of this cycle of lives. A man is not necessarily reincarnated in human form, but depending upon the gravity of his sins, may be reborn as a horse, sheep, bird, dog, or cold snake fated to crawl in the dust.

The Pythagoreans, who had been called the successors of the Orpheans and credited with developing their theories, held to the unique doctrines of samsaric reincarnation and Universal Breath.

Honda could detect a trace of the latter principle in King Milinda's concept of life and the soul; he had long meditated on Indian philosophy. It also bore a resemblance to the mysticism of ancient Shinto.

Compared to the fairy-tale cheerfulness of the *jataka*, tales drawn from the various lives of the Buddha, in Theravada Buddhism, the Western theory of reincarnation, darkened by gloomy Ionic melancholy, depressed Honda in spite of the fact that both came from the same source. Consequently he tended to heed Heraclitus who had claimed that all things were in flux.

Enthusiasmus and *extasis* merged in this philosophy of transitory unity, according to which one was all, one came from the all, and all from the one. In the area which transcended time and space, ego disappeared, unity with the universe was easily accomplished, and man was able to become through this divine experience every thing. There, man, nature, bird, animal, forests rustling in the breeze, streams sparkling with the scales of fish, cloud-capped mountains, blue seas dotted with islands – all were able to disengage themselves from their earth-bound existence and unite in harmony. It was such a world that Heraclitus talked about.

The living and the dead,
The awake and the sleeping,
The young and the old are all one and the same.
When the ones change, they become the others.
When those shift again, they become these.

God is day and night.
God is winter and summer.
God is war and peace.
God is fertility and famine.
He transforms into many things.

Day and night are one.
Goodness and badness are one.
The beginning and the end of a circle are one.

These lines represent the sublimity of Heraclitian thought, and when Honda came into contact with it, was blinded by its brilliance, he experienced a certain liberation; but at the same time he was cautious lest he remove too hastily the hands with which he covered his dazzled eyes. For one thing, he was afraid of going blind; for another, he felt that he was still too immature in his sensitivity and ideas to accept such boundless illumination.

14

For this reason Honda averted his eyes for a while and concentrated on his studies of the theories of samsara and reincarnation that had been revived in seventeenth- and eighteenth-century Italy.

Tommaso Campanella, a monk living in the sixteenth and seventeenth centuries, believed in the theory of the life cycle and reincarnation. This heretic and rebellious philosopher was welcomed in France after spending twenty-nine years in prison. There he was happy and much honoured during the last years of his life. When Louis XIV was born, he dedicated to him an *éloge* in which he claimed that the royal birth was proof of his theory of reincarnation.

Campanella learned the Brahman theory of samsara and transmigration from Botero and there discovered that the souls of the dead transmigrated even into monkeys, elephants, or cows. Borrowing the Pythagorean belief in the immortality of the soul and in reincarnation, he designated the inhabitants of his principal work, *Città del sole*, to be 'wise men who had originally come from India to escape the pillage and atrocities of the Mogul'. 'Pythagorean Brahmans', he called them, yet he left their belief in samsara ambiguous. Campanella himself claimed that after death the human soul did not go to hell, purgatory, or heaven.

It is said that his Caucasian Sonnets vaguely suggest the theory of samsara. In these poems, he expressed his emotions of sorrow. 'I cannot believe that my death will bring improvement to mankind; frequently, even if misfortune be averted, evil prospers more than ever. Human senses survive eternally after death; such senses simply forget the suffering endured during life in this world. If we cannot even know whether our former lives were spent in torture or in peace, how shall we know anything of the afterlife?'

In contrast to the jubilation Honda had witnessed in Benares, the Europeans who discoursed on reincarnation were especially depressed by the adversity and sorrow of this life. Furthermore, they did not seek joy in a hereafter, but hoped merely for oblivion.

On the other hand, the eighteenth-century philosopher Giovanni Batista Vico, a ferocious opponent of Descartes, advocated reincarnation and a return to eternity, and his bravery and militancy in his struggle made him a forerunner of Nietzsche, who held the same views. Honda read with pleasure one passage from Vico, in which he praised the Japanese as being heroic, even though he had but a vague knowledge of Japan. 'The Japanese eulogize the heroic man as did the Romans at the time of the Punic Wars. They are fearless in military affairs and speak a language similar to Latin.'

Vico interpreted history through his concept of recurrence. In short, he maintained that each civilization came to its final phase with 'Premeditated Savagery', which is far worse than the earlier 'Natural Savagery'. The latter signifies a noble naïveté, but the former indicates cowardly cunning and insidious trickery. Thus the venomous 'Premeditated Savagery' or 'Civilized Savagery' must necessarily perish, after centuries of progress, by a renewal of 'Natural Savagery'.

Honda felt that an example was to be found in the brief history of modern Japan.

Vico believed in the order of the universe as propounded by Catholicism; yet he was close to the theory of causation through karma. 'God the creator', he said agnostically, 'and the created are separate entities. The *raison d'être* and essence of things are individual in each entity; therefore, the created is an entirely different entity from the godhead as far as its essence is concerned.'

If one holds the created – that which appears to be an entity – to be dharma and atman and if one regards its *raison d'être* to be karma, then deliverance is simply attaining the entity of the creator on another dimension.

Vico claimed in his theology that God's creation changed 'internally' into the created and 'externally' into matter, and thus the world was created in time. He also said that the human spirit, being God's reflection, was able to grasp the concept of infinity and eternity and was immortal. It is not confined by the body and consequently is not limited by time. But he did not provide an answer to the question why the limitless being was shackled by limited things, claiming this to be unknowable. But this is the very point at which the wisdom of the theory of samsara and reincarnation should begin.

On reflection, it is surprising that Indian philosophy, persistently insisting on the power of knowledge, did not reject fantasy or dreams and never developed its own agnosticism.

15

When Honda discovered that a Western tradition of reincarnation had been feebly handed down by lone and solitary thinkers, he mused that it was only natural that King Milinda, who had ruled north-western India in the second century BC, seemed to have quite forgotten the Pythagorean philosophy of ancient Greece when he met the Elder, Nagasena, and plied him with questions. He was most interested in, and at the same time sceptical of, the more profound Buddhist theories of samsara and transmigration.

The first volume of *The Questions of King Milinda*, as it appears in the Japanese translation of the Buddhist canon, opens with the following description of the ruler's capital:

> Thus I have heard: In one of the regions colonized by the Greeks, there is a city called Sagara. It is a great centre for commerce and foreign trade and is marked by purple mountains and clear water, parks, woods, and fields, forming a pleasant, natural paradise on earth; and its inhabitants are devoutly religious. Furthermore, their enemies have all been driven away, so that they feel not the slightest insecurity or oppression. The king's castle is surrounded by fortifications, a variety of ramparts, majestic, forbidding side gates, high white walls, deep moats, and the protection provided is complete. The city's squares, crossroads, and market-places are most aptly designed: beautifully decorated stores are

filled with countless invaluable merchandise. Several hundreds of charitable hospitals add dignity to the city, while several thousand mansions and high pavilions tower like the Himalayas high in the clouds. And in the city streets, throngs of people are visible, men like pines, women like flowers, priests, warriors, farmers and traders, serfs – people of all classes pass by in groups.

All the citizenry welcomes scholars and teachers of various religions and doctrines. Thus, Sagara appears as a nest for elders and academicians of all persuasions. Also in the streets stand eave to eave both large and small dry goods merchants who handle goods woven in Benares called *khotumbari* and all other kinds of goods and fabrics. Lavish fragrance wafts from the flower and incense market, purifying the air of the city. Other shops handle wishing pearls and divers other gems and goods of gold, silver, copper, or stone. It is as though one has stepped into a dazzling mine of jewels. Then, as one turns in another direction, there are great stores for grain and warehouses full of priceless merchandise, shops with all manner of food and drink and cakes; nothing is lacking. In short, Sagara rivals Uttarakuru in wealth, and its prosperity compares well with that of Arakamandar, the city of heaven.

Extremely self-confident and excelling in elocution and debate, King Milinda was contemptuous of Indians as being intellectual chaff. And it was in the midst of this ravishing and glorious city that he met the Elder, Nagasena, for the first time, a sage superior in intellect to the King.

'O Wise One, when I call you Nagasena, exactly who is this Nagasena?' asked the King.

The Elder answered with a question: 'What do you think Nagasena is?'

'O Wise One, I think Nagasena is what exists within a body, a life or soul which enters it as wind or breath.'

The King's reply reminded Honda of the Pythagorean theory of the Universal Breath. That is to say, *psyche* in Greek originally meant 'breath', and if human psyche was breath, man was sustained by air, and thus the whole universe was maintained by air and breath. Such was the Ionian theory of natural philosophy.

The Elder further asked why it was that the breath of one who blows a conch, flute, or horn never returned once it was released, and yet the blower did not die. The King was unable to reply. Thereupon Nagasena made a statement which pointed up the fundamental difference between Greek and Buddhist philosophy.

'The soul is not breath. Inhaled and exhaled, breath is merely the body's latent energy or power.'

Honda immediately felt he could anticipate the dialogue that would follow; it did in fact appear on the next page.

The King asked, saying; 'Oh Wise One, is anyone and everyone reborn after dying?'

'Some people do, some do not.'

'What sort of people would they be?'

'Those who have committed sins will be reborn; those who are sinless and pure will not be reborn.'

'Are you going to be reborn, O Wise One?'

'When I die, if I am attached to life in my heart, I shall be reborn; but if not, I shall not be reborn.'

'I understand.'

From this point on, a zealous desire for learning was kindled in King Milinda's heart, and pertinaciously he posed question upon question concerning samsara and transmigration. The King pursued the Elder with the spiral investigation of Greek dialogue, asking for proof of the 'selflessness' of Buddhism and the question why men who possess no 'self' go through samsara, and concerning the essence that is subject to the law of samsara. Because if samsara occurs through a sequence of causes and effects – a good cause producing by reward a good effect, a bad cause a bad one – there must be an eternal host substance responsible for causal actions. But atman, which was recognized in the days of the *Upanishads*, had been categorically denied in the Abhidharma teachings that characterized the school to which Nagasena belonged. Because of the doctrine and because of his ignorance of the elaborate system of the Consciousness Only school that developed later, Nagasena merely answered: 'There is no samsaric subject as essence.'

But Honda saw an indescribable beauty in the parable which Nagasena used to explain samsara and transmigration, that of a sacred taper, whose flame is not quite the same in the evening, at midnight, and at dawn, and yet not different either as it continues on the same wick burning throughout the night. The karmic existence of an individual is not substantive existence but merely a succession of phenomena similar to the flame.

And so Nagasena taught that time was the existence of samsara itself, almost in the same manner as the Italian philosophers who espoused it many centuries later.

16

It was only natural that King Milinda should choose a Buddhist as his companion in these dialogues, for the ruler, being a foreigner, was necessarily excluded from Hinduism. One not born within the Indian caste system, sovereign or not, was arbitrarily rejected by this religion.

Honda's first encounter with the words 'samsara' and 'reincarnation' had occurred thirty years before, at the house of Kiyoaki Matsugae, where, having listened to the sermon of the Abbess of the Gesshu Temple, he had on his own read the *Laws of Manu* in the French translation of Louis Delongchamps. These laws, which were compiled sometime between the second century before and the second century after the birth of Christ, inherited the idea of samsara established at the beginning of the eighth century BC in the *Upanishads* with their belief in the unity of Brahma and atman. The *Brihadaranyaka Upanishad* states:

> Indeed the person performing a good deed will become benevolent and one performing a bad deed will become evil; one becomes pure by pure acts and black by evil acts. Therefore it is said: A human being is composed of *kama*, or 'desire'; by following *kama*, one creates will; by following will one creates karma; and through karma, samsara comes into existence.

In retrospect, Honda's experience in Benares might have been predestined since that day when, at nineteen, he had become familiar with the *Laws*. The *Laws of Manu* encompasses all of religion, morality, custom, and law, beginning with the creation of heaven and earth and ending with samsara. During their rule of India, the British wisely permitted these laws to continue in effect as practical rules for the Hindus who resided there.

After a second reading of the *Laws*, Honda was for the first time able to touch upon the origin of the jubilation and adoration that he had witnessed in Benares. He read in the impressive first chapter the description of the birth of Brahma, the ancestor of the entire world, where it is told how a divinity coming into being spontaneously expelled the chaos of darkness and began to shine. First he created water and placed a seed in it. The seed grew and became a golden egg as brilliant as the sun. A year later, he broke the egg and from it Brahma was born. And the water that had nurtured the god was that of Benares.

The principle of reincarnation expounded in the *Laws of Manu* classifies human rebirth as being roughly of three kinds. Three natures govern the bodies of all sentient beings: wisdom (*sattva*), which is joyous, serene, and filled with pure, shining emotions, is reborn as a god; ignorance (*rajas*), which likes business enterprises, which is indecisive and tends to follow dishonest works and is addicted to sensuous pleasures, is reborn as man; and anger (*tamas*), which follows a life of indolence and dissipation, slothfulness, cruelty, unbelief, and evil, is reincarnated as an animal.

Transgressions that bring about transmigration into animals are itemized in detail: the murderer of a Brahman will enter the body of a dog, pig, donkey, camel, cow, goat, sheep, deer, or bird; a Brahman who steals money from another Brahman will be reborn a thousand times as a spider, snake, lizard, or aquatic animal; one who invades the bed of a noble person will be born a hundred times as grass, bush, vine, or flesh-eating animal; one who steals grain will become a rat; a honey filcher will become a horsefly; a milk thief will be born as a bird; a herb scrounger will be a dog; a meat stealer will be reborn as a condor; a thief of fat meat will become a cormorant; a salt filcher will transmigrate as a cricket; a robber of silk will be a partridge; a linen stealer will be reborn as a frog; a cotton thief will become a crane; a cow poacher will be an iguana; a filcher of incense will become a muskrat; a vegetable thief, a peacock; a stealer of fire, a heron; a furniture thief, a wasp; a horse thief, a tiger; a woman abductor, a bear; a stealer of water, a cuckoo; and a fruit poacher, a monkey.

17

Nonetheless, the Theravada Buddhism of Thailand was sustained by the naïve doctrines of the *jataka*, or 'birth stories', in the Southern Buddhist Canon that retained much of the flavour of the original Pali texts. It was not even considered strange for Shakyamuni, who had made no transgression as a bodhisattva in his former lives, to be reborn as a rat or a golden swan.

The southern teachings current in Thailand were unknown in Japan until the late nineteenth century. Within one to two hundred years after the death of the Buddha, they were divided into many schools, usually called the Eighteen Theravada Sects; and their teachings, brought to Ceylon by Mahinda under the rule of King Ashoka in the third century BC, are still practised there and in Burma, Thailand, and Cambodia.

In the Theravada Canon, written in Pali, the minute regulations set forth in the *vinaya*, or 'rules' section, still regulate the daily lives of Siamese cenobites. Monks are subject to two hundred and fifty precepts, nuns to three hundred and fifty.

Honda was anxious to learn about the Thai concept of samsara and transmigration, how it differed from the Yuishiki doctrine that attributes the existence of the exterior world to inner ideation, and what sort of characteristics it possessed. Whatever the little Princess's belief, he wanted to know what ideas of samsara were entertained by the ubiquitous saffron-robed monks in Bangkok. He read voraciously.

Thus it was that he discovered that the doctrines of the Eighteen Theravada Sects had originated in the Abhidharma school to which Nagasena, the Elder who had conversed with King Milinda, belonged. As for the dissemination of the *Questions of King Milinda*, certain scholars claim that the work was probably compiled in north-western India, where there were then Greek colonies, and later travelled eastward to the region of Magadha where it was transcribed into Pali. Ultimately, with the addition of some material, it reached Ceylon and spread from there to Burma and Thailand, becoming the *Milindapanha* of the Thai canon.

We may thus assume that the particular Thai concept of samsara is approximately the same as that advocated by Nagasena. The basic tenet of this sect is that the karmic essence that causes samsara is thought or will. This is consistent with the *Agamas* and is very close to primary Buddhist thought. The followers of this sect claim that in terms of motivation there is basically neither good nor evil in men or matter in the external world. What makes them good or bad is completely the product of mind, thought, or will.

So far so good. But in explaining 'selflessness', or *anatman*, the Abhidharma school proceeds from the fact that the whole material world is *avyakrita*, 'unrecordable' as either good or bad – neutral. For instance, imagine a carriage. Despite the fact that all the constituents of this carriage are simple material elements, they can turn into an instrument of crime if the driver runs over a man and escapes. Thus, as mind and will are causes for transgressions and karma, man is fundamentally *anatman*, 'without self'. However, thought rides in the vehicle of the body and produces samsara and reincarnation through the six karmic causes: passion, anger, wrong views, indifference, non-anger, and correct views. Thought is the cause of samsara, but it is not the migrating body. What this body may be is never explained. The hereafter is merely a continuation of this world, and the taper light burning during one's final evening in this world is the birth light of the next life with which it is linked.

On reflection, Honda seemed to understand better what must have been going on in the mind of the little Thai Princess.

With every rainy season, the rivers in Bangkok overflowed, the divisions between road and river, river and rice paddies immediately vanished. Roads became streams, and rivers boulevards. It was surely not an unusual event, even in the mind of a child, that a flood of dreams should invade reality, that past and future, breaking their dikes, should overflow into this world. The green spears of rice plants peeked out of the flooded paddies, and the waters of river and paddy were both bathed in the same sun, both reflected the same masses of summer clouds.

Similarly, a flood of past and future might have occurred subconsciously in the mind of Princess Moonlight, and the isolated phenomena of this world, like islands dotting the vast stretch of water clearly reflecting the moon after the rains, might be the more difficult of the two to believe. The embankments had been broken down and all divisions had disappeared. The past had begun to speak freely.

18

Honda now felt that he could easily return to the Yuishiki theory that had so puzzled him in his youth. He could grasp the system of Mahayana Buddhism that was like some magnificent cathedral now that he had the help of the lovely enigma he had left behind in Bangkok.

Nevertheless, the Yuishiki doctrine was a dazzlingly lofty religio-philosophic structure by which Buddhism, once it had denied atman and soul, provided a most precise and meticulous explanation of the theoretical difficulties concerning the migrating body in rebirth and reincarnation. Like the Temple of Dawn in Bangkok, this consummately complex philosophical achievement pierced the vast expanse of the blue morning sky, which, in that mysterious time before sunrise, was filled with cooling winds and glimmering light.

The contradiction between samsara and *anatman*, a dilemma unresolved for many centuries, was finally explained by Yuishiki doctrine. What body recurs from life to life? What body is liberated in the Pure Land paradise? What can it be?

To begin with, the Sanskrit word for Yuishiki, *vijnaptimatrata*, 'consciousness only', was used in India for the first time by Asanga. Asanga's life was already half shrouded in legend by the time his name became known in China at the beginning of the sixth century through the *Chin kang hsien lun*, or 'Treatise of Vajrarishi'. The Yuishiki theory originated in the Mahayana Abhidharma sutras, and as we shall see, one *gatha*, or 'verse', in these writings constitutes the core of Yuishiki ideas. Asanga systematized Yuishiki principles in his main work, the *Mahayanasamparigraha shastra*, 'A Collection of Mahayana Treatises'. It is pertinent to note that Abhidharma is a Sanskrit word indicating the last of the tripartite Buddhist canon comprising sutras, rules, and scholastic treatises and is practically synonymous with scholastic treatises.

Ordinarily we function in life through the mental operation of the so-called six senses: sight, hearing, smell, taste, touch, and mind. But the Yuishiki school established a seventh sense, *manas*, which in its widest import applies to all mental powers that perceive self and individual identity. But it does not stop there. It further advocates the concept of *alayavijnana*, 'the ultimate consciousness'. Translated by 'storehouse consciousness' in Chinese, *alaya* stores away all 'seeds' of the phenomenal world.

Life is active. *Alaya* consciousness functions. This consciousness is the fruit of all rewards, and it stores all seeds that are the results of all activity. Thus that one is living indicates that *alaya* is active.

This consciousness is in constant flux like a foaming white waterfall. While the cascade is always visible to our eyes, the water is not the same from minute to minute. New water incessantly pours by, streaming and surging, sending up its misty vapours.

Vasubandhu expatiated on Asanga's theory, and in his *Trimshikavi jnaptikarika*, or the 'Thirty Eulogies to Yuishiki', stated: 'Everything is in constant flux like a torrent.' This was one sentence that the twenty-year-old Honda had heard from the lips of the old Abbess of the Gesshu Temple and had kept locked in his heart, though he had not been quite himself at the time because of Kiyoaki.

Furthermore, this thought was connected with his trip to India, with the memory of the two waterfalls plunging precipitously into the Wagora at Ajanta, of the streams which had struck his eyes the moment he stepped out of the *vihara* that he felt someone had just left.

And in those probably final and ultimate falls at Ajanta reflected a mirror image of the Sanko waterfall at Mount Miwa where Honda had met Isao for the first time and of the cascade in the Matsugae garden where he had encountered the old Abbess.

Now *alaya* consciousness is implanted by all seeds of all results. Not only the results of the seven senses we have already spoken of and their activity during life, not only the results of mental activities, but also the seeds of physical phenomena that are the objects of such mental activities are implanted in it. Implanting the seeds into the consciousness is called 'perfuming', in a manner similar to the way incense permeates clothing, the process being referred to as *shuji kunju*, or 'seed perfuming'.

The process of reasoning will differ depending on whether one regards this *alaya* consciousness as pure and neutral or otherwise. If it is assumed to be neutral, then the power which generates samsara and reincarnation must be an external, karmic force. All temptations, all things that exist in the external world, or all illusions of the senses from the first through the seventh constantly exert influence on the *alaya* through the power of karma.

According to the doctrine of Yuishiki the seeds of karmic power – karmic seeds – are indirect causes, or 'auxiliary karma', and the *alaya* consciousness itself is both the migrating body and generative power of samsara and reincarnation. Asanga claimed that this idea would eventually lead to the logical conclusion that *alaya* consciousness itself was not completely pure, that, being a mixture of water and milk, as it were, its adulterated ingredients generated the world of illusion while the pure part brought enlightenment. The karmic seeds of good and evil it contains will materialize in the future according as they are the reward for good or bad acts in the past. This is the difference between the doctrines of the Yuishiki and the Kusha schools, for the latter stresses the external power of karma. Yuishiki developed its unique concept of the world structure based on the idea that the seeds of the *alaya* consciousness generate this consciousness and form natural law (like causes produce like effects) and that these seeds by means of karmic seeds produce moral law (different causes produce different effects).

Alaya consciousness is thus the fruit of sentient beings' retribution and the fundamental cause of all existence. For example, the materializing of a man's *alaya* consciousness means simply the existence of that man.

Thus, *alaya* consciousness makes the delusions of the world in which we live. The roots of all knowledge, embracing all objects of perception, make these objects materialize. The world is composed of the physical body and its Five Roots,* the natural or material world, and 'seeds', that is, the energy that makes all mind and matter materialize. The self, which we tenaciously think of as being our actuality, and the soul, which we presume to continue to exist after death – both are born from the *alaya* consciousness, which is the creator of all phenomena, and therefore both return to this consciousness; all is reduced to ideation.

Yet according to the term *yuishiki*, 'consciousness only', if we think of an object as actually existing in the world and assume all to be merely the product of ideation then we are confusing atman with *alaya* consciousness. For atman under given conditions is a constant entity, but *alaya* consciousness is a ceaseless 'flow of selflessness'.

In his *Mahayanasamparigraha shastra*, Asanga defines three kinds of 'perfuming' pertaining to those seeds which cause the world of illusion to materialize after being perfumed by the *alaya* consciousness.

The first is the seed of name. for instance, when we say that a rose is a beautiful flower, the designation 'rose' distinguishes it from other flowers. In order to ascertain how beautiful it is, we go up to a rose and take cognizance of how different it is from other blooms. The rose first appears as 'name'; the concept gives rise to imagination, and when imagination comes into contact with the real object, its fragrance, colour, and shape are stored away in memory. Or it is possible that the beauty of a flower we have seen without knowing its name has moved us to desire further information about it; on hearing the name 'rose' we conceptualize it. Thus we learn meanings, names, words, and their objects, as well as the relationships among them. All things we learn are not necessarily beautiful

*The five organs of the senses: eyes, ears, nose, tongue, and body as roots of knowing. (Translators' note.)

names nor always accurate meanings, but everything we acquire by perception and thought has been since time immemorial stored away in memory and brings forth worldly phenomena.

The second seed is that of attachment to self.

When the seventh of the eight consciousnesses, *manas*, gives rise in the *alaya* consciousness to egotism with its differentiation between self and others, that egotism insists on an absolute individual self; by eventually moving the other six consciousnesses it produces a series of 'perfumings of self'. Honda could not but think that both the formation of so-called consciousness of self in modern times as well as the fallacy of egotistic philosophy found their origins in the second seed.

The third is the seed of the *trailokya*.

Trailokya means the 'three worlds' and signifies the entire world of illusion consisting of sensuous desire, form, and the formlessness of pure spirit. *Lokya* represents cause. This seed, which is the cause of the three worlds of suffering and delusion, is the seed of karma itself. The difference of fates, the partiality of fortune and misfortune depend on the merit and demerit found in this seed.

Thus it was clear that what migrated in samsara and reincarnation, what passed from one life to the next was the vast flow of selflessness of the *alaya* consciousness.

19

But the more Honda learned about Yuishiki theory, the more he had to know how *alaya* consciousness caused the phenomenal world to appear. For according to Yuishiki concepts, cause and effect dependent on *alaya* occurred simultaneously at a given instant, and yet alternately. For Honda, who could think of cause and effect only in terms of time sequence, this idea of simultaneous, yet alternating causes and effects of the *alaya* consciousness and the phenomenal world was exceedingly difficult to grasp. Yet it was clear that in this concept lay the basic difference between the interpretation of the universe by all of Mahayana (including the Yuishiki school) and that of Hinayana Buddhism.

The world of Theravada Buddhism was like the rainy season in Bangkok when the river, rice paddies, and fields presented an unbroken limitless expanse. The monsoon floods now must have occurred in the past too and would occur in the future as well. The phoenix tree with its vermilion flowers blooming in the garden was there yesterday and therefore would doubtless be there tomorrow. If it was certain that existence went on, say, even after Honda's death, similarly his past would certainly continue smoothly into the future in repeated reincarnations. Unquestioning acceptance of the world as it was, the natural tropical docility so like the land which accepted the floods, was characteristic of Theravadins. They teach that our existence continues from the past, through the present, to the future; past, present, and future resemble the vast brown waters of a river bordered by mangroves with their aerial roots, its flow heavy and languid. The doctrine is called the theory of constant existence in past, present, and future.

Contrary to this, Mahayana Buddhism, especially the Yuishiki school, interpreted the world as a torrential and swift rapids or a great white cascade which never pauses. Since the world presented the form of a waterfall, both the basic cause of that world and the basis of man's perception of it were waterfalls. It is a world that lives and dies at every moment. There is no definite proof of existence in either past or future, and only the present instant which one can touch with one's hand and see with one's eyes is real. Such a world concept is unique to Mahayana Buddhism; reality exists in the present only, there being no past or future.

But why should this be called 'reality'?

If we can recognize a narcissus by seeing it with our eyes and touching it with our hands, at least the narcissus and its immediate environment exist at the moment of touching and seeing.

That much is confirmable.

But then, if we are asleep and if a narcissus is placed in a vase by our pillow during the night, can we prove the existence of the flower at every moment during our sleep?

Thus, if our eyes are gouged out, our ears, nose, and tongue cut off, if we depart our body and our consciousness is extinguished, does the world of the narcissus and its environment continue to exist?

But the world *must* exist!

The seventh consciousness, *manas*, may affirm or deny the world, depending on its attachment to self. Honda could say that since there was a self, that as long as that self continued to perceive, even after the loss of all five senses, there existed about him his fountain pen, vase, ink bottle, red glass pitcher and on it the white cross of the window frame forming a smooth curve reflecting the morning light, his copy of the *Compendium of Laws*, paperweight, desk, wall panel, framed pictures – his world which was a carefully arranged extension of these small objects. Or he might say that as long as self-consciousness (the self) existed and perceived, the world was nothing more than a phenomenal shadow, a reflection of the ego's perceptions; the world was nothing and therefore non-existent. Thus the ego would with arrogance and pride try to treat the world as its own, like a beautiful ball to kick about.

But the world *must* exist!

Yet in order for it to do so, there must be a consciousness that will produce it, make it exist, make the narcissus be, that will guarantee the existence of these things at every moment. This is the *alaya* consciousness, as constant as the North Star, which is awake at every moment during the long dark nights, making such nights exist in fact, incessantly guaranteeing reality and existence.

But the world *must* exist!

Even if all consciousnesses to the seventh should claim that the world were non-existent, or even though the five senses were completely destroyed and death occurred, the world would exist as long as there was *alaya*. Everything exists through *alaya*, and since it does, all things are. But what if *alaya* were extinguished?

But the world *must* exist!

Therefore, *alaya* consciousness is never extinguished. As in a cascade, the water of every moment is different, yet the stream flows in torrential and constant movement.

Thus, *alaya* consciousness flows eternally in order to make the world exist.

For the world *must* at all costs exist!

But why?

Because only by the existence of the world – world of illusion – is man given the chance of enlightenment.

That the world must exist is thus the ultimate moral requisite. This is the supreme answer of the *alaya* consciousness as to why the world must be.

If the existence of the world – the world of illusion – is the ultimate moral requisite, *alaya* consciousness itself, which produces all phenomena, is the origin of that moral requisite. But the world and *alaya* consciousness, or *alaya* and the world of illusion that gives birth to phenomena, must be said to be interdependent. For if *alaya* does not exist, the world does not come into being; but if the world is not, *alaya* is deprived of samsara and reincarnation in which *alaya* itself is the migrating essence, and the way to enlightenment will be forever closed.

Thus it is through this highest moral requisite that *alaya* and the world are mutually dependent; the existence of the *alaya* consciousness depends on the very necessity that the world exist.

Yet only the immediate present is reality, and if the ultimate authority that guarantees momentary existence is *alaya*, that *alaya* that brings about all worldly phenomena exists at the point where time and space intersect.

Honda was able to grasp, albeit with difficulty, that here was born the unique Yuishiki theory of cause and effect being at once simultaneous and alternate.

Now for Buddhist theory to be authentic, there must be textual proof that it is part of the teaching of Gautama Buddha, and the Yuishiki school found just that in the following *gatha*, the most difficult in Mahayana Abhidharma sutras.

All dharma are stored in consciousness,
And consciousness is stored in all dharma.
The two become mutual causes
And always mutual results.

Honda interpreted this passage as meaning that according to the law of continuous cause and effect characteristic of the *alaya* consciousness, the world observed at the momentary section of the present might be described as being sliced like a cucumber into momentary slices of present that are observable one after the other.

The world is born and dies at every instant, and on each momentary cross section appear three forms of endless births and deaths. One is ‘seeds producing the present world’, then ‘the present world “perfuming” the seeds’, and last, ‘seeds producing seeds’. The first is the form in which the seed causes the present world to materialize, and naturally it includes momentum from the past. There is a trail from the past. The second shows the present world being ‘perfumed’ by *alaya* seeds and becoming future phenomena. Naturally uneasiness over the future casts its shadow. But it does not mean that all seeds are 'perfumed' by the present and produce present phenomena. Some seeds, even though being tainted, are merely succeeded by other seeds. These are the third kind of seed. And their causes and effects alone do not occur simultaneously, but follow a time sequence.

The world manifests itself through these three forms, and everything occurs in an instantaneous present.

But the first and second seeds are born anew simultaneously, influence each other, and perish in the same instant. The momentary cross sections, inherited only by these seeds, are discarded as the seeds move from section to section. The structure of the human world is formed of thin slices of instants, infinite in number, pierced through by the skewer of the seeds of the *alaya* consciousness. And the thin slices representing so many instants are both pierced and discarded in each minute segment of time.

Samsara and reincarnation are not prepared during a lifetime, beginning only at death, but rather they renew the world at every instant by momentary re-creation and destruction.

Thus the seeds cause this gigantic flower of delusion called the world to bloom at every point in time, abandoning it at the same instant. But the succession of seeds producing seeds demands the help of karma seeds, as we have said. These karma seeds come from the 'perfuming' of the momentary present.

The true meaning of Yuishiki is that the whole of the world manifests itself now in this very instant. Yet this instantaneous world already dies in the same moment and simultaneously a new one appears. The world which appears one moment is transformed in the following and thus continues on. Everything in the entire world is *alaya* consciousness.

20

When Honda's thinking had evolved this far, everything around him took on an unanticipated appearance.

This particular day, he happened to have been invited to a villa in Shoto in the Shibuya district concerning a prolonged lawsuit and was waiting in the second-floor reception room. No lodgings were available, and when the plaintiff came up to Tokyo on matters of litigation, he stayed at the house of some wealthy man from his home region. The owner had long since left Tokyo for Karuizawa to avoid the bombings.

The administrative suit was being conducted with a leisureliness that stood above time. It had, in fact, been initiated by a law promulgated in 1899, and the origin of the dispute itself went back to post-Restoration days several decades earlier. The accused in this case was the government, and even the defendant's title had changed from Minister of Agriculture and Commerce to that of Agriculture and Forestry with the reorganization of the cabinet. Lawyers representing the plaintiff covered several generations, and now, if Honda, who had been entrusted with the case, won, according to the original agreement one third of the entire land accruing to the plaintiff would be his remuneration. However, he did not expect that the litigation would be over in his lifetime.

Thus he came to the Shibuya villa only to pass the time, using the work as a pretext. In reality he came in anticipation of the polished rice and chicken that his client usually brought as a gift from the country.

The client, who should have long since arrived, was not there yet. He was no doubt having difficulty with the trains.

The June afternoon was too warm for his civilian uniform and gaiters, so Honda opened the tall, oblong English window and stood by it to catch some air. Having had no military experience, he could not to this day manage his gaiters properly, and they tended to slip off his legs and to bunch around his calves, giving him the sensation of dragging a pilgrim's bag around his legs when he walked. His wife Rié always feared that the loose gaiters might get caught in the crowded streetcars and trip him.

Perspiration seeped through the lumpy areas of the gaiters today. The vulgarly shiny summer uniform, made of some staple fibre, retained every crease, and Honda knew that the back of his jacket must be puckered into ugly wrinkles from sitting. But it was no use straightening it.

From the window, he could see all the way to the Shibuya Station area bathed in June light. The residential parts of the immediate vicinity had survived relatively intact, but the area from the foot of the plateau up to the station was freshly bombed ruins spotted with half-destroyed concrete buildings. The air raids that had razed the area had occurred only the week before, on the nights of May twenty-fourth and twenty-fifth, 1945, during which a total of five hundred B-29s had fire-bombed various residential parts of Tokyo. The odour of the conflagration still remained, and the memory of the hellish scene still lingered in the light of day.

The odour, like that of a crematorium, was mixed with more ordinary smells such as those from kitchens or bonfires, commingling with the pungent tang of chemicals as in a pharmaceutical factory or machinery. The smell of burnt-out ruins was already familiar to Honda. Fortunately his house in Hongo had not yet been touched.

In the continuous metallic whine of bombs drilling through the night sky above, followed by a series of explosions and the release of fire bombs, he could always hear something inhuman, something like the voices of women cheering somewhere in the sky. Honda realized later that these were the cries of the damned.

In the burnt-out ruins, the debris had turned rusty, and the crushed roofs had remained untouched. Pillars of various heights stood everywhere like blackened pickets, and ashes crumbled from them to dance in the faint breeze.

Here and there something glittered brightly – for the most part, the remains of shattered panes of glass, glass surfaces burned and warped, pieces of broken bottles that reflected the sun. These little fragments harvested all the June light they could gather to them. Honda beheld for the first time the brilliance of the rubble.

The concrete foundations of houses were clearly limned under the crumbled walls. High and low, each was lit by the afternoon sun. For this reason, the entire ruin had the appearance of a type mould for a sheet of newsprint. But the predominant shade was the light reddish brown of a flowerpot, not the gloomy grey unevenness of a newspaper mould.

There was little greenery, for the area had been mostly commercial. Some half-burned trees were still standing along the streets.

Many shattered office buildings had paneless windows on this side, through which one could see the light reflecting in the glass on the far side, and the window frames were blackened probably by the soot that had been deposited by the shooting flames.

It was a sloping area with a complex mesh of back streets on different levels. The concrete stairs and steps that remained led expectantly to nothing. Nothing remained either above or below them. In the field of rubble too there was no starting point, no destination; only the stairways adhered to direction.

All was quiet, but there were faint stirrings and things would rise softly. When he looked, it seemed like some hallucination, in which blackened corpses ravaged by countless vermin began to stir. They were ashes caught in the breeze, rising everywhere. There were white ashes and black ashes. Some floating ash adhered to a crumbling wall and rested there. Ashes of straw, ashes of books, ashes from a second-hand bookstall, ashes from a quilt maker's shop, floating about individually, commingling indiscriminately, moving, shifting over the face of the devastation.

An area of asphalt road gleamed blackly with water spurting from a ruptured main.

The sky was strangely spacious and the summer clouds immaculately white.

This was the world presented to Honda's five senses at this very moment. His plentiful savings had enabled him to accept only those legal cases that suited him during the war, and the study of samsara and reincarnation which entirely filled his leisure time seemed designed for the purpose of making this devastation manifest. The destroyer was Honda himself.

The vast panorama of devastation before his eyes, resembling the end of the world, was not the end itself, nor was it the beginning. It was a world that imperturbably regenerated itself from instant to instant. *Alaya* consciousness, perturbed by nothing, accepted this expanse of reddish ruin as one world, relinquishing it the next moment, accepting in the same way other worlds in which the colour of destruction deepened with every day, with every month.

Honda felt no emotion as he compared this sight with the city as it had been. Only when his eyes caught the bright reflections of the fragments of broken glass in the ruins and he was momentarily blinded did he understand with the sureness of his senses that the glass, the whole ruin would disappear the next instant to make way for another. He would resist catastrophe with catastrophe, and he would deal with the infinite disintegration and desolation with ever more gigantic and all-inclusive instantaneously repeated devastation. Yes, he must grasp with his mind the instant-by-instant, inevitable total destruction and prepare for the carnage of an uncertain future. He was elated to the point of trembling with these refreshing ideas that he had gleaned from Yuishiki doctrine.

21

When his talk with the client was over, Honda took his gifts and started out for Shibuya Station. There had been reports of a large-scale bombing of Osaka by B-29s. Of late, rumours were frequently heard that western Japan was now the main target. Tokyo seemed to be having a momentary respite.

Honda thought of walking a little further as long as it was light. At the top of Dogen Hill was located the former estate of Marquis Matsugae.

As far as Honda knew, the Matsugae family had sold eighty acres of its total land-holding of one hundred and ten to Hakoné Real Estate Ltd, in the early twenties. But half of the money obtained at that time was lost in short order when the fifteen banks it had been placed in collapsed. The adopted heir of the family, a profligate, quickly disposed of the remaining thirty acres, and the present Matsugae house was reputed to be an ordinary place built on something less than an acre. He had driven by the gate, but had not entered now that he had completely lost touch with the family. Honda was vaguely curious to know whether the house had disappeared in the air raid last week.

The road running along the burned-out buildings of Dogen Hill had already been cleared, and climbing the slope presented no difficulty. Here and there he could see where people had begun to live in their simple air-raid trenches which they had covered with half-burned lumber and pieces of zinc sheeting. It was close to dinner time, and smoke from the cooking fires was rising. Someone was replenishing a pot with water spouting from an exposed conduit. The sky was filled with the beautiful glow of evening.

From the top of the slope to the upper boulevard, the entire area of Minami Daira-dai had once been a part of the hundred-and-ten-acre Matsugae property. The former estate had recently been divided into small lots, but now it had again been transformed into a vast, unbroken ruin, reacquiring under the spacious evening sky the grand scale of bygone days.

The single remaining building belonged to a detachment of military police, and soldiers with arm bands were constantly going in and out. Honda vaguely remembered that the edifice had once stood next to the Matsugae estate. And sure enough, the next moment he recognized the stone pillars of the Matsugae gate beyond.

From it, the remaining acre appeared extremely small, for the property had been divided among many tenant houses. The pond and the artificial hill in the garden appeared as poor miniature replicas of the once magnificent lake and the maple-covered mountain of the old estate. There was no stone wall in the back, and as the wooden fence had burned down, the expanse of devastated neighbouring lots lay in view all the way to Minami Daira-dai. He realized that the plot had been reclaimed by filling in the former extensive pond.

An island had once occupied the centre of the lake, while a waterfall poured into it from the maple-covered mountain. Honda had once crossed over to it by boat with Kiyoaki and from there had recognized the figure of Satoko clad in a light-blue kimono. Kiyoaki had been in the flower of his youth, and Honda too had still been young, much more so indeed than he remembered. There something had commenced and something had ended. But no traces remained.

The Matsugae estate had been restored by the ruthless, impartially destructive bombing. The contours of the land had changed, but across the desolate expanse Honda could still single out the location of the pond, the shrine, the main house, the Western-style wing, and the driveway in front of the porch. The outlines of the Matsugae house that he had frequented were clearly etched in his memory.

But under the billowing evening clouds the innumerable shrivelled zinc fragments, broken slates, shredded trees, melted glass, burned clapboard, or the exposed chimneys of fireplaces standing lonely like skeletons, doors squashed into lozenge shapes – all were dyed a deep, rusty red. Collapsed and prostrate on the ground, their wild shapes that defied norms seemed like strange nettles sprouting from the land. The eeriness was further heightened by the evening sun which added to everything a distinctive shadow.

The sky was the vermilion of silk kimono lining with tufts of cloud scattered about. The colour had penetrated to their very core, and their ravelled edges radiated like golden threads. He had never seen such a sinister sky.

Suddenly he discerned in the vast ruin the figure of a woman sitting on a garden stone which had survived. The back of her somewhat shiny trousers made from lavender silk kimono material was transformed to *lie-de-vin* by the evening sun. Her black gleaming hair done in a Western style was wet, and her huddled figure appeared tormented. She seemed to be crying, but her shoulders were not shaken by sobs; she seemed to be suffering too, but her back gave no indication of anguish. She sat hunched up as though petrified. Her motionlessness lasted too long for someone merely lost in thought. Honda judged from the lustre of her hair that she was probably middle-aged, perhaps the owner of one of the houses that had stood there, or possibly a relative.

He realized he should have to offer assistance if she had been overcome by some indisposition. As he drew closer, he saw a black handbag and cane which she had placed beside the stone on which she was sitting.

Honda put his hand on her shoulder and shook it discreetly. He half feared that if he used any strength the form would collapse into ashes.

The woman looked obliquely up at him. The face frightened Honda. From the gap that showed at the unnatural hairline he realized that the black hair was a wig. The harsh vermilion of her lipstick stood out against the powder which had been thickly applied to cover the wrinkles and the hollows of her eyes; it was drawn on in the old-fashioned court style, a peaked upper lip and a tiny lower one. He recognized the face of Tadeshina beneath this indescribably aged mask.

'You're Mrs Tadeshina, aren't you?' said Honda without thinking.

'Who could you be?' said Tadeshina. 'A moment, please,' she added, hurriedly taking her glasses from her breast. He could see the Tadeshina of former days in her sly attempt to gain time by opening the sides and putting them over her ears. Under the pretext that she needed her glasses to see, she hurriedly tried to place him.

But the ruse was not successful. Even with the glasses, the old woman saw only a stranger standing before her. For the first time uneasiness and an old aristocratic prejudice – a mild chilliness she had learned to simulate so skilfully over the years – appeared on her face. This time she spoke with stiff formality.

'You must excuse me. I have quite lost my memory of late. I really have no idea...'

'I'm Honda. Thirty years ago I was a classmate of Kiyoaki Matsugae's at the Peers School, and I used to come to the house all the time.'

'Oh, Mr Honda! How good it is to see you! I don't know how to apologize ... I'm sorry not to have recognized you. Yes, Mr Honda, indeed. You look just as you did in your younger days. Oh, what a...'

Tadeshina hurriedly put a sleeve to her eyes. Her tears in former days had always been suspicious, but now the make-up under her eyes immediately soaked them up like a whitewashed wall in the rain, and a generous supply overflowed almost mechanically from her bleary eyes. Such tears, as abundant as an overturned tub of water, totally unrelated to either joy or sorrow, were much more believable than those of thirty years ago.

Nevertheless, her senility was preposterous. On her skin, hidden under the thick white powder, Honda could see the moss of decrepitude that covered her entire body, and yet he sensed her extraordinary mind still working diligently like a watch ticking away in the pocket of a dead man.

'It's good you're looking so well. How old are you now?' asked Honda.

'I'm ninety-four this year. I'm a little hard of hearing, but other than that I have my health and no ailments; my legs are strong, and I manage to get around alone with a cane. My nephew's family are looking after me, and they don't like to let me go out alone. But I don't really care when or where I die, so I like to get out as much as possible while I still can. I'm not at all afraid of the air raids. If I'm hit by a bomb or incinerated I'll die without any pain and without causing anybody any trouble. You may not believe it, but I feel envious of the bodies lying by the roadside these days. When I heard that the Shibuya area had been burned in the bombardment the other day, I simply had to see the site of the Matsugae estate. I slipped out of my nephew's house. What would the Marquis and the Marchioness say if they were alive to see this state of affairs! They were fortunate enough to die before experiencing any of this misery.'

'Fortunately my house hasn't been burned yet, but I feel the same way about my mother. I'm glad she died while Japan was still winning.'

'Oh dear! Your mother's gone too ... I am terribly sorry to hear that, I had no idea...'

Tadeshina had not forgotten the emotionless, gracious civilities of her former days.

'What's become of the Ayakuras?'

After putting the question, Honda immediately regretted it. As he had expected, the old woman hesitated noticeably. However, whenever she showed any visible sign of emotion, it was usually lacking in sincerity and simply for exhibition.

'Yes, after Miss Satoko entered the orders, I left the Ayakura family, and since then I've only attended Lord Ayakura's funeral. The Viscountess, I believe, is still alive, but after his lordship passed away she sold the house in Tokyo and went to relatives in Shishigatani in Kyoto. Her daughter . . .'

Honda felt a quivering in his heart and asked involuntarily: 'Do you ever see Miss Satoko?'

'Yes, I've seen her three times in all after the funeral. She's always so kind to me when I visit her. She even invites me to spend the night at the temple. So sweet and gracious . . .'

Tadeshina took off her clouded glasses, quickly removed a coarse tissue from her sleeve and held it over her eyes for some time. When she took it away there was a dark ring where the powder had come off.

'Miss Satoko's well then?' said Honda again.

'She is, indeed. And – how shall I say? – she's more beautiful, more pure than ever, and her beauty becomes more serene as she grows older. Please visit her some time, Mr Honda. Do, she'll be so pleased to see you.'

Honda abruptly recalled that midnight drive from Kamakura to Tokyo alone with Satoko.

She was another man's woman, but she had been almost oppressively feminine then.

She had already had a foreboding of things to come ultimately and had expressed her readiness in preparing for them. Honda recalled, as vividly as though it had happened yesterday, that thrilling moment just before dawn when her profile had been framed by the car window with the foliage in the background flying past.

When he came back to reality, Tadeshina's face had lost its pretence of deference and she was scrutinizing him. Wrinkles like the lines in tie-dyed silk surrounded her bow-shaped lips, but now at either side her mouth was slightly pulled up in the semblance of a smile. Suddenly, in the two eyes – old wells in patches of snow – the pupils moved horizontally with a suggestion of the old coquetry.

'You were in love with her, weren't you? I knew it.'

Honda flinched, more at the vestiges of Tadeshina's coquetry than from displeasure at such a conjecture after so many years. To change the subject, he turned his thoughts to the gifts he had received from his client. It occurred to him that he might share a portion with her; a couple of eggs and a little chicken.

Tadeshina expressed her guileless joy and appreciation just as he had expected she would.

'Oh, my, eggs! How unusual to see eggs these days! I feel as if I haven't seen one for years! Heavens, eggs!'

The meandering, complex thanks that followed made Honda realize that the old woman must be given scarcely any decent food. He was further surprised when she again took out the egg that she had put away in her shopping bag. Holding it up against the fading twilight sky, she said:

'Rather than taking this home – you must excuse my poor manners – I would rather just eat it here . . .'

As the old woman spoke, she looked regretfully at the egg against the darkening sky. It smouldered in her trembling old fingers as the fading light touched its delicate, cold shell.

For some time Tadeshina caressed the egg in her hand. The noise in the area had abated, and only the faint sound of her dry skin rubbing against it was audible.

Honda ignored her search for a sharp corner against which to crack the shell. He was reluctant to help her in an action which was somehow objectionable. Tadeshina broke the egg unexpectedly skilfully on the edge of the stone on which she was sitting. Carefully bringing it to her mouth in order to lose none of its content, she gradually lifted her face and poured it between her gleaming dentures gaping at the evening sky. The lustrous roundness of the yolk passing her lips was fleetingly visible, and her throat emitted an extremely healthy swallowing sound.

'My, this is the first nourishing food I've had in a long, long time. I feel revived. I feel as though the beauty of my youth has come back. You might not believe it, Mr Honda, but I was a famous beauty in my day.'

Her tone had suddenly become frank.

There is a time of day immediately before dusk when the outline of every object becomes sharply delineated. It was just that moment. The lacerated edges of wooden beams in the wreckage, the freshness of the rents in the shredded trees, and the curled zinc sheets with their puddles of rain water – everything appeared almost unpleasantly vivid. In the extreme west only a horizontal line of scarlet was to be seen in the sky between two or three towering black burned-out buildings. Flecks of scarlet were also visible through the windows of the ruined structures. It was as if someone had turned on a red light in a deserted and uninhabited house.

'How can I thank you? You have always been such a tender-hearted man, and you are still so kind. I have nothing to give you, but at least...'

Like a blind woman, Tadeshina hunted through her bag. Before Honda could stop her, she had taken out a volume bound in the Japanese style and thrust it into his hand.

'At least I want to give you this book. I have always treasured it and carried it with me. It is an efficacious sutra given me by a priest to ward off harm and illness. I am so happy to have run into you and to have been able to talk about bygone times. You'll probably be going out on air-raid days, and there are bad fevers about. But if you carry this sutra with you, you are sure to avoid any disaster. I should like you to keep it as a token of my appreciation.'

Honda held the book up reverently to show his thanks and looked at the title on the cover. It was barely legible in the evening light.

Mahamayurividyarajni, 'Sutra of the Great Golden Peacock Wisdom King'.

22

Ever since that day, Honda could scarcely contain his desire to see Satoko, but he knew that the urge came in part from Tadeshina's remark that she was still beautiful. He was deathly afraid of seeing a 'ruin of beauty' like the ruins of the city.

But the war situation was deteriorating daily, and it was difficult to obtain train tickets unless one had connections in the Army, and a pleasure trip was out of the question.

As the days passed, Honda opened the *Peacock King Sutra* that Tadeshina had given him. He had never had the opportunity of reading any Esoteric Buddhist sutras before.

The opening passages gave explanations and rules for use in small, almost illegible print.

To begin with, the Peacock Wisdom King occupied the sixth position from the southern end of the Susiddhi Court in the Womb Mandala. As he is attributed the power of begetting all Buddhas, he is also called the 'Peacock King, Begetter of All Buddhas'.

When he consulted the Buddhist documents he had so far collected, Honda found that the deity had clearly originated in Hindu *shakti* worship. Since *shakti* rites were directed toward Kali, wife of Shiva, or toward Durga, the statue of the bloodthirsty goddess he had seen at the Kalighat in Calcutta was indeed the archetype of the Peacock Wisdom King.

When he discovered this, the sutra that had come into his possession by accident suddenly became of interest to him. Along with the use of *dharani** and mantra in Esoteric Buddhist rites, the old deities of Hinduism had invaded the world of Buddhism by resorting to all sorts of transformations.

Originally the *Sutra of the Peacock Wisdom King* was believed to have been an incantation spoken by the Buddha, and it was supposed to ward off snakes or cure poisoning from their bites.

According to the *Peacock Sutra*:

> When one Kissho, who had not been long ordained, was preparing kindling for the monks' bath, a black snake came out from under a strange tree and bit his right toe. He fainted and fell to the ground, his eyes turned up, and he foamed at the mouth. Ananda went to where the Buddha was and said: 'How can he be cured?' Whereupon the Buddha answered, saying: 'If you hold the *Sutra of the Incantation of the Great Tathagata Peacock Wisdom King*, clasp the monk Kissho in your arms, and make the proper hand signs as you chant the mantra, the poison will be harmless. Neither sword nor cane will be able to inflict injury. It will fend off all calamities.'

Not only snake poison, but all fevers, all wounds, all pain and suffering were reputed abolished by this sutra. Simply chanting it was sufficient, and the mere thought of the Peacock Wisdom King did away with all fear, enemies, and calamities. Therefore, during the Heian period, only the Elder of the Toji and the Abbot of the Ninna Temple in the Imperial line were permitted to perform the Esoteric Buddhist rites of this sutra. During such ceremonies, fervent prayers were offered against all possible situations, from natural calamities to pestilence and childbirth.

The Peacock Wisdom King in the illustration was a gorgeous and sumptuous figure as though the personification of the peacock itself, so different from the

*Magic formulas. (Translators' note.)

bloody image of Kali, his prototype, with her protruding tongue and her necklace of severed heads.

His magic formula was said to imitate the cry of the peacock – *ka-ka-ka-ka-ka-ka-ka-ka-ka-ka-ka-ka-ka* – and the mantra, *ma yu kitsu ra tei sha ka,* meant 'Peacock fulfilment'. Even the special hand gesture, which was called the 'sign of the Buddha Begetter, the Peacock Wisdom King', and which was made by joining the two hands back to back, the two thumbs and the two little fingers pressed together, was both a description and imitation of the peacock's majesty. The gesture represented the shape of the peacock, the little fingers being the tail and the thumbs the head, and the rest of the fingers the feathers. The way the middle six fingers moved as the incantation was chanted depicted a peacock dancing.

A blue Indian sky trailed behind the Wisdom King on his golden peacock mount. A tropical sky with its impressive clouds, its afternoon ennui, and its evening breezes, all necessary for spinning a gorgeous and colourful illusion.

The golden peacock was seen from the front, standing firmly on its two legs. It had opened its wings and was carrying the Wisdom King on its back, guarding him by spreading its magnificent fan tail which stood in place of a halo. The king was sitting in the lotus position on a white lotus flower placed on the back of the peacock. Of the king's four arms, the first on the right held an open lotus; the second, the peach-shaped fruit of karma; the first hand on the left was held over the heart, its upturned palm supporting the fruit of good fortune; and the second, a peacock tail of thirty-five feathers.

The Wisdom King posed with compassionate countenance, and his body was extremely fair. The skin visible under silk gauze was enhanced by such magnificent jewellery as the crown on his head, the necklace around his neck, the earrings hanging from his ears, and the bracelets at his wrists. A cool weariness lingered on the heavy lids of the half-open eyes as though the deity had just awakened from an afternoon nap. Imparting boundless mercy and saving people without number might produce in one an emotion similar to the idle sleepiness that Honda had discovered in the bright, vast expanses of India.

In contrast to this absolutely white and serene image, the extended feathers of the peacock that acted as a halo were dazzlingly polychrome. Of the plumage of all birds, that of the peacock was closest in hue to the evening clouds. Like an Esoteric Buddhist mandala that rearranges a chaotic universe into an orderly one, the feathers presented the methodical organization of the riotous disorder of colour seen in the evening clouds, their amorphousness, and the play of light upon them, in a geometric and patterned brocade. Gold, green, indigo, purple, brown – such dusky brilliance, however, indicated the end of the evening glow when the disc of the setting sun itself was no longer visible.

The tail feathers lacked only scarlet. If there were such a bird as a scarlet peacock, and if the Peacock Wisdom King had been seated upon it, tail fully open, he would be none other than the goddess Kali herself.

Honda believed that such a peacock must have appeared in the evening clouds in the sky above the ruins where he had encountered Tadeshina.

PART TWO

23

'You've planted some beautiful cypresses,' said Honda's new neighbour. 'It used to be so barren and treeless here.'

Keiko Hisamatsu was an imposing woman.

She was close to fifty, but her face, rumoured to have undergone plastic surgery, retained an overly taut, shiny youthfulness. She was one of those exceptional Japanese who could speak informally to either Prime Minister Yoshida or to General MacArthur; she had long since divorced her husband. At the moment she had a lover, a young American officer in the Occupation Forces who worked at the camp at the foot of Mount Fuji. She had repaired her long-neglected villa at Ninooka in Gotemba and would occasionally come for a rendezvous or, as she said, 'to write leisurely answers to long-neglected letters'. Her villa stood next to Honda's.

In the spring of 1952, Honda celebrated his fifty-seventh birthday. For the first time in his life, he had acquired a villa. Guests had been invited from Tokyo for the opening that was to take place on the morrow. He himself had come a day early to oversee preparations and had invited his neighbour Keiko to inspect the garden that measured something more than an acre.

'I've been looking forward to the completion of your house as if it were my own,' said Keiko, walking over the dead, frost-wet lawn, lifting her thin high-heeled shoes step by step like a waterfowl. 'This grass was planted last year. How well it has taken. You set up the garden first and then took your time with the house. Only a true lover of gardens could do that.'

'I had no place to stay, so I commuted from Gotemba to lay it out,' replied Honda, looking like some Parisian concierge in his heavy, slightly ravelled cardigan with a silk scarf wrapped around his neck against the cold.

Honda felt a certain discomfort with women like Keiko, who had lived a life of leisure. It was as though his pettiness were being seen through – the meanness of working and studying through life and now at the onset of old age suddenly trying to learn how to relax.

His being here, the proprietor of a villa, had been made possible by an antiquated section of a little-known law issued under the Imperial Seal on April 18, 1899, and entitled 'Concerning the return of nationally owned lands, forests, and fields'.

In July of 1873, a land-reform decree was issued, and government officials had gone from village to village attempting to ascertain the ownership of various holdings. Fearing they would be taxed, owners denied possession of certain tracts, and thus a great number of private holdings and commonages had become unattached and had been transferred to the government.

Much later, in view of the clamorous voices of regret and resentment, a law was passed in 1899, the second article of which stated that applicants for the return of land were required to prove previous ownership by producing at least one of seven records. One was called a 'state document'. And the sixth article of the code stated that all pertinent legal action would come under the jurisdiction of the Court of Administrative Litigation.

Many such suits were instituted in the 1890s, but the Court of Administrative Litigation permitted only one hearing, with no opportunity for appeal. And since there was no provision for supervision of the legal process, everything was done in a most leisurely fashion.

In any village in which communal lands had been confiscated because of a thoughtless lie, the Oaza, or administrative division, became the plaintiff in administrative litigation. Even if the village had been amalgamated into a township, the Oaza could claim possession and remain as an 'owner district'.

In the case of a certain village in the district of Miharu in Fukushima Prefecture, a suit was instituted in 1900, in which the government and the plaintiff went about the business most leisurely. Over a period of fifty years, the defendant had changed from Minister of Agriculture and Commerce to Minister of Agriculture and Forestry, and, one by one, successive lawyers in charge of the litigation had died, only to be succeeded by others. In 1940, a delegate from the district of the plaintiff village came to Tokyo to see Honda, who was already a well-known lawyer, and deposited the hopeless case in his hands.

The fifty-year deadlock was broken by the defeat of Japan in the war.

According to the new constitution executed in 1947, special courts were eliminated and the Court of Administrative Litigation was abolished. All administrative cases in process were transferred to the Tokyo High Court and treated as civil suits. As a result, Honda won the case without difficulty. It was nothing more than pure luck – being at the right place at the right time.

In accordance with the agreement which had been handed down through the years, Honda received as his fee for winning the case one third of all lands returned to the village. He had the choice of accepting this real estate or of converting it into cash at the going rate. He chose the latter. Thus he came into the sum of thirty-six million yen.

This event changed the very roots of Honda's life. During the war he had gradually grown bored with a lawyer's lot, and while retaining the widely respected name of the Honda Law Offices, he left all work to his younger partners and put in only an occasional appearance. His social life changed and so did his thinking. He could not take his good fortune seriously, coming so suddenly as he had into possession of close to forty million yen, nor could he be serious about the times that had made such a miracle possible. Therefore he decided to take the whole thing casually.

He considered dismantling and rebuilding his residence in Hongo, which would have been much better off burned in the raids, but he was already too disillusioned with the city to construct anything new there and expect it to last for ever. Anyway, it would be burned to the ground in the next war.

His wife Rié preferred to sell the property and perhaps live in an apartment rather than to continue on in the big old house by themselves. But Honda took the pretext of her sickliness for building a villa in a remote, sparsely populated spot where she could rest.

The couple went to see some land in the Sengokuhara area in Hakoné with an introduction from an acquaintance, but when they heard of the excessive dampness in the region they were frightened off. Guided by the chauffeur of the hired car, they drove over Hakoné Pass and explored the summer resort area of Ninooka in the Gotemba section that had been developed some forty years before. There were many villas belonging to former dignitaries. But after the war, they had closed their gates to avoid the American Occupation Forces near the Fuji Manoeuvring Terrain and the inevitable women who followed them. Honda was told that in an area west of the villa district there was some barren land that had once belonged to the government but that had been turned over without charge to the farmers of the region as a result of the land reform. One could make a good buy there.

The entire area at the foot of Mount Hakoné was not covered by the volcanic lava as was that around Fuji. But it was barren land unfit for growing anything except perhaps cypresses. The farmers did not know what to do with it. Honda was delighted with one property where pampas grass and sagebrush covered a slope that gently descended to a valley stream. Mount Fuji was clearly visible.

Upon inquiry he found the price to be very reasonable and therefore did not follow Rié's suggestion to give the matter further thought. He made an immediate down payment for a parcel of a little over four acres.

Rié said that she did not like the unspeakably sombre harshness of the land. She was afraid of melancholia. She knew instinctively that she had no use for such feelings in her old age. But to Honda, who was dreaming of pleasure, it was this very gloominess that was indispensable to him.

'It's nothing. If we clear the area and plant some greenery and put up a house, it'll be almost too cheerful,' he had said.

Hiring carpenters from the area to build the house and employing people there to plant the trees and do the landscaping was a slow process, but it kept the expenses down. Honda retained from former days his habit of considering indiscriminate expenditure vulgar. Nevertheless, the pleasure of leisurely guiding a guest around and showing off his extensive property was surely an emotion born long ago in his boyhood when he had frequented the Matsugae estate. He did not mind the chilliness of early spring which stung the skin with the frigidity of the lingering snows of Hakoné, because it was the chilliness of his own garden; by the same token, the loneliness of only two people casting faint shadows on the expanse of lawn pleased him, because it was the loneliness of his own property. He felt as though he were grasping the real luxury of private ownership for the first time. Furthermore, it pleased him that he had come to it not through fanaticism, but completely by means of his own logical thinking and good timing.

Keiko's overly handsome profile held no trace of coquetry or reserve. She had the ability to make any man beside her – even the fifty-seven-year-old Honda – feel as though he were a mere stripling. It was a woman's power to impose on a fifty-seven-year-old man the apparent cheerfulness and sunniness of a youth bound by pure hypocrisy and vanity, one who kept up appearances at all costs, though uneasy and respectful with women.

From Honda's point of view, age was nothing to be taken into account. Until he was in his forties he had been conscientious about the plusses and minuses of age. Now, however, he had an actually casual and carefree idea of it. He was not surprised when sometimes he happened to discover clear signs of true childishness in himself, in his fifty-seven-year-old body. Old age was, somehow, a kind of declaration of bankruptcy.

He had grown terribly concerned about his health and terrified of his self-indulgence in emotion. If the function of reason was control, the urgent necessity for it had passed. Experiences were nothing but cleaned bones on a dinner plate.

Keiko stood at the centre of the greensward, contrasting the view of Hakoné to the east with that of Fuji to the north-west. She exuded a stateliness which was best described as regal; the fullness of her suit coat, her erect neck, everything conveyed the air of a commanding general. Her young officer must surely be subjected to all manner of orders, including ones not so easy to execute.

Compared to the clear, snow-dotted ridges of Hakoné, Fuji, half covered by clouds, appeared ephemeral. Honda noticed that some optical illusion made it now higher, now lower.

'Today I heard a nightingale for the first time,' said Honda, looking through the fragile withered upper branches of the thin cypress trees that he had purchased in the neighbourhood and transplanted to his property.

'Nightingales come in mid-March,' said Keiko. 'You'll be able to see cuckoos in May. You can see as well as hear them, mind you. This is probably the only place that one can see and hear cuckoos at the same time.'

'Let's go in. I'll build a fire and make some tea,' Honda suggested.

'I brought some cookies,' said Keiko, referring to the package she had left in the vestibule a short while ago. The Hattori Clock Shop at the corner of Owari-cho on the Ginza had been turned into a PX after the war; and Keiko, having free access to this facility, usually bought her gifts there. English-made cookies familiar to her since prewar days could be purchased there inexpensively. The thin, hard, plum jam sandwiched in them served to connect the afternoon teas of her childhood with those of the present.

'I have a ring I should like you to appraise,' said Honda, starting to walk.

24

Fragrant daphne still in bud surrounded the terrace, and the birdhouse built in one corner bore the same type of red tile roof that covered the main house. When they saw Honda and Keiko approaching, the tiny sparrows that had flocked around the feeder darted away chirping, as though pricked by needles.

Just inside the entrance stood another door with a stained-glass centre, and to either side were windows latticed with orange panes like those of Dutch mansions in the late Edo period. One could indistinctly see inside through them. Honda liked to stand here and look at the interior sinking in the wistful colours of the evening sun, an interior he himself had meticulously designed, with its thick beams purchased from a rural house and transferred intact, the chaste North-German antique chandelier, the panelled doors with simple line drawings of Otsu folk painting, footman's armour, and a bow and arrows – all bathed in the fading yellow light, exuding the feeling of some gloomy still life, as if some Dutch painter like Jan Treck had done a Japanese scene.

Honda invited Keiko to enter. He seated her in the chair by the fireplace and tried to light the kindling, but it would not catch. Only the fireplace had been planned by a specialist from Tokyo; it was well designed and never let the smoke reverse and flow back into the room. But whenever he tried to build a fire, Honda always realized that he had never in his life had the opportunity of mastering the simplest techniques or knowledge. Indeed, he had never even handled basic materials.

It was strange to learn this at his age. He had never once known leisure in his entire life. Thus he had obviously never made any contact with nature, with the waves of the ocean, with the hardness of trees, with the weight of rocks, and with the tools like ship's fittings, nets, or hunting rifles that workers came to know through their work, and the aristocrats, conversely, were familiar with through the graciousness of their living. Kiyoaki had turned his leisure not toward nature but only toward his own emotions; if he had matured, he would have grown into nothing but idleness.

'Let me help,' said Keiko, bending down with dignity, after watching Honda's ineptness for some time, the tip of her tongue protruding between her hard lips. Her hips appeared almost limitless to Honda's upturned eyes. The blue celadon colour of her tight skirt, filled like a gigantic vase of the Yi Dynasty, was enhanced by the cut of the suit that had a sharply narrowed waistline.

As Honda had nothing to do while Keiko occupied herself with fire, he left the room to fetch the ring he had mentioned. When he returned, savage vermilion flames were already slithering up the logs, and pieces of kindling were gnashing their teeth in the coquettishly clinging smoke, while sap secreted from the freshly cut wood sizzled. The brick lining of the fireplace flickered in the firelight. Keiko calmly brushed her hands and observed the result of her efforts with obvious satisfaction.

'How is this?'

'I'm impressed,' said Honda, extending his hand into the firelight and handing the ring to Keiko. 'This is the ring I mentioned a while ago. What do you think? I bought it as a present.'

Keiko withdrew her fingers with their red manicured tips from the area of the flames and scrutinized the ring in the fading light from the window.

'A man's ring,' she said.

It was formed of a dark green, square emerald encircled by gold finely sculpted to depict a pair of protective *yaksha* with impressive half-bestial faces. Keiko moved the ring from her fingertips, probably to avoid the reflection of her red nails, and holding it between her fingers, slipped it on her index finger. Although a man's ring, it was the size for some delicate, dark-skinned finger; it was not overly large even on her.

'It's a good stone. But with old emeralds the inside fissures always effloresce in the long run. There's danger of fragility when the cloudiness rises from underneath. This one shows that condition. But still it's a good stone. And the carving is unusual. It'll be valuable as an antique.'

'Where do you think I bought it?'

'Abroad?'

'No, in the ruins of Tokyo. At Prince Toin's shop.'

'Oh yes, those days ... But no matter what financial trouble the Prince might have had, for him to open an antique shop ... ! I've been there two or three times myself. Everything interesting turned out to be something I had seen at relatives' long ago. But the shop had to close. I heard that the Prince was never there; the former steward who was acting as head clerk was running the show and stealing all the profits. Not a single member of royalty has started a successful business after the war. No matter what the property tax, they should have safeguarded what possessions they had left. There was always some promoter who would talk them into something. Especially Prince Toin, who had always been a soldier. He reminds me of the poor samurai who all went bankrupt after the Restoration.'

Then Honda told her the history of the ring.

In 1947, Honda heard that Prince Toin had lost his title after the war and had bought up art objects cheaply from members of the former nobility overburdened with property taxes. He had opened an antique shop for foreigners. The Prince would not have remembered him even if Honda had gone to see him, but he had been moved to look in at the shop out of sheer curiosity without identifying himself. In a glass case, he discovered the ring of Princess Chantrapa, which the Siamese prince Chao P. had lost in the dormitory of the Peers School thirty-four long years before.

It was obvious that the ring, which had been believed mislaid at the time, had in reality been stolen. The sales clerk, of course, did not disclose the origin of the object, but it must have come from the house of some former noble. The man who had had to sell it must have been a student at the school when Honda was there. He was moved by an old sense of justice to purchase it, wanting to return it himself somehow to the original owner.

'Then are you going to Thailand to give it back? To clear the name of your alma mater?' teased Keiko.

'I intended to some day. But it's not necessary now. The Princess has come to Japan to study.'

'A dead girl here to study?'

'No, no, Chantrapa the second – Ying Chan, I mean,' said Honda. 'I've invited her to the party tomorrow. I intend to put the ring on her finger then. She's seventeen years old, with beautiful black hair and bright eyes. She speaks Japanese quite well; she must have studied hard before leaving her country.'

25

The next morning Honda awoke alone in the villa, and for protection against the cold, donned a woollen scarf, a cardigan, and a thick winter coat. He crossed the lawn and walked to the arbour at the west end of the garden. More than anything else he had been anticipating watching Fuji at dawn.

The mountain was tinted crimson in the sunrise. Its tip glowed the colour of a brilliant rose stone, and to his eyes it was a dreamlike illusion, a classical cathedral roof, a Japanese Temple of Dawn.

Sometimes Honda was confused as to whether he sought solitude or frivolous pleasure. He lacked something essential to become a serious pleasure-seeker.

For the first time somewhere within – and at his age! – a desire for transformation had awakened. Having earnestly observed other men's reincarnation without so much as turning an eye, he had never brooded over the impossibility of his own. And now that he was reaching an age when the last glow of life revealed the expanse of his past, the certainty of its impossibility heightened the illusion of the possibility of rebirth all the more.

He too might do something unexpected. To this day all his actions had been predictable, and his reason had always cast its light one step ahead, like a flashlight held by someone walking along a dark road at night. By schemes and predictions he had been able to avoid surprising himself. The most frightening thing was that all mysteries, including the miracle of transmigration, finished by being cut and dried.

He needed to be surprised. It had become almost a necessity of life. If there were a special right in scorning reason and trampling it, he had the rational self-conceit to think that it was permitted only to him! He had to involve his stable world in some amorphous turmoil again, in something with which he was not at all familiar!

Honda knew very well that he had lost all physical qualifications for that. His hair had grown thin, his sideburns were streaked with white, and his stomach had swollen like remorse itself. All the characteristics of early old age which he had considered so ugly as a youth now marked his body unsparingly. Of course, even when young, he had never regarded himself as handsome, like Kiyoaki, but he had not thought himself to be particularly ugly either. At least he had not found it necessary to place himself among the negative numbers in a world of beauty and to construct his equations in consequence. Why was it that now when his ugliness had become so obvious, the world about him was still beautiful? This was indeed far worse than death itself; the worst death!

It was twenty minutes past six. Two thirds covered by snow, Fuji had brushed off the colours of dawn and stood against the blue sky in sharply etched beauty. It was almost too clearly visible. The texture of the snow was delicate, full of the sensitive tension of its undulations. It called to mind the fine play of lean muscle. Except for the lower slopes, there were only two slightly reddish black patches near the top and near the Hoei summit. The blue sky was hard and cloudless; had he thrown a rock, the sharp sound of stone hitting it would have echoed back.

This Fuji influenced all dispositions, controlled all emotions. It was the pure white essence of questionability itself that rose before him.

Honda's hunger sharpened in the tranquillity. He looked forward to his breakfast of bread purchased in Tokyo and the soft-boiled egg and coffee he would make as he listened to the chirping of the birds. His wife was due to arrive with Princess Ying Chan at eleven o'clock to begin preparations for the party.

After breakfast he returned to the garden.

It was close to eight. Little by little small wisps of cloud had begun to rise like snow drifting on the other side of Mount Fuji. They spread stealthily, as if to spy on the near side, extending their tentacles as they progressed. Suddenly they were swallowed up by the ceramic blue sky. These seemingly insignificant ambushes were not to be ignored. Such clouds tended to regroup up to noon, repeating their surprise attacks and eventually covering the entire mountain.

Honda sat absent-mindedly in the arbour until about ten o'clock. He had stored away the books that all his life had never been far from him and was dreaming of raw materials from which life and emotion had not been filtered out. He sat motionless, doing nothing. A cloud, which had appeared faintly to the left and which soon stopped at the Hoei summit, raised its tail like a leaping dolphin.

His wife, who he insisted be punctual, arrived at eleven o'clock in a clamorous taxi. Princess Ying Chan was not beside her. 'Oh dear, you're alone!' said Honda at once to this bloated, sour woman as she removed several packages from the car.

Rié did not answer for a minute, but raised her eyelids like heavy sunshades.

'I'll explain later when I've more time. I've had so much trouble. Help me with these packages first.'

Rié had waited until the designated time, but Princess Ying Chan had not made her appearance. This was after two or three telephone calls. She had finally phoned the only available contact, the Foreign Student Centre, and was told that the Princess had not returned to her dormitory the night before. She had been invited to dine at the home of some Japanese family where a new student from Thailand was staying.

Rié had been worried and had considered delaying the time of her own arrival at the villa. But she had no way of informing Honda, since they did not yet have a phone. Instead, she had hurried to the Foreign Student Centre where she left a note written in English with the caretaker, carefully explaining with a map how to get to the villa. If things went well, the Princess should arrive by the time the party started in the evening.

'Well, if that was the trouble, you could have asked Makiko Kito to help find her.'

'But I couldn't possibly impose on a guest. Even she would have a hard time locating a girl from a foreign country she doesn't know at all and then bringing her all the way over here. And besides, you can't expect a celebrity like Makiko to go out of her way. She probably thinks she's doing us a favour just by coming.'

Honda fell silent. He would reserve judgement.

When a picture is removed from the wall where it has long hung, it leaves a fresh whiteness the exact size and shape of the frame. The resulting image is pure, to be sure, but it is quite out of step with its environment; it is too strong, too insistent. Now that Honda had retired from his professional activities on the bench he had left all matters concerning justice to his wife. The whiteness of the wall was always claiming: I am just, I am right, who could possibly blame me?

To begin with, it was the wealth into which Honda had unexpectedly come and the ugliness of age which Rié had begun to notice in herself that had removed the framed portrait of the quiet submissive wife from the wall. As her husband grew rich, Rié became afraid of him. But the more fearful she was, the more arrogant she became, showing unconscious hostility to everyone, talking constantly of her chronic kidney ailment, and yet more than ever wanting affection. This desire for love made her even more homely.

As soon as she arrived at the villa and had carried the packages of food to the kitchen, Rié began noisily to wash Honda's breakfast dishes. She was sure her fatigue would aggravate her illness and was preparing the excuse of being made to work too hard though no one had ordered her to do so. She kept doing what was harmful to her health, expecting Honda to stop her. If he did not do so now, things would be difficult later.

'Why don't you rest a while and do that later?' he said kindly. 'We have plenty of time. Ying Chan really causes a lot of trouble, doesn't she? She was saying she wanted so much to help. After all that, I have to pitch in at the last minute.'

'Your help will make things worse.'

Rié returned to the living room wiping her wet hands.

In the dusky chamber where a patch of afternoon sun lay by the window, Rié's eyes under her puffy lids looked like the small holes in a woman's Nō mask. The regrets of a barren woman, uncured, worsening over the years, a body bloated with regrets like a billowing tarpaulin. 'I am right, but I'm a failure.' The unchanging gentleness she had shown her deceased mother-in-law had come from this self-reproach. If she had had children, if only she had had many children, she would have been able to melt her husband with the accumulation of their soft, sweet flesh. But deterioration had long since begun in a world where propagation was denied, just as a fish cast up from the sea on an autumn afternoon gradually rots away. Rié shuddered before this rich husband of hers.

Honda had thoughtfully ignored the distress of his wife, who was always hoping for the impossible. Now he could not bear the truth that he craved that too and in so doing was reduced to her level. But this fresh abhorrence made the existence of Rié quite important.

'Where did Ying Chan stay last night? Why did she stay away? There's a housemother at the Foreign Student Centre and supervision is probably strict. Why did she? Who was she with?' said Honda, pursuing his thought.

It was simply uneasiness. It was the same daily unsettled feeling, the precise category of emotion he experienced mornings when he shaved himself badly or nights when he could not find a comfortable position for his head on the pillow. It was a far cry from concern for a fellow human; it was somewhat detached and yet it seemed to conform to an urgent necessity in life. He had felt as though some foreign object had been cast into his mind, something like a small black Buddha image carved in black ebony from the Thai jungles.

His wife continued to prattle on about insignificant details such as how to receive the guests and which rooms should be given to those who were spending the night. All that was of no interest to Honda.

Gradually Rié became aware that her husband's mind had wandered. In the past she had never felt any suspicion about her husband when he ensconced himself in his study, for it was certain that his law studies had bound him there; but now his absent-mindedness signified the burning of an invisible flame, and his silence betokened some kind of scheme.

Rié's eyes followed her husband's gaze in an effort to find the source of his distraction. But there beyond the window lay only the garden with its dead grass on which two or three little birds had come to sport.

The guests had been invited to come at four, since Honda wanted them to see the view while the sun was still in the sky. Keiko came at one with an offer to help. Both Honda and Rié were pleased with this unexpected assistance.

Among all her husband's new friends, strangely, it was only to Keiko that Rié opened up. She felt intuitively that Keiko was not an enemy. The reason was Keiko's kindness, her great bosom and huge hips, her calm speech. Even the fragrance of her perfume seemed to lend a sort of security to Rié's innate modesty, like the official red seal of approval stamped conspicuously on certificates hung in bakeries.

Seated next to the fireplace Honda, mellowed, opened the morning paper that Rié had brought from Tokyo, listening absently to the women's conversation in the kitchen.

The headline on the first page was: ENTIRE ADMINISTRATIVE TREATY APPENDICES, according to which sixteen American Air Force bases were to be retained after the Japanese-American peace treaty went into effect. Printed to one side was a talk by Senator Smith expressing American determination – OBLIGATION TO PROTECT JAPAN. WILL NOT TOLERATE COMMUNIST AGGRESSION. On the second page American economic trends were reported under the title DECREASE IN CIVILIAN PRODUCTION: NEW REVERSAL RESULTS FROM ECONOMIC SLUMP IN WESTERN EUROPE, which appeared in bold print and showed definite concern.

But Honda's mind was constantly brought back to Ying Chan's absence. He conjured up all sorts of situations and his unshackled imagination made him uneasy. From the most ominous to the most obscene, reality had the multi-layered cross section of wood agate. He had never seen reality take such form in so far as he could recall.

Honda was startled by the loud crackling of the newspaper as he folded it. The page facing the fire was hot and dry. He idly mused that it was impossible for a newspaper to be so hot. The sensation was strangely bound with the sluggishness that lingered deep in his slackened body. Then the flames curling over a fresh log suddenly reminded him of the funeral pyres at Benares.

Keiko appeared in a large apron and said: 'How about serving sherry and whisky and water, and perhaps some Dubonnet for aperitifs? Cocktails are too much trouble. Let's not serve them.'

'I leave everything up to you.'

'And what about the Thai princess? We should have a few soft drinks in case she doesn't indulge.'

'She might not come,' Honda answered placidly.

'Oh?' Keiko said calmly and withdrew. Her impeccable courtesy made her perspicacity rather uncanny. Honda thought that one would often overestimate a woman like her because of this elegant nonchalance.

Makiko Kito was the first to arrive. She was accompanied by her pupil Mrs Tsubakihara, in whose chauffeured car they had driven over the Hakoné mountains.

Makiko's reputation as a poetess was at its height. Honda had no standards for measuring poetic values; but when he heard Makiko's name repeated by the most unexpected people, he realized how highly she must be regarded. Mrs Tsubakihara, from a former *zaibatsu* family, was about fifty, the same age as Makiko. But she showed deference to Makiko as if she were a goddess.

Mrs Tsubakihara was in perpetual mourning for her son, a Navy ensign, who had died seven years ago. Honda knew nothing of her past, but she seemed like a sad bit of fruit pickled in the vinegar of grief.

Makiko was still beautiful. Her pellucid skin showed signs of ageing, but it retained the freshness of lingering snow; and the creeping grey in her hair, untouched by artificial colouring, gave the stamp of sincerity to her poetry. Her behaviour was natural, but she emitted a sense of mystery. She never overlooked strategic presents or dinner invitations to important personalities. She won over those who might speak ill of her. Though all real emotion had long since dried up, she preserved a lingering hint of sorrow and the illusion of being alone.

Compared to her grief, that of Mrs Tsubakihara seemed immature. The comparison was indeed cruel; Makiko's aesthetic sorrow, which had been distilled into a mask, produced masterpieces, while the fresh, unhealed grief of her disciple remained in a raw, unformed state, providing no inspiration for the creation of moving poetry. Whatever slight reputation Mrs Tsubakihara enjoyed as a poetess would at once disappear were it not for Makiko's support.

Makiko extracted poetic emotion from the raw grief of this constant companion, drawing forth an abstracted sadness that no longer was the possession of anyone and labelling it with her own name. Thus, the unworked gem of sorrow and the skilled craftsman combined to bring forth innumerable masterpieces – mufflers that succeeded in concealing the ageing necks that carried them year after year.

Makiko was irritated to have arrived early.

'The chauffeur drove too fast,' she said, looking at Mrs Tsubakihara beside her.

'Quite so. The traffic was not so congested as we expected.'

'Let's see the garden first. We were looking forward to that,' she said to Honda. 'Please don't bother, we'll just take our time and stroll about and maybe write a little poetry.'

Honda insisted on showing them around and took along a bottle of sherry and some titbits, intending to serve them in the arbour. The afternoon had grown warm. Beyond the garden, which narrowed as it sloped gently to the valley, one could see Mount Fuji to the west. It was veiled by the cotton clouds of spring, and only the snow-clad summit was sharply limned against the azure sky.

'By summer I plan to have a swimming pool built in front of the terrace where the birdhouse is,' Honda explained on the way.

But the ladies' response was chill, and he suddenly felt like a clerk at some inn escorting guests on a tour of the premises.

Artists and their ilk proved most difficult for Honda to deal with. He had resumed relations with Makiko at the time of the fifteenth memorial service for Isao in 1948. Japanese poetry had not been the cause, as one might have expected. The former perfunctory relationship of counsellor and witness (even though it held undertones of conniving) had actually blossomed into friendship, for they both held unvoiced affection for Isao. Honda was at a complete loss for words and had thus broached the inane subject of a swimming pool. Makiko with her pupil at her side stood facing the spectacle of Mount Fuji in the spring.

He knew that the women did not quite feel contemptuous of him, yet he realized they felt easy enough with him to act without constraint. He was outside their circle, alien to their way of life. He could easily imagine Makiko speaking to someone involved in a difficult case: 'Mr Honda's a friend of mine. No, he doesn't write poetry. But he's very understanding, and he's excellent in both civil and criminal cases. I'll speak to him for you.'

But within, Honda was afraid of Makiko, and she probably was just as frightened of him. She had revived the old association with him in order to protect her name. Honda had no illusions as to her true character; he knew that she was quite capable of bearing false witness, of telling at the critical moment the most thoroughly believable lies.

Other than that, Honda was likeable, unobjectionable to the women. How freely they talked in front of him, whereas they at once hid behind innocuous social chatter when Rié approached. Honda liked to observe these once beautiful, but no longer young women, their perpetual sad conversations, their confusion of their own sensuality with the past, memories and realities encroaching one upon the other, and their habit of distorting nature and reality to suit their whim. He also liked their ability to bestow automatic lyricism on everything beautiful they saw, like a bailiff stamping every piece of furniture he finds. As if this were a way of protecting themselves from whatever beauty they might perceive. Honda liked to see them romp and gambol like two inspired waterfowl who, having stumbled clumsily onto land, slip back into the water, exhibiting forthwith unexpected grace and nimbleness as they swim and dive with abandon. When they composed a poem, they would display unreserved freedom in mental sunbathing, quite without fear of the resultant exposure. It brought to mind the young Princess and the old ladies at Bang Pa In.

Would Ying Chan really come? Where had she stayed the night? Concern suddenly inserted a rough wooden wedge into his mind.

'What a beautiful garden! Hakoné to the east and Fuji to the west. It's a crime that you dawdle around without writing a single poem. While we're forced to produce poetry under the polluted skies of Tokyo, you read law books here. What an unfair world!'

'I gave up on legal books long ago,' said Honda, offering them some sherry. The movement of kimono sleeves and the graceful motion of their fingers as the two women accepted the sherry glasses were extremely lovely. Actually Mrs Tsubakihara slavishly aped Makiko, from the gesture of lightly holding up her sleeve to the way she curled her ringed fingers when picking up the glass.

'How happy Akio would have been to see this garden!' said Mrs Tsubakihara, mentioning her dead son. 'He adored Mount Fuji, and even before entering the Navy, he had a framed photograph of it in his study so he could always look at it. Such clean-cut, youthful tastes.'

Every time she mentioned his name, the ripple of a sob touched her cheeks, as though a precision mechanism existed in the depth of her heart, automatically activated at every reference to him, independent of her wishes, and producing an unvarying facial expression. As an emperor's name is always mentioned with a reverent expression, the fleeting trace of sobs was practically synonymous with the name Akio.

Makiko had spread a notebook on her lap and composed a poem.

'You've already written one!' exclaimed Mrs Tsubakihara, looking jealously at her teacher's bent head. Honda looked too. The slim, white, fragrant nape that had once attracted young Isao lingered like a fading moon in his eyes.

'That's Mr Imanishi. I'm sure it must be!' cried Mrs Tsubakihara, looking at the man crossing the lawn. Even from that distance, the white forehead and tall figure walking in the characteristically infirm manner, trailing its long shadow, were recognizably his.

'How horrible! He's sure to start that vulgar talk again. He'll ruin our enjoyment straightaway,' said Mrs Tsubakihara.

Yasushi Imanishi was about forty and a specialist in German literature. He had introduced the younger German writers during the war and now indiscriminately wrote all kinds of essays. Currently he was dreaming about the *Millennium of Sex* that he was going to write, but as yet there was no sign of his having done so. Probably he had lost interest in writing it now that he had discussed with everyone the details of its contents. What relevance the *Millennium*, which was altogether weird and gloomy, could hold for him no one could say. He was the second son of the head of Imanishi Securities and was living the comfortable life of a bachelor.

His face was pale and nervous, but he was congenial, talkative, and both the financial world and left-wing writers found him amusing. He really felt that he had discovered for the first time in his life something that suited his personality in this post-war iconoclastic period directed against established authority and convention. This was the struggle taken up by rugged, pale intellectuals. He advocated the political significance of sexual fantasy, which he had adopted as his specialty. Until then, he had been merely a Novalis-like romanticist.

Women liked the manner he had of gallantly spicing his aristocratic ways with obscenities. Those who called him degenerate were only revealing that they were holdovers from feudal days. At the same time, Imanishi never failed to disappoint serious progressives by his silly future map of the *Millennium*.

He never spoke in a loud voice. For that presented the danger of taking matters from the area of delicate sensuality and transforming them into ideology.

The four guests passed the time in the arbour basking in the afternoon sun, while they waited for the others to arrive. The gurgling sound of the stream running just below insisted on intruding itself into their awareness. Honda could not help but remember the words: 'Everything is in constant flux like a torrent.'

Imanishi had called the kingdom of his fantasy 'The Land of the Pomegranate'. He had named it after the small, ruby-red bursting seeds. He claimed that he travelled to his kingdom asleep and awake, and everyone asked for news of it.

'What's happening in "The Land of the Pomegranate" these days?'

'As usual the population is well under control. All sorts of problems arise because of the high incidence of incest. A single woman is often aunt, mother, sister, and cousin to the same man. As a result, half the babies are incredibly beautiful, while the other half are ugly and deformed.

'The beautiful children of both sexes are separated in infancy from the ugly ones and assembled in a place called "The Garden of the Loved Ones". The facilities are magnificent, a veritable paradise on earth. An artificial sun constantly gives out exactly the ideal number of ultraviolet rays. No one wears clothes, and all devote themselves to swimming and other physical exercises. Flowers bloom in profusion, and small animals and birds are never caged. The children there eat good nourishing food, but never grow fat, for they are checked weekly by medical examiners. They can only grow more and more beautiful. But reading is strictly forbidden. It spoils natural beauty, so the taboo makes sense.

'But when they reach adolescence, they're brought from the garden once a week to become objects of sexual amusement for the ugly ones outside. After two or three years of this sort of activity, they are destroyed. Don't you think it's true brotherly love to terminate life while beautiful people are still young?

'The creative powers of all artists in the land are utilized to develop various means of slaughter. That is to say, there are theatres throughout the country devoted to sexual murder, in which the beautiful boys and girls are cast in all manner of roles where they are tortured to death. They re-create all sorts of mythological and historical personalities who were sadistically murdered while young and beautiful. But of course there are many new creations too. They are nobly murdered in magnificent, sensual costumes, with splendid lighting, brilliant stage settings, and wonderful music; but usually they are toyed with by members of the audience before they are quite dead, and after that the bodies are consumed.

'The graves? The graves are right outside "The Garden of the Loved Ones". It's a beautiful place, and ugly deformed people stroll among the tombs on moonlit nights, lost in romantic moods. As statues of the beautiful ones are erected as gravestones, there's no cemetery in the world with so many beautiful bodies.'

'Why do they have to kill them?'

'Because they're soon bored by living people.

'The people in "The Land of the Pomegranate" are infinitely wise. They know very well that there are only two roles for humans in this world: those who remember and those who are remembered.

'Now that I have told you this much, I must inform you about their religion. Such custom is based on religious belief.

'They don't believe in rebirth in "The Land of the Pomegranate". Because God is manifest at the supreme instant of sexual climax, and the true nature of godliness lies in its unique appearance. There is no possibility that one would become more beautiful after rebirth, and that means that resurrection would hold no meaning. It's unthinkable that a faded shirt should be whiter than a brand-new one, isn't it. So the gods of "The Land of the Pomegranate" are used once and thrown away.

'The religion of the country is polytheistic, but in a temporal sort of way; and countless numbers of gods squander their total physical existence, disappearing once they have expressed this highest moment in eternity. Now you know: "The Garden of the Loved Ones" is a factory for making gods.

'To transform history in this world into a chain of beautiful events, the sacrifice of gods must continue infinitely. Such is the theology. Don't you think it's rational? Furthermore, the people display absolutely no hypocrisy; so beauty and sexual attractiveness are synonyms. They are very well aware that only through sexual desire may one approach God; that is, beauty.

'One possesses a god by means of sexual desire, and sexual possession occurs at the climax of pleasure. But an orgasm does not endure, therefore possession can mean only one thing: the unification of the unenduring with the ephemeralness of the object of sexual desire. The surest method is the elimination of this object at the moment of climax. Therefore, the people of the country are clearly aware that sexual possession is consummated in murder and cannibalism.

'It is certainly wonderful that this paradox of sexual possession controls even the economic structure of the country. The fundamental rule of possession is "to kill the loved one", which means that completion of any possession signifies simultaneous termination of possessing, and continued possession is a violation of love. Physical labour is permitted only to create beautiful physiques, and the ugly are exempted from it. Actually industrial production is completely automated and does not require human power. The arts? The only arts are found in the infinite variety of the murder theatre as well as in the erection of statues to the beautiful dead. From the religious point of view, sensual realism is the basic style, and abstraction is completely rejected. Incorporation of "life" in the arts is strictly forbidden.

'The approach to beauty is through sexual desire, but what records this moment of beauty for all eternity is memory ... Now you have a rough understanding of the fundamental structure of "The Land of the Pomegranate", I think. The basic concept is memory, and in a manner of speaking, memory is national policy.

'Orgasm, a phenomenon something like a corporeal crystal, is further crystallized in memory, and following the death of the god of beauty, one can recall the highest degree of sexual excitement. The people live only in order to reach this point. Compared to this heavenly jewel, the physical existence of human beings, whether the lover or the beloved, the killer or the killed, is only the means of reaching this point. This is the ideal of the country.

'Memory is the sole matter of our spirit. Even should a god appear at the climax of sexual possession, then that god becomes "the remembered one", and the lover becomes "the one who remembers". Only through this time-consuming process is the presence of the god really proved, is beauty attained for the first time, and is sexual desire distilled into love that is independent of possession. *Hence, gods and humans are not separated in space, but there is a time lag between them.* Here lies the essence of temporal polytheism. Do you understand?

'Murder sounds harsh, but it is necessary for purifying memory and distilling it into its strongest concentrated element. Besides, these ugly, deformed inhabitants are noble, truly noble. They are experts in altruism; they live for self-denial. These lovers-cum-murderers-cum-rememberers live their roles faithfully, they remember nothing about themselves, but live only in adoration of the memory of the loved ones' beautiful death. Remembering becomes the single task of their lives. "The Land of the Pomegranate" is also a country of cypresses, beautiful mementoes, and mourning; it is the most peaceful and quiet place in all the world, a country of recollections.

'Every time I go there, I think I never want to return to a place like Japan. The land is full of the sweetest, tenderest elements of humanity. It is a country of true humanism and peace. They have no such savage custom as eating the flesh of oxen and pigs.'

'I would like to ask you one thing. You say that they eat human flesh, but what parts of the human body do they consume?' Makiko asked, amused.

'You know very well without asking,' said Imanishi in a quiet, subdued voice.

Honda thought it more than comical that a former judge could listen without flinching to such manner of talk. He had never even dreamed that a man like Imanishi could ever exist. Had Cesare Lombroso, the criminologist, met him, he would have ordered him immediately banished from society.

Honda was repelled by Imanishi's sex-oriented interests, yet he himself indulged in another kind. If this were not a product of Imanishi's imagination, they should all be inhabitants of the sex millennium of the gods. It was a divine theatrical farce that God had made Honda live on as one who would remember, killing off Kiyoaki and Isao as those to be remembered. But Imanishi had stated that there was no rebirth. Samsara might be an idea standing in opposition to resurrection, and its characteristic might be its guaranteeing that life occur only once. In particular, Imanishi's theory that there was a time lag between human existence and God, and that man could meet God only in memory forced Honda to look back upon his own life and his travels; it evoked something vast and vaguely nostalgic.

What a man Imanishi was!

He intentionally exposed to the sun black inner deformities and was even pleased in so doing. He staked all on the sophistication of his nonchalant face, describing his blackness to others as though it did not concern him at all.

Honda, having long been a part of the legal world, concealed in his heart a certain romantic respect for the self-confident criminal. To be truthful, the confident criminal was extremely rare. Indeed, he had never met anyone who could be so classified except Isao.

It followed that Honda concealed feelings of hatred and contempt for repentant offenders.

Which was Imanishi?

He was probably never repentant, but he quite lacked the nobility of the principled criminal. By his vanity and sophistication he was trying to embellish the meanness of a man who has confessed and thus sought to achieve the advantage of both confession and sophistication. The ugliness of this transparent anatomical model! Honda, nevertheless, persistently refused to recognize the fact that he was somewhat attracted to Imanishi, that the invitation he had extended to him to come to the villa was rooted in a kind of envy for his courage. Furthermore, that he concealed this was not because of his conceit and fortitude in demeaning himself to the baseness of one who has confessed, but doubtless because of his fear of Imanishi's X-ray eyes. Honda had secretly labelled his own fear the 'sickness of objectivity'. It was the ultimate hell, filled with pleasurable thrills, into which a cognition that refused to act was finally precipitated.

The man has eyes like a fish, thought Honda, glancing surreptitiously at Imanishi's profile as the latter was talking triumphantly to the women.

Only after the sun had dyed the clouds to the left of Mount Fuji had all the guests assembled.

When the four made their way from the arbour to the house, Keiko's American lover, the Army lieutenant, was helping her in the kitchen. Shortly, the ageing erstwhile Baron and Baroness Shinkawa arrived; then at intervals, Sakurai, a diplomat; Murata, the president of a construction company; Kawaguchi, an important newspaper man; Akiko Kyoya, a singer of French songs; and Ikuko Fujima, a traditional Japanese dancer. Such a motley group of guests would have been unthinkable in Honda's former household. Honda's heart, too, was heavy: Ying Chan had not put in an appearance.

26

Former Baron Shinkawa was seated in a chair by the fireside from which point he coldly observed the other guests.

He was now seventy-two. Grumbling and complaining without fail whenever he left home, he could not forego the joy of going out; at even his age his love for parties had not diminished. He had been very bored during the period of the post-war purges and had fallen into the habit of accepting all invitations. This had continued on into the post-purge years.

But now everyone considered him and his garrulous wife to be the most boring of guests. His sarcasm had lost its bite, and his epigrammatic expressions had become long-winded and shallow. He was never able to recall people's names.

'That ... what was he called? ... remember ... he was often depicted in political cartoons ... don't you remember? ... a small, fat man, round as a butterball ... what was his name? ... a very common one ...'

His listener could not help but recognize Shinkawa's losing battle with the invisible monster of forgetfulness. This quiet, but tenacious animal would occasionally withdraw only to reappear at once, clinging to Shinkawa, brushing his forehead with its shaggy tail.

At last, he would give up and continue his story.

'... anyway, this politician's wife was a remarkable woman.' But the episode in which the most important name was missing no longer held any flavour. Each time he would stamp his foot in sheer vexation, so anxious was he to impart to others the flavour of the tale he alone could savour. It was then that Shinkawa would be aware of a mendicant-like emotion, one he had previously never experienced. In his struggle to find someone to appreciate his simple punning jokes, as though begging for understanding, he had unconsciously become obsequious.

He was pathetically compelled to tear down the refined pride he had so long possessed, and gradually his prime concern became the assumption of an attitude of contemptuousness – something that he had exhibited most casually on the tip of his nose like cigar smoke in former days. But at the same time, he took great pains to avoid revealing this hidden contempt to anyone. He was fearful that he might not receive other invitations.

In the midst of a party, he would occasionally pull at his wife's sleeve and whisper in her ear:

'What a despicable pack. They don't know the first thing about how to speak of the indelicate in a refined way. Japanese ugliness is so complete it's almost impressive. But you mustn't let them suspect how we think.'

Shinkawa's eyes suddenly became glazed before the flames in the fireplace; he recalled the garden party at the Marquis Matsugae's some forty years ago, proudly remembering that there too he had felt nothing but contempt for his host.

But only one thing had changed. In former times, the object of his contempt could do him no harm; but now just being there profoundly wounded him.

Mrs Shinkawa was vivacious.

At her age she increasingly found an indefinable interest in talking about herself. Her search for listeners harmonized beautifully with the attempt to abolish class distinctions that was now in style. She had never once been concerned about the quality of her audience.

She paid exaggerated compliments to the singer of French songs as though she were talking to royalty, in return for which she obtained a hearing. She shamelessly praised Makiko Kito's poems and then imposed her own tale on the poor woman – once she had been complimented by an Englishman who had called her a poet. He had made the remark when she had compared the late summer clouds over Karuizawa to a Sisley painting.

Now, moved by some uncanny intuition, she began to talk about the garden party at the Matsugae estate as she joined her husband by the fireplace.

'As I think back, those were stupid and uncivilized times when expensive parties entailed nothing more than having a few geisha dance and make music at home. How unimaginative people were then. I must say Japan has made quite a bit of progress: the barbarous customs are gone and it's ordinary for wives to be included in social affairs. Look at them, the women at this party are no longer silent. Conversations that took place at garden parties used to be excruciatingly boring, but now the women converse very wittily.'

But it was doubtful whether she had ever listened to anyone's conversation, either now or at any time in the past forty years. She had never tried to talk about anything except herself. Mrs Shinkawa suddenly left her husband's side. She cast a glance into a dark mirror mounted on a wall. Looking-glasses never frightened her. They all functioned as waste-baskets into which she could discard her wrinkles as she stood before them.

Jack, a first lieutenant in the Quartermaster Corps, was working hard. The guests looked with pleasure at this member of the 'Occupation Forces' who was so gentle and loyal. Keiko treated him grandly, with incomparable regal skill.

Sometimes Jack would extend an arm and encircle her from behind, mischievously touching her breast. She permitted herself a calm, wry smile as she clasped his hairy, ringed fingers.

'Such a child. He's incorrigible,' she said in a dry, didactic tone, looking around at everyone. Jack's posterior encased in his Army uniform was capacious, and the guests would compare it with Keiko's majestic buttocks, arguing which was the larger.

Mrs Tsubakihara was still talking with Imanishi. She was taken aback to meet for the first time someone who completely scorned her precious sorrow, but she did not change in the least the idiotic expression of mourning on her face.

'No matter how much you grieve, your son will not come back to life. Besides you've a balloon in your heart so filled with grief that nothing else can possibly get in. It gives you a secure feeling, doesn't it. Let me be rude a bit more: you're convinced that no one else will do you the favour of filling your balloon, so you fill it yourself with home-made sorrow-gas that you pump into it at a moment's notice. That releases you from the fear of being bothered by any other emotion.'

'What a horrible thing to say! How cruel...'

Mrs Tsubakihara looked up at Imanishi from the handkerchief in which she muffled her sobs. He thought the look in her eyes was that of an innocent little girl who craved to be raped.

The president of the Murata Construction Company was offering a hyperbolic compliment to Shinkawa, hailing him as a great patron in the financial world. Shinkawa was irked to be assigned to the same category as the vulgar builder. Murata had erected immense billboards bearing his name on all the company's construction sites; the self-advertising was everywhere. But no one looked less like a construction expert. A pale, flat face revealed his background as a reformist bureaucrat of pre-war days. He was an idealist who lived parasitically off others. No sooner had he stopped clinging and achieved independent success in business than he discovered a bright, vast ocean where his inherent crassness could disport itself without restraint. Murata had made the dancer Ikuko Fujima his mistress. Ikuko was wearing a sumptuous kimono interwoven with silk and lacquer threads, and a five-carat diamond blazed on her finger; when she laughed, she held her neck and back rigidly erect.

'An extremely fine house, sir, but if you'd let me build it for you, I could have saved you a lot of money. What a shame,' Murata repeated at least three times to Honda.

The diplomat Sakurai and the senior reporter Kawaguchi were discussing international problems, standing on either side of Akiko Kyoya. Sakurai's fish-like skin and Kawaguchi's, marked by age and spoiled by saké, provided a good contrast between the two and their careers. One was cold- and the other hot-blooded. They were discussing weighty problems, as men are wont to do in the company of women, in an effort to impress the singer Akiko. She, on the other hand, was completely oblivious to the subtle rivalry and inane vanity, constantly helping herself to the canapés, glancing alternately with her melancholic, dark eyes at the dishevelled white hair and the overly groomed head. She pursed her mouth into the shape of an O and tossed one titbit after another between her goldfish lips.

Makiko Kito took the trouble of going up to Imanishi and saying: 'You have the most peculiar tastes.'

'Must I get your permission every time I make love to your pupil? It's as though I were making love to my mother, I feel a kind of sacred tremor. At any rate, I'll never make the mistake of making love to you. What you think of me is written all over your face. I'm the type that repels you sexually more than any other, right?'

'You know very well you do.'

Makiko felt relieved and spoke in a most charming voice. Then she laid a strip of silence between them, that resembled the black edge of tatami matting.

'Even if you should succeed in making love to her, you could never assume the role of her son. Her dead son is extremely sacred and beautiful to her; she is a holy priestess serving him.'

'Well, I don't know. To me everything looks suspicious. It's blasphemy that a living person should continue harbouring pure emotions and expressing them.'

'That's why I say she is serving the pure sentiment of the dead.'

'Anyway she does it out of her necessity to live. That already makes it suspicious.'

Makiko narrowed her eyes and laughed in sheer repulsion.

'There isn't a real man at this party,' she said. With that she left Imanishi as Honda called to her. Mrs Tsubakihara was seated on the edge of a bench built into the wall, crying as she leaned back. Outside, the night air was extremely cold, and condensed droplets of moisture trickled down the panes.

Honda intended to ask Makiko to take care of Mrs Tsubakihara. If her tears stemmed less from her painful memories than from the small amount of liquor she had consumed, she could well be a sentimental drinker.

Rié, her face pallid, approached Honda and whispered in his ear.

'There's been a strange noise. It started a little while ago in the garden ... I wonder if I'm hearing things.'

'Did you look?'

'No, I was afraid to.'

Honda strode to one of the windows and cleared the steam from the pane with his fingers. Beyond the dead grass, above the cypresses, hung a spectral moon. A wild dog was snooping about, dragging its shadow after it. Stopping and curling up its tail, it threw out its furry white chest that shone in the moonlight and howled mournfully.

'That's it, isn't it?' Honda asked his wife. The cause of her childish fear had been too easily revealed and Rié did not immediately agree, but merely smiled a vague, indecisive smile.

As he listened further, two or three dogs responded from beyond the cypress grove.

The wind had increased.

27

It was midnight. From the window of his second-floor study, Honda watched a small, ghostly moon traverse the sky. Ying Chan had not put in an appearance. The moon had come instead.

The party had come to a close near midnight. Only the overnight guests still remained, gathered in a small circle. Gradually they withdrew to their assigned bedrooms. After the two guest rooms upstairs, came Honda's study, which in turn adjoined the master bedroom. Once she had seen the guests off, exhaustion had settled in, numbing Rié's body to the very tips of her swollen fingers. She had retired to her bedroom after bidding her husband good night. Alone in the study, Honda still saw the backs of his wife's hands which were so swollen they gave off a dull sheen. Rié had triumphantly shown them to him.

The malice spreading inside had pushed outward, swelling her skin, erasing the angularity of her hands, which had taken on a strangely puffy, childish appearance that stayed with him a long time. He had suggested a private celebration in their bedroom on the occasion of the house-warming, but he had been turned down. If his suggestion had not been vetoed, what would have happened? Something desolate must flow under that nauseous subcutaneous fat of kindness and sympathy.

Honda looked about his Western study, with its pretentious bright window and its clean desk. When he really worked hard, the study was never like this. Then it had an unmanageable disorderliness, like that of living itself, and it smelled like a chicken roost. Now, on the arty desk fashioned from a single zelkova plank an English writing set of Moroccan leather had been placed. In the pen plate were several pencils neatly sharpened, all in a line, embossed letters freshly shining like the insignia on cadets' collars. There was also his bronze alligator paperweight – inherited from his father – and an empty letter box of meshed bamboo.

He rose frequently and crossed over to wipe the panes in the bay window with its curtains still open, for the moon shining through the glass was clouded and distorted by the heat in the room. He was certain that unless the moon were permitted to stay clear, the emptiness and disgust that flooded his heart would expand and expand, and the dark turmoil would be transformed into sexual desire. It astonished him to discover that it was just such a landscape that awaited him at the end of his life's journey. The dog's mournful bark sounded again, and the fragile cypress trees creaked in the wind.

It was some time since his wife had gone to sleep in the next room. Honda switched off the light in the study and walked over to the bookcases that flanked the wall of the guest room. Quietly he took down a number of Western books and piled them on the floor. What he had himself labelled the 'disease of objectivity' now overcame him. The minute he surrendered to it he would be forced to antagonize all society which until now had been on his side.

But why? he wondered. This too was a part of the varied aspects of human behaviour which he had objectively observed from the bench or from the lawyer's seat for so many years. How could it be that observing from those vantage points was perfectly legal, but looking as he would now a violation of the law? Observation in that manner had made him the object of approval by society, while watching like this was subject to reproach and contempt. If this were a crime, it was probably because he derived so much pleasure from it. Yet his experience as judge had taught him the pleasure to be found in a clear mind, devoid of private desire. And if that enjoyment was noble because it was not accompanied by any quickening of the pulse, could it be that the essence of criminality lay in the palpitation of the heart? This innermost response of a human being, this palpitation in the face of pleasure – could that be the most significant ingredient in any violation of the law?

All this was sophistry. As he pulled the books from the bookcase, Honda felt a throbbing in his heart similar to that of a young boy, and he was made sharply aware how weak and vulnerable his very existence was *vis-à-vis* society. He was alone and helpless. The forces that had held him high as on a scaffolding had now been removed. Like the sand trickling in an hour-glass, the inexorable endless descent had started. In that case, law and society were already his enemies. Had he possessed a little more courage and were this not his own study but some corner of a park where young grass grew or perhaps a dark by-road speckled with the lights of houses, he would then in reality become a most shameful criminal. People would jeer: 'The judge became attorney, and the attorney a criminal!' They would say that here was a man who had never stopped loving the court throughout his life!

Once the books were removed, a small hole appeared before him in the wall. The dusty, dark space was just large enough for his face. The dusty smell suddenly filled Honda's heart with keen memories of youth, striking the meagre red sparks of the secret pleasures of childhood. He remembered the texture of the dark-blue velvet coverlet mixed with the odour of the toilet. The first obscene word he had discovered in a dictionary. All the melancholic, foul odours of boyhood. He discovered in his throbbing heart the faintest caricature of the noble passion that had urged Kiyoaki toward final catastrophe. Whatever it was, it was a single dark passage that connected the nineteen-year-old Kiyoaki and the fifty-seven-year-old Honda. As he closed his eyes, an illusion sprang up, in the darkness of the bookcase, of scattered particles of red flesh flying about like a cluster of mosquitoes.

The guest room next to his study was occupied by Makiko and Mrs Tsubakihara. Imanishi occupied the chamber beyond. Honda had definitely sensed some sort of communication between the two rooms; he had heard doors opening surreptitiously and then the sound of muffled voices, scolding whispers, similar to spatterings on the surface of water. The noise stopped and then began again. Something was being precipitated on the plane that inclined into the depth of night, as though an ivory die were cast and were rolling down a tilted board.

He had an idea of what was taking place. But what met his eyes was more than he had imagined.

In the adjacent guest room twin beds had been placed parallel to the wall with the secret opening. The bed directly below the hole was almost completely out of his view, but the other was entirely visible. The night lamp was on, but the bed itself was veiled in shadow.

Honda was startled to see in the pale light a pair of wide-open eyes staring into his. They belonged to none other than Makiko.

She was sitting on the far bed clad in a white night kimono. The collar of the robe was primly closed, and her silvery hair shone dimly in the light that came from one side. She had cleansed her face of cosmetics, and its whiteness of former days had not changed. It still was clear and cold. Her age was revealed in the round shoulders where the plump flesh had drooped, but for the most part her confidence in the imperviousness of her being, never threatened through the long years, was obvious in the regular breathing of her breast. It was as if the essence of night were seated there, clad in white. Honda felt as though he were looking at Mount Fuji on a moonlit night. The gentle slope at the foot of the mountain was covered in the flowing creases of the blue-lined blanket. Makiko's lap was half hidden under the coverlet on which she languidly leaned her arm.

Her eyes, that appeared at first to have caught Honda's peeping gaze, were not really turned toward the hole. They were lowered and were gazing at the bed placed against the wall.

Seeing only her eyes, one would be convinced that Makiko was concentrating on the creation of a poem as she gazed into some river which happened to lie just beneath. It was that time of night when the human spirit could grasp a certain vivid turmoil in the air and would struggle to crystallize it. In making the effort, one's eyes would become like those of a hunter about to shoot. Seeing only her eyes, one could but feel the sublimity of her soul.

Makiko was not looking at a river or a fish, but at human forms writhing on the shadowy bed. Honda elevated his head until he struck the top of the bookcase in an effort to see down through the small peephole. He could in this way observe what was taking place on the bed beyond the wall. A man's thin, pale thighs were twined about those of a woman. Immediately below him were two heaps of withered flesh hardly bursting with vigour, swaying slowly like aquatic animals as they made contact. They gleamed damply in the faint light; the devourer was unmistakably being devoured; obvious trickery was going hand in hand with sincere tremors. Two mounds of moist pubic hair touched and separated; and a white patch where the light struck the woman's belly, as if a piece of white tissue had been inserted between the two bodies, pierced Honda's awestricken eyes.

Whatever the situation, Imanishi had shamelessly exposed the pitiful thighs of an intellectual in heat. True to his theories, the cheerless, rippling oscillation of his flat buttocks, between which appeared a wasted coccyx, was merely a momentary illusion. His obvious lack of sincerity angered Honda.

Compared to him, Mrs Tsubakihara was earnestness itself; he could see her hands stretched out like those of a drowning woman, her fingers desperately grasping at Imanishi's hair. At last, she called her son's name. It was a suppressed, faint cry:

'Akio, Akio. Forgive me...' Her words were muffled in sobs, but Imanishi was not affected in the least.

Honda, suddenly recognizing the solemnity and loathsomeness of the situation, bit his lips. It was now clear. Whether Makiko had ordered her to perform or not, it was obviously not the first time that Mrs Tsubakihara had been involved in this sort of exhibition for Makiko and probably only for her. This was the essence of the teacher–student relationship between Makiko and Mrs Tsubakihara, their contempt and dedication.

Honda looked at Makiko again. She was looking down serenely, her silvery hair shining and floating over her head. They were of a different sex, but Honda realized that Makiko was his exact counterpart.

28

The next day was beautiful and sunny. The Hondas had invited their three overnight guests and Keiko to drive in two separate cars to the Sengen Shrine at Fuji-Yoshida. Except for Keiko, they all planned to depart for Tokyo from there, and Honda had locked up before leaving the villa. Just as he was closing the door, he had the sudden premonition that Ying Chan would come during his absence; but that was most unlikely.

Honda had just been reading the *Honcho monzui*, 'Compositions of Elegance Composed in Japan', which Imanishi had brought for him. Of course, he had wished to read the 'Essays on Mount Fuji' by Yoshika no Miyako and had asked Imanishi to get him a copy.

'Mount Fuji is located in the province of Suruga; its peak, as if sharpened, towers high into the heavens.' Such descriptions held little interest, but then a passage followed that struck Honda so strongly that it had long remained in his memory; he had not had the chance of reading it again since then.

An old man recounted: On the fifth day of the eleventh month in the seventeenth year of Jokan (AD 875), officials and people gathered to hold a celebration in accordance with tradition. The sun emerged around noon, and the sky was extremely beautiful and clear. As the spectators looked up to the summit of the mountain, they saw two beautiful women in white garments dancing together. Both were floating more than a foot above the peak. All the inhabitants of the land saw them.

It was not strange that such optical illusions should occur on a fine day at Mount Fuji, for it often produced various chimera. Frequently a quiet wind at the sloping foot of the mountain would develop into a strong gale at the top, carrying a mist of snow into the blue sky. It was probably this snow dust that had appeared in the form of two beautiful women to the inhabitants' eyes.

Fuji was cold and self-assured, but through its confident coldness and whiteness it permitted all possible fantasies. In ultimate frigidity is vertigo, just as delirium characterizes the extreme of reason. Fuji was a mysterious ultimate of perfection and its beauty verged on a vague lyricism. It was at once infinite and finite. It was quite possible that two beautiful women in white garments had danced there.

In addition, Honda was charmed by the fact that the spirit enshrined at the Sengen Shrine was a goddess called Konohana Sakuya.

Mrs Tsubakihara, Makiko, and Imanishi rode in Mrs Tsubakihara's car, and the Hondas and Keiko took the limousine Honda had engaged for his return to Tokyo. This was a natural arrangement, but Honda had vaguely wanted to be in the same car as Makiko and experienced a pang of regret. He had wanted to sit next to her and look into the intense eyes he had seen the night before, the eyes of a huntress ready to launch her arrow.

The drive to Fuji-Yoshida, however, was not an easy one. The national highway, the former Kamakura Road, climbed over the Kagosaka Pass from Subashiri and passed northward along Lake Yamanaka. It was mostly unpaved and mountainous. The prefectural boundary between Shizuoka and Yamanashi ran along the ridge of Kagosaka.

While Keiko and Rié sat next to each other and made their small woman-talk, Honda looked out the window with childlike earnestness. Keiko's presence was very useful in forestalling Rié's complaints. Rié had become like a bottle of beer that overflowed the moment the cap was removed. Since morning she had been objecting to the idea of driving back to Tokyo, insisting that not since childhood had she taken such a long, meaningless, and extravagant drive.

This same Rié became quite docile, even charming, as she talked with Keiko.

'You don't have to worry about kidney trouble,' Keiko said bluntly.

'Do you think so? When I hear you talk like that, I'm rather encouraged. It's strange. I get angry when my husband speaks to me sweetly with his dishonest, exaggerated sympathy and pretended concern.'

Probably out of tact, Keiko would never come to Honda's defence when Rié attacked him.

'Mr Honda has no head for anything but logical thinking, and there's nothing you can do about it,' said Keiko.

Once across the dividing line, one could see that the northern slope of the mountain was completely blanketed in hard-frozen snow that, in contracting, had become etched in a snakeskin pattern. It resembled the backs of Rié's hands when the swelling subsided.

At the moment, however, Rié had become more bearable to Honda. To be with two women who, in his hearing, were talking so unflatteringly – especially when one was his own wife – somehow provided him a passing feeling of contentment.

Beyond the Kagosaka Pass, a heavy layer of snow lay over everything, and the ground in the sparse grove at Lake Yamanaka looked as if it were covered by frozen *crêpe de chine*. The pine needles were yellow, and only in the water of the lake was the colour bright and clear. As he looked back, the white surface of Fuji, the origin of all the whiteness in this area, was glowing as if it had been brushed with oil.

It was about half past three in the afternoon when they arrived at the Sengen Shrine. As he glanced back at the three passengers emerging from the black Chrysler, Honda experienced an ominous feeling as if he were watching corpses suddenly rising from a black coffin. This morning it was imperative for the three that they wipe clean the memory of the previous night. But confinement in the close quarters of the limousine for the entire journey had made the episode even more odious, like the waters of abdominal dropsy that accumulate immediately, no matter how frequently they are tapped. The three blinked as though bothered by the glare from the snow at the roadside. Nevertheless, Makiko was standing rigidly erect. Honda was repelled by the sight of Imanishi's sallow, unresilient skin. He had blasphemed against the beauty of that tragic fantasy of the flesh, of which he had spoken so elatedly the previous day; this had been proven by his complete lack of qualifications as a lover. He compounded the outrage by his conviction that his ugliness would remain undetected.

In any event, Honda had witnessed it. The one who sees and the one who had unknowingly been seen were already conjoined at the limits of this double world. Makiko glanced up at the gigantic stone torii with 'Mount Fuji' carved on a framed rock and again took out the notebook she always carried for jotting down her poetical thoughts. A delicate pencil was permanently attached to it by a purple string.

Helping each other, the six walked along the damp, snowy path leading to the shrine. Here and there the sun penetrated through the branches, highlighting patches of snow. The lofty limbs of the old cryptomerias continued to release their dead brown needles that fell on the little heaps of tenacious snow. There was a misty light that made it seem that they were enveloped in a greenish haze. At the far end of the path a red torii surrounded by snow came into view.

This sign of divinity evoked in Honda the memory of Isao Iinuma. Again he looked at Makiko. Momentarily he felt he could forget her eyes at midnight, now that she was imbued with divine power. Isao, adored by those changing eyes, had perhaps been slain by them.

Keiko maintained a calm and self-possessed attitude no matter what she saw.

'How beautiful! Wonderful. How Japanese!' she said expansively.

Makiko actually seemed to wince on hearing her conclusive way of speaking and glanced at her somewhat fretfully. Rié detachedly watched from her position at the rear.

Each tottering step Mrs Tsubakihara took along the path to the shrine gave her the appearance of a sorrowful crane with drooping feathers. She offhandedly refused the assistance profferred by Imanishi and placed her hand on Honda's arm. She was in no mood to compose poetry.

Her grief was too genuine to be a pose, and Honda was almost touched as he gazed down at her doleful profile. His eyes met Makiko's who had chosen that instant to glance from the other side at her dejected disciple. As usual, Makiko had discovered poetry in the woman's sad face lit by light reflecting from the snow. She composed a poem.

When they reached the sacred bridge that crossed the road to the top of Mount Fuji, Mrs Tsubakihara spoke to Honda in a quavering voice.

'Please forgive me. When I think that this is the shrine of Mount Fuji I feel as though a smiling Akio should be meeting me. He was so fond of Fuji.'

Her grief was strangely vacant; sadness seemed to blow through the empty woman like a gust of wind swirling through a vacant arbour. And she was almost inordinately quiet, quite like after a séance – devastation in the wake of the ghostly spirit. Her dry cheeks in the shadow of strands of hair appeared absorbent, like pieces of rice paper. Quietly, unhindered, her sorrow seemed to flow freely in and out through them almost like breath.

Observing this scene had made Rié forget her own illness. She was the very picture of health. Honda in such moments suspected that his wife was a hypochondriac, that even her swelling was probably not genuine.

The party finally reached the great red torii that towered nearly sixty feet high. When they had passed through it, they found themselves directly in front of the pavilion where the sacred dances were performed; it was surrounded by soiled snow that had been piled in front of the red gate. Sacred rope was strung along three sides of the pavilion under the eaves, and from the tops of the tall cryptomerias a ray of clear sunshine fell on the sacred strips of paper *gohei* which stood out against the unpainted offering table on the floor. The pavilion up to its latticed ceiling was lit by the reflection from the snow, but the sunlight that reached the paper was especially bright. The strips swayed lightly in the breeze.

Momentarily Honda felt the pure white paper to be alive.

Mrs Tsubakihara's tears broke the spell. No one was particularly surprised by the sound of her sobs.

No sooner had she caught sight of the holy paper than she was stricken with fear. She ran to the front of the red main shrine guarded by reliefs of Chinese lions and dragons, and prostrating herself in prayer, burst into tears.

Honda no longer wondered why her grief had not healed so long after the war. He was witness to the secret whereby, as yesterday, it was revived and freshened.

29

The next day, Keiko telephoned from Ninooka in Gotemba. Honda was out. Rié was home in bed, still exhausted from the party. When she heard it was Keiko, however, she came to the phone.

Keiko had called to relate that Ying Chan had come to Gotemba that day alone.

'When I was walking the dog, I saw a young lady wandering about the gate of your villa. Somehow she didn't look Japanese. I called to her, and she said she was from Thailand. She told me she had been invited by Mr Honda but that she had been prevented from coming. She arrived today because she thought that everyone was still here. I was surprised at her cheerfulness; but she had come alone all that way, and I felt sorry that she had to go back again. I offered her some tea at home and took her to the station. I've just returned from seeing her off. She said she would apologize to Mr Honda after she got back to Tokyo. But she claims she doesn't like to use the telephone. Talking in Japanese on the phone gives her a headache. She's very charming. Her hair is so black and her eyes so large.'

After chattering on, Keiko thanked Rié for the party again, added that she was busy preparing a poker game that night for her American officer and his friends, and then hung up.

Rié faithfully reported the entire conversation to Honda when he arrived. He listened, grimacing as if inhaling smoke. Of course he did not tell his wife that he had dreamt of Ying Chan that night.

One of the advantages of age was knowing how to be patient. Still he did have some social obligations in addition to work. He could not wait forever for the unpredictable Ying Chan. He could have entrusted the ring to his wife, but wanting to present it himself, he carried it in the inside pocket of his suit coat.

Some ten days later, Rié reported that during his absence Ying Chan had made a visit, the purpose of which had not been altogether clear. Dressed in her mourning kimono, Rié had just been leaving the house to attend the funeral of a former classmate when she saw Ying Chan entering the gate.

'Was she alone?' asked Honda.

'Yes, she seemed to be.'

'It's too bad she made the trip. We'll have to invite her to dinner or something next time.'

'I wonder if she'll come,' Rié said with a vague smile.

Honda was fully aware that a telephone call would create psychological problems for Ying Chan. Thus he arbitrarily selected a date and sent her a ticket to the Shimbashi Theatre, leaving it up to her whether she came or not. The road company of the traditional Osaka puppet theatre had opened in Tokyo; he wanted her to see a performance. He sent her one of the matinée tickets he had bought, intending afterwards to take her to dine at the Imperial Hotel, which had recently been returned by the Occupation Forces to Japanese management.

The particular performance that day was *Mount Kagami* and *The Monkey Leader of Horikawa.* Having previously experienced her irresponsibility, he was not surprised when Ying Chan failed to put in an appearance. Sitting alone, he leisurely watched the scene known as 'Women's Quarters'. During the long intermission before the presentation of *Horikawa*, he strolled out to the garden. It was a fine, clear day and many people had come out to enjoy the fresh air.

He was impressed to see that the appearance of the audience here had, compared to several years ago, improved considerably of late. Perhaps it was because there were many geisha, but kimonos had become more sumptuous and ostentatious as memories of the terrible ruins faded. Women's tastes in these post-war days had become especially colourful, no matter what their age. There was a decidedly more opulent display of bright fabrics than in the audiences of the Imperial Theatre during the twenties.

If Honda had been so inclined, he could have selected the most beautiful of the young geisha and become her patron. It would be a pleasure to buy her anything she requested and enjoy her coquetry, tenuous as a spring cloud . . . those tiny feet so neatly clad in white custom-made *tabi.* She would be a perfectly dressed doll in her kimono. All this could belong to him. But he could at once foresee the conclusion. Boiling water of passion would overflow and the dancing ashes of death would fly up to blind him.

The charm of this theatre lay in the manner in which the garden gave on to the river; there during the hot summer months one could enjoy the cool breezes wafting up from the water. But now the river was stagnant, and barges and garbage floated slowly downstream. Honda well remembered the rivers in Tokyo during the war with the bodies of those killed in the bombing drifting along. There was no longer any factory smoke, and the water had become ominously cleansed, reflecting the strangely blue sky overhead said to occur at the moment of death. In comparison, this muddied, polluted water was the very symbol of prosperity.

Two geisha were leaning against the balustrade, enjoying the river breeze. One was wearing a silk kimono with a small design scattered with cherry petals and a Nagoya cherry-pattern obi in black. It was most probably hand-painted. She was tiny with a round face. The other exhibited a taste for colour in her choice of clothing. A cold smile played on her face from the bridge of her nose, which was slightly too high, down to her thin lips. The two kept up an incessant chatter, punctuated by exaggerated exclamations. Two curls of smoke mounted from their cigarettes – imported brands with gold tips – which they held between fingers that never fluttered in surprise.

Honda soon realized that they were surreptitiously looking at the opposite bank. The former Imperial Japanese Naval Hospital with its statue of some erstwhile admiral still on display had now been turned into an American military hospital and was filled with soldiers wounded in the Korean War. The spring sun gleamed on the half-open cherry blossoms in the front garden, under which young soldiers were being pushed in wheelchairs. Some walked with the aid of crutches, while others strolled about with only their arms in pure white slings. No voices called from across the river to the two exquisitely dressed young women, nor was there the sound of cheerful American whistles. Like a scene from another world, the opposite bank bathed in brilliant sunshine was completely quiet, manned as it was by the forms of maimed young soldiers purposely pretending nonchalance.

The two geisha obviously enjoyed the contrast. Covered in white powder and silk, indulging in spring idleness and extravagant living, they feasted on the spectacle of those who only yesterday had been the proud victors with their injuries, pain, dismembered arms and legs. Such subtle malice and exquisite viciousness were their specialty.

From his vantage point as a bystander, Honda could discern the extravagance of the contrast between the theatre garden and the scene on the far bank. Over there existed the dust, blood, misery, injured pride, irretrievable misfortune, tears, heartache, and the mangled male sexuality of the soldiers who had controlled Japan for the last seven years; while on this side, women of the defeated country paraded their over-refined, arrogant sensuality, relishing the blood of the erstwhile conquerors drenched in their own perspiration. They were flies eating at the wounds, spreading the transparent black wings of their *haori* like the wings of magnificent black butterflies. The river breeze was of no use to bring them together. It was easy to imagine the frustration of the Americans, who had so futilely shed their blood to create this useless brilliance to which they had no access, to engender the vanity and extravagance of this insensitive display.

'It really doesn't seem to be true,' Honda heard one of the women remark.

'Yes. They're too miserable to look at. Foreigners are so big and all the more pitiful in that condition. But misery is mutual. We have gone through a lot.'

'Well, that is what they get for biting off more than they can chew,' the other woman coldly declared. They watched with intensified interest, but this soon passed and faded. As if in competition they each produced compacts and squinted obliquely into the mirrors as they powdered their noses. The heavily scented powder, caught by the river breeze, sifted down along the hem of their *haori*, to be carried even to the sleeve opening of Honda's coat. He noticed that the little mirrors, though covered with a thin film of powder, still managed to cast a wan reflection on the bush at his feet, quite like the fluttering of tiny ants.

The faint ringing of a distant bell signified that the curtain was about to rise on the next act. Only the final part of *Horikawa* remained. As he turned his steps back toward the theatre, resigned that Ying Chan would not put in an appearance this late, Honda suddenly realized that he had experienced a sensual pleasure in her wonderful absence. Ying Chan was standing inside, half hidden in the shadow of a pillar; it was as if she were trying to avoid the light streaming in.

Honda's eyes had not yet adjusted themselves to the obscurity and all he saw was the black of her hair and the luminous darkness of her large eyes as though they were a blur of opacity. Her hair oil gave off a strong fragrance. Ying Chan smiled, showing a blurred whiteness of lovely teeth.

30

That evening they had dinner at the Imperial Hotel. It had been devastated. The Occupation Forces had claimed to understand the creative genius of Frank Lloyd Wright, but they had not hesitated to cover the stone lantern in the garden with white paint. The pseudo-Gothic ceiling of the dining hall was even more gloomy and in worse repair than ever. The only patches of freshness were provided by the white linen cloths that glistened ostentatiously on the rows of dining tables.

When Honda had ordered, he immediately drew from an inner pocket the small box and placed it directly in front of Ying Chan. She opened it and cried out.

'It was inevitable that the ring should be returned to you.' Speaking in the simplest language, Honda told her its history. The smile that flickered over her features as she listened did not always coincide with his narration, and it occurred to him that she might not be comprehending all he was saying.

Her breasts, visible above the level of the table, were, quite unlike her face which was childish, magnificently developed, like those of a figurehead on a ship. He knew without seeing that the body of one of the goddesses in the Ajanta murals lay beneath the simple student's blouse across from him.

The deceptively light but solid flesh seemed to have the weightiness of some dark fruit ... the almost stifling black hair and the ambiguous, wistful lines from the slightly flared nostrils down to the upper lip ... She seemed to be just as casually oblivious to the words that her body spoke as she was when she listened to Honda's recital. Her enormous, jet-black eyes transcended intelligence, and they somehow gave her the appearance of being blind. What mystery of forms! That Ying Chan should present to him a body that one sensed was overly fragrant was due to the spell of the distant jungle which reached as far as Japan. Honda felt that what people called blood lineage was perhaps a deep, formless voice that pursued one eternally. Sometimes a passionate whisper, sometimes a hoarse cry, it was the very origin of all beautiful physical forms and the wellspring of the charm they emitted.

When he placed the dark green emerald ring on Ying Chan's finger, he had the sensation that he was witness to the moment when the deep, far-off voice and the girl's physical being were at long last perfectly fused.

'Thank you,' said Ying Chan with a fawning smile that might have marred her dignity. Honda realized that it was the expression that always appeared when she felt sure that her selfish feelings were understood. But no sooner did he try to capture it than the smile was already gone like a swiftly withdrawing wave.

'When you were a child you claimed to be the reincarnation of a Japanese boy I knew very well; you annoyed everyone by insisting that Japan was your real home and that you wanted to return. Now that you are here and that ring is on your finger, it means that for you too a great circle has been joined.'

'I don't really understand,' answered Ying Chan with not a trace of emotion. 'I don't remember anything of my childhood. I really don't. They all tease me about having been slightly mad and laugh at me when they tell what you've just been saying. But I've completely forgotten everything. I went to Switzerland as soon as the war broke out and stayed there until the end, and the only thing I remember about Japan is that I used to love a Japanese doll someone gave me.'

Honda felt an urge to tell her that it had been sent by him, but checked himself.

'My father told me that Japanese schools were good, so I came here to study. Recently I've had the idea that perhaps when I was a child I was like a mirror reflecting everything in people's minds, and I simply said what occurred to me. For instance, if you had an idea, it might have been reflected in me. That was probably what happened, I imagine. What do you think?'

Ying Chan had the habit of terminating a question with an English rising inflection. Her ultimas reminded Honda of the sharply curling tails of the golden serpents at the tips of the red Chinese-tile roofs of Thai temples reaching into the blue sky.

Honda was suddenly aware of a family at a nearby table. The head, probably some businessman, his wife and their grown sons were having dinner. Their fine clothes notwithstanding, he could discern something vulgar in their faces. He surmised that they had become wealthy through the Korean War. The faces of the sons were particularly flabby, like that of a dog that has just been awakened, and their lips and eyes reflected a complete lack of breeding. They were all noisily sipping their soup.

From time to time, the sons would nudge each other and steal a glance at Honda's table. Their eyes were mocking: an old man having dinner with a concubine that looked like a schoolgirl. Their eyes seemed to have nothing better to say. Honda could not but recall Imanishi's exasperating inadequacy that midnight in Ninooka and compare it to himself.

There are rules more severe in this world than those of morality, Honda felt at such moments. Unsuitable lovers were punished by the fact that they would never be the source of dreams, but merely evoke disgust in others. The people of those times when one knew nothing of humanism were surely much more cruel to all ugly creatures than modern man.

After dinner Ying Chan excused herself to go to the powder room, and Honda remained alone in the lobby. He suddenly felt relaxed. From that moment on, he could enjoy Ying Chan's absence without compunction.

A question sprang to his mind: he had not yet learned where Ying Chan had stayed the night before the house-warming.

She did not return to the lobby for some time. He remembered the occasion when the little girl had relieved herself at Bang Pa In surrounded by her ladies. Then he recalled the naked Princess bathing in the brown river along which coiled the roots of mangroves. No matter how hard he had stared, he had not been able to make out the three black moles he had expected to find on her left side.

Honda's wants were quite simple, and it would have been incorrect to label his emotion 'love'. He wished only to look at the completely naked form of the Princess, aware that the once flat breasts had ripened, thrusting out like the heads of fledglings peeping from their nest; to see how the pink nipples pouted discontentedly and how the brown underarms lay in faint shadow; to watch the manner in which the underside of her arms carried wave patterns like a sensitive, sandy shore; to be aware of how every step toward maturity progressed in the dusky light; and then to quiver in the presence of that body, comparing it to that of the little girl. That was all. In her belly, floating in pure softness, the navel would be deep-set like a small coral atoll. Protected by thick hair instead of *yakshas*, that which once had been sober, hard silence would now be turned into constant, moist smiles. The way her beautiful toes would open up one by one, the way her thighs would shine, and the way her mature legs would extend to support earnestly the discipline and dreams of the dance of life. He wanted to compare all of those with her figure as a little girl. This was to know time, to know what time had wrought, what time had ripened. If those moles were not to be found on her left side after careful inspection, he would then fall in love with her completely and finally. Transmigration stood barring the way to his love, and samsara held his passion in check.

Awakened from his dreams by Ying Chan's return to the lobby, Honda suddenly voiced what was occupying his thoughts. Despite everything, his words were sharp with the pangs of jealousy.

'I forgot to ask. I heard that you stayed out all night before the party at Gotemba without reporting in at the Foreign Student Centre. Was it at a Japanese house?'

'Yes, it was,' Ying Chan responded without hesitation, sitting in the armchair next to Honda's, hunching her back a little and scrutinizing her beautiful legs that she held neatly together. 'A Thai friend is staying there. The family all insisted I spend the night, so I did.'

'It must be an entertaining household with a lot of young people.'

'Not exactly. The two sons, the daughter, my Thai friend, and I all played charades. The father heads a big business concern in South-east Asia, so they're very kind to South-east Asians.'

'Is your Thai friend a boy?'

'No, a girl. Why?'

Again Ying Chan abruptly raised the last syllable of her question.

Then Honda expressed disapproval that she had made so few Japanese friends. He warned her that living abroad made no sense unless she cultivated a variety of people in the country where she was studying. As she might possibly be uncomfortable having dinner with him alone, he offered to bring some young friends along the next time, unconsciously scheming for another opportunity to see her. He extracted from her a promise that at the same day the following week she would come to the lobby of the Imperial at seven o'clock. The thought of Rié made him hesitant to invite her to his own house.

31

He returned home. He got out of the car and felt the drizzle moisten his temples. The houseboy met him in the vestibule and informed him that Mrs Honda was tired and had retired early. He also reported that a persistent guest had insisted on waiting more than an hour and was in the small living room to which the houseboy had been obliged to usher him. Did he recognize the name Iinuma? asked the youth. At once Honda surmised that the man had come to ask for money.

It was four years since Honda had last seen Iinuma at the fifteenth anniversary memorial service for Isao. At that time it was obvious that Iinuma was quite without funds after the war. Yet he had been favourably impressed by the tasteful, simple memorial service held at a shrine.

Honda had at once thought it was about money, for recently people who had not visited him for years would turn up for no other reason than to ask him for funds. Unsuccessful lawyers, former attorneys who had become vagrants, unsuccessful court reporters – all came flocking. Each had heard of Honda's good fortune and each seemed to think he had some right to a share, since Honda had come into the money by sheer luck. He responded only to the requests of the truly humble.

When he entered the reception room, Iinuma rose from the chair and made a deep obeisance, showing the back of his wilted suit up to the nape of his grey-haired neck. Playing the role of a poor man suited him more than poverty itself. Honda urged him to sit down and ordered the houseboy to bring whisky.

Iinuma offered an obvious lie, saying that he had been just passing by and could not resist the urge to see Honda. One glass and he pretended to be drunk. As Honda started to pour another drink, he held the glass with his right hand and respectfully supported the bottom with the left. This struck Honda unpleasantly. A rat often held his loot in just such a fashion. Then Iinuma found a cue to start his harangue.

'Well, it seems to me that "following the reverse course" has come to be the cliché of the day. But the government will start revising the constitution by next year at the latest, I think. The reason everybody's talking about the revival of conscription is because there are really grounds for it. But the infuriating thing is that the foundation can't be brought out in the open and is still underground. By contrast, how do you like how powerful the Reds are getting? How about the disorders in the anti-draft demonstration in Kobé the other day? They called it an "anti-draft youth rally", but the strange thing was that a lot of Koreans took part. They fought against the police with not only rocks, but hot pepper, Molotov cocktails, bamboo lances, and everything else. I heard that some three hundred students, children, and Koreans invaded Hyogo Police Station and demanded the release of the ones who had been arrested.'

He wants money, Honda thought, paying little attention to what Iinuma was saying. But, he deliberated, he must let Iinuma know that no matter how the New Dealers controlled things with their socialistic policies, no matter how much noise the Reds made, the basis of the private property system would never be shaken.

The drizzle outside the window seemed to thicken as though a multilayered curtain of rain was enveloping the house. He had seen Ying Chan off to the Foreign Student Centre in a taxi. Since then the thought had not left his mind that this spring rain must have seeped into her simple room in the students' quarters and made it damp. What sort of subtle effect would the humidity have on the girl's body that had matured in the tropics? How did she sleep? Facing the ceiling and breathing hard? Or coiled up with a smile on her lips? Or on her side like the golden reclining figure of Shakyamuni in the Nirvana Hall, arm under head, supine, showing the brilliant soles of her feet?

'The General Rally for the Banishment of Oppressive Laws by the Kyoto Branch of the General Council of Japanese Labour Unions has got violent too,' continued Iinuma. 'At this rate, May Day this year isn't going to be any too peaceful; you just can't predict how much violence will break out. Red students take over school buildings in the universities and have confrontations with the police. And this, sir, right after the signing of the Japanese–American Peace Treaty and the Mutual Security Pact. How ironic.'

He wants money, thought Honda.

'I'm all in favour of Prime Minister Yoshida's idea about declaring the Communist Party illegal,' Iinuma went on. 'Japan's in turmoil again. If we let things go on, now that the Peace Treaty is signed, we're going to be thrown headlong into a Communist revolution. Most of the American troops will be gone, and how are you going to control a general strike? I lose a lot of sleep over Japan's future. *What's learned in the cradle is carried to the grave* is true even now.'

He wants money, Honda kept thinking. But even after several more drinks Iinuma still did not bring the subject up.

He talked briefly about his divorce two years ago, then suddenly changed the subject to bygone days, and started on a dogged confession how he would never in his life forget the obligation he felt toward Honda, who had given up his judgeship and volunteered to conduct Isao's defence without remuneration. Honda could not bear the thought of Iinuma talking about Isao and he hurriedly interrupted.

Iinuma suddenly took off his jacket. The room was not warm enough to be uncomfortable, but Honda presumed that he was drunk. He took off his necktie next and unbuttoned his white shirt, unfastening even his undershirt to expose a chest which had turned red from the alcohol. Honda could see the almost completely white hairs scattering the light like so many needles.

'To be honest with you, I came to show you this. I have no greater shame. If I could, I would have preferred to hide it from you all my life, but I have been thinking for some time that I would reveal it only to you and let you have a good laugh. I thought only you would really understand me, even my failures. You would know what kind of man I am. I'm honestly and truly ashamed, when I compare myself to my dead son who died so nobly. I have no words to express adequately the depth of my shame at still being alive like this.'

Tears ran down his cheeks, and his words came pell-mell:

'This is the scar from when I tried to commit suicide right after the war. My mistake was thinking I might not succeed in committing seppuku, so instead I plunged a dagger into my chest, but missed my heart. I bled like a pig, but I didn't die.'

As though showing off, Iinuma caressed the scar that glistened a purplish blue. As a matter of fact, even Honda could see that something had been irreversibly terminated. Iinuma's ruddy, coarse skin had puckered, surrounding the wound and closing it clumsily, underscoring the unsuccessfulness of the attempt.

However, Iinuma's obdurate chest, now covered with white hair, still was proud of what it had once been. Honda finally realized that it was not at all money for which he had come, still he did not feel ashamed for having misjudged his purpose. Iinuma had not changed. Honda found it understandable that even such a man as he should be compelled to distil and crystallize a desperate, soiled, and humiliating deed, that he should strive by so doing to transmute shame into a rare gem, and that he should gradually be overcome by the desire, the need to display it to a trustworthy witness. Whether he was serious or merely pretending, the fact remained that the purple scar on his chest was in the final analysis the only precious thing that remained in his life. Honda had been selected for the unwelcome honour of being witness to this noble action of many years ago.

Iinuma, seeming to have rapidly sobered, put on his clothes, apologized for having overstayed, and extended thanks for the drinks. He was about to leave when Honda stopped him. Wrapping up some fifty thousand yen in bills, he thrust the packet into the pocket of Iinuma's seedy coat despite the protestations of his visitor.

'In that case,' said Iinuma finally, thanking Honda with extreme formality, 'I accept your kindness with gratitude. It will be a privilege to use it to help revive the Seiken School.'

Honda accompanied him to the entrance in the rain. Iinuma's silhouette disappeared through the side gate beneath the pomegranate leaves. It reminded him, for some reason, of one of those countless nocturnal islands that dot the gloomy waters around Japan. An outlying island with no water except the rain – mad, wild, starving.

32

Far from the peace he had expected on placing the ring on Ying Chan's finger, Honda was filled with fear.

He was concerned with the difficult question of how to conceal himself to view her nude. How wonderful it would be if, unaware of him, she would move about full of life or take her self-indulgent ease, revealing every secret in her heart, being completely natural. How wonderful to observe like a biologist every detail. But should his presence be known, then everything would at once collapse.

A perfect crystal of quartz, a glass bowl in which nothing exists but the free play of lovely, subjective being. Ying Chan should be in just such a bowl.

Honda was certain that he had played a part in the crystallization of Kiyoaki's and Isao's transparent lives. In them he had been the extended helping hand, even though it had proven ineffectual and useless. The important thing was that Honda himself had been unaware of his role; he had played his part quite naturally, as a matter of fact quite idiotically, though he himself was convinced that he had been intelligent about it. But after he had become aware! After a torrid India had unsparingly taught him, what help could he have rendered to life? What kind of intervention, what engagement could there be?

Furthermore, Ying Chan was a woman. Hers was a body which filled the cup to its very brim with the unknown darkness of charm. It seduced him. It attracted him constantly toward life. For what purpose? he wondered. He did not know, but one of the reasons was probably that the life to which he was attracted was destined to involve others through the charm it exuded; it was fated to destroy its own roots. Another reason was that he was obliged to realize completely this time the impossibility of involvement in another's life.

Of course Honda was convinced that having Ying Chan in a transparent crystal would constitute the core of his pleasure, but he could not separate that from his innate desire for investigation. Was there no way by which he could harmoniously reconcile these two contradictory tastes and overcome Ying Chan, this black lotus that had bloomed from the mud of life's flow?

In this respect, it would have been better if she had shown some clear sign of being the transmigration of Isao and Kiyoaki. Then Honda's passion would be cooled. Yet on the other hand, had she simply been a girl who had nothing to do with the mystery of rebirth Honda had witnessed, he would not have been so strongly attracted to her. Perhaps the origin of that strength which sternly held his passion in check and that of the extraordinarily powerful attraction existed together in the same samsara. The source of awakening and the origin of samsara and delusion were both samsara.

As he thought of it, Honda strongly wished that he were a man approaching the end of life, someone propertied and totally complacent. Honda knew a number of such people. Many were discernment itself in turning a profit and rising in the world or in struggling for power; they were adept in grasping the psychology of formidable competitors. Yet when it came to women they were completely ignorant, even though they had slept with several hundreds. Such men were satisfied to surround themselves with the screens of women and flatterers whom they bought with their money and power. Like loons, the women would sit around, showing only one side of their faces. Such men are not free; they're in a cage! thought Honda. They sit in cages made of things that only *their* eyes can see, that void the world and shut it out.

Other men are somewhat wiser. They are rich, powerful and more aware of human nature. They can know everything about a man, they can penetrate to the core of things by interpreting the slightest surface indication. Super-psychologists who master the taste of life by the bitterness of smartweed vinegar. Whenever they wish they can order the trees and rocks and shrubs shifted in their beautiful little yards, they possess diminutive, refined gardens made of well-organized and well-arranged extractions of the world and life: gardens of real connoisseurs. Such precincts consist of rocks of deception, crape myrtle of coquetry, horse-tails of guileness, washbasins of flattery, small waterfalls of loyalty, and the craggy rocks of countless betrayals. They sit the whole day before such allegorical plots, soaking themselves in the quiet pleasure of having disarmed the world and life of all resistance. Yet like a pricelessly rare teacup filled with foaming light-green tea they firmly grasp in their hands the bitterness and superiority of cognizant men. Honda was not such a man. He was neither self-satisfied nor secure. And yet he was no longer ignorant either. He had seen only the borderline between the knowable and the unknowable; still it was enough to make him aware. And uncertainty was an incomparable treasure that man could steal from youth. Honda had already taken part in the lives of Kiyoaki and Isao, and had seen forms of fate where it was completely meaningless to extend his hand. It was as if he had been deceived. From the standpoint of fate, living was like being swindled. And human existence ... signified nothing but the lack of fulfilment, and that he had thoroughly mastered in India.

Nevertheless, the absolutely passive life or life's ultimately ontological form which is not commonly revealed had attracted Honda too much. And he was tainted by the extravagant concept that without such forms there was no life. He quite lacked the qualifications of a seducer. For seducing and deceiving were futile from the standpoint of fate, and 'the will to seduce' was itself futile. When one recognized that there was no other form of living except to be naïvely deceived by fate alone, how was it possible to interfere? How could one even glimpse the pure form of such existence? For the moment, one could conceive of such a being only in its absence. Ying Chan, who was self-sufficient in her universe, she who was a universe in herself, must be isolated from him. At times, she was a kind of optical illusion, a corporeal rainbow. Her face was red and her neck orange, her breasts were yellow and she had a green stomach, blue thighs, indigo calves, and violet toes. Above her head was an invisible infra-red heart, and below her firmly planted feet were the invisible ultra-violet footprints of memory. The extremity of the rainbow had fused with the heaven of death. She was a rainbow bridging the firmament of death. If 'not knowing' was the first factor in eroticism, the ultimate had to be the eternally unknowable ... death.

When the unexpected amount of money came into his possession, Honda thought like everyone else that he would spend it for his own gratification, but such money was useless for his most essential pleasure. Participation, caring, protection, possession, monopoly – all these things required money, and money had its use; but Honda's pleasure rejected all of them.

He knew that in inexpensive joys lurked thrilling pleasure. The feel of wet moss on the tree trunks in the grove where he had hidden himself, the subtle scent of dead leaves on the ground where he had knelt on a May night of the previous year in the park. The fragrance of young leaves was pungent and lovers lay dishevelled on the grass. Auto headlights came and went ruthlessly on the road around the grove. Their beams illuminated the coniferous trees that were like the columns of some shrine and then would tragically and swiftly sweep down the shadowy shafts one after the other; he had shuddered as the light swept over the grass. Momentarily it picked out the almost cruelly sacred beauty of white turned-up underclothes. Only once Honda saw a ray of light pass directly across a woman's face with dreamy eyes. As he had glimpsed the reflection of a speck of light, they must surely have been open, if only partially. It was a ghastly moment when the darkness of human existence was abruptly unveiled, and he had inadvertently seen what he should not have.

To match his tremors with those of the lovers, to synchronize his palpitations with theirs, to share their fear, and at the end of such uniting, to remain an outsider who saw but was not seen. Celebrants of this furtive spying lurked here and there under the trees and in the bushes like crickets. Honda was one of these nameless men.

Young men and women ... bodies entwined ... white lower parts exposed. Tenderness of hands moving where the shadows were deepest. White buttocks of men moving like Ping-Pong balls. The almost legal authenticity of their sighs.

Yes, when the headlights momentarily peeled off the darkness of existence, the woman's face had been unexpectedly illuminated. But it was not the ones being observed who were startled, but those who watched behind the trees. When the distant and lyrical siren of a patrol car resounded far outside the night park, where the reflections of neon signs glowed like embers, the watched women did not leave off their debauchery, and their men infallibly raised their virile torsos like young wolves.

On one occasion Honda had lunched with an experienced lawyer, who passed on a bit of gossip he had overheard at some police station. The nasty scandal had never appeared in the papers. It concerned a highly respected man prominent in legal circles, who enjoyed the prestige and respect due to his eminent position. He had become an habitual voyeur and had been apprehended by the police. He was sixty-four years old. A young policeman asked for his personal card, ruthlessly demanding an account of the old man's offences. The hapless lawyer was literally shaking with shame as he was forced to reconstruct in detail the setting of his voyeurism. During this time he was sternly lectured by the officer. As soon as the young policeman learned of the offender's high social status, he ridiculed the poor man for his own amusement, emphasizing the incredible gap between the prestige he enjoyed and the sordidness of his crime. He was fully aware that it was humanly impossible to bridge such a chasm, and yet he had tortured the man. Under the upbraiding by someone young enough to be his grandson, the old man had become obsequious, hanging his head and incessantly wiping his sweaty forehead. After being stuffed with mud slung by one so low in the governmental bureaucracy, he was finally discharged. Two years later he died of cancer.

How would he have behaved? Honda wondered.

Honda was supposed to know all about the secret of how to bridge such a hopeless abyss. The secret formula from India should have proven effective.

Why hadn't the old judge been able to explain the nature of his pleasure by using legal jargon? – a pleasure so strong that it brought tears to the eyes, the most modest pleasure in life. But even though Honda pretended to listen casually and to regard it as a piece of amusing gossip, he could not help wondering throughout the meal whether there were not some deeper motivation behind the subject his colleague had brought up. He took care to smile contemptuously at the critical points just like the narrator, but he was confused by the cruel contrast between the solemnity of the pleasure produced and the misery it evoked. Such an act was as worthless to the world as a wornout pair of straw sandals; yet solemnity was concealed in its very core, and that was true of any kind of pleasure. As a result of that hour-long ordeal, he had completely renounced the thrill of his habit. Fortunately, that side of him was known to no one.

It could not be that he was oblivious to danger, because he had overtly humiliated his own reason. The real adventure of a dangerous action is reason, and courage too came from that.

If money could not guarantee security and purchase for him real thrills, then what could he do to grasp fresh life at his age? And yet his hunger for living seemed never to decrease but rather to sharpen with age.

Thus, though he did not wish it, it would be necessary for him to use some sort of intermediary. Even if Ying Chan should by some chance sleep with him, as long as what he really wanted was something she could never show him, then it would be imperative that he employ some roundabout, artificial method to obtain what he needed so much.

Tortured by these thoughts and unable to sleep, he would take out the *Sutra of the Great Golden Peacock Wisdom King*, which had for some time remained undisturbed, accumulating dust on his bookshelf.

At times he murmured the mantra that stood for the achievement of the peacock: *ma yu kitsu ra tei sha ka.*

It was merely a game of conundrums. If he had survived the war because of this sutra, then life sustained by such means seemed all the more worthless.

33

Keiko showed great interest in the story of the *Sutra of the Peacock Wisdom King*.

'You say that it's efficacious against snakebite? Then I'd love to learn it. There are lots of snakes in my garden at Gotemba.'

'I remember just a little of the opening passage. It goes: *ta do ya ta icchi mitchi chiri mitchi chiribiri mitchi.*'

Keiko laughed. 'Sounds like the song "Chiribiribin".'

Honda felt a childish vexation at her flippant reaction and fell silent.

Keiko had brought along a student from Keio University whom she introduced as her nephew. He was wearing an imported suit and an expensive imported wristwatch. He had narrow eyebrows and thin lips. Honda was startled to realize that his own eyes, when looking at this frivolous modern young man, had involuntarily taken on the censorious stare typical of the members of the old kendo team.

Keiko maintained her self-composure at all times. She gave directions to everyone in regal, placid tones. Any request made of her was followed by elaborate instructions.

Honda had found this out two days before when he had taken her to lunch at the Tokyo Kaikan to celebrate her return to the city. He mentioned his wish to introduce Ying Chan to some suitable boy, 'aggressive' if possible. The one word gave the whole ploy away to Keiko.

'I see,' she said. 'It's inconvenient for you that she's a virgin. I'll bring you my incorrigible nephew the next time we meet. You won't have to worry about any aftermath with that boy. Later you'll be able to play the role of the gentle, sweet, overly kind confidant and enjoy her at your leisure ... what a wonderful plan!'

When Keiko said 'wonderful', the wonderfulness always seemed to vanish. In pleasure she completely lacked emotion – had she been a prostitute she would have had to pretend. She was too methodical.

Keiko embarked upon an explanation of her nephew's modishness – his name was Katsumi Shimura. She told Honda that he sent his measurements to New York and through an American friend of his father's ordered Brooks Brothers suits for every season of the year. This anecdote alone told much about the young man.

While the story of the *Sutra of the Peacock King* was being retold, Katsumi gazed off into the distance, obviously bored. The lobby of the Imperial Hotel was like the entrance to a tomb with low projecting rocks cutting off the mezzanine; in the shop occupying a corner of the lobby gaudily coloured American magazines and paperbacks bloomed in disarray like withered flowers left in a graveyard.

Aunt and nephew closely resembled each other in their inability to listen seriously to what anyone else might be saying. In the nephew's case this was due to mere rudeness, while in the aunt's it seemed to be part of her good manners. Keiko would have listened with the same casual indifference to confessions horrible enough to freeze a normal person to the very marrow.

'The trouble is ... I don't know for certain that Ying Chan will really show up,' said Honda.

'You've developed a phobia about that ever since the house-warming. Let's just relax and wait. If she doesn't come, we can still have fun. The three of us will go to dinner. Katsumi is not particularly the type to be overly anxious.'

'Oh, yes ... well, that's right,' Katsumi answered vaguely with his typically over-crisp intonation.

Abruptly Keiko removed a stick of solid perfume from her handbag and rubbed it on her earlobes, from which hung jade ear-rings.

As though on signal, all the lights in the lobby went out.

'Tisk! A power failure,' exclaimed Katsumi. What was the point of saying the power had failed when it already had, thought Honda. Some people spoke only as an apology for their laziness.

Keiko, of course, said nothing. The perfume was returned to her bag and the catch clicked in the darkness. The sound seemed to open into a deeper darkness. In the gloom the firm, opulent, sovereign flesh of Keiko's hips seemed to expand secretly and limitlessly with the spreading fragrance of the scent.

The silence was only momentary. As though pushing aside the darkness, the artificially vivacious conversation of the ship-wrecked immediately began.

'During the occupation,' said Honda, 'the American forces had priority on the use of what little electricity there was, so we couldn't help but have blackouts. Yet I'm surprised it goes on.'

'Recently during a massive power failure,' added Keiko, 'I was passing through Yoyogi when I saw that only the American Yoyogi Heights was brightly lit; that one section floating over the darkness of the entire area made it seem like a town of people from another planet. It was beautiful but eerie.'

It was dark, but the headlights of the traffic in the streets beyond the pond in the front garden cast light up to the revolving doors of the entrance. One door was rotating from the momentum of someone departing and the headlights shone like luminous stripes in underwater darkness. Honda felt himself quiver slightly as he recalled the scene in the park at night.

'You can breathe so freely and easily in the dark,' said Keiko. Honda wanted to ask: And what about the daytime? Keiko's shadow loomed up and sped across the wall. A bell-boy had brought candles and when they were placed in ashtrays on several tables the lobby became a veritable cemetery flickering with lights to welcome back the dead.

A taxi drew up at the entrance. Ying Chan entered, dressed in a lovely canary-yellow dress. Honda was astounded at the miracle: she was only fifteen minutes late.

Ying Chan was beautiful in the candlelight. Her hair melted into the darkness; the many flames flickering in her eyes and the brilliance of her teeth were even more lovely than in electric light. The front of the canary-yellow dress rose and fell with each breath, exaggerating the shadows.

'Do you remember me? I am Mrs Hisamatsu. It's been some time since we met in Gotemba,' said Keiko. Ying Chan did not even thank her for that occasion and only nodded charmingly.

Keiko introduced Katsumi, who offered his seat. Honda knew at once that the boy had been strongly impressed by Ying Chan's beauty.

She casually opened her hand on which she wore the emerald, but not in any effort to show it off to Honda. In the candlelight the stone reflected a green like the wings of some iridescent insect that had just flown in. The protecting *yakshas*' impressive golden faces were angry and full of shadows. Honda interpreted the fact that Ying Chan had worn the ring as an expression of her sweetness.

Keiko immediately spotted the jewel and without ado drew Ying Chan's hand to her.

'How unusual. Is it Thai?'

She could not have forgotten her close inspection of the stone at Gotemba, but her manner was so natural and convincing it quite seemed to have slipped her mind.

Staring into a candle flame, Honda silently wagered with himself whether Ying Chan would tell that it had been a gift from him.

'Yes, it's from Thailand,' said Ying Chan simply. He was relieved by the answer and charmed with the graceful naturalness of the entire episode he had created.

As though she had already forgotten about the ring, Keiko, taking the initiative, arose.

'Let's go to Manuela's. Since we shall be going to a nightclub anyway, we might just as well have dinner there. The food is quite good.'

Katsumi was driving a Pontiac that had been purchased under some American name. It would take them less than two minutes to reach their destination.

Ying Chan sat beside the driver, and Honda and Keiko rode in the back. Keiko's bearing when getting in and out of cars was spectacular. As far back as she could remember, she had always had the habit of climbing in before anyone else. She never sidled along on skirted hips to the far seat, but would aim at the place where she would be sitting and in one motion, without hesitation, deposit there her amphora-like buttocks.

Ying Chan's long black hair cascaded over the back of the seat, and from behind it was especially magnificent. It reminded Honda of black ivy hanging from the ramparts of some deserted castle. During the day, the inevitable lizard would be resting in the shade...

Miss Manuela owned a small, fashionable nightclub in the basement of a building across from the Japan Broadcasting Association. The brunette Eurasian dancer cheerfully greeted her faithful customers as soon as she recognized Keiko and Katsumi coming down the staircase in the vanguard of the little party.

'Oh, welcome! Katsumi, too! You're very early tonight. Feel free to take over.' At this early hour no one was to be seen on the dance floor, and only music came across its emptiness like a north wind scattering the fragments of light from the mirror ball as if they were scraps of white paper flying about on midnight streets.

'Wonderful! We have the club to ourselves!' said Keiko, stretching her sumptuously ringed hands into the dark space. Over this sweeping exclamation, the gleaming wind instruments sounded sadly.

'Oh, don't bother,' said Keiko, stopping Miss Manuela, who, in place of the waiter, was on the point of taking orders for drinks. 'Do sit down.' Katsumi stood up and offered her a chair. Only after he had done so did Keiko introduce Ying Chan and Honda, and referring to the latter, added: 'This gentleman is my new friend. I've acquired a Japanese taste.'

'That's fine. You're really too Americanized. It's better to get rid of some of that American odour.'

Miss Manuela pretended to sniff around Keiko in an exaggerated way, and Keiko responded theatrically by acting ticklish. Ying Chan laughed heartily at these antics and nearly upset a glass of water on the table. Honda was a little perplexed, and he and Katsumi glanced at each other. On reflection, he realized that this was the very first time their eyes had met.

Keiko, as if suddenly remembering, recovered her dignity.

'Did you have trouble when the power failed a while ago?' she asked fatuously.

'Of course not. We serve only by candlelight,' Miss Manuela answered with a lordly air; and white teeth gleaming in the gloom, she turned her friendly smile to Honda.

Members of the orchestra would greet Keiko when they left their seats, and she would answer by waving her white hand. Everything rotated around her.

The four had dinner, and while Honda did not enjoy eating in dark places, he had no alternative. The blood oozing from his slice of chateaubriand should have been bright red, but it appeared dismally dark.

Customers began to increase in number. Honda was aghast when he imagined how others would regard him, acting young in a place of entertainment such as this. The sooner the revolution the better; people were saying there would be one.

Honda was caught by surprise when his three companions simultaneously arose. The two women had stood up to go to the powder room and Katsumi had risen in accordance with prescribed etiquette. Katsumi sat down again, and the man of fifty-seven and the other of twenty, left together in the midst of music and dancing, remained silent, looking in different directions, having nothing to say.

Suddenly Katsumi spoke up rather hoarsely: 'She's charming.'

'Do you like her?'

'I've always been taken by dark, petite, and glamorous types that can't talk Japanese very well. How shall I say? ... I probably have somewhat peculiar tastes.'

'Really?' Honda responded with a soft smile, yet he was repelled by Katsumi's words.

'What do you think about the body?' he asked.

'Well, I've never given it much thought. Do you mean sensualism?' the young man answered glibly, quickly lighting Honda's cigarette with his Dunhill lighter.

'For instance, suppose you have a bunch of grapes. If you grasp them too hard they'll be crushed. But if you hold them just so as not to bruise them, then the fullness of the skin will put up a subtle resistance to your fingers. That's what I mean by "body".'

'I think I understand,' answered the young student thoughtfully, eager to act as an adult, doubtless bolstering his self-confidence with the weight of his memories.

'Fine if you do. That's all I meant,' said Honda, terminating the conversation.

Later Katsumi asked Ying Chan to dance; they returned to the table after three consecutive numbers.

'I couldn't help but remember your theory about the grapes,' Katsumi said to Honda with a look of innocence.

'What are you talking about?' Keiko asked. The conversation faded into the noisy music and was lost.

Honda never tired of watching Ying Chan dance, though he himself did not know how. In movement she was free of the handicaps of living in a foreign land and her natural disposition was happily revealed. Her slim neck, relatively small for her body, moved well. Her ankles were delicate and quick. She danced on her toes, and under her swaying skirt her beautiful legs, like two tall palms on a distant island, moved swiftly. Languidness and vitality constantly alternated; hesitation and liveliness shifted at every instant, and while she was dancing her smile never disappeared. When she whirled around at Katsumi's fingertips during a jitterbug number, her body had already turned, but the gleam of her white teeth still remained visible like a half moon.

34

The world was filled with ominous portents.

A riot broke out in front of the Imperial Palace on May Day. The police shot into the mob and the situation deteriorated. Six or seven demonstrators formed a group and attacked an American car, turning it over and setting it on fire. An assaulted policeman abandoned his white motor-cycle, which was immediately burned. An American sailor, who had fallen into the moat around the palace, popped up and down in the water because whenever he lifted his head demonstrators threw stones at him. Flames sprang up all over the square in front of the palace. During the riot American soldiers stood guard with fixed bayonets at the General Headquarters in Hibiya and at the Meiji Life Insurance Building.

It was an extraordinary event. No one believed that things would end here, and everyone suspected that other, larger-scale riots must be in store for the future.

Honda did not go to his office in the Marunouchi Building that day and did not actually see the demonstration, but when he heard about it on the radio and read the details in the newspapers he felt the situation to be serious enough. He had spent the wartime period rather uninvolved, yet now in peace he could not ignore what was happening about him. He felt insecure with the three customary ways of investing money and resolved to consult about the future with a friend who advised him on financial matters.

The next day, unable to sit still at home, he set out for a walk. The early-summer sun was shining; nothing seemed out of the ordinary. Avoiding the old store that sold serious material such as legal books, he entered a shop in the front of which magazines were displayed in random piles. He had formed the habit over the years of always going to bookstores on his walks.

The multitude of titles on the spines soothed him. Everything was stored away in the form of concepts. Human love and desire, political unrest were all committed to writing and lined up in tranquillity. Furthermore, one could find anything one desired, from books on knitting to international politics.

He did not know why he felt so relaxed on entering a bookshop; it was a habit formed in childhood. Kiyoaki and Isao had had nothing like it. How had it come about? he wondered. Did he feel insecure unless he constantly surveyed the entire world? Was it obstinacy that would not let him recognize facts that had not been recorded in print? According to Stéphane Mallarmé, sooner or later everything would be expressed in writing. If the world ended up in a great beautiful book, it would never be too late to dash over to the bookstore after it had all been printed.

Yes, yesterday's events were already finished. Here there were no flames from Molotov cocktails, no shouts, no violence. One could not even sense the distant repercussions of bloodshed. An amiable citizen trailed by a child was hunting through the books; a fat woman in a light green sweater holding a shopping bag arrogantly asked if the latest issue of some women's magazine had not yet come out. In the back of the store a vase with an arrangement of irises – a hobby of the storekeeper – had been placed below a framed piece of unskilled calligraphy which read: 'Reading is nourishment for the heart.'

Honda circled around in the congested store, bumping into customers. As he could find nothing he liked, he went to the shelves on which popular magazines were displayed. There a young man in a sports shirt, apparently a student, was engrossed in a magazine. From a distance, Honda could see that he had been staring at a single page with extraordinary earnestness. Approaching on the right side of the youth, he casually glanced at the leaf.

He saw a poorly printed, opaque blue photogravure of a naked woman sitting tied with a rope and leaning to one side. The boy never took his eyes from the magazine which he held in his left hand.

Honda noticed that the youth was strangely rigid – the neck, profile, and eyes were somehow unnaturally strained like those of a figure in some Egyptian relief. Then he saw clearly that the youth's right hand which was thrust into his trouser pocket was violently and mechanically moving.

Honda left the bookstore at once. His stroll had been spoiled.

– Why had he had to do such a thing in front of people? Didn't he have the money to buy the magazine? If that were so, I would have paid for it myself and given it to him. Yes, why didn't I do that right away? I really shouldn't have hesitated to give him the money.

But Honda's thoughts changed in the interval between two electric poles by the roadside.

– No, I don't believe that that was the case. If he really wanted the magazine, it was cheap enough for him to buy just by pawning his fountain pen.

The magazine should not have been purchased and taken home. From this point on, Honda's imagination ran riot. For some reason the youth did not quite seem to be a total stranger.

Not wishing to go home and face his wife with such thoughts on his mind, he chose a roundabout way and continued straight on instead of turning when he came to the corner of the Methodist Church.

Probably the reason the youth had not taken the magazine home was not at all because his family was strict or because he had no place to hide it. Honda arbitrarily came to the conclusion that the young man lived alone in a rooming house. It was obvious that as soon as the youth returned home the loneliness eagerly awaiting him would jump at him like a house pet; and he would have been afraid to open the picture of the trussed and naked woman, to share his pleasure with the loneliness. There, probably, waited the absolute freedom of the prison which the youth had himself constructed. In the tiny space, barren and square, in the dark nest filled with the smell of semen, he must have been afraid to face the naked blue woman writhing under the tightening rope that crushed her breasts, her nostrils spread like the wings of a dove. It was like committing murder to face a tightly bound woman in such perfect freedom. Thus he had chosen to expose himself to the public gaze. He had wanted to project himself into the role of a man tied by the ropes of people's eyes and to face the woman bound in danger and humiliation. The odious conditions he had chosen represented the *sine qua non* as subtle and delicate as silk thread that is concealed in all sexual love.

The seductions of a very special, extraordinarily sweet vulgarity ... The boy would not have been consumed with desire for the girl had she been a beautiful photographic model. Sexuality that storms day and night like a gale through the metropolis. A great dark over-abundance. The streets across which shoot the flames of Molotov cocktails. The great underground canal of hidden sexual passion. When Honda saw the imposing stone pillars of his house, standing since his father's days, he realized he would have to live in a fashion very different from the way his father had lived out his old age. When he pushed open the side gate and saw the great white magnolia flowers in full bloom on the tips of their tall branches, he suddenly felt the fatigue of his walk and wished he could devote the rest of his life to creating haiku.

35

Honda suggested a talk with Keiko and Katsumi, in as much as he had to pick up a box of cigars which he had asked her to get. Katsumi drove to meet him at his office building. It was an early summer afternoon and the sun was strong.

Genuine Havana cigars were unavailable, but tobacco products from Florida could be purchased at the PX. Since Keiko would be shopping for cigars at the former Matsuya department store, now the PX, Katsumi informed him they were to meet her there.

Honda could not himself enter the PX, of course. He had Katsumi stop in front, and they watched the exits from the car window. Outside the white-curtained PX windows numerous caricaturists loitered about, hounding the American soldiers who emerged. The young soldiers, apparently back from Korea, put up little resistance as they amiably stood to be sketched. Among them an American girl wearing blue jeans, probably on a shopping trip, was sitting on the brass rail of a window having her portrait done.

It was an interesting scene to watch while killing time in the car. The serious-faced American soldiers, looking quite professional, posed for the drawings with no feelings of shyness before the spectators. It was hard to tell which was the customer. Spectators surrounded them, and as soon as someone grew tired of watching and left, another immediately took his place. The rosy faces of the tall Americans stood out like the heads of statues above the mass of bystanders.

'She's late,' Honda commented to Katsumi as he got out of the car to stretch his legs in the sunlight.

He joined the crowd to look at the American girl. Hardly pretty, she was swinging her blue-jeaned legs. She wore a shortsleeved plaid blouse that looked like a man's shirt. A shaft of light falling through the buildings fell diagonally across half of her freckled cheek and was regularly deflected by the movements of her jaw as she chewed a wad of gum. She was not particularly cold or arrogant. The curious stares had not affected her natural poise in the slightest, and the deep-set brown eyes, as if propped open, gazed blankly into space almost without moving.

She looked at the people as though she were watching the air; such a girl might be someone Honda was looking for. When he realized it, he felt a sudden stir of interest like rapidly curling ends of hair that have been set on fire. It was then that a man standing next to him spoke. He had been glancing at Honda's face for some time. 'We've met somewhere before, haven't we?' he said at length.

Honda saw a shortish rodent-like man in a seedy suit. His hair was cut straight at the temples, and his restless eyes held the glint of an ominous obsequiousness. At once Honda felt uneasy.

'Who could you be? I'm sorry, but I don't seem to . . .' he said coldly.

'Don't you remember? We're peeping chums under the trees in the park,' he said, stretching to whisper in Honda's ear.

Despite his efforts not to, Honda paled.

'What do you mean?' he said coolly. 'You've mistaken me for someone else.' A bitter sneer instantly appeared on the little man's face. Honda knew that this sneer was like cracks in underground strata that sometimes had the power of instantly toppling great buildings. But at the moment there was no real proof. And still better, Honda no longer had any prestige to guard. It was thanks to this sneer that he clearly realized his present lack of social position.

Honda shouldered the man aside and began to walk toward the entrance of the PX. Opportunely Keiko appeared.

She came out, breasts high, dressed in a purple suit and followed by an American soldier whose face was almost completely hidden behind a mountainous armful of paper bags. Honda thought it might be her lover, Jack, but it was not.

In the middle of the pavement, Keiko introduced Honda to the soldier, and referring to the latter, explained: 'I don't know his name, but he was kind enough to offer to help carry my packages to the car.'

Seeing Honda talking with an American soldier, the little man hastened away.

A huge, brilliant golden brooch, like the metal of the Great Order of the Chrysanthemum, shone on Keiko's breast. She marched straight up to the car where Katsumi was respectfully waiting in the May sunshine. He held the door open and playfully bowed her in.

The soldier handed the paper bags one by one to Katsumi, who staggered, barely able to hold them.

It was a fine spectacle. The crowd in front of the PX stood watching with gaping mouths, quite forgetting the caricaturists.

When the car started to move, Keiko waved to the courteous soldier and he responded. So did two or three other men in the crowd.

'What popularity!' Honda commented rather flippantly to show himself how quickly he could recover from the traumatic episode.

Keiko laughed contentedly and said: 'There is kindness to be found everywhere.' In great haste she took out a handkerchief heavily embroidered in the Chinese style and blew her nose loudly like a Westerner. The nose showed no signs of damage afterwards. It was as high and magnificent as usual.

'That's because you sleep naked every night,' said Katsumi who was driving.

'What a rude thing to say! As though you've ever seen me . . . By the way, where shall we go?'

Honda was apprehensive about walking around the Ginza area lest they run into the small man again.

'Let's go to that new ... what's the building? ... at the corner of Hibiya,' he said irritably, unable to remember.

'You mean the Nikkatsu Hotel?' said Katsumi. And soon, glimpsing the soiled mustard colour of the river through the crowd, they crossed the Sukiya Bridge.

Keiko was most kind and also intelligent, but that she lacked a certain gentleness was obvious. Of any subject – literature, art, music, or even philosophy – she spoke with her extravagant feminine, pleasure-loving enthusiasm as though she were talking about perfume or necklaces. She never actually paraded her erudition in art or philosophy, and her knowledge was not necessarily well balanced; but in some fields her information was quite thorough.

As he recalled, upper-class women of the late nineteenth and early twentieth centuries were either stuffy self-appointed virtuous types or brazen minxes, so Keiko's well-roundedness surprised him. But he could foresee trouble for the man who became her husband. She was never cruel, but in her one sensed a certain intolerable fastidiousness in little things.

Could that be a defence? But for what purpose? To be sure, she had never been raised in such a way that she would require armour. She had never found it necessary to fight the world. Rather, the world always showed her deference, and one felt in her a kind of purity that was overpowering in its authority.

Keiko was congenitally incapable of distinguishing between affection and favour, and thus anyone she granted a boon might assume that she loved him.

This occasion was no exception. On the mezzanine overlooking the lobby that resembled a new rugby field, Keiko, a glass of sherry before her, began giving instructions. Honda was overwhelmed. It was as though he were listening to a lecture in a course on French cooking on how to prepare a fowl named Ying Chan.

'You've seen her twice since then. How were things? How far do you think you can go?' she asked Katsumi first. Then she pulled out a large box of cigars, which she seemed to have forgotten about until that moment, and silently placed it in Honda's lap.

'How did it go? I think the time's almost ripe.'

Honda traced the pattern on the cigar box with his fingers. It reminded him of the paper currency of some small European country, its gold coins and pink ribbons embossed in golden letters on a green background. He was conjuring up the aroma of cigars; he had not smoked for some time. Simultaneously he sharply repelled Katsumi's words. Nevertheless, he was surprised when he discovered himself enjoying the repugnance like an omen of something.

'Did you at least kiss her?' asked Keiko.

'Yes, once.'

'How was it?'

'How was it ... ? Well, I took her back to the Foreign Student Centre and kissed her just a little behind the gate.'

'Yes? And how was it?'

'She seemed pretty flustered. It was probably her first time.'

'That doesn't sound like you. Couldn't you have gone further?'

'But she's special. She's a princess.'

Keiko turned to Honda. 'The best way,' she said, 'would be for you to take her to Gotemba. Why don't you say you're throwing a party and invite her to stay overnight? As late as possible. She can't very well turn you down because you know she's stayed out other nights; and besides, she has to make up for the party she stood you up on. If she's alone with Katsumi she'll be on her guard, so you must go with them. Of course, Katsumi will drive. You can tell her that I'll be waiting in Gotemba. It won't be true, but I won't be inconvenienced . . . When you reach your villa she'll find it strange that no one else is there. But even so, a foreign princess can't possibly run away, so it must be left to Katsumi. You can leave her to him for the night and wait for your *canard à l'orange* to be ready.'

36

It was midnight at Ninooka in Gotemba. After putting out the fire in the fireplace, Honda took his umbrella and strolled from the living room out to the terrace.

There, in front, the swimming pool had already taken shape, and the rain was beating on the rough concrete. It was far from completed, and even the ladder was not yet attached. In the light from the terrace the rainy concrete was the colour of greyish liquid. The swimming pool was being constructed by workers from Tokyo, and progress was necessarily slow.

It was obvious even in the nocturnal darkness that the swimming pool was not adequately drained. Honda decided he must tell the contractor when he returned to Tokyo. The many puddles in the bottom of the pool were pelted by the rain, producing ripples that wretchedly captured the reflections of light from the distant terrace. Night fog rose from the western end of the valley and hung motionless in the middle of the green. It was extremely cold.

The unfinished pool had begun to look like a gigantic grave pit, big enough and more for a legion of skeletons. Actually it did not *begin* to appear, it had never been anything else. The water would splash up if skeletons were dropped to the bottom and then grow calm, and the dried bones would immediately soak up the water and become glossy and fresh. Old-time Japanese, on reaching Honda's age, would have thought of building a treasury storage-house celebrating longevity. Honda was building, of all things, a swimming pool! It was a cruel attempt to float his sagging decrepit flesh in an abundance of blue water. Honda had acquired the habit of spending money only for games full of malice. How the Hakoné mountains and the summer clouds reflecting in the water of the pool would brighten his old age! And what a grimace Ying Chan would make if she ever discovered that he had built it precisely because he wished to see her naked body at close hand in the summer.

Honda started to return to lock the doors, when, raising the umbrella, he glanced up at the lights on the second floor. Four windows were still bright. They were in the two guest rooms adjacent to the study next to which Ying Chan was staying. Katsumi occupied the room beyond that.

Despite the umbrella, raindrops soaked his trousers and seemed to penetrate to his knees. In the night chill tiny red flowers of pain secretly blossomed in his various joints. He imagined them to be something like miniature *higan-bana*. The bones that in his youth had modestly hidden in his flesh playing out their roles were now in his old age beginning more and more to claim existence. They had begun to sing and complain, breaking through the deteriorating flesh and attempting to escape from the stubborn darkness of the body. They were constantly watching for opportunities to dash into the outside world where they could bask in the sun as freely as the young leaves, rocks, and trees that enjoyed sunshine all the time. Doubtless they knew that the day was not far off when they would realize their dreams.

Watching the lights on the second floor, Honda suddenly became warm as he thought of Ying Chan disrobing. Did bones take on heat? Had the red flowers in his joints developed hay fever? Honda quickly locked the doors, turned out the lights in the living room, and stealthily went upstairs. He entered from the bedroom door so that he could proceed noiselessly to the study. He felt his way to the bookcases in the darkness. His hands trembled as he removed one after the other the thick foreign volumes. At last he put his eyes to the peephole in the back of the case.

Ying Chan entered the circle of dim light humming a song; he had never craved for any moment so much as this. It was the yearning one felt while waiting for a calabash flower to bloom on the verge of a summer evening. It was the moment at which a slowly opening fan revealed its complete picture. Honda was going to see Ying Chan in a state that as yet had been seen by no one. This was what he wanted more than anything else in the world. By his act of watching, this unseen condition was already destroyed. Being seen by absolutely no one and being unaware of being seen were similar, yet basically different.

Ying Chan had been surprisingly calm when she arrived at the villa and learned that the plans for the party were untrue.

From the time of their arrival Honda had worried about the explanation he must make. Katsumi had left all that to him in order to remain blameless in the matter. However, explanations were unnecessary. When Honda started a fire in the fire-place and gave her a drink, Ying Chan smiled happily and asked no questions. She might have thought that she had misunderstood his Japanese when she had originally been invited. Invitations extended in a foreign language often lead to misunderstandings and confusion. The reason Ying Chan had renewed acquaintance with Honda when she first came to Japan was because the Japanese ambassador to Thailand, having heard from others about Honda's former connections with Thai royalty, had written a letter of introduction. He had requested that Honda speak Japanese as much as possible so that the Princess might improve her command of the language.

As he watched Ying Chan, who seemed quite unaware of any danger, Honda was filled with a kind of pity. She was crouching by a fire in a strange country, involuntarily involved in a conspiracy of the flesh that was far from tender. The flames reflected on the sides of her bronze cheeks, and her hair seemed to smoulder. Her constant smile and her beautiful white teeth produced in him an indescribable sense of pity.

'When your father was in Japan, he was always frozen in winter. He couldn't wait for summer. You must feel that way too.'

'Yes. I don't like cold weather.'

'Well, it'll last only a little longer. In two months it will not be very different here from summer in Bangkok. As I look at you now I remember your father in cold weather. And I remember when I was young,' said Honda, going to the fireplace to flick the ash from his cigar. He stole a glance at Ying Chan's lap from above. Whereupon her knees that had been open closed like sensitive mimosa leaves.

All three had pushed aside the chairs and were sitting on the rug in front of the fire, and Honda could see Ying Chan in her various postures. She could, for example, sit nobly erect in a chair or relax on her side, her lovely legs crossed on the floor, playing the seductive Western woman. But sometimes she would suddenly break these patterns and surprise Honda, as when she had first come to the fire. She had hunched her shoulders from the cold, thrusting out her chin, miserably burying her neck; the way she talked and waved her thin wrists in the air suggested a certain Chinese-type shallowness. She had gradually drawn closer to the fire and sat facing it like the women who sold fruit in the deep green shade of the tropical afternoon markets with the blazing sunlight before them. With both legs rigid, hips suspended in the air, she bent over so that her voluptuous breasts and full thighs pushed against each other. The centre of gravity lay at the contact point of crushed breast and thigh, around which her body swayed slightly in an incredibly vulgar manner. At such times the tension of her flesh was concentrated in her buttocks, her thighs, her back, in all the ignoble places of her body, and Honda sensed a sharp odour of wilderness like that created by the heaps of dead leaves in the jungle.

Katsumi feigned calmness, and the patterns of the cut-glass brandy tumbler reflected on his white hand, but he was obviously irritable. Honda disdained his sexual desire.

'It'll be all right tonight. I'll have your room very warm,' said Honda, forestalling the question of her staying overnight before it came up. 'There'll be two big electric heaters. Thanks to Keiko's connections we were given an electric capacity as big as the one at Occupation Forces' quarters.'

But Honda did not explain why this Western-style house did not have a Western heating system or even a Korean or a Chinese one. People had suggested a wall system using coal instead of oil, which was so difficult to obtain. His wife too had liked the idea, but Honda had not agreed. Wall heating consisted of passing hot air through double walls, and it was essential for him to have walls of only one thickness.

He had pretended to his wife that he was making the trip alone, claiming he wanted to do some research undisturbed. Her words when he was about to leave, ordinary considerate words, had remained in his mind like curses: 'Don't catch cold. It's frigid at Gotemba. On a rainy day like this it'll be colder than you think. Take good care of yourself.'

Honda put his eye against the peephole. His eyelashes, turning inward, pricked his thin eyelids.

Ying Chan had not yet changed her clothes. The night kimono that had been laid out still lay on the bed. She was seated in a chair in front of the mirror and was earnestly gazing at something. He first thought it was a book, but it was much smaller and thinner and looked rather like a photograph. Curious to know whose picture it was, he tried all angles, but he could not manage to see it.

She was humming a monotonous melody to herself. It sounded like a Thai song. Honda had heard such popular tunes in Bangkok, sung in the high, squeaky tone of a Chinese fiddle. It suddenly brought back memories of the brilliant metal links in the chains around the banks at night or the boisterous scenes of the canal markets in the mornings.

Ying Chan put the photograph in her purse and walked two or three steps toward the bed; that is, toward the peephole. Honda's heart leaped. It seemed as though she would break through the wall and attack him. But instead, she jumped up on the farther of the two beds which was still covered by a spread and leaped from it to the one by the wall, which had already been made up for her. He could only see her legs.

Ying Chan bounced two or three times on the bed, turning with each leap in a different direction. He could see that the seams of her stockings were twisted.

Her beautiful legs were encased in gleaming nylon; her calves were smooth and tapered to firm ankles. Her soles were still in contact with the mattress, and she bounced by lightly bending her knees, her fluttering skirt momentarily exposing areas far above her knees. On the upper part of her stockings, where the texture was different and the beige darker, garter buttons like pale green peas were visible. Farther up, the bare dark skin of her thighs was like a dusky dawn sky seen through a skylight.

As she jumped, Ying Chan appeared to lose her balance, and the legs before his eyes began to fall to the right as if to disappear; but she descended from the bed without mishap. This was probably her childish habit of testing an unfamiliar bed.

Next she inspected the details of the night kimono Honda had put out for her. She placed it over her dress and looked at herself from all angles in front of the mirror. Then she removed it and settled down in the chair before the mirror. With both hands she grasped the clasp of the gold necklace behind her neck and skilfully undid it. She raised her fingers before the mirror and started to take off the ring, but then stopped. For Honda, watching her mirror image, Ying Chan's slow movements and her expression were as if under water or possibly manoeuvred by remote control.

Instead of taking off the band, she raised her hand high toward the ceiling light. The man's emerald ring, conspicuous on her finger, sparkled greenly, and the monstrous faces of the golden protector *yakshas* glowed.

Finally, reaching back with both hands, she began to undo the small hook above the fastener of her dress. Honda held his breath,

Ying Chan stopped her movement and turned her face toward the door on the right. It was being unlocked with the spare key Honda had provided and Katsumi was opening it. Honda bit his lip, vexed by the bad timing. If Katsumi had come two or three minutes later, Ying Chan would have had her clothes off.

The sudden apprehension of the innocent girl was transformed in the dim round frame of the peephole into a painting of a critical moment. She did not yet know who might be coming through the door. Perhaps a great white peacock would strut arrogantly in, filling the room with the fragrance of lilies. And the flutter of its wings and its cries, like the squeaking of a pulley, would transform the entire room into the quiet hall of the Rosette Palace that one afternoon...

But what entered the room was an overly affected mediocrity. Katsumi did not so much as excuse himself for opening the door without knocking, but awkwardly mumbled that not being able to sleep, he had come to talk with her. The girl, resuming her smile, offered him a chair, and the two began a long conversation. Katsumi spoke flatteringly in English and Ying Chan became suddenly talkative. Peeping through his hole, Honda yawned.

Katsumi placed his hand on hers, and as she did not withdraw it, Honda watched intently. But he could not maintain the position for long, for it strained his neck.

He leaned against the bookcase and tried to follow what was going on by the sounds. The darkness released his imagination, and in his thoughts things progressed step by step much more rationally than what was really happening in the room. In his imagination Ying Chan's disrobing had already begun, and her brilliant nakedness had flowered. When she raised her left arm and smiled, the three moles appeared on her left side, symbols of the stars in the seductive tropical night sky, symbols of his proscription. He covered her eyes, and the image of the stars immediately shattered in the darkness.

There was a stir.

Honda hastily put his eye to the hole and in so doing bumped his head on the corner of the bookcase. The noise worried him more than the pain, but the situation on the other side of the wall was beyond any concern about small noises.

Katsumi was holding on to a resisting Ying Chan. The two bodies struggled in and out of the circular field of the peephole. The girl's dress was unzipped and her brown, perspiring, angular back with brassière straps was visible. She freed her right hand and lashed out with clenched fist. The green emerald sparkled like a flying beetle and scraped along Katsumi's cheek. He drew back, putting his hand to his face. Soon there was the noise of him opening the door and leaving the room. Ying Chan was out of breath. Looking about, she dragged away one of the chairs, probably to prop against the door.

Honda panicked. Katsumi, who pretended to be so mature, was really a spoiled child, and he might well come by to borrow a first aid kit for his cheek.

Honda went to work at once. One by one he returned the thick books to the bookcase and with the meticulousness of a criminal checked that none of the titles had been replaced upside down. He verified that the door to the study was locked, turned off the heater, and stole back to his bedroom. He changed into pyjamas, threw his clothes on the dresser, and crept into bed. He was prepared to act like someone interrupted in sleep when Katsumi's knock came at the door.

This became an experience of Honda's unknown 'youth'. The swiftness and nimbleness of a dormitory student who has violated the rules and crept back to bed with an air of innocence. Though he lay quietly, his heart palpitated so rapidly that the pillow, alive, seemed to jump up and down. It did not quiet for some time.

Katsumi was probably hesitating whether to come to see him or not. This long hesitation must be the result of calculation, the weighing of the advantages and disadvantages of an impulsive visit. While he was waiting, but not really expecting Katsumi, Honda fell asleep.

The rain had stopped by morning and a golden brocade of sunlight cascaded through the gap between the curtains over the east window.

Honda wrapped a scarf about his neck and in his thick gown went down to the kitchen, intending to prepare breakfast for the young people. He found Katsumi already sitting in a chair in the living room neatly dressed.

'Well, you're up early,' Honda called halfway down the staircase, glancing swiftly at his pale cheeks.

Katsumi had already built a fire in the fireplace. He did not actually seem to be hiding his left cheek, and Honda was disappointed not to see a large scar in the firelight. There was a light scratch that could be explained away by any simple story.

'Won't you sit down for a while?' Katsumi indicated a chair as though he were the host.

'Good morning,' Honda said again in greeting and sat down.

'I felt I ought to talk with you alone. I got up particularly early,' said Katsumi as if he had done Honda a great favour.

'And ... how was it?'

'Good.'

'What do you mean "good"?'

'Just as I expected.' The young man smiled, suggesting something profoundly significant. 'She looks like a mere child, but she really isn't.'

'Did it seem like the first time for her?'

'I'm the first ... My successors will be green with envy, I'm sure.'

It seemed needless to pursue the matter further, and Honda changed the subject. 'By the way, did you happen to notice, she has some peculiar marks ... on her left side ... three, almost artificially magnificent moles all in a line. Didn't you see them?'

A momentary confusion crossed Katsumi's smug face. Many answers were possible, and there was the question of saving face too. He quickly concluded that the telling of lies had better be sacrificed for a more important occasion. It was interesting to speculate on the many possible responses passing through the young man's mind. Suddenly Katsumi leaned back on his chair with an exaggerated gesture of surprise.

'You win!' he said in a high voice. 'You're a hard man, Mr Honda! I'm losing my grip. I was fooled by her English when she seemed to say that it was the first time. You know her body already!'

It was Honda's turn to smile suggestively.

'I'm asking whether you saw the moles.'

The young man answered tensely. He was being pressed to test his feigned composure. 'Of course I saw them. They were slightly wet with perspiration and all three of them moving together in the dim light. With her dark skin they had a sort of mysterious and unforgettable beauty.'

Honda went to the kitchen and prepared breakfast of coffee and croissants. Katsumi volunteered to help, but his anxiousness to do so was quite uncharacteristic of him. As if forced by a sense of obligation, he set out the plates, asked Honda where the teaspoons were kept, and arranged them on the table. For the first time Honda felt something akin to friendship bordering on pity toward the young man.

They argued about who should take the breakfast to Ying Chan's room. Claiming the host's prerogative, Honda placed the dishes on a tray and slowly carried it upstairs.

He knocked on Ying Chan's door. There was no answer. Putting the tray down on the floor, he opened the door with a duplicate pass-key. Wedged shut by something on the inside, it was difficult to force.

Honda looked around the room filled with morning light. She was gone.

37

Of late Mrs Tsubakihara had been meeting Imanishi frequently.

She was quite blind. She was unable to form intelligent opinions about men. Nor could she judge one by sight and tell what kind of person he was ... pig or wolf or vegetable. And such a woman was trying to write poetry of all things.

If awareness of suitability was the indication of a proud love affair, no one could appease Imanishi's self-consciousness as much as this woman, blind to any kind of suitability. She had begun to love the forty-year-old man like a son.

No one was further than Imanishi from possessing physical youthfulness, freshness, or courage. He had a weak stomach, sallow, unresilient skin, and was quick to catch colds. His long body, devoid of developed muscles, was like a long, limp sash, and he swayed when he walked. He was, in other words, an intellectual.

It should have been very difficult to love such a man, but just as Mrs Tsubakihara turned out bad poetry with such ease, so had she fallen in love with no difficulty whatever. In anything and everything, her lack of skill was brilliant. Her docility and self-admitted love of criticism made her listen happily to Imanishi's constant personal rebukes. In all things she espoused the concept that criticism was a short-cut to improvement.

As a matter of fact, Imanishi had something in common with her. He was not annoyed by her girlishness when she talked so seriously about literature and poetry in the bedroom, and he himself chose the same setting to make his ideological confessions. A strange mixture of profound cynicism and immaturity lay behind the sickly youthfulness that flashed across his face from time to time. Now Mrs Tsubakihara believed that he liked to say things to hurt people because he was pure.

The couple always met at a spruce little inn recently built on the Shibuya Hill. Each room formed an independent building separated from the others by a small stream running through the garden. The woodwork was fresh and clean, and the entrance inconspicuous.

About six o'clock on June sixteenth their taxi pulled up in front of the Shibuya Station and, halted by the crowds, could proceed no farther. The inn was only five or six minutes away by foot, and Imanishi and Mrs Tsubakihara left the car.

A massive chorus singing the 'Internationale' overwhelmed them. Banners fluttered in the breeze: 'Down with the Law on the Prevention of Subversive Activities!' From the bridge of the Tamagawa Line a large banner was suspended: 'Yankees Go Home!' The faces of the people swarming over the square were flushed, cheerful, and light-hearted in their rush toward destruction.

Mrs Tsubakihara was frightened and hid behind Imanishi, who despite himself felt drawn by fear and anxiety toward the crowd. Light streamed meshlike through the legs of the mob surging across the square, the thump of footsteps increased like a sudden shower, then screams pierced the chorus and the sound of irregular clapping grew louder – all happened simultaneously as the riotous night descended upon the massed demonstrators. It reminded Imanishi of the extraordinary shudder he invariably experienced at the onset of his frequent colds with the concomitant rise of fever. Everyone had the horrible sensation of being skinned like rabbits and of having their raw red flesh suddenly exposed to the air.

'Cops! Cops!'

The sound of voices spread and the crowd scattered in confusion. The chorus of the 'Internationale' which had been a massive wave broke into fragments that lingered here and there like puddles after rain. And these were routed by cries as the rush-hour crowds and those singing inextricably commingled. White police vans roared up, stopping by the statue of the Faithful Dog Hachi in front of Shibuya Station, and members of the police reserve in dark blue helmets popped out of the vehicles like a flock of grasshoppers.

Clutching Mrs Tsubakihara's hand, Imanishi ran for his life with the crowd that was struggling to get away. When he reached a store front on the opposite side of the square and had caught his breath, he was astonished by his unexpected capacity for running. He too had been able to run! he realized. Thereupon unnatural palpitations abruptly began and his chest ached.

Compared to his own, Mrs Tsubakihara's fear, like her sorrow, was somewhat stereotyped. Clutching her purse against her breast, she stood at his side as though she would faint at any moment. The purple neon lights reflecting on her powdered cheeks seemed to transform her fear into iridescent shell work. But her eyes never wavered.

Imanishi slipped cautiously along the front of the store and looked across the rolling square in front of the station. Amidst the welling shouts and screams, the great illuminated clock on the station building serenely recorded the time.

A doomsday fragrance was rising. The world was turning red like the eyes of someone in want of sleep. Imanishi felt as though he were listening to the strange noises of silkworms in their raising room nibbling furiously away at mulberry leaves.

Then in the distance flames shot up from a white police van. Probably a Molotov cocktail. Angry red tongues and screams rose with the white smoke. Imanishi realized that he was smiling.

At length as they started to walk away from the scene, Mrs Tsubakihara noticed something hanging from Imanishi's hand.

'What do you have there?'

'I just picked it up.'

He opened what seemed like a dark rag as he walked along and showed it to her. It was a black lace brassière, distinctly different from the type Mrs Tsubakihara used. It must have belonged to a woman exceptionally confident of her breasts. It was a large-size strapless kind, and the whale-bone woven into the cups exaggerated the bulkiness of the two haughty, statuesque hollows.

'How horrible! Where did you pick it up?'

'There, a minute ago, when I ran over to the store. I noticed something clinging to my foot. It must have been stepped on. It's all covered with mud.'

'The dirty thing! Throw it away!'

'But how strange! How very peculiar.' Imanishi was delighted with the attention of the curious pedestrians passing by and proudly exhibited the brassière as he walked along.

'How could something like this fall off? Do you think it's possible?'

Of course it was not. Brassières, even the strapless type, were firmly fastened by several hooks. No matter how low the neckline, the brassière could simply not get undone and spill out. Buffeted by the crowd, the woman had torn it off herself or someone else had. The latter instance would be unlikely, and it was more plausible that the woman had done so of her own volition.

For what purpose, he had no idea. At any rate, amidst the flames, the darkness, the shouting, a pair of large breasts had been sliced off. Only their satin shell had come away, but the strong, resilient fullness of the flesh was clearly attested by the black lace moulds. The woman had purposely shed her brassière with pride. The halo had been removed, and the moon now appeared somewhere in the turbulent darkness. Imanishi had picked up only a halo, but by this act he seemed to capture – more so than if he had picked up the breasts themselves – their warmth, their cunning elusiveness, and memories of lust came swarming like moths about a lamp. Imanishi casually put the brassière to his nose. The smell of cheap perfume had permeated the fabric and was still strong despite the mud. He supposed she must have been a prostitute specializing in American soldiers.

'What a horrible man you are!'

Mrs Tsubakihara was genuinely angry. His spiteful words always held some note of criticism, but such a sordid act was mean and unforgivable. And this was not criticism but rather a snide insult. She had taken the measure of the cups in a glance and recognized Imanishi's implied disdain for her own ageing, withered breasts.

Once away from the square in front of the station nothing had changed on the road from Dogen Hill to Shoto along which small, hastily built shops stood cramped in the ruins of the bombing. Already at this early hour drunkards were loitering about, and neon lights hovered like schools of goldfish above their heads.

'I must hurry to destruction; unless I do, hell will return,' thought Imanishi. As soon as he had escaped from the danger, the ordeal flushed his cheeks. With no further reproach from Mrs Tsubakihara, he had already let the black brassière slip from his fingers to the road where the stagnant air was hot and humid.

Imanishi was obsessed with the idea that unless destruction came to him soon, the hell of daily life would quicken and consume him; if destruction did not come at once he would for yet one more day be subject to the fantasy of being consumed by dullness. It was better to be caught in sudden, complete catastrophe than to be gnawed by the cancer of imagination. All this might then be unconscious fear that unless he put an end to himself without delay, his indubitable mediocrity would be revealed.

Imanishi could see signs of world destruction in the most insignificant things. Man always finds the omens he wants.

He wished that revolution would come. Leftist or rightist, it made no difference. How wonderful if it would carry someone like him, a parasite of his father's insurance company, to the guillotine. But no matter how he might proclaim his own shame, he was not sure whether the masses would hate him or not. What would he do if they interpreted his confession as a sign of repentance? If a guillotine were to be built in the bustling square in front of the station and days came when blood flowed in the midst of all this mundaneness, he might by his death be able to become 'the remembered one'. He pictured himself being placed beneath the cutter – scaffold of lumber wrapped in red and white cloth like a lottery booth, adorned with banners announcing a special summer sale in the commercial district, and a large price tag 'Special' pasted on the blade. He shuddered.

Mrs Tsubakihara tugged at his sleeve as he walked along lost in fantasy, calling his attention to the gate of their inn. The maid waiting in the vestibule guided them in silence to their usual room. Once they were alone, Imanishi, still in turmoil, became aware of the gurgle of the stream.

They ordered a plain chicken dish and saké. While they waited through the usual time-consuming preparations of the inn, they usually indulged in some kind of physical exchange. But today Mrs Tsubakihara forced him into the washroom and made him wash his hands thoroughly, letting the tap water run as he did.

'Go on. Go on,' she said.

Imanishi did not at first grasp why he was made to wash his hands so repeatedly, but from her serious expression he gathered that it was because of the brassière he had picked up.

'No, you must wash them better.' She frantically covered his hands with soap and opened the tap wide, disregarding the noise and the splashing on the copper sink. Finally Imanishi's hands felt numb.

'Don't you think that's enough?'

'No, it's not. What do you think will happen if you come near me with hands like that? Touching me means touching the memory of my son that is in me. You'll profane Akio's sacred memory, the memory of a god ... with your dirty hands ...' Turning quickly away, she covered her eyes with a handkerchief.

Rubbing his hands together under the gushing water, Imanishi glanced obliquely at her. If she began to weep, that was a sign that whatever it was had passed and that she was prepared to accept anything.

'I wish I could die soon,' said Imanishi sentimentally as they sat drinking saké together later.

'So do I,' agreed Mrs Tsubakihara. Her skin, as transparent as rice paper, showed the faint crimson of approaching intoxication.

In the next room where the doors were open the rising and falling contours of the light blue silk quilt gleamed as if it were quietly breathing. On the table slices of abalone with artificial pink in the dusky folds floated in a bowlful of water. And food was simmering in an earthenware pot.

Without speaking, Imanishi and Mrs Tsubakihara knew that they were both awaiting something – probably the same thing.

She was enraptured with the thrill of sin and its attendant expectation of punishment for these secret meetings behind Makiko's back. She imagined Makiko entering the room, brandishing the brush dipped in red ink with which she corrected poems. 'This won't do as poetry. I'll watch. Now try to create poetry with your whole being. I am here to teach you, Mrs Tsubakihara.'

Typically Imanishi had wished to carry the affair to its culmination right before Makiko's disdainful eyes. That first night at Ninooka in Gotemba was the climax of his dream which his affair with Mrs Tsubakihara must again attain. At the very summit of the climax, Makiko's penetrating eyes had fixed on them both like cold stars. At any cost, her stare was necessary to him.

Without her eyes Imanishi could not be rid of a feeling of pretence in his union with Mrs Tsubakihara; they could never escape the complex of being an illicit couple. Those eyes belonged to the most authoritative and dignified of matchmakers, eyes of a perspicacious goddess shining in a corner of the dusky bedroom, they had united and yet rejected them, forgiven and yet disdained them. Such eyes controlled acquiescence by a mysterious and reluctant justice that was set aside somewhere in this world. Only under them was the basis of the couple's union justifiable. Away from them, the lovers were merely withered grass floating on the waters of phenomena. Their union was an ephemeral contact: a woman, the captive of an irretrievable and illusory past, and a man craving for an illusory future that would never come. It was like the dead clicking of Go stones in their container.

Imanishi felt that Makiko was already seated immobile, waiting, in the adjacent chamber into which the light of this room did not shine. The feeling of her presence became more and more urgent, and he felt that he must confirm it. He went to the trouble to check, and Mrs Tsubakihara posed no question, probably feeling the same way as he. In a corner niche of the small room of four and a half mats an arrangement of purple irises floated like flying swallows.

As usual when they had finished their lovemaking, they indulged like two women in endless small talk as they lazed about. Imanishi, now sexually released, spoke of Makiko in his worst derogatory manner.

'Makiko's using you. You're afraid you can't be a poet in your own right if you split with her. As a matter of fact, that might have been true up to now, but you must realize that you've got to an important turning point. Unless you free yourself from the influence, you'll never be good.'

'But if I'm conceited enough to be independent, I know my progress in poetry will stop too.'

'Why have you decided that?'

'I haven't decided, it's true. Maybe it's just fate.'

Imanishi wanted to ask whether her poetry had ever actually improved, but his good breeding would not permit such an impertinence. Yet the words he used to pry her free from Makiko held no sincerity. He had the feeling that Mrs Tsubakihara had answered fully aware of that.

At length she pulled up the sheet and, after tucking it around her neck, recited one of her recent poems, turning her eyes toward the dark ceiling. Imanishi criticized it immediately.

'It's a nice poem, but I don't like the petty, smug feeling it gives of dwelling on the mundane; it lacks universality. The reason is probably the last phrase. "The blueness of the deep pool" lacks imagination. It's too conceptual. It's not based on life.'

'Yes, I suppose you're right. I feel hurt if I'm criticized right after creating a poem, but in a couple of weeks I can see its weaknesses. But you know, Makiko praised this one. Unlike you, she said the last part was good, though she thought that "blueness *is* the deep pool" might be more in keeping.'

Mrs Tsubakihara's tone was condescending, as though she were pitting one authority against another. In high spirits she began gossiping in detail about her acquaintances, and that always pleased Imanishi.

'The other day I saw Keiko. She told me something interesting.'

'What?' Imanishi was immediately intrigued. He twisted from his position on his stomach and clumsily dropped long cigarette ash on the sheet around her breast.

'It's about Mr Honda and the Thai Princess,' said Mrs Tsubakihara. 'The other day he secretly took her and Keiko's nephew Katsumi, who is the Princess's boyfriend, to his Ninooka villa.'

'I wonder if the three of them slept together.'

'Mr Honda wouldn't do anything like that! He's the quiet, intellectual type. He probably wanted to play the generous matchmaker for the two young lovers. Everyone knows he adores the Princess, but they couldn't even carry on a sensible conversation with such a difference in age.'

'And what was Keiko's role in the affair?'

'She was nothing more than an innocent bystander, actually. She happened to be at her villa in Ninooka. Jack was off duty and spending the night there. Suddenly, three o'clock in the morning, there was a knock at the door and the Princess dashed in. Keiko and Jack were awakened from a sound sleep; but no matter how much they coaxed, the Princess absolutely refused to explain the situation. They were at wits' end. The Princess asked them to let her stay the night, and they did. Keiko intended to get in touch with Mr Honda in the morning, she said.

'With all of that, she got up late and rushed Jack back to camp after a cup of coffee. As she was seeing him off in a jeep at the gate, Mr Honda came to the villa looking as white as paper. Keiko laughed and said it was the first time she had ever seen him so upset.

'She knew he was looking for Ying Chan and, wanting to tease him a little, asked what he was up to so early in the morning.

'He said that Ying Chan had got lost, and his voice even quavered. After a while, when Mr Honda started home – he had given up the search – Keiko told him that Ying Chan had spent the night with her. Mr Honda blushed like a schoolboy – and at his age! – and said: "Did she really!" He sounded ever so happy.

'When Keiko took him to the guest room and he found the Princess still sound asleep, he nearly collapsed with relief. Ying Chan had not been awakened by all the commotion. She was buried in her black hair, her pretty mouth a little open and her long eyelashes closed. The exhaustion that had been so obvious on her face four or five hours before when she had rushed to the villa was now quite gone, and an innocent youthfulness had returned to her cheeks, and her breathing was peaceful and regular. As if in a pleasant dream she coquettishly turned over in her bed.'

38

Princess Ying Chan was once again unavailable for Honda. The moonless rainy season went on and on.

That morning, when he had seen the sleeping girl's face, he had not wanted to awaken her. Having asked Keiko to look after her, he returned to Tokyo. Ashamed of himself, he did not see the Princess nor did he hear from her.

When this apparently calm and peaceful period commenced, Rié began to show signs of jealousy.

'We don't hear from the Thai Princess these days,' she would casually observe during a meal. Her words carried a certain sarcasm, but her eyes were earnestly probing.

Rié had begun to draw free-association paintings on a white wall which reflected nothing for her.

Honda was in the habit of brushing his teeth regularly mornings and evenings. He noticed that his toothbrush was frequently changed, well before it was worn out. He presumed that Rié, probably having purchased a stock of brushes of the same type, colour, and hardness, changed them as she saw fit. But the changes seemed too frequent, and though it was of little consequence he brought the matter to her attention.

'How stingy you are! Isn't it funny for a millionaire to be saving on something like that!' she had answered, almost stammering in her anger. Not comprehending the reason for her fury, he had let her alone. But later he realized that the toothbrushes were changed the mornings after nights when he came in late. Apparently Rié surreptitiously changed them after he had gone to bed. The following day she would carefully inspect the base of each shiny bristle of the old brush to determine whether there were traces of lipstick or the faint fragrance of a young woman and then discard it.

Honda's gums bled sometimes for one reason or another; and though he did not yet need a full denture, he occasionally complained of pyorrhea. How did Rié interpret the pink stains that sometimes discoloured the roots of the bristles?

He was merely conjecturing, but there were times when Rié seemed like a kind of obsessed scientist devoting herself to creating some new compound from the oxygen and nitrogen in the air. She seemed bored with her free time, and yet her eyes and senses were sharp. Though complaining incessantly of headaches, she constantly patrolled with nervous steps the many corridors of the old house.

Once when the subject of the villa happened to come up, Honda remarked that he had built it so that she could recuperate from her kidney condition.

'Are you telling me to go to that graveyard by myself?' she had said in tears, misunderstanding.

She was right in recognizing Honda's love for Ying Chan that had begun ever since he had gone to Gotemba alone; she had come to this conclusion from his silence about the girl. But she never supposed that he had not seen her since then. She mistakenly assumed that he was seeing her in secrecy and therefore wanted to erase the name from Rié's thoughts.

Such tranquillity was uncanny. It held the false stillness of a hideout for some fugitive emotion afraid of its pursuers. Rié intuitively felt that some exclusive, secretive banquet had been arranged to which she would never be invited.

What was happening?

She had judged correctly also when she thought something had occurred, although Honda himself felt that everything was finished.

Since Rié had completely stopped going out, Honda began to leave the house more frequently than ever, even though he had no purpose. He felt suffocated by the constant presence of his wife who always stayed in under the pretext of illness.

As soon as Honda left the house, Rié would suddenly come alive. Theoretically she should have been worried about the purpose of his unexplained outings, but she had been able to reconcile herself with her now familiar fears. Thus jealousy had become the basis of her freedom.

It was the same as love; her heart was always ensnared, trammelled. She tried to practise calligraphy for a change, but involuntarily her hand would write characters related to the moon ... 'moonshadows' ... 'mountain in the moonlight'.

It was repulsive to her that a girl as young as Ying Chan should have such large breasts. She would conjure up from the characters for 'mountain in the moonlight' that she had inadvertently composed a pair of mountains in the shape of breasts quietly bathing in moonlight. This was related to her memory of the Twin Hills in Kyoto. But no matter how innocent, Rié feared anything that evoked memories. She had seen the Twin Hills on a high-school trip; and when she recalled the sway of her own small breasts perspiring under the white summer uniform, she felt herself curl up.

Concerned with Rié's fragility, Honda had wanted to engage several servants. Rié made the excuse that her worries would be multiplied if she had to oversee so many people, and she had only two maids in the kitchen. The work there that she had loved for many years was now considerably lessened; besides it was not good for her legs to be standing for any length of time on a chilly floor. She had no alternative but to stay in her room. She took up sewing. The drawing room draperies were threadbare and she ordered some silk brocade from Tatsumura in Kyoto. From the fabric with its print of patterns copied from those in the Shoso-in at Nara, she sewed new curtains.

Rié lined the material carefully with a thick black cloth to cut out the light. Honda noted this as she worked.

'You'd think we were still at war,' he teased. As a result, she became even more obstinate in completing what she had begun.

She was not concerned about light leaking out from the inside, but about moonlight seeping in.

Rié stealthily read her husband's diary when he was out and was infuriated when she could find no mention of Ying Chan in it. Out of reticence, Honda had developed the habit of not writing anything romantic in his diary.

Among her husband's documents she found an extremely old record entitled 'Dream Diary'. *Kiyoaki Matsugae* was written on it. The name was familiar to her, for Honda had frequently mentioned it. But he had never spoken about the diary, and of course, this was the first time she had set eyes on it.

Looking through it, she was amazed at the absurd fantasies. She carefully replaced it. Rié was seeking no fantasy. The only thing she believed could cure her was the truth.

When, on closing a drawer, a kimono sleeve is caught, the seams of the sleeve and the bodice will tear as one walks away. As similar experiences were repeated, the sleeves of Rié's heart were torn to bits. She was captivated by something, yet her heart was empty and listless.

The rain continued day and night. She could see from the window the wet hydrangeas. The pastel violet balls of flowers floating in the gloomy day appeared as her own soul gone astray.

There was nothing more insufferable than the idea that Princess Moonlight existed in this world. It was shattered because of her.

Rié had lived her whole life without once knowing the terror of emotions. Thus she was surprised by the eruption of the riotous feelings of solitude within her. The barren woman had given birth for the first time, but to something monstrous.

Thus it was that Rié learned that she too had imagination. What had never been used, what had rusted in a corner of her long and tranquil life was suddenly unearthed out of necessity and polished and sharpened. At any rate, anything born of necessity is accompanied by bitterness, and her propensity toward flights of fancy held no sweetness.

Imagination based on reality might have opened and freed a mind, but that which attempted to come as close to the truth as possible demeaned and dried it up. Furthermore, if that truth did not really exist, everything would at once be transformed into futility.

But imagining a crime in which there was some truth would do no harm. Rié's imagination was a double-edged sword. She believed that there was truth somewhere and she desired that it not exist. Thus her jealous imagination was trapped by its own self-denial, and yet could not tolerate its own existence. Just as excessive acidity in the stomach gradually eats away the stomach walls, so her imagination eroded the root of its own imaginativeness, and at the same time she was driven by a desire to be saved that was a scream for help. Truth. If there were truth, she would be saved! The desire that appeared at the end of such a one-sided obsessive search inevitably began to resemble an urge for self-punishment. Because that truth – if it really existed – would crush her.

But punishment sought and obtained naturally holds a sense of unfairness. Why should an attorney be punished? That would be a reversal. When what she craved finally came to pass, instead of the delight of fulfilment, dissatisfaction and anger would flare up. Even now she could feel the heat of the burning stake. She must not allow such injustice to occur. She must not expose herself to such incomparably exquisite pain. Suffering from doubt was already enough; why should she pile the pain of recognition upon it?

Desiring to search out the truth, and yet to deny it, wanting to deny the truth, yet seeking only salvation in it. Such emotion went forever around in circles, just as the stray traveller on a mountain road, intending to go forward, somehow always returned to the point he started from.

It was like being enveloped in fog where in one area the details are uncannily distinct. One follows a ray of light only to discover that the moon is not there, rather it is at one's back and what one sees ahead is its reflection.

Yet Rié had not completely lost all sense of self-examination. Sometimes disgusted with herself, she wanted to cover her face in shame. Yet she felt that it was none of her fault that she had turned into an ugly, unlovable being because of her husband. She felt that her husband had really changed her into something despicable because he had no desire to love her. When she arrived at this realization, hatred welled up in her breast like a gushing spring.

But in her state, she tended to avoid the truth of the matter that even if she had not been turned by jealousy into one so repulsive, there were other causes that had transformed her into what she now was, that even had she stayed unchanged she would no longer have been loved. Her husband was perforce to be despised, but from his own need to turn away from her charms, he could not help but change her into an unlovable creature.

Rié had taken to gazing for long periods into her mirror. Wisps of stray hair emphasized the unloveliness of her cheeks. Everything about her seemed artificial, including the swelling of her face.

Since she had become aware of the bulging years ago, she had made up rather heavily. She disliked the way her eyes looked hooded, and she would apply dark eyebrow pencil and thick powder. When they had been younger, Honda had teased her by calling her 'Moonface'. She was irked at being chided about her affliction, but the night he called her 'Moonface' his affection had been particularly warm, and thinking her handicap had probably increased his feeling, Rié had begun to take pride in her face. But on reflection, the sexual passion inspired by her oedema contained a certain, subtle cruelty. To be sure, on such nights his lovemaking was passionate, but in view of his admonition that she remain absolutely passive, he might have been entertaining the illusion of a several-day-old corpse with her swollen face.

The reflection in the mirror was a living ruin. Under her lustreless hair, a sinewy malice appeared on her moonlike features like the ribs of a round fan. Her face had gradually turned into one not of a woman, and whatever feminine roundness it had, persisted only in the swelling. Even that was the cold, faded, tiresome roundness of the moon in daylight.

To apply beautifying make-up now would only signal defeat. But being ugly was also a defeat. She had lost all desire for repairing the defects in her present face; so the dents remained dents, the ugliness ugliness, and everything continued tranquilly like the rise and fall of sand dunes. Rié thought that it might just not be her husband's fault that she was unable to tear herself away from jealousy, but the fault of the enormous boredom that enveloped her like heavy bedding. She felt that she would need a frightening amount of strength to push it away and indolently did nothing about it. But if she was so lazy why could she find not even momentary peace?

Rié suddenly remembered the winter beauty of Mount Fuji, which she had been able to see from the second floor of the house soon after her marriage. She had been told by her mother-in-law to bring down the dinner service reserved for the New Year's celebrations and had gone obediently up to the storage room on the second floor. She had seen Fuji from there. She had tied a red cord across her sleeves to keep them down as new brides did.

Rié noticed that the rain had stopped and the evening light was limpid. Thinking to dispel her worries by looking at Fuji, she went up to the storage room on the second floor for the first time in many years. She climbed over the stacked guest bedding and opened the window with its opaque glass panes. The post-war sky, unlike that of former days, was bright, but an isinglass cloudiness had settled everywhere. Fuji was not visible.

39

Honda awakened with a need to urinate.

Tattered ends of interrupted dreams.

He had felt like strolling about a small residential district of Tokyo with its rows of little hedged gardens. The houses were tiny, and in front of them bonsai had been placed on shelves in the yards; some had small flower patches bordered with shells. The gardens were damp and filled with the inevitable snails. Two children sat facing each other on the edge of a veranda drinking warm sugar water and savouring wafers with broken corners. It was one of those Tokyo districts from which such scenes had now totally vanished. He had come to a dead-end alley surrounded by hedges. A decrepit wooden wicket gate stood at the farther end.

When he opened the wicket and stepped in, it proved to be the bright front garden of an old-fashioned hotel, and a garden party was in progress. The manager with a Ronald Colman moustache came forward and bowed respectfully.

Just then the brilliant, pathetic sound of bugles rose from the buffet tent, the ground suddenly split asunder, and Princess Moonlight clad in a golden dress emerged on the wings of a golden peacock. The assembly applauded as the peacock flew over their heads making a bell-like sound with its wings.

Princess Moonlight's shiny, brown thighs astride the golden peacock exposed her privates, and in short order she sent down a shower of fragrant urine onto the upturned faces of the onlookers.

Why had she not gone to the toilet? Honda wondered. He must scold her for such outlandish manners. He entered the hotel in search of a bathroom.

Inside, the building was completely still and contrasted with the commotion outdoors.

The door of each room was unlocked and slightly ajar. Honda opened each one and saw that every room was empty except for a coffin on the bed.

A voice told him that that was the toilet he was looking for.

Unable to contain himself longer, he entered a room and tried to urinate into the coffin, but he could not out of fear of committing blasphemy.

It was at that point that he awakened.

Such dreams were merely the pitiful signs of old age when the urge to urinate came at shorter and shorter intervals. After returning from the toilet, completely awake and clear-headed, he was taken up with recapturing the broken threads of the dream. He knew that there was undeniable happiness to be found there.

He wished to recapture the feeling of radiant joy by making it go on. In it a brilliantly pure, unreserved delight existed to the fullest. And the joy was real. If, even in a dream, Honda could not think that the joy of capturing an unrepeatable segment of time in his life was real, what else could reality be? When he glanced up to the sky he caught sight of the transformed figure of the Peacock Wisdom King set in a complete harmony of affinity and sympathy, soaring astride the golden peacock. Ying Chan was his.

The next morning even after he awakened, the happy feeling distinctly persisted, and Honda was in high spirits.

Of course, the dream that he had had in his second sleep was so vague and shapeless that he could not possibly recall it. He could only remember that it had contained none of the happiness of the first. But the brilliant light in this latter had pierced the accumulation of the second dream that was like a snowdrift and had stayed in his memory until morning.

All day he again thought of Ying Chan, using her absence as a lever. He was astonished when he realized that something like the passion of the youthful first love he had never known infused his fifty-seven-year-old body.

On reflection, falling in love for him was not only extraordinary, but rather comical. By having closely observed Kiyoaki Matsugae, he knew full well what sort of man should fall in love.

Falling in love was a special privilege given to someone whose external, sensuous charm and internal ignorance, disorganization, and lack of cognizance permitted him to form a kind of fantasy about others. It was a rude privilege. Honda was quite aware that since his childhood he had been the opposite of such a man.

He had often observed the contrariness of human fate that let one individual participate in history out of ignorance and another fail to because of eagerness. Thus he believed that the greatest reason for not obtaining what one wished lay in the desire to obtain. Because Honda had never wanted money, millions had come to him.

That was how he thought. His inability ever to obtain anything was not the result of any shortcoming or innate flaw in himself, nor was it some bad luck he carried with him. It was his habit to formulate everything into laws, to universalize. So it was no small wonder that he set out to circumvent this particular one. It was his manner to do everything by himself, thus he could easily play both the role of legislator and violator. In other words, he limited what he wanted to what he could never get. If by chance he obtained the object of his desire, it invariably proved worthless. Thus he strove to attribute all manner of impossibilities to this object, to put it at as great a distance as he could. In other words, he kept a passionate apathy in his heart.

In the case of Ying Chan the shrouding in mystery of this thick-petalled Thai rose was achieved almost completely after the incident that night in Gotemba. It consisted in relegating her to some unattainable place, somewhere his perception could never penetrate. (In the first place, the length of his arm and that of his perception were the same.) The pleasure one gets by seeing necessarily presupposes some unseeable sphere. Honda felt that he had seen to the ends of the world during his experience in India. And he wanted to know the feeling of an indolent animal licking its resin-smeared fur and relaxing in a pool of sunshine, sending its prey someplace where the claws of perception could never reach. In trying to simulate such an animal, was he not trying to imitate God?

It was unbearable for Honda that his carnal desires should so perfectly overlap with his desire for perceiving; and he knew very well that love would never be born in him unless he could separate the two. How could a rose spring up between a pair of gigantic trunks entwined and ugly? Love should not open up like a parasitic orchid on either one with their shameless hanging roots, nor from his insipid desire for perception, nor from his rank fifty-seven-year-old lust. It was necessary that Ying Chan should exist beyond the reach of his desire for perceiving, that he deal only with the impossibility of his desire.

Absence was the best for this. It was indeed. It was the only pure, perfect material for his love. Without absence the nocturnal beast of perception would immediately begin to glare and soon tear everything apart with its sharp claws. Biting into the unknown, transforming everything into familiar corpses, stepping into the morgue of perception – this frightfully boring disease had once been cured by India, had it not? What India and Benares had taught him was that, escaping the ultimate of perception, Ying Chan like a single remaining rose should be locked tightly away at the back of a dusty ebony shelf; he could pretend to know it already so that it would escape the eyes of his perception. That Honda had achieved. He had locked the cupboard himself, and it was by his will that he did not open it.

Long ago Kiyoaki, fascinated by the completely impossible, had committed an impropriety. But Honda created the impossible so that he would commit no violation of it. For the minute he attempted a violation, beauty could no longer exist in this world.

He remembered the freshness of the morning when Ying Chan had vanished. A part of himself had been driven by fear, yet another part had enjoyed the situation. Even after he had discovered that she was no longer in her room, he did not panic and at once summon Katsumi. He was totally engrossed in savouring her ubiquitous lingering fragrance.

It had been a beautiful sunny morning. The bed was rumpled. He detected in the minute wrinkles in the sheet evidence of where her feverish body had tossed and turned in her distress. Honda picked up a curly wisp of hair hidden under the swells of the blanket that was like a nest where some lovely little animal had suffered. He looked to see if there were traces of Ying Chan's transparent saliva in the hollow of the pillow that still held its innocent indentation.

Only then had he gone down to tell Katsumi.

Katsumi had turned white. Honda had no difficulty in concealing the fact that he was not at all surprised.

They decided to join forces to search for her.

It would be untrue for Honda to deny he was then entertaining the thought of Ying Chan's death. He did not believe she was dead, but in this sunny interval in the rainy season death wafted even in the wasted fragrance of the morning coffee. Something tragic enclosed the morning like a fine silvery edging. It was the proof of grace Honda had dreamt about.

Though he had absolutely no intention of doing so, he suggested to Katsumi that perhaps they should notify the police and enjoyed seeing the extremely alarmed expression this evoked.

Honda visualized with a thrill Ying Chan's body floating in the swimming pool that reflected the blue sky. He went out to the terrace and looked into the rain puddles in the excavation. He felt that the glass that demarcated the real from the unreal had been completely shattered that moment and that he could thus easily step into the world of the unknown. The universe could be anything that morning. Anything was possible: death, murder, suicide, even universal destruction right in the midst of the bright fresh panorama.

As he and Katsumi descended the narrow lane across the soaking lawn toward the mountain stream, Honda enjoyed, in a swift flight of imagination, a foreboding of his once considerable social prestige collapsing amidst great fracas if a suicide scandal were to appear in the newspapers. But this was ridiculous exaggeration. The incident had taken place only between Katsumi and Ying Chan, and no one in the world knew anything about Honda's peep-hole.

For the first time in many days one could see Fuji beyond the garden. It was already a summer mountain. Its snowy skirts had been hoisted unexpectedly high, and the colour of the earth in the morning sun glowed like rain-soaked brick.

They looked in the stream; they searched in the cypress woods.

When they left the grounds Honda suggested that Katsumi go to Keiko's house where he just might find her in. This he obstinately refused to do, offering instead to check by car along the road to the station. He was terrified of facing his aunt.

Honda himself was hesitant about visiting Keiko at such an early hour, but it was unavoidable in this instance. He pushed the bell. Surprisingly, she appeared, make-up completed and dressed in an emerald-green dress and a cardigan.

'Good morning,' she said quite normally. 'You're looking for Ying Chan? She came over here while it was still dark. She's asleep now in Jack's bed. Lucky Jack wasn't here. What a scene if he had been. Since she seemed upset, I gave her some chartreuse and let her sleep. After that I was wide awake, so I just stayed up. What a horrible man you are! But I asked no questions about what happened. Would you like to see her lovely face while she's sleeping?'

Honda, still extremely patient, controlled his desire to see Ying Chan. Neither she nor even Keiko had contacted him.

He was waiting for madness to take complete possession of him.

Reason was threatened by an extreme of anxiety, and just as the old fox in the farce *Fox Hunt* jumped at his prey although he was quite aware of the danger of a trap, Honda was waiting for the moment when he would be driven into blind self-destruction despite his experience and knowledge, accomplishment and skill, reason and objectivity – or rather, he was waiting for the moment when the accumulation of them all would drive him to it.

Just as a boy must wait for maturity, so a fifty-seven-year-old too had to attend his own ripening; and that was toward catastrophe. When all the trees in the withered November thickets had lost their leaves and the underbrush had yellowed and when in the clarity of the winter sun the place appeared as white and dry as the Pure Land, like the snake gourd, a single spot of crimson among dead vines, he fervently awaited his ripening toward catastrophe.

Whether what he sought was a flamelike lack of discernment or death, Honda's age made it difficult for him to know. Someplace, he knew not where, something was being slowly and carefully prepared. And now the only thing certain in the future was death.

At his office in the Marunouchi Building, when he heard a young law clerk receiving a private telephone call, shielding it so that his superiors would not know, Honda was overcome by intense loneliness. The call was obviously from a woman, and the young man, concerned about those around him, pretended reluctance; but in the distance Honda could almost hear the clear, attractive voice of the young woman.

Probably the two shared a secret language and communicated with each other by using business jargon. Honda suddenly conceived a plan for firing the young man whose eternally well-groomed hair, romantic eyes, and arrogant lips were all so unbecoming to a law office.

The best time to catch Keiko, who spent her days going to luncheons, cocktail parties, and formal dinners, was now at eleven o'clock in the morning. After having overheard the young clerk, Honda was loath to make the call from the small office in his loud voice. Saying he was going to do some shopping, he went out.

The shopping arcade in the Marunouchi Building was one of the few places where pre-war Tokyo still lingered on, and Honda enjoyed window-shopping at the haberdasheries or selecting paper for calligraphy. Gentlemen, obviously pre-war types, were hunting for reasonable purchases that would not be too hard on their pockets; they walked cautiously to avoid slipping on the mosaic floor that was particularly slippery after the rain.

Honda called Keiko from a pay phone.

As usual she did not answer at once, but he was positive she was at home. He pictured her magnificent, opulent back; she must be in her slip putting on make-up after having selected her attire for the luncheon party and was oblivious to the telephone.

'I'm sorry to keep you waiting,' she said in her rich, leisurely voice. 'I've been thoughtless not to call. Have you been well?'

'Quite well, thanks. I wondered if we could have lunch sometime soon.'

'Oh, how kind! But you really want to see Ying Chan, not me.'

Honda was at once at a loss for words and decided to wait for Keiko's lead. 'I'm sorry I've troubled you. By the way, she never contacted me after that night. Have you seen her?'

'No, not since then. I wonder what she's doing. Isn't she taking exams or something?'

'I don't think she studies much.'

Honda was amazed by his own ability to carry on the conversation so calmly.

'But you want to see her anyway,' began Keiko. Then she thought for a moment. The interval of silence was neither heavy nor important. White powder was probably floating in the shafts of morning light falling through the bedroom windows. Honda knew that she was not the kind of woman to feign mystery, so he waited, leaving everything up to her.

'I shall pose a condition, I think,' she said.

'What is that?'

'Ying Chan escaped to my place and she trusts me completely. So if I tell her that I shall be present too, she won't turn you down straightaway. Is that all right?'

'What do you mean is it all right? I was going to ask you to do precisely that.'

'I really want to let you see her alone, but for a while ... Where shall I call to give you the answer?'

'At my office. I've decided to go there every morning from now on,' replied Honda and hung up.

The world was transformed from that moment on. How could he bear to wait for the next hour, the next day? He made a little wager with himself: if Ying Chan wore the emerald ring when she met him, that would mean she had forgiven him; if she did not, that would signify the opposite.

40

Keiko's house was situated in the higher section of Azabu and was deep-set with a driveway that led up to the entrance. There was a semicircular Regency façade built by Keiko's father in memory of his youth in Brighton. One warm afternoon toward the end of June, Honda had accepted an invitation to tea and entered the mansion with the feeling of returning to pre-war Japan.

Following a typhoon and thunder and rain, suddenly in the summer light, unusual for the rainy season, the quiet woods on the front grounds seemed to store remembrances of an entire period. He thought he was returning to nostalgic old music. This kind of mansion, now almost the only one remaining in the burned ruins, had become even more privileged, sinful, and gloomy by reason of its solitariness. It was just as though remembrances left behind by the times were to have their impact suddenly heightened with the passing of the years.

A formal invitation had come to him announcing that Keiko's house had been released by the American Occupation Forces, and that she wished to give a tea to celebrate the occasion. She did not touch on the matter of Ying Chan. Honda came bearing a bouquet of flowers. While the house had been confiscated, Keiko had lived with her mother in a separate dwelling that had once been the steward's, and she had never invited guests to visit in Tokyo during that time.

A servant in white gloves met him at the door. The circular entrance hall was high-domed. The cryptomeria doors on one side were painted with cranes, while on the other they opened on to a spiral staircase of marble that led to the second floor. Halfway up the stairs, in a dark niche, stood a bronze Venus with eyes demurely lowered.

The doors with the Kano-style cranes, both half open, led to the drawing room. He found no one there.

Light from a row of small windows brightened the room, and the panes were old-fashioned crystal surfaces that refracted rainbow colours. Further to the interior, one side recessed into a niche. Golden clouds had been painted all over the wall, on which hung a narrow scroll with calligraphy. A chandelier was suspended from the Momoyama-style latticed ceiling. All the small tables and chairs were splendid Louis Quinze – *d'époque*. The upholstery of each chair bore a different design; altogether they formed the sequence of a *fête champêtre* by Watteau.

While Honda was examining the chairs, a familiar fragrance came to him, and turning around, he saw Keiko standing there in a fashionable double-skirted afternoon dress of heavy mustard pongee.

'How do you like them? Aren't they antediluvian?'

'What a perfectly splendid mingling of East and West!'

'My father's taste rather ran to this sort in everything. But don't you think they're well preserved? The confiscation of the house couldn't be avoided, but I ran around and did what I could so that it wouldn't be destroyed by ignoramuses. Since they used the place for Army VIPs, they turned it back to me quite undamaged, as you can see. There are childhood memories for me in every corner. It was lucky that some of the country bumpkins from Ohio didn't run the place down. I wanted you to see it today.'

'And where are your other guests?'

'They're all in the garden. It's hot, but the breeze is pleasant. Won't you come out?'

Keiko made no reference to Ying Chan.

Opening a door in one corner of the room, she stepped out onto the terrace that led to the garden. In the shade of the large trees cane chairs and small tables were scattered about. The clouds were extremely beautiful, and the colours in the women's clothes heightened the green of the lawn. Flower-like hats swayed to and fro.

Upon approaching the group Honda realized that it was composed of old women; furthermore, he was the only male guest there. He felt out of place as he was introduced. Each time the pink hands, blotched and wrinkled, were extended, he hesitated to shake them; he was depressed by the accumulation of hands; they darkened his heart like a cargo of dried fruit in the hold of a ship.

Western women, apparently unaware of the gaping zippers on their backs, swung their broad hips and cackled with laughter. Their sunken eyes with brown or blue pupils were focused on things he could not locate. When pronouncing certain words they would open their dark mouths so wide that he could see their tonsils, and they gave themselves to the conversation with a kind of vulgar enthusiasm. One of them, snatching up two or three thin sandwiches with red manicured fingers, turned suddenly to Honda and announced that she had been divorced three times and wanted to know whether the Japanese divorced a lot too.

The colourfully dressed guests strolled about the grove to escape the heat and were visible through the trees. Two or three of them emerged from the entrance to it. There was Ying Chan accompanied by a Western woman on either side.

Honda's heart pounded as though he had stumbled. This was it, this palpitation was important; thanks to it, life had stopped being solid dead matter and was transformed into a liquid, even gaseous state. Just seeing her had done him good. Sugar cubes melted in tea at the instant of this palpitation; the buildings all became unsteady; all the bridges bent as if they were candy; and life became synonymous with lightning or with the wavering poppy in the wind or with the swinging of a curtain. Extremely self-centred satisfaction and unpleasant shyness intermingled as in a hangover, projecting Honda with one thrust into a dream world.

Escorted by two tall women, Ying Chan in a sleeveless salmon-pink dress, her black hair lustrous as jet falling over her shoulders, suddenly came out of the grove into the sunlight. Honda took double pleasure in being reminded of the Princess's picnic at Bang Pa In, when she had been attended by the old ladies.

Keiko, unnoticed, was standing at his side.

'How do you like that? Don't I keep my promises?' she whispered in his ear,

A childlike insecurity welled up in Honda, and he was afraid that he could not possibly go through with the scene unless he depended completely on Keiko for help. Step by step, a smiling Ying Chan approached this incomprehensible fear. He was flustered by his concern to control his emotion before Ying Chan should reach him, but the closer she came, the more it grew. Honda was tongue-tied before he even tried to speak.

'Just act as though nothing ever happened. You'd better not mention anything about Gotemba,' Keiko whispered in his ear again.

Fortunately Ying Chan's progress was interrupted in the middle of the lawn when another woman stopped her to chat. She seemed not to have noticed him as yet. Ten or fifteen yards away she swayed on the branch of time like a beautiful orange that could be reached in seconds, ripe, heavy with fragrance and juice. Honda examined everything about her: her breasts, her legs, her smile, her white teeth. Everything had been nurtured under the burning summer sun, yet inside, her heart was surely impenetrably cold.

When Ying Chan finally joined the group in the circle of chairs it was still uncertain whether she had really not noticed Honda or was pretending not to have.

'It's Mr Honda,' Keiko said encouragingly.

'Oh?' said Ying Chan, turning around with a perfectly relaxed smile. Her face in the summer light was revived and her lips were more relaxed and smiling. Her eyebrows flowed, and in the amber brightness of her face her large, black eyes were luminous. Her face was enjoying its season. Summer had relaxed her as though she were stretching self-indulgently in an ample bath. The naturalness of her pose was complete. As he visualized the hollow between her breasts under her brassière perspiring as if in a steam room, he could feel the summer concealed deep within her body.

When she extended a hand her eyes were expressionless. Honda took it somewhat shakily. She was not wearing the emerald ring. Though the wager he had made was with himself, he realized now that he had wanted to lose, to be coldly rejected. He was surprised to note than even rejection gave him a pleasant sensation and did not at all disturb his audacious reveries.

Ying Chan took up an empty teacup, so Honda stretched his arm and touched the handle of the antique silver teapot. But the heat of the metal made him hesitate. He probably was motivated by a fear that the destination of his action would be interrupted by a fog of insecurity, that certainly his hand would tremble, and that he might do something terribly clumsy. A servant's white-gloved hand immediately came to his rescue and relieved him of his concern.

'You look well, now that summer's here,' he finally managed to say. While he was quite unaware of it, his manner of speaking was more polite than usual.

'Yes, I like summer.' Smiling softly, Ying Chan answered as if out of a text-book.

The old ladies around her, manifesting their interest, asked him to translate the conversation. The fragrance of the lemon on the table and the smell of old bodies and perfume put Honda's nerves on edge, but he translated the conversation. The old ladies laughed meaninglessly, commenting that the Japanese word for summer made them feel decidedly warm, conjecturing about a possible tropical etymology for the word.

Intuitively Honda felt Ying Chan's ennui. Looking around, he saw that Keiko had already gone. Boredom was increasing in Ying Chan like a silent animal sadly rubbing itself against the sultry grass. This intuition of his was the only bond with her. She moved gracefully, smiling and talking in English, but he gradually began to feel that she wanted perhaps to tell him about her boredom. It was a kind of music made by the accumulation of the summer melancholy of her flesh, from her heavy breasts down to her beautiful light legs. It was constantly in his ears, high and low, like the faint hum of insects flitting in the summer sky.

But it did not necessarily mean that she was bored with the party. Rather, the aura of ennui filling her body could have been her natural state that the summer had revived. She was obviously quite at home in this ennui. Retreating slightly into the shade of a tree, she spoke with vivacity, holding her teacup surrounded by old ladies who addressed her as Your Serene Highness. She suddenly took off a shoe and with one sharp, stocking-clad toe casually scratched the calf of her other leg with the exquisite balance of a flamingo, holding the teacup perfectly steady and not spilling a single drop into the saucer.

Momentarily Honda was confident that he could slip into Ying Chan's heart straight and smoothly, even if he were not forgiven.

'That was quite a feat.' Honda found a momentary interval in the conversation and spoke in Japanese.

'What?'

Ying Chan raised questioning eyes. There was nothing more charming than her mouth, which, when given a riddle, responded with an instant 'What?' like a bubble floating on the surface of the water, making no effort to solve it. She did not at all mind unintelligibility, so he should have the same sort of courage. He had prepared a note written in pencil on a page torn from a little memorandum.

'Please see me alone,' he said. 'During the day is all right. Only an hour will do.

How about today? Can you come here?' He handed her the paper with the time and place written on it.

Ying Chan deftly avoided the observant eyes of the ladies and glanced at the paper in the sun. Her momentary effort at evasion made Honda happy.

'Are you free?'

'Yes.'

'Will you come?'

'Yes.'

Ying Chan's 'yes' was almost too distinct, but it was accompanied by a beautiful smile that at once softened her answer. It was clear that she was thinking of nothing.

Where do love and hatred go? Where do the tropical cloud shadows and the violent rains that fall like stones disappear to? To be made to realize the futility of his suffering was stronger than being made to realize the futility of his occasional happiness.

Keiko had disappeared, but now she returned leading two guests into the garden from the drawing room as she had done when Honda arrived. One old woman, on seeing the beautifully kimonoed figures, one in light and the other in dark blue, made hard and rasping sounds of admiration with her parrot-like tongue. Honda turned to look. It was Makiko attended by Mrs Tsubakihara.

Honda had been rapturously gazing at Ying Chan's jet-black hair suddenly blowing in the wind like a sail, and the arrival seemed particularly untimely. As they approached, the two greeted Honda first of all. 'How lucky you are today,' said Makiko coldly, looking around at the old ladies. 'The only thorn in a bouquet of roses!'

Of course, the two women were introduced to the Westerners and amenities were exchanged, but they were pleased to return to Honda, with whom they talked in Japanese.

When the clouds shifted and the shadows deepened on her hair, Makiko said: 'Did you see the demonstration on June twenty-fifth?'

'No, I only read about it in the papers.'

'So did I. They threw Molotov cocktails everywhere in Shinjuku, and some police boxes were burned down. It was a terrible riot, I hear. At this rate, I wonder if the Communists won't take over.'

'I don't think so.'

'But things seem to get worse every month: even home-made guns are appearing. I imagine that the Communists and the Koreans will soon turn the whole of Tokyo into a sea of flames.'

'We can't do much about it, can we?'

'You'll have a long life because you don't worry,' said Makiko. 'But looking at the world these days, I wonder what would have happened if Isao had lived. I started to write a series of poems called "June Twenty-fifth". I wanted to write poetry at the lowest level, one on which it would be impossible to create; I'd been looking for material that could never be turned into poetry when I finally hit on this.'

'You say you hit on it, but you didn't go to see it yourself.'

'A poet has long sight, unlike people like you.'

It was unusual for Makiko to talk in such a relaxed fashion about her own poetry. But her attitude was a kind of priming. She looked around and smiled into Honda's eyes.

'I hear you were pretty upset in Gotemba the other day.'

'Who told you?' Honda asked, unperturbed.

'Keiko,' said Makiko calmly.

'Come to think,' she continued, 'it might have been an emergency, but Ying Chan has a lot of nerve barging into someone's house in the middle of the night and banging on the lovers' bedroom door. Jack's a lovely boy to treat her so kindly. He's really a well-bred and charming American.'

Honda was confused. He was certain that Keiko had said that morning: 'Lucky that Jack wasn't here. What a scene if he had been.' And now Makiko was talking as though he *had* stayed the night. It was either Makiko's misunderstanding or Keiko's lie. The discovery of Keiko's meaningless little falsehood gave him a secret feeling of superiority that he was reluctant to share with Makiko. He wanted to avoid the absurdity of getting involved in women's gossip. Furthermore, Makiko had thought nothing of perjuring herself in front of judges. Honda never lied, but at times he had the habit of ignoring some paltry truth gliding away in front of him like trash flowing down a little gutter. It was a small vice that dated from the days of his judgeship.

As he attempted to change the subject, Mrs Tsubakihara came sidling up as though seeking Makiko's protection. He was surprised that her face had become so drawn in the short time since he had last seen her. Her sorrowful expression itself had a wasted look, her eyes were hollow, and her lips, garishly painted orange, made her utterly grotesque.

With a smile in her eyes, Makiko suddenly lifted her disciple's round white chin with one finger and showed it to Honda.

'She gives me such a difficult time, threatening me with her ideas of suicide.'

Mrs Tsubakihara let her chin rest on Makiko's finger as though she wished to remain for ever in that position, but the latter immediately removed it. Mrs Tsubakihara, looking across the lawn where an evening breeze was beginning to rise, half spoke to Honda in a thick voice: 'But without talent how can one go on living?'

'If the untalented had to die, everybody in Japan would be dead,' Makiko responded in amusement.

Honda observed this exchange with a shudder.

41

At four o'clock two days later, the appointed hour, Honda was waiting in the lobby of the Tokyo Kaikan. If Ying Chan came, he intended to take her to the roof garden restaurant which had opened that same summer.

The lobby was a convenient place to wait inconspicuously for someone. The easy chairs upholstered in leather were spaciously arranged and he could spread the bound newspaper in front of his face. In an inside pocket Honda had three hand-rolled Monte Cristo Havanas which he had obtained after a long wait. Ying Chan would doubtless be there before he could smoke them all. No sooner had he seated himself in a chair than the windows darkened; his only concern was that the showers might come and they might be unable to have dinner in the roof garden.

Thus a rich fifty-seven-year-old man awaited a Thai girl. The realization ultimately saved him from his fear, and he felt that he had returned to a normal daily life. He was a kind of harbour and not by nature a ship. The only natural state of his existence, that of waiting for Ying Chan, was re-established. It was almost the form of his very soul.

An older man of means who did not seek the simpler male pleasures. He was a troublesome being, and he easily made the decision to exchange the earth for his boredom; but on the surface he was the embodiment of modesty, a spirit that preferred to lie low in a delimited, hollow area. He had the same attitude toward history and eras, miracles and revolutions. Sitting on a covered abyss as though on a toilet, he simply smoked his cigar and waited. He depended on his opponent's will for a decision and only under such conditions did his dream for the first time assume a distinct shape. Then, though only through a peep-hole, he saw the ambiguous form of ultimate happiness. Could death take him to extreme happiness in this condition? If so, Ying Chan must be death.

Honda was ready to play the cards of apprehension or despair he held in his hand. This time of expectant waiting was like black lacquer inlaid with countless mother-of-pearl pieces of uncertainty.

From the cellar-like Grill Rossini on the same floor, the tinkling sound of silverware could be heard as tables were set in preparation for the dinner hour. Like the knives and forks in the waiters' hands that had not yet been separated, emotion and reason commingled in Honda; and not a single plan (a malicious tendency of reason) had been made – his will was still uninvolved. The pleasure which he had discovered at the end of his life entailed such an indolent abandonment of human will. As he thus relinquished it, the determination to engage himself in history that had so obsessed him since youth was also suspended in space, and history hung detached somewhere in mid-air.

A circus girl soaring on her trapeze through the blinding height of timeless, dark hours, the skirt of her white skin-tight tunic fluttering ... Ying Chan.

Outside the window it had grown dark. Two transients and their respective families were exchanging interminable greetings beside Honda; they lasted so long that he felt almost faint. A young couple, apparently engaged, were stonily silent like two manic depressives. Through the window he could see the stir of tree branches along the street, but the rain seemed not to have come. The wooden binding of the newspaper felt in Honda's hands like an extremely long shinbone. He smoked the three cigars. Ying Chan did not appear.

At long last he ate a reluctant meal and made his way to the Foreign Student Centre. His behaviour was against all good sense.

He entered the simple, four-storeyed building in Azabu. In the entry hall two or three dark-skinned, sharp-eyed youths in short-sleeved shirts of a large plaid were reading poorly printed South-east Asian magazines. Honda went to the front desk and asked for Ying Chan.

'She's out,' the clerk answered automatically. The response seemed too quick to be genuine. As Honda asked two or three questions the sharp-eyed youths all stared at him. The stifling night air made him feel as though he were in the waiting room of some little tropical airport.

'Could you tell me her room number?'

'It's against the rules. You can see the students only in this lobby and only by their consent.'

When Honda gave up and left, the young men returned to their magazines. Brown ankles jutted out sharply like thorns from all the pairs of crossed legs.

He could walk freely through the front garden, but no one was there. The sound of a guitar came from a brightly lit room on the third floor, and the windows were open wide to the humid weather. A melody sung in a high but soft voice resembling a high-pitched Chinese viol twined around the sounds of the strings like a yellowed vine. Listening to the sad voice, Honda recalled the unforgettable nights in Bangkok just before the war.

If only he could slip in, he wanted to go through every room, for he did not believe that Ying Chan was out. She was everywhere in the humid evening darkness of the rainy season. In the faint fragrance of flowers that had probably been cultivated by foreign students, in the distinct yellow gladioli or the pale violet of the Roger's bronze leaf intermingling in the dark ... Minute elements of Ying Chan floating all about gradually coalesced into shape and solidified into her being. He could sense her even in the faint whir of mosquito wings.

Most of the windows were dark. Only one room at the corner of the third floor cast a bright radiance through moving lace curtains. Curious, Honda gazed at the window. Someone was standing just inside looking down at the garden. The wind caused the curtains to flutter and he caught a fleeting glimpse. It was Ying Chan wearing a slip. Involuntarily he ran toward the window and came directly under a street lamp. Ying Chan seemed shocked on recognizing him. Immediately the light was turned off and the window was closed.

Honda leaned against the corner of the building and waited a long time. The minutes dripped away and the blood throbbed in his temples. Time dripped like drops of blood. He pressed his cheek against the thin blue moss growing on the concrete, letting it cool his hot old cheeks.

After a while, a rustling like that of a snake's tongue sounded from the third-floor window. It was slowly opened, and something soft and white fell at Honda's feet. He picked it up and opened a piece of crumpled white paper. Inside was a wad of cotton large enough to fill his palm. It seemed to have been pressed into a compact mass, for as he released the outer wrapping it swelled like something alive. Honda fumbled with the layers of cotton. Inside lay the emerald ring protected by the golden *yakshas*.

He glanced up to the window again, but it was tightly closed and there was not the faintest ray of light.

When he left the Foreign Student Centre and came to his senses, Honda realized that he was only a couple of blocks from Keiko's. Customarily he did not use his car for his rendezvous. He could summon a taxi, but he decided to punish himself by walking in spite of the pain in his back and hips. Even if she were not in, he could not possibly go straight home without first knocking at her door.

Were he young, he would have cried aloud as he walked. If he were young! But he had never cried when he was young! He had been a promising youth who thought he should use reason to bring success to himself and others instead of wasting time in shedding tears. What sweet sorrow, what lyrical despair! He permitted himself to feel like this only in a hypothetical past tense. By so doing, he eradicated all authenticity from his present emotion. If only sweet romanticism were allowed to one of his years! But neither now nor when he had been young had his make-up permitted anything of sweetness to himself. His only recourse was to daydream about a different kind of self in the past. How different? It had been quite impossible to become a Kiyoaki or an Isao.

If Honda's imagination let him dream that he would have been of this or that personality were he only young and thus served to protect him through the years at every dangerous emotional point, then his reluctance to recognize his present emotional condition was probably the result of such self-denial in his youth. At any rate, it was impossible for him to cry aloud as he walked – not when he was young and not now. In anyone's eyes this old gentleman in his Burberry coat and Borsalino would appear to be just a nocturnal stroller, whimsical, solitary.

Thus, as a result of the unpleasant self-consciousness that made him refer to all emotions only indirectly, Honda had become so safe that he no longer had to worry about self-consciousness. It had become possible for him to act on any impulse or any desire, however shameless. If one studied his every action, one might conclude incorrectly that he was a man who acted on impulse. His hasty trip to Keiko's house along this nocturnal road, threatened at any moment by heavy showers, was one of his idiotic impulses. As he walked, he felt the urge to thrust his hand down his throat and, as though drawing a pocket watch from his vest, extract his heart.

It was improbable that Keiko would be home at this hour of the night, but she was.

Honda was at once shown into the resplendent drawing room. The Louis Quinze chairs with their straight backs would not let him relax, and he felt he was about to pass out from sheer exhaustion.

The cryptomeria doors were half open just as they had been the other day. The night solitude in the drawing room was enhanced by the overpowering brilliance of the chandelier. Through the window he saw the lights of the town twinkling through the far end of the grove in the garden, but he did not have the energy to walk over and out. It was better to endure the demoralizing heat and disintegrate in perspiration.

He heard Keiko's footsteps as she descended the spiral marble staircase to the entrance hall. She was wearing a colourful mumu with a long train. She entered the drawing room and closed the door with the cranes behind her. Her black hair was standing erect as if in a storm, flying about, shapelessly swollen, making her face with its light make-up appear unusually small and pale. She walked around among the chairs and sat down facing Honda in front of the niche with its mural of golden clouds. Cognac had been placed on the small table between them. Beneath the hem of her dress peeked her bare feet in bedroom slippers adorned with bouquets of dried tropical fruit. The red lacquer of her toenails was the same colour as the large hibiscus flowers on her black mumu. Nevertheless, the abundance of dark hair standing on her head in front of the golden clouds added immeasurably to the gloom.

'Please excuse me. My hair looks mad. Your sudden visit upset even that. Unfortunately I just washed it a little while ago. I was going to set it tomorrow. You men don't know about such ordeals. But is something wrong? You look pale.'

Briefly Honda told her what had happened, but he was disgusted to be speaking like a defence lawyer. He could not escape the habit of describing logically, inductively, even in this matter of such burning urgency. His words were useful only for arranging events into some sort of order. He had wanted to appeal to her by wordless, senseless screams for help. At least he had until he entered the house.

'The moral of the story is not to rush into things, it would seem,' said Keiko. 'I told you to leave everything to me. I don't know what to do either. Even so, Ying Chan was very, very rude. I wonder if that's the way in the South where she comes from. But I know that you're quite taken with her capricious manners.' She offered him cognac and said: 'And what are you suggesting I do?'

She did not sound at all annoyed, but displayed her characteristic melancholy enthusiasm.

Honda was slipping the ring on and off his little finger. 'I would like you to return this to Ying Chan and ask her to accept it. The separation of this ring from her body makes me feel as though the relationship between her and my past is permanently severed.'

Keiko was silent, and Honda feared that she was angry with him. She held the glass of cognac at eye level and watched how the once rippling liquid gradually slipped down the concave surface of the snifter, forming viscous transparent cloud patterns. Her large eyes under the black mountain of hair were almost frightening. Her serious expression was too natural for someone trying to suppress a sardonic smile. Honda thought that her eyes were like those of a child who has watched the crushing of an ant. 'I came to ask you merely to do that,' he said encouragingly. 'That's all.'

He was gambling on an extremely trivial exaggeration. Where could he find pleasure except in a kind of ethical principle not to neglect the ludicrous? He had picked Ying Chan out of this garbage pail of a world, and though he ached to possess her he had not so much as laid a finger on her. He was seeking to intensify this idiocy to the point where his lust would intersect the orbits of the stars.

'Why don't you forget about the girl?' said Keiko finally. 'Just the other day I heard she was dancing cheek to cheek with some vulgar student at a *thé dansant* at the Mimatsu.'

'Forget her? I can never do that. Leaving her alone is allowing her to mature.'

'And I suppose you have the right to stop her from maturing. How about your previous feeling that you didn't want her to be a virgin?'

'I thought it would change her overnight into a completely different woman. But that failed, thanks to your stupid nephew.'

'He's quite a fool, isn't he,' said Keiko, breaking into laughter. She examined her long nails through her glass in the light of the chandelier. They were painted with red lacquer and shone through it, glowing within the convexity like a small, mysterious sunrise.

'The sun's coming up, see!' said Keiko, indicating her glass. She was drunk.

'A cruel sunrise,' Honda murmured, ardently wishing that the fog of shabbiness and irrationality would completely envelop this overly bright room so that he would be unable to see a thing before him.

'What would you do if I turned you down?'

'My future would be completely black.'

'What an exaggeration!' Keiko put the glass on the table and thought a while longer. She murmured something about always being in the position of helping others. After a while she said:

'The real problem deep down is always childish. When a man makes up his mind, he'll set off on an African expedition to look for a single misprinted stamp.'

'I think I'm in love with Ying Chan.'

'Oh dear!' Keiko laughed loudly, quite unconvinced.

There was a decisive note in her voice when she spoke again. 'I understand now. You need to do something absolutely simple and silly right now. For instance,' she lifted the hem of her mumu a little. 'For instance, how about kissing the arch of my foot? It'll cheer you up . . . studying the foot of a woman you don't love at all. Don't worry, I've just taken a bath and I'm quite scrubbed. It won't hurt you.'

'If this is in exchange for my request, I'll be glad to oblige right now.'

'All right, go ahead. It'll do you good to try something like that just once . . . in view of your well-known pride. The credit side of your reputation will be even further enhanced.'

Keiko was obviously carried away by her passion as a preceptor. She stood directly under the splendid chandelier and with both hands brushed back her abundant hair, causing the sides to wave like elephant's ears.

Honda tried in vain to smile. He looked around and slowly bent down. The pain in his hip increased sharply, so that he crouched and prostrated himself on the carpet with grim determination. From this viewpoint, Keiko's sandals resembled religious paraphernalia guarding the firmly planted, slightly sinewy arches of her feet. Clusters of brown, tan, purple, and white dried fruit hung over the vermilion toenails. As Honda put his lips close to the sandalled feet, they artfully drew away. Ultimately, unless he lifted the hem of the hibiscus skirt and thrust his head underneath, his lips could not reach the arches of her feet. Putting his head inside, he found that the mumu was filled with the faint warm fragrance of perfume. Suddenly he was in unknown country. When he raised his eyes after having kissed Keiko's feet, the light was all dark vermilion through the flower print, and two beautiful white columns with pale patterns of veins stood before him. In the distant sky hung a small black sun sending out dishevelled black rays.

Honda twisted clear and stood up with difficulty.

'There. I've done my part.'

'And I'll do mine,' said Keiko, accepting the ring with a serene smile becoming to her age.

42

'What are you doing?' Rié called from the house to her husband, who had still not come in for his breakfast.

'I'm looking at Fuji,' he answered from the terrace. The voice remained directed not toward the room but rather toward the mountain beyond the arbour at the western edge of the garden.

It was six o'clock of a summer morning, and Fuji was flushed the colour of wine. Her contours were hazy. Like powder painted on the nose of a child in preparation for a summer festival, a brush mark of snow was visible around the eighth station.

After breakfast, Honda went out again, wearing only a pair of shorts and polo shirt, and lay down beside the swimming pool under the brilliant morning sky. He playfully scooped up some water.

'What are you doing?' Rié called again as she cleaned away the breakfast things. This time he made no answer.

From the window Rié glared at this evidence of madness in her fifty-seven-year-old husband. In the first place, she did not like the way he was dressed. A man in the legal profession should never wear shorts. His stiff, emaciated white legs stood out below them. She did not fancy his shirt either. As if in punishment for wearing a polo shirt without possessing the virile fullness of youth, the sleeves and back drooped limply. She had come to the point where she took interest in seeing just how far her husband would go in his follies. It was a sort of perverse pleasure as in bearing down on an aching tooth.

Sensing through his back that his wife had given up and retreated to her room, Honda gazed to his heart's content at the beauty of the morning scene reflected in the pool.

Cicadas had begun to sing in the cypress grove. Honda raised his eyes. Mount

Fuji which had had an alcoholic flush had now turned a rich purple. It was eight o'clock, and in the graduated greens of the foothills floated the faint contours of woods and villages. As he looked at the deep blue of Fuji in summer, Honda invented a little game he could enjoy alone. It consisted in visualizing a midwinter mountain in midsummer. After staring at the dark blue Fuji for a while, he would then suddenly shift his gaze to the blue sky on one side; the after-image on his retina would turn completely white and momentarily he could see a pure milky mountain in the blue sky.

After discovering the way to create this illusion, Honda came to believe that there were two mountains. Beside the summer Fuji there always existed a winter one; in addition to the real image, an essence of the mountain, pure white, also existed. As he shifted his gaze to the swimming pool, he saw that the reflection of Hakoné occupied a much greater area than that of Fuji. The mass of mountain covered with green was hot and stifling. Birds flying through the sky reflected in the water and a familiar nightingale visited the feeding box.

Yes, yesterday he had killed a snake near the arbour. It was a striped one some two feet long, and he had killed it by crushing its head with a rock so that it should not frighten the guests expected today. The little massacre had occupied his entire day. Blue-black steel springs, the image of the smooth, writhing body of the snake struggling against death lingered in his mind. Knowing that he too could kill something gave him a gloomy sense of power.

And the swimming pool. Again Honda stretched his hand and troubled the surface of the water. The reflection of summer clouds shattered into fragments of frosted glass. The pool had been completed six days before, but no one had yet used it. Honda had been here with Rié for three days, but under the pretext that the water was cold he had not once been in.

His sole reason for constructing the pool had been to see Ying Chan naked; nothing else mattered.

The sound of hammering could be heard in the distance. Keiko's house was being remodelled. Since her place in Tokyo had been released by the Occupation Forces, Keiko came less and less to Gotemba, and somehow her relationship with Jack had cooled. Honda's new house had stimulated her sense of competition, and she had started to remodel her own on a grand scale, almost to the extent of building a new one. She maintained that she would not be able to live in it during the summer and would probably spend the season in Karuizawa.

Honda, leaving the swimming pool to avoid the sun that was growing gradually stronger, with difficulty opened the beach umbrella planted in the middle of a table. He seated himself on a chair in the shade and again directed his gaze to the surface of the water.

The morning coffee still provided a numbing sensation at the back of his head. In the bottom of the twenty-seven by sixty foot pool, white lines showed through the ripples of blue paint, reminding him of the lime markings and mint-scented saromethyl ointment inextricably associated with the athletic competitions of his distant youth. A clean white line was drawn geometrically on everything, and from it something started and something ended. But the memory was faulty. Honda had had nothing to do with athletic competition in his youth.

Rather the white line reminded him of the centre marking running down a highway at night. He suddenly remembered the little old man who had always carried a cane on his night excursions into the park. The first time he had met him on a sidewalk swept by the dazzling headlights of automobiles, the old man was walking with his chest thrust out and an ivory-handled cane on his arm. If he had walked normally the cane would have dragged on the ground, and he had raised his bent arm unnaturally high so that his posture was even stiffer. The fragrant May woods lay to one side of the walk. The little man looked like some retired Army officer carefully concealing his now valueless decorations in the inner pocket of his jacket.

The second time he had happened on him in the darkness of the woods, Honda had observed in detail the cane's function.

When lovers met in the woods the man would usually press the woman back against a tree and begin to caress her. Seldom was the reverse true. And so when a young couple was thus involved the little man would take up his position on the opposite side of the trunk.

In the darkness not far from where Honda happened to be, he could see the cane's U-shaped ivory handle gradually edging around the tree trunk. He peered into the darkness, watching the floating white shape. When he discovered that the handle was ivory, he knew at once to whom it belonged. The woman's arms encircled the man's neck, while his arms met behind her back. The oily hair on the back of the man's head glistened in the beams of the passing headlights. The white handle roamed for a while in the darkness, and then as though having determined its course, it brushed the hem of the woman's skirt. Once the garment was hooked, the cane lifted it skilfully and quickly with one sweep up to her waist. The woman's white thighs were exposed, but he did not make the mistake of being found out by touching them with the cold ivory.

Then the woman whispered: 'No, no.' And finally: 'It's cold.' But the man, in seventh heaven, made no answer, and the woman seemed not to notice that his arms were completely occupied in embracing her.

This cynical and debasing mischief, this dedicated selfless cooperation always brought a smile to Honda's lips whenever he recalled it. But when he remembered the man who had spoken to him some time ago in broad daylight at the entrance to the Matsuya PX the slight edge of humour was replaced by a chilling sensation of fear. It was outrageous that his pleasure might disgust others and thereby subject him to their everlasting repugnance and further that such disgust might one day grow to be an indispensable element of pleasure.

Chilling self-disgust fused with the sweetest allurement ... the very denial of existence joining with the concept of immortality that can never be healed. This unhealable existence was the unique essence of immortality.

Returning to the edge of the swimming pool, he bent down and took the flickering water in his hands. This was the feel of the wealth he had acquired at the end of his life. As he felt the darting arrows of the aestival sun striking his bended neck, it was as though he were the target of the enormous malice and derision of the fifty-seven summers of his life. It had not been such an unfortunate existence. All had been guided by the oar of reason, and the reefs of destruction had been skilfully avoided. To claim that he had not had a happy moment would be pure hyperbole. Nevertheless, how boring the voyage had been! It would be closer to his true feelings if he dared exaggerate and say that his life had been spent in complete darkness.

To declare his life unrelieved black seemed to express a certain acute empathy toward it. (There was no compensation, no joy in my association with you. Though I not once asked for you, you imposed your tenacious friendship and coerced me into this outlandish tightrope-walking called living. You made me frugal with my infatuations, gave me ridiculously excessive possessions, transformed justice into wastepaper, converted reason into mere furniture, and confined beauty to its shabbiest form.) Life strove mightily to exile orthodoxy, hospitalize heresy and trap humanity into stupidity. It was an accumulation of used bandages soiled with layers of blood and pus. Life was the daily changing of the bandages of the heart that made the incurably sick, young and old alike, cry out in pain.

He felt that somewhere in the brilliant blue of the sky over this mountainous region were concealed the gigantic, supple white hands of a sublime nurse engaged in futile daily treatments and demanding chores. The hands touched him gently and again encouraged him to live. The white clouds floating in the sky over Otomé Pass were dazzlingly new, almost hypocritically hygienic white bandages that had been strewn about.

Honda knew that he was sufficiently objective about himself. To other people, he was among the most wealthy lawyers and in a position to enjoy a leisurely old age. This was a reward for having dispensed impartial justice, and there was no record of graft to mar his long life as judge and attorney. Thus he was regarded, if with some envy, at least with no reproach. It was one of those belated remunerations that society sometimes bestows on a persevering citizen. At this point in life, if his little vice were to come out in the open, people would dismiss it with a smile, regarding it as one of those harmless human foibles in everyone. In short, he had everything that was desirable in the eyes of the world, except perhaps children.

The couple had talked about adopting a child, and they had been urged to do so by others, but Rié had grown reluctant to discuss the matter and Honda too had lost interest after he had come into his property. He suspected that people were just after his money.

Voices came from the house.

He listened, wondering whether a guest might have arrived so early in the morning. But it was only Rié talking with Matsudo. Soon the two came to the terrace and looked out over the undulations of the lawn.

'Look,' said Rié. 'The lawn over there is so uneven. When you look at Fuji that slope by the arbour is the most conspicuous area of all. The uneven grass will be an embarrassment. A prince is coming, you know.'

'Yes, madame. Shall I mow it again?'

'Would you please.'

The chauffeur, a year older than Honda, walked to the end of the terrace to get the mower from the little storage room where the garden tools were kept. Honda had hired Matsudo not so much because he liked him, but because he appreciated the experience the chauffeur had driving government cars throughout the war and even after it.

His extremely sluggish manner, his faintly arrogant way of speaking, and the absolutely calm attitude of a man whose daily life was based entirely on the principle of safe driving – everything irritated Honda. (You think you can succeed in life simply by being as discreet about things as you are in driving, don't you? Well, you're wrong.) As he watched the old chauffeur he realized that Matsudo probably believed his employer to be the same kind of discreet person that he was. And Honda felt offended as though the chauffeur were drawing a rude caricature.

'Sit down here. You have plenty of time,' Honda called to Rié.

'Yes, but the chef and waiters will be here soon.'

'They'll be late as usual.'

After hesitating slightly, like a thread loosening in water, Rié re-entered the house to fetch a cushion. She feared that her kidneys might take cold from the iron chair.

'Chefs and waiters and ... I can't stand those people ruining the house,' she said, seating herself in the chair next to Honda.

'If I were like Mrs Kinkin and loved flamboyance, how I should have enjoyed this style of living!'

'You bring up such ancient subjects!'

Mrs Kinkin had been the wife of the most celebrated lawyer in Japan not long after the turn of the century. A former geisha, she was famous for her beauty and extravagance. Frequently she could be seen riding a white horse. And she raised eyebrows by wearing long geisha kimonos to funerals. When her husband died, she committed suicide, desperate that she could no longer live in the luxury to which she was accustomed.

'I hear Mrs Kinkin kept pet snakes and she always carried a little one about in her purse. Oh, I forgot. You said you killed one yesterday. It would be terrible if a snake appeared while the Prince is here.' She called to Matsudo who was walking away with the lawn mower: 'Matsudo! If you find a snake, get rid of it, but please don't let me see it.'

Watching the movement of her throat as she shouted, there where age was so ruthlessly illuminated by the reflection of the pool, Honda suddenly remembered Tadeshina, whom he had met in the ruins of Shibuya during the war. He recalled the *Sutra of the Peacock Wisdom King* that she had given him.

'If you are bitten by a snake, all you have to do is to chant this spell: *ma yu kitsu ra tei sha ka*.'

'Really?' Without a trace of interest, Rié sat back in the chair again. The sound of the mower engine which began immediately permitted them the choice of silence.

Honda took for granted the pleasure his old-fashioned wife showed about the forthcoming princely visit, but he was surprised at her calmness when she learned about the expected arrival of Ying Chan. For her part, Rié was hoping that her long suffering would come to an end if she were to see Ying Chan at her husband's side.

'Tomorrow Keiko will be bringing Ying Chan along to the opening of the swimming pool, and they'll stay with us overnight,' Honda had said casually, and she had experienced a kind of tingling pleasure. Her jealousy had been so deeply fraught with uncertainty that her distress, dissipating with every second, was like waiting for thunder after seeing a flash of lightning. What she had feared had fused with what she so anxiously awaited, and the realization that she need wait no longer cheered her.

Rié's heart resembled a river sluggishly flowing through a vast and desolate plain, eroding its banks. And now, about to enter the unknown sea, it contentedly deposited its muddy sediment at the river mouth. It was here that it would cease being fresh water and would be transformed into the bitter saline sea. If one increases the volume of an emotion to its limits, its nature changes of its own accord; the accumulation of suffering which had seemed to destroy her was suddenly transformed into a strength for living – an exceedingly bitter, exceedingly stern, but suddenly expansive blue strength – the ocean.

Honda had not noticed that his wife had been changing into an unrecognizably bitter and hard woman. The Rié who had tortured him by her ill-humoured, silent quest was in fact no more than a chrysalis.

On this bright morning she felt that even her chronic kidney ailment was considerably better.

The distant, lazy sound of the mower made the eardrums of the silent couple vibrate. It was a silence totally alien to that of the picturesque old couple who no longer needed to converse. With some exaggeration Honda interpreted the situation in this way: they were two bundles of nerves leaning against each other and in so doing just managed to avoid collapsing to the ground with a metallic crash. It was as though they were both, with difficulty and in silence, acquiescing to their condition. If he had committed some brilliant crime, he would at least have been able to feel that he was soaring a little higher than his wife. But his pride was deeply hurt when he realized that both his wife's suffering and his own joy were of the same stature.

The second-floor guest-room windows reflecting on the surface of the water had been opened to let in the air, and the white lace curtains were fluttering. Tonight Ying Chan was expected behind that window, the one from which she had once climbed to the roof in the middle of the night and nimbly jumped down to the ground. The act made him think that she could only have sprouted wings. Had she not really flown away when he had not been watching? How could one be sure that Ying Chan astride a peacock, unobserved by him, had not freed herself from the bondage of this existence and been transformed into a being beyond time and space? He was clearly enchanted by the lack of any proof that she had not and the impossibility of ascertaining that indeed she could not. When he reached this conclusion he realized the mystical nature of his love.

The surface of the swimming pool seemed as though some fisherman had cast a net of light over it. His wife was silent, her little swollen hands so like those of a Japanese doll lay on the edge of the table half covered by the shadow of the beach umbrella.

Honda could immerse himself in his thoughts.

The reality of Ying Chan was limited by the Ying Chan he could observe. She was a girl with beautiful black hair and a constant smile and a penchant for not keeping promises, yet a very determined young woman of impenetrable emotions. It was certain that the Ying Chan one saw was not all there was. For Honda, longing for the Ying Chan he could not see, love depended on the unknown; and naturally perception was related to the known. If he drove his perceptions on and with them plundered the unknown, thereby increasing the area of the known, could his love be achieved? No, it would not work that way, because his love strove to keep Ying Chan as far away as possible from the talons of his perception.

Since youth Honda's hunting dog of perception had always been extremely astute. Thus the Ying Chan he knew by seeing corresponded to his powers of perception. Nothing but his ability to perceive made her existence possible.

Therefore his desire to see Ying Chan in the nude, a Ying Chan unknown to anyone, became an unattainable desire divided contradictorily into perception and love. Seeing already lay within the sphere of perception, and even if Ying Chan was not aware of it, from the moment he had peeped through the luminous hole in the back of the bookcase, she had become an inhabitant of a world created by her perception. In her world, contaminated by his the moment he laid eyes on it, what he really wanted to see would never appear. His love could not be fulfilled. And yet, if he did not see, love would forever be precluded.

He wanted to see a soaring Ying Chan, but bound by his perceptions, she did not soar. As long as she remained a creature of his perceptions she could not violate the physical laws governing them. Perhaps, except in dreams, the world where Ying Chan soared naked astride a peacock lay a step beyond and did not materialize because Honda's perception itself became a screen and was defective, an infinitesimal obstruction. Then how would it be if he got rid of the obstruction and changed the situation? That would mean the removal of Honda from the world which he shared with Ying Chan, in other words, his own death.

It now became clear that Honda's ultimate desire, what he really, really wanted to see, could exist only in a world where he did not. In order to see what he truly wished to, he must die. When a voyeur recognizes that he can realize his ends only by eliminating the basic act of watching, this means his death as such.

For the first time in his life the significance of suicide for a cognizant man carried weight in Honda's mind.

If he denied perception as his love directed and tried to escape from perception infinitely, attempting to take Ying Chan to a territory beyond its reach, resistance by perception meant sure suicide. It would mean Honda's exit from a world contaminated by perception, with Ying Chan left behind. But at the very moment of his departure she would stand radiantly before him; nothing was so predictable as this.

The present world was one Honda's perceptions had created and thus Ying Chan inhabited it too. According to the precepts of the Yuishiki School, it was a world created by Honda's *alaya* consciousness. But the reason he still could not give himself completely to this doctrine was because he was too attached to his perceptions and was unable to agree to consider their root as the eternal *alaya* consciousness that discards the world one instant without regret and renews it the next.

Rather Honda thought of death as a game and was intoxicated by its sweetness. Incited by his perceptions, he dreamed about the supreme bliss of the moment of suicide, when the Ying Chan who had been seen by no other person would appear in all her brilliant, pure amber nudity like a resplendent moon rising.

Didn't 'fulfilment of the Peacock' mean precisely this? According to the *Rules for Depicting the Peacock Wisdom King*, the *sammaya-gyo*, or the distinguishing symbol that represents the divinity's main vow, is described as a half-moon above the Peacock's tail; and above that a full moon is depicted. Just as the half-moon waxes into the full moon, so the learning of the Law is fully achieved.

What Honda wished might indeed be this Peacock fulfilment. If all love in the world were as incomplete as the half-moon, who would not dream of the full moon rising above the Peacock tail?

The sound of the mower stopped and a voice was heard from the distance: 'Is this enough?'

Like a couple of bored parrots on their perch, the Hondas turned awkwardly to look toward the voice. Matsudo stood there in his khaki overall, and Fuji was already half hidden in the clouds behind him.

'Well, don't you think that's sufficient?' Rié said to her husband in a low voice.

'I suppose. We can't ask too much of the old man,' responded Honda.

With both hands he formed a big circle of approval, and Matsudo, understanding, slowly rolled the mower back to the house. The sound of a motor came from the gate on the Hakoné side and a station wagon entered the grounds. It was the car from Tokyo bearing the chef, three waiters, and an abundant supply of food.

43

Honda had not yet invited the older inhabitants in the neighbouring houses despite the fact that he was the newest comer to the View-on-Fuji Villas at Ninooka. The older inhabitants had kept away from their villas, frightened by rumours that public morals had been corrupted by the bars that had opened for the American soldiers near Gotemba. These establishments had brought in their wake call girls and pimps and low-class prostitutes who wandered about the training grounds armed with Army blankets. This summer the owners had begun to trickle back, and Honda had invited some on the occasion of the opening of the pool.

The oldest villa owners were Prince and Princess Kaori and the aged widow of Kanzaemon Mashiba, founder of the Mashiba Bank. Mrs Mashiba had announced that she would bring along her three grandchildren. There were several other guests from the area. In addition to Keiko and Ying Chan, Imanishi and

Mrs Tsubakihara were expected from Tokyo. Makiko had replied quite early that she would be travelling abroad. Under ordinary circumstances Makiko would have been accompanied by Mrs Tsubakihara on her trip, but this time she had chosen another disciple as her companion.

Once a servant became a permanent employee, Honda was amused to note, Rié could drive her rather mercilessly, though she never gave up her sweet smile for outside help such as the chef and the waiters. She spoke politely and showed consideration in everything, anxious to prove to herself and others that she was beloved by one and all.

'Madame. What are we to do about the arbour? Shall I prepare drinks there too?' asked one of the waiters, already dressed in his white uniform.

'Please do.'

'But it will be difficult for just the three of us to cover so much ground. Would it be satisfactory if we just left ice in the thermos bucket and requested the guests to help themselves?'

'Surely. The ones who stray as far as the arbour will probably be young couples anyway, and it might be just as well not to disturb them. Be doubly sure not to forget the mosquito repellent when it starts to get dark.'

Honda was truly shocked to hear his wife speaking in such a manner. Her voice was pitched unnaturally high and her words floated on the air. The frivolity she had presumably despised more than anything in the world over the years now so infused her voice and words that he suspected her of sarcasm.

The alert movements of the waiters in their white uniforms seemed to have charged the household with straight lines. Their well-starched jackets, their youthful efficiency of movement, their apparent respectfulness, and their professional polish turned the household into a strange and refreshing world. All private matters were swept aside, and arrangements, consultation, commands, and orders flew about as if they were indeed the butterflies in whose shape the white napkins had been folded.

A buffet had been set up beside the pool to permit the guests to eat in their swimming suits. The familiar appearance of the house had instantly changed. Honda's treasured desk, covered with a white tablecloth, now served as an outdoor bar. Although he himself had directed the alterations, once underway they turned into a kind of violent transformation.

Driven back by the gradually intensifying sunlight, he watched everything in amazement. Who had planned all this? And to what end? To spend money? to invite impressive guests? to play the role of the complacent bourgeois? to boast of the completed swimming pool? As a matter of fact, this was the first private pool in Ninooka either before or since the war. There are many generous people in this world who will forgive another's wealth if only they are invited to his house.

'Dear, please put these on,' said Rié, bringing him a pair of dark-brown summer worsted trousers, a white shirt, and a bow tie with tiny brown polka dots. She placed them on the table under the beach umbrella.

'You want me to change here?'

'Why not? There are only the waiters. Besides I'm going to ask them to take an early lunch break now.'

He took up the bow tie, the extremities of which were shaped like gourds. Holding one end between two fingers, he playfully held it up to the light of the swimming pool. It was an informal, miserable, limp strip of fabric. It reminded him of the procedure of the 'summary order' of a police court. 'Notification of summary procedure and demur of the accused.' It was Honda himself who most detested the approaching party ... except for one ultimate kernel, one scintillating point of hopelessness.

Old Mrs Mashiba was the first to arrive with her three grandchildren. These consisted of an unmarried girl and her two extremely ordinary, bespectacled, and studious-looking younger brothers, one a senior and the other a sophomore in college. The three immediately retired to the dressing rooms where they changed into swimming suits. The grandmother, wearing a kimono, remained under the umbrella.

'While my husband was alive, especially after the war, we fought at every election. I always voted Communist just to spite him. And then I was a great admirer of Kyuichi Tokuda.'

The old widow adjusted her kimono collars incessantly or nervously tugged at her sleeves like a grasshopper ducking its head and rubbing its wings. She was reputed to be a completely unconventional and entertaining person; hidden behind mauve glasses, sparkled prying eyes, relentlessly speculating on the finances of one and all. Exposed to her cold gaze, everyone felt as if he were her dependent.

The three young people who returned dressed for swimming possessed bodies typical of good families, modest and sleek-limbed. One after the other they jumped into the water and in a relaxed way began swimming. Honda regretted above all that Ying Chan was not to be the first to enter the water in his pool.

Soon Rié came from the house escorting Prince and Princess Kaori, who were already in their bathing suits. Honda apologized for having been unaware of their arrival and for not having come up to greet them. He scolded Rié for not warning him; but the Prince merely shook hands, dismissing the whole matter, and went into the water. Mrs Mashiba watched this exchange with a bemused look as though she were observing boorish people. After the Prince had circled the pool once and climbed up on the edge, she spoke to him from where she was in her shrill voice: 'How young and manly you are, Prince! Ten years ago I should have challenged you to a race.'

'I may not be up to you even now, Madame. Just swimming fifty yards and I'm already out of breath, as you see. Anyway, how wonderful that we can swim in Gotemba, though the water's a trifle chilly.'

He shook the drops from his body as though sloughing off ostentation. Black dots spattered on the concrete.

The Prince himself had not noticed that people sometimes regarded him as cold because of his great efforts to behave on all occasions with the nonchalance and informality that had come after the war. When it was no longer necessary to maintain dignity, he became confused about human relationships. Confident because of his elite position that he had the right to dislike tradition more than anyone else, he slighted those who held it in esteem in this day and age. That might have been all right if when he remarked that someone showed no progressiveness it had not come to mean the same thing as when he had commented in former days that someone was too low-born. The Prince rated all progressives, as he did himself, as 'sufferers in the fetters of tradition'. Thus, paradoxically, the next step would have him thinking of himself as a commoner.

When the Prince removed his glasses before swimming, Honda saw his face for the first time without them. They were for him a rather important bridge to the world. When his bridge was removed, his plain face held a certain vague melancholy, partly because of the glare. It was a melancholy where the gap between long-gone nobility and the present was somehow confused, out of focus.

In contrast, the Princess, slightly plump in her bathing suit, was imbued with natural grace. When she floated on her back and raised one arm and smiled, she looked like some innocent, lovely waterfowl happily swimming against the background of Hakoné. One could but assume that she was one of those rare people who knew what happiness was.

Honda was mildly irritated by the Mashiba grandchildren who, having emerged from the water, now surrounded their grandmother and were conversing politely with the Prince and Princess. The subject of the young people's conversation was exclusively America. The oldest girl talked about the fashionable private school where she had studied, and her younger brothers only about the universities where they were going once they had graduated from their respective Japanese colleges. Everything was America. Television was already widespread there ... how nice if that were true of Japan ... but at the present rate it would probably be over ten years before they enjoyed television here ... and on and on ...

Mrs Mashiba did not like conversations about the future. She interrupted immediately.

'You're all laughing at me, thinking I'll not be here to see it anyway. Very well, then. I'll appear as a ghost on your screens when you're watching every night.'

The manner in which the grandmother ruthlessly controlled the young people's conversation was extraordinary, as was the way the youngsters immediately fell silent and listened the moment she spoke. Honda thought they were like three intelligent rabbits.

The host was becoming skilled in greeting his guests as they appeared one after another in their bathing suits at the entrance to the terrace. On the other side of the pool, flanked by two couples from neighbouring villas, Imanishi and Mrs Tsubakihara clad in street clothes raised their hands in greeting. Imanishi was wearing an aloha shirt with a large print design in which he was completely out of character, while Mrs Tsubakihara wore her usual black kimono of silk gauze that resembled a mourning outfit. She was striving for effect: a single ominous black crystal set in the brilliance of the swimming pool. Honda saw through her right away and concluded that Imanishi had put on his ludicrous shirt to flout his simple mistress who was always trying to play roles quite unsuited to her.

Lagging behind the animated guests in their bathing suits, the couple slowly walked along the edge of the water that made their black and yellow reflections rock.

The Prince and Princess knew Imanishi and Mrs Tsubakihara well. The Prince frequently attended post-war meetings of the so-called cultural elite and was on sufficiently friendly terms with Imanishi to talk quite informally with him.

'That amusing man has just arrived,' he remarked to Honda.

As soon as Imanishi was seated, he took out the crumpled wrapper from a pack of imported cigarettes, threw it away, and drew out a new package. When he had stripped off the wrapping, he tapped the bottom and skilfully extracted a cigarette. 'I can't sleep at all these nights,' he said perfunctorily as he put it to his lips.

'Are you worried about something?' the Prince asked, placing the plate from which he had just been eating on the table.

'Not especially. But I've got to have someone to talk to in the middle of the night. We talk and talk until morning, and when the sun comes up we feel like committing suicide. Then we solemnly take sleeping pills. But we wake up and nothing has happened. The morning's the same as ever.'

'What sort of conversations do you have night after night?'

'There's ever so much to talk about if you know that this is going to be your last. We cover every possible subject in the world. What we've done, what others have done, what the world has experienced, what mankind has gone through, or things a forgotten continent has dreamt of for several thousands of years. Anything will do. There are all kinds of subjects. The world is going to end tonight.'

The Prince looked most interested and questioned further.

'But if you're alive the next day, what do you talk about then? You've covered everything.'

'That's no problem. You just talk it all over again.'

Amazed by this answer that sounded as though Imanishi were putting him on, the Prince fell silent.

Honda stood to the side listening. He did not know how serious Imanishi was. 'By the way, whatever happened to the Land of the Pomegranate?' he asked, recalling the weird tale he had once heard.

'Ah...' said Imanishi, turning his cold eyes on him. His face looked more dissipated than ever these days, and it contrasted strangely with the colourful Hawaiian shirt and the American cigarettes, creating, Honda felt, the impression of a certain type of interpreter who worked for the Occupation Forces. 'It's been destroyed! It exists no more.'

This was his usual manner of speaking and the statement in itself did not surprise Honda. But if the millennium of sex, once called the Land of the Pomegranate, had perished in Imanishi's illusions, it also had to disappear in the mind of Honda, who hated these fantasies. It existed no more. Imanishi was guilty of slaughtering the fantasy, and Honda could imagine how he must have been intoxicated by the fanciful bloodletting in destroying the kingdom he had created. He could picture the harrowing scene that night. He had created by words and destroyed by words. Although the kingdom had never possessed reality, still it had once manifested itself somewhere, and now it was destroyed by cruel whim. Seeing Imanishi's drug-roughened yellowish brown tongue lick his lips, Honda vividly pictured imaginary mountains of corpses and rivers of blood.

Compared to the desires of this sallow weakling, his own wants were far more quiet and modest. Yet they were equally impossible of fulfilment. Seeing Imanishi who showed not a trace of sentimentality and hearing him announce with his typically affected nonchalance the destruction of the Land of the Pomegranate, Honda was pierced to the core by the frivolousness of it all.

But his thoughts were immediately interrupted by Mrs Tsubakihara speaking in his ear. The fact that she whispered in a particularly low voice bespoke the fact that she had nothing of importance to relate.

'This is just between you and me. You know that Makiko's in Europe, don't you?'

'So I hear.'

'I'm not talking about the trip itself. I just wanted to tell you that she didn't invite me to go with her this time. She took some vulgar and untalented pupil along. But of course I'm not criticizing that. Only she didn't tell me anything about her going. Can you believe it? I went to see her off at the airport, but I was so overcome I couldn't say a word.'

'I wonder why she didn't mention it. The two of you were practically inseparable.'

'We were not only inseparable, she was my goddess. And my goddess deserted me.

'It's a long story, but when her family was in great difficulty after the war – her father, a poet too, was an officer – I came to her assistance before anyone else. I asked her advice in everything. I concealed nothing from her. And I think I lived and wrote poetry just as she wished me to. The feeling of body and soul joined to a goddess kept me alive, though I was a mere shell after I lost my son in the war. My feelings didn't change at all even after she became so famous, but the only bad thing was that there was too much of a gap between her talent and mine. Or rather it became even clearer than ever to me after I was deserted that I had not had a shred of talent to start with.'

'That's not true, I'm sure,' said Honda, to be polite, squinting in the light from the swimming pool.

'No, I know it now perfectly well. There's no harm in facing it, but it's clear to me that she must have known from the very beginning. Can you think of anything more cruel? Knowing that I was completely without talent, she led me around by the nose, made me obey all her commands, and sometimes patted my back and used me as much as she wished. Then she discards me like an old shoe and goes off to Europe with some other wealthy, fawning disciple.'

'Let's put aside the question of your talent. Makiko possesses outstanding ability and you know that's always accompanied by ruthless cruelty.'

'Just as a goddess is cruel ... But, Mr Honda, how can I go on living after being deserted by a goddess? Without the one who knew my every thought and deed, what can I do?'

'How about religion?'

'Religion! It's no use believing in some invisible god who possesses no risk of treachery. It won't work if I can't have one who watches over me and tells me to do this and not that, who leads me by the hand in every action, and from whom I can conceal nothing, before whom I am purified and feel no shame.'

'You'll always be a child … and a mother.'

'Yes, Mr Honda, I shall indeed.'

Already tears were brimming in Mrs Tsubakihara's eyes.

The Mashiba children and two new couples were in the swimming pool at the moment. Prince Kaori joined them, and they tossed about a large rubber ball with green and white stripes. The sound of splashing water, the shouting, and the merry laughter added brightnesss to the diffused light in the pool. The swaying blue surface was whipped up, breaking into a flurry of whitecaps. The water that had been licking quietly at the corners of the pool was now rent by the muscular shining backs of the swimmers, who made deep gashes in its sparkling surface. These instantly closed again and were transformed into quivering swells that engulfed those in the pool. The spray that rose among the shouting on one side produced countless oily rings of light on the other, all elaborately contracting and expanding.

The green and white striped ball, the instant it flew among the swimmers, appeared in chiaroscuro. The colour of the water, the tones of the bathing suits, even the people playing there were unrelated to human feelings of any depth. Yet this amount of water and its movement, the laughter and the shouts of the people, somehow all evoked a feeling of tragedy in Honda's mind. He wondered why.

Could it be because of the sun? He looked up to the sky where the light appeared distorted by the deepness of the blue, and began to sneeze. Just then Mrs Tsubakihara addressed him in her familiar tearful voice, muffled by the inevitable handkerchief that covered her face:

'What a good time they're having! Who would have imagined during the war that this would ever be possible. I wanted so much to have Akio experience this … at least once.'

It was after two when Rié escorted Keiko and Ying Chan onto the terrace in their swimming suits. After having waited so impatiently and for so long, Ying Chan's appearance seemed to Honda much too routine.

Keiko, in a bathing suit with black and white vertical stripes, seemed voluptuous from across the pool. It was difficult to believe that she was nearly fifty years old. The Westernized life she had led from her childhood had helped to produce long and shapely legs totally unlike those of other Japanese women. Her carriage was excellent, and when seen in profile talking with Rié her curves flowed with statuesque majesty, and the sovereignty of buxom flesh was apparent in the symmetry of the swelling breasts and buttocks.

Ying Chan provided an ideal contrast beside her. Clad in a white suit, she was holding a white rubber bathing cap in one hand and pushing back her hair with the other in a relaxed pose, one leg extended beyond the other. In her manner of placing her leg slightly forward, visible from a distance, was a kind of tropical asymmetry that excited people. Strong and yet slim, the long thighs supporting a well-developed torso somehow imparted a feeling of precariousness. In this she was most different from Keiko. In addition, the white suit brought out the brownness of her skin. The encased breasts and their dusky ripeness reminded Honda of the fresco at the Ajanta cave temple depicting the dying dancer. From this side of the pool he could clearly see her teeth gleaming whiter than her bathing suit when she smiled.

As she drew nearer, Honda stood up to greet this girl he had so eagerly awaited.

'Now everyone's here,' said Rié, hastening over, but he made no reply.

Keiko greeted the Princess and waved to the Prince in the pool.

'I'm exhausted after the experience,' she said in her rich, smooth voice, showing no sign of fatigue. 'I'm too bad a driver to take the car from Karuizawa to Tokyo, pick up Ying Chan and come all the way over to Gotemba. We're lucky to be here at all. I wonder why all the cars steer clear when I drive. It's like driving in no man's land.'

'They're obviously impressed by your dignity,' said Honda. For some reason, Rié laughed nervously.

In the meantime Ying Chan, oblivious to everyone, stood with her back to the table, her hands playing with her white cap, enchanted by the water tossing in the light. The inner surface of the white rubber cap gleamed occasionally as though it were oiled as she toyed with it. Honda was utterly captivated by the sight of her body, and it was only considerably later that he finally noticed something green glittering on one finger. It was the emerald ring with the golden guardian deities.

The instant he saw it, Honda's joy knew no bounds. It was a sign that she had forgiven him and that the Ying Chan who wore the ring had become the Ying Chan of former times. The rustling of the forest at the Peers School in Honda's youth, the two Siamese princes and the melancholy of their eyes, the announcement of Princess Chantrapa's death which had been received toward the end of summer in the garden at the southern villa, the long flow of time, the audience with the young Princess Moonlight in Bangkok, the bathing at Bang Pa In, the ring that had surfaced again in post-war Japan – the entire past was woven into a golden chain that linked up with his longing for the tropics. Only when she wore the ring did Ying Chan form a series of brilliant melancholy leitmotifs constantly stimulated in his intricate memories.

He heard the humming of bees close to his ear and caught the fragrant odour of the breeze that reminded him of roasted wheat, the unmistakable scent of summer. The Hondas were not particularly fond of flowers, and the garden had none of the beauty of Fuji's summer plains where pinks and gentians bloomed. But in the fragrant wind the scent of these fields and the dust stirred by the American Army manoeuvres, at times dyeing the sky above yellow, delicately commingled.

Ying Chan's body was breathing at Honda's side. Not only that, but it welcomed summer as if hypersensitive to its special infection; she was infected by summer from head to toe. The texture of her skin resembled the glow of some strange Thai fruit sold on the market-place in the shade of the mimosa. It was a bare body that in time had ripened and matured, signifying some accomplishment or promise.

As he reflected, he realized that the last time he had seen her unclothed was when she was seven, twelve years ago. The childish, slightly distended belly, which he remembered so vividly, had now flattened, but as if in compensation, the little flat chest had developed voluptuously. As she was preoccupied with the noise in the pool and was standing with her back turned toward the table, Honda could observe in detail the cords which, tied at the nape of her neck and falling down both sides, connected at the hips, the area in between forming a lovely straight line of bare back down to the crevice of her buttocks. Just above he could see the descending curve hesitate briefly at her coccyx, like the quiet basin of a small waterfall. The covered buttocks had the roundness and exquisiteness of a full moon rising. The cool of night seemed contained in the exposed flesh, while brightness appeared to radiate from the hidden flesh. The parasol barred her smooth skin with light and shadow; one arm in the shade was like bronze, but the other in the sun was like the polished surface of Chinese quincewood. Yet the skin, repelling both air and water, was not merely smooth, it had the moistness of amber orchid petals. The bone structure, which at a distance appeared delicate, was actually strong and well proportioned, though small.

'Well, shall we go in?' said Keiko.

'Yes, let's.' Ying Chan looked back vivaciously and smiled. She had been waiting for these words.

Then she placed the white swimming cap on the table and raised her arms to put up her lovely black hair. The quick, rather negligent movement afforded Honda, who was in a good position, the opportunity of seeing under her arm the lower part of her side. The top of the suit was cut like an apron, and the part over her breasts had a cord passing through it and around the back of her neck, where the two ends were tied and then caught by loops at the back. The bib was cut low enough to reveal the rise of her breasts, and her sides were hidden only by the narrow sashlike ends which formed the loops for the cords at the back. Therefore, though the lower side was always visible, when her arms were raised, the narrow strips of fabric were displaced, fully exposing parts previously hidden. Honda saw that the firm expanse of skin there was no different from other areas. Not a single imperfection or blemish. She was unperturbed even in the sun, and not a suggestion of a mole was discernible. Joy welled within him.

Ying Chan forced the gathered mass of hair under the bathing cap and set out for the swimming pool with Keiko. By the time Keiko realized that she was still holding her cigarette and had returned to the table, Ying Chan had already entered the water. Assuring himself that Rié was nowhere about, Honda whispered in Keiko's ear as she stooped to crush her cigarette in the ashtray:

'I see she's wearing the ring.'

Keiko said nothing, but winked knowingly. Little wrinkles, usually invisible, appeared at the corners of her eyes.

While he was gazing rapturously at the two swimmers, Rié returned and seated herself at his side. Intently watching Ying Chan leaping like a porpoise out of the sparkling water and plunging back in, a smile on her face, Rié said in a grating voice:

'With a body like that she ought to have a lot of children.'

44

In the library that night Honda could not interest himself in the usual books.

In a seldom-opened desk drawer he found a copy of *Court Proceedings*. For lack of anything better to do, he started reading. It concerned the sentence delivered in January, 1950, designating Honda as the legal possessor of his present holdings.

He opened the large file, which was bound by a black cord, on an English escritoire covered with Moroccan leather.

Main clause: Decision no. 9065 of 15 March 1902 by the Ministry of Agriculture and Commerce and National Forestry, whereby nationally owned land is nonreimbursable is hereby reversed. The defendant shall return to the plaintiff those national forests itemized elsewhere. Legal costs are to be borne by the defendant.

Nothing was more miraculous than the fact that the forests and mountains in a region of Fukushima prefecture, which originally had had no connection whatever with Honda, should now comprise the bulk of his wealth and support the disintegration of old age. Although it so happened that he had achieved victory, it had little to do with the original suit that had been brought in 1900, turned down once in 1902, then tenaciously pressed for half a century regardless of the vicissitudes of history. The cryptomeria forests, which people never frequented at night, and their damp undergrowth had again and again repeated their natural life cycle to afford him the manner of life he led today. How would some stranger passing through the forest early in the century have felt if, moved by the nobility of the treetops thrusting into the blue sky, he were to discover that their only *raison d'être* was to support a man's follies fifty years later?

Honda listened. The sounds of insects were still rare. His wife had gone to bed in the adjacent room. The house was pervaded with the coolness that suddenly follows the coming of night.

The party to celebrate the opening of the pool had ended about five o'clock, and all the guests except Keiko and Ying Chan were to return to their own homes. But Imanishi and Mrs Tsubakihara obstinately refused to leave. They had come with the intention of staying overnight. As a result both dinner and sleeping arrangements had had to be replanned. Mrs Tsubakihara was oblivious to the inconveniences she created.

The Hondas, Keiko, Ying Chan, Imanishi, and Mrs Tsubakihara made their way to the arbour, where they stayed for some time.

Honda's original project had been to assign Keiko to the outer guest room and reserve the inner one next to the study for Ying Chan, but the change of plans required that he assign the second room to Imanishi and put Keiko in with Ying Chan. That scotched the scheme to use the peep-hole to observe Ying Chan sleeping alone. With Keiko there she would certainly be more reserved.

The words and phrases of the court documents conveyed no meaning to him.

Sixthly, in item 15 of Instruction no. 4, 'Others shall be recognized as *de facto* owners under the regulations of the Tokugawa government and those of each fief' signifies that in addition to the cases of recognized possession set forth in items 1 to 14, when it can be ascertained that possession was generally recognized, the property may be returned to the recognized owner. 'General recognition' means...

He looked at the clock and saw that it was already five or six minutes past twelve. Suddenly his heart stopped as if he had stumbled over something in the darkness. Hot, indescribably sweet palpitations commenced.

They were familiar to him. When he had lurked in the park at night, when what he had been expectantly awaiting was about to happen before his eyes, his heart would begin to palpitate as if pestered by a swarm of red ants.

An avalanche. A sombre avalanche of honey that, overpowering everything with its suffocating sweetness, crushed the pillars of reason; all emotions were transmuted into these mechanical, rapid palpitations. Everything melted. It was useless to struggle against them.

Where did this avalanche come from? Somewhere there existed the secluded dwelling of carnal desire, and when it sent forth orders from afar, no matter how defective the antenna, it stirred sensitively; and abandoning all, one instantly responded. How alike were the voices of pleasure and death! When one is summoned, all work at once becomes unimportant. As on a ghost ship abandoned by its crew, be it the entries in the log, the uneaten food, the half-polished shoes, the comb left before the mirror, or even the partially knotted ropes – everything breathes of the mysteriously departed men, everything is left as it was in the haste of departure.

The palpitations were signs of welling desire. Manifestly only ugliness and disgrace lay in store, yet these palpitations had the richness and the brilliance of a rainbow; something indistinguishable from the sublime burst forth.

Something indistinguishable from the sublime! That was the villian. Nothing was more unattractive than the fact that both the force moving one to the noblest or most just of deeds and that inspiring the most obscene pleasure and the most ugly of dreams should spring from the same source and be accompanied by the same warning palpitations. Base desires merely cast base shadows, and if the temptation of sublimity did not flash in these initial palpitations, a man could still maintain a calm pride in life. Perhaps the root of temptation lay not in carnal desire but in this pretentious illusion of silvery sublimity, this vague and mysterious half-hidden peak among the clouds. It was the birdlime of 'sublimity' that first ensnared a man and then made him yearn with unbearable impatience after the vast light.

Honda, unable to endure it longer, stood up. He peered into the obscurity of the adjacent bedroom to be sure that his wife was asleep. Again he stood alone in the bright study. Since the dawn of history he had been alone in this study, and he would still be alone in it when history came to an end.

He extinguished the light. The moon was bright, and the furniture took on vague contours; the desk made of a single piece of zelkova wood gleamed as though its surface were covered with water.

He leaned against the bookcase on the wall dividing the study from the next room, listening for signs of movement. He could hear something, but it did not seem to be that they were still up and talking. It was conceivable that, unable to sleep, they might be conversing, but not a single distinct word filtered through to him.

Honda removed some ten Western books from the shelf to free the opening of the peep-hole. The number of books and the titles were always the same. They were invariably old leather-bound tomes with gilt lettering on law in German that had come to him from his father. His fingers could tell each and every one by the difference in thickness. The order in which he removed them never varied. He could guess the exact weight of each and he knew the odour of accumulated dust. The touch and the weight of these solemn and imposing volumes and the precision of their arrangements were the indispensable formalities of his pleasure. There was no more important ceremony than that of reverently removing these stone walls of concepts and transforming the grim pleasure he would have in reading them into his wretched infatuation. Carefully, making no noise, he lowered each volume to the floor. With each book the pounding of his heart increased. The eighth was a particularly heavy tome. When he pulled it out, his hand felt numb from the dusty golden weight of the pleasure he experienced.

He completed the task faultlessly and then placed his eye to the peep-hole without bumping his head. The subtlety of this skill was also of great consequence. How important each of these trifling matters seemed! As in some ritual, no detail could be omitted so that he might glimpse this other brilliant world. He was a lone priest left in the darkness. Strictly adhering to the ceremonial procedures long rehearsed in his head – he was plagued by the belief that if he should forget any part of the ritual the whole structure would collapse – he carefully put his right eye to the hole.

One of the bedside lamps seemed to be lit and a dim light mottled the room. He had been clever to have Matsudo move the wall bed so that both now stood in his field of vision.

In the dusky light inextricably entangled limbs writhed on the bed immediately before him. A white plump body and a dusky one lay with heads in opposite directions, exhausting their wanton desires. It was a position naturally assumed when the mind tied to the flesh and the brain that engendered love attempted to obtain balance by reaching out to the farthest point in order to taste the wine fermented by that love. Two heads of black shadowy hair were intimately pressed against two black pubescent mounds also filled with shadows. The annoying wisps of dishevelled hair strewn across the cheeks had become signs of love. Smooth, burning thighs lay in intimate contact with smooth, burning cheeks, while the soft bellies heaved like moonlit inlets. He could not hear distinct voices, but a sobbing, neither pleasure nor sorrow, vibrated the length of the torsos. Breasts now abandoned by the partners innocently turned their nipples toward the light, trembling at times as though under an electrical charge. The depth of the night concealed in the aureoles around the nipples, the distance of the pleasure that made the breasts shudder, testified to the fact that every atom of their bodies was still isolated in maddening aloneness. They were feverishly striving to come closer, toward a greater intimacy, to fuse one into the other, but to no avail. Far away Keiko's red-lacquered toes flexed as if she were dancing on a sheet of hot iron, and they merely trod the empty twilight.

Honda realized that the room was filled with cool mountain air, but he felt as though the centre of a furnace lay beyond the peep-hole. A shining furnace. He regretted that Ying Chan's back that he had examined so carefully during the day at the pool, perspiration flowing slowly down the spine, was turned toward him. Shortly the perspiration was diverted from its channel and trickled down the dark flank against the bed. It seemed as though he could smell the fragrance of some rich, ripe tropical fruit that had just split open.

Keiko shifted her body slightly to be on top, and Ying Chan tilted her neck, thrusting her head between Keiko's shining thighs. Naturally her breasts came into view. Her right arm encircled Keiko's hip, while her left hand gently caressed her belly. Intermittently little nocturnal lappings could be heard licking the banks of the harbour.

So beautiful was Ying Chan's sincerity that he was seeing for the first time that Honda even forgot to be surprised by this so treacherous conclusion to his love.

Her closed eyes were turned toward the ceiling, and her forehead was half buried in Keiko's sporadically convulsing thighs. Keiko's mimosa-like hair almost completely covered her lovely, peaceful nostrils, now no longer cold and narrow. Ying Chan's bow-shaped upper lip was open and moist, and a busy sucking movement extended from her delicate chin to her cheeks that gleamed darkly. Presently Honda saw a line of tears flowing like some living animal from the shadow of her long eyelashes along her tightly closed eyes and down her cheek.

Within the limitless movement of waves everything was directed toward an as-yet unknown summit. The two women seemed to be desperately striving to reach ultimate limits neither had ever dreamt of or hoped for. Honda felt as if there were some unknown pinnacle poised in the space of the dark room like a brilliant crown. It was probably the Thai full-moon diadem suspended there above the two writhing women; only Honda's eyes were able to envision it.

The bodies of both women alternately extended and contracted and then collapsed as they buried themselves again in sighs and perspiration. The crown floated indifferently in the space which their straining fingers almost reached. When the envisioned summit, that unknown golden limit was manifest, the scene was completely transformed, and Honda could see the two women entangled beneath his gaze only in their suffering and torture. They were battered by the dissatisfaction of the flesh, their gathered brows were filled with pain, and their hot limbs seemed to writhe as though trying to escape from what seared them. They possessed no wings. They continued their futile thrashings to escape from their bonds, from their suffering; and yet their flesh firmly retained them. Only rapture could bring release.

Ying Chan's beautiful, dark breasts were drenched in perspiration, the right one crushed and disfigured beneath Keiko's body, while the left, heaving vigorously, lay voluptuously on her left arm with which she was caressing Keiko's belly. On the constantly trembling mound the nipple slumbered, and with the perspiration the sphere glowed as if bright with rain.

At that moment Ying Chan, perhaps jealous that Keiko's thigh had freedom of movement, raised her left arm high and grasped it as though to claim it as her own. She placed it firmly over her head as if she could do without breathing. The imposing white thigh completely covered her face.

Ying Chan's whole side was exposed. To the left of her bare breast, an area her arm had previously concealed, three extremely small moles appeared distinctly, like the Pleiades in the dusky sky of her brown skin that resembled the dying evening glow.

Honda was shocked. It was as if his eyes had been pierced with arrows.

Just as he ducked his head and was about to leave the bookcase, he felt a light tap on his back. On withdrawing his head he discovered Rié standing there in her nightdress, her face frighteningly pale.

'What are you doing? I suspected as much.'

Honda felt no guilt as he turned his perspiring forehead to his wife. He had already seen the moles.

'Look. Look at the moles...'

'Are you telling me to peek?'

'Go ahead. It's just as I thought.'

Caught between dignity and curiosity, Rié hesitated for some time. Ignoring her, Honda walked to the bay window and seated himself on the built-in bench. Rié put her eye to the peep-hole. Having been unable to see his own posture when he had done the same thing, Honda could not bear to witness the demeaning position of his wife. Nevertheless, they had come to the point of sharing the same deed.

He looked for the moon concealed by a cloud through the metal screen in the bay window. Behind the cloud, edged in light, the moon sent forth beams in all directions and cloud clusters trailed away in similar stateliness. The stars were few, and he saw only one shining brightly, scarcely touching the tops of the cypress trees.

When Rié had done peeping, she lit the lamp in the room. Her face was shining with joy.

She walked to the bench and sat down. Already she was cured.

'I'm stunned ... Did you know about that?' she said in a warm, low voice.

'No. I just found out.'

'But you said it was just as you thought.'

'That's not what I meant, Rié. I was talking about the moles. Some time ago you raked through my study in Tokyo and read Matsugae's diary, didn't you?'

'*I* hunted through your study?'

'It doesn't matter. I'm asking if you read Matsugae's diary.'

'I ... I don't remember. I'm not interested in other people's diaries.'

When Honda asked her to bring him a cigar from the bedroom, she obediently followed his command. She even lighted it, shielding it with her hand from the wind that came through the window screen.

'The key to transmigration is in Matsugae's diary. You saw them too, didn't you? The three black moles on her left side? Those moles were originally on Matsugae.'

Rié, thinking of other things, was indifferent to what Honda was saying. She probably thought her husband was looking for excuses. Honda pressed her, wishing them to have the memory in common.

'Well, you did see them, didn't you?'

'I can't say. But the scene was horrible. You never know about people, do you?'

'That's why I'm saying that Ying Chan is the reincarnation of Matsugae.'

Rié gazed at her husband with pity. It was only natural that a woman who believed herself cured should try in turn to act as such. This woman who had so savagely confirmed reality was now ready to infect her husband with the roughness that burned her skin like salt water. Rié was no longer the Rié of old. Although she had once desired to transform reality she had wisely learned to believe in it. She had learned that without changing herself, the world could be transformed through observation. She rather looked down on her husband's world, without realizing that she had in fact become a co-conspirator by having been a voyeur too.

'What's all this about reincarnation? How ridiculous! I didn't read any diary. At any rate, I've finally calmed down. Your eyes must have been opened too, but I was suffering from something that didn't exist at all. I was wrestling with an illusion. Now that I realize it, I suddenly feel tired. But everything turned out for the best. There's nothing to worry about any more.'

The two were sitting at either end of the bench, an ash-tray between them. Honda, concerned that Rié might be cold, closed the window; the smoke from his cigar slowly eddied up under the light. They were silent, but the silence was not the same as that which had occurred that morning.

Their hearts were bound together by the odiousness of what they had observed, and Honda felt momentarily how good it would have been if they could have been like so many other couples in the world, if they could flaunt their impeccable moral rectitude like immaculately white aprons across their chests, sit at table three times a day and proudly eat to their satisfaction, if they could assume the right to disdain other things in the world. But in reality they had merely been transformed into a couple of voyeurs.

Yet each of them had not seen the same thing. Where Honda had discovered reality, Rié had found out her illusions. The process whereby they had reached this common point was the same for both in that they had not yet recuperated from their fatigue and their work had been futile. What remained now was mutual consolation.

After a while Rié yawned so widely one could see to the back of her mouth.

'Don't you think we should start thinking about adopting a child?' she said most appropriately, combing back her dishevelled hair.

Death had flown from Honda's heart the moment he had seen Keiko and Ying Chan together. Now there was reason to believe that he might be immortal. 'No', he said with determination, plucking a piece of tobacco from his lip, 'it's better to live by ourselves. I prefer not having any heir.'

Honda and Rié were no sooner awakened by a violent pounding on the door than they smelled the smoke.

'Fire! Fire!' a woman was shouting. When the couple, joining hands, ran out the door, the second-floor corridor was already filled with swirling smoke, and the person who had roused them was gone. Covering their mouths with their sleeves, the two ran coughing and choking down the stairs. The pool with its water flashed through Honda's mind. They would be safe only if they could reach it without delay.

As they burst out on to the terrace and looked at the pool, they saw Keiko holding Ying Chan and crying to them from the far side. That the fire was already sweeping through the house was obvious, for though the lights had not been turned on, the reflections of the two women were none the less clearly visible on the surface of the water. Honda was amazed by the personal appearance of both Keiko and Ying Chan. Their hair was dishevelled, but both were wearing the dressing gowns they had brought with them. Honda was clad only in his pyjamas and Rié was wearing her night kimono.

'I woke up coughing because of the smoke. It must have come from Mr Imanishi's room,' said Keiko.

'Who knocked on our door?'

'I did. I knocked on Mr Imanishi's too, but he hasn't come down. What shall we do?'

'Matsudo! Matsudo!' Honda shouted, and the chauffeur came running along the edge of the swimming pool.

'Mr Imanishi and Mrs Tsubakihara are in there. Can't you go and help them?'

They looked up and saw flames shooting out of the second-floor windows along with dense white smoke.

'That's impossible, Mr Honda,' the chauffeur said, carefully considering the situation. 'It's too late now. Why didn't they get out?'

'They must have taken too many sleeping pills,' Keiko remarked. Ying Chan buried her face in Keiko's breast and began to cry.

Apparently the roof had caved in, for flames shot high into a sky filled with flying sparks.

'What are we to do with the water?' said Honda helplessly, looking at the swimming pool that was so reddened with reflected flames and sparks that it would seem that in touching the water one's hand would be burned.

'Yes, I think it's too late to put out the fire, but perhaps we should douse the valuable pieces in the living room. Shall I bring a bucket?' asked Matsudo without making a move.

Honda was already thinking of something else.

'How about the fire department? I wonder what time it is now.'

No one had a watch. They had all been left behind.

'It's three minutes past four. The sun will be up soon,' said Matsudo.

'How provident of you to have thought to bring your watch,' Honda said sarcastically, regaining his assurance as he discovered he was capable of sarcasm even in such circumstances.

'It's an old habit. I always sleep with my watch on,' placidly answered the properly dressed Matsudo.

Rié, dazed, had seated herself in a chair next to the folded beach umbrella.

Honda saw Ying Chan remove her face from Keiko's breast, hastily fumble through the breast pocket of her dressing gown, and take out a photograph. The gloss of the picture was enhanced by the flames. Glancing distractedly at it, he saw that it was a completely nude Keiko leaning against a chair.

'I'm glad this was not burned,' said Ying Chan, smiling. As she looked up at Keiko, her white teeth gleamed in the light of the flames. His memory functioned amidst a welter of thoughts, and Honda recalled the scene just before Katsumi had broken into her bedroom. This was the same treasured picture that Ying Chan had been looking at then.

'Silly,' said Keiko, tenderly putting an arm round her shoulder. 'What did you do with the ring?'

'The ring! Oh, I've left it in the room,' Honda heard her say distinctly. He was seized by a fear that the flaming silhouettes of his two friends might appear in the far windows of the second floor, screaming in terror. They were most certainly dying there. Probably they were already dead. This might well be why the fire gave the impression of quietness despite the grating and roaring.

The fire engine still had not come. Honda thought of the telephone in Keiko's house which was being remodelled and sent Matsudo running over to call the Gotemba Fire Station at Nimaibashi.

The holocaust had enveloped the entire second story, and the first floor was filled with smoke. As the wind happened to be coming from the direction of Fuji to the north-west, smoke did not blow toward the pool, but the dawn chill crept up the spines of the onlookers.

The fire changed at every instant. Mingling with sounds like colossal footsteps amidst the flames came the intermittent noise of things bursting. With each sound Honda associated some burning object: now a book, now the desk. He visualized pages turning over, swelling like roses.

The volume of fire increased in proportion to the smoke. The heat could be felt even on this side of the swimming pool, and the rising hot air carried up cinders and sparks. During the short time before they turned to ash, the cinders were gold, reminding one of the flutter of golden wings of fledglings leaving their nest. It seemed as though things were departing. In one area of the sky radiant with soaring flames, the outlines of the cloud banks hidden in the dusky light of dawn were now defined.

A roaring, probably caused by falling beams on the second floor, rose from the house. Then a section of outer wall was rent by flames, and a window frame engulfed in fire fell into the pool. The subtle decorative flames imparted to the falling black object the momentary illusion of being a window of the Marble Temple in Siam. A sizzling pierced the air as the frame plunged into the water. They jumped back from the pool.

The house, gradually losing its outer walls, took on the appearance of a gigantic burning bird cage. Tatters of delicate flame fluttered from every chink and every crack. The house was breathing. It was as though the source of a deep and vigorous life breath existed within the flames. From time to time the shape of some familiar piece of furniture, some former lifelike shadow would appear in their midst, but it would collapse instantly covered in brilliance and turn into joyfully dancing flames.

The upsurging fire would suddenly shoot out like a snake's tongue only to disappear again into the smoke, while red faces of flame would suddenly appear from the dense black fumes. Everything happened with incredible rapidity, fire and fire joined hands, smoke wrapped about smoke, all attempting to reach a single summit. The upside-down burning house dropped mixtures of flame deep into the swimming pool, and the limpid dawn sky was visible through the tips of fingers of fire.

The wind changed direction and smoke blew toward the pool, sending the spectators further from the water. Although they could not detect it with certainty, and although no one mentioned it, they knew surely that the odour of burning human flesh was present in the smoke, and they covered their nostrils with both hands.

Rié suggested that it would be best to go to the arbour since dew was falling. The three women, turning their backs on the fire, started toward the arbour across the lawn just mowed the previous day. Honda remained alone.

He felt insistently that he had seen this somewhere before.

Flames reflecting in the water ... burning corpses ... Benares! How could he not have dreamed of recapturing the ultimate he had seen in that holy land?

The house had turned into kindling and life had become fire. All triviality had returned to ash and nothing but the most essential was important, and the hidden, gigantic face had turned up its head abruptly from the flame. Laughter, screams, sobs were all absorbed in the clamour of the flames, the crackling of wood, the distorted panes of glass, the creaking of the joints – sound itself was enveloped in an absolute quiet. Roasted tiles cracked and fell, one by one the fetters were released, and the house turned into a brilliant nakedness hitherto unknown. The light cream section of outer wall on the first floor which had not yet burned suddenly wrinkled and turned brown; and at the same time, the fire thrust violently through a light smudge of smoke. The smooth speed of transformation into flames and their shiftings in finding an escape were unimaginably exquisite.

Honda brushed sparks from his shoulders and sleeves. The surface of the swimming pool was covered with embers and ashes that swarmed like duckweed. But the brilliance of the fire penetrated everything, and the purification of the Mani Karnika ghat was reflected mirror-fashion in this small, limited area of water, in this sacred pool created for Ying Chan's bathing. What was different here from the funeral pyres reflected in the Ganges? Here too were fire and wood, and the two human bodies, slow to burn, were doubtless writhing and threshing in the flames. They no longer felt pain; the flesh merely imitated and repeated the forms of suffering as it resisted destruction. Such were the two corpses. This was precisely the same as that clear fire in the evening dusk at the floating ghat. Everything was being rapidly reduced to constituent elements. Smoke rose high into the sky.

The only thing missing was the face of the sacred white cow that had turned and stared straight at Honda from the other side of the flames.

When the fire engine arrived, the fire had already died down. Nevertheless, the firemen conscientiously hosed the house. A rescue was attempted, but they found the two corpses completely incinerated. The police arrived and requested Honda to verify the scene of death. But as the staircase had collapsed, it was difficult to reach the upper floor, and Honda gave up. On being told of the habits of Imanishi and Mrs Tsubakihara, the officer in charge commented that the cause of the fire had probably been their smoking in bed. If they had taken sleeping pills about three, then the time of the drug's maximum effect would have coincided with the onset of the fire, doubtless starting from a lit cigarette dropped on the quilt. Honda did not accept the idea of suicide. When the officer spoke of 'double suicide', Keiko, listening at one side, broke into unrestrained laughter.

When things settled down a bit, Honda would have to present himself at the police station to make a deposition. He was sure to be busy today. He must send Matsudo out to purchase food for breakfast, but it would be some time yet before the stores opened.

As there was no other place to go, everyone gathered in the arbour. In her faltering Japanese Ying Chan brought up the subject of a snake she had seen as she ran from the fire. It had appeared on the lawn and slithered away with unusual speed, the distant fire glinting on its oily brown scales. Listening to her, all of them, especially the women, felt even more the penetrating chill of the air.

Just then, Fuji, the colour of red tile at dawn, one sparkling brush mark of snow near its summit, appeared before them. Even under these circumstances Honda's eyes shifted involuntarily from the red mountain to the morning sky immediately beside it. The habit was almost unconscious. He could clearly see the distinct form of a winter Fuji.

45

In 1967, it happened that Honda was invited to a dinner party at the American Embassy in Tokyo. There he met the head of the American Cultural Centre in Bangkok. His wife, somewhat over thirty, was Thai, and people said that she was a princess. Honda was sure that she was Ying Chan.

Ying Chan had gone home shortly after the fire at Gotemba in 1952 and Honda had had no news since then. Momentarily he believed that she had unexpectedly returned to Tokyo after fifteen years as the wife of an American. This was not impossible, and it would be quite typical of Ying Chan to pretend not to know him at all when she greeted him at their introduction.

He looked at her several times during dinner, but the woman obstinately spoke no Japanese. Her English was that of a native American. Deeply engrossed, Honda made completely irrelevant answers on several occasions to the woman seated next to him.

Following dinner, liqueurs were served in another room. Honda approached the lady who was wearing a rose-coloured dress of Thai silk and for the first time had the opportunity of talking with her alone.

He inquired if she knew Ying Chan.

'I do, indeed! She was my twin sister. But she's dead now,' she said brightly in English. Impulsively he asked how she had died, and when.

The lady said that after she returned from her studies in Japan, Ying Chan's father discovered that she had benefited little from her stay, and he had tried to send her to the United States to study. But Ying Chan had not agreed and had chosen to live in her residence in Bangkok surrounded by flowers. She died suddenly in the spring at the age of twenty.

According to the lady-in-waiting, Ying Chan was alone in the garden, standing under a phoenix tree with its smoky vermilion flowers. Although there was no one else there, she was heard laughing. The lady-in-waiting thought it strange that she should be laughing all by herself. Clear, innocent sounds that rose in the sunny blue sky. The laughter ceased and almost at once turned into shrill screams. The lady-in-waiting rushed up to find Ying Chan on the ground, her thigh bitten by a cobra.

It was an hour before the doctor arrived. In the interval, her muscles slackened and she lost all motor control. She complained of sleepiness and double vision. Spinal paralysis set in and she began to salivate. Her breathing slowed while her pulse quickened and became irregular. Ying Chan had gone into final convulsions and died before the doctor arrived.

THE DECAY OF THE ANGEL

Translated by
Edward G. Seidensticker

1

The mists in the offing turned the distant ships black. Even so it was clearer than yesterday. He could pick out the ridges of the Izu Peninsula. The May sea was calm. The sunlight was strong, there were only wisps of cloud, the sea was blue.

Very small ripples broke on the shore. There was a certain distasteful quality, before they broke, about the nightingale colours at the bellies of the ripples, as if they had in them all the unpleasant varieties of seaweed.

The churning of the sea, day after day, a daily repetition of the churning sea of milk in the Indian legend. Perhaps the world would not let it rest. Something about it called up all the evil in nature.

The swelling of the May sea, endlessly and restlessly moving its points of light, a myriad of tiny spikes.

Three birds seemed to become one at the top of the sky. Then, in disorder, they separated. There was something wondrous about the meeting and separating. It must mean something, this coming so close that they felt the wind from each other's wings, and then blue distance once more. Three ideas will sometimes join in our hearts.

The black hull of a small cargo ship, its funnel mark a mountain over three horizontal lines, gave, in the heaping up of its mass, a sense of grandeur and sudden growth.

At two in the afternoon the sun withdrew into a thin cocoon of clouds, a whitely shining worm.

The horizon was a blue-black hoop of steel perfectly fitting the sea.

For an instant, at a single spot in the offing, a white wave sprang up like a white wing and fell back again. And what would that mean? It had to be some grand signal, or perhaps a grand whim.

The tide came slowly in, the waves were rising, the land lay before the most powerful of assaults. The sun was behind clouds and the green of the sea took on a somehow angry darkness. A long white line stretched across it from east to west in a sort of gigantic inverted triangle. It seemed to twist itself loose from the flat surface and, near at hand, towards the apex, fan-like lines lost themselves blackly in a black-green sea.

The sun came out again. Again the sea gave smooth lodging to the white light, and, at the ordering of a southwest wind, numberless shadows like the backs of sea lions moved northeast and northwest, limitless schools of waves aloof from the shore. The flood was held under strict control by the distant moon.

Mackerel clouds half-covered the sky, their upper line quietly severing the sun.

Two fishing boats were putting out to sea. There was a cargo boat farther out. The wind was stronger. A fishing boat came in from the west, as if to signal the opening of a ceremony. It was a poor little boat, and yet, wheelless and legless, it advanced with a proud grace as if sweeping in full-skirted.

By three the mackerel clouds were thinner. On the southern sky clouds fanned out like the tail of a white turtle-dove to throw a deep shadow over the sea.

The sea: a nameless sea, the Mediterranean, the Japan Sea, the Bay of Suruga here before him; a rich, nameless, absolute anarchy, caught after a great struggle as something called 'sea', in fact rejecting a name.

As the sky clouded over, the sea fell into sulky contemplation, studded with fine nightingale-coloured points. It bristled with wave-thorns, like a rose branch. In the thorns themselves was evidence of a smooth becoming. The thorns of the sea were smooth.

Three ten. There were no ships in sight.

Very strange. The whole vast space was abandoned.

There were not even wings of gulls.

Then a phantom ship arose and disappeared towards the west.

The Izu Peninsula was shrouded in mist. For a time it ceased to be the Izu Peninsula. It was the ghost of a lost peninsula. Then it disappeared entirely. It had become a fiction on a map. Ships and peninsula alike belonged to 'the absurdity of existence'.

They appeared and disappeared. How did they differ?

If the visible was the sum of being, then the sea, as long as it was not lost in mist, existed there. It was heartily ready to be.

A single ship changed it all.

The whole composition changed. With a rending of the whole pattern of being, a ship was received by the horizon. An abdication was signed. A whole universe was thrown away. A ship came in sight, to throw out the universe that had guarded its absence.

Multiple changes in the colour of the sea, moment by moment. Changes in the clouds. And the appearance of a ship. What was happening? What were happenings?

Each instant brought them, more momentous than the explosion of Krakatoa. It was only that no one noticed. We are too accustomed to the absurdity of existence. The loss of a universe is not worth taking seriously.

Happenings are the signals for endless reconstruction, reorganization. Signals from a distant bell. A ship appears and sets the bell to ringing. In an instant the sound makes everything its own. On the sea they are incessant, the bell is forever ringing.

A being.

It need not be a ship. A single bitter orange, appearing no one knows when. It is enough to set the bell to ringing.

Three thirty in the afternoon. A single bitter orange represented being on the Bay of Suruga.

Hidden by a wave and appearing again, floating and sinking, like a ceaselessly blinking eye, the bright dot of orange floated slowly off towards the east through the ripples in near the shore.

Three thirty-five. Sombrely, a black hull appeared from the west, from the direction of Nagoya.

The sun was behind clouds, like a smoked salmon.

Tōru Yasunaga looked away from the thirty-power telescope.

There was no sign yet of the cargo ship *Tenrō-maru*, due to make port at four.

He went back to his desk and absently scanned the Shimizu shipping notices.

Expected arrivals of non-scheduled ships, Saturday, 2 May, 1970.
Tenrō-maru, Japanese, 16:00. Taishō Shipping Company. Agent, Suzuichi. From Yokohama. Berth 4-5, Hinodé Pier.

2

Shigekuni Honda was seventy-six. He often travelled alone now that his wife Rié was dead. He chose easily accessible places that would not overtax him.

He had visited Nihondaira Heights below Fuji, and on his return had stopped by the Mio Grove and seen such treasures as the cloth, probably from Inner Asia, said to be a fragment of the angel's robe; and as he started back towards Shizuoka he found himself wanting to be alone for a time on the shore. There were three runs every hour of the Kodama Express. It would be no great matter if he were to miss his train. The return trip to Tokyo took only a little over an hour.

Stopping the cab, he walked with the help of a cane the fifty yards or so to the Komagoé shore. He asked himself, as he gazed out to sea, whether this would be the Udo Beach identified in the fourteenth century by Ichijō Kanera as the precise spot of the angel's descent. He thought too of the Kamakura coast of his youth. He turned back. The beach was quiet. Children were playing, and there were two or three anglers.

His attention on the sea, he had not noticed earlier, but now his eye caught, the rustic pink of a convolvulus below the breakwater. In the sand along the breakwater a great litter of garbage lay scoured by the sea winds. Empty Coca-Cola bottles, food cans, paint cans, non-perishable plastic bags, detergent boxes, bricks, bones.

The dregs of life on land cascaded down and came against infinity. The sea, infinity not met before. The dregs, like man, unable to meet their end save in the ugliest and filthiest of fashions.

Straggling pines along the embankment sent out blossoms like red starfish. To the left a radish patch put out forlorn little four-petalled white blossoms. Small pines lined the road. For the rest there was a solid expanse of plastic strawberry shelters. In vast numbers, under quonset huts of plastic, strawberries trailed their fruit over stone terraces among a profusion of leaves. Flies crawled along the saw-blade edges of the leaves. Quonset huts, as far as he could see, unpleasantly white, jammed in, one against another. Honda noticed – he had not before – a small tower-like structure among them.

Just in from the prefectural highway on which the cab had stopped, it was a two-storey hut on a disproportionately high concrete platform. It was too tall for a watch shelter, too poor for an office building. Three sides were almost unbroken expanses of window.

Curious, he stepped into what appeared to be the yard. White window frames were heaped in great disorder on the sand. Fragments of glass faithfully caught the clouds. Looking up, he saw in a second-floor window what seemed to be shades for telescope lenses. Two huge iron pipes, rust red, protruded from the concrete platform and buried themselves in the earth. Uncertain of his footing, Honda made his way across the pipes and started up a flight of decaying stone steps.

At the foot of the iron stairs leading to the shelter was a shaded signboard. In English:

TEIKOKU SIGNAL STATION

And in Japanese:

SHIMIZU OFFICE OF THE TEIKOKU SIGNAL
AND COMMUNICATIONS COMPANY

Notice of arrivals, departures, and moorings
Detection and prevention of accidents at sea
Land-to-sea communications
Marine weather information
Receiving and dispatching of ships
Various other matters related to shipping

The peeling white paint of the characters, here and there worn thin, with the name of the company in an antique hand, pleased Honda. The smell of the sea poured forth, quite without restraint, from the list of duties and functions.

He looked up the stairs. All was quiet.

Below and behind him, to the northwest, beyond the prefectural highway and the town, where pinwheels caught the light over carp streamers on new blue-tiled roofs, lay the complex of Shimizu Harbour, a crisscrossing of cranes on land and derricks on ships, white silos of factories and black hulls, iron bleached by the sea winds and thickly painted chimneys, one mass stopping at the shore, the other coming in from the several seas; there in the distance was the mechanism of the harbour laid bare, meeting at the appointed spot, glaring across the line. And the shining dismembered snake of the sea.

Fuji rose far above the hills. Only the summit was visible, as if a great sharp white boulder had been flung up through the uncertainty of the clouds.

Honda stopped to look.

3

The concrete platform was a water tank.

Water was pumped into it from a well and stored for irrigating strawberries. Teikoku Signal had seen the possibilities of the high platform and put up a wooden shelter. It was ideal for sighting ships from Nagoya to the west or Yokohama to the east.

Normally four signalmen worked eight-hour shifts. One of them had long been ill, however, and the other three took turns at twenty-four-hour duty. The first floor was the office of the superintendent, who from time to time came from the downtown office. The three signalmen had only a bare-floored room, some four yards square and surrounded on three sides by windows, on the second floor.

Attached to one window was a desk with a view on the three sides. Facing south was a thirty-power telescope, facing the harbour facilities to the east were fifteen-power binoculars, and at the southeast corner, for night signals, was a one-kilowatt beam. Two telephones on the desk at the southwest corner, a book shelf, maps, signal flags arranged on high shelves, and to the northwest a kitchen with a closet and a cot completed the furnishings. In front of the eastern window was a steel electric pylon, its porcelain insulators repeating the colour of the clouds. The power line ran down to the beach, where it was caught by a second pylon. A turn to the northeast took it to a third, and so around the coast, a diminishing curve of silver towers, to Shimizu Harbour. The third pylon was, from this vantage point, a good marker. A ship came into the harbour, and one knew as it passed the third pylon that it was approaching Basin 3-G, which included the piers.

Even now identification was by naked eye. So long as vagaries in cargoes and currents ruled the movements of ships, they would continue to come in too soon or too late, and a certain nineteenth-century romanticism would not disappear from welcoming parties. There was a need for more precise observations to tell the customs and quarantine officials and the stevedores and pilots and laundries and provisioners when to put out their welcoming flags. There was a still greater need for a just arbiter to decide which was to take precedence when two ships came in together and competed for the last berth.

That was Tōru's work.

A fairly large ship had appeared. The horizon was already obscure, and it took a quick and well-trained eye to determine a ship's origins. Tōru went to the telescope.

In the clear atmosphere of midsummer or midwinter, there would be an instant when a ship would move rudely in over the high threshold of the horizon; but in the mists of early summer such an appearance was a gradual separation from the inchoate. The horizon was like a long, white, soggy pillow.

The size of the black cargo ship seemed right for the 4,780-ton *Tenrō-maru*, and the stern bridge also corresponded to what the registry had told Tōru. The wake was white and clean, as was the bridge. There were three yellow derricks. What was the round red mark on the black funnels? Tōru strained his eyes. He made out the character for *tai*, 'large', in a red circle. Taishō Shipping, no mistake about it. All the while the ship kept up a speed of twelve and a half knots, and threatened to outrun the telescope. It was like a fly crossing a round window screen.

He could still not make out the name. He was sure that there were three characters, and foreknowledge told him that the first was *ten*, 'heaven'.

He returned to the desk and telephoned the agent.

'Hello. This is Teikoku Signal. You should be ready for the *Tenrō-maru*. It's just coming past the pylon. The cargo?' Tōru conjured up an image of the waterline dividing the ship into red and black. 'I'd think about half full. When will the stevedores be out? At five?'

That would give them an hour. The number of places that must be informed had grown.

Tōru moved busily back and forth between the desk and the telescope, and made some fifteen calls.

The pilot station. The tugboat *Shunyō-maru*. The pilot's house. Various provisioners. The Port Service Patrol. Customs. The agency once more. The Harbour Management Section of the Harbour Control Office. The Office of Statistics for weighing the cargo. Shipping offices.

'The *Tenrō-maru* is coming in. Hinodé four-five. If you will, please.'

The *Tenrō-maru* was already at the third pylon. As the image moved past land it was distorted by heat shimmerings.

'Hello. The *Tenrō-maru* is coming into three-G.'

'Hello. This is Teikoku Signal. The *Tenrō-maru* is in three-G.'

'Hello. Customs? The police, please. The *Tenrō-maru* has come into three-G.'

'Hello. The *Tenrō-maru* is in three-G. Sixteen fifteen.'

'Hello. The *Tenrō-maru* came in five minutes ago.'

Ships not from abroad but from Nagoya or Yokohama were more frequent at the end of the month than at the beginning. Yokohama was one hundred and fifteen nautical miles away, nine and a half hours at twelve knots. Tōru had no duties except to be on watch for an hour or so before a projected arrival. There were no other arrivals today save the *Nitchō-maru* at nine in the evening, from Keelung.

Tōru always felt a little dejected when he had finished a round of calls. The harbour would be suddenly alive. He would light a cigarette as he watched the stir from remote isolation.

Actually he should not be smoking. The superintendent had had a sharp word or two when he had first noticed a boy of sixteen with a cigarette in his mouth. Afterwards he had said nothing. No doubt he had concluded that inattention was the more profitable policy.

Tōru's pale, finely carved face was like ice. It conveyed no emotion, no affection or tears.

But he knew the happiness of watching. Nature had told him of it. No eye could be clearer or brighter than the eye that had nothing to create, nothing to do but gaze. The invisible horizon beyond which the conscious eye could not penetrate was far more remote than the visible horizon. And all manner of entities appeared in regions visible and accessible to consciousness. Sea, ships, clouds, peninsulas, lightning, the sun, the moon, the myriads of stars. If seeing is a meeting between eye and being, which is to say between being and being, then it must be the facing mirrors of two beings. No, it was more. Seeing went beyond being, to take wings like a bird. It transported Tōru to a realm visible to no one. Even beauty there was a rotted, tattered skirt. That had to be a sea never defiled by being, a sea upon which ships never appeared. There had to be a realm where at the limit of all the layers of clarity it was definite that nothing at all made an appearance, a realm of solid, definite indigo, where seeing cast off the shackles of consciousness and itself became transparent, where phenomena and consciousness dissolved like plumbic oxide in acetic acid.

Happiness for Tōru was sending his eyes into such distances. There was for him no more complete a throwing off of the self than in seeing. Only the eyes brought forgetfulness – save for the image in the mirror.

Tōru himself?

A sixteen-year-old who was quite certain that he did not belong to this world. Only half of him was in it. The other was in that realm of indigo. There were consequently no laws and no regulations that governed him. He but pretended that he was bound by the laws of this world. Where are there laws regulating an angel?

Life was strangely simple. Poverty and deprivation, the contradictions of society and politics, troubled him not in the least. Occasionally he would let a soft smile float to his lips, but it had in it nothing of sympathy. It was the final sign rejecting humanity, an invisible arrow released from the bow of his lips.

When he tired of looking at the sea, he would take a hand mirror from the desk and look at himself. In the pale, well-shaped face there were beautiful eyes, always brimming with midnight. The eyebrows were thin but proud, the lips were smooth and firm. But the eyes were the most beautiful feature. There was irony in the fact that his eyes should be the most beautiful part of his physical being, the fact that the organ for establishing his own beauty should be the most beautiful.

The eyelashes were long, and the eyes, utterly cruel, seemed at first sight to be lost in a dream.

This orphan, one of the elect, different from other men, had complete confidence in his own immaculateness, whatever evil he might work. His father, captain of a cargo ship, had died at sea, and his mother had died soon afterwards, and he had been taken in by an impoverished uncle. A year in a prefectural training centre upon his graduation from middle school and he was licensed as a third-class signalman and hired by Teikoku Signal.

Tōru knew nothing of the hard calluses built by outrage at poverty, like lumps of amber hardening from sap that oozes through wounded bark. His bark had always been hard. A thick, hard bark of contempt.

The joy of seeing, where everything was self-evident and given, lay only at the invisible horizon, far beyond the sea. Why need there be surprise? Despite the fact that deceit was delivered at every door every morning without fail, like the milk.

He knew his own workings to their smallest parts. His inspection system was flawless. There was no unconscious.

'If I had ever spoken or moved from the smallest subconscious impulse, then the world would have been promptly destroyed. The world should be grateful for my awareness of myself. Awareness has nothing to be proud of but control.'

Perhaps, he sometimes thought, he was a hydrogen bomb equipped with consciousness. It was clear in any case that he was not a human being.

Tōru was a fastidious boy. He washed his hands any number of times every day. Constantly scrubbed at, they were white and dry. To the world he seemed no more than a clean, tidy boy.

He was indifferent to disorder outside himself. It seemed to him a symptom of illness to worry about wrinkles on another's trousers. The trousers of politics were a sodden, wrinkled mess, but what did that matter?

He heard a soft knock on the door downstairs. The superintendent always opened the badly fitting door as if crushing a matchbox and came stamping up the stairs. It would not be he.

Tōru slipped into sandals and went down the wooden stairs. He addressed the pinkish form at the undulant window, but did not open the door.

'It's still early. He might be as late as six. Come back after dinner.'

'Oh?' Frozen for a moment in contemplation, the undulant form moved off. 'I'll come back, then. I have lots of things to talk about.'

'Yes, do.'

Tōru shoved the stubby pencil he had for no reason brought with him behind his ear and ran back upstairs.

As if he had forgotten his caller, he gazed into the gathering dusk.

The sunset would be behind clouds, but it would come at six thirty-three, still more than an hour away. The sea was turning grey, and the Izu Peninsula, for a time out of sight, came dimly back, as if outlined in ink.

Two women made their way among the plastic houses, baskets of strawberries on their backs. Everything beyond was the sea, like unwrought metal. Just in line with the second pylon a five-hundred-ton cargo ship had been at anchor all afternoon. It had left early to save dockage, apparently, and then lowered anchor for a leisurely cleaning. The cleaning evidently finished, it was once more weighing anchor.

Tōru went into the kitchen, which contained a small washstand and a propane burner, and warmed his dinner. The telephone rang. Harbour Control. A message had come from the *Nitchō-maru*, confirming that it would arrive at nine.

After dinner he read the evening paper. He became aware that he was waiting for his caller.

Seven ten. The sea was enfolded in night. Only the white of the plastic houses, like a coat of frost, seemed to resist.

A pounding of light engines came through the window. The fishing fleet had put out from Yaizu to the right, making for the sardine banks off Okitsu. Green and red lights amidships, perhaps twenty of them, moved past, fighting for the lead. The quivering of the lights upon the sea gave visual manifestation to a primitive beating of hot-bulb engines.

The night sea was for a time like a village festival. It was like a rolling mass of festival-goers, each with a lantern in hand, pushing noisily for a dark shrine. Tōru knew that the boats would be talking to one another. Rushing, fighting for the threshold of the sea, dreaming of a huge take, vital and aggressive, fish-scented muscles shining, they would be talking to one another through speakers, out there on the sea.

In the quiet after the stir, the automobiles on the prefectural highway kept up a steady drone. Tōru heard a knocking on the door. It would be Kinué again.

He went down and opened the door.

Kinué, in a pink cardigan, stood in the light. She had a large white gardenia in her hair.

'Come in,' said Tōru, with manly vigour.

Giving him a smile of delicate reluctance such as a great beauty might permit herself, Kinué came in. Upstairs she put a box of chocolates on Tōru's desk.

'For you.'

'You're too good to me.'

A crackling of cellophane filled the room. Tōru opened the oblong golden box and, taking a chocolate, smiled at Kinué.

He always treated her as if she were a great beauty. She took a seat beyond the signal light. Tōru seated himself at the desk. At a fixed and discreet distance, they took up their positions as if prepared to flee down the stairs.

When he was at the telescope he turned out all the lights; but otherwise it was bright from fluorescent ceiling lights. The gardenia in Kinué's hair took on a lustrous white glow. The ugliness beneath was rather splendid.

It was an ugliness that no one could miss. It cut off comparison with mediocre ugliness that could, given the right time and place, become beauty of a sort, or ugliness that revealed a beauty of spirit. It was ugliness, and could be described as nothing else. It was a bounty from heaven, a perfect ugliness denied to most girls.

But Kinué was constantly troubled by her beauty.

'The good thing about you,' she said, worried about her knees and tugging at her short skirt, 'the good thing about you is that you're the only one who never makes a pass at me. Of course you *are* a man, and I can never be too sure. I must warn you. If you ever do make a pass at me I won't come and see you any more. That will be the end. You promise that you at least never will?'

'I vow it most solemnly.'

Tōru raised a hand in pledge. He had to be very earnest in such matters when he was with Kinué.

Every conversation was preceded by the pledge. Once it was made, her manner changed. She threw off uneasiness, her seated figure relaxed. She touched the gardenia in her hair as if it were breakable. She smiled from its shadow, and, with a sudden, deep sigh, began talking.

'I'm so unlucky I could die. I doubt if I can ever expect a man to understand what it means for a woman to be too beautiful. Men do not respect beauty. Every man who looks at me has the most contemptible urges. Men are beasts. I might have more respect for them if I hadn't been born so beautiful. The minute a man looks at me he turns into a beast. How can I respect a man? A woman's beauty is tied right away to the ugliest things, and for a woman there is no worse insult. I don't like to go downtown any more. Every man I pass, every last one of them, looks at me like a slobbering dog. There I am walking quietly down the street and every man that comes up to me has a look in his eyes that says I want her I want her I want her. Every one of them with a look in his eyes that can only be put into those words. Just walking through it all wears me out.

'On the bus just now someone made a pass at me. I hated it.' She took a little flowered handkerchief from her cardigan and dabbed elegantly at her eyes.

'He was a good-looking boy, right beside me. From Tokyo, I'd imagine. He had a big Boston bag on his knee, and he was wearing a visor cap. From the side he looked a little like —' and she mentioned the name of a popular singer. 'He kept looking at me, and I said to myself, Here it comes again. The bag was all soft and white like a dead rabbit. He poked his hand under it so no one else could see, and then stretched out a finger and touched my leg. Right here. On the thigh, and high up on it too. I was surprised, let me tell you. And it was worse because he was such a clean, nice-looking boy. I screamed and jumped up. The other passengers were all looking at me and my heart was beating so, I couldn't say anything. A nice lady asked me what was wrong. I was going to say to her this man made a pass at me. But he was all red and looking at the floor, and I'm too good-natured. I couldn't tell them what had happened. It wasn't any duty of mine to cover up for him, but I said I thought there must be a nail, people should be careful about this seat. Everyone said it was very dangerous and looked very bothered and stared at the cushion. It was a green one. Someone said I should turn in a complaint, but I said it didn't matter, I was getting off at the next stop. And I did get off. My seat was still empty when the bus pulled away again. Nobody wanted to risk it. All I saw was black hair shining under the visor cap. That's my story. I can congratulate myself on not having harmed anyone. I was the only injured party, and I'm glad. That's the fate of a beautiful person. Just accept all the ugliness in the world and hide the wound and die without letting out the secret. That's enough. Don't you suppose a beautiful, well-shaped girl has the best chance of getting to be an angel? I'm telling you, no one else. You can keep a secret.

'Yes, it's true. Only a beautiful woman can really know, and she sees it in the eyes of a man, the ugliness of the world, the way the real shape of a human being gets lost.' Each time Kinué used the word 'beautiful' it was as if she were mustering up all the saliva she had in her and spitting it out. 'It's a beautiful woman that keeps hell at a distance. She gets these nasty things from the other sex and spite from her own, and she smiles and calls it fate. That's what a beautiful woman is. It's really a shame. Nobody knows what a shame. It's a misfortune only somebody as beautiful as she is can understand, and there's not a single person that can really sympathize. It makes my skin crawl when another woman says she wishes she were as beautiful as I am. Those people will never understand our misfortunes. Never. How can they be expected to understand the loneliness of a jewel? But then a diamond is always being washed clean by dirty greed and I am always being washed clean by dirty ideas. If people really knew what it is like to be beautiful, why all the beauty parlours and plastic surgeons would go broke. The ones who think it's good to be beautiful are the one who aren't. Isn't it the truth?'

Tōru was rolling a hexagonal green pencil between his fingers.

Kinué was the daughter of a wealthy landowner. She had been somewhat strange since an unfortunate love affair, and she had been in a mental hospital for six months. She had a curious syndrome described as delirious depression or depressed intoxication or something of the sort. There had been no serious outburst since, and it had settled into a conviction that she was the most beautiful girl in the world.

Because of the delusion, she had been able to break the mirror that so tormented her and fly off into a mirrorless world. Reality became malleable, selective, a seeing of what was desirable and a rejection of everything else. The guiding principle would for most people have been a tightrope inviting almost certain disaster, but it brought her no complications and no sense of danger. Having thrown the old plaything of self-awareness into the garbage can, she had started to make a new plaything of wonderful ingenuity and intricacy, and now she had adapted it perfectly to her needs and set it to work like an artificial heart. When she had finished shaping it, Kinué had attained perfect happiness; or, as she would have put it, perfect unhappiness.

Probably the romantic misfortune had come about when a man made mention of her ugliness. In that instant Kinué saw the light down her only road, the defile open to her. If she could not change her own looks, then she must change the world. She set to work on her own secret plastic surgery and achieved a reversal, and a gleaming pearl emerged from the ugly, ashen shell.

Like a beleaguered soldier finding an escape, Kinué came upon a basic but elusive link with the world. With that as her fulcrum, she stood the world upside down. A most extraordinary revolution. Exquisite craftiness in taking for misfortune what in her heart she desired above all.

His way of holding a cigarette somewhat old for his years, Tōru leaned back and stretched out long legs in blue jeans. He found nothing the least novel in her discourse, but he gave not a sign that he was bored. Kinué was very sensitive to her audience.

He never made fun of her as her neighbours did. That was why she visited him. He felt in this mad, ugly woman five years his senior a comrade in apartness. He liked people who refused to recognize the world.

If the hardness of the two hearts, the one protected by lunacy, the other by awareness – if the degree of hardness was about the same, then there need be no fear of wounds, however much they brushed against each other. Nor need there be a fear of carnal brushes. Kinué was now most off her guard. When Tōru got up with a creaking of his chair and moved towards her in great strides, she let out a shriek and ran for the door.

He was hurrying to the telescope. His eye glued to it, he waved a hand behind him.

'Work to do. Go on home.'

'I'm sorry. I didn't mean it. I really believe you're not like other men, but you caught me by surprise. I've had such awful things happen to me, and when a man stands up all of a sudden I think it's happening again. You must understand that I live in constant fear.'

'It's all right. Go on home. I'm busy.'

'I'll go. But–'

'What is it?' His eye still on the telescope, he sensed that she was hesitating at the top of the stairs.

'I – I have a great deal of respect for you. Well, goodbye.'

'Goodbye.'

There were footsteps and the sound of a closing door. Tōru followed a light with the telescope.

He had glanced out of the window as he listened to Kinué and caught a sign. Though it was cloudy there were lights scattered up and down the west Izu hills; and when the sign of an approaching ship came in among the lights of the fishing boats there came a faint, suspicious change like a spark in darkness.

The *Nitchō-maru* was not due for almost an hour. But one should not trust ships to keep their appointments.

Off in the obscurity, in the circle of the telescope, crawling along like a bug, were the lights of a ship. One cluster became two. The ship had changed direction, and the stern and prow lights separated. To judge from the distance and the lights at the bridge, it would not be a fishing boat of some hundreds of tons, but the *Nitchō-maru*, a good forty-two hundred tons. Tōru already had a practised eye for reckoning the tonnage of a ship from its length.

As the telescope followed them, its lights moved away from the distant lights of Izu and the fishing boats. With grand confidence it pressed forward on its sea route.

It came like shining death, casting bridge lights into the water. By the time he could clearly make out in the night, sketched in port and stern and deck lights, the form of a ship, that special form of a cargo ship, like a complex old ceramic piece, Tōru was at the signal light. He adjusted it by hand. If his signals were too fast, the ship would have trouble making them out, and if they were too full, the southeast pillar of the building might block out a part of them. And because recognition and quickness of response were moreover not easy to foresee, timing was not at all easy.

Tōru turned on the switch. Light leaked faintly from the old blinker. There were binoculars on top of it, like the eyes of a frog. The ship floated upon a round space in the dark night.

Tōru sent out three hallos. Dot-dot-dot-dash-dot.* Dot-dot-dot-dash-dot. Dot-dot-dot-dash-dot.

There was no response.

He again signalled three times.

A dash. It was like an oozing from beside the bridge.

He could feel the resistance of the distant shutter.

'Your name?'

Dot-dash-dash-dot, dot-dash-dot-dash-dot, dash-dot-dot-dot-dash, dot-dash, dash-dot-dot-dot.

After that initial dash, the name of the ship, phantomlike.

Dash-dot-dash-dot, dot-dash-dash-dot, dot-dot-dash-dot, dash-dash, dot-dot-dash, dash-dot-dot-dash, dash-dot-dash-dash-dot.

*Translator's note: the code is that used by the Japanese for the Kana syllabary.

It was the *Nitchō-maru*, without question.

There was a wild restlessness in the long and short lights, as if in among the clusters of solid lights a single light were mad with joy. The voice calling out from afar over the dark sea was like the voice of the madwoman. A metal voice crying out sadly though not sad, pleading an agony of joy. It only reported the name of a ship, but the infinitely disturbed voice of light also conveyed in each fragment the irregularity of an overexcited pulse.

The signals would probably be from the hand of the second mate, on watch. Tōru could sense in the signals from a bridge the feelings of a second mate returning home. In that distant room, heavy with the smell of white paint, bright with the brass of compass and wheel, there would be the weariness of the long voyage and the lingering sun of the south. The return of a ship, battered by winds and its own cargo. A professionalism containing a masculine languor. A trained swiftness, and all the red-eyed intensity of a homecoming. Two bright lonely rooms faced each other across the dark sea. And as communication was struck up, the existence of another human spirit out in the darkness was like a ghost-light in the sea itself. It would have to anchor offshore and come in tomorrow. Quarantine closed at five, and would not open until seven in the morning. Tōru waited until the ship had passed the third pylon. If there were later inquiries, he need only give the hour.

'The ones from foreign ports are always early,' said Tōru to himself. He sometimes talked to himself.

It was approaching nine. The wind had dropped, the sea was quiet.

At about ten he stepped outside for a breath of air to fend off sleep.

There was still traffic on the prefectural highway. The lights around Shimizu Harbour to the northeast blinked nervously. Mount Udo, which on clear days swallowed the setting sun, was a dark mass. There was drunken singing from the dormitory of H. Shipyards.

Back inside, he turned on the weather report. There would be rain and a high sea and bad visibility. Then came the news. American operations in Cambodia had incapacitated headquarters, supply points, and hospitals of the Liberation Front until October.

Ten thirty.

Visibility was already bad, and the lights of Izu had disappeared. It was better, thought Tōru sleepily, than a bright moonlight night. On moonlight nights it was difficult to make out ship lights in the glare of the water.

Setting the alarm clock for one thirty, he lay down on the cot.

4

At about the same time Honda, at his house in Hongō, was having a dream.

He had gone to bed early and, exhausted from the journey, soon fallen asleep. Perhaps under the influence of the pine grove he had seen that day, the dream had to do with angels.

Flying over the pine grove of Mio was not an angel but a multitude of angels, male and female. The dream made good use of what Honda knew of Buddhist writ.

Dreaming, Honda told himself that the writ was true. He was filled with clean happiness.

There are angels of the Six Worlds of Desire and the sentient beings of the several Worlds of Form. The first are the better known. Since the angels in Honda's dream were disporting themselves, the males with the females, it seemed likely that they were from the Worlds of Desire.

They carry lights of seven colours, fire, gold, blue, red, white, yellow, and black. It is as if giant hummingbirds with rainbow wings were weaving in and out.

The hair is blue, the teeth flash white as they smile. The bodies are softness itself, cleanness itself. The gazes are unblinking.

The male and female angels of the Worlds of Desire come constantly up to one another; but the angels of the third world are content to hold hands, of the fourth to exchange thoughts, of the fifth to exchange glances, of the sixth and highest to exchange words.

It would be such a gathering, Honda told himself. There were scattered flowers, there were delicate perfumes and music. Honda was enrapt at this introduction to their several worlds. He knew that, though angels are sentient beings superior to humans, they still have not escaped the cycle of birth and rebirth.

It seemed to be night and yet it was bright afternoon, it seemed to be day and yet there were stars and there was a down-turned crescent moon. There were no human figures if one excepted Honda himself. He wondered if he might be the fisherman who at Mio tried to steal the angel's robe.

Buddhist writ has it thus: 'Male angels are born at the knees of male archangels, and female angels at the shoulders of female archangels; and they know of their earlier places of birth, and they drink at the heavenly stream of sanctification.'

Soaring up, dipping downward, the angels seemed to be making sport of Honda. With arched feet they came within brushing distance of his nose. He traced the white flower-fingers, and those that went behind the neck of the face smiling at him – it was the face of the Thai princess Ying Chan, crowned with flowers.

The angels were taking less notice of Honda. Coming near the dunes by the sea, they dipped under the lower branches of the pines. Honda was unable to take in everything. He was dazed by the whirling glitter. Heavenly flowers of white rained ceaselessly down. The sound of heavenly flageolet and lute. Blue hair and skirts and sleeves and scarves of raw silk, draped from shoulders down over arms, trailed in the breeze. An immaculate white bosom lingered for a moment before his eyes, the clean sole of a foot withdrew into the distance. A beautiful white arm, lighted by a rainbow, brushed past his eyes as if seizing at something. In that instant he saw the hollow of a gently opened finger, and, floating in it, the moon. Rich white arms permeated with a heavenly scent opened wide and soared skyward. The gentle lines of hips, outlined clearly against the blue sky, trailed like wisps of cloud. Then from afar a pair of unblinking black eyes came pressing down upon him, and, with a soft toss of a white forehead, reflecting the stars, the figure plummeted away, ankles raised.

Among the male angels he could clearly pick out Kiyoaki and a stern Isao. He tried to follow them, but, in the constantly shifting pattern of rainbow lights, he could not hold any one figure for more than an instant, however smooth its path.

Looking at the spot where he had seen Ying Chan, he wondered whether time might be more complex in the Worlds of Desire, and, changing form phantasmagorically, the past and the present might occupy the same space. The quiet little tragedy faded wistfully away even as new links seemed to be forming.

Only the pines were of this world. Their needles were etched in detail, the trunk of the red pine against which Honda leaned was rough and hard to the touch.

Honda presently came to find the constant motion irritating and even unbearable. He was still watching, as if from beneath a giant deodar in a park. A park of humiliation. Automobile horns in the night. He watched on and on, reducing everything to a common element, the most sacred and the most sordid of things. He made everything the same. Everything was the same. From start to finish. In deep depression Honda opened his eyes and tore away the dream, as a man swimming in from the ocean might tear away clinging seaweed and fling it down on the shore.

He could hear his watch ticking softly in the hamper at his pillow. He turned on the night light. One thirty.

He feared that he would be awake until daylight.

5

Aroused by the alarm clock, Tōru went by habit to the washstand and scrubbed his hands. Then he went to the telescope.

The cushion at the viewer was warmly, repellingly damp.

He kept his eye a slight distance away. He could see nothing.

He had set the alarm for one thirty against the possibility that the *Zuiun-maru*, due at three, might come in early. He looked again, and saw nothing. From about three the sea came to life. Swarms of fishing boats approached from the left, their motors thumping and their lights fighting for the lead. For a time the sea below him was like a street fair. The boats were hurrying back for the morning market in Yaizu from the Okitsu sardine banks.

He took a chocolate and went to warm himself a bowl of noodles. A call came from the Yokohama signal station. The *Zuiun-maru* had been delayed and would not be in until four. He could have slept longer. He yawned several times. The yawns seemed to force their way up from the farthest depths of his lungs.

Three thirty, and there was still no sign of the ship. To drive away the more and more insistent drowsiness, he went downstairs and outdoors and took long breaths of cold air. The moon should be rising, but it was cloudy and there were no stars. He could see only rows of red lights at the fire escapes of an apartment complex and, much farther off, a blaze of lights around Shimizu Harbour. A frog croaked softly and the first cock caught a hint of dawn in the cold air. The layers of clouds to the north were faintly white.

He came back indoors. It was five minutes till four. The first glimpse of the *Zuiun-maru* drove away sleepiness. The morning twilight was coming on, the plastic strawberry houses were like a snowy landscape. He had no trouble identifying the ship. He aimed the blinker at the red port light and the name promptly came back. In the dawn light the *Zuiun-maru* glided slowly into 3-G.

At four thirty there was a very faint flush over the clouds to the east. The line between sea and land was clear, the water and the reflections of the fishing boats took form and place.

At the desk, in light barely strong enough for writing, Tōru wrote over and over again, to no purpose: *Zuiun-maru, Zuiun-maru, Zuiun-maru.* The light was stronger by the moment. He glanced up, and could make out folds of waves.

The sun rose at four fifty-four. Tōru went to the east window and pulled back the glass to let in the beauty of the last moments before sunrise.

Just over the spot where the sun would rise, delicate clouds drew in deep relief pleats exactly like the folds of a skirt, as if there were a chain of mountains over the sea. Layers of rose-coloured clouds trailed above, with here and there apertures of an ashen green. Below the ridge of mountains clouds of light grey surged up like the sea. The mountain relief caught the rose glow down to its lower skirts. Tōru could almost see dots of houses on the far slopes. Above them was a vision of a rose coming into bloom.

It was from here, he said to himself, that he had come. From the mirage land, visible occasionally through openings in the dawn sky.

The morning breeze was chilly, the groves below the window had taken on a fresh green. The porcelain insulators on the pylons stood out white in the dawn. Eastward and eastward the line of pylons stretched, towards the distant point of the sunrise. But the sun did not come out. Just at the moment of sunrise the rose faded and was sucked up into blue clouds. In place of the vanished rose, clouds scattered like silk threads; but there was no sun.

It finally made its appearance at five past five. From an opening in the dark grey clouds at the horizon, just above the second pylon, came the first glimpse of the sun, carmine, melancholy, as if it were not rising but setting. The top and the bottom were cut off by a screen of clouds, like shining lips. An ironic smile of thin lips rouged in carmine floated briefly among the clouds. Thinner and thinner, fainter and fainter, they left a sardonic smile that was there and not there. The higher stretches of the sky carried a warmer, brighter light.

By six, when a ship with a cargo of sheet iron came in, the sun was astonishingly high, a ball of light dim enough for the naked eye. In its weak light, the sea to the east was a cloth of gold.

Tōru called the tugboat and the pilot's house.

'Good morning. The *Nitchō-maru* and the *Zuiun-maru* have come in. Yes, please.'

'North Fuji? The *Nitchō-maru* and the *Zuiun-maru* are in. Yes. At four twenty, the *Zuiun-maru*, three-G.'

6

The change of shifts came at nine. Tōru left the chocolates for his successor. The weather forecasters had gone astray. It was a beautifully clear day. The sun as he waited for his bus was too bright for eyes that had not had enough sleep.

The road off towards the Sakurabashi station of the Shimizu Railroad had once gone through paddies, but they had all been filled in and subdivided. The bright flats were a tasteless jumble of new shops, like Main Street in an American country town. Getting off the bus, Tōru turned left across a brook. Beyond was the two-storey apartment house where he lived.

He went up a stairway with a blue awning and opened the door at the end of the second floor.

It was as he had left it, neat and tidy, two rooms with kitchen, six mats and four-and-a-half mats, dim behind shutters. Before he opened the shutters he went to turn on the heater for the bath. He had a bath of his own, albeit a small one, heated by propane.

Worn out from looking, Tōru, who had no occupation but to look, leaned against the windowsill to the northwest and looked at the Sunday-morning bustle in the new houses beyond the orange grove. Dogs barked. Sparrows flitted among the orange branches. On south verandas men who finally had houses of their own were sprawled on rattan chairs reading newspapers. He caught glimpses of aproned women inside. The newly tiled roofs were a violent blue. The voices of children were like splinters of glass.

Tōru liked to look at people as at animals in a zoo. The bath was ready. Always after work he had a long bath and scrubbed every hollow of himself. He only had to shave once a week.

Naked, he creaked across the washing platform and got in without washing. No one would use the bath after him. He had set the thermostat, and it had missed by no more than a degree or two. Warmed, he got out and washed at his leisure. When he was tired and short of sleep, a cold sweat came out on his face and at his armpits. He stirred up a good suds and scrubbed industriously at his armpits.

The light from the window slipped down blue-white over his upraised arms and caught the left nipple, beside an armpit now hidden in suds. He smiled. He had been born with three inlaid moles, like the Pleiades. From he did not know when, they had seemed to him like proof in the flesh that limitless bounties were his.

7

Honda and Keiko Hisamatsu were perfect companions in old age. When he went walking with Keiko, everyone took them for an affluent, well-matched husband and wife. They could see each other every other day or so and not be bored. They worried about each other's cholesterol count and haemorrhoids and possible malignancies, and caused doctors much amusement. They changed hospitals with great frequency, suspicious of all doctors. They even had an understanding on trivial economies. They were assiduous students of the psychology of the old, their own aside.

They had even struck a balance in irritability. The one would take on a discreet objectivity when the other was a victim of meaningless irritation, and each fed the other's pride. They nursed each other's lapses in memory. When either would forget what he had just said or say quite the opposite, the other (why it could as easily have happened to him) would politely refrain from laughing.

They were both a little vague on things that had happened these last ten or twenty years; but in ancient matters having to do with family and the like they competed in precision as if reading from a golden record. And often they would become aware of the fact that, neither of them listening to the other, they had been lost in concurrent soliloquies.

'Sugi's father – he was the founder of Sugi Chemical. It's since become Nihon Chemical. His first wife was from an old family in his home town, name of Honji. It didn't work and she took back her maiden name. Then she remarried, a second cousin. She was a nasty one, and she bought a house right beside his in Kagomachi. Then some diviner everyone was talking about – what was his name – anyway he told her the well was in a bad direction. So she did exactly what he told her and put up a shrine looking out from the garden. People came to pray at it in swarms and hordes. It only lasted until the air raids, but –' That was the sort of soliloquy in which Honda came to indulge himself.

And this is the sort of thing Keiko would say: 'She was the daughter of a mistress, and that made her a half sister of Viscount Matsudaira. She fell in love with an Italian opera singer and got disinherited and chased him off to Naples and he ran out on her. She tried to commit suicide. It was in all the papers. A cousin of Baron Shishido's wife, Baron Shishido would have been her uncle, anyhow it was the Sawado family this cousin married into. She had twin boys, and no sooner had they turned twenty than they were killed in traffic accidents one right after the other. They were models for *Twin Buds of Sorrow*. It's very famous. You may have read it.'

The audience was never attentive to this unravelling of genealogies, but that made no difference. Inattention was better than the look of boredom that came with attention.

They had in common an ailment which they wished no one else to know of: old age. Everyone wants to talk about his ailments, and it was clever of them to have found the right listeners. What made them a little different from most couples was that Keiko felt no need for dissimulation or youthful airs.

Fussiness, bias, hostility towards youth, excessive attention to detail, fear of death, indiscriminate irritability, these things Honda and Keiko found in each other, but not in themselves. And when it came to obstinacy, each was provided with a stock that quite balanced the other's.

They were very tolerant of young women and very intolerant of young men. They loved to complain about the young, and the Zengakuren and the hippies did not escape their lances. Smooth skins, rich black hair, a dreamy, bemused look, all of these were anathema, because attributes of the young. It is a sin for a man to be young, said Keiko, and Honda was pleased.

If old age was the reality most unpleasant to have to accept and most continuously to be lived with, then Honda and Keiko had each made the other a refuge from the reality. Their intimacy was not juxtaposition but a brushing past in the rush for a refuge. They exchanged empty houses and hurried to lock the doors behind them. Alone inside the other, each of them would breathe easily.

Keiko thought of her friendship with Honda as faithful adherence to Rié's last testament. As she lay dying, Rié had taken Keiko's hand and beseeched her to look after Honda. She thus saw to her husband's future in the most sagacious manner.

One fruit of the union had been a trip to Europe the year before. Keiko became a substitute for Rié, who had obstinately refused to go. Rié had loathed the thought of travel abroad and, each time he had suggested it, had asked Keiko to go in her place. She knew perfectly well that her husband did not like to travel with her.

In the winter Honda and Keiko went to Venice and Bologna. The cold was a bit trying, but they found the quiet and decay of hibernal Venice enormously to their liking. There were no tourists, the freezing gondoliers had no business, bridges would emerge one after another like ashes of ruined dreams. In Venice was the end at its most beautiful, beauty being gnawed to a skeleton by sea and factory. Honda caught cold and ran a high fever. The swiftness with which Keiko found a doctor who could speak English, the thoroughness of her ministrations, made Honda see that a companion in old age is a necessity.

On the morning his fever abated, his gratitude found expression in boyish embarrassment. 'All this gentleness and maternal affection. I can see why the girls love you.'

'The two are not the same at all.' In fine spirits, Keiko feigned anger. 'I am only kind to friends. To be liked by women I have to be cruel. If the girl I liked best were running a fever like this, I'd have to throw over all my worries and run out on her. I'd rather die than have the sort of arrangement most of them do, living together as if they were husband and wife and taking care of each other in old age. There are plenty of haunted houses where mannish women are living with shrinking maidens of dreadful fidelity. Mushrooms grow in the dampness and that is what they feed on, and they spin soft cobwebs and sleep in them in each other's arms. The mannish woman is always a worker, and so there they are cheek to cheek, figuring out their taxes. No, it's not the sort of romance I want to be part of.'

Thanks to the ugliness of masculine old age, Honda was an amply qualified sacrifice to this dauntless resolution. Such are the unexpected blessings of old age.

By way of recompense, perhaps, Keiko poked fun at Honda because he carried with him a small wooden cenotaph in Rié's memory. He had kept it secret; but when his fever went over a hundred he began leaving final instructions, sure that he was in the last throes of pneumonia. One was that she take the cenotaph back to Japan.

'That sort of love makes a person's flesh crawl,' said Keiko, not at all gently. 'She didn't want to come, and so you dragged her along against her will.'

On the morning of his recovery Honda found the clear sky pleasant, and the tongue-lashing an added pleasure.

It was not clear to him, even after Keiko's ungentle remarks, what he was asking of Rié. She had been a chaste wife to the end, of that he had no doubt; but there were thorns in all the hollows and on all the corners of the chastity. The sterile Rié made always manifest the reservations Honda himself had about humanity. His unhappiness she made her happiness, and she immediately saw what was behind an occasional show of gentleness and affection. Even farmers were taking their wives abroad these days. Given Honda's affluence, his proposal was a very modest one. Her refusal was extraordinarily stubborn. Sometimes she even shouted at him.

'What are London and Venice and Paris to me? I'm an old woman, and what do you expect me to get out of it, being dragged around to places like that?'

A young Honda would probably have been put off by such brusqueness; but the old Honda wondered whether his proposal to take his wife abroad had really had in it any sort of affectionate solicitude at all. Rié had become accustomed to look with suspicion upon evidences of affection, and Honda had fallen into a similar habit. Perhaps his travel plans had embodied an urge to play the role of the virtuous husband. Making everything its opposite, making his wife's resistance into womanly diffidence, her coldness into concealed ardour, he had sought evidence of his own benevolence. And perhaps he wanted to turn the whole voyage into a celebration marking the passage of some stage or other in life. Rié immediately picked out the vulgar motives behind his fabricated benevolence. She pleaded illness, and presently the averred illness became real. She drove herself into physical pain. Travel was out of the question.

Bringing the cenotaph with him was a post-mortem tribute to her honesty. If Rié had seen her husband tucking the cenotaph into his briefcase (the premise was of course a contradiction), how derisively she would have laughed! Today all manner of sentimental affection was permitted to Honda. And the one who permitted it was the new Rié.

On the night of their return to Rome, as if by way of compensation for her services in Venice, Keiko brought to their suite in the Hotel Excelsior a beautiful Sicilian girl she had picked up on the Via Veneto, near the hotel. The two enjoyed themselves the whole night through in Honda's presence.

Later Keiko said: 'Your coughing was wonderful. You weren't entirely over your cold. You coughed all night, the strangest sort of coughing. I can't tell you how wonderful it was listening to that funny old cough while I had that marble body to enjoy in the next bed. It was background music better than the best I could have bought. I felt as if I were doing something or other, I don't quite know what, in a fine, luxurious tomb.'

'You were listening to the skeleton.'

'That's it. I was between life and death. Their intermediary. But you're not to say that you weren't having a good time yourself.' Keiko was quite aware that Honda had come over and felt the girl's foot.

In the course of the trip Keiko taught Honda how to play cards. Upon their return she invited him to a canasta party. After lunch four tables were put up in the parlour.

With Honda were Keiko and two White Russian women. One was old and the other a portly person in her fifties. It was a gloomy, rainy afternoon. Honda could not understand why Keiko, who was so fond of young girls, should invite only old and ageing women to these parties. There were only two men besides Honda, a retired businessman and an elderly teacher of flower-arranging.

The Russian women had been in Japan for several decades; and it was a source of surprise to Honda that their only Japanese consisted of vulgar pidgin uttered in very loud voices. They sat down to cards immediately after lunch. The Russians promptly retouched their faces with rouge and lipstick.

Since the death of their husbands, also White Russians, they had continued to operate a family enterprise manufacturing foreign cosmetics. They were very niggardly, but they did not mind spending money on themselves. Taken with persistent diarrhoea on a trip to Osaka and wanting to avoid the embarrassment of countless trips to the lavatory on the way back, they had chartered a plane, and on their return to Tokyo been taken to a hospital where they were known.

The old woman, her hair dyed brown, was wearing a turquoise pullover and a spangled cardigan, and her pearl necklace was too heavy. She was bent, but the fingers that took up the compact and lipstick were still powerful, so powerful that the wrinkled lower lip was pulled to one side. She was a fierce battler at the canasta table.

Her favourite subject was death. Her last canasta party, she was sure. By the next one she would be dead. She would await protests when she had made her declaration.

The intricate design of the cards scattered over Italian parquetry quite dazzled the eye; and on her powerful finger an amber-coloured cat's eye bobbed over the lacquer faces like a fisherman's float. Crimson fingertips on splotched hands like the belly of a shark that had been stranded for some days on a beach rapped nervously at the table.

With a graceful fanning of cards, Keiko expertly shuffled the two decks. The decks were left face down after each player had received eleven cards, and a single card was left face up beside them. It was the three of diamonds, a sort of lunatic freshness in its red. Honda caught his breath. He saw three moles, stained in blood.

The special sounds of a card game: laughter as of a table fountain, sighs, little cries of astonishment. It was a zone where there need be no inhibitions in such matters as chuckling, uncertainty and unease, the craftiness of old age. It was like night in a zoo of emotions. Cries and laughter came from all the pens and all the cages.

'It's your turn.'

'No, it's yours.'

'Doesn't anyone have a canasta yet?'

'But I'll be scolded if I play out of turn.'

'She's a very good dancer. Go-go too.'

'I've never been to a go-go hall.'

'I have. Just once. Like an insane asylum. Have a look at an African dance some time. It's the same thing.'

'I like to tango.'

'I like the old dances.'

'The waltz and the tango.'

'The old dances are so graceful. These new ones are like spooks. The men and the women all dressed the same. And the colours. Like a nicky – you say?'

'A nicky?'

'You know. All sorts of colours in the sky.'

'Oh, a *niji*. A rainbow.'

'Yes. A *niji*, that's what it's like. Men and women, all sorts of colours.'

'But a rainbow is beautiful.'

'Rainbows will soon be animals too, at this rate. Rainbow animals.'

'Rainbow animals.'

'I haven't much longer. I want just one more canasta before I die. That's all I want, my very last wish. My last canasta, Mrs Hisamatsu.'

'Don't say it again, Galina.'

This curious exchange made Honda, whose hand came to nothing at all, think of waking up in the morning.

What he had seen first each morning since turning seventy was the face of death. Sensing the arrival of dawn in the faint light at the paper doors, he would be awakened by a strangling accumulation of mucus. During the night mucus accumulated into a red-black mass and nurtured its own nightmarish stiffness. Someday someone would perform for him the service of taking it between chopsticks and cleanly lifting it away.

The lump of mucus, like bêche-de-mer, would inform Honda afresh each morning that he was still alive. And with the awareness of life it would bring a fear of death.

Honda was in the habit of giving himself over to a flow of dreams each morning. Like a cow, he would ruminate.

The dreams were bright and sparkling, much fuller of the happiness of life than life itself. Gradually dreams of boyhood and youth came to predominate. In a dream he would taste the hotcakes his mother had made one snowy morning.

Why should a meaningless little episode be so insistent? No doubt precisely because it was a meaningless little episode remembered hundreds of times over a half century. Honda could not himself understand the hold on his memory.

The last traces of the old breakfast room had probably disappeared, so often had the Hongō house been rebuilt. A fifth-year student in the secondary course at Peers, Honda had on his return from school – it would have been a Saturday –

gone with a friend to call at a faculty house, and so proceeded homeward, hungry and without an umbrella.

He usually came in through the kitchen door, but today he went around to look at the snow in the garden. The matting to protect the pines from the winter cold was flecked with white. The stone lanterns were capped with white brocade. His shoes squeaking across the snow, he caught a distant glimpse of his mother's skirt at the knee-high window of the breakfast room. He was at home.

'You must be hungry. Come on in, but brush the snow off first.'

His mother pulled her kimono tight together. Taking off his coat, Honda slipped into the *kotatsu.* As if she were trying to remember something, his mother blew on the embers. She brushed a wisp of hair up away from the ashes.

'Wait just a minute,' she said between breaths. 'I have something good for you.'

Placing a small pan on the embers, she rubbed it with greased paper. She poured neat circles of batter on the hot grease.

It was the taste of those hotcakes that Honda so often remembered in dreams: the taste of honey and melted butter that snowy afternoon. He could remember nothing more delicious.

But why should that one detail have become the germ of a memory he was to carry through life? There could be no doubt that this unwonted fit of gentleness on the part of his severe mother had added to the enjoyment. There was a strange sadness entangled with the memory: the profile of his mother as she blew on the embers; the glow on her cheeks as they lighted up, with each breath, embers that were not permitted to warm the parlour of this frugal house, dusky even in the light from the snow; the play of light and darkness, shadows coming over his mother's cheeks each time she took a breath. And perhaps concealed in the intensity of her motions and the rare display of gentleness was a pain that she had refused all her life to give voice to. Perhaps it had come transparently and immediately across to him, in the full round flavour of the hotcakes, through the untrained young palate, in the sense of affection. Only thus could the sadness find explanation.

Sixty years had gone by, as an instant. Something came over him to drive away his consciousness of old age, a sort of pleading, as if he had buried his face in her warm bosom.

Something, running through sixty years in a taste of hotcakes on a snowy day, something that brought knowledge to him, dependent not on an awareness of life but rather on a distant, momentary happiness, destroying the darkness of life at least for that moment, as a light far out on a dark moor destroys an infinity of darkness.

A moment. Honda could feel that nothing at all had happened in the interval separating the Honda of sixteen from the Honda of seventy-six. An instant, time for a child in a game of hopscotch to hop over a ditch.

He had seen often enough how the Dream Diary kept so faithfully by Kiyoaki had come true. He had had evidence enough of the superiority of dreams to waking. But he had not thought that his own life would ever be so filled with dreams. There was happiness in the dreams that poured over him like floods over Thai paddy lands; but they had only nostalgia for a past that would not return to set against the delicious fragrance of Kiyoaki's dreams. A young man who had not dreamed had become an old man who dreamed occasionally, and that was all. His dreams had little to do with symbol or with imagination.

This chewing-over of dreams as he lay in bed each morning came in part from a fear of the arthritic pains that were certain to follow. With the memory of yesterday's scarcely endurable pain in the hips, the pain this morning would move to his shoulders and sides. He did not really know until he got out of bed where it would be. He did not know while he still lay in bed, flesh withered and bones creaking in the gelatinous remains of dreams, in thoughts of a day that was certain to bring nothing of interest.

It was a chore even to reach for the house phone he had had installed some five or six years before. He would have to endure the housekeeper's shrill morning greetings.

He had kept a law student in the house after Rié's death, but he had soon come to find the youth irksome and sent him away; and since then there had been only Honda and two maids and a housekeeper in the big house. The women were constantly changing. At odds with the slovenliness of the maids and the dishonesty of the housekeeper, Honda became aware that his sensibilities were not up to the modish habits and words of today's women. However diligently they might work, all their mannerisms, up-to-date locutions like 'fun game' and 'well, sorta', a door opened without proper ceremony, a loud guffaw without a respectful hand over the mouth, a mistake in honorifics, gossip about television actors, all of them brought physical revulsion. When in his inability to control it he would let slip a word of complaint, he could be sure that the woman would be gone the next day. He would vouchsafe a complaint to the masseuse he called almost every night, and a domestic tempest would ensue. The masseuse had acquired the fashionable predilection for being called 'Ma'am' and would refuse to answer if not so addressed; but Honda could not do without her.

However frequently he might complain, there was dust on the parlour shelves. The master of flower-arranging who came for a weekly lesson also spoke of it.

The maids would invite errand boys in for cups of tea, and the whisky he valued so highly was being drunk up by he did not know whom. Occasionally he would catch a burst of insane laughter from far down a hallway.

His ear branded by the housekeeper's morning courtesies, he would have trouble bringing himself to order breakfast, and the sticky clinging of feet to the mats in the corridor as the two maids opened the shutters irritated him indescribably. The hot-water faucets were forever getting stopped up, and an empty toothpaste tube was never replaced until he ordered it to be. The housekeeper kept a good enough watch on his laundry and cleaning, but it took a laundry tag scratching at his neck to tell him that that was the case. His shoes were polished but the sand was carefully preserved within, the catch on his umbrella was left unrepaired. He had been unaware of such details while Rié lived.

The smallest tear or scratch and an article was discarded. There were unpleasant scenes.

'You tell me to have it repaired, but there isn't a place in town that would repair it.'

'All right, go ahead and throw it away, then.'

'It's not all that valuable.'

'Whether it's valuable or not has nothing to do with the case.'

There would be instant contempt for his penuriousness in the woman's eyes.

Such incidents made him more and more dependent on Keiko.

Keiko had become energetic in her pursuit of Japanese culture. It was her new exoticism. For the first time in her life she began to go to Kabuki, and she would compare inept actors with famous French actors. She began to learn Nō music and make the rounds of temples in pursuit of Buddhist art.

She was always asking him to go to likely temples with her, and once he had been on the point of suggesting the Gesshūji. But it was not a temple for a lighthearted outing with Keiko.

Not once in these six decades had Honda visited Satoko, Abbess of the Gesshūji. Though he had heard that she was still alive and well, he had not once exchanged letters with her. In the war years and after, he had any number of times been taken by an impulse to call on her and apologize for his neglect; but always misgivings had been stronger, and he had kept his silence.

He had not for a moment forgotten the Gesshūji. But as the years of silence went by, a self-imposed restraint grew stronger, a feeling that the Gesshūji was too precious, that he must not after all this time invade her sanctuary with memories, or look upon her in her old age. He had heard from Tadeshina in the bombed-out ruins of Shibuya that Satoko was only more beautiful, as a spring is more limpid. Nor was he himself beyond imagining the ageless beauty of the ageing nun. He had heard an Osaka friend describe it in awed tones. But Honda was afraid. He was afraid to see a relic of past beauty, and he was more afraid of present beauty. Satoko would by now of course have reached a level of enlightenment far beyond Honda's reach, and were Honda in his old age to visit her he would cause not so much as a ripple upon the tranquillity. He knew that she was beyond being intimidated by memories. But the image of Satoko, safe in indigo armour from all the slings of memory, seemed when he looked through the eyes of the dead Kiyoaki another germ of despair.

And it weighed on him to think that he must visit Satoko as Kiyoaki's representative, bearing memories.

'The sin is ours, Kiyo's and mine, and nobody else's,' she had said on the way back from Kamakura.

Sixty years had gone by and the words were still in his ears. Were he to visit Satoko she would probably after a quiet laugh talk easily about the chain of memories. But the journey was too much for him. Old and ugly and stained with sin as he was, the complications seemed only to increase.

The Gesshūji itself, gently enveloped in a spring snow, was layer by layer more distant, with memories of Satoko, as the years passed. More distant, but not with a distance as of withdrawing into the heart. As he sought to remember it, the Gesshūji was on a snowy pinnacle, like a temple in the Himalayas, its beauty turned to harshness, its softness to a day of wrath. The ultimate in clarity, a moon temple quite at the ends of the earth, dotted a single dot with the purple cassock of an ageing and ever more delicately beautiful abbess, seemed to send off an ice-light, as if it stood at the very limits of awareness and reason. Honda knew that he could be there in no time by aeroplane or express train. But the Gesshūji had become not a temple for a man to visit and look upon, but a ray of moonlight through a rent in the extremities of his consciousness.

It seemed to him that if Satoko was there then she must always be there. If he was chained to eternal life by consciousness then she must be up there an infinite distance from his hell. Doubtless she could see through it at a glance. And he felt that the deathless hell of a straitened and fear-ridden consciousness and her celestial immortality had struck up a balance. He could wait three hundred years, a thousand years, to see her.

He made all manner of excuses, and in the course of time all the excuses in the world came to seem like excuses for not visiting the Gesshūji. He was like a person denying beauty that was certain to bring destruction. His refusal to visit the Gesshūji became more than procrastination. He knew that to visit it had become an impossibility, perhaps the narrowest of the gates in his life. If he were to insist upon a visit, might the Gesshūji not withdraw from him, disappear in a mist of light?

All the same he came to think that, matters of an undying consciousness aside, senility had ripened the moment for a visit. Probably he would make his visit as he was about to die. Satoko had been a person whom Kiyoaki must meet at the risk of his life; and a young and beautiful Kiyoaki calling out still to Honda forbade a meeting unless Honda, witness to the cruel impossibility, gambled his own life. He could meet her if he met death too. Perhaps, in secrecy, Satoko too knew of a time and awaited its coming. An ineffably sweet well of memory flowed over the ageing Honda.

That Keiko should be here with him was a little incongruous.

He had rather strong doubts about Keiko's understanding of Japanese culture. There was something admirable all the same in her expansive half-knowledge. She quite avoided pretence. She went her rounds of the Kyoto temples, and, like artistically inclined foreign ladies stuffed with misconceptions from a first visit to Japan, she would shrill forth her pleasure at objects that no longer interested most Japanese, and arrange them in false nosegays. She was fascinated with Japan as with the Antarctic. She would spread herself out with all the awkwardness of a stockinged foreign lady as she viewed a rock garden. All her life she had known only Occidental chairs.

She was in genuine intellectual heat. She fell into the habit of holding forth with her own peculiar notions about Japanese art and literature, albeit neglecting a detail here and there.

It had long been one of her indulgences to invite the foreign ambassadors in turn to dinner. Now they became the audiences for her proud lectures on Japanese culture. Older acquaintances had not dreamed that Keiko would one day honour them with discourses on gold-leafed screens.

'But they're passers in the night with no sense of gratitude at all.' Honda warned her of the futility. 'They'll go on to their next posts with not a thought left in their heads for this one. What's the point in even seeing them?'

'The birds of passage are the ones you don't have to be on your guard with.

You don't have to worry about ten years from now, and a new audience every night is rather fun.'

But she was taking herself seriously, congratulating herself in a naïve way on furthering international cultural exchange. She would learn a dance and immediately unveil it before ambassadorial guests. It gave her strength to know that her audience was not likely to detect the flaws.

However assiduously Keiko might refine her knowledge, it was not up to plumbing the darkness where stretched the deepest roots of the Japanese. The dark blood springs that had agitated Isao Iinuma were far away. Honda called Keiko's store of Japanese culture a freezer full of vegetables.

Honda had become recognized at the embassies as Keiko's gentleman friend. He was always invited with her to dinner.

It angered him when at one embassy the footmen were in formal Japanese dress. 'Displaying the natives, nothing more. It's an insult.'

'I don't feel that way at all. Japanese men look better in Japanese clothes. Your dinner jacket does nothing for me at all.'

When, at a diplomatic black-tie dinner, the guests would start for the dining room with a gentle stir, the ladies in the lead, and the flowers on the table would throw deep shadows from a forest of silver candlesticks, and outside there would be quiet summer rain, the shining sadness of it all was most becoming to Keiko. She allowed not a flicker of the ingratiating smile so common among Japanese women. There was grand tradition in the grand glowing back of the retreating figure. She even had the husky, melancholy voice of the old Japanese aristocrat. In the company of ambassadors whose weariness was showing through the gilt and of cold-blooded counsellors each with its own special affectations, Keiko was alive.

Since they would be separated at the table, Keiko spoke to him quietly in the procession. 'I brought up *Robe of Feathers*. But I've never been to Mio. Take me there some day soon. There are so many places I've never been.'

'Any time. I've just been to Nihondaira Heights, but I wouldn't mind going again. I'll most happily be your escort.'

His stiff shirt insisted on pressing at his chin.

8

At the opening of *Robe of Feathers*, two fishermen, one of them the deuteragonist, are engaged in conversation. 'The boatmen call out as they make their way up the tempestuous Mio channel.' There comes a description of the journey. 'Suddenly, a thousand leagues off, the friendly hills are enshrouded in clouds.' A fine long robe of silk hangs on the pine at centre rear. Hakuryō starts off with it, thinking to make it his own. The protagonist, the angel, appears. He ignores her pleas that he return it. She is desolate, unable to fly back to the heavens.

'Hakuryō clutches the robe. She is helpless. Her tears like the dew in her jewelled hair, she weeps. The flowers fade, the five signs of the decay of the angel come forth.'

On the express from Tokyo Keiko was humming the prologue. 'And what,' she asks with sudden earnestness, 'are the five signs of the decay of the angel?'

Honda was well informed. He had looked into the matter of angels after that dream. The five signs are the five marks that death has come to an angel. There are variations, depending on the source.

Here is the account in the twenty-fourth fascicle of the *Ekottara-āgama:* 'There are thirty-three angels and one archangel, and the signs of death in them are fivefold. Their flowered crowns wither, their robes are soiled, the hollows under their arms are fetid, they lose their awareness of themselves, they are abandoned by the jewelled maidens.'

And *The Life of the Buddha*, fifth fascicle: 'There are five signs that the allotted time has run out. The flowers in the hair fade, a fetid sweat comes from under the arms, the robes are soiled, the body ceases to give off light, it loses awareness of itself.'

And the last fascicle of the *Mahāmāyā-sūtra:* 'And at that time Mahā gave forth in the heavens five signs of her decay. Her crown of flowers wilted, a sweat poured from under her arms, her halo faded, her eyes came to blink without pause, she lost all satisfaction with her rightful place.'

So far the similarities are more striking than the variations. The *Abhidharma-mahāvibhāsā-sāstra* describes the five greater signs and the five lesser signs in considerable detail. The five lesser signs are first.

As an angel soars and pirouettes it usually gives forth music so beautiful that no musician, no orchestra or chorus can imitate it; but as death approaches the music fades and the voice becomes tense and thin.

In normal times, day and night, there floods from within an angel a light that permits of no shadows; but as death approaches the light dwindles sharply and the body is wrapped in thin shadows.

The skin of an angel is smooth and well anointed, and even if it immerses itself in a lake of ambrosia it throws off the liquid as does the leaf of a lotus; but as death approaches, water clings and will not leave.

At most times an angel, like a spinning wheel of fire, neither stops nor is apprehensible in one place, it is there when it is here, it dodges and moves and throws itself free; but when death approaches, it lingers in one spot and cannot break free.

An angel exudes unblinking strength, but as death approaches the strength departs and blinking becomes incessant.

Here are the five greater signs: the once-immaculate robes are soiled, the flowers in the flowery crown fade and fall, sweat pours from the armpits, a fetid stench envelops the body, the angel is no longer happy in its proper place.

It will be seen that the other sources enumerate the greater signs. So long as only the lesser ones are present, death can still be put off, but once the greater signs appear the issue is not in doubt.

In *Robe of Feathers*, one of the greater signs has already made its appearance, and yet the angel will recover if the robe is returned. It may be imagined that Zeami allowed himself a poetic hint of decay and decline and did not worry about the meticulous letter of the law.

Honda remembered with extraordinary freshness the five marks of decay in the Kitano Scroll, a national treasure he had seen long before in the Kitano Shrine. He had a photographic copy which called up something, a song of horrid foreboding, perhaps, to which he had earlier been deaf.

In a garden blocked off by the beautiful foundations of a Chinese pavilion, crowds of angels are plucking on zithers, beating on drums. But there is no suggestion of vitality, the music has fallen to the dull buzz of a fly on a summer afternoon. Pluck though they may, beat though they may, the strings and skins are slack and tired and decayed. There are flowers in the forward parts of the garden, and among them a grieving cherub presses its sleeves to its eyes.

Death has come too suddenly. Incredulity is written on beautiful, otherwise inexpressive white angel faces.

Within the pavilion are angels in postures of disarray. Some seek ineffectively to cut graceful arcs with their sleeves, some are twisting and writhing. They stretch their hands languorously over finite spaces but cannot touch, their robes are senselessly dirty, filth pours from their bodies.

What is happening? The five signs have come. The angels are as princesses with no escape, caught by the plague in a close, tropical garden.

The flowers in their hair are limp, their inner spaces are suddenly bloated with water up to the throat. The gathering of soft, graceful figures has at some point been pervaded by a transparent decay, and in the very air they breathe there is already the smell of death.

These sentient beings who by the mere fact of their existence lured men into realms of beauty and fantasy must now look on helpless as, in an instant, their spell is stripped away like flaking gold leaf and swept up in the evening breeze. The classically elegant garden is an incline. The gold dust of all-powerful beauty and pleasure drifts down. Absolute freedom soaring in emptiness is torn away like a rending of flesh. The shadows gather. The light dies. Soft power drips and drips from the beautiful fingers. The fire flickers in the depths of flesh, the spirit is departing.

The brightly chequered floor of the pavilion, the vermilion balustrades, have faded not at all. Relics of grandeur, they will be there when the angels are gone.

Beneath shining hair beautiful nostrils are turned upward. The angels seem to be catching the first fore-scent of decay. Petals twisting beyond clouds, azure decay colouring the sky, all pleasures of sight and of spirit, all the joyous vastness of the universe, gone.

'Good, good.' Keiko sounded a full stop. 'You are so well informed.'

Nodding vigorously, Keiko touched a fashionable bottle of Estée Lauder to her ears. She had on pantaloons with a serpentine pattern and a blouse of the same material, a chamois belt reversed at the hips, and a black cordovan sombrero of Spanish make.

Honda had been somewhat startled by the ensemble when he had first caught sight of her at Tokyo Station, but he refrained from commenting upon her chic.

Five or six minutes more and they would be in Shizuoka. He thought of that last sign, a loss of awareness of place. He who had had no such awareness to begin with lived on. For he was no angel.

Vacantly, Honda remembered a thought he had had in the cab that had brought him to the station. He had asked the driver to hurry, and they had taken the expressway from West Kanda. An early-summer drizzle had been falling, he could not have said for how long. They made their way through the rows of banks and brokerages at fifty miles an hour. Huge, solid, the buildings spread great wings of steel and glass. Honda said to himself: 'The moment I die they will all go.' The thought came to him as a happy one, a sort of revenge. It would be no trouble at all, tearing this world up by the roots and returning it to the void. All he had to do was die. He took a certain minor pride in the thought that an old man who would be forgotten still had in death this incomparably destructive weapon. For him the five signs of decay held no fear.

9

There was one matter weighing on Honda's mind as he escorted Keiko to the pine grove at Mio. He feared ruining her good spirits by showing her the utter vulgarity to which this most beautiful of Japanese scenic spots had been reduced.

It was a rainy weekday, but the huge parking lot was jammed with automobiles, and the dirty cellophane in the souvenir shops caught an ashen sky. They did not seem to bother Keiko in the slightest.

'Beautiful. Perfectly lovely. Smell the fresh air and the salt. The sea is so near.'

As a matter of fact the air was strangled with gasoline fumes and the pines were on the point of asphyxiation. Honda felt better. He had visited the place some days before, and he had known what Keiko would see.

Benares was sacred filth. Filth itself was sacred. That was India.

But in Japan, beauty, tradition, poetry, had none of them been touched by the soiled hand of sanctity. Those who touched them and in the end strangled them were quite devoid of sanctity. They all had the same hands, vigorously scoured with soap.

Even at the pine grove of Mio, angels in the empty skull of poetry answered to the unspeakable demands of men, and were forced into myriads and myriads of twists and turns, like circus performers. The cloudy skies were traced as if with a mesh of silver high-tension wires by their dances. In dreams men would meet with only the marks of the decay of angels.

It was past three. 'The Pine Grove of Mio. Nihondaira Prefectural Park.' The rough-scaled bark of the tree was enshrouded in the green of moss. Above a gentle flight of stone stairs, the pines sent rude bolts of lightning across the sky.

The blossoms, veils of green smoke that even the branches of strangling pines will send forth, shut off a lifeless sea.

'The sea!' said Keiko joyously.

Honda did not trust the joy. There was a little of her party manner in it, of flattery for the villa at which she was a guest. Yet exaggeration can spawn pleasure in something that is nothing at all. At least the two of them were not lonely.

Outside a pair of shops, their cantilever shelves bulging with red Coca-Cola cartons and souvenirs, stood a pair of photographer's dummies with apertures for two faces: Jirōchō the boss of Shimizu Harbour, in a pale grove of pines, and Ochō, his lady friend. Jirōchō's name was on the triangle of the umbrella he cradled in his arm. He was in travel dress, with a walking stick, light-blue mittens and leggings, and a hitched-up kimono in narrow blue and white stripes. Ochō had a high chignon, and wore a black satin kimono and an obi of yellow Hachijō plaid.

Honda urged Keiko on towards the grove, but she was entranced by the dummies. She repeated Jirōchō's name over and over to herself. She knew nothing about him except his name, not even the elementary fact that he was a famous gambler; and Honda's lecture on the subject left her yet more entranced.

The nostalgic hues, the fresh, wild vulgarity, quite enthralled her. Wherever she might search in her own life with its distant harvest of the carnal, she could catch no sound so wild and sad in its vulgarity. Her great virtue was that she was without preconceptions. What she had never seen and never heard of was, the last bit of it, 'Japanese'.

Almost angrily, Honda sought to break up her love affair with the dummy.

'Oh, stop it. You're making a fool of yourself.'

'You think the two of us still have the luxury of being fools?'

Serpent-twined legs spread wide, hands on hips, Keiko struck a pose as of an Occidental mother scolding a child. There was anger in her eyes. He had besmirched the poetry.

Honda surrendered. They were beginning to attract a crowd. The cameraman came running up with a tripod and a red velvet cloth. As Honda dodged behind the dummy to avoid curious eyes his face appeared at the aperture. The crowd laughed, the diminutive cameraman laughed, and, though it seemed not entirely appropriate that Jirōchō should be laughing, Honda laughed too. Keiko tugged at his sleeve and took his place. Jirōchō had changed sex, and so had Ochō. The merriment was louder. Honda was drunk. He had known much of peep holes, but he had not had the experience of mounting a guillotine for the pleasure of boisterous masses.

The cameraman took rather a long time with his lens, perhaps because he had become a cynosure.

'Quiet, please.' The crowd was quiet.

Honda's austere face protruded from the low-slung hole over the yellow plaid. Stooped, hips thrust out, he had taken up his pose at the peep hole in Ninooka. Behind the scene of these humiliating antics a subtle quick change took place as, indifferent to the crowd's laughter, Honda confirmed that his whole world hung on the act of observing. He resumed this role, and the viewers became the viewed.

There was a sea, there was a great pine, its trunk roped off: the pine of the heavenly robe. The gentle, sandy slopes leading up to it thronged with spectators. Under the cloudy sky the several colours of their dress were uniformly sombre, the wind in their hair made them look like a rotting upturned pine. There were clusters of people, there were couples off by themselves; and the great white eye of the sky crushed down upon them. And in the wall that was their foremost rank laughter was forbidden. They gazed at Honda with a stony blankness.

Women in kimono, shopping bags in their hands, middle-aged men in badly cut suits, boys in green-chequered shirts and plump-legged girls in blue miniskirts, children, old men, Honda saw them gazing at their own death. They were waiting for something, some occurrence so amusing that it must have its own grandeur. Lips were relaxed in good-natured smiles. Eyes were aglow with a naked bestiality.

'Quiet!' The cameraman raised his hand.

Keiko promptly withdrew her head from the hole. She stood before the multitude stately as a knight commander. Jirōchō, shaking her head, had become a person in serpentine pantaloons and a black sombrero. The crowd clapped. Keiko calmly wrote down her address for the cameraman. Several young persons, having decided that she was a famous actress from an earlier day, came up for her autograph.

Honda was exhausted by the time they reached the pine.

It was a giant pine on the point of death, spreading its arms in several directions like an octopus. Rents in the trunk had been filled with cement. People disported themselves around a tree that lacked even a proper supply of needles.

'Do you suppose the angel was in a swimming suit?'

'Is it a he-pine? Is that why the woman picked it?'

'She couldn't reach the top.'

'Not much of a pine, when you get a good look at it.'

'But isn't it nice they've managed to keep it alive. Just feel the sea wind.'

And indeed the pine leaned more aggressively to sea than a sea-trained pine should have, and the sea scars on its trunk were numberless as on a beached hulk. Towards the sea from the marble enclosure a pair of binoculars stood perched on a fresh vermilion bipod like a tropical bird. The Izu Peninsula loomed whitely beyond. A large cargo ship was passing. As if the sea had set out its wares for sale, a circle of driftwood and empty bottles and seaweed marked the high tide.

'Well, there you have it, the spot where the angel danced the heavenly dance to get back her feathered robe. There they all are getting their pictures taken again. That's the way to do it. Don't even look at the pine, just get your picture taken. Do you suppose they think it makes so much difference that they should be at a spot where something remarkable happened and stay long enough to get a shutter clicked in their faces?'

'You take it too seriously.' Keiko sat down on a stone bench and lit a cigarette. 'It's beautiful. I'm not in the least disappointed. It may be dirty and the tree may be about to die, but it has a spell. If it were all pretty and dreamy the way it is in the play, then it would be a lie. The naturalness is very Japanese. I'm glad we came.' So Keiko seized the lead.

She enjoyed everything. That was her queenly prerogative.

In the vulgarity, as heavy and all-pervasive as a sultry sand-laden wind during the summer rains, she happily, gaily saw her sights, and she took Honda with her. On their return they looked in on the Mio Shrine. At the eaves of the sanctuary, on a rough framed board, was a votive painting in low relief of a newly built passenger ship. Sending out its wake over a blue sea, it seemed exactly right for a harbour shrine. Against the rear wall of the sanctuary was a large fan-shaped board on which was carved the cast for a Nō performance. It had been given six years before in the Dance Pavilion.

'A ladies' day. *Kamiuta, Takasago, Yashima*, and then *Robe of Feathers*.' Keiko was impressed.

In the aftermath of the excitement she picked up and ate a cherry from under one of the trees that lined the path.

'See what I'm doing. I'm inviting death.'

His steps somewhat uncertain, Honda began to regret that vanity had kept him from bringing his stick. Panting and gasping, he had fallen behind when Keiko called out the warning.

Low on the rope that joined the trunks of the trees, numbers of identical signs waved in the breeze.

'Danger. Poisonous insecticides. Do not pick or eat.'

The branches, heavy with fruit from faint pink to blood red, were clustered with little knots of paper that carried prayers and petitions. Some of the cherries had been picked to bare seeds by the birds. Honda suspected that the signs were empty threats. And he knew that a small dose of poison was not enough to carry off Keiko.

10

Was there nothing more to see, was there nothing more to see, asked Keiko. Though exhausted, Honda ordered the driver to go back to Shizuoka by way of Mount Kuno. They stopped before the signal station Honda had seen some days earlier.

'Doesn't it strike you as a rather interesting building?' Honda looked up from the profusion of portulaca at the stone base.

'I think I see a pair of binoculars. What's it for?'

'It keeps watch on ship movements. Shall we look inside?'

Though curious, neither had quite the courage to knock.

They had climbed the stone steps that encircled the base and were at the foot of the iron stairway when a girl brushed past them with a clanging of iron, so near a miss that one of them called out a warning. Kicking up her skirts like a yellow tornado, she passed so quickly that they did not see her face; but she left all the same an impression as of a fleeting distillation of ugliness.

It was not that she had a bad eye or an objectionable scar. It was just that a hangnail of ugliness for an instant obstructed the view and went against all the careful, delicate ordering known as beauty. It was like the darkest of dark, fleshly memories rasping against the heart. But if one wished to view her in a more quotidian manner, she need be no more than a shy maiden returning from a tryst.

They climbed the stairs and paused at the door to catch their breath. It was half open. Honda pushed his way inside. The room seemed empty. He called up the narrow stairway to the second floor. Each time he called he was seized by a violent fit of coughing.

There was a creaking at the top of the stairs. 'Yes?' A boy in an undershirt looked down.

In surprise, Honda noted the blue flower hanging over his forehead. It seemed to be a hydrangea. As he looked down, the flower fell and rolled to Honda's feet. The boy was startled. He had forgotten the flower. It was brownish and worm-eaten and badly wilted.

Keiko, still in her sombrero, surveyed the scene over Honda's shoulder.

Though the stairway was dusky, it was apparent that the boy had a fair, handsome face. An almost disquietingly fair face, it seemed, despite the fact that the light was behind it to send down its own light. The need to return the flower his excuse, Honda carefully but briskly made his way up the steep stairs, his hand against the wall. The boy came halfway down to take it.

Their eyes met. Honda knew that the cogs of the same machine were moving both of them, in the same delicate motions at precisely the same speed. Honda's duplicate down to the finest detail, even down to an utter want of purpose, was there as if bared to a cloudless void. Identical to his own in hardness and transparency despite the difference in their years, the delicate mechanism within this boy corresponded precisely to a mechanism within Honda, in terror lest someone destroy it, the terror hidden in its deepest recesses. In that instant Honda saw a workerless factory polished to a perfection of utter bleakness, Honda's mature self-awareness in juvenile form. Producing interminably without consumers, endlessly throwing away, horribly clean and perfectly regulated for heat and humidity, rustling forever like a flow of satin. Yet there was a possibility that the boy, though he was Honda himself, misunderstood the machine. His youth would be the reason. Honda's factory was human from an utter want of humanity. If the boy refused to think of his own as human – that was all right. Honda rested in the confidence that though he had seen all of the boy, the boy could not have seen all of him. In the lyrical moods of his youth, he had been wont to think the machine the culmination of ugliness; but that was only because a youthful miscalculation had confused fleshly ugliness with the ugliness of the machine within him.

The ugliest of machines, very youthful, very exaggerated, romantic, self-advertising. But that was all right. Honda could so name it today with the coolest of smiles. Exactly as he could name a headache or a pain in the diaphragm. It was nice that the ugliest of machines should have so beautiful a face.

The boy was of course unaware of what had happened in that instant.

Halfway down the stairs, he took the flower. He crushed the source of his embarrassment in his hand.

'Damn her.' He spoke to himself. 'I'd forgotten all about it.'

Most boys would have flushed. It interested Honda that no transformation at all came over the white composure.

The boy changed the subject. 'Is there something I can do for you?'

'Not really. We're tourists, and we wondered if we might have a look around for our edification.'

'Please. Come on in.'

The boy bowed quickly from the hips and laid out slippers for them.

It was cloudy, but the naked outdoors seemed to be sweeping them suddenly from a dark attic to an open moor. Some fifty yards to the south were Komagoé Beach and the dirty sea. Honda and Keiko knew well enough that old age and affluence dispel reticence. Soon they were seated as if at their own verandah on the chairs pushed towards them. Yet the words that followed the boy back to his desk were very ceremonious.

'Go ahead with your work, please, quite as if we weren't here. Would you mind, I wonder, if we were to take a look through the telescope?'

'Please. I don't need it at the moment.' The boy threw the flower into the wastebasket. After a noisy washing of hands the fair profile was bowed over the notebook on the desk as if nothing had happened; but Honda could see curiosity swelling the cheek like a plum.

He invited Keiko to have a look through the telescope and then had a look himself. There were no ships, only a heaping of waves, like a culture of black-green bacteria squirming purposefully under a microscope.

The two were a pair of children soon tired of their toy. They had no particular interest in the sea. All they had really wanted was to intrude for a moment upon a stranger's life and work. They looked around them, at the several instruments echoing the stir of the harbour, distantly and sadly but faithfully, at 'Shimizu Docks' and the name of each dock in large black letters, at the wide blackboard listing the ships in port, at the books ranged on the shelf, *Shipping Ledger*, *Registry of Japanese Shipping*, *International Codes*, *Lloyd's Register of Ship-owners 1968–69*, at the telephone numbers on the wall, those of the agent and the pilot and the customs and quarantine stations and the provisioners and the rest.

All these details had about them, undeniably, the smell of the sea, the light of the harbour some two or three miles distant. From whatever distance, a harbour announces its languorous turbulence in its own sad metallic tones. It was a gigantic, lunatic zither, sprawled out by the sea and sending an undulant image over the sea, sounding and for a time echoing destruction on all the seven giant strings of its docks. Entering the boy's heart, Honda dreamed of the sea.

Sluggishly pulling in, sluggishly tying up, sluggishly unloading – what an endless compromise it was, this trancelike mating of the sea and the land. They were joined in mutual deceit, the ship wagging a seductive tail and pulling coyly away again with a threatening bleat on its whistle, moving away and then coming in again. What a naked, unstable mechanism!

From the east window he could see the confusion of the harbour frozen under a smoky mist, but an unshining harbour was not a harbour, for a harbour is a row of white teeth bared tensely at a shining sea. The teeth of piers eaten at by the sea. It had to shine like a dentist's office and smell of metal and water and antiseptic, with cruel derricks pushing down overhead and antiseptics sinking the ships into a motionless sleep, and perhaps, from time to time, a trace of blood.

The harbour and this little signal room. The image of the harbour taken and firmly impounded as toll, until he could almost fancy that it was a ship grounded high on the rocks. There were more than a few likenesses to a dental office: the simplicity and the efficient disposition of the instruments, the freshness of the whites and the primary colours, the readiness for a crisis that could come at any time, the warped window frames gnawed at by the sea winds. And the watch, solitary in the field of white plastic, carrying on an intercourse almost sexual with the sea, through the day and through the night, intimidated by harbour and ship, until gazing became pure madness. The whiteness, the abandonment of the self, the uncertainty and loneliness were themselves a ship. He felt that one could not stay at it long without getting drunk.

The boy pretended to be lost in his work. But Honda knew that in point of fact he had no work when there were no ships in sight.

'When is the next ship due?'

'About nine in the evening. This has been a slack day.'

He answered with an air of bland efficiency; and his ennui and curiosity came through like strawberries through plastic walls.

It may have been a matter of pride for the boy not to make himself more formal – in any case he put on nothing over his undershirt. In the hot air, still even with the window open, there was nothing unnatural in his way of dress. The fair body, with no fullness of flesh but with rather a sort of botanical slenderness, sent the immaculate shirt down from the shoulders in two circles and thence over the roundness of the stooped chest. It was a body with a firm coolness about it, and no suggestion of softness. The profile, aristocratic eyebrows and nose and lips, was well formed, as on a somewhat worn silver coin; and the eyes with their long lashes were beautiful.

Honda could see what the boy was thinking.

He was still embarrassed about the flower in his hair. He had had no trouble covering the embarrassment as he received his guests, but he was spun up in it as in a swirl of red threads. And since they had of course had a glimpse of the girl's ugliness he had to put up as well with misunderstanding and concealed smiles of solicitude. The cause of it all was in his own magnanimity. It had inflicted an incurable wound upon his pride.

Of course. One could scarcely believe that the ugly girl was his paramour. They were altogether too ill-matched. One had only to look at the frangibility of the earlobes, like the most delicately wrought glass, and at the supple whiteness of the neck to know that the boy was one who did not love. Love was alien to him. He washed his hands industriously after crushing the flower, he had a white towel on the desk, he was constantly wiping at his neck and armpits. The freshly washed hands on the ledger were like sterilized vegetables. Like young branches trailing out over a lake. Aware of their own elegance, the fingers curved haughtily, intimate with the supernal. They clutched at nothing material, and their business seemed to be with the void. They seemed to stroke the invisible, but without humility or petition. If there are hands to be used only for addressing the infinite and the universe, they are a masturbator's hands. I have seen through him, thought Honda.

Beautiful hands for touching the moon and the stars and the sea, meant for no practical work. He wanted to see the faces of the persons who sought to hire them. When they hired a man, they learned nothing from such tiresome details as family and friends and ideology and transcripts of grades and state of health. It was this boy himself they had hired, knowing none of these things; and he was unmixed evil.

Look at it if you will. Unmixed evil. The reason was simple. The insides of the boy were wholly and utterly those of Honda himself.

An elbow against the table at the windowsill, pretending to gaze unblinkingly out to sea, under a natural covering of senile gloom, Honda from time to time stole a glance at the boy's profile, and felt that he was seeing in that glance his own life.

The evil suffusing that life had been self-awareness. A self-awareness that knew nothing of love, that slaughtered without raising a hand, that relished death as it composed noble condolences, that invited the world to destruction while seeking the last possible moment for itself. But there was a ray of light in the empty window. India. India, with which he had had his encounter as he became aware of evil and wanted to flee it for even an instant. India, which taught that there had to exist in response to moral needs the world he had been so intent on denying, enfolding in itself a light and a fragrance which he had no devices for touching.

But his own inclinations all through his long life had been to make the world over to emptiness, to lead men to nothing – complete destruction and finality. He had not succeeded; and now at the end of it, as he approached his own separate finality, he had come upon a boy sending out identical shoots of evil.

Perhaps it had all been an illusion. Yet, after missteps and failures, he could congratulate himself on an ability to see through pretence. His vision, so long as it was not obstructed by desire, did not fail him. Most especially in what did not suit his deeper inclinations.

Sometimes evil took a quiet, botanical shape. Crystallized evil was as beautiful as a clean white powder. This boy was beautiful. Perhaps Honda had been awakened and bewitched by the beauty of his own self-awareness, which had sought to recognize neither self nor other.

Somewhat bored, Keiko was putting on lipstick. 'Perhaps we should go?'

Faced with the old man's equivocation, she took on protective colouring from her dress and began slipping around the room like a great languid tropical serpent. Her discovery was that the shelf nearest the roof was divided into some forty compartments, and each of them contained a dusty little flag.

Drawn to the bright reds and yellows and greens of the loosely rolled flags, she stood gazing up at them for a time, arms folded. Then, suddenly, she laid a hand on the sharp, gleaming ivory of the boy's naked shoulder.

'What are these flags for?'

He pulled back in surprise. 'We're not using them just at the moment. They're signal flags. We only use the blinker. At night.'

He pointed at the signal light in the corner of the room. Hurriedly his gaze returned to the desk. Keiko looked over his shoulder at sketches of ship funnels. He paid no attention.

'May I see one?'

'Please.'

He had been hunched as low as possible over the desk. Now he stood up and moved to the shelf, avoiding Keiko as he might avoid a hot jungle undergrowth. He passed in front of Honda. Standing on tiptoes, he took a flag from the shelf.

Honda had been lost in his own thoughts. He looked at the boy, arms outstretched beside him. A faint sweet smell flooded Honda's nostrils. There were three moles on the left side of the chest, yet whiter, until now covered by the undershirt.

'You're left-handed,' said Keiko, not one for reticence.

The boy darted a glance of annoyance at her as he took down the flag.

Honda had to be quite sure. He came nearer the boy. The arm was folded once more, like a white wing; but at each motion two moles were darkly hidden behind the hem of the undershirt, and a third was exposed. Honda's heart raced.

'What a beautiful design. What is it?' Keiko spread out a flag of chequered yellow and black. 'I'd like a dress made of it. What do you suppose the material is? Linen?'

'I wouldn't know about the material,' said the boy roughly, 'but it's an "L".'

'"L". For "love".'

The boy went back to his desk, now openly annoyed. 'Take your time,' he mumbled, as if to himself. 'There's no hurry.'

'So this is an "L". Not at all what I would expect an "L" to be. Let's see, now. "L" should be a murky green. Black and yellow chequers are entirely wrong. Heavier and stronger, like knights at a joust. A "G" maybe?'

'"G" is yellow and blue vertical stripes,' said the boy, somewhat desperately.

'Yellow and blue vertical stripes? Entirely wrong. "G" is as far from vertical stripes as it can be.'

'I'm afraid we're keeping you from your work. Thank you very much indeed. I hope you won't mind if I send candy or something from Tokyo? Do you have a card?'

Surprised at this rather exaggerated politeness, Keiko put the flag on the desk and went to take her sombrero from the little binoculars at the east window.

Honda laid his card politely before the boy. The boy took out a card of his own with the address of the signal station. 'Honda Law Offices' on the card before him seemed to dispel his suspicions.

'You seem to have heavy responsibilities,' said Honda casually. 'Can you manage all by yourself? How old might you be?'

'Sixteen.' It was a brisk, businesslike answer that deliberately omitted Keiko.

'Very useful work. Keep at it.' Each syllable formal and precise through his false teeth, Honda cheerfully motioned Keiko towards the door and started to put on his shoes. The boy saw them downstairs.

Back in the car, Honda felt too tired to look up. He directed the driver to a hotel on Nihondaira, where he had taken rooms for the night.

'I want a quick bath and a massage.' Then, casually, he said something that left Keiko open-mouthed. 'I'm going to adopt that boy.'

11

Tōru was feeling irritable and restless.

He had idle visitors frequently enough. The building seemed to arouse curiosity. Most of them had children and came in at the children's urging. Tōru would lift them up to the telescope, and that would be that. This pair had been different. They had come as if trying to pry into something, and left as if they had stolen something. Something that Tōru himself had not been aware of.

It was five in the afternoon. Rain was threatening, and darkness came early.

The long line of indigo across the sea was like a great badge of mourning. It gave an air of repose. A single cargo ship was visible, far to the right.

There was a telephone call from Yokohama informing him of a sailing. There were no other calls.

It was time for dinner, but he was not hungry. He turned on the desk light and leafed through pages of ship funnels. They were good for driving away boredom.

He had his favourites among them, and reveries about them. He liked the mark of the Swedish East Asia Line, three yellow crowns on a white circle, and he liked the elephant of Osaka Dockyards.

On the average of once a month a ship bearing the elephant came into Shimizu. The white elephant over a yellow crescent on a black ground was visible from a considerable distance. He liked that white elephant riding in from the sea on its moon.

He liked the Prince Line of London, a coronet with three rakish feathers. When a Canadian transport came in, it seemed to him that the white ship was a gift and the mark was a brisk greeting card.

None of these marks was a continuing part of Tōru's consciousness. When they came within range of the telescope they were with him for the first time. Like bright cards scattered over the world, they had been part of a gigantic game in which he had not been a participant.

He loved only distant images that were no reflections of himself. If, that is to say, he loved anything.

Who and what might the old man have been?

Here in the room he had only been someone for that spoiled, overdressed old woman to bother; but now a separate presence remained behind, that of a quiet old man.

Tired, erudite, intelligent old eyes, a voice so low that Tōru had had difficulty in catching it, a politeness that almost seemed to verge on ridicule. What was he enduring?

Tōru had never before met anyone quite like him. He had never before seen the will to dominate take such quiet form.

Everything should have been old knowledge; and yet there was something in the old man that caught on a corner of Tōru's awareness like a rock snag and would not give way. What might it be?

But presently cool arrogance returned, and he ceased to speculate. The old man was a lawyer in retirement. That was enough. The politeness was a professional manner, nothing more. Tōru detected and was ashamed of a tendency in himself towards rustic wariness.

Getting up to warm his dinner, he threw a wad of paper into the wastebasket, and caught a glimpse of the withered hydrangea.

'Today it was a hydrangea. She poked it in my hair as she left. Yesterday a cornflower. The time before a gardenia. The wanderings of a demented mind? Or have they some meaning? Maybe it's not just her idea. Maybe someone puts a flower in her hair every day and she carries some sort of signal without knowing it? She always does all the talking, but next time I have to ask her.'

Perhaps there was nothing of the accidental or the random in events that took place around Tōru. Suddenly it seemed that a fine pattern of evil was taking shape around him.

12

Honda was silent through dinner, and Keiko was too startled to talk.

'Are you coming to my room?' she asked as they left the table. 'Or shall I go to yours?'

Always when they travelled together they went after dinner to the room of one or the other and talked over whisky. If either pleaded fatigue the other understood.

'I'm not feeling as tired as I did. I'll be with you in maybe a half-hour.' He took her wrist and looked at the number on her key. She found endlessly amusing the pride he took in this little public display of intimacy. He could be amusingly intimate one instant and sombrely, threateningly judicial the next.

She changed clothes. She would make fun of him. But she reconsidered. She saw that she could make fun of him without restraint when the matter was a serious one; but it was a law between them that the frivolous must always be serious.

They sat at the small table by the window. Honda ordered the usual bottle of Cutty Sark. Keiko was looking at the swirls of mist outside. She took out a cigarette. Cigarette in hand, she wore a sterner, tenser expression than usual. She had long ago given up the foreign affectation of waiting for him to light a match. He had always disliked it.

Abruptly she spoke. 'I'm shocked, utterly shocked. The idea of taking in a child you know nothing about. I can think of only one explanation. You've kept your proclivities hidden from me. How blind I've been. We've known each other for eighteen years and I never suspected. I see now. There can be no doubt about it. We've had the same urges all along, and all along they've brought us together and made us feel secure, comrades and allies. Ying Chan was just a stage property. You knew about her and me, and were playing your part. A person can't be too careful.'

'That isn't it at all. She and the boy are identical.' He spoke with great firmness.

Why, she asked over and over again. How were they identical?

'I'll tell you when the whisky comes.'

It came. She had no choice but to await his words. She had lost the initiative.

Honda told her everything.

It pleased him that she should listen so carefully. She refrained from the usual overgeneralized response.

'You have been wise to say and to write nothing about it.' Whisky had produced a voice of smooth charity and benevolence. 'People would have thought you mad. The trust you have built up would have collapsed.'

'Trust no longer means anything to me.'

'That's not the point. Something else you've kept hidden from me is your wisdom. No, a secret as violent as the most violent poison, capable of everything horrible, a secret that makes any sort of social secret seem like nothing at all. You could tell me that there are three lunatics in your immediate family, you could tell me you have sexual inclinations of a most curious sort, you could tell me the things most people would be most ashamed to tell me. It would be a social secret, nothing at all. Once you know the truth then murder and suicide and rape and forgery are easy, sloppy things. And what an irony that a judge should be the one. You find yourself caught up in a ring bigger than the skies, and everything else is ordinary. You have discovered that we've only been turned out to graze. Ignorant animals, out on loose tether.' Keiko sighed. 'Your story has cured me. I think I have fought rather well, but there was no need to fight. We are all fish in the same net.'

'But it is the final blow for a woman. A person who knows what you know can never be beautiful again. If at your age you still wanted to be beautiful, then you should have put your hand over your ears.

'There are invisible signs of leprosy on the face of the one who knows. If leprosy of the nerves and leprosy of the joints are visible leprosy – then call it transparent leprosy. Immediately at the end of knowledge comes leprosy. The minute I set foot in India I was a spiritual leper. I had been for decades, of course, without knowing it.

'Now you know too. You can put on all your layers of makeup, but someone else who knows will see through to the skin. I will tell you what he will see. A skin that is too transparent; a spirit standing dead still; flesh that disgusts by its fleshiness, deprived of all fleshly beauty; a voice that is hoarse; a body stripped of hair, all the hair fallen like leaves. We will soon be seeing all the symptoms in you. The five signs of the decay of the one who sees.

'Even if you don't avoid people, you'll find, slowly, that you are being avoided. Unknown to themselves, those who know give off an unpleasant warning odour.

'Fleshly beauty, spiritual beauty, everything that pertains to beauty, is born from ignorance and darkness and from them alone. *It is not allowed to know and still to be beautiful.* If the ignorance and darkness are the same, then a contest between spirit that has nothing at all to hide them and flesh that hides them behind its own dazzling light is no contest at all. Beauty is only beauty of the flesh.'

'Yes, it is true. It was true of Ying Chan,' said Keiko, light reminiscence in her eyes as she looked out at the mists. 'And that I suppose is why you told neither Isao the Second nor Ying Chan the Third.'

'A cruel sort of solicitude, I suppose, from a fear of obstructing fate. It kept me from speaking. But it was different with Kiyoaki. I did not then know the truth myself.'

'You want to say that you were beautiful yourself.' She cast a sarcastic eye from his head to his feet.

'No. I was industriously polishing the instruments to let me know.'

'I understand. I am to keep it absolutely secret from the boy until he is twenty and ready to die.'

'That is correct. You only have to wait four years.'

'You are quite sure you won't die first?'

'I hadn't thought of that.'

'We must make another appointment with the Cancer Research Institute.'

Glancing at her watch, Keiko took out a small box filled with multicoloured pills. She quickly selected three with her nail tips and drank them down with Scotch.

Honda had kept one thing from Keiko: that the boy they had met today was clearly different from his predecessors. The mechanism of his self-awareness was as apparent as if it lay behind a window. He had seen nothing of the sort in the other three. It seemed to him that the internal workings of the boy and his own were as alike as two peas. It was impossible that such could be the case – and yet, might the boy be that rarity, someone who knows and is all the more beautiful for knowledge? But that was impossible. If it was impossible, then, carrying all the proper marks, the proper age and the three moles, might the boy be the first instance of a cleverly wrought counterfeit set down before Honda?

They were beginning to feel sleepy. The talk moved to dreams.

'I very seldom dream,' said Keiko. 'Even now I sometimes do dream of examinations, though.'

'They say you go on having dreams of examinations all through your life. I haven't had one in ten years.'

'That's because you were a good student.'

But it seemed altogether inappropriate to be talking with Keiko of dreams. It was like talking to a banker about knitting.

Finally they went off to their rooms. Honda had the sort of dream he had denied ever having, a dream of an examination.

On the second floor of a wooden frame schoolhouse, rocking so violently that it might have been hanging from a branch of a tree, Honda, in his teens, took up the answer sheets being passed briskly down rows of desks. Kiyoaki, he knew, would be two or three seats behind him. Looking from the questions on the blackboard to the answer sheets, Honda felt very sure of himself. He sharpened his pencils to chisels. He had the answers immediately. There was no need to hurry. The poplars outside were swaying in the wind.

He awoke in the night and every detail of the dream came back to him.

It had without question been a dream of an examination, and yet Honda had had none of the harried feelings that should go with such dreams. What had made him dream?

Since only he and Keiko knew of their conversation and it was not Keiko, then it had to be Honda himself. But he had not had the slightest wish to dream. He would not have made himself dream without consulting his own wishes in the matter.

Honda had of course read many books on Viennese psychoanalysis; but he could not accept the principle that one's wish was to betray oneself. No: it was more natural to believe that someone outside was keeping a close watch, and importuning.

Awake he had volition and, whether he wished it or not, was living in history; but somewhere back in the darkness was someone, historical perhaps, nonhistorical perhaps, setting him against dreams.

The mists would seem to have cleared and the moon to have come out. The window, a little too tall for the curtain, was shining at the bottom a faint silver-blue, like a shadow of the giant reclining peninsula beyond the waters. So India would look, thought Honda, to a ship approaching from the Indian Ocean at night. He went back to sleep.

13

10 August.

Beginning his shift at nine in the morning, Tōru as always opened the newspaper once he was alone. No ships were due until afternoon.

The paper was filled with stories of the industrial wastes that had floated ashore at Tago. There were some fifty paper mills at Tago, but Shimizu had only one, and that a small one. The prevailing currents were moreover eastward, and industrial wastes rarely came into Shimizu Harbour.

It seemed that the Zengakuren had come in considerable numbers for anti-pollution demonstrations. They were much beyond the range of even the thirty-power telescope. Things beyond the range of the telescope were of no relevance to Tōru.

It was a cool summer.

The sort of summer day was rare when the Izu Peninsula comes clearly forward and thunderclouds boil in a clear sky. The peninsula was in mists, the sunlight was dim. He had seen pictures taken recently from a weather satellite. Suruga Bay seemed to be always half hidden in smog.

Kinué stopped by in the morning, an unusual time. She asked if it would be all right to come inside.

'I'm all alone. He's gone to the main office in Yokohama.'

There was fright in her eyes.

During the early summer rains he had taxed her considerably with the practice of bringing flowers for his hair, and for a time she had stopped coming. Now her visits were frequent again. She had stopped bringing flowers, but the fright and insecurity that were the excuse for the visits were more and more exaggerated.

'The second time. It's the second time, and a different man each time.'

The story began the moment she sat down. Her breathing was heavy.

'What happened?'

'Someone is after you. When I come to see you I always make sure that no one sees me. If I didn't I might cause complications. If they were to kill you it would be my fault, and I'd have no choice but to kill myself.'

'What are you talking about?'

'The second time, I tell you. That's why I'm so worried. I told you about last time. Remember? It was the same this time, but a little different. I went for a walk on Komagoé Beach this morning. I picked some beach lilies and then I went down to the water, and was looking out to sea with nothing very much on my mind.

'There aren't many people on Komagoé Beach, and I do get tired of having people stare at me. I love looking out to sea. I feel so relaxed. I sometimes think that if I put my own beauty on one side of the scales and the sea on the other they'd balance perfectly. So it's as if I'd turned my beauty over to the sea, and had no worries left.

'There was no one there. Just two or three people fishing. Maybe because he wasn't catching anything, one of them kept staring at me. I pretended not to notice, but that stare was on my cheek like a fly.

'I doubt if you can understand how awful it makes me feel. Here it is happening again, I say to myself. My beauty taking off on its own, robbing me of my freedom. It seems like something apart from me, beyond my control. Here I am, bothering no one, just wanting to be left alone, and it's off making trouble. It's a sign of true beauty, I know. But beauty's the worst sort of nuisance when it's off on its own.

'It's excited a man again, I say to myself. I barely have time to think how I hate it, and there it is, all busy tying a man up again. He's been an innocent bystander and now all of a sudden he's an ugly beast.

'I've stopped bringing you flowers, but I like putting flowers in my own hair when I'm by myself. I was singing and I had a pink lily in my hair.

'I don't remember what I was singing. Isn't it odd, when it was just a little while ago. But I think it must have been a sad, faraway sort of song, right for my beautiful voice. It's such a bore. The stupidest song in the world is beautiful when I sing it.

'Finally the man came up to me. He was young, and so polite it made me want to laugh. But there was something dirty in his eyes. He couldn't hide it. His eyes were like glue on my skirt. He talked about all sorts of things. But I was able to protect myself. You needn't worry about me. I was able to protect myself. It's you I'm worried about.

'He tried to confuse me by talking about all sorts of other things, but he kept coming back to you. He asked what sort of person you are, and how hard you work, and whether you are nice to people. I told him, of course. I told him that you are the kindest, most industrious person in the world. One thing seemed to surprise him. When I said you're superhuman.

'I knew by instinct. It was the second time, remember? Almost the same thing happened a week or ten days ago. Somebody suspects something about the two of us. Some awful person who hasn't shown himself has heard about me or maybe seen me from a distance, and he's lost his senses over me, and he's hired someone to spy on me, and wipe out a man he thinks might be fond of me. Insane love is coming nearer and nearer. I'm terrified. What will I do if harm comes to you through no fault of your own, just because I'm so beautiful? There's a conspiracy of some sort, I know it. A conspiracy hatched up by hopeless love. Some man is so rich and powerful that it's terrifying, and as ugly as a toad, and he's stalking me from way off, and he's out to get you.'

Not pausing for breath, she was trembling like a leaf.

One blue-denim leg across the other, Tōru was smoking a cigarette. He was wondering what the point to it all might be. Kinué's dramatic imaginings quite aside, he was certain that someone was investigating him. Who would it be? And why? The police? But he was guilty of no offence more serious than smoking while still a minor.

He would think the problem over by himself; and in the meantime he would help the imaginings by giving them a logical turn.

He spoke solemnly. 'Probably it is as you say; but I would have no regrets at all if I were to be murdered for the sake of a beautiful woman. Somewhere a rich and powerful and ugly man is waiting like a tiger to pounce on someone pure and beautiful. And his eye has landed on the two of us.

'You have to know what you're doing when you fight a person like him. He has his nets out everywhere. The thing to do is pretend you're not resisting and take plenty of time and seek out his weak points. The thing is to muster your strength and strike when you know what his weak points are.

'You must never forget for a moment that pure beauty is the enemy of the human race. His great advantage is that he has the whole race on his side. He won't let up for a minute until we've knelt down and admitted that we're human beings too. And so when the time comes we have to give in and pray to his gods. Unless we pray like mad he'll murder us. And when we do he'll relax and let us see his weak points. We have to hold out till it happens, all the while hanging on to our own self-respect.'

'I understand perfectly. I'll do exactly as you say. But you must help me. This poisonous beauty of mine has me always feeling that I might stumble and fall. If the two of us go together hand in hand, why, we might wash the whole human race clean. And then the world would be a paradise, and we'd have nothing more to be afraid of.'

'Exactly. Everything is all right.'

'I like you better than anyone else in the world.' She blurted out the words as she backed through the door.

Tōru always enjoyed her absence. When such ugliness became absent, how did it differ from beauty? Since the beauty which had been the premise for the whole conversation was itself absent, Kinué continued to pour forth fragrance after she was gone.

It sometimes seemed to him that beauty was crying in the distance. Just beyond the horizon, perhaps. It called out in a high voice, like a crane's. The call echoed and disappeared. If it took human form, it did so for but an instant. Only Kinué, a snare of ugliness, had captured the crane. And had long been feeding it with self-awareness.

The *Kōyō-maru* came in at three eighteen in the afternoon. No other ship was due until seven. Including nine ships awaiting berths, there were twenty ships in Shimizu Harbour.

Offshore in Third Area were the *Nikkei-maru II*, the *Mikasa-maru*, the *Camellia*, the *Ryūwa-maru*, the *Lianga Bay*, the *Umiyama-maru*, the *Yōkai-maru*, the *Denmark-maru*, and the *Kōyō-Maru*.

At the Hinode Pier, the *Kamishima-maru* and the *Karakasu-maru*.

At the Fujimi Pier, the *Taiei-maru*, the *Hōwa-maru*, the *Yamataka-maru*, and the *Aristonikos*.

On buoys at Orito, a lumber port, the *Santen-maru*, the *Donna Rossana*, and the *Eastern Mary*.

Because of the danger, a single tanker, the *Okitama-maru*, was at a pipe in the Dolphin Area, reserved for tankers. It was on the point of sailing.

Large tankers with crude oil from the Persian Gulf anchored in the Dolphin Area, smaller tankers with refined oil could come into the Sodeshi Dock, at which there was a single ship, the *Nisshō-maru*.

A rail spur led from Shimizu Station past a number of berths and lonely customs warehouses deflecting the intense summer light, and deeper into the summer grasses, where from between warehouses the light on the sea told in derision of the end of land, and yet on and on as if it were meant for casting old steam engines into the sea. Then, suddenly, the crooked, rusty track came out upon the shining sea, and at its terminus was what is called the Railroad Dock. It was host to no ships at all.

Tōru had just entered the *Kōyō-maru* on the register for the Third Area.

It was anchored offshore, and loading operations would have to wait until the next day. There was no great urgency in sending out word of its arrival. At about four there came a call asking if it had in fact arrived.

At four there was a call from a pilot. Eight pilots worked in shifts, and the call was to inform him of the next day's assignments.

*

Time heavy on his hands, Tōru gazed out to sea through the telescope.

But as he gazed the uncertainty and the phantom of evil brought by Kinué came back to him. It was as if a dark filter had been slipped over the lens.

Indeed it was as if a dark filter had lain over the whole of this summer. Subtly, evil had come over the light, to dim the radiance and to thin the strong shadows of summer. The clouds lost their sharp outlines, the sea was a blank, the Izu Peninsula invisible on the steely blue-black of the horizon. The sea was a dull, monotonous green. Slowly, the tide was coming in.

Tōru lowered the telescope to the waves on the beach.

As they broke, a spray like the dregs of the sea slipped from their backs, and the pyramids of deep green changed, rose and swelled into an uneasy white. The sea lost its serenity.

Even as it rose it broke at the skirts, and ragged spots of white from its high belly like a call of inexpressible sorrow became a sharply smooth yet infinitely cracked wall of glass, like a vast spray. As it rose and broke, the forelocks were combed a beautiful white, and as it fell it showed the neatly arrayed blue-white of its crown, and the lines of white became a solid field of white; and so it fell, like a severed head.

The spread and the falling away of foam. Little patches of foam trailing off to sea like lines of water bugs.

Foam trailing off over the sand like sweat from the back of an athlete at the end of his exertions.

What delicate changes passed over the white monolith of the sea as it came in upon the shore and broke. The myriad confusion of thin waves and the fine partings of the foam became in desperation an infinity of lines spewed out over the sea as from silkworms. What a subtle evil, overcoming by sheer force even as it took itself this delicate white.

Four fifteen.

The sky in its upper reaches was blue. It was an affected, pompous sort of blue. He had seen a similar blue in the library, in a collection from the School of Fontainebleau. Composed all lyrically with just an apology for clouds, it was not a summer sky at all. It was laid over with a saccharine hypocrisy.

The lens had left the shore, and was turned on the sky, the horizon, the sea.

It caught a sheet of spray that seemed to hurl itself into the very heavens. What could it be up to, this single point of foam flinging itself above the rest? Why had it been elected?

Nature was a cycle, the whole to the fragment, the fragment back to the whole. Compared to the fleeting cleanness of the fragment, the whole was dark and sullen.

And was evil a matter of the whole?

Or of the fragment?

Four forty-five. Not a ship in sight.

The beach was lonely. There were no swimmers, and only two or three anglers. The sea without ships was worlds away from dedication and service. Suruga Bay lay utterly sober, without love and without joy. There had to be ships sliding in and out, cutting razor lines of white through this sluggish, flawless perfection. A ship was a weapon of cool contempt against the perfection, gliding over the thin taut skin of the sea and wounding it. Yet going no deeper than the surface.

Five o'clock.

The white of the waves become for an instant the colour of a yellow rose, to tell that evening approached.

He saw two black tankers, large and small, making for sea to the left. The fifteen-hundred-ton *Okitama-maru*, which had left Shimizu at four twenty, and the three-hundred-ton *Nisshō-maru*, at four twenty-three.

They were like mirages in the mist. Not even their wakes were distinct.

He lowered the lens to the shore.

As they took on the colour of evening, the waves were stern and hard. The light had more and more the colour of evil, the bellies of the waves were uglier.

Yes. The waves as they broke were a manifest vision of death. It seemed to him that they had to be. They were mouths agape at the moment of death.

Gasping in agony, they trailed numberless threads of saliva. Earth purple in the twilight became a livid mouth.

Into the gaping mouth of the sea plunged death. Showing death nakedly time and time again, the sea was like a constabulary. It swiftly disposed of the bodies, hiding them from the public gaze.

Tōru's telescope caught something it should not have.

He suddenly felt that a different world was being dragged forth from those gaping jaws. Since he was not one to see phantasms, there could be no doubt that it existed. But he did not know what it was. Perhaps it was a pattern drawn by micro-organisms in the sea. A different world was revealed in the light flashing from the dark depths, and he knew it was a place he had seen. Perhaps it had something to do with immeasurably distant memories. If there was such a thing as a previous life, then perhaps this was it. And what would its relation be to the world Tōru was constantly looking for, a step beyond the bright horizon? If it was a dance of seaweed caught in the belly of the breaking waves, then perhaps the world pictured in that instant was a miniature of the mucous pink and purple creases and cavities of the nauseous depths. But there had been rays and flashes – from a sea run through by lightning? Such a thing was not probable in this tranquil twilight sea. There was nothing demanding that *that* world and *this* world be contemporary. Was the world he had had a glimpse of in a different time? Was it of a time different from that measured by his watch?

He shook his head. As he fled the unpleasant sight, the telescope too became unpleasant. He moved to the fifteen-power binoculars in another corner of the room. He followed the great hull of the ship leaving the harbour.

It was the *Yamataka-maru* of the Y.S. Line, 9,183 tons, bound for Yokohama.

'A Yamashita ship has just left, bound in your direction. *Yamataka, Yamataka.* It's now seventeen twenty.'

Having telephoned his message to the main office in Yokohama, he returned to the binoculars and once more followed the *Yamataka-maru*, its masts now disappearing into the mist.

The mark was a single black line near the top of a persimmon-coloured ground. Y.S. LINE in large black letters on the hull. White bridge, red cranes. The ship was in desperate flight from the circle in the telescope. Sending white lines from its prow, it moved out to sea.

It was gone.

There were bonfires in what had been strawberry patches below the window.

The plastic shelters which had until about the end of the summer rains covered the whole expanse had all been taken away. The strawberry season was past. Cuttings for forced cultivation were off at the fifth station of Fuji welcoming a man-made winter. They would return late in October, to be ready for the Christmas market.

People were working among the foundations and on black paddies from which even the foundations had been removed.

Tōru went to get dinner.

He had a simple dinner at his desk. It was nightfall.

Five forty.

A half moon came from the clouds, high in the southern sky. Another moment and the half moon, like an ivory comb dropped down into the sky, was indistinguishable from a cloud.

The pines along the sea were black. It was already dark enough to make out the red tail-lights of the anglers' cars parked on the beach.

Children were swarming over the road through the strawberry patches. Strange children of the evening. Weird children, coming out into the dusk from nowhere, cavorting insanely through the fields.

The bonfires sent up tongues of flame beyond.

Five fifty.

Tōru glanced up. He caught a ship mark quite indistinguishable to the ordinary naked eye, and reached for the telephone. Such was his confidence that his hand went for the telephone even before he had verified the mark.

The ship's agent answered.

'Hello? This is Teikoku Signal. The *Daichū*. I've just sighted it.'

It was like a smudge drawn by a dirty finger across faint pink on the southwest horizon. As if examining a fingerprint on the glass, he picked it out and identified it.

The register told him that the *Daichū-maru*, 3,850 tons, was a lauan transport, one hundred metres long, speed 12.4 knots. The only ships capable of more than twenty knots were international freighters. Lumber ships were slower.

He felt particularly close to the *Daichū-maru*. It had been launched the spring before from the Kanazashi Shipyards here in Shimizu.

Six.

In the pink offing, the dim form of the *Daichū-maru* was edging past the *Okitama-maru*, leaving the harbour. It was a strange moment when an image oozes from a dream into everyday life, an actuality from an abstraction – a poem becomes corporate, a fantasy an object. If something meaningless yet ominous is through some process taken into the heart, there is born in the heart an urgency to give it shape, and so a something comes to exist. Perhaps the *Daichū-maru* was born of Tōru's heart. An image indistinct as the sweep of a brush had become a gigantic hull of some four thousand tons. And the same thing was forever happening, somewhere in the world.

Six ten.

Foreshortened by the angle of its approach, it raised its two derricks like the horns of a great black beetle.

Six fifteen.

It was quite clear now to the naked eye, but it hesitated black on the horizon like an object forgotten on a shelf. The distance was accordioned, and it stayed on and on, a black beetle left on the shelf of the horizon.

Six thirty.

Through the lens, diagonally, he could see the funnel mark, a red 'N' in a circle on a white ground. He could make out piles of lauan.

Six fifty.

Now broadside in the channel, the *Daichū-maru* was showing red mast lights against a cloudy twilight sky which no longer held a moon. It slipped past the *Okitama*, making its miragelike way out to sea. There was a considerable distance between them, but the lights were caught in foreshortened perspective; and it was as if, out on the dark sea, the embers of two cigarettes were brushing and parting.

In from a foreign port, the *Daichū-maru* had two great iron rails on its deck to keep the lauan from falling overboard. In such quantities that the waterline was not showing, great trunks burned by the tropical sun lay piled one on another, like the bundled corpses of huge, powerful brown slaves.

Tōru thought of the new regulations for waterlines, junglelike in their details. Waterlines for lumber vessels were of six varieties, summer, winter, winter North Atlantic, tropical, freshwater summer, and freshwater tropical. The tropical category was further divided into tropical by zone and tropical by season. The *Daichū-maru* fell into the former, and under the 'special regulations for deck lumber transport'. Tōru had memorized with fascination the lines that define the tropical zone.

From the east coast of North America along the thirteenth parallel east to sixty degrees west longitude; thence directly to ten degrees north by fifty-eight degrees west; thence along the tenth parallel to twenty degrees west; thence along the twentieth meridian to thirty degrees north; thence to the west coast of Africa ... thence to the west coast of India ... to the east coast of India ... to the west coast of Malaya ... thence along the southeast coast of Asia to the tenth parallel on the coast of Vietnam ... from Santos ... the east coast of Africa to the west coast of Madagascar ... the Suez Canal ... the Red Sea, Aden, the Persian Gulf.

An invisible line was drawn from continent to continent and ocean to ocean and what was within was named 'tropical', and so, suddenly, a 'tropical' made its appearance, with its coconuts, its reefs, its cobalt seas, its storm clouds, its squalls, the screams of its multicoloured parrots.

Trunks of lauan, splashed with the scarlet and gold and green labels of the tropics. Heaped-up logs of lauan: they had been wet by tropical rains and they had reflected warm starlit skies, they had been attacked by waves and eaten by the shining bugs of the deep; and they could not dream that they were headed at the end of the journey for the boredom of everyday life.

Seven.

The *Daichū-maru* passed the second pylon. The lights of the harbour were aglow.

Since it had come in at an odd hour, quarantine and unloading would have to wait until the next morning. Even so, Tōru made the usual calls: the pilot, the police, the harbour superintendent, the agent, the provisioners, the laundry.

'The *Daichū* is coming into three-G.'

'Hello? This is Teikoku Signal. The *Daichū* is coming into three-G. The cargo? The line is barely showing.'

'Shimizu Provisioners? This is Teikoku Signal. Thank you for everything. The *Daichū* has just come into three-G. It's off the Mio lighthouse at the moment.'

'Shizuoka Police? The *Daichū* is coming in. Tomorrow at seven, if you will, please.'

'The *Daichū*. *D-a-i-c-h-ū*. Yes, if you will, please.'

14

Off duty on an evening in late August, Tōru had finished his dinner and bath. He went out to take the cool of the south wind under the blue awning of the veranda, still warm from the heat of the day. There were doors all along the shabby veranda, which he reached by iron stairs.

Immediately to the south was a lumber yard more than a hundred yards square, its huge cross-section dark under lights. The lumber sometimes seemed to Tōru like a great silent beast.

There was a crematory in the grove beyond. Tōru would like to have seen a flame that could show itself in the smoke from such an enormous chimney. He never had.

The summit of the dark mountain to the south was Nihondaira. He could see the streams of automobile lights on the road leading up to it. There were clusters of hotel lights, and the red lights of television towers.

Tōru had not been to the hotels. He knew nothing of the affluent life. He did know that wealth and virtue were incompatible, but he had no interest in making the world virtuous. Revolution could be left to others. There was no concept for which he had a greater dislike than equality.

He was about to go inside when a Corona pulled up at the stairs. He could not make out the details, but he was sure he had seen it before. He was startled when the superintendent got out.

A large envelope clutched in his hand, the superintendent lurched up the stairs, as he always did when he came to the signal station.

'Yasunaga is it? Good evening. I'm glad I caught you at home. I've brought something to drink. Let's have a drink and a talk.' He did not mind being overheard.

Overwhelmed by this unique visit, Tōru reached for the door behind him.

'You're very neat.' The superintendent seated himself on the cushion Tōru offered, and, wiping at his forehead, looked around him.

The building had been finished only the year before. It was as if the dust had not been allowed to gather. There was a maple-leaf pattern on the frosted glass of the aluminium-sashed windows, inside which were paper doors. The walls were lavender, the wood of the ceiling was of almost too good a grain, waist-high at the door was a frosted pane with a bamboo pattern, and the doors between the rooms too were decorated in unusual patterns. The tastes of the occupant demanded the newest wares.

The rent was twelve thousand five hundred yen a month, and two hundred fifty yen besides went each month into a common maintenance fund. Tōru thanked the superintendent for the half of the rent paid by the company.

'But aren't you lonely, all by yourself?'

'I'm used to being alone. I'm alone at the station too.'

'That's true, of course.'

The superintendent took a bottle of Suntory Square from his bag, and side dishes as well, shredded cuttlefish and prawn crackers. If Tōru had no glasses, he said, cups would do as well.

Something unusual was afoot. It was not the superintendent's practice to come calling upon subordinates thus provisioned. The visit could mean no good. Since Tōru had nothing to do with the accounts, it was not likely that he was about to be charged with fiscal venalities; but he must have made a grievous blunder without himself being aware of it. And here was the superintendent pressing liquor upon the boy he had scolded for his addiction to tobacco. Tōru was reconciled to dismissal; but he knew well enough that, even without a labour union, it was a world in which industrious young men were not to be treated roughly, though they might be no more than signalmen third class. There were plenty of other jobs, if he took the trouble to look for them. In control of himself once more, he glanced at the superintendent with something like pity. He was confident that he could meet with dignity whatever came, even if it be notice of his dismissal. Whatever his adversary might think, Tōru knew that he was a jewel not easily come by.

Refusing the whisky the superintendent pressed upon him, Tōru sat in an airless corner, his beautiful eyes alight.

He might be alone in the world, but he lived in a small castle of ice, quite free of the ambition and greed and lust upon which people lose their step. Because he disliked comparing himself with others, he was quite free from envy and jealousy. Because he had cut off the road to mundane harmony from the outset, he quarrelled with no one. He let people think of him as a gentle, harmless, cuddly white bunny. The loss of a job was the smallest triviality.

'I had a call from the main office the other day.' The superintendent was drinking to build up courage. 'I wondered what it might mean, and it turned out to be a summons from the president himself. Let me tell you I was surprised. I went into his office wondering what would come next, and I have to admit that I was shaking in spite of myself. And there he was, all smiles. Have a seat, he said. I knew the news wasn't going to be bad, but it turned out not to be good and not to be bad either as far as I myself was concerned. What do you think it was? Well, it had to do with you.'

Tōru's eyes were fixed on him. The news proved to be quite beyond his imagining. Dismissal had nothing to do with the case.

'Wasn't I surprised, though. It had come through an older man who had done a great deal for the president. There's someone who wants to adopt you. And it's up to me to make you agree, even if I have to force you. That's quite a responsibility, coming from the president himself. Someone's put a high price on you. Or it might be that someone knows a good article when he sees it.'

An intimation came to Tōru. It had to be the elderly lawyer who had left his calling card.

'I should imagine his name is Honda.'

'That's right. How did you know?' The superintendent was astonished.

'He came once to look at the station. But it seems odd that he should want to adopt me after just the one time.'

'It seems that he's made two or three very careful investigations.'

Tōru frowned. He remembered the tidings from Kinué. 'Not a very pleasant sort of thing to do to a person.'

The superintendent hurried on in some confusion. 'But it's all right. He found out that you're a model young man. Not a mark against you.'

It was not so much the elderly lawyer Tōru was thinking of. It was that spoiled, Westernized old woman, from a world utterly alien to Tōru, spreading her scaly powder like a gaudy moth.

The superintendent kept Tōru awake until eleven thirty. Sometimes, his knees in his arms, Tōru would doze off; but the superintendent, now in his cups, would shake him and go on talking.

The man was a wealthy and famous old widower. He saw that it would far better serve the interests of the Honda family and of Japan to adopt a truly talented and willing young man than to take in a dolt from a high-placed family. He would hire tutors as soon as the adoption had been accomplished, to put Tōru into the best preparatory school and university. The prospective father rather hoped that Tōru would choose law or business, but the final choice must of course be his own, and the father would be quite unstinting with his help. He did not have long to live, but there were no family complications, and the whole of his estate would go to Tōru. Could any proposal be more attractive?

But why? The question tickled at Tōru's self-respect.

The other person had jumped over something. It corresponded, by wonderful coincidence, to something Tōru himself had jumped over. It seemed to the other and to Tōru himself that the irrationality of it all was natural; and the ones who had been taken in were the common-sense ones in between, the president and the others.

The news came to Tōru as nothing to be surprised by at all. He had been prepared for a curious denouement the moment he had met the quiet old man. He was confident that no one would find him out, but the faculty of not being caught by surprise had given him the confidence to pass generous judgement on wholly outrageous mistakes about himself and to swallow the results. If in the end they came to nonsense, they were the results of beautiful error. If a confusion in the world's awareness was taken to be a self-evident premise, then anything could follow. The view that all the benevolence and malevolence directed at him were based upon error brought a blinding of self-respect, and self-denial as the final conclusion to cynicism.

Tōru had only contempt for inevitability, and to him volition was nothing. If he imagined himself caught up in an antiquated comedy of errors, he had ample reason. There could be no doubt that nothing was more ridiculous than the anger of a volitionless person who thought his volition was being trampled on. If he behaved in a coolly rational manner, then to say that he had no particular wish to become an adopted son amounted to the same thing as saying that he was quite prepared to become an adopted son.

Most people would immediately have become suspicious of the inadequate reasons offered. But that was a matter of weighing the appraisal of another against one's self-esteem, a road which Tōru's thoughts did not choose to travel. He compared himself with no one. In the measure, indeed, that the proposal was child's play lacking inevitability and became something very like the whim of an old man, the element of the inescapable grew more tenuous, and the proposal easier for Tōru to accept. A person without fate or destiny is not bound by the inescapable.

The proposal came, in sum, to aims masking themselves as educational endeavour.

An ordinarily proud and high-spirited boy could have said: 'I'm no beggar.'

But that sort of protest had about it the smell of boys' magazines. Tōru had the more enigmatic weapon of a smile. He accepted by denying.

As a matter of fact, the play of light, when he investigated his enigmatic smile in a mirror, sometimes made it seem like that of a young girl. Perhaps a young girl in some distant land, speaking some incomprehensible language, had just such an enigmatic smile as her only route of communication. He did not wish to be understood as saying that the smile was girlish. Yet it was not a man's smile. It had in it a quality as of a bird waiting in its nest at the most delicate moment, free of either coquetry or timidity, between hesitation and resolution, preparing because of an adversary for a crisis as of walking a dark path. Between dark and dawn, neither road nor hill could be made out, and each step might mean drowning. It sometimes seemed to Tōru that it was a smile he had inherited from neither of his parents, but acquired rather from a young girl, a stranger, he had met in his distant youth.

Nor was it conceit that made him think so. He could see himself from corner to corner and the confidence that the most perceptive of persons could not see him as he saw himself was the basis of his self-respect; and so long as it was to the Tōru seen by others, the offer of alms was an offer to a shadow of the real Tōru, quite incapable of wounding his self-respect. Tōru was secure.

But were the motives of the man so incomprehensible? There was nothing in the least incomprehensible about them. Tōru understood perfectly. The victim of boredom is quite capable of selling a world to a rag-picker.

*

His knees in his arms, Tōru was nodding sleepily. He had made up his mind. But good manners demanded that he defer his assent until the superintendent could be a little prouder of the sweat he had expended.

He was happier than ever with his faculty for not dreaming. He had lighted mosquito repellent for the benefit of the superintendent, but the mosquitoes were at his own feet and ankles. The itching shone through his drowsiness like moonlight. He thought vaguely that he must again wash the hands with which he was scratching.

'Well, I'm afraid you're sleepy. You have every right to be. The night's practically over. Dear me. Eleven thirty already. I've stayed much too long. So the story sounds good to you? You agree?' As he stood up to leave, the superintendent laid a persuasive hand on Tōru's shoulder.

Pretending to have awakened only now, Tōru said: 'Yes. I agree.'

'You agree?'

'I agree.'

'Thank you, thank you. I'll take care of everything else. Think of me as your father. All right?'

'Yes. I'd be very grateful if you would.'

'But it will be a loss for the station, letting a good boy like you go.'

He was far too drunk to drive. Tōru went for a taxi and saw him home.

15

Tōru was off duty the next day. He spent the day at a movie and watching the ships in the harbour. He was on duty from nine the next morning.

After a number of typhoons, the late-summer sky for the first time displayed summery clouds. He was more attentive than usual to the clouds, thinking that this would be his last summer at the station.

The sky that evening was beautiful. Lines of cloud hovered over the ocean like the god of storms himself.

But the grand, orange-tinted forest of clouds was decapitated by yet another layer of clouds. Here and there the powerful muscles of the storm clouds were flushed over with shyness, and the blue sky behind poured over them in an avalanche of high azure. This layer was dark, that shone like a bright bow.

It was the nearest and highest layer of clouds. In exaggerated perspective, the layers that trailed off behind seemed to descend in steps beyond the clear sky. Perhaps, thought Tōru, it was a fraud perpetrated by the clouds. Perhaps the clouds, making a show of perspective, were deceiving him.

Among clouds like antique white clay images of warriors were some that suggested dragons twisting angrily and darkly upwards. Some, as they lost their shape, were tinged rose. Presently, they separated themselves into bland reds and yellows and purples, and their stormy powers left them. The white shining face of the god had taken on the ashen hue of death.

16

Surprised to learn that Tōru's birth, on 20 March, 1954, came before the death of Ying Chan, Honda ordered further investigation. He went ahead with the adoption proceedings all the same.

He regretted that he had learned from her sister only that her death had come in the spring, and that he had not sought more specific information. Inquiring at the American Embassy about the residence of the sister, who had returned to America, he sent off two or three queries, but not the smallest fragment of information came in response. He had a friend in the Foreign Office make inquiry through the Japanese Embassy in Bangkok, but the only reply was that an investigation was in progress. There followed silence.

He could think of any number of devices if he did not mind the expense; but, with badly misplaced frugality and the impatience of old age, he neglected looking into the matter of the princess's death even as he pushed forward with arrangements for the adoption. It seemed too much trouble.

The nerves of the Honda of 1944, uneasy about classic monetary principles, were probably still young and resilient. Now, when the classic common sense was falling apart, Honda clung to it stubbornly, and the result was a quarrel with a financial consultant fifteen years younger than he.

This last quarter of a century he had all the same amassed a fortune of perhaps two million dollars. The million that had come to him in 1948 he had cleanly divided into three parts, which he had put into stocks, real estate, and savings. The portion in real estate had increased tenfold and the stocks threefold and the savings had diminished.

He had not lost his taste for the stocks preferred by old gentlemen who, in wing collars, played billiards at English-style clubs. He was not free from the tastes of an age when the mark of class was to be the holder of 'elegant, reliable' stocks like Tokyo Fire and Marine, Tokyo Electric Power, Tokyo Gas, and Kansai Electric Power, and to have a contempt for speculation. Yet the uninteresting stocks that exclusively made up his portfolio had tripled in value. Because of the fifteen-percent tax deduction for dividends, he paid scarcely any taxes at all from his dividend income.

Tastes in stocks were like tastes in neckties. Wide, gaudy, modish prints were not for an old man. If he did not reap the benefits of bold tastes, neither did he take the risks.

In the decade since 1960 it had become possible, as in America, to guess a man's age from the stocks he owned. The bright celebrities among stocks were day by day becoming more vulgar, day by day taking on the look of the hoi polloi. The makers of small transistor parts, recording annual sales of ten billion yen, with stocks once fifty yen a share now touching fourteen hundred – they were altogether too ordinary.

While paying careful heed to his taste in stocks, Honda was quite insensitive to taste in real estate.

He had made a very good profit from the houses he had put up in 1953 for

American soldiers near the Sagamihara Base. In those days it took more money to build houses than to buy land. Upon the advice of his financial consultant, Honda at first ignored houses and bought up some ten acres of unimproved land at a hundred yen or so per square yard. Each square yard was now worth perhaps twenty thousand yen. Land for which he had paid three million yen was now worth perhaps seven hundred and fifty million.

This was of course a windfall. He had had good luck with some of his land, rather poorer luck with other, but none of it had lost value. He regretted now that he had not left half that million dollars' worth of forest land as it was.

His experience in making money had been a strange one. He could, to be sure, have made tenfold more if he had been bolder; but he could not think that he had come the wrong way. His prudence had guaranteed against loss. Yet there were small regrets and feelings of dissatisfaction. Pushed to their conclusion, they amounted to a dissatisfaction with his own innate nature; and a certain morbid lyricism was an inevitable result.

Honda had achieved security by clinging to his old-fashioned principles even though he was quite aware of the sacrifices they required. He worshipped the trinity of classical capitalism. There was something sacred about it, the harmony of liberal economics. It was symbolic, it had in it the slow, studied intellectual arrogance and sense of balance the gentlemen of the home country had towards colonies still in the primitive insecurity of monoculture.

Such things survived in Japan, then? As long as the tax laws remained unchanged, and enterprises continued to depend on sources of money other than their own capital, and as long as banks continued to demand land as security for loans, the giant article in pawn known as the land of Japan would have no part of the classic principles, and land prices would continue to rise. Inflation would cease only with the end of economic growth or with a Communist government.

While perfectly aware of these facts, Honda remained faithful to the old illusion. He took life insurance, and became an almost foolish defender of a currency system that was day by day falling to pieces. Perhaps a distant mirage of the age of the gold standard, when Isao was living so passionately, remained with Honda.

It had been long ago that the beautiful dream of harmony so dear to the liberal economists had faded, and the dialectical inevitability of the Marxists too had come to look rather peculiar. What was supposed to die had increased and multiplied, what was supposed to grow (it did grow, of course) changed into something quite different. There was no room left for pure doctrine.

It was simple to believe in a world headed for destruction, and had he still been twenty Honda himself would perhaps have so believed; and the very refusal to collapse kept the person who had to slip over life like a skater and presently die constantly on the alert. Who would be so foolish as to skate if he knew the ice was cracking? And if the ice was quite certain not to crack, then a person was denied the pleasure of seeing others fall in. The only question was whether the ice would crack or not while one was skating, and Honda had not a great deal of time left to skate.

And while he was about it, his holdings gradually increased from interest and various sorts of profit.

People thought at any rate that their holdings increased. If they kept ahead of inflation they did increase. But something that increased by laws fundamentally in opposition to those of life could exist only by eating away at what stood on the side of life. Growing profits were the incursions of the white ants of time. A slight increase here and there brought the gentle, steady gnawing.

And then one became aware of the fact that time bearing profits and time for life were of a different nature.

These were thoughts that inevitably went through Honda's mind as he lay awaiting daylight, altogether too awake, and indulged in the sport of chasing thoughts.

Interest accrues like moss over a great plain of time. We are not up to pursuing it forever. That is because our own time leads us relentlessly downhill to a cliff.

It had been a still-young Honda who thought that self-awareness was entirely a matter of the self. It had been a still-young Honda who had named 'self-awareness' the awareness of a reality like a dark, thorny sea cucumber floating in the transparent cask of the self. 'Like unto a violent torrent, ever flowing, ever changing.' He had apprehended the principle intellectually when he was in India, but it had taken him thirty years to make it a part of himself.

As he grew older, awareness of self became awareness of time. He gradually came to make out the sound of the white ants. Moment by moment, second by second, with what a shallow awareness men slipped through time that would not return! Only with age did one know that there was a richness, an intoxication even, in each drop. The drops of beautiful time, like the drops of a rich, rare wine. And time dripped away like blood. Old men dried up and died. In payment for having neglected to stop time at the glorious moment when the rich blood, unbeknownst to the owner himself, was bringing rich drunkenness.

Yes. The old knew that time held intoxications. And when the knowledge came there was no longer enough liquor left. Why had he not stopped time?

Even though he reproved himself, Honda did not think that it had been because of his own laziness and cowardice that he had not stopped time while he could.

Feeling the approach of daylight through his eyelids, Honda indulged in a soliloquy.

'No, there was never for me a moment when I had to do it, stop time. If I have something that might be called a destiny, then it has been in this inability to stop time.

'There was for me nothing that might have been called the pinnacle of my youth, and so no moment for stopping it. One should stop at the pinnacle. I could discern none. Strangely, I feel no regrets.

'No, there is still time after youth has gone by a little. A pinnacle comes, and then the moment. But if the eye that discerns the pinnacle is called an eye of awareness, then I must offer a small objection. I doubt that anyone has been more diligent than myself in putting the eye of awareness to work, more relentless in keeping it open. It is not enough for detecting the pinnacle. The help of destiny is needed. I am quite aware that few have been given that in shorter supply than myself.

'It is easy to say that strength of will kept me back. Was that really the case? Is not the will the leavings of destiny? Between will and determination, are there not inborn differences, as between castes in India? And is not the poorer one the will?

'I did not think so when I was young. I thought that human volition sought to make history. And where did history go? That stumbling old beggar woman.

'Some are all the same endowed with the faculty to cut time short at the pinnacle. I know it to be true, for I have seen examples with my own eyes.

'What power, poetry, bliss! To be able to cut it short, just as the white radiance of the pinnacle comes into view. There comes a foreknowledge in the delicate excitement offered by the slopes, in the changing distribution of the alpine flora, in the approach of the watershed.

'Just a little more and time will be at the peak, and without pausing it will begin its descent. Most people beguile the downward course by taking in the harvest. And what is that? The trails and the waters are only plunging downward.

'Endless physical beauty. That is the special prerogative of those who cut time short. Just before the pinnacle when time must be cut short is the pinnacle of physical beauty.

'Clear, bright beauty, in the knowledge that the radiant white pinnacle lies just ahead. And unhappy purity. In that moment the beauty of a man and the beauty of a gazelle are in wonderful correspondence. Raising its horns proudly, raising the hoof of the white-spotted leg ever so slightly in the face of the denial. Replete with the pride of the farewell, crowned with the white mountain snows.

'It would not have become me to raise my hand in farewell to those who were below, where time still ran on. Had I raised my hand in sudden farewell at a street crossing, I would only have stopped a cab.

'Perhaps, unable to stop time, I had to be content with stopping a succession of cabs. For the purpose, and that only, with firm resolve, of being taken to yet another place where time does not stop. Without the poetry and the bliss.

'Without the poetry, without the bliss! That is the important thing. And I know that only in them lies hidden the reason for life.

'Even if time is stopped there is rebirth. That I know too.

'And I must deny Tōru the terrible poetry and bliss. That must be my policy.'

Honda was by now quite awake. With dull pains here and there and with mucus in his throat to tell him that a new day had begun, he became captive of the need to bring together again things that had fallen apart while he slept. As if opening an old folding chair, he brought himself out of bed. The room was light. It was his practice to give notice of his having awakened through the interphone, but today he preferred not to. Instead he took a lacquered box from the shelf, and from it the report on Tōru he had had from the detective agency.

Report on proposed adoption
Number M-2582
Client 1493: Mr Shigekuni Honda
20 August, 1970

Dainichi Investigating Agency

Tōru Yasunaga, born 20 March, 1954; aged sixteen

Permanent residence: 6–152 Yui, Ihara-gun, Shizuoka Prefecture

Present residence: Meiwasō, 2–10 Funabara-chō, Shimizu, Shizuoka Prefecture

Character and deportment:

The subject is highly intelligent, with the unusual I.Q. of 159. As against 47 percent of examinees with an I.Q. of a hundred, only .6 percent have an I.Q. of over 140. It seems regrettable that such a talented boy should have lost his parents early and, reared by an uncle in straitened circumstances, have been forced to stop his education at middle school. A knowledge of his own abilities, moreover, has not been allowed to go to his head. He has acquitted himself of his rather simple and routine duties with the utmost conscientiousness and diligence, and his modesty and good manners have won him the affection of his colleagues and superiors. Since he is only sixteen, it is too early for a great deal to be reported on his behaviour, but it would seem that his ministrations to a demented girl named Kinué who is the sport of the neighbourhood have nothing to do with sex but are evidence of a gentle, charitable humanism. She looks up to a youth younger than herself as a god.

Interests and hobbies:

He would seem to have no pronounced interests. On holidays he goes to the library or to a movie or watches the ships in the harbour. Usually by himself in these pursuits, he would seem to have solitary inclinations. One may perhaps explain his addiction to tobacco despite the fact that he is still a minor as a result of the solitary and routine nature of his work. Smoking would seem to have had no effect on his health.

Marital status:

He is of course single.

Ideological tendencies and associations:

Perhaps because he is still so young, he has shown no interest in extreme political movements. He would on the contrary seem to have a distaste for politics and political movements. The company is without a union, and he has taken part in no movement towards unionization. He is a voracious reader despite his youth, and his interests would seem to be wide. He owns almost no books, but is a devoted user of libraries who relies on remarkable powers of memory to master what he has read. There is no evidence that he has been addicted to extremist writings of either the left or the right. The evidence is rather that he has sought knowledge of a general and varied kind. He sees comrades from his middle-school days occasionally but would seem to have no close friends.

Religious and other beliefs:

The family is Buddhist, but the subject himself seems to have little interest in religion. He belongs to none of the newer religious sects. He has resisted strong pressure from their adherents.

Family:

Investigations to the third generation on both sides of the family have revealed no evidence of mental illness.

17

Honda chose a day late in October for Tōru's first lesson in foreign table manners. The small parlour was set for a banquet in the French style, complete with caterer and butler, and Tōru wore a new navy-blue suit. He was informed that he must sit well back in the chair and bring it close to the table, that he must not put his elbows on the table or lean too low over his soup, and that he must keep his arms close to his sides. There followed instructions in the disposition of the napkin and the taking of the soup, with the spoon tilted towards the mouth for purposes of avoiding noise. Tōru followed all the instructions carefully, repeating over and over again sequences that did not come easily.

'Foreign table manners may seem a trifle stupid,' said Honda, 'but when they come in an easy, natural way they give a person a sense of security. Evidence of good breeding gives a person status, and by good breeding in Japan we mean a familiarity with the Western way of doing things. We find the pure Japanese only in the slums and in the underworld, and may expect them to be more and more narrowly circumscribed as time goes by. The poison known as the pure Japanese is thinning, changing to a potion acceptable to everyone.'

There can be little doubt that Honda was thinking of Isao as he spoke. Isao knew nothing of Western table manners. Such elegant accessories were no part of the grandeur of his world. And so Tōru, still sixteen, must be taught Western table manners.

Food was served from the left and drink from the right. Knives and forks were taken in order from the outside. Tōru looked at his hands like one engulfed in a torrent.

The instructions continued. 'And you must make polite conversation while you eat. That puts your table companion at ease. You must be careful about timing your swallows, because there is a danger, when you talk with food in your mouth, of spitting something out. Now, then. Father' – Honda referred to himself as 'Father' – 'will say something to you, and you must answer. You must think of me not as your father but as a very important man who might be able to do a great deal for you if he likes you. We are acting out a play. All right, now. "You are studying hard, I see, and you have your three tutors all speechless with admiration; but it seems a little odd that you should have no real friends."'

'I don't feel any great need for them.'

'That's no answer at all. If you give that sort of answer people will think you queer. Now, then. Give me a proper answer.'

Tōru was silent.

'It won't do. Studying will do you no good if you don't use common sense. This is the sort of answer you should give, as pleasantly as can be: "I'm studying so hard that I really don't have time at the moment for friends, but I'm sure I'll have some as soon as I start prep school."'

'I'm studying so hard that I really don't have time at the moment for friends, but I'm sure I'll have some as soon as I start prep school.'

'That's it, that's it. That's the style. And all of a sudden the conversation turns to art. "Who is your favourite Italian artist?"'

There was no answer.

'Who is your favourite Italian artist?'

'Mantegna.'

'No, no. You're far too young for Mantegna. Probably your table companion has never heard of Mantegna, and you'll make him uncomfortable, and give an unpleasant impression of precociousness. This is how you answer. "I think the Renaissance is just wonderful."'

'I think the Renaissance is just wonderful.'

'That's it, that's it. You give your table companion a feeling of superiority and you seem all cute and charming. And he has an opening for a long lecture on things he only half understands. You must listen all aglow with curiosity and admiration even though most of what he says is wrong and the rest is old hat. What the world asks of a young person is that he be a devoted listener, nothing more. You're the winner if you let him do the talking. You must not forget that for a moment.

'The world does not ask brilliance of a young person, and at the same time too firm a steadiness arouses suspicions. You should have a harmless little eccentricity or two, something to interest him. You must have little addictions, not too expensive and not related to politics. Very abstract, very average. Tinkering with machinery, or baseball or a trumpet. Once he knows what they are, he feels safe. He knows where your energies can go. You can even seem a little carried away by your hobbies if you want to.

'You should go in for sports but not let them interfere with your studies, and they should be the sports that show off your good health. It has the advantage of making you look a bit stupid. There are no virtues more highly prized in Japan than indifference to politics and devotion to the team.

'You can graduate with the highest marks in your class, but you have to have a sort of vague stupidity that puts people at their ease. Like a kite full of wind.

'I'll tell you about money once you're in prep school. You're in the happy position for the moment of not having to worry about it.'

As he lectured to the attentive Tōru, Honda had the feeling that these were really instructions for Kiyoaki and Isao and Ying Chan.

Yes, he should have spoken to them. He should have armed them with the foreknowledge that would keep them from flinging themselves after their destinies, take away their wings, keep them from soaring, make them march in step with the crowd. The world does not approve of flying. Wings are dangerous weapons. They invite self-destruction before they can be used. If he had brought Isao to terms with the fools, then he could have pretended that he knew nothing of wings.

He had only to say to people: 'His wings are an accessory. You needn't trouble yourself about them. Just keep company with him for a while, and you'll see that he's an ordinary, reliable boy.' Such tidings could have been remarkably effective.

Kiyoaki and Isao and Ying Chan had had to make do without them, and had been punished for their contempt and arrogance. They had been too proud even in their sufferings.

18

The three tutors were all highly gifted students from Tokyo University. One taught sociology and literature, one mathematics and science, and one English. It was known that in 1971 the prep-school entrance examination would have more essay questions and fewer short-answer questions, and that there would be more emphasis on English dictation and Japanese composition. Tōru was suddenly set to English newscasts. He took them on tape and repeated them over and over.

Here is a question on geography and the movements of the heavenly bodies:

In what position is Venus present longest for morning observation? Indicate on the chart. What is the shape of Venus when viewed in this position? Please indicate which of the following you believe to be the correct answer:

1. The east half is light.
2. The west half is light.
3. It is shining in a thin crescent, like the moon.
4. It is round.

What is the position of Mars when it is visible in the southern evening sky? Please indicate on the chart.

What is the position of Mars when it is visible in the southern midnight sky? Please indicate on the chart.

Tōru immediately circled 'B' on the chart, and so answered the first question successfully. He chose the third possibility for the second question, circled 'L' for the third question, and, finding spot 'G' at which the sun, the earth, and Mars were in a line, circled it.

'Have you been asked this question before?'

'No.'

'Then why were you so quick?'

'I see Venus and Mars every day.'

Tōru answered quite as if he were a child describing the habits of his pets. As a matter of fact Venus and Mars were like the mice that occupied the signal station. He knew all about their feeding habits.

It was not, however, as if he felt nostalgic for nature or regretted the loss of his telescope. He did have a sense of that uncommonly simple work as his own, and the world beyond the horizon was a source of happiness for him; but he did not feel in the least deprived by the loss of them. It was his task, from now until he was twenty or so, to explore a cave with an old man.

Honda had taken pains to choose as tutors bright, companionable, talented young men of a sort Tōru might look to as models. He made a slight miscalculation in the case of Furusawa, Tōru's literature teacher. Much pleased with Tōru's disposition and intelligence, Furusawa would take him to nearby coffee houses when they were tired of their lessons, and sometimes they would go on long walks together. Honda was grateful for these services and liked the cheerful Furusawa.

Furusawa did not at all mind saying unpleasant things about Honda. Tōru enjoyed them, though he was careful not to nod too quick an assent.

One day the two of them walked down Masago Rise past the ward office and turned left towards Suidōbashi. The street was torn up for a new subway line, and Kōrakuen Park was hidden behind construction towers. The twilight of late November came through the framework of a roller coaster as through an empty basket.

Passing trophy shops and sports shops and short-order restaurants, they had come to the Kōrakuen gate. Two rows of lights over the red gate flashed from left to right: 'We will no longer be open in the evening after 23 November.' So the shining nights would soon be over.

'How about it?' asked Furusawa. 'How about a good shaking in a teacup?'

'Well.' Tōru thought of himself in a dirty pink teacup, now rather lonely and short of customers among its blinking little lights. He thought of himself being so shaken and twisted by it that objects became streaks of light.

'Well, do you want to or don't you? You only have ninety-two days left till the examinations, but I'm sure you have nothing to worry about.'

'I'd rather have a cup of coffee.'

'Such dissipation.'

Furusawa led the way down the steps of a coffeehouse called the Renoir. It was across the street from the third-base side of the baseball stadium, which was like a huge trophy pouring forth darkness.

The Renoir was larger than Tōru would have expected from the outside. The tables were generously spaced around a fountain. The lights were soft and the carpet was beige. There were few other guests.

'I had no idea there was such a place so close to home.'

'A cloistered maiden like you wouldn't.'

Furusawa ordered two cups of coffee. He offered Tōru a cigarette, upon which Tōru leaped.

'It's not easy to keep it out of sight.'

'Mr Honda's much too strict. It's not as if you were an ordinary middle-school boy. You've been out in the world. He wants to make a child of you again. But you just have to wait till you're twenty. You can spread your wings once you're in the university.'

'Exactly my own idea. But I have to keep it to myself.'

Furusawa frowned and laughed a pitying laugh. It seemed to Tōru that he was trying to be older than twenty-one.

Furusawa wore glasses, but his good-natured face was very engaging when he smiled, and wrinkles formed around his nose. The horns were bent, and he was forever shoving the glasses back up on his nose, the gesture with his forefinger as if he were reprimanding himself. He had large hands and feet, and he was considerably taller than Tōru. He was the gifted son of a railway worker. Hidden in him was a spirit like a squirming red lobster.

Tōru had no urgent wish to destroy the image Furusawa had of him, as another son of the poor, holding onto the windfall that had come to him. Others, all of them, painted free pictures of him, but it was their freedom. What was most certainly his own was contempt.

'I don't really know what Mr Honda is up to, but I should imagine he's making a guinea pig of you. But that's all right. He has a big fat estate, and you don't have to dirty your hands the way other people do clawing your way to the top of the garbage heap. But you do have to hang on to your self-respect. Even if it kills you.'

'Yes,' answered Tōru succinctly. He refrained from saying that he had a great deal of self-respect in reserve.

He was in the habit of tasting his answers. If they seemed sentimental he bit them back.

Honda was off at a dinner with some legal colleagues. Tōru would have something to eat with Furusawa before they went home. He was required, whatever else might happen, to have dinner with Honda at seven every evening when Honda was at home. Sometimes there were other guests. The evenings with Keiko were the greatest trial.

His eye was cool and clear when he had finished his coffee. But there was nothing to see. He looked at the half circle of coffee dregs. The bottom of the cup, round like the lens of a telescope, obstructed his view. The bottom of this world showed a clean white face of porcelain.

Turned half away, Furusawa suddenly spoke as if throwing the butt of his words into the ashtray. 'Have you ever thought of suicide?'

'No.' Tōru was startled.

'Don't look at me like that. I haven't thought of it all that seriously myself. I don't like the weak and the sick sort of people that commit suicide. But there is one variety I accept. People who commit suicide to establish themselves.'

'What sort of suicide is that?'

'Are you interested?'

'A little, maybe.'

'Then I'll tell you.

'Take a mouse that thinks it's a cat. I don't know how, but it does. It's gone through all the tests and concluded that it's a cat. Its view of other mice changes. They are its meat, that's all, but it tells itself it refrains from eating them just to hide the fact that it's a cat.'

'A rather large mouse, I suppose.'

'It doesn't matter. It's not a question of size but of confidence. It's sure that the concept "cat" has taken on the guise "mouse", nothing more. It believes in the concept and not the flesh. The idea is enough, the body doesn't matter. The happiness from the contempt is all the greater.

'But then one day' – Furusawa shoved his glasses up and drew a persuasive line beside his nose – 'but then one day the mouse meets a real cat.

'"I'm going to eat you," says the cat.

'"You can't," replies the mouse.

'"And why not?"

'"Cats don't eat cats. It's impossible as a matter of instinct and as a matter of principle. I'm a cat myself, whatever else I may look like."

'The cat rolls over laughing. It laughs so hard it's clawing the air and its white furry belly is heaving. Then it gets up and starts to eat the mouse. The mouse protests.

'"What are you eating me for?"

'"Because you're a mouse."

'"I'm a cat. Cats don't eat cats."

'"You're a mouse."

'"I'm a cat."

'"Prove it."

'So the mouse jumps into the laundry tub, all white with suds, and drowns itself. The cat wets a forepaw and has a lick. The suds taste horrible. So it leaves the body floating there. We all know why the cat goes off without eating the mouse. Because it's not something for a cat to eat.

'That's what I'm talking about. The mouse commits suicide to establish itself. It doesn't of course make the cat recognize it as a cat, and it didn't think when it killed itself that it would. But it was brave and perceptive and filled with self-respect. It saw that there are two parts to mouseness. First is that it is a mouse in every physical detail. Second is that it is, for a cat, worth eating. Those two. It has long ago given up in the first matter, but in the second there is still hope. It dies in front of the cat without being eaten, and it establishes itself as something that cats don't eat. In those two respects it has proved it wasn't a mouse. That much. To prove besides that it was a cat is simple. If something that had the form of a mouse wasn't a mouse, then it can be anything else. And so the suicide is a success. The mouse has established itself. What do you think?'

Tōru was weighing the parable. He had no doubt that Furusawa had polished it by telling and retelling it to himself. He had long been aware of the disjuncture between Furusawa's genial appearance and his inner workings.

If only Furusawa was concerned, there was nothing to worry about; but if he had detected something in Tōru to make fun of, then Tōru must be careful. Tōru sent out a probing mental hand. It came upon nothing dangerous. Furusawa had sunk deeper and deeper into himself as he talked; he could not see out from so far below the surface.

'And did the mouse's death shock the world?' Furusawa was no longer paying attention to his audience. Tōru saw that he had only to listen as to a soliloquy. It was a voice of slow, moss-covered pain, such as he had not before heard from Furusawa. 'Did the view the world had of the mouse change in any way? Did the true word spread that there existed something that had the form of a mouse but was not a mouse? Was there a crack in the confidence of the cats? Were the cats sufficiently concerned to obstruct the spread of the word?

'Do not be surprised. The cat did nothing at all. It had forgotten. It was washing its face and settling down for a nap. It was full of catness, and not even aware of that fact. And in the sluggishness of its nap it became with no effort at all what the mouse had so desperately wanted to become, something other than itself. It could become anything, through inaction, through self-satisfaction, through unconsciousness. The blue sky spread over the sleeping cat, beautiful clouds drifted by. The wind carried to the world the cat fragrance, the heavy snores were music.'

'You're talking about authority now.' Tōru felt compelled to put in a word of recognition.

Furusawa's face broke into a good-natured smile. 'Yes. You're very quick.'

Tōru was disappointed. It had ended up as the sad sort of political parable the young are so fond of.

'You'll understand some day yourself.' Although there was no danger of being overheard, Furusawa lowered his voice and brought his face close to Tōru's. Tōru remembered the smell of his breath, forgotten for a time.

Why had he forgotten? He had smelled Furusawa's breath frequently enough in the course of their lessons. He had not been especially repelled by it; but now he was.

There had been no touch of malice in the story, and yet it had somehow angered Tōru. He did not choose to reprove Furusawa for it, however, and feared that to do so would be only to lower himself. He needed another reason, a quite adequate one, for disliking and even being angry at Furusawa. So the smell of his breath became unendurable.

Oblivious to what was happening, Furusawa went on: 'You'll understand, one of these days. With deception as its starting point, authority can only sustain itself by spreading deception. It's like a germ culture. The more we resist, the greater are its powers for endurance and propagation. And before we know it we have the germs in ourselves.'

They left the Renoir and had a bowl of noodles nearby. Tōru found it far more appetizing than a dinner with his father and all those dishes.

As he ate, eyes narrowed against the steam, Tōru was measuring the degree of danger in his relations with this student. He could not doubt that there was sympathy between them. But somehow the harmony was muted. It was possible that Furusawa had been hired by Honda to test Tōru. He knew that after one of these expeditions Furusawa presented a report on where they had been and a bill for his expenses. Honda had of course asked that he do so.

They passed the Kōrakuen again on their way back, and again Furusawa suggested a ride in the teacups. Tōru assented, knowing that Furusawa wanted a ride. The teacups were just inside the gate. No other customers appeared, and presently, with reluctance, the attendant turned on the switch for just the two of them.

Tōru got into a green cup, and Furusawa chose a pink cup a considerable distance off. They were decorated with a cheap flower design reminiscent of teacups on special sale somewhere out in the suburbs, at the too brightly lighted front of a tableware shop.

The cup started moving. Furusawa was suddenly close, and then, shoving his glasses up on a smiling face, he darted off again. The cold Tōru had felt at the seat of his trousers became a cold blast. He turned up the speed. He liked to have it so fast that he could feel nothing and see nothing. The world became a gaseous Saturn.

When the cup had come to a stop, shaking gently from the inertia, like a floating buoy, Tōru stood up. Dizzy, he sat back down again.

'What's the trouble?' Furusawa came smiling towards him over a platform that still seemed to be moving.

Smiling back, Tōru remained seated. It displeased him to have the world, until now all a blurr, importunately line up its sordid details, the peeling posters and the backs of Coca-Cola signs, like great red electric heaters.

19

'Furusawa took me to the Kōrakuen,' said Tōru at breakfast the next morning. 'We had a ride in the teacups, and then we had Chinese noodles for dinner.'

'That's nice,' said Honda, showing his false teeth. It should have been the bland, insubstantial old smile that went with false teeth; but Honda seemed to be genuinely pleased. Tōru was wounded.

Since he had come to Honda's, Tōru had known every morning the luxurious pleasure of scooping up the meat of an imported grapefruit, cut into sections by a thin curved knife. The rude abundance of juice, in the faintly bitter, glossy white meat of fruit ripe to bursting, sank into his lazy morning gums with its warmth.

'Furusawa has bad breath. I can hardly stand it when we're studying together.' Tōru smiled an equivocal smile.

'I wonder why. Do you suppose he has stomach trouble? But you're too fussy. You can put up with that much. You're not likely to find a more able tutor.'

'I suppose not.' Retreating a step, Tōru finished his grapefruit. A carefully scrutinized piece of toast gave off in the November morning light a glow as of well-tanned leather. Tōru watched the butter melt into it, and then took a bite, careful to follow the instructions he had had from Honda.

'Yes, Furusawa is a good man,' he said after the first bite. 'But have you looked into his ideas?'

It pleased him to see confusion of the most vulgar sort come out on Honda's face.

'Has he said something to you?'

'Nothing specific. But I can't get over feeling that he either has been or still is involved in some political movement.'

Honda was startled. He trusted Furusawa, and was sure that Tōru liked him. From Honda's point of view, Tōru's warning was based on confidence and understanding; but from Furusawa's it was clearly the report of a secret informant. It amused Tōru to observe how Honda would dispose of this delicate ethical problem.

Honda saw that he was not to pass the light judgement he usually passed upon good and evil. Judged against a broader humanity of which Honda was fond of thinking, Tōru's behaviour was ugly; but judged against the image Honda had for Tōru himself, it passed muster. Honda was at the point of confessing that what he looked for in Tōru was ugliness.

To put Honda at his ease and offer occasion for mild reproof, Tōru tore off a childish mouthful of toast, spreading crumbs liberally on his knee. Honda took no notice.

It would not do to reprove Tōru for the element of meanness in this first mark of trust he had vouchsafed. On the other hand Honda's old sense of ethics demanded that he inform Tōru of the impropriety of turning informant, whatever the reason; and so something rather petty was by way of coming into this happy breakfast scene.

Their hands bumped awkwardly as they both reached for the sugar bowl.

A sugar bowl bright with betrayal in the morning sunlight. Feelings of guilt for having reached out simultaneously. It wounded Honda to think that this had been the first suggestion of a parental bond.

Tōru was pleased at more than this open confusion. He could see the hesitation as Honda found himself unable to preach the obvious lesson: that one must show more confidence in and respect for a person whom one has even tentatively called teacher. For the first time the controversy within Honda and the evil hidden in his educational policies became clear. Tōru felt like a liberated child spitting out a watermelon seed.

'Well, leave it to me. You just go on doing as you've always done. Don't worry yourself over anything but your studies. Leave everything else to me. The first thing is to get you through your examinations.'

'How right you are.' Tōru smiled a beautiful smile.

Honda deliberated for a day. The next day he asked an acquaintance in the Public Security Division of the Metropolitan Police to investigate. A report came some days later. Furusawa had been a member of an extremist student faction. Honda invented a trivial pretext for dismissing him.

20

Tōru occasionally wrote to Kinué, and got long answers. He had to be careful when he opened them, because each one contained a pressed flower for the season. Sometimes she would apologize for having sent a hothouse flower, there being no wildflowers in bloom.

Wrapped in paper, the flower would be like a dead butterfly. There was pollen for wing dust, letting one imagine that when it lived it had flown. Dead wings and dead petals are the same. The remembrance of colour that has flown through the sky, and the remembrance of colour in stillness and resignation.

Only after reading the letter did he recognize one fragment, dry and brown like the skin of an Indian, strong red threads torn and jagged from having been pressed flat, as the petal of a red hothouse tulip.

The letters were the endless confession she had brought to the signal station. And she always offered in much detail a description of her loneliness for Tōru and her wish to come to Tokyo. He always replied that she must be patient, however many years passed. He would find an occasion to summon her.

Sometimes he almost thought, after having been away from her for so long, that she was beautiful. And immediately he would laugh. Yet he was coming to see what the mad girl had meant to him.

He needed lunacy to dim his own clarity. He had to have someone beside him who would see as something quite different all the things he saw with such clarity, clouds or ships or the gloomy old hallway of the Honda house, or the schedule of all his lessons until examination day posted on the wall of his room.

Tōru sometimes longed for liberation. The direction was clear. It must be the direction of uncertainty, the realm behind this clearly defined world, a realm whose phenomena were flowing over a waterfall.

Kinué unconsciously played the role of the gentle guest who brought freedom into the cage.

Nor was that all.

She brought balm for certain itches within him. He itched to do injury. His heart was a sharp drill protruding from a sack, itching to cut someone. Having cut down Furusawa, it was looking for someone else. Its cleanness, free of the least speck of rust, must sooner or later turn savage. Tōru saw that he could do something other than observe. The awareness brought tension, and Kinué's letters brought rest from it. Because of her madness she was beyond his harming.

The strongest bond between them was his certainty that he could not himself be wounded.

A successor to Furusawa was found, a student of the most ordinary common-sense sort. Tōru hoped that within the next two months he could get rid of the other tutors as well, for he did not want to seem in their debt when he had passed his examinations.

But caution held him back. Honda would begin to have certain suspicions were Tōru to waste his energies on such minor personages. He could come to discount Tōru's complaints, and, accepting the faults complained of, find fault in the complaints themselves. And the secret pleasure would disappear. Tōru concluded that he must be patient. He must wait until someone far more worth wounding appeared. Whoever it was would provide a way, albeit an indirect one, of wounding Honda himself. A way that left no room for resentment. A clean, unsullied way of Tōru's very own, leaving Honda with no one but himself to blame.

And who would come into his life, like a ship on the far horizon? As the ships had first taken firm shape in Tōru's mind, so would his victim appear one day, a shadow neither ship nor mirage, unsuspecting and vulnerable, following the dictates of the drill in his heart. Tōru came almost to have hopes.

21

Tōru entered the preparatory school of his choice.

In his second year there came a proposal, through a suitable mediator. A certain person had a marriageable daughter he thought Tōru might be interested in. Tōru had reached the legal age of consent, but he was still only eighteen. Honda laughed the proposal off. The other person was persistent, however, and the proposal came through another mediator. Since the second man was an eminence in the legal world, Honda could not turn him away unconditionally.

Honda longed for something: a young bride who would be twisted with grief at the loss of her twenty-year-old husband. She would wear the pale, beautiful hues of tragedy; and so, at no expense, Honda would have another meeting with a pure crystallization of beauty.

The dream was rather out of accord with his educational policies. Yet if there had been no margin at all for the dream, and if there had been no sense of crisis, Honda would scarcely have bothered with policies calculated to give Tōru a long and beautyless life. What Honda feared was what Honda hoped for, what Honda hoped for was what Honda feared.

The proposal was repeated at appropriate intervals, like water dripping through a floor. It amused Honda to be visited by this eminence and to hear his desperate plea. He thought it too early to tell Tōru.

Honda was fascinated with the photograph the old man brought. The girl was eighteen and a beauty, with a thin delicate face that had in it nothing of the bright and modern. There was beauty in the faint air of bewildered resentment with which she faced the photographer.

'Yes, she is very beautiful. And is she strong physically?' asked Honda, the intent of his question quite the opposite of what his friend must have supposed it to be.

'I can assure you that I know her very well. She is much stronger than this picture would lead you to believe. She has had no serious illnesses. Health is of course the most important thing. It was her father who chose the picture, and I think he chose a rather old-fashioned one.'

'She is of a cheerful disposition, then?'

'Not, I fear, if that expression contains a suggestion of frivolity.'

It was an equivocal response. Honda wanted to meet the girl.

It was clear that the proposal had taken Honda's wealth into account. Only that could explain the eagerness for an eighteen-year-old bridegroom, however talented he might be. The tempting object must be snatched up before someone else saw its possibilities.

Honda was perfectly aware of all this. And if he were to accept the proposal, the obvious reason would be to control the urges of a difficult eighteen-year-old. But Tōru here before him seemed quite under control already. So the interests of the two parties were more and more divergent, and Honda saw no reason at all to pursue the talks. He felt a certain curiosity about the contrast between the parents and the beautiful candidate herself. He wanted to see greedy self-respect give way. The family that made the proposal was of much prominence, but such considerations no longer troubled Honda.

A dinner party was proposed at which Tōru and the girl would be present. Honda declined. Instead he and the person who had brought the proposal had dinner with the girl's family.

For two or three weeks the seventy-eight-year-old Honda was in the grip of temptation. He had seen the girl at dinner, and they had exchanged brief remarks. He had received several more photographs. Hence the temptation.

He had not given a favourable answer, nor had he reached a decision; but his ageing heart was the victim of impulses which his reason could not control. The wilfulness of old age gave him the itch. He longed to show the pictures to Tōru and see his response.

Honda did not himself know what had possessed him, but happiness and pride were at work in the temptation. He knew that if in fact he were to inform Tōru of the proposal he would have passed the point of no return. But wilfulness did not see reason.

He longed to see all the results of the match, of bumping the two of them together, a white billiard ball and a crimson. It would be good if Tōru was fond of the girl and it would be good if she was fond of him. She would mourn him when he died, he would be aroused by her greed and come to see humanity for what it was. Either would for Honda be a pleasing result. A sort of festival.

Honda was much too old to have solemn thoughts about the nature of human life. He was at an age when he could justify malicious games. Whatever the malice, death was near, to make amends. He was at an age when youth was a plaything, humanity a collection of clay dolls, an age when, putting ceremony to his own uses, he could turn honesty and sincerity into the play of the evening sky.

When others were as nothing, surrender to such temptations became a kind of destiny.

Late one evening Honda called Tōru into his study. Mildewed by the summer rains, it was the English-style study he had inherited from his father. Honda disliked air-conditioning, and there was a faint glow of sweat on Tōru's white chest. It seemed to Honda that a doomed white hydrangea was in bloom before him.

'It will soon be summer vacation.'

'But exams come first.' Tōru bit at the chocolate mint Honda had offered.

'You eat like a squirrel.' Honda smiled.

'Oh?' Tōru too smiled, the smile of one whom it is not possible to injure.

Looking at the pale face, Honda thought that this summer sun must burn it to a crisp. It was a face that did not seem in danger of pimples. With a studied casualness, he opened a drawer and laid a photograph on the table before Tōru.

Tōru was rather splendid. Honda missed no detail. Tōru examined it with the solemn attention of a guard examining a pass. His questioning eyes looked up at Honda and back again at the picture. Then came boyish curiosity, and he flushed to the ears. Putting the photograph back on the table, he plunged a rough finger into an ear.

'She is very beautiful,' he said, a touch of anger in his voice.

Very, very splendid, thought Honda. There was something poetic in the youthfulness of the response (and it had been in a moment of crisis). Honda forgot that Tōru had responded as he had wanted him to respond.

It was a complex amalgam, as if Honda's self-awareness had itself for an instant played a boyish role, hiding confusion with a touch of roughness.

'Would you like to meet her?' Honda asked quietly.

He coughed somewhat nervously, hoping that the next response would be as appropriate. Tōru sprang lightly to his feet and went over to beat on Honda's back.

'Yes.'

The word was almost a growl. Taking advantage of the fact that his father could not see, his eyes were aglow as he said to himself: 'The wait has been worth it. Here is someone worth injuring.'

Yet farther on, beyond the window, it was raining. A sad, lonely rain, like a black liquid, giving the bark of the trees a steamy glow in the light from the window. At night the subway trains, here running on elevated tracks, shook the ground. The bright lights in the windows as the train plunged underground again brought a vision to Tōru, still beating on his father's back. There was no sign tonight of a ship.

22

'Suppose you keep company with her for a while. If you don't like her you just have to say so. There is no commitment.'

Tōru went to dinner one night when summer vacation had begun. After dinner, upon a suggestion from her mother that it might be nice to show him her room, Momoko Hamanaka led him upstairs. It was a large Western room, girlish from corner to corner. Tōru's first experience of the utterly girlish. It was luxuriantly pink. There was girlishness in every detail of the wallpaper, the dolls, the accessories. They quite breathed a beguiling young charm. Tōru took a seat in an armchair. The thick multicoloured cushion made sitting difficult.

Momoko had a mature look, and yet there could be no doubt that all these details were of her own choosing. The cool pallor, somewhat blanched, was in keeping with old-fashioned features not too deeply carved. The solitary earnestness made her the only object at odds with the beguiling charm. Her beauty was too formally perfect; and as in the formal perfection of a paper crane it had in it something ominous.

Her mother brought tea and withdrew. The two had met several times before, but for the first time they were alone. That fact did not produce new tensions.

Momoko was safe in the knowledge of having obeyed instructions. He must awaken her to danger, thought Tōru.

He had been put off by all the solemn attentions during dinner. But his annoyance was about to leave. A match was being made. Delicate love was being picked up in pincers, tinted. The bon-bon had already been put in the oven. To Tōru it made no difference whether he had gone in of his own accord or been put in. He had no reason to be dissatisfied with himself.

The first thing Momoko did when they were alone was to choose an album from four or five numbered ones and offer it to Tōru. Thus he was made aware of her essential mediocrity. He opened it on his knees, and he saw an infant in a bib, its legs spread wide. Pants were swollen with diapers, like a Flemish knight's. The dark pink of a mouth not yet filled out with teeth. Tōru asked who the infant might be.

Momoko's consternation was rather wondrous. She glanced at the album and put a hand over the picture and snatched the album from him. Clutching it to her breast, she turned to the wall. Her breathing was heavy.

'How perfectly dreadful. The numbers were wrong. I didn't mean for you to see this one. Whatever will I do?'

'Is it such a secret that you were once a baby?'

'Aren't you cool. Like a doctor.'

Calm again herself, Momoko replaced the album. Tōru was sure, from his misstep, that in the next album he would see Momoko at seventeen.

But the next album was most ordinary, pictures from a recent trip. Each picture showed how popular Momoko was. It was a record of tedious happiness. Far more than to pictures of a recent trip to Hawaii, Tōru was drawn to Momoko in the garden beside a bonfire, one evening the previous fall. The bonfire was a rich, sensuous vermilion. Crouched beside it, Momoko had the grandeur of a witch.

'Are you fond of fires?' he asked.

He caught hesitation in her eyes. He had a strange confidence that she had been menstruating as she sat looking into the fire. And now?

How pure abstract malice would have been if it had been free from sexual attraction! He saw that this new challenge would not be as easy as dismissing his tutor had been. But he had confidence in his coldness, however much he might be loved. It lay in the indigo realm within him.

23

Reluctant to leave Tōru by himself, Honda took him to Hokkaido that summer. Their schedule was an easy one. They did not want to tax themselves. Keiko, for whom it had become difficult to travel with Honda, went off by herself to Geneva, the Japanese ambassador to Switzerland being a relative. The Hamanakas wanted to have two or three days with the Hondas, and so the two families took rooms in

Shimoda. Overwhelmed by the summer heat, Honda rarely left his air-conditioned room.

It was agreed that they would have dinner together each night. The Hamanakas came for Honda. Where was Momoko, they asked. She had come a little earlier, said Honda, and was out in the garden with Tōru. And so the Hamanakas sat down and waited for the young couple to return.

Honda was standing by the window, a cane in his hand.

It was all very stupid. He was not hungry, and the menu was an impoverished one. He knew without going to the dining room that vulgar family merriment awaited him. And Hamanaka table conversation was tedium itself.

The old had politics forced upon them. Even though he ached in all his joints, a man of seventy-eight could hide his want of interest only under a show of wit and good humour. A want of interest was important all the same. It was the only way to win out over the idiocy of the world. The unconcern of a beach receiving each day the waves and the driftwood.

Honda thought that, purse-lipped and surrounded by lackeys, he had yet a little life in him, a little sharpness with which to hinder the purse-lipped days and the lackeys; but it had deserted him. All he really had was an overwhelming sense of folly, and of a vulgarity that melted into a monotone. How myriad were the manifestations of the vulgar. The vulgarity of elegance, the vulgarity of ivory, the vulgarity of holiness, the vulgarity of the craze, erudite vulgarity, the vulgarity of the academic pretender, coquettish vulgarity, the vulgarity of the Persian cat, the vulgarity of monarchs and beggars, of lunatics, of butterflies, of blister beetles. Reincarnation was retribution for vulgarity. And the chief and indeed the only source of it all was the wish for life. Honda himself was without doubt a part of it. What distinguished him was his uncommonly keen sense of smell.

He glanced sideways at the ageing couple before him. Why had the two of them come into his life? The superfluity of their presence ran against his sense of order. But there was no help for it now. There they were, smiling on his sofa, as if prepared to wait a decade or so.

Shigehisa Hamanaka, aged fifty-five, was the former chief of a feudal clan in the northeast. He sought to cover the now-empty pride of family in Bohemianism, and had even written a book of essays, *The Chief*, which had been a modest success. He was the president of a bank, the head office of which was in his old fief, and he had made a name in the pleasure quarters as an old-style man of taste. There was still a full, rich head of black hair over the gold-rimmed glasses and the almond-shaped face, but the stronger impression was of vapidity. A confident raconteur, he always allowed an appropriate pause before a witty conclusion. A clever talker who made a great point of skipping the preliminaries, a person of gentle irony who never forgot his respect for the aged, he would not have dreamed he was a bore.

His wife Taeko too came from the military aristocracy. She was a fat, rough-featured person, and fortunately the daughter looked like the father. All Taeko could talk about was family. She had seen neither movies nor plays. She passed her life before a television set. They were very proud of the fact that their other three children were married and on their own, and only Momoko remained.

Old-fashioned elegance had thus become shallowness. It was more than Honda could bear to hear Shigehisa talk permissively of the sex revolution, and to hear Taeko's shocked responses. Shigehisa used his wife's old-fashioned responses as a part of his act.

Honda wondered why he could not be more tolerant. He knew, as it became more and more of a burden to make new acquaintances, how difficult it was to muster a smile. Contempt was of course the emotion that came first, but even that was rather a lot of trouble these days. He thought how much easier it would be to respond with spittle than with words, even as the words came to his lips, but words were the task that remained. With them an old man could twist the world as he might squash a willow lattice.

'How young you look standing there,' said Taeko. 'Like a soldier.'

'A very inappropriate simile, my dear. You must not liken a judge to a soldier. I have never forgotten an animal trainer I once saw in a circus in Germany. That is what Mr Honda is like.'

'A far more inappropriate simile, I should think, my dear.' Taeko was dreadfully amused.

'I am not striking a pose, you must believe me. I am standing here so that I can see the sunset and the young people in the garden.'

'You can see them?'

Taeko came and stood beside Honda, and Shigehisa too, with dignity, left his chair.

The garden was spread below the third-floor window. It was circular, bordered by a walk that led down to the sea, and there were two or three benches among the shrubs. A few family groups were returning, towels over shoulders, from the pool a level below. They cast long evening shadows over the lawn.

Momoko and Tōru were walking hand in hand halfway along the circle. Their shadows stretched far out to the east. It was as if two great sharks were biting their feet.

Tōru's shirt was full in the evening breeze, and Momoko's hair was blowing. They were a most ordinary boy and girl; but to Honda they were as insubstantial as gossamer mosquito nets. The shadows were the substance. They had been eaten away by the shadows, by the deep melancholy of a concept. That was not life, thought Honda. It was something less easy to excuse. And the terrible fact was that Tōru probably knew.

If the shadow was the substance, then the all too transparent something clinging to it must be wings. Fly! Fly over the vulgarity! The limbs and the heads were a superfluity, too concrete. If the contempt in him was only a little stronger, Tōru could fly off, the girl's hand in his; but Honda had forbidden it. Honda longed with all the powers of his senile impotence to put his envy to work and give the two of them wings; but not even envy burned very hot in him any more. Only now did he see it for what it was, the most fundamental emotion he had felt towards Kiyoaki and Isao, the source of all lyricism in intellectual man, envy.

Very well, then. Suppose he were to think of Tōru and Momoko as the basest, the least tempting morsels of youth. They would act, fall into each other's arms, like a pair of puppets. He only had to move a finger. He moved two or three of the fingers on his stick. The pair on the lawn walked towards the cliff path.

'Just look at them, would you. Here we are waiting, and it seems they mean to go farther away.'

Taeko stood with her hand on her husband's elbow. There was a touch of excitement in her voice.

Facing the sea, the young couple went through the shrubbery and sat down on one of the rough wooden benches. Honda could see from the angle of the heads that they were looking at the sunset. A lump of black came out from under the bench. Honda could not make out whether it was a cat or a dog. Momoko stood up in surprise. Tōru, standing up beside her, took her in his arms.

'Well, now.' The voices of her parents, watching through the window, floated up gently as dandelion floss.

Honda was not watching. The cognizant one was not watching through his peephole. There at the bright window, he was half enacting in his heart the movements his awareness had ordered, directing them with the strength of all his faculties.

'You are young, and you must give evidence of a far stupider vitality. Shall I put thunder into you? A sudden flash of lightning? Shall we have some queer sort of electric phenomenon: perhaps send flames darting from Momoko's hair?'

A tree stretched its branches spider-like towards the sea. They started to climb it. Honda could feel the tension in the pair beside him.

'I shouldn't have let her wear pants.' Taeko seemed on the edge of tears. 'The little hussy.'

They entwined their legs around the branches and swung up and down. Leaves scattered towards the ground. One tree among the others seemed to have gone mad. The two were like a pair of great birds against the evening sky.

Momoko jumped from the tree first. But she did not jump boldly enough, and her hair was entangled in one of the lower branches. Tōru followed her and sought to disentangle it.

'They're in love.' Taeko, in tears, nodded again and again.

But Tōru was taking too long. Honda knew immediately that he was deliberately entangling the hair more tightly. The delicately overdone efforts brought a twinge of fear. Secure in these ministrations, Momoko sought to pull away from the branch. The pain was sharp. Pretending to make matters unintentionally worse the more he tried, Tōru mounted the low branch like a jockey. Momoko pulled at the long rope of hair, her back to him. She was weeping, and her hands were at her face.

From the third-floor window, across the wide garden, it was like a scene in wax, a quiet little pantomime. The grandeur was in the evening light, an avalanche falling off to the sea, in the high glow of the light glancing off towards the sea from the clouds, relics of sun showers through the afternoon. Because of the light, the trees and the islands in the bay, closer and closer, spread colour on hard, thin lines. The clarity was terrible.

'They're in love,' said Taeko once more.

A bright rainbow arched over the sea, like an outcropping of the sunlight in Honda's heart at the idiocy of it all.

24

Excerpts from Tōru Honda's diary.

I cannot excuse the several mistakes I am making in the matter of Momoko. That is because one must proceed from clarity, and the smallest element of miscalculation produces fantasy, and fantasy produces beauty.

I have never been a sufficiently ardent devotee of beauty to believe that beauty produces fantasy and fantasy miscalculation. When I was still new at the signal station, I sometimes misidentified a ship. Especially at night, when it is difficult to calculate the distance between mast lights, I would sometimes take a puny little fishing boat for an international freighter, and send out a signal asking it to identify itself. Unaccustomed to such formal treatment, the fishing boat would sometimes flash back the name of a movie star. It was not however a thing of great beauty.

Momoko's beauty of course meets all the objective standards. Her love is necessary for me, and I must give her the blade with which to cut herself. A paper knife will not suffice.

I know well enough that the more firmly insistent demands come not from reason or will but from sexual desire. The detailed demands of sex are sometimes mistakenly thought logical. I think that, lest I confuse the two, I must have another woman for sex. That is because the most subtle and delicate wishes of evil are not for a physical wound but for a spiritual. I know well enough the nature of evil within me. It is in the insistent demands of awareness itself, awareness transformed into desire. Or to put the matter differently, it has been clarity in its most perfect form acting out its part in the darkest depths.

I sometimes think it would be better if I were dead. For my plans can be realized on the far side of death. For there I can find true perspective. To do it while still alive is more difficult than the difficult. Especially when you are only eighteen!

I find it very hard to understand the Hamanakas. There can be no doubt that they want us to be engaged for five or six years, and that they will presently exercise their option and bring the two of us together, fully recognized members of society, in high matrimony. But what guarantee have they? Should they have such confidence in their daughter's beauty? Or is it that they put high hopes on payments for breach of promise?

No, I doubt that they have made any real calculations at all. They take the crudest, most common-sense view of relations between man and woman. To judge from their gasps of admiration when they hear my I.Q., I should imagine that all their energies go into the study of talent, and especially talent with money.

Momoko telephoned from Karuizawa the day I got back from Hokkaido. She wanted to see me and so I must come to Karuizawa. I have no doubt that her parents were behind it. There was just a touch of artificiality in her voice, and so I made bold to be cruel. I replied that since I was deep in studies for my university entrance examinations I was unable to accept her kind invitation. And when I hung up I felt a quite unexpected twinge of sadness. Denial is itself a sort of concession, and it is natural that the concession should bring a shadow of sadness over one's self-respect. I am not afraid of it.

Summer is almost over. I am very much aware of its passage. As strongly as words can express. There were mackerel clouds and cumulus clouds in the sky today, and a faint touch of sharpness in the air.

Love should follow along, but my emotions must not follow anything.

The little present Momoko gave me in Shimoda is here on my desk. It is a framed bit of white coral. On the back, in two pierced hearts, it carries the inscription: 'From Momoko to Tōru.' I do not understand how she can go on being prey to these childish tastes. The case is filled with little bits of tinfoil that float up like the white sands of the sea when you shake it, and the glass is half frosted with indigo. The Suruga Bay I have known is compressed into a frame five inches square, it has become a lyrical miniature forced on me by a girl. But small though it is, the coral has its own grand, cold cruelty, my inviolable awareness at the heart of her lyric.

Whence come the difficulties in my being? Or to put it another way, the ominous smoothness and facileness of my being.

I sometimes think that the ease of it all comes from the fact that my being is a logical impossibility.

It is not that I am asking any difficult questions of my being. I live and move without motive power, but that is as much an impossibility as perpetual motion. Nor is it my destiny. How can the impossible be a destiny?

From the moment I was born on this earth, it would seem, my being knew that it flew in the face of reason. I was not born with any defect. I was born like an impossibly perfect human being, a perfect film negative. But this world is full of imperfect positives. It would be a terrible thing for them to develop me, change me into a positive. That is why they are so afraid of me.

The source of greatest amusement to me has been the solemn injunction that I be faithful to myself. It is an impossibility. Had I sought to follow it I would immediately have been dead. It could only have meant forcing the absurdity of my existence into unity.

There would have been ways if I had not had self-respect. It would have been easy, without self-respect, to make others and myself as well accept all manner of distorted images. But is it so very human to be hopelessly monstrous? Though of course the world feels secure when the monstrous is reality.

I am very cautious, but I am greatly wanting in the instinct for self-preservation. And I am so brightly wanting in it that the breeze through the gap sometimes makes me drunk. Since danger is the ordinary, there is no crisis. It is very well to have a sense of balance, since I cannot live without a miraculous sort of balance; but suddenly it becomes a hot dream of imbalance and collapse. The greater the discipline the greater the tendency towards violence, and I grow weary of pressing the control button. I must not believe in my own docility. No one can know what a sacrifice it is for me to be gentle and docile.

But my life has been only duty. I have been like an awkward novice sailor. Only in seasickness and nausea have I escaped from duty. The nausea corresponded to what the world calls love.

For some reason, Momoko is reluctant to come home with me. We talk for an hour or so after school at the Renoir. Sometimes we have our innocent fun in the park, riding the roller coaster. The Hamanakas do not worry a great deal about having their daughter come home late if it is not after dark. Though I sometimes take her to a movie, of course, I must let them know in advance that we are going to be later. There is not much pleasure in these public dates, and so we also have our assignations, brief ones.

Momoko came to the Renoir again today. She may seem old-fashioned, but she is just like any other girl in the unpleasant things she has to say about her teachers, in gossip about her friends, in talk, all contemptuously masked with indifference, of the scandalous behaviour of movie stars. I humour her a little, showing a manly tolerance.

I lack the courage to write further, for my reservations on the surface seem no different from the unconscious reservations of all other teen-agers. Whatever my perversity, Momoko does not feel it as such. So I let my feelings have their way. Unintentionally, I become sincere and honest. If I really were, then the ethical contradictions in my being should be exposed like mud banks at low tide; but the troublesome ones are the banks not yet exposed. As the waters recede they pass a point at which my frustrations are no different from the frustrations of any other young person, the sadness that furrows my brow draws a line no different from that on the brow of any other. It would not do for Momoko to catch me there.

I have been wrong in thinking that women are tormented by doubts as to whether they are loved. I have wished to plunge Momoko into doubt, but the swift little beast has eluded capture. It would do no good to tell her I do not love her. She would think I was lying. My only recourse is to bide my time and make her jealous.

I sometimes ask myself if I was not somehow changed by the dissipation of my sensibilities in welcoming all those ships. There had to be some effect on me. Ships were born of my consciousness and grew into giants and had names. Only so far were they my concern. Once in port, they were of a different world. I was too busy receiving other ships. I did not have the art to become alternately ship and harbour. That is what women demand. The concept of woman, become sensible reality, would in the end refuse to leave port.

I have known secret pride and pleasure in seeing the concept on the horizon gradually take shape. I have put my hand in from outside the world and created something, and I have not tasted the sensation of being brought into the world. I have not felt myself brought in like laundry brought in before a shower. No rain has fallen to give me existence within the world. On the verge of intellectual drowning, my clarity has been confident of proper sensual rescue. For the ship has always passed. It has never stopped. The sea winds have turned everything to spotted marble, the sun has turned the heart into crystal.

I have been self-reliant to the point of sadness. I wonder when I first fell into the habit of washing my hands after each brush with humanity, lest I be contaminated. People have diagnosed the habit as uncommon fastidiousness.

My misfortune has clearly had its origins in nonrecognition of nature. It is natural that I should not have recognized nature, for nature, containing all rules, should be an ally, and 'my' nature has not been. I have accomplished the nonrecognition with gentleness. I have not been spoiled or pampered. Always feeling the shadow of persons clamorous to do me injury I have been careful about expenditures of gentleness certain to do injury to others. One may see in the care a very human sort of solicitude. But mixed in with the very word 'solicitude' are unpleasant shreds of weariness.

I have thought that, in comparison with the nature of my own being, the affairs of the world, delicate and complicated international problems and the like, have not been problems at all. Politics and art and ideology have been so many watermelon rinds. Only watermelon rinds left on the seashore, mostly white but tinged with the faint pink of sunrise. For though I have hated the vulgar, I have recognized in them the possibility of eternal life.

Incomprehension and error have seemed preferable to a relentless probing of my depths. This last means indescribable rudeness and discourtesy, not possible without the nastiest hostility. When did a ship ever understand me? It was enough for me to understand. Spiritlessly, punctiliously, it gave me its name and without another word slipped into harbour. It has been fortunate for the ships that not one of them was aware of the situation. Had any one of them shown the slightest misgivings, in that instant it would have been wiped out by my consciousness.

I have put together a delicate machine for feeling how it would be if I were to feel like a human being. The naturalized Englishman is more English than the native Englishman, they say; and I have become more of an expert on humanity than a human being. More, in any case, than an eighteen-year-old. Imagination and logic are my weapons, more precise than nature or instinct or experience, quite waterproof in awareness of and accommodation to probability. I have become a specialist in humanity, as an entomologist might become a specialist in South American beetles. With odourless flowers I have explored the ways in which human beings are captured by the odour of certain flowers, caught up in certain feelings.

So it is to see. I have seen from the signal station how an international freighter sets its sights from a certain distance out at sea, and makes towards shore at twelve and a half knots with the most urgent dreams of home. That was mere probing, my eye was really turned on an invisible realm far beyond the horizon. What is it to see the invisible? That is the ultimate vision, the denial at the end of all seeing, the eye's denial of itself.

But sometimes I fear that all these thoughts and all these plans of mine begin in me and end in me. It was so, in any event, at the signal station. All the images flung into that little room like fragments of glass cast their light upon the walls and ceiling and left no trace behind. Is it not the same with other worlds too? I must be my own support and go on living. Because I am always floating in air, resisting gravity, on the borders of the impossible.

Yesterday in school one of our more ostentatiously erudite teachers taught us a fragment of a Grecian lyric:

Those born with the bounty of the gods
Have the duty to die beautiful,
Not dissipating the bounty.

For me, for whom the whole of life is a duty, this particular duty does not exist. Because I have no knowledge of having received a bounty.

Smiling has become a heavy burden, and so I have taken it upon myself to be out of sorts with Momoko for a time. I leave room for the perfectly ordinary view, even while offering a glimpse of the monster, that I am a sulky, frustrated boy. And because it is an unrelieved piece of acting, because it is altogether too stupid, I too must have a measure of passion. I have looked for a reason. I have found the most plausible one. It is the love born in me.

I almost burst out laughing. For I had become aware of the significance of lovelessness as a self-evident premise. It is in the freedom to love indiscriminately at any time. Like a truck driver napping in the summer shade, certain that the moment he awakens he can drive off again. If freedom is not the essence of love but its enemy, then I have friend and enemy in hand at once.

My sulkiness seems to have been convincing. That is most natural, for it is the form taken by love that is free, asking while denying.

Momoko promptly lost her appetite. She looked at me with a worried face, as she might look at a pet bird. She had the vulgar notion that happiness is to be apportioned to all, like a big loaf of French bread. She did not understand the mathematical principle that happiness for one must be unhappiness for another.

'Has something happened?' It was an inappropriate question coming from those elegant lips, on that face shaded over with quiet tragedy.

I laughed vacantly and did not answer.

It was the only time she asked the question. She was soon lost in her own talk. It was the part of the faithful listener to be silent.

She noticed the middle finger of my right hand, which I had injured on the buck in gymnastics class that day. I saw the relief on her face the moment she saw the bandage. She thought she had found the cause of my ill temper.

Apologizing for not having noticed earlier, she said with a great show of concern that it must hurt a great deal. I answered brusquely that it hurt scarcely at all.

As a matter of fact it did not. I was unable to excuse her for finding such a simple explanation. And it displeased me that, despite the fact that I had been at pains to hide the bandage from her, she had taken so long in finding it.

I turned off her sympathies with stronger and stronger assurances that it did not hurt in the least. With an expression on her face as of having seen through all the pretence and all the feigned bravery, she was more and more insistently sympathetic, having convinced herself that she must extract an admission from me.

She insisted upon going off to a drugstore immediately for a fresh bandage. The old one was already a dirty grey, and dangerous. The stronger my denials the greater her awareness of my powers of abnegation. Finally we went off together and had the bandage changed by a lady who was obviously a former nurse. Momoko looked aside in terror, and so I was able to hide the fact that the wound was only a scratch.

How was it now, she asked earnestly.

'The bone is showing.'

'No! How horrible!'

'You needn't be alarmed,' I said sullenly.

She was terrified at a casual hint that the finger might have to be amputated. The extravagant horror showed all too clearly her sensual egotism, but it did not displease me.

We talked as we walked along. As usual, the chief burden of conversation was hers. She was happy in the warmth, the brightness and the propriety of her home. It irritated me that she felt not the slightest doubt about her parents.

'I should imagine that your mother has spent quiet nights with another man or two. She's lived a long time.'

'Absolutely not.'

'How do you know? There were things that happened before you were born. Ask your brothers.'

'It isn't true.'

'And I imagine your father has a pretty woman off somewhere.'

'No, no. Absolutely not.'

'What's your proof?'

'You're dreadful. No one has ever said such dreadful things to me before.'

We were on the point of a quarrel, but I did not like quarrels. Sullen silence was called for.

We were on the sidewalk below the Kōrakuen pool. As always, it was teeming with people in search of inexpensive pleasure. Few of the young people could have been described as well dressed. They were in the ready-made shirts and machine sweaters of the fashionable provincial set. A child suddenly squatted down in the middle of the street and began picking up beer caps. It was scolded by its mother.

'Must you be so nasty?' Momoko seemed near tears.

I was not being nasty. It was kindness on my part not to tolerate smugness. I sometimes think I am a fearfully moral beast.

We had turned as our stroll took us, and were at the gate to the Kōrakuen garden of the Mito Tokugawa family. 'The gentleman troubles himself on the world's behalf; only then does he take his pleasure' – hence the name Kōrakuen, 'Garden of After-Pleasure'. Near though it is, I had not before visited it. The sign informed us that the garden closed at four thirty and that tickets were not sold after four. It was ten minutes till four. I urged Momoko inside.

The sun was directly ahead as we went through the gates. The insects of early October were singing.

We passed a party of perhaps twenty people on their way out. Otherwise the paths were empty. Momoko wanted to hold my hand, but I showed her the bandage.

Why, with precarious emotions, were we walking in the late afternoon like lovers, down the quiet path of the old garden? I had of course a picture of our unhappiness in my heart. A scene of beauty threatens the heart, gives it fever and chills. Had she been of sufficient sensibility, I would have liked to hear her rambling on in a delirium. I would have liked to see her lips parched with the horror of having met the unfathomable.

Seeking complete solitude, I walked down past the Waterfall of Awakening. It was dry and the pool was cloudy. The network on its surface like a mesh of threads was from water striders. Seated on a rock we gazed down into the pond.

I could see that she at length found my silence threatening. I was confident that she did not know its source. I had introduced an emotion experimentally, and was fascinated to see it producing agnosticism in another. Without emotion we can link together in any number of ways.

The surface of the pond – rather the swamp – was screened off by leaves and branches, but here and there it caught the rays of the western sun. The inappropriate light set off the accumulation of leaves on the shallow bottom like an unpleasant dream.

'Look at it. If you were to turn a light on them, our hearts would be just as shallow and dirty.'

'Not mine. Mine is deep and clean. I'd like to show it to you.'

'How can you say you're an exception? Give me your proof.'

An exception myself, I was irritated at another's claim to be an exception. I did not see in any case how mediocrity could claim to be an exception.

'I just know it, that's all.'

I could sense well enough the inferno into which she had fallen. She had not once felt the need to prove herself. Soaked in a bliss that dripped sadness, she had dissolved everything from the girlish gewgaws to love itself in the obscure liquid. She was up to the neck in the bathtub of herself. It was a dangerous position, but she was not prepared to ask for help, and indeed refused the helping hand. To wound her, it was necessary to drag her out of it. Otherwise the blade would fall short, deflected by the liquid.

There were autumn cicadas in the evening groves, and the roar of the subway came through the calls of the birds. A yellow leaf dangled from a spider web on a branch far out over the swamp, catching a divine light each time it revolved. It was as if a tiny revolving door were floating in the heavens.

We gazed at it in silence. I was asking what world would be opening beyond the dark gold each time it turned. Perhaps, as it revolved in the busy wind, it would give me a glimpse of the bustle in some miniature street beyond, shining through some tiny city in the air.

The rock was cold. We had to hurry. There was only a half-hour till closing time.

It was a walk as irritating as a hangnail. The quiet beauty of the garden was caught up in the restlessness of sunset. The waterfowl on the pond were astir, the pink of the bush clover beside the wasted iris had faded.

The closing hour was our pretext for hurrying, but it was not our only reason. We were afraid of the mood of the autumn garden, sinking into our hearts; and we wanted the swiftness of our pace to turn up voices inside us more shrilly, like a record that is revolving too fast.

We stood on a bridge along the circular path. There was no one else in sight. Our shadows stretched out over the moving carp, with the shadow of the bridge. We turned our backs to the pond, out of distaste for the huge patent-medicine sign beyond. We were facing a little round artificial hillock tangled with dwarf bamboo, and the net flung by the setting sun upon the groves beyond. I felt like the last fish resisting the violent light and refusing to be caught in the net.

Perhaps I was dreaming of another world. I felt as if a moment containing death had brushed past the two of us, high-school students in pale sweaters on a bridge. The sexual fullness of love suicide crossed my heart. I am not one to call for help, but if help were to come, I thought, it would come only with the end of consciousness. There would be joy in the rotting of consciousness there in the evening light.

The little pond to the west was choked with lotuses.

Like jellyfish in the evening breeze, the lotus pads blocked off the water. Covered with a powder, the green leathery pads buried the valley below the hillock. They softened the light radically, catching the light of other pads, the delicate shadow of a maple branch. They wavered uncertainly, competing for the evening light. It was as if I could hear them in faint chorus.

I saw how complicated their movements were. The wind might come from one direction, but they did not bow obediently in the other. One spot was forever in motion, another obstinately still. One pad would show its underside, but the others would not imitate it. They bowed sluggishly, painfully, to the left and right. Winds that brushed the surfaces and winds that loitered along the stems produced immense disorder. I was beginning to find the evening breeze chilly.

Most of the pads were fresh at their centres but eaten by rust at the edges. The decay seemed to spread from the spots of rust. There had been no rain for two days, and there were brown water stains at the concave centres. Or dead maple leaves.

The sun was still bright, but from somewhere darkness pressed in. We exchanged brief remarks. Though our faces were near, it was as if we were calling out to each other from far off in an inferno.

'What is that?' As if in fright, Momoko pointed to a cluster at the foot of the hillock, a tangle of rich red threads.

It was a cluster of shining spider lilies, a powerful red.

'It's closing time,' said the old attendant. 'Hurry up, please.'

Our afternoon at the Kōrakuen brought me to a decision.

It was a trivial decision. If I was to wound Momoko not in the flesh but in the spirit, then there was an urgent need for another woman.

To make Momoko taboo was at the same time a responsibility and a logical contradiction. And if my carnal interest in her was the hidden source of my rational interest, then my dignity was left with nothing to stand on. I must wound her with the shining sceptre of 'love that is free'.

To have another woman did not seem difficult. I went to a go-go hall on my way home from school. All I had to do was dance as I had learned to at the houses of friends, whether skilfully or not did not matter. I had several friends who had a healthy routine. Each day after school they would spend an hour or so alone at a go-go house before settling down after dinner to studies for entrance examinations. I went with one of them, and persevered over Coca-Cola after the hour had passed. A countrified girl with thick make-up spoke to me, and I danced with her. She was not, however, what I was after.

I had heard from my friend that there were certain to be 'chastity eaters' at such a place. One would imagine rather older women, but such is not always the case. Women are sometimes interested in education even when they are young. A surprising number of them are goodlooking. Their pride dictates against submitting to a sexual virtuoso. They prefer to become tutors and leave a lasting impression on young hearts. The interest in young male purity derives from the pleasure of leading into temptation; and yet, because it is quite clear that the women themselves have no sense of guilt, the pleasure must derive from leaving the man with the guilt which has carefully been nurtured elsewhere. Some are bright and happy, others of a melancholy turn. There is no standard, but they are all like hens warming eggs of sin. They are less interested in hatching the eggs than in cracking the heads of young roosters.

In the course of the evening I made the acquaintance of one of them, a rather well-dressed girl of twenty-five or twenty-six. She said I must call her Nagisa, 'Miss Brink', and did not tell me her real name.

Her eyes were almost uncomfortably large, and she had thin, malicious lips. Yet there was in her face a warm richness as of a rustic orange. Her bosom was a startling white and she had good legs.

'Really!' That was her favourite expression. She was not at all reluctant to ask questions herself, but she greeted every question in return with a 'Really!'

Since I had told Father that I would be home at nine, there was only time for dinner. She drew a map and gave me a telephone number and said that since she lived alone there was no need for shyness.

I want to be as precise as possible about what happened when, some days later, I went calling. Because the event itself is so filled with sensual exaggeration and imaginings and disappointments and the events are so distorted, a person departs from the truth in the very effort to be cool and objective; and if he seeks to portray the intoxication, he falls into conceptualizing. I must take up all three, sexual pleasure and the trembling curiosity of a new experience and an oppressive disharmony that could be either sensual or rational. I must cleanly separate them, allowing none to encroach upon the others, and I must transplant them, perfect and undamaged. The task will not be an easy one.

She seemed at first to have overestimated my shyness. She reassured herself repeatedly of the fact that I was 'new to the experience'. I did not want to appear under false colours, nor, on the other hand, did I want to be one of those young men who seek to attract a certain sort of woman with their inexperience – not after all a very attractive trait. And so I assumed a delicate arrogance, which was nothing but shyness cloaking itself in vanity.

The woman seemed torn between a desire to put me at my ease and a desire to excite me; but she was really thinking of herself. She knew from experience that over-ardent instruction can make the young person stumble. That was the reason for her sweet reserve. It was the perfume with which she had carefully touched herself. I could see a little gauge wavering in her eyes.

Since it was quite obvious that she was using my eagerness and curiosity to arouse herself, I was reluctant to have her look at me. It was not that I was feeling particularly shy; but I made the gesture as I brushed her eyes shut seem like a demand of shyness. I suppose that thus rolling in the dark a woman feels only the wheel that runs over her.

It goes without saying that my feelings of pleasure were over as soon as they began. I was much relieved. Only with the third try did I feel anything like real pleasure.

And so I saw: pleasure has an intellectual element in it from the start.

Which is to say: a certain distance is established, a play of pleasure and awareness is established, calculation and reckoning are established, and so, until one is able to look clearly down upon one's pleasure from without, as a woman looks down at her breasts, there is no pleasure. To be sure, my pleasure took a rather thorny shape.

But the knowledge that the shape of something attained to after considerable practice lies concealed in the initial brief and insubstantial satisfaction was not good for my pride. That very first something was not at all the essence of impulse, it was the essence of concept, long in the making. And the intellectual operations of pleasure thereafter? Do they perhaps make the slow (or precipitous) collapse of concept a small dam, and use the electric power to enrich impulse bit by bit? If so, the intellectual road to the beast is very long.

'You're great,' said the woman afterwards. 'You have real possibilities.'

How many ships has she seen out of harbour with that same bouquet?

I am avalanching.

Yet I have nothing at all to do with the collapse and ruin of self. This avalanche, wilfully destroying family, house, doing injury, bringing shrieks from an inferno, is something that the winter sky has caused to fall gently upon me, and it has nothing to do with my own basic nature. But in the instant of the avalanche, the softness of the snow and the hardness of the cliff change places. The agent of disaster is the snow and not the self. It is the softness and not the hardness.

For a very long time, indeed since the beginning of natural history, my sort of heart, a heart of irresponsible hardness, has been ready. Most commonly, in the form of a stone. In the purest form of all, a diamond.

But the too-bright sun of winter penetrates even into the transparency of my heart. It is at such times that I see myself with wings that have no obstacles, and I see too that I shall do nothing at all with my life.

I shall probably achieve freedom, but freedom akin to death. None of the things I have dreamed of will come to me in this world.

Like the winter view from the signal station on Suruga Bay, when I could see even the reflections from the automobiles on the Izu Peninsula, I can see with these eyes every detail of the future.

I will no doubt have friends. The clever ones will betray me, and only the stupid ones will remain. It is strange that betrayal should come to a person like me. I suppose that everyone, faced with my clarity, feels the urge to betray. There can be no greater victory for betrayal than to betray such clarity. Probably all the people who are not loved by me are confident that they are so loved. The ones who are loved by me will probably guard a beautiful silence.

The whole world will wish my death; and, each trying to outdo the others, seek to prevent it.

My purity will presently wander beyond the horizon to that invisible realm. Probably at the end of unbearable pain I shall seek to become a god. The pain! I will know all of it, the pain of absolute silence, of a world of nothing at all. I will crouch trembling in a corner, like a sick dog. And the happy ones will sing songs around me.

There is no medicine for it. No hospital. It will be written in tiny gold letters, somewhere in the history of the race: that I was evil.

I vow it: that when I am twenty I will cast Father into hell. I must start making plans.

It would have presented no difficulty at all to go walking arm-in-arm with Nagisa where I had promised to meet Momoko. But I did not wish so hasty a solution, nor did I wish to see Nagisa stupidly intoxicated with victory.

She had given me a little silver chain and medal inscribed with her monogram, 'N'. It would not do for school or home wear, but I wore it around my neck when I met Momoko. I knew from the bandage incident that it was not easy to attract Momoko's attention. Despite the cold, I wore an open shirt and a V-neck sweater, and made sure that my shoe was badly tied. The medal was sure to fall out and catch the sun when I retied it.

It was a considerable disappointment that though I tied my shoe three times Momoko did not notice the medal. The inattentiveness came from complete confidence in her own well-being. I could not, for my own part, make too obvious a show.

In desperation I took Momoko swimming at the heated pool of a large Nakano sports centre. She was delighted at this little reminder of our happy summer days in Shimoda.

'You're a man, aren't you?'

'I believe so.'

This classical exchange between man and woman was taking place here and there beside the pool, where one of those Harunobu scenes, men and women indistinguishable, was being posed in the nude. There were long-haired men indistinguishable from women. I have the confidence to fly symbolically over the head of sex, but I have never felt the urge to melt into the other sex. I have no wish to be a woman. The very structure of woman is the foe of clarity.

I had had a swim and was sitting on the edge of the pool. Momoko was leaning towards me. The medal was no more than three or four inches away.

Finally it caught her eye.

She took it in her hand.

'What does "N" stand for?' Finally she asked the question.

'Guess.'

'Your initials are T.H. What might it be, I wonder.'

'Think about it for a moment'

'I know. It stands for Nippon.'

I felt rather let down. I began putting myself at a disadvantage by asking questions in return.

'It was a present. Who from, do you think?'

'"N". I have relations named Noda and Nakamura.'

'And why would I be getting presents from your relatives?'

'I know. It's for "north". It did occur to me that the design around the edge was like a compass. You got it from a shipping company or something. At a launching. North, for a whaler. Right? Am I right? A whaler, and it was sent to your signal station. No doubt about it.'

I cannot be sure whether Momoko really thought so, or whether she was trying to put herself at ease, or whether she sought to conceal her uneasiness in a play of innocence. I had lost the urge, in any case, to tell her she was wrong.

And so my operations turned to Nagisa. She was a phlegmatic sort, and I could appeal to her bland, harmless curiosity. If she had time to spare, I said, she might like to see my young fiancée from a distance. She accepted immediately. She asked me over and over again whether I had slept with Momoko. She seemed very interested in the practical application her pupil had made of her lessons. I told her when I was to meet Momoko at the Renoir and made her promise to act like a stranger. I knew that she was not one to keep a promise.

I was aware that shortly after our arrival Nagisa had arrived and taken a seat behind us, on the other side of the fountain. Silently and lazily, like a cat, she seemed to be glancing at us from time to time. Since Momoko was the innocent one, the understanding between Nagisa and myself was suddenly closer, and it was as if most of my remarks were being directed at her. The silly expression 'physical bond' took meaning.

I was sure that she could hear us through the murmur of the fountain. In the awareness of being overheard, my words took on a certain appearance of sincerity. Momoko was delighted that I was in such good spirits. She was congratulating herself, I could see, that we got on so nicely, though she did not know why.

Tired of conversation, I took the medal from my collar and bit at it. Far from reproving me, Momoko laughed happily. I caught a taste of silver, and against my tongue it felt like an indissoluble pill. The chain brushed my lip and chin. It was pleasant all the same. I felt like a bored dog.

Through the corner of my eye I saw that Nagisa had stood up. I knew from Momoko's wide eyes that she was standing beside us.

Suddenly a red-nailed hand was tugging at the medal.

'You're not to eat my medal.'

I stood up and introduced the two.

'I'm sorry to have interrupted you.' Nagisa walked off. 'I'll see you later.'

Momoko was blanched and trembling.

It was snowing. I spent a tedious Saturday afternoon at home. There is a window at the landing of the Western staircase. Only from it do you get a good view of the street. My chin on the sill, I knelt looking out at the snow. It was a quiet street even on ordinary days, and today the automobile tracks were blotted out.

There was a dim light from the snow. Though the sky was dark, the light of the snow signalled a strange time of its own, different from the time of day. Behind the house across the street it settled into hollows between the blocks of a concrete fence.

An old man, umbrella-less, in a brown coat and black beret, came up from the right. There was a pronounced swelling towards the bottom of his coat. He was embracing it. It would seem that he had a parcel of some sort which he wanted to keep dry. I could see a gaunt, hollow face under the beret, quite out of keeping with the stout figure.

He stopped at our gate. There was a low gate beside the main one. I thought he would be some unusually impoverished caller with a request to make of my father. He looked around him, however, not bothering to brush the snow from his now white coat and making no motion towards coming in.

The swelling disappeared. A parcel fell to the ground, as if he had laid a great egg. I gazed at it. At first I could not make out what it might be. A spherical object of many colours glowed darkly from the snow. I saw that it was scraps of fruits and vegetables in a plastic kerchief. The kerchief bulged with bits of red apple, orange carrot, pale green cabbage. If he had gone out to throw them away, then he must be a strict vegetarian who lived alone. In such quantities, they gave the snow a strange, fresh spectrum. Even the bits of green cabbage seemed to breathe with a strangled breathing.

Riveted on the bundle, my eyes fell behind the old man as he walked off. He took tiny steps through the snow. I saw him from behind. Even taking into consideration the hunched shoulders, the coat was shapeless and unnatural. It was still swollen, though not so much as before.

He walked off. He was probably unaware of it himself, but five or six yards from the gate something fell from his coat like a great ink spot.

It was a dead bird, a crow, apparently. Or perhaps a turkey. I even thought I could hear the sound of the wings as it struck the snow; but the old man walked on.

The bird was a puzzle. It was a considerable distance away, blocked by the trees in the garden and further obscured by the snow, and there was a limit to my powers of vision. I thought of going for binoculars or going out to look, but an overpowering inertia held me back.

What sort of bird was it? As I looked at it, for almost too long a time, it came to seem not a bird but a woman's hair.

Momoko's sufferings had begun, like a conflagration from a cigarette. The perfectly ordinary girl and the great philosopher are alike: for both, the smallest triviality can become the vision that wipes out the world.

As planned, I became the petitioner. I sought to cajole her, and I followed her lead in saying the most dreadful things about Nagisa. She wept as she told me I must put an end to the affair. I said I would like nothing more, but needed her help. With some exaggeration, I said I would need her help if I was to break off with that devil of a woman.

She agreed to help me, but on one condition. I must throw away the necklace, and she must be witness to the act. Since it was nothing to me, I agreed. The two of us went to the bridge in front of Suidōbashi Station. I took it off and handed it to her, and told her to throw it with her own hand into the filthy canal. She flung it from her, arching it high into the sunlight of the winter evening. It hit the stinking water over which a barge was just then passing. She fell on me, her breathing as heavy as if she had just committed murder. Passers-by looked at us curiously.

It was time for my special night classes. I left her, with a promise to meet on Saturday afternoon.

*

I had Momoko write to Nagisa a letter of my dictating.

I wonder how many times I used the word 'love' that Saturday afternoon. I said that if I loved Momoko and Momoko loved me, then we must plan together to avert disaster, we must write a fraudulent letter.

We met at a bowling alley by the Meiji Gardens. After several strings, we went out hand in hand through the warm winter afternoon, through the shadows of the bare gingko trees, and into a new coffeehouse on Aoyama Avenue. I had brought paper and stamp and envelope.

Applying the anaesthetic, I whispered of love as we walked along. In the course of time I had turned her into a person no different from the mad Kinué. She breathed easily only under the most obvious misconception, that our love was unchanging.

The two of them are alike in their denial of reality, Kinué in her belief that she is beautiful, Momoko in her belief that she is loved. Momoko needs help with her delusion, however, while Kinué needs no word from outside. If only I could raise Momoko to the same level! Since there was in the wish a pedagogical urge – love, so to speak – my protestations of love were not wholly without substance. But was there not a methodological contradiction in having an affirmer of reality like Momoko become a denier? It would not be easy to have her, like Kinué, do battle with the whole world.

But while reading the sacred formula 'I love you' over and over, endlessly, a change comes to the heart of the reader, I could almost feel that I was in love, that some corner of my heart was drunk in the sudden and abandoned liberation of the banished word. How similar the tempter is to the flying instructor who must go flying with a beginner!

Momoko's other requirement, altogether appropriate for a somewhat old-fashioned girl, was no more than a purely 'spiritual' affirmation, and all that was needed to satisfy it was a word or two. Words, casting a clear shadow on the earth in their passage – might they not have been the essential I? I had been born to use words thus. If so (these sentimental locutions greatly annoy me, of course), then perhaps the basic mother tongue I have kept hidden is after all the language of love.

While the patient himself is ignorant of the truth, his family goes on telling him that he is certain to recover. So, with the most intense earnestness, I whispered over and over to Momoko of love, there in the beautiful network of shadows from the winter trees.

Once we were at our ease in the coffeehouse, I told her of Nagisa's nature, as if I were asking her advice and following it. I described in outline certain stratagems likely to be effective. I of course created my Nagisa with complete licence.

Since Momoko was my fiancée and loved me, Nagisa was not the sort of woman likely to be moved by a plea that she give me up. Such a plea would only arouse her contempt and lead her on to greater unpleasantness. She was a woman who did battle with the word 'love' and sought to bring it down by assault from the rear. She had resolved to leave her brand on boys who would one day be good husbands and fathers, and so to jeer from the shadows at marriage itself. Yet she had her amiable defects. She gave no ground in her hatred of love, but she had a certain strange sympathy for a woman who was struggling to make her way. I had heard her describe several representatives of the species. The argument most likely to move her was that she was obstructing not love but money and security.

So what should we do?

'Make me a girl who does not love you but needs you for your money.'

'Precisely.'

The thought greatly excited Momoko. What fun, she said dreamily.

The excitement that had replaced her gloom was altogether too bright and open. It put me out of sorts.

She continued. 'And of course there is a grain of truth in it. Mother and Father make a great secret of it, and I have never said anything myself; but we're not all that well off. There was trouble in the bank and Father took responsibility and all the land at home is mortgaged. Father is such a good-natured man. He was the victim.'

She was as entranced with the effort to make herself into a mean, crass woman (certain that she could never be one) as a young girl with her part in the school play. This is the letter which, to that end, I devised for her there in the coffeehouse.

Dear Nagisa,

Because I am about to make a request of you, please read my letter through to the end. The truth is that I want you to stop seeing Tōru.

I will tell you the reasons as honestly as I can. Tōru and I would seem to be tentatively engaged, but we do not love each other. I do think of us as good friends, but my feelings go no deeper. What I really want is affluence and freedom, married to an intelligent husband who has no difficult family problems. In this I am following my father's wishes. Tōru's father has not much longer to live, and when he dies Tōru will inherit the whole of his estate. My father has his own interests in the matter. There have been difficulties at the bank, of which we do not speak, and we are somewhat pressed financially, and need the help of Tōru's father and of Tōru himself once his father is dead. I do love my mother and father, and if Tōru's affections were to turn elsewhere it would mean the end of all my plans and hopes. And so, to put the matter quite bluntly, the marriage is of very great importance for financial reasons. I have come to think that there is nothing more important in this world than money. I do not see anything dirty in it, and I think expressions like 'love' and 'affection', leaving it out of consideration, are misplaced. What may for you be a moment's dalliance is a matter of the greatest importance for my whole family. I am not saying that because I love Tōru you must give him up. I am speaking as a more mature and calculating girl than you may think.

This being the case, you are mistaken if you tell yourself that it will be all right for you to go on seeing Tōru in secret. The secret is certain to leak out, and it will not do to have Tōru think me a woman willing to close her eyes to everything for the sake of money. It is precisely for the sake of money that I must watch over him and preserve my pride.

You must not show this letter to Tōru. It has taken all my resolution to write it. If you are an evil woman, then show it to him and make it your weapon for getting him away from me; but you will have to live the rest of your life with the knowledge of having taken from another woman not love but her very living. We must dispose of the matter with cool heads, since the emotions of neither of us are involved. I feel quite capable of killing you if you show this letter to him; and I doubt that it will be an ordinary sort of murder.

Most sincerely,

MOMOKO

'The ending is good.' Momoko was still excited.

'If I were to see it anything could happen.' I smiled.

'I'm not worried.' She leaned towards me.

I had her address the envelope and put a special delivery stamp on it, and we went off hand in hand to mail it.

Today I went to Nagisa's apartment and saw the letter. Trembling with anger, I snatched it from her and ran out. At home later that night, I went into Father's study and, heartbroken, showed it to him.

25

Tōru began preparatory school at seventeen, two years later than most boys, and he would enter the university at twenty, in 1974, when he reached legal maturity. During his third year in preparatory school he had no recess from studies for the university examinations. Honda cautioned him against overwork.

One autumn day in that third year Honda dragged a protesting Tōru out for a weekend of nature. Tōru did not want to go far from home, and so they followed his wishes and drove to Yokohama for a look at the ships, his first in a very long time. The plan was that they would have dinner in the Chinese quarter of Yokohama.

Unfortunately the sky of early October was clouded over. The sky is high and wide over Yokohama. They got out at South Pier. The sky was an expanse of rough mackerel clouds, with only here and there a spot of white. Like the aftertone of a bell, there was a touch of blue beyond Central Pier. It seemed on the verge of disappearing.

'If we had our own car I could drive you. A driver is a useless expense.'

'Not yet. I'll buy you one, I promise, when you get into the university. It will only be a little longer.'

Sending Tōru off to get tickets for the terminal building, Honda leaned on his stick and looked wearily up at the stairs he must climb. He knew that Tōru would be willing enough to help him, but did not want to ask.

Tōru was happy from the time they reached the harbour. He had known that he would be. Not only Shimizu but every harbour was like a crystalline medicine that worked an immediate cure on him.

It was two in the afternoon. The register for nine in the morning had been posted: the *Chung Lien II*, Panamanian, 2,167 tons; a Soviet ship; the *Hai-i*, Chinese, 2,767 tons; the *Mindanao*, Philippines, 3,357 tons. The *Khabarovsk*, a Soviet ship bringing numbers of Japanese passengers from Nahodka, was due at two thirty. The view of the ships was good from the second floor of the terminal building, slightly higher than their decks.

They looked out over the prow of the *Chung Lien*, and the stir in the harbour beyond.

It was not unusual for the two of them, as the seasons passed, to stand thus side by side in confrontation with grandeur. Perhaps indeed it was the position best for the Hondas, father and son. If the 'relationship' between them consisted in using nature as a mediator between their separate awarenesses, knowing that evil results from a direct meeting, then they were using nature as a giant filter to turn brine into potable water.

Below the prow of the *Chung Lien* was the lighter anchorage, like an accumulation of bobbing driftwood. Marks and signs on the concrete pier forbidding automobiles suggested the aftermath of a game of hopscotch. A dirty smoke drifted in from somewhere, and there was an incessant chugging of engines.

The paint had flaked from the dark hull of the *Chung Lien*. The bright red of the rust-preventive painted a pattern around the prow like an aerial map of harbour installations. The rusty stockless anchor clung to the hawse pipe like a great crab.

'What is the cargo, all done up in neat, long bundles? Like spindles.' Honda was already scrutinizing the stevedores at work on the *Chung Lien*.

'Boxes of some sort, I'd imagine.'

Satisfied that his son knew no more than he, Honda turned his attention to the shouts of the stevedores and labour such as he had not known in his life.

The astonishing thing was that the flesh, the muscles, the organs (the brain aside) given to a human being should through the whole of a long life of indolence have been blessed with health and a superfluity of money. Nor had Honda wielded great powers of creativity or imagination. Only cool analysis and solid judgement had been his. He had made money enough through them. He felt no pangs of conscience at the sweating stevedores he saw in action or in pictures, but he did feel a nameless irritation. The scenes and the objects and the movements before him were not the reality of something he had touched and taken profit from. They were a barrier, an opaque wall forever laughing derisively at both sides, daubed all over with smelly paint, between him and some unseen unreality and the unseen people taking profit from it. And the figures so vivid on the wall were themselves in the tightest bondage, controlled by someone else. Honda had never wanted to be thus in opaque bondage, but he had no doubt that they were the ones who had their anchors like ships, deep in life and being. Society paid recompense only for sacrifice. Intelligence was paid in measure proportionate to the sacrifice of life and being.

But there was no point in worrying at this late date. All he had to do was enjoy the movements before him. He thought of the ships that would come into the harbour after he was dead, and sail off for sunny lands. The world overflowed with hopes of which he was not part. If he were a harbour himself, however hopeless a harbour, he would have to give anchorage to a number of hopes. But as it was, he might as well declare to the world and to the sea that he was a complete superfluity.

And if he were a harbour?

He glanced at the single little boat in Honda Harbour, Tōru here beside him, engrossed in the unloading operations. A boat that was exactly the same as the harbour, rotting with the harbour, refusing forever to leave. Honda, at least, knew it. The ship was cemented to the pier. They were a model father and son.

The great dark holds of the *Chung Lien* were agape. The cargo overflowed the mouths of the holds. The figures of stevedores in brown sweaters and green bellybands of goldthreaded wool were half visible on the mountains of cargo, their yellow helmets bobbing as they shouted up at the cranes. The myriad iron lines of the derrick shook with their own shouts, and as the cargo wavered precariously in the air it blotted out and then revealed again the gold-lettered name of the passenger ship tied up at Central Pier.

An officer in a white cap was supervising the operations. He was smiling. It would seem that he had shouted a loud joke to encourage the stevedores.

Tired of the unloading operations, the father and son walked to a point from which they could compare the stern of the *Chung Lien* with the prow of the Soviet ship.

The prow was astir with life, the low stern was deserted. Ochre vents pointed in several directions. Rough piles of garbage. Ancient casks with rusty iron hoops. Life jackets on white railings. Ships' fittings. Coils of ropes. The delicate white folds of lifeboats under ochre covers. An antique lantern still burned under the Panamanian flag.

The stillness was like that of a Dutch still life, tinged over with the sadness of the sea. It was as if napping with its private parts exposed to the forbidden gaze of landsmen, all the long hours of tedium aboard ship.

The black prow of the Soviet ship with its thirteen silver cranes pressed down from above. The rust of the anchor clinging to the hawse pipe had streaked the hull with red spider webs.

The ropes tying them to land marked off great vistas, three crossed ropes each, trailing beards of Manila hemp. Between the immovable iron screens moved the unresting bustle of the harbour. Each time a little tug with old black tyres hanging at its side or a white streamlined pilot boat moved past, it would leave a smooth track in its wake, and the dark irritability would for a time be soothed.

Tōru thought of Shimizu as he had studied it alone on holidays. Something was wrested from his heart each time, he would feel something like a sigh from the great lungs of the harbour, and as he covered his ears against the shouting and roaring and grating, he would taste simultaneously of oppression and liberation, and be filled with a sweet emptiness. It was the same today, though his father had an inhibiting effect.

'I think it was a good thing,' said Honda, 'that we broke off with the Hamanaka girl early in the spring. I can talk to you now that you have gotten over it and seem so lost in your studies.'

'It doesn't matter.' Annoyed, Tōru put a touch of boyish melancholy and gallantry into his words. They were not enough to stop Honda. Honda's real purpose lay not in apology but in the question he had long been wanting to ask.

'But that letter. Doesn't it strike you as altogether too stupid? Wasn't it really too much to have a young girl speak openly of what we had been perfectly aware of and closed our eyes to? Her parents made all sorts of excuses, and the man who first came with the proposal had nothing to say at all when he saw the letter.'

It displeased Tōru that Honda, who had until now not touched upon the matter, should be speaking so plainly, almost too plainly. He sensed that Honda had taken as much pleasure in breaking the engagement as in making it.

'But don't you suppose all the proposals that come to us are the same?' Elbows on the railing, Tōru did not look up. 'Momoko was honest, and so we were able to take early measures.'

'I quite agree. But we mustn't give up. We'll find a good girl yet. But that letter –'

'Why should you be so worried about it now?'

Honda gave Tōru a gentle nudge with his elbow. Tōru felt as if he had been jabbed by a bone. 'You had her write it?'

Tōru had been expecting the question. 'Suppose I did. What would you do?'

'Nothing at all. The only point is that you have found a way of getting through life. We must describe it as a dark way, with no sweetness in it.'

Tōru's self-respect had been affronted. 'I would not want to be thought sweet.'

'But you were very sweet while it was all in process.'

'I was doing as you wanted me to do, I should imagine.'

'Yes.'

Tōru shuddered as the old man bared his teeth to the sea wind. They had reached a point of agreement, and it brought Tōru to thoughts of murder. He could easily enough let them have their way by pushing Honda over; but he feared that Honda was aware of even that impulse. It left him. To have to live was blacker than the most cheerless black. To have to see every day a man who sought to understand, and did understand, the deepest thing inside him.

They had little more to say. After a round of the terminal building, they stood for a time looking at the Philippine ship on the far side.

Directly in front of them was an open door to the crew's cabins. They could see the scarred linoleum, glowing dully, and, around a corner, the iron rail of a stairway leading downward. The short, empty corridor of the quotidian, of frozen human life, never for a moment away from human beings, on whatever remote seas. In the great white transient ship, that one spot was representative of a dark, dull afternoon corridor in every house. In a vast, unpeopled house as well, where lived only an old man and a boy.

Honda ducked. Tōru had just made a violent motion. Honda caught a glimpse of the word 'Notebook' on the rolled-up tablet Tōru had taken from his briefcase. He flung it past the stern of the Philippine ship.

'What are you doing?'

'Notes I don't need. Scribblings.'

'You'll be fined if they catch you.'

But there was no one on the pier, and on the ship only a Philippine sailor who looked down at the sea in surprise. The rubber-bound tablet floated for an instant and sank.

A white Soviet ship with a red star on its prow and the name 'Khabarovsk' in gold letters was being brought against the pier by a tugboat with masts the colour of a thorny broiled lobster. There was a cluster of welcomers at the rail, their hair blowing in the wind. Some were on tiptoes. Children on the shoulders of adults were already shouting and waving.

26

The very question was indignant when Keiko asked Honda how Tōru meant to spend the Christmas of 1974. Since the September incident, the eighty-year-old Honda had been afraid of everything. His incisiveness had quite left him. He seemed to cower and tremble perpetually, to be a victim of unrelieved disquiet.

This state of affairs was to be explained not only by the September incident. They were now in the fourth year since Honda had adopted Tōru. Through most of those years Tōru had seemed quiet and docile, and there had been little change in him; but this spring he had reached maturity and entered Tokyo University, and everything was changed. He had suddenly come to treat his father as an adversary. He was prompt in putting down every sign of resistance. After Tōru had hit him on the forehead with a fire poker, Honda went to a clinic for a few days to have the wound treated – he told the doctors that he'd had a bad fall. Thereafter he was most attentive in reading and deferring to Tōru's wishes. Tōru was studiously rude to Keiko, whom he recognized as Honda's ally.

From long years of avoiding relatives who might be after his money, Honda had no allies prepared to sympathize with him. Those who had opposed the adoption were pleased. Everything had turned out as expected. They set no stock whatsoever by Honda's complaints. He was only trying to arouse sympathy. Their sympathies were rather with Tōru. Such beautiful eyes, such impeccable deportment, such a devoted sense of filial duty – they could only conclude that a suspicious old man was maligning him. And indeed Tōru's manners were above reproach.

'There seem to be troublemakers around. Who can have told you such a silly story? Mrs Hisamatsu, I'm sure. She's a nice person, but she believes everything Father tells her. I'm afraid he's pretty far gone. He has delusions. I imagine that's what happens when you spend so many years worrying about money; but he treats even me, right here under the same roof, like a thief. After all, I am young, and when I talk back he starts telling people I'm not good to him. The time he fell in the garden and hit his head against the root of the plum tree – remember? – he told Mrs Hisamatsu I'd hit him with a poker. She actually believed it, every last word of it, and that doesn't give me much room to fight back.'

He had that summer brought the mad Kinué from Shimizu and installed her in the garden cottage.

'Her? Oh, she's a very sad case. In my Shimizu days she helped me this way and that. She wanted to come to Tokyo because at home everybody made fun of her and the children were always chasing after her and shouting at her. So I persuaded her parents to let me have her. They'd kill her if they put her in an asylum. Yes, she's crazy, no doubt about it, but she's harmless.'

Casual acquaintances among the elders of the family were much taken by Tōru, but they were courteously and skilfully turned away when they sought to enter his life. They were inclined to lament that a man once so keen and intelligent as Honda should have fallen so hopelessly into senile delusions. They had long memories, remembering that windfall of more than twenty years before. Envy was at work.

A day in Tōru's life.

There was no longer a need to look at the sea and await ships.

There was no need to attend classes either, but Tōru did so to inspire confidence. He went by automobile, despite the fact that the university was a ten-minute walk away.

The habit of rising early had not left him. Judging from the light through the curtains that a quiet summer rain was falling, he would go over the ordering of the world he controlled. Were the evil and the arrogance going like clockwork? Was no one yet aware of the fact that the world was wholly under the control of evil? Was order being preserved, everything proceeding after the laws, with not the smallest spot of love to be detected anywhere? Were people happy under his hegemony? Had transparent evil, in form a poem, been spread over their heads? Had 'the human' been carefully wiped away? Had careful arrangements been made for every sign of warmth to be ridiculed? Was spirit quite dead?

Tōru was confident that if he but laid a beautiful white hand upon it, the world would succumb to a beautiful illness. And it was natural too that he should expect windfall to follow unanticipated windfall. For reasons that he did not know, an impoverished signalman had been chosen as the foster son of a rich old man, and an old man with one foot in the grave. One of these days a king would come from some country or other and ask to adopt him.

Even in the winter he would run to the shower room he had had installed next to his bedroom and have a cold shower. It was the best thing for waking a person up.

The cold water would liven his pulse, lash at his chest with its transparent whip, thousands of silver needles would stab at his skin. He would take it against his back for a time and turn to face it again. His heart had still not quite made friends with it. It was as if a sheet of iron were pushing at his chest, as if his naked flesh were encased in a tight suit of armour. He twisted and turned, like a corpse dangling from a rope of water. Finally his skin had awakened. Young skin stood there regally, turning off the drops of water. At that moment Tōru raised his left arm and looked down at the three moles like three shining black pebbles in a cascade. They were the sign of the elite, visible to no one, hidden under a folded wing.

He dried himself. He breathed deeply. His body was flushed.

It was the duty of the maid Tsuné to bring his breakfast the moment he called for it. Tsuné was a girl he had picked up in a Kanda coffeehouse. She obeyed all his orders.

It was only two years since he had first known a woman, but he had quickly learned the rules for making a woman serve a man who did not love her. And he knew how to spot instantly a woman who would do what he told her. He had dismissed all the maids likely to follow Honda's wishes and hired women whom he had discovered and slept with, and given them the title 'maid', using the English word. Tsuné was the stupidest one among them, and the one with the largest breasts.

When breakfast was on the table, he poked at a breast by way of good morning.

'Nice and firm.'

'Yes, in very good shape.' Tsuné answered respectfully if expressionlessly. The heavy, dark flesh itself was respectful. Particularly deferential was the navel, deep as a well. The beautiful legs were somehow incompatible with the rest of Tsuné. She was aware of that fact. Tōru had seen how, as she brought coffee past on the uneven floor of the coffeehouse, she had brushed her calf against the lower branches of the starving rubber plant, like a cat rubbing against a bush.

Tōru thought of something. Going over to the window, he looked down into the garden, the chest of his bathrobe open to the morning breeze. Even now Honda scrupulously respected the hour for his morning walk, just after he was out of bed.

Tottering along on his stick in the stripes of November sunlight, Honda smiled and managed a good morning Tōru could barely hear.

Tōru smiled and waved. 'I'll be damned. The old man's still alive.' That was his good morning.

Still smiling, Honda skirted a dangerous steppingstone. He did not know what would come flying down upon him if he were so incautious as to say more. He had only to endure this moment of humiliation. Tōru would be out of the house at least until evening.

'Old people smell bad. Go away.' Honda's offence had been to come too near.

Honda's cheek twitched with anger, but he had no recourse. If Tōru had shouted at him, he could and would have shouted back. But Tōru had spoken softly and coolly, gazing at Honda with his clean, beautiful eyes, a smile on his pale face.

Tōru's dislike seemed to have grown through the four years they had been together. He disliked everything, the ugly, impotent flesh, the useless chatter that covered the impotence, the tiresome repetitiveness, five and six times over, the automatism that became fretful at the repetitiveness itself, the self-importance and the cowardice, the miserliness and the self-indulgence, the pusillanimity in the constant fear of death, the complete permissiveness, the wrinkled hands, the gait like a measuring worm, the mixture of arrogance and obsequiousness on the face. And Japan was teeming with old people.

Back at the breakfast table he kept Tsuné on duty to pour his coffee. He had her put in sugar. He complained about the toast.

It was a sort of superstition that the success of a day depended upon a smooth beginning. The morning must be an unflawed crystal. He had been able to endure the boredom of life at the signal station because observation did not damage self-respect.

Once Tsuné said: 'The manager of the coffee shop used to call me Asparagus. Because I am long and white, he said.'

Tōru replied by pressing his lighted cigarette against the back of her hand. Stupid though she was, Tsuné thereafter minded her words. Especially when she served him at breakfast. The four 'maids' took turns on duty. Three of them looked after Tōru, Honda, and Kinué, and the fourth was off duty. The one who served Tōru his breakfast was the one he received in his bed at night. When he had finished with her she was dismissed. No one was permitted to spend the night with him. They thus enjoyed his favours once every four days, and were allowed to leave the house once a week. Honda secretly admired the tightness of the control and the want of dissension. The maids followed Tōru's orders as if to do so were in the nature of things.

He had taught them all to call Honda 'the old master', and otherwise trained them impeccably. Occasional callers would say that nowhere else these days did they see such beautiful and well-trained maids. Tōru left Honda wanting for nothing even while humiliating him.

Having made himself ready for school, Tōru always looked in at the garden cottage. Carefully made up, wearing a negligee, Kinué always received him from the chaise longue on the veranda. Her newest coquetry was illness.

Tōru would sit on the veranda and face the ugly woman with the warmest, most sincere gentleness.

'Good morning. And how are you feeling this morning?'

'Not too bad, thank you. I doubt if there is anything more beautiful in this world than the moment when a beautiful woman with only the strength to make herself up, all weak on her couch, receives a caller and manages a feeble "Not too bad, thank you". The beauty of it all waves like a heavy flower, and it is there on her eyelids as she closes her eyes. Isn't it? I think of it as the one thing I can do for all your kindness. But I'm very grateful. You're the one kind man in the world who gives me everything and asks nothing in return. And now that I'm here I can see you every day and don't have to go out. If only your father weren't here.'

'Don't worry about him. He'll give up and die one of these days. The September business has been taken care of and everything is going fine. I think next year maybe I can buy you a diamond ring.'

'How nice! That's what will keep me alive, the thought of it. But today I'll have to make do with flowers. The white chrysanthemum in the garden is my flower for today. Will you pick it for me? How nice. No, not that one. The one in the pot. That's it. The big white one with the petals all drooping like threads.'

Heedlessly, Tōru broke off the white chrysanthemum so carefully tended by Honda. Like an ailing beauty, Kinué turned it languorously in her fingers. Then, with an all-too-fleeting smile on her lips, she put it in her hair.

'Be off with you. You'll be late for school. Think of me between classes.' And she waved him good-bye.

Tōru went to the garage. He started up the Mustang sports car he had had Honda buy him that spring upon his entry into the university. If the absent, romantic engine of a ship could cut through waves so cleanly, kick up such a wake, then why could not the six delicately alert cylinders of the Mustang scatter the stupid crowds, cut through the masses of flesh, scatter splashes of red as the other scattered splashes of white?

But it was held in quiet control. It was coaxed and wheedled into a gentle pretence of docility. People admired it as they admire a sharp, shining blade. It forced a smile from its beautiful hood, paint all ashine, to assure them that it was not dangerous.

Capable of a hundred and twenty-five miles per hour, it debased itself by keeping to the twenty-five-mile speed limit as it made its way through the Hongō morning crowds.

The September third incident.

It began with a little spat Tōru and Honda had in the morning.

Through the summer Tōru had been happily rid of Honda, who had taken refuge from the heat at Hakoné. Reluctant to rebuild after his Gotemba villa burned down, Honda had left the land as it was and, always sensitive to the heat, spent his summers at a Hakoné inn. Tōru preferred to stay in Tokyo and drive here and there, to the mountains and the sea, with friends. Honda returned to Tokyo on the evening of September second. He saw Tōru for the first time in some weeks. There was clear anger in the eyes that greeted him from the sun-blackened face. Honda was frightened.

Where was the crape myrtle, he asked in surprise as he went out into the garden on the morning of the third. The old crape myrtle by the garden cottage had been cut at the roots.

Kinué, who had been in the main house, had moved to the cottage early in July. It had been from fear of Tōru after the poker incident that Honda had first taken her in.

Tōru came out. He had the poker in his left hand. His room was a remodelled parlour. It had the only fireplace in the house. Even in summer there was a poker on the nail beside it.

Tōru of course knew that the mere sight of it would make Honda cower like a whipped dog.

'What are you doing with that thing? This time I'll call the police. Last time I kept quiet because I didn't want publicity, but it won't be so easy for you this time.' Honda's shoulders were quivering, and it had taken all his courage to speak.

'You have a stick, don't you? Defend yourself with that.'

Honda had been looking forward to the crape myrtle in bloom, its blossoms shining against a trunk smooth like the white skin of a leper. But there was none. The garden had been made over, he knew, in the Ālaya, the Storehouse, into a different garden. Gardens too must change. But in the instant that he so felt, uncontrollable anger came from another source. He cried out, and even as he cried out he was afraid.

The summer rains had ended and the heat had come after Kinué had moved to the cottage. The crape myrtle was in bloom. She disliked it, she said. It gave her a headache. She started saying that Honda had planted it there to drive her mad; and so Tōru cut it down after Honda's departure for Hakoné. It was as simple as that.

Kinué herself was out of sight, far back in the dusky recesses of the cottage. Tōru offered Honda no explanation. There would be no advantage in it.

'I suppose you cut it down?' said Honda, more softly.

'That I did.' Tōru's answer was cheerful.

'Why?'

'It was old and useless.' Tōru smiled a beautiful smile.

At such times Tōru would lower a thick glass door before his eyes. Glass that came down from the sky. Glass made from exactly the same material as the limpid morning sky. Honda knew that no shout, no word would reach Tōru's ears. Tōru would only see false molars. Honda already had inorganic teeth. He was already beginning to die.

'I see. It makes no difference.'

All through the day Honda sat still in his room. He barely touched the food that the 'maid' brought. He knew what she would report to Tōru.

'The old man's being awful sulky.'

Perhaps the sufferings of the old man did in fact come to nothing more than sulkiness. Honda could see in them foolishness beyond defending. It had all been his own doing and not Tōru's. There was no need for surprise at the change in Tōru. Honda had seen at the first glance the 'evil' in the boy.

But at the moment he wanted to measure the depth of the wound inflicted on his self-respect by what he had asked for.

Honda disliked air-conditioning and was at an age when he feared stairs. He had a large twelve-mat room on the ground floor, looking out over the garden to the cottage. Built in the medieval *shoin* style, it was the oldest and gloomiest room in the house. Honda ranged four linen cushions in a row. He lay down and then sat up on his heels. With all the sliding doors pulled shut, he let the heat accumulate. Sometimes he would crawl to the table for a drink of water. It was as warm as in full sunlight.

Time went past along the indefinable line between waking and sleeping, like a nap at the ultimate end of anger and sadness. Even the pain in his hips would have been a distraction, but today there was none. He was only exhausted.

An unfathomable disaster seemed to be coming down on him, only made worse by the fact that it had precise, delicate gradations, and, like a subtly compounded potion, was having the predicted effect. Honda's old age should have been free of vanity, ambition, honour, prestige, reason, and above all emotion. But it wanted cheer. Although he should have forgotten all feeling long ago, black irritation and anger continued to smoulder like a bed of embers. Stirred, they sent off a reeking smoke.

There was autumn in the sunlight on the paper doors, but isolation contained no signs of movement, of change into something else, like the change of the seasons. All was stagnation. He could see them clearly in himself, anger and sadness that should not have been there, like puddles after a rain. The feeling born this morning was like a bed of leaves ten years old, and new each instant. All the unpleasant memories poured in upon him, but he could not, like a youth, say that his life was unhappy.

When the light at the window told him that evening was near, sexual desire stirred in the crouching Honda. It was not a sudden onset of desire, but rather something tepid that had gestated through hours of sadness and anger and coiled round his brain like a red worm.

The driver he had used over the years had retired, and his successor had been guilty of certain indecisions. And so Honda had sold his automobile and now used rented cars. At ten he called a maid on the interphone and asked her to order a car. He took out a black summer suit and a grey sports shirt.

Tōru was out. The maids looked with curiosity upon the nocturnal departure of the eighty-year-old Honda.

When the car turned into the Meiji Gardens, Honda's desire had become something like a faint attack of nausea. Here he was again, after twenty years.

But it was not sexual desire that had burned in him all through the ride.

His hands on his stick, more erect than usual, he had been muttering to himself: 'I only have to endure it six months more. Just six months more. If he's the real thing.'

That 'if' made him tremble. If Tōru were to die in the six months before his twenty-first birthday, everything could be forgiven. Only the awareness of that birthday had made it possible for Honda to endure the arrogance. And if Tōru was counterfeit?

The thought of Tōru's death had been a great comfort. In his humiliation he had concentrated upon Tōru's death, in his heart already killed him. His heart was quiet, happiness welled up, his nose twitched with tolerance and pity when he saw death, like the sun through isinglass, beyond the violence and cruelty. He could be drunk on the open cruelty of what is called charity. Perhaps that was what he had found in the light upon the vast, empty Indian plain.

He had not yet detected in himself symptoms of a fatal illness. There was nothing to be alarmed about in his blood pressure or his heart. He was confident that if he lasted another half year he would outlive Tōru, perhaps by only a few days. What quiet, secure tears he would be able to shed! Before the foolish world, he would play the part of the tragic father deprived of the son he had come upon so late in life. He could not deny that there was pleasure in looking forward to Tōru's death, in looking ahead to it with the quiet love, oozing sweet poison, of one who knows everything. Tōru's violence, beguiling and lovable, seen through the time ahead as through a Mayfly's wing. People do not love pets that will outlive them. A short life is a condition for love.

And perhaps Tōru was fretting at a prospect like a strange, unheard-of ship suddenly appearing on a horizon which he had been scanning for days. Perhaps a foretaste of death was moving him, irritating him. The possibility brought unbounded gentleness over Honda. He felt that he could love not only Tōru but the whole human race. He knew the nature of human love.

But if Tōru was counterfeit? If he was to live on and on, and Honda, unable to keep up with him, to waste away?

The roots of the strangling desire within him were in the uncertainty. If he was to die first, then he could not refuse the basest of desires. He might all along have been destined to die in humiliation and miscalculation. The miscalculation about Tōru may itself have been the trap laid by Honda's destiny. If a person like Honda had a destiny.

The fact that Tōru's awareness was too much like his own had long been a seed of disquiet. Perhaps Tōru had read everything. Perhaps Tōru knew that he would live a long life, and, reading the determined malice in the practical education given him by an old man confident of his early death, had plotted his revenge.

Perhaps the eighty-year-old and the twenty-year-old were even now engaged in close combat over life and death.

Night in the Meiji Gardens, for the first time in twenty years. The car had turned left from the Gondawara entrance and was on the circular drive.

'Keep going, keep going.' Each time Honda gave the order he added a cough, like a bothersome accessory.

Egg-coloured shirts appeared and disappeared among the night trees. For the first time in a very long while, Honda felt that very special throb in his chest. Old desire still lay piled under the trees like last year's leaves.

'Go on, go on.'

The car turned right behind the art gallery, where the groves were thickest.

There were two or three couples. The lighting was as inadequate as ever. Suddenly there was a glaring cluster of lights to the left. In the middle of the park the entrance to the expressway gaped with a multitude of lights, like a deserted amusement park.

To the right would be the grove on the left side of the art gallery. The night trees cut off the dome, and branches poured out over the sidewalk, a tangle of firs, plantains, pines. Even from the moving car he could hear the insects in the clump of agaves. As if it had been yesterday, he remembered the ferocity of the mosquitoes in the thickets and the sound of slapping against naked skin.

He dismissed the car at the parking lot by the art gallery. The driver glanced at him from under a narrow forehead. It was the sort of glance that can sometimes work collapse. You may go, Honda said again, more strongly. Pushing his stick out on the sidewalk ahead of him, he climbed from the car.

The parking lot was closed at night. A sign said that access was forbidden. A barricade blocked off the entrance. There was no light in the attendant's shelter, and no sign of life.

Looking after the car, Honda walked down the sidewalk past the agaves. They flung out harsh leaves, a pale green in the darkness, quiet, like a clump of malice. There were few passersby, only a man and woman on the sidewalk opposite.

Having come as far as the façade of the art gallery, Honda stopped and looked at the great empty scheme in which he found himself. The dome and the two wings rose powerfully into the moonless night. The rectangular pond and the white gravel of the terrace, long streaks of light from the lamps cutting off the dim white of the gravel like the line of the tide. To the left loomed the round wall of the Olympic Stadium, its now-dark floodlights high against the sky. Far below, lamps, like a mist, touched the outermost branches of the trees.

In the symmetrical plaza, which contained no shadow of desire, Honda felt as if he were at the centre of the Womb Mandala.

The Womb Mandala, one of the two elemental worlds, is paired with the Diamond Mandala. Its symbol is the lotus, and its Buddhas manifest the virtue of charity.

The womb has also the meaning of inclusiveness. Just as the womb of the beggar woman held the embryo of the Lord of Light, so the muddied heart of the ordinary man holds the wisdom and mercy of all Buddhas.

The perfect symmetry of the shining mandala holds at its centre the Court of the Eight-Petalled Lotus, abode of the Lord of Great Light. Twelve courts stretch out in the four directions, and the abodes of the several Buddhas are fixed with delicate and detailed symmetry.

If the dome of the art gallery, high in the moonless night, was taken for the central court, then the avenue where Honda stood, separated from it by the pond, was perhaps the abode of the Peacock Lord, to the west of the Court of Emptiness.

With the Buddhas disposed geometrically on the golden mandala transferred to the dark groves of the symmetrical plaza, the expanse of gravel and the emptiness of the sidewalk were suddenly filled, merciful faces were everywhere, dizzying in the full light of day. The more than two hundred holy faces, and more than two hundred of the Diamond Mandala as well, were shining in the groves, and the ground was ablaze with light.

The vision faded as he walked off. The night was filled with the singing of insects, cicada voices stitched the shadows like needles.

The familiar path was still there through the groves, to the right of the art gallery. He remembered with longing that the smell of the grass and of the night trees had been an indispensable part of desire.

He felt the return of a sharp sense of pleasure, as if he were crossing a tideland, at his feet the workings of fish and shellfish and starfish and crustaceans and seahorses, as at night on a coral reef, the water lapping warm against the soles of his feet, in danger of being cut at each step by the pointed rocks. Pleasure dashed ahead, the body was unable to follow. Signs, indications, were everywhere. As his eyes grew accustomed to the dark he saw white shirts scattered through the groves, like the aftermath of a slaughter.

There was a previous caller in the shadows where Honda hid himself. Honda could tell from the dark shirt if from nothing else that it was a veteran peeper. The man was so short, coming only to Honda's shoulders, that Honda at first took him for a boy. When he made out the grizzled head, the moist breathing so near at hand seemed heavy and stupid.

Presently the man's eyes left their object and were trained on Honda's profile. Honda looked studiously away, but he had felt that the short grey hair bristling from the temples was somehow related to a disconcerting memory. He struggled to bring it out. The usual cough rose to his throat, though he fought to keep it back.

A certain confidence came into the man's breathing. Raising himself to his full height, he whispered in Honda's ear.

'So we meet again. You still come, do you? You haven't forgotten?'

Honda turned and looked into the rodent eyes. A memory came back from twenty-two years before. It was the man who had stopped him in front of the Ginza PX.

And he remembered with fear how coldly he had treated the man, asserting mistaken identity.

'You needn't worry. Here is here and there is there. Let's let bygones be bygones.' This way of forestalling Honda's thoughts added to the uneasiness. 'But you'll have to stop that coughing.' He turned to look busily off beyond the tree trunks.

Breathing more easily as the man moved some distance away, Honda looked into the grasses beyond the tree. The throbbing had departed, however. It had been replaced by uneasiness and, again, anger and sadness. Self-forgetfulness withdrew as he pursued it. Though the spot was well suited for viewing the man and woman on the grass, there was a false quality about them, as if they knew they were being watched and were acting parts. There was none of the joy in seeing, there was neither the sweet pressure from the recesses of scrutiny nor drunkenness of clarity itself.

Though they were only a yard or two away, the light was too dim for him to make out details or the expressions on the faces. There seemed to be a screen between him and them, and he could approach no nearer. He hoped that if he went on looking the old throb would return. One hand against the trunk of the tree, one hand on his stick, he looked down at the couple.

Although the little man showed no disposition to interfere with his sport, Honda went on remembering things he should not have remembered. Since his own stick was uncurved, he could not hope to imitate the virtuosity of the old man who used his stick to lift skirts. The man had been old then, and no doubt he was dead by now. No doubt rather large numbers of the old men in the 'audience' had died in the course of these twenty years. And not a few among the young 'performers' too would have married and gone away or died in traffic accidents or from juvenile cancer or high blood pressure or heart and kidney ailments. Because movements and transfers are far brisker among the performers than in the audience, some of them would be in apartment clusters in bedroom towns an hour or so by private railway from Tokyo, ignoring wives and children and abandoning themselves to the joys of television. And the day was at hand when some of them would join the audience.

Something soft brushed his right hand. A large snail was making its way down the tree.

He pulled his hand gently away. The flesh and the shell in succession, like the celluloid of the soap dish after the sticky suds, left revulsion. From just such a tactile impression the world could melt away, like a corpse in a tank of sulphuric acid.

Honda looked down again at the man and woman. There was almost a pleading in his eyes. Make me drunk, the earliest moment possible. Young people of the world, in ignorance and silence, let me get drunk to my heart's content on the forms of your passion, which have no room for the old.

Sprawled out in the singing of insects, the woman raised herself and put her arms around the man's neck. The man, who was wearing a black beret, had his hand deep under her skirt. Her fingertips moved energetically over the wrinkles of his shirt. She was twisted against his chest, like a spiral stairway. Panting, she raised her head and kissed him, as if she were gulping down medicine.

As Honda gazed, so intently that his eyes ached, he felt a surge of desire, like the first rays of the morning sun, from depths until then empty.

The man reached into his hip pocket. The thought that in the very middle of desire he feared being robbed brought a sudden chilling of Honda's own desire. The next instant he was doubting his eyes.

The object the man took from his pocket was a spring knife. His forefinger touched it and there was a sound as of a rasping snake's tongue. The blade gleamed in the dark. Honda could not be sure where the woman had been stabbed, but there was a scream. The man sprang up and looked around. The beret had slipped back. For the first time Honda saw the hair and face. The hair was a pure white, and the emaciated face was that of a sixty-year-old, wrinkled to every corner.

The man brushed past Honda, now in a state of shock, and ran off with a speed that belied his years.

'Let's get out of here,' muttered the rat-like little man in Honda's ear. 'There's going to be hell to pay.'

'I couldn't run if I wanted to,' said Honda weakly.

'Too bad. They'll suspect you if you don't get away.' The man bit his fingernail. 'Maybe you should stay and be a witness.'

There was a whistle, a rush of footsteps, and a stir of people getting to their feet. The beam of a flashlight came from surprisingly near in the shrubbery. Policemen were standing around the woman, discussing the problem in loud voices.

'Where'd he get her?'

'In the thigh.'

'It's not much of a cut.'

'What sort of man was he? Tell us what sort of man he was.'

The policeman who had been crouching beside the woman with his flashlight in her face stood up.

'An old man, she says. He won't have gone very far.'

Trembling, Honda pressed his face against the tree. His eyes were closed. The bark was damp. It was as if a snail were crawling over his face.

He opened his eyes narrowly. He could feel the beam from the flashlight. Someone shoved at him, from so low that it had to be the little man. Honda stumbled from the shelter of the big tree. His face almost fell against one of the policemen. The policeman grabbed his wrist.

A reporter for a weekly magazine specializing in scandal happened to be at the police station. He was delighted at news of the stabbing in the Meiji Gardens.

The woman, her leg heavily bandaged, was asked to identify Honda. It took three hours for Honda's innocence to be established.

'I'm absolutely sure it wasn't this old gentleman,' said the woman. 'I met the other one a couple of hours ago on a street-car. He was an old man, but he dressed very young, and he was a good talker, a good mixer, you might say. I'd never have dreamed he could do such a thing. That's right. I don't know the first thing about him, his name or where he lives or what he does or anything.'

Before the woman confronted him, Honda was firmly tied up and his identity was established and he was forced to reveal the circumstances that had brought a person of his standing to the park at such an hour. It was a nightmare, that precisely the foolish story he had heard upward of twenty years ago from his old legal friend should now be his own experience. They all seemed to have the lucidity of a nightmare, quite divorced from reality; the shabby police station, the dirty walls of the interrogation room, the strangely bright light, the bald head of the detective.

He was allowed to go home at three in the morning. A maid got up and suspiciously opened the gate. He went to his room. He was troubled by bad dreams.

He came down with a cold the next day and was a week getting over it.

The morning he began to feel a little better, Tōru paid an unexpected visit. Smiling, he put a weekly magazine by Honda's pillow.

It carried this headline: 'Troubles of His Excellency Mr Judge-Voyeur, Falsely Accused of Stabbing.'

Honda took up his glasses. There was an unpleasant throbbing in his chest. The article was astonishingly accurate, even carrying Honda's real name. This was the climactic sentence: 'The appearance of an eighty-year-old voyeur would seem to indicate that the control of Japan by the aged extends even to the world of deviates.'

The statement that his proclivities were not new but that for some twenty years he had had numbers of acquaintances among the voyeurs made Honda sure who the informant had been. The police themselves must have introduced the reporter to the little man. A suit for libel would only add to the embarrassment.

It was a vulgar incident that deserved to be laughed away; but Honda, who would have hoped that he no longer had prestige and honour to lose, saw in the loss of them that they were in fact still present.

It seemed certain that for rather a long time people would associate his name not with his spiritual and intellectual endowments but with the scandal. People were not quick to forget scandals. It was not moral indignation that made them remember. For encapsulating a person a scandal was the simplest and most efficient container.

The stubbornness of the cold told him that he was crumbling physically. To have been a suspect was an experience which, in the complete absence of intellectual dignity, seemed to bring a collapse of flesh and bones. Knowledge, learning, thought, could do nothing for it. What good would it have done to confront the detective with the fine details of the concepts he had acquired in India?

Henceforth Honda would take out his calling card:

'Shigekuni Honda.'

'Attorney-at-Law.'

People would insert a line in the cramped space between the other two:

Shigekuni Honda
Eighty-Year-Old Voyeur
Attorney-at-Law

And so Honda's career would be compressed into a single line.

'Former judge, eighty-year-old voyeur.'

And so the invisible edifice which Honda's awareness had built through his long life had collapsed in an instant, and a single line was inscribed on the foundation. It was as concise as a white-hot blade. And it was true.

After the September incident Tōru moved coolly to have things his way.

He took as his lawyer an old lawyer with whom Honda had feuded, and consulted with him upon the possibility of having Honda declared incompetent. An examination would be required to establish mental debility, but the lawyer seemed confident of the results.

And as a matter of fact the change in Honda was clear. After the incident he stopped going out and he seemed afraid of everything. It should be easy enough to establish the symptoms of senile delusions. Tōru had only to appear before a court of domestic relations and have Honda declared incompetent, and the lawyer would be appointed his guardian.

The lawyer consulted a psychiatrist with whom he was on good terms. Behind Honda's much-publicized misconduct the psychiatrist drew a picture of senile unease. Two ailments emerged, 'vicarious sexual desire', an obsession like a fire reflected in a mirror, not to be made light of, and incontinence resulting from senility. Everything else could be left to the legal system, said the lawyer. He added that it would be good if Honda were to begin spending his money unwisely, in such a way as to give rise to fears that the estate might be endangered, but unfortunately there were no such tendencies. Tōru was in any case worried less about money than about power.

27

Late in November a splendid engraved invitation, in English, came to Tōru from Keiko.

There was a letter with it.

Dear Tōru,

I have been very bad about keeping in touch.

Everyone seems to have made arrangements for Christmas Eve, and so I am having a premature Christmas party on the twentieth. I have until now always invited your father, but I have had to conclude that because of his advanced years an invitation this year would be a disservice, and I am inviting you instead. I think we should keep the matter secret from him. That is why I have addressed the invitation to you.

I fear that to say so will be to reveal too much of myself, but the truth is that since the September affair I have found it difficult to invite your father, out of deference to the other guests. I know it will seem to you that I am a bad friend, but in our world it is the final stroke when the private becomes public. I must be very careful.

My real reason for inviting you is that through you I want to continue relations with the Honda family. I will be delighted therefore if you can accept this invitation.

And so do please honour me by coming alone. Among the other guests will be several ambassadors and their wives and daughters, the Foreign Minister and his wife, the president of the Federation of Economic Organizations and his wife, and numbers of other pretty ladies as well. You will see from the invitation that it is to be black tie. It would be a great help if you could let me know soon whether or not you will be able to attend.

Yours sincerely,

KEIKO HISAMATSU

One could if one chose see the letter as a rude and haughty one, but Tōru smiled at the thought of Keiko's confusion after the September incident. He could read between the lines. Keiko, so proud of her immorality, retreated trembling behind bolted gates in the face of scandal.

But something in the letter aroused Tōru's delicate guard. That Keiko, so staunch an ally of his father, should be inviting him – might it not be to make sport of him? Might her intention in introducing him to all those pretentious guests as the son of Shigekuni Honda not be to excite them and so embarrass not Honda but Tōru himself? That was it. There could be little doubt.

Tōru's combative instincts were aroused. He would go to the party as the son of the notorious Honda. No one of course would touch upon the matter. But he would shine as a son unapologetic for a notorious father.

The sensitive spirit would move silently among them, a faint, beautiful, somehow sad smile on its lips, the skeletons of family scandal (such beastly little affairs), no doing of its own, ranged beside it. Tōru could see all the pale poetry. The contempt and interference of the old would push the girls irresistibly in Tōru's direction. Keiko's calculations would prove faulty.

Not owning a tuxedo, Tōru had to put in a quick order for one. He slipped into it when, on the nineteenth, it was delivered, and went over to show Kinué.

'You look very good in it. Lovely. I know how much you wanted to take me dancing in it. What a pity that I should always be so ill. What a real pity. And that's why you've come to show me. How very kind of you. That's why I like you.'

It was obesity that had rendered Kinué immobile. She was in the best of health and she got no exercise, and in these six months she had fattened beyond recognition. The heaviness and immobility gave more immediacy to her illnesses. She was constantly taking liver pills, and she would gaze from the chaise longue through the trees at the blue sky, so soon to be lost. Her perpetual refrain was that she was not long for this world, and she was a great trial for the maids, whom Tōru had told that they were in no circumstances to laugh.

What Tōru admired was the cunning with which, offered a set of conditions, she would outflank them and raise defences which would give her the advantage and reinforce her beauty and perhaps add a touch of the tragic to it. She had immediately sensed that he did not mean to take her out. So she had put her illness to the uses of the situation. Tōru thought he had things to learn from this so stubbornly guarded pride. She had become his teacher.

'Turn round. Oh, it's very nicely cut. The shoulder line is beautiful. Everything looks good on you. Just like me. Well, you must forget all about me tomorrow evening and enjoy yourself. But when you're enjoying yourself most, think for just a moment of the sick girl you've left at home. But just a moment. You need a flower in your lapel. If only I were strong enough I'd go and pick it for you myself. Maid, please. The winter rose, the red one, if you will.'

She had the maid pick a crimson rosebud just coming into bloom, and herself put it in his buttonhole.

'There.' With the most languorous, evanescent of fingers, she pushed the stem through. She tapped the glossy silk of the lapel. 'Go out into the garden and let me have another look at you.'

The corpulent figure seemed to be breathing its last.

At the appointed time, seven in the evening, Tōru pulled up in his Mustang, as directed by the map, at a wide, white-gravelled drive in Azabu. There were no other cars yet.

Tōru was astonished at how old-fashioned Keiko's mansion was. The lamps under the trees set off a circular Regency front. There was something rather ghostly about the place, the effect intensified by red ivy blackened by the night.

Tōru was ushered in by a white-gloved butler past the circular domed hallway to a parlour in the rich Momoyama style, and there seen to a Louis XV chair. He was rather ashamed to find himself the first guest. The house was brilliantly lit but still. There was a large Christmas tree in one corner. It seemed out of place. Left by himself when the butler had taken his order for a drink, he leaned against the old-fashioned paned window and looked out through the trees at the lights of the city and a sky turned purplish by neon.

A door opened and Keiko came in.

The brilliant formal dress of the septuagenarian before him quite robbed him of speech. Sleeves trailing to the hem of the skirt, her evening dress was beaded over its whole surface. The shifting colours and patterns of the beads from the neck down over the skirt were such as to dazzle the eye. At the bosom, the wings of a peacock in green on a gold ground, waves of purple over the sleeves, a continuous wine-coloured pattern down over the waist, purple waves and gold clouds on the skirt, the several boundaries marked in gold. The white of the organdy ground was set off by a threefold Western pattern in silver net. From the skirt emerged the toe of a purple satin slipper, and at the always proud neck was an emerald Georgette stole, draped down over the shoulders and reaching to the floor. Below her hair, cut shorter and closer than usual, hung gold earrings. Her face had the frozen look of one that had more than once been ministered to by plastic surgeons, but the parts that still remained under her control seemed to assert themselves all the more haughtily. The awesome eyes, the grand nose. The lips, like red-black bits of apple beginning to rot, tortured into a yet more shining red.

'I'm terribly sorry to have kept you waiting,' she said brightly. The face with its sculptured smile came towards him.

'My, but you're looking grand.'

'Thank you.' Briefly and abstractedly, in the Western fashion, she showed him her well-shaped nostrils.

The aperitifs came.

'Perhaps we should turn down the lights.'

The butler turned off the chandelier lights. In the flickering of the Christmas tree, Keiko's eyes flickered, as did the beads on her dress. Tōru was beginning to feel uneasy.

'The others are late. Or is it that I am too early?'

'The others? You're my only guest this evening.'

'So you were lying about the others?'

'Oh, I'm sorry. I changed my plans. I thought I would have my Christmas alone with you.'

'I think I'll ask to be excused, then.'

'Why?' Seated quietly, Keiko made no motion towards stopping him.

'Some sort of plot. Or a trap. Something in any case you've talked over with Father. I'm tired of being made fun of.' He had disliked this old woman from their first meeting.

Keiko was motionless. 'If it were something I'd talked over with Mr Honda, I wouldn't have gone to so much trouble. I invited you because I wanted to have a good talk with you, all by ourselves. It is true that I lied to you, because I knew you wouldn't come if you knew you were to be my only guest. But a Christmas dinner with only two people is still a Christmas dinner. Here we are both of us in party dress.'

'I suppose you want to give me a good lecturing.' Tōru was angry at himself for having let her make her excuses.

'Nothing of the sort. I just want to talk with you quietly about some things Mr Honda would throttle me for if he were to find out. They are secrets that only Mr Honda and I know. If you don't want to listen, well, that is that.'

'Secrets?'

'Just sit down there quietly, if you will.' An elegantly sardonic smile on her lips, she pointed to the somewhat worn Watteau garden party on the chair Tōru had just vacated.

The butler announced dinner. Opening doors Tōru had taken to be a wall, he ushered them into the next room, where the table was set with red candles. Keiko's dress jingled.

Not one to encourage conversation, Tōru ate in silence. The thought that the skill with which he managed his knife and fork was the result of Honda's assiduous tutelage enraged him all over again. Tutelage to make people think him a long-time adept of a cravenness he had not known until he met Honda and Keiko.

Keiko's fingers at knife and fork, beyond the heavy baroque candlesticks, absently quiet and diligent, like an old woman at her knitting, were a young girl's fingers brought into old age.

The chilled turkey was tasteless, like the dry skin of an old man. The chestnut stuffing and the cranberry jelly had for Tōru the sourly saccharine taste of hypocrisy.

'Do you know why you were so suddenly sought after to become heir to the house of Honda?'

'How should I?'

'Very easygoing of you. You haven't wanted to know?'

Tōru did not answer. Putting down her knife and fork, Keiko pointed through the candle smoke at his tuxedo front.

'It's all very simple. It's because you have three moles on your left chest.'

Tōru was unable to hide his surprise. Keiko knew of those three moles, the root of his pride, which through all his life should have attracted the attention of no one but himself. An instant later he had brought himself under control. The surprise had come from the fact that, by chance, the symbol of his own pride had coincided with a symbol of something for someone else. Though the moles may have set the something in motion, that need not mean that he had been found out. But Tōru had underestimated the intuitions of the aged.

The surprise so clear on his face seemed to give Keiko greater confidence. The words poured forth.

'See? You can't believe it. It was all too foolish, too nonsensical from the start. You have told yourself that you have managed everything coolly and realistically, but you swallowed the nonsensical premises whole. Who would be so foolish as to want to adopt a complete stranger on a single meeting just because he had taken a liking? What did you think when we first came with the proposal? We made all sorts of excuses to you and your superiors, of course. But what did you really think? It puffed you up, I should imagine. People like to think they have their strong points. You thought that your childish dreams and our proposal matched admirably? That your strange childish confidence had been justified? That's what you thought?'

Tōru was for the first time afraid of Keiko. He felt not the slightest constraint because of class, but there are persons endowed with a special nose for scenting out worth. They are the angel-killers.

The conversation was interrupted by dessert. Tōru had let the moment for an answer pass. He knew that he had under-estimated his adversary.

'Do you think that your hopes and those of someone else coincide, that your hopes can be smoothly realized for you by someone else? People live for themselves and think only of themselves. You who more than most think only of yourself have gone too far and let yourself be blinded.

'You thought that history has its exceptions. There are none. You thought that the race has its exceptions. There are none.

'There is no special right to happiness and none to unhappiness. There is no tragedy and there is no genius. Your confidence and your dreams are groundless. If there is on this earth something exceptional, special beauty or special evil, nature finds it out and uproots it. We should all by now have learned the hard lesson, that there are no "elect".

'You thought, didn't you, that you were a genius beyond compensation. You thought of yourself, didn't you, as a beautiful little cloud of evil floating over humanity.

'Mr Honda saw it all the minute he saw your moles. He decided in that instant that he must have you with him, to save you from the danger. He thought that if he left you as you were, if he left you to your "fate", you would be killed by nature at twenty.

'He tried to save you by adopting you, by smashing to bits your "godlike" pride, by drilling into you the world's rules for culture and happiness, by making you over into a perfectly ordinary young man. You did not recognize that you had the same starting point as the rest of us. The sign of your refusal to recognize was those three moles. It was affection that made him adopt you without telling you why he wanted to save you. The affection, of course, of a man who knew too much of the world.'

Tōru was more and more uneasy. 'Why do you say I will die at twenty?'

'I think probably the danger has passed. Let's talk about it in the other room.'

A bright fire had been lit in the fireplace. Below the mantel, a gold-clouded alcove in the Japanese style with a Kōtatsu hanging, two small golden doors opened to reveal the fireplace. Tōru and Keiko sat before the fire, a small table between them. Keiko repeated the long story of birth and rebirth she had had from Honda.

Tōru listened, gazing into the fire. He started at the faint sound of a collapsing log.

Clinging to a log with its smoke, the flame would twist and grow, and then show again in the darkness between log and log, its bed rich with a bright, still repose. Like a dwelling, the small floor dizzying in its reds and vermilions was deep in quiet, marked off by a rough frame of logs.

Sometimes the smoke bursting through the sombre logs was like a grass fire far out on a night plain. There were great vistas in the fire, and the shadows moving in the depths of the fireplace were a miniature of the flames of political upheaval tracing shadows across the heavens.

As the flames died down on one log, an even expanse of quiet vermilion would show itself from under a delicate tortoiseshell bed of ashes, trembling like a heap of white feathers. The firm bind of logs would collapse at its foundations. Then, maintaining a precarious balance, it would burn up like a great rock in the air.

Everything was flowing, in motion. The quiet chain of smoke, so stable, was forever breaking up. The collapse of a log that had finished its work brought a sort of repose.

'Very interesting,' said Tōru, rather tartly, when he had heard the story to the end. 'But where's the proof?'

'Proof?' Keiko hesitated. 'Is there proof for the truth?'

'When you say "truth" it sounds false.'

'If you demand proof, I should imagine Mr Honda has preserved Kiyoaki Matsugae's diary all these years. You might ask to see it. He wrote only of dreams, and Mr Honda says all of them have come true. But maybe it doesn't matter. Maybe nothing I've said has anything to do with you. You were born on March twentieth and Ying Chan died in the spring, and you have those three marks, and so it would seem that you are her reincarnation. But we have not been able to find out exactly when she died. Her twin sister said only that it was in the spring, but she seems unable to remember the exact day. Mr Honda investigated in any number of ways, but without success. If she was bitten by a snake and died later than March twenty-first, you go scot free. The spirit wanders around for at least a week. So your birthday has to be a week after she died.'

'Actually I don't know my own birthday. My father was at sea and there was no one to take care of the details, and the date of registration was put down as the birthday. But I was born before March twentieth.'

'The earlier it was, the dimmer the possibility,' Keiko said coldly. 'But maybe it doesn't matter anyway.'

'It doesn't matter?' Tōru showed signs of indignation.

Quite aside from whether or not he believed the terrible story he had heard, to be told that it did not matter seemed to him like a naked denial of his reasons for being. Keiko had the ability to make a person seem like an insect. It lay behind her unchanging gaiety.

In the light from the fire the multicoloured evening dress was sending off deep, rich hues. It arched and coiled around her like a rainbow in the night.

'Maybe it doesn't matter. Maybe from the outset you were a fraud. In fact I myself am rather sure that you are a fraud.'

He glanced at her profile. She had spoken into the fire as if presenting a petition. There was no describing the splendour of that profile, set aglow by the fire. The fire in the eyes enhanced the proud high bridge of the nose. It sent everyone else into childish fretfulness. It dominated relentlessly.

Thoughts of murder came to Tōru. How could he upset this woman, leave her pleading for her life? Were he to throttle her, to shove her head into the flames, he was sure she would look back at him with a proudly burning face, a grand mane of fire swirling around her. Tōru's self-respect was hurting, and he feared her next words, likely to bring blood. What he most feared was blood pouring from an open wound in his self-respect. Its haemophilia would not permit the flow to be stopped. And so he had until now used all emotions to draw a line between emotion and self-respect, and, avoiding the danger of love, armed himself with countless thorns.

Keiko seemed intent, quietly and ceremoniously, on saying what had to be said.

'We will know for certain that you were a fraud if you don't die in the next six months. We will know that you are not the regrowth of the beautiful seed Mr Honda was after, and that you are what an entomologist would call a simulator. I doubt myself that we have to wait a year. It does not seem to me that you are doomed to die in six months. There is nothing inevitable about you, not a thing a person would hate to lose. There is in you not a thing to make a person imagining your death feel that a shadow had come over the world.

'You're a mean, cunning little country boy of the sort we see sprawled all over the place. You want to get your hands on your father's money, and so you arrange to have him declared incompetent. You're surprised, aren't you? I know everything. And when you have money and power, what do you propose to seek next? Success? Your thoughts don't go a step beyond those of any mediocre boy. The only way Mr Honda's training has gone wrong is that it has done nothing more than bring out your essential nature.

'There is nothing in the least special about you. I guarantee you a long life. You have not been chosen by the gods, you will never be at one with your acts, you do not have in you the green light to flash like young lightning with the speed of the gods and destroy yourself. All you have is a certain premature senility. Your life will be suited for coupon-clipping. Nothing more.

'You cannot kill Mr Honda or me. Your sort of evil is a legal sort of evil. All puffed up by illusions born of abstract concepts, you strut about as the master of a destiny even though you have none of the qualifications. You think you have seen to the ends of the earth. But you have not once had an invitation beyond the horizon. You have nothing to do with light or enlightenment, there is no real spirit in flesh or in heart. At least Ying Chan's spirit was in the shining beauty of her flesh. Nature has not had a glance for you, it has not had a glimmer of hostility towards you. The person Mr Honda is looking for has to be one to inspire jealousy of nature at its own creation.

'You're a clever boy, no more. If someone pays your expenses you swim through the entrance examinations and a good job is waiting for you at the other end. A model student for the Education Fund. Propaganda material for the do-gooders who say that if material wants are taken care of, all sorts of hidden treasures will emerge. Mr Honda was too good to you, and gave you too much confidence. He prescribed the wrong dose, that is all. Give you the right dose and you'll be back on the track. Make you the secretary to some vulgar politician and you'll wake up. I'll be happy to introduce you to one, at your convenience, any time.

'You will do well to remember what I have said. You have seen and think you have seen it all; but it is no more than the little circle in a thirty-power telescope. You would have been happier, I suppose, if we had let you go on thinking that was the whole world.'

'It was you who dragged me out of it.'

'And what made you come so happily was the thought that you were different.

'Kiyoaki Matsugae was caught by unpredictable love, Isao Iinuma by destiny, Ying Chan by the flesh. And you? By a baseless sense of being different, perhaps?

'If destiny is something that takes hold of a person from outside and drags him after, then the other three had destiny. And has anything caught you? Only we, Mr Honda and I.' Letting the green and gold peacock on her bosom take the fire as it would, Keiko laughed. 'We are two bored, cold, cynical old people. Can your pride really permit you to call us destiny? A nasty old man and woman? An old voyeur and an old lesbian?

'You may think you have taken stock of the world. The ones who come summoning a boy like you are the ones who have taken stock of the world. The one who drags out the conceited purveyor of awareness is the veteran practitioner of the same trade. No one else would have come knocking on your door, you may be sure. You would have gone through life without the knock, and the results would have been the same. Because you have had no destiny. The beautiful death was not for you. It was not for you to be like the other three. The drab, dreary heir, that is the role for you. I invited you tonight to let you learn all about it.'

Tōru's hand was trembling, and his eye was on the poker beside the fire. It would have been easy to reach for it, pretending to stir the fire. He would arouse no curiosity, and then he had only to swing it. He could feel the weight of it in his hand, he could see the blood spurting over gold chair and gold doors. But he did not reach out. He was fearfully thirsty, but he did not ask for water. The anger that enflamed his cheeks seemed to him like the first passion he had known. It remained shut up within him.

28

Remarkably, Tōru came to Honda with a request. He wanted to borrow Kiyoaki's diary.

Honda was reluctant to lend it, but even more reluctant not to.

He let Tōru have it for two or three days. They became a week. On the morning of the twenty-eighth, when he had resolved to have it back, he was startled by an outcry from the maids. Tōru, in his bedroom, had taken poison.

It being the end of the year, the family doctor was not available. Honda had to take the risk of publicity and call an ambulance. There was a wall of onlookers when the ambulance came shrieking up. They were eager for another scandal from a house that had already provided one.

Tōru remained in a coma and there were convulsions, but his life was not in danger. He felt severe pains in the eyes, however, when he regained consciousness. Impediments developed in both eyes, and he totally lost his sight. The poison had attacked the retina, which had deteriorated beyond hope of recovery.

The poison was industrial wood alcohol, stolen under cover of the year-end confusion from a factory that belonged to a relative of one of the maids. The maid, who followed Tōru unquestioningly, wept and insisted that she had not dreamed he would drink it.

The blind Tōru said almost nothing. After the turn of the year Honda asked him about the diary.

'I burned it just before I took the poison,' he answered briefly.

His answer when asked for an explanation was much to the point.

'Because I never dream.'

Honda asked for Keiko's help any number of times while all this was taking place. There was something strange about her. It was as if she alone knew the motive for the attempted suicide.

'He has twice the pride of most boys. I should imagine he did it to prove he's a genius.'

When pressed, she admitted that she had revealed everything at her Christmas party. She said she had done it out of friendship, but Honda replied that he wished to see no more of her. He thus announced the end of a beautiful friendship that had lasted more than twenty years.

The declaration of incompetence was revoked, and now it was the blind Tōru who needed a guardian. Honda drew up a notarized will and named the most reliable guardian he could think of.

Tōru dropped out of the university, remained shut up in the house, and spoke to no one except Kinué. The maids were dismissed, and Honda hired a woman who had had experience as a nurse. Tōru spent most of the day in Kinué's cottage. All through the day Kinué's soft voice could be heard through the doors. Tōru did not seem to weary of making reply.

His birthday passed on the twentieth of March. He showed no sign of dying. He learned to read Braille. When by himself he listened to records. He could recognize birds by their songs. One day, after a very long silence, he spoke to Honda. He asked that Honda let him marry Kinué. Though aware that her insanity was hereditary, Honda gave his permission immediately.

Decay advanced, the signs of the end appeared quietly. Like hairs tickling his neck when he came back from the barber shop, death, forgotten most of the time, would come tickling when remembered. It seemed strange to Honda that, though all of the preparations for receiving it had been made, death did not come.

Honda had been aware during the excitement of a certain heaviness in the region of his stomach, but he did not, as the old Honda might have been expected to, rush off to a doctor. He diagnosed the trouble as indigestion. He continued to have little appetite after the New Year came. It was not like him to pass it off as only a result of the troubles, nor was it like him to take emaciation as a result of mental anguish.

But it had come to seem that there was no distinguishing between pain of the spirit and pain of the flesh. What was the difference between humiliation and a swollen prostate? Between the pangs of sorrow and pneumonia? Senility was a proper ailment of both the spirit and the flesh, and the fact that senility was an incurable disease meant that existence was an incurable disease. It was a disease unrelated to existentialist theories, the flesh itself being the disease, latent death.

If the cause of decay was illness, then the fundamental cause of that, the flesh, was illness too. The essence of the flesh was decay. It had its spot in time to give evidence of destruction and decay.

Why did people first become aware of that fact only as old age came on? Why, when it buzzed faintly past the ear in the brief noontide of the flesh, did they note it only to forget it? Why did the healthy young athlete, in the shower after his exertions, watching the drops of water hit his shining flesh like hail, not see that the high tide of life itself was the cruellest of ills, a dark, amber-coloured lump?

For Honda now, life was senescence, senescence was life. It was wrong that these two synonyms should forever be libelling each other. Only now, eighty-one years after he fell into this world, did Honda know the perverse essential at the heart of every pleasure.

Appearing now on this side and now on the other of human will, it sent up an opaque mist, the defence of the will against the cruel and terrible proposition that life and senescence are synonymous. History knew the truth. History was the most inhuman product of humanity. It scooped up the whole of human will and, like the goddess Kali in Calcutta, dripped blood from its mouth as it bit and crunched.

We are fodder to stuff some craw. In his shallow way, Imanishi, who died in the fire, had been aware of it. For the gods, for destiny, for history, the only human endeavour imitating the two, it was wise to leave man unaware of the fact until he had grown old.

What fodder Honda had been! What unnutritious, tasteless, dusty fodder! Instinctively refusing to become palatable, he now at the end of it all wanted to stab the mouth of his devourer with the tasteless bones of his awareness; but he was certain to fail.

Tōru went blind in an attempt at suicide. His twenty-first birthday came and went. Honda had no further wish to look into possible traces left behind by the person, unknown, dead at twenty, who was the true reincarnation. If there had been such a person, very well. Honda no longer had the energy to look into that person's life, nor would it have become him to make the effort. The movements of the heavenly bodies had left him aside. By a small miscalculation, they had led Honda and the reincarnation of Ying Chan into separate parts of the universe. Three reincarnations had occupied Honda's life and, after drawing their paths of light across it (that too had been a most improbable accident), gone off in another burst of light to an unknown corner of the heavens. Perhaps somewhere, some time, Honda would meet the hundredth, the ten thousandth, the hundred millionth reincarnation.

There was no hurry.

Why hurry? He did not know even where his own rut was taking him. So concluded Honda, a man who had not been in a hurry to die. What he had seen at Benares was human indestructibility as the fundamental essence of the universe. The other world did not lie quivering beyond time, nor did it lie shining beyond space. If to die meant to return to the four elements, to dissolve into the corporate entity, then there was no law holding that the place of birth and rebirth need be no other than here. It was an accident, an utterly senseless accident, that Kiyoaki and Isao and Ying Chan had all appeared beside Honda. If an element in Honda was of exactly the same quality as an element at the other end of the universe, there was no exchange procedure, once individuality had been lost, whereby they could purposely come together through space and time. The particle here and the particle there have precisely the same significance. There was nothing to keep the Honda of the next world from being at the farther end of the universe. When, after the string had been cut and the beads scattered on the table, they are strung in another order, the one indestructible rule, provided no beads have fallen under the table, is that their number must be as before.

Eternity does not come into being because I think I exist: Buddhist doctrine now seemed to Honda mathematically sound. The self was the order of beads determined by the self and therefore without validity.

These thoughts and the almost imperceptible decay of the flesh went together like the wheels of a cart. It was all right, even pleasant, to put the matter so.

In May or thereabouts he began to suffer from pains in the abdomen. They were very stubborn, and sometimes spread to the back. While he was still seeing Keiko, ailments inevitably came into the conversation. He would speak casually of some serious ailment, and with a great stir she would lay it out on the carving board. A stabbing sort of kindness competing with an amiable tendency to exaggerate, she would assign to it all the malignant medical terms she could think of, and he would be off to a hospital in a spirit of something like jest. Now that he was no longer seeing Keiko, he had to an astonishing degree lost this sort of enthusiastic disquiet. Pain such as he was able to endure he left to the ministrations of his masseuse. Even the thought of a doctor was wearing.

Indeed general debilitation and rhythmical attacks of pain brought new powers to think. His ageing brain had lost all ability to concentrate, but now it returned, and pain even worked aggressively upon it, to bring certain vital faculties other than the purely rational to bear. At the age of eighty-one Honda attained to a wondrous and mysterious realm that had before been denied him. He knew now that a more comprehensive view of the world was to be had from physical depression than from intelligence, from a dull pain in the entrails than from reason, a loss of appetite than analysis. The addition of a single vague pain in the back to a world that had been to the clear eye of reason a minutely detailed structure, and cracks began to appear in the pillars and vaults, what had seemed like hard rock proved to be soft cork, what had seemed to have solid form turned to inchoate jelly.

Honda had by himself reached that honing of the senses, achieved by few in this world, to live death from within. When he looked back upon life from its far side other than as a journey over a flat surface, hoping that what had declined would revive, seeking to believe that pain was transient, clinging greedily to happiness as a thing of the moment, thinking that good fortune must be followed by bad, seeing in all the ups and downs and rises and falls the ground for his own prospects – then everything was in place, pulled tight, and the march to the end was in order. The boundary between man and object disappeared. The portentous ten-floor building in the American style and the fragile human beings who walked beneath it had as a condition that they would outlast Honda, but as a condition of equal importance that they would fall, like the crape myrtle so rudely cut down. Honda no longer had cause to sympathize, and he had lost the imagination that gives rise to sympathy. The loss had been easy, for he had always been short on imagination.

Reason still worked, but it was frozen. Beauty had become a phantom.

And he lost that greatest ill of the spirit, to will and to plan. In a sense that was the great liberation provided by pain.

Honda heard the chatter that envelops the world like gold dust. Conditional talk, noisily claiming permanent residence.

'Let's go to a hot spring, Grandfather, when you're feeling better. Would you like Yumoto, or would Ikaho be better?'

'Let's have a drink when the contract is signed.'

'Let's.'

'Is it true that now is a good time to get into the stock market?'

'When I grow up can I eat a whole box of cream puffs all by myself?'

'Let's go to Europe next year.'

'In three years I'll be able to buy a boat from my savings.'

'I can't die till he grows up.'

'I'll get my retirement pay and we'll build an apartment house and have a quiet old age.'

'Day after tomorrow at three? I don't know whether I can make it or not. No, you have to believe me, I really don't. Suppose we say you'll be there if you feel like it.'

'We'll have to get a new air-conditioner next year.'

'It's a real problem. Can't we at least cut down on entertainment expenses next year?'

'They say you can have as much tobacco and liquor as you want when you're twenty.'

'Thank you. It's very kind of you. Next Tuesday evening at six.'

'That's just the point. That's the way he is. Just wait two or three days and he'll be around with a sheepish look on his face to apologize.'

'Good-bye. See you tomorrow.'

Foxes all, walking the path of foxes. The hunter had only to wait in the thicket.

It seemed to Honda that he was a fox with the eyes of a hunter, walking the path of the foxes even though he knew that he would be caught.

Summer and ripeness were approaching.

It was mid-July when Honda finally stirred himself to make an appointment at the Cancer Research Institute.

On the day before the appointment he had one of his rare looks at television. It was a sunny afternoon, the summer rains having just lifted. There was a shot of a swimming pool. In the unpleasantly artificial blue of the water, young people were splashing and jumping and swimming.

The faint, fleeting scent of beautiful flesh!

To deny the flesh, to see them as skeletons disporting themselves by a pool in the summer sun, was ordinary, dull. Anyone could do it. Anyone could deny life, see through to the bones beneath the youthful surface. The most mediocre of persons could do it.

What revenge could there be in that? Honda would end his life without having known the feelings of the owner of beautiful flesh. If for a single month he could live in it! He should have had a try. What must it be like, to wear such a beautiful covering? To see people fall down before it. When admiration passed the gentle and docile and became lunatic worship, it would become torment for the possessor. In the delirium and the torment were true holiness. What Honda had missed had been the dark, narrow path through the flesh to holiness. To travel it was of course the privilege of few.

Tomorrow he would have a thorough examination. He did not know what the results would be. He should at least be clean. He had the bath drawn before dinner.

The middle-aged housekeeper, formerly a nurse, whom he had employed without consulting Tōru, was an unfortunate woman, twice widowed, but she was a model of kindness and devotion. Honda had been thinking that he must provide for her in his will. She even saw him to the bathtub lest he fall, and left behind the frays of her concern like cobwebs in the dressing room. Honda did not like being seen naked by a woman. He took off his bathrobe before the steaming mirror. He looked at himself. His ribs were in sharp relief, his stomach sagged, and in its shadow hung a shrivelled white bean; and so down to whitish shins from which the flesh seemed to have been stripped away. The knees were like swellings. How many years of self-deception would it take to find rejuvenation in this ugliness? But he was able to console himself with a long smile of commiseration at the thought of how much worse it would be if he had been beautiful in the first place.

The examination took a week. He went to the hospital for the results.

'You must come in immediately. The sooner you come in the better.' So it had happened. 'We didn't catch a trace of it all those other times, and it seems unfair to have it jump out all of a sudden without warning. A person can't be too careful.' The doctor smiled a beatific smile, as if reproving Honda for some dereliction. 'But there seems to be no more than a benign growth on the pancreas. All we have to do is cut it away.'

'It wasn't the stomach?'

'The pancreas. If the gastroscope pictures turn out I'll show them to you.'

The diagnosis had coincided with his own personal one. He asked a week's reprieve.

He wrote a long letter and had it sent special delivery. It was to inform the Gesshū Temple that he would be visiting on July twenty-second. Since the letter would arrive on the twentieth, the day after posting, or the twenty-first, he hoped that the Abbess might be persuaded to receive him. He described his career over the past sixty years and apologized for not having awaited an invitation. The matter, he explained, was rather urgent.

On the twenty-first, the morning of his departure, he went out to the cottage.

The housekeeper had pleaded that he take her with him to Nara, but he had said that he must make the journey alone. She gave him elaborate instructions. She packed his suitcase with warm clothes to protect him from air-conditioning. It was almost more than an old man could lift.

She also gave elaborate instructions for his visit to the cottage. It seemed to Honda that she might be apologizing for what she considered oversights on her part.

'I must tell you that Mr Tōru wears that one white kimono like a bird its feathers. Miss Kinué is terribly fond of it, and when I tried to take it off and wash it she bit my finger, and so there it is still on him. Mr Tōru is, as you know, a very undemanding person, and it doesn't seem to bother him at all to wear that one kimono day and night. You must be prepared for it. And then, I don't know quite how to say it, the maid who takes care of the cottage says Miss Kinué vomits a great deal and has strange eating habits. She seems delighted that she should really be sick. I wonder. Anyway, you must be prepared.'

She probably did not see how Honda's eyes shone at this oracle telling him his line would be cut off from the eye of reason.

Pushing at his cane, Honda sat down on the veranda. The door was open. He had been able to see into the cottage from the garden.

'Well, Father,' said Kinué. 'Good morning.'

'Good morning. I'm off to Kyoto and Nara for a few days and I wanted to ask you to look after the house.'

'A trip? How nice.' Uninterested, she returned to her work.

'What are you doing?'

'Getting ready for the wedding. Do you like it? Not just for me, for Tōru too. People say they've never seen a more beautiful couple.'

Tōru, in dark glasses, sat silently between the two.

Honda knew nothing of Tōru's inner life since he had lost his sight, and he kept his always limited powers of imagination under control. Tōru lived on. But nothing was more capable of conveying heaviness to Honda than this lump of silence no longer a threat.

The cheeks below the dark glasses were paler and the lips redder. Tōru had always sweated heavily. There were beads of sweat at the open neck of the kimono. He sat with legs crossed and left everything to Kinué, but the effort of putting Honda aside was evident in the nervousness with which he scratched his leg and wiped at his chest. There was no strength in the motions. It was as if he were moved by strings from the ceiling.

Though his hearing was apparently keen, he gave no sign that he was taking the outside world in through his ears. No doubt other people, save only Kinué, would have had the same impression, but however confidently the visitor approached, he was for Tōru a discarded scrap of the outside world, a rusty can overgrown by the summer grasses.

Tōru had no contempt, no resistance. He sat in silence.

Though known to be fraudulent, the beautiful eyes and smile had brought him the tentative recognition of the world. Now the smile had left him. There might be some comfort if even regret or sorrow were visible, but he showed emotion to no one except Kinué, and she did not speak of what she saw.

The cicadas had been noisy since morning. Through the branches of the neglected garden, the sky shone like a string of blue beads. The cottage seemed even darker than usual.

The tea garden was reproduced in the circles of dark glasses that would in any case have turned away the outer world. There were no flowering trees now that the crape myrtle was gone from beside the stone basin. The shrubs among stones that did not quite add up to a landscape and the light through the trees were caught in the glasses.

Tōru's eyes no longer took in the outside world. The scene outside, no longer related to vision and awareness, filled the black lenses in intricate detail. It seemed strange to Honda that all he saw was himself and the little garden behind him. If the sea and the ships Tōru had seen all through the day and their strong funnel marks were an intimate part of his awareness, then behind the glasses and the eyes moving whitely from time to time, the images must be locked in forever. If for Honda and for everyone Tōru's inner workings had become forever a mystery, then it need not surprise them that sea and ships and funnel marks too were shut up within.

But if they belonged to a world outside of and irrelevant to Tōru, they should be sketched in detail on the lenses. Had Tōru perhaps completely merged the outer world and the inner? A white butterfly flew across the dark glass picture.

Tōru's heels looked up from the skirt of his kimono. They were white and wrinkled as those of a drowned corpse, and patches of dirt were scattered like bits of foil over them. The kimono had gone quite limp. Sweat drew clusters of yellow clouds at the neckline.

Honda had for some time been aware of a strange odour. He saw that the dirt and oil on the kimono had mixed with the sweat into the smell as of a dank canal that young men put out in the summer. Tōru had lost his fastidiousness.

And there was no smell of flowers. The room was strewn with flowers, but they gave off no odour. There were red and white hollyhocks everywhere, no doubt ordered from a florist, but they were several days old, and dry and wilted.

Kinué's hair was garlanded with white hollyhocks, not inserted into the hair but leaning this way and that, held unevenly in place by rubber bands. As her head bobbed they sent forth a dry rustling.

She would stand up and sit down again, decorating Tōru's still rich hair with red hollyhocks. There was a band around his head. She would poke three and four dry red hollyhocks into it and then, like a student of flower arranging, stand back and survey the results. Flowers falling over his ears and cheeks should have been an annoyance, but Tōru had abdicated control of the regions above his neck.

After a time Honda went to dress for the journey.

29

Having learned that the road to Nara was now excellent, Honda took a room in Kyoto. He stayed at the Miyako Hotel and hired a car for noon on the twenty-second. The clouds were out of keeping with the heat. Showers seemed likely up in the hills.

So he was here, thought Honda, content. Sensations came as through screens to his weary body and heart, beneath old-fashioned unbleached linen. He had brought a blanket as defence against the air-conditioning. The shrilling of the cicadas in the Keagé district near the hotel sank through the windows.

He made a firm resolution as the car started off. 'Today I am not going to see skeletons beneath flesh. They are only a concept. I will see and remember things as they are. It will be my last pleasure, my last effort. My last good look. I must look. I must take in everything, with an unoccupied heart.'

The car passed the Sambōin Temple at Daigo. From the bridge at the Kajūji Temple it turned onto the National Nara Highway, and from Nara Park on to the Tenri Highway. In an hour it was at Obitoké.

Honda had noticed numbers of Kyoto women with parasols, not often seen in Tokyo. Some of the faces beneath were shining, some – because of the designs on the parasols, perhaps – were dark. Some were beautiful shining, some were beautiful dark.

As they turned from the southern outskirts of Yamashina they were in suburban wastes, a region of small factories burning in the summer sun. Waiting with several women and children at a bus stop was a pregnant woman, warm in a bold Western print. The faces wore a certain stagnation, as of tea leaves floating on the torrents of life. Beyond was a dusty tomato patch.

The Daigo district was a clutter of all the dreary details of new construction, to be seen throughout Japan: raw building materials and blue-tiled roofs, television towers and power lines, Coca-Cola advertisements and drive-in snack bars. Among heaps of rubble below cliffs where wild daisies stabbed at the sky were automobile dumps, blue and yellow and black, piled precariously one on the other, the gaudy colours molten in the sun. At this sad accumulation, kept hidden at most times by the automobile, Honda thought of an adventure story he had read as a child, and of the heaps of ivory in the swamp where elephants go to die. Perhaps, sensing the approach of death, automobiles too gather at their own graveyards. In any event, the brightness, the openness, the want of shame seemed to him quite automobilish.

From Uji the hills were for the first time green. A billboard proclaimed 'Delicious Chilled Sweets'. Bamboo leaves arched over the road.

They crossed Moon Bridge in Uji and were on the old Nara Highway. They passed Fushimi and Yamashiro. A sign informed them that Nara was twenty miles distant. Time went by. At each marker Honda thought of the expression 'mile-stones on the way to the grave'. It seemed to him inconceivable that he would return over the same road. Sign followed sign, marking clearly the road he must travel. Nineteen miles to Nara. A mile nearer the grave. He opened a window, stealing an inch from air-conditioning, and the cicadas were ringing in his ears, as if the whole world were sounding in solitude under the summer sun.

Another filling station. More Coca-Cola.

The beautiful green embankment of the River Kizu stretched far away to the right. It was deserted, roily clouds defining its handsome groves. Blue patches glowed in the sky.

And what, thought Honda vacantly, might it be? The green platform was like a doll stand. The turbulent clouds made it seem that dolls had been lined up and then lost. Or perhaps transparent rows of dolls were still there. Would they be mortuary images? Perhaps images of darkness shattered by a tempest of light still left traces against the sky; and that was why the embankment was so grand, so solemnly respectful. It raised into the sky the light left behind by rows of dolls. Or perhaps the light which he seemed to see was the negative of a bottomless darkness.

He was aware of eyes once again seeking to go behind objects. They were what he had banned as he left the hotel. If he let them have their way the concrete world would once again collapse like a dike from the hole pierced by his glance. He must persevere yet a little more. He must hold it yet a little longer, the work of glass so delicate and ready to break.

The Kizu lay to their right for a time, its many shoals below them. A power line sagged down over it, as if melted and bent by the heat.

Presently the road turned to cross the Kizu on a steel bridge, and a sign told them that Nara was only five miles away. They crossed numbers of white country lanes bordered by grasses that had not yet sent forth plumes. The bamboo thickets were dense. The young bamboo leaves filled with sunlight as with warm water wore a soft, golden sheen, like the pelts of fox cubs, against the silent black of the evergreens.

Nara came into view.

As they descended through the pines along the hills, the great, soaring, protecting roof of the Tōdaiji and the golden kite tails at its gables were Nara.

The car moved through quiet streets, past plain, awning-shaded old shops with white gloves and other wares hung out for sale. They came to Nara Park. The sun was stronger, the cicada calls that hammered at the back of Honda's head were intenser. White spots on summer deer floated up through dappled sunlight.

Turning onto the Tenri Highway, they passed through shining fields. To the right from a casual little bridge a road led to Obitoké and Obitoké Station; to the left, another to the hills at the base of which lay the Gesshūji. Fringing the paddies, it was now paved, and the drive to the lower gate was an easy one.

30

They could perfectly well drive to the mountain gate, a considerable distance up the hill, altogether too far for an old man to walk, said the driver, looking up at the yet fiercer sun in the cloudless sky; but Honda refused, and told him to wait at the lower gate. He had to know for himself Kiyoaki's sufferings of sixty years before.

Leaning on his stick, he looked down from the gate, his back to the shade that invited from within.

Songs of cicadas and crickets filled the air. Into such quietness was woven the roar of automobiles on the Tenri Highway, beyond the fields. There were no automobiles on the road before him. White gravel delicately lined the shoulders of the road.

The serenity of the Yamato Plain was as it had always been. It lay flat as the world of man. Obitoké shone in the distance, its roofs like little shellfish. A trace of smoke hung over it. Perhaps it now had small factories. The inn where Kiyoaki had lain ill was at the foot of a flagstone slope such as was probably to be found in the village even now; but he thought it would be useless to look for the inn itself.

An endlessly blue sky arched over village and plain. Clouds trailed tatters of white satin like mirages from the misted hills beyond. The upper lines cut into the sky with a clear, statue-like beauty.

Honda squatted down, overcome by heat and fatigue. He felt as if the malign light from the sharp blades of summer grass were stabbing at his eyes. He felt that decay had been smelled out by a fly that brushed past his nose.

With his eyes he reprimanded the driver, who had climbed from the car, and, worried, was coming towards him.

He was beginning to doubt that in fact he could reach the mountain gate. His back and his stomach were aching. He waved off the driver and went inside the gate, determined to be healthy for as long as the man was watching. Gasping for breath, helped by the curves, he made his way up the uneven gravel road, catching through the corner of his left eye the bright yellow of moss, like a sickness, on the trunk of a persimmon tree, and, on his right, the lavender heads of bellflowers from which most of the petals had fallen.

The shadows that blocked off the road ahead had a sort of mystic quiet. The uneven road, which would be a river bottom in a rain, shone where the sun struck it like mineral outcroppings, and whispered with the coolness of its shadows. There was a reason for the shadows, but Honda doubted that it was in the trees themselves.

He asked himself and his stick at which shadow he might rest. The fourth shadow, already invisible from the automobile, quietly invited him. Coming to it, he sat, almost collapsed, on a chestnut root.

'In the beginning,' thought Honda, as if of undisputed reality, 'it was decided that I would rest on this day at this moment in the shade of this tree.'

Sweat and insect songs, forgotten while he was walking, surged forward as he sat down. He pressed his forehead against his stick. The pressure of the silver head drowned out the pain throbbing in his stomach and back.

The doctor had told him he had tumour of the pancreas. Smiling, he had said that it was benign. *Smiling, benign.* To stretch out hopes on such words was to trample on the pride of a man who had lived through eighty-one years. Honda considered refusing surgery when he returned to Tokyo. If he did, however, the doctor was certain to bring pressure upon 'near relatives'. He had already fallen into the trap. He had fallen into one trap when he had been born into this world, and there ought not to be another trap waiting at the end of the way. He must laugh at it all, thought Honda. He must pretend to hope. The sacrificial kid in India had gone on struggling for so long after its head had fallen.

The eye of the troublesome supervisor no longer upon him, Honda leaned on his stick and reeled extravagantly as he made his way up the slope. He began to feel as if he were being funny. The pain left him and his step was brisker.

The smell of summer grasses filled the air. Pines were thick along the road. Leaning on his stick, he looked up at the sky. In the strong sunlight the cones among the thick branches were etched scale by scale. He came to an abandoned tea patch on the left, matted with spider webs and creepers.

There were strips of shadow ahead. The nearer ones were like the slats of a damaged blind, the farther ones were richly black, gathered in threes and fours, like sashes for mourning weeds.

A large pine cone lay fallen on the road. On the pretext of picking it up, he sat down on a giant pine root. His stomach was heavily, painfully hot. The fatigue, unable to find an outlet, bent like a rusty wire. As he toyed with the cone, fully opened and dried, the tea-coloured scales put up a powerful resistance to his fingers. Dew-flowers dotted the way, their blossoms wilting in the sun, delicate traces of greenish lavender among leaves like young swallows' wings. The great pine tree against which he leaned, the celadon of the sky above, the clouds like leavings from a broom – everything was ominously, threateningly dry.

Honda could not identify the insect songs that filled it all. A sound like the drone bass of all insects, a sound like a gnashing of teeth in a nightmare, a sound like an aimless echoing against the ribs.

He stood up again, and again he wondered whether he would reach the mountain gate. As he walked on, he could only count the number of shadows ahead. How many more shadows could he make his way past in the intensity of the heat, the torment of the slope? But he had already passed three since he had begun counting. A shadow stretched halfway across the road. Should he count it as a full shadow or only half a shadow?

Where the road curved gently to the left there were bamboo thickets. They were like settlements in the world of man. The delicate young leaves crowded thickly one against another, some light as asparagus, some black with a powerful malice and perversity.

As he sat down and wiped at the sweat once more, he saw a butterfly, the first. It was an outline in the distance, and cobalt freshly adorned the russet of the wings as it came nearer.

He came to a marsh. He rested under the strong green of a chestnut on the bank. There was not a breath of air. A dead pine tree lay like a bridge across a corner of the yellow-green marsh, the surface of which was disturbed only by the tracks of water striders. Around it shimmered tiny ripples, disturbing the dull blue reflection of the sky. The dead tree was a reddish brown to the tips of its needles. Propped up, it appeared, by branches in the marsh bottom, the trunk was above water, rusty red in a sea of green, its original shape still intact. It continued without a doubt to be a pine tree.

He started off again, as if following the hairtail butterfly that darted out happily from among the still plumeless grasses and foxtails. The tarnished green of the cypress grove across the marsh spread to the near side. Little by little the shadows were thicker.

He could feel the sweat coming through his shirt and soaking the back of his suit coat. He could not be sure whether it was a healthy sweat from the heat or a cold, oily sweat. In any event he had not sweated so profusely since he had reached old age.

Where the cypress grove gave way to a grove of cryptomeria, there stood a lone *nemu* tree. The soft clusters of leaves in among the hard needles of the cryptomerias were like wraiths, like afternoon slumber. They made him think of Thailand. A white butterfly from the *nemu* led him on his way.

The road was steeper. The mountain gate would be near. The cryptomerias were thicker, and a cool breeze came from among them. Walking was now easy. The bands across the road had until now been the shadows of trees. Now they were strips of sunlight.

The butterfly cut an uncertain path through the darkness of the cryptomeria grove. It drew a low line across ferns shining liquidly in sunlight to the black gate within. For some reason, thought Honda, all the butterflies hereabouts flew low near the ground.

He passed the black gate. The mountain gate lay ahead. So finally he was at the Gesshūji. He had lived these sixty years only to come again.

Gazing at the prow-shaped pine that served as a carriage stop, Honda found it hard to believe that he was here. He felt strangely refreshed, even reluctant to reach his destination. He stood at a pillar of the mountain gate, which was flanked by two much smaller and lower gates. Sixteen-petal chrysanthemums were stamped on the ridge tiles. On the left pillar was a neat, lady-like sign identifying the temple as the Gesshūji, under the protection of the Imperial House. On the right pillar was a dim inscription in relief: 'Peace on Earth. Within is Housed the Imperial Recitation Text of the *Prajñāparamitāsūtra*. A Fortress of the Law of His Benign Majesty.'

There were five stripes on the egg-coloured earthen wall to indicate the high rank of the temple. Across yellowish gravel, steppingstones led to the doorway in a chequered pattern. Honda counted them with his stick, and when he had come to ninety he was at the closed doors. In the recessed grip his hand touched a chrysanthemum and clouds cut from white paper.

The farthest corner of the interior came back to him. He stood motionless, forgetting to announce himself. Sixty years ago the young Honda had stood on this same doorstep before this same door. The paper would have been changed a hundred times in those years, but a clean white expanse blocked the way now as it had that cold spring day. Though the grain of the wood was perhaps a little more prominent, it showed little sign of the wear of the winds and the snows. Only an instant had passed.

Ill at the Obitoké inn, Kiyoaki had staked everything on this trip to the Gesshūji. Feverish, he would still be waiting for Honda's return; and what would he think when he saw that in that instant Honda had become a bent, immobile old man?

A steward probably in his sixties, dressed in an open-necked shirt, came to receive him. He needed help in negotiating the last high step. Leading him to a suite of rooms, eight mats and six, in the main hall, the man said politely that they had received his letter and perused its contents, and motioned him to a cushion laid out with geometric precision on a mat with a figured border, white on black. He did not remember the rooms from six decades before.

On the scroll in the alcove, in the style of Sesshū, a dragon twisted and writhed among storm clouds. Below it was a crisp, tidy little arrangement of wild carnations. An old nun in a white kimono of cotton crepe and a white obi brought red and white sweets and cold tea on a rimmed tray. Through open doors green floated in from the garden. There was a thick growth of maples and arbovitae, and beyond it a white gallery; and nothing more.

The steward talked of this and that, and the moments passed. Honda sat quietly in the breeze. The sweat and the aching had left him. He felt that rescue had come.

He was in a room of the Gesshūji, which he had thought it would be impossible to visit. The approach of death had made the visit easy, had unloosed the weight that held him in the depths of being. It was even a comfort to think, from the light repose the struggle up the hill had brought him, that Kiyoaki, struggling against illness up that same road, had been given wings to soar with by the denial that awaited him.

The shrilling of cicadas remained in his ears, but here in the dusk it was cool, like the dying echo of a bell. The old man talked on, making no further reference to the letter. Honda could not bring himself to ask whether he would see the Abbess.

He began to fear that the empty passage of the moments was a circumspect way of informing him that the Abbess would not receive him. Perhaps the old steward had seen the article in the weekly magazine. Perhaps he had advised her to plead an indisposition.

Honda did not feel timid about seeing her, guilt-ridden though he was. Without the crime and the guilt and the mortality he would not have had the courage for that climb. He now saw that the scandal had given him his first dark prompting. Tōru's attempted suicide, his blindness, Honda's illness, Kinué's pregnancy, had all pointed to the same spot. It was true: they had frozen into a cluster and forced him up that burning road. Without them he could only have looked up at the radiance of the Gesshūji upon a distant summit.

If, after so much, the Abbess were to refuse him because of the incident, he could call it fate. He would not see her in this life. He was sure all the same that he would see her one day, even if he was denied a meeting on this last spot in this last hour in this world.

Cool repose replaced fretfulness, resignation sorrow, to make the passage of time bearable.

The old nun appeared again, and whispered something in the steward's ear.

'Her Reverence has informed us that she is ready to see you,' he said, in the accents of this West Country. 'Come with me, if you will, please.'

Honda wanted to believe his ears.

The green light from the northern garden was too strong, and for a moment he did not recognize it; but it was here, sixty years before, that the Abbess's predecessor had received him.

He remembered the bright review of the seasons on that earlier screen. It had been replaced by a plain screen of wattled reeds. Beyond the veranda burned the green of a small tea garden, alive with cicadas. Beyond a profusion of maples, plums, and tea bushes were the red buds of an oleander. The summer light fell sharply upon the white spears of dwarf bamboo among the steppingstones, repeating the white light from the sky above the wooded hills.

A beating of wings seemed almost to strike the wall. A sparrow flew in from the gallery and on again, its shadow wavering against the white wall.

The door to the inner apartments slid open. Before Honda, who had brought his knees together in stiff formality, the old Abbess appeared, led by a white-clad novice. The pale figure in a white kimono and a cloak of deep purple would be Satoko, now eighty-three.

Honda felt tears come to his eyes. He was powerless to look up at her.

She faced him across the table. The nose was the finely carved nose of those years before, and the eyes were the same beautiful eyes. Satoko had changed utterly, and yet he knew at a glance that it was Satoko. The bloom of youth had in a jump of sixty years become the extreme of age, Satoko had escaped the journey through the gloomy world. A person who crosses a garden bridge from shadow into sunlight may seem to change faces. If the beautiful young face was the face in the shadow, such, no more, was the change to the beautiful old face now in the sunlight. He remembered how, as he left the hotel, Kyoto faces had seemed bright and dark under parasols and how one could predict the quality of beauty from the brightness and darkness.

For Honda it had been sixty years. For Satoko had it been the time it takes to cross a garden bridge from shadow into sunlight?

Age had sped in the direction not of decay but of purification. The skin seemed to glow with a still light; the beauty of the eyes was clearer, shining through something like a patina. Age had crystallized into a perfect jewel. It was cold though diaphanous, roundly soft though hard, and the lips were still moist. There were wrinkles, deep and innumerable, but they were bright as if washed clean one by one. There was something brightly forceful about the tiny, somewhat bent figure.

Hiding his tears, Honda looked up.

'It was good of you to come,' said the Abbess pleasantly.

'It was rude of me to introduce myself without warning, and it is very kind of you to see me all the same.' Wanting above all to avoid familiarity, Honda found himself using the stiffest of greetings. He was ashamed of the phlegm-choked old voice. He forced himself on. 'I addressed myself to your steward. I wonder if he was kind enough to show you my letter.'

'Yes, I saw it.'

There was a pause. The novice took advantage of it to withdraw.

'How the memories come back. As you can see, I am so old that I cannot be sure of lasting the night.' He took courage from the fact that she had read his letter. The words came more easily.

The Abbess laughed and seemed to sway gently. 'Your interesting letter seemed almost too earnest.' Like the steward, she spoke the West Country dialect. 'I thought there must be some holy bond between us.'

The last drops of youth leaped up within Honda. He had returned to that day sixty years before, when he had pleaded youthful ardour to the Abbess's predecessor. He discarded his reserve.

'Your revered predecessor would not let me see you when I came with Kiyoaki's last request. It had to be so, but I was angry. Kiyoaki Matsugae was after all my dearest friend.'

'Kiyoaki Matsugae. Who might he have been?'

Honda looked at her in astonishment.

She might be hard of hearing, but she could not have failed to hear him. Yet her words were so wide of the mark that he could only believe he had been misunderstood.

'I beg your pardon?' He wanted her to say it again.

There was no trace of dissimulation as she repeated the words. There was instead a sort of girlish curiosity in her eyes, and below them a quiet smile. 'Who might he have been?'

Honda saw that she wanted him to tell her of Kiyoaki. Scrupulously polite, he recounted his memories of Kiyoaki's love and its sad conclusion.

The Abbess sat motionless through the long story, a smile always on her lips. Occasionally she would nod. She listened with care even as she gracefully took the cold refreshments the old nun had brought in.

Calmly, without a touch of emotion, she said: 'It has been a most interesting story, but unfortunately I did not know Mr Matsugae. I fear you have confused me with someone else.'

'But I believe that your name is Satoko Ayakura?' He coughed in the urgency of his words.

'That was my lay name.'

'Then you must have known Kiyoaki.' He was angry.

It had to be not forgetfulness but unabashed prevarication. He knew that the Abbess had reasons enough to pretend ignorance; but that a woman far from the vulgar world, of her venerable state, should lie thus openly gave grounds for doubting the depth of her convictions. If she still carried with her all the hypocrisy of that other world, then there must be doubts about the validity of her conversion when she entered this one. The dreams of sixty years seemed betrayed in that instant.

His persistence passed a reasonable limit, but she did not seem to resent it. For all the heat, her purple cloak was cool. Her eyes and her always beautiful voice were serene.

'No, Mr Honda, I have forgotten none of the blessings that were mine in the other world. But I fear I have never heard the name Kiyoaki Matsugae. Don't you suppose, Mr Honda, that there never was such a person? You seem convinced that there was; but don't you suppose that there was no such person from the beginning, anywhere? I couldn't help thinking so as I listened to you.'

'Why then do we know each other? And the Ayakuras and the Matsugaes must still have family registers.'

'Yes, such documents might solve problems in the other world. But did you really know a person called Kiyoaki? And can you say definitely that the two of us have met before?'

'I came here sixty years ago.'

'Memory is like a phantom mirror. It sometimes shows things too distant to be seen, and sometimes it shows them as if they were here.'

'But if there was no Kiyoaki from the beginning –' Honda was groping through a fog. His meeting here with the Abbess seemed half a dream. He spoke loudly, as if to retrieve the self that receded like traces of breath vanishing from a lacquer tray. 'If there was no Kiyoaki, then there was no Isao. There was no Ying Chan, and who knows, perhaps there has been no I.'

For the first time there was strength in her eyes.

'That too is as it is in each heart.'

A long silence ensued. The Abbess clapped gently. The novice appeared and knelt in the doorway.

'Mr Honda has been kind enough to come all this way. I think he should see the south garden. I will take him there.'

The novice led her by the hand. Honda stood up as if pulled by strings, and followed them through the dark rooms.

The novice slid open a door and led him to the veranda. The wide south garden was before him.

The lawn, with the hills behind it, blazed in the summer sun.

'We have had cuckoos since morning,' said the novice.

The grove beyond the lawn was dominated by maples. A wattled gate led to the hills. Some of the maples were red even now in the summer, flames among the green. Steppingstones were scattered easily over the lawn, and wild carnations bloomed shyly among them. In a corner to the left were a well and a well wheel. A celadon stool on the lawn seemed so hot in the sun that it would surely burn anyone who tried to sit on it. Summer clouds ranged their dizzying shoulders over the green hills.

It was a bright, quiet garden, without striking features. Like a rosary rubbed between the hands, the shrilling of cicadas held sway.

There was no other sound. The garden was empty. He had come, thought Honda, to a place that had no memories, nothing.

The noontide sun of summer flowed over the still garden.

25 November 1970

THE END
The Sea of Fertility